CW01548175

THE ADVERSARY
JAMES R. BOWMAN
FOUR HORSEMEN OF THE APOCALYPSE SAGA: BOOK ONE.

Published by

MELROSE
BOOKS

An Imprint of Melrose Press Limited
St Thomas Place, Ely
Cambridgeshire
CB7 4GG, UK
www.melrosebooks.com

FIRST EDITION

Copyright © James R. Bowman 2009

The Author asserts his moral right to
be identified as the author of this work

Cover art by Peter Pracownik
www.peterpracownik.com

ISBN 978 1 907040 08 5

All rights reserved. No part of this publication may be reproduced, stored in a retrieval system, or transmitted, in any form or by any means electronic, mechanical, photocopying, recording or otherwise, without the prior permission of the publishers.

This book is sold subject to the condition that it shall not, by way of trade or otherwise, be lent, re-sold, hired out or otherwise circulated without the publisher's prior consent in any form of binding or cover other than that in which it is published and without a similar condition including this condition being imposed on the subsequent purchaser.

Printed and bound in Great Britain by
Athenaeum Press Ltd. Gateshead, Tyne & Wear

This publication has been printed on paper that has been manufactured and harvested from sustainable forests.

Contents

ACKNOWLEDGEMENTS

THIS BOOK IS DEDICATED TO EVERYONE WHO has influenced me over the years. Most know who they are but if I were to list them all, we'd need another book just for that. There are, however, certain individuals who warrant a special mention; so I would like to take this opportunity to thank them for everything they have done and for enriching my life in so many ways. In no order of importance I would like to start with my mum and dad, who have always allowed me the freedom to make my own choices (picking me up from the tarmac and treating my wounds when I make the wrong ones). Their love and support has been unconditional and this is for them. It is also for my wife, Sue, who has put up with me for the last twenty-one years. Her love, support and belief have kept me going when things were at their darkest. Another woman who has made her mark on me is Xifu, D; who taught me about humility and my place in the grand scheme of things. Much of her teaching is incorporated into my story and, as each day passes, more and more of what Sue and I learnt from her becomes a reality. Thanks to Brenda and Co (they know who they are) and to Barbara Archer, my proofreader, whose advice and inspiration gave me a direction to travel in and some of the tools to travel with; to Peter and Nicola for their vision of the Horsemen and for painting an exceptional cover; to Costas Coffee (all of them) in Ipswich for putting up with me camping in the corner of their stores and hiding behind my laptop these past few years; the Port of Felixstowe, who have been good to this family in ways they'll never fully appreciate; and finally, a special mention to whatever invisible and elusive entities have helped contribute to this tale (as my loving wife believes that there is something otherworldly helping me to write this). So, for everyone I haven't mentioned and who contributed their something to this book, however small, thanks for being there when I needed you; and for those who hindered, for being there when I didn't.

Introduction

OVER THE YEARS, THERE HAS BEEN ONE phrase, used in almost every industry and utilized worldwide. A phrase that seems to repeat itself with a frequency that has rendered it virtually pointless, and that is: *Looking at the big picture*. Now, over the course of both my mundane and various career moves, I still find myself hearing that phrase being paid lip service to quite a lot of late. The thing with the big picture though, is *whose* big picture anyone is looking upon at any given time; whether it is the same picture as them; whether someone is color-blind maybe, and seeing a monochrome shade of this picture; or just generally unable to fathom what it is they are looking at in the first place: a big, small or an entirely different picture. I have often wondered just what this alleged picture actually is and what it is people see, for rarely have I seen a group of people who can all sing off the same hymn sheet for any length of time without quarreling about it. Opinions seem to be as varied and as widespread as grains of sand in a desert – one for every man, woman and child even. Certainly now, more than ever, apparently, we see our leaders and those who move discreetly – and some not so discreetly – behind the scenes operating to agendas of their own: agendas which seem equally diverse and widespread and not always for the benefit of those whom they serve.

The Adversary

Now call me archaic, or hidebound, or anything you like; but ever since I was mentally aware of such things I have often wondered why humans can't seem to get along. We are a species of beings the same as bees are a species, termites are a species, and so too are ants; yet for such insignificant things in the eyes of most humans (I hasten to add not mine), how is it *they* manage to exist in vast numbers while at the same time resist the urge to kill, steal, abuse, rape, lie to and in fact *not* do to each other all the things we humans have perfected to a fine art. It seems our big picture has fragmented into an infinite number of obscured shards and other than an absence of crazy glue to put them back together, no one is sharing their shard and it's been so long now that there is probably no one left who even has a clue what this big picture once looked like. The mother of all jigsaw puzzles and no one is sharing their piece (literally).

Through experience and some thoroughly engaging encounters with some equally fascinating people (some of whom have scared me half to death, I might add), I have sought a way to glue the shards of what little *I know* of the big picture into some semblance of a whole, and share it with as many other people who might be interested. Maybe they have a shard that complements it and, hopefully, whilst up until this moment they were unsure what to do with it, perhaps it now makes more sense to them and can help them move forward with renewed purpose.

From early days when humans sat around fires and began communicating, they told stories to each other. The wise men and women educated their charges by combining knowledge into their stories, and this practice has continued to this very day. Yet knowledge is subjective: what is relevant to one may mean nothing to another. Accepting this, I ask you to simply enjoy the story and make of it what you will. If you enjoy reading it half as much as I enjoyed writing it, then it has attained its purpose. If it inspires you to consider things you hadn't before, or simply look at things a little differently, then it will have done its bit for evolution.

Lastly, I look forward to seeing you all along the journey. Who knows, maybe we'll even get to see something of this big picture while we are still able to appreciate it.

James R Bowman

PROLOGUE

VIEW FROM A PRECIPICE

NOON, MOUNTAIN STANDARD TIME, LATE AUGUST, HOTEVILLA
MOTHER VILLAGE, ARIZONA.

THE LAND SHOOK. AND NOT FOR THE first time either. It had resonated like a dance drum skin on several occasions over the last few years and the wizened and weatherbeaten elderly elder had noticed it. Many from the kiva had spoken of it, but few believed what it heralded – unlike him.

'It has begun at last!' He spoke the ominous words aloud as if the hot desert air would carry them skyward to all those who needed confirmation of what they perhaps already suspected. His voice crackled like the rolling of some old parchment but for all that, there was still power there. It was deep and resonated from within his being and barely moved his lips.

'May the creator and Maasaw have mercy upon us if they so choose, for what is coming will have none.' The elderly elder, the *Kikmongwi*, one of the last of his kind, squatted down froglike, bare feet flat on the ground, with his wiry body swinging between his own knees while at the same time he placed both leathered palms down on the scorched earth. Driving his fingers into the soil, he literally pulled himself down even further until his walnut-tanned and now tilted head was mere inches from the ground. Remaining perfectly still, he listened.

There were none left alive who could hear what he heard, and even if there were they would not have liked what he was hearing at that very moment. He heard the sound of transition. Something was coming from Tokpela (the Hopi first world). He looked up suddenly, like a jack rabbit scenting a coyote. He scrunched up his aged yet still crystal clear eyes and focused intently upon some distant spot in the west, and a wry smile creased further – if that was at all possible – his already craggy and lined features.

'I sense you coming, you old trickster, and I will be ready for you, for this is our world and you are *not* welcome,' he chuckled humorlessly before continuing, 'ah, but how well you know the *bahanna* (the Native American slang and not so pleasant term used for describing the white people). You know that now, of all times, with their minds being closed and their loss of faith in anything but themselves, they will not see you, even when you stand among them.' He paused and looked around as a breeze ghosted over his flesh. 'Not for some time, hey, trickster? But it won't take long, will it?' he added quietly, sadly picturing the carnage he knew would follow.

Standing slowly, for he was way past his ninetieth summer and just how far past mattered little to him now, he pressed the small of his back until he heard the satisfying crack of bone. Then, sighing in relief at the sensation, he made his way back to his fields. There were matters to attend to before the trying and dying times ahead fell upon the land like nightfall.

3 p.m. Greenwich Mean Time, August, St George's Hospital, Newcastle, UK.

The explosions resounded again and again and like them, Tomas threw himself backwards again and again, his body reacting on pure instinct as the scene played over for him alone. Scream after scream tore from his throat as flames and shrapnel sizzled around his flesh. Reliving the moment over and over every time he closed his eyes was taking a tremendous toll on both his body and most of all, upon his battered soul. The distinctive smell of ozone and charred meat assailed his senses along with the brief but pitiful cries of the dying. He knew, in that part of his mind which had miraculously remained detached from the devastation going on around him, that the majority of those in his vicinity were already dead and for the most part, they were silent.

He was still screaming as he woke. A pair of worried looking yet experienced nurses stood either side of him, supporting him and gently, though firmly, restraining him from leaping out of the bed and doing himself further injury. It didn't help his confusion as his wild, staring and not fully conscious gaze took them in. They were twins; what were the odds? Tomas continued to thrash in his sheets as the dream, with the now added faces of the nurses included, took hold of him once more and pulled him back into its lethal embrace.

'Mister Smith! Mister Smith! Will you wake up, please. It's all right now; it was just a bad dream. Mister Smith. Are you okay?'

Tomas flopped once more, like a beached fish drawing its last gasp. From the fragments and dying vestiges of his nightmare he wondered once more just who this Mister Smith was for he had heard the name used before, and then he lay still again. The continuous tone on the monitor told them all they needed to know.

'Code Blue, Code Blue, will somebody get that bloody crash cart back in here again. Now!'

Fifteen minutes later and the regular blip on the monitor assured them he was back once more, having defied the odds of yet another incredible resuscitation.

'We might as well leave this thing in here. What's that now? Six times he's gone under. How does he keep coming back?' Gill asked hopelessly.

Gail, the other one of the twins, knew it was a rhetorical question and as such didn't bother to reply straight away; they had started asking it of each other after the third time he had crashed a few days earlier. All under the same circumstance too: waking from a nightmare that must scare him so much his heart just gives up. They figured that death seemed to calm him just enough for them to restart him and terminate the dream. 'I know what you mean,' Gail answered eventually, though knowing she didn't need to, but the mysterious Mister Smith – she doubted that was his real name too considering the military types who had brought him in – still bothered her as well.

'The question isn't how it is, it's *why* it is.' They padded down the antiseptic-smelling corridor towards their next assignment, hands thrust into the pockets of their crisp white uniforms. 'Something keeps scaring the shit out of him so much so that when he sleeps he would rather die than confront it, and we just keep bringing him back to face it all over again. Do you ever get that feeling we're just torturing the poor bastard?'

'Gail!' Gill exclaimed in mock severity 'Shame on you! Talking like that. We *are* saving his life. That's what we do and it's what we'll keep doing until he's better.' But even as she said it Gill didn't look too convinced herself.

'Saving it for what, though?' Gail whispered quietly, again as much to herself as it was in response to her friend. Neither they, nor any other person entering or leaving the room of Mister Smith saw the archaically armored figure incongruously standing patiently and, with a look of some small concern, watching proceedings from the corner of the room.

Two days later and one more crash and it seemed that the enigmatic Mr Smith had stabilized; he even became quite chatty as his health miraculously returned – much to the surprise and differing opinions of the medical staff. Throughout Tomas's sojourn at the hospital there had been an armed guard on the door at all times but at 9 p.m., just shy of two weeks after his admission, the body of Mr Smith vanished

10 A.M., SUNSHINE SKYWAY BRIDGE, TAMPA, USA.

The morning traffic had lessened to a tolerable chaos by the time Geoff arrived at the midway point of the bridge. He knew it was the mid-point because he passed it every day on his way to and from work and had done so this past five years religiously. But what made it more obvious today was the fact that he was not alone at the mid-point. At the apex of the Skyway Bridge, where the cables almost met, pulling down from each of the two towers, there were parked at least thirty cars. Having arrived from either direction, they parked where they stopped, effectively blocking any further traffic from passing over.

The cacophony of horns and curses began as predicted, but it didn't bother Geoff. Nothing mattered any more since waking from the dream the previous night. It had been *so* real. *She* had been so real. On waking, Geoff had wept at being separated from her once more, and the old wounds tore open all over again. He remembered the funeral with a clarity he wished he couldn't recall. He remembered the endless visits to the hospital and towards the end how he had slept by her bedside. He didn't want to remember her that way; he wanted to visualize her the way she appeared to him last night. Seeing her in all her beauty made the images of her wasted and gaunt frame vanish like the morning mist out on the bay. But that was all done with now. She had promised him so much and shown him a way to be with her again.

Geoff looked around with eyes that registered little beyond his own intentions, but he did see several other people he knew, albeit tenuously. They saw him too and waved a pleasant if somewhat distracted greeting. Geoff waved back politely, as ambivalent about it all as they evidently were. To all intents and purposes, it looked like a social gathering at the bridge. Maybe a new ship was coming by, or it was a good spot to watch dolphins. Maybe even, they were there to explore the claims of the power of the Tampa Triangle. Only they weren't. As the moments passed, it became clear that it was no innocent ensemble. One by one, without any apparent care in the world and as if it were the most natural thing to do, they mounted the railing, climbing with chillingly serene smiles on their faces. Seventy-three people – Geoff included – men, women and even children, made their way to the edge of the bridge, whereupon with no hesitation whatsoever, they proceeded to throw themselves off, casting themselves out into oblivion.

For long minutes after the last person had silently fallen from view there was nothing but the mournful sounds of The Eagles playing on the local radio station wafting out from someone's car stereo. A light breeze picked up and along with it a pale mist wafted through the abandoned cars where, had there been anyone left alive to see it, a petite blonde woman also drifted from side to side, weaving gracefully through the cars, as though she were on wheels herself. With her pale, billowing hair blowing oddly against the breeze – as though an invisible force tugged at her – she was as out of place as the event itself moments before. If she knew what had just happened, she didn't show it, but somehow, all the same, she seemed equally pleased and saddened by something simultaneously. Each expression warred for dominance on her delicate and hazy features, yet neither succeeding. But no sooner had she passed the last abandoned vehicle than another gust blew across the bridge, and with it, she too vanished.

CHAPTER ONE

FOUND

LESSONS IN LIFE COME IN ALL SHAPES, sizes and colors. They also tend to come at the most interesting, as well as, more often than not, the most inconvenient of times. The universal cosmic law of *If it can, it will* invariably comes into play at those times. Now, there are, as a general rule of thumb, two sorts of principal education in the world. There are those lessons that life and the world itself provides; and then there is the other sort – the more familiar sort. They are the antiquated styled lessons we bombard our youth with today, teaching them diligently the uncanny ability to repeat parrot fashion the archaic ideas and opinions of others, of older and mostly long-dead souls whose legacy, rightly or wrongly, just goes seemingly on and on. These past voices then reiterate their work to our students, ingraining them with all the mistakes, prejudices and misrepresentations garnered from our chequered and somewhat dubious past, and instilling them into our potential future so we can make all the same mistakes our ancestors made all over again in all new and inventive ways. For, however useful we think those lessons are – and to be fair some of them are actually even handy in the really real world, though not too many of them – it's those lessons that life itself doles out that tend to be the really bloody important ones.

What makes these lessons so relevant is because, if you don't pay attention

1

to them and act upon them when they are presented, the consequences are more often than not fairly disastrous. It's those disastrous consequences that, should you survive them, will reinforce that particular life's lesson with a gravity that leaves a lasting impression, the experience adding itself to your DNA memory banks and stimulating mental growth; which means to the average (and even not so average human) that each small or massive thing we learn should subsequently lead to tiny leaps in mortal evolution, or at least hopefully, because only some sort of karmic masochist continually makes the same stupid mistakes over and over again. The day Neolithic man first put his hand in the fire and got it burnt, he learnt there and then not to do such a stupid thing twice. And it isn't something that you can tell someone what it is they should or shouldn't do: that particular someone's pride usually steps in then and convinces them that they know better, so most souls have to go through the process of finding out themselves. It's almost an initiation of sorts but unfortunately not all souls pass the test. There is a saying that encompasses that ideal: that of *Good judgment comes from experience, experience comes from bad judgment*.

Hence, the key phrase to pay close attention to in all this is: *should you survive it*; because some of these life lessons are notoriously harsh and can actually be quite fatal if not heeded soon enough, though such is Nature, she's not known for her compassion after all. Do stupid things: expect severe consequences. Just ask the man who crawled into the cave in the middle of bear country, with no apparent thought at all about what might already be in there. Nature does not suffer fools gladly – a fact that at least one soul had just painfully discovered as the severed head that was currently lying upturned in the gutter, and whose now sightless eyes that gazed blankly into oblivion, would have attested. It would have given anything for a second chance at the particular life lesson that saw it residing in the wet and undignified spot it found itself in. Snow-covered and blood-smeared, it was rapidly merging with the rest of the flotsam and jetsam of roadside accumulation, swiftly becoming just like so much frozen road kill. It had been a harsh lesson learnt and unfortunately, *not* one it was going to get a second chance at rectifying.

The lesson that had brought about the circumstance surrounding the disembodied head was that of *assumption*. Most people had heard the old adage about how not to *assume*, as it made an *ass* out of *u* and *me*. For the recently removed head, assumption had simply made it so much dead meat.

The still-warm corpse that belonged to the head was twitching the last of its wasted life away beneath its filthy blanket as its nervous system tried to work out just what was missing and why the signals it was sending to its brain just went one way and nothing came back. It had made one too many assumptions this night. Its error was that it considered the man that currently stood over it as an easy mark. But as the poor sod found out, looks are deceiving. More so in this century, it seemed to the minion who presently inhabited the man. Its last venture upon the mortal realm had been during the Crusades. His kind had been rife back then and had sported amongst the humans with bloody abandon; trouble was though, there had been more guardians back then and his brethren had been all bar wiped out, or at least very nearly. A lucky few had managed to escape through a density portal when one of the master's assassins arrived to deal with the aforementioned and thoroughly hated guardians. The minion hadn't hung around long enough to see the outcome but he didn't hold out much hope for the fat headed, fat bellied and ignorantly interfering humans.

The human man, however, currently hosting the reminiscing minion, was looking down at his bloody handiwork. He wasn't fat at all, quite the opposite in fact. He was dangerously skinny, almost to the point of emaciation, and in the poor lighting of the alley, the corpse that had recently been a whole man hadn't seen the details of his face and body, it saw only the expensive looking suit and shoes. He had noticed straightaway that the dopey old man wasn't wearing a coat. What was he thinking at that time of the morning and in such shitty weather as they were having? *Shame really, I could have used a new coat*, the-soon-to-be corpse thought. Had he but known it, that was his first clue as to his forthcoming lesson. But the cold and desperation pushed that clue and all other helpful logic from the mugger's mind. It just reinforced to

3

him how stupid the old man was – an easy mark. For where expensive clothes were, he figured, there was usually money, maybe some jewelry and maybe, if he was really lucky, even a mobile phone or MP3 player. He could sell those easily enough. But had the light been just a touch more revealing, he would have changed his mind in a heartbeat and hunkered back down in his blankets, burying himself as far away from being noticed as he could, praying that the thing that had walked into his alley, the thing that had once been a mortal man and was now something totally alien, walked on past and didn't look at him. But it wasn't and he didn't. The lesson was about to be learnt.

The minion knew it was close, for other than the fact its master had told it that it was close, it had actually begun to *sense* its prey. It felt it as a slight tingling on the periphery of its mind so it knew it had arrived in the right area. Its master had told it that the man it sought was likely to be moving and living amongst the down-and-outs of society, for the human was making concentrated efforts at avoiding detection by his own people, and the minion should start its search there. First things first though: it needed a body. It had found the first human it came to that was unfortunate enough to be out when the minion had slipped through the density portal opened for it by its master, and it had slid into the human's thoughts with an almost obscene ease. The odds of finding such a host on the first try should have been astronomical but the minion felt its luck was in this day.

It had possessed the sordid little man within moments, made easier by the sheer morass of corruption contained within its mind. Had it taken enough time to consider the aura of the mortal, it would have seen the murky browns and putrid yellows with flashes of a foul black shooting through it like fractured lightning. The minion began to see images – images that had the mortal authorities been even remotely aware of, they would have seen the human incarcerated faster than his feet could have touched the ground. A hundred years ago and it would have seen him lynched by a howling mob – *much more entertaining*, thought the minion, with a cruel glee.

The creature now within the human smiled a rictus grin at the prospect, tearing the flesh about the corners of the mouth as it did so, and it applauded the sick deviant it had inhabited as a kindred spirit. Especially with the graphic and steady stream of mental images now available to the new occupant, divulging the many ways he entertained *his children*, as he thought of them. All these and so much more was contained within the now exposed mind of the decrepit sexual predator. Who would have known it to look at him, though? Whip-thin and slightly graying, with pale, freckled skin with several dark, hair-sprouting moles marring his features. He was sickly pale, with cold damp flesh that had rarely, if ever, seen the sun beyond its face and hands, and maybe forearms at a push. At first glance, dressed, he looked so regular and normal, but on any prolonged or closer examination he actually disturbed people. But other than this genetic burden – one that had prevented him from ever marrying, having any real friends and even fewer acquaintances – his fragile appearance offered him one benefit, and it was this one aspect he used to his full advantage, that of just how harmless and benign he appeared: a smiling, sickly sweet, well-dressed little old man, but one with a voice like liquid honey. It was his compensatory gift, and that alone in his solitary life had served him well enough.

Memories told the creature that because of this gift, along with his uncanny ability to coerce others, its host was a peddler. A merchant of sorts. Only this modern day peddler dealt with property and offered financial products to what he *had* considered was the immensely gullible public and he used this role to infiltrate numerous homes; finding it a most lucrative way to *research* prospects for his own extracurricular activities. Not any more, he didn't, though. He was now an unwilling and extremely terrified passenger, trapped in his own body and experiencing pain like he could only have imagined before; fully aware of everything that he did and felt, but totally helpless and unable to prevent any of it. The possessor smiled again. Now that was what it considered *bad karma*.

The creature enjoyed the torture it inflicted upon its host, all the sweeter for the centuries of denial it had suffered since last tasting mortal life. First it tore out the eyes of its host, not needing the fleshy accouterments, for it utilized its own much more acute and wide-ranging senses, so, grabbing its face with its old yellow, slightly nicotine-stained yet still manicured nails, it tore through the skin of its forehead and dragged inexorably on downwards, piercing the moist, rheumy and definitely squishy eyeballs as it came to them, relishing their wet, gelatinous feel in its hands as it mashed them between its fingers. The anguished and agonized screams sent shivers of pure pleasure through the creature, spurring it on to further sensations. It lashed out and smashed a nearby window and with no care whatsoever for the consequences, grabbed a shard of broken glass and proceeded to stab, slash and slice face, hands, arms and legs; laughing with a ripped raw and savaged throat, unused as it was to the sound issuing forth from it. A sound no human could have made. The sound carried far on the chill night air and people, asleep in their beds, heard the sound subliminally and without understanding, and pulled their blankets tighter about them while shivers of fear pulled their skin tighter and their dreams turned momentarily dark and terrifying.

But the creature knew it couldn't afford to play with the human for long as they had a tendency to die before their usefulness was up, and that meant having to find another. It also knew that its master would take a dim view of such dalliance – very dim – so it shuffled off into the frozen night, leaving its host screaming pitifully in the unfathomably deep and putrid abyss of its own skull.

For hours throughout the night it meticulously trawled the icy and snow-laden streets of Ipswich, guessing that only the unfortunates and the dispossessed would be abroad during that early period between midnight and dawn, and in such foul weather too – weather its master had forewarned them to expect. It found several street dwellers but none of them were the one it sought. Growing impatient, it trudged mechanically from the dockside region where it had begun its hunt and was now crossing from Lower Brook Street to Upper Brook Street and shambling past shops as it did so. Wet and snow-covered, it hastened into the narrow alleyway of St Stephens Church Lane, and had almost shuffled to the end, before the blanket-wrapped individual appeared, stepping suddenly out in front of it from a darkened doorway where it had concealed itself, brandishing its tiny weapon: a small five-inch lock knife. Their eyes locked in what seemed an eternity and a destiny passed between them as the minion laughed and horror filled the mugger's eyes for a split second as the minion lunged at the knife wielder.

Moments later the skinny, possessed man was on his way again, hands dripping blood and heading towards the cold, mist enshrouded graveyard ahead and the shiny glass shopping centre beyond it. Driven in its purpose, the creature continued its search.

Two days earlier saw another bedraggled man staring at a railway schedule with a look of annoyance. Tomas wasn't entirely sure where he was heading. He had simply bought the first ticket to the furthest place from where he was presently. And that was in Gateshead, just outside the Team Valley, where he had kept a tiny flat. Jumping on the metro system at the Metro Centre shopping complex which his flat overlooked, Tomas headed directly for the station, where he would then board the next train departing, wherever it was going, which as it turned out was a long way south, all the way down to Ipswich, with an apparent change at Doncaster. That was fine; it suited him well enough and he was counting the stops between where he was and his final destination. *Too many*, he muttered to himself. *There's just too many bloody chances for one of those dickheads to get on, and that's gonna make it a long fucking journey watching every Tom, Dick and Harriet who boards in case they're one of them.* Tomas was a loose end, and his former employers didn't like them on the loose so they always sent teams out to tie them up. He knew this, having tied a few himself; but Tomas didn't know who exactly they would send, so he would have to stay vigilant. *Keep it together, Tom. Wait for the opportunity to present itself. One always does and you'll know it soon. Just don't piss about when it does. Those bastards are close. I just know it. I can almost smell them, feel them breathing down my blasted neck and I don't fucking like it, no, sir, not one fucking bit.*

He paid his money and grabbed his old military issue rucksack, hoisting it expertly over one shoulder, and with a last look behind him, seeing nothing overly suspicious except some paramedics tending someone who had collapsed, he jogged off towards his platform. He hadn't wanted to keep the rucksack, which bounced against his back as he ran, though he said it every time he packed it away for future use. Too many memories were attached to it in truth, but increasingly and most importantly now, it was the fact it had his name and number stamped the length of it. He knew he should have dumped it years ago but had never gotten around to it, and as those years passed Tomas grew less and less happy about it advertising who he was. But it had been full of his emergency bug out kit, for moments just like he was having.

Tomas eventually found a seat opposite a man who looked even worse than he did, which was impressive going as far as he was concerned. He knew that since he had left the hospital just a few hours ago – though somehow it now seemed longer – his appearance hadn't been exactly high on his priority list. He had lost a little weight for sure. That was to be expected and he noticed that little gem only when he had tried dressing for the first time in the few weeks since the event – as his mind termed it, not yet comfortable with the word explosion, nor how he recovered so completely, so fast; at least bodily – his mind would take a trifle longer, he felt – and finding his favorite combats a little baggy in places that hadn't been before. *The coma diet. Wonder if it'll ever catch on. Though no doubt some scrawny size zero waif in California has already had a go.* Tomas barked a disgusted laugh that turned into a morose grumble, muttering incessantly to himself as he gathered his stuff, tightened his belt and made good his escape. His dark brown hair had grown and he now sported an equally dark and scraggly beard with matching moustache – ideal, he thought, if he was going back in theatre off in the Middle East somewhere as he so frequently did, but it drew unwanted attention on the public transport. Tomas noted how people looked at him sideways; turning their noses up subconsciously at what they considered was a member of the great unwashed, beneath them and no doubt dangerous. Tomas grinned evilly to himself. *Well, they are half right anyway*, though the beard and moustache – both were interspersed with the odd grey hair here and there and were unkempt and greasy – were the least of Tomas's worries at that moment. Apparently they had stopped shaving him as the hospital grew – with a suddenness that went just as unnoticed as did Tomas – increasingly busy as each day passed. His face, once considered ruggedly good-looking though not quite handsome, was now haggard and drawn, with dark circles beneath his hooded eyes, and a slight yellow pallor flushed his normally tanned skin. He knew he had looked worse and definitely felt worse, so he pushed on. A perpetual frown had etched itself upon his already weather-wrinkled forehead, as though since waking he was permanently burdened or deep in thought. Tomas thought he was the epitome of burdened, much of which, however, was self-inflicted by his newly found friend – his conscience. He would, though, have considered himself gifted, blissfully happy and doubly blessed if he only knew what awaited him.

After leaving the hospital in Newcastle, somewhat hurriedly and much to the surprise of the nursing staff, who had only resuscitated him again some two days earlier from his seventh cardiac arrest, he had grabbed whatever he could and planned to dive headlong into the underground world of the socially dispossessed and street dwelling people, oblivious of whatever condition he had; hoping, or so he thought, to lose himself amidst the already lost and forgotten as well as avoiding the prying and possessive hands of his former employer. Enough was enough but they never wanted to hear that, feeling they had proprietary rights over all and everything regarding former special operative and equally former Major Tomas John Arthur Walker. But Tomas felt otherwise. Abandoning his rank, albeit honorary, and all privilege associated to it, he had handed in his resignation, meticulously typed and very concise – such was his way – and delivered it personally. But they hadn't believed him or even wanted to listen to him. Smiling the condescending smiles of those who think they know better, they simply tossed it into a drawer and told him to take all the time off he needed and they would talk about it later. For Tomas though, there wasn't to be a later. The explosion had put paid to that.

The Adversary

Tomas had grown very disillusioned over the last few years of his *career*, though career was not technically the right word: it was more a self-imposed indenture that just happened to pay him for killing people in a sort of muddied and self-justified legal kind of way. Or so he was told. Not that it was about the money: Tomas truly enjoyed what he did, which was why in his early years he had been so damn good at it. But now – he couldn't put his finger on what it was exactly that bugged him – the years of ruthless and invariably pointless slaughter had finally caught up with him and had started to unearth the thing he was totally convinced he hadn't owned. A conscience. This also led him to start breaking rules he had stoically and rigidly held for the last three decades. These had been little rule breakages at first, sliding in over his last few years of service, but nothing disastrous. That happened during his final year and it was a biggy. The fundamental rule that simply said not to get involved in any way shape or form with the mark or their relatives. But she had been the wife of the man he had been ordered to kill, and every fibre of his being told him it was wrong and could only end badly. But for good or ill, he found he just couldn't help himself. It was as though she was comprised of every aspect of every fantasy he had ever had. She had been distraught at the funeral and it had broken Tomas's heart to see her in such pain. He watched himself helplessly go to her, speak to her and be a shoulder for her. Tomas had been kind. He stepped in and comforted her as much as possible over the ensuing weeks. And over the six months following, they had grown closer and closer and Tomas knew a joy he thought he would never know. To the man whose life had been devoted to dealing death and serving his government, a whole new sensation was starting to get the better of him and he truly believed that it was the elusive and oft-maligned sensation that apparently made the world go round – that of love. He really wished later that he hadn't heard of that particular emotion, for it brought with it in unequal amounts twice the pain as it had pleasure – another sensation Tomas was unfamiliar with and would have been happy to remain ignorant of for the rest of his life, however long that was destined to be.

His mother had been overjoyed but his father at first wasn't so sure.

Having served queen and country himself he took a disapproving stance of Tomas's *betrayal* of his duty for a *woman*, abandoning, as he saw it, Her Majesty's finest. Times had been different when he had met Tomas's mother and he never missed a chance to say so. Duty must always come first, family second. For a while Tomas had agreed. But he had seen all too clearly how his family had suffered under both his father's and his own military lifestyle. Father and son had rarely seen each other during Tomas's youth, as both man and boy were both away somewhere at any given time: his father on some mission or other and Tomas away at school. But with the birth of Gwen, his baby sister, things changed. It was a fact that still amazed Tomas: firstly that his father was at home long enough to sire anything; and secondly that his mother had even allowed such carnal activities, her being as she was, almost obsessively religious. But his father had opted to stay home more all the same. Perhaps a daughter had touched him where a son never had. But over the years Tomas realized his family was no more dysfunctional than many others – the majority of families had their baggage. But disapproval aside, Walker senior hadn't stood in his son's way, accepting events he had no control over any more. It was, however, the one day when the four of them were due to meet for dinner that things took a serious turn for the worse.

Tomas had stayed in Newcastle after his last mission because that was where his new fiancée's family still lived and where she had grown up, and if he could, he wanted to keep her off the radar of his employers. How they hadn't discovered what he was up to yet amazed him for a long time, knowing they wouldn't take too well to his union with the widow of one of their targets, who would normally, as part of Tomas's routine clean up, be dead too. But Tomas blindly and conveniently forgot that part, happiness like he had never known turning him into a grinning idiot. Tomas's family came up country to stay with him and they were meeting at a favorite restaurant just outside Eldon Square in Newcastle City and Laura, his delicate blonde bride-to-be, was the last to arrive. When she did, they took their seats outside, making the most of the last of the August sunshine. But they had barely ordered drinks when the first explosion tore through the restaurant. The second and third sent smashed glass, shattered timbers and all other manner of lethal flying fragments ripping through the outside terrace with an air-blistering destructive force, shredding and decimating beyond recognition anything in their path. So powerful was the blast it was actually embedding pieces of oven and cutlery in the buildings opposite. One hundred and thirty-four people died instantly, vaporized by the blasts; and another forty-seven, including pedestrians, drivers of passing cars and occupants of the adjacent buildings were severely wounded, twenty-six of whom would later die in hospital. The remaining survivors would never be the same again, thanks to their crippling wounds and burns. So severe were they that nine more of them would be dead by the end of the year.

Three of the instantly disintegrated were Tomas's parents and future wife, though Tomas was unaware of that fact for the ten days he lay unconscious in intensive care, broken, burnt and left for dead himself. They had found him underneath a scorched and half-melted filing cabinet that had shielded him from much of the blast and it was a mystery as to how the object had been blown that far and not obliterated him itself, but medical matters pressed and soon put paid to that speculation, and he became just another enigma. An enigma brought in by silent soldiers, one of whom camped himself permanently outside his hospital door. Whoever he was, the powers-that-be wanted to make sure he went nowhere and no one got in without full vetting and searching. Tomas's clothes were so scorched and torn by the blast that he remained unidentified for his entire stay and he had absconded before the administrative staff even started looking into who he might have been. But staff shortages and overworked and underpaid doctors and nurses, as well as an unsubtle hint from the military brass to drop it, soon gave them more to worry about than tracking some John Doe's next of kin, so he slipped through the net once more, remaining anonymous as the eponymous John Doe. It was that anonymity that helped save the shattered remains which was all that was left of his now hollow life.

The media reported the carnage as an accidental gas leak and that it was a tragedy on an unparalleled level. The world wanted to believe that it was terrorists but when nobody laid claim to it they had to settle, reluctantly though, for a mere accident, citing the event as one of, if not the worst fatalities of its kind in not only Newcastle's history, but of Great Britain's as a whole. But by the time Tomas had regained consciousness, the news had slipped past, it as it does and moved on to fresher, meatier stories.

Tomas's recovery was swift. So swift in fact that it caught even the medical staff on the hop. One minute he had been plumbed into the life-saving machinery; the next, he was extricating himself from it and demanding an explanation of how he came to be there from the stunned nurses who had been attending him. His wounds had healed so fast and so clearly that an investigation was mounted as to his initial diagnosis and how he came to be in the ICU in the first place. But nobody answered his questions and it was during this time of confusion that Tomas made his assumptions and subsequently took his leave to verify them – much to the consternation of the rapidly-transferred armed guard decamped outside his door to keep an eye on him – who after Tomas made good his exit, found himself decamped in Alaska. Tomas had heard the nurses talking when they thought he was asleep, and had gotten the gist of what had occurred. *Gas leak my arse. Some fucker's going to pay for this. Why did I tell them I was leaving? I should have seen this coming, you stupid blind idiot, Tomas. Curse those bastards and yourself while you're at it, Tomas, for being such a plonker!* Tomas wept and raged silently as he made good his escape. He knew he would have to be fast because the moment they realized he was missing from hospital, the bloodhounds would be out and they would hit all the obvious places such as his home first of all, which was unfortunately right where he had to go. There were some things he needed before disappearing, and stupidly enough he had kept them there. *Of all the daft, crazy and fucking amateurish places*, Tomas kept berating himself repeatedly as he made ready to leave.

Tomas moved with all the speed and expertise his ravaged and battered body would allow him, for although his wounds had healed externally, his body – as he discovered – was still weak and frail from the experience. A lack of any real food and two weeks of relative inactivity will do that to anyone. But Tomas was no stranger to hardship and he pushed his body beyond its limits in order to achieve his goals. It was with moments to spare that he made it out of his diminutive rented flat with the clothes he stood up in and a few essentials he kept in a rucksack for just such occasions. He knew the taxi ride in his hospital gown might raise a few eyebrows but there was no helping some things; he just said he was off to a fancy dress party and hoped the cabby bought it.

He was in and out in less than ten minutes, but after the hour it took to get from the hospital to his flat, it was time enough for the bastards he worked for – *used to, anyway*, Tomas reminded himself angrily – to catch him up, and there were at least four who were going to start the payback for murdering his family and trying, unsuccessfully for them, to murder him; for as sure as eggs were eggs two unmarked black SUVs screeched to a halt outside his apartment block and two people from each leapt out and ran to where Tomas only moments before had speedily and unobtrusively exited, dressed, and bug out pack in hand.

Tomas knew too well that there were no such things as accidents and the little charade that put him in the hospital and his family in the morgue smacked of the type of heavy-handed tactics they employed when they were pissed. Tomas had tripped the switch he had rigged to the shaped devices within his flat and left the contacts in place within the door surround. *Bang goes my deposit*. Tomas chuckled humorlessly at his wry comment and jogged away into the afternoon. It was timed for twenty seconds, giving whoever was stupid enough to break into his place ample time to get themselves slap bang in to the middle of the blast zone. Tomas was considerate that way: he didn't believe in wounding or maiming unnecessarily. Having quite vocally disagreed with the NATO representatives about reducing the caliber of their weapons, he refused to go along with it. Wounding one so another had to stop and take care of them? *What a load of bollocks. That still leaves two soldiers alive who when he recovers, him and his mate will shoot your arse, more so as he's likely to be pissed for being shot in the first place.* Tomas liked his targets dead, irrevocably so. His father had taught him, along with decades of experience, that dead people didn't shoot back, track you down, follow you or try to make your life any more difficult than it no doubt already was. In this case, nor did they report back about their discovery, which was that Tomas was alive, if not so well, and on the loose. Of course, their absence would do that for them but it gave Tomas a day or two and he made the most of it. He had made it barely three hundred yards down the road, heading towards the metro stop, when he heard the concussive blast of the three claymores he had primed going off. *That'll leave a bruise in the morning, I suspect*, Tomas chuckled coldly to himself as he stepped on board the bus.

Tomas hadn't relaxed at all, not even when he had finally sat down on the train and the steady rumble of steel wheel on steel track began its cathartic, soothing and constant rhythm as it picked up speed. He studied the other passengers closely, scowling as he scrutinized their faces, looking for any sign they weren't who they pretended to be. Surely they hadn't gotten wind of his movements already and placed someone on the very train he now found himself on? His paranoia had started early and didn't show any signs of going anywhere in the immediate future. Several of the passengers had shut their eyes already and settled in for the long ride before the train had even left the station; others were busy about their own business and paid him no heed at all. Eventually, satisfied that he was alone amongst civilians, Tomas turned his attention to the furtive looking and scruffily dressed man opposite him. There was something about him that Tomas couldn't quite figure, though he really didn't look well for one thing.

'What's your name, son?' Tomas asked with as much concern as he could muster.

'What?' Furtive looked about, unsure he had heard correctly and that the scary man opposite him was in fact talking to him.

'It's not *what*, it's pardon. Don't they teach you anything these days?' Tomas shook his head sadly. 'I said, What's your name?'

Furtive looked even more worried, if that was at all possible, and what color he had left drained from his face. 'M... Mitchell. Mitchell Deeks. Why?'

Tomas smiled, trying to look reassuring and failing dismally. To Deeks, his effort had a similar effect to that of the crocodile saying to an antelope, 'Why won't you come in for a swim?'

'Well, Mitchell, it looks like a long boring journey and I thought we might pass some of it in light conversation. Why don't you tell me a little bit about yourself? What brings you to be riding this particular train this day?'

'Are you fucking gay or something?'

Tomas kept staring at Deeks but the smile vanished. Tomas's face became as chiseled stone and Deeks pressed himself back into his chair, knowing the moment he said it that it was the wrong thing to say and he should by rights either be bleeding profusely by now or needing to be much further away from the man before him than he could actually get. That had been much of Deeks's problem in the past and was what had brought to him his current lowly position. The fact his mouth said stuff before his brain had sanctioned it was no way to go through life, not for very long anyway.

'You really ought to be careful with that mouth of yours. Here I am, trying to be friendly, and you have to try and ruin it, but...' Tomas sat back and relaxed, making a show of it to put Deeks somewhat at ease, at the back of his mind wondering why he was bothering with the worthless waste of space at all. He drew a blank and put it down to spending too long unconscious, not talking to anyone and missing any current news. His psyche felt the need to converse and Deeks was the captive choice, '...I'm feeling rather forgiving, so we'll pretend you didn't say that and start again, shall we?'

Deeks nodded, realizing he had just dodged a bullet.

'So, where were we?' Tomas recapped softly. 'You were about to tell me why you are heading south of the border.'

Deeks nodded and licked his cracked lips several times, his gaze flicked around the carriage like it was receiving a jolt, and Tomas finally figured the pasty faced youth's problem. He was either coming down or off some drug or other. Tomas leant forward and stared into Deeks's eyes. The pupils confirmed it. Sitting back again, Tomas encouraged the young man to speak with an impatient wave of his hand.

'I… err… well, I have friends in Ipswich…'

Tomas raised his eyebrows, thinking that the prospect of this individual actually having friends was tenuous at best, but he said nothing and let him continue.

'They got me a place down near them. There's a hostel near the docks that helps people like me.' He didn't embellish what *people like me* meant and Tomas didn't pursue it. 'They'll… that is my friends, they'll help keep me clean…' Deeks rubbed his nose as though it suddenly irritated him, '…if you get my drift, man.'

Tomas did, sadly. He'd seen the effects on too many good people who simply couldn't cope with some of the dreadful things they had both seen and done. It was an easy escape, but it turned into a very slippery slope and few ever made it back up, at least not intact.

'So, what? They put you up at this hostel? That's nice of them. Your friends got money?'

Deeks shook his head and explained how his social worker had sorted it out for him. They had even filled out all his forms for him and all he had to do was sign his declaration when he got there and hand over his paperwork, which he duly fished out of the grubby backpack he had stuffed between his feet, to show Tomas as though it were a trophy or something equally valuable.

'So it *does* cost you then?' Tomas glanced at his paperwork and saw that it was something like one hundred and eighty pounds a week for the privilege. *Nobody helps anyone for the sake of it these days: there's always a price and it isn't always money.*

'Yeah, well no, not exactly. I gotta use me benefits so it all gets sorted for me, like. I'm not very good with money.' Deeks laughed a high, nervous girly sound. 'Simple and all really, and they're expecting me either later today or tomorrow, but I got this early train so I should be there this evening. I give them this…' He retrieved his papers from Tomas, '…and sign their whatever, and I get a room and meals. Not bad, eh?' Deeks seemed quite proud of his little arrangement.

The germ of an idea began to form in Tomas's mind.

'No, not bad at all.'

They managed the change at Doncaster and Tomas helped the struggling Deeks find his connection and seat, marveling how he had even made it to the first train, let alone how he was going to find his way from one end of the country to the other. This was the longer part of the trip. The hours trundled boringly by until Tomas, having brought some ropey sandwiches at a vendor before boarding, dug them out and passed one to Deeks. He nodded gratefully, pulled a face that saw the sandwich as some sort of challenge, and put it to one side as he stood up again.

'Sorry, man, nature calls, if you get my drift. I'll be back in a min.'

Tomas watched as Deeks shouldered his dog-eared backpack and weaved his way down to where the train's toilets were, apologizing to nearly everyone he passed as he bounced off them or brushed against them, so unsteady on his feet was he.

Some twenty minutes later he still hadn't made it back, and Tomas grew concerned. *Surely the little toerag hasn't done a runner? I didn't scare him that much, did I?* Maybe he did, but something icy slid along Tomas's spine and settled uncomfortably in his gut, telling him a different story entirely. Shaking his head forlornly, Tomas rose and, grabbing his pack, he set off in the direction of the wayward Deeks.

Outside the toilet door stood an angry looking suit. Some city slicker with all the charm of an oily mackerel. He was thumping on the door and hurling abuse to whoever might have been listening. Tomas closed his eyes briefly, seeking that calm, cold area he found was absolutely necessary when talking to assholes like this. They were naturally a naked flame to his volatile combustibility and it was all he could do not to throttle them on sight. When he opened them again, the Italian suited and cheap, fake jewelry wearing twerp was still hammering on the door. Tomas rolled his shoulders and stepped up in front of him, causing him to stop his thumping mid-swing. He narrowed his piggy eyes as though he couldn't believe what Tomas had just done.

'Fuck off!' the suit drawled and Tomas laughed. The crowd that had gathered about Slick automatically backed up a step without even knowing why they did it. Tomas's hand shot out like a striking cobra and grasped Slick's wrist. A casual Aikido move later and the mouthy suit wearing idiot was on his knees, the other hand trying futilely to release the iron grip Tomas had on him. In fact the more he tried to free himself, the tighter Tomas squeezed until the suit gave up and rolled over, whimpering.

'Good! I thought you were never going to shut up.' But before dealing with the mewling pup at his feet, Tomas turned to the rubberneckers who had gathered and he leveled his indomitable gaze at them all one by one. 'I suggest you all take this cretin's somewhat colorful advice to go about your business. This facility is now closed until further notice.'

A voice shouted from the back, 'Who the fuck are you, then?'

Tomas zoomed in on the direction of the heckler's voice. 'Very brave, aren't you, but I'm the one that's just closed it, and by all means, you are more than welcome to come past me to try and reopen it.' Tomas twisted Slick's wrist for effect and he obligingly screamed right on cue. 'But I really wouldn't advise it.' Tomas's voice and demeanor had taken on a dangerous edge, one that presaged imminent violence, but these were just civilians and they stood little chance against him, even in his weakened state. They simply didn't possess the ruthless capability to inflict damage on another human the way he did. But he didn't want matters to escalate to that extent. It was tiring him out rapidly just holding Slick in place.

Fortunately, the words of bravado were just that: a pathetic little effort at protest just to appease the crowd. Satisfied they had at least made an effort, they dispersed quickly enough, leaving Tomas and Slick alone in the compartment between the carriages where the toilet was located. Slick looked up with watery and fearful eyes, finally accepting he was at the mercy of the grim looking man towering over him. Tomas wondered what to do with him, but his hesitation only gave Slick's limited imagination more time to conjure up a myriad of scenarios, all of which involved copious amounts of pain.

'If I let you go...' Tomas almost felt the relief from Slick at hearing those words, '...I trust you will keep your mouth shut and go back to your seat.'

Slick was nodding even before Tomas had finished. Tomas let him go and Slick grabbed his abused wrist and cradled it to his chest. Tomas caught sight of his bottom lip quivering as he did so.

'You're not crying, are you?' Tomas let as much derision seep into his voice as he could muster, sneering at the boy before him who pretended to be a man. Slick looked up, red eyed. He had indeed been crying, realizing just how close he had come to having his wrist broken by Tomas with the same level of thought as most people had about swatting a bug.

'Get up, will you, and consider this a lesson.' Another of those wonderful life lessons. Slick scrambled to his feet, still clutching his throbbing append-age. 'Lose the ridiculous suit and two-dimensional attitude. The next time you talk down to someone with that towering ego you seem to possess, be ready for the consequences, for as sure as the day is long and night follows that day there *will be* consequences. There always are, and some of them, as you just found out, hurt a lot more than others. The world does not revolve around you and your needs, however much you might think it does. Now you, *fuck off* before I change my mind about you.'

Slick didn't need telling twice; he scuttled away fast enough. Tomas watched him go and imagined that if Slick had possessed a tail, it would be so far between his legs about now he would be able to scratch his nose with it. The moment he was alone though, Tomas turned and pressed his ear to the toilet door. Nothing. That wasn't good. Tomas checked and it was still locked. Silence from inside a locked train toilet didn't bode well at all and Tomas suspected the worst.

A quick glance left and right just to make sure he was still alone, Tomas applied some of his years of experience with doors and seconds later, the toilet door was swinging inwards. Tomas's fears were realized as he took in the scene before him. Quickly stepping in and closing the door behind him, ensuring nobody else saw what he did, Tomas checked Deeks for a pulse, checking both the carotid artery in his neck and the vein in his wrist for confirmation. Nothing. Deeks's eyes were still open but glazed beyond sight now, and the needle hanging limply from his distended forearm vein told all Tomas needed to know. *So much for you staying clean then. That lasted a long time, you prat.* Tomas scrubbed his hand over his unshaven face as he thought about his next move, his meaty hand idly scrunching his lips and beard as he considered his options. With a last look at Deeks, the idea that had germinated in Tomas's mind earlier took root and began to sprout.

Mitchell Deeks stepped off the train at Ipswich Station and with no urgency, made his way off the platform and hailed a taxi the moment he was outside. By the time the cleaner had screamed at the grizzly scene that greeted her when she opened the toilet door, Tomas was nearly at his destination. The police found the battered body of a man slumped in the toilet, his face so badly beaten and lacerated he wasn't even going to be identified by dental records, and the skin on his hands had been cut and seared by what they could only assume was some sort of sharp implement and flame device, eradicating the finger prints. A search of the body revealed nothing more as to the man's identity except a name that was printed on the green rucksack that was found with him: a certain T Walker, along with what looked like a military serial number. It seems this soldier had met with a rather unpleasant end; no doubt the victim of drug dealers or other low life, and the syringe they also found sticking out of him reinforced that hypothesis. It would ensure that the verdict of death by misadventure quickly closed his file once and for all.

Tomas had retained his numerous passports and watertight bag filled with cash from several countries – not much of each, but enough to get by for a week or two when he had switched rucksacks with Deeks. He had to be fast: Slick wasn't the type to keep his big mouth shut for long once he was outside the immediate threat of danger to himself. One of the stupid people, all mouth and trousers and no substance. Tomas wasn't usually in one place any longer than a week or two anyway, nor did he intend to be in Ipswich as long as that even. Just a few days: long enough to solidify his presence as Mitchell Deeks, get his name around a bit, and then Tomas would just disappear one night. That way, by the time the powers-that-be had identified the corpse on the train, which they soon would with DNA (no doubt Deeks had a record of some sort) and the fact that he was someone other than the late lamented Tomas Walker got back to those looking for him – Tomas would be well away again by then, with a trail growing colder than the godforsaken weather he found himself in at present.

ᚦᛖᛗᚨᚾᛟᛗ ᚱᛋᚠᚱᛋ

The minion's main problem was that it didn't really have a clue as to what its prey actually looked like. No one did, not even his master, which meant it was a more time-consuming exercise having to actually investigate every homeless soul it came upon. Too many bodies later and it was growing frustrated. The minion also knew it had to take shelter during the daylight hours so as to not draw any, as yet, unwarranted attention to itself. The only solid information it had was that with its own enhanced senses, it would see the aura that surrounded the mortal. For apparently, this pathetic flesh sack was allegedly one of the last guardians of mortalkind. The minion's master, a powerful entity known only to those who served it as the Adversary, had spent the last thousand years systematically tracking down and annihilating every last guardian born to the Earth and destined to rise to her defense in the event of dire peril to her and her people. It was believed that up until three months ago, they had all perished so the Adversary commenced the next phase of his plan. But unbeknown to everyone, two more suddenly came to the Adversary's attention. That had definitely *not* been part of his plan and he wasn't happy.

Minions had been dispatched to a small island upon the Earth known as Britain, and more had been sent after the other guardian. The one the minion now sought had moved faster than anticipated. One moment it was in the north of the country, then it was on the move. One minion narrowly missed it at the hospital, where it had located its quarry. It had some difficulty, but it had followed its prey to the railway station, where before it could board the train after its quarry, its host had succumbed to a heart failure. By the time it had abandoned its now dead and useless skin suit and found another, the train was long gone. Knowing its destination, however, another minion was sent directly there ahead of the prey, but as of yet, he had not materialized. It needed to narrow its search parameters again for the town was larger than anticipated. The creature scoured every nook and cranny it came across and had trudged far and wide in its search. A grizzly trail of bodies had been left in its wake. After all, it hadn't been told *not* to kill anyone else, just as long as it killed its quarry. Having been deprived of such fun in the mortal realm for so long, it was enjoying itself. It hadn't discriminated in its victims – men, women and children had all succumbed to its pleasures. The feel of flesh rending beneath its fingers was exquisite and the sound of bones snapping sent jolts of pleasure coursing through its spirit. But none of these were its intended quarry and it knew that it had to locate him soon. For one, this body was failing; and for two, it mustn't fail. In the minion's world, failure wasn't an option that was even entertained. A fate considered much worse than mere death awaited the minion should it not succeed. It had seen the result of one such failure, with the minion being slowly turned inside out with flesh shredding and bone pulverizing slowness, and then the ravens and crows were set to feed upon the wet entrails, organs and meat. After they had fed, the minion was then slowly turned back, resurrected and proceeded to go through it all again. The possessed man shuddered as the demonic minion within it did so.

Not having located its prey, the minion tried another tack. It made its way back to the dock side where it had started and was about to try the opposite direction when it suddenly felt an electric tingle ripple all over it. Its prey was close. Much like two magnets that oppose, the feelings grew stronger the closer the two objects came. Its quarry was close, very close. It dropped the dismembered arm it currently held, throwing it back onto the snow-covered corpse it had yanked it off, and made all haste toward the marina area of the dock. *Soon, my lord*, it thought as it ran, *soon*.

Snow didn't really bother Tomas as such, but it had started to irritate him over the years. He had spent more than enough time crawling through it, over it and under it to ignore its bone chilling touch, at least for a time anyway. It hadn't stopped snowing since he had gotten off the train. Not even a sky-emptying downpour, but a long, drawn out, insipid series of flurries that for the most part just melted as they hit the already wet ground. But as the temperature dropped, more and more had begun to settle.

He had checked in at the hostel and, just as Deeks had said, he signed his declaration, watching for any signs that his new identity had been blown. But the staff simply smiled and waited patiently for him. Tomas found himself wondering at the idiot that owned up to any of the questions they asked, but he kept his musings to himself, smiling back in return and handing over the duly signed document. He had practised Mitchell's signature a couple of times before slipping up the side passageway of the hostel and entering the hostel itself by its side door. Done with the tricky stuff, Tomas dumped what he had left of his stuff, which was all he could fit in Deeks's smaller bag, onto the bed in his first floor room, which he found overlooked the street. Tomas spent an hour or so relaxing, or trying to, by just staring out of the window, watching the cars come down to the division in the road, either turning right or left at the series of pedestrian crossings that were barely visible now under the blanketing snow. One hour became six, the cars outside growing fewer and fewer, as Tomas's mind roamed aimlessly, revisiting past events that had led him to his current predicament, as he did most nights in the absence of sleep. His years of training and life-or-death assignments had taught him to sleep so lightly that even a particularly loud insect could wake him. Since the explosion and his imposed coma, where every night his mind had been tortured by the horrors that had led him to that moment, Tomas had found it even harder to sleep. Every time he closed his eyes he was assailed by swarms of disembodied faces, their mouths stretched in silent screams and the eyes filled with accusation. Recently his parents and fiancée had begun to add themselves to the swarm, but prior to that his mind had been filled with the faces of all those he had both murdered on behalf of his bosses, and those who had died through his failure to act. Both played havoc with him, tormenting him with their anguished gazes. They would start small and grow larger and larger as they hurtled towards him at dizzying speeds until Tomas was convinced they were going to slam into him. Mentally, he would flinch from the impending impact which never came. Upon opening his mind's eye again, those ones would be gone, but there would be yet more and more faces spinning towards him from every direction. Every night without fail. If they carried on this way, Tomas knew that soon enough he would be joining them and they would finally have their revenge.

Three-fifteen in the morning and it was only the growling of Tomas's stomach that brought him out of his reverie. The building was silent and upon rising and risking a peek into the hallway, Tomas saw it was also in relative darkness. Assuming the establishment might frown upon late night snacking in their kitchen area, Tomas decided he would slip out and track down some all-night kebab houses. Every town had them, he discovered. Why should this one be any different? Plus, he reasoned, food and an early morning run might tip the scales for his ghosts and set him up for a bit of light, postdawn slumber.

The morning air was chill and crisp to say the least. His breath ghosted from him in warm clouds, thick and grey until it lost the fight with the icy air and vaporized. *Bloody hell, this is like soddin' Siberia out here. I just knew I should have taken Laura away to the Caribbean like I suggested and got married there. If any of this shit had happened there at least I'd be in the bloody warm.* Tomas wasn't really cold though, not in the regular sense. He actually knew well just how cold Siberia was, having carried out an assignment there once that had nearly killed him. It was one of his earlier sniper kills, or was at least supposed to be. A Russian General had embezzled something in the region of fifteen million dollars, which – as could be expected, had upset someone higher up – and was planning to outfit some Chechnian para-military group with all the weapons they could use. But Tomas had found him first. Twelve days and nights he had spent out in the frozen wastes, avoiding detection from helicopters, soldiers with dogs, and an errant pack of wolves that took a liking to him for some reason and had chased him for two days until, eventually getting bored with that game, they had vanished into the chill mists, their haunting and plaintive howls rapidly fading. But if he thought getting in through the general's neurotic, if in the end pointless defenses was hard, it was nothing compared to getting back out again. Tomas liked to be certain of his kills – it was a personal thing – so he had taken to point-blank eliminations wherever possible, and when the general failed to make himself a target, Tomas was left with little choice in the matter. As luck would have it, in the general's compound, chosen specifically for its isolation and inaccessibility, it had been possible. Tomas took out six guards from over five hundred yards away within the space of four minutes. He had timed it so that the circuit they were on gave him a further ten before their counterparts returned. Tomas, in his white thermal ghillie suit, covered the distance in eight minutes. He was helped by the persistent snowfall that had started three days earlier. But, although it covered his tracks and scent, it had hindered his aim and visibility. He also knew that he was in danger of frostbite and hyperthermia if he stayed out much longer. He reached the fence and slipped through with minimal cutting, thanking the powers-that-be that the general hadn't been as paranoid as to utilize a generator and electrify the fence. Planting as many charges as he could in the two minutes remaining, Tomas waited for the other guards. Twin Hochlers with suppressors came to Tomas's hands as he slung his fifty-caliber rifle behind his shoulder. These babies were his weapon of choice, short barreled for close-up work and easy concealment. Moments later, he was running across the yard that led to what his initially unwilling informant had told him was the general's main HQ, with said informant now telling tales to fishes at the bottom of the Adriatic, thus ensuring he didn't double-cross anyone – Tomas left as little as possible to chance. Tomas was always amazed at what people were willing to divulge when pieces of their anatomy were exposed to steam for a prolonged period of time. He didn't really like torture even though he was good at it, but time had been short then and he needed answers quickly. Slowly inflicted third degree burns made Gregory very talkative indeed. If he promised to draw the schematic and tell all he knew, Tomas promised to cool his burns. He never actually said how. By the time Tomas reached his waist, both legs now trembling and raw, Gregory didn't care. He knew what bits were next to burn and that just tipped him over the edge. Then so did Tomas.

Two rounds into the back of the general's head and fifteen through his back and chest ensured he wasn't getting up again. Planting the rest of his charges, Tomas hoped it was enough of a diversion to enable him to reach the general's private chopper that hastily taken satellite imagery had indicated was kept there. As it transpired, it was more than enough time but unfortunately for him, the chopper was only partially fuelled. He hadn't made it much further than thirty miles from the compound before he had to ditch it before it ditched him. Another fifteen days was what it had taken him to trek back on foot to where his extraction point was, *was* being the operative word as he was eight days late. But, as luck had it, and you needed some luck in Tomas's line of work, it was where he had hidden his satellite phone – the only way he had to contact an evac team without the benefit of reaching civilization. That was simply too far on foot. He would never reach anything remotely useful before the cold killed him.

Moderate hyperthermia and stage one frostbite were all he had when the team found him. The wolves had returned the third day while Tomas waited, and had proved to be really useful. The meat was a bit stringy but nutritious all the same, and Tomas had learnt just how warm their fur actually was. He hadn't really wanted to kill any of them, hoping they would simply leave him alone, but it was a harsh world and everything needed to eat. Them and him. He chose the three that seemed to hold back the most, pegging them for the omegas. Those who were at the bottom of the wolves' pecking order. Three skillful shots in rapid succession, and they were down. The rest dispersed, panicked by the sudden turn of events. The dead ones were skinned and meat-stripped before the others returned to investigate. Tomas wasn't overly fond of humans – that much was apparent – but alone and isolated in the Russian wilderness, Tomas felt safe enough to vent his emotions for the wolves he had killed. He wept the entire time he removed their fur and apologized for another day after, speaking to the wolves, beseeching them for what he had to do to them, begging their forgiveness. It tore his soul, and their lupine faces added themselves to his nightly list of ghosts.

Tomas stretched and limbered up in the Ipswich predawn light before setting off. He didn't really have any direction in mind – his run would serve as a reconnoiter for where he was and what surrounded him, as well as some much-needed exercise for his abused body that both anticipated and objected to it in equal measure. Tomas always believed that the first two miles were the worst as his muscles limbered up and expanded. His lungs, which struggled at first – *Being blown up will do that to a person*, Tomas mused as he ran – soon inflated and began their job of pumping oxygen around his battered system as his second wind kicked in. By the fourth mile Tomas was settling into his stride, albeit shakily. He had passed the quayside construction sites and had jogged over the roundabout at the end of the road. Passing a lit up hotel on his right, he continued forwards. There were, not surprisingly, few people about. The odd car crunched past as its tyres compressed the virgin snow that hadn't yet abated, and its ghostly lights came and went in the preternatural morning darkness. Tomas pressed on and veered right at a spectacular looking building that was seemingly made entirely from black glass. Following its curve, Tomas admired it briefly as he ran on. Taking another left, he found himself passing a police station and even that seemed lifeless and dejected as it sat upon the corner of the road with few lights visible. Tomas had little time for the regular police but he presumed they served a purpose in making the public at least feel they were protected, even if they weren't really. *The policebo effect*, Tomas mused as he ran. It looked an uninviting and cheerless sort of building, as did most police stations, and Tomas ran on, right again and up the incline and past the Wolsey Theatre, where his innate direction sense turned him right once more. Tomas reasoned that by keeping his turns now to the right, he would eventually wind up back close to, if not exactly where he started, though he noted disappointedly that he hadn't seen any all-night or early-morning food vendors – not even a greasy burger van – and his stomach was starting to object once more. He slowed down at a boarded up and ugly looking grey building that squatted in the middle of nowhere next to an older building called the Regent Theatre. Tomas considered it a strange combination of architecture and thought it looked like some giant public toilet. Keeping it to his left, Tomas veered down a smaller street with a Chinese restaurant on the corner. But just as he passed a taxi office on his left, a sensation much like having a bucket of ice water dropped on his head fell over Tomas in much the same way. He juddered to an abrupt halt, turning around carefully as he drew in several deep lung-filling breaths, regulating his rapid breathing as fast as he could while his eyes described a three-hundred-and-sixty-degree arc. *Bloody hell! I'm way out of shape. There's no way I should be panting like this with just a few miles under my belt.* Tomas bent forward and rested his hands on his knees, keeping his legs straight as he did so. But *what the hell was that?* The strange sensation swept over Tomas again and this time he leapt away, seeking cover. He saw a small alley beside a shuttered jewelers. Union Street, the sign said, and he plunged into the concealing darkness it afforded. An abandoned or simply parked car sat hulking at the end of the alley and Tomas saw that where it turned sharply left, two more were parked.

His nose told him it was the rear of a kebab shop. He had smelt that familiar scent on more than one occasion: old cooked meat. *Well, meat by default, anyway.* Tomas wrinkled his nose and inhaled deeply, savoring the salty and juicy aroma, conjured as much by his imagination as by the contents of several someone's discarded meals. Only now, it made his stomach growl once more, even louder than before, and his mouth began to salivate slightly. Obviously they had thrown away their meal earlier that night. Perhaps realizing they were late for somewhere and too late to eat, they tossed their Styrofoam cartons of kebab aside, and the cold air had acted like a refrigerator, preserving the freshness of the discarded meat and pitta bread.

But the icy, drenching sensation swept over Tomas for a third time. As he ducked down yet again, his hackles rose on the back of his neck. A casual glance down saw the hairs on his arms and backs of his hands start to lift as though he was suddenly charged with a surplus of static. *This doesn't feel good. What the fuck is going on here?* Tomas looked up carefully, leaning out to the side of the car. As the front and rear windshields were thick with snow he couldn't see through them but he saw no one else. No sign of movement or any sound of anyone approaching. *This is too fucking weird.* But Tomas hadn't stayed alive as long as he had because he didn't pay attention to his instincts. Instincts that were at that precise moment all bar screaming at him that he was in immediate peril. He just didn't know from what. *If I run, I make myself a target for whatever is lurking out there, and I'll be damned if I'm doing that. The bastard can come to me, whoever it is.* Tomas spared a second to check the sky and his watch. Five ten. Still a couple of hours before daylight even started to make an appearance. Tomas risked a dash to the back of the shop and the security of hunkering down between the two parked cars there. It put his back to something solid and gave him a rough one-hundred-and-eighty-degree view. *With breakfast thrown in too. Can't be all bad.* Tomas grabbed the nearest carton and investigated its contents. His work had taught him not to be overly fussy about where his next meal came from and he knew that he could make even the strongest constitutions faint at some of his choices. He didn't even like to think too much about them himself. Still, it was all nourishment and that was what was important to the body and could make all the difference between life and death. *Especially in this bloody weather.* He pulled out a handful of 'stuff' and gave it a cursory inspection. *Not quite what you were expecting, old son, but it's better than a poke in the eye with a sharp stick. And if my bloody stomach doesn't shut up soon, it'll give me away to half the damned town.* On cue, it growled once more. Tomas looked down at it and scowled, as if it understood his ire, and shoved the contents of his hand into his mouth, ignoring any potential blue furry bits, and began to chew. *Chilli sauce and mayo? Damn! Some people have no taste at all.* Eyes scanning constantly for the source of his *feeling*, Tomas ate.

Two very cold and uncomfortable hours passed and still nothing happened. He had felt the icy drenching sensation twice more and each time he fully expected his stalker or stalkers to suddenly appear, weapons in hand. But truth was, in all his years of hunting men, he had never experienced prescience like this. The sun had started to creep up behind some of the buildings, but it really needn't have bothered. The pale and insipid grey diffused light it gave off did little for the frozen morning. The charcoal clouds that hung moodily and heavily in the sky absorbed the majority of the light before it could make it to the ground, leaving whatever was left to dilute itself across the land. *So much for fucking global warming. I thought shit was supposed to be getting hotter, not bloody colder. This sorry little country hasn't had a winter like this for some time and there's gonna be chaos if it doesn't let up. The damn place grinds to a shuddering halt with a couple of inches of fall.* Tomas rolled his eyes skyward. *Looks more like a few feet's worth up there.*

Tomas didn't rush up; he probably couldn't have even if he wanted to after the prolonged stasis but instead, he put his body through the series of exercises he utilized when sniping. Exercises that loosened and flexed muscles that had been held rigid or immobile for too long. They were subtle and didn't require much movement and wouldn't betray a position. Very similar to pilates, Tomas expanded and contracted muscles, ensuring he could move freely when he chose to. He had seen experienced men die because they were still cramped from their firing position when things had turned ugly in the blink of an eye and they couldn't respond in time. There were no second chances in his line of work. Seven forty-two and Tomas had had enough. Feeling agile enough to make a move, he stood slowly, hooded and cold stung eyes watching for the slightest of movements that would betray him to those who sought him. Yet for all his routine exercises, he still felt bones and muscles pop and complain at his abuse of them. *I know it's a damn cliché, but I really am getting too damn old for this shit.*

One or two cars, with their headlights still on, crawled down the narrow road and Tomas heard them before he saw them, pulling into the road he had been overlooking. He watched them until their tail lights disappeared around a distant corner.

A low whisper by Tomas's ear sent sheets of the icy dread he had felt earlier, washing over him in nausea-inducing waves. It was ten times worse than what he had felt before and it was all Tomas could do to hang on to the contents of his impromptu breakfast.

'Veeerreee gooood, Tommmasss… verrreee goood indeeed.' The sibilant hiss that passed for a voice grated in Tomas's ears as though a bowsaw was being pulled back and forth through his head. Tomas winced and screwed his face up in pain. 'Feeew ever notissssss we watch themmm.'

Tomas looked around with panic now. Where was this voice coming from? Diving from his hiding place, Tomas stumbled out into the street, caring little for his safety now, for they – whoever they were, had obviously found him. Confrontation was all he had now.

'The massster has sent meeee to finnd yooooo, Tomassss. I feeel yoooo and your thoughts arrrrr minnne.'

Tomas slammed his back against a wall, as much for support as it was for security. The solidity of the brick gave Tomas a boost, enough to call out a challenge of his own.

'Show yourself, you spineless bastard! If you know anything about me at all, you'll know I don't do your sad little mind games.' Tomas's hand kept dropping to the missing and very much missed leg holster where his Glock used to be. *Old habits could be a pain in the ass sometimes.* Tomas snarled mentally to himself. It wasn't so much the absence of the weapon that irritated him; just that he automatically sought it for the solution to his problem. Of course, the fact it *wasn't* there anyway only added to his annoyance.

'In due cooorse, Tomasssss. Firsssst I will savor yoooorrrr feeaaar.' The voice ripped through Tomas's mind with all the care and consideration of a cluster bomb in a greenhouse. Shards of fragmented glass scorched through his head with every one of the dozen or so voices that made up the one that spoke to him. It seemed to come from every direction all at once, combined from the voices of several people who were all talking just out of sync with each other. Discordant and abrasive to the ear.

'You hiddd wellll, Guardiannnn, buttt now your timmme issss done. Yooooo arrre oouurrrsss.' Tomas flinched as he absorbed the pain and made a decision of his own. He ran.

As he ran, Tomas tried to make sense of the insane words that had assailed him. Hide? Guardian? Theirs? Who were they? What the hell did they mean about being a guardian? A guardian of what? And who exactly was he hiding from other than his employers? Because as sure as water was wet, that voice didn't belong to anyone or anything he was familiar with in all his years of service. Was it a new weapon? If so, it was as sure as shit effective. Not much in the mortal realm bothered Tomas but that voice really didn't sound as if it belonged to anything presently existing within it, and that did bother him.

His quasi religious upbringing recalled tales of devils and demons. More precisely, it was his religious studies' tutor at school and the oft-quoted lectures from his beleaguered mother, spouting tales of scripture at him every time he stepped out of line. Needless to say, he heard quite a few, but he hadn't believed in them then. Why should he now? But he hadn't heard *that* voice back then. Maybe if he had, he would have been a different person and paid some heed to his mother's warnings of where his life would end up. *A bit too late for that now, I guess.* Regret tinged Tomas's thoughts as he part ran part slid across the crossroads at the end of the road. Tomas had more or less regained his bearings and he figured the hostel was only a few hundred yards ahead of him. Passing Chinese and Indian restaurants, shops and offices all in their early morning darkness before their workers surfaced to populate them, he skidded over another crossroads and veered left into Angel Close. And it was just as he entered the car park adjacent to a local swimming bath and just before an imposing looking church, that the gale hit him. The wind hit full on and with so much force it took Tomas's feet from him, making him land on his back with an *oomph* as the breath was driven from his lungs. The now howling gale was unrelenting and was determined to prevent him rising as he tried to do so. Buffeted from all sides by icy blasts, he had to turn his head from side to side just to draw in air to breathe. Caught within and a part of the roaring elemental gale that pummeled his body and ears was the voice from earlier, laughing with an almost hysterical glee at Tomas's efforts. The sound in his ears was akin to standing at the base of a waterfall. It was a constant roar of pure elemental fury that sought to rob Tomas of his senses as much as hammer his body. Tomas heard subliminal screams encapsulated within the torrent of sound, as if the wind itself was made up from millions of screaming souls. Maybe it was.

A glance around him and Tomas's worst fears were realized. Nothing else was affected by this localized tornado. He saw refuse and crisp packets lying unaffected on the ground not twenty yards from where he fought against the attack, for there was little doubt that this was what it was – an attack. Tomas had heard of such things being experimented on since before the First World War. And he knew also that most governments even now had divisions and vast resources dedicated to developing what they called OPP – Offensive Psychic Powers. Sure, they worked on defensive ones too, but like most military concepts, they always considered attack the greater defense. Using a common euphemism, they could communicate their usage of these living weapons without alerting the public to their covert schemes. Sometimes it was easiest to simply hide out in plain sight. After all, everybody had heard the term *black ops*. Little did they know it had a double-barreled meaning. Tomas had very little to do with them in his former life, except he knew that they existed and he had read a little about them. This was what they would have called a *psychic attack*. But never in his wildest dreams did he think it would be as powerful as this or that they would turn that particular resource to hunting him.

'Yoooouuu neeeed to have more ressspeccct, Tomasss. Yooouu cannot run from ussss. Theeerrre issss nowhere on thissss ball of muddd you callll a world that yooooo cannn hide from usssss. Tooodayyy yooooo dieeee!' Tomas fought to look up as the grating voice spoke to him again. It felt like shards of ice were being driven into his spine, one vertebra at a time. Looking up finally, he saw the skinny and emaciated man standing before him. Standing beside the monument to Thomas Slade, a local seafaring man, in front of the door to the church tower. Wind and dirt smashed into Tomas's face and stung his skin and eyes as he struggled to focus on the man. Through watery and grit filled eyes even Tomas could see that there was something wrong with him. Not just wrong, but *wrong*. There was a fundamental wrongness about this individual that poured yet more liquid nitrogen down Tomas's back. But he didn't have time to consider what it was, before the thing spoke again. But as it spoke Tomas saw the significance then of the old woman held tight against the thing's side. Tomas also saw the bloody and clawed hand gripping her by the throat.

'Die easeeee, Tomassss. Yooouuu do nottt want tooo beee responsible for any more innocent deaths. Think of your familllleeee.' Tomas only had a second to ponder what the man meant about any more innocents, when he saw him grip and twist the old woman's throat. With a brief strangled scream and a swift wrench, he tore her head from her shoulders and tossed the body to one side, where it hit the ground with a sickening, bone-crunching thud. The minion then lobbed the dripping head to Tomas. Caught in the vortex around Tomas, it spun a few times before landing bloodily at his feet and staring up accusingly at him. The thing laughed at Tomas's reaction as it saw the look of horror and self-loathing, reinforced with the burden of guilt it knew Tomas felt wash over his features as he stared back at the old woman's head.

The vortex increased to almost cyclone conditions and Tomas was struggling now to remain standing. He leant forward into the gale and could even touch the ground with one hand as the force of the air supported him, but it was only a matter of time before it did more than that. Tomas knew he had mere seconds before it picked him up bodily like so much chaff, and threw him to his doom. Tomas felt fear then. Not the dread fear he had grown used to about his government tracking him – they would be men and women, human, fallible, and not as good as him. Those he could deal with as an occupational hazard. What he faced now was something far greater than that: something other than mortal, and that drew his primal fears from the dark recess where he had secreted them as he grew from child to manhood. The fears of children about bogey men and things under the bed were nearly always banished by the logical, rational world of adulthood, as though by simply denying their existence, therefore it would be so. Because everyone did it, that lent it credibility. So the human race went about its business oblivious to and in terminal denial of the things like that which stood before him: things that were, it seemed, all too real.

With Tomas's fear came an acceptance of those very things he had denied. Things he had spent his life vehemently shying away from. All he knew was that day, that moment. After death? Who cares? Tomas hadn't. Until now. Images flooded his mind like a dam had burst; and everything he had ever heard, seen, read or had been told, assailed his struggling synapse. Amidst the deluge of images, one face grew prominent and it wasn't one he had ever consciously seen before. But unlike the horror he found himself surrounded by, this face seemed beneficent, understanding and a little annoyed. Then it too spoke.

'Come to me!' The voice resonated in his head like a church bell, clear and in perfect pitch. Like music. But it wasn't so much a command as it was a supplication. But before Tomas could make any sense of it, the wind abruptly dropped and he fell flat upon his face, throwing his hands out at the last minute to break his fall before he broke something else. Tomas's senses weren't so dulled by events that he had forgotten the thing before him, and with a practised grace, he sprang back to his feet, ready for whatever might happen next. The creature was still before him but this time, instead of the expression of arrogant joy at Tomas's pending demise, it now wore a look of abject confusion. Tomas guessed that what had just occurred hadn't been on the thing's agenda and it was perplexed by the rapid shift in circumstances. Tomas took the few seconds of confusion to calm his own mind and take several deep breaths to relax his body. The wind had been colder than anything he had ever experienced and as it tore through his clothes it bit at the shrapnel scars, which hadn't yet fully healed on his body. The new skin pulled and itched and it hadn't liked the icy wind raking over it. His lips were still blue and Tomas rubbed his hands vigorously to get the blood flowing again. It was only in the absence of the cold that he realized just how close to death he had come in the icy cyclone.

'*Come to me.*' That was what the voice had said. It still echoed in his mind. And as it did so, it drew other images from his memory. Images of the West Country. Of fields and trees; leafy, winding roads and an image of the Tor, down in Glastonbury. Tomas hadn't been south for many years. The last time had been on one of his many silencing missions. Industrial espionage was one of the prime reasons Tomas was utilized and this one particular executive had crossed that invisible line between international business relations and treason. And irrespective of whether he saw it that way or not, his employer did. And that was what mattered to Tomas. He and the executive, Bill Haynes, had spoken long into the night about the rationale of what he was doing, and Tomas actually found it thoroughly plausible. Of course, the next day, when Bill's wife came down to find herself a widow, the reasons no longer mattered. Tomas had made coffee for himself and the recently-widowed, as she came down that morning, found him sitting in her beautifully constructed, ancient pine-and-brick country kitchen, sipping his coffee.

Her eyes moved with an amazing speed, taking in firstly Tomas, then the still, slightly bleeding corpse of her husband lying on the brick floor a few feet away. She looked back to Tomas with that expression that knew the inevitable was coming but felt the need to try anyway. She stammered tearfully, as she couldn't contain her grief and fear as she spoke her case for life. She tried to convince Tomas that Bill hadn't told her anything about anything. Tomas finished his coffee as she blurted it all out. Calmly placing his mug down, Tomas quietly apologized and before she could react, put two rounds in her chest and one through the bridge of her nose. She fell without another sound.

Tomas had stood, looked down at the dead couple, and put three more rounds into each. It was amazing what some people recovered from. They lived in Bridgewater and that was the last time he had been to that part of the world. Suddenly Tomas felt the urge to revisit.

Firstly though, there was the thing that stood between him and his backpack up in his room. It wasn't much, but it would expedite his journey south. He considered going through the skinny man as it didn't seem too tough, but why take the chance? Tomas turned to run back the way he had come – there was another way around the bath house and either would take him to the hostel entrance. But no sooner had Tomas turned and had taken two steps in the opposite direction when he felt the air brutally knocked from his lungs as both feet from the emaciated creature landed squarely upon his back, driving him down face first into the filthy slush covered ground of the car park. Experience threw Tomas into a roll as he hit, which was just as well, as a foot stamped hard down on the spot where his head should have been. Tomas kept rolling and came up in a fighting crouch, facing the now snarling creature that had once been a man and was now only a thing just a few feet away from him. Tomas saw for the first time the true extent of what had become of the creature before him.

'What the...?' The thing leapt and Tomas feinted left before rolling right; and the creature sailed past, issuing a hideous shriek of frustration as it raked out its claws and caught only fresh air. Tomas backed up out of range and took stock of the unprecedented and totally surreal situation. Running was out of the question: this thing seemed too fast for that. The only option left for the immediate was through it. The creature spun and regarded Tomas with a hate-filled expression. The lack of eyes and the ruined sockets only made it all the more menacing and grotesque. A mouthful of broken teeth and blood spat out torrents of abuse and threats at Tomas with a voice like broken glass, and that scaled every range – so much so it had dogs barking at one point. Tomas winced slightly but words didn't really hurt, and he smiled slightly as he found his calm return whilst watching the minion scream and gesticulate.

Tomas rolled his shoulders and squared his feet, dropping his centre of gravity and solidifying his body, as he had been taught by his army fitness instructor, who had had more Aikido black belts tucked away than he could wave a stick at, though he never wore them or had anything on show to demonstrate his prowess. He simply said he didn't need to. He knew, that was enough.

The thing that had once been a man hissed and spat like a scorched cat and Tomas simply laughed at it. The minion wasn't used to this reaction: it was used to fear and terror, not humor. No matter, it would soon be over and the master would reward it. It had found the quarry and it would die, for no mere mortal could stand toe to toe with a servant of the Adversary plucked directly from the Domain, and hope to live.

'Time to dieee, mortaaaal!'

Again Tomas laughed and the minion cocked its head sideways, birdlike and quizzical, not at all pleased about how its prey was behaving.

'You have to be joking, right?' Tomas responded with genuine curiosity. 'If you know anything about me, you'll know I don't do dying, least not when someone else says so and not while I have a breath left in my body. Trust me: I go, you go.'

'Brave words, mortal,' it hissed, 'but you do nottt know whattt faces you.'

Tomas chuckled and looked the minion up and down. *Time for a bit of psychology.* 'Got a good guess, you worthless piece of shit, but if you think you're the man for the job, you are sorely mistaken. Bigger and uglier people have tried and failed, plus I've seen more meat on a vegetarian's toothbrush than what's attached to your frame, and if you think you can take me with your bare hands you're even more deluded than I gave you credit for. You might be good with defenseless little old ladies, which I might add is one thing you'll be paying for, but for me: I've been shot, stabbed, poisoned and even blown up. The fact I'm still here ought to tell you something, you scrawny little runt. Now are you going to do something or do you intend to talk me to death or wait until I die of boredom?'

Sure enough, the minion's face screwed up in response, hate and fury warring for dominance on its ruined features. Tomas had seen the strength that belied its appearance as it had dispatched the old woman – he would have to watch that. But angry things make stupid mistakes and it seemed this thing had an ego – an easily bruised one at that – and any second now it was going to do the stupid thing Tomas was waiting for. Tomas lightened his breathing and subtly assured himself of his footing, knowing he was only going to get one shot at this. Again, Tomas rolled his shoulders, loosening the muscles there and, smiling benignly, he waited.

The minion was livid and a crimson haze had begun to obscure its vision. Rage at this mortal's defiance had caused the body it inhabited to hemorrhage. It wasn't going to last much longer. Rage and fear of failure at this close juncture drove it forward with a howl of pure venom. Hands like claws were outstretched as it rushed the waiting Tomas. For there was no longer any flesh upon the fingers – just bony digits where the skin and muscle had been gnawed off, much to the anguish of the body's impotent passenger, who felt every bite. Then the bones were filed against brick and pavement to turn them into the razorlike barbs that were now directed at Tomas, eager to stab and tear at his flesh too. The minion could almost feel the sensation of his quarry's soft organs impaled upon its talons. But for all its inhuman strength and ancient knowledge, it didn't know truly who it faced. Arrogance blinded it to the death in its quarry's eyes. For although it was a killer by its nature, so too was Tomas. Those who had seen him behave as he was at that moment would have been very concerned. Those who had faced this countenance of Tomas Walker rarely saw much else again afterwards. When it necessitated it, he was a cold, disciplined and ruthless killer, unlike the howling creature rushing him, though Tomas was taken aback by its speed: it was fast for something so decrepit looking.

Milliseconds before the creature reached him, Tomas exploded into action like a giant striking cobra. Stepping into the minion's charge whilst retaining his solid body mass, Tomas snapped out his right arm; hand out, heel first. The soft pad of his hand, now reinforced by the two bones of forearm and driven by the muscles of his entire body, smashed into the minion's face in an unexpected blow that sent bone and teeth spraying in all directions. Most importantly though, it turned the nasal bone into an organic dagger, which rammed home straight into the brain of the body. The head stopped immediately and the body had little choice but to follow its momentum. The legs flew upwards and then gravity took over. Tomas assisted it by slamming the body down hard and was rewarded by the satisfying sound of several bones snapping under the brutal impact, the neck being one of them. The body, for all it was worth now, was truly dead. It moved now purely at the will of the minion that inhabited it, but even that was momentarily stunned by the sudden turn of events. Absently it knew it could still manipulate the corpse to its will, but in truth it would need another vessel, and soon, if it was to complete its mission. But it was still too confused by Tomas's reaction to fully appreciate the severity of its condition. It didn't even see the boot that was plummeting towards its face with lethal speed. The heel crunched clean through the skull as though it were simply a large melon. Bone and brain matter splashed out and discolored the already dirty slush of the ground. Tomas, however, was taking no chances that the thing was going to get up again so he repeated the move several times until all that was left above the shoulders was a crunchy puddle. It didn't stop the body though and it writhed and flopped like a grotesque landed fish. Bony talons still reached for Tomas in futile desperation. Tomas stepped back and watched it for a second before solving even that issue. Several firm kicks later, and the broken body lay still enough to satisfy him. Tomas looked at it for several minutes as he organized his travel plans.

'I'm not sure what you were, old son. I'm not even sure I want to know, but if you can still hear me, you tell whoever it was who sent you as you go screaming back to whatever hell you crawled out of, that you don't fuck with Tomas Walker, fucker.' With a parting kick Tomas turned and ran off. He didn't want to be associated with the grizzly mess when day broke properly and the stinking corpse was invariably found. He was in no mood for police or questions. Within the hour he expected to be on a train and heading south.

As it began to snow again, Tomas cursed and pulled his collar up against the chance of wet flakes slipping down his already sweaty back. 'Bloody weather,' Tomas muttered as he jogged back to the hostel. Slipping in unobtrusively, he gathered what belongings he wanted to take and slipped back out into the cold grey morning, quickly losing himself in the increasingly heavy snowfall. He never saw the woman who stepped out of her car after pulling in only moments after Tomas had jogged out of sight and who, upon seeing the strange shape laying on the path, had gone over to investigate. Tomas also failed to see the same woman twitch as though she had been shocked. Her head convulsed twice and then she stood unnaturally still, only her hair moving in the icy breeze. Warm clouds of breath spewed from her mouth. Breath, breath and breath, then…nothing. Her chest simply stopped rising and falling with the rhythmic pulse of life but her next move was to reach up and drag her long and red-painted nails down her face, raking her flesh and taking her eyes with them. Tomas never heard the inhuman scream of agony and loss, rage, fear and frustration as he made his way with all haste to the nearest railway station.

ᚦᛗᚨᚠᚾᛣᛗ ᚱᛋᚠᚱᛂ

This journey had been uneventful; a fact Tomas was thoroughly grateful for. With all he had to think about, assimilate and try to comprehend about the last thirty-six hours, he really didn't want any more excitement for a while. A long while, preferably. At some point, which had slipped by unnoticed by the preoccupied Tomas, it had stopped snowing, though it was hard to get too excited as it had only turned into a miserable and totally depressing sleety rain. It had been a long and thought provoking journey, made longer by the snoring of the two men opposite him. He had slept in barracks and tents and even under the stars with men who snored, but they paled against these two. Every time he kicked the seat to interrupt them, they paused, snorted and were silent for all of five minutes before they commenced all over again, the decibel level slowly increasing until one or the other snorted, grunted then started all over again. These were big, portly, bordering on obese, ruddy cheeked tweed wearing men who Tomas assumed were part of the agricultural community. Farmers most like, and after the initial humor of how stereotyped they were, their animalistic grunting began to grate. Surely they weren't going to sleep all the way? But they did and it did little for Tomas's humor when he finally disembarked. He wasn't even sure which station he had gotten off at at first – he simply had to get off and get some air, plus he couldn't tolerate the hideous noise from the two men any longer. Tomas kept his head down and avoided all the CCTV cameras he could see as he left the station. Those he couldn't avoid, he just obscured his face from as he made his way out of the nearest available exit. The rain only added to his foul demeanor as he soon found himself sodden and wishing for the snow to come back. At least, Tomas figured, snow didn't make you quite as wet as the driving rain he found himself hustling off in.

By the time he had made his way out of the built up parts of town and was yomping up some deserted country lane, Tomas came to realize just why the West Country was so lush, verdant and simply so damn green. *It's so bloody wet! I hate it. What is it with me and weather? If it's not snow it's rain, if not rain it's hail or some other equally unsavory shit falling out of the sky on me. If I wasn't already bloody neurotic, I'd be inclined to think this was personal.* As Tomas wrung water out of his coat under the shelter of some spreading oak for the umpteenth time, he mumbled to himself once more: *I'd have been bloody drier if I'd swum here.*

After two wet and uncomfortable days of journeying with shanks's pony, Tomas found himself on the outskirts of Glastonbury wishing it had a station so he could have saved himself all this faffing about, comparatively uncertain as to how he came to be there anyway as he was sure it wasn't his intended destination. He thought he was heading towards Bridgewater. *Hmmm. Close but no cigar. Musta made a wrong one somewhere. Your internal GPS must be on the fritz, old son; that's what you get for walking and thinking when you should just concentrate on where you're going, Tom, you Muppet.* But Tomas knew that he had a lot to think about – deep thoughts about serious things. He hadn't killed in some time and the memory of what he had done to the creature that had stalked and attacked him back in Ipswich disturbed him on a level he never knew he possessed. The fact that it wasn't a man, or even human any more, was apparent, or should have been to anyone with a more open mind than he had. Tomas, however, had seen the devastating results of a wide range of chemical and bacterial agents when they had been utilized against the numerous groups and individuals his former employers considered appropriate, and their effects could be misconstrued for something supernatural. *It's possible, I suppose.* But he had never seen anything like what he fought. *What chemical made a person do that to themselves? And for that level of injury. He seemed to feel no pain either. Had to be drugs of some description though – one of those new chemical cocktails that the fucking idle rich kept getting invented on an almost weekly basis to use as recreation. Yeah, that's got to be it. Speed or some kind of amphetamine laced with dog food or who knew what. Perhaps even some sort of hallucinogen or nerve agent.* Considering the mess and damage he had left behind, maybe the authorities would investigate. Tomas smiled wryly to himself at that thought. *Then again, maybe not.* Deep down in Tomas's psyche he already had his suspicions, but his rational mind refused to voice them for fear of making them a reality. *You're probably losing it, Tom, that's all there is to it. You have got to get a grip – you may not be so lucky next time, and you ought to stop talking to yourself, too.* Tomas chuckled loudly to himself then at the thought of berating himself in the third person, and slogged on in the unrelenting drizzle. Two days' hiking and sleeping rough came and went in a blur for the former operative. So preoccupied with recent events, he let his legs function on autopilot and take him where they would. Tomas suddenly remembered seeing a town sign a mile or two behind him – he wasn't sure – but he was sure it read: Glastonbury.

Not only did he find himself on the edge of the ancient and evocative town, but he also found himself inexplicably standing before the majestic and globally renowned Glastonbury Tor. Tomas knew it for what it was. There weren't many people who hadn't heard of it, in fact, but few had stood before it like Tomas was now. In fact, it was the first time Tomas had actually stood before it himself. He'd flown over it on many an occasion when spending time at Salisbury; and for all his worldly travels and for all the places he had seen, as the sun began to set behind the Tor – as it did from Tomas's current vantage point – it seemed the most incredible sight. It was all he could do to just stand there and stare at it. Ensorcelled as he was by the corona of light cast by the setting sun and illuminated behind the stone edifice, Tomas completely forgot about the rain, even as it ran in chilly rivulets down his neck. He also failed to notice the incongruity of the fact that it was hacking down with rain and the sky should have been thick with dirty, ash grey clouds. How was it that the sun managed to appear through it all, just there and just then to provide him with this mystical light show? Tomas was filled with enigmatic images of knights and the warriors of Arthur's England; of Merlin and Morgan; Guinevere – for whom his little sister had been partially named – and Isolde. All that was missing were rousing trumpets and glorious choirs exhorting their majesty. Tomas's imagination made up for that, though. The mystical isle of Avalon called to him, entwining him with invisible strands of diaphanous desire, and without his conscious mind even realizing what his body was doing, Tomas was putting one foot before the other, and before too long, he was making his way up the muddy and slippery slope of the Tor itself.

Tomas slipped and instinctively threw out a hand to steady himself, but his feet had other ideas and he dropped unceremoniously onto his butt and began to slide back down the rain drenched slope. Something sharp snagged Tomas's hand as it scrambled for purchase, and tore a long gash across his palm. Tomas cursed and pulled it protectively to his chest: an action which did little to slow his descent. With a last effort, Tomas slammed his boot heel down and it thankfully caught on a grassy hump before his now bruised behind thumped over it.

'Shit! Fuck! Goddamn it… what the hell am I doing here anyway? Why —'

'Be quiet, Tomas, and stop moaning. While you're at it, stop swearing. Get up, turn around and continue to the top, as you were doing so well.'

Tomas stopped all right. He swiveled his head round as far as it would go, both ways. Even an owl would have been impressed. Tomas sought the origin of the voice but all he was met with were the continuing blank stares of slowly-chewing sheep. He looked down the Tor and leant back to look up. There was nobody to be seen, anywhere.

'Oh no, not again,' Tomas whimpered to himself. A lesser man might have broken down then and succumbed to his fate, but Tomas was made of, thankfully, sterner stuff, and with a glance at his torn hand he shook the surface blood free, licked the wound clean, and spat out the bloody mess. And after tearing a makeshift bandage from one of the three shirts in his pack, Tomas braced himself to carry on downwards. Eyes narrowed to determined slits, he drew in a deep breath and set out. This time, he was choosier about his hand and footholds, which saw him reach the bottom in better condition than if he had continued his freefall.

'This is most tiresome, you know. I have gone to great lengths to get you here. The least you could do is continue to the top as asked.' The voice sounded weary and nothing like the sibilant hissing of the other one, but Tomas was taking no chances and as soon as his feet reached level ground he was off running. Not far from the base was a muddy area set aside for cars to park, for those who liked to drive to the Tor rather than take the long walk. Tomas was halfway across it when he risked a look back, just to see if someone or something was following him. He breathed a ragged sigh of relief that there wasn't, but he had done the one thing he always told himself off for doing, which was look back when you should be looking where you're going when moving at speed.

In the split second he had taken his eye off where he was going, someone had erected a steel wall directly before him and Tomas ran full on into it.

'Oooof, urghh.' Splash. The wind was again blasted from Tomas's body and he was dumped back onto his bruised rump, though it was somewhat cooled from the deep puddle he landed in, filthy water sloshing him all over. Tomas just sat there, with brown rivulets trickling down his face, as his body fought to regain its equilibrium.

'Now why do you make me have to come after you? I credited you with more sense than you are presently showing; not to mention that it can't be very pleasant sitting in that puddle like that. Here, take my hand! Let me help you up.'

The source of the voice was directly before him and Tomas scrubbed puddle water from his eyes to see who or what was talking to him. What he saw standing there made his jaw drop and his mind take several backward steps in tactical retreat as it tried to make sense of it. Had it not, insanity may have swallowed him whole there and then. Tomas saw the hand extended and what it was attached to. Tomas's body took over where his mind left off and he found himself scrambling backwards through several more puddles in a bid to put some distance between himself and what he was looking at. But Tomas was disheartened when it too took several powerful strides to once again loom over him. 'I really suggest you take my hand and get up from there before someone sees you.'

Tomas looked frantically past the figure overshadowing him to see three other people entering the car park – one man alone and a young couple who were giggling and talking quietly together, all three paying Tomas no attention at all. Nor the predicament he was in. Tomas looked back at the figure standing patiently over him with the hand still on offer, and asked the first question his questing mind could formulate. 'What are you?' From a huddled spot at the back of his mind, Tomas was vaguely disappointed by the high pitch and fear that caused his voice to tremble and squeak. Tomas had seen a lot of late and even his colorful past couldn't allow his mind to accept what it was looking at.

'Is that the best question you can come up with… after all these years of doubt and disbelief and vehement denial? I despair. Maybe the others were right and this is pointless. But I would not be here now if I didn't disagree and hold out some level of hope that you are the man we seek. Now, come take my hand and get up. I'd rather not talk to you sitting there in the mud like an animal. You're not an animal, are you?'

'I... err... I'm not, no.' Tomas felt his mind begin to claw its way back, sufficient at least to formulate the words he sought. *I take back my earlier comments, Tom! You have already lost it and this is just a figment of your fractured, deluded mind.* Tomas spoke softly inside the confines of his mind, firm in the belief it was where he would be spending the rest of his days.

The entity before him shook its head sadly. 'You haven't lost it yet, Tomas Walker, though the day is not yet over and many things can still be arranged.'

Tomas looked anywhere but at the speaking entity. 'You're in my head. You're not real, so just go away and leave me alone!'

'Really? I'm not real? So what exactly did you run into?'

Tomas's eyes flicked around in his head, the whites showing more prominently than before. 'I tripped.'

Tomas cast his glance over to the trio of hikers, much like a drowning man might cast a line hoping someone would grab it and reel him to safety. He wasn't so lucky. 'Hey! You over there! Can you see him?' Tomas pointed wildly at the entity but the couple just looked at him as though he were some sort of leper. They muttered together and abruptly veered away from the madman sitting in the puddle and waving his arms about. The other, an older man, just looked curiously at Tomas. A mixture of pity and concern graced his weathered expression; but he didn't look at the space the entity currently occupied – not one solitary glance. It was proof enough for Tomas.

'There! See? You have to be in my head. Those people don't see you, therefore you don't exist.'

The entity actually looked bewildered, staring first at Tomas and then at the spectators, or spectator, as the other two had hustled away quite sharpish. 'I don't believe it; you're actually rationalizing me? You were quite happy to consider what that minion was, only a few days ago now, the one that attacked you, remember? But you can't get your head around me? After all you were taught at that school you attended and all your mother told you when she read to you as a child, sitting upon your bed, patiently answering all your questions. You *do* remember that, don't you?'

Tomas did, but how did this entity know it? Though if Tomas put two and two together he would have had his answer already. But mortal minds weren't ready to accept as much phenomena as Tomas had experienced over the previous seventy-two hours and his was taking a little time out. This naturally made his leaps of assumption a bit slow in coming.

'Post-traumatic stress disorder?' Tomas suggested hopefully, praying that in diagnosing himself the image might disappear. But again, no such luck.

'Sorry, but no. Now I really need you to get up and get a hold of yourself. I'm real enough, believe me. But we have to talk, just not about your mental state and the PTSD you don't have. Though it's not to say you don't have problems, there are other, considerably bigger ones than yours, and it's those we need to talk about, sooner rather than later.' Once more the entity reached out a helping hand, which again Tomas just looked at. He knew that whilst he refused to touch it, he couldn't be real. But once he took the proffered hand and it proved to be as solid as his own, then he would have no choice but to accept who and what stood before him.

'Are you okay, chief?' The hiker who had looked at Tomas with sympathy earlier had wandered over and now stood as close to Tomas as the entity. In fact only a few feet separated the two. The man was in his early sixties by Tomas's estimation, and he looked up at the old man as though he had just pulled him back from the brink of somewhere particularly lethal. The man was wearing a yellow waterproof, red woolly hat, and jeans. Thick socks tucked into sturdy walking boots completed the image. But it was the kindly face with the scraggly grey beard that Tomas stared at, smiling lamely.

'You need a hand, pal?' Tomas saw the concern that creased his smiley eyes and the toothy grin that bisected the beard. He couldn't believe he was being rescued. 'It ain't any good you sittin' in that there mud like that; a wet arse ain't all that funny not unless you is a bit peculiar. You're not a bit peculiar, are you?' Tomas absently shook his head.

'Good, though it ain't like we don't get right funny old grockles down 'ere some days. Place seems to attract 'em like flies to you know what.' His rolling West Country accent gave his speech an almost hypnotic, musical quality. But the help Tomas needed was in the form of verification, and he needed it badly.

'You can see him, right? Him! There!' Tomas waved an erratically pointing digit at the entity, who just stood, arms folded over its massive chest and smiling down at Tomas smugly. But the ageing hippie just smiled down at Tomas with as much sympathy as he could muster after looking both left and right, then shrugging.

'Sorry, pal, 'fraid not. Can't see a soul but you, but hey, don't take offense like. Each to their own, I say. If you're seein' people who ain't there, well that's just fine by me. We get a lot of them down 'ere too. In fact there's a load of 'em back in town convinced, I tell ya, that they talk to dead people and all other kinds a folk. There's one who chats with some Egyptian top knob or somesuch, and others who natter to Mayan chiefs, Chinese philosophers, Native Americans and even one to Odin himself.' The hippie shook his head and chuckled good naturedly. 'How is it though that they never chat to regular folks, like Bill the baker or Fred, the man who emptied the shitholes? It's always some king, queen, prince or ancient shamanic type. You gotta wonder, don't ya? Who do you see?'

Tomas just stared at the now broadly-smiling entity before him before answering,'You don't really want to know, trust me. If you can't see him, we'll leave it at that. Probably for the best, anyway.' Tomas was suddenly weary, the fight gone from him.

'Fair enough. Now can I offer you a lift somewhere? I'm back off to Totnes meself but I can drop you somewhere along the way if that'll be of any help.'

Tomas was about to answer that that would be great, but before he could get a word out, the entity spoke first.

'Tomas! Shut up! You don't want a lift. Say no thank you to the nice old man and let him be about his business: he doesn't have long left.'

Tomas stared wide-eyed at the entity in sudden alarm at the last comment, then back to the ageing hippie. 'I... er... no, no thank you, I'm good. I must have slipped and hit my head, that's all.' *Hard,* Tomas grumbled to himself. 'Are you sure you can't see anyone there?' Tomas tried one last time in desperation before his sanity finally left him on some extended vacation. Tomas averted his gaze from the disapproving stare the entity was leveling at him as he asked his last question, and waited for the hippie to respond.

'Sorry, chum, no can do. But if you're okay I'll leave you to it, then. But my personal recommendation is not to sit in puddles for too long; it obviously has a strange effect on you. Good luck, and see you on the other side.' With a wave, the hippie turned away and strolled back to an equally aged red Ford Fiesta.

Sooner than you think, I reckon.

'Now, now, Tomas, who are we to determine the fate of another?' This time it was Tomas's turn to look bemused as he regarded the figure still patiently standing before him.

'Anyway, fun time over. It's time we got down to business, and I've humored you long enough. Now are you going to take my hand and allow me to help in a dignified sort of way, or am I going to have to treat you like a child and drag you out by the scruff of your neck? Your choice, last chance.' The hand came forward once more.

'Here goes nothing.' Tomas reached out and grasped the hand.

Now Tomas was unclear exactly what happened next. He remembered the warm, dry contact of his hand against the solid flesh of the entity, sadly confirming the reality of it, and then there was a rush of warmth, a blinding golden flash and a thunderous boom, both so loud and bright that it left Tomas's eyes blinded temporarily and his ears ringing. When both senses returned to normal a few moments afterwards, Tomas found himself in darkness, though not total darkness. Just to add to his misery, the entity was still with him, sitting cross-legged upon the ground a few feet away and glowing softly. Just enough light came off him to illuminate them both. Tomas groaned, shook his head and sank down opposite. Belatedly noticing that he was now in fact dry and warm, Tomas again stared wide-eyed at the entity, who smiled back, acknowledging Tomas's discovery and pointing to a spot on the ground before them from where sprang up a small blue flame. It grew and grew until it was the size of a small camp fire, and it threw off enough heat to take any further chill from Tomas's bones; though he absently noticed that it burnt no fuel and left no scorch mark on the soil. It just sort of, floated there.

'Neat trick,' Tomas remarked dryly.

'Thought you might like it. You feeling any more stable now? Up for a little chat?'

Tomas nodded, not trusting himself to say too much as he anchored his psyche to the inside of his skull once more.

'Good. Now the excitement has passed, I'm inclined to start with a few introductions, though I know who you are. You *have* to be wondering who I am.'

'I was going to say that you must be brighter than you look, but in light of you being all glowy already, perhaps I won't bother,' Tomas responded dryly.

The entity laughed softly. 'Nice to see your humor returning; you're going to need that.'

Tomas raised his eyebrows as though he'd heard that line before, and it rarely boded well for him when he did. Trouble was, it had an adverse effect on Tomas's humor when he thought he was about to get screwed. 'Suppose you get on with it. Who are you then and where the fuck are we now?'

The entity glowered at Tomas's sudden attitude adjustment, but let it slide without rebuke. 'To answer one then the other; I am Michael, War Master of the Celestial Host, Chief Herald of the Empire and Ruler of the

Warriors of the Fourth Province. You, however, probably know of me as Archangel Michael.'

Tomas's expression was unreadable but stunned surprise lurked just beneath the surface, though before he could say anything, Michael continued, 'As to the where, well I thought a spot of peace and quiet might be called for, away from prying eyes and ears. We sit atop Silbury Hill at present, and considering the gravity of what we need to discuss, the fewer beings who overhear us the better. Plus... I quite like it here.' Michael sat back and waited for all that to sink in before continuing – curious to see as to how Tomas was going to react.

'Okay. Michael. Just Michael? Is that like Madonna, Prince or Sting? Why don't people do surnames these days? What's the big deal really?' Tomas sensed he was about to ramble. The enormity of what he had just been told had not fully registered yet, though he had suspected as much. But denial held the full impact from him, so he just shut up. Michael, however, took it as his cue to carry on, ignoring Tomas's inane question for what it was.

'Now I know you're not a historian, theologian or even much of a scholar, but I know you know a little about your people's past.' Tomas nodded slowly as Michael continued, 'Well, you don't document things too well. It seems the truth and the facts are things to manipulate subject to who is doing the recording and, to be honest, you've gotten so much of it wrong it's a miracle you've survived as long as you have as a race. There are things abroad that should have annihilated your kind already but by the grace of a few individuals whom I'll touch upon later; your species has slipped below the radar for the last few thousand years. But your luck on that front has just come to an end.'

Tomas was curious now by the tone of Michael's voice. Gone was the light but slightly frustrated timbre; it was now the manner of someone who had something truly serious to say. He had heard the same voices from generals and government officials when they ordered some really serious mission, one that had wide-ranging and potentially catastrophic consequences.

Tomas wasn't really sure he wanted to hear any more, for he was pretty sure he wasn't going to like it. 'Fair enough. Now I'm sure you hear this a lot, but what brings you down to my little shitpile of a life, grant me a fucking personal appearance and all, disrupt my already crappy existence and bother me in person, as if my life isn't fucking weird enough already?' Anger. Tomas recognized it in his response. It was a secure bastion for him and he had spent a large part of his life hiding within it. So long, in fact, he didn't know if he could exist without it. It was akin to armor for him and it prevented the scum and detritus of the world from reaching him, but what Tomas hadn't noticed over the years, at least not until he faced the prospect of sharing his life with another, was that it prevented him from interacting with that selfsame world in a way that actually connected him to it. Years of detachment and aloofness distanced him from his fellow humans and had dampened his natural empathy to the point of virtual non-existence, so much so that when he was faced with matters concerning them, he grew indifferent and cold – and angry. A part of him knew it was wrong and he didn't know why he did it, but it was so ingrained in him he realized he didn't know how to *not* be angry any more. Of course, recent events hadn't helped in that department much either. Blown up by his own people, his family wiped out as callously and as easily as a human armed with a canister of bug killer sprays an insect; then to cap it, he finds himself tracked, stalked and attacked by a thing – a creature from somewhere Tomas would rather not think about, who somehow possessed a human and sought his pain-filled and bloody death. So Tomas felt somewhat vindicated in his responses; and being so filled with such an angry retaliatory rage, all logical and rational reason was, for now at least, beyond him.

Michael's frown deepened and the steeldust grey of his eyes turned thunderous. In the space of a heartbeat, Tomas saw how the entity before him could transform from a benign-appearing albeit heavily armed being who conformed with many of the preconceived ideas of what an archangel should look like (though Tomas did note, a little after the fact, that he didn't have any wings or the frequently depicted halo), into an awesome warrior whose countenance was designed to inspire fear. His light intensified and Tomas felt a dangerous tension fill the air. He got the distinct impression he had hacked him off somewhat. *Bloody hell, I wonder what he's like when he's really pissed?*

'You don't want to find that out, Tomas...' but before he could continue, Tomas flared up himself. Michael seemed to know how to push his buttons and rummaging round in his head was definitely one of them.

'Will you keep out of my fucking head! I don't how they do it where you come from, but where I come from what's in there isn't fucking public property. They are my thoughts so keep your fucking nose out or...'

Tomas's blazing reaction had apparently found one of Michael's buttons. He stood up like a roaring God. His previous lack of wings was soon compensated for as several snapped out from behind him, surrounding him with a dazzling corona of retina-searing glowing golden feathers. Already possessing a Herculean physique, he almost doubled in size, as if he had absorbed a ton of steroids. His flesh blazed from within and blue fire rippled off him like a living sheath. A massive meaty hand shot out like fork lightning and grabbed Tomas by the throat and lifted. Tomas was yanked up so fast he thought his head was going to pop right off his spinal column. Michael pulled him in close until they were almost nose to nose, before yelling at him in a voice like the engine of a jet aircraft firing up in his face.

'Enough!' Michael's bellow nearly ruptured his eardrums and the force of it resembled the cyclone he had been trapped in days before. 'Do not try my patience, mortal! There are two ways we can do this and you really wouldn't like one of them. Your life will not end with your tongue ripped out, nor will it inhibit what is expected of you. I was not against this plan, unlike many of my brethren, who see your kind as a waste of time and effort, fully deserving of whatever fate you have brought upon yourselves. Unfortunately, that particular fate now involves the rest of us, and you *humans* are required to participate. You in particular.'

The way Michael said the word human, Tomas realized then the gulf between the being that was with minimal effort, all bar strangling him several feet off the ground; and himself. Tomas likened it to one of those WWF wrestlers holding a kitten up by the throat, so helpless did Tomas suddenly feel. At least while he still could feel. Sensation was slipping away from him as he hung by his neck and his spinal cord was slowly stretched. He wanted to say something in protest, but all he managed was a garbled croak. But that and the fact his face had turned purple must have snapped the enraged Michael out of his terrifying outburst. He dropped Tomas as though he were suddenly white hot. And Tomas, for his part, dropped to the ground like a sack of bones, gasping and clutching his throat.

'You have *no* idea who or what we are, you puny mortal, so do not presume to even *think* about threatening me. I will do as I see fit in these matters. We are at war, you silly little creature, and the enemy has had too long to ingratiate himself amongst your kind. If I need to see what goes on inside your tiny skull, I will do so. Do you understand me?' Tomas just nodded as his throat was too raw still to do much more than croak.

'Your species has no real comprehension of what we are or what we are capable of. You imagine we exist by some ludicrous fabrication drawn from the minds of a few individuals who perhaps had the misfortune to have slightly more insight than the rest of your species. In your kind's case, a little knowledge was a fatally dangerous thing and it has allowed the dilemma we all now face to come to pass.'

Tomas just croaked and lay where he fell, rubbing his crushed neck, way past caring what the talking nightlight was blathering on about. Michael stopped talking and looked down at Tomas properly for the first time since dropping him. A flash of pain and sadness flickered over Michael's features as he realized, belatedly, what he had done, and knew that he shouldn't have.

'You see? This is what your kind does to ours, and you and I are not the worst of them.' Michael knelt by Tomas and slowly prised his hands away from his throat so he could inspect the damage. Tomas couldn't have stopped him if he wanted to: Michael's strength was phenomenal. But he did notice that Michael's wings had vanished again and his glow had softened to that of the earlier diffused glow. 'We bring out the worst in each other somehow and I don't know the why or how of it, but that's what happens. Look, I'm sorry about that...' Tomas just stared back: there was little else he could do. '...Here, allow me.' Michael laid the same hand over Tomas's neck as he had used to lift and crush it. A soft violet glow emanated from beneath his skin and it spread out to surround Tomas's bruised and battered neck. A few seconds was all it took and Michael sat back, resuming the spot he occupied when they first arrived. Tomas slowly sat up, examining and flexing his neck and throat, which no longer hurt at all. It was as good as new, well, sort of, at least as good as it was before being crunched. Tomas was satisfied if not entirely happy about the episode.

'Thanks, I think. Which sounds odd to me, thanking you for fixing something you very nearly broke in the first place.'

Michael at least had the good grace to seem contrite as he lowered his head shamefully while Tomas spoke. He looked up when Tomas stopped speaking, eyes hooded, wondering what he was going to do or say next. When Tomas didn't speak, Michael took it as his cue to apologize properly.

'Forgive me. I shouldn't have lost my temper like that. It has been too long since we interacted with mortalkind – and then it wasn't exactly success- ful – that we, or in this instance, I, seem to have forgotten how to treat you. Much like you and your animals, I suppose. You mistreat them because you can. You consider them inferior to you so you treat them as such. We are more similar than we would like to think, or admit. It's a wonder we managed to evolve at all.'

Tomas knew it wasn't all the angel's fault; he could be an antagonistic bastard himself at times. That came just as easy to Tomas as breathing, only this time he had picked the wrong time, and individual, to put his parts on with, and had paid the price for it. That was a memory that would stay with him for a long time to come. Sitting down himself, facing Michael, they were back to square one. Then, after sighing deeply, Tomas spoke first.

'So what's this all about, Michael. You mentioned a war. Our people spend most of their waking existence at war with someone or another. I suspect that's human nature. Put two people in the same room and before long they'll be fighting. Disagreeing about something, probably religion.' Tomas was silent for a second as that thought sunk in. 'That does seem to cause the majority of our problems. Ironic, don't you think?'

Michael nodded slowly and deliberately, appreciating it perhaps more than Tomas knew. But he knew also that he was there to explain their more immediate problem as best he could to this human, so he took a deep breath and started, unsure of how he was going make the enormity of what he had to tell him believable, for he could hardly believe it all himself.

'It's probably not a coincidence that you cite religion as your biggest problem, because on so many levels I suppose it is. But that is, in a convoluted way, our fault to begin with. We set you up, filled you full of ideas – not all good ones I hasten to add – and then we let you go.' Michael's voice was sombre, almost regretful and wistful. It was as though by talking about it he could go back and redress the problem. He knew he couldn't do that though, so he sighed, leant forward and looked hard at Tomas.

'There is no way I can bring you up to speed on your planet's history in the short time we have available. Suffice to say the last ten thousand years haven't been ones we are very proud of.'

Tomas felt the germ of a handful of questions starting to form on his lips but he bit them back. If time was of the essence, then he would listen to the briefing and keep his mouth shut: what harm could a few minutes of silence do him? Tomas was about to find that out.

'Creatures roamed your world millions of your years ago, that were fearsome to behold. You have recently termed them dinosaurs and categorized them in the early history of your world as giant reptiles. That is partly true, but not all them were the peabrained monsters you have portrayed them as. Many of them were sentient beings, exiled from other worlds long before man came onto the scene. They were exiled for a reason. Their crimes were so heinous and unacceptable to the higher races and to the Absolutes, that they were to never call a living planet home ever again. But it is a large multiverse and some found their way back here.'

Tomas's mind was spinning. Archaeology and paleontology were being turned on their heads in the space of a few sentences by a walking myth in its own right. He dreaded with every molecule what Michael was going to say next but at the same time he was transfixed with a curiosity that astounded even him. He was hearing something profound from the lips of a being that the majority of the world denied the existence of – even the churches and organized religions of the world, and this had to be worth hearing. So Tomas leant forward too, encouraging Michael to press on.

'These creatures, for want of a more precise description, used their vast powers and, believe me, they were vast, to summon others of their brethren. The Winslow meteorite crater, as you call it, was the impact site of one of the exiled gaols. Fragments of its structure are now scattered across your world, insidiously resonating their dark energy out, infecting the populace with the evil inherent in many of them. That changed your world then. These creatures accepted the sacrifice inherent in their grand scheme, and you are finding many of their remains, still. Several hundred survived the cataclysm and the ice age that followed, and it was they who set about engineering humanity from the mixed gene pool that existed on this juvenile planet.'

Tomas was agog. This was a creation myth that would have tongues wagging for another millennium and have scholars as well as theologians pulling their hair out and screaming *heresy* until they asphyxiated. But without the aid of time travel, what did they really know? Some poor git spent his life dedicated to his theory, and when nobody could actually disprove it, it became credible and part of future learning, just by default. It may not have been right, but what did that matter as long as it fitted in with the thinking of the time? So that was close enough, apparently. Theory: the word should be removed from the planet's language for all the crap it has gotten its inhabitants into. Michael watched Tomas, looking for some sign that what he was saying was registering, and when Tomas encouraged him to continue, he took

59

it that it *was*, and picked up his tale where he left it.

'Hundreds of centuries passed and they remained unnoticed by us, for we were not expecting them to even be this close to us, let alone scheming and plotting; interfering with your growth and evolution. But by the time we grew aware of your species, the exiles had done much of their work. They had set themselves up as gods: powerful entities who influenced your kind in savage and sorcerous ways. Who knows what would have become of you had we not intervened when we did. There were numerous battles fought all over your world and many of them have made into your mythology and literature, though not many of them are technically accurate. But poetic license, as you call it, seems to have been preferable to the truth. Your species has an uncanny ability for misinterpretation. What you call Chinese whispers over the last ten thousand years have done your kind no favors whatsoever. When you developed free will...'

Tomas perked up at that seemingly ambiguous and throwaway comment. 'What do you mean *developed*? Didn't we have it to start with? Isn't it a human prerogative?'

Michael shook his head, his face betraying the difficulty he was having condensing and simplifying what he considered was a lengthy and impossible subject for one of Tomas's lowly mortal capability. 'Perhaps it would have wound up that way, but your evolution to the state you find yourselves in now isn't necessarily the way you would have evolved had you been left to your own devices. Much like my own kin and those who preceded us, your genetic potential was still in a latent flux while your planet grew to maturity.'

Tomas's eyes started to glaze over a little at what Michael was implying. He was so far out of his depth here it was almost beyond belief. This seemed akin to explaining thermodynamics to a river shrimp: okay, so it understood hot and cold, but more than that...?

'You still with me?' Michael had noted Tomas's blank expression, but Tomas nodded anyway and encouraged him to continue. Maybe it would all fit into place later, when his stretched synapse had taken time to assimilate what he was hearing.

'Very well. The creatures your scientists have called dinosaurs, weren't, as I said before, all you think they were. Many of them were fell creatures, evil beyond your ability to comprehend, and they knew how to manipulate DNA and the molecular structure of the fabric of your world. Many of them eventually taught your kind to do similar things.'

Michael scowled as though he hadn't liked or agreed with that strategy, adding it to the seemingly long list of their other crimes.

'In a nutshell, your kind were designed and grown, brought on to become a slave race for the exiles.' Michael saw the horror in Tomas's eyes at what that meant. 'Easy, Tomas.' Michael raised a calming hand before explaining what that meant.

'You are physically no different than you would have eventually become, but free will wasn't a part of your initial make-up. We encouraged that later after the great battle that saw your people liberated and many of the exiles returned to their various gaols, dead or so defeated they ran before they could either be captured or killed. It shames me that many are still technically on the loose...' Tomas's eyes widened again, '...but they have been untraceable for so many centuries now that my brethren have all bar forgotten about them.'

'What about this free will thing you started on about? Easy with the rest, let me get my head around one thing at a time, assuming I can even do that, but let's give it a whirl. What's the worst that can happen? No, don't answer that, just the free will bit – please.'

'You'd be surprised how many times that has been said and instantly regretted, Tomas, for I assure you, there is worse out there that would give your wildest nightmares nightmares. But for now, as I was saying, free will. When your species was set free, we stepped in to govern you and you saw us as yet more gods. But over the millennia that followed, and as you grew to an acceptable sentience, factions developed and your species went to war with itself over whose deity was superior, and this escalated at an unprecedented rate. You surpassed even our period of barbarism. With such bloodshed came numerous power plays, from both your kind and mine. We deemed this totally unacceptable and after many great and heated councils, it was ruled by the Absolutes and the greater majority – thank the host – that we withdraw completely from your world and leave you to grow your own way. We did this by seeding the idea amongst you that there was only *one* deity… one great and mighty ruler of all you would come to know. We did this in the mistaken belief that if there was only one deity, you could not diversify and war amongst yourselves about whose was superior, seeing as there was only supposed to be one. Look how wrong we were, yet again.'

This time, Tomas could understand Michael's sadness and point of view. It didn't sit well with Tomas either. But he did understand the free will clause then. Maybe humanity would have been better off without it.

'So, if I've got this right, you're saying that by allowing humanity free will, we have chosen to reinterpret all we have been given to believe, and twist it to our own ends…reinventing and manipulating doctrine and rules to suit those who are doing the twisting. And the big prize at the end of that, that there is no God. You made that bit of world-changing information up to get out of your responsibilities? Did I get that about right? I'm not quite sure how that sounded out loud.'

But Michael nodded and lowered his head shamefully. 'Close enough,' he said finally. 'Your species began to fall into two distinct categories, though even before that your dual natures were apparent to us. But we hoped, naively, that they would assimilate and the greater good would overcome your cruel and oft times evil base natures. How wrong were we!'

This time, it was Tomas's turn to nod.

'I presume you have heard of our brother, Lucifer?' This woke Tomas up with a start. This was a name he knew almost as much as Michael's, and hearing it rarely meant anything good was afoot. So he asked cautiously, suspicion dripping from his voice, 'Why? What does this *Lucifer* have to do with what's happening? 'Cos you know that's not a name spoken in the highest regard very often down here. Usually it's only by the heavy metal brigade or some deluded devil worshipper who has seen one too many movies.'

Michael sat back and rested his palms on the ground, as though relaxing after a particularly difficult task had been completed and he now faced an easier one. He rolled his head on his shoulders, loosening muscles in his neck and shoulders, before talking again – a habit Tomas found uncannily familiar. 'Much and nothing.'

Tomas frowned at the cryptic answer. 'Look now. This isn't the time to go getting all mysterious and start babbling in riddles like what your kind is renowned for. Just give me a straight answer: it's about all I can handle right now. Simple and straightforward. K I S S – Keep It Simple, Stupid. That's what my old chap used to say and that's how I like it. Technical can come later.'

'Fair enough, but it isn't such a simple explanation.'

'Typical. It rarely is, but try anyway.' Tomas sat back and emulated Michael.

'Very well. To cut another extremely long story short, Lucifer was amongst the ruling council of elders, as much as I and my brothers and sisters were also. There were sixty-four in total. Sixty of us and four honorary slots for the Absolutes.' Michael saw the curious look from Tomas at the mention of these Absolutes, knowing he had spoken of them before. 'I'll come to who they are shortly, trust me.' So Tomas acquiesced, uneasily.

'When your dual natures manifested and it was seen that unless something was done about you, your planet was going to fail and the entire system would collapse; we felt that we should intervene...'

'Again,' Tomas slipped in sardonically. Michael scowled at the rebuke but carried on all the same, knowing Tomas wasn't far off the mark, though that didn't make it any easier for the big archangel to bear.

'...and steer matters back on course. That said, Lucifer and twenty-nine others volunteered to *step down* and set up an alternative council. A council that was one complete planet back and one designed with the sole purpose of controlling and managing your darker sides. Your good souls would continue to evolve forwards; but the repeat offenders and those not yet ready for the trials they were set to encounter here on Earth, along with those who committed atrocities and who railed against your spiritual growth, they needed to go elsewhere.'

An image flashed in Tomas's mind and the automatic answer of his mother came unbidden, softly to his lips. 'Hell?' Tomas suggested quietly, not really expecting the answer he got.

'Yes and no.'

Tomas bit back a sharp retort at the archangel's ambiguity. 'Look, what did we agree? Less of the bloody riddles.'

Michael scowled at Tomas's language: it was clear he didn't approve of a lot of his more colorful vocabulary. *Tough shit*, thought Tomas out of spite. Michael scowled again, obviously still reading Tomas's mind even after being asked not to. The former soldier smiled cruelly and with an icy glee at the discomfort he caused the archangel. *'Two can play at that game, old son,'* Tomas thought to Michael. *'You'll find I'm a quick learner.'* Tomas smiled mentally but Michael just smiled back and answered him out loud in a voice with all the finality of a morgue door slamming shut.

'You'll have to be. Your life depends on it.'

Tomas had been waiting for the juicy bit that answered some of the question about what it all had to do with him. At least he now knew his life hung in the balance. All he needed to find out now was how and what he could do about it.

'Nice. It always seems to be my life as the ultimate price. Why can't it just be something a little less pertinent for once? It's always all or bloody nothing. It doesn't matter who it is shouting the odds; the price is always my bloody life.' Tomas shook his head and scrubbed his hands over his face. Fatigue was creeping up on him now as the adrenaline of his more recent revelations had begun to ebb. Powerful, deadly, yet sensitive fingers manipulated the muscles of his cheeks and neck as though he could rejuvenate them, at least long enough to hear out the mythological entity sitting opposite him, atop a mysterious hill in the middle of nowhere. *Be careful what you wish for,*

Tom: this is probably what you get for saying you were tired of your life and the mundanity of it all. There's nothing fucking mundane about this. It's like I just fell into the goddamn fucking Twilight Zone. Maybe I'll wake up back in the hospital soon and find this has all been just some horrible, realistic and a far too fucking lucid dream.

Michael spoke softly, then with a voice that could rip steel doors off their hinges, and Tomas sat back involuntarily, suddenly on edge at the barely suspended menace that dripped from every word the archangel spoke.

'I'm only going to say this once more, Tomas, before I rip that tongue from your head. There is no need for you to utilize such graphic expletives on such a regular basis. It is neither big nor clever. Now I appreciate social habits and the need to put on a charade for others, but I am not so easily impressed. Language is one of the areas where your people have ground to something of a halt. Think back to your earlier literary exponents and see how they worshipped language and explored its many and numerous variations, and compare that to your present-day scribes. I'm afraid there is no comparison. Who is your present-day equivalent to William Shakespeare, for one example?' Tomas tried to say something but Michael stopped him. 'No, don't try to answer: you'll only sully the words with something puerile and inane. But trust me when I tell you that whatever we require of you, as I said before, it could still be accomplished without a tongue in your head. Your call.'

'I'll do my best, though I can't promise a total abandonment of too many years of bad habits. But I'll give it a go if it makes you happy. Meet you halfway, if you will. What do you say? Can I keep my tongue a bit longer? After all, there may be a few ladies who'll miss it.' Tomas wanted to keep his voice light but he knew it fell on deaf ears and Michael just glowered at him much like a parent looks with exasperation on their naughty child. Tomas grinned mischievously and thought a change of subject might slide him past this particular gripe, so he steered it back to their earlier subject.

'Okay, so tell me about this Lucifer chap. I take it he's the one responsible for all this chaos?' Tomas once more leant in to Michael, overdoing his interest in the answer.

'Yes and no.' Michael grinned back evilly at Tomas, knowing the answer would annoy him all over again, but Tomas didn't bite this time, though Michael did see his jaw clench and his teeth press tighter together as he continued his crocodile smile.

'Really? How does that work then?' Tomas answered with an overexaggerated civility which wasn't lost on Michael, who seemed to enjoy the game on some deeper level.

'He is not directly responsible, but due to his mysterious absence, another has taken control and assumed power in Lucifer's stead. That, my friend, is where our problem lies. A being we know only as the Adversary has usurped the council and has initiated a series of events that we were too arrogantly blind to see until too late.'

Tomas leapt upon the last two words. 'What do you mean, *too late*? If it's too bl…too late, then why are we even having this conversation?' Anger almost made Tomas slip in an expletive but he caught himself, though he found himself growing steadily and increasingly curious as to just what was happening in the greater beyond. Michael looked pained at Tomas's question and hesitated answering him. 'What's up? What have I said now?' Tomas asked, concerned now at Michael's reaction.

Michael stood and paced a few feet away from Tomas before turning back to face him, hands clasped militarily behind his back as he looked down upon the scruffy human.

'This is pointless. There is just so much you need to know and I… we don't have the time to cover all there is. You must understand, Tomas, much of what I am telling you has occurred over millennia, not just the last few months. There are plots within plots and weaves within weaves. There have been defections on both sides because of what the Adversary has done and is proposing to do. The multiverse stands upon the brink of a change so mind-bendingly vast and destructive that even those who went on ahead of us can barely comprehend the audacity of it. And they want me to explain it to you in a matter of hours. I'm not sure who is the craziest here: them for suggesting it, me for trying to do it or you for wanting to know more about it. None of it looks as though it's going to end well, but like you humans have been known to say; more bad things are likely to happen when good people do nothing.'

Tomas had picked up on a few words yet again and questioned them, oblivious to the archangel's defeated tone. 'You mean *universe*, surely?'

Michael seemed to come back to himself and focused on Tomas again, steely blue eyes weighing him shrewdly before he spoke. 'No, Tomas, I mean what I say. Simply this: universe implies there is only one, whereas multiverse says correctly that there are many, many verses out beyond your sphere of understanding. There are even many beyond ours. You have no idea how insignificant we all are in the grand scheme of things. But better that, than to face what will happen should the Adversary succeed.'

Tomas felt very small suddenly and fear gripped his belly again at the expression on the archangel's face and the way Michael delivered his last words: they had a dread finality to them. There was a question left hanging there, just waiting to be asked, and Tomas knew he was going to have to ask it.

'Go on then. What will happen should this Adversary succeed?' Tomas screwed his face up in anticipation of the answer much the same as though he were waiting for a blow to the head. In fact, the answer was not dissimilar in its effect.

'There is no easy way to phrase the enormity of it so that you will comprehend it; but in essence, every planet, in every solar system, along with every star in every galaxy, will have the living energy sucked from it. Look up, Tomas, and tell me what you see.'

Michael waved a hand and before Tomas's eyes, the sky turned dark and his vision was full of stars. The constellations sparkled and flashed like diamonds cast upon a velvet backdrop, and Tomas knew that many of those twinkling lights were suns in distant parts of space that may not even exist any more even as their dying light was still traveling to them. But Tomas diligently surveyed the magical scene before him and answered simply, 'Stars?'

Astrologically, it was an inadequate answer. There was so much more there and so little mortalkind understood. For all their technology and telescopes, radio antennae and high-tech gadgetry, we were just pissing in the wind, guessing at the majority of what we saw and making more assumptions and theories than were really good for us; and to Tomas's mind, about things that were of no relevance to the vast majority of the populace whatsoever. Okay, so there was bacteria in moondust, or not – it didn't matter. It didn't feed the starving or answer the next sustainable fuel question or reverse global warming. To Tomas's way of thinking, it was simply a way for a handful of antisocial intellectuals to spend their countries' wealth and avoid getting a real job. He never got the whole *space* thing, not when nobody even had half a clue as to what was at the bottom of our own oceans. Michael, however, rolled his eyes as though he expected no better an answer, and made the vision disappear once more.

'And all you see there, Tomas, is as though you were looking up at it from the inside of a grain of sand. A grain of sand in desert so vast you could not even comprehend it.'

It was Tomas's turn to scowl now. 'You say that a lot. Apparently we don't seem able to comprehend very much, according to you, but I think you might be surprised at just what we can get our tiny minds around. After all, it's only been a few hours and I've pretty much gotten used to you. Well, sort of, but I get it. It's big, and…?' Tomas's voice was edgy; his words were steel coated with annoyance. He didn't like being treated like an inferior youth. Tomas had an uncanny knack for adaptability and he felt himself adjusting to the surrealism of his predicament with a speed that secretly surprised even him. It was almost as if he had finally found the calling his life had been in training for. Almost.

'And, my friend,' Michael finished for him, 'the Adversary has discovered a way to destroy it and absorb that energy for himself. Now if you think we are powerful, you have yet to see a Drakarim in all its glory…'

'A what?' Tomas interjected at yet another new addition to the saga.

But Michael ignored his plaintive and equally peeved reaction, '... or meet the Absolutes, though that will be rectified soon enough, but there are beings out there who make us look like your own Neolithic cavemen by comparison. But should the Adversary succeed, he will overshadow even them, growing to an omnipotent state whose power will know no bounds. You can't imagine what a creature with that sort of power would be capable of. Bad doesn't even start to describe the horrors the multiverse would face and, just to add to our woes, it all starts right here, with the death of your world. Here is where the cataclysmic chain reaction begins, though I should say *begun*, unless we can stop him; or more to the point, unless you stop him.' Tomas's jaw dropped and his eyes bugged out at what the now smug looking archangel just implied. 'Well, you did ask.'

The rollercoaster ride of discovery Tomas found himself hurtling along on didn't show any signs of slowing up just yet, but a touch of realism plateaued it momentarily. A rumbling stomach that was convinced its throat had been cut brought Tomas back down to earth.

'Don't suppose you've got a sandwich stashed about your person somewhere, have you? All this revelatory stuff is hungry work, apparently, and for the love of me, I can't even remember the last decent meal I had.'

Although it wasn't food, the look of shock and embarrassment on Michael's face was almost satisfaction enough. *Almost*. Tomas began to wonder how much of his life was governed by that word. *Almost*. Tomas cast his mind adrift while the angel responded to his request for food and found that much of his world owed a little something to *almost*. Latterly it was the fact he had almost died. Almost but not quite *and that was unfortunate for whoever was responsible for that*. For, lodged implacably at the forgotten recess of his mind, secured in the area with the warning signs that read: do not enter, dangerous, enter at your own risk and a plethora of other equally graphic warnings, was the seed of vengeance. Whoever had done the deed was going to pay in ways that hadn't even been invented yet and Tomas was going to enjoy every brutal and pain-filled second of it. There was to be no quick, over-and-done-with explosion for them. Oh no, it was going to be drawn out and laborious; leaving absolutely no doubt whatsoever what it was they were screaming in agony for. Tomas pulled away from that thought quickly: it didn't do to dwell in there. He slammed the door shut, leaving it pounding on the inside for release like some reluctant prisoner. But he didn't do it quickly enough to prohibit Michael getting a look at the darker side of his companion. Not that it was merely dark; it was more like a black hole, devoid of anything, and sucking any and all light that was foolish enough to come too close, straight down its hungry gullet. Tomas knew he could lose his sanity in there in a heartbeat if he allowed that side of him even the tiniest toehold on his psyche. Michael didn't say anything. What was there to say? He knew Tomas was dangerous – that much was apparent by the more obvious history. But Michael also knew Tomas to be one of the last guardians of the world and to be one of those, an element of what they were guarding against was required. For how could evil be recognized without understanding what evil is. It was the guardian's role in each lifetime to stand against such darkness; only the Adversary had been meticulous in eradicating the planet's guardians throughout time, dispatching them in each incarnation and ideally preventing them from procreating and seeding their DNA and guardianship to their descendants. Tomas was an enigma on that front and Michael frowned as his reservations about using him came flooding back. They had suddenly appeared in the celestial warrior's consciousness and angels were dispatched immediately to track them down. These scouts fell swiftly to the enemy as they too had sensed Tomas and the other guardian, and the enemy had directed minions to kill them at all costs. It was only by Tomas's own hand that he had escaped the clutches of one of the Adversary's assassins and brought himself within the sphere of awareness of Michael – though the big archangel hoped the twins were having as much luck, if not more, with the other one as he was having with the mortal who was tucking into the food he had provided belatedly. Michael kept forgetting the fragility of Tomas's species and their rapacious appetites, not just for food. They devoured everything in their path like swarms of destructive locusts. Except unlike locusts, who had their place in the natural order and were controlled, albeit in part by humanity itself, humanity had no such restraint and nor did it have any natural predators. Not until now, anyway. They were in for something of a surprise.

Tomas finished, sat back and belched, rubbing chicken fat from his lips and face with the back of his hand, then wiping them on his filthy jeans.

'Feel be er for that?' Michael asked, not really interested.

'Is the Pope Catholic?' Tomas responded automatically, and Michael shrugged.

'Hard to say, really. I suppose it needs a definition on Catholicism. Suffice to say, I imagine he believes he is and that's what counts, I suppose.'

Tomas just stared at him until he found his tongue again. 'Forget I spoke. I don't want another theological debate just yet: my mind's in enough trouble as it is. Why don't we just wrap this up and see where that leaves us. You were about to tell me what exactly it is you want me to do, not that I reckon I'm going to be much help in this fu— , sorry, screwed up disaster of biblical proportions. But tell me anyway – curious minds are literally dying to know.'

Tomas sat back, replete, and waited for Michael to start up again with his summarized lecturing. Michael sighed, knowing his infinite patience was being tested by this mortal and knowing also that he failed himself for letting him get to him. It was a sign of the times, it seemed, that everything was breaking down and even the elevated races were succumbing to the drain the Adversary was leveling against the cosmos. Michael knew that before too long, they would be powerless to stop him and even the Absolutes would fall. When that happened, it was all over.

'Contrary to what you may have believed about our omnipotence, we weren't. We could not be in all places at once; nothing, as far as we know, can. It seemed to be a convenient contrivance of your kind to instill fear and awe amongst your populace. Still, that said, we could soon find out events as we utilized lesser entities to keep track of things. Much like your generals would have used an adjutant to advise and carry out menial tasks to keep things moving, so did we. So did Lucifer. But it seems that Lucifer's second had aspirations above his station.'

'So? Couldn't happen to a nicer fella. That's what you get for being a sneaky lying son of a bitch in the first place. Some other sneaky lying son of a bitch always wants to shove you out of the way and get a piece of the action themselves. We call it politics.'

'Yeah, well, like I said before, where do you think you got most of your ideas from? We didn't always set the best example, but that's the way of it, unfortunately. There's no going back to put it right: all we can do is try to set matters right from now before the Adversary, whoever he really is, finally kills your world and starts the chain reaction, which, if I didn't mention it before, is irreversible.'

Tomas just gaped at Michael as though he was crazy: he couldn't believe he had just said what he had. It was like some incredulous fairy tale and he expected *him* to stop it? That was the icing on the cake. 'And what? You want me to stop it? You have got to be fucking kidding me!'

Michael roared like a volcano and all light, sound and sensation vanished for Tomas. Even his last outburst paled into mere annoyance by comparison. It was as if a sun had exploded on the hill top, and Tomas cried out in agony as his vision disappeared in a magnesium flash of searing agony, then darkness. Every molecule in his battered frame resonated with the fury of Michael as he shouted at Tomas with all the wrath of a vengeful supernova. 'Do I sound as if I'm kidding, you ridiculous, insignificant mortal?'

And for all Tomas's stubborn bloody mindedness and antagonistic tendencies, he realized as he had never realized before, just how frail, pointless, and as Michael said, insignificant he truly was. A cloak of humility fell over him, smothering him with sensations he never even knew he was capable of; at least not since he was a child. He had been caught bullying a weedy little fellow because he couldn't climb a tree. Norris was smaller and weaker than him by far and Tomas's father had found out about the bullying. Tomas had never seen him so angry and after several good lashes of his belt, ensuring he wouldn't be sitting comfortably for several days, he was then dragged by his storm god of a father the full mile and a half it was to Norris's house where, to the boy's parents' astonishment and subsequent pleasure, Tomas had been made to make a full and sincere apology. After that, he didn't see the light of day for a full two months, he was so grounded. But it wasn't the punishment or the humiliation that bothered Tomas – even at eleven he accepted pain and discomfort in his stride – it was the fact he had disappointed his father in such a bad way. That sensation of failure; it was that all over again only magnified a hundred times, that Tomas felt before the twin sun scrutiny of Michael's blazing eyes. But beyond his own remorse, Tomas got to see the other side of these creatures and they were truly fearsome to behold. Whatever reputation they had was honestly deserved. And just for a fraction of a second, Tomas believed his life was over and Michael had been tipped over whatever edge they possessed.

'Sorry,' Tomas ventured after a few attempts at finding his voice. It came out small and barely audible. Like a pin dropping in a vast, dark and empty auditorium. The world returned with as much pain as it had vanished under and Tomas groaned.

'Welcome back, Tomas. I wondered if the real you was still alive in that hardened shell you have existed within for so long. I hope that taught you that I do not kid, nor do I exaggerate and, yes, we do expect something from you and yes, your life will be at stake. Now considering the number of lives in the multiverse that are also at stake, is yours such a great sacrifice?'

Tomas couldn't meet Michael's gaze, not yet. He was still a raw wound of exposed emotion and the sudden exposure of his shame and innermost memories hurt him more than he cared to let on. But he managed an answer all the same.

'No, I suppose not.'

'No, you suppose correctly. I would take your life in a heartbeat if I thought it would end this travesty, but it will not. There is a chance, though not much of one I must admit, that you might actually succeed in your task;

but I wouldn't get my hopes up just yet. You are going to need to make a choice, Tomas. That is the asset and liability of free will. You must choose to do this voluntarily and by your own free will. But in order to do that, you need a certain amount of facts. That is the law. So here I am giving them to you as fast as I can in the hope some of them actually sink in to that thick head of yours – sufficient for you to make this crucial decision. Now, are you up to me carrying on? Or are you going to behave like an asshole again? Tell me now so I can just put you out of both your and my misery and get back on with protecting my people and the multiverse.'

'Carry on, please.' This time Tomas did meet Michael's gaze and there were tears there. Tomas couldn't contain them any longer, nor could he stem the flow of emotion that he had suppressed both before and after the explosion that had taken his future, his parents and his fiancée. He had believed he could contain it all and move on. Again he was mistaken and Michael had annihilated the last dam Tomas had in place. 'I am sorry, Michael, really I…' The dam broke and so did Tomas.

Michael quickly stepped forward and as his glow increased with each step, his rack of multihued wings unfolded, more than mortal eye could count or comprehend; and with massive arm and enfolding wings, Michael protectively wrapped Tomas in both as he wept.

Tomas woke feeling unlike anything he had ever felt before – clear headed, refreshed and rejuvenated on a level he couldn't even begin to fathom. He looked back at his recently dredged memories: the ones that caused him so much pain, and he felt a detachment that allowed him perspective and perhaps, even, healing. Sitting up, Tomas looked around for Michael, wondering if that too had been part of his dream. It wasn't, for there was the archangel, standing with his armored back to Tomas and looking out over the afternoon-sunlit countryside. He sensed Tomas's rousing and turned, smiling benevolently as he did so.

'Feel better?' His voice held genuine concern and none of the menace of earlier.

'Actually, I do.'

'Don't sound so surprised, Tomas. We are still capable of feats that help rather than hinder your race.'

Tomas blanched and grinned humorlessly. 'Yeah, I'm sure you are. Guess I'm living proof of that but if you tell anyone I cried like a girl I'm gonna have to kick your arse. We clear?'

Michael smiled. 'Yeah, we're clear, Tomas.' He held out a hand, much the same as when he first encountered him. 'Friends?'

Tomas didn't hesitate this time. 'Friends it is.' He pulled himself upright and rolled his neck and shoulders as he stood, loosening muscles that had tightened there. After a few more stretching exercises, Tomas felt about as good as he had ever felt, all things considered. Turning to Michael once more, Tomas pressed for the rest of what he had to tell him. 'So there's more, I gather. More I need to know to make this choice? Not that it's really necessary. I'll do it. Whatever it is, I'll do it or at least give it a go.'

Michael nodded and gestured for Tomas to sit once more. 'I'm sure you will, Tomas, and it gladdens my heart that you have chosen so, but I need to tell you these last few details to comply with the law. The Absolutes will have my wings if I skip the details; and if you think I'm scary, wait till you meet them.'

'You know what? You have an uncanny knack of making me feel better one minute and scaring the shit out of me the next. You gonna tell me about the Absolutes now, or is that another surprise?'

Michael laughed an almost musical sound and it would have had choirboys and priests crying from the rapture and joy inherent in that sound. 'Ha, no, not yet, Tomas, but soon. For they are on their way here and you will find out for yourself whether they deem you suitable for the task you will have chosen to accept.'

Suddenly Tomas wasn't so sure that agreeing to take on Michael's charge was such a good idea after all, and he started to mentally list his reservations.

'Relax, Tomas. Remember this. They are on our side, thank the stars. Now to round off your cosmology lesson. Remember I told you about the planet being young?' Tomas nodded dutifully. 'Well that was a long time ago and now she is in her twilight years.'

Tomas's eyes widened again. 'What are you saying now? That the planet's old and on her way out?'

Michael shook his head and chuckled at the analogy. 'By the stars, no. Perhaps I phrased that wrongly. She is about to give birth; an event that could take place either anytime soon or in another millennium. Either way, it is a vital process, for it moves the solar system forward...as it does in every galaxy when a world gives birth. This is the cycle of continuity and progress. Much the same as all species on this world. You breed, die, and your descendants carry on moving forward. The same applies to worlds.'

Tomas hadn't been brilliant at science. Astrology definitely wasn't one of his strong points and he found himself struggling with the mechanics of what Michael was telling him.

'The sun is ablaze, if you hadn't already noticed.'

'No need to take the piss now, is there? That much I can figure out, thanks. Now would you like to carry on, or you got any more sarcastic observations you'd like to share?'

'No, not as yet. However...' Michael began to pace again, gesticulating as he got into flow about stars and space, '...every blaze needs fuelling, and for the sun to continue it needs fuel on a large scale. What will feed the flames for the next cycle is Venus and Mercury as they shift through their orbits. Your moon will move to replace Mercury and this Earth will move to replace Venus, Mars replace Earth, and so on and so forth. We will evolve to join the Drakarim and the Unc'anharaphim while your race should, by then anyway, have evolved enough to take our place in the first orbit. The child your Earth will deliver will remain to be the moon for Mars – their magnetic fields regulating the climate changes that will occur as their density readjusts itself.'

'Whoa, whoa, just whoa a minute, will you? Unc and what? Density regulation? Are you just doing this for fun now? That's just a bit too much info for my tiny mortal mind to get to grips with in one sitting. Let me recap to see if some of that mud you flung stuck. The planets are all going to shuffle up one and kick two into the sun to recharge it for a while longer. But unless I'm very much mistaken, won't that kill everyone anyway? It doesn't sound like a simple movement. We get a bit of climate change here and the shit hits the fan. This sounds considerably worse.'

'It is, and it's not.' Tomas scowled, for Michael was at it again. 'Those who have evolved sufficiently will remain with the Earth. She will take care of her inhabitants – you need not yet worry about the details of that – and those who have not progressed will be gated through the density portals to Mars for their awakening on the new Earth, as it will become.'

Tomas frowned as a few pieces slotted together and made a little sense. 'Mars. This is the same Mars you are implying is Hell? Hell is an actual planet, one that is right next door?' Michael nodded, curious as to where Tomas was going with his line of enquiry. 'How is it that we can't see all that fire and brimstone going on then? We just landed a Phoenix probe up there. Wouldn't it be able to see something?'

Michael smiled as he saw the opening he needed to make his explanation easier.'Density. You queried it a moment ago. Like light, sound, gas and rocks here on Earth, you can only see and perceive what falls within your density spectrum. Gases are out of your physical spectrum so you can't directly touch them unless you tamper with them. Same with air. You feel its effect but can't see it. If you punch the air it doesn't hurt, but if you punch a rock, which is considerably denser, you might break something and it won't be the rock. You following me?'

Tomas nodded and flicked his eyebrows upwards as if to say 'Yes, yes, I'm not entirely stupid'.

'Good. Now on every level, from your molecular stage upwards, you are made of the same stuff as this world. Water, minerals, calcium and carbon and so on and so forth. You are not made of anything from Mars or any other planet in this or any other verse. So, like light waves, you can only perceive that which falls within your density spectrum. There are several miles of Mars's surface that you do not, cannot, nor will ever be able to see, unless you learn to master density. And your species is a long way from that little discovery, and the way you're going, you're getting further and further away with each passing day.'

Tomas scratched his head as he struggled to reconcile the physics of what he was hearing. Michael saw his effort and added an example for him.

'The sun is central to this solar system, so there is the greater density, the greatest directed force. The closer you get to the core of the system, the greater the density – much the same way as you feel the pressure when you dive beneath the oceans. How far can you go before you are crushed by the weight? Not too far, I suspect. Adversely, the further you get from the centre of a thing, the lesser the density and the more gaseous a thing becomes, at least to your perception. A child from Earth could flick boulders the size of houses for miles if he was one planet back without density alteration. Likewise, the biggest man on Earth would break his bones if he struck an infant one planet closer to the centre of the system.'

Tomas conceded Michael's point and decided to press on, regardless of his understanding. 'Okay, so how does this affect things?'

Michael accepted the question as permission to continue. 'When Mars takes over here, the Adversary, we believe, wants as many souls there as possible, and by draining the souls from this world, he hastens your planet's demise. This has been going on for too long unabated and we approach a critical time when he and his armies will be able to take corporeal form here, in this density range. The carnage then will be unimaginable. As it stands, only the prime rulers and upper echelon beings can manifest here, as I have before you now. It takes great effort to open density portals to let greater numbers through, and that requires power. Souls equal power. Did you know that some six hundred thousand of your people are reported missing every year? And that's just the ones you know about. You can actually treble that figure. Then there are those under the Adversary's influence who are perpetuating your problems through war, disease and religion, where even more die. The more that die, the more his cause is aided to weaken your own defenses and those of the planet. She is almost incapable of defending you. Should she weaken any further, it will be all she can do to sustain your lives. Does that put things in some sort of perspective for you?'

'Wow. Why didn't you just say all that to start with?'

It was Michael's turn to scowl now and shake his head at the irrepressible and sardonic nature that emerged from Tomas when he perceived the chips were down. Michael added to his rapidly vanishing humor, 'That is before he even finds the suicides.'

'The what?'

'The suicides. It's when a person —'

'I know what a suicide is, goddamn it, but why are you mentioning it like it's a tangible thing? Surely, dead is dead no matter how they do it or have it done to them, isn't it?'

Michael turned suddenly serious and clasped his hands behind his back once more: a sure sign of the gravity of the topic he now faced. 'There is a place within every world where the power of the soul is gathered when it takes its own life. It circumvents the natural order and has nothing to do with burning in Hell, or being damned forever, as many of your institutions foolishly decree it. It isn't something to be punished; it is something to be pitied and sad for, for they are removed from the cycle until the planet moves forward, deemed too fragile in spirit to exist. They go neither forward nor back but are held within the Labyrinth that surrounds the Core. Occasionally though, one or two bright souls manage to garner themselves a second chance and slip free of the maze. They manifest in numerous ways we've discovered and there doesn't seem to be any pattern as to their choices. They become fey and mysterious creatures, not entirely part of this world as humans know it, but close enough for them to move amongst you undetected. Some more than others are curious as their buried memories flare sufficiently to connect them to you, but not enough to control their natures. These often seem as mischievous entities and should be treated with care, for they are powerful, Tomas. Prolonged proximity to the Core and an ephemeral existence between worlds gives them access to abilities even we cannot comprehend.'

Tomas couldn't believe what he was hearing: yet another alternative mythology to what he had always assumed was a religious fact. *So much for that shit. Looks like the Christians and all the rest of the God botherers around the world are in for a bit of a shock, and we must have only scratched the surface of what all this really means, though I'm not too sure I want to know much more – this is fucked up enough already.* He cast a guilty look at Michael, who was looking at Tomas disapprovingly and rolling a dagger that seemed to have appeared out of nowhere, skillfully around in his meaty hand with an expertise that left Tomas in little doubt he knew how to use it.

'It is this gathering of souls held within the Labyrinth we believe the Adversary is after as we speak,' Michael continued steadily, watching Tomas all the time, 'for it would empower him enough to break the stalemate we have him held at right at this moment.' Suddenly Michael spun away and stalked to the edge of the hill top and looked skyward. 'We balance upon a sword's edge and the battle could go either way. It is for this reason we come to you now, one of the last guardians of this world, for it is only *you* who can deliver the blow that sunders his grip on this dying planet, for it is *your* planet, *your* duty. You must allow her, your mother and creator, the time and ability to rally her strength, and us ours, for the final push that will deliver victory to our hands and defeat to the Adversary.'

Tomas sat in silence for a few minutes as the enormity of what he had just heard sank in, at least as far as it was going to. 'No pressure then,' he said finally.

Tomas stood in silence himself for five minutes or so as the gravity of it all nestled on his shoulders like some dark and oppressive vulture, its black, intelligent eye staring at him with accusation and apprehension. What would he do? Would he even do anything? Could he? Tomas knew he had already accepted his lot and had told Michael that only a few moments beforehand. But was that merely a reaction to an overwhelming body of evidence being presented to him in fully three-dimensional and Technicolor glory, or was it that he felt he had nothing to lose by not succumbing to Michael's heavily weighted and politely phrased request? He didn't know; he couldn't think straight. His mind was full of sticky webs that linked one thing to another but obscured it at the same time, though one little fact did pop up and nag him.

'You said I'm one of the last of these so-called guardians? That implies there are more. Who are they, then, and why haven't you told me about them? Surely I'm likely to need all the bloody help I can get.'

Michael turned back to Tomas and a look of indecision crossed his annoyingly perfect features and his bright blue eyes darkened for a second. Tomas was good at reading people and he knew in that instant that Michael either didn't want to tell him or was about to lie to him in a convincing sort of way. 'You are correct in your assumption, Tomas: you are not the only guardian. There is another. One who we hope will be assisting you in their own way but, suffice to say, they will not be aiding you in person, not in this endeavor, but their quest is just as important as yours, maybe even more so. But do not let this knowledge affect what it is that you have to do, for that will not help at all and may even hinder your progress. I can say no more.'

'Can't or won't?'

'Both.'

Tomas accepted this is as much as he was able: he could see by the set of the archangel's jaw he wasn't likely to get anything else out of him just yet. He would try another tack, though, and see where that got him. 'Fair enough, but another question arises from this subject. What happened to the rest? If we are so bloody important and supposed to fight world-shattering evil like this, how come the rest got their arses kicked, just leaving me and this other? That's gotta be the story for now, surely? Maybe there is something I can glean from it that might help, maybe stop me falling foul of the same thing that befell them. What do you think?'

'I don't know.' Michael was naturally suspicious and the fact Tomas was now digging for information rather than just reacting to what he was being told put the archangel on the back foot.

'They weren't all heroes, Tomas, though some were and history has documented them. Unfortunately, not all with the accuracy they deserve, but they were heroes nonetheless. You will have heard of a few of them as they have slipped into your mythology and stories, passed down over generations. One of the more recent manifestations of one of the lost heroes is Arthur Pendragon. I suspect you have heard that name.'

Tomas blinked furiously. Had he heard correct? Arthur? King bloody Arthur? 'You saying he was real?'

Michael nodded. 'Oh yes, very real. Your storytellers were inspired by the reality of the man but they would have been unaware of just how much they were influenced. Dreams, flashes of insight and whispers in the night. We can be subtle when we wish to be, you know.'

'You lot prompted those stories? Why?'

'To inspire you all to rise to the potential you ignore. It was hoped the chivalry and valor would do what the spirituality failed to do. But the fusion of the two may reach that dormant spark within you all and set it ablaze. It seemed to have worked a little: the story still seems popular. He was one of your ancestors, you know.'

That did it. Tomas couldn't contain his laughter any longer. His incredulity had been stretched way beyond its previously considered boundaries and this topped it off. King Arthur of the stories was his bloody relative. That was just bloody terrific.'What then? Does that make me some lost king, then?'

Michael shook his head and looked at Tomas a little worriedly, as though he had pushed the mortal's sanity a trifle too far.

'No, Tomas, it doesn't, but try not to put too much stock in what you know. It is merely a genealogical fact. Bloodlines. Throughout time there have been guardians, and they have stood against the darkness wherever it raised its head. That is what they are destined to do. In some lifetimes, they have no need to step up and live their lives in peace and relative tranquility. But it is their blood that the Adversary has focused on. He has set out to eradicate the bloodlines and prevent any further guardians being born. We don't know how, but they missed you and the other. For that, we are grateful.'

'What other?' Tomas slipped in innocently, trying to catch Michael out.

'You'll have to do better than that, Tomas. Do I not look as though I've been around a while? I didn't get to live this long by being stupid and gullible.'

Tomas just shrugged and grinned coldly, as though saying he had to try. 'Fair enough, but why did he miss me and this alleged other?' Tomas tried another tack. 'What makes us so special?'

'Now that is a good question. One we don't have an answer for. You are an enigma, Tomas, you and the other guardian. Suffice to say we are grateful you both slipped the Adversary's net. It has given us a fighting chance: one we thought had passed us. The mystery of your survival and heritage will have to wait for another time: one that should we survive this, will be worth worrying about. But until then —'

'One thing at a time, right?' Tomas knew enough about getting his priorities straight; to accept that Michael was right. His ancestry could wait until less pressing times.

'Right.'

Tomas got up and stretched, popping the kinks out of his suddenly weary frame. The weight of responsibility fell heavily on his shoulders and the enormity of what was happening to him began to take its toll. He paced a bit, back and forth, stretching his limbs and spine as he did so, interlacing his fingers and pressing them out, knuckles cracking like firecrackers on the fourth of July. Even Michael winced.

'You know, I still can't really believe all of this...' Tomas's sudden exclamation cut through the still air like gunfire. Michael was stunned, suddenly aghast at what he was hearing, and the prospect of having wasted the last few hours of valuable time bringing Tomas around to the bigger picture caused him to experience a momentary surge of panic. '…But much of what you say makes a strange kind of sense,' Tomas continued, and Michael let out a sigh of relief. 'And seeing as my life pretty much sucked before, whatever it is I have to do can't be any worse than the life of misery I was facing. At least I can go out trying to do something remotely useful, and if I fail, then I haven't lost anything by trying. What do you think?'

'I think that you are ready to meet the individuals who will be taking over from me: the ones who will accouter you for your task and steer you in the right direction.'

This time it was Tomas's turn to stare, spinning suddenly to lock gazes with the archangel. He strode across the hill top until they were just inches apart, and even though Michael stood a head taller than Tomas, the smaller man was no less intimidating. Nor was he intimidated in return by the archangel's looming presence.

'Now what do you mean: taking over from you? Where the bloody hell are you going? You get me roped into this scheme then just bugger off? Nice one. Isn't this the sort of behavior that got you into trouble in the first place?'

Michael smiled down at the feisty mortal and thought that just possibly, with every shred of luck he possessed, he might just be the man for the job. Not that they had any other options, but it was a good sign all the same.

'I have to go, Tomas. I have legions of my own to command and the enemy does not rest. We must meet him whenever and wherever he appears, and our numbers are spread thin enough as it is, what with more and more portals being activated across your world.'

The blank look reappeared on Tomas's face as Michael started on about portals. The archangel then stopped abruptly. He cast a speculative look at Tomas and a cluster of emotions flashed across his countenance. Tomas caught a few. Pity, sadness, resignation and guilt. Guilt? Tomas didn't like that one much: he had seen that particular look before. Usually before he was sent off on some sort of mission he wasn't expected to return from.

'You don't think I'll have much of a chance of success, do you?'

'You are perceptive, Tomas. Too perceptive perhaps, and my own feelings betray me, it seems. But no, I don't think you have much hope. You are but one man against an enemy you can't even begin to comprehend. In truth, it was hoped there would be more of you left but we must make do with what we have and be grateful for that.'

'Thanks. Make a guy feel wanted, why don't you? I can't help it if you all let the others get themselves offed by this Adversary character. You should be more accepting of small mercies and be pleased he missed me, though I can't imagine how – I haven't been exactly low profile in my past. Considering my profession, I would have thought I was an easy target.'

Michael agreed. 'So would we, but it seems you were concealed by some sort of mystical shield even we don't understand. There was a power there that had not been felt for millennia, but it was dissipated too fast to recognize by the explosion that took your family. It seems your brush with death negated the shield when you technically died. Those few seconds were enough to light you up like a beacon. The enemy sensed you, as did we, and it was just a matter of who would get to you first.'

Tomas cracked a harsh laugh. 'Looks like they got the better of you again, doesn't it? Though if that scrawny effort was the best they could come up with they shouldn't be too hard to take down.'

'Perhaps the short notice we both had saved your life, for that was merely a possessed. A lesser minion in the flesh of a mortal. It is the only way they can interact with this world. Even that was rare, but now...' Michael was suddenly wistful, '...they appear everywhere and in increasing numbers. It is fortunate your heroic genes shone through and you prevailed against it.' Michael rested a massive yet gentle hand upon Tomas's shoulders as he spoke, the praise genuine and instilled with as much pride as the archangel was capable of. But even those few supportive words made Tomas uncomfortable, for he was ill-accustomed to praise of any sort; it was merely expected of him to do what he was ordered to. If he succeeded, all well and good; if he failed... well he was either dead or would shortly be, and his replacement would step in. There was always a replacement, just waiting for you to screw up. Dead men's shoes. It was no way to live and Tomas was glad he was free of it, or at least as free as he was going to get.

'Yeah, well, I don't feel very damn heroic right now but thanks for the vote of confidence.'

Michael gripped his shoulder a little tighter to emphasize his words. 'There is as much evil in you as there is the capability for good – that much is apparent to one such as I – but you chose not to succumb to that dark nature; you rose above the insidious temptation to accept defeat or the false promises of the Adversary to act for their side.'

Tomas was confused: he didn't remember any temptation being offered. Michael picked up the thread of Tomas's question before he asked it.

'It wasn't an open invitation, Tomas, but it would have occurred during your life as a killer. Had you fallen prey to the Adversary's offers, you would still be killing and thoroughly enjoying your role. Your life could have gone either way and it is often easier to accept the dark path than to stand against it. It takes strength. Strength of both purpose and character, unafraid to stand alone against your peers if you disagree with them. For as much as you are a race of people, you are also individuals and should not be afraid to express that individuality if you feel strongly enough about something. You seem to have an innate compre-hension for what is right and what is wrong. It is what separates you.'

Tomas was squirming. He didn't or hadn't seen it that way at the time and wasn't even sure how he saw it now. Right and wrong was simply a matter of perspective.

'You chose correctly though, Tomas, however you justify it. Instinct, sixth sense, your higher self – however you call it – it is that part of you that remains infallible, sacrosanct and pure. That is a good power to possess in the evil times ahead, Tomas.'

'I don't have any powers, Michael, I am just a man. That is unless the ability to put away copious amounts of beer without suffering a hangover is a power.'

Michael laughed then, in his rich and musical baritone, which had the contagious effect of making Tomas smile too, and soon enough he was laughing along with the big angel. Then, with a slap across the shoulder blades that nearly sent Tomas hurtling off the hill top, Michael became serious once more.

'No, Tomas, it isn't a power, but it is good you retain your sense of humor in the face of such adversity. May it serve you well on the hard road set out before you; I suspect you'll need it.'

Tomas couldn't have agreed more. Based on what Michael had told him, he might as well just slice his own throat there and then and get it over with.

'Do not think such things, Tomas.' Michael was genuinely horrified. 'To do so would hand the Adversary almost certain victory. You see, the deciding blow that vanquishes him must come from a guardian of this world. We thought all was truly lost until you both appeared, but to allow the Adversary to win by you taking your own life would be truly unthinkable. You have given us hope where none existed.'

And for a second, Tomas began to feel a glow unlike anything he had felt before; that is until Michael spoke again. 'But the truth of the matter is, we do not expect you to even get close enough to land a blow, let alone *the* blow. The odds against you are virtually insurmountable, for you must succeed where armies of angels have failed.'

Tomas spun away and stalked the hill top, not sure what to do next. Stop, start, sit down or stand up. He was up and down like an emotional rollercoaster with the task set out before him. One minute he was a godsend, the next a mere punctuation.

'Screwed if I do and screwed if I don't,' Tomas growled eventually.

'Pretty much.' There was no point in Michael dissembling.

'Nice. I suppose you have a plan B if I don't do whatever it is you don't expect me to do.'

For the first time since meeting him, Michael was speechless.

Tomas continued, 'Terrific, this is just getting better by the minute. The more I find out the less I'm liking this, not that I was liking it much before-hand, but I'm dreading asking the next question.'

Michael raised an eyebrow as if to say 'Ask anyway'.

'Do I get a weapon or somesuch? If I'm to land a blow on anything, some sort of ordnance might not go amiss.' Tomas held his arms out. 'I'm a bit light these days. They made me hand everything back in, spoilsports! It took me ages to get used to not sleeping with my Hochlers at arm's reach. Still miss them, to be honest.'

As though Tomas had completed a riddle and qualified for the next level of some surreal reality game, Michael beamed. 'Now that is something we can help you with. As I said earlier, I have other commitments, but…' Michael drew the massive broadsword that he wore and he held it aloft. Instantly it burst into a bright blue flame that soared skywards, '…you asked about the Absolutes and I promised to tell you more about them, though I rather figure you already know who they are, or will when you see them.'

Tomas grew instantly wary. 'See them? They're coming here?'

But Michael had closed his eyes and was concentrating on the cobalt flame of his sword. It grew brighter and arced upwards as though it were trying to pierce the stratosphere. Tomas was impressed and cautious both at once, for a beacon like that could draw unwanted attention as easily as it drew those it was intended for.

Tomas wasn't sure what alerted him, or inspired him to even turn to look, but turn he did. He looked to the east. Unerringly way off in the distance something moved against the skyline – something moving with incredible speed, and it was heading directly for them. Michael lowered his sword and the flame vanished. Resheathing the cold, unblemished steel, Michael joined Tomas and watched the speck grow rapidly in size until it divided itself like cells. One becoming two, then two becoming four. It was at four it stayed and Tomas's chest tightened involuntarily as a suspicion grew within him – one he didn't want to acknowledge but was finding increasingly difficult to avoid as the four figures drew inexorably closer. *Oh shit! Oh shit! Oh shit! Oh shit!*

'Very eloquent, Tomas, but, you are not wrong with the intent behind the sentiment. You should be in awe, for few souls ever get the personal attention of all four Absolutes – not unless they have been doing something they shouldn't have and judgment needs passing. That hasn't happened since Kalith was exiled back when your people were still thinking about building the pyramids. No, Tomas, awe is good, but they will take care of your needs from here on in.'

Tomas cast alternating glances between Michael and the four riders – for riders is what they were and they were all galloping towards him, mounted upon thundering steeds whose hooves churned up the very air as if it were solid earth. He fancied he could even hear them pounding down as they powered forwards. But it wasn't the horses that transfixed Tomas, so much as their riders. Each as different from the other as Tomas was from them, but all radiated power on so many levels. Tomas was left feeling virtually obsolete.

Michael was right about one thing though. Tomas did know who these Absolutes were. He wished he didn't, for it brought him closer to the precipice of his sanity than he had ever been before. Even Michael appeared mundane by comparison. Yet none of Tomas's observations, which he had no doubt Michael fished from his head, stopped the archangel announcing them with the majestic voice of some herald of hallowed antiquity. His voice resonated across the land and Tomas was certain that anything, man or beast, that heard the announcement stopped dead in their tracks to pay homage.

'The fate of worlds now rests with you, Tomas, and I wish you the greatest fortune, the strongest of arms and the courage of your convictions. Know that we will aid you in whatever way we can, but for now, stand humbled and show the proper respect, for *the Four Horsemen of the Apocalypse* cometh.'

CHAPTER TWO·

PREPARATIONS

I F THE LAST FORTY-EIGHT HOURS OF TOMAS'S life had been an exercise in
surrealism, it took a turn then, and not for the better. What he saw had
his mind spinning out of control and for one brief, panicked moment,
he thought he was going to lose the last remaining vestiges of his already
stretched sanity. Tomas found that his mind was reaching out, desperately
seeking a handhold back in the world he knew; or at least what was left of it.
But his mental fingers could find no purchase and he began to slip down that
rocky slope.

The already dubious presence of the archangel had put Tomas in the
state of mind where he expected a padded room to materialize at any moment,
solidifying the stark realization it had all been some extreme, drug-induced
hallucination, brought about by exceeding his pain medication after the
explosion, the explosion which ripped his world and, apparently, his sanity as
well, away from him. Pinching himself through his pockets, he came to the
grim conclusion he was awake and, despairingly, he realized there was also
no immediate sign of his padded room. *Damn! There's never one when you
want one.*

Whilst this inner turmoil coursed through Tomas, his exterior stood
impassive, staring up at the spectacle unfolding before him. Riding towards

him through the air were four very imposing individuals, so far removed from what he knew he could comprehend, that it made the angel's arrival seem quite acceptable.

'Close your mouth; you look like an imbecile.' Michael stood, watching Tomas.

'Ugh?' was about all Tomas could manage. He saw the archangel's lips move, but the blood rushing in his ears drowned out the words.

'I said, close your mouth.' Michael reached out one long and perfectly formed finger and lifted Tomas's chin upwards. There was an audible clack of teeth meeting teeth, and the sudden shock of his head rattling brought Tomas back to what remained of his senses. Switching his gaze between the angel and the imminently arriving Horsemen, Tomas heard himself stating the obvious.

'They're real?'

Michael shook his head resignedly and sighed deeply. 'Of course they are real; they are the Absolutes. Theirs is the governance of this solar system from inception to completion. They are the beginning and the end; the alpha and the omega, if you will. It is a responsibility that weighs heavily, more so than even ours. Bear one harsh fact in your mind: if they are concerned, things are indeed dire.'

'Any more surprises I need to know about? Or are you finished screwing with my head now? Not that I think it could handle much more anyway, this is just *too* much.' Tomas scrubbed his hands through his hair and dragged them down over his face, partly in the vain hope that when he looked up again, the vision before him would be gone. Unfortunately it wasn't. In fact it was closer than ever. He watched as the riders touched down gently, their mounts snorting clouds of hot breath as they circled briefly, coming to a perfectly trained halt. The quartet turned their penetrating gaze upon Tomas and he felt it as a tangible thing, his legs almost buckling under the gravity generated by those otherworldly eyes. But it was under extreme pressure he had lived his life, and his own inner steel began to reassert itself, granted slowly, but nevertheless surely. After the sudden shock of the day's quite profound revelations, the old Tomas found his mettle and gazed back, taking in the figures before him: the legendary Four Horsemen of the Apocalypse. *Okay then*, he thought, *let's see where this goes. See what plan they've got up their armored sleeves for me. But one thing's for damn sure: if they think I'm going off like some sacrificial offering, they've got another think coming entirely, Four Horsemen of the bloody Apocalypse or not.*

Death dismounted first. Tomas had little difficulty in distinguishing him from the other riders. He recognized War as well: there truly was no mistaking the personification of all things Warlike. It was Famine and Pestilence he couldn't work out which was which. *I'm sure I'll find out in due course, though*, Tomas mused as Death made his way across to stand before him and Michael. He wondered why Death bothered with a horse at all, for folded at his back, like some gigantic raven, was a huge pair of midnight-black wings projecting over each shoulder to lend a menacing air to an already menacing persona, and like the ravens, they glistened blue-black as the rising sun glanced off their feathery surface. It was as if the light was almost reluctant to touch them for fear it would be sucked up and extinguished. Giving the wings closer scrutiny, Tomas saw that not all the feathers were actual feathers. Interspersed amongst them were what looked to be *steel* feathers. It was the closest thing Tomas could imagine to armored wings. *Impressive.* It matched the rest of Death's garb: less the robed look, more of the black knight. Though he still sported the cowl and cloak, it was more of an accessory than a full look. Even with the cowl up covering most of his helm, Tomas was able to discern the skeletal features of his face plate. *That's sneaky. Perhaps that's what people have seen to think he's a skeleton, and if that's all anyone has seen, then what's behind that visor? What's the true face of Death? And more to the point, would I want to see it anyway. Jeez, would anyone? Though once maybe I might have done. When I was so lost in my work, I would have challenged the bastard for his job. I can't believe I even survived those dark days.* Beyond the visor, only a pair of glowing eyes was visible. Burning like distant stars deep within the cowled helm. Tomas wasn't sure he wanted to see much more than that now: he wasn't the man he used to be.

Appearing in Death's armored hand, as though it had always been there – although Tomas could have sworn he didn't have it when he dismounted – was the infamous scythe, which at least answered another age-old question as to whether he actually used one of those unwieldy things. *But who would have gotten that good a look at him for the mythology to have built the way it had? Someone obviously lived to tell the tale; good effort. Guess it just goes to show you there's always some truth to these myths.* The myth stood before him in all his bleak and ominous glory. The weapon caught every shred of light as the blade swung gently in his grasp. It looked so sharp and positively lethal that it seemed to cut the light itself as it moved, splitting and refracting light into smaller rays. Another facet of Death's mythology stood patiently behind him, for like the tale, Death did indeed possess a pale horse. It was the most ghostly shade of grey Tomas had ever seen. Its eyes were inky pools within a misty surround and it was huge – easily the biggest horse Tomas had ever seen. It was the sort of animal that shire horses would have descended from. And other than an initial snort upon its arrival, coupled with a brief pawing of the earth with its massive steel-shod hoof, it stood so perfectly still, it could have been carved from granite. It put Tomas in mind of the Da Vinci drawings of horses: such defined musculature. The ultimate supernatural horse for the ultimate supernatural being. Then Death spoke. His voice ripped fire down Tomas's nerves and he very nearly dropped to his knees; again. It was like standing next to a jet engine that was throttling up, only the noise was *inside* his head.

'Well met, Michael…' Glancing over, seeing Tomas's plight, Death shook his head slightly. '…Mortals should never have to encounter the Horsemen directly like this; they are incapable of withstanding our physical presence. However, as these are unprecedented times I suppose allowances must be made.' Tomas's face was screwed up in agony, His hands were clasped over his ears, for all the good it did, and if he could have found his voice, he would have screamed. Death nodded almost imperceptibly. 'That should be better, mortal, you can stop whimpering now.'

Indeed it was. Tomas removed his hands from his ears, distantly noting there was blood upon his palms. *That's it, I'm never going to be able to hear another thing. Damn, that hurt. These bloody things are supposed to be on my side; so far they've caused me more grief than the poxy enemy. This had better improve fast or I'm outta here and to hell with the lot of them.* Death turned his implacable gaze upon Tomas and tilted his head slightly, uncannily birdlike. Tomas felt the gaze like freezing cold air blasting against him.

'And where will you go, little mortal? Believe me when I tell you that unless we succeed you will have no need to go searching for Hell: *it* will find *you.* At that point, I think you will find us preferable – infinitely preferable.'

Death turned his attention back to Michael then, Tomas forgotten as though he were no longer there. While the archangel and Death conversed, Tomas took a moment to recover his equilibrium and take in the other Horsemen. They all sat on their mounts in the practised manner of experienced warriors. *I suppose they spend a lot of time in their saddles: after all, they are the Horsemen. You don't get a title like that by walking.* Tomas first studied War. He was wearing even more armor than Death and looked formidable indeed. Like Death, his armor was dark; it was as though it had been made from gun metal itself. The dull steel look of death-dealing machinery. *That's some horse*, thought Tomas, *having to carry around an armored car like that.* He sat upon an enormous barrel-chested roan, some eighteen hands high by Tomas's estimation. He knew only enough about horses to get by – he'd never had a lot to do with them, other than the occasional meal. But this one looked as though it could look after itself, and run both forever and over anything foolish enough to mess with it. The horse's crimson eyes regarded Tomas with something akin to equine contempt. Tomas sensed nobility to the creature and he felt small under its scrutiny. Its rider, as best as Tomas could ascertain, carried only one weapon that he could see: a huge broadsword which projected its wire-wrapped hilt over one massive armored shoulder. It was then that Tomas noticed the etching upon War's armor. It was as though every weapon ever built, both old and new, was engraved there. Tomas knew weapons – they were his stock in trade – but there were even some he had never seen before and looked as though they could even be from the future. They were all engraved upon him. The harder Tomas looked at it, the more he could see. They seemed to move and flow about his person like living, liquid steel. Images were appearing on the almost seamless armor, acting out scenes from battles throughout history. It was almost hypnotic as the etchings twisted and moved over and through the steel. Tomas particularly liked the numerous spines that protruded from his steel-clad body, making close-quarter grappling just as lethal for any opponent foolish enough to get that close. He was a walking, though not so much talking, embodiment of humanity's warring nature. *Impressive. He looks like one well-hard son of a gun, literally.* Tomas fully appreciated this personification, almost identifying with him. *God knows how he moves about in that armor – he looks like a Chieftain tank on legs.* Tomas grimaced then at the irony of his thought. *Suppose I best get out of the habit of saying that, seeing as God obviously doesn't know much of anything going on here these days.*

Like Death's visor, Tomas was unable to pierce the gloom of War's helm. His eyes were invisible, but he got the impression though, that he was seeing well enough as his head rotated slowly like a giant steel owl, scrutinizing the surroundings, watching for any sign of ambush or trouble. *Who better?* Tomas thought. His own military experience would probably have had him doing the same.

Turning his attention to the other two now, they were not what he expected from entities who personified Pestilence and Famine. One was a tall and slender man, seemingly of middle years. His dress and demeanor reminded Tomas of the ancient nobles of Spain, though in truth, he could have originated anywhere. But that was how Tomas reconciled it in his mind. His face held an expression of boredom and indignation; a well-groomed moustache and goatee completing the image. Were it simply that, Tomas would have considered him less than imposing, except it wasn't. The low rising sun, which initially sat behind them, had risen higher and in doing so, Tomas could now see the ice sparkling from his attire. *It's not just his clothes!* Tomas realized with a start. It was on his skin too. Pale, blue-tinged skin, with eyes like chips of turquoise ice. The Horseman caught Tomas looking and smiled. It was all teeth and sincerity. His cheeks wrinkled up as he beamed down at him. Leaning forward and crossing his forearms across the pommel, he spoke; but unlike Death's, his voice was fluid and melodious, slightly tinged with the Spanish that Tomas expected.

'Please…' He waved a distracted hand at his deathly sombre comrade, who paid him no heed and continued his conversation with Michael, '…allow me to introduce myself and my cohorts, for it certainly seems like they will not. They can be very rude, I'm afraid, though you'll have to excuse them – in their line of business there's not a lot of call for pleasantries. I am Famine. The stoic fellow to my right is War. He doesn't say a lot, but my advice would be to listen carefully when he does…' War's helm swiveled round to spare him a quick steely glance before continuing his vigil and Tomas felt the disapproval even from the distance he stood at. '…Yes, well, moving on then, to my left, my severe companion here by process of elimination is Pestilence. Don't mind her slightly strained expression – she takes her role very seriously – but it is worth the wait for when she does smile, it's like the sun coming out from an eclipse. Happens about as much too.' He was rewarded with a stare from Pestilence this time – a gaze that would have drilled holes through diamonds. Tomas looked closer at Pestilence. She was an interesting figure. She looked like an experienced warrior crossed with a geisha crossed again with steppe horseman; with fur-rimmed helm boots and great cloak. There were no wings looming over her shoulders but there were the hilts of two swords. Tomas guessed they were katanas by the shape of the hilt. She looked as though she knew how to use them too. She could have been the daughter, or wife even, of the likes of Genghis Khan or Attila the Hun. *There are definitely a few horses' worth there.* As with War, he could see numerous semi-concealed weapons ensconced about her person and upon her mount. All of them, bar Death, seemed to carry a bow or two of some description. Tomas turned back to Famine, who had been regarding Tomas even as he had been regarding them. 'So, what weapon do you favor? Death has got his scythe; War has got...well, everything, it seems; and Pestilence has those twin blades across her back. What does it for you?' Famine smiled again – a chilly yet at the same time reassuring smile that Tomas found endeared the Horseman to him. He watched as Famine held out his hand, and from nowhere a vicious looking weapon appeared. It took Tomas a moment to recognize it as a halberd, though not one he was familiar with: this one looked decidedly nastier.

'Never was one for letting an enemy get too close; this helps somewhat.' Tomas believed him – the blade was catching the morning light and its keen edge was clearly evident. A barbed spike protruded from the top. Again, closer scrutiny slipped past the superficial exterior, impressive as it might be. It wasn't something that he could put his finger on, but looking at the Horseman before him – who at first glance seemed out of place in the quartet and somewhat effeminate even – now, holding the halberd, his demeanor had shifted slightly and Tomas got a different impression entirely: one of imminent danger – violent and explosive. Famine's smiley eyes had intensified into icy, frozen maelstroms. Tomas felt the temperature drop lower and lower, the longer he held Famine's gaze. His feet started to lose sensation. Looking down at them, he saw the ground had frozen solid and had commenced cracking and splitting. The frost had spread from the haft of the halberd where it touched the ground. Tomas heard the ground pop and crack as it contracted in the sub-zero temperature.

'*Never* underestimate anyone, Tomas, however they may appear to you. There are many dark and malevolent creatures out there who are as sublime and as beautiful as anything you could imagine. Visions of them have driven men and even angels to their deaths. They will have powers you cannot even begin to comprehend let alone stand against. Allow me to demonstrate further.' With that, the air about Famine shimmered, distorting him and blurring his image for a heartbeat. When the air stilled again, he was tanned, his hair black, and fire surrounded him. His eyes too were aflame. The cold air was instantly replaced with such an extreme heat that Tomas found it almost impossible to breathe. Black flames leapt up from the halberd and sweat began to pour from Tomas. He felt that he was going to black out any second – never had he experienced such heat. The world began to swim.

'Enough! Famine is quite correct. However, we have lingered here too long as it is. The cloak that protected you and kept you hidden from the enemy's eyes as well as our own is no more. That means that they can find you much as we did. There could be a thousand minions heading this way as we speak. Much depends on how big a threat you are considered.' Death walked as he talked, finishing his comments as he mounted his steed.

'Look, this is all very flattering and all, but I'm still at a loss as to how big a threat I can be. You constantly remind me that I'm just a *mortal*, apparently nothing special, so just why would the enemy, whoever that might be, this Adversary character, send an army to do me in? It's nice to feel important but this is getting carried away. I'm not the man I was. All I want is to be left in peace. Is that too much to ask for?'

Apparently it was, as all eyes turned to Tomas. Mountains would cringe and try to scuttle off under the combined stares of these entities. Tomas instantly regretted his outburst. Death turned to Michael and in a voice that had all the finesse of a steel door slamming shut upon a very deep crypt, he addressed the archangel, 'You *have* told him the reason behind this, I take it? He does know he is the only one left capable of fulfilling the Covenant?'

Michael simply nodded and continued to glower at Tomas. Death then turned to Tomas. 'A mortal hand must strike the deciding blow for humanity. And we never said you weren't special. For your species to continue with its independence you have to stand against all adversity. This is your test, if you will. Failure is extinction. Michael has told you this, surely?'

Death looked between Tomas and the archangel. Michael nodded once more. Tomas looked abashed but continued all the same, though a deep part of him knew that arguing with these four was akin to digging through a mountain with a toothbrush. Not only pointless and doomed to failure but quite possibly the most stupid thing to do – ever.

'I know what you think, but you can't want me, of all people, There must be other mortals infinitely more qualified for this role than me. I'm betting that the world's religious leaders have candidates by the bus load, all preordained and whatever, having spent their lives dedicated to such a momentous occasion ever arising. Now, here it is and you pick me? What about them?'

Stunning Tomas temporarily with a voice deep and heavily accented, was the voice of War. He had turned to face Tomas and removed his helm as he did so. Tomas saw a hard face, as black as coal, with eyes as white and piercing as twin suns, and a myriad of fine battle scars threaded across his grim visage. His voice, it occurred to Tomas, was that of one of the African nations. He had visited so many, his mind couldn't sort out which, handicapped as he was by his current predicament. But he did remember Famine's advice and kept his mouth shut.

'This is not about religion, Tomas, it is about survival. Religion has absolutely *nothing* to do with this. Those who practise it are so indoctrinated and blinkered now, that they would die in denial of what was tearing them to pieces even as it did so. It has been the ruin of your species, as you no doubt already know. It has fractured your people irreparably. We need a warrior, not a priest or any of that ilk. Yet that warrior must possess the qualities of both the priest and the soldier. I assure you the meek will *not* inherit anything except an early death. We need a warrior, a pragmatist, yet somebody who also possesses morals. Somebody who stands an iota of a chance in succeeding. You may not like it, you may try to deny it, but you Tomas, you are that man. Your life has led you to this moment. Everything you have done, however insignificant, however distasteful – all of it has been to prepare you for this moment. That was why you trained, was it not, to be prepared for any number of eventualities? Consider this one of them.' War's voice then rose, booming like thunder. He roared at Tomas, 'Now get a grip on yourself. You're a soldier; behave like one. Consider these your orders. Your petty feelings have no place here; your own self-pity is inconsequential. Your people and your world need you,Tomas. Are you going to turn your back on the greatest fight of their existence? Are you going to let them die – let *everything* die, just so you can feel better about yourself?' War paused for effect, letting the first part sink into Tomas's psyche. Then he continued, 'Or will you fight? Will you stand as the light against the darkness, prepared to do all you can to drive it back?'

Tomas felt War's words drive into his very soul, a thing he had long since banished to a dark recess. It was dragged kicking and screaming into the light and scrutiny of War's speech. It felt very small and ashamed, yet at the same time it felt exhilarated by the prospect of redemption and a sense of pride at its own self-worth – something he hadn't felt in a very long time. Tomas stood straighter and pulled his shoulders back. Tears sprang unbidden to his eyes and as he tried to speak his voice betrayed him, cracking and breaking with suppressed emotion. He managed words on his third attempt.

'I am sorry, I've been in this downward spiral for so long I'd lost sight of who I was; only what I had become. Of course I will stand; how could I not, if I am truthful with myself. Too long have I spent lying to myself that at some point, I'm not even sure when it happened, but I fell for the lie and began to believe it. You are right.' Tomas then laughed. 'Of course you're right: you are the Absolutes, The Four Horsemen of the bloody Apocalypse. What do want me to do then?'

At that moment, before anybody could speak, a wind sprang up, sudden and intense. Tomas had to shield his eyes and brace himself against it lest he be blown from the hill. The Horsemen were immovable and untouched, only their cloaks flapping gave any indication they were affected at all. Then as abruptly as it arose, it was gone. Tomas looked up then and drew an involuntary gasp. Surrounding the hill upon which they stood, had to be at least several hundred angels, all shapes, colors and sizes, accoutered in an eclectic mix of armors. All carried weapons and all looked very determined. A few that Tomas could see were even wounded, showing signs of recent battle. One of the host separated itself and glided up to kneel before Michael.

'Lord Michael, forgive our untimely and undignified arrival, but I bear dire news and your counsel is required.' The angel bowed its head and waited for a response.

'Speak, Gariel. What is so dire as to send you all to me directly?'

Gariel looked up. 'My lord, an army has materialized upon the great plain at the site of the Henge. They have seekers with them and it is our belief that they have picked up the scent of the mortal.'

Gariel turned to spare a glance for Tomas: a swift appraisal to determine if he was worth his warriors dying for. He returned his attention to Michael before Tomas could interpret the look he received. He didn't know if it was disappointment or hope. But Tomas vowed not to let them down. Michael was still thinking – some parts out loud.

'I don't know how they could have tracked you here so fast. This hill is still protected by the ancient powers, and it should have concealed us for longer. Even from seekers.'

Tomas walked over to Michael and looked between him and his lieutenant. 'What are seekers, anyway?' He waited for an answer, which Gariel deferred to Michael to answer.

'They are demonic bloodhounds. Basically, if they get a scent, usually from blood, they can track an individual anywhere. And I mean anywhere. I didn't think they had your scent, seeing as we found you so promptly.'

Tomas looked at the two small cuts upon his palm. He didn't think much of it when he took out Bony in the alley, but his tooth must have nicked him. Then he recalled the night he'd spent within the protective stone circle whilst traveling to Glastonbury. He'd taken shelter there one night, where he had inadvertently cut his hand on a baked bean can he'd found and had to tear open for lack of a tin opener.

'Something you want to share with us, Tomas? Something that might shed some light on this before I go to deal with this incursion?'

Tomas gave up what he suspected. Michael nodded and issued his orders to the host to prepare for battle.

'It is enough for a seeker; the Henge is amplifying the aura generated by your spilt blood. It is akin to a beacon for them. Unfortunately, they are too close to us here for my liking, and hopefully our paths will cross again, Tomas. I also wish you speed and good fortune with your mission, for I believe this is only one more of many such incursions into this world, and it is one more too many. They must be stopped before humanity becomes too aware of what is befalling it. Worldwide panic would only benefit the Adversary.' Tomas agreed: he was an advocate of the quiet solution. 'Though I fear that if the Adversary is strong enough to send his minions here directly, we are already too late.'

'Let's hope not, shall we? It would be a shame to let this Adversary get away with it without a fight and now you've got me fired up for one, I'd like to stick a proverbial spanner in his works, if you get my gist.'

Michael did, and for the first time since meeting the big archangel, Tomas saw him genuinely smile.

'Good for you, Tomas. Yes, I too would like to see that.' Michael reached out his hand to Tomas, who extended his own to grip Michael's wrist. Feeling the warmth and pressure from the contact, Tomas was bolstered all the more. 'Farewell, Tomas, the Horsemen will look after you from here.'

Relinquishing his hold upon Tomas, and without another word, the archangel spun, snapped open his impressive wings, and with a glance and a nod to Gariel, the pair took off like a pair of ground-to-air missiles. Seconds later, in a cacophony of beating wings, the host took flight behind them. In less time than it took to blink, they too were gone.

Tomas felt at a momentary loss. The absence of Michael left him feeling a little vulnerable. For all that the archangel had forever changed his life and brought him into a battle that left him feeling several shades of insignificance, he also emanated safety and security: that as long as he was with him things would be okay. Tomas then experienced another sensation as the past memory of the last time he had felt that warm secure feeling – as a child in the arms of his father – came over him. This opened a floodgate of emotions, long since repressed, but Tomas had no idea how many and how suppressed they were until they assailed him. Warmth spread throughout his body and his chest constricted uncomfortably as the lump rose to his throat. It was all he could do to hold back the tears that threatened to unman him in front of the Horsemen. Wave after wave as memory after memory rose unbidden to the surface. Tomas never realized how much he bitterly regretted their last conversation. Words spoken in anger; he'd stalked off without a backwards glance for the man who raised him and taught him about life. A father who would have, given the need, sacrificed his life for his son with absolutely no hesitation. This last thought was very nearly the breaking of him, but it was with a Herculean effort that Tomas managed to control his emotional upsurge, desperately rationalizing the fact it was an after-effect of Michael's leaving. The archangel obviously generated this feeling of wellbeing; his sudden departure gave Tomas no time to compensate for the void it left.

'Are you well, Tomas?' Famine asked, concern tingeing his Spanish accent. 'What ails you?' Tomas looked up at the riders, tentatively meeting their combined stare.

'I'm fine, just having a moment. It's a lot to take in, after all.' He looked up at each one, letting the magnitude of who sat before him wash over him, and trying to consign his awe to a more manageable level. 'It's not every day this sort of thing happens, which is just as well, I suppose. Okay then, I think I've got my thoughts in some kind of order now so I suppose we ought to get down to the nuts and bolts. What is it and how exactly do you want me to go to my death?'

Famine sat back and laughed. Pestilence glowered at him with evident disapproval. War never batted an eyelid; he just continued to watch Tomas as though he were examining, testing him – looking for cracks. But it was Death who spoke next, and Tomas wasn't sure, but even for Death, he thought he heard a resigned note of inevitability to his voice.

'Why do you think you are going to your death?'

Tomas gave him a look of amusement and shook his head, as if to say 'What a stupid question'. 'Because that's what Michael said. Along the lines that I am unlikely to survive such a confrontation, but I have to go through the motions to fulfill this free will Covenant or whatever. So, of my own free will I will have a go at this Adversary. Get me close enough and I'll give him something to think about, and then after he's wiped the floor with me, it'll be up to you guys to finish off whatever's left. Sound about right?'

'You're a bit of a pessimist, aren't you?' Famine piped in. 'A sort of goblet half empty type of guy, yet normally I'd be inclined to agree with you. A mortal up against one of the strongest of Lucifer's contingent. He would be a hard match even for Michael, and that on a normal day. But this isn't a normal day. He's considerably stronger now, but you're a hero…'

This time it was Tomas's turn to laugh. 'Thanks, ha. That makes me feel much better. I told Michael what I thought about them. Blowing smoke up my arse isn't going to make me impervious to being ripped to bits in a heartbeat, but the sentiment's appreciated. Look, I've said I'll do it; you haven't got to sell it any more. Just get me there and let's get on with it.'

War joined in the debate at that moment. His resonating African accent was almost hypnotic and it almost commanded any who heard it to stop and listen. 'History has been populated with heroes, sacrificing themselves for the greater good, doing the right thing for the good of their people, facing indomitable odds, knowing that there was little to no chance, yet doing it anyway. Such actions differentiate heroes from normal men. Such actions are worthy of honor and valor. You are one such mortal, quite possibly the last. The blood of heroes runs true in your veins: mortals who have stood to the call and risen above their fellows to face the greatest of all challenges. The list is long and salubrious. Yet it was not merely death they sought, but victory. Though it may cost them, it did not lessen their fight. Do not die so easily – the battle is not so easily lost; nor is it over until the last breath leaves you.'

'You've said that little speech before, haven't you?'

For the first time, a hint of a smile lifted a corner of War's mouth. 'Once or twice. Why? Did it work?'

Tomas shook his head slowly from side to side. 'Not really. I've heard it before, or at least something similar. Usually delivered by people who were planning to run in the opposite direction and diving for the safety of their nuclear fallout shelter umpteen miles below ground while other people do their dying for them.'

'You seem very cynical for a man of your profession. Is it not the role of the paid soldier to expect such treatment?'

Tomas had been through this debate many times and he realized it still didn't sit well with him. 'So it might be, but that doesn't mean it sits any better for the knowing. Most of those who give the orders aren't worth a sack of horse shit; after all, you can grow food with shit. All they do is take – but don't get me started on politics and especially politicians. It's a sad fact that those who could run things, don't. Those who can't – seem to. Why is that? It's a crazy screwed up world. Ending it might not be a bad thing. Clean slate and all that. Trouble is, some clown would survive and try to do it all again, in the same stupid way.' Tomas scratched his head diffidently: he'd been known to go on for hours about how things needed to change and who was at fault. It was his stomach growling again that interrupted his train of thought. 'Don't suppose any of you guys…' seeing Pestilence suddenly, '…and girls, have got any food on you? I seem to have developed an appetite.'

Tomas cast an apologetic glance towards Michael, who had provided him with his last meal only a few hours ago; but to his stomach it felt like days. Famine smiled as he answered and Michael rolled his eyes in disbelief as if to say 'World-shattering and unprecedented events and all he thinks of is food!'

'Bear with us a little longer. I'm sure you won't keel over, and we'll take care of that for you a little later.'

Tomas wasn't sure he liked the way that sounded, but he let it go for the moment, opting instead to pursue his initial objective: how he was going to die at the hands of the Adversary. 'Fair enough, it did have the ring of a condemned man's last meal anyway. C'mon, let's do this thing. Give me a gun, or whatever, I'm not fussed.' Tomas gestured for War to toss something over to him, but War never moved. 'What's up now? You want me to do this thing or not?'

'If only it were that easy. Don't you think we would have done something more by now? Use your mind, Tomas, and stop being such an ass,' Famine interjected before War could speak. His face had darkened dangerously at Tomas's flippant attitude. 'The Adversary is a supernatural being; surely you don't think anything as mundane as a gun could harm him? No, he's only vulnerable to supernatural weapons . No mortal, or mortal's weapon, can harm him, as you so wrongly suggest. It will take something more.' *Considerably more* Famine whispered to himself below Tomas's hearing as he studied the human tragically through hooded eyes.

'If that doesn't sound like a suicidal mission then, I don't know what does. Some sort of hero I might be. Willing, I'll concede, but supernatural? Definitely not. That somewhat reduces my chances of success then, wouldn't you say? And you wonder why I seem so blasé about it. It's not like I haven't been on assignments that at first glance looked decidedly one way. I've always found a way out: it's what I do. You want me to use my mind? How's this?' Tomas adopted a resolute stance, hands on hips. 'That gun you carry – it's a weapon of war, meaning it's yours. Doesn't that make it a supernatural weapon? So why couldn't I use that? The round that kills him will be sufficiently supernatural too, wouldn't it? I'm not afraid of death…' Tomas looked at Death sitting astride his horse, so far remaining silent. '...Even less now actually, now that I've met him in the first person. You said you wanted someone pragmatic; I'm that too. So that's my plan – simple, straightforward and to the point. You drop me off wherever I need to go, and I'll get on with it. How does that go with your plan?' Tomas looked between them. Their expressions were unreadable but he sensed some unspoken communication taking place. 'You did have a plan?' Tomas added, for the increasing silence didn't fill him with confidence. It took him back to his earlier thought that he was simply an offering, an expedient necessity in order to fulfill the needs of their Covenant. Long minutes passed before Famine spoke again.

'You are partly right, Tomas; we never expected you to survive and I'm sure you appreciate our honesty. We still don't. But your fortitude has inspired us to consider the possibility of success. Pestilence is a good judge of character and she sees something in you that inspires her – and let me tell you, that doesn't happen often.'

'Do not talk about me as though I am not here; you know how that annoys me, Famine.' Pestilence almost hissed. 'Do not presume to put words in my mouth also simply because I chose not to flap my lips with the same regularity that you seem to enjoy flapping yours. I said that with the right weapon he might come out of it alive, if not in one piece. There is strength in him that is lacking in many mortals, a great many, hence our current predicament. I say we give him what assistance we can and allow the mortal the opportunity to prevail, he is the progeny of Guardians after all is he not?'

Tomas was mesmerized. Her voice *was* like audio honey. Pestilence was soft spoken. It juxtaposed with her fierce warrior-like exterior, and when she spoke, it softened her serious expression and lit her up like a lotus blossom showing its face to the sun for the first time. Tomas's memory shot him back to his time in Korea and many a hot tropical night spent in the company of Madam Misu's willing girls. It was one of his more pleasant undercover assignments but they paled into harpies against Pestilence when she spoke and looked at him. He couldn't reconcile her inherent beauty with her embodiment, Pestilence. It conjured images of disease and rotting flesh, black death and Ebola. He'd seen the results of both and they weren't pretty.

'Tomas!' Famine's address brought him back to reality with a start. 'Are you familiar with the Temple of Solomon at Megiddo?'

Tomas nodded, recalling another government-paid-for excursion. This time it was on a secondment to MOSAD, the Israeli secret service. Their intelligence was first rate, but due to certain political and diplomatic restrictions, they required an outsider to carry out this particularly nasty little detail.

'I stayed there once; the fortress though, not the temple. I don't remember there being a temple – just ruins – but some gun runners were using it for a rendezvous point. I use gun runners with some poetic license, they weren't exactly guns, and Pestilence would have been interested in the effects of their chemical merchandise, but I digress. I was their contact, or so they thought. It was my job to close them down – permanently – if you get my point. It went off without a hitch – which makes a welcome change – and I had a pleasant week in Jerusalem after that. Saw the sights, then slipped off home. That was – let me think – some six and a half years ago now, easily. As I recall: unless they've tidied up, so much ruins and rocks in the middle of nowhere. I am aware of its historical significance. I was well briefed, but I thought all that Armageddon stuff was so much religious dogma and linguistic by-play with its older names. What was it?' Tomas looked into the distant past. 'Har Megiddo – the hill of, or something like that. Gradually became Armageddon: the site of the last great battle, from what I can remember. What about it, anyway?'

'Solomon was, amongst other things, a gifted magician and he knew a lot more than history credited him with, and it seems that there were quite a few enchantments secreted into the architecture and which have wormed their way deep into the Earth. He had allusions, it seems, about immortality; and returning to rule from his resurrected fortress, in his resurrected body, fully intent on resurrecting his kingdom along with it.'

'That's a lot of resurrections. I take it that by the lack of that happening, he suffered from something of a resurrection dysfunctionality?'

Famine groaned, the only one to register Tomas's poor humor, before continuing his explanation. 'The Adversary was and is, it seems, playing a long game indeed. We have become aware of only a tiny part of his plan; that is possible thanks to War's gentle persuasion with several minions we captured. It seems that they plan to raise Solomon's fortress at Megiddo – an impregnable and very defensible foothold upon this world – for the Adversary has need to be there.'

'I didn't have this guy down as the needy sort,' Tomas quipped, and drew a scowl from Death, or at least that was how he interpreted the stare Death leveled at him.

'That need – whatever it is – is sufficient for us to deny him; but it was the fact that the Adversary himself intends to manifest at this fortress, which gave us our opportunity: the opportunity to insert humanity's chosen warrior and attempt to nullify the Covenant. Failure or success is immaterial; the attempt will have been made. It should allow us to intervene directly before he becomes too strong for us.'

Tomas snorted in derision. 'Are you serious? Is that possible?' When no denial was forthcoming, even from the loquacious Famine, Tomas began to feel some trepidation about what he was up against. 'What do you mean as well when you say "should"? Don't you know for sure?'

This time Famine did look pensive, which did even less for Tomas's confidence. 'No, we don't know for certain. As you have been made aware, this is unprecedented. Your gesture may be entirely fruitless.'

'Thanks, I'm feeling better by the moment about all of this. There was I thinking I was in expert hands, hands that had a watertight and cosmic plan to guarantee success. At least to not have my death become any more meaningless and to not have been entirely in vain?' More blank looks. 'Apparently not then. What with your reputation and an army of angels, or whatever they are, to back it up, and all it rests upon is "should". Not even my old bosses sent an agent out based on that; and they had little value for life, especially their own people. Everyone was expendable as long as it got the job done. Looks like I still am.'

Famine leant forward and adopted a philosophic pose but kept his icy gaze upon Tomas, who had decided to sit down on the grass, hands searching his pockets by habit for the cigarettes he had given up many, many years before after finding out how much DNA could be ascertained from a discarded butt and how easily a sniper can spot a lit end in the dark over distance. But the habit of looking never left him when his hands had nothing better to do. Dew settled upon his faded jeans, but damp jeans were a minor discomfort, after years of training to ignore such minor inconveniences. But it had been a trying night and it was starting to catch up with him. An involuntary yawn gave him away to his companions.

'You need to have more faith, Tomas; we are not entirely without resource. You must have had some at some point. Did you not have intentions once to join the religion of your mother and serve in that institution?'

Tomas stiffened instantly at the evoked memory and his reply was curt and brooked no misunderstanding. 'I was still at school then and that was a very long time ago and another lifetime altogether. That Tomas Walker is very dead and, trust me, he won't be resurrecting himself anytime soon. He's seen and done far too much for that, so don't even go there.'

Tomas was never really sure why the thought of being a priest filled him with such anger, but it did and he took that as a positive justification he'd made the right choice. The Horsemen remained impassive in the face of Tomas's annoyance, and that just annoyed him more. The detached manner drove it home to Tomas just how alien these beings were to the insignificant and emotional mortals. These legendary Horsemen dealt with the ending of worlds and the mighty task of ensuring that all the species, however many more there were, all complied with the cosmic rules set down at the beginning of all things. Why then, should they be overly concerned that they pushed a few buttons within Tomas, a mortal – less than a grain of sand in the galactic equation. Tomas tried to fathom just how many people had died since they rose up on two legs. It was an incalculable figure as some one hundred and fifty thousand people, if not more, died each and every day. There simply weren't enough noughts. Now it looked like another equally improbable figure was going to be applied to the demise of the rest. And on top of all that, it seemed that *he* had a prominent part in actually *stopping* it from happening. *Or at least trying to, I suppose, for however long I get to live through it anyway. Ah well, it's not like I had anything else pressing to do.* Tomas tried calming himself before speaking again; he had always believed that angry people were stupid people, letting that base emotion override common practical sense. Angry people usually ended up dead very quickly. Cooler heads prevail. He repeated a Buddhist chant he had learnt years before, several times, until his breathing settled back into a relaxed pattern once again.

'So tell me about this resource that you are not without. How exactly is that going to help me, and does it involve food? 'Cos my stomach is starting to think my throat's been cut. Even living rough on the streets I got to eat more often than this. You might not need food but us mortals do, I'm afraid, and you said you were going to address that.'

Famine smiled at Tomas, though it had more of the crocodilian aspect to it and Tomas wasn't sure he was going to like whatever was going through his mind. He watched as Famine dismounted and strode over towards him. 'You are quite correct, Tomas, now get up!' Famine reached him before he could rise and the Horseman extended a hand to assist him. Tomas gripped his wrist; Famine did likewise and showing little to no effort, pulled. Tomas was lifted clean off his feet and it felt like his shoulder was very nearly dislocated in the process. 'Sorry about that. I forget how frail you mortals are. It's not often I get to manhandle one. Still, you're on your feet, that's what counts. Now, about your growling intestines. Let's see what we can do about that.' Tomas had no idea what to expect, but what he didn't anticipate was Famine's next move. With a speed that belied thought, the mighty gleaming halberd had appeared in the Horseman's hand, which spun it through a dazzling series of maneuvers. It came to rest in a horizontal position, the blade directly facing Tomas's chest.

'Now wait a mi —' Tomas exclaimed, horror suddenly showing in his eyes as he saw what Famine intended. Wham. The blade slammed into Tomas, right up to the haft, the remainder of its two-foot blade protruding from his back. Tomas looked down wide-eyed at it, disbelief written all over his expression. His mouth tried to form words, but nothing came. He began to feel his knees buckle and just before blackness smothered him, wrapping him in sweet oblivion, an explosion of light engulfed him. Tomas then screamed as his body found its voice. Light and energy ripped through him. He felt every molecule burst into incandescent flame. Seared beyond pain, his mind sought escape from the agony and it promptly fled. It was seconds or years later – Tomas couldn't tell – but he found himself looking down upon the tableau unfolding upon the mist-shrouded hill. He saw the English countryside all around – skeletal trees and dew-covered fields, a light coating of frost upon everything as winter forged on. He saw foxes and badgers going about their early morning business; and heard the cawing of the crows as they flocked about their nests high in the tree tops, vying for mates and the best nesting positions. But it was the scene upon Silbury Hill that drew his gaze back. He saw himself standing transfixed before another being who was holding a deadly looking pole, arm out, impaling the man before him. Himself, Tomas realized with horror. Without knowing how or understanding how he could be watching himself from so high up, he swooped down in a panic, desperate to stop what was happening to him, but he seemed to be incapable of getting close enough. He was, however, close enough to see his expression. The eyes were white, rolled up in his head, and his face was contorted in a rictus of pain. His limbs had stiffened like a million volts were passing through him. Maybe they were. He couldn't feel anything in his current state. He watched as Famine pulled the weapon free. It made an awful sucking sound as the flesh gave up the blade. It seemed that the consciousness of Tomas couldn't share the body with Famine's blade, for the moment it was pulled free, Tomas was snapped back into his body so fast, the world passed in a blur. It took a few seconds for his eyes to adjust to being in his head again, and the view they afforded. The first thing they saw was a smiling Famine. Leaning nonchalantly upon his now vertically positioned pole arm, Famine spoke, and Tomas heard it through cotton wool from some distance away, or that was how it felt, until his hearing settled back down from the blood pounding in his ears.

'That feel any better?' The question was asked in all innocence, but Tomas was still feeling the blade crunching through his sternum and ripping out the muscles of his back. Tomas sucked in several great lungfuls of cold morning air as he inspected the wound. Or the wound he expected to find, only he couldn't find one. Scrambling in his clothes he felt the flesh of his chest, but there was nothing there – only the lightly scarred and lightly tanned as well as moderately hairy chest. Even his clothes were uncut. Tomas looked up at Famine, the silent question in his confused expression showing he didn't understand what had just happened and was hopeful that an explanation was about to be forthcoming.

'I am Famine, remember? *Famine*? Come on, Tomas, make the leap. Mine is the governance of all that requires nourishment and sustenance. From planets down to the smallest of insects, I embody all the causes of such. Extreme cold and extreme heat prohibit life, from every creature to all manner of crops and plant life. That is the simplest way of putting it. The technical details would take a lifetime to convey so we'll leave it at that. Consequentially, the reverse is also applicable. I can provide infinite nourishment. Which is precisely what I have done. I have imparted a fraction of my own power into you, fusing it with your DNA and genetic make-up. Henceforth, you will have no need for sleep or the necessity to partake of food and water – unless you choose to. Your task should not be inhibited by having to stop to eat and sleep.' Tomas just stood bug-eyed as he took in what Famine was telling him. 'I know it's a lot to take in right now so try not to worry overly about it. Suffice to say, you shouldn't be whining about being hungry again, so we can get on with the next step. I hope you know how to ride.'

Tomas was struggling to keep up with the moment. *Don't worry? I've just been impaled on two foot of steel, booted out of my body and summarily told I'll never need to eat again; and he doesn't want me to worry? Sure, what have I got to worry about? Other than the fact that with friends like these I'm not sure I actually need enemies.*

His mind gradually caught up on the conversation and he latched onto the last word he heard. 'Ride? I know I'm going to regret this, but ride what where?' Tomas heard his own voice and he realized there was a note of acceptance creeping into it. This last stunt had tipped his already struggling mind over some precipice. A *whatever* mindset had asserted itself, firm in the belief he couldn't be surprised any more. It was simply safer to just go along with whatever they had in mind for him and get matters over with. He did, though, berate himself and determined to not ask any more stupid questions: the answers were often unexpected and painful. When he focused his attention back on the Horsemen, War was pointing to something behind him. Tomas turned warily, preparing for the worst. What he wasn't expecting was the magnificent animal standing calmly behind him just a few feet away. He turned to look directly into the slate grey eyes of a grey stallion easily as huge as those of the Horsemen – wide of chest, supported by powerful legs. It regarded Tomas with an innate intelligence that said he was being studied as much as he was studying the horse. The first thing to pop into Tomas's head was that it looked like some thunderous storm cloud on legs. *Storm; that would be a fitting name for you, boy.* The horse whickered and nodded its head in front of him, snorting out hot breath, which Tomas thought ironically had the smell of ozone. It was as though the horse had read his mind and accepted the name. *There's a lot of that going lately.* Upon closer examination Tomas saw a little flash of white on the horse's forehead. *Had that been there a moment ago?* Or had the horse picked up on the name and added it as a sign of approval? Tomas looked back to the riders and smiled – a boyish smile that took several years off his time-worn face. It was like the boy being given his first puppy. That strange chemistry that takes place when a living thing is gifted to another. There was no other feeling like it. It wasn't the same with inanimate objects, not even fast cars. There was something deep and connecting about being given an animal – a bond instantly created. That was how it was with Tomas and Storm; he felt a connection as he gazed into the slate grey eyes very like the crackle of lightning. Tomas, still grinning like a loon, looked back to his new companion, only to find that it was now accoutered for war and travel – saddled and armored in a similar fashion to War's roan. But coupled with the buzz of the gift, Tomas also felt a twinge of trepidation.

'Did I mention it had been some years since I'd ridden?'

War reassured him. 'Fear not, Tomas, Storm will take care of you; he's quite capable.'

Tomas was stunned. How did they know he'd thought to call him that?

'He just told us.'

'Look, I know it's all in a day's work for you guys, but would you mind not strolling through my mind and answering my thoughts? Have some respect, will you? I'm sure that somewhere it is considered impolite to invade another person's mind without their consent, hmm?'

The four riders looked amongst themselves, as though silently discussing something – him no doubt. Then Death turned to Tomas and simply said, 'Very well. It will be as you request, though should you choose to communicate with us mentally, we will hear you. Does this satisfy you?'

Tomas nodded, then walked over to Storm. He rubbed his neck and generally made a fuss of the incredible animal. Storm even seemed to like it: he whinnied excitedly once more and stamped his hoof a few times, turning his head to whuffle Tomas's cheek with his warm, moist, bristly nose. This elicited the first chuckle of genuine mirth and pleasure from Tomas – the first in a long time, he realized.

The voice of Death cut through his reverie as though the deadly scythe itself had sliced through his thoughts. 'We need to be away now. Mount up, Tomas, we have a long way to go and we are restricted in our manner of travel, for caution in alerting the enemy. We must ride the sky rather than open a portal, and this takes time. We need to rendezvous with Raphael and his army, who are currently encamped upon the Jezreel Plain, awaiting our arrival.'

'There's an army camped out in the desert? Earlier Michael said he didn't want humanity alerted too soon about this. We're not backward, you know; we have things called satellites which monitor the world's hot spots. The Middle East is one such hot spot. Don't you think it might cause some panic if it picked up a bloody great angelic army camped out within a few miles of civilization? I thought you guys were intelligent?'

'That mouth of yours is going to get you in deep trouble one day.'

Tomas laughed. 'Just how much more trouble do you really think I can get into that I'm not already up to my neck in?'

Famine chuckled at Tomas's retort and Death shot him a quick look, but even Pestilence had the slightest of smiles on her beautifully severe face at Tomas's ironic observation.

'Tomas,' Death started. 'We have mastered density manipulation. There is nothing in your technology that can detect us. They will be out of phase until they are ready to appear, for now, and they are observing the activity taking place at Megiddo.'

'What activity?' Tomas asked, his confidence returning slowly along with his curiosity.

'That,' Death said, a hint of annoyance in his already dour voice, 'is what we go to determine. Now mount up and prepare yourself.'

The order was given in such a way that Tomas inherently knew not to press any further. He may be an ally, but he was under no illusion that they thought little of him and considered him a necessity at best. Had they been able to circumvent him they would have. It wasn't that they were purposely cruel, he concluded: simply so far above humanity that they regarded humans with the same contempt that the average human regarded an animal.

As Tomas took the few steps towards Storm, Pestilence sidled her own grey over to them, though to say her mare was grey was anomalous: it was more a silvery shade, like brushed steel. She regarded him coolly as he stroked Storm's neck in a bid to reassure the big horse that his intentions warranted no cause for its concern – though to be truthful, the reassurance was more for Tomas's sake than the horse's. It had been sometime since he had ridden, as he had told the Horsemen. What he had neglected to mention was that he had fallen off several times and the horse had taken an instant dislike to him and had bitten him at every available opportunity. Storm bent his head back to watch Tomas place his foot in the stirrup and take the reins. He studied his new rider until he was mounted, remained still until he felt him settled, then whinnied once more. Pestilence's horse responded in kind. The subtle communication went sailing over Tomas's head. The thought of communicating horses didn't occur to him in the slightest. Frankly, he found it took most of his concentration now just to remain upright and composed astride the beast. *It wouldn't do to be falling off and looking a pillock in front of these guys.*

Pestilence sidled up close to Tomas, affording him a waft of her heady perfume, and in her lilting Asian accent instructed him briefly on riding techniques: how to sit more comfortably, what to avoid doing in order to lessen muscle cramps. She tightened his gear in the appropriate places and, once finished, cast a critical eye over his posture. Satisfied that all was well, she silently turned to join the others.

'Thank you,' Tomas said quietly, just enough for her to hear.

Pestilence stopped and looked back at him. 'Thanks are not necessary, Tomas: we do what we must to ensure your arrival and ability to complete your task. No more, no less. We all do our duty. It is the way.'

'All the same, it seems a lot considering all I'm to do is to go and die like a good little mortal. That is what you expect, isn't it?'

She looked sad at Tomas's cynical words.'You mortals put too much stock in pessimism. Yes, you should always expect the worst, prepare for it and plan for it. Do not be deluded into believing all is well with everything. Faith has much to be accountable for. It has prevented humans from preparing, blindly burying their heads in the belief that something that no one has ever seen will save them. You may well surprise yourself, Tomas. Like many humans, you are stronger than you know. Expect the worst, for when it does not appear then it is only for the better. Find the balance between the two. Everything exists in harmony. Even to riding the horse you sit upon. Be part horse, part man. Anticipate his actions as he will anticipate yours. Move with his movements, not against them; the ride will be smoother. The same concept applies to all things.'

Tomas was silent for a moment, taking in all she had said. It had been the most she had said since they had arrived. 'All that aside, tell me: you don't think I'll survive this assignment, for want of a better name for it – suicidal mission might be better – but that's a bit too negative.'

'In truth – no.' Their eyes locked briefly and Tomas felt he was spiraling down into hers. She blinked and the sensation passed, but not before Tomas glimpsed an insight into the austere rider. He felt a deep abiding sadness suppressed below the surface. And got the impression that she would rather be anywhere, or anything other than the cosmic embodiment of sickness and disease. Especially now.

'I appreciate your honesty, but now I'm all settled to go, shouldn't we be off? The prospect of getting to warmer climes is appealing, as I'm freezing my arse off on this hill and I'm not looking forward to the journey. I get the impression it'll be colder up there than down here.'

Pestilence shook her helmeted head. The fur that circumnavigated the brim swished in the chilly air, sending little droplets sparkling away into the morning mist.'Whilst you ride Storm, you will be impervious to the elements, as are we. Neither wind nor rain, or cold or heat will bother you, though I do caution you to hang on tight. Catching you should you fall may be problematic.'

With that last warning, Pestilence turned and rejoined her comrades. They all turned then as one and saluted Tomas.

'Hold on tight, Tomas. We ride for Megiddo.' Upon the last word, which still hung in the air, the Four Horsemen of the Apocalypse spurred their mounts forward. Storm took off, barely a heartbeat behind them. Several powerful strides later they reached the edge of the hill top, and even though Tomas knew what to expect, his mind and reactions were still unprepared for the disconcerting take-off. His body was subconsciously geared for the horses to drop off the side of the hill but instead, they leapt out into the void. He partly wished that he had closed his eyes at that moment, for the sight of horses' hooves pounding along on nothing but fresh air and rapidly gaining height was one of the most unnerving experiences he had the misfortune of being a part of. Occasionally one of the Horsemen looked back to ensure he was still there, hanging on. Tomas grinned thinly back to them, muttering and cursing to himself when they turned away again. But after thirty minutes or so of steady ascent, and breaking through the cloud barrier, they seemed to level out and things got a little smoother. *Damn. This is just so bloody odd. The last time I had this view I was looking out the window of a 747.* Tomas laughed then, as he imagined the faces of some bored passenger, casually glancing out of their window to see five riders on horseback, galloping along faster than they were flying. Riding across cloudscapes as though they were green fields.

Famine dropped back to see if he was okay. 'Hanging in there, Tomas?' Surprised that he could hear Famine so clearly, Tomas nodded and smiled but said nothing. 'Good. I expect this will take some getting used to.'

Now there's an understatement to end them all. But Tomas didn't think Famine was looking at the long view. 'Not for long though, hey? After all, I'm unlikely to be making a return trip, am I?'

Famine had no witty answer to that, for he knew the truth of what Tomas was saying, so with a curt nod he spurred his horse on and rejoined the other three, leaving Tomas to his thoughts. Thoughts which had turned darkly inward, mulling his own prospects over.

At least death will be some sort of release: the fate of humanity rests on my shoulders and I already know I'm going to fail. It's bloody expected of me. One last mega failure to add to all the ones that are lesser by comparison, but failures all the same. So many people depending on me and I seem destined to let every one of them down. It's at times like this, Tomas thought sourly, *life really sucks.*

Chapter Three

Imbolc

GWEN STEPPED OUT OF THE SANTA FE mini-market and immediately wished she hadn't left her coat back at her own store. The icy cold air gusting through the holes in her knitwear led her to think that she couldn't have gone far wrong with a thicker sweater either. Gwen shivered as another gust of what she called *a lazy wind* put goose bumps on her goose bumps. She called it that, as she had explained to her friend once: *It's a lazy wind because it doesn't bother to go around, it just goes right through.* It made her more aware than ever that she had foregone her underwear as well today. *That'll teach me;* el natural *doesn't really work in winter – though I suppose if I got my sorry ass out of bed a bit earlier I might be able to remember these things instead of simply where the coffee is. But I do so like my bed, it's a shame to have to get out of it all.* Gwen silently berated herself for her slothfulness. Having jumped up and grabbed whatever came to hand, Gwen had poured her coffee in to her traveling mug and run out of the house, bed head and no make-up. But Gwen could get away with that look where others would fail dismally. Ever since she had been a girl, she had been the envy of most of her school-friends. They'd always said she had the figure of a dancer. Some of the more cruel ones said it was a boy's body, but she was lithe and agile. Her breasts had developed early, but only to such a size that she had no need for bras or other support. They supported themselves quite well on their own. This didn't win her many friends, and the fact that she could look fresh faced without any make-up just annoyed them more; girls could be truly evil if they put their minds to it and several did. Those had been harsh schooldays. It was no small wonder she played truant for so much of them. Summer and winter, she spent climbing trees in the local park. And at five foot one and a bit, there wasn't a lot of spare body fat to keep the cold out when sat up a tree in nothing but a school uniform. Her mother had never even noticed when she took to taking extra clothes with her during the winter months.

When invariably the same friends grew up, slowly expanding and deteriorating due to their lifestyles: kids, marriage and just being bloody idle, she had stayed her same youthful looking self, remaining much as she had when she was at school. Only older. Gwen was a firm believer in growing older, not necessarily up. This little fact had lost her what tenuous friendships she had experienced with those same school-friends. *Gits!* The increasing distance and isolation from them got her to start thinking seriously about travel. And travel she did, ditching art college where she had somehow wound up, packing her meagre belongings; and with few goodbyes she was gone. Europe, India, Sri Lanka, Tibet, Brazil, Mexico and eventually into the US, where she had enjoyed many a pleasant year, not to mention one or two not so pleasant ones. But she pushed those memories down: now wasn't the time to dwell on them. *How I never got sold into slavery is a bloody miracle. What was I thinking? Single blonde female, hiking around the world on her own. I might have been worth a camel or two. That just proves I'm crazy, not to mention lucky. A girl's gotta have some luck these days, with so many creeps out there.*

It was, however, this day's freezing temperature that kept her moving and not dredging up any more of her past – certainly no more than she needed to. Gwen muttered to herself that she didn't need to as much as she was. And yet – odd memories had been slipping in and out of her mind a lot recently and she found them an unwanted distraction. Gwen attributed them to the high altitude and the cold weather. Focusing on the task at hand whilst shivering involuntarily, again , Gwen picked up her pace across the lot and made a beeline for her little car. It had been warm enough in her store, but when she got dressed this morning, she had been so distracted by these odd memories and dreams, she had somehow forgotten she was visiting Dolores today. How she managed that was another mystery, because she had been visiting regularly for over a year now. She hadn't remembered until it was too late and she was pulling up at the store. Now she was paying the price for those inadvertent memories having disturbed her delicate morning routine. *I don't know what's going on in my head these days but it's starting to take the piss now, though this'll teach me to pay more attention to stuff in the past than what I'm doing in the present – Focus, Gwen girl, for God's sake: you've got too much to do today! Thank heavens for the girls: I'd be stuffed if they weren't there. Days like this I wonder if I'm cut out for this shopkeeping lark. I've never been a morning person, but just lately it's got out of hand. Reminder to chat to Res about it: I'm sure she's got the answer and I bet I won't like it.* Gwen chuckled to herself at the prospect of Dolores's reaction, for she was always full of sage advice and enjoyed handing it out.

As Gwen shuffled across the parking lot, avoiding the slush and desperately trying not to get her Ugs wet, for she loved her Ugs, having had them for some years now, and the last thing she wanted to do was get them ruined in the filthy water. So she carefully navigated the puddles as she watched the other customers coming and going, all struggling in the Santa Fe winter. The thing about being several thousand feet above sea level was that the air was thinner, making it feel considerably colder. Some days the air hurt to breathe and its thinness generated so much static electricity that it played merry hell with the women who swanned about, all trying to look like catalogue models. Having spent hours getting their hair just so, the moment they stepped outside it sprang out in all directions, like stepping onto a

Van Der Graff generator – much to their annoyance and Gwen's constant amusement. They amused her for other reasons too, for as much as someone could be a product of their environment, they were that. The southwestern influence was prevalent in just about everything in Santa Fe. Brimming with Pueblo and Navajo imagery as well as the Spanish and Mexican; from the adobe buildings, chillis and even down to the luminaries or farolitos – essentially paper bags with little candles in which adorned many homes and lit up pathways – which some people were now putting out on the run up to Christmas. *Just like home: people get earlier and earlier with their decorations no matter what they are.* Gwen pondered the similarities briefly but there were simply so many minute things that, together, created the ambience that set this city apart from all the rest, which is what attracted Gwen to it originally. It did though, seem to try and stereotype its inhabitants. Gwen, not being one for conformity, noticed this almost straightaway and had purposely shied away from the subconscious uniform that many of the women who lived and worked within the artists' community had adopted: that of the cowboy boot, long colorful skirts and western style high-waisted jackets. Gwen conceded it looked nice, a bit frontier mixed with a bit Native American and rolled into traditional American female sensibility; but it wasn't her. She had been called a hippie chick – Little Miss Flower Power and all other variations upon a theme. Not that she cared – she was in fact quite proud of her individuality. But it appeared that many who moved here from all over the world seemed to succumb to the unwritten dress code – some sooner, others later, but most, eventually. Gwen had learnt early in life that, however free and easy something appeared, there was always an undercurrent of conformity, of regulations and rules. There was always someone seemingly in charge, ensuring things got done their way. It was subtle, but the world was full of these manipulative individuals, trying to shape people and events to meet their minds' ideal. Gwen figured she was either paranoid or especially observant, for she refused to become embroiled in these invisible entrapments. When it began to look like life was being interfered with again, she would up sticks and leave. She could see it happening here, but there was an attraction to the land that seemed to hold her stronger than her own instincts. *Another odd thing for the list.*

Having made it unscathed to her car, Gwen had pulled out onto the road and was roaring off as fast as she dared considering the treacherous conditions, back to her own adobe-styled house. She still called it a house: a remaining idiosyncrasy left over from her British heritage. In truth, it more resembled a glorified mud hut with timbers poking out. Even though it was state of the art inside and historically in keeping with the indigenous peoples and environmentally conducive, it never failed to give her that Neolithic feeling when she went home at the end of the day. She had affection-ately named it her *cave*. It amused her friends: Dolores and her two shop assistants Jennifer and Madeline. *Maybe it's just for them I stay here. Them and the mountains, the desert and the feeling that the land wants me here. I must be getting softer in the head.* Gwen chuckled to herself. The sweet sound of her laughter echoed in the confines of her Jeep Wrangler – whose loosely fitted soft top was letting in cold air as fast as her warm air-con was trying to do the opposite. As much as she moaned about the arty-farty women hereabouts, they couldn't affect her enough to make her forget just how beautiful the New Mexico desert and surrounding Sangrea de Christo mountains were; not forgetting her favorite retreat, Hyde Memorial Park. She loved her time away up in the trees. She would tolerate the women's sideways glances and whispered mutterings a bit longer, though she knew she had been saying that for the last three years too. *Suppose I'll say it a bit longer then, and do what I always have and leave it up to the Goddess to determine where she wants me next. So home it is. Jen and Maddy can survive without me for a bit longer. I am the boss after all. I'll make it up to them and bring them those sickly chocolate mocha lattes they like so much, and some lemon pound cake. Damned if I know how they pile it in without piling it on; still, good luck to them. If you've got it, use it, I say.* The day's niggles so far settled down in her mind, Gwen settled in for the remainder of the drive home to pick up her coat and bits, singing along, somewhat out of tune, to Buffy Saint Marie and Robbie Robertson; content for the time being, humming as she made the round trip, even still singing tunelessly to herself as she arrived back in town for the promised supplies. Laden with steaming beverages, Gwen skidded out onto the road and headed for the town square.

Dolores Begay, or Res to those who knew her well, was her friend pretty much since the day she had arrived in Santa Fe. Dolores, her mother and her grandmother were all of the Long Turtle clan and had lived in Santa Fe all their lives. Dolores worked part-time for her cousin, who held a pitch on the porch of the Governor's Palace – a place where Native Americans had been trading almost since it was built, which was some time ago, for the building had been recognized as one of, if not the, oldest public buildings in the US. The Pueblo and the Navajo had been around as long as anyone currently living there could remember, and in the desert for centuries; even bequeathing their pitch to their children to continue. It was a tenuous living, but it was all there was for some. Dolores and her cousin were two of the fortunate ones: both held down several jobs to make ends meet. When she covered for Joshua Stonerook, her cousin, he went off and did house maintenance; when they swapped back, she did housekeeping for some of the wealthier families, some as far away as Albuquerque and Taos.

Ever since Gwen's arrival in town, she had been helping Dolores out. It started out as a debt repaid, for it was Dolores and her family who put Gwen up for what ended up being three months. Initially it was only to be a week or two while she found a place of her own, but the trio enjoyed the arrangement and it just seemed to go on and on. It would have probably continued were it not for what happened one odd afternoon: her own place found her. But now, it was just fun. It gave Gwen a break from the tedium of shop work and it helped Dolores out. Occasionally she would have to run her grandmother into Albuquerque for hospital appointments. During summer it was a thoroughly enjoyable time out for Gwen: she met all manner of fascinating people. Her favorite time there was during the Earth Day celebrations each year. The world, his wife and their dog, literally, came out for that and the atmosphere was phenomenal. However, it was days like this one, when it was colder than a cold thing – though the hot soup and tea she had brought was a godsend – that it wasn't quite so much fun. *Freezing your butt off and losing all sensation in your appendages as that icy wind whistles around your nether regions; lovely! The things I do for friendship.* But Gwen's conscience pricked her then, for Res' grandmother wasn't taking the cold well. That was the reason for today's excursion and Gwen's cover: a lovely old lady who everybody called Grandma Yellow Deer. Her actual name was Eleanor, but according to Dolores, no one had ever been heard using it, and she was considered by many to be a true wise woman. Her forte was weather, but she was no mean healer either, and a few months back she had predicted a winter unlike any the people had ever seen. *I hope this weather is as bad as it's gonna get*, thought Gwen, not being a fan of the cold, as she parked the Jeep in the square. *But I can't shake the feeling that it's not and that something much worse is coming.*

Grandma Yellow Deer hadn't looked well when she saw her last and it was cause enough for concern. She was eighty-six years old and looked as though she had earned every year of life. Her history was etched within every line of her weathered and parchment-thin skin. But even though her body had become frail quite rapidly of late, her eyes still looked as though they would bore holes through mountains and could read your every thought. Which occasionally she did. *Now that is unnerving. Lovely old gal. Lovely – but bloody scary sometimes.*

Dolores was busy with a customer when Gwen arrived, so Gwen mouthed a silent 'hello' and held up the Styrofoam cups, which steamed slightly in the cold air. Dolores acknowledged her with a flash of her big brown eyes and an almost imperceptible nod. Gwen backed up and parked herself down on a nearby bench to wait, watching and listening to Dolores go through her sales pitch, feeling her mind drift again. She had heard her go through this often enough in that haunting voice of hers. Gwen just loved the accent and knew she could listen to her friend tell stories for hours upon end – and had. It cast Gwen's mind back to when she was a little girl herself and she had listened, rapt, as her mother had told her stories. Not of animal spirits, Gitche Manitou the Great Spirit, White Buffalo Calf Woman and a host of other equally fantastic tales, but they were powerful stories nonetheless. And they now were part of all she had left of her parents. *Memories*. She had been told that they and her brother had died mysteriously in some macabre explosion, something that should never have been able to happen, according to the coroner. The odds of such a localized blast doing so much damage was highly improbable at best, but even though no further explanation was forthcoming, it didn't alter the outcome. They were all dead and that was all there was to it.

The will finalized itself almost and the financial loose ends were all tied up. Gwen didn't do a lot, leaving it mostly in the hands of her father's solicitor; she just answered questions, ticked boxes and signed in all the appropriate places. A few weeks later and it was all over. And for as sad as Gwen was about the loss, it solved her business and housing issue well enough. It was a strained sadness brought about by guilt. She knew she should be sad but couldn't quite manage it fully. She hadn't seen any of them for some considerable time, especially her distant brother. He just seemed to vanish into smoke and the only way she knew she had a brother at all was the odd reminder from her parents; and even that eventually stopped. So she had been able to pay off the shop she now ran as well as the property that went with it. Mortgage-free and solvent. She thanked her mum and dad daily for that. In memory of them, she had called her small New Age store 'Earth Angel'. It was a nickname her mother had given her as a baby, apparently. Gwen didn't remember it, but her mother had told her the story often enough. It had come from an old record that her father had first asked his future wife to dance to. Both Tomas and Gwen had been conceived out of wedlock. Her parents always told them that they had been difficult days back then. Her parents met when they could, when her father's duties would permit. That and other concerns had driven her mother to guiltily turn her life over to the Church toward the latter part of her life. It was in part the thought of how her mother had gone *a bit strange*, that made Gwen turn her thoughts to the other strange woman in her life. The former owner of her shop and home. *Now she was a right peculiar one. This place must attract them like some huge geophysical magnet. Maybe that's also why spiritual places always seem to be up mountains or at height, attracting those who don't fit in with what society deems 'normal'. Pah, who wants to be normal anyway? Certainly not me.*

It was her first Earth Day, and Gwen was thoroughly loving it. The Pueblo dancers, the floats and just the total atmosphere. It was magical and ethereal both at once. Sights, smells and an audiovisual spectacular. Gwen had found herself reclining under one of the trees in the town square, taking a pull on a bottle of ice cold MGD, when the little old lady had walked up, hands clasped before her, and stated quite emphatically in a wheezy but strong voice, 'There you are. I've been looking for you.'

Gwen looked around her, thinking the old girl was talking to someone else, but there was no one else nearby, only her. 'Sorry, can I help you? Are you lost or something, because I think you may have just mistaken me for someone else.'

The wizened old lady smiled a surprisingly toothy smile. *Good grief! Looks like she's breaking them in for a mule. How does she talk with them in there?* They were a prodigious set of gnashers all right, but she spoke clearly enough, even if little of it made any actual sense to Gwen, but she listened patiently.

'I've been here too long, and my time is up – but it must go to the right person and you look *just* like her.' *Like who?* 'Now why don't we go and have a little chat over a nice cup of tea and let me tell you all about it. By the way, my name is Mrs Callaghan, but you can call me Cynthia.'

Gwen said okay, and stood, feeling almost compelled to follow her. In hindsight it was even stranger that she should have done what she did. But within forty-eight hours, she was one hundred and forty thousand dollars short and the proud owner of a three-bedroom adobe home on the city's edge, and new owner of the New Age gift store a block down from the vegetarian mini-mart. How anyone could have given her a mortgage was another small miracle, but they had. And Gwen had been able to pay it off shortly afterwards with the estate proceeds, but for all that, it was no less surreal. The shop not only came with full inventory, but two employees: Jennifer and Madeline. *Now they are two genuine mysteries, but bless them both. I'd be lost without them – but they must be out of the same stable as the dotty old bird who sold me the store.*

Gwen's stroll through memory lane was interrupted by the customer leaving. Dolores sighed deeply and rocked back onto her heels, one hand rubbing a stiff neck as she balled the other into a fist and blew hot air into it.

'Yata-hey, Gwen,' Dolores greeted her friend gratefully as she took charge of her latte, sipping and moaning in pleasure with equal intensity. 'That was a hard one.'

'Yata-hey, Res. Sorry I didn't get here earlier – long story involving my stupidity, and, I think I just broke the land speed record getting back into town. Lucky I didn't get a ticket. I called ahead to make sure Ernest had the soup and bread ready and warm.' Gwen inclined her head in the direction of the woman's receding back as she fished out the aforementioned lunch and handed Dolores hers. 'She buy much?'

'Yeah, eventually,' through mouthfuls of chunky vegetable soup and warm cornbread, 'though she wanted to know the ins and outs of everything. It's amazing I've got any voice left. This helps.' Dolores held up her soup to emphasize. 'She was here two hours before you arrived and I've been talking non-stop. Still, she bought just over five hundred dollars' worth so it was all good. Don't worry too much now if you have a quiet afternoon – today is paid for.'

'I've told you before, Res, you'd be brilliant at giving talks properly.

Look how many times you have to do it. Why not get paid for doing that alone? You should give the college a call. Maybe even the centre over in Old Town. Don't they want speakers?'

Dolores looked wistful a moment as though the notion appealed, but she shook her head slowly, the raven-black braid at her nape swishing gently back and forth, and the abalone-and-turquoise chips she had tied into the braid clicking as they swung. Gwen looked at Dolores. She was one of those who had followed the fashion trend of the region, but being Hopi, and with those dark mysterious eyes and skin as red as the desert itself, she carried it off with a natural grace the others couldn't hope to emulate. The abundance of silver and turquoise at her wrists, the fetish carvings she wore and especially the huge squash blossom necklace, just enhanced the image. Standing, Dolores pulled on her ankle length beaded sheepskin coat. That alone would have fetched several thousand dollars if it had been in a store, but she hadn't bought it; she had made it herself, taking just over two years. First curing and stitching the hides, then meticulously beading the back, shoulders and lapels. Dolores was a twenty-first century Hopi, but she retained her traditionalist values against a difficult upbringing. Her grandmother flew in the face of convention but somehow she seemed to get away with it. In the most part it was because she was so respected and loved by anyone who had the fortune to know her. There wasn't a nasty bone in her body.

'The coffee was lovely, the soup as good as ever and even the cornbread *was* still warm. Ernest bakes the best cornbread outside Grandma's kitchen.' Another truism, for Grandma Yellow Deer made the best cornbread in the southwest, at least that's what everyone told her. Gwen wasn't inclined to disagree: it was gorgeous. Moist and as yellow as the sun, with juicy pieces of corn interspersed throughout. Many a cold night had passed with that and her famed spicy chilli bean soup. She had no doubt the old girl would take the recipe to the grave with her as well, just to spite Ernest, who had been badgering her for a decade now to give it to him, under the guise that it would be a shame to lose such a valuable national treasure. But Dolores and Gwen thought he was just desperately jealous.

'You know I could sit and yarn with you for hours. Great Spirit knows, we haven't done plenty of *that*, but I must go fetch Grandma. Her hospital appointment is at two, which leaves me about an hour and a half by my reckoning.' Dolores never wore a watch – there wasn't room on her wrists for one thing – but it never failed to amaze Gwen how she kept almost perfect time. It was as though she had an internal time clock that kept her on schedule.

'Spot on, Res, that's a knack I really could use. Half the time I don't even know what day it is, let alone what time. If it weren't for you, Jen and Maddy keeping me on the straight and narrow I'm not sure even the Great Spirit and the Goddess combined would have a clue when and where I am. It's all been getting worse of late. I've been so distracted by sudden surges of buried memories of my past.' Gwen raised her eyebrows and struggled with a wan smile. 'Though apparently not buried enough. What do you reckon, Res? Am I finally losing it?'

Dolores frowned, marring her normally flawless and serene expression. The look she gave Gwen was one of concern and Gwen was instantly worried. She'd seen that look on her friend's face before, and it hadn't boded well then either. 'Grandma too; she has been remembering all her family since the Kachinas came last. I was worried, yes, but not as much as I am now – now that you are reliving your past as well. Have you spoken to the girls about this?'

Gwen said she hadn't, and slipped into one of the comfortable silences she shared with Dolores. Dolores though looked at her feet and scuffed her boots absently against the wood of the porch as she contemplated her own thoughts. Several rebellious gusts of icy air danced and spun around the two women briefly; eliciting shivers and curses from Gwen. But for Dolores, her shivers weren't just for the cold. They were the shivers of prescience. The sensation felt by many prior to something momentous taking place. Unfortunately, like so many of these things, it seemed stronger with malevolent activity than with the benign.

'What really concerns me though is that Grandma is rarely wrong,' Dolores said eventually, 'and she has been saying that the Kachinas are *coming back*. Wolf, Ogre and many more. I do not know what this means, but she has been muttering this in her sleep for several weeks now. I had originally thought it was due to the forthcoming Powamu ceremony in February. Maybe the Crow Mother's appearance would calm her and these dreams would pass. Now, as I say, I do not know. What do you think, Gwen?'

Gwen knew a little about the Kachinas: she had seen several dances and carried some of the cottonwood carvings in her store. In fact she had a lot in her store from the local craftsmen and women of the Zuni, Hopi, Acoma and other Pueblo tribes. The one thing she did know was that there were some two hundred and fifty of these supernatural beings in the Hopi pantheon. Not all of them were nice; the Ogre Kachinas especially not, or as they were known, the *Nataskas*. These were used to terrify the children at the dances if they were disobedient; but some of the older stories she had heard from the elders implied that they were much more fearsome and destructive. It would be a sign of very bad things indeed should the *Nataskas* return in their own form. And that was an understatement.

'I don't know, Res. It's a bit far-fetched really, in this day and age, I mean. It's probably just a coincidence that me and Grandma are having flashbacks. These old memories have to surface at some time, I suppose. That's all they're doing with me. Grandma? Well, she is old, Res, after all.'

Gwen grimaced, hoping her expression would lighten her friend's now thoughtful mood, but it didn't seem to. Dolores appeared as grave as before so Gwen tried to change the subject. 'It's quarter to now, so you've got an hour and a quarter to play with. Get off with you. I'm fine really; just letting my imagination get the better of me. You go get Grandma to her appointment and I'll see you about five at the store. Jen and Maddy have got a few appointments of their own booked in for tonight, and I said I'd be there for teas and coffees.' Gwen reached out and clasped her friend by the shoulders and, gently turning her in the direction of Gwen's Jeep, which Dolores borrowed, she propelled the Hopi woman with affection towards it. Dolores allowed herself to be ushered off and it finally brought her smile back.

'Yes, Mother,' Dolores fawned, knowing that Gwen hated that, but knowing also that she did have a tendency to mother everything she encountered. Maintaining it was genetic: her own mother used to do the same with everyone she met. 'It's a Walker thing', she would say. With a final wave, Dolores completed her short walk and climbed in to the Jeep, firing it up and turning the stereo on. Gwen could hear Douglas Spotted Eagle even as the car pulled out of the square; the haunting flute music carrying on the breeze.

Gwen pulled up the little cushioned stool and settled down for a quiet afternoon with her book. With her flask of soup beside her she sat and let her mind roam once more. It wasn't a conscious choice, but it seemed easier than fighting the compulsion to dredge up the plethora of random images that assailed her. The first series of images that coalesced into a coherent mental picture was that of her first day at the store; greeted as she was by her two newly adopted assistants, both smiling broadly as she parked her Jeep and strolled over to the door. Jennifer Deveraux, blonde hair falling like a golden waterfall to her waist, her fringe sweeping gently to the left, exposed her big blue eyes, vibrant and glistening. They had the effect of making the New Mexico sky appear cloudy. Shapely and petite, she stood only an inch or two taller than Gwen. She was dressed in faded denims and pink angora sweater. The neckline plunged alluringly and exposed her flawless skin – Gwen thought a tad too much – but she seemed to carry it off without looking cheap. A large silver-set moonstone hung at her throat and it seemed to pulse with a life of its own; beckoning the eye to it the same way the sea calls to the soul, tempting the unsuspecting to plunge into its mysterious depths.

With an exertion of her willpower Gwen turned to the other woman who stood at the doorway to greet her. Madeline Cortez: she was everything Jennifer wasn't. Tall and well built with a cascading mane of the darkest auburn hair ever. In one light it seemed as black as night, in another it flared the deepest red, almost as though it were actually smouldering and merely waiting for the signal to burst in to flame again. Where Jennifer was pale, Maddy – as she preferred to be called – was dark. Her mocha skin reflected her Latin American heritage. Gwen never did know exactly where she originated – they never spoke of their homes – but it could have been anywhere where dark sultry women hailed from. The Dominican Republic, Cuba, Latin America or even as far as Spain itself. When pressed, all she would say was 'Oh, I'm from all over', and that was about that. Jennifer wasn't much different. She was cagey about her exact birthplace but her southern accent limited the option a bit more. Beyond that, Gwen knew very little except that they were always about. They were at the store every day before her, with fresh coffee brewing and warm croissants ready. They had a small apartment only one block over. Gwen had visited it once and was stunned. For two apparent single girls, who appeared so casually flawless, it was virtually empty. No TV or ornaments, only two beds, a lounge and a serviceable kitchen. The bathroom was basic as well, and conspicuous by its apparent lack of the usual girly enhancing products. They just shrugged and their explanation was just as sparse. 'We don't need a lot. And as for looks? Well, I guess we're just lucky that way. Maybe it's in the genes.' They were certainly an enigma, and unlike any other females she had ever known, but she had grown to love them like sisters all the same. And talented. Gwen had never seen the likes. Maddy was probably the most gifted Tarot reader she had ever encountered and people would flock from all over the region to see her. Some even flew in from neighbouring states. That kept the girls solvent and they insisted that Gwen only pay them a cursory salary for the sake of the IRS. As for Jennifer, she had a thing going with her psychometry. She received a stipend from the local and state police for her services. Her

ability to locate missing things and even people had earned her a reputation too as well as a tidy bank balance. Not that they needed money: they
rarely bought anything. On the other hand, they drew people to the store
like moths to a flame and thankfully, they found plenty of things in store to
spend their money on. Gwen often joked that she would adopt the girls as
sisters properly one day and the last time she had said that they both stopped
what they were doing, looked at each other seriously, then at Gwen and said
together, 'We'll hold you to that, Gwendoline Walker.' That had been a little
over two weeks before. Gwen had been a bit creeped out by that for a few
seconds, but then the moment passed and all was as it had been.

The sound of Douglas Spotted Eagle's flute wormed its way into her
daydream and it took a few seconds of hearing it for her to fully realize
what it meant. The Jeep should have been long gone by now. Why could
she still hear it? Gwen was fully snapped back to the present by that revelation, her mind instantly taking in her immediate environment, seeking any
imminent danger. Seconds passed and she was satisfied that she was in no
immediate peril. Expanding her awareness, mentally seeking the source of
the music, Gwen jumped up, her stomach sinking with that familiar feeling
that something was wrong. However much she hoped to the contrary, she
just knew it to be true. Quickly throwing the Navajo blanket over the wares
on display, she called to the man next to her, 'Keep an eye on this, will you,
Miguel?' The man who always sat next to her when she did her turn for
Dolores nodded all was in hand, as it was whenever she asked. 'Thanks, I'll
be back in a minute.'

'Pro noblem, Gwen. You know that's Latin for everything's fine.' He
chuckled to himself, for he always said the same thing, and Gwen smiled
as she jumped off the porch and began to run in the direction that she last
saw the Jeep go. But she hadn't gotten more than a dozen paces before the
screams started. Skidding to such an abrupt halt at the unearthly sounds,
Gwen very nearly went head over heels on a particularly icy patch. But she
still had to know what was happening. Walking now instead of running,

leaning forward in order to see before her body reached the corner, what she saw made her gasp in shock and disbelief.

There were people running down the street towards her and past her. Running in what could only be described as panic and terror. Gwen could see why, beyond their fleeing forms. Looking upwards, Gwen watched amazed as the sky darkened ominously. Not only by natural means, but by flocks of birds, large and small, filling the sky alongside swarms of insects. *Insects? How could that be? It's bloody winter; there shouldn't be an insect for months yet. What the hell's going on?* She saw her Jeep a hundred yards in front of her, Dolores apparently still within it, but making no move to get out and run. Gwen began to make her way towards her, pushing past screaming and running people, much like a salmon battling upstream. Then she saw why they were running. *How could this be?* Was she seeing things? Though she soon ruled that idea out. *Obviously not, judging by the way everyone's running. But it can't be, it just can't. They're not real.* Several giant Kachinas were looming in the distance and heading this way at a frightening pace, their terrifying and ominous shadow driving all before them to flee in terror.

'They are very real, Gwen, just as real as you or us. That is why the animals do their bidding against their own will and nature. We must help them; it is time, Gwen.'

At the sound of the lilting southern accent, she had spun to see both Jen and Maddy standing behind her. Just standing there as though they had been there all along.

'How did you get here? How? Wha —' Maddy put a finger to her lips, gesturing for Gwen to stop talking, seeing as she was making a hash of it. A hundred questions were hurtling around in Gwen's head but none of them would form up and come out of her mouth in anything that resembled coherence. 'But I —'

'Not now, Gwen. One thing at a time. First, let's help these peoples. Two- and four-legged.'

Gwen blinked her eyes a few times and took several quick breaths to steady her racing consciousness before speaking again. 'They're Kachinas, bloody huge and very real looking Kachinas! How is this possible, Jen? What the bloody hell is going on?'

Jen spared a quick glance to Maddy. 'Long story, one we promise to go through with you if we survive this.'

'What do you mean, if we survive this?' Gwen felt her grasp on reality begin to slip slightly and her head felt all light and swimmy, as though she were about to faint.

The towering figures of the Wolf, Bear and Ogre Kachinas could be seen from a great distance, denoting just how big they really were to be visible from town. But they were not the immediate threat. That was coming from the animals that were now pouring into town. Wolves together with deer, badgers, foxes, coyotes. Not to mention the scuttling forms of scorpions and the very flesh creeping spiders that leapt and ran up and over all in their path, biting and stinging indiscriminately. All manner of vermin were swarming into the streets and buildings too. Screams could be heard and occasionally someone would come crashing out of a shop window, desperate to escape, covered in undulating fur. Or worse – screaming in agony for a few brief seconds until the rats, mice or spiders poured into their throats and silenced them. Seconds later the stripped or bloated corpse would be left sprawled in the street, flesh either shredded or garishly swollen and dissolving internally from so much venom; and the furry swarms flooded off, looking for their next victim. The roars and howls, barks and screeches were getting louder as the stampede of ravaging animals poured into the built up areas. Gwen saw people caught in the onslaught, impaled on wicked looking antlers. Several were decapitated as black and brown bears stood and swatted at those trying to escape. Others went down beneath the slavering and fang-filled maws of the wolves – experts at hunting and bringing down prey much bigger than themselves. Walking amongst them were lesser sized Kachinas, in part resembling the dancers who portrayed them, except these were real, solid, something akin to flesh and bone but looking horrifically more malevolent. What flesh she could see was a putrid green like that of a decomposing corpse. For all that, though, they were no less lethal. They carried vicious looking weapons and were not slow in using them. Within moments the ground was slick with the blood of those too slow to flee or too stunned to accept what was happening until it was too late. The deadly torrent of animals and those that drove it were less than forty yards from Dolores now and she still hadn't tried to get away. The haunting flute music from her stereo was still playing and it cast a surreal atmosphere on the tableaux unfolding before them. Gwen turned to her friends in desperation, looking at their calm yet concerned expressions. They seemed to be waiting for her to say or do something.

'What can I do?' Gwen virtually shouted at them in her rising panic.

'Gwen, do you accept our help with your own free will? Are you prepared to do whatever it takes to prevent this? Will you make the ultimate sacrifice?'

'What? Sacrifice? What are you saying? Sacrifice what? Myself? But —'

Again, Jen and Maddy silenced her. They moved to stand either side of her and placed one hand each upon her shoulders. They stood, three women against the tidal wave of brutal, animal ferocity that was thundering towards them. 'Gwen, you must choose now! You must decide if you are willing to give up everything to save these creatures, and you must decide now, or Dolores and all these people will die. Horrible wasteful deaths. You can stop this, we will help you, but you must choose, *Now!*'

Gwen felt their fingers grip her like steel bear traps as she was forced to face the torrent of teeth, claws and blood. She watched horrified as the first wave of animals broke like the ocean upon the shore over Dolores. Sitting rigid in the Jeep, it afforded her some initial protection and bought her a few seconds' reprieve. It was buffeted by powerful bears, their teeth grating and salivating hungrily upon the windshield and side windows as they sought to get at the warm flesh and blood within. More wolves had bounded over the roof, their claws scratching at the vinyl roof, but as they pounded on to within feet of Gwen, she saw flocks of crows descend and begin to rip at the roof, cawing rapaciously. They would be through in seconds. Gwen was out of time. She had to choose now or it would be too late.

'Okay! I'll do it. Whatever you want, just make them stop!' Gwen screamed out her acceptance and with the last syllable hanging in the air, time seemed to slow. The air thickened to the consistency of tar. Gwen could see the eyes of the creatures, rolling white and livid. Enraged beyond comprehension at their inability to move.

'We have little time, Gwen. I have bought us a few seconds. Let us go fetch Dolores, for her time hasn't yet come.'

Gwen had no idea what Maddy was on about, but her sense of the practical asserted itself: whilst the animals weren't moving and she was, that was good enough. She would worry about how later. The three girls ran between snapping wolves and slavering bears, stepping over and around the smaller but no less ferocious animals. It was the queerest sensation for Gwen could see the eyes of the animals following her, their jaws working in the weirdest of slow motions. They reached the Jeep and pulled the passenger door open. With that sudden movement, Dolores seemed to come to. Her eyes went wildly spinning at the sight before her and she passed out, slumping forward just as Gwen reached in and grabbed her.

'Help me. She's too heavy; I can't budge her.' Jen moved Gwen out of the way and took hold of Dolores. Now if the Kachinas and the animals weren't strange enough for Gwen, the sight of little delicate Jennifer manhandling Dolores and carrying her away down the street to safety as though she were no more than a child, sent the last vestiges of her sanity running screaming for a dark safe corner in the secure recesses of her mind.

'It's your turn now, Gwen. You must break the enchantment cast upon the creatures by the Kachinas. They are still not strong here in this world. However, you are a part of this world, and as such your will should be the greater. For the moment. It is within you, Gwen; you must dig deep to release it. Do it now, Gwen. We can't hold them much longer.' *How are they holding them at all?* She could see that much was true. Several of the wolves and a couple of the larger bears had begun to forge their way forwards, walking haltingly as they struggled against the thick air. Air that shimmered about them like rippling transparent treacle. Gwen looked between her two friends, looking for any sort of a clue.

'But what do I do?' Taking a faltering step towards the animals, she kept one eye on them and one back on Jen and Maddy, searching for any indication of how she was to do this thing.

'You'll think of something, Gwen. You have to: it's your destiny.'

Destiny? Now what are they on about? Gwen looked once more at the wolves and again at her companions, then took a deep steadying breath and strode up to the lead wolf. Were it not for the fact it was still moving slowly and inexorably forwards, it would have passed for a stuffed one. Okay, here goes nothing. Gwen reached out a hand and placed it upon the wolf's head as though she were petting it. She simply said the first thing that came to her.

'Stop! Stop now. I command it in the name of the Goddess!' On cue, there was a blinding flash of light and a silent concussive explosion that blasted Gwen off her feet and sent her sprawling backwards. Having landed awkwardly, it took her a few seconds to regain her balance and her equilibrium, and for the lights to stop spinning before her eyes. She sat up in perfect time to come nose to wet nose with the huge shaggy wolf she had touched, its vivid yellow eyes mere inches from her own, and she could feel its mind burrowing into hers, questing, searching for something. She could smell its breath as it panted, and the odor of its wet fur. Gwen's mind began to swim with images of mountains, trees and waterfalls. Of rivers and then of wolf cubs. Other wolves drifted into her field of vision then, all sitting in that inimical wolf fashion, regarding her with curiosity and a frightening intelligence. The smells of pine and fresh mountain air assailed her nostrils. Gwen blinked and the image intensified when her eyes were closed. It was as though she were up on the mountain herself. Opening them again, she saw that the wolf had sat, like the ones in her vision. Back legs skewed out to one side, the big furry tail slowly beating the ground beside it. Head cocked to one side, it regarded the small two-legged female before it. Gwen spared a quick glance beyond it, looking for the Kachinas, but there was no sign of them. Whatever she had done, it had been sufficient to send them packing. Part of Gwen's mind tried to rationalise that maybe they had never been there in the first place. Just her overproductive mind giving her hallucinations, though a smaller, but no less insistent part spoke to her about the complete opposite. It had gained some credibility as she looked into the eyes of the wolf before her, for more images flooded into her head. These ones, however, were not so pleasant. She saw the Ogres and the Wolf Kachinas smashing through the forests, herding all creatures before them. In voices that defied description they ordered the wildlife to do their bidding – it felt like a blanket had been thrown over her will, suppressing it, succumbing it to the urges of the malevolent Kachinas. Any that fought the unnatural compulsion were destroyed. It brought tears unbidden to Gwen's eyes as she saw how many had died at the hands of the Dark Spirits. Something in Gwen's soul died with them as she experienced their agony.

Just as she thought that she could take no more and blackness had begun to edge in around her consciousness, oblivion looming just out of reach, the wolf blinked and the mental assault came to an abrupt end. Gwen fell forward exhausted, and she would have hit the tarmac of the road hard, were it not for the big shaggy wolf moving forward to catch her. Gwen scrunched into the shoulder of the animal. Instinctively throwing her arms around its massive neck to support herself, she buried her face in to its ruff and cried.

What she couldn't see at that moment was that all the animals involved in the provoked attack had ceased their rampage. Birds of every description alighted upon all the rooftops and watched intently. Herds of deer and coyotes all stood together. Bound by a force that removed any dissension amongst them. They waited. A great breath was held and all eyes were on the odd couple: the two-legged female and the four-legged pack leader. She had spoken a word and the fog that shrouded their minds had lifted. This was a conversation worth hearing.

Gwen eventually sat up. Her eyes were red with prolonged crying. She had never experienced such an outpouring of emotion, not even when her parents had died. This was primal, dragged from deep within her, the part that humans tended to bury as they lost their connection to the natural world around them and became indifferent to the plight of what they considered lesser creatures. Sitting back up and drawing several ragged breaths to steady her nerves, Gwen realized that she had not relinquished her hold upon the wolf, nor had it pulled away from her embrace. With a feeling of compassion that nearly had her crying all over again, the wolf licked Gwen's face, running its previously lolling tongue up the tracks of her tears, twice upon each cheek, then it leant back and regarded her once more. Gwen spoke to it then, softly as one would to a beloved pet.

'You shouldn't be here, you know!' Gwen saw intelligence and recognition in its eyes, but what she didn't expect, was a reply.

'I know this, two-legged, but we were not ourselves. We came against our will and our will is strong. This is not a good thing.' It paused for a heartbeat, then it added, 'How is it you speak wolf?'

Gwen almost laughed out loud. Instead she replied, 'I was just wondering the same thing actually. I have no idea what just happened. Who were those things herding you and wreaking havoc? How is it I stopped this and how can I understand you and you me? Tell me I'm not dreaming!'

The wolf looked at her askance and said in a dry yet bemused tone, 'You are not dreaming. I am the speaker for the ground dwellers here.' He looked skyward and barked a couple of yelps to the rooftops, whereupon a large black crow swept down and alighted upon Gwen's inadvertently outstretched arm. She hadn't raised it for that purpose, but to protect her face as it caught her off guard with its shadowy dive. It cawed a few times and by the last caw, Gwen understood what it had said too.

'I see. The people of the sky were affected just the same by these creatures. Of course you were; you wouldn't have done what you did otherwise, would you?'

'No, two-legged land-bound, we would not have. It was a good thing what you did, though you should have done it sooner, before many of my brethren fell!'

Gwen felt a stab of guilt, however irrational, for she couldn't have anticipated this catastrophe. It seemed that the crows felt otherwise. Their belligerence seemed somehow fitting for them in a crow sort of way. Gwen had always imagined them as the bouncers of the bird world. If birds had clubs then they worked the door.

'It's gone now though. It's all over. You can return to your wilds.' But the wolf and the crow both corrected her on that point. 'One at a time, please: this is hard enough already without having to separate one voice from the other.'

The wolf spoke next. 'They are still out there, two-legged – the unnatural ones. These are the dark sprits of our ancestors' legends, returned to exact vengeance. We cannot fight them; they are too powerful for us. You must do this thing. You stopped them once, but they will return. They are not gone.' Gwen was about to protest but the wolf forestalled her. 'I know your soul, two-legged, I have seen it. You are the Handmaiden of the Mother. A strength abides within you and there is no deceit. We trust you. You are a sister to the land-bound.'

'And to the sky-born,' the crow added. Then with a move so fast – Gwen had no time to avoid it – the razor sharp hooked beak of the crow flashed out and with a cruel twist, tore a chunk from Gwen's arm. She squealed and nearly dropped the massive corvid, but its impenetrable black eye held her firm. It then pecked its own leg, then the outstretched paw of the wolf. Blood welled from all the wounds, as would be expected. What

Gwen didn't expect was the crow hopping along to let its own blood flow into the wound upon her arm, then it hopped back as the wolf placed its shaggy paw upon the wound, letting its own blood mingle. Once that was done the crow cawed out an exultation and the entire rooftop burst into life and sound. It was terrifying and exhilarating both at the same time. The cacophony was immediately joined by the wolves, coyotes and all other land dwellers.

'It is done, little sister. You are a part of our circle now. You will be spoken of in our legends to come. Walk in harmony, two-legged; it is time we were away. This place is too strange and alien for many of us and I feel the fears returning.'

Gwen was about to agree when the magic was exploded by the deafening wails of several police sirens. Before the animals could turn and flee, a dozen police cars came screeching in to the square and skidded to a side on halt. *This is just like the movies*, Gwen thought with an eerie detachment. She watched as the sheriff's men leapt from their vehicle with all the expected drama and gung-ho trigger-happy behavior expected of boys with guns. Gwen could see an impressive array of weapons trained upon them all, mainly focused in the centre, upon her and the wolf, for there were simply too many targets otherwise. Nothing moved. A thousand eyes were riveted upon the new arrivals. Gwen sensed a few snarls and some general disapproval. Perhaps they had seen these two-leggeds out with their weekend guns. A wave of anger at these so-called hunters flared within her and it was picked up by Jen and Maddy, who had stood silent up until now.

'Don't do anything silly, Gwen, not now. These men are as innocent in their way as the wild folk. Ignorance is no excuse to punish them. I can feel it building inside you. You have released something dangerous, Gwen, and now you need to control it. Now isn't the time to let it free. Be calm and let us guide you.'

Gwen stood, releasing her hold upon the wolf reluctantly, and allowing the crow to glide a few feet away to bounce upon the top of a parked car. The wolf just stared at the men, a combination of contempt and pity showing in his golden eyes. The sheriff, bull horn in hand, shouted his demands to the women. 'Move aside or we will be forced to open fire. Those are dangerous beasts, killers, and need to be destroyed before they kill any other humans. They might even be rabid.'

Gwen couldn't contain it any longer and she openly laughed at their ludicrous bahavior, and their equally ridiculous premise. Any excuse to get their guns off.

'I don't think so, Sheriff. I suggest that you and your men be the ones to pack up and go away: everything is in hand here, thank you very much. It doesn't need several overgrown boy scouts with guns to solve this. I grant you, we can't undo what's been done, but shooting won't undo it either. It's a long story and maybe one day you'll hear it, but for now, please, just go away.'

It seemed polite enough to Gwen's ear, but apparently it had somehow gotten misinterpreted somewhere between her and the sheriff, and he seemed to hear something completely different, for he grew immediately enraged. Snatching up his bull horn, he bellowed out his indignation.

'You were warned! Open Fire!' The noise was deafening as all the weapons that were leveled at them spat their lethal missiles. Molten lead roared towards them, death inherent in every shot. But it seemed to Gwen that the air thickened again like before, and the bullets were traveling in slow motion. She spared a quick glance to Jen, who winked and raised her outstretched palm.

'You too, Gwen. We can help you channel your energy!'

Gwen did likewise.

The police couldn't believe their eyes when they saw the three women raise their hands and instantly, the bullets and molten lead shot from the pump shotguns exploded into a cloud of multicolored butterflies and wafted off towards the wild lands beyond the town.

'Fire again; Fire at will!' The sheriff was on the verge of apoplexy.

Again, the girls raised their hands and uttered a simple 'no', and again the sky was filled with rainbow-hued insects. Hundreds of shots later and a lot of butterflies, the police stopped shooting. Whilst they stood and looked to each other for some sort of explanation, the wolf simply nodded his shaggy head towards Gwen, turned and loped off. Gwen heard two voices in her mind: those of the wolf and the crow.

'I am Kavan of the wolves. Call me if you need help!'

The crow added its own name. 'I am Shan of the sky-born. You may call me also for aid. If I hear it, I will come.'

Gwen didn't know what to make of it, so she merely thanked them with her mind and hoped that they understood. A brief acknowledgement told her they did.

The police watched in utter confusion as the sky-born took wing and arrowed off towards the mountains and forests beyond. Within minutes the streets were deserted once again, as though the animals had never been there. The only sign that anything untoward had taken place was the destruction of property and the unfortunate dead bodies left behind. The sheriff and his deputies were standing stock still, wide-eyed and slack jawed, each looking to the other for some sort of rational explanation. No one spoke at first: there weren't that many words that came close to describing what had just happened. The sheriff himself, a veteran of some twenty years on the force, was at a loss as to what he was going to put in his report. In fact he was unsure how he was ever going to come to terms with the whole episode. It was at that moment that one of his deputies gave them all a way out.

'We missed! That's it, isn't it?'

Another picked up on the thread. 'Yeah.' His southern drawl was slow and unsteady at first, but as he got his head around it, the idea grew fatter and more believable than what had just happened. 'I had the sun in my eyes, so I must have fired high.'

Another. 'Me too. I must have put faulty rounds in the shotgun. Maybe they were wet, you know, all smoke and noise.'

Much nodding went around the police then as they all got their stories straight, because it just had to be. It couldn't have been the mystical spectacular that had just unfolded: those things just didn't happen outside the movies.

Jen called out to the sheriff, 'Perhaps you boys should all be on your way now. The fun is over and I'm sure there are a lot of scared people out there in need of some reassurance. Yawl surely the people to do that. We'll take care of matters here if you want to send for an ambulance or two to take care of these poor people.'

Her gentle southern voice was almost hypnotic to the stunned policemen. When they hesitated, Jen slowly repeated it, only this time it was delivered with a different cadence. This time, it was less of a suggestion and more of a command. Issued by someone who was used to her commands being obeyed with little opposition. Again they hesitated, heads reluctantly turned to the sheriff for his approval, but it was clear in their eyes that they really wanted to go, and sooner rather than later would be good. The sheriff took off his hat and rubbed his sweaty head before making his decision. With all the speed of a sloth running a marathon, the sheriff made a choice, and luckily for him, it was the right one. 'Okay, Ma'am, if you're sure.'

Jen placed her hands on her hips and struck a pose as if to say 'Of course I'm sure, now go!' The sheriff replaced his hat and adjusted the chin cord, then with as much authority as he could muster, he ordered his deputies to pull out and rendezvous back at the station for further orders. The three women stood and waited until the last tail lights from the retreating cars had disappeared, before Gwen collapsed in an ungainly heap upon the road. She sat as though her bones had been removed, more resembling a rag doll than a living, breathing woman.

'This is no time to rest, Gwen. Here, let us help you.'

Gwen looked up from her prone position to see both Jen and Maddy reaching down to her, offering their hands to her to pull her up. Limply placing hers in theirs, she was lifted clean off her feet by the two girls, nearly pulling her shoulders from their sockets.

'What the…' This second display of strength reminded Gwen that there was more to these two than she had ever known. Having watched them effortlessly carry Dolores to safety, how had they appeared at her side from nowhere? They were simply there, where there had been only empty space seconds before, she was sure of it. There was no way on earth they could have gotten from the store to her side like that. The flurry of questions that had been stilled during the encounter with the police began to reassert themselves, and she looked between the two women who she no longer knew, mentally deciding which question had the most importance to ask first.

'Why aren't we dead and where did all those butterflies come from?' Maddy just smiled annoyingly. 'And don't be smiling at me like that: I don't even have a word for what I'm feeling right now, but it's not very pleasant. I don't take kindly to being lied to and…'

Maddy waved a casual hand and Gwen's mouth continued to move but no sound issued. Jen and Maddy stood and watched their friend as she spoke, or at least went through the motions, casting slightly amused looks between them, waiting. It took several seconds before Gwen realized that they were taking no notice of her rant whatsoever.

'Gwen, save your breath,' Jen advised. 'We understand your obvious annoyance at being probably the only one who doesn't know what's happening. An explanation is also overdue, but certain things had to occur before one could be forthcoming. Today qualifies for that. But here amidst the general populace isn't the place for it. They've had enough shocks for one day; they need to let the dust settle before the crap really hits the fan. You, on the other hand, need to calm down and put aside your preconceived notions of how the world works and what your place is within it.'

Gwen tried to ask what the hell she was on about, but it was much like a silent movie without the subtitles. Only this time, Gwen realized there was no sound. Her eyes flew open in fear and she grasped her throat in panic, as though the gesture would make any difference. It didn't. Maddy smiled again, but quickly stopped as she sensed Gwen's growing discomfort. The horror of being unable to make any sort of vocalization was playing across Gwen's features. With a repeat gesture, her ability to communicate was restored, but now Gwen remained silent, and glowered at the two strangers before her. Too enraged to speak coherently anyway, she needed to calm first before she gave these two a piece of her mind – what there was left of it.

'We have given you back your power of speech, for now,' Jen warned, waggling a finger at Gwen like a disapproving school ma'am, 'but it is conditional you stop fuming, and pay attention. Matters have moved on, and there are certain items that need to be addressed, and soon. Things will go easier and faster if you hold that viper's tongue of yours and utilize that latent intelligence you possess.'

Gwen knew she was being rebuked and insulted in equal measure. She also knew that she was seeing a whole new side to her friends that she hadn't even imagined existed. They emanated power and authority in such vast quantities that world leaders would have been intimidated by them. Gwen, however, had always had a problem with authority. It seemed to bring the worst out in her, but even she capitulated to these two women. So all she did was simply agree.

'Okay.' With her concession, Gwen began to notice other details around her. It was as though her consent raised a veil which seemed to have fallen over her. For a few seconds she couldn't reconcile what she was seeing. Then it hit her. This was winter. The square had been dusted with snow and slush, and icicles hung from the trees. At least they did a few hours ago. Now, the grass was clear, lush and verdant. The trees were free of ice and were in fact blossoming. Spring had descended upon Santa Fe during the middle of January. She watched in rapt fascination as flowers sprang up through the grass where only hours ago, there was snow. As she watched, she removed her jacket and scarf, subconsciously aware that the temperature too had increased in line with what she was witnessing. With a spongy, not quite associated to her surroundings feeling, Gwen asked a question in a voice that seemed small and afraid, overawed by all that was going on.

'I know it's repetitive, but what's happening? I mean, what's really happening? This…' Gwen pointed at everything in general, '…this isn't right. How can this be?' Gwen knew her questions fell short of what her mind craved by a country mile, but it was all she could manage. But the spongy feeling increased, and along with it came a feeling of spinning. Moments later Gwen's disorientation had escalated to a point where her mind refused to take any more and promptly switched off. Gwen crumpled in an almost slow motion action, and the lights kindly went out.

She woke to the soft, heady smells of blossom and new grass. Fragrant flowers sent wafts of their delicate scents to mingle with the others. Before she opened her eyes, Gwen was briefly transported to the meadows near her home in England, where she used to run to when she couldn't bear school during the summer months. Lying out amongst the wild flowers and butter-flies, Gwen imagined that she was merging with the very ground, becoming at one with the natural order. So still would she lie, that on more than one occasion grass snakes and adders would slither over her, intent upon their own agendas. Field mice clambered up onto her, investigating her clothing, even taking threads that had been loose. Rabbits, one fox, a weasel and even the odd mole had happened upon her during her excursions. At the time she hadn't thought it strange, only wonderful and totally natural. Now, her mind was reconfiguring the memory, implying that there was more to it than she had ever believed possible. Her present predicament came rushing back to her then and she sat bolt upright so fast, it made her dizzy all over again.

'Easy, Gwen, take it slow. Here, drink this.' A bottle of water was placed in her hands, which reflexively grasped the cool bottle. She took a long pull, then hiccupped twice before drinking some more. Eventually, sated, Gwen looked at the two women who had passed themselves off as friends. She flashed through the many nights that they had shared doing the girly slumber party thing. Sleepovers with a chick flick for the DVD, a bottle of wine or two, and lengthy discussions concerning many of the male populace as well as some more cerebral issues, though they usually degenerated as the night wore on. Instantly those memories were dashed by the day's events. Her trust was shredded and lay in torn fragments at her feet. Feeling more herself, she turned to her former companions and requested a rational explanation for their bahavior. It was, it seemed, turning into a day of disappointments.

'I see you are feeling a bit better after your little nap: something akin to your old self. An interesting phrase, but more about that later. For now, are you up to a little chat? There are a few things you need to know.'

Gwen adopted an exaggerated look of surprise. 'No shit! I expect there are several things I need to know. Starting with just who you too really are. You *aren't* just two convenient shop assistants, are you?' Gwen knew the moment the question left her lips that she didn't really want to hear the answer, but unfortunately there was no avoiding it.

'No.'

'Thought not.' Gwen sighed at the knowledge. 'You've been taking me for a mug these past years, having a good laugh at my expense no doubt, pretending to be my friends but when my back is turned you're up to heaven only knows what. Can you imagine how such a feeling of betrayal hurts?' The emotion began to creep through the anger Gwen was feeling and her eyes welled up, causing the world to take on a distorted and ethereal quality as she looked out through salty tears.

'Firstly and most importantly, you must believe us, Gwen, when we tell you that we are still your friends. We love you. We have never stopped, and nor will we. However, you must realize that everybody has their secrets. It doesn't alter the fact of who we are; it's just our particular secret is a tad larger than most people's. Though like so many things, an individual can only know what it is capable of and likely to excel at when it actually tries and does it. Until then it could live under the belief that it is normal and unexceptional. You, Gwen, are neither. Your ignorance of what you are and our secrets have much in common – as you are soon to find out.'

Gwen listened, fighting an urge to interrupt with more, she realized, inane questions about matters she didn't understand. Instead she let Jen continue her explanation, seeing where it went. 'Have you ever wondered about your affinity with wildlife? Your mother never had one, nor your father. Why you are a vegetarian? Your parents weren't. Why in all the world did you settle here in New Mexico? Why do you find such a kinship with the Native Americans? These and so many other questions can be answered comparatively easily. We could sit here for days and go over each one; over all the events and choices that have steered and guided your life up to this moment. You are Gwen, the sum of your experiences. For the most part, you don't need us to tell you any of this. In your heart of hearts you already know the answer. But how many times have we sat up late and debated the power of coincidence and fate? Whether there is really such a circumstance as being in the right place at the right time. You are always where you need to be when you need to be there. Humanity has a phrase that says that there are more things under heaven than can be understood, or something like that, but essentially it's true.'

Jen stopped and took a drink from her own bottle of water. While she did, Maddy picked up the thread and continued, 'There are people with incredible gifts. Their evolutionary journey has accelerated them ahead of many others, and these souls perform certain tasks. Imagine them, if you will, as prefects; monitors for the sake of humanity. Though not all are consciously aware of the role, those that are often find themselves the focus of ridicule and persecution.'

'I understand all that, but without seeming selfish, what has it got to do with me?'

'These monitors, for want of any other title, need something to monitor, wouldn't you say? No, don't answer; let me. They monitor those individuals who are destined to do great things. In every generation there are these individuals, though they don't know who they are. Nor are they likely to, unless called. None have been called in an age. It would take something of epic proportions and having catastrophic consequences to consider making such a call. It seems that we have surpassed such time. Matters are beyond calling. Warriors have been dispatched to locate and actually fetch the destined ones.'

Gwen felt another question that she didn't want to hear the answer to rise in her throat, and it was out before she could stop it. 'Destined to do what, exactly?'

Maddy looked to Jen and vice versa. An unreadable look passed between the two that had Gwen wishing all the more she hadn't asked that.

'There's no easy answer to that. Suffice to say for the moment – whatever it takes.'

'Whatever it takes to do what? You know how I hate it when people start rambling on in riddles. Why can't some people just damn well say what it is they've got to say without running it around in circles until it means nothing and they've effectively said nothing. It's bad enough that politicians do it. Most of them wouldn't know how to speak the truth now if their lives depended on it. They've dissembled for so long it has become as natural as breathing. It's like that saying "How do you know a politician is lying? Their lips are moving". I expect it from them, *not* from you. Now will you just say what you mean; I'm struggling enough with this already. C'mon, be fair!'

Again the look passed back and forth. It was like watching a tennis match as Gwen followed the gaze back and forth. Then it hit her. 'You're talking to one another, aren't you? Telepathically?' Gwen blurted excitedly, her own predicament temporarily forgotten over the revelation at what her so-called friends could do.

Maddy simply nodded; and Jen closed her own eyes and looked down, weighing in her own mind just how she was going to make what she had to say credible enough for Gwen to swallow without her freaking out again. Jen looked up, adjusted her clothing and ran her hands through her hair, flicking it back so it sat right where it did before she interfered with it. But the ritual complete, she began to speak. Maddy reached out and Gwen let her take her hands in hers as, outraged as she was, the comfort it gave outweighed her annoyance.

'I'm cutting a very long story extremely short here so bear with this. The blanks will be filled in later, I promise. For now, suffice to say you have been chosen, destined, if you will, to be the vessel.' Jen saw Gwen's frown at that so she embellished. 'Since the Earth was young, and long before humanity, we have served the planet as her avatars. Maddy and I represent the elements of this world. Myself for air and water, Maddy for fire and earth. We acted directly where she could not. We are the scalpel where she would be too devastating. We have always known a third might be required, but we never anticipated it actually happening, so we are almost as surprised as you.'

Gwen made a face that said in no uncertain terms were they as surprised as she was, but she remained silent and gestured for Jen to continue her tale. 'No one knew who the vessel would be, not even the Earth. It simply manifested itself in each generation of humanity. Guardians were chosen and they continued through each successive bloodline. Again, they may not have known their role unless they were called to act. Not every generation called. Hundreds of years have passed since any had to act, and then, not for the doom that faces us now...'

Gwen couldn't help but leap in at that last bit. 'Doom? What bloody doom? You never mentioned doom, oh no. I'd remember a word like doom: it has a certain impacting quality about it.'

Maddy squeezed Gwen's hands to interrupt her flow before it could pick up any momentum. 'Guardians were chosen, as I said, to protect the vessel. Whatever force led you here was fortuitous indeed. You remember the lady who sold you the store? Of course you do. It might surprise you to know that she was a guardian, but she was killed, brutally, shortly after leaving here, as were many other guardians. Let your imagination do its worst – matters are that dire. It seems that there are few guardians left. Those individuals who weren't called still tended to gravitate towards greatness. Two of your ancestors, to whom you owe an addition to your bloodline, are none other than Boudicea and the woman who was eventually portrayed as Guinevere in the romances. But they weren't called. They were not to become the third in the Trinity. You are.'

Gwen pulled away from Maddy before she could stop her this time, shooting her a look of 'Back off a minute'. Whilst she was unconscious, they had moved her to the centre of the square under the comparative shade of one of the trees; Gwen leant back against one now and looked long and hard at the two women. A tinge of barely-contained hysteria was evident in her strained voice.

'You're telling me you've been around since the dawn of time and you now want me to join you? Do you know how that sounds? Really?'

Jen shrugged her shoulders sympathetically. Gwen knew that they had some idea of the enormity of what they were telling her. What they didn't know was how she would handle such news. Gwen thought she was handling it fairly well, all things considered. There was still the option that *they* were off their trolley and not her; that much of what just happened was due to some mass hallucination brought about by a sudden outpouring of natural radiation or gas.

'We have a pretty good idea of how it sounds, yes, though the dawn of time is a bit melodramatic. It hasn't quite been that long.'

Maddy piped at that. 'Though there are some days when it feels a lot longer. But I shouldn't complain: it hasn't been all bad. A lot of it *has*, I grant you, but not all of it.' Maddy looked at the expression of uncertainty on Gwen's face, warring with outright disbelief. 'You need something a bit more definitive, don't you? We have so little time to convince you. Maybe desperate times require desperate actions. What say you, Jen?'

Jen nodded. 'I'm inclined to agree, but here isn't the place – we could use somewhere secluded. These poor people here have had enough shocks for one day. We need to let them recover before they get any more, which is likely, though that is in your hands, Gwen.'

'Mine? Don't you go laying the blame for this on me. I had nothing to do with it!'

'Granted, though I suspect it was you they were after and, subject to your acceptance of certain truths, you may prevent any further bloodshed. Personally though I think it might be a bit too late to avoid that, but we must try all the same.'

Maddy and Jen stood, both offering a hand to Gwen to assist her in rising, but she looked at the hands as if they were a pair of poisonous snakes.

'Thanks, but I can manage. I may appear calm and rational but I assure you I'm not. I still don't trust you two, not after what you've done and what you apparently seem to be capable of. I'm not entirely over the bullets to butterflies thing yet. I've never felt so betrayed in my life. I thought you were my *friends*.'

Gwen's plaintive accusation struck home with the girls and they finally gave in to their own consciences. Tears bubbled forth like mountain springs and their masks of authority slipped a fraction. The pain glimpsed beneath caused Gwen to catch her breath as a lance of empathy struck her. Gwen knew then, that with everything that had happened this day, it wasn't the intention of these girls to hurt her. It seemed to hurt them as much, having to put her through this. They were as tormented by having to give the explanation to her, as she was in dealing with the implications of said explanation. She had always sought phenomena to substantiate many of the New Age beliefs she perpetuated in her store. Witnessing it first hand was another thing altogether and she had overreacted. Knowing that now didn't make it any easier; her own guilt at having given her friends such a hard time wracked her even as she watched her friends break down and cry before her. Ancient beings they may be, but she had lived with them for years now, as close as any family could be. That was what they were: family. Standing, Gwen went to them and upon reaching them, she spread her arms wide and encircled the two blubbing girls. 'I'm so sorry. I've been a right shit.'

Making the admission triggered Gwen's own tears as the emotion of the moment overtook her. Her voice cracking and failing, she tried to tell them how sorry she was for giving them such a cold shoulder. The girls, in the same weepy voices, tried to say they understood, but too soon it all fell apart and the conversation dissolved into the three of them, arms encircling each other, all crying their eyes out together, heads pressed into each other's shoulders.

They wept like this for several long minutes, each finding their own catharsis from the release. When they were in a fit state to find their voices again without breaking down, which they did after three attempts, they pulled their faces back from each other but didn't break the embrace. The trio stood and gazed at each other's red puffy faces and it was Jen who managed to speak first.

'We are sorry too, but we understand. It hasn't been easy for anyone. It's a lot to take in, but please, know this one thing, first and foremost: we are your friends and have always had your best interests at heart. We had fervently hoped that this would never have to happen, but it has. It's always the same – the less you understand, the more you fear – the more you understand, the less you fear. Once you understand what it is that is expected of you, you'll accept it with little to no fear. We wouldn't do anything to intentionally hurt you. You are as a sister to us in more ways than you could possibly realize, though you will. Maybe we could go to that place you like so much, up the other side of Hyde Memorial Park, near that rock the shape of a mushroom?'

Gwen was startled. She had never taken the girls there. It had been *her* refuge. 'How did you know about that? I've never taken anybody there. Have you been spying on me?' Gwen felt her indignation begin to rise again, but kept it in check. She was glad she had when Maddy explained how they always kept an eye on her, for her own protection. It was why they were with her and as matters progressed elsewhere, or, rather, went downhill, her safety became more of an issue. Today's events were testimony to that. They begged her forgiveness and that set Gwen off again. Tearfully, she forgave them and agreed to go to Toadstool Rock, as she called it. They would take the Jeep once they had seen Dolores safely home. She lived on the way to the park and in all likelihood, there would need to be some explaining to Grandma Yellow Deer. When Gwen mentioned this little fact to the girls, even they blanched. Ancient beings they might be, embodiments of the elements, but Grandma Yellow Deer was another power altogether. Her reputation was equally formidable, and both Jen and Maddy grimaced at the thought of trying to explain to the canny old Hopi wise woman just why her day had been so disrupted. Inwardly, all three secretly wished for the Kachinas to come back, for that seemed a much safer option than what they presently faced. Placing the still-unconscious form of Dolores into the Jeep, they headed off out of town, just as the first ambulance turned up to tend to the dead and try to make some sort of sense from what they saw.

CHAPTER FOUR

STORMS

TWIN STORMS WERE RAGING ACROSS THE FACE of the Domain – a torn and tortured land that was more commonly known throughout the multiverse as Hell. The first of these storms was an impressive elemental outpouring that ripped and devastated all it came into contact with, howling and lashing out at anything that was foolish enough to be outside and upright while it scoured the land. Buildings, trees and even rocks suffered under its relentless onslaught. But it was those who dwelt upon the surface of the land who suffered most, while those who dwelt beneath simply cowered in fear at the maelstrom roaring above them. This storm was also highly adaptable, donning the cloak of whatever region it swept through, lending its own awesome strength to some already hostile and lethal environments; and gathering up shards of ice the size of ploughshares and spinning them into monstrous razorlike tornadoes, only to fling them back out again, decimating anything in its path. Desert winds, laden with flesh-stripping sand and leaving trails of blasted, stripped white bones scattered in their wake. Firestorms and acid rain. Tidal waves of liquid methane. And erupting volcanoes, spewing out a lethal cocktail of molten rock and searing ash. All this devastation and planetary violence roared out across the Domain, leaving death and chaos behind them as they continued on their rampage.

The second storm was only slightly less elemental but just as effective in its destruction of life and inspiration of fear. The main difference between the two was that the first storm would eventually blow itself out and the planet would calm. This other storm was growing stronger daily and threatened to not only scourge the Domain, but to sweep out across the cosmos, bringing with it a fiery doom for everything it encountered. It would be a storm the like of which the multiverse had never before imagined, let alone witnessed. This storm though, had a name. It was known as the Adversary, the Bringer of Endless Night. Much like a super cell in earthly storms, he grew in power and strength at a spectacular rate, but this rapid growth only had the effect of making him more volatile and violently unstable, as his patience, self-control and previously rigid iron will failed to keep pace. Today was one such day. Anything with one iota of sense ran for cover in much the same way as if they were outside; only they ran faster from the Adversary. In fact, many fled outside as it was preferable to take their chances with the weather rather than face the Adversary's wrath. On days like this though, there were probably fewer hiding places from him than from the storm outside, and for those that lived upon and within the Domain it was an altogether unpleasant and unfortunate problem that was only going to end badly, whichever they faced.

The residents of Lucifer's palace, which now, along with all his other possessions, belonged to the Adversary, were running every which way as the demon lord strode his corridors, glowering like a thunderhead. His current destination was his throne room. *His* throne room. But that thought didn't cheer the Adversary today. So highly charged was he this day that tapestries, centuries old, combusted and fell to the marble and semi-precious stone corridor floor as he passed, ending their long existence as ash upon the amethyst. Sculptures that were older than humanity came crashing down, smashed to fragments as he vented his fury upon them as he barreled onwards.

And yet, even with his facial features contorted in rage as they presently were, there was no shortage of imposing features, but it was the eyes in particular that grabbed and captivated anyone looking upon the Bringer of Endless Night. They blazed with a raw power as if fuelled by a raging volcano within. As powerful as those without. A dark light and ebony flame spilled from those fiery orbs, casting a baleful glow and black malevolent shadows wherever they swept. They were most definitely *not* the eyes you wanted turned upon you. Being the object of attention from that penetrating and incandescent gaze had unmanned many from the lowliest minion to the highest ranking demon lords. A simple glance on a regular day was akin to being whipped with razor wire, and today was anything but regular.

Since the Adversary had stepped up and usurped his liege lord Lucifer, it had been whispered that here was the true power behind the throne – the hand that had guided Lucifer, a puppet ruler since the inception of the Covenant and the forming of the Domain. Here was an entity that grew in power and cruelty sympathetically, as his reign went from strength to strength. Many of the ruling lords had already succumbed to his dominion – some grudgingly, others eagerly, but succumb they did; though there were one or two very powerful and ancient arch demons that still had reservations and withheld their pledge. His thoughts turned immediately to Be'elzebub, who was continually absent and refused all summons for him to return. It was this thorn amongst many that particularly enraged the Adversary this day. He believed that they should *all* bow to him and do his will, instantly, without question, no exceptions. He should not have to *ask* them anything. Obey or die: as simple as that. *And that is exactly how it will be too,* the Adversary growled to himself, the moment his power had grown sufficiently. the He could feel the newly arrived souls swelling him, their life force feeding him like a massive tick growing larger and increasingly bloated as he fed. The souls were as blood to the Adversary. *Soon!* he thought as he stampeded onwards, swatting an unsuspecting minion who had made the fatal mistake of stepping out in front of him. Not dissimilar to stepping out in front of a speeding express train, except the express train didn't stop, back up and hit you a second time. Several minions had perished this day for simply being in the wrong place at the wrong time. Several more wouldn't have the use of various limbs for some considerable time either. They would grow back or mend, depending on how close they were to the Adversary's sword at the time. He didn't really care.

He had promised his underlings power unlike anything they had formerly known, but many were concerned whether or not the increasing difficulty in staying alive around their new liege was truly worth the promise, for all the power in the cosmos meant zip if you were sliced to ribbons simply for being in the same vicinity as the Adversary. It was this prospect that had creatures of every shape, size, color and anatomical configuration, many hideous beyond mortal man's comprehension, running, slithering and flapping for safety as fast as their appendages could transport them – an increasingly difficult task considering that the Adversary was everywhere these days, howling and screaming about one thing or another. Today's tirade was just another in a long list of explosions. If he continued in this fashion, there would be little Domain left to rule. Still, by the time he had reached the great hall he had run out of minions to swat. The first things he saw were the massive golden double doors to the throne room. They were ajar. *They've been in here without permission?* The Adversary was outraged all the more. *His servants are just far too willful. They seem to obey only the orders they think need obeying. Lucifer has been far too lax in his discipline. Oh, how that will change!* he fumed, as his gaze was drawn through to where the monstrous jeweled throne squatted. It was an ugly thing that seemed to have too many sharp edges, and the overabundance of jewels made it look crass and tasteless. It sat atop a dais that more closely resembled a Mayan pyramid. Steps accessed it on three sides. It sat upon it like the pus-filled head of a boil. The Adversary threw the two golden doors wide open as though they were non-existent; whereas in actuality, they stood some sixty feet in height, and were wide enough to drive a half-dozen chariots through side by side. Added to the fact they were solid gold and at least two feet thick, it was an impressive feat by any standards. These doors had been in place at Lucifer's palace since it was built. They were the sole reminder to the ex-archangel of his previous existence. Each door had been fantastically carved with two hundred three foot by three foot panels, and another four hundred on the opposite side. The scenes were so vivid as to a₁ ₁ear almost lifelike. They were scenes of the creation of the universe: the birth of worlds and the ascent of the *Children of Thought* or Ch'drnOmThophilim – angels, as humanity came to know them, and the elder gods before that. The mysterious Drakarim, with their twinned race, the Unc'anharaphim, were depicted also: the fierce Drakarim, powerful and majestic dragons; alongside the aesthetic and mystical Unc'anharaphim with their single spiral horns raised skyward. Both races were shown right up to their equally mysterious disappearance. So spiritually powerful were these doors that in the early centuries of Lucifer's reign, pilgrims came from all over the cosmos to gaze upon their wonder. They became so powerful, imbued with the reverence of all those who stood in their presence, that their vibration began to manifest on other worlds; even upon the Earth, where the race of men, who were still in their relative infancy, began to feel them as well as be influenced by them. Their spiritual and provocative power can be seen even today for one such artist, Lorenzo Ghiberti, subconsciously influenced by Lucifer's doors, built and designed, over a period of fifty-one years, what has become known today, thanks to a compliment from Michelangelo, as the Doors of Paradise, currently located at a historic monastery in Florence. If only Ghiberti could have seen where his masterpiece was originally influenced from, he would have had nightmares for the rest of his life. Today, with the Adversary bearing down on them, paradise couldn't have been further away. And it was showing no signs of coming back anytime soon.

In this instance, it was the originals that slammed back into the walls with a resounding crash as the Adversary burst in and inadvertently crushed yet another minion who, up until that moment, had considered itself safe behind them. Striding up towards the raised dais, he mounted the twenty-one steps in two great leaps, spun and threw himself into the throne. Drawing a deep breath, chest expanding heroically, the Adversary roared out his frustration, rattling doors, walls and windows with its ferocity. Several long and very loud minutes passed this way.

It seemed that in this final venting, the Adversary calmed somewhat, at least sufficiently for him to sit back and draw several more relaxing breaths. In this slightly more passive state it was possible to discern the origin of the Adversary for, calmed, he appeared nothing less than the beautiful and smoldering image of a Pre-Raphaelite archangel. It was a much-discussed mystery of how this entity had remained concealed for so long, for unbeknownst to all bar Lucifer and the Adversary himself, he had been removed from all records, everywhere. Thus he could serve with an anonymity that afforded a greater freedom. He was the visual embodiment of a solar deity, and even though he could assume many forms, this was his preferred one. Perfect features and Herculean physique. A vast mane of wavy, sun gold hair framed a face that contained the best features of both sexes. Flawless skin, so smooth it could have been carved from porcelain; full lips that would have been the envy of any male or female, and they spoke of a sensuality that defied comprehension. He would have been considered perfection incarnate, except for a few small points of note that ruined the illusion. The sheer outpouring of hate from those eyes had formed a ridge across the top of the nose, giving an air of brutality to the expression that upon a closer inspection made it seem quite ugly. The sensuous mouth was ruined by the cruel twist that seemed perpetually in place, distorting the full crimson lips, and, coupled with the protruding canines that pressed down into the bottom lip, it put a dark and feral twist to the entire visage. Of course the Adversary didn't see it that way: he was more self-absorbed than Narcissus ever was. And should anyone be brave enough to look at the Adversary overly long, they would catch glimpses of his great spread of golden wings, held slightly out of phase for ease of movement, yet ever poised for immediate action. It was hard at the best of times to ascertain just how many there were: sometimes it seemed as though there were more than his body could accommodate; another time, one huge span of golden metallic avian perfection. Like those of a monstrous golden eagle.

This day, the Adversary was girded for war in an elaborate combination of Greco-Roman styles; sporting gilded shoulders and engraved breastplate, bracers and greaves, the latter decorated with carved warriors in combat. Magnificent jeweled armbands made his already bulging biceps appear even larger. His warrior's kilt exposed legs that more resembled polished walnut trees, so muscled and tanned were they. Completing the ensemble, slung at his hip, was the infamous jeweled scimitar that had been the bane of numerous minions that day. Many past enemies had fallen before it, and prior to the Adversary's ownership, it had been the personal blade of Lucifer himself. Legend had it that it could sever rocks from mountains and leave a glass-smooth surface beneath. Diamonds could be sliced upon its keen edge like ripe fruit. There was little in the multiverse that could stand against it; and rumor abounded that it was a gift from the Four Horsemen of the Apocalypse themselves to Lucifer when he chose to step down and help redress the balance. Only the blades of the Horsemen could withstand its power. As former ruler of Hell it was Lucifer's symbol. Now, on the other hand, it was the Adversary's not so diplomatic alternative to any who disputed *his* rule.

Adopting a meditative posture, with elbows resting upon his knees, the Adversary linked his long, well-formed fingers together. Pyramiding the two forefingers upon which he rested his chin, he began murmuring a lilting incantation that only he could hear. Instantly a soft rose gold glow began to manifest against one wall of the palace hall, a scant few paces from where the Adversary currently sat. Several seconds passed before a large crystalline structure began to shimmer into being, solidifying as the chant continued. It resembled a very large, double terminated Herkimer diamond that stood up on its end. As the light died away it made it possible to see the crystal's occupant, much like a fly trapped in amber. Frozen in impotent and futile rage, lay the former lord and ruler of the Domain, Lucifer, equally former and paramount Archangel of the Celestial Order; higher even than Gabriel and holder of the sobriquet, Bringer of Light – his own beatific face captured in impotent rage at the betrayal by one of his own, and not only that, but his most trusted friend. Correction. Former friend. It occurred to Lucifer at that moment, that there were a lot of *formers* these days and likely to be many more before this was all over. He stared out, limited to the view afforded by the direction his gaol faced and that which now fell within his peripheral vision. Although much of it was distorted by the crystalline facets of his prison, he could still make out the figure of his former friend, adviser and assassin – now his gaoler, tormentor and, definitely, his enemy.

It was this field of vision that the Adversary rose and casually strolled over to stand within. Hands clasped behind him like a general scrutinizing a new recruit, he paced back and forth a few times without ever taking his eyes off the ex-ruler, savoring the pleasure of knowing the pain and fury that must be coursing through Lucifer at both his own predicament, and being within feet of his captor and tormentor, yet powerless to do anything but stare and listen to the insane drivel spewed forth by him whenever he felt the need to gloat.

'I'm so pleased you opted to stay with us for a while. My apologies if the accommodation is perhaps a trifle cramped, but we must all make sacrifices, mustn't we!' The Adversary feigned listening to an imaginary response before continuing. 'What was that? Why, thank you, we do pride ourselves upon the level of hospitality we offer our guests – both short-term...' knowing how the dungeons currently brimmed with *short-term* guests, '...and our longer residents, such as yourself. Though I must add, I'm a little disappointed with the capabilities of your household staff. It's a wonder you've managed to hold things together here for as long as you did. I sent one of your more *allegedly* competent servants to perform a simple task. I have to say that I'm a trifle embarrassed to say that it *failed*!' The last word was roared out at Lucifer, who, incapable of doing otherwise, stood motionless as the now red faced Adversary screamed at him, spittle flying from his open mouth and his face instantly contorted by an unimaginable outpouring of rage. Then, faster than a heart beats, it was gone. In place of the madness was the angelic face of calm and serenity. 'However...' the Adversary continued, as though he had not been interrupted at all, '...little matter, for my plan progresses apace. Soon, not to be too clichéd, it will be too late for anyone, *anyone...*' he roared again with an unstable emphasis; and again he calmed, '...to stop my cataclysm, least of all one puny human. It would have been nice though to have wrapped it all up neatly. Humanity's death and that of their miserable planet will empower me even beyond your pathetic dreams. I can't imagine why you didn't want this for yourself aeons ago; it was within your capability...' The Adversary put his ear to the crystal as though listening to a voice only he could hear. 'What's that? You're a spineless toady and not worth the energy holding your molecules together? Well yes, I'd have to agree with that. But once I've found and freed the ancients, their release will be the catalyst that spells the doom for you and those whores' spawn that seem to think humanity and this cesspit of a system is worth a crap. Believe me, it's not. You and those of the Celestial Host are nothing more than lackeys to an absent and uncaring lord. An unfeeling entity who's no more a God than I am; though we both know that's no longer technically true, for when I've taken care of that mud ball and events are in motion, *I will be a God*. Then we shall see what we shall see.'

The Adversary had partaken in numerous conversations like this with Lucifer, who, though he had heard this rant more times now than he could count, was still infuriated by them. He may be physically trapped but it did not stop his blood from boiling with suppressed fury. Unfortunately, the wards set upon his prison were powerful indeed and he was completely ineffective in battling them. As helpless as a fly in a hurricane.

'Hah! What was God thinking?' the Adversary continued, striding away from his ex-liege, as though bored with looking at him, yet knowing he was a captive audience for his tirade. 'Or was God thinking at all? After all there has been plenty of time to deal with those insignificant insects, *but no*, instead of death, they are given *free will*! I have never understood that: humanity was always an incapable race. Just look at them now, destroying each other at a fantastic rate of knots, though of course with some substantial help from yours truly...' The Adversary buffed his talons upon his breastplate in a show of feigned humility and false modesty. 'No doubt they would complete the job on their own, left to their own devices, but it is still too slow for me, so really all I'm doing is speeding up the inevitable, putting right that which should never have been started...' The Adversary was growing enraged again as he spoke. So too did his voice increase in power and volume. '...Rules, balance and those interfering high and mighty Horsemen, stamping their rigid and meticulous rules upon everything. *Enough!* I say. I will stand for it *no more!*'

The Adversary had begun to glow brighter and brighter as his megalomaniacal rant escalated into maniacal laughter, and the light seared Lucifer's unblinking eyes. He was still laughing as he strode from the hall and his voice grew fainter and fainter as he described what he would do, until Lucifer was left in silence. Closing his mind off to the pain caused by the scorching light, magnified through the crystal, Lucifer again futilely pondered how he could have allowed this travesty to happen, how he could have missed Zaramael Et Arim's decent into madness. Zaramael Et Arim, the true name that Lucifer had known him by since they chose to rule the Domain what seemed an eternity ago. They were as close as brothers throughout their earlier years. It wasn't until the ascent of humanity that they had their first ever disagreement about the merits of their evolution. True, Zaramael had always considered it a mistake to raise humanity, but for millennia he supported Lucifer, even against his own views; that was what friends did. But perhaps it was the prospect of an eternity of anonymity that had fuelled this narcissistic insanity. This plan to free the Nephillim from their prison, break the eighth seal and actually *kill* a planet. It was unheard of throughout time. And it seemed he was going to succeed in his plan. Yet – why was this one mortal so important that he had to send a minion to destroy it? Surely, if matters were so advanced, one more mortal would have made little difference? Unless this mortal *could* have an impact; could be a fly in Zaramael's proverbial ointment. Lucifer sincerely hoped so. He had been subjected to so many of these episodes of late, but this was the first time a specific mortal was mentioned. After all, he had killed so many already, it could only be hoped that whatever bug had climbed up Zaramael's ass and was causing him all the pain of a cluster of burst hemorrhoids, it continued to do so. Maybe there was even a way to extricate himself from his current predicament. Lucifer knew as well as any, however, that events would unfold as they would and only time would tell. And that, thought Lucifer wryly, was one thing he presently had plenty of.

CHAPTER FIVE

METAMORPHOSIS

SOMEWHERE, TOMAS WASN'T SURE WHEN EXACTLY, BUT between leaving the shores of Great Britain and descending towards the Syrian shoreline, he had come to find a sort of peace. A disjointed calm unlike anything he had ever experienced before. It wasn't so much a meditative calm, brought about by deep breathing or chanting. Tomas knew about that. He had spent some time in Tibet with some Buddhist monks – nine weeks to be exact. A Chinese operative was hiding out somewhere in the region and it was Tomas's job to hide him on a more permanent basis. This fellow had been playing both sides and had effectively upset everyone by eventually selling them both out to the North Koreans. All the intel pointed to him being in the region, but not what he was doing or where exactly. Tomas had to do some digging of his own; and not just holes for the monks. During the period he spent with the monks, they collared him for heavy lifting and fixing the one car they ran about in; though to be fair, in response, they tutored him in simple breathing and meditative techniques, and how to sit for days on end if need be without hardly moving, which, much to their chagrin no doubt, served him well on sniper stake outs. But this calm wasn't like that. It was much more profound, stilling an inner turbulence that had been with him since his earliest memory. It was what drove him – it was only his constantly striving forwards that kept it from consuming him. Whatever *it* was, *it* wasn't moving now. Perhaps there was some truth to what they told him: peace only comes to the soul when that soul fulfills its destiny. Until then, it is constantly seeking, striving for its purpose. Apparently, Tomas's was to die. And oddly, he was fine with that.

Galloping over the hundreds of miles of dreamlike cloud lands, he had come to terms with what was expected of him. To die in order to save humanity. It wasn't like he hadn't been ordered to do this before. It was always there, the possibility that he would fail to return from any of the assignments he undertook. If caught, he would be disowned by whichever government was utilizing his singularly unique ability at the time. If tortured, again, he was under no illusions that he would be expected to die before giving up any information, sensitive or otherwise; and if at all possible, take his own life first. Dead men rarely talked. Tomas didn't think that any government had gotten the hang of necromancy yet, but in light of recent events, who knew?

His whole life up to this moment had almost been like a trial run, honing and perfecting his craft for the day he would have to do what was expected of him now. He recalled the thoughts of only a few hours ago, about how he might wake at any moment in his padded room, pumped full of all manner of hallucinatory and anti-psychosis medications. *Wishful thinking, that. Instead, here I am, grimly clinging to a flying horse, rocketing through the sky towards my inevitable death with the Four Horsemen of the Apocalypse. It's hard to say, but I don't think we've invented drugs that could match this yet.*

Tomas chuckled at his thoughts as they flew. Metaphors were spilling from him thick and fast as he rationalized the direction his life had just taken. He thought that he was burying some of his demons. Now he was probably going to be butchered by one. How man had demonized so many things, he couldn't understand – categorizing them and boxing them, renaming them so they could be explained by his meagre intellect. That was how humanity got by: if it couldn't explain something, it simply gave it another name and boxed it away. Conformity was now a classification for how somebody fitted and acted within any given society. Conformity, to an extent, also determined how somebody else believed, or not, as to whether you were fit to exist within their society. A thousand years ago, if he had spoken of the fact that he had held a long conversation with one of the archangels, he would have been heralded as a prophet; revered and followed by many. Nowadays, he would have been locked up and drugged up, probably even electroshocked – humans could still be barbaric when it suited them – with no end of intellectual boffins shaking their collective heads and sucking in breath over their cigar- and port-stained teeth, spouting any number of theories, many ending in some sort of *osis* or *ology*, about who had written what paper that correctly diagnosed his particular disorder, or at least which one was closest. *Usually good enough for most humans. They're damn good at pounding square pegs into round holes. I'd bloody well like to see what explanation they'd have for this if they could actually see it. Maybe we've passed the point of no return and the balance has shifted to the opposite direction? I don't know,* Tomas sighed as he rode. Storm flicked his ears in response to Tomas's mood. *Seems that gulf between the fantastic and the scientific has grown of late. Humanity seems to have lost its magic almost completely. How on earth did we let it get so bad? Where did it all go wrong? Damn, it's not that I was ever a frekkin' believer, but if those monks can get me to look at things differently, openly – though I don't think they had this in mind – surely Joe public can pull it back from the brink? Maybe this is a wakeup call.*

The calm that Tomas was experiencing seemed to open his objectivity considerably more than he was used to. The former world of Tomas Walker, government operative, was so black and white it even held no room for simple things like right and wrong. It was merely: live and carry out orders, survival being the priority by a hair's breadth. Now – everything had become so many various shades of grey. He had dropped many archaic preconceptions in light of recent events. How could he hold on to the rules for a world that barely existed in the way he had come to know it? Humanity lived blinkered to all but the obvious about it. Focused on the two degrees in front of it, it failed to comprehend the impact that the other three hundred and fifty-eight degrees were having. *I think I'd better stop this internalizing; I'm getting so deep now I'm even losing myself a bit. Focus, Tom. You've got one last mission to carry out. Let's see if we can't give this Adversary a run for his money. 'Cos if he thinks I'll be an easy mark, he can think again.*

Clouds soon gave way to blue sky, and then the Syrian coast gradually came into view. Or at least that's what he presumed it would be. In his military mind, it would have been the logical place if they flew as the crow did. Tomas gritted his teeth and spurred Storm to catch up with the lead rider, Death. Pulling alongside, Tomas sought news on their forthcoming strategy.

'I take it we'll be coming in low to avoid radar detection, if they haven't picked us up already?'

Death barely turned his head to Tomas in acknowledgement. 'We don't appear on your feeble radar, Tomas. You must get it through your head that we are so far beyond your technology… though you are inadvertently correct about one thing. We will be coming in low, but we will be riding most of the way to Megiddo. For it is not through concerns of mortal detection, but from the enemy. Our presence is palpable. By utilizing our abilities like this, it makes us even more visible. Therefore we intend to use them as little as possible, for even though we are formidable, our powers lessen as the Adversary's grow, and we do not want to face an army just now. The numbers might go against us at the moment.'

Tomas was getting fed up being treated like some child by these beings. They may be all-powerful, but they had little respect for humans, it seemed. And it seemed for him, even less. 'Look, Death, you have to understand one thing. I don't know what you are capable of, and frankly I'm caring less and less as each moment passes. So stop treating me like some idiot. I'm more than a little capable of understanding tactics – I've formulated more than enough of my own in the past. If you shared a bit more, maybe I'd stop asking pointless questions; but as I seem to be out of your loop, I'm having to make this up as I go.'

Whilst they had been talking they had in fact descended to a lower level, so much so, the hooves of the horses occasionally flicked up spume from the crests of waves. Tomas looked down, and almost wished he hadn't. At high altitude, he'd lost track of just how fast they were moving – now he had a point of reference – the sea – it came crashing back to him. It wasn't like he hadn't gone supersonic before, only the last time, he'd been *inside* something, not riding *outside* on its back. *Ah, crap. I hope horses have got good brakes.* Looking up, Tomas could see the beach enlarging by the second. At this rate, they were going to put a groove in it about a mile long. But as though reading his mind – again – they began to slow, alighting on the beach as gently as sea spray from the lightly lapping waves. So gentle in fact, that they left no hoofprints at all in the wet sand. Tomas started scanning the immediate area, much the same way War was, though Tomas figured he saw much more; for his part he could see people, locals going about their business, oblivious to the surreal quintet gathered upon their beach. Once again, Tomas found questions burning within him as stared at the faces of the passers-by, and he turned to Death to voice one of them. 'I take it that they can't see us yet. Density, right?' without turning.

'Right, but it is not being seen by humans that concerns me right now. War, are we secure?' Tomas spun in the saddle to see the indomitable giant give a last scan before replying that all was clear. It appeared that they had arrived undetected. Then came the 'but'. There was always a 'but', and Tomas had found it rarely meant good news.

'…But, even though there are no actual minions in the nearby vicinity, I can sense a considerable number of possessed. I suggest we make haste before the more sensitive amongst them are alerted to our presence.'

Tomas considered this, then their destination. 'By my reckoning, the Jezreel plain is going to be a few days' ride from here even as the crow flies. If we're going by land we should get a move on. I trust you know the way?' This time, all four riders turned and looked at Tomas. Tomas, for his part felt quite pleased with himself as he managed to look back at all of them without flinching from their weighty consideration. But then Famine broke the spell by laughing out loud and slapping his thigh in good humor.

'Good man, Tomas. Found some of that old steel, I see. How are you feeling after your first flight? Did you like my gift to you? How are you feeling now?'

'To be honest, I haven't given it much thought. I've had more on my plate than whether I needed to service one end or the other. Both have often been, in my opinion, an inconvenience in my line of work.'

Famine looked a little crestfallen.

'Don't pout, Famine; did we not want this human to adapt to the situation in which we have thrust him? What good would he be if he was overawed by the simplest of things?' Pestilence's reminder cheered the normally exuberant rider back to his former self, who acknowledged the right of it. It was the pragmatic voice of War that cut through the genial banter, reminding them of their purpose.

'I have no wish to put our more recent limitations to the test by waiting to see who finds us. Perhaps we should move out: a moving target is much harder for them to concentrate on. Not only that, but the sooner we get to Raphael, the sooner Tomas can get on about his task.'

It wasn't the cheeriest thought Tomas had ever heard, but he was right all the same. 'You're right; there's no time like the present. Let's get this done. Do we need to use roads or are we just gonna go through stuff?'

Death just shook his head forlornly. 'The roads will suffice; they go in the direction we need, and as I said before…'

'I know, Death, I'm only pulling your chain. You're far too serious, you know. It's a misuse of power to go through things, and will only alert those unsavory types. You see, I do listen. Shall we?' Tomas spurred Storm ahead a few feet and looked back. 'You coming then or what?' as Tomas heeled Storm, who faced front, rearing briefly onto his hind legs and pawing the air. Not bothering to see if they followed or not, Tomas could hear Famine chortling to himself behind him.

'Storm! Stop showing off to those others and let's get a move on.' But

Tomas was smiling as he said it, secretly pleased that his horse shared his viewpoint. It seems that even supernatural creatures have a sense of pride and humor.

'I definitely think that you and I are going to get along. For how long is another matter entirely, but hey, let's make the most out of it, shall we?'

Storm responded to Tomas's voice with a whinny of his own and leapt away, giving the brisk easterly breeze a run for its money.

As they pounded silently and wraithlike through the streets, Tomas saw how matters had deteriorated since he was here last. Bodies littered the sidewalks. He saw what War had called the possessed, tearing at the bloating corpses. Rubble was strewn everywhere as no end of explosions had rocked the districts. *What was happening here? Or was it not just here, was it everywhere?* Matters seemed far worse than Tomas had imagined, for up until now, all he had to go on was the word of these entities. Suddenly the reality of the horror they faced dawned on Tomas in startling Technicolor. Clouds of flies hung in the putrid air. But what stunned Tomas more, was the fact these bodies were just ignored. He saw men and women passing on the streets simply stepping over the ruined carcasses as though they were any other type of garbage. As another explosion rocked the ground and sent clouds of dust and debris blowing out of the decrepit building just ahead of them, Tomas reined in – with seconds to spare, it seems, as a second blast tore the façade from the building and peppered the wall opposite with shrapnel and hurtling debris. The Four Horsemen drew level and looked meaningfully to each other.

'Hey, pack that in. I'm here too, you know. Quit talking to each other like I don't exist. Damn, that's just so bloody typical of you lot. All hell's breaking loose and you instantly forget I'm here.' This got their attention. Death's head spun to glower at Tomas so fast he was sure it was going to go all the way around before fixing on him.

'Better. Now my instinct is to get out of the way of these explosions. Firstly, are we immune from harm with this density thing or are we going to have to avoid getting blown to kingdom come?' Before any of the Horsemen could answer, Tomas continued, 'Because, two things come to mind. Firstly, that was bloody close, so does someone know we are here or was it coincidence? Secondly, if we are not immune to getting our arses scattered across the landscape, then we ought to bug out of this built up area quick smart and to hell with who sees us. The lesser of two evils really, if you ask me. I've been blown up once, thanks, and I don't much fancy doing it again anytime soon.'

'The mortal has a point —' War began, but was unceremoniously cut off.

'He has a bloody name too! Tomas, in case you've forgotten.' Tomas was rapidly losing patience with his imposed feeling of insignificance. War gave Tomas a glance that very nearly seemed apologetic.

'Tomas has a point.' War watched Tomas nod his acquiescence before continuing. 'We stand to lose out whichever route we take. Not wishing to point out the obvious, but we either decrease our density to insubstantiality to avoid further harm, which gives us away; or we take to the skies, avoiding this rat's trap, and we give ourselves away. Someone knows we are here without a doubt. It would appear that we have a leak in our camp. The Adversary is expecting us.'

Another explosion shattered the silence that had fallen over the quintet as they considered their limited options. Only this time it was a block back; the falling masonry posed no immediate threat this time.

'I know you hate my seemingly inane questions, and I know this isn't really the time for another one, but I gotta wonder: Why doesn't this elusive God just come on back and put a stop to this little insurrection? Surely it's gotta be easier than this.'

Famine snorted with barely suppressed indignation. 'If only it were that easy. It would certainly make our lives that much simpler, but try this on for size: Man builds a locomotive, the track and several carriages to go with it. He fuels it, starts it rolling, then, when it's built up a maximum operating speed, he stands before it with his hand outstretched, ordering it to stop. What do you think happens next?'

'Splat?' Tomas ventured.

'Exactly. The multiverse isn't really all that different. Just because someone made a thing, it doesn't mean that that someone can easily stop it. Equally similar to trying to dismantle it at full speed: undo the wrong bit at the wrong time and disastrous consequences can occur.' Famine sat back and folded his arms, satisfied with his analogy.

'Just how much more disastrous can things get?' Tomas responded cautiously.

'I never said it was an infallible process, but presuming you don't care about the consequences, which the Adversary, it would seem, doesn't, then here we are. Not only that, as I'm sure you've heard, no one knows where this God is. I've been around some time and I've never had an encounter, not even a glimpse, and I'm an Absolute.'

'Arse. So it really is down to us then. Hope you don't mind me asking, but just seeing as we're in the middle of a war zone, some celestial backup wouldn't have gone amiss.' Tomas's last words were emphasized by a hail of bullet fire ripping into the buildings just behind them, sending stone chips and ricochets zinging past their heads. 'I think that's our cue to get the flock outta here.' Tomas turned to face Death. 'You seem to make the important decisions here, so it's your call. Upwards or through? We're screwed whichever but if we don't do one of them soon, that ragged little army of semi-automatic wielding possessed are going to win some brownie points the moment they round that corner back there. Now you may be bulletproof but I am most definitely not.' Two more explosions ahead of them caused Tomas to duck as yet more debris whizzed overhead and dinged off War's armor. This prompted some reaction.

'We need to deal with this, Death. Allow me.' Turning his horse on a dime, War galloped to the junction from whence the gunfire originated. Another burst flew from somewhere out of sight and bounced off War's armor with the similar sound to pouring marbles into a can. He never flinched; he merely unslung the sword from across his back and by the time it was in his hands and facing the alley, it had become a massive cylindrical barrel, with what looked to be a least a dozen smaller ones inset. Then War pulled the trigger. It both looked and sounded like a jet engine firing up. Tomas had once seen an A10 tank buster up close. This was similar in many aspects, but he had never seen one hand-held before. It truly was some beast of a weapon; it looked like it ought to have been standing on a tripod or something similar. How he even held on to it was a miracle, but then again, he was War after all. The noise was deafening as it fired up and disgorged its rain of leaden death. Tomas noticed through the sound of doom, that there was no return fire. Nothing human could stand before that, not even possessed. It would be a surprise, in fact, if any building beyond them had remained intact after such a barrage. Tomas guessed that they had to be at least fifty-millimeter shells. It seems War wasn't taking any chances. As he watched, War spun the sword-cum-gun and it shifted into something else. The metal flowed into the form of what Tomas recognized as a Javelin LF ATGW. Tomas had seen plenty of the anti-armor fire-and-forget weapons. He had used more varieties than you could wave a stick at. Tomas could only imagine what War had seen to employ the anti-tank guided weapon. Fortunately, he didn't have a problem with having to reload, and several concussive explosions later, War was back amongst them.

'You probably just destroyed some valuable ancient ruin with all that firepower.'

'Ancient by whose standards? Anyway, that should keep them occupied for now, but there is no such thing as a quiet explosion. More will come flocking to the disturbance. I would say we have about ten minutes to do whatever it is we are going to do, before reinforcements arrive. I can't guarantee what form they will be in. If it's minions, we could be in trouble, with Tomas here.'

Death pondered something. 'Very well. I had planned to do it at Megiddo, where there would be less time for any repercussions or for something to go wrong.'

Tomas didn't like the direction this conversation was heading and he began to get a bad feeling in the pit of his stomach – usually a sure sign something unpleasant was amiss.

'Guys? Do what? Why are you looking at me like that? I've seen that look before, usually just before —'

Tomas never had the chance to finish his sentence, for at blistering speed – for which Tomas never stood a chance of seeing, let alone avoiding – the three remaining Horsemen, War, Pestilence and Death, had all drawn weapons and, as one, thrust them into Tomas, in much the same way that Famine had done earlier. The twin swords of Pestilence. The enormous Sword of War, which as Tomas looked down, stunned, he saw protruding from him from throat to gullet. And of course the still- gleaming scythe of Death. All of them were sticking out of him like some macabre magician's act, only without the box. Tomas couldn't speak; it was all he could do to just look up and down dumbfounded at what had just happened to him. A feeling of pressure began to build within him, and Tomas's eyes began to bulge in barely constrained panic. Following the pressure, came pain, unbearable pain. Tomas gritted his teeth together so hard he was sure they were going to shatter any second. Rational thought left him as his thresholds were arrived at, shattered and surpassed; convinced there was going to be another explosion – him – as the pressure continued to build, bringing with it yet more pain. Tomas knew he could take pain as part of his training, but this: it was unlike any pain he had ever experienced. Nor could he imagine how it could be humanly achieved. Every molecule was being torn asunder and incinerated at the same time. Through all this, the Horsemen sat implacable, their weapons skewering him mercilessly. He could take no more. Squeezing his eyes shut against the pain, he screamed. As he vented his own agony, ripping from his raw throat, he felt a cooling wind buffet him, diminishing the searing agony. It was like standing at the nexus of a hundred wind tunnels. Forces immeasurable tore at his face, skin and clothing.

His scream died. So too did the gale, almost simultaneously. Tomas opened his weeping eyes, genuinely amazed to find himself alive and even still sitting upright upon Storm. The first thing Tomas was able to focus his eyes on were his hands. For a split second, it looked as though his hands were underwater: the skin seemed to ripple and shift. Then it was gone and all was as it was, though with one fundamental difference – there were no razor sharp pieces of steel sticking out of him. Finding his voice, dragged from a throat ripped raw, Tomas had to know what had just occurred and just as importantly – why he wasn't dead. *Maybe I am but I didn't think death would hurt quite as much as that, though.*

'Wha– ' Tomas coughed, and tried again. 'What did you just do to me?' he asked, looking imploringly at the three resolute expressions regarding him much like the results of a science experiment. They looked to see what he would do next. Only Famine seemed unconcerned, if anything, slightly amused at Tomas's discomfort. Death answered him.

'For one thing, Tomas, you may take solace in the fact that you are a true guardian, as destined. Any other mortal could not have withstood what just happened to you. One of us interacting with them maybe, but not three of us.'

'Thanks. That's nice to know,' Tomas interjected bitterly, 'but couldn't you have just *told* me that?'

Death shook his head, causing the raven-black cowl to waft gently side to side. The grim visage of his helm continued to stare at him, the rictus grin almost mocking him and his predicament. 'No, unfortunately not. Your kind has beseeched an absent god for too long, vainly hoping that your numerous and quite frankly, sorry prayers are answered, solving all your not entirely insurmountable problems for you. Not going to happen. There is nothing there to hear you. Only us. The Enemy and the Angelic Host, even the Drakarim, no longer hear you —'

Again Tomas interrupted as his strength, quite surprisingly, returned.

'Wait a minute. That's a bit harsh, isn't it? People need something greater than themselves to believe in, something to feel it's all worth it; and you shouldn't insult and disrespect them for that!'

Again Death answered with all the patience and inevitability of the grave itself, his voice as chilling and resounding as a falling guillotine. 'It is not disrespect, Tomas, nor is it insulting. It is *fact*. Since man has risen and fought wars, he has beseeched numerous deities for aid and protection. This was not originally encouraged by the Angelic Host, who very early on, adopted the forms you knew, as many of your elder deities, but they grew to like it. Some, more than others. This proved to be problematic and divisions began to form amongst the host. So, when you reached a certain point in your sentience, it was considered prudent for all concerned to focus your misguided devotions in one direction only. This didn't go down well with some, but the majority won out. Yet it seems even that failed.'

Tomas was beginning to wonder where this was going. *That's all I get these days: bloody lectures.*

Death continued, 'Throughout your species' past, there have been incursions by the enemy; your wars show the success of many of these – though not to this extent. This is something else altogether. The guardians rose to the call of your people, but they in turn called for aid, beseeching the long-absent and unhearing figurehead that the Celestial Hosts had perhaps, in hindsight, mistakenly steered you towards. For as expected, there was no assistance from the quarter. With no assistance forthcoming, inevitably your warriors died – '

War interjected with a note of urgency in his voice. He had been watching and listening, as was his habit. Something was coming. 'Not to hurry you up at all – but, *could you hurry it up*? We'll be having some unwanted company any moment now, but I appreciate Tomas needs to know this and I'll buy us what time I can, but give him the summarized version if you will. I'll be much happier surrounded by Raphael and his army.' War turned and headed in the direction of the disturbance.

'Very well then…' Death sounded almost peeved at having to reduce his speech. He seemed to like delivering them and it seemed his companions had tired of hearing them. '…Where was I? Oh yes, your warriors died, unprotected by the deity they had put their hope, belief and faith in to protect and save them. We are here to ensure that that mistake is not perpetuated. As a final guardian, and with matters considerably more catastrophic than they have ever been before, it seemed prudent to give you more than empty prayers to protect you. You are aware of Famine's gift to you? Well, those of War, Pestilence and myself are not dissimilar. Our attributes, or a fragment thereof, have become yours. In order for you to complete your task, or at least be in with a chance, however slim – we have removed certain obstacles from your path. Famine's gift you know…'

Several explosions rocked the nearby building, causing choking clouds of dust to swirl into the street where the group stood. When it cleared, War was trotting towards them and shouldering his sword across his back. Looking pointedly at Death, he queried, 'You finished yet?'

'No.'

War shook his head despondently and settled next to Famine and Pestilence, to wait. 'We've got a few moments longer, which seems just as well. As much as I enjoy a good fight, this isn't fighting. It's slaughter. Killing possessed is more of a mercy killing; those poor souls have no idea what awaits them.'

Death's look said 'Do you mind?' 'Thank you. Now will you pass over the sword to Tomas? He'll need that.' Turning back to Tomas he added, 'You saw how War used it; it will now serve you in the same capacity. Your will is its action. It will also gird you for combat in any garb you require, even to enhancing your strength where needed. Your body will be your main weapon – the sword will help you protect it – though, of course, it may be susceptible to other influences. For example, it may be at risk from disease, venom and poisons: tools of the trade for the enemy. Strength alone will not prevail there. The gift of Pestilence protects you from all but the most potent venoms. Remember, as we grow weaker, the Adversary grows in strength – and vice versa. Unchecked, he will soon be a match for us on this world. *And that will not do!*' This last was delivered with such vehemence from the Grim Reaper, Tomas was momentarily taken aback by its force. *Obviously not pleased about that concept. Still, can't say I blame him about that: the end of all things seems a bit final.*

'What about you? What's your gift?' Again the temperature seemed to drop around the Absolutes, causing Tomas to shiver even through Famine's assurance.

'Mine is the governance of Death. While I live, you shall not die. Any wounds you receive should heal rapidly. I will also bond Storm to you.' Death reached out a gauntleted hand and grasped Tomas by the bicep. If there was such a thing as a liquid nitrogen bear trap, then that was what clamped onto Tomas. He felt a bone searing heat for a heartbeat, and then it was gone. So too was his coat and sleeve below the grip zone. On his bare arm was the branded, stylized image of a horse; and the smell of charred flesh. His. Tomas somewhat belatedly yelped in a gesture of pain, as it should have hurt a lot more than it actually did.

'Stop whining! You humans seem to be very good at that. Does it hurt?' Tomas replied in the negative. 'Are you in any way discomforted?' Again, no.

'Good, so that's out of the way. Choose a form for the sword to take that you are happy with, and will it so.'

Tomas barely understood what was asked of him, his learning curve was going to be swift and brutal, it seemed. Tomas, though, liked the idea of the sword and visualized it backslung the way War wore it. In less time than it took to think it, he felt the unfamiliar weight hanging from his back, scabbard and all.

'Good. Get used to it; it will be your greatest ally in the dark time to come.' Storm whinnied at this, as though put out that it wasn't him being Tomas's greatest ally. 'Now we should depart…'

189

'...Finally, that outpouring of energy lit us up like the Fourth of July. Every minion for miles around will be descending on this spot any second now. I've set as many traps as I can to slow them down, but you know what they're like: they'll just crawl over their dead to get to us. I suggest we density down, keep low, and head for the hills. We may need to find another route to the rendezvous; the obvious way will be blocked by now. Keeping to the wilderness, we can minimize much of the collateral damage to the population; they've got problems of their own after all. Though I fear a confrontation may now be inevitable at this point.'

Tomas felt a tingle as Death reduced their density in order to pass through solid matter and travel as the crow flies to the hills beyond the town. Tomas rubbed his brand unconsciously and Storm turned his head back to look at his rider, flicking his ears with an intelligence that spoke of misgivings for his passenger.

'Bloody marvelous, even with all these gifts you've just laid on me, even Storm thinks I'm likely to get myself killed sooner rather than later.'

The Four Horsemen, just before they spurred their own mounts to run, cast Tomas a look that for the most part was unreadable, but he was sure he detected a distinct feeling of *probably*.

It was still a disconcerting sensation several hours later as Tomas and the Four Horsemen had nearly cleared the devastated ruins of what was once civilization; to have mortar and other various explosives going off all around you, and to have white hot masonry and shrapnel screaming through your insubstantial body. On more than one occasion the group had found it necessary to increase their density and retaliate, which Tomas was pleased to see, utilizing extreme prejudice. The Sword of War began to respond to his summons with quicker reaction times on each call. The last two times were in the form of his old favorite, the Hechler and Koch semi-automatic machine pistol. Two pitched running battles gave Tomas his first true glimpse of the minions of the enemy. Hideous and malformed creatures, many displaying such "hellish" traits as scales, horns, insectoid bodies and ragged leathery wings. Not forgetting their sharklike fangs and razor talons – the last of which Tomas had seen rend concrete and sever the iron reinforcements within like they were string.

Other than themselves, who Death was convinced had had to have been betrayed by someone close in order for their enemies to know exactly where they were likely to be; Tomas had seen several groups of humans, desperately defending themselves from these abominations. The streets were littered with the bodies of these valiant fighters, for they were no match against the supernatural strength and arcane power of these minions. He saw one particular group of humans direct a hail of machine gunfire at an approaching horde, but their rounds seemed to bounce harmlessly off them, causing no more than the smallest flesh wound. Tomas couldn't stand by and see them slaughtered – breaking from his comrades and with the shouts of Death echoing in his head to get back, he willed Storm into a gallop, pounding down the rubble strewn street, past the charred remains of cars and people's homes. He cast a passing thought to the contorted and mutilated dead that littered the road as much as the rubble did, empathy lending his rage weight.

Hearing horses' hooves from behind them must have been the absolute last sound they expected to hear; that, and the sight of Tomas, galloping towards them upon an armored horse. Tomas had emulated War as best as he could for the short time he had to practise, girding himself in dull grey steely armor. It had to be the most bizarre sight that the local populace had ever seen. Certainly since the last crusade anyway. The doughty fighters cowered as Tomas, now in full charge, emerged from a dust cloud like a wraith from the past, and leapt the scrappy barricade they had erected. Landing like an expert, which was more down to Storm than anything Tomas did, and skidding to a halt before the charging minions, Storm reared up and pawed the air impressively, causing the lead minions to break stride to avoid being brained by a pair of flashing steel-shod hooves. Tomas willed to hand an SA80A2 assault rifle with under-barrel grenade launcher. Then, with the precision and practice of so many years coming back to him these past hours, he pumped three grenades into the horde, with devastating effect. They expected the usual noise and irritation that they barely felt from mortal weapons. What they hadn't anticipated was the fact that Tomas's weapon was of *very* supernatural origins. His shells took them completely by surprise, especially the half-dozen he blew into bloody chunks. The rest, still stunned by the explosion, hesitated a second too long. Tomas let rip a prolonged burst of continuous fire into those remaining, quickly dispatching them and sending them to join their decimated comrades. Turning afterwards to face the stunned and bewildered defenders, Tomas hailed them. Forgetting that he was English, he simply spoke to them, but apparently his gifts took care of the inconvenience of linguistics, his voice echoing mysteriously from the confines of his steely helm.

'Take my advice and leave, now. Don't bother with trying to fight. I promise you that you can't win against these. Believe me as well, when I tell you that these are no secret weapons from your enemies; these creatures are the real deal and they do not discriminate – East, West, Northern or Southern, black, white, yellow or red. You are human; that is enough for them. They will tear your flesh and you will die. The end, and thank you. So get your shit together and run like the devil himself is chasing you, because I can assure you, he *might* be, and his minions certainly *are*.'

'Take us with you,' one pleaded, but Tomas backed Storm up a couple of paces.

''Fraid not, pal. You really don't want to be going where I'm going; you want the opposite direction. Head for the coast and get a boat. Where I'm going there is only more death. Now *run* and take as many of your people as you can before any more appear, looking for their friends.'

With a last look at the ragtag group, knowing that their chances of survival were bleak, his efforts probably only delaying the inevitable, Tomas wheeled Storm about and trotted back the way he had come from, unaware how his legend had just started as his dull steel armored back vanished into the choking dust filled air. Willing the sword away, he rejoined his own group.

I think I'm getting the hang of this sword thing, Tomas thought to himself cheerlessly. Becoming a master of destruction again wasn't something he was particularly proud of. The sound of his horse's hooves clopping on the flagstones of the city street alerted his companions to his imminent return. Tomas got the immediate impression that they weren't happy.

'That was reckless and pointless; they will only succumb to another raiding group. Your task in saving humanity lies elsewhere and on a much grander scale than a few desperate refugees.'

Tomas stopped abruptly and spun in his saddle to face down Death, who had fired the rebuke at him the moment he was in earshot. An equally cold and steely gaze hardened the features on Tomas's face, features drawn tight in barely suppressed fury. Death's metallic rictus grin faced Tomas back, unmoving, uncaring. But a sudden fury surged through Tomas, its blaze illuminating some thoughts that had so far been shadowy and elusive. Instant clarity drove his mouth to overrule his normally more cautious brain, for his control hadn't been all it used to be of late, and, tossing that control aside, he let rip.

'I've worked something out about you. Your incessant monotone about the "big picture", how my role is critical to it and the greater good should override all lesser matters: that's been all *you* so far. Well, *I* think it's something else altogether. I've spent enough years taking lives, but it was on a small scale compared to this. When it comes to the human race being extinguished, it's another matter entirely. *All* life is relevant then, and if I can save any, then I bloody well will. Granted, I was basically a hired killer for the Government, I make no bones about that, but since my near-death experience...' (Tomas knew it went back further than that but the explosion had catalyzed it for him.) '...I have come to realize that it's the principle of saving *all* life where possible that's important. Standing up for what's right, doing what needs to be done. Helping the underdog. It's what makes us human. Those that walk by or deny involvement are also our problem, but even they deserve saving, if it is what's required. For all you know, those few "refugees" may go to provide the solution to this debacle.'

Death listened to Tomas's tirade with his usual equanimity. The reply was icily delivered. Seemingly ignoring the main part of Tomas's fiery rebuke, he seemed focused on the opening sentence.

'What is it that you think you have learnt about me, Tomas?' The voice was even more menacing than usual. So much so, even the others turned to cast questionable looks in their direction. They too were curious now to see what Tomas had learnt to anger the Reaper so, for in all their time together, they knew that took some doing. 'What do you think you know?'

The air seemed to still. Even the smallest particles wafting in the air seemed to hang, suspended in time, waiting for Tomas's answer. Tomas was too annoyed to stop now, too committed to this course of action.

'I think that you are afraid!' Tomas spat, with a sneer of derision.

'Afraid?'

'Yes, bloody well afraid. Afraid of the future. Afraid of the uncertainty of your place within it. *You* said this was unprecedented. *You* said that this could rewrite the entire multiverse. That means you stand to lose as much as us. You stand to die, as we do. And that is what I think you are afraid of. You've been so long ensuring the demise of others, the prospect of your own imminent death is an alien thing. It's not me who's lost his grip on reality, but you. It's for the people like them that we are fighting in the first place.' Tomas thumbed the direction of those he had just saved. 'Forget the big picture for five minutes; it's the little details that you need to see again.'

Vindicated, Tomas waited for the furious maelstrom of Death's reply, and not really caring either. But long seconds later, it still hadn't happened. Instead – to Tomas's amazement and even the other three Horsemen's, who knew their companion well enough – all Death said was, 'Don't run off like that again, least not without us. Now, can we press on? We've still got a distance to go and there will only be more minions abroad, now that the sun is setting.'

Dumbstruck, Tomas heeled Storm to follow Death. War quietly took point again. Pestilence and Famine, just as silent, dropped back and acted as rear guard.

Conversation went into hiding after Tomas's and Death's confrontation. It appeared that Tomas had struck a nerve. And after a millennium of being secure in the knowledge that one was going to outlive pretty much everything, coming face to face with one's mortality must have been a sobering thought. The nerve was now very much exposed and over the course of their journey, Tomas began to experience a strange sensation. It seemed that his conscience was rebuking him. Of course the nerve was exposed. What did it have to fear? There was nothing to concern it – it probably didn't even know it was exposed. Tomas began to feel ashamed of his outburst, responding in anger to Death's apparent insensitivity, but he could be accused of the very same insensitivity. However ironic it might be, Death, along with the Horsemen, were still conscious, sentient beings. Their only exception was their longevity and comparative uniqueness in the multiverse.

Three messy and brutal encounters later, the Horsemen and Tomas found themselves resting in the lee of a natural outcropping. Where the wind had howled over centuries, it had worn a vertical bowl shape in the rocks – effectively concealing them from any aerial observation. It wasn't that they needed to stop, but a particularly large band of minions were ahead of them and prudence seemed best served in letting them pass.

Tomas was still troubled by the uneasy silence that had befallen the group, so while the riders consulted each other on what strategy best suited their next stint, Tomas wandered away slightly, dismounted, and stretched his legs. Placing his hands in the small of his back, he pushed in, popping a few vertebrae in the process. Although he was a bit stiff with muscles unused to the activity, Tomas found he was in no pain – not like he should have been with the extensive riding and recent increase in having to fight for his life. *At least these gifts are useful for something; I'd probably want a wheelchair by now. I just hope they don't take them back suddenly. I'd be in big trouble then. Someone would have to stretcher me out.* But Tomas knew his thoughts were only a diversion from what really bothered him: his "disagreement" with Death. It soured the remaining moments of his life. Tomas accepted the fact he was going to die, but to go to it like this, with bad feeling between entities he had started to consider friends, odd though that felt – friends with the Four Horsemen of the Apocalypse – but that was all he could call it. Finding a large rock, Tomas sat and relaxed his mind and went through his muscle relaxing exercises, sitting, apparently perfectly still, but putting each muscle group through subtle stretches and regulating his breathing. He found himself watching a night stalking desert spider. Having waited until the rigorous heat of the day had cooled, it now emerged and began to hunt. Tomas saw it creep towards an unsuspecting lizard, foolishly exposed and chilled down, sluggish and slow. Tomas felt a moment of remorse for the creature whose brief life was about get considerably briefer. Transferring his own concerns to the tableaux before him, Tomas wondered what went through the lizard's mind each day. Did it think about such lofty thoughts as theological discourse? Did the lizard society have such things as gods? Were their gods in fact, large hairy spiders? Were these voracious hunters worshipped by the lesser creatures, the same principle applied upwards and so forth? After all, humanity had its ancient pantheons, which were as far above humanity as potentially the spider is above the lizard. *It makes a warped sense, really. Our gods scared the shit out of us humans; and spiders do a similar thing, both to the lizard and many humans too. But if they think that about spiders, what do they think of us?* Tomas recognized he was in a very big theological spiral there, and not one he was intellectually qualified to answer, for it went on and on *ad infinitum*. The end was merely speculation, though a teacher had made the point to him once, and it always stuck with him.

'Tomas,' she started, 'remember the microbe.'

He remembered thinking, the what?

'The microbe: the one that lives upon your flesh, with you, every day. Look at the callouses upon your palms. Those hard areas are where you have killed the microbes through repetitive work. Did you think of their society when you did this? I expect not. Much the same as your creator. Are you considered in all matters? Possibly not. Does the microbe truly know what it dwells upon? Who knows? But put yourself in its place. Imagine you have to explain to them about people, that it might live on a hand, on an arm attached to a body. They don't even look like us. Where is the analogy? Were they our size, they would be feared as flesh-eating monsters. Then try to explain our socio-political cross-cultured species. Our sports and so on and so forth. This is a very big subject, Tomas, but simply think of yourself as the microbe and you have an idea of your place in the grand scheme of things.'

If only she could see him now, though he doubted she would smile. She rarely smiled at him; usually she was berating him for being male and stupid. He hoped it was an affectation, for he liked her, even when she told him off. He would have liked to tell her that he remembered her lessons.

Habit made Tomas think he was thirsty and could use a cool drink, but after a moment's consideration, he realized that he wasn't thirsty at all. Nor was he hungry, tired or anything else for that matter. The enormity of the gifts of the Horsemen crashed in on him then. He had been thinking of himself as human up until then, but was he now? Was he more than human or less than? So much of this was like an episode of *The Twilight Zone*. He half expected to see the show's host, Rod Serling, walk out from behind a rock, in his suit, and begin to talk about him and what had happened to him so far. Of course, he didn't, but it didn't stop Tomas from feeling a sudden pressure in his chest. That 'Oh my God, what have I done?' sort of pressure.

Without looking up, Tomas was snapped out of his reverie by the sense that he was no longer alone. Oddly, he even knew who it was who stood behind him. But Tomas emphasized his ability by swiftly drawing his Hochlers and pointing behind him, unerringly at the chest of the being that stood there.

'Ah, Death. What can I do for you, that I'm not already doing? Something other than die for a good cause?' Tomas grimaced. It had just blurted out. For too long he had put up the bitter cynical barrier around himself, so determined to keep people out that he did it without thinking.

That wasn't what he wanted to say at all.

'I see you are getting along with the Sword of War. Considering it has rarely been apart from its master since its birth, it seems to like you, though I would appreciate you *not* pointing it at me. There are few things in the multiverse that can equal me…' Death hesitated briefly before continuing, '… *were* few things – since the Adversary commenced his grand plan, I believe that has changed – but the Sword of War was always one of them. I would not care to test my limits at this time.'

Tomas considered the request for a few seconds, then nodding slowly, he obliged. Tomas's face, if Death could have seen it, was contorted in confusion. He knew he had something to say to the Grim Reaper, but he didn't know how. All he managed was a curt, 'Couldn't you cough or something before sneaking upon people. You won't have to test anything then.' Tomas was realizing, now more than any other time, that anger was a parasite and it was reluctant to let go once it had insinuated itself. Tomas had carried his for a very long time.

'Death does not "cough" for anyone, but I will reconsider how I approach you.'

Tomas wasn't sure if he had read the direction that this conversation was going in, but he felt that, like him, Death had something to say also and seemed to be having as much trouble in saying it as him too. With an exertion of will Tomas didn't think humanly possible, he stood and turned to face Death. At six feet one inch, Tomas wasn't generally used to having to look up at people who stood before him. Surpassing seven feet, Death loomed a bit, but Tomas met his gaze unswervingly. Drawing a deep breath, he said it.

'We have to talk!'

'Yes.'

Tomas felt the dam give then. Having made one move, the next came easier. 'I'm sorry!'

He didn't know what to expect at that moment. The steel face plate of Death's helm stared back at him. The twin suns that seemed to be his eyes, hidden within, stared back and seemed to bore into Tomas's soul. Long seconds passed like this, neither moving. To Tomas, those seconds felt more like days.

Then Death spoke. 'So am I.'

Death reached out a big gauntleted hand and placed it lightly on Tomas's shoulder. A surge of power flowed from the contact, like soft lightning. Tomas pushed on, for fear that if he gave in to the emotion generated from the contact, he would stop talking and break down. *That* wouldn't do at all.

'It was an ill-considered comment, both to make and to make in front of your colleagues. I let my self-righteous anger get the better of me and I shouldn't have. You are a myth, a legend.' Tomas spread his arms to give the sense of the enormity of what he was implying. 'The personification of the most terrifying thing known to man, and I wrongly assumed that for all that, you have no thoughts or feelings – just duty. Part of me felt it was a selfish duty. Were it not, you would have left this battle to the angels and not gotten involved yourself. I was wrong, I see that now.' Tomas lowered his head in a gesture of humility.

'Not entirely,' Death replied. 'When I say we, I really mean I, have separated ourselves from any direct involvement with your kind for so long that we, I, have become indifferent to your struggle. To the individuality of your souls. For even though many of your kind choose to follow certain doctrines, you are still individuals, striving, reaching for the intangible. You were right to save those people; maybe it was destined you should do so. We have both had much to dwell on this day and we are the richer for the sharing of it. Thank you for reminding me of why we exist, Tomas – and it is my fervent wish that you, in fact, *do not die* on this mission, for I believe we may have much to discuss when this matter is resolved.'

Tomas merely nodded his agreement. The lump in his throat prohibited him from speech at that particular moment. Fortunately he was spared the need to, for another voice carried to them, that of War.

'They have passed. We can continue in relative peace. At least for a time, anyway.' Tomas spared a fleeting glance back to see how the spider fared. It appeared that the lizard wasn't as torpid as the spider thought; it had leapt away and was now breathing hard halfway up a rock, flicking its tongue out. Possibly at the spider. *Good for you!* Tomas thought. *Just because it may be inevitable, there's no need to make it easy for them.* Being bigger and more powerful didn't necessarily guarantee success – obviously the lizard had a trick or two up its tiny scaly sleeves – but in the hunter prey game, the roles almost never reversed. The prey was always the prey and the hunters likewise. You never saw gazelle stalking and eating the lions – now wouldn't that be a turn up for the books! But could they be taught to not fear the lion? Would that be a start up the evolutionary ladder for them: to not actually be a hunter – after all they were vegetarians – but to not be prey any more? Maybe the removal of fear was all it took for all species to evolve. Fear drove so much of what was wrong with the world. It was fear that led to wars, fear of another having or taking what belonged to them, or having more, or ultimately, fear that another believed in something that may or may not be true and accurate, merely that it was different, and humanity feared that which was different.

'In your own time, Tomas!' Famine's voice brought an abrupt halt to Tomas's mental meanderings, which in one way he was disappointed about, for he felt himself on the verge of some sort of epiphany. Even so, it cleared some misgivings he had been thinking about.

'Coming. Just thinking how I'm looking forward to yet more horseriding. Mmm, can't wait.' Tomas rubbed his stretched thighs as he walked back to Storm and mounted up, settling himself in anticipation of another long hard gallop.

'Sarcasm? Surely not from you, Tomas?' Famine chuckled back at him. 'Hope you two sorted everything out: we don't have the luxury of ill feeling at this stage in the proceedings; we need absolute trust amongst ourselves. Any chink in that armor could give the enemy a chance to insinuate themselves and drive the wedge in good and proper. Worse part is, as their strength grows, you probably wouldn't even notice it was them feeding you your thoughts and not yourself. Remember, that's how the possessed get that way.'

Tomas took the rebuke-cum-warning and glanced quickly at Death, who had mounted and was already putting distance between them.

'Yeah, we're good, thanks. All sorted. How much further?' Tomas reined in beside Famine as they cantered up to the others.

'Still a little way as yet; we have to make diversions we hadn't intended, to minimize our exposure to the enemy. Essentially, we're taking the long way round.'

'I know I'm new to this mystical shit, but, as we've made ourselves known to the enemy already, why not say fuck it, there must be a quicker way to get to Megiddo – some sort of short cut. Surely you guys don't ride and fly everywhere all the time? It isn't like we've kept that low a profile, is it? How many arse kicking sessions have we had since arriving? Enough, I'd say, to let them know where we are, don't you think?'

Pestilence interjected, 'You are right, Tomas, you are new to this. Let me explain it to you in terms you will understand – again. We are involved because the end of all things is upon us. As this world grows weaker, so do we, and so does the Celestial Host. The enemy grows in strength, however. Should we open a portal to Raphael, the energy flare that that would give off, not only here, but at the encampment, would alert the Adversary not only to our whereabouts, but to that of Raphael's army, which so far, is undetected. We do not want them detected until you are away about your own task. Only then will our army materialize and attack, its purpose: to provide distraction hopefully sufficient to buy you as much time as possible to fulfill your destiny.' Pestilence didn't speak often, but when she did, for some reason, Tomas felt like a schoolboy being told off for doing something stupid.

She continued, 'Should we all fail at that point, much will hinge on the other, perhaps too much.'

Tomas came instantly alert at the last part of Pestilence's rebuke. 'What other? I thought you said I was the last. What haven't you told me now?'

'There are lots of things we haven't told you; it would take many of your lifetimes to impart all that we know. Even then, you would always be lacking the experience of what we have seen and dealt with. For now, I suggest you concentrate on what you do know, rather than what you don't.' She wasn't going to be drawn into elaborating on the slip, if slip it was. Tomas couldn't tell with her. Maybe it was intentional to make him feel he wasn't alone in his hopeless task after all.

War's voice again carried to them. 'Stop talking and start riding. We need to ride hard and fast through the night. Maybe then we'll avoid the other small army of minions heading this way. It seems we upset someone behind us by evading their trap.'

Marvelous: minions behind and minions in front. No doubt there were bloody minions to either side as well and here we are, riding through a hostile territory in order to go to face some more even nastier minions, and Big Chief Minion himself. Why aren't destinies simple? Tomas sighed deeply as he pondered this, putting heels to Storm. The five horsemen sped out across the rough terrain, heads low and cloaks flapping behind them, but for all their speed and stealth, dark malevolent eyes watched the quintet. After a few moments to ensure the riders were a safe distance ahead, six tall, massively built humanoid figures rose from the rocks where they had secreted themselves, and began to lope across the sand, maintaining a constant distance behind the riders. Slavering fangs and razor talons glinted in the moonlight as the Hounds of Fenris pursued their quarry. But these were no ordinary hounds; these still wore the insignia of their former lives. Lives before their capture, before their torture and subsequent transformation into the beasts they now were. The six former angels of Raphael's scouting troop were now the willing and eager servants of the Dread Wolf Lord Fenris, their minds subverted and rendered docile by the corruption of their change. The powerful hounds now had only one mission: to find and kill the Four Horsemen of the Apocalypse, and the one called Tomas Walker. They were close now. When next the riders stopped, they would attack. Driven by the knowledge and the promise of elevation within the Wolf Lord's ranks, the hounds drew ever closer to their prey. Along with promotion came the promise of more power, for that seemed to be how the Domain's inhabitants ranked themselves – by power. The more you possessed, the higher you rose. These tempting treats drove the Hounds of Fenris, the former warriors of the Angelic Host, to snap and claw even amongst themselves in a bid to be the first to reach the Horsemen, and the thought of sinking their slavering fangs into their bodies obliterated all thoughts and memories of their former lives from their now clouded minds. Their only thought was kill and reward, kill and reward. Driven by this imperative, they picked up their speed.

Chapter Six

Propagation

Gwen was beginning to wonder just why they had to hike *so* far from civilization for their demonstration. After all, the spot they proposed was her favorite and she had picked it with the express purpose of being as far as possible from any other humans. It wasn't that she was particularly xenophobic or humanaphobic, if such a word or condition existed, but there were just some days that she never wanted to see another human again for as long as she drew breath. Those days, she would pack up all she could carry – sometimes even her tent and sleeping bag, and trek up here for some Gwen time and to calm herself back to an acceptable level. She could scream if she so chose, which occasionally she did, and no one would hear her. It was very cathartic, nearly as good as punching something. She simply had to expel whatever had built up inside her. Once, she had punched a mossy looking tree in pure frustration – only to find it wasn't quite as mossy as it looked. She had cracked a bone in her hand that day. Jen and Maddy had no sympathy for her when she eventually came back and held up her hand forlornly.

'That's what you get for hitting trees; it serves you right, if you ask me. I hope it hurts.' It did, for a good ten days after. Gwen didn't hit trees again after that. She kept a punchbag hanging in her garage, which she took her frustrations out on now. Serving a dual purpose, it calmed her and kept her fit at the same time. Which was just as well, Gwen realized, after a traumatic day like she had just had, nearly having her ears chewed off by a very irate Grandma Yellow Deer. The girls had backed out of there as quickly as possible once it was evident that Dolores was now simply sleeping, and unharmed. They had driven to the park's car park and abandoned the Jeep there and started walking. Gwen knew how far it was, and it was apparent that the girls did too, having spied on her each time she came out here, though they said it wasn't spying – rather it was more a case of protecting. They insisted that they had kept a respectful distance, but were in range should trouble occur.

'What trouble? There's nothing out here but me, the trees and maybe a few animals. Give me the animals any day. At least you know where you stand with a bear – whether it wants to eat you or not. It's just people you can't trust.'

The girls just shrugged, for there was little argument from them as far as that went.

The day was still cold and Gwen was glad she had picked up her coat, but her Ugs were fast deteriorating – they weren't designed for hiking in the woods – and she muttered frequently about it. All the girls did was to assure her it would be okay. If things worked out as they hoped, footwear would be the least of her worries. Gwen wasn't sure if that was all that reassuring. The more she ran it through her head, the less confident she felt about their impromptu excursion. Gwen also knew from the one time she had encountered a ranger up near her retreat, that gunshots were unlikely to be heard either.

The trees had a certain mystical quality to them at this time of year, for even though many of them were evergreen, they seemed to know it was winter. The frosty sparkles on the leaves of the ferns; and the red mulch from the cedars, which gave the ground a moody contrast to the deep greens, managed to give off a magical woodland feel. Ancient gnarly roots twisted and twined around the occasional rocky outcropping. Some were even deep enough to shelter in should the walker be caught in one of the sudden storms that could spring up without warning at certain times of the year. Gwen distracted herself with the familiar sights of the forest as they drew closer to Toadstool Rock. Gwen couldn't imagine what had happened to this stony outcropping to leave it in this formation, but it was a distinct umbrella shape, almost as though water had worn it away, but she couldn't imagine enough water this far up to do such a thing and not wear away the foliage. It was too big for someone to have carried up here. It was just one of nature's mysteries, she supposed. Looking across to Maddy and Jen, she figured that they were another of nature's mysteries, for they seemed totally unaffected by the weather. Granted, they never really overdid the warm clothes – they always seemed to be warm to the touch, but this day, they were hiking through a winter forest, barefoot and only wearing thin and not very long summer dresses. Yet, for all its insanity, they seemed more in place here like that, than they did back amongst civilization. This seemed more their element – the wild and untamed – which, she figured, kind of summed them up quite well.

'You two do know that it's going to be dark soon, and we'll never get back to town in time. The temperature is already dropping and you're not really dressed for this, are you?' Maddy skipped ahead and twirled around a tree, laughing as she did so. *That's it; they've flipped and I'm out here with a couple of nutters.* Maddy leant back against the trunk of a mossy cedar and placed one foot up on the bark. She ran both hands through her flaming mane and held it up, exposing her swanlike neck. Gwen thought she looked more like some sort of tree spirit then, the sort that tempted mortal men out into the woods, never to be seen again. Seeing her there, many would think that there were worse ways to go.

'Gwen, dearest, have you not worked it out yet?'

'Worked what out? That either you or me is off their trolley? That much I've considered. The fact that you're not normal is increasingly apparent as well. Let me guess. We're not going back tonight, are we?'

Maddy shook her head and smiled benignly.

'And don't smile like that either. It's not charming any more; in fact it's quite unsettling now. I only mention this because we didn't bring any supplies for a camping trip. You know, essentials like food? Water? Shelter? Any of the above ring any bells in that pretty head of yours?'

Jen laughed then and joined Maddy a few steps ahead. 'Gwen, will you stop worrying? We've already said that no harm will befall you. Surely that's enough to simply enjoy the forest and the company of your friends. Relax. Don't worry about us. I assure you, this weather won't bother us one little bit. It's not even really cold yet, look...' Jen held out her slender arms, '...can you see any goose bumps?'

'Well... no actually, but that's beside the point. It's just not natural.'

'Ah, that's where you are wrong, Gwen. It is in fact more natural than you can possibly imagine. When you were born, were you born with clothes?'

'No, but I wasn't born with fur either. Things that live in the cold are usually covered in the stuff. I'm not, nor are you.'

Jen put her hands on her hips and tilted her head at Gwen – a gesture Gwen had seen on many an occasion. It meant she was going to lecture her again.

'Gwen, how do you move your limbs?'

Gwen stopped walking and considered the question, wondering where she was going with this one. 'I suppose, they just move because my mind says so.' Gwen's open expression implied that was that. Did they want any more? It seemed they did.

'More, Gwen, there's more to it than that. Think how fast your mind works, manipulating muscles through electrical impulses, exciting the molecules and guiding them to obey your every command, however complicated. I'm sure the medical people have a much more detailed version of how those simple operations occur, but the crux of it is in your mind. So is temperature: it is the control of your molecules. Your mind keeps them warm therefore you are warm, however cold it is. Many of the older cultures have a degree of mastery of this. It is *very* natural for it is *your* mind, *your* body, *your* control. How unnatural can that be?'

Gwen didn't know how to answer – it made total sense.

'Expanding from that control of your own molecules – through frequency manipulation – comes the ability we call telekinesis. It is simply tuning the radio of your mind to the frequency of whatever it is you are trying to move, as though you were tuning in to a radio station. When the two sync, you get music. With telekinesis, when your mind comes into sync with the object, it becomes an extension of you, granting you the ability to move it the same way and same speed that you move any limb on your body.'

'So, that's why the weather doesn't bother you?' Gwen tested, though suspecting that there was considerably more to it than that. She wasn't going to be disappointed.

'More or less. Now why don't we press on. The sooner we get to the clearing, the sooner we can explain properly. All your questions will be answered then, if that's all right with you.'

Gwen knew she was outnumbered in this and they were just humoring her, trying to ease the enormity of what was happening. She knew she wasn't the boss any more out here: they were. She was now the novice, the neophyte. *Sacrifice?* 'So are we planning to be out here long then?' A last attempt to try and figure an agenda, but they were still having none of it.

'We'll be out here as long as it takes, but like I said,' Jen reinforced, 'we'll look after you.'

Gwen smiled thinly and knew that they knew what she thought about that.

The rest of the journey was uneventful apart from Gwen's occasional question, and she was running out of sane sounding ones, but the girls weren't answering any of them, sane or otherwise. They just strolled through the darkening forest like it was a stroll on a sunny day. One or both sometimes would walk beside her and hold her hand in a familiar and strangely comforting way; other times, they would leap away and dance about the trees and bushes like a pair of mischievous schoolgirls who had slipped away from the teacher. But eventually, like all journeys, this one ended as they stepped through the treeline into the familiar surroundings. About half an hour before arriving, Jen had slipped away and Maddy didn't let on why. But to Gwen's amazement, when she broke cover, the first thing she saw was Jen, sitting before Toadstool Rock, blanket spread out on the oddly snowfree grass, a series of small fires blazing in a ring about the rock. On the blanket, Gwen saw bottles of water and piles of fruit, bread that was still steaming – her mind couldn't process that little gem – and a selection of cheeses was also apparent.

'Thought you might be hungry – told you we would look after you. Once fed, and cozily warm, we'll get down to why we're here. Seem reasonable?' Gwen just nodded dumbly as Maddy led her to the flickering fairy ring. Gwen soon found that she had to divest herself of several layers of her clothes, for it was, as Jen said, cozily warm within. Taking her Ugs off and depositing them to one side to, hopefully, dry; she placed her coat, sweater and one of the tee shirts she wore on top. Sitting barefoot in her faded jeans and kami top, she tucked in to the surprising repast.

'This tastes like Ernest's bread?' as she munched on warm, buttery cornbread with a soft cheese spread upon it.

Jen smiled excitedly and nodded, her own mouth full.

'How on earth did you manage to do that? It's still warm, for Pete's sake,' Gwen continued.

When she had finished her mouthful, Jen answered just as enigmatically as before, 'You do ask a lot of questions, Gwen, which is odd when you already have an inkling of the answers. How did we get to you so fast when the animals appeared? No, don't try to answer that; we'll show you shortly. How's that?'

Gwen wasn't so sure. During the meal, she had been having serious second thoughts about all of this. It was fast becoming too weird for comfort. She had sought phenomena all her life, but now she was faced with it, she found she was scared. That was the word she had been avoiding all the way up here: scared. Gwen had read enough pagan lore to let her imagination run free a bit. Here she was in the woods with two mysterious women who were growing increasingly scarier by the minute. They were like strangers to her, for they no longer behaved like the girls she knew. A whole new side to them was manifesting and it hinted at danger and an irreversibility that would affect her life for evermore. She didn't know if she was up for that sort of change. She enjoyed the routines she had; they had stabilized her and for the first time in who knew how long, Gwen thought she was putting down roots. What she didn't know, was just how truthful a statement that was going to turn out to be.

Jen and Maddy watched Gwen carefully, silently communicating between themselves about her suitability, but in the end they concluded that she was the one, the conduit, and she had accepted the role back at the square. After all, the power did flow through her. Were she *not* the chosen one, nothing would have happened and things might be going a bit differently about now. Yet, for all her acquiescence so far, Gwen still had that scared bunny look – what was termed in animals, the fight-or-flight reflex. Gwen's looked very much like flight. But matters had gone too far to turn back now; she needed to see this through, to understand what she had accepted.

Fed and watered, Jen cleared the remains of their meal away, though where it went, Gwen had no idea, but go it did. And by this time too, it was also fully dark. A thin sliver of the moon barely lit anything, so the only light came from the circling fires, and it cast macabre shadows, leaping and flicking in and out of her limited visibility. Maddy stood first and walked a way out in to the clearing: far enough that Gwen lost virtual sight of her, barely able to discern her shapely silhouette. Jen stood, stretched and told Gwen to sit still and watch. But Gwen had determined that as soon as Jen joined Maddy in the dark she was off. Already slipping her Ugs on, she knew she could pick up her coat and be gone in a heartbeat. The moment Jen stepped from the circle of firelight, Gwen was up and running. Or at least she tried to be. Firstly, she hit the sticky air that she had seen before in the square holding the animals fast. Then the word hit her.

'*Stay!*' The force of the word hit her like a wet mattress moving at thirty miles an hour. Gwen was lifted off her feet and hurled back through the air in a pseudo slow motion manner, as the dense air cushioned the impact. It was the oddest – as well as a painful feeling – slammed between two invisible forces. The air driven from her lungs by the impact made the world swim disconcertingly; and as she landed with an undignified thump, back on the grass before the toadstool, the air returned to normal and she rolled several feet before coming to a tangled, sprawled stop.

'Now get up, please, and sit still, like we asked you to do. We didn't take any pleasure from having to do that, but you were asked nicely. This behavior is beneath you. We asked you to trust us. You need to understand certain things, Gwen, and it's not just our opinion. It seems you have been chosen by a power greater than us. It's simply better for you to know what is happening to you in advance, don't you think?'

Gwen nodded slowly, a horrified look still etched upon her features at the preventative steps taken to stop her running. This was real. Her slightly battered body and very battered mind finally accepted that this was much bigger than her and that if beings of obvious power wanted her to be involved, then perhaps she should see it through. Especially as it turned out that running was a wasted exercise. 'Okay, you've got me! I won't run again, here, see?' Gwen pulled off her Ugs and threw them out of reach, along with her coat. 'How's that?' Gwen could see the glow of the girls' eyes from where she sat, even if she couldn't see their bodies. It was as though two massive feral cats were watching her from the darkness. They didn't answer, but strangely… the thought hit her like an epiphany – *Ha! How much more strange could it get? Crikey, what am I thinking? They just did magic on me, bloody hell. Magic! It's real. Oh hell, if that's real, what else is real? What else is out there?* Gwen was about to find out how strange as she turned her attention back to the girls again. She could still see their eyes glowing, but she was sure they weren't that big before, or that far apart. And getting bigger by the looks of things. *Oh no! What now?* Gwen backed right up against the toadstool, in the vain hope that the overhang would shelter her from whatever was taking place before her in the darkness. The more she looked, Gwen realized it couldn't be the girls, for it now appeared as though two cars were parked out there with their headlights on, but, hang on, why were they going upwards? And since when did cars have golden headlights with vertical slits in them? The lights began to weave from side to side before her, still ascending and growing further apart until one pair was off to the far left, the other, the far right.

Gwen wasn't sure what happened next, but a sphere of light began to grow around her. Magnesium white, it grew brighter and brighter. It took a few seconds for Gwen to realize that it was the toadstool itself. Gwen leapt forward with a horrified squeal, alternating her gaze between the two pairs of hovering lights and the incandescent toadstool. But it was on the alternating glance to the floating lights that the illumination did its trick and she saw what they truly were. She simply stared slack mouthed and wide-eyed for several seconds before promptly passing out. Again.

As she lay unconscious, her mind swam with fantastic images of creatures she had only ever dreamed of. They were all around her, smothering her, and this feeling of suffocation brought her back to reality with a start. As her eyes focused again, all she could see was a wall of metallic, iridescent red scales the size of shields, flashing before her through every hue of red imaginable. They surrounded her but did not constrict her, so Gwen was able to turn about and look around her. She wished then she had stayed unconscious, for looming over her were two enormous reptilian heads the size of large trucks. The golden swirling headlight eyes were fixed on her diminutive form.

Gwen couldn't work out where she was in relation to their heads at first. Then as the initial shock wore, not off, but down a bit; she found that she was cozened in the coils of a glistening red scaled tail.

'It seems she's awake again, Jen.' The voice was booming in her ears, but it was Maddy's voice, gentle in her mind. Gwen lay there, too stunned to do much – not that there was an awful lot she could do, considering where she found herself, but look up in awe at the two great draconian faces looking down at her. The other face was as white as fresh snow, but as it moved, Gwen saw that it was more pearlescent, and flashed through more colors than the most precious opal. Her dimly remembered physics told her that white held every other color within it, so it made a kind of sense. But they were *dragons!*

It was difficult to tell what they were thinking as they gazed upon her recumbent form. Were they smiling? Or were they like crocodiles? – a mouth full of enormous teeth just looking like they are smiling, usually just before they eat you.

'We're not going to eat you, Gwen, don't be silly.' This time, the voice was only in her head and it was definitely Jen's. 'What do you think? Not something you see every day, is it?'

That did it for Gwen. She just burst into bouts of hysterical laughter. *Not something you see every day? That's a good one, I've been living with two dragons that look like Victoria's Secret Models, and now they decide to share? Damn! How many more were there out there?*

It seemed the girls had maintained their mental link with Gwen and answered her thought for her. 'We are it, the only two, you'll be pleased to know, and before you ask, there are only a few individuals who know about us in our mortal form, including you, now.'

'But why are you sharing this with me? Fantastic as it is, there are so many hows and whys going through my head I can't even start to ask them.'

'We know, but most of them will be answered as time progresses. Patience is something you are going to have to develop. That is always assuming we survive the coming storm. Humanity has weathered many before, but this is so unlike those others. This is serious. That's why we were sent to find you. You, Gwen, our beloved sister, are to set a precedent, the likes of which has not been known since this multiverse was born.'

'What?' was about all Gwen could manage at first. Then she added, 'Would you mind kindly putting me down now; I don't think I'm going to faint again, at least not yet.'

'That's good, but why is this all so hard for you take in? I mean, you run a New Age store, one that's called Earth Angel; you're friends with Native

Americans who have shared some of their most private rituals and ceremonies with you, and are familiar with many more. You've even spoken to a wolf and a crow just recently. Are you not a blood sister to them now?'

Gwen looked at the fresh wound on her arm and recalled the surreal conversation that brought it about. There were in fact, a lot of dead people back in town to testify to her encounter. 'But it's all just so *fantastic*. How can any of this be real? It's like I'm reading one of those books I stock, full of elves, fairies and bloody Atlanteans. I used to think they were on something, or were having flashbacks or something. Maybe there's some truth to it all now.'

A bass rumble emanated from the throat of the dragon that was Maddy. 'No, not a lot really. Maybe lost genetic memory or pure wishful thinking based on much older legends. Like your King Arthur story. By the time it was romanticized to fit the age, it barely resembled what really happened. Legends have a way of doing that. Take us, for example – a lovelier pair of innocent girls you couldn't wish to find…'

Gwen snorted derisively and added a 'yeah, right', which earned her a little squeeze before she was deposited back on the grass.

'Hey! Easy with the little human. I've been battered enough for one night, thanks.'

'…Anyway, as I was saying before I was insulted, we have been portrayed and identified in just about every culture across the entire planet. Every civilization has stories of dragons. For the most part it was us, but we didn't do a hundredth of what was attributed to us, though it made a good story. Though on saying that, our brethren have been known to visit, and some of those may have overstepped the mark. But not since Babylonian times, as I recall. That was about the last time I remember feeling their presence.'

Gwen sat down and put her head in her hands and scrounged her fingers through her hair, dreading the next question that she knew she had to ask. It was almost expected, but equally she didn't want to hear the answer. In light of her life over the last twelve hours or so, it was going to be something radical.

And just to cap things, she was getting a headache: the sort that pushed a hot poker into the backs of your eyes from the inside out and made the rest of your head feel as though it was in one of those medieval torture devices that screwed no end of metal rods into your head. Gwen looked up through her lids, barely moving her head, and nearly jumped again as the face of Jen, the white dragon, was looming down to sniff her. Then her long, snakelike, blue forked tongue lashed out around her, tasting her and the air about her. 'It's started, hasn't it?'

Gwen looked up this time, though it was a struggle. 'What's started?' she asked despondently, the pain taking a miserable hold on her.

'The pain. I'm guessing it's not the first of these headaches you've had. Am I right?'

Gwen nodded weakly. This time the pain was escalating much faster than it usually did and her medicine cabinet was some miles away. She groaned and rolled onto her side, pulling her knees up into a fetal position, groaning some more as the pain sent waves of sickly heat cascading across her body.

'We were hoping to resolve this matter with you before it became an issue. Seems matters are even more advanced than we thought. There is a permanent cure for these headaches, Gwen. It is called acceptance.'

But Gwen only groaned further, as the telepathic voice of Maddy resonated through her already tender skull.

'Not so loud, please. Accept what? What have you done to me?' Gwen managed to get out her questions before another wave incapacitated her again. *Shit! Where did this come from? One minute I'm fine, the next my skull is being squeezed like a lemon.*

'These are conflict headaches. When your destiny conflicts with what you are actually doing. The greater the conflict, the greater the pain. It seems you are still fighting your destiny, Gwen, and as yours is pivotal to the cataclysm at hand, your pain will probably kill you.'

Gwen screamed then as her pain flared again. She began tearing at her clothes as wave after wave of inner heat surged through her. It wasn't like she was wearing much anyway, but the kami top and the jeans went, leaving her in her skimpies. Then even they had to go. If she could have unzipped her skin and languished in her bones, she would have done.

'Make it stop!' Gwen was writhing uncontrollably, her nails digging into her skull, so much so that one broke, and blood was evident through her blonde hair.

'The only thing we can suggest, Gwen, is to fully accept your destiny, wholeheartedly and of your true free will. Deceit will be recognized and the pain will increase. Unfortunately, explanations will have to come after rather than before, as we would have liked.'

But Gwen had heard enough. 'For God's sake, will you stop talking and tell whoever I need to tell that I accept.'

It stopped.

Or at least it stopped getting worse. Gwen lay on her back, perfectly still, one knee raised and her hands still entangled in her hair. She lay like this for a good twenty minutes as she slowly regained her bearings. The only outward sign she lived at all was the steady breathing, the rise and fall of her chest. Her naked chest, which Gwen slowly came to remember as lucidity returned to her with the gradual abatement of the pain. So too did the recollection of how she came to be in that state.

'Did I just do what I think I did?' Gwen asked when she felt her voice return.

'I don't know,' Jen responded, in her usual voice. It wafted across the night air and caressed Gwen's ears as though she lay next to her. 'What is it you think you've done?'

Gwen opened her eyes slowly. It was still dark and she could just make out the outlines of trees, silhouetted against the moody night sky. Gwen hadn't noticed, but the toadstool had gone out as well; it had dimmed to its original rocky look. Conspicuous by their absence as well, were the two dragons. But as her eyes became accustomed to the gloom she saw that Jen and Maddy, walking lithely across the clearing towards her, were their comparatively normal selves except they too, were naked. 'I think I've just committed myself to something I'm probably going to live to regret.'

Maddy responded with the one comment Gwen didn't want to hear. 'We hope you live to regret it as well. In fact, it would be nice if we all get to live to regret your choice. For that to happen, we need to finish your education.'

'What do you mean, finish? I didn't know I'd started. I thought I only just accepted this.'

Maddy and Jen slipped down beside Gwen. Maddy began stroking Gwen's hair and Jen slid an arm around her shoulders, pulling her closer until their skin touched. 'In part.' Maddy sighed, knowing how hard this was going to be for all of them. '*You* accepted our help back in the square and it opened you up to the Earth. *You* survived the contact as the power flowed through you, but the biggest change is yet to come, and your heart had to accept that wholly. It is only unfortunate that we couldn't break it to you gently, before destiny took that choice from us. It was touch and go there for a moment though – even we couldn't tell if you were agreeing just to ease the pain, or were genuinely accepting your role in the upcoming battle. It's a good job the Earth knew the difference.'

Gwen perked up somewhat at the mention of the word *battle*. 'What battle?' Gwen looked at each girl in turn, waiting to see which one provided the explanation. 'You never mentioned anything about a bloody battle.' There were more questions clambering for answers, but she couldn't get them out; she couldn't even get her mouth and mind working in conjunction with each other sufficiently for a coherent sentence to come out. But her face told the girls as much as they needed.

'No, we didn't.' Jen picked up the narrative from Maddy then. 'Though what do you think the presence of the Kachina spirits we fought earlier heralded? It is because of a battle so great straining to explode that you have been raised to fulfill your destiny.'

Gwen shook her head as though to clear a fog over her mind. It seemed to be getting progressively harder to both think and speak clearly. Gwen recognized the feeling as being similar to the time she had tried a friend's Diazepam for a giggle. It had the same sensation, for her at least, of knocking back a bottle of tequila, or two. She ended up as good as useless for the best part of sixteen hours because of it. Gwen could feel the same creeping lethargy insinuating itself in her head and limbs.

'Destiny? Isn't that another word for the fact that your life is no longer your own and all choice has been removed?' Gwen asked, resignation coloring her every word. 'I get the distinct impression that I've been railroaded into accepting this and choosing whatever it is I've chosen. Now, I have the weird idea that I've been drugged. I haven't though, have I?' The vehemence at the last was palpable in Gwen's voice – she didn't like being manipulated: it brought out the confrontational side of her. All her brief life, Gwen had always sought to remain a free spirit, answerable only to her own will and not subject to the will of others. This was beginning to feel very much like somebody else's idea.

'It is, Gwen, it always has been. And before you fly of the handle, let me finish.' Maddy still stroked her hair and was still lying seductively naked next to her, but her tone had changed to that of the school ma'am, correcting a misguided child. *Which I annoyingly have to concede I am, but that doesn't make it any easier to swallow*, Gwen mused and closed her eyes again as she was softly, but firmly chided.

'As we have said before, this is your destiny. And you are right to one extent that choice is limited, but there is a but.' Maddy wriggled a little closer to Gwen. 'It's like all things in life. You may be steered in a direction you did not opt for, either through work or relationships, financial limitations or any other number of reasons, but the fact of the matter remains that within those parameters there is still choice.'

Again Gwen tried to disagree and Maddy silenced her. 'Let me try another analogy: you drift along life's river; you must deal with staying afloat and what interacts with you from the riverbank. Yet through all this, you are still susceptible to the current of the river. It propels you. When you reach a fork and the current takes you left or right, it is not of your choosing: you merely deal with the consequences and adapt to the change. You do not rail at the river for its choice in which direction you ended up taking. Maybe, had you gone the other way, it would have ended in a particularly nasty waterfall culminating in your premature death. Such is life. For however important your choices are, it is equally important how you deal with the choices made for you. In this instance, the Earth chose for you. Do you believe that she would have done so lightly? Or without compensation?'

This watery explanation had somewhat doused her simmering anger. For as though she wanted to lash out, to blame someone, something for her predicament, what Maddy said made complete sense. Gwen had always maintained that fate guided her and she just went along with it, sending her where she needed to go, providing her with what she needed. By adhering to this philosophy, she believed that was how she ended up in Santa Fe in the first place. The enormity of what that implied struck her. The Earth had steered her life through all its twists and turns, educating her in the knowledge she needed to be the girl she was today, where she was today, facing the choice she had made today. Gwen gave up, and flopped flat onto the grass. It was making her head ache again, even through the lightness and spongy feeling. Gwen smiled all the same, looking up at the two beautiful girls, who in turn, looked down upon her. 'I give in. You're right, the Earth's right. I've seen the signs for years and paid them little to no heed. It has been brewing for a while, hasn't it?'

Jen nodded sadly and lay down alongside Gwen, head propped up on one hand, her elbow resting in the grass alongside Gwen's head. Jen started to trace spirals on Gwen's belly with a long, well-manicured fingernail. Gwen's pale skin reacted by raising the blood to the surface, showing where Jen traced. It was also slightly ticklish, but in a nice, slightly rude way. Gwen closed her eyes and let herself enjoy the sensation. Maddy did the same the other side of her, and in addition, she began to sing quietly, yet hauntingly. Gwen couldn't identify any words – they were more sounds than real words

– but the melody was hypnotic. Then Jen added her own voice and Gwen was transported. Stretching languidly like a spoilt cat, Gwen lost all sense of time as the girls expanded their tracing to encompass her legs, up over her breasts and down her arms. Over and over they went. Gwen wasn't sure when it happened, but at some point during proceedings, one of the girls had leant over and kissed her. It just seemed the natural thing to do. Gwen, so thoroughly caught up in the rapturous feeling, responded in kind. She barely felt the hand that slipped between her thighs, only the sudden increase in pleasure which elicited several little gasps from her. Her breathing was becoming labored as the girls continued their teasing exploration of her body. The kisses became more frequent and more fervent. As matters escalated, the trio soon became a writhing mass of female flesh, entwined and thoroughly lost in each other's bodies. Moans and gasps became more and more heated as they took each other to new heights of pleasure, using their bodies, hands, fingers and tongues. It was a bonding session that Gwen wasn't going to forget in a very long time.

Hours passed this way, and it was just before dawn, as the sun began to creep over the horizon, that matters reached a crescendo and Gwen's world became a swirling mass of lights as her body could take no more and peaked in a mental and physical way. Wave after wave crashed over her as though she were caught in an oceanic spray of liquid light. She gasped and cried out in an ecstasy she had never before experienced, and was unlikely to again. It was like being drawn deep into the Earth and then exploding like a newborn star. Every fibre of her being was torn asunder and renewed, over and over again, stripped to her core and turned inside out, then reassembled to have it happen again. It was a joy she never wanted to end. But end it did, draining her so entirely she was truly like an empty vessel, and Gwen slept then. Slept while the Earth filled that emptiness with something new.

It was the smell of food cooking that brought Gwen back to the world she had left behind. Slowly, she opened her eyes – just a hint – to determine if it was day or night. The dazzling sun told her it was day. At least I haven't slept too long. *Oh my God! What did I do last night?* As memory returned, Gwen became more and more aware of her surroundings, of the fact she was still naked, and that she was not alone.

'It looks as though someone is stirring, Jen.' Maddy's voice reassured her that she was still in the company of friends; they hadn't left her alone in the woods after *that*. 'It's food. I swear that woman instinctively knows when there's food to be had.'

Gwen opened her eyes fully then, followed by a bone cracking and muscle popping stretch, one that any cat would be proud of. Realizing she was still naked, Gwen smiled sheepishly and looked around for her clothes, but couldn't see them anywhere.

'Err, girls. Where are my clothes?' though as she asked, she noticed that neither Jen nor Maddy had dressed either. Subconsciously, she admired their lithe, well-toned bodies and the seductive curve of the backs that swept down to shapely buttocks, which topped long, muscular legs. These were bodies which she had gotten to know *very* well only a few hours before. She blushed again as she was assailed by images and memories of events involving those body parts. Gwen was open minded about such matters though, having experimented when she was in college. She was content she knew where her sexual preference lay, but there was something binding and ritualistic about last night, seemingly more of a natural bonding than simply crude sex for sex's sake. She had never thought of the girls that way before; well, she corrected, not with any intent at least. It was undeniable that they were gorgeous, worthy of admiration, but they were her friends and her employees and that was that. Though apparently that *wasn't* just that any more.

They were going about the mundane business of cooking and tidying up the little campsite, as naked as they were the night before, seemingly oblivious to the incongruity of it. Somehow, in the dark it didn't seem so strange; in the light of day though, it felt a bit weird. Not unpleasant, she amended to herself. There was a definite catharsis to being naked in the woods in broad daylight – probably why there were so many naturalists – but it was still just a bit weird after all. She looked between the two for an answer to all that had occurred – any sort of answer would probably help at this delicate stage – but all they did was smile at her and offer her a bowl of fruit and some scrambled egg on a wooden platter. Gwen took this without question. Even though they hadn't spoken a word since she had awoken, her stomach suddenly reminded her of how hungry she was. She always got the munchies after… She blushed at the sudden memory of the previous night's activities. Diverting herself from those lewdly embarrassing thoughts, she started to pick over her food, hoping the girls would offer some sort of clue to the morning's events.

'Okay, so you don't want me getting dressed yet, I get that, though you gotta understand, I'm not entirely comfortable with this daylight nudity thing – all it'll take is some meandering hiker to come stumbling through here and he'll think all his Christmases have come at once. I have a reputation here and I'm *trying* to build a business.'

Still no reply was forthcoming, so Gwen carried on. 'I won't be happy to find myself in the papers with some scandalous headline like *Local Busineswoman Romps in Woodland Lesbian Escapade,* or somesuch nonsense.' Then it occurred to Gwen suddenly that she needed to be at the store. She had lost all track of the day and it had clean slipped her mind. 'What time is it?' she panicked, nearly dropping her food. 'Have I slept long? I've got to get to the store!' Gwen shoveled steaming egg in to her mouth as she waited for the answer, eyes frantically scanning for her elusive clothes.

She nearly sprayed her egg across the clearing when they finally spoke. 'It's about two in the afternoon; you've been asleep for three days!'

CHAPTER SEVEN

AL'MAYAKIN

AZAROTH SURVEYED THE HORIZON. HE SCANNED IT with an intensity that could almost *will* what he was looking for to appear, though, as of yet, what he sought had not shown itself. Very little had appeared, in fact. There had been some of the humans' flying machines roaring overhead, but they did little to disturb him. Like many of the Adversary's generals, he was keeping his army lower in the density field, beyond any mortal's ability to see, to avoid premature detection, only manifesting it when the need arose. But as to his purpose in the desert – so far, it was eluding him. This fact alone frustrated the arch demon more than anything else at that moment; for although he was a formidable hunter, and patience was a major attribute to being as successful as he, this particular hunt went against his better instincts and was testing his patience to the extreme. Were it not for the threats of the Adversary, he would be back in his own realm ensuring his own lands were secure. And yet… Maybe it was the promise of unimaginable power that had finally convinced him to risk everything, here, now. The prospect of ruling a multiverse instead of merely his own insignificant, by comparison to the Earth, desert realm within the Domain – maybe it was only that which had provided sufficient impetus to betray his former lord, Lucifer, and throw in his lot with the Adversary, though that unfortunately meant doing the bidding of his new master. But being entrusted to be the one to kill the Legendary Four Horsemen of the Apocalypse: that went way beyond and above the call of any duty.

But Azaroth was nothing if not adaptable. He would treat this like any other hunt and try not to be too intimidated by what he was entrusted to do. *I'm caught between a rock and a sharp place – four very sharp places, if I'm honest. I'll be lucky to walk away from this unscathed. Though walk away I shall. At any cost.*

Schemes within schemes, plans within plans. These were a regular occurrence within the Domain, and several were often in motion at any given point in time – it was the intrusive thought of the current intricacies that made Azaroth chuckle as very few things could. They lightened his increasingly foul humor. His amusement manifested as a deep grating sound that emanated from his barrel chest, a sound much like rocks tumbling down a hillside. The Adversary had sent *him* to do this thing, but Fenris, the recently released Wolf Lord and apparent pet of the Adversary, seemingly had ambitions that drove him hard as well, though he thought few knew anything of his plans and intentions. How wrong was he! Fenris was still finding out about how things functioned in the Domain, having been absent for so long. Odin and Tyr had done a passably successful job of containing the rapacious wolf for so long. Now Lucifer was interred in his old gaol, Azaroth thought it somehow quite fitting. It had been the Wolf Lord who had – luckily, in Azaroth's opinion – captured a flight of Raphael's scouts and turned them; ripping information from them as easily as he would skin a rabbit, which he loyally, just like any good dog should, turned over to the Adversary, who in turn again, had sent Azaroth to complete the task – this to the barely restrained fury of Fenris. His rage could be heard in the neighbouring kingdom. Then, Azaroth had captured one of Fenris's hounds, just as they had detected the infernal Horsemen shortly after they had been sighted arriving in what the humans called Syria. After his scouts had brought the creature back, Azaroth tortured and killed it with as much pleasure and single-mindedness as Fenris had done originally to the angels, though not before he had learnt all he needed to know from the now permanently deceased scout. Fenris's hounds' senses were exceptionally sharp, but they were nothing compared to the arch demon's. Even before the great division, formation of the Covenant and subsequent descent with Lucifer, his skills at tracking had been prodigious. With time, they had only improved. Azaroth had *felt* the foul presence of the Horsemen the moment they touched down on the soil of this barren land. It was a powerful resonance: that tingle of restrained magical energy, even though they were trying to remain inconspicuous. Though he could not detect their exact location, he knew their destination now. That was enough, placing himself between them, and it would be sufficient. A good hunter would let his prey come to him. It was an art he prided himself on. Millennia of honing his senses to detect subtle and minute shifts in the density fields of whatever world he bestrode gave him an edge few others possessed. In the mind of Azaroth, not even Lucifer himself was as good. He could feel their power like a disturbance in his mind. His senses were spread like a finely woven web and the Horsemen were like a struggling fly. As the sensation grew stronger, he knew they drew ever closer to him. The strange part in all this, though Azaroth corrected his thought at that: *the stranger part*, was the fifth sensation he was experiencing. It had appeared in his mind mere hours after they arrived. Something had happened and he did not know what. He was told that a mortal had joined their company and was to be destroyed at all costs. What was odd, though, was that he shouldn't be able to sense him the same way he did the Horsemen. They were supernatural beings, the mortal wasn't – or at least that used to be the case: he felt different now, somehow more than mortal, but at the same time similar to the Horsemen. It was as though he were an extension of them. Something had happened since they had arrived. Something that no one had anticipated. Not even the Adversary, it seemed, knew of this turn of events. Azaroth hated surprises with a depth that held no bounds. He had cultivated a cadre of spies that had infiltrated just about every ruling house within the Domain, primarily to avoid any unwanted surprises and staying one step ahead of whatever game was afoot. Adding to Azaroth's frustrations was the threat hanging over his head from his one-time associate and now his liege lord, that to fail was not an option to be taken lightly. To be threatened in this way spoke more of the importance of this mortal than he was given to believe. For although the Adversary grew in power and paranoia as each day passed, this was the first time he had resorted to such direct and brutal tactics to get his point across. No, this was no ordinary hunt: his prey were already extraordinary and with the addition of this mortal, things had shifted uncomfortably, coming close to being very messy indeed. Azaroth didn't like messy. Ordinarily he would back out of this and reassess his options. Only this time, he wasn't given any choice in the matter. Should he dare to go back unsuccessful, he would consider himself fortunate to share the same fate as his former master. *Un*fortunate didn't bear thinking about, though he couldn't avoid *but* think about it. It made him very edgy indeed.

Though the Adversary had been prone to exaggerate from time to time, one thing that was said that held true was that this desert, situated upon this miserable ball of mud, would resemble his own homeland. It did. Just. Though it was nowhere near as hot or treacherous, the bare, scorched rocks did make a passing resemblance. But he wouldn't even loose his own spawn here; for this land was far too timid for them. They couldn't afford to grow soft, for they were his heirs, destined to rule should anything happen to him. On his home world, in his realm, there were geysers of molten lava, lakes of liquid rock and rivers of acid. The air here was not thick with noxious vapors, flammable gases and ash. Nor did the winds reverberate with the screams of the dying – a sound he fervently missed, but hoped to hear again *very* soon.

His realm was particularly hostile; great battles raged continually as the rival factions jockeyed for superiority. Littered with the bloated corpses and dismembered limbs of the fallen, the battlefields drew swarms of the monstrous ravens that nested and bred in the mountains. Those not lucky enough to be killed outright suffered the pleasure of being eaten alive by these creatures, with tearing beaks that could disembowel with a stroke and pierce skulls with a single blow to rip out the soft tissue within. Of course, there was always the hope that he could spend some time here after this matter was dealt with.

Maybe he could make it feel a little more like home then. His scouts had reported a city not too far away. There would be plenty of screams then as he and his legions swarmed upon the unsuspecting mortals. Though maybe he would warn them, slip in the stiletto of panic, just to let the anticipation of imminent death sweeten the meat.

Upon his initial arrival with the army, a day after he had sent scouts abroad to prepare the site and a little over two days previous, Azaroth and his legions had materialized directly before an armored convoy. A snaking line of what appeared to be several metallic boxes filled with the soft, fleshy humans was weaving across the desert. No doubt running away; it was what humans did best, after all. Azaroth's knowledge of this realm was limited, not having visited often due to the Covenant; but the last time he had spent any time here, man had only just mastered the horse as a beast of convenience. The convoy stopped abruptly and disgorged several humans, who began shouting at each other excitedly. Many of these humans ran to the front of the boxes and pointed something desperately at the nightmares that were stepping through the portal before them. These odd containers were something new to Azaroth and his curiosity was momentarily piqued. Though the moment the soldiers began shooting their insignificant bullets at the fiends that had stepped through the portal, seemingly out of apparent thin air before them, their fate was sealed. The few minutes of mutual surprise at encountering each other passed. Azaroth's minions swarmed over the tanks and armored personnel carriers like ants over jam. Steel was torn apart like paper and the humans were ripped screaming from their illusion of safety. Then their bones were ripped likewise from their bodies. Several fell to Azaroth's own particular brand of viciousness. He felt it had been too long since he had felt bone, sinew and entrails sliding through his talons. It was also a feeling he found he missed: his own talons rending flesh, not having to use the puppetry of some human possessed skin sack. Azaroth reveled in their tortured cries of mercy, abruptly silenced as their lives were snuffed out. He watched as their tiny minds broke as easily as their puny bodies as they beheld what was slaughtering them.

Realization rose in them like bubbles beneath water, only to burst along with their sanity as they broke the surface. His army of demonic minions, ranked in their thousands, with more spilling through the portal even as the vanguard dispatched the mortals, spread out across the landscape like a sea of death.

Azaroth licked the last remaining viscera from his talons, snapped out his own ravenlike wings and took flight. Two great downdrafts later and he was gliding across the battlefield to a nearby hillock – one that offered a vantage point to the direction in which the Horsemen were expected. From there, he spied a pinnacle of rock, thrusting upwards like some massive stone lance that had pierced the Earth. At least that was the analogy Azaroth liked. Flapping from the crest to the summit took only a few moments, though it was a good three miles away. Utilizing the natural thermals, Azaroth rose majestically and landed with just as much grace atop the stony finger. Taloned feet gripped the rock and one hand tore up chunks of stone as it too gripped for balance as the demon lord squatted low, folding his raven wings over his head to shade his face as he focused his sight on the horizon again. One muscular and slightly scaled arm supported his warrior's frame whilst the other shielded his eyes further. Like some predatory beast, Azaroth had sat atop the pinnacle for two days, entrusting the dispersal of his legions to subordinates, for Azaroth, as a rule, preferred to hunt alone. It had been the Adversary's idea to utilize the legions. Azaroth had accepted them graciously, though silently railing at the hindrance they would be, and at the subtle implication of the gift.

'I want no chances taken, do you understand me, Azaroth? *None.* The mortal must die. I don't care how many legions you use to accomplish this; will you see this done for me, old friend?' The Adversary had placed a comradely yet powerful hand on Azaroth's shoulder and squeezed. He still bore the marks, and even suspected that he would bear them for evermore, such was the power behind the touch. It was terrifying even for the likes of him, an arch demon, to feel the power in that grip as well as seeing the burning intensity in his old friend's fully obsidianlike eyes. It was as though the Adversary's Herculean frame was struggling to contain the power he was amassing within.

His muscles bulged with power, and it was though the energy threatened to rip flesh and pull him apart at the seams. Power veritably throbbed from the Adversary, and Azaroth came to realize then that this being was no longer his friend; it was a pretense. He was as far above him as he was to an insect. Acceptance was hard, but necessary to survival in the Domain, and it was this acceptance that kept him alive where others had perished. He was in the presence of a God now – of that there could be little doubt, there was so much power. Not only was it terrifying, it was intoxicating. Even were Lucifer to be freed now, he doubted that he would have the power to stop the Adversary. Azaroth could almost taste its heady potential. It was the energy of one soon to shatter the Covenant and for the first time in the combined history of the entire multiverse, elevate himself to near omnipotence, if not more so. How powerful would he become? Azaroth knew there was only one reply, and in a voice as calm, controlled and steady as ever, which belied the uncertainty; and something he would never admit, which was fear, bubbling beneath, he said, 'Of course I will, Zaramael. Do we not go back to the beginning together? And am I not one of – if not *the* greatest – hunters in the Domain? Excepting yourself of course. Was it not I who captured the last herd of Unc'anharaphim for Lucifer's stables? One mortal should pose little threat.'

Azaroth knew that these were no idle claims: he was an exceptional hunter and he *had* captured the unicorns, although he omitted the fact that it was at considerable loss of life, and very nearly his own too. But they both knew he was as far behind his *former* old friend as humans were to Drakarim. And even though he accepted the legions with a bow, inwardly Azaroth snarled, for it was an insult to his prowess. It was the Adversary's way of both reminding him of his place and keeping an eye on him, for there were undoubtedly spies amongst the ranks of minions, and probably none of his own.

These thoughts rankled with Azaroth and had been a constant distraction since leaving the Domain. The brief altercation when they arrived proved to be a fleeting diversion, but that was over soon enough, and then the dark brooding thoughts returned. That was no good for his concentration, so he had removed himself from that which reminded him of his obligations and where he could focus on the hunt. It was just before sunrise on the third day when he felt what he had been waiting for. *There you are!* His consciousness had been ranging as far as he was presently able to on this world, for as yet, his powers were still restricted and tied to the Domain. *Soon, very soon, my powers, thanks to the Adversary, will have grown sufficiently to dominate this miserable planet. Then there will be a reckoning the likes of which even the Domain has never seen.* This was a thought Azaroth relished, for as well as power, the Adversary had promised Azaroth dominion of the Earth when his new regime commenced. It was as well Azaroth never knew that the Adversary had promised it to many of his generals. The strongest alone would be the subsequent ruler. For now though, the Horsemen approached and it was a good sign that they had not sensed his probing sight. The information from Fenris's captured hound proved true: the Horsemen were indeed heading for Megiddo. Azaroth's astral form had stood only a few hundred horse lengths from the group and not been detected. The Adversary was right about another matter: one that diminished the powers of the Horsemen as he grew in his – another factor that worked in his favor. But he wouldn't let that make him overconfident. *One problem at a time.* There was an added bonus too: they had to fight through hordes of possessed and Hounds of Fenris were closing on their trail. They would reach them long before Azaroth would. He would let them do the grunt work. Maybe they would even kill one of them. He wasn't too proud to take the credit for another's work; it wouldn't be the first time. Then he would finish off whatever was left. Maybe this wouldn't be such a bad hunt after all. Smiling to himself at the rewards he would receive for this, Azaroth stood and turned, spreading his wings as he did so.

Gliding down off the pinnacle, Azaroth rejoined his legions, folding his great wings and walking amongst them, many of whom were fighting amongst themselves for amusement and food. Rations were not in abundance here for they had traveled light, not anticipating a long hunt; and since the mortals had been finished off shortly after the initial battle, they took sustenance wherever they could and from whoever was unfortunate enough to fall. Finding his second-in-command was easy. He was a massive and brutal looking individual, and had a reputation even amongst the warriors of the Domain. He was originally a pet of Lucifer. The Dark Lord had kept him since what the humans called the Neolithic period. They called him Karcon. He stood a good seven feet tall, with shoulders thicker than the legs of two men, and was lightly covered in a coarse black hair. Thick brows on a protruding forehead gave him a brutal expression at all times. Tombstones for teeth filled his wide mouth and he had carved many of them to points in order to better tear at flesh with them. Over the aeons spent with Lucifer, he had learnt many things that belied his savage exterior and he was far more intelligent than his appearance portrayed.

'Karcon!' Azaroth bellowed across the sea of warriors. He saw the big Neanderthal get up and wade through the soldiers as easily as he would walk through long grass, swatting those too slow to move first. Having killed three just walking to stand before Azaroth, he lowered his head in obedience at his present and, he was told, temporary master.

'Azaroth, *my lord*. You summoned Karcon?' the beast growled.

The title was spoken with barely concealed contempt and Azaroth knew the ancient warrior had little respect for him, but orders were orders and he was obeying them, just. Karcon raised his eyes to meet Azaroth's, and the arch demon gazed into unfathomable pools of liquid green. Karcon had wide, unblinking eyes set apart across his broad face and which maintained a safe distance from the evidently broken, flat nose. It was as though he had been hit in the face with a very flat and very hard object too many times, pushing in and spreading his facial features below his jutting brow. Other than being vicious, violent, cruel and malevolently intelligent, Karcon had been gifted with a degree of power, for such was the reward system of the Domain. Coupled to this he had also been granted the ability of flight. Karcon had ripped a pair of wings from one of the Celestial Host during battle many centuries before and had them magically grafted onto himself by Lucifer's enchanters in the Domain. They were a deep green that matched his piercing gaze and he was excessively proud of them, showing them off whenever he got the chance, believing that they enhanced his image to whoever he addressed. Much like a peacock trying to impress a rival. Their beauty contradicted the serrated scimitar that hung at his hip and the spiked twin-headed mace that hung at the other – mace heads that still had scraps of bloody flesh stuck to them after the encounter with the humans.

'Yes, I summoned you, Karcon, and it wasn't to gaze upon your ugly face or those ridiculous parrot wings you keep flapping, so put them away before I tear them off and feed them to you. I want you to pay attention.'

Karcon's face turned darker than a thunder head and he had to exert every shred of self-control he had learnt, to not leap at the arch demon and kill him where he stood. That pleasure was destined to come after this hunt. And the Adversary had promised that he, Karcon, could have that pleasure. Imagining all he would do to the arrogant Azaroth had kept him occupied whilst his illustrious leader had been away. Karcon looked forward to that more than Azaroth could imagine. But he folded the wings away all the same.

'Good. Now I have located the Horsemen, a day's march from here, but I don't want to wait a day. I want you and the winged legions to go on ahead and confront them. It should only take a few hours for you all to get there. I will lead the foot troops at a forced march and should join you soon enough. I will give you their location.' Azaroth closed his eyes and transmitted the visual details to Karcon, implanting all he had seen into the warrior's mind as though he had seen it himself. If possible, the Neanderthal's eyes went wider still at the implantation. He was never comfortable with others in his head, though having been in there, few were ever comfortable going in Karcon's again after seeing what went through his warped and troubled psyche. Thus he had few masters in his long existence. After Lucifer had tired of him, Zaramael had taken him under his wing and used him to further many of his schemes. Karcon enjoyed the Adversary's work. It allowed him to do what he loved to do best. Kill.

'There is a human with the Horsemen. Do what you will with the others, but I want the human's head intact for the Adversary and I wish to devour his remains myself. I am entrusting you to return these things to me. Can you be trusted, Karcon?'

'Of course, mighty Azaroth. I am yours to command.'

The lie came easily to Karcon: he had been lying to demons for longer than he could remember. It had been part of his usefulness; his Neanderthal brain only gave away whatever he was thinking at the time, nothing more. So to those who could smell deceit, he came up genuine every time. But Azaroth wasn't considered the greatest hunter of the Domain for nothing. *You small minded barbarian; you lie so smoothly, I can see why the Adversary uses you. No doubt you have further orders concerning me after this, but we will have to see about that, won't we? I have some plans of my own, little pet, and you are not part of them.* Outwardly, Azaroth merely smiled his predatory smile and acknowledged the claim with a nod. 'Of course you are. Now you have your orders. Go prepare my legions; you leave as soon as the sun reaches its zenith.'

Lowering his eyes and head slightly, before moving away, the Neanderthal snorted a question back to Azaroth. *Of all the nerve!*

'Why don't you open a gate like you did to get here, and we all go? Victory assured, yes?'

Azaroth couldn't believe the audacity of the creature, questioning *him*. 'Because, you insubordinate bastard, I don't want to alert the Horsemen any more than I have to. They are unaware of us at the moment. A gateway would alert them, allowing them to do the same and possibly escape. Do *you* want to explain that to the Adversary? How *your* suggestion allowed his enemy to remain free?'

'No,' was all the Neanderthal said. Furious at itself, he turned away without another word. Neither did Azaroth pursue the matter, simply letting it go.

Karcon lumbered off to gather the winged legions together and give them their instructions and to begin the chants of battle: the ancient rites that focused their strength and minds on the fight and nothing else. By the time they reached the Horsemen, they would be virtually unstoppable – so driven to kill, they would fight even beyond the most mortal of wounds. If they could hold a weapon, they would wield it.

The winged legions were selected for their brutality and were primarily made up of captured humans, altered and enhanced by diabolical methods to boost their lethal prowess. These warriors were equivalent to cavalry for the Demon armies. They would descend on the advancing forces like a rain of death from above. There was little defense to their attack, for their maneuverability in the air gave them an advantage, and as Azaroth had planned for them, they would be attacking out of the sun, blinding the Horsemen until it was too late. A motley selection of barbarians stolen from history; their ranks were filled with gladiators of ancient Rome, Vikings from Scandinavia, Picts and Celts. There was even a contingent of Mayan jaguar warriors, African tribesmen and desert nomads of the time of the great Khan. These souls were chosen for their single-minded brutality and ability to kill, each given the wings they had to tear from a living angel in order for their promotion to these diabolical ranks. These were Lucifer's own battalions, usurped by the Adversary, and were considered some of the best in the Domain. Azaroth thought it a pity he wasn't going to be there to see the initial encounter. But prudence was the better part of curiosity. You didn't get to live as long as he had by being reckless.

It had been hard to contain their excitement at being on the Earth again at first, having been stolen out of their own times centuries before. They had been unable to return before now, for the ability to open portals to the various worlds was limited to only those of exceptional power, those of the upper echelons. This applied to both those of the Domain and those of the Celestial Host. Exceptions to this rule were the Drakarim, the Unc'anharaphim and the Four Horsemen. Seeing as there were no more Unc'anharaphim and nobody had seen a Drakarim for millennia, it only left the Horsemen and they were soon to be extinct too. The Adversary had granted Azaroth the power to open portals where previously he had been incapable – and he reveled in the new-found gift. It opened all manner of opportunities to the arch demon. He only had this matter to contend with first, and then the fun would truly start.

Azaroth ordered his ground-based warriors into their battalions and appointed their sub-commanders, whose role it would be to ensure all kept up; those who didn't would become rations. Having wings and being an arch demon meant he could keep pace with them effortlessly, so he returned to his pinnacle for a little introspection after he had set the warriors running. They howled and whooped as they set off, keen for battle, blood and glory. Of course, not being high on the intelligence ratings made them ideal soldiers for lost-cause battles: they didn't really care much. They existed to fight and kill. It was what they did best. Even so, the fact they were going up against the Four Horsemen was withheld from them. Azaroth didn't want to give them any cause to hesitate. Not being clever didn't necessarily mean they were stupid.

A flash of movement caught the arch demon's attention, so he swooped down to investigate. There would be ample time to catch up with his troops. For the moment he was enjoying the solitude and relative peace. What he had seen was a fortunate human who had survived the initial onslaught of his fellows, though fortunate probably wasn't the first word to come to his mind, having been trapped beneath an armored car for two days without food or water, listening as his comrades were torn asunder and devoured. Then the pain kicked in as he realized his own predicament. Eventually, he had managed to scramble himself out from the wreckage and begin to crawl away, hopefully in the direction of salvation. He had to crawl, for his legs were still pinned beneath the twisted metal. A flapping sound behind him made him turn, fully expecting to fend off some daring buzzard. Instead, the last sight he beheld was definitely not a buzzard – they had learnt the hard way not to come too close to the carnage left by the minions. What he saw in lieu of that was the fang filled mouth of Azaroth, rapidly descending upon him with his jaw unhinged and salivating, seconds before it closed over his head. Sheer terror prevented the unfortunate soul from hearing the wet crunch as his skull was bitten in two.

ᚦᛗᚨᚠᚾᛟᛗ ᚱᛋᚠᚱᛋ

Tomas and the Horsemen were negotiating some fallen rocks just as they were about to ascend a small rise when War, who was already halfway up the rise, raised a warning hand. They stopped instantly, coming alert and drawing weapons with a speed that still managed to surprise Tomas. Desperate to know what the problem was, but trained to keep his mouth shut and maintain silence, Tomas tried the other method of communication now available to him.

'What is it?' He tried thinking to Death. *'What has he seen?'*

Death had heard him, it seemed – much to Tomas's amazement – responding without taking his gaze from War. *'I am not sure, but it can't be good, based on all our encounters so far. Word must have traveled by now of our arrival here. I suspect even our destination has been ascertained.'*

Tomas quickly went through his mental inventory, a practice he had already become accustomed too. He manifested his armor, adding a few personal touches as he became more and more familiar with the process. It wasn't all steel now; Tomas had modified parts with Kevlar body armor to give him some extra maneuverability. It should have been an eclectic mix of archaic and modern, but Tomas blended the colors together, blacks and browns with a Kevlar-lined, tan cloak. He secretly liked the look of the others and was fulfilling a boyhood fantasy. He knew it was unnecessary, but he allowed the little vanity. At least it was armored, he justified to himself. Lastly, the Sword of War came to his hand in readiness. Pestilence and Famine spared him a cursory glance of approval before doing likewise. War trotted back to the group and flicked his visor up. Penetrating eyes stared out at them, and Tomas saw it was a grave expression. It wasn't good news. Instinctively, Tomas started his gentle muscle loosening exercises, flexing and contracting muscles, ensuring they were supple and ready, though he wasn't expecting to hear what he did, about what they were getting ready for.

'Demons. And lots of them too. Seems news travels faster than I thought.' War began adjusting his own weapons as he continued, 'I had hoped we would have made it to Raphael before we ran into any serious trouble and it doesn't look to get any more serious than this.'

Storm sidestepped closer to War as Tomas asked just how serious.

'The Adversary has sent Azaroth, Lucifer's hunter. I suspect his arrogance at his own hunting abilities has clouded his better judgment. That, or he has other things on his mind, but he has grossly underestimated our powers. Firstly, he has sent a swarm of winged cavalry to take us; they should be here within the hour at the speed they are coming. An inconvenience. Secondly, he has hoped to put us on the defensive and make this a decisive stroke. They come with the sun at their backs. Thirdly, there are several thousand more foot soldiers running closely behind. They will be here in perhaps six hours or even less, depending on how hard Azaroth pushes them. Knowing him, he'll kill them all to get here as fast as possible. Fourthly —'

Tomas held up a gauntleted hand to stem the tide of doom and gloom. 'Wait a minute; just how many of these are you going to go through? I mean… bloody fourthly? I'd had enough at firstly. Can we not just deal with one problem at a time? Wouldn't now be a good time for a gate?'

Pestilence started to speak coolly in her husky voice and Tomas prepared himself for another lesson.

'Gateways are traceable, Tomas. No doubt Azaroth purposely avoided opening one directly onto us for fear of alerting us to it. Maybe then we would have gated away, but by confronting us directly, should we use a gate now to Raphael, he would trace it to our army and force us to give away its location to the enemy. It is better we tackle this another way.'

'You mean directly, don't you?' He sighed, Tomas knew his life was going to be comparatively short in this conflict, but he didn't think it would be over quite so soon, or assisted by those who were supposed to assisting him. But before they could answer, Tomas just had to know what fourthly was. War obliged.

'Fourthly is more immediate really, for there are at least six hounds behind us. Now they will be upon us in minutes, if my estimation is correct. I knew they were coming but I wanted the ridge behind us first. So much for that plan. Are you sure there isn't something you're not telling us, Tomas? The

Adversary is going to a lot of trouble to see you dead.'

'A lot of people want me dead; guess it's my dazzling personality and winning charm. I've pissed a lot of people off over the years. I've gotten used to it. You tend to not make many friends in my business. But what about these dogs then? What's so bad about them?'

War shook his head ruefully and just for a second, Tomas thought he heard him laugh in his helm before speaking again. 'Tomas,' he said, his bass tone tinged with exasperation, 'it might be easier to imagine that everything we speak of is a hundred times worse than it sounds and wants to kill you in a thousand different ways before eating your organs. Trust me; these aren't dogs as you think. You've heard of werewolves, haven't you?'

Tomas nodded dumbly.

'Well these make those look like puppies, but try not to worry about them: Famine and Pestilence will take care of them. We on the other hand, have some flies to swat and a lesson to give. It does not pay to disregard the Four Horsemen so easily.'

Death concurred and as soon as Famine and Pestilence had wheeled away to deal with the hounds, he summoned his scythe to his hand. In a blur it transformed into the biggest and most elaborate crossbow Tomas had ever seen. Its stock was ebony and highly carved with symbols and runes. Black steel cables ran up to the shining silver crescent that was the bow itself. That too, was etched and engraved with fantastic images and runes. Even the quarrels co-ordinated with the weapon. Black fletched and silver tipped.

'Impressive,' Tomas admitted, 'if not a bit antiquated. You'll need to be some archer to pick them off with that before they close on us.'

Tomas glanced across to War, who was testing the pull on his own massive longbow. The arrows for that beast were more like small spears with fletching. *This is gonna need some fancy twenty-first century solutions otherwise we are going to be up to our necks in demons before they pick off enough, and I know just the thing.* Dismounting and dematerializing Storm to his new home on Tomas's arm, he quickly adapted his helm, to that of the SWAT style tactical helmets along with a pair of shaded ballistic goggles, so he could look towards the sun without blinding himself. Lastly, he pulled his shemagh scarf back around his mouth to keep the sand from billowing up into his throat and choking him when he fired. He was certain the demons weren't going to stop and pat him on the back before they pulled him apart. With that thought in mind, he willed the sword to take the form of a Javelin LF anti-tank weapon, something he wouldn't normally be able to use so freely on his own, but the Sword of War made it light and manageable. It had proven to be particularly effective against armored vehicles and maybe even some of the older tanks, especially with the high explosive armor-piercing shell. Some of those critters hurtling towards them were certainly armored enough and built like tanks. Just as well Tomas wasn't averse to the concept of overkill. Looking every inch like someone who wanted a fight now, he had picked up several small arms as they left the city. Wearing thigh rigs on both armored legs, he had knives stuffed all over and had even managed to pick up several grenades. It was another thing he wasn't averse to – utilizing whatever the dead had. He figured that it wasn't any use to them, and they weren't likely to object.

Flicking the laser guided range finder – another little gadget he had willed alongside the cumbersome missile launcher – to two thousand meters, Tomas yet again found himself surprised by what the sword could do. He fully expected to have to dump the missile launcher on the ground, for they were incredibly heavy, though effective. Instead, Tomas found that he could hoist it to his shoulder, thoroughly surprised at how light the sword made it. Usually ground mounted, it was normally a hefty bit of kit. But this wasn't any normal weapon. Far from it. It was the Sword of War.

What an asset! It meant that he was more agile with it than he should have been. Though it had been introduced some years before, it was still one of the best ATGWs going. *Maybe I should have picked something a bit smaller or even ground mounted it like usual. What was I thinking?* But Tomas didn't have the time for rhetoric or to mull over his choice of weapon and what to do with it for long – what was done was done. Though it could be fired in buildings, he still had a momentary reservation as to what the blast was going to do to him, holding it on his shoulder as he was. Looking through the lens, he could see the cloud swarming towards them. Their bodies were black voids against the ambient temperature of the air that surrounded them. Lowering it again until they were closer, he looked back to try and see if Pestilence and Famine were still in sight, but they had disappeared. All he saw was the heat haze of the desert which swallowed them up. He hoped they were okay. It was odd, but though he hadn't known these entities for long, it felt like it had already been an age. He had accepted the recent discovery of their existence almost as easily as the news of a new species of bird being found. Well, he conceded, there was a little more to it than that, but all things considered he had taken it fairly well; and since that traumatic meeting he had grown to appreciate their viewpoints even if not fully understanding their perspective; and he found he missed their company, the light jovial banter of Famine in particular. Tomas suspected he had a wicked sense of humor, and for one of the Four Absolutes, he thought it was the most outrageous thing he had ever heard of. He expected sombre and dour. All morose business, though Death had that look down to perfection already. For the first time in his life, Tomas realized he actually enjoyed the presence of others. Or at least these others. Maybe it was their distance from mundane subjectivity, a definitive practicality they exhibited that he could appreciate, one that mirrored much of Tomas's own thoughts. He also realized that he wanted to hang around with them a bit longer, for there were just so many things he accepted that he didn't know. It was like being a rookie all over again, only worse. His thoughts were brutally interrupted by War hastily laying out the plan for after the battle. Tomas turned to face the Horsemen then, though keeping the Javelin pointed at the swarm.

'What do you mean *after* we defeat these minions? Damn!' Tomas retorted, as much to himself as to the Horsemen, after spinning to face War, amazed that they would even think that far ahead. One problem at a time, he had said, surely? Had they not seen what he had? Tomas was getting irritated at himself now. Taking a few calming breaths again. *Of course they have. No doubt they've seen even worse in their time, Think positive, Tomas, you've got the Four Horsemen with you. Get your head back into the zone. Detach, Tomas, Detach. Where's that bloody ruthless bastard that used to live here?*

'You're making me ask so many bloody questions. I'm getting on my own nerves. But if I read you right, you expect us to beat that?' inclining his head towards the imminent swarm. He looked between Death and War. Implacable expressions met his astonished one. Seems they did. 'Fair enough, so what about after?'

As War began preparing his arrows and Death began fitting the two-foot-long quarrels to the crossbow, War outlined their possible escape route. This, the way War described their plight, seemed like their only option. Tomas quickly became invisible as Death seemed to vehemently disagree, citing the fact that what War proposed was as bad as gating to Raphael and just as irresponsible. It hadn't been sealed all this time for nothing.

'Guys? Sorry to butt in, but two things: can we worry about whatever or wherever it is you're worried about *after* we kick these guys' arses; secondly, as they're nearly here and we are only three, not even five, are we ready for this or have you got something up your armored sleeves?'

War smiled a particularly scary smile then. 'I'm always ready for a fight, Tomas, you should know that.'

Then Death added his own confirmation. 'I am Death. I am the Absolute. I am the reaper of souls; and it is time the enemy learnt what it truly means to confront Death and the Horsemen of the Apocalypse.' He raised the crossbow skyward just as War pulled back on the string of his own weapon, the bow creaking under the immense strain as it tensed for the shot. Both were poised, waiting for the swarm to fall into range. Though the swarm probably did several hundred meters prior, it would just be more destructive the closer it came. Tomas still had his doubts though, finding it hard to shake them completely no matter what they said.

'That's all very well; it certainly sounds impressive, but it doesn't alter the fact that there are hundreds of them and only three of us. Even with five we would be hard- pressed.' Tomas, though, would have found small comfort had he actually seen Famine and Pestilence ride up to them and silently rein in behind them. Neither dismounted; they simply changed weapons, as their comrades had.

'Don't get me wrong. I'll give it all I've got but I don't rate our chances much.' Tomas checked their progress on the range finder on the Javelin. Three thousand meters and closing fast. Moving through the final checks and flicking the safety off, two thousand six hundred meters.

'Good to see we haven't missed all the fun.' The voice of Famine made Tomas start. But he didn't turn at first, concentrating on the range finder. Added too, was the fact Tomas found it increasingly difficult to keep turning this way and that with a rocket launcher attached to his shoulder. Two thousand three hundred meters. But curiosity and a strange concern got the better of Tomas and he wanted to know how it went back there. But he didn't take his eyes off the target as it drew inexorably closer. He was beginning to make out individual forms now and they didn't look happy at all.

'You and Pestilence all right? Any problems?' Famine laughed out loud at the thought, all the time going about the business of arming himself accordingly.

'Good grief no, old boy, they didn't know what hit them. I've no idea where they get their ideas from about us, but there are six dogs back there that now know better. Or if you're counting them by body parts, there are about forty-seven dogs. Pestilence vented a bit of spleen on them. In fact I very nearly stood back and watched. She was amazing to behold. If I wasn't already several degrees below freezing, it would have given me the chills.'

At this last, Tomas craned his neck for a glance. Sure enough, Famine resembled someone dipped in liquid nitro. White, glistening and frosty. Generating a creeping mist of his own mist, like one of those liquid nitro canisters. Both Famine and Pestilence had now adopted missile weapons of their own and were busy loading them up. Famine's was a bow similar to War's and Pestilence sported a smaller, more compact black horn bow

– more suitable for use from horseback. Tomas was put in mind of the steppe horsemen from the time of Genghis Khan. Deadly and accurate. A quiver of yellow fletched arrows hung at her hip, with white ash and frost fletched ones at Famine's. *Very co-ordinated,* Tomas thought wryly. *Seems they like to look the part as well as actually represent it. Black, yellow, white and red* (Tomas recalled the crimson cloak of War), *representing the four colors of man as well. No coincidence, I bet.*

That was all Tomas had time for. A quick check on the view finder showed one thousand nine hundred meters. That was close enough. Tomas pulled the trigger.

The vapor trail of the wire guided missile was the first and only indicator the swarm got that this was something they should be concerned about. Azaroth had assured Karcon that mortal weapons would do them no harm, though the Horsemen would more than make up for it. So when the mortal fired the smoking tube at them, few moved. Little did they know that it was the Sword of War, a very supernatural weapon, with equally supernatural effects. Tomas discovered another benefit then: reloading. Or not.

The Sword of War simply provided shot after shot. So Tomas fired several more times before the first struck. The swarm never saw the second or subsequent missiles. The first shot blew a hole in the flying nightmares big enough to give them instant cause for concern. The incandescent flames licked out hungrily, obliterating those in its immediate reach. The concussion from the explosion sent the rest pinwheeling in to each other, knocking several from the sky. The explosion had the added effect of bunching up the demons into convenient clusters. Clusters, which as it happened, made for bigger targets.

More than pleased with the initial effect, Tomas fired off several further shots either side of the first, blasting demons from the sky like clay pigeons. It was devastating. Winged corpses plummeted from the sky, smoking and torn as the fell to the Earth, only to smash further upon the rocky ground below. The Horsemen were no less destructive, for though they may have only appeared to use conventional weapons, the hundreds of shafts that flew from them were far beyond mortal capabilities. Tomas had seen guns fire fewer rounds per second than these warriors. Demons fell like rain as the sky darkened with their onslaught. Famine's targets were hit by a double whammy, for not only did the barbed shaft cause irreparable damage, the sub-zero capability of his shafts froze solid whatever they seemed to hit, sending demons screaming – or at least they would have, had they not been frozen solid – to the ground and shattering like broken glass on impact. But more were still coming. Many more. Half as many again had fallen back behind the forerunners, using them as shields to take the brunt of the attack. They swooped low and fell beneath the deadly volleys. Their powerful wings stirring up clouds of choking dust and sand, giving them some protection in the concealment as they powered towards the warriors like a flight of monstrous jet propelled vultures, emerging from the dust cloud too close and too low for missile weapons. The Horsemen, experienced warriors, calmly and smoothly switched to their favored blades and braced for impact. Tomas, his heart thudding in his dry mouth, knew now that matters had passed that point of no return. No amount of thinking or talking was going to affect matters at this stage in the game – only action. Thought became deed as Tomas's instincts took over. It seemed as well, as he remembered he was the only one not mounted, that the Sword of War was helping him out. He had never felt so invigorated and alive; being on foot didn't faze him as much as it should have done. Nor had his reflexes ever been as responsive as they seemed to be, almost anticipating his foes' next move. The sword switched at a thought to his Hechler and Koch HK33, fully equipped with the forty-round mags – which, for his supernatural weapon – would not run out. With a scream of defiance, Tomas let rip into the front rank of swooping and hollering demons, tearing them to shreds. Bits of demon and clumps of feathers were blasted away as the searing rounds took their toll. But even though he decimated many, their speed and momentum carried them through the barrage to fall upon the warriors. In less time than it took to think about the switch from gun to sword, it was done and the fantastic blade clove into the first demon. Parrying several vicious attempts to decapitate him as the desperate hand-to-hand combat ensued, Tomas waded in. A part of his mind was resigned to whatever outcome fate had in store for him; another part thoroughly enjoyed the carnage that erupted all around him. He found himself grinning like a wild animal. Oblivious to flailing limbs and splashing blood and ichor that hissed and bubbled against his mystical armor, he swung the sword like he was felling trees, with little grace but proving to be highly effective. The ring of steel upon steel was deafening as he clashed with demon after demon.

Tomas felt several stunning blows rattle off his armor, which brought him back from the brink of some kind of battle madness. Shaking his head to clear the ringing in his ears and the red mist from before his eyes, courtesy of a glancing blow to his helm. The deliverer of said blow hadn't anticipated failure and was thoroughly surprised when Tomas spun in a crouch, his outstretched arm propelling the Sword of War in a backhand sweep that smashed through the minion's hip, upwards through its spine and exiting in a spray of ribs and entrails. The malevolent eyes still bore in to Tomas as the dying torso fell to the side, leaving the disassociated legs to briefly pump their life fluids out before collapsing to the bloody sand. Had he not ducked fractionally when he did, either through his own instinct or by a prod from the sword, he might be several inches shorter now. Tomas switched then from rampaging berserker to icy cold controlled killer, accepting that blind fury was likely to get him killed quicker than a more methodical approach.

Were it simply humans he was up against and had they seen him before his epiphany, they may have thought him simply dangerous but doomed all the same. It was an unsustainable rampage that would sooner or later allow an enemy within range, and when that happened no amount of armor would keep their blades from his body. But something seemed to have woken within Tomas: a battle awareness that lowered the temperature in his immediate vicinity. With a terrifying economy of movement Tomas systematically decimated all within sword range. Humans would have known better then and run. One to one with this warrior could now only end one way. But these weren't humans; they were minions of the Domain. Their every fibre existed for this type of combat. Their bodies were living weapons: horns, teeth, claws and talons. This before the grizzly array of weapons they carried. Weapons which so far had only managed to nick at best, and slide off at worst, the mystical armor that seemed to flow and repair itself about the human. Moments before, he had been swinging randomly, massacring anything that came close enough to strike, but now he moved with a deadly grace and a speed that elevated him above any mortal capability. Moving from simply defense to a lethal offense, Tomas began *pursuing them* – pushing them back even as they strived to overwhelm the quintet.

Tomas was transfixed on those only within his immediate range. Those that chose to attack his companions were pushed from his mind: they could look after themselves – or so he hoped. Tomas ducked and swerved as two slashing scimitars moved the air and brushed the top of his helm. Two minions had leapt at him, one from the right and one from the left, attempting to pincer him with their crossed blades. Catching one on his own blade, a deft twist of his wrist sent the minion sprawling behind him. Tomas now faced one with only seconds before the other was up and attacking him from behind. Tomas rolled his shoulders and spun the blade around his wrist, firming his grip on the wire wrapped hilt. Feinting to the right, Tomas's blade licked out and opened the cheek of the minion before him, enraging him further. Instinct warned Tomas of the assailant behind him and he stepped smartly to the left just as its blade rolled off his armored ribs. Tomas hooked the minion's sword arm with his own and wrenched upwards. Hearing the satisfying sound of bone cracking and seeing the sword fall from nerveless fingers, Tomas smashed the back of his gauntleted fist into the face of the stunned creature. The spikes which appeared with a thought on the back of his hand took out the eyes and drove into the brain. The creature was dead before its legs folded beneath it. Without another thought, Tomas spun the body into the path of the other minion. It was all the distraction he needed and it too died as Tomas strode past it, looking for the next opponent. He didn't have far to look as hundreds more forged towards him.

Finding a second's reprieve, Tomas willed to his hands his weapons of choice, that of his favorite twin Hochlers, the MP5A3, one of the favored weapons of his comrades-in-arms within the SAS. Since the embassy siege, he had developed further respect for the little German-manufactured machine pistol. Tomas kept his on automatic and with both weapons spewing hot metal at a good eight hundred rounds per minute, he cleared himself a respectable opening in the minions' ranks. Tossing in a few of his pilfered grenades made it even bigger, though the grenades not being of supernatural origin, they did little more than annoy the minions, though they served as a useful distraction before Tomas waded in to further the carnage.

War had abandoned his bow. Instead he spun with brutal efficiency a single bladed, two handed battle axe. The blade itself was almost as long as the haft, its rune-etched blade tearing through anything and everything before it. Weapons, armor, bone – nothing lived that stood before it. War bestrode the battlefield like a giant. His armor had moved beyond that of medieval plate to something else entirely. He was still armored, except now it encased him from head to foot like a second skin, flowing over every contour of his massive bulk. His cloak of finely woven red chain mail flew behind him as he moved. The hem was fitted with hundreds of minute blades, so as he spun and swirled it behind him, it too became a weapon, slashing those who sought to attack from behind. Famine and Pestilence were having an equally devastating time of things. It seemed as though the Adversary had some poor intel. There was nothing diminished about these four. Famine leapt and danced amongst the minions like a whirlwind. Had someone upended a helicopter into the fray, using its rotor blades as a weapon, it couldn't have done more damage than Famine and his spinning halberd. The primary difference of course, is that a helicopter wouldn't be laughing like a madman as it went about its grim business. Pestilence was no less successful, her own twin katanas carving swathes through the minions. What her swords missed, her booted feet found. Her progress could be marked by the silvery traces of light left in the wake of her windmilling swords. She too laughed as she killed. For like Famine, who utilized his own icy capabilities to neutralize his enemies as well as the halberd, Pestilence did likewise, inflicting and afflicting her foes with equal abandon. Many fell screaming to the ground, wracked by a concoction of foul diseases that had escalated to their potential in a heartbeat. Few things in the universe could withstand a concentrated full-on dose of bubonic plague and leprosy, accelerated and concentrated by Pestilence herself, or when she mixed the lethal cocktail with a whole array of other, more modern diseases. Their screams were terrible, ripped from swollen and agonized throats. Many of the diseases Pestilence wielded were horrendous enough on their own and most had been the bane of humanity since the earliest of days; but combining them and multiplying their effects a hundredfold was truly hideous to behold. Her victims fell before her by the score. And continued falling. Every sword stroke dealing more than one means of destruction.

Death himself moved through the demons like a hurricane. He was a tornado of black and silver, a lethal whirlwind of absolute annihilation. With every sweep of the massive scythe, demons were sent hurtling in all directions. Those that weren't sliced on the wicked edge were smashed into the next world by the sheer power of the entity. He moved with such speed that it was hard to keep track of his shadowy form. But there was a plan, a design to the way the Horsemen fought. They knew their craft well.

Tomas was unaware of the maneuver instigated by the Horsemen, but before he realized it, he had been split from the group and had taken a contingent of minions with him. Had he seen the aerial view he would have seen the Horsemen divide the minions expertly, like so many sheep. The smaller groups of minions were easier to deal with than one larger mass and before long – Tomas had no idea how long – he found himself with fewer and fewer opponents. Parrying their attempts with contemptuous ease, Tomas managed a few seconds to roll his shoulders, pushing the increasing strain from them, though he was pleasantly surprised to find himself nowhere near as fatigued as he feared he would be. Obviously the gifts of the Horsemen and the benefit of the Sword of War were at work here, but Tomas wasn't complaining as he gritted his teeth and laid into another batch of howling demons.

Several hours later, however, despite all the gifts and enhancements, the tip of his sword rested on the sodden ground, his burning shoulders unable to hold it up any more. Breathing as raggedly as a man who had just run several marathons back to back, and as the adrenaline left his body, Tomas found himself standing – thankfully – alone and unmolested. The tightly sprung muscles bunched through the concentration of battle gradually uncoiled, leaving him feeling drained. He struggled to raise his ballistic goggles to rest upon the peak of his helm, wiping the spattered gore away as he did so, while he surveyed the carnage around him. Pulling his bloody shemagh down to get more air, the putrid smell hit him full on. Unaccustomed to such a rank, vomit inducing stench, Tomas turned and threw up, retching a few times until his stomach had nothing left to give. Standing back up and, dragging the back of his now spikefree hand across his mouth, he turned to see the Four Horsemen making their way towards him, stepping over dismembered, frozen and decomposing corpses. *Even the crows aren't gonna want these stinking things: it's like they've been dead a year already.* Looking at the riders, he saw that, other than being as gore spattered as himself – and even that seemed to vanish as he watched – they seemed calm, composed and as controlled as ever. It was as though they had never been involved in a battle at all. Tomas was feeling like he had been rolled down a very steep and rocky mountain. It might be that he couldn't be killed easily thanks to the gift from Death, but he didn't mention anything about bruises and broken ribs. As the flush of battle left him, Tomas began to feel every hit that he had ignored whilst trying to stay alive during the onslaught.

'Bravo, Tomas!' The voice of War carried over the charnel field. 'You acquitted yourself spectacularly. To be honest, we half expected to be picking your ruined carcass out of this mess; we had no idea you had it in you still.' War was clapping his gauntleted hands together. So too was Famine. The tall, whip-thin Horseman was grinning from ear to ear as he picked his way amongst the bloating corpses, stepping delicately as though he was loath to get any of their putrefaction on his now clean and frost-glistening boots.

'Thanks – I think. It's nice to know you had such confidence in me. Oh no, that's right, you *don't*. As I recall, you seem to think I'll be lucky to make it to the rendezvous. I guess this just goes to show you that you shouldn't judge books by their cover. However, I don't want to do that again anytime soon. How long were we at it?' Tomas didn't wait for any immediate answers before chattering on, 'Weren't there some more due any time now? I'll be buggered if I could face another one let alone another army. I can safely say I'm fucked.' Tomas leant forward, resting his weight upon the pommel of the protruding sword, as much for effect as to actually steady himself. All he really wanted was a bloody big steak, chips and a pint. That and to sleep for a month.

'You are unfortunately correct, Tomas. The remains of Azaroth's army lie just beyond the ridge. I'd estimate we have no more than ten minutes or so before they crest the rise and see what has become of their comrades. I suggest we ride with all haste for Al'Mayakin and pray we can outrun them.' Within moments, they had summoned their steeds and Tomas was employing every shred of willpower he possessed to mount his own without falling off the other side. He had never felt so drained. Death explained that it was his body adapting to the changes as they were used for the first time. The sword had used him brutally as the need had arisen. But without much sympathy, he was also told he would get used to it and it would wear off shortly. Letting Storm do all the work, the quintet sped off in the direction set by War. Their destination was an ancient and abandoned fortress that nobody other than the Four Horsemen, it seemed, knew existed.

'I hope the damn thing is still there and we're not off on some wild goose chase. I really don't want to have fight again so soon; it's all I can do to hang on here,' Tomas spoke mentally to Death, too weary to even talk. *'I'm also so very glad they split their forces: we'd be in shit creek about now, otherwise. So I take it you've got a plan for when we arrive?'*

Death considered his response for a moment before speaking, his voice booming in Tomas's sore head, which made him wince and screw up his face with the effort. 'Not really a plan as such. Though it pains me to have to open this fortress tomb, we have little choice. I have sent a summons to Phanuel at Megiddo to spare some of his warriors to assist us; he assures me that he will get to us as soon as possible without alerting the sentries at the Adversary's tower. We must hold out for as long as we can. That – I am afraid, is the entire plan we have for now.'

Tomas sighed deeply at the apparent futility of it all. Two steps forward, three back. His life of late just seemed to be one obstacle after another, and many of these obstacles wanted to tear him limb from limb.

Speeding across the desert towards the fortress entailed them crossing several main roads, one of which must have been one of the major arterial routes; of which most had been deserted, excepting the occasional burnt out wrecks of various vehicles – some coming, some going, all destroyed. In this instance, however, they rocketed past a convoy of M1 Abraham tanks. Tomas recognized the sound of the fifteen-hundred-break-horsepower jet engines, and these were designated to the US military. There were eight tanks and three personnel transports plus a couple of Hummers interspersed between them. Trouble was, they were heading in the direction that the demonic foot soldiers were coming from.

'We have to stop and warn them!' Tomas virtually shouted at Death as the galloping Horsemen showed no sign of stopping or alerting the troops.

'We do not have the time to alert everyone we see, plus, how do you think that we would be received by the warriors? I do not have the time or the patience to argue credibility with a human when there are several thousand demons only minutes behind us. It is what you humans call collateral damage. They have weapons. Perhaps they will survive as we are the intended quarry of Azaroth's minions.'

'Do you really think that's likely?' Tomas shot back. 'There have to be at least sixty people there. Remember what I told you back in the city?' Death recognized the rhetorical question and remained silent. 'It is what makes us who we are; we are judged by our actions, not only our words. There's too bloody many who talk a good yarn but actually do fuck all. Sorry, old son, but that's not me. If you don't want to scare the shit out of them then I'll do it.'

With no further warning, Tomas reined in, Storm skidding to a halt, sending clouds of sand billowing up into the air. 'You just go on and get that bloody fortress ready; we will be right behind you. I expect you can still communicate with me at a distance, so make sure you guide us in and be ready with some of that covering fire we threw at the aerial lot – I have a feeling we'll need it.'

Death had no expression he could read, just the steel skull leering at him from within the midnight cowl, but Tomas saw the almost imperceptible nod. That was it; Death and the other three Horsemen tore off like a quartet of exocets. Within seconds they had vanished from sight, not just due to their phenomenal speed but by phasing their density out too. Tomas was left alone. Sitting on Storm, armored like a mix of medieval warrior and frontline infantry man, his black Kevlar-lined cloak draped across his steed's rump, Tomas mentally ran through how he was going to approach this. Spinning Storm on his back legs, the pair ran like the wind across the desert to get ahead of the tanks before the minions appeared. It was going to be tight, he knew; but he couldn't leave them to die, at least not without some warning or some chance. The tanks were moving at about seventy miles per hour, governed as they were, unable to reach their top speed of a hundred miles per hour. Trouble was, their jet engines didn't like the sandy conditions much – they played havoc with their turbines – and it was a costly and time-consuming process to get them shipped back to the States, where they were painstakingly refurbished. But for all their power, they were no match for Storm. Tomas skidded to a halt on the tarmac and waited for the convoy to spot him, keeping one eye out on the horizon behind him for the first sign of the demon army.

After the initial shock of the convoy commander – at seeing a strangely garbed man sitting upon a horse in the middle of the road, apparently calmly waiting for them – the next bit of news blew his mind. A half a dozen two-and-a-quarter-ton tank barrels, as well as the mounted machine guns, were leveled at Tomas. The anonymous gunners all watched him with unveiled suspicion. Their ballistic helmets and goggles were sand-covered and betrayed nothing of the expressions of the soldiers underneath. Tomas really didn't want to test his *gifts* against that much firepower, should they consider him a crackpot.

'Who did you say you were again?' the CO asked, his southern accent apparent as well as the disbelief in his voice. Tomas knew he had seconds to convince him.

'Major!' Tomas recognized the speaker's rank and addressed him with as much respect as his withering patience would allow. 'I really don't have the time to brief you as much as you would like about what is about to crest that rise behind me. Suffice to say, it's big. It will kill you and your men in the most painful, unimaginable ways possible; and those lovely tanks of yours will be about as much use as a chocolate welding torch. I don't know what you've seen so far, but unless you turn tail with me now, you won't be seeing much more. You may not survive even now – I don't think your vehicles will go fast enough to outrun them – but there is a fortress hopefully not too far away that may provide us with a chance. Here, there's none. Get your men onto the tanks with all the ordinance they can carry. Leave the trucks and the hummers, and make sure all the tanks are pointing behind us; we may be able to slow them up and buy us a few minutes. But we must go – now!'

'Look, son, we've seen plenty on this tour, but you have *got* to take the biscuit. Out here looking like I don't know what, sitting on your pretty horse and spouting some kind of shit about I don't know what. But if you think I'm abandoning vehicles and following you anywhere just on your say-so, you have got another think coming. Now I suggest you ride off from wherever you came from and let us get on with what we do best.'

Tomas couldn't believe what he was hearing, though he could sympathize with the major to some extent – after all, Tomas himself had taken some convincing and he *still* wasn't entirely happy with things. But knowing what he did and what he had just gone through, he had to make this man see sense, and fast. There was only one way he could think of.

'Look, Major… whatever your name is. If I can prove to you beyond all shadow of doubt, will you do as I ask without question? Because you gotta believe me: all I'm trying to do is save our collective arses. I promise to explain it all to you when and if we reach safety, or at least comparative safety. But you'll have to trust me implicitly. I know it'll go against all your training but think of your men: it's their lives we're talking about here as well. All I need you to do is get up here behind me and I'll do the rest.'

The major hesitated. He *had* actually seen quite a bit of *weird shit* these last few weeks. He hadn't been happy with a lot of it, though there was little to be happy about all round. *What the heck. What's the worst that can happen?* he thought resignedly. He barked some orders to his second and swung expertly up behind Tomas.

'Used to weekend out on my daddy's ranch. Been riding since before I could walk.'

Tomas was pleased: it only meant then he had himself to worry about. 'Hold on tight then: this might be a little different.'

Before the major could utter another word, Storm spun and was away. Within the rush of the wind, Tomas could hear the major screaming behind him. Just as Storm broke the sound barrier with a concussive boom, the major became instantly silent. They had reached the crest before the demons and, without breaking the silhouette of the ridge line too much, the major saw just what Tomas had warned him about.

'That sure is gonna be some explanation, son. I hope we live long enough for you to tell it. Can you get us back as quick as you got us here? We need to move while I still have some vestige of my sanity remaining to me, 'cos this horse and you are sure pushing what little I have left.'

Tomas didn't hesitate, and much in the same manner as their journey to the ridge, they found themselves back at the convoy. Pragmatic as ever, the major wasted no time even though he must have had a hundred questions and, sliding off Storm, he ran to the convoy whereupon he began hollering orders until his voice broke. There were men scurrying everywhere. Tomas was gratified to see the efficiency of the soldiers. They obeyed without question even though they too no doubt had a myriad of questions of their own about how a horse had moved as fast as it had and just what their commander had seen to make him as animated as he was. But within only a few minutes, the eight tanks were laden with soldiers, turrets turned smoothly behind them, loaded and ready to fire.

'Let's go; follow me!' Tomas led the way, setting off in the original direction he had been heading before this detour. He called mentally to Death, who responded that they were heading in the right direction and were only a few miles away. Tomas relayed this to the major and sent them on their way; hanging back himself, for only he could affect the minions with any permanent results. No matter how many rounds the tanks fired, they would only slow them; though it might be enough to buy them breathing room until Phanuel arrived with the cavalry.

The massive engines thrummed as they propelled the tanks across the rugged desert terrain. The few miles stretched disturbingly as they had to deviate from a direct course, to enable the vehicles to get around some of the more extreme areas. The demon army had crested the ridge and was now bearing down upon the fleeing humans, only a few miles behind them, and they were closing fast. It was just as well the engines drowned out all sound, because if the soldiers could have heard the howls and terrifying screams of the eager minions, most would have taken their own lives there and then rather than face them. Tomas stopped and turned and, urging the soldiers on, he spun up his Javelin and rapid fired several rockets into the vanguard. Turning and galloping to the lead tank before the first exploded, he heard the rest go off and hoped that it had slowed the closing minions for a few seconds longer.

'The moment we reach the fortress, Major, I want all the men to get off and get inside as fast as they can. Then we need to send as many rounds into that lot as possible before they get too close, in order to get the men out of the tanks. Can you do that?' The major didn't bat an eyelid at how he could even hear Tomas as he and his horse easily kept pace with a tank doing sixty miles an hour. All he did was nod that he understood.

Barely a mile separated the forces now and those at the rear of the group could make out several of the lead creatures. But the terrain was still too unpredictable to allow them to open fire. It was all they could do to hang on. But even as that thought went through Tomas's mind, the very thing he feared happened. He saw a marine go off the side. It was only his training that allowed him to survive the fall, but it wasn't without cost. He had obviously broken something, because he didn't get up and there was a shard of something sticking out at an odd angle from his thigh. Tomas heard his screams and turned Storm dramatically to intercept the fallen man. Much of Tomas's military career had been just about him. All others were expendable as far as he was concerned, but recent events had given him cause to change his view on that. Now, he refused to give those bastards anything. Certainly not one of his own if he could possibly avoid it.

War was waiting for the tanks as they pulled up at the fortress. Tomas had told him what he wanted them to do and War had concurred. He bellowed his orders to the soldiers who – and even the major – instantly leapt to obey them. He knew military authority when he heard it, and there was none higher than War himself. The M1s, with expert military precision, elevated their barrels to the trajectory that War, fully conversant with their terminology, issued to them. Thus the process went smoothly.

Tomas leapt from Storm's back before the big destrier had come to a complete halt. He landed beside the fallen man, who was groaning and rolling about in obvious agony. Tomas saw the bone sticking out, slick and white. It was a clean break, thankfully.

'This is probably gonna hurt more later,' Tomas said to the man, just before he slugged him: a right hook that knocked the man clean out. Once he was still, Tomas grabbed the leg and pulled. At the same time, he pushed the broken bone back in, realigning the two parts as best he could. Whipping his shemagh off, Tomas tied it around the wound. Glancing up, he could see the minions were only a few hundred yards away. It was either shoot or lift the man over the horse. *'I don't suppose you mind bending down, Storm? The saddle is a bit high to get this guy over,'* Tomas thought to his companion. The highly intelligent stallion bent its foreleg dutifully, allowing Tomas to drape the man over it, swinging himself up just as several arrows came sailing past him, one skidding off his ballistic helmet.

'Shit!' Tomas heeled Storm, but the big stallion already knew what was expected of him and he accelerated away with all the power he possessed, muscles bunching as he leapt away, which, as it turned out, was just as well. The explosions just behind him put paid to the arrows as the M1s began synchronous firing, one after the other. By the time the last one had fired the first was firing again. They were to do this until either they ran out of shells or the horde got too close to enable the men to get out safely, whichever happened first.

Speeding towards the fortress, Tomas got his first real look at Al'Mayakin. It was a lot bigger than he expected for some reason. Fortunately, it was well situated atop a largish hill; they needed all the advantage they could get if they had to defend it against invasion. It had good sized stone walls. Tomas reckoned they had to be about forty feet with regular crenulations along the top. One good sized gate lay in the center and that was where the tanks were ituated. *Those Templar Knights certainly knew how to fortify something.* The moment Tomas drew up, several men rushed out to grab their fallen comrade and carry him back inside. Tomas noticed that they seemed unnaturally subdued. *I bet they've seen just who they are shacked up with. It isn't every day you find yourself face to face with Death and the Four Horsemen of the Apocalypse. One of those boys has got to be a God botherer; he'll spot them for who they are a mile off. Mass is never gonna be the same for them again. I just hope they live long enough to go to another one.* 'You wanna get these boys in; those shells are just irritating them!'

War nodded and gave the order. Within moments all the soldiers were through the gate and taking up positions on the battlements, setting up all the ordnance they had brought with them.

Famine came out then and suggested Tomas get in; he had an idea that involved the now redundant tanks. 'Give me a hand, War, old chap; I want to stack these in front of the gate, as close as we can get them.' As soon as Tomas had closed the gate behind him, he heard the sound of steel against steel from the other side. Fearing the worst, he ran to the battlements and looked over. He wished he hadn't. His eyes were drawn in equal measure to what War and Famine were doing, and the sea of demons that was bearing down on them. *Oh, crap!* Tomas watched as War and Famine stacked the tanks, one on top of the other, stunned at the display of strength and power. Those things were quite a few tons apiece and they tossed them like sacks of flour. Tomas had witnessed a couple of displays of their martial prowess now, and all it left him with were more questions about just what they were capable of if they turned their minds to it. They were the Horsemen of the Apocalypse after all, and if only four entities could bring it about, then they had to be pretty powerful.

Famine had shifted to his fiery persona; aiming his halberd at the tanks, and a wave of heat pulsed off him. It slammed into the steel vehicles and the residue washed up the walls, nearly taking Tomas's eyebrows off with the searing temperature. Only his quickened reflexes saved him from an embarrassing incident. The heat grew and grew, building to such intensity that it was impossible to look at without your eyes shriveling in their sockets. It built until the tanks simply melted like so much butter. In a heartbeat Famine had changed again – reverting to his icy aspect – and this time he blasted the molten steel as it hung suspended in liquid form still in the air before it fell splashing to the sand below; slamming blizzardlike into it and cooling the molten metal onto the door and walls, effectively plugging and armor plating the only entrance and exit to the fortress. It was a phenomenal display of power and Tomas realized that he *really* didn't know just what these beings were capable of. Humbled, Tomas stepped back and took a last lookout at the demons before he began moving amongst the men stationed there. *What are they waiting for?* They saw what he saw, and they hadn't had the benefit of his brief and concentrated education. They had to be terrified. He would have been. But he felt a rising sense of pride at how well these men held it together. He was still scared, he realized; and more than moderately unhappy with the situation he found himself in, but at least he had had the element of surprise removed from him by the Horsemen. He moved amongst the marines, trying to put as many at ease as best he could. No easy task, considering what they faced. Just how did you explain that an army of demons, straight out of Hell – *which, by the way, is real and is about to wipe the universe out –* is out there, just a few hundred yards away and it wants to eat your eyeballs straight out of your head. Tomas just hoped that no one asked the one question he dreaded.

'Sir?' one marine asked, 'What is it we're fighting, sir? They don't look… right, somehow.'

That was the one question he didn't want. *Bloody typical. Why can't I keep my thoughts to myself? How do I tell him without scaring him shitless? The truth? Pah, I don't think so…* Tomas chuckled to himself. He could imagine that going down a storm. *Best make something convincing up for now. We'll do the truth if we all survive.* But before Tomas could weave something feasible to keep the young man sane and calm for a bit longer, the moment was lost as Death had moved silently upon them. He spoke before Tomas. And he told the cold hard truth. No cushion, no sugar, no nothing. Bam! There it was. Laid out in all its grim reality by none other than the grimmest Reaper himself. Tomas just looked between the soldier and Death. *Maybe they do deserve to know; maybe it's just me who really wishes he didn't know what was going on.* Several others had perked up at the arrival of the midnight-clad warrior with the giant scythe. Tomas could see the fear in their eyes. Just as it had been in his. They knew that this was no Halloween stunt; that this figure, along with the others, was the real thing. That those out there were exactly what he said they were. Tomas watched sadly as more than a few pulled out crucifixes and rosaries and other various charms and sacred paraphernalia. There were crossings and mutterings aplenty as Death laid it out before them.

Tomas couldn't take any more. He silently turned his back on them and went down to the central courtyard, where War and Famine were just dismounting after flying over the walls. That little stunt had not gone unnoticed either. What had he gotten the major and his men into? More importantly though, Tomas realized, why weren't the enemies attacking?

'They are waiting for Azaroth to arrive. Now we are here, and out of their immediate reach, they need new orders. This is not what they were expecting. I also suspect that Azaroth will be interested to know what has appeared here. Very interested indeed.' Famine had come up behind Tomas and with that annoying habit he had, plucked the last thought from Tomas's mind.

'What have I told you about doing that? My thoughts are to remain my own unless I reach out to you. I was under the impression we were clear on the subject.'

Famine held up both hands in a mock supplication, knowing full well he had overstepped a boundary.

'My apologies, friend Tomas. Old habits and all that. You are quite right. However…' Famine continued as though nothing had happened, the incident forgotten already, '…if Phanuel doesn't arrive before Azaroth attacks, we may have a slight problem.'

Tomas didn't like the way Famine emphasized the word *slight*. To him it sounded like a *major fucking disaster*. 'I know I don't really want to ask – every time I do, it just keeps getting worse – but, forewarned is forearmed and all that shit. Go on. Why might we have a problem?' Tomas unconsciously grimaced, fully expecting something heinous. He wasn't disappointed.

'Back when humanity was in its infancy, the Nephillim moved amongst you and taught many a forbidden lore. It has been the bane of you mortals ever since, but one of those forbidden arts was that of star summoning.' Tomas retained his blank expression in case Famine assumed he had a clue what he was on about, which he didn't. 'I see. Well, you've heard the tale about comets and shooting stars being heralds and omens of misfortune?' Tomas nodded; that much he knew. 'There is truth buried in that old superstition, as there are in many of them. Cutting a long story short, and you should be grateful it's me telling you this and not Death – he spins this out for days. I've heard him. Anyway, many of these meteors are, much to our eternal shame, prisons for those who broke the Covenant and were subsequently exiled into the void, forbidden to ever put a foot upon a living planet again, banished for eternity, or at least until the end of this cycle. Trust me, that's a long time even for an eternal being. The Nephillim taught humans how to summon these prisons – an ancient spell involving the magnetic fields of your world. You see, the meteors are primarily ferrous based – iron. The sorcerer was able, as part of the charm, to bind the demon to his will in payment for release. You have many legends that tell of this, the most famous being that of the Djinn. Anyway, one of these demons: a particularly nasty individual, Nakir the Black – he didn't just get that sobriquet for his color, though he was black as pitch, scaled as I recall, with eight eyes. He was attributed with introducing the arachnids to your world but that's another tale. He wasn't the most co-operative upon his release, killing the one who summoned him, as well as several Nephillim and an awful lot of humans. He wreaked havoc upon this land. His influence is still in evidence today – another long story.' Famine looked thoughtful for a moment before continuing, 'I do believe it was Uriel who finally defeated him, eventually imprisoning him again in the one thing that can affect both the Celestial and the Damned equally – iron. There again it appears in your mythology.'

Tomas just took his word for it; his mythology was a little rusty. 'Is this going to be a long story? Just in case you've forgotten, we've a battle to prepare for.' The strained smile Tomas wore took the sting out of the comment.

'Point taken. I shall endeavor to keep to the salient points. Now where was I? Ah yes, iron prisons. No sooner was he trapped, than he and his prison were spirited away by persons unknown, though we suspect it was the Nephillim yet again. Should you survive all this, you'll learn more about them; terrible creatures. Anyway, it was later discovered here, at this ancient Templar stronghold, which started life as an ancient pagan site of worship. There are nexus points beneath us where the dragon lines cross.'

Tomas frowned. 'What the bloody hell are dragon lines? Don't go throwing stuff in like that; I'm struggling to keep up with you as it is. Academia and history were never my strong points; you need my little sister for that. She used to love it.'

Famine looked thoughtful for a moment as though recalling something. 'Yes. Gwendoline. You're probably right. She would.'

Famine left the enigmatic comment open, not pursuing it, much to Tomas's chagrin. That was twice now she had been referenced with no explanation. He would have to take it up with them, but at a later point: they had more pressing matters requiring their attention.

'…But dragon lines are the interconnecting lines of force that energize this world. You would call them ley lines, I believe,' Famine continued.

'How do you know of Gwen?' Tomas was too curious as to why the Four Horsemen should know of his sister to let it go, but Famine wasn't about to be distracted and carried on as though he had not heard Tomas's question.

'As well as the Djinn, your legends also tell of otherworldly beings being affected by iron. The magi of the Romans knew of this too. By the time they came to crucify the man they called Jesus, enough evidence had been gathered about him to determine his otherworldly status. Hence they pierced his hands and ankles with iron nails, and then stabbed him with an iron spear. Iron, it was the bane of many back then. But in their perpetual search for knowledge, the Templar Knights eventually came across this place, and the iron tomb of Nakir. Unfortunately for them but fortunately for the rest of humanity, their magical prowess wasn't all they thought it was, and in their futile attempts to tap into whatever power emanated from the tomb, all they managed to do was summon the base consciousness of Nakir, and this is what made it so dangerous, for it forged a link between this realm and the Domain. It probably stemmed from Nakir's desire to return there, who knows; but energy was magnified by the nexus points crossing, creating a field of dark light around the tomb, corrupting all those within its range. The corrupted Templar Knights immediately fortified this pagan chapel, bolstering its defenses and rededicating it to the Dark Angel. They then began to spread their own corruption, killing indiscriminately, disobeying every command from their superiors. Parts of your earlier crusades can be put down to them, such antagonists. There was rumor, though it has yet to be substantiated, that several lower minions were brought through the gateway from the Domain. Whether they remained inside or made it to the outside world is unclear. But, thanks to the man you call the Pope, the Pope of that time anyway – the early 1300s – whose not so pious paranoia and jealousy of the Templar Order drove him to condemn *all* of the Templar Knights, not just the corrupted ones. They were subsequently rounded up, most of them eventually captured and burnt at the stake for heresy.' Famine spat demonstrably: he obviously thought little of the human's definition of heresy. 'Though their fiery deaths were not before some rather unpleasant torture. So engrossed by their need to make an example of the allegedly desecrated Temple Knights they exercised their creativity in that department. This place, however...' He gestured towards the fortress. '...was momentarily forgotten, and there were still several knights left on permanent guard duty here when we arrived, with the Archangel Uriel, to deal with the situation. They were well fortified inside, defending their artifact possessively. This, in a warped sort of way, served our purpose. We needed guardians to ensure it wasn't disturbed. Uriel made them permanent guardians. Life eternal, protecting the tomb and its passageways. We then sealed the tomb, shifting its density out of phase with this world so that it would never be found, though on a smaller scale than before, and painstakingly removed all trace of its existence throughout history in the hope that it would remain unnoticed until this world passed away in due course. To the outside world it would look like any other hilltop. But alas, we needed this fortification and, however hazardous it might be in there within the dark field, it'll be considerably more hazardous out here when Azaroth arrives and he launches his attack.'

Tomas didn't look happy at all. He called it simply his pessimistic streak, but it had kept him alive on more than one occasion and what was this *before* he just mentioned? There were benefits to seeing the worst in things; not that this current situation could be called beneficial, or could get any worse; but it did need pointing out.

'You don't suppose that whatever is in there felt something change when you opened this place up again, do you? And, just to add to our woes, is likely to come out and investigate?' Tomas took his helmet off and ran his hands through his matted hair then down across his face, feeling the stubble of several days' growth. *Shit! I must still look as bad as I did when I was on the streets; I wonder how many greys are in this now.* Tomas hadn't looked at his reflection since leaving hospital, and he knew he looked rough then. God knows what he must look like now. *Perhaps I ought to sort my shit out.* Then he thought about his likelihood of survival, and thought better of it. *Bollocks. Why bother? Who's gonna be looking at me, anyway? The only thing likely to see my mug is more probable to want to tear it off and eat it than say Hmmm, you really could use a shave, you scruffy human.* The thought amused Tomas and a wry smile crept onto his craggy face. He barely heard Famine say, 'Possibly.' Tomas sighed at the prospect. *Bloody marvelous. That's all we need.*

Tomas left Famine conferring with his cohorts as they planned some sort of strategy. Tomas had had enough for one day. As far as he was concerned no amount of strategy was going to extricate them from this one. With his luck, Phanuel would turn up just as Azaroth finished with them. No, there really weren't any get out of gaol free cards in this scenario. Perhaps that was what put him in such a foul humor. He had always left himself a way out before. In fact it was the first thing he set up. This was just a shambles, lurching from one crisis to another, almost as if they were making it up as they went along. Tomas walked amongst the marines, listening to snippets of their conversations. They were scared, probably for the first real time in their lives – certainly in their military careers. There was something predictable and acceptable about facing another human. A soldier had something in common with another human, but this was different. It was akin to facing another species altogether. Tomas had seen this enemy up close and personal, closer than he would have liked, truth be told. Maybe some of them had been human once, but time in the Domain had changed them, and not for the better. His musings had taken him up to the battlements again, where he could see the army of Azaroth spread out before him. *So many; there's no way on earth we are going to withstand that.* The morass of demons rippled and flowed like an inky sea of doom. Occasionally one would rise up and exhort itself with a bloodcurdling scream. A marine had moved across the stones to stand beside Tomas, silently sharing the dismal view before he spoke.

'Excuse me, sir. Sorry to interrupt your thoughts and all, but me and the boys were wondering, are they really —' Tomas knew the question before the private had finished, secretly grateful for the interruption from his own dismal thoughts.

'Yes they are, and my advice is to try and not think about it too much. Just think of them as a hostile that wants you dead. Any more than that and it'll just fuck you up. Trust me.'

The haunted look in Tomas's eyes forestalled any further pursuance of that line of thought in the marine, but he could see that he still had questions. Tomas stood, statuelike, waiting for the next one.

'Sir —' the marine began again after a few minutes.

Tomas stopped him again. 'Call me Tomas, not sir; I used to work for a living.' Tomas saw the recognition of the fact he had served in the change of expression on the marine: he felt then he was talking to one of his own. That would get back and maybe make them feel slightly more at ease. Truth be told, Tomas had never taken to ranks even though he had been granted one for expedience's sake, enabling him to move amongst many of his potential targets with comparative ease. But he doubted that his limited bonding would have any lasting effect. 'Before you continue, son, make sure you want to know the answer. It's been my experience of late that there are very few *good* answers, and trust me when I tell you I've done my share of asking questions – many of which I wished I hadn't after I'd gotten the answer. They didn't bring me any peace. And if it's peace of mind you're looking for, then I'd keep shtum.'

The marine struggled whether or not to ask, but something familiar in his eyes told Tomas he was going to ask anyway, irrespective of the answer. 'Si – Tomas. Seeing that lot out there, do you think we can survive this?'

Tomas stayed silent at first, looking from the fervent expression on the young man's face and alternating it with long hard stares at the sea of demons encamped only a few hundred yards away from them. He could even smell their foulness from where he stood. It didn't look good, he had to admit. But he knew he couldn't lie to the marine. So, with a heavy heart and a resigned sigh, he gave him his answer. *No*. The word echoed in his mind. 'What do you think, son? Were you trained to accept defeat from superior numbers so easily?'

The marine stood thoughtful for a second, considering what Tomas had just said and how it worked with what he had seen beyond the wall. 'But, Tomas, we weren't trained for that. We were trained to tackle people. Terrorists, insurgents, and other armies, you know, *normal* enemies, if there is such a thing. But those aren't normal. The big guy in black called them demons. Demons, for Christ's sake. What are we supposed to do against them?'

Tomas noted how the soldier couldn't bring himself to call Death by the name he knew him to really be. The big guy in black – neat. But in the end, it made little difference. They were demons all right and even though they had no business being here, they shouldn't think that all humanity was simply going to lie down and roll over. These boys would show that to them to the last. Once matters got underway, he had no doubt they would do whatever was required of them. No one would falter in their duty – they were too good for that – but this was what gave the enemy its edge. The horror of the anticipation. Waiting was always far worse than doing. It gave the imagination far too much time to mess with people's heads. Maybe that was it. Why wait? Tomas had an idea.

'Yeah, they're demons. So what? At least it's bloody obvious what they want and that they are the enemy, not like some misguided moron who looks like anyone else and wants to blow himself up, taking as many with him or her as possible. In the name of what? Some futile cause? Don't they know that they are *all* futile? Nobody ever wins; they never have. In all our 250,000-ish years of humanity. How can anyone fight against a mentality like that? It's just stupid. Fucking religion! It's got so much to answer for.' Tomas calmed himself before he got carried away. 'Help is coming; all we have to do is hold these mothers here for as long as possible. We might not win – I can't kid you about that – but on the other hand, we just might. Fifty-fifty; reasonable odds in my book. And even if we don't, we'll have given a damn good account of ourselves. Now…' Tomas realized he didn't know the man's name; that would have to change. He'd know them all before anything else happened to them. They would be remembered.

'What's your name, son?'

'Potter, sir… sorry, Tomas. It's a habit, I guess. George Potter the second. The third is back home and should be about four months now.' It brought a welcome and absent smile to the young man's face and it lightened Tomas's spirit to see it. *Such a pity.*

'Well done, Potter; you'll make a fine father, I bet. Do me a favor and keep yourself alive long enough to bring that little one up. Now, what's the best form of defense?'

The question threw Potter for a moment, but after a few seconds' consideration he responded with a good answer, bearing a question of his own. 'My football coach used to say that a lot. Was it a good offense?' hoping it was the right answer. He was rewarded with a chilling smile from the stern man before him. Potter hadn't known this man for long – just for a few minutes at best – but when Potter saw that smile, he mentally filed him away as someone very dangerous indeed. Tomas's dark eyes flashed with sudden animation. The white teeth stood out amongst the greying stubble of his beard, giving him a distinctly predatory look. And just for a split second, Potter wasn't sure who to be more afraid of.

'C'mon, Potter, we've got a lot to do – and little time to do it. Why don't we go and find the big guy in black.'

Chapter Eight

Triskelle

'WHAT?' IT WAS ABOUT ALL GWEN COULD manage. Her ability to talk coherently had momentarily left her. In fact, all rational thought had left her petite body. She couldn't work out what to do with her hands or seem to be able to co-ordinate them with her mouth. A light breeze blew, raising goose bumps on her presently unfeeling skin. Gwen couldn't decide whether to explode or carry on eating and wait for the punchline; so she simply stood and stared at them, frozen, plastic fork halfway to her mouth, empty now, as the egg had fallen to the grass. It was hard enough to keep scrambled egg on a fork when it had her full attention. Long seconds passed before the power of speech returned to her, albeit gradually. Though emotions vied for attention within her, her speech still only managed to come out in a flat monotone. Gwen couldn't put her finger on what emotion best suited her for what she was going through. Jen and Maddy seemed to be taking some perverse pleasure in her stunned predicament. She gave up with the food; her hunger had vanished like so much morning mist with the revelation.

'Girls! Tell me you're kidding; tell me I haven't been crashed out here in the bloody woods, naked, for three days.'

Jen nodded as though it were the most obvious thing in the world to have done. Standing opposite Gwen, only a few feet away. 'Yep. Though I'd forgotten how much you mutter in your sleep. Very insightful. Remind me to sit you down one day and go through some of the odd titbits with you and then,' Jen smirked, 'you can confirm just how true they are. Some bits even made Maddy blush. And who is Jason again?'

Gwen was horrified and it obviously showed on her face, though this just seemed to amuse the girls all the more, for they started giggling amongst themselves. Gwen found a bit of fire and she threw her platter to the ground, though the effect was lost as she stamped her naked foot, looking quite ridiculous. It seemed the girls had a warped sense of humor, making fun of her this way, but Gwen's anger quickly turned tearful. She had gone along with these two with more than enough faith, and after all was said and done, they still tried to provoke her. It was just too much to take and she dropped to the ground, burying her face in her hands, and started to cry. How had things gone from comparatively normal to this disaster so suddenly? They must have drugged her, though she couldn't recall taking any, but what would she know? She'd only taken drugs the once, and they were some skanky looking mushrooms. All they managed to do was make her sick, so she wasn't what you could call an expert on symptoms and signs. Now here she was, naked, deep in the woods, far away from all she knew, her business in jeopardy, and no obvious way out. The dragon thing was probably her hallucinating – part of their drug-induced plan to break her. They had succeeded; she had no more to give. The fire that blazed within her – what gave Gwen her feisty character – finally, sadly, went out.

'I give up,' Gwen sobbed. 'Just don't kill me, please. You've had your fun, now let me go, *please.*' Gwen had dropped to her haunches and was slowly rocking on her heels; elbows tucked in and her forehead resting on her knees. She didn't see Jen and Maddy slip up either side of her and drop to their knees. Gwen squealed in surprise when the two girls put their arms about her. She tried to struggle away from them. Irrational fear had replaced the usual pragmatic Gwen, but the girls held her firm.

'Gwen! Please, relax.' Maddy had a note of concern in her own voice at Gwen's outburst. Squirming in their grip, Gwen was desperate now to get away from them but she couldn't move. They held her down no matter how she bunched her legs to spring away. With a quick push, they drove Gwen back off her heels and dropped her onto her bottom, where she landed with a squeal of surprise and moderate pain as she had landed on her plastic fork and it wound up sticking into the meat of her buttock. This seemed to break her train of thought from flight to fight. Her spark rekindled vengefully.

'Ow! Shit! Christ, that hurts.' Gwen turned to remove the broken plastic utensil from her bruised flesh. Seeing that she had calmed momentarily, the two girls let go, though they were poised to restrain her further if she made a bolt for it.

'Calm down, Gwen, you silly thing; we're not going to hurt you, kill you or do anything else to you for that matter. There are some things we need to explain to you, to be fair, and we had hoped that your mind had adjusted well enough. Maybe you needed more sleep.'

'*More* sleep? You *are* taking the piss now,' Gwen shot back. 'Three bloody days! How much more sleep do you think I need?' Gwen resigned herself to not being able to get up so she sat back, wincing as her stabbed posterior squashed up on the ground, but definitely calmer now. It was then that she noticed the spirals. 'You've bloody well tattooed me in my sleep?' They were all across her abdomen and down her legs. Gwen saw a myriad of tiny pale blue spirals. She began to examine the rest of her body. They were all over her, faint but definitely there. Her rage began to build again and she started to rise, shrugging Jen's hand off her shoulder, but as she turned to do the same to Maddy she saw the baleful look in the tall redhead's eyes. Unless she was hallucinating again – which she doubted, considering how she was feeling – Gwen came face to face with a pair of blazing reptilian eyes. Black vertical pupils set in a liquid gold surround, they pinned like her like a bug in a specimen tray as they bore into her mind. She stared transfixed at the tiny flames licking out from the corners of her eyes.

'Sit down, Gwen!' Even her voice had changed. Deeper and more sibilant. It resonated with a power that Gwen felt vibrate through her very bones. Gwen sat, her own eyes wide and fearful, red rimmed from her recent tears. She looked to Jen quickly, checking to see if the other girl had changed. She hadn't. In fact, Jen was smiling as benignly as ever, and if Gwen wasn't mistaken, a look of pity played across her serene features.

'I'm sitting, okay? I'm sorry. Look, I'm sitting. What do you want from me?' Gwen's nervous, edgy voice served to somewhat pacify the fiery woman before her.

Maddy stood and walked off a few paces before turning back to Gwen. The fire in her eyes had gone out and had returned to normal, but she wasn't smiling. And Gwen had the distinct realization then that it didn't bode well for any forthcoming good news.

'Your prolonged sleep was a necessary testing, Gwen, to ascertain your genetic compatibility with the Earth and to prepare the way for the next phase of your journey. Without her assistance, your molecular make-up wouldn't be able to sustain the transition. In short, the Earth has altered your deoxyribonucleic acid and increased your chromosomal content. It seems that in doing so, it has disrupted your mental and emotional capabilities. We had hoped that you would adapt better, certainly faster, for your next step will in all likelihood be even more traumatic than this one.'

Gwen was horrified, and this started her crying again. She couldn't believe what she was hearing. 'You've been messing with my DNA?' she sobbed. Her mind was registering all the information slower than usual, it seemed. Her ears seemed to be full of cotton wool and her own words sounded spongy to her. Glancing over Maddy's shoulder, she felt that the trees had started to sway in a most disconcerting manner, round and around. No, it wasn't the trees; it was her. With a pop, she passed out.

Gwen came to gradually. Like a swimmer caught deep below the surface, she could see the light playing on the surface; but try as she might, she found it hard to reach. Her mind swam furiously, desperate to break the surface before the emotional turmoil she swam in drowned her. Distant voices seeped through to her consciousness. Recognizing them as her companions, Gwen concentrated on trying to hear what they were saying. But try as she might, it was just so much gibberish; though two words did manage to slip through, and with them, Gwen surfaced.

'She's awake.'

Against her will, for she felt as weak as a newborn kitten, Gwen was lifted up into a sitting position again and something cool was pressed to her lips. Refreshing liquid trickled down her dry throat and relieved her dry, cracked lips. Coming fully back to her senses, Gwen gasped. Whatever it was they were giving her was absolutely fantastic and she drank greedily.

'Easy, little sister, easy. Not too much at once: you'll give yourself a head rush.'

Gwen was reluctant to heed the warning until one of the girls –Jen – pulled the goblet away from her moist and searching mouth. Finally opening her eyes fully, Gwen saw that nothing had changed around her, yet everything seemed brighter and more colorful than before. She ran her tongue around her lips, making sure none of the drops escaped her.

'Wow! What was that?' Gwen's eyes fixed on the goblet that Jen held as though she could will it back to her mouth. But Jen simply shook her head and the magical liquid, goblet and all, simply vanished.

'That, my dear, was a little-known beverage, mostly consisting of nectar but with a few other little things thrown in for good measure, totally natural though. Don't worry, we haven't drugged you, if that's what you're thinking. You were, weren't you? Hopefully that brew will bring some clarity to you.'

Only a few seconds had passed but she did feel better. Gwen smiled – an embarrassed sort of twist to her usually ditzy grin – and she found herself much more relaxed than after her earlier awakening.

'How much do you remember about our conversation before your little three-day nap and mini-meltdown?'

Gwen scrunched her hands through her hair again as though it would help her memory, mentally wandering through her mind's filing system, which wasn't much better at best than tossing things into the various already cluttered corners of her head.

'Not much really: something about acceptance, destiny and pow…' As she spoke, the words prompted a surge of buried memories, recently swept into a darkened corner by Gwen's subconscious as it seemed a bit too much to tackle at the time. Part of her had hoped she wouldn't have to tackle them again at all. So much for that.

She was bombarded with images of slavering wolves, giant Kachinas and smashed corpses, lying strewn across the street. Then the memory of two enormous dragons slammed into the forefront of her mind. Gwen looked back and forth then, rapidly between the two girls. They retained their silence, though it was clear they could virtually *see* the memories flooding back to her, based upon her own mix of shock and horror playing merry hell with her features.

'We need to be serious now, Gwen, as you apparently remember what has happened to you to date. You will also appreciate that matters are going a little against the expected norm.'

'You could say that, and all this has something to do with me, I take it?'

'Yes! To do with you and partly because of you. You've seen first-hand what has started to happen. It is not only happening here, but all over the world. It's only going to get worse. Before too long, matters will be irredeemable. Now, we've laid the groundwork with you, but the final choice has to be yours. You accepted your destiny three days ago. You recall the pain in your head subsiding?' Gwen nodded. 'But that acceptance only brings us to this moment.'

Gwen sensed with a deepening anxiety that there was more to come, though she had seemingly passed a point she hadn't been aware of – because she felt relaxed and steady, eager in fact for more information, even knowing it was probably more doom and gloom. Her turbulent psyche was gradually finding a purchase in reality again. Though that reality had irrevocably changed, Gwen found she didn't really mind. She hadn't been overly fond of the previous one anyway. Her earlier trepidation was being gradually replaced with enthusiasm, a keenness to know more, and what her place in all this was. She was soon discovering the true meaning of ignorance being bliss.

'Go on!' Gwen encouraged. 'I've had about all the shocks I'm going to have. I think that it's either the nectar, or, that I'm actually ready to hear this. Either way, I've got to know what I am, what you think I am, and what is expected of me.'

'Very well,' Maddy exclaimed, casting a quick glance to Jen, making sure she concurred. Jen nodded that she should continue.

Maddy took a deep breath and started. 'You recognize the fact that Jen and I are dragons. We are of a race known as the Drakarim. We were the oldest of the four races.'

Gwen couldn't stop herself butting in. 'Four races? Who are they, then?'

With the patience of a teacher instructing a child, Maddy deviated to accommodate her curiosity. 'Us, the Drakarim; our twin race who branched away at the beginning of our rise – the Unc'anharaphim; the Ch'drnOmThophilim; and yourselves. One you know as dragons, the second as unicorns and the third as angels. But try not to concern yourself too much with them for now. Suffice to say, there have been times when certain individuals have been elevated to positions above that which they were born to. A few of your kind have evolved to join the ranks of the Ch'drnOmThophilim, but that is another tale for another time; as well as far too many of your kind being taken by the Nescarii and subverted to their foul ways.'

Gwen butted in again. 'Nescarii? Doesn't that make five? You just said there were four, including us. Are you trying to confuse me? 'Cos I don't think you'll have to try too hard.'

'Yes and no. The Nescarii are what the inhabitants of the Domain have termed themselves, to differentiate themselves from their brethren, the Ch'drnOmThophilim. You would know them as demons.'

Gwen mouthed a silent 'ah', not wishing to pursue that avenue just yet. Rolling her finger to Maddy, she gestured she should carry on.

'You…' Maddy started again, exasperation just starting to creep in to her teacher's level tones. Gwen was good at getting her to bite every now and then, maintaining that she took matters a little too seriously. This was definitely one of those times, but the residual effect of the nectar was still tingling through her system, making Gwen a little mischievous. The closest to this feeling was once, when she was a girl, having to take a trip the dentist – somewhere she hated. She had to have a wisdom tooth taken out and they had sedated her partially before the operation. During one particular case of verbal diarrhea, she had nearly bitten off the dentist's finger. But, as she recalled, there was no pain and that was the important bit, '…have the opportunity to rise above your species now. That is the choice you must make. We are the avatars of this world, and we are currently just two. Yet now, matters have escalated to such desperate proportions, it is unlike any other time in the history of the known multiverse, whereupon the Earth, weakened as she has become under the onslaught, has been caught off her guard so much so that she is unable to rally herself to fight back. Another must do so on her behalf. It is for that reason alone that we now need to be three. For the first time *ever*, another is called. You, Gwen, must choose to become the third avatar.'

Gwen was grinning inanely before Maddy even finished.

'Fine,' Maddy turned to Jen, placing her hands on her hips in that age-old posture of female irritation.

'You've given her too much. Look at her! She's in no fit state to make such an important decision. We really don't have time for this, you know. We —'

'Shut up, for crying out loud. You're giving my arse a headache.' Gwen frowned at her own analogy, not having a clue what *that* meant, but she continued regardless. 'Giddy I may be, but I'm quite capable of making my own choices. I don't know if it's the nectar or somewhere in between, but I've never felt more free; unencumbered by the practical and logical starchiness I must have inherited from my folks. Anyway, things were getting boring back there, if I'm really honest. Don't get me wrong: it's not that I didn't like everyone or the store. I loved all of them – you, it – but... I'm not the best at settling down. Frankly, I don't know how I managed to stay in one place for as long as I did, have, am...oh you know what I mean.'

Maddy looked for a second like she was going to say something. Her mouth opened, then she thought better of it and closed it again, looking momentarily unsure.

Gwen took the pause as her cue to carry on. 'I mean, it's not every day you get to talk to wolves and stop bullets in midair, is it? No, it's not,' Gwen answered for them before either could speak, and forged on. 'I know it's not every day as well, that the likes of me, one cute English storekeeper, gets to do something like this – something profound. If what you say is right, then I'm needed. It's actually nice to be needed for a change. Not simply needed just because I supply people with objects or the odd coffee, but *really* needed. I like that.'

Gwen shook her head then, in a happy, dizzy, fly-buzzing-around-her-head sort of way. One that had the strange effect of endearing people to her when she did it. It wasn't the reaction they had expected and probably for the first time in longer than even they could remember, they were speechless. Gwen hopped from one foot to the other, gently clapping her hands alternately in front of her and behind her, smiling and looking from one to the other. She cut such a comedic figure, capering about like she was, and naked to boot, that it broke the precarious tension and sent the two avatars into fits of giggles.

'Now you seem to have lightened up a bit...' Gwen continued, smiling to herself and thinking that she had never felt so uninhibited. (She really ought to get the recipe for that nectar; she could make a fortune. And everyone would be a lot happier for it.) *Always assuming it was a legal concoction. Some prissy, anally retentive git in the Government would still try and ban it, though. I swear those miserable bastards want everyone to be just as miserable and hacked off as them. They certainly do enough to piss everyone off already – what's another one to add to the list? Tossers. I swear it's a conspiracy.* '...maybe you can tell me then exactly what being an avatar entails.' This time it was Jen's turn to look stern. Gwen thought they must take it in turns – sort of good cop, bad cop – though her happy thoughts soon vanished, just like a balloon popping, when Jen spoke.

'Firstly, you have to die!'

All of Gwen's previous vindication came flooding back. 'Hah! I knew you were up to no good, and I'll be damned if I didn't let you drug me *again*. I must be some sort of pillock.' She started to back slowly away from the girls, whose eyes were darting left and right, trying to figure out where she was going to run to. Though streaking through the woods didn't exactly fill her with enthusiasm or brimming confidence, at least she might stay alive a bit longer.

'Relax, Gwen. You really must get a grip on this fight-or-flight reflex you seem to have. It's not death in the physical sense. We're not going to beat you over the head with a blunt object, if that's your worry. It's like the death card in tarot: it's change or transformation. The *cute English storekeeper* will be no more, as such. You'll no longer be the proprietor of Earth Angel either; you'll hand it over to another's keeping, much in the same way as it was handed over to you. Dolores will make a fine shopkeeper, don't you think?'

Gwen stilled her urge to flee, but narrowed her gaze to scrutinize the girls suspiciously. 'You mean you're *not* going to kill me then? But you are going to give all my stuff away, my hard-earned and worked-for stuff?'

Both Jen and Maddy shook their heads simultaneously, rolling their eyes skyward as if to say 'Silly girl'.

Gwen saw the look and responded hotly, repeating her words in a poor mimic of Jen's lilting southern accent. '*Firstly you have to die*! What the bloody hell was I supposed to think? It doesn't really leave a lot to interpret, does it? It's not like firstly you have to die means, *would you like sugar with that?* No! It means you bloody well have to die! Of course I'm going to run away. Do I look stupid?' Gwen was standing ankle deep in grass, naked in the middle of the woods, jabbing her forefinger at two casually-dressed girls, who stood smiling at her.

Jen spread her hands wide in a gesture of resigned innocence. 'Well, yes, actually.'

Gwen froze. Without moving, she gave herself the once-over. She had to agree with them. Her expression said more than words. Slowly lowering her arm and folding her wrists over each other behind her back, Gwen kicked one foot through the grass.

'Fair comment. Okay, I admit it did look a little bit like dummy spitting. I'm sure it's all this standing about with my bits swinging in the wind that does it. That's my excuse and I'm sticking to it.'

Maddy walked over and placed a comradely arm around her shoulders. Slowly she turned her and led her back to the fire pit, which by now had burnt down to a few smoldering embers. Maddy winked at it and it roared back into life, blazing merrily away on what appeared to be nothing but rocks and stones.

'There is a phrase, Gwen, one that you have heard before. It says that to give up everything – potentially then, you have everything. So it will be with you. Look at us. Are we unhappy? Do we ever seem to lack anything? No, for all the Earth is ours – so too will it be yours. You will become more than mortal, Gwen, and you will be able to do many extraordinary things. Now sit down again and take a breather: you've had a little too much excitement in too short a time. Here – have a drink.'

Maddy passed Gwen some water and waited patiently while she obeyed. Jen had joined them again and sat on the grass next to Gwen, folding her supple legs underneath her. She started to twiddle with Gwen's hair, in a way she often had when they sat in the store – she would braid little bits while Gwen sat and did paperwork. It was a feeling of familiarity, and Gwen started to relax again. The girls saw the tension slowly ebb from her taut frame, rigid shoulders dropping as her wired muscles unwound.

'Better?' Jen asked softly, for she sat only a few inches from her friend, legs touching as she stroked and fondled Gwen's head and hair. Not in a sexual way this time, but in that indescribable way that brings a sense of comfort and security. Gwen nodded sheepishly, all too aware of her recent behavior. It all seemed so irrational in hindsight and her head swam with memories of her yo-yoing emotions. It was all so surreal, like something she had read about in one of her paperbacks. It was the sort of chain of events that only ever happened to someone else, not her. Though not any more, it seemed. She was about to embark on the adventure of a lifetime if any of what they said was true. Oh, it all sounded fantastic, and Gwen was appreciative to at least still be alive, though even that was about to change, apparently. *I hope it doesn't hurt. I wonder if there's any more of that nectar up for grabs. I'm sure that with enough of that in me I won't feel anything.* With bravado she didn't really feel, Gwen steeled herself to do whatever it was that they required her to do, telling herself repeatedly that it was for a good cause.

'Okay, I feel better now. What do we do next?' It was at that point though, that Gwen realized that something was missing. In fact, the more she thought about it, she realized that it had been missing for some time. The sounds of the forest. The creaking of the trees and the sound of the birds. Squirrels barking as they capered amongst the high branches, and no end of other sounds that made up the constant cacophony of the woodland. She sat in silence now and that – more than anything she had seen or heard since she had arrived at Toadstool Rock – bothered her.

'Why is it so quiet?' Gwen found she was whispering, as though to speak any louder would disturb the eerie silence.

'Why are you whispering?' Jen whispered back conspiratorially, leaning to better share the secret. Before Gwen could answer though, Maddy dropped to her knees beside them both and leant in towards them. And in a hushed tone, she had Gwen look around.

'Gwen, look at the forest edge, slowly and quietly, and you'll see why.'

Slowly, ever so slowly, she began to study the treeline, focusing intently on what she didn't know. But as she concentrated, images began to appear. Hundreds of pairs of eyes looked back. She was being watched in return. The branches were jam-packed with all manner of birds, sitting silently – even reverently – together, riveted upon the clearing and the three two-leggeds within. Gwen gasped as she saw bears and mountain lions, badgers, coyotes and wolves, squirrels and deer; and what she took for grassy clumps were in fact knotted bundles of snakes, all entangled yet calm, watching with their intense reptilian gaze. It was fascinating and terrifying all at once. If Gwen had any doubts about the two girls even up to that point; seeing the animals there, together, dispelled them like a gale force through mist. Creatures that should be attacking and eating each other sat side by side like the best of friends. As her eyes adjusted, she could see further and further into the woods beyond and there were still more of them. There had to be hundreds and hundreds. Whole herds of deer, millions of birds. A disorientating sensation swept over Gwen, causing her to close her eyes and grab her head with a grimace of unexpected pain. Both girls were instantly attentive, cradling her and speaking soothingly.

'Let it go, Gwen, let it go. You're not ready for that yet. You're only halfway there. Let it go.' The pain diminished slightly along with the dizzy swimming sensation that had come over her unexpectedly. In a weak but still awed voice Gwen sought the answers to a myriad of questions that had sprung unbidden to her slightly overwhelmed mind.

'There are so many whats and hows, I don't know where to start. I'm guessing that we are the why.'

Maddy nodded. 'Your mind is reaching out to them already, but it's not quite up to that task. Trying to see through a hundred thousand pairs of eyes will give anyone a pain in the head. In fact, these animals are here to greet the new avatar: you, Gwen. They all came to be the first to see the birth of the one who will nurture them and protect them, succor them in their time of need, and defend them from all who would do them harm. They will become a part of you and you of them. Because you have part-way undergone your connection to the Earth, your mind was susceptible to the draw of the animals. Their need and desire pulled at your unconscious, fragmenting it into a hundred thousand minds. Your eyes saw from all of theirs at once. Fear not though, for after your rebirth, you'll find that a much more pleasurable sensation.'

Gwen was a little frightened by Maddy's explanation but also relieved, assuring herself that a little fear was a healthy thing and that everything would become apparent soon enough. Jen whispered in her ear, keeping her voice low so as to not rattle her delicate sensibilities any further. 'We need you to lie down now, Gwen, flat on your back as though you were doing snow angels. Arms wide and legs spread.'

Gwen blushed uncontrollably.

'Behave yourself, you minx, we're not doing that again.' The humor in Jen's voice relaxed her a little, but she was still nervous. Her stomach tied itself into several knots.

'No matter what happens now, Gwen, you need to relax. I know it sounds lame and we've probably repeated the fact so many times already, but it's true. The more relaxed you are now, the easier it will be. Especially for you. Close your eyes. The next time you open them, you'll see the world as an entirely new place and it'll break your heart. Focus on our song and breathe deeply.' With that, Jen started to sing. Not real words but sounds that appeared like words. It was almost another language and the sounds made the skin on Gwen's arms and legs prickle like a small electric current had been passed through her. She realized then that it *was* another language. The language of Magic. It was a language she had yearned for all her life. Hearing it was as though a missing piece of her soul had finally been found. Seconds after Jen had started to sing, Maddy picked up the melody and repeated it in counterpoint. The effect was phenomenal, amplifying the sensations coursing through Gwen's mind and bringing tears unbidden to her closed eyes.

She never saw the seven intricately cut stones push their way out of the ground around the trio, ringing them with spiral carved stone menhirs. Chunks of crystal protruded from their granite structures and caught, reshaped and subsequently scattered whatever light hit them. Tiny sparks of light flitted between the crystal, and spirals on the rocks and the subtle subdermal spirals indelibly imprinted into Gwen's body. As each sparkling mote flashed upon her skin, the pale turquoise spirals began to glow from within. After only a few seconds of this pyrotechnic display Gwen was almost invisible, cocooned within a halo of soft blue light emanating from her glowing spiral markings. It would have fascinated her had she been able to see it, for she had long been an exponent of the significance and importance of spirals in the governance of the Earth and all around it. The ancients obviously knew this, for why else would it be seen on so many relics and historic archaeological finds. Stone circles, art, jewelry and even within caves.

The chanting singsong melody of the girls continued, wrapping Gwen in a musical sheath to the total exclusion of the outside world. All she now knew was warmth pulsing from her core, and the tingle of the magic – as she liked to think of it – dancing across her flesh. Time began to mean little to her as the harmony carried her along. She could have been lying there for hours or days for all she knew, so entranced by the internal and external stimulation. *External?* This was new. Gwen thought that they weren't doing the touchy feely stuff again? But the more she concentrated on the touch, the less it felt like hands or fingers. It felt more like some snake was coiling about her leg. Legs? And getting higher? She knew she shouldn't open her eyes: they had said so. Maybe it would break the rhythm of whatever they were doing. But Damn! They were getting higher. Any second now they would reach her... Gwen gasped as whatever was coiling itself up her thighs pushed itself gently into her. That was it – she was going to open her eyes and see just what the hell was going on. A wave of indescribable pleasure ripped through her, temporarily cutting off rational thought. This was wrong. Gwen started to panic and when she tried to open her eyes she found she couldn't even do that. Her mind said she wanted to but her body refused to obey. As self-preservation began reassert itself, Gwen tried to bring her arms and legs in to protect her vulnerable body. They were firmly pinned down, as though she had been crucified upon the ground – staked out, star shaped, just like in some old western movie. Gwen tried to scream then; vocalize the horror she imagined was being perpetrated against her, but the moment she parted her lips to yell, a tendril-like thing pushed its way into her mouth and began to force itself down her throat, just as those below her waist pushed up higher into her again. More coiled over her chest, constricting her breathing. Every time she breathed in the coils moved further down her throat. She couldn't move, fight, scream or prevent the invasion. Her mind was howling at her that she was about to die: to effectively drown on dry land as her body was invaded by who knew what. Lights began to flash before her closed eyes as the last remaining vestiges of lifegiving oxygen left her wracked body. Had she been able to see herself lying there in the woodland clearing, she would have seen thousands of tendrils, resembling prehensile tree roots, thrusting out of the earth around her and binding her to the ground, over and over until she was virtually invisible beneath them. Then, as the life Gwen knew began to diminish, seconds before she lapsed into sweet oblivion, the tendrils began to sink back into the earth, taking Gwen with them. Heartbeats later, she had totally vanished, leaving no trace that she had ever been there at all. Gwen, the tendrils and even the disturbed grass had all vanished. Jen and Maddy stopped singing and sat in a contemplative silence for a good ten minutes after, just looking at the spot their friend had occupied only moments beforehand. Slowly and quietly, the decorative and energized stones sank back into the loamy soil from which they had originally arisen. They too vanished completely. Quietly and deliberately, Maddy and Jen tidied the makeshift campsite. Eventually, when they were satisfied that all traces of their presence had been removed, they manifested their hiking clothes back on. Jen tidied her hair as a matter of habit, not through any real need, but it made her feel better.

'Might as well head back home,' Maddy suggested in hushed tones. 'She won't be back for a while. I imagine Dolores could do with a hand adjusting to her new life. I suspect it's all going to come as something of a shock.'

Jen agreed, nodding sympathetically. 'I also suspect, my redheaded friend, that there are some very edgy people back in town, trying to piece together just what has happened to their ordered existence. I reckon we should have a go at diffusing any potential situations. People have a way of going off the handle when something untoward happens to them. They might even get it into their heads to do something stupid.'

Maddy flashed Jen a concerned look which said 'Really? Do you think they would?'

'They're humans, Maddy. It's in their nature to overreact and retaliate with excessive violence. They don't understand what's happening to them, and that lack of understanding makes them unpredictably predictable, if you take my meaning.'

'I do, and I think you might be right, though I don't know that we'll accomplish much. Once people get a bee in their bonnets, they're historically hard to discourage.'

'Well, let's do what we can. I like this little town. It would be a shame if it all went horribly wrong and we had to move somewhere else. Did you keep her car keys? I don't think they need to see two dragons swooping in on them just yet. It might be better to arrive normally. Anyway, I happen to quite like that CD Gwen has playing in there at the moment.'

Maddy laughed even as she shook her head forlornly. 'You're incorrigible! Momentous events are taking place all around us, the world is probably ending, and all you want to do is listen to Robbie Robertson.'

Jen shrugged as if to say 'And?' Maddy gave up, tossed her mane of red hair off over one shoulder as she rummaged in her pocket, and produced a set of keys. She tossed them to Jen, who caught them deftly.

'You drive!' Maddy called back over her shoulder as she wandered off towards the car park, where the Jeep sat.

They were right in their assumption. The moment the girls pulled up at the town square again, they were immediately confronted by several irate police officers demanding an explanation to both their most recent whereabouts and what their involvement was with the massacre three days prior. It took most of their combined powers of diplomacy and coercion to convince them that what they had experienced was something far beyond their capability to handle, and that emergency measures should be instigated to protect those individuals still living and working in the immediate vicinity. They explained that they had been away doing similar for the outlying areas, and Gwen was still out there doing what she could. With a mental nudge, the policemen bought the tenuous explanations though they seemed at a loss as to what to do next, for this really was something they weren't geared up for. It didn't conform to any of the procedures they had in place. The girls didn't like to "nudge" them too much, but the police did need a prod in the right direction and had to be galvanized into the correct course of action: mainly getting everyone together and getting the hell out of Dodge. There was no telling how long it would be before whatever had attacked before, would decide to attack again. With themselves and Gwen temporarily out of circulation, they would all be vulnerable and completely defenseless. Frankly, the girls were stunned the enemy hadn't already wiped out the town. The ferocity of the first attack had been expected, but Gwen was more of a priority than the town. It was part hope and part acceptance that the town may or may not be there when the girls got back. They both sighed in relief when they saw it still stood.

They helped with the clean-up operation for a day, before finding Dolores. She took everything rather well considering the circumstances surrounding them, and vowed to continue the work started by Gwen during her few years as custodian. She confessed that the circumstances now made some sense of Grandma Yellow Deer's most recent dreams. The girls didn't pursue it, for they had great respect for the elderly wise woman and her foretelling. They ran through the books with Dolores, making sure she was happy with all the wholesalers and the bills, for both the store and the house. The Native American woman had been stunned for several hours when she had been given the news of what she was to inherit. Dolores felt that it was all so much of a waking dream but Maddy assured her it wasn't though it would take some getting used to, but asked her not to worry too much because they would help where they could. There were more immediate and infinitely more important things to be concerned about. There were few assurances and little solace to be had, but what they had, they gave to Dolores and her grandmother. Maddy and Jen, a most pragmatic pair, both acknowledging the dangers and the hand of the Great Spirit at work, would be vigilant and do all they could for as long as possible. Satisfied that they had achieved as much as feasible in the short time they had to prepare the townsfolk and the new owner of Earth Angel, they left Santa Fe on the morning of the third day, and headed back up to the woods.

Maddy and Jen didn't know what to look at at first. What should have been a familiar drive to the oft-visited car park and woods soon became a journey into the unknown. Had they not known better, they would have sworn that they had slipped back in time to a more primordial era. Hyde Memorial Park, as it was known previously, no longer existed, it seemed. Something much more vast and brooding had taken its place over the course of forty-eight to seventy-two hours. Huge trees had burst forth, and bromeliads the size of cars hung from their trunks and upper branches. Ferns that could have hid elephants covered the ground, vanishing into the darkness of the immense forest. Jen and Maddy were avatars of the Earth and, as such, they feared very little upon it, but even they felt a touch of trepidation as they drove in, for as Maddy pointed out, the forest was closing ranks behind them as they got further in. There was, it seemed, no turning back.

'Interesting, don't you think?' Jen commented as the Jeep bounced over a bulging root that pushed up across the road. Maddy had to agree. In truth, they didn't know what to expect as a consequence of their actions. All that was transpiring was, as they had told Gwen, so unprecedented. Winding their way up many of the trees and spanning the gaps in between, were wickedly barbed ropes of bramble and dog rose, with stems as thick as mooring rope and covered with spines the size of daggers. As archaically beautiful as the forest now looked, closer inspection revealed it to be infinitely more deadly. Now stopping in the small clearing that used be a sizeable car park, Jen and Maddy abandoned the Jeep and commenced on foot. They saw the lethal undergrowth writhe and twist before them, almost daring them to enter. They looked at each other, silently communicating their concerns. But they needn't have worried, for the moment they drew close enough, the writhing tendrils parted like a bead curtain, revealing a mossy pathway beyond. The moment they put foot to the path, the briars snapped shut behind them like a monstrous organic and sentient bear trap. For all the intimidating display of menace and danger the forest put on when they had first arrived, the path itself was a journey of amazement and beauty. Plants long since extinct flourished. Massive flowers with the most vibrant and intoxicating aromas. Huge fruits of every shape and color hung from branches big enough for two people to walk along side by side. The girls adjusted their clothing to suit their new environment. Short halter dresses and bare feet were the order of the day for them as they strolled casually along the meandering pathway. They were ensorcelled by this "new" ancient forest. The wildlife had certainly taken to it. It could be seen in droves, darting and running through the undergrowth. Occasionally an animal would stop and stare at the visitors. Recognizing them on a deep level for who they really were, the curious animals bowed slightly in acknowledgement and moved on, secure in the knowledge of their total safety. The sounds of birds wove a musical accompaniment as they walked. There was little doubt that this forest was alive, not just with wildlife, *but in itself*. It was a living entity and the girls respected that. A fitting residence for the next earthly avatar. A huge stag, complete with an impressive rack of antlers, stopped mid-flight and stared at the girls. Proud and majestic, it appraised the visitors. Yet for all its own royalty – owner of a bloodline any king would be proud of – it lowered its great head and bowed in silent reverence and respect to the two avatars. Jen and Maddy bowed their heads back in acknowledgment. With a last glance from its intense liquid brown eyes, the deer leapt away and vanished once again into the forest: a wraith that flowed like mist amongst the trees, agile for one of his size and musculature.

The sound of burbling and trickling water caught their attention next. A silvery splashing brook had materialized alongside the pathway and was growing in size the further and deeper they ventured. As they stopped to investigate it, they saw flashes of silver and gold darting below the surface as schools of fish explored their own newly acquired environment. Toads could be seen wandering around the mossy embankment along with frogs and newts. Maddy was enchanted; she didn't know where to look next without seeing some new wonder. Clouds of butterflies and dragonflies filled the air above them, as multihued as any rainbow. Whatever was happening to Gwen was having a direct effect on the surroundings. The closer they got to the area where they had left her, the more profound it became – for they both, Jen and Maddy realised, no longer had any idea where they were in relation to the forest they knew before – they simply walked now at the mercy of the meandering path, resigned to the fact that they would eventually be deposited where they needed to be. The girls recognized many of the features that they had spoken of with Gwen during some of the quieter moments in the store. What she had described as her ideal woodland was now manifesting around them in all its verdant glory.

Progressing onwards with their journey, they saw the babbling brook grow to stream size then up into small river proportions; not particularly deep, but wide enough to move over the landscape and make an impression. Every now and again it would deviate from the path and vanish into the trees, some of which were so vast and sprawling that their root system spanned the watercourse like a bridge, and the river flowed through and beneath it. Bees swarmed around the upper branches. Hives formed and clouds of workers were busy gathering the copious amounts of nectar from the myriad of flowers. Jen commented on the fact that it must make the most wonderful honey and licked her lips appreciatively. She had a bit of a weakness for honey: it satisfied a sweet tooth she vehemently denied she had.

Yet for all their exploration of what the forest revealed to them, what they didn't see was what the forest still hid from them – and that was just how much and how far it had grown. It had spread out and encompassed the original Hyde Memorial Park like the latter was a pot plant in the midst of a forest. Losing track of all time in the semi-permanent twilight of the dense foliage, the girls eventually found themselves in a small clearing; though small wasn't exactly the right word for it as it was the size of a sports hall but this was filled with huge clumps of spongy moss. Enormous geodes had been pushed up and cracked open, revealing the sparkling crystal formations within. They knew they were at their destination, for before them was the biggest tree either of them had ever seen. It dwarfed even some of the huge Redwoods for girth and it surpassed the Brazil nut tree for height. It loomed over Toadstool Rock, making it look like a real fungus. The rock, however, had split. It had cracked in half and the origin of the river sprung forth from within it, creating a good sized pool which the little river ran off from. In the middle of this pool, though it was more like a small lake, was a raised island of grass – the same area of grass that they had left Gwen lying on before she disappeared beneath it. It now sat in the midst of the pool like a reverent shrine. Chalky lines of pale blue spirals could be seen interlacing through the long grass like some ancient hill drawing. Knowing instinctively that they had arrived at the right place, Jen and Maddy sat themselves down on the soft mossy outcroppings and prepared themselves for a bit of a wait.

'I like this grove, Jen,' Maddy commented, her eyes roving around the secluded woodland sanctuary, as they sat listening to the abundant birdsong and general animal chatter. 'Why don't we have anywhere like this?'

Jen laughed and gave Maddy an affectionate shove. 'Because up until now, where could we have gone where humans wouldn't come venturing

292

and trying to get into? Nowhere would have been sacred. And if we had guarded it the way Gwen has this forest, they would have been all the more determined to gain access under the guise of "exploring", "studying". No, they weren't ready for such places as this. Now, with all that is happening, their world is about to – if it hasn't already – change irrevocably. The Adversary has inadvertently brought about an evolutionary metamorphosis for humanity. No matter who wins now, nothing will ever be the same again.'

Maddy could do nothing but agree with Jen's stating of what she had already known. 'So that means we can have somewhere now?'

'If you like, Maddy, but you and I both know that there is so much for us to do that we would never find the time to enjoy the benefit of having it.'

Maddy shrugged. 'I don't know. You know how that desert looks in summer. I'm sure there is a secluded canyon I could call home. Even you could find a little retreat out there. Or, you know how I've had a soft spot for Death Valley. It's not too far away and you don't get many humans wandering around out there, even before this.'

Jen shook her head resignedly, looking at her friend with affection, yet at the same time with the weary look of one who has spent so many long centuries in the same person's company; so much so, a familiarity with how they thought was as ingrained in them as much as their own thoughts. 'How many times have I heard you say this, now? Why don't we wait and see if we even have a world to call home first, 'cos if the Adversary finds whatever it is he's looking for and we don't stop him, then none of it will matter, will it?'

Deflated but realistic, Maddy had to concur. With a deep sigh of her own, for she had always been the more romantically inclined of the pair of them, she accepted what her sister told her and knew it for the stark truth; though it didn't hurt to have dreams, she thought to herself sadly.

'Fair comment, Jen, but enough talk. We should start the song now, I can feel the Earth calling, and she's almost ready.'

Jen giggled at the comment. 'You make her sound like an oven ready meal.' And just for a moment, they both succumbed to the humor of the image, hearing an imaginary 'ping' and the ground spitting out a well-basted and steaming Gwen. But it was hard to try and *not* imagine where the sage and onion had gone.

It was late in the afternoon when the two draconian avatars of earth, fire, air and water began their song of power, their voices raising the vibration of the grove to an electrostatically charged environment. The creatures of the wood added their own counter-harmony to the girls' voices. It became a song the likes of which had never been heard before, nor was ever likely to be heard again. Its power reached out in ever increasing sound waves, pulsing from the forest like the ripples from a pebble dropped into a pool. Only this time, no physical embankment was going to prohibit their passage. Every single living thing on the planet became aware on a level that caused a moment's pause in what they were doing – enough to acknowledge that something had changed, but not as to what.

The song continued into the early evening and it was just as the moon had waxed to its zenith that the sound of wood cracking and splitting began to be heard. Maddy started several little fires going, placing them where the geodes were growing, letting their crystals magnify the light around the grove. It created a spectacularly magical effect.

The sound of creaking and splitting wood continued for about an hour. They stopped singing as the sound abated. Then, with a thunderous retort, the huge tree cracked open. A vertical rent appeared, starting a foot from the ground and finishing some seven feet above. The bark had peeled back to either side, giving the rent a distinct vulval look. A mist began to slip out of the opening and creep along the ground. Swirling around the little fires and dabbling along the water's edge, it lent the whole scene an air of magic and mystical anticipation.

Many of the animals, like before, had come to see what was transpiring. Their own instincts told them that it was a transcendent moment, never to be repeated. This experience would be passed down through their genes to their own young for evermore after this night. Another little evolutionary change for the immediate wildlife.

Jen and Maddy rose, and with the ethereal delicacy of their nature, stepped over to the dark, moist entrance of the tree's core. There they waited patiently, knowing it was only seconds away. Time was measured now in heartbeats. The primal rhythm pulsed within them all, the blood coursing through their bodies keeping time to the natural flows that throbbed within the magical forest. It was almost a countdown to the moment that Gwen would make her reappearance within the living world. Ba-boom, ba-boom, ba-boom, the cumulative hearts beat. Then, upon the thirteenth beat, a glistening, lightly emerald hued foot extended from the darkness; immediately followed by the calf, the thigh, and then the woman herself – a vision of natural perfection: her eyes bright and liquid, her hair lustrous, her breasts pert and defined, and flawless skin, for being tinged slightly green wasn't considered a flaw. Gwen stepped out fully into the night and drank in the atmosphere. She closed her eyes and spread out her arms as if to embrace everything. A shaft of moonlight materialized around her, bathing her in its silvery glow. Her skin flashed and sparkled like the scales of a magnificent fish, cascading every color over her body like mother-of-pearl flashing in the sun.

Then the moment passed, and she relaxed. The shaft of moonlight filtered in to the rest, and what could pass for normality in this fantastic place returned. For a moment, Gwen looked at everything as though she had no idea of where she was, or how she had come to be there; even to looking directly at Jen and Maddy like she had never seen them before. Tilting her head to the side, birdlike, first left, then right, Gwen blinked; and with the one movement of her now double lids, memory came crashing back in, filling the void her transition had created within her. Everything that had happened to her from the moment in the town square came flooding through her, bringing her right up to the moment she now stood within.

'Come here, Gwen, come sit for a moment. I imagine this is all very disquieting and you may need a moment to reorganize your thoughts. You know, get your bearings.' Gwen allowed Maddy to lead her by the arm to one of the spongy mossy seats and she sat, with no real idea of what she was doing. The girls could see her assimilating her thoughts by the way her eyes flashed, but her body just reacted like an automaton.

'How are you feeling?' Jen ventured, hoping that some gentle conversation would help her friend return to herself.

Gwen looked up slowly as though there was a subtle time delay in her hearing what she did and her ability to respond. 'I, er... I.' Gwen shook her head lightly and coughed. Maddy instantly reached over with a manifested stone goblet of cool water from the little lake. Gwen registered the movement slowly, but took the goblet and drank. Slowly at first, then with a growing need. She finished six goblets in all before she tried to speak again.

'I think, that all things considered, I'm actually quite fine.' Even her voice had taken on a slightly more enriched and melodious tone. Gwen noticed this and her hands flew to her throat, thinking that something might be wrong, but there was nothing there to cause or indicate any need for concern. She tried speaking again, as much to hear her voice and get used to it, as it was to actually hear the answers. But as she spoke, she took in her surroundings and then the questions flowed much more freely.

A good hour later, Gwen had run out of her most immediate and pressing questions and was beginning to relax a little. In fact she was fast becoming quite enamored with "her" grove and all it contained. 'It's all so fantastic really; little bits of what happened in there keep flashing up and clarifying themselves. I get a rush of details and it's like I'm there again. Amazing, just so bloody amazing.'

The girls had noticed though, that one thing was conspicuous by its absence: that which she had now become.

'Gwen? Did you see anything else during your sojourn? Anything draconian?'

Gwen looked thoughtful for a moment, then nodded slowly. 'Yes I did, now you mention it. I saw another like you two: the same liquid golden eyes, only this one was more of an emerald green in color. There were roots and ivy milling about her claws and entwining up her forelegs. I remember that it was...' The final memory slotted into place and Gwen's face froze in awe and amazement. '...That was me?' she squeaked eventually.

Maddy and Jen nodded, smiling encouragingly as they did so.

'I'm a... green... I'm a green...'

'Say it, Gwen, it's okay.'

Gwen looked between them again and gave it another go. 'I'm a green dragon?'

The girls beamed, then each jumped up and hugged Gwen like the sister she had now become.

Gwen sat back then, seemingly more relaxed, and sipped her water. Her thoughts took a turn inwards then, for as much it was incredible, the implications of what she now was and how she now looked crept up on her. Looking at her wiggling green toes she mused on trivial things, like wearing sandals again, shopping, and those general day-to-day things that entailed her mingling with the public.

It's a all a bit eco, and if I was in California I might get away with it. But being green and covered in pale blue spirals might prove a tad difficult anywhere else. It's going to play havoc with my social life. Gwen laughed out loud then, surprising her companions and eliciting a look of concern. *What social life? Bloody hell, I don't think I've had one of those since Jefferson, that son of a bitch.* As Gwen reminisced on her former lover, the man she had left England with all those dim and distant years ago, tendrils and plant fronds began to whip and twitch around her, picking up her agitation. *That complete and utter tosser! I hope he's got some nasty sexual disease now – crabs or syphilis or something equally nasty and virulent. That'll teach him to put himself about like that.*

They had been in Ohio, her first point of contact with the US, for about six weeks and things looked rosy. They had big plans. His parents had a small business with a reasonable annual turnover, and Jefferson had long-term ideas that would see it grow to several times beyond its current capabilities. They would have been sitting pretty and Gwen couldn't have been happier, though in hindsight, Gwen couldn't believe how blinded she had been. Her rose-colored spectacles had shielded her from Jefferson's other long-term plan, which, as she found out the hard way, was to shag his way through as many women as he could get his grubby little mitts on.

She had met Jefferson in London, where he had been killing time between conventions. It had been a whirlwind romance. Even though she thought such things only ever happened in books, this time it really was happening to her and she still had trouble believing it. Swept off her feet by the slick, smooth talking farm boy from good old Ohio, she was captivated when he suggested that she go back home with him. She dumped everything – already disillusioned with college. She packed a rucksack, grabbed her passport and whatever money she could lay her hands on, and ran. But their rosy future turned bleak when a horrific road accident took both his parents just short of two months after they returned home, thrusting Jefferson into the role of managing director of his father's firm. He had barely had time to mourn when he took command. He simply wasn't ready for the pressure, so he took his "stress management" out on just about every female he came across. Gwen caught him one Saturday afternoon, about three weeks after the funeral. She had turned up unexpectedly at the office – the car had packed up so she took a cab back to let him know. He had triple A recovery so he could get it picked up off the freeway where she had abandoned it. He wasn't easy to find at first so she asked a few people if they'd seen him. Last known destination was heading to the stockroom for inventory; they said he had told them not to bother him as he would be concentrating. He'd been there for about an hour. Oh, he was concentrating all right. Her first view was of his pale, sweaty ass pumping in and out for all he was worth with the reception-ist, Diane something or other. *Diane slut*, Gwen amended to herself.

Her mousy brown hair was flopping over her eyes as she was bent over several sacks, her butt poking up just like the proverbial bike rack, squashing out with every thrust; oversized breasts swinging back and forth in rhythm to his pounding. Moans and gasps were competing with his exhortations. *You dirty little whore, c'mon, give it to Papa!* Those words had stuck with her and were the first things she heard in her mind whenever she thought of the cockroach. They would have looked quite funny if she wasn't so pissed. Reaching in quietly, suppressing her fury and outrage, partly at herself for not spotting the signs sooner, she scooped up the pile of discarded clothes and backed out quietly before they saw her. They certainly hadn't heard her, rutting like animals. Knowing they were both naked in the stock room gave her an idea that cheered her up a little. She closed the door, quietly locked it and broke off the key. As she left, after clearing out his safe for what Gwen considered was her due, she hit the fire alarm. To this day, she would have liked to have seen their faces when the firemen broke down the door to let them out. With the air-con blasting cold air out and after the sprinklers had soaked them, they should have been a sorry state. Gwen took the first Greyhound out and, as luck would have it – or in retrospect maybe not luck but something else – it was destined for Albuquerque, New Mexico. The rest, as is said, is history. So much for men.

'So, is this going to fade at all?' Gwen's abrupt question startled the two girls, who were still hovering anxiously, concerned that even though she had come back physically, her mind may have not made it back. 'Or am I going to be green for the rest of my life?'

'Sorry?' Jen responded, quickly regaining her thoughts from assuming the worst.

'I mean,' Gwen continued as though she had never been answered, 'you're not white and Maddy's not red, so why the bloody hell am I green? It doesn't seem entirely fair.' Gwen pouted, yet before either could respond to her query, Gwen clapped her hands together and jumped up grinning. The girls looked worried again.

'I've got it! I'm not ripe yet! That's it, isn't it? I'm like a little green tomato. Maybe I should curl up in a drawer for a week or two. Will I go red or yellow?'

'Are you quite finished?' It was Maddy this time, almost stamping her foot. Exerting her authority. Both Gwen and Jen turned to look at the annoyed looking redhead. Gwen had the good grace to look contrite, bowing her head slightly, though she kept her eyes on Maddy, giving her a coy, shy look.

'Sorry, Miss, won't do it again, Miss.' Keeping her knees together, Gwen scrubbed one foot back and forth like she was putting a cigarette out. Holding her hands behind her back completed the image. Maddy threw up her hands in consternation and stomped off several feet, muttering. Jen smiled and knew that Gwen was just winding up the easily baited Maddy.

'I take it you are actually okay, Gwen. Not too traumatized by it all?'

Gwen looked up then, straight in to Jen's eyes so there could be no misunderstanding. 'I'm fine, really. Shocked, surprised, a bit giddy I suppose. It is, after all, a lot for a girl to take in. But if you are referring to my marbles, well, they are all there. However many there were before this anyhow. So, joking apart now, am I going to stay green?'

'Not if you don't want to,' Jen assured her in her most reassuring tone. 'But that said, there are some things you need to master. And quickly.'

'Go for it. After the last few days or weeks or however long I've been gone again, I'll have a go at anything.'

Maddy rejoined them and took her seat again, glowering at Gwen. She hated being wound up and set off like some clockwork toy. Gwen always said she took things a little too seriously and Gwen made it a point to demonstrate that at every opportunity. Almost without fail, Maddy bit.

'You saw us in our draconian forms, so how do you think we get all that in here?' Jen patted herself on the chest and waited to see what Gwen came up with.

'Pass. Next question.' Gwen shrugged. 'I have no idea. Dehydration?' She ventured.

Maddy groaned, looking askance at Gwen, who shrugged as though butter wouldn't melt in her mouth.

'What? How the hell should I know? I'm not a physicist or a biologist. It doesn't seem possible to get all that into that.' Gwen mimicked something big being squashed into something considerably smaller, by flinging her arms out then bringing them back in to hold something tiny in her hands. 'I imagine you are going to tell me though, otherwise it would be conversation going nowhere, wouldn't it? Please!' Gwen implored, 'Don't be treating me like a mental case. I'm fine now, but I'm still as impatient as I was and even though I've just gone through some incredible shit, which…' She forestalled their imminent interruption, '…I know – it will all become apparent in due course. But for now, I'm finding I have a need for some simple facts, not science lessons. And don't be asking me questions about what you want to tell me. I hate riddles and they make me crabby, correction, crabbier than I already feel. So please, again I ask: just tell me what I need to know to get a handle on all this. Don't beat around the bush, no pun intended.'

It was the most coherent speech that Gwen had come out with for a while and it took the girls aback. They had been dealing with denial, fear, paranoia and no end of other human emotions all vying for attention within Gwen. This had the semblance of rationality and they both felt a weight lift. Maybe there was hope after all.

'Very well. The abridged version it is. But do stop us if there are any questions: much of what we tell you has to be mastered by you, not just known about.'

Gwen nodded and waved impatiently for them to continue. Jen stood, adopting unconsciously the role of the teacher. She began to speak as though she were instructing a class. Gwen assumed it was another of her incarnations and sat back to listen. As she did so, without any conscious thought, she reached up and an obliging branch dipped down, depositing a big juicy apple in her outstretched hand. Jen stopped and watched, stunned. Her mouth paused halfway through shaping a word. Gwen took a bite of her apple and with a little spray of juice, she mimed a 'what?'

Jen mimed back, holding the apple, with a question of her own. Suddenly Gwen realized what had happened and she blanched, looking in horror at the apple as though it had crawled into her hand of its own volition.

'I don't know how I did that, honestly. I wasn't thinking about it except that I really fancied one right then. Wow. Neat trick.'

'Gwen, you are now capable of many such neat tricks. Obviously your subconscious has adapted to your new role; it just maintains to adapt your conscious mind to accepting what and who you now are. You are Gwen, the avatar of nature. The living embodiment of flora and fauna. The natural world responds to your will as easily as you lifting an arm to scratch your ear. Your thoughts are their actions. The same principle applies to your body now. It is as malleable as your thoughts.'

Gwen scrunched up her face as though she was concentrating on understanding what Jen just said. 'You are saying, right, that I can change my body by thinking about it?'

Nodding. 'Basically, yes. Its simple name would be molecular manipulation and density compression or expansion.'

Gwen looked agog and shook her vibrant and lustrous locks in a mock confusion.'If that's the simple term, you can keep the technical one to yourself. What's that in idiot terms? I'm not up on the science part that much. I know the basics to an extent but complex stuff I never really got along with.'

Jen smiled. She knew Gwen's dislikes. 'You're a shape shifter. You can be anything that this planet contains. You have the capability to rearrange your molecules to conform to whatever your mind requires. It is an exterior process though; you are still yourself within, whatever form you adopt. Likewise, as you demonstrated a few minutes ago, you can also manipulate the flora to your mind's will.'

Gwen looked thoughtful as several memories spun up within her. Disjointed images from her incubation. She knew that they weren't hers but she couldn't decipher what they were trying to impart to her. They were hazy, messy, as though she were seeing someone else's thoughts through a crystal ball. But amongst it all, Gwen felt certain impressions. It felt as though she was now the repository of an accumulated wealth of information, provided by any number of souls over the course of the Earth's lifespan. *Maybe I'll add my little bit to whoever comes next. That won't be much then.*

'I don't know, you'll have to bear with me but I think that I'm kind of remembering stuff that I didn't have before...' She grimaced slightly at the memory. 'I'm seeing a woman – tall, lithe, almost willowy, long white robes, I think. Crap!' Gwen looked mortified. 'Sorry, I sound like one of those people who invents mystical looking spirit guides or the likes; but I'm not, I assure you. I remember her thoughts, if that makes any sense. Let me see.' She paused while she organized what she wanted to say so it made sense to her as much as to those who would hear it.

'I think she is saying that I can "borrow" molecules from all around me. Does that make sense?'

Maddy beamed and came rushing over, and gave Gwen an impromptu hug.

'Thanks, Maddy, but what does it mean?'

Maddy sat back and pondered for a second how she would explain it all. There were no easy options, so she bit the bullet and went for it. 'Well, in a nutshell...'

Maddy was interrupted by a groan from Gwen. 'Very droll,' Gwen moaned at the unintended pun. 'Nutshell? Get it?'

Maddy rolled her own eyes skyward, smiled wanly that she did, and tried to carry on. 'Absolutely everything is comprised of highly charged molecules, all resonating at their own individual frequencies and speeds. They are in all objects, water, even the air. You now, as with all the higher races to an extent, have the ability to add and subtract the number of molecules you need at any given time. If you opt to take your draconian form, which you now possess, by the way.' Gwen's facial expression told Maddy all she needed to know about that little revelation. 'I take it you've seen that in one of your new memories too?'

Gwen nodded dumbly. She *had* seen several disturbing images of flight and of seeing a pair of massive emerald hued reptilian wings where her arms should have been. It had been a most disconcerting yet oddly exhilarating experience.

'Good. Now to continue – all your little spherical molecules are held together by a force, a current, a charge. Call it electricity but it is fundamentally more vital than that. It is the force that holds your molecules together and binds them, constructing the physical form and all that goes with one. Blood, bone, tissue, sinew, veins, and the list is endless. They all rely on this life force. Once the alternator or generator that is you...' Maddy poked Gwen in the chest, eliciting a disgruntled 'ow', '...stops supplying the energy, or put another way, death, the electromagnetic field that holds the molecules together ceases and the binding capability stops; the molecules just drift away from each other in every random way imaginable. Decomposition is the result. No power, no life. You've seen no end of those TV doctors give the patient a jolt when they have a cardiac arrest. Well, it's the same thing. It's like giving a car a boost. You can now manipulate that force. The looser your molecules the less dense you become. Eventually you would become gaseous if you loosened them too much. Alternatively, you can compress those you have and become heavier than lead and harder than diamond. You would become as immovable as a mountain should you require it to be so.'

Gwen was assimilating this news as fast as she could; the implications were astounding. The more she thought about it though, the more questions sprang into her head.

'This all sounds like so much science fiction. Why haven't our scientists figured this out yet? It all sounds so simple. Like me tuning the radio of my mind into the frequency of whatever it is I want to connect with. Hey,' Gwen squeaked excitedly, 'like that branch with the apple on. I didn't even really think about that. It just... sorta happened, if you follow me. Shit, I'm blabbering now. Calm down, Gwen,' she muttered to herself.

'You're right, Gwen.' Jen picked up the thread of the conversation then. 'It is a logical science; the trouble, of course, is *knowing how* to tune in to something. That's another matter altogether. You can do this because you are now genetically superior to your fellow humans. You are now Drakarim.'

The process was almost visible on Gwen's face. Her flawless brow furrowed briefly as she put the pieces together; and they were coming together, with frightening clarity.

'So what does that mean, "genetically superior"? I'll keep my hair when I'm old, or what? What exactly have I become?' Gwen couldn't help but wonder how many more times she was going to ask that.

'Drakarim, Gwen, are the eldest of the four higher races, as we explained to you before. They have moved even closer to the fiery hub of this spiraling solar system. Closer even than the angels. This means they have evolved even further physically. Whereas before, as a mortal, you had only a double helical DNA strand and a mere forty-six chromosomes...'

'Mere?' Gwen snapped. 'You make it sound like we're a bunch of amoebas. Ah, look at the little single-cell organism,' she whined in a peeved sort of way, letting the girls know she didn't like being condescended to, nor should they do it to others. Especially her.

'...Well, you have a few more now,' Jen continued smoothly. 'Four hundred and twenty-two more to be precise; and if you can imagine your double helical DNA strand as one of thirty-two others, giving sixty-four strands in total, that's what you have now. Mortals to you now *are* as close as that amoeba to you, and that's not being condescending; it's a fact. One you'll have to get used to, I'm afraid.'

Gwen was stunned. She didn't feel any different. She had become something from a fantasy story. She was a genetically altered fucking dragon! Not even human any more. Gwen was numb. Her emotions had seized up on her. What was she to feel about this? *I know I volunteered to do this – but what have I done to myself? I'm not even Gwen any more. I can't be; I'm not human.* Gwen's mind was reeling at this new bit of information. But there was no going back now; she had to get a handle on it, and fast. *Starting with my bloody clothes; enough is enough.*

'If that was your potted version, I think I'll hold back from the detailed one for a while. What I do want, however, is my damn clothes. By your reckoning, I've been out here and naked for ten days or so. That's quite enough, don't you think?'

'So what do you want to wear?' Maddy returned, putting the ball back into Gwen's court.

'What have you got?' Gwen batted back, used to this tennis type conversation.

'Actually, Gwen, it's more like what have *you* got. Have you not been listening?'

'What?' Gwen shot back, getting annoyed again at the ambiguous and riddle-like statements of her so-called friends. They wanted her to do something but couldn't manage a straight answer when pressed. 'Look. I'm a bit frazzled at the moment. Can you just take some pity on little old me and just tell me what you're trying to say?' She dropped her shoulders and gestured to them imploringly to give up what they knew.

'Do you remember what I said five minutes ago about molecular manipulation? If so, Gwen, my little fruitbat, close your eyes and manipulate some molecules. Choose something you are familiar with. Try your sweater, jeans and your Ugs. Imagine you are wearing them. Visualize yourself in them.'

She did. A light tingling rippled over her body and caused her to open her eyes and see what had happened.

'Oh my God! That's incredible!' Gwen didn't know which bit of herself to look at first. Her favorite sweater was there, and it felt so real. Jeans and Ugs both were fitting her as though they were made especially for her, which in a way, they were. She clapped both hands on her buttocks and admired the way her jeans hugged her rear. 'Does my butt look big in these?'

The girls clapped their approval at Gwen's initial success. Jen held up a hand and water from the pool leapt up to gather around her outstretched fingers. She rolled the water around in the air, pulling it this way and that, and then she flattened it, compressing its molecules into disc shapes. This had the effect of creating a floating, ever so slightly rippled, watery mirror.

'Take a look.'

Gwen wasted no time twirling and spinning before the mirror, checking her reconditioned figure. She got up close to have a better look at her face and skin. Other than the slight green hue and pale blue spirals, it looked fresh and toned. Even the tiny crow's feet that she had noticed forming, had gone. *I didn't look this good at eighteen. Gwen, you lucky girl, this is one perk you can certainly live with.* It was as though Jen had picked up on her thoughts, moving to stand beside her. They both looked at their reflections. Each looked no older than twenty, but by Jen's reckoning, she and Maddy were several thousand years old, if not older. And they still looked stunning; Gwen was amazed.

'Can I do anything about this green shade though? I suspect I'll look a bit seasick in certain lights.' Gwen secretly thought she looked a bit like the wicked witch from the *Wizard of Oz*, only without the pointy hat and dodgy nose. It made her smile a little.

Jen told her to try the same thing as she did with her clothes. And she managed it with equal effect. She squealed and hopped with excitement, just like a ten-year-old at Christmas having been given every present they had asked for and then some. Gwen was scrutinizing herself like she had never seen her reflection before. 'I'm sorry to seem overwhelmed by this, but it's incredible, and you're telling me that I'm going to look like this for a very long time?'

'I don't like to say forever, considering the crisis we are currently in the midst of, but essentially, yes. You are reborn, Gwen, quite literally. You have become the epitome and living embodiment of nature. The sap that flows through your body now will perpetually rejuvenate you. You are as perfect as you can be and will stay that way for as long as the Earth endures – which won't be much longer unless we get down to business. After all, there was a reason this was done to you, and it wasn't so you could gaze at yourself all day.'

Gwen felt the gentle rebuke by a warming of her cheeks. 'You're right. I'm sorry; I've been incredibly selfish about all of this. Chucking my toys *way* out of the pram. It's been all about me, hasn't it.' The rhetorical question wasn't lost on the girls, and they nodded sadly. 'All I've thought about is what I've lost, not what the rest of humanity stands to lose. So…' Gwen stood straighter, more determined than at any other time she could recall, '…I've accepted my fate, my destiny or whatever it is I have now. So I guess it's about time you told me what it is that is expected of me.'

Without thinking, Gwen made to sit down. used to having her sofas in the store. As she moved, several roots rose up from the soil and tied themselves into a chair shape. A slightly surprised Gwen sat in her makeshift furniture. Giving it a quick once-over, she tried to create the same for the girls. Two more chairs wove themselves into existence and the girls sat.

'Very good, Gwen. It is as well you are a quick study. Let's hope you adapt as well away from your grove.'

For the next hour Gwen badgered them about "my grove" and where her new power would be the strongest. And they in turn broke the news to her about the nature of her quest. This stemmed the tide of her questions like a tap being abruptly turned off. All the elation that had started to stir her in ways she had never dreamt of – well actually *had* dreamt of but never expected them to come anywhere near true – evaporated like so much smoke. Her very natural high came crashing down around her ears. She mentally weighed up the implications of what they told her, her mind turning over like a book having its pages flipped. But not on any one of them could she see the answer she so desperately sought. Within several heartbeats, she had run out of options. Gwen began to pace the grove, her bare feet scuffing through the wet grass at the edge of the pool. With a nervous habit she had never let go,

Gwen began to chew on her little finger. The enormity of what they had just asked of her began to assert itself and her earlier panic started to rise in her breast again, threatening to stop her breathing altogether.

'I have absolutely no idea where to start!' Gwen finally blurted out to the girls, who had waited patiently for their friend, but this wasn't the news they wanted to hear.

'You have to know something, Gwen,' Jen protested, 'you were the chosen one for the Earth. Does nothing stir in your memory now? What with all you've gained, has it not unlocked the answer?' Both Jen and Maddy, for the first time Gwen could recall, looked concerned, genuinely concerned. Gwen was stunned, angry and terrified all at once. And not for the first time she realized: *the ups and downs of this are more likely to kill me than anything at this bloody rate. Get a grip, Gwen old girl. Breathe, that's first.* She took several long deep calming breaths, regulating her erratic heartbeat and relaxing suddenly bunched muscles. Slumping down on a mossy pad, Gwen tried to tackle it from another direction.

'How is it that you don't know its whereabouts? Or for that matter, how is it the Earth herself doesn't know? Surely of any of us, it would be her.' Gwen looked desperately between the two but they only shook their heads sadly to the negative. 'Crap! Well, I just don't know. How do you hide something like that?' Gwen had started to fidget again, putting her left foot on top of her right, monkey fashion, toes gripping the other foot. That was the least obvious sign of Gwen's agitation. The more blatant indication was the undulating and writhing foliage that was giving the forest a malevolent demeanor, reflecting its mistress's anxiety.

'Gwen, you must understand, it was hidden long before the Earth grew to the sentience she now possesses.' Maddy had stood and had picked up the pacing started by Gwen. 'She hid it to protect herself from just this type of predicament. Let's face it, if it was that easy to find, we probably wouldn't be having this discussion now. Nor would the Adversary be in the position he – through pure ill fortune – finds himself in.' There was no denying the logic to hiding the damn thing, but some clue would be useful, Gwen thought, her irritation just making the forest rustle all the more.

'It's amazing really, isn't it, when you get right down to it. You railroaded me in to this big transformation – ' They started to protest but Gwen held up a silencing hand and they held back their expected argument. 'I've sacrificed my humanity, my life and everything I was, to assist in this great calamity, only to find that the one thing you had me do it for puts us absolutely no further forward than we were before we did it. Why didn't you just ask me before? I could have told you then I had no idea.' The venom was taken out of the comment by the beatific smile Gwen wore. She knew that she had reached a point where rollercoaster had reached the end of the ride. Beset by irony and conflict on all sides, she knew the only way forward was going to be a physical search. Whatever clues or ideas she might have would have to be tackled by her direct presence. And that meant a serious amount of traveling in a decreasingly short time. It really was, how long is a piece of string? The Adversary could complete whatever it was he was up to at any moment. Then what? The End? Just like that?

Sitting for what seemed like hours, though in truth it was only a few moments, Gwen tried to formulate a plan. She had to put on a brave front, for there really was no going back now. She was good at ignoring what she didn't like and pressing on with what she did. Stubborn and mule headed had been a couple of the names she'd had applied to her. There wasn't much to like here – the end of the world and all that – but it was, for the moment at least, outweighed by things that she did like. Certainly for the time being.

Her mother always said: First things first. She wasn't going to go searching anywhere unless she got a handle on what she could do. Adversary or no, she needed at least rudimentary capabilities if she was to get by out in the big bad world. That meant trying the shape shifting thing that the girls had mentioned. After all, if things were as bad as they made out, there probably weren't any planes flying. Not commercial ones anyway. So birds might not be a bad place to start. Resolved. For now, Gwen stood and approached

Maddy with a determination she didn't fully feel, but was adamant that she would be seen as having. Stopping before the girls, legs braced and arms folded: 'Right then, we're not going to do much sitting on our collective asses and blowing smoke up mine to make me feel better. There are some things you need to show me if we're to go gadding about on this wild goose chase.'

Another crash.

'We?' Jen and Maddy looked surprised for a second before their grim visage took over again. 'Sorry, Gwen, but there are other matters that we have to attend to; this quest will be yours alone. We won't be coming with you.'

If the rugs beneath Gwen were as numerous as cats' lives, then she was on her last legs. Just when she thought that she was over the big shocks: *Wrong again. Maybe I ought to just expect the worst of everything every time. That way I won't be disappointed. This is* not *going the way I had planned.*

'Marvelous. Kick me a bit more. Why don't you? How long did you two have to get used to what you are? A bit longer than me, I bet. This is getting ridiculous. Back, forth, and back again. It's bloody well like passing your driving test on a Monday, and on Tuesday being told you have to chauffeur the Royal Family around, in an unfamiliar car on foreign roads. I mean, how do you handle something like that? I'll tell you how,' Gwen continued. 'Not very bloody well, that's how.' Her mood didn't improve when they just smiled at her. *That's all they fecking well seem to do: smile at me like I'm some kind of pet that's learning to perform its tricks. I'm not some performing seal or the like.*

'Well I'm not a pet, do you hear me? I'm not. Stop grinning like that – it's driving me round the bloody bend. What,' she growled, 'what do you find so amusing *now?*'

'What else? You – you ditzy object. Why are you blathering on about pets? We know you're not one of them; they do as they're told. But *that's* not in your make-up, is it?'

Gwen shook her head in tacit agreement, though she felt slightly manipulated at that point and her suspicious nature took over again. 'What are you getting at then? What are you saying now? I'm having a moment here, and I can't figure out why you don't take me seriously any more.'

'We do, Gwen, believe me we do.' Maddy and Jen flanked Gwen and herded her to the centre of the clearing. 'That's why we think you'll make a formidable dragon. You need to know your secondary form; it's who you are now.' It hadn't even occurred to Gwen that she would have to assume this other shape. Her mind had accepted the fact but only in a tenuous, sort of surreal kind of way. The abrupt change of subject put her off her pace. They were good at reading her moods and steering her back on course. Gwen nodded her agreement and let Maddy continue her *lesson*. 'So why don't I go first, then you try to copy me, okay?' But for Gwen's nervous annoyance, she couldn't help but be thrilled at the prospect of "going dragon". Her stomach started to turn somersaults and she found herself grinning like a simpleton. This was the first time since her *cocooning* – as she had come to think of it – that she had seen the dragon forms of her companions. Other than being incredibly exciting, it would still the final nagging doubt in the back of her mind. The one that said she was hallucinating after too many wild mushrooms.

In less time than it took to think her thoughts, Maddy had swiftly executed her change. Gwen was impressed at the speed she had done it. *God! I'll never do it that quick. I'll probably end up looking like a big iguana or something.* Inwardly amused and terrified at the same time, Gwen walked out into the clearing, looking around her to see if she had enough room. Mentally, and without any direct intent, she imagined the trees moving back out of the way, and to her total amazement, that's just what they did. Amidst rustling and crackling of branches and leaves, about sixty feet of treeline backed up, creating a much wider clearing. A voice in her head spoke clearly to her, as though the speaker were at her ear. It spoke words of encouragement and was accompanied by a very strong sensation of love. Warmth and affection that mere words had no conception of. It swathed Gwen in an aura of wellbeing and made her breast swell with a love and pride of equal intensity.

'Your mastery of your new abilities is so instinctive, Gwen. Well done! Bear that in mind in future, for it will aid you more than rational thought. Let your intuition guide you. Perhaps that knows where you will need to concentrate your search.' It was Jen's gentle southern tones that spoke to her. It put her in mind of the difference in her old radio, of how the sound was monotone and flat, whereas the voice in her mind came through in nine point one surround sound. It was almost four-dimensional. 'For now though,' she continued, her tone firming ever so slightly, 'I want you to concentrate on Maddy. Close your eyes and visualize her in your mind. Picture every scale; every muscle, horn and fang. Create an image in your mind. Of course, you'll want to pick your shade. Green, I expect, but the details are yours, *ma Cherie*. But once you have it fixed firmly in your mind...' Jen's voice was fluid, as watery and musical as the rivers she presided over. It was almost hypnotic but it held Gwen's full attention, and she focused on every nuance and magical syllable as it echoed within her skull.

'Okay, I've got the image there. I can see it. It's looking right at me with those glorious golden swirling eyes you have, and its long reptilian tongue is flicking out at me, tasting the air.' Gwen felt Jen's mind touch again, soft yet powerful. It was as though her mind could snuff her out with barely a cross thought, so potent was its presence.

'...And once you have the image there – move your consciousness into it. Imagine you are behind those golden eyes and looking out. Take a deep breath and fill your lungs with the sweet woodland air; taste the multitude of scents that abound. Be the dragon, Gwen; be it.'

Gwen opened her eyes and after a sudden rush of vertigo passed her by, she realized that she was, or at least her head was, some considerable distance off the ground.

'*Oh – my – God!*' Gwen thought back out to the girls, or at least so she hoped. *'This is just bloody fantastic.'* She swung her own massive head around to check herself out. She flapped her wings experimentally and much to her joy and surprise, they actually rose and fell at her command. Her tremendous forelegs were like her arms and she inspected the sword-length talons on her car-sized feet. It took her another good hour of this scrutiny to fully acquaint herself with her new form. But once she had given herself a thorough inspection Gwen felt pleasantly comfortable as the huge fern-green earth dragon.

'So this is what I am now? At my cellular level, I'm genetically a Drakarim?'

'You most certainly are, Gwen, *ma petite*, a most impressive one at that. Well done!' Jen swiftly adopted her own ice-white dragon form and there – for the first time in the history of the solar system and of this sequence of planets, the trinity of avatars were together, standing as one in the first sacred grove of the avatar of nature.

The atmosphere was palpable, charged with raw primal power. The air became thick with the magic emanating from the three. They were living conduits to the Earth herself and the power she wielded. Even in her weakened state it was awesome. The devastating force of the oceans, the winds and of the volcanoes and mountains. She could feel it all thrumming through her bones. She was connected to these forces in a tangible and very real way. Intuitively feeling her own power. That of every living thing that swam, crawled, walked and flew. Everything that grew from the living soil. Every single blade of grass to every fragrant blossoming flower on the vine in the highest tree of the most distant jungle. She felt connected to her core. She expanded to the size of the planet in an instant, only to shrink to the size of a grain of sand in the next. She experienced the microcosm and the macrocosm in as many heartbeats as it took to say it.

Gwen lost track of time as the images flowed through her and around her, binding her to all she saw. From the most diminutive and minute to the most expansive, she touched it all. Gwen knew then more than she had ever known anything in her brief life, that nothing was insignificant; that everything was an intrinsic part of the weave. The warp and weft of the delicately balanced collection of life on Earth. And if she thought that was sufficient to blow her mind, she hadn't counted on the Earth herself making her presence known. There was a concussive shock wave like she had stood on a nuclear warhead and it had gone off beneath her. The wave resonated up her legs and with a blinding flash in her mind, she felt and saw *all* the dragon lines that permeated the Earth: the lines of force and lifegiving power that mortals termed "ley", taken from the old English term, but which were nothing less than the veins of the Mother. Gwen wanted to express her joy, astonishment, elation and wonder in words, but she couldn't find any that could do justice to what she was experiencing. What came from her was nothing short of a cry of exultation, torn from her gigantic lungs and ripped from her throat, that sent every bird skyward and stopped creatures dead in their tracks for hundreds of miles around. The townsfolk in nearby Santa Fe, Albuquerque and even distant Brazil stopped, curious as to the ululation that raised the flesh on the arms of those that heard it and felt it. It was the first cry of the earth avatar and its sound would resonate out for all time, as the shock wave from her cry rippled out over the planet's surface, connecting with every living thing out there, bonding and binding with all on a cellular level – touching everything on the Earth before cascading off and out into the cosmos.

Jen and Maddy, in their draconian forms, stood back from Gwen in a sign of both respect for her ascendance, and out of awe for the untapped wellspring of unadulterated power Gwen seemingly possessed – another factor that was unprecedented. They had no idea of her limits or potential. Nor at that moment did Gwen, swept along as she was by the outpouring of emotion and energy from the Earth. It built within her like a pressure cooker and Gwen knew of no way to expel it before she exploded. The only thing she could think of was to bunch her muscular hind legs and extend her huge leathery wings, veiny membranes catching the minutest of breezes. She flexed her talons and with an explosive thrust, she shot herself skyward, so fast, she created several sonic booms as she tore through the sky. Upwards and upwards she screamed – only stopping when the sky turned from a vibrant blue to the hazy black of space itself.

Coming to her senses somewhat, Gwen was exhilarated at her new-found abilities and the connection forged with the planet and all upon it. With that connection, however, came a new feeling: a profound sense of purpose and possessiveness. This was *her* world. The Adversary, if he did but know it, had made a powerful new enemy this day and Gwen vowed to herself as she soared high in the atmosphere of her world, that she would do all she could to thwart the machinations of this demonic pretender.

'Return to us, Gwen!' The twin voices of Jen and Maddy reverberated though her skull with, she noted, a hint of concern coloring their call. Relishing the power of flight, Gwen arrowed downwards towards her grove and the clearing way beneath her. Of course, it never occurred to her that she would send no end of military installations into a tailspin as they tracked her sudden arrival and subsequent disappearance. As though they didn't have enough problems already. Poor old New Mexico had yet another Roswell in the making. She was a UFO all right – the *Ultimate Flying Object*, Gwen thought wryly.

She returned to her grove, making a better landing than she thought she would considering the fact she had never done it before. It wasn't something she had considered when the moment inspired her impromptu flight. Once on the ground though, Jen and Maddy spent the rest of the afternoon with her, practising some of the more peculiar shapes she might employ. Birds, fish, insects and even plants. Mostly in the hope that her intuition might provide some insight into the nature of her quest, and where that which she must seek might be found. But nothing presented itself. The sun eventually set on the most strange, yet amazing day of Gwen's life. She only hoped she lived long enough to appreciate the sweet memory. A memory she would treasure in the dark days to come.

The trinity relaxed by the pool in the clearing. Gwen was quite adept by now at adjusting her clothing and she had been having a mighty fine time donning various ensembles to find one she felt "avatarish" in, but she couldn't decide on any one thing. So, settling for her own clothes for the time being, she munched on an apple – kindly provided by the forest along with a number of other woodland delicacies – and asked the question that had been haunting her.

'Tell me again, just so I can get it fixed in my mind what it is I've got to find. I've tried to think about it throughout this afternoon but I keep coming up blank.'

Maddy swiped the dribbles from a particularly juicy nectarine from her lips before speaking. The little humanistic trait made Gwen chuckle. Such human mannerisms from two creatures so otherworldly and powerful that they seemed so out of place now. 'It is simply, Gwen, nothing other than the First Tree. The original tree that seeded all that we now have. The tree that appears throughout human culture. The tree of life, tree of knowledge, Yggdrasil the world tree, so on and so on. The one and only tree that can kill or cure the Earth, depending on who finds it first. We pray that it be you, Gwen.'

So do I. Bombarding the girls with questions about the whys and the hows after an hour bore no fruit either about its previous locations and why the Earth herself didn't know its whereabouts. Gwen mulled over what and where she might have to go to locate such a thing. The enormity of the task and what they expected of her was almost overwhelming, and the prospect of scouring thousands of square miles of jungle for one tree didn't fill her with joy either. *There has to be a way, or a place: something we've missed. Something that has slipped from the records. Knowing my bloody luck it'll be in somewhere obscure like Atlantis or Avalon or somesuch, and look how much luck humanity has had in finding them.* Gwen snorted in disgust. *Instinct they say. Well, they obviously don't know my track record with that particular ability, or lack thereof, though I suppose I ought to have more faith in it now, all things considered.*

At some point during the conversation, Jen excused herself, citing an important errand that needed attending to. Jen crossed over to Gwen and hugged her; long and with an intensity that brought a lump to Gwen's throat and a knot of panic to her stomach. It was the type of hug that friends did when they thought they would never see each other again. Where was she going? Or equally importantly, where did she think Gwen was going? When they broke apart, Gwen held on to her newly acquired sister and looked her straight in her cobalt blue eyes, searching for some meaning to this display of parting.

'You are coming back, right?' Gwen asked, her voice catching as she spoke, tripping over the emotions that she barely held in check. But Jen smiled, almost reassuringly, and hugged her again.

'I hope so, though if I do, you may not be here when that happens, Gwen. Don't forget that you too have an important mission to undertake now and I doubt you'll be able to complete it without leaving this grove. But I've done all I can to prepare you; so too has Maddy, and you mustn't be afraid if we have to part. This is war, Gwen, with cataclysmic consequences, and we must do all we can. I have to find Raphael now and bring him up to date on you and your role now in the fabric of the cosmos. Your arrival will hearten the warriors and fill them with renewed hope in the times ahead. You do understand, don't you, Gwen? Please tell me you do.'

Put that way, Gwen did. She realized she was having an irrational reaction to the separation. It was just the thought of setting off alone with all new abilities and no one to guide her while she learnt just what she was capable of. They had learnt from birth over aeons; she had only had days. Maddy joined the pair and an emotional group hug ensued. There were tears; but eventually even they abated and they stood back from each other. Acceptance had been reached and Jen backed up and took her silvery white dragon form, and with a last meaningful and love-filled look from the great swirling golden eyes, she bunched herself up and launched herself skyward so fast, to the eye, that one second she was there, the next she was gone. Just the rustle of leaves and swaying of branches as she tore past them, marked her passing.

Gwen had a thought then, or perhaps it was more of an urge. Maybe it wasn't even her thought but the subtle intimation of the Earth herself – but the result was the same. *I need to meditate,* Gwen concluded, *somewhere right out of the way. Away from human interference; and see what this alleged intuition they rate so highly comes up with, if anything, otherwise I've no bloody idea where to start. And I need to get my nose into some books before I embark on this wild tree chase. They pray that I'm the one who finds it,* Gwen repeated their earlier hope to herself, *but at this point, no one's praying bloody harder than me.*

CHAPTER NINE

ANTITHESIS

A NGELS MAY HAVE BEEN IMMUNE TO MANY things when residing on the Earth, but one of the things they were no longer immune to – was a dry throat. The dust kicked up by several thousand restless feet filled the air and managed to get just about everywhere. Unfortunately, this only added to Raphael's increasingly foul humor. His armored, sandaled feet were pacing back and forth with a ferocity that threatened to wear a groove into the very bedrock he paced upon. Occasionally he would stop and take a long drink of cooling, dust clearing water, dragging the back of his hand across his mouth – to clear what he spilt down his chin – in a most barbaric fashion for one who personified the noblest of golden warriors. It caused a smile of barely concealed humor to creep onto Uriel's face as he sighed resignedly and shook his head of glistening auburn curls at his comrade's irrational behavior. This, of course, only made Raphael's face darken all the more as he glowered at his companion-in-arms who sat, still smiling irritatingly at him. He needed another drink. Maybe that would cool his inner turmoil.

Several earthenware jugs had been placed close by. A thin layer of rime coated their exterior as a minor enchantment kept the water and bowls of fruit that sat near them refreshingly cool in the scorching desert heat.

Raphael drank deeply. Thirst barely quenched and still far from refreshed, and after having recommenced his pacing – now with an unclogged throat – he started to mutter; but his gaze kept flicking to the smiling Uriel. It was as though he was taunting him. Something snapped then in the raging archangel, and with a growl of pent up frustration and a mighty swing of his brightly shining golden sword, he swept through the clay jugs and smashed them to smithereens, sending water and fragments of jug hurtling and splashing in all directions. Uriel waved a casual hand and anything that inadvertently splashed his way just bounced harmlessly off the mystical barrier he coolly manifested.

'Arrgghh! Is that all you have to do all day? Sit there and polish that pig sticker of yours? Why are you not raging at the Adversary's lack of spine and his refusal to meet us upon the field, where we can finally resolve this matter and put things back the way they were?'

But Uriel wasn't about to be baited by Raphael; he'd been here before – many times – and the results were always the same. Uriel had long ago reasoned that for all his companion's peaceful intentions, all he really wanted was a good scrap. And he was like a bear with a sore head until he got it.

'Peace, Brother,' Uriel spoke soothingly. 'Save your energies for the battle which both you and I know will come soon enough.' Uriel had been reclining upon a nearby rock, idly watching his brother pace like a caged animal, and at the same time he honed a huge and most impressive sword, lightly drawing the oiled stone along the blade's edge to remove any nicks and imperfections, though due to its very nature, any imperfections were gone by the second stroke of the stone; and the blade remained supernaturally sharp. But it was more for the familiar feel of the process than any remedial work; it was cathartic and almost meditative to the massively built angelic warrior. Uriel was known as the Archangel of the Flaming Blade, and during battle the blade did just that. He was a beacon amidst darkness as he cut swathe after swathe through the ranks of the demonic armies. He was known to be so intimidating during battle, that lesser and lower level minions simply died where they stood as their gaze fell upon the archangel, such was his power. The lucky ones merely fled in abject terror. For the really unlucky ones, they fell beneath the blazing sword's caress and the searing touch of the righteous blade. Its cut caused more than just death. It caused every cell within the hapless soul to burn with the intensity of the sun. It happened so fast, that to the observer, the recipient simply exploded in a puff of blazing ash, forever annihilated from the cycle. No redemption, no regeneration, no more existence. Not even the opportunity to return to the most distant planet and start the cycle of life over. The only other weapon to have such an effect was the scythe of Death himself. It was a rough deal being a minion of the Domain. Certainly at the lower levels, where the majority began their servitude, it was harsh – either facing the wrath of the archangels and their legions and dying; or deserting and fleeing back to the domain, where they were subjected to a fate far greater than death on the battlefield – always assuming they were caught, for the Domain was a big place and renegade demons could hide out there for an eternity if they were clever and very, very careful. Few in the world understood the nature of many of the demonic minions of the Domain. Many didn't start their life that way. Many are and were prisoners of war, captured warriors of the Celestial Hosts. Time and torture gradually subverted them to the cause of Lucifer and the lure of the Domain's many temptations. The rest were captured mortals, stolen from the Earth and cast into bondage. Slaves and conscripts. Lacking any power, they would be unable to leave the Domain, but once familiar with the rules of survival there, they could amass power by the death of others and by reward from their new liege lord, whoever that may be. These lords could be both kind and cruel. It made for a delicate lifestyle and kept everybody walking on eggshells in order to stay alive.

If a demonic lord could be bothered, he would send out hunters for these renegades. It served as both sport and as an exemplary lesson in discipline. Lucifer was lord of the Domain and had a tenuous connection with virtually all souls that existed there, and could have located these deserters if he chose, but he let his lords govern their own territories and vassals. That served to amuse him more.

The way Uriel blazed upon the battlefield gave these lesser souls every opportunity to avoid him. However, there were no end of other willing angelic warriors more than happy to oblige in his stead, though he was undoubtedly a hard act to follow.

Raphael was only frustrated rather than truly deranged, Uriel knew this. He also knew that it was for several reasons too. And each one just compounded the other and fuelled his rage all the more, making him painfully aware of his impotence at rectification. For one, he was the archangel responsible for maintaining the vigil upon the ancient Megiddoan fortress amongst other things – a duty in which he had obviously been lax in these past centuries, for various and seemingly now, insignificant reasons. But so had many of the other celestial guardians been equally absent from their duties. Raphael wasn't alone in his dereliction, but it didn't stop his own guilt eating him up. He was a hair's breadth away from flagellating himself with razor wire, for it had been his slip that allowed the Adversary to gain a foothold on this plane at the site of an ancient portal to the Labyrinth. History had forgotten, either by accident or design, the principal location of the mystical maze. It had appeared throughout mortal history in various countries and many held it as an integral part of their mythology. But few knew its true origin. Again, the ancient races had imparted this knowledge and several thousand years of oral tradition had bastardised it much the same way as many other legends had been. So it was difficult to pinpoint now, but there had once been and apparently still was a powerful junction beneath this fortress – a multiple crossing of the dragon lines that ran deep in the Earth. Belief held that it was this factor that drew the ancients to build there in the first place. The ancient and now lost races, like the Anasazi of Canyon De Chelly, and the Mayans and Zapotecs of South America – they too carved their homes where the dragon lines flowed at their most potent, though it was still a mystery where these ancient peoples vanished to, and what knowledge they took with them. Even the angels hadn't been privy to that information – a fact which burnt many up with curiosity, still.

The Megiddo fortress had once enabled entities of power to access the legendary Labyrinth: the great maze that surrounded the core and granted access to the Mother – via the Soul Gates – that surrounded the centre, though access via a soul gate didn't necessarily mean that they would make it through the maze to the core. The Mother didn't grant her audience lightly. It was this fact that led many earth-worshipping practices to adopt the Labyrinth as a powerful emblem of their beliefs.

Megiddo was one of seven sites located at various sacred places across the globe. For all that it was one of seven, it was actually the oldest of the gates and considered, even, to be the first. The most powerful. This was no doubt why the Adversary had concentrated his will upon it. Raphael felt the weight of his failure daily. And each day it grew heavier, amassing in direct proportion to his anger. He had a burning desire to lash out at something other than simply jugs of water. It was as if by the strength of his arm alone, he could put right the whole sorry mess. The lack of anything to hit ground upon him as well, and set him teetering precariously upon the edge that he was now on. He had taken to pacing to try to expel some of the guilty energy that was coursing through his body, but it had little effect; and his patience, usually deeper and steadier than the mightiest of rivers, was running a little shallow now.

'You need to calm yourself, Raph, and curb that viper's tongue of yours. You know full well the capability of my sword, not to mention that it has saved your scrawny neck on many an occasion.' Uriel stroked the blade with the stone a few more times for effect. The crystal clear ringing of stone off steel even sounded mighty and impressive as the stone rang off the end of the blade. At this point Raphael at least stopped stalking back and forth and stood still – the first time for several hours – and fixed his piercing gaze on his companion briefly before flicking away again. His normally flawless and beatific brow was furrowed as he watched the water bearers replace the jugs and cast the cantrip over them that chilled the water; hastily going about their task and avoiding the blazing eyes of the archangel, lest they draw his attention to them. Quickly completing their chore, the bearers ran off as fast as they could. An angry archangel wasn't the most stable and safe thing to be around. Today, Raphael was anything but stable.

'I – am – calm,' he fumed in moderately normal tones. '*This* is calm,' he spat. 'Trust me, you'd know the difference. Damn!' Looking back over his shoulder at the still-growing fortress of Megiddo, he asked the question he had been asking since they had arrived. 'Why don't they send out their army and be done with it? They send just enough to hold us at bay, without committing their full legions, while the rest scurry about in there like so many blasted ants, forever adding to its fortifications. I hate to imagine what else they are up to in there. We need to get in sooner rather than later, Uriel. Yesterday at the latest, preferably sooner than that.'

Uriel nodded his silent agreement as he too looked towards the massive expanding construction of the Adversary. There was no disputing that fact; before it was too late.

'I thought Michael was due to be here by now with the means to conclude this, or at least expedite it. I swear, he can never be on time and if anyone was likely to miss the final judgment, it would be him. He'd turn up just as everything finished and wound down and he'd come out with that greeting he always uses: "What did I miss?" If he turned up when he was supposed to, he would know exactly what he missed. Argh!' Raphael threw a beleaguered hand in the air in exasperation at Michael's behavior. 'Why do I bother? He'll never change. It's just that this situation has put me so far out, everything gripes now.' Raphael stomped back and forth like a caged animal.

Uriel had to agree with that too. It was good that Raphael recognized his recent shortcomings; it would help him resolve them. Recognition was always fifty per cent of the battle. 'You'll make yourself ill like this, Raph.

We need your sword too much to have you burn yourself into a state of apoplexy. You need to be calm and stable, and not let your rage get the better of you – lest you suffer a reversion. And that, we really don't need, nor do you. Those who've been afflicted by it haven't recovered yet. Maybe they won't.'

This caught Raphael's attention, for since the Adversary had set the balance askance by his tyrannical plan, strange ailments had been manifesting amongst the hosts – both of the celestial legions and those of the Domain. The results were not pleasant for either. For a member of the celestial legions, reversion meant a slide into mindless bestiality. Unthinking and uncontrollable, they turned on their own kind as they savaged anything within their immediate proximity, and if they survived long enough to see one orbit of the moon, for those on the Earth, they then slid even further. Cellular degeneration began to take them back to the most basic of life forms. So far, those that had suffered from the malaise had either died in combat or subsequently died of the transformation. There seemed to be no cure for this and those who were afflicted were growing in numbers, as they became more and more driven by their emotions.

Raphael stopped in his tracks and looked long and hard at his companion, who was studying him in return, looking for the telltale signs of reversion: protruding brow, pronounced canines and an increase in facial and bodily hair; subtle at first, then increasing as the disease took hold. Even Pestilence had been unable to halt this epidemic. The disturbance to the eternal cycle had disrupted even the uncanny abilities of the Horsemen too, it seemed; for similarly, disease had taken hold across the globe and Pestilence struggled to contain it as more and more of the Adversary's minions broke through and invaded the mortal world with their physical presence, tearing humanity to pieces. Cities were turned into charnel houses overnight and refugees swarmed over the continents, desperate to flee from their own particular nightmare. Even the animals fled and this caused as much turmoil as anything when swarms of humans encountered swarms of fleeing dogs, cats, rats and even crows, as well as a multitude of other creatures. Chaos ensued on a scale that was unprecedented.

Picking a fight with Uriel had seemed at first to be a way of releasing some of his pent up anger, or so Raphael thought, but the darkly armored archangel had deflated him without even raising a hand. Reversion. It was the one thing that many, including Raphael, actually feared. It had a most sobering effect on him. Dropping his shoulders and releasing the tension that wound within him, he walked across and sat on an adjacent rock to Uriel's and laid his sword down beside him.

'I don't know how you do it, Uriel, keeping so calm the way you do. Doesn't the audacity of this creature set your blood to boiling? All I have to do is think about it for a few moments and I feel the rage begin to build.'

Uriel too sheathed his weapon. Unlike Raphael, he didn't feel happy to relinquish it from his person, though all archangels had a symbiotic bond to their weapon of choice, and it could come to hand in less time than it took for a heart to beat. Even so...

'Of course it does,' Uriel responded with understanding. 'As you know, Lucifer and I set up the Domain together when he chose to govern it, and many of my closest friends went with him. He asked me to join him too, you know.'

Raphael's eyes went a little wide with surprise. He hadn't and there were few secrets amongst the upper ranks of archangels, so close were they. But he let Uriel continue all the same. 'So when this usurper rises and makes a mockery of all the Domain stands for, it grates against every fibre of my being. I do not even know if Lucifer still lives – we were like brothers once. Closer, if that could be possible. Yet even Lucifer, with the familial bond we shared, kept a secret so great that it burdened him to the point of forgoing his position amongst the elevated, and opting to rule the Domain.' Raphael knew there had to be more to that tale than met the eye, but now wasn't the time to ferret that out; it would have to wait for a more appropriate time, if one ever came again.

Uriel continued, 'I would remove this upstart and see my friend once more, well and free from his troubles. Likewise, I do not believe humanity deserves this manner of intervention. We should not have abandoned them the way we did. Look what they have become, unguided. See what they have destroyed.' Uriel just tipped his head outwards indictaing everywhere. 'But for all these things, Raph, I am only one being. You are only one being. Powerful we may be, but we cannot resolve this without the aid of others, so it serves me not at all to beat myself up about what I cannot change. I must go along with the flow of events and trust to forces greater than myself that resolutions present themselves.'

Raphael still didn't look entirely convinced, though some of what Uriel had said had gotten to him.

'But we cannot hold out much longer, Uriel. Our numbers are spread so thin already and there are more of the enemy every day – humanity cannot defend itself with the modern weapons they possess. There is not enough iron in their ammunition to do any good. All it does is sting the enemy and slow their progress; they might as well use sticks.'

Uriel understood the plight that humanity suffered under and wondered just what situation they would be in now had the Nephillim not escaped and taught mortals more things than they needed to know: ancient magics and about weapons and of matters of the flesh. Though he had dwelt on this dilemma for eons, it did no good: the Nephillim were still loose somewhere in the world, though thankfully not all of them. The bulk of their brethren were still incarcerated, but the seven who were out were bad enough. Uriel attributed the Adversary's finding of the Megiddo gate to these traitorous former angels. They had been free since before the formation of the Domain and even came close to destroying the Covenant before it was formed. They had been causing trouble intermittently ever since across the Earth. Uriel had vowed recently that should he survive this war, he would make it a personal quest to track them down and rid the multiverse of their foul contaminant once and for all.

Uriel sat in a contemplative silence for a moment before continuing, calming the rage that had started to grow within him at the thought of the Nephillim.

'Added to this, Raph, I know where Michael went and who he is due to return with. I believe that should this plan be successful, we will have a much greater chance of defeating the ravening hordes that run riot across this jewel of a world.' However, the same brow-furrowing crease of concern adorned Uriel's forehead as he looked out at the eastern sky, wondering where their brother had gotten to. Raphael was right about one thing: Michael was long overdue.

'What I don't know, though, is what the Drakarim are up to. The avatars have been absent for some time now with an agenda of their own and they have been ensconced somewhere in North America for at least the last hundred years that I know of. I can only hope they know what they are doing, for their aid is sorely missed.'

Raphael had remained silent as Uriel spoke. He heard what he was saying but the archangel had given him much to think about. It made him realize that his head had been blinkered during the recent troubles. There was more taking place than he had attended to. That wouldn't do. Uriel was right, annoyingly again, that he had been driven by his emotions, overbearing guilt and self-pity. It was a surefire route to reversion. With a starburst of revelation, it occurred to him that not only had he been mentally absent from affairs, but during that time, he hadn't seen Gabriel anywhere. The icy archangel was rarely absent from matters of portent. This certainly qualified as one of them but the more Raphael thought about it, the more he realized he hadn't seen him for a long time.

'Do you know where Gabriel is?' Raphael asked Uriel, catching the warrior on the hop with the question, for his mind was pondering the absence of the avatars.

'Do you know what? I don't,' Uriel remarked, surprising himself by the realization. 'But now that you mention it, I haven't seen him for several years now. I'd be pushed to place where exactly I did see him last.'

Uriel came alert suddenly, leaping to his feet and surprising the now finally reclined Raphael. He watched his friend with some concern regarding his sudden animation. Uriel's hand automatically went to the hilt of his sheathed weapon. A touch of reassurance.

'This is not good, Raph. You're right, he has been absent for a time now, too long, and his legions would be most expedient about now, not to mention those two deadly swords of his. It used to blow my mind when he and Pestilence used to spar. It was nigh on impossible to separate the two, so fast did they entwine, blades flashing in a lethal union of steel on steel. The sound generated from their sparring was almost musical.'

Raphael had to agree. He too had witnessed the sparring sessions. Pestilence was passionate about her swordwork and loved every moment; it could be seen on her face, which was usually controlled and serene. Yet when she fought, it became animated and wild. Her expression would terrify as much as her swordwork.

But Gabriel's expression never wavered. It remained impassive no matter what the situation. He fought efficiently and coldly, as though he were made of ice. Nobody had ever seen the archangel lose his temper or even show any excessive emotion. It made it difficult to fathom what went on behind his icy grey eyes, what schemes and machinations unfolded within. His eyes matched his demeanor; they were a slate grey, like chips of iced seawater. Yet for all their pale dilution, they seemed to look directly into your heart and ascertain the truth there. He ordered the death of millions with the same disdain and contempt he would have had disposing of an apple core. If it was what it took, then that was what he did. The question was, why he was absent now, of all times. Uriel resolved to ask Michael, if and when he ever returned.

'If you ask me, Gabriel was something of a show-off when he fought,' Raphael grumbled sourly to Uriel's back. The archangel was alert now, eyes fixed on the distant horizon, but he still heard the quip.

'Your mood is making you sound petty, Raph. That almost sounds like envy. You're not coming down with a dose of cardinal sin, are you?'

Raphael's face was a picture. Indignation written all over it. 'Don't be trite, Uriel; it's just that we don't see warfare in the same way. There is no passion in him. It's just a series of maneuvers designed to kill in the most expedient way. I think sometimes it is completely feasible for him to switch sides and fight for the enemy with little to no emotional detachment. But all said and done, we have all become too good at the one thing we abhor most. Given the choice, I would gladly hang this cursed blade upon the wall and never lay a finger on it ever again.'

Uriel's voice drifted back to Raphael, interrupting his sombre mood. 'Not something you're going to get to do today, I'm afraid. But you are right about Gabriel; it is difficult to ascertain his motives and some days even his loyalties. But for now, I'd settle for just knowing his whereabouts.'

To alleviate his increasingly maudlin mood, Raphael asked Uriel what he was looking at.

'I have a feeling, my friend, that Michael is on his way as we speak.' Uriel squinted into the setting sun at a speck that was growing as he watched it. 'In fact, I do believe that it is him now.'

Raphael stood smoothly, moving to stand next to Uriel, and watched as the speck grew into the winged figure of their comrade, rocketing towards them like some inbound missile. At the last possible moment, he back winged and landed in a cloud of dust.

'Great,' Raphael mumbled as he turned his face away before getting another mouthful of desert. 'I've just washed out half a ton of sand from my throat. I didn't need another.'

Michael landed with expert precision and folded his silvery rack of wings away, before dematerializing them completely. He stood like an angelic god of war – bare arms, biceps bulging, laced with a myriad of criss-cross cuts, his breastplate dented and creased from several and quite substantial impacts. The helm he doffed was equally dented and his breathing was slightly labored. Uriel tilted his head quizzically at Michael's appearance.

'What did I miss?' Michael asked, looking between his two associates.

'Trouble?' Uriel asked coolly. Prodding the dented rib armor for emphasis.

'Told you!' Raphael said a little smugly. 'Every flaming time.'

Michael turned to him and silently asked the 'what every time?' question.

Raphael just shook his head. 'Never mind. Where have you been anyway? Weren't you due ages ago?'

'I ran into a few of the Adversary's minions. Quite literally. They slowed me for a bit, but I enjoyed the exercise though. That aside, I expect he's here by now. Is he in?'

'Is who in?' Raphael asked genuinely. 'Were we expecting someone?'

Both Michael and Uriel swiveled their heads to stare avidly at Raphael.

'What? If you don't see fit to tell me what you're up to, the only recourse I have is to ask you. My crystal ball's a bit clouded these days.' But as Raphael looked at Michael, he could see that he wasn't overly impressed. In fact he looked pretty deflated.

'I left him with the Four Horsemen; they were due to meet here. Considering my slight diversion I thought they would have been here before me.' Michael scrubbed his bear paw sized hands though his damp hair. Uriel thought he looked tired.

'I can only hope that they are merely delayed much like I was, and not fallen afoul of the Adversary's hordes. They know of Tomas; it was only fortune that I got to him first. I gather the Adversary sent some lesser minions after him. We should be grateful for his complacency, for it allowed Tomas to get away.'

Raphael had to ask, 'So who is this Tomas character, and why wasn't I made aware of this development?' Raphael's lip had started to protrude again at this imagined slight.

'Raph,' Michael started wearily, 'what sort of secret would it be if I went around telling everyone? Plus, before you go off into one, Uriel only knows because he was there when the message came in that he had been located. Time was of the essence, for the enemy had located him too, and we simply had to get to him first. No insult was intended in keeping you out of the loop, believe me. Anyway, you seemed to have enough on your plate at the time, though for all that hard work and effort, it all seems to have come to naught if he isn't here.'

Raphael cooled a little at the explanation; he was far too sensitive these days, jumping down the throats of everybody who seemed to have it in for him. Maybe Uriel was right. Maybe he was feeling the first symptoms of reversion.

'That still doesn't answer my question of who this Tomas is,' Raphael said, the note of petulance still evident in his usually placid and controlled voice.

Michael brought him up to speed as quickly as he could. All the while, his eyes flicked to the horizon in the hope that the Four Horsemen and his charge would come galloping in. But the sky remained empty, save for the few brave carrion birds, circling aimlessly. Eagerly awaiting their next meal.

'It is obvious then that something has happened to delay them, but we cannot afford to wait upon their arrival. The Adversary has had ample time to sow the seeds of dissolution and destruction; we can spare him no more. The Horsemen are capable, are they not? If they can get here they will; if not, then maybe they will send word.' Uriel's words cut through the haze of anxiety that had enveloped Michael and he relaxed visibly, albeit for only a second or two.

'I have no doubt as to the capabilities of the Horsemen, but at the end of the day, they are only four; what if the enemy truly did have advanced knowledge of our plan and sent legions to intercept them? After all, if we can find them, so could they.'

'*Michael!*' Uriel's tone brought the bedraggled archangel up short. 'Do not beat yourself up about this. It's enough that Raphael is wallowing in self-pity and some type of belated guilt trip. Enough is enough. We are all a part of the cause of this disaster, but we cannot change the past by moping. All we can do is act to effect a change to the future and make damn sure we do not make the same kinds of mistakes again. That means dealing with the matter at hand: ousting the Adversary from Megiddo and breaking his armies, closing the Soul Gate, and sending his sorry ass back to the Domain once and for all.'

Duly chastised, the two warriors looked at Uriel as though seeing him for the first time in a while, then they grinned toothy smiles that brought light to the darkest places, and they embraced as brothers and as warriors, with much mutual backslapping and assurances.

'Damn, I hate it when he's right like that. But there's no denying it: we must continue regardless of all the bad news and grim omens.'

Raphael looked at Michael suspiciously. He saw that that there was more bad news lurking beneath the surface of his brother. He also saw the reluctance to spill it lest he depress them all once again. But Raphael was like a dog with a bone, persistent to the point of sadistic.

'There's more, isn't there? More you're not telling us?'

Michael nodded sadly. 'It is like we don't have enough problems – but if you insist. Wait! Is that Phanuel I see?'

Raphael stepped up to stand immediately before Michael, obscuring his view with his own face, which had darkened again to the thunderhead before the storm.

'Stop dissembling, Michael. Let's hear it all while we are about it. How much worse can matters get anyway?' Raphael wished he hadn't tempted fate with his last comment when Michael spoke again; he simply wandered away and plonked himself down on the rock Uriel previously occupied and groaned, with his head in his hands.

'Fenris is loose!'

Uriel's eyes widened into a 'what?'

Michael nodded and continued, the initial shock over, with: 'That's not all. The gaol he was trapped in has become the gaol that now holds Lucifer captive and at the Adversary's mercy. It is only a small mercy that he at least lives still.'

Uriel asked in hushed tones, shock taking his voice, 'How did you find this out?'

Michael indicated his battered armor. 'You don't think a minion could get close enough to do this, do you? No, I caught one of their generals: some creature called Zethrial. Apparently he was seconded to Fenris to liaise between the Adversary and the Dread Wolf Lord who, it seems, has amassed a sizeable army of hounds, ravaged from the Adversary's own regiments initially to boost his pack. Now he is turning every prisoner he takes. Some have even come from humanity. The Adversary is employing portal traps to catapult any unwary soul straight into the Domain. I don't know how many of these he has but it means he is utilizing Lucifer's enchanters to supply him, for only they knew the enchantment for their creation.'

Uriel looked stunned beyond words. Sadness crept onto his features, that seeped into his bones and made his shoulders drop momentarily in despair and dejection.

Now, matters seemed about as bad as they were going to get for the time being when Michael broke the grim news to his companions. They stood in comparative silence, each lost in their own thoughts. Uriel poured several goblets of chilled water and drained his swiftly before topping up again, silently wishing it were the most potent of wines, so that it would erase what he now knew, certainly for a while anyway.

Then the shock wave hit. The rippling wave of energy flowed across the desert like a tsunami; nothing escaped its touch as it flowed into and over everything in its path with a speed that caught absolutely everything by surprise. It hit the three archangels full on and caused all of them to suck in breath like they had been dipped in an icy river. Yet when it passed them by unharmed they looked to each with a curiosity none of them had ever experienced before.

'What just happened?' Uriel asked, the first to find his voice. The others just shook their heads. Raphael and Michael were looking around for both the source and for anything that might be following it – but all they saw were the curious faces of their brethren milling in as much confusion as themselves.

Phanuel glided over and alighted by the trio. His own expression seemed torn between concern for what was taking place, and something else that made the usually stoic commander seem as though he were balanced on razors.

'I've no idea what that was, but as no one seems hurt, I can't think about that now. I've just been contacted by Death. He is holed up in the Al'Mayakin fortress and under siege by several legions of Azaroth's minions. They have Tomas with them, apparently, but could use some assistance as soon as possible. I'm taking my flight of archers and a thousand warriors to their aid; it is only an hour from here if we go now.'

'Do you think that energy wave and Death's situation are connected, Phanuel?' Uriel asked the pragmatic archangel commander. He was a superb warrior and headed up the finest archers in the entire Celestial Host, and was known for his level head and objective opinions. The politics of the Covenant meant little to him; he simply enforced its rules, and he did it well. But he shook his head at the question.

'No, I don't believe they are, but there is definitely a power afoot that wasn't there before the wave. I can feel it. A deep sense of something enormous, though whether it is for good or ill, I cannot tell. Though I expect we will find out soon enough the way things are going, hey?' That did seem to be the way of things at present.

'Very well, we'll deal with things here. Go. See if you can extricate old bony ass from whatever predicament he's gotten himself into, and get them back here as quickly as possible, preferably with their charge still intact. It's too detailed for now, Phanuel. I'll explain when you get them back.' Phanuel nodded, and spun smartly. Taking two steps and snapping his wings out, he tore off to gather his warriors. And in what seemed to be only a matter of minutes, a cloud of celestial warriors filled the sky and made for Al'Mayakin.

The sun had set fully now, and the silvery orb of the moon was beginning her journey across the night sky. Still waxing, it shed a wan light across the desert of the Jezreel valley, bringing a chill to the air and casting mysterious shadows that seemed to dance of their own volition. Where the desert had been awash with color throughout the day, now, it seemed to all wash away, leaving it in a monochromic nightscape – just greys, whites and blacks. The surreal landscape then became a hostile living thing in its own right. Eyes of rock and shadow watched everything, casting an indifference to either side, neither aiding nor inhibiting, but simply watching. Watching and waiting.

The Fortress of Megiddo was abuzz with shadows and activity of its own. Torches could be seen aplenty as the inhabitants worked on long into the night, never stopping. Those who fell or tired were immediately replaced by fresh bodies. From the position of the archangel's vantage point, they watched helplessly as their enemy went about his foul design. The archangels had opted to wait until dawn before they launched their attack, for it was a time between light and dark that the minions abhorred for some reason. The prospect of the rising sun enraged them; it also put it at the backs of the attackers, giving them an added advantage as the enemy had to look directly into the sun's rays – not something they liked. Nor something the archangels cared a shred about. The night had been a frenzy of preparation. The dire news had galvanized them in a way that made them feel even guiltier about their lack of effort. Realizing that a creeping malaise had sapped the Celestial Host without their knowledge, slowing them and holding them back, the energy wave had broken whatever spell had overcome them and the warriors all felt renewed and invigorated.

Though many remained unaware of the cause of both symptom and cure, it had piqued the curiosity of the archangels. Raphael pondered it continually until both Michael and Uriel told him to shut up for five minutes and let their bleeding ears rest. With less than an hour to go before the sun rose and heralded the attack, many were still eager for the fight to come and had rested little. As soon as the lifegiving and life affirming sphere, that fiery orb we call the sun, fully crested the horizon, the Angelic and Celestial Host would attack like they had never attacked before.

With less than thirty minutes before the sun was fully up, the three resident archangels gathered for a final briefing. They stood upon the crest of the ridge that would see the first rays and gave them a perfect vantage to assess the battle lines and formations that they had worked on through the night, moderately satisfied that they had arrayed their troops as best they could with what resource they had available. Michael was still muttering about Tomas and that they should have heard from Phanuel by now, and Raphael kept muttering about Michael and the origin of the mysterious wave.

'For the first time in I don't know how long,' Uriel started, breaking their inane banter and focusing their attention on him, 'I'm actually looking forward to this battle in order to simply shut you two clucking mother hens up for five minutes. Hopefully the sound of steel ringing on steel and the screams of their dying will finally drown you out.'

'That's not fair, Uriel,' Michael retorted indignantly. 'These are important factors that need discussing. Contingency must be made now that the prophecy involving the mortal contribution has been affected. Matters rest now upon a blade's edge and this battle, if not the entire war, could now go any way.' Uriel raised both hands pleadingly before Michael, keen to stop his argument before it gained any momentum, and he got to hear it all again.

'I know, Michael, I know. Believe me, I even agree with you on these points, as I do with Raph,' he added quickly before his fiery friend started up as well. 'But we should focus now on this battle and let the fates show us a sign. Even without our intervention, fate always has a way of delivering options and surprises right when they are both needed and least expected. I know you both prefer the proactive approach, but there are times when even we must sit back and react to events, for it would seem that these are monumental times. Events such as we are witnessing, you know full well, are bigger than any of us. For once, *we* are the pawns in a much larger game...'

Michael was looking over Uriel's shoulder at something as he spoke, which had started to irritate him. 'Are you even listening, Michael, or are you so wrapped in your own reasoning that you refuse– '

'Shut up, Uriel. You're right, okay? But for now, shut up and tell me what that is up there.' Michael pointed skyward to a speck that was getting bigger by the second and apparently aiming directly for them at breakneck speed. It was increasingly difficult for them to focus on the object as it came out of the sun, and even the archangels had to shield their eyes after staring too long into it. Raphael drew his sword and hoisted his shield, for all the good it would do. But it never hurt to be prepared.

'Easy, Raph. I don't sense the enemy, nor do I think it is any man-made weapon.'

None of them got the chance to utter much more as a sudden gale sprang up around them, covering them with sand and debris. The powerful winds tore at their cloaks and hair and came close to overbalancing them. The trio threw their arms up over their eyes to shield them from the worst, turning their heads slightly to avoid swallowing more than they already had. Then, as fast as it had risen, it dropped. Blinking and spitting sand, they looked up to see the biggest, swirling liquid gold eyes they had ever seen, mere feet from them and regarding them with something akin to humor.

'Do you greet all your visitors with a display of naked steel, Raphael? Or has it been so long that you no longer recognize me?' The voice was deep and resonant, echoing around their ears and through their minds. But for all its awesome power and majesty, Uriel still smiled as he recognized the timbre and subtle accent of the gigantic white dragon that sat upon its haunches before them.

'Milady Jenharim. Of course we recognize you; how could we not? It was merely the surprise of your visit that took us momentarily unawares. For I was only just thinking about you. We are about to commence a battle charge upon our mutual enemy, so you'll forgive us if we are a bit on edge. Raphael, put that away.'

He did, and fast. Immediately followed by a bow so low, in armor, they thought he might topple head over heels. 'My lady, please forgive me. These have been fraught times, but it is no excuse to draw a weapon against your gracious self. I accept whatever penance you deem fit.'

The dragon laughed then. A sound much the same as a cascading waterfall, but they detected the mirth within it, immediately followed by a blinding white flash of spiraling energy, and as the dancing motes cleared from before the eyes of the archangels, there, standing before them, was the beautiful figure of the Drakarim, known to the angels as Lady Jenharim; known to the world at present as Jennifer Deveraux and known to history as the Eternal White Dragon, avatar of the sea and sky.

She stood before them in a tight fitting, yet fluid dress of silvery scales that caught every color of the rainbow as she moved. It gradually shredded away about her knees, leaving her bare shins and feet visible. Her flowing locks wafted around her like a halo or corona, as though she commanded her own personal breeze for the effect; which, actually, she did. It was always good to make an impression.

'Welcome to our camp, Lady. Is this an untimely social visit or is it no coincidence that you appear to us now in our moment of need?' Michael asked, finally finding his tongue and allowing the battle commander he was to reassert itself.

'All of the above and none of them, actually.' As she spoke Jen took in the scene below her, assessing the battle herself and sensing the futility of it. The fortress looked impregnable and probably too late to be taken by siege. 'I bear news of great importance actually, news that may lighten your apparent burdens.'

It was only moments now before the horn was due to sound, signaling the attack, and it was obvious by their demeanor that they were keen to know if her news affected the charge.

'No, unfortunately it is nothing that will forestall your attack, but it may lend heart to your flagging spirits.'

Uriel tilted his head, birdlike, and implied she go on.

'Well, I don't suppose you happened to feel the shock wave earlier, by any chance?'

Raphael immediately became animated and he stepped closer, like an excited schoolboy, eager for a gift. 'We did. It had a most propitious effect upon the warriors, seemingly cleansing them of a disheartening malaise, Well, not just them, but all of us. What was it?'

'It was, my lord Raphael, the birth cry of the latest member of our sisterhood. We have found and accepted the sacrifice of the latest avatar. Gwendoline Walker, the new avatar of nature. She completes the trinity and has become the Handmaiden of the Earth herself.' Jen smiled at the expression and emotions that vied for space on the faces of the archangels. Shock, concern, pleasure, surprise, wonder. So many in such a short space of time.

It was Raphael who found his voice first. 'This is truly a time of wonders. I was only telling these two moments before your timely arrival that we need to step back and let the fates provide an answer. It seems that one has been offered.'

Uriel raised his eyebrows and looked at his friend with wonder. Shaking his head lightly, Uriel smiled and turned back to Jennifer. 'That is good news indeed, but will she complete her given role then in time?'

Raphael turned to stare at Uriel again, the look of wonder quickly replaced with another, not so impressed look. For Uriel again seemed to know something he didn't.

'What do you know now that I don't, Uriel? What secrets have you been keeping yet again?'

Uriel rolled his eyes as if to say 'Oh no, not again' without taking his gaze from the vision that was Jennifer. Uriel quickly explained that he had spent more time in the library than Raphael had. Several thousand years earlier, it had come to his attention that an equally ancient prophecy had been discovered and it involved a third avatar. Uriel had approached the two existing ones and discussed its implications. The who, how and when. And what they would need to do should they be called. But as the years passed into centuries and centuries to millennia, the avatars took the scroll and the prophecy was eventually forgotten by Uriel until now, and the presence of the White Dragon – she brought it all flooding back. Raphael harrumphed in disgust at being omitted again.

'Why didn't you tell somebody else? Seeing as you forgot all about it.'

'I did, Raph. I told Gabriel.' Those few words then had a most peculiar effect, as though a key had been turned, but as of yet, they weren't sure what lock or door it turned in. But there was the germ of thought there and tenuous connections were made.

'Well,' Raphael asked after a moment's pause, 'what is it she needs to do? You're a git for that, Uriel, leaving people hanging on, trying to work out just what it is you're trying to tell them.'

'You have little patience these days, Raph,' Uriel replied automatically, his mind not quite catching up with the conversation, momentarily lost elsewhere. Then he came back and looked right at his friend and brother. 'But to put you out of our misery, she needs to find the First Tree. And considering the epidemic of reversion that seems to be gaining a foothold, the fruit of the tree could make the difference between victory or defeat. Life or Death.'

Raphael gave his friend a look that said 'Why didn't you say that in the first place?' and Uriel cuffed him on the shoulder by way of friendly affirmation. 'Now you know. In fact, now we all know. But why does that name sound familiar?'

Michael was about to answer when a loud roar went up from the direction of the Megiddo fortress, interrupting the chat on the ridge. Raphael looked down to see Nathaniel, the warrior who had stepped in for Phanuel during his absence, raise his horn and issue the blazing challenge. Unfortunately, it wasn't the surprise attack they would have liked. The spies of the Adversary were becoming far too numerous and far too efficient. Something would have to be done about that.

Jen turned to the archangels. 'Need a hand?'

They looked at her as one and she stood, innocent looking, raising her arms and interlocking her fingers. And turning them back on themselves, she pushed out and cracked her knuckles in anticipation. Her expression became all business. They smiled in anticipation of the expressions on the faces of the minions when they came face to face with a real live Drakarim. For many of the Domain, the Drakarim were just legends and few had ever seen one since they disappeared from the affairs of the multiverse. Uriel grinned. His pleasure at the prospect of time with Jennifer, in whatever capacity, overwhelmed him. He would rather more intimate time, but to a veteran of many wars, fighting with this lovely creature would be just as stimulating.

'Absolutely, Milady, it will be an honor and a pleasure to fight alongside you.'

Raphael and Michael saluted her each with a clenched fist slammed onto their breastplates.

'Okay then,' Jennifer crooned, 'let's go send these parasites back to whatever hole they crawled out of and make them wish that they had never emerged in the first place.' As all three archangels saluted her again with the fist to the heart, she shimmered back to her mighty draconian form and roared out a challenge that reverberated around the entire valley.

'That'll give them something to think about!' The voice of Jen

– sounding as amused as one could just prior to battle – echoed in their minds. 'Brace yourself.'

They duly turned away as the powerful haunches of the dragon propelled her skyward, showering the archangels in a vortex of desert sand. She swooped down over the Angelic Host, which sent wave after wave of cheers coursing through them at the sight of her magnificence. The warriors were even more fired up now, seeing their new fantastic ally.

'Time to go show the enemy that matters will not continue to go smoothly for them. Strength and victory, my brothers. May your arm smite many this day and may we all live to tell the tale.' A last look passed between the three archangels and with no more words to be said, they snapped their own wings open and followed Jennifer to the battlefield.

For all their spying and inside information about the impending attack by the Celestial Host, what the Adversary's forces didn't count on was Jennifer. The presence of the terrifying white dragon swooping down from the sky filled the minions with a trepidation that was not best felt at the start of a battle. With her great fang-filled maw agape, talons extended and wings swept back like a plummeting falcon, she screamed down upon the front ranks of minions like lightning from heaven. Blasting them with her icy breath weapon, she froze the front ranks solid as her power of the ice storm slammed into them. What didn't freeze immediately was raked from the ground and torn asunder as she ripped them from the earth and banked upwards for another pass, scattering their remains over their now terrified brethren. More cheers rose from the angels as Michael took wing with his flight of aerial cavalry. First blood was theirs, and the angels were champing at the bit to get in to the fray. They didn't have long to wait as the minions' own aerial force lifted up to meet Michael's. But unlike the graceful and agile warriors of the Celestial Host, the minions were more cumbersome and disorganized. Their winged warriors were hideous vulture-like creatures, with long, grey, fleshy necks, six bony arms and cadaverous features. Their bodies more resembled insects than men. But for all their abnormal appearance, they sported plenty of weaponry as well as long filthy claws and mouthfuls of vicious barbed teeth.

Jen had turned with uncanny maneuverability in the air and had decimated several hundred more with another two further devastating passes. By now, the foot soldiers, led by Uriel and Raphael, had closed the gap between the defenders and themselves. The clash could be heard for miles as the two forces slammed into each other. Many of the front ranks of minions had turned and attempted to flee, but the press from behind prevented any retreat. Most died where they stood. Morale had been shot the moment Jennifer had attacked them and the impetus of their attack died along with them. Bodies were falling from the sky in another demoralizing rain of death, landing amongst their own and killing more than a few who weren't prudent enough to get out of the way.

It fast became a rout, which turned quickly to a slaughter. Less than a fifth of what had turned out to defend had managed to return to the relative safety of the fortress. Cowards and deserters were not treated well by the Adversary or his generals. So even though they survived the attack, their fate was still uncertain and would invariably end up with their deaths at the hands of their own.

It was a short-won victory and served to raise the spirits of the host, giving them hope; and any victory these days was a good one. But later that afternoon, when the archangels gathered to discuss the day's events, the fact that they were basically no further forward took the wind from their sails a touch. Then, not only did they lose the wind, they lost their sails as well when Phanuel returned even later that evening – the Four Horsemen of the Apocalypse and around fifty human marines in tow – with devastating news. Michael stormed off, furious, uttering words and phrases that should never grace the lips of one such as he.

And it was all anyone could do to calm the outraged Raphael, for what with all that had transpired without his knowledge already, the idea that there was a sacred temple with the concealed remains of an ancient and incredibly evil being interred there, hidden from not only the world but the upper echelons of the Celestial Host too, so incensed him, that Uriel thought he was going to revert there and then. Nathaniel and Phanuel tended to the troops and saw to the defenses, just in case the minions rallied and attempted a night assault. Eventually, even Raphael left, citing that he was going to 'chop rocks' for there weren't enough minions in the Domain right now to make him feel better about hitting them. He stormed off, whining about secrets and lies. It left Jennifer and Uriel, for the time being at least, alone – a fact that Uriel was not in the least displeased about.

�473ᛞᛟᛗ ᚱᛋᚠᚱᛋ

Zaramael's fury was reinventing itself exponentially. It had risen to levels previously unheard of, even in the Domain. Vast sections of Lucifer's palace had been smashed and melted during one particularly temperamental outburst, so much so, that it had to be cordoned off for subsequent repair as it was now considered unsafe structurally. Minions were busy laboring away even now to complete the work. Some of them had died already for venturing too far from the relative safety of the crumbling palace they were supposed to be rebuilding. The Adversary had become restless as well as dangerously homicidal in a volatile, explosive sort of way and had little time or mercy for anything that happened to be in the way of him or his sword when he went prowling his new home. A home which was still technically Lucifer's; so too was the sword but the Adversary had considered it all his own even before the coup, for it was his magicks that had helped forge it in the first place and it was how he managed to get it away from Lucifer when he took charge.

But that was the past. Now however was a different matter entirely, and suffice to say that the fact that some things were not going the way he hoped they would, was an understatement. Surprisingly to the Adversary, many of his plans were encountering difficulties, and most were so unforeseen it was what made it so unbelievable. He was apparently surrounded by fools and failure at every turn, and now he found that his army was routed at Megiddo, at his own Fortress. *My own Fortress! Arrgghh.* Though again, it wasn't technically his either; it belonged to the sorcerer Solomon, but he had been missing too long to worry about now. But the thought of the magic wielder caused a rage to flare in the Adversary and another chunk of masonry felt his wrath and was sent spinning away. *How is this possible? Why am I surrounded by incompetents?* Progress at Megiddo was beginning to grate on his already frazzled nerves too, which by normal – or what passed for normal in the Domain – circumstances wouldn't have made him blink. But by absorbing so much power of late, his concentration was suffering, his temper was a hairtrigger and, to add to his problems, he was finding his mental capacity struggling to assimilate to increased input; fuelling his paranoia and neurosis all the more. His predicament was, of course, due to no fault of his. His advisors and generals were failing him at every turn: feeding him misinformation; irregular reports; not divulging important and relevant intelligence where appropriate; and definitely not reporting the increasing number of reportable failures and defeats. His warriors and expanding army were spreading across the face of that miserable planet, spreading chaos and anarchy wherever they went. The number of souls coming to him now was incredible, though it could and should still be more. The possessed too, were growing in numbers, for those demons and minions still unable to take physical form on the Earth wore the pathetic skin suits of humanity to carry out their corruption; but they were only barely adequate for the infernal creatures to move around in, for they lived only a limited time before they rotted and fell apart under the diabolical influence of their host. *Fragile, ridiculous species.* This sort of eradication should have been carried out long before they grew to any kind of sentience. How those moronic and small-minded individuals who supported their ascendance could even entertain these creatures living in the same multiverse as the likes of him, stunned him beyond sensible comprehension. He couldn't begin to articulate his contempt and disdain, so mortified was he. His fists and sword usually did that for him these days. They seemed to get the message over in a more definitive and usually permanent sort of way.

Of course, his current woes were none of his fault. How could they be? He gave the orders; it was those others who failed him and let him down – those who undermined his authority and made a mockery of him by not completing simple tasks when issued.

Azaroth. He had failed in a grand way. One damnable mortal. One insignificant speck of human detritus and he, a veritable god by comparison, one who had walked the multiverse when it was still young, had been incapable of killing him. Okay, so this mortal was in the company of the Four Horsemen and they were capable – *But they were only five against a thousand.* He roared. More masonry went the way of the dodo as another powerful swipe ripped several hunks out of a nearby wall. The details were still fuzzy, for Azaroth hadn't yet reported back to him in the flesh – probably a wise move, all things considered, for in the Adversary's current state of mind, it would be a short report.

Striding across the Grand Hall when he eventually arrived at his destination, the Adversary kicked the remains of the last messenger aside. The ripped-off limbs left sticky slime trails on the smooth marble floor as they slid to smack wetly into the wall. Delivering bad news was a dangerous task at best, but delivering it to the Adversary these days was just suicidal. Oddly enough, there were no longer any volunteers for message duty. It now fell to those minions who were generally out of favor with their lord or commander. It was a lose-lose situation: deliver the message and probably die, fail to do so and die anyway for desertion and treason. This led to a phenomenal amount of toadying and sucking up by the minions, desperate to remain in favor.

Cursing, muttering and intermittently screaming to himself, the Adversary paced the palatial hall. Avoiding the small craters that now dotted the floor – as these now cooled pools of molten liquid marble became more prolific– as the Adversary's temper flared and his fiery footsteps dissolved the rock beneath him. This was another reason he now found himself alone more and more these days. He had incinerated too many advisors who made the mistake of relaying bad news or giving unfavorable advice, standing too close to him when they did so. The range of these spontaneous explosions varied, subject usually to the severity of the news received; but due to his rapid accumulation of power they were somewhat unpredictable. Though he was gaining more control of this newly acquired power each day, it didn't always work. Taking a few calming breaths, the Adversary closed his eyes and envisaged his lieutenant, Azaroth. Projecting his consciousness out, he sped across time and space towards him. For if he wouldn't come to the mountain, then, much to Azaroth's imminent displeasure and utter horror, the mountain would go to him.

Blissfully unaware of what was about to befall him, Azaroth reclined in the heat, soaking up the moderate warmth of the midday sun. It was nowhere near as warm as his own realm, but it sufficed nonetheless. The insipid warmth of the fiery orb fell upon him as he gnawed on some charred flesh. What it had been before its roasting was anybody's guess. Azaroth didn't care either way; he was hungry and that was all there was to that. But whatever it was, it was now the meal of the demon lord – bones and all – who very nearly choked on it when the image of his master appeared directly before him, glowering with barely concealed displeasure. The awesome visage of the Adversary towered over Azaroth, standing – or hovering as it was, a few inches off the ground – with powerful arms folded across its rippling chest, one long, black talon tapping gently upon his massive and perfectly formed bicep. The blazing eyes bore into the desperately scrambling demon, who was clambering to perform the requisite bows and obediences to his lord, but failing dismally. The Adversary's voice cut through his mind like razor wire being pulled through his head.

'Get up and explain yourself, Azaroth, and for your sake, it had better be good.'

Azaroth stood, endeavoring to regain some composure, though there was little chance of that now. He was fuming inside at being caught out the way he had been; he must be slipping. But what enraged the hunter more, was how easily the Adversary had circumnavigated his wards, as though they were no longer there. Azaroth always set up wards around his person when he was at ease: they warned him well in advance when and who was approaching him. They had saved his life on numerous occasions, except now, apparently.

Azaroth launched into the details of how the current situation had come about. Of how the renegades had taken up a desperate refuge in some old ruin a few miles away, and how his minions were routing them right now. In fact they were due to return even as they spoke. But the Adversary brushed away the details in favor of one in particular.

'You've killed the human then, I take it?' The Adversary looked around the immediate vicinity, making a show of looking for some evidence – a trophy, maybe. Perhaps his head? Some bones? His heart even? Anything? The lack of any immediate response told the Adversary more than mere words could convey.

'I'll take that as a no, then. So why not?' The tone of his lord was still cool, though that was probably more disturbing to Azaroth than had he been raging.

'My lord Adversary, it seems that the mortal has taken up with the Four Horsemen, and they were still more formidable than previously anticipated. More resourceful it seems, for it was they who took the mortal to ground in the ruin, where they have ensconced themselves like burrowing grubs.'

The Adversary frowned a little and swiveled his head to get a better look at the surroundings he was standing within. Without looking at Azaroth, he asked, 'Where exactly is this "ruin" you speak of? This terrain looks uncannily familiar, for some reason I cannot place. Why is that, Azaroth?'

Azaroth didn't know. He had never been here before himself and one ruin looked much the same as any other, surely? The Adversary ranged his mind out further, taking in the grim scene of the battle of the ruin. He wasn't expecting the sight before him. Nor did it fill him with merciful thoughts.

Returning to Azaroth, he studied the nervous demon before him, looking for complicity or any indication that he was lying or attempting to deceive him. All he saw was monumental arrogance; a superior blasé attitude from one who was used to getting his own way and unused to failure, though he had the grace to exhibit the appropriate fear at his eminent presence. Though he had never been up against the Horsemen directly, it was still barely excusable. No one had ever dared before now, but these were unprecedented times. The sight of the small chapel fortress triggered something lost in the dark recesses of the Adversary's memory; as did the sight of the battered and bedraggled remnants of his force fleeing across the desert back towards them, fending off some angelic warriors and, fortunately for Azaroth, this sight took the murderous thoughts from him. There was more to this scenario than the Adversary first thought and he found he needed answers more than he needed the feel of Azaroth's warm entrails sliding through his fingers.

'I think you'll find your forces have been decimated, Azaroth. I saw the remains of the Celestial Host out there. I'm suspecting that the renegades had help in their escape.' Azaroth's eyes went wider still at the word. 'Yes, escape. They are no longer there and the moment has passed. Hmmm? Any thoughts?'

Azaroth had none. His mind was spinning cartwheels, trying to make sense of what his lord was telling him. *They failed?* It was inconceivable. As he looked, stunned at the words of the Adversary, he ranged his own astral form out to see for himself the truth of what he was hearing. His heart sank as the limping survivors struggled back, fighting a rearguard from a flight of the Celestial Host, who were harrying the fleeing demons. Azaroth was disappointed to see Karcon amongst the survivors; he disliked the creature intensely and trusted him even less. His loss would *not* have been a blow. It was a shame they hadn't all just died and be done.

'Deal with those angels and return to me here. I desire a moment to think.'

Azaroth was keen to oblige, for he was getting a second chance at redemption here and he knew it. The respite from being out beneath the Adversary's scrutiny gave him a moment to think, too. He could also vent some of his now considerable annoyance upon the warriors of the Celestial Host. They would take the brunt of his fury. And did. All Karcon saw as he desperately held off two warriors with his own broken sword and one he had ripped from a fallen demon, was a dark blur, as the mighty Azaroth powered into the surprised angels. Their screams were terrible as Karcon saw a whole new side to his surrogate master. Azaroth was fury incarnate and the seven angelic warriors stood no chance against him. Three of them never even saw the huge bastard sword coming, as it smashed through them like stalks of corn. The other four fell to Azaroth's talons as he eviscerated and decapitated them with a howl of infernal pleasure, relishing their deaths as though it were a delicacy to be savored. The remains of their ruined corpses steamed upon the desert floor as Azaroth turned his darkly blazing gaze upon his lieutenant. Between ragged breaths, the big Neanderthal, who had watched the brief battle with relief and interest, wondered if he would be so easy to kill after all. He would have to rethink his plans.

Azaroth said nothing to the demon or to the remainder of the survivors, for these carrion were below his direct contact. Instead, he merely glowered at them with barely restrained murder in his eyes. Then, after a moment's consideration, Azaroth took off, flying back to the Adversary, who was only an apparition at the moment; but it wouldn't do to make him any more furious than he already was by having to chase his ass.

'My lord,' Azaroth coughed as he landed back upon the ridge where he had left the Adversary contemplating. 'They are taken care of, and the remnants of the force will be here shortly. I cannot understand how this happened, my lord. I cast a shield over our warriors. Nothing should have been able to affect them: only something of an equally dark force should have been able to dispel it, and, it would have had to have been in the proximity of our warriors to do so. None there were powerful enough. Such magicks are not the province of the Horsemen – that much I know – which was why I chose to employ such a powerful enchantment.'

'Yet apparently there *was* something there, and I have a suspicion as to what it was. Come with me, Azaroth. We will put paid to this mystery and determine your next move.' But as he finished speaking, Karcon and his ragtag group of demons appeared from behind an outcropping and stopped short of Azaroth and the Adversary, dropping to their knees, well, those that could. Some simply dropped dead, overcome by their wounds and by the sight of the Adversary. Others didn't have knees at all yet they abased themselves as best they could. The sight of Karcon forestalled the Adversary's departure and the Dark Storm turned to address him, pointing a talon directly at Karcon's heart, or at least where it should have been. If asked, the big creature would maintain he didn't have one.

'*You!*' the Adversary roared before resuming at a more acceptable level. 'You wretched creature, explain your failure, and why have you returned unsuccessful? Explain also why you did not simply die in service to your lord rather than return in disgrace.'

Karcon stepped forward and told the tale as best he could, for speaking in long bouts wasn't his strong point. Hitting things was what he did best.

'My... my lord,' he faltered as he began, 'we took the outer walls and drove them underground, where they held the narrow entrance against us by bringing the rocks down. By the time we had breached the pathetic defense and engaged them, aid arrived from behind, which at first proved to be more of a distraction than a problem, due to the shield. But then a strange thing happened and the shield vanished. It was our downfall and the hated Phanuel led his cavalry against us. Their javelins and spears took many before they hammered us like so much iron against the anvil of the Horsemen. These creatures were the only survivors other than myself, who for my part, fought until the end. These wretches *hid* beneath the dead until the main body of the Celestial Host, along with the Horsemen and their humans, opened a gate and fled. I have nothing to do with them; they simply followed me back here. If you wish me to impale myself upon a blade, give me one that's not broken and I'll gladly give my life for you, my lord.' Karcon held out his big gnarly hands in supplication, waiting for a sword to be placed there. Azaroth drew his blade and was about to hand it to Karcon when the Adversary stopped him. Azaroth nearly growled his frustration at being so close.

'Wait, Azaroth. His words have the ring of truth and his willingness to die bears them out. Maybe he can be utilized for another task. His failure is nothing compared to yours, it was not *Karcon* who let the mortal escape, nor was it *Karcon* who I entrusted this task to. It was *you*, if I recall, so do not be so quick to end his life when it should be yours that be forfeit.'

Neither saw the smile play across Karcon's ugly features, though it was so misshapen, few would have called it a smile even if seen full on. Painful wind, perhaps...? 'What is your name, warrior? By what are you called?' the Adversary asked the still groveling Karcon. Though he knew it already, it was best to retain the pretense before Azaroth, lest he suspect their duplicity.

'Karcon, great lord. Karcon the magnificent, due to my recently acquired wings, my lord.' Karcon spread his emerald green angel's wings in demonstration of his title.

'I see. Taken from the enemy, I presume?'

Karcon nodded encouragingly.

'Good. As it should be. Azaroth!' The Adversary turned to the arch demon and gave instruction to promote Karcon to his official second – a move designed to enrage and humiliate the arch demon. Of course, it was fortunate that Karcon had even survived the assault, but that was why the Adversary had chosen him: he was notoriously hard to kill.

'As you wish, my lord.' Azaroth could have throttled the groveling creature where it squatted and cheerfully fed it to the Adversary, had he been there in the flesh; so incensed was he at this turn of events. It was rapidly going from bad to worse.

'Then, Karcon, I want you to kill these miserable cowards. I will not tolerate such craven actions. When you are finished wait here for my return. Azaroth, give him your sword!' When he hesitated, though it was only for a fraction of a second, the rebuke was fearsome, even for an apparition. 'Do it now or face my wrath, you disobedient scum!'

Azaroth felt the force of the Adversary's will in the very fabric of his being, so potent was it. If he continued to grow at the rate he was absorbing power, it wouldn't be long before he was able to extinguish life with the same thought that held his image before them now. Life would get very tense then. Azaroth, however, handed his weapon to the smug looking Karcon, and turned his back on him – a move of faith, though he kept his astral eye fixed on him, waiting for treachery. But none came. Instead, he turned to carry out his instruction while the Adversary continued his previous conversation with Azaroth in a tone that made him wonder if they had been interrupted at all.

'Let's go take a look at this ruin of yours, for if it is what I think it is, your disfavor with me degenerates further than you can imagine, *old friend.*' The last two words had a ring about them that put the hackles up on the neck of Azaroth. They rang of past tense, of formerly known as. There was a finality to the way he said it that disturbed him greatly. What was this ruin and why was it so important to him? He would find out soon enough. The Adversary promptly vanished, leaving Azaroth to unfurl his great raven wings and launch himself at speed in the direction of the ruin, lest he leave him waiting for his arrival, though he began to wonder just how much more shit he could be in that wouldn't get him killed.

Azaroth landed softly before the devastated walls, at the breach his warriors had created. It was there the image of the Adversary awaited him. His expression didn't offer any encouragement that this was going to be a wild goose chase or somesuch. He'd found something he didn't like. Azaroth looked at the ruins, looking for something that distinguished them from any other. He almost missed the graven markings above what remained of the linteled entrance to the underground chambers Karcon spoke of. His heart sank deeper still, if that was at all possible. It was so deep it was almost subterranean now. The word *Nakir* could be made out. Then, like with the Adversary, a distant memory was dragged kicking and screaming to the forefront of his mind. With it a realization of just what he had allowed to transpire by his complacency over one measly human. And, why his enchantment was fractured. Much to his disbelief, matters had just gotten considerably worse. He concluded he was cursed somehow. He had to be.

The Adversary saw the realization of what had happened dawn on Azaroth's face. He let it sink in good and proper before he let rip into him, straining to contain his explosive rage and retain a modicum of decorum for the ruler he was aspiring to be.

'I see you know what that was.' It was not a question but a confirmation. Azaroth simply nodded. 'You know what's in there and where it goes, so, where do you think the human is now?' The last was a question, and one the Adversary wanted an answer for, but Azaroth was lost momentarily in thought at the implications of this turn of events and how they might affect him. The Adversary took this for insolence and roared at Azaroth with the hurricane force he had used earlier. That got his attention again.

'*It goes to the Domain, you sniveling, useless, worthless, putrid piece of Karak shit!*' The blast nearly lifted him off his feet. Yet it wasn't the force that annoyed him; it was the insult. A Karak was a beast of burden that was bred and dwelt within the Domain, employed in swampy regions for heavy lifting. The prime reason that they existed in the temperate swamps was because of their waste. Their shit was so foul, it had to fall beneath the equally foul water as soon as possible to prevent it from poisoning anybody unfortunate enough to be in its immediate proximity. The smell alone had been known to kill weaker beings. Were it not for their almost unlimited strength and their basic mental capacity, these beasts would have been wiped out long ago. Yet there was one odd thing about them – their roast flesh was some of the most juicy, sweet and tender in the entire Domain. It beggared belief how something so utterly repugnant, lethal and noxious as what sloshed about their four intestines, to eventually pass out of their backsides – could exist in flesh that tasted so good, both cooked or raw. To be called after their shit was a low insult, reserved for the lowliest of creatures, and it scored the mark the Adversary intended. Azaroth's face became thunderous. It was only with a gargantuan exertion of will that he kept his voice even.

'Surely, *my lord Zaramael*, a mortal in the Domain will not survive long, if indeed he even survived the transition. Density manipulation for lesser creatures is usually fatal. Those that do exist there, do so at our sufferance.' Azaroth imbued the title of his liege with as much contempt as he could muster, using his given name to lend it weight.

'Think, you moron. If he passed through the gate, then he must have either been empowered to do so, or he was taken through. Both options will adjust him to the Domain's density, for only beings of a certain level of power can operate such a gate. The consecrated bones of a being such as Nakir forge powerful links with the Domain. It was what made his crypt so sought after. It vanished several hundred years ago and none from Lucifer's realm could take physical form here long enough to seek it out. There are only so many beings in the multiverse with enough power to hide the likes of this. The Four Horsemen and the Drakarim. And as I see no dragons hereabouts, I'm guessing that the Horsemen opened it, and in order to know where it was to open it, it stands they must have been the ones who closed it and hid it. Please keep up. And it was the mortal passing through it that caused the failure of your spell; the energy release of the portal nullified it. Do you see my problem now, Azaroth? The problem your failure has left me?'

He didn't really. In his mind, the problem was gone. The domain was no place for the unwary, let alone some wayward mortal who had inadvertently landed himself there. In Azaroth's mind, he was as good as dead.

'We don't know where it comes out, do we? For all we know he could have fallen into a frozen methane ocean or onto the razor sharp rocks of the Tartarus Mountains. Perhaps even into one of the lava oceans. Let's face it, there are a thousand places – a thousand thousand places in fact, where he could have met his doom. How do we know he's even alive? Let it go.'

The Adversary was losing what little patience remained to him. Were Azaroth not the excellent tracker he bragged to be, he would have torn him limb from limb for the sheer pleasure of it, reanimated him and done it all over again until the urge went away. As it was, he needed him – and at the same time despised the fact he needed him.

'I have no more time to spend here educating you, Azaroth. Fetch Karcon and return to the Domain. Do what you can to find this human and rid me of him once and for all.' The image of the Adversary leant in close to Azaroth's face, scant millimeters away, and he spoke in the most chilling tones he had ever heard.

'Fail me again and I promise you this: you will live as a boneless sack of flesh for all eternity, for I will personally remove every bone within your sorry body, after breaking every one first. They will then be pulled slowly from your living corpse and you will feel every one coming out, from your skull to your spine. Then I will start on your internal organs. This will happen every day until I say otherwise. Do I make myself clear?'

He did.

'I will not fail you again, mighty Zaramael. You know I live to serve.'

The Adversary stood back and looked at his vassal, long and appraisingly. 'Do I really? Well prove it. Find the human and bring me his head!'

Azaroth bowed and asked the one question he immediately regretted asking the moment the words left his mouth. 'Where would you have me start, my lord? The Domain is a large place.'

'That's why I sent you to kill him here, when I knew where he was, you imbecile. Now there is a whole planet to comb. It's your task. You figure it out. But I want it done by the full moon of this world. Much depends upon it. Including your continued existence pain free.'

Azaroth looked up and concentrated on the sky and the stars beyond. He calculated he had about three weeks' Earth time before his deadline ran out. Not long enough to cover an entire planet. He needed a plan B. No time like the present; he would achieve nothing more here other than more threats and abuse. Enough was enough, even from the Adversary. It wasn't too late to replace him with another whilst Lucifer was still incapacitated. *Hmmm! Food for thought.* With that, Azaroth bowed low to the image of his lord and made his obeisances as he turned and left, flapping gracefully away, back to the hated Karcon. The Adversary watched him go for a moment himself, before winking out and returning to his stationary body, standing motionless in his palatial hall. To the casual observer, it looked as though the Adversary was merely standing and thinking – though few were so incredibly stupid as to stand and casually observe the arch demon, at least not within arm's or even sword's reach. Certainly not if they expected to live for much longer.

After a few seconds' reorientation to reacquaint himself with his body, the Adversary bellowed out for another of his vassals – a sound that put every other thing in range of the sound on instant alert. For not only was there one volatile maniac on the loose, but he had just called for another one. It was going to get messy again; they just knew it.

'Asmodeus!' was all he roared. Caring not if he was in the vicinity to hear it. Simply expecting him to respond. Most creatures of power within the ruling echelons of the Domain had their names attuned in such a way that should anyone speak them, they became aware of who was speaking. If they got really bored, they could extend that ability to the other realms and influence the speaker, should they so desire, for good or ill. Usually ill. That was much more fun.

In this instance, he was not kept waiting long, nor did he need to issue a second summons, for that would have reduced his mood from already foul, to something that didn't warrant consideration. With a resounding crash, the double doors to the great hall slammed open with enough force to loosen the hinges on one of the huge, solid doors, leaving it hanging askew. This did nothing to alleviate the humor of the Adversary as the being known as Asmodeus stormed in to the hall.

He was a great hairy, barrel-chested demon resembling an ancient malevolent Khan figure, draped in several shaggy bearskins falling from his huge, broad shoulders. A few still bore their owners' skulls, filled with row after row of golden wire wrapped teeth and fangs. They still seemed alive and animated as the big demon's muscles moved and flowed beneath them. The dark grey and leathery skin of his huge belly hung over a wide belt – which supported baggy leggings tucked into dark leather boots, though what they were the leather of was uncertain, for they were thick scaled, like some huge lizard. Facially, Asmodeus was much akin to the bears he wore. Coarse black hair covered most of the surface of his face except for the glowing yellow eyes and the gaping maw of his mouth, which like the skulls, was full of adorned fangs and tusks, attended occasionally by the long black flicking tongue that emerged to scent the air. He was something of a cross with bear, boar and crocodile, exhibiting all the vicious traits of each. From the head down, it was hard to differentiate where his furred helm, with its two spiraling horns, stopped and his shaggy mane of hair started. Rumor had it that he never removed it – and even slept in it, rutted in it and, though no one could actually attest to witnessing the event, even bathed in it. Framing all this fur and fang was an impressive twin pair of blue-black leathery wings – a malignant fusion of dragonfly and bat. Each membrane of the sprawling wings ended with a vicious looking claw at its tip, and the poison they carried was potent enough to kill a Karak in less time than it took to defecate.

Another object Asmodeus was rarely seen without was currently gripped tightly in the huge and equally hair-covered right hand. His renown with this weapon was legendary within the Domain and the gigantic double headed axe had myths all of its own. So large that it took two minions to carry it, its twin blades shone golden and were as large as two shields. One blade was honed razor sharp and due to several strategic grooves in it, sang when it was arcing through the air. Often it was the last sound any creature foolish enough to stand before the bearlike warrior ever heard. It almost cried as it took life. The other blade had an evil serrated edge that tore and rendered flesh to ragged shreds, causing wounds that should the unlucky cur actually survive a confrontation, would never heal cleanly, leaving a permanent and messy reminder of who not to antagonize. Asmodeus wielded this awesome weapon as though it were no more than a hatchet. In his left hand was a sloshing horn of noxious smelling ale. His appetites ran to excess on all accounts. Battle, whores, ale and sleep. Not necessarily in that order.

'What do you want, Zaramael? I heard this noise and thought it was my ass at first, then I recognized it as your voice. Not so dissimilar.' Asmodeus grumbled something else to himself and lumbered over to the one remaining chair left intact after the Adversary's earlier tantrums. Squashing his bulk into the chair, he belched and took another great swallow of the ale, spilling as much down his face as he poured in. Emptying the flagon, he tossed it aside, lifted himself up on one cheek and broke wind explosively.

'Aaahhh, that's better. Now what did you want, boy? I've a busy schedule.' The Adversary was verging on apoplectic hysteria; he hadn't been spoken to this way since he deposed Lucifer and commenced his cataclysmic plan. Most feared for their lives too much. Not so Asmodeus. He was older than the Adversary by aeons. And it was believed he even witnessed the great exodus of the Drakarim, though he never admitted that he did, but nor did he deny that he hadn't. It all added to the air of mystery he maintained.

'Your insolence will be your undoing one of these days, old man. It is only fortunate that we go back aways and I am indebted to you. But those favors are running low and I would tread more shrewdly, were I you.'

Asmodeus squinted at the Adversary, as though unsure of what to make of him, or more likely suffering the effects of too many ales too early in the day. That would be barrels as well.

'You summoned me here to threaten me? I can get that back home without tending to your needs. If you wanted to do that, why not carry on bellowing like the Karak you sound like?' Asmodeus sniffed and scrunched his face up in disgust. 'And this place smells much like a Karak farm,' at which point he sniffed himself, 'though that might be me. Who cares? But I'm guessing you wanted something other than my awesome company. Am I right?'

The Adversary began to pace his own hall, much as he had before, though only without dissolving the marble flooring. It was a testament to his slowly growing self-control, though it was usually shortlived as the incoming power overwhelmed him again.'Your company is tolerated, along with your rank odor and insolence, only for as long as you continue to obey my commands – lest you find your parasite-infested carcass ensconced alongside your former master.'

Asmodeus just laughed, as one would laugh at the pretensions of a young boy trying to be a man, and one who had heard it all before. 'Sorry, Zaramael. Can't help myself. Of course I understand your position. However, *boy* rulers come and go. They always have, they always will. It seems to be the way of things everywhere. That interesting period on Earth when the Romans conquered much of the known world demonstrates that very well. Changing left, right and center they were, all because they pissed off those who supported them. Always remember, son: value those who help you on the way up. If not, they'll kick the living shit out of you on the way back down. A free lesson, *oh great and shiny one*,' Asmodeus drawled in mock obsequiousness.

That did it. That tipped the Adversary beyond the edge.

'You mock me?' His voice was colder now than the frozen methane oceans. The Adversary began to grow in height and rage, while Asmodeus just sat and watched him. But enough was enough.

'Calm down, for Belial's sake. You'll pop something. Though I may not crawl at your feet like those other toadies you surround yourself with, you have my support and that of my legions. But my advice is take it easy on the absorption. You're becoming far too sensitive and volatile. After all, just look at this place; it's a mess. You may not like the manner of my counsel, but that's too bad. My words are the balance to all that sucking up you get. I won't lie to you, least not yet anyway, not while those promises you made stay made. It's better to serve one I can put up with rather than one who pisses me off with his increasingly pitiful rule. It's also better than ceasing to exist. Where's the fun in that? I'd miss my ale and whores too much. The sound of their bones cracking as they are taken, their succulent flesh sundering beneath my claws, damn, I'm erect just at the thought of it. Do a better job and I'm there, old friend. Now, for the last time, what do you want?'

'Keep your filthy cock under control, you sadistic bastard,' the Adversary snapped back, though not with any real aggression. The old goat was right: it was refreshing to hear a voice of reason and it helped him wrestle the dark fog of rage that overcame him with increasing frequency as he took on more and more. 'I have a task for you. Azaroth, may his balls rot and fester, has allowed a mortal to enter the Domain and I want, no, I *need* this human annihilated, expunged from existence.'

Asmodeus waved a dismissive claw. 'Then have Azaroth deal with it. There are humans dumped into the Domain on a daily basis. Why should one more get up your nose so much?'

The Adversary shook his great golden head and walked back and forth again, his hands clasped behind him, more to prevent them wrapping themselves about the throat of Asmodeus. He was a simple creature and failed to see the bigger picture more often than not and he hated having to explain it to him. But explain it he did, as though he were telling a child.

'So you think he might be the one destined to stop you? Do you really think one human could stop you at this point?' Asmodeus listened but he rarely heard anything he didn't want to hear. 'The prophecy is so old that not even Lucifer believes it any more, correction, believed it. I keep forgetting he's gone now.'

The Adversary stopped and looked at Asmodeus – a meaningful look that made the old bear repeat what he had just said to himself, and then the proverbial penny dropped. Asmodeus moved to stand before the Adversary. He moved pretty fast for a hulking behemoth of a creature – a condition he cultivated to throw his enemies off balance until the moment came. Then they were really surprised.

'He's not gone, is he? That's why I'm here, isn't it? You young fool, what have you done?' Much of Asmodeus's casual attitude came with the knowledge that his former liege was no more. Discovering that it was not the case brought him up short and brought a note of trepidation to his voice.

'Lucifer did in fact keep a copy of the prophecy,' said the Adversary. 'He took it seriously enough, I can assure you.' The Adversary cast a dark and condescending look at Asmodeus. 'Forget your whores, forget your fucking appetites and for one second pay attention to what I am telling you, unless you think that you can whore and drink with your own head shoved up your ass and that axe of yours shoved down the wet hole that will be your neck.' Asmodeus gave a quick bow of assent and allowed his lord to continue. 'I can't trust Azaroth and I suspect that I will have to deal with him soon enough. For now, I can't have the object of the prophecy here, in the same domain as Lucifer. While he was on Earth they were sufficiently separated, but not now. One of them has to go and as I don't know where the infernal human has ended up yet, that leaves Lucifer. I need someone I can trust to do this, but until I find someone, you'll have to do. He is more than a potential danger; he is a sign of weakness, my weakness. That *I* allowed, however indirectly, this mortal to enter *my* realm, will be seen as a failure. Should the other lords get wind of this before I have accumulated sufficient power for it to not matter, things could become problematic. The fact it would be disastrous is an understatement. Which brings me to the secondary part of your task.'

'By Baphomet's hairy balls, there's more? I think you are starting to take advantage of my good nature, Zaramael.' Asmodeus stomped back and forth across the hall, occasionally casting speculative glances at the Adversary, just to make sure he was still there and this wasn't some huge charade. He was and it wasn't. The Adversary was beyond deadly in his seriousness. Giving up his predilection for walking around in pointless circles, Asmodeus stalked over to stand before his protégé, the demon he had taught subterfuge to and helped eradicate his name from history to better perform his duties as Lucifer's agent. It was at moment that Asmodeus realized the Adversary had grown. He now towered over Asmodeus. Whereas before, the hairy demon had been considered a giant amongst his peers, he felt small now as he stared into the abysses that were the eyes of the Adversary. And he didn't like it one little bit.

'You're getting bigger too. You're obviously getting more than you are letting on about from this arrangement. How about you sharing some of the spoils around with those who support you? If there is power to be had, I for one want some of it. Should the lords find out the true state of affairs, there'll be hell to pay, and I want all the edge I can get.'

'Do this thing for me,' the Adversary cajoled, knowing he had Asmodeus back where he wanted him. The lure of power was a strong motivator in the Domain. 'And I will let you feel the ecstasy of the living force as it flows from the dying Earth. I will let you taste the sweetness of her death, and it will put you off your whores and drink forever. Nothing comes close to the sensation. There is no narcotic anywhere in the multiverse to compare with it. Kill this human and deliver this thing for me and it will be yours to drink your fill. What say you, Asmodeus, *old friend*?' The Adversary folded his arms across his chest and looked down upon his mentor and vassal, and waited patiently for the reply he knew was coming.

'Very well, you've talked me into it. What do you want me to deliver? I'll have my best scouts abroad within the hour to start the search for this mortal. They'll comb the Domain. Don't worry, we'll find him.' Asmodeus waited for the details of the delivery, but his face dropped and he took an involuntary step backwards from the Adversary when he told him, looking him up and down as though he were some imposter.

'Lucifer!'

The Adversary faced Asmodeus and smiled a most chilling smile, filling the bearlike demon with unimaginable dread. He barely found his voice. *'You've still got him – here? Are you mad?'* he hissed. His golden glowing eyes had widened in shock that the former lord of the entire Domain was still within these walls. 'Surely though, he is at least dead?'

The Adversary shook his head slowly. 'Careful, old man. The last being to call me mad is over there – and there and there.' The Adversary pointed to several body parts strewn across the hall and up the wall. The slight smile of inner mirth had not left the Adversary's face and it disturbed Asmodeus as much as the revelation. *Perhaps he is truly mad. How much power can one being take, after all?* he thought closely to himself as he looked at the being before him, for even stray thoughts were no guarantee of safety with his increasing powers. Even though Asmodeus was ancient, and had a myriad of personal enchantments shielding him at all times from the prying minds of his enemies – for a ranking demon had no "friends" at his level – the Adversary was an unpredictable force now. There was no telling what he was capable of. Asmodeus was watching the Adversary, who seemed to have gone a bit distant, staring off into space as though he was looking at something that only he could see. Asmodeus wasn't sure if he should say anything, leave, or what – either one of them was bound to be the wrong choice – so he just stood and waited. Long moments passed before the Adversary spoke again, and then it was as though nothing had interrupted his earlier thoughts.

'Yes, I still have him here and no, he's not dead. It was a tough choice,

I must admit, but he has been part of the Domain so long, I thought it best to wait until I have sufficient power to sustain this world before destroying its former ruler – just in case there were any repercussions to his demise.'

Asmodeus was still stunned at this. 'There'll be bloody repercussions all right if this ever gets out. Can you trust all the minions here? They were Lucifer's before yours, and loyalty is a very precarious thing here.'

The Adversary looked momentarily troubled at that. He had killed quite a few of Lucifer's personal servants for that very reason, but how many more were there? Had any others seen the crystalline gaol of Lucifer? He hadn't materialized it many times, but walls here had both eyes and ears. Maybe he would have to eradicate the rest and start over entirely. Messy but probably safer until he ascended beyond having to concern himself with such petty matters. His thoughts of carnage were interrupted by Asmodeus.

'So where am I supposed to be taking him, then? It had better be somewhere good.' A note of resignation had deflated the usually irascible arch demon, and the Adversary turned to stare bemusedly at the shaggy demon's discomfort and deflated tone.

'Cheer up, you old goat. Of course it's somewhere good. Who do you think I am?' Asmodeus knew it to be rhetorical and wisely kept his mouth shut. 'I want you to take him to Daemos. It is a small and seldom-used rock which Lucifer kept for his own personal entertainment. It has restricted access: mainly him and now me, and the only place that anyone other than Lucifer himself could get there, is via a hidden portal which lies beyond the Graven Forest on the shores of Charon's river, at the base of the Tartarus Mountains.'

Asmodeus didn't look convinced. His mind was calculating the distance and the likelihood of all the possible things that could go wrong en route. They were many. 'Why not just open a portal and take him there direct? Surely that would limit the hazards?'

The Adversary shook his great head as he sauntered over to stand before the hairy general, a long black talon extending on his right hand as he neared Asmodeus. Standing before him, the Adversary placed his left hand upon the shoulder of the now nervous demon, and with the right, began to lightly trace the razor talon over the fat, hairy and grey-scaled belly in front of him. The Adversary spoke in gentle tones to Asmodeus, as though he were talking to some senile old codger.

'Asmodeus, Asmodeus. How is it you have lived so long? Have you spent so long thinking with your cock that your mind has putrefied? Or are you so ale-sodden that the festering lump between your disgusting ears has atrophied? Either way, you, of all people, know that should I open a portal to the cavern entrance, it will leave a signature. A traceable signature for the more astute of my enemies. It matters not that it originates here, but it matters a great deal if they should discover the whereabouts of the entrance. I had gone to great pains to secure the area several thousand years ago. You have no idea how many sorcerers I had to kill to ensure it stayed the secret we wanted it to be. That portal is one of a kind, and until I decide what to do with Lucifer, I don't want it tampered with. Now, before I send you on your way, there is a crevasse upon Daemos. It's very deep, I assure you. There are several of Lucifer's enemies still down there who can attest to its depth. Or could at least if they were not long dead. Dump him in there; he can talk to them for a while.' He paused in his tracing and stood back to look at the great quivering belly. Asmodeus, curious as to what he was looking at, tried to look as well, but couldn't see over the horizon of his girth, though he soon found out.

'Of course, you'll need to know the exact location and the enchantment to activate the portal. But I need to be confident that it remains a secret, which is why I have engraved it upon your flesh. It will ensure that only you can activate it. You need not read it; simply walk through.'

During this explanation Asmodeus began to scream as searing glyphs and sigils began to brand themselves onto the flesh where the Adversary had traced. The acid touch of his talons had sliced deep and the blood flowed freely over the top and spilt onto the marble floor, hissing where it touched.

'Now I suggest you go get yourself cleaned up and have your legions ready to travel by sun up. You have a long way to go, and not long to do it, for I want him there as soon as possible. I'm sure a being of your caliber will have no trouble multitasking, and in your instance, that means doing more than one thing at once. Walking and breathing do not count.' The Adversary roared with laughter. He always laughed at his own humor, for he considered himself quite amusing at times; though few others did, for it was usually at their expense as the Adversary killed, maimed or tortured them. It always involved pain of some description anyway.

The laughter of the Adversary and the screaming of Asmodeus were both cut short as a commotion from without grew in volume and proximity. Something big and very pissed off was rapidly approaching the great hall. There was much roaring and smashing going on, punctuated with occasional screams as the Adversary's guards tried and failed to prevent whatever it was getting any further.

'What now?' Both Asmodeus and the Adversary looked towards the weighty doors of the hall, which were presently closed but not secured. They waited calmly, though Asmodeus was drawing ragged breaths as the agony slowly abated from his recent branding, and he too looked with some trepidation in the direction of the roaring cacophony. They didn't have long to wait.

The poor doors that had taken such punishment since the Adversary had moved in were no stranger to rough handling, but even they finally gave up their Herculean battle to cling to the framework as the cause of the ruckus came thundering into the great hall. It seemed that anger had overridden sense in this impressive demon. This giant amongst demons was the creature known as Shemyaza the Strong. In his current state he even dwarfed the Adversary, who was standing calmly – at least on the exterior. Inside he was imploding with rage at this intrusion and the manner in which it had been executed. Shemyaza entered with such devastating force that both doors were ripped from their massive hinges and sent spinning end over end towards Asmodeus and the Adversary. But a casual gesture from the new ruler of the Domain sent both doors veering off to embed themselves in the marble and granite walls, where they vibrated with the impact. The Adversary was not really a connoisseur of art, so the travesty perpetrated upon those golden doors was lost on him, but the fact that they were his doors more than made up for it. Yet still he remained motionless and silent as the brutal looking Shemyaza ate up the ground as he strode across the hall, stopping only when he was mere feet from the Adversary. Asmodeus, who had seen what his lord was capable of, and knew his very limited temper of old, prudently began to back up away from the spatter area. By his reckoning, this was Shemyaza's third mistake of the day. This monster was supposed to be a general in command of a hundred thousand. In Asmodeus's opinion, he had all the brains of a lobotomized Karak.

'Why was I not summoned to this counsel? I arrive at the fortress of Asmodeus to be told he has been summoned before you. In this war, we should all be privy to whatever plans are afoot, should we not, usurper?' Fourth mistake, grimaced Asmodeus. This wasn't going to end well. Without raising his head, or his eyes, the Adversary spoke to the chest of Shemyaza as though it were his head. *Need to go a bit lower to find his brains though*, thought Asmodeus wryly. He sat himself back down on the seat he had occupied earlier and began to examine the still bubbling scorch marks emblazoned upon his own belly.

'So I take it,' the Adversary began softly, 'that you feel quite strongly about this. So strongly in fact, that you saw fit to burst into my private hall and interrupt a private meeting that you were specifically *not* invited to. Odd as it may seem to you, my intellectually challenged Shemyaza, not all my affairs are to be sanctioned by you. Do I seem reasonable so far?'

Shemyaza wasn't expecting this response at all. Asmodeus truly wondered just what sort of reaction he had expected. He couldn't have thought to intimidate the Adversary? That would have been insane. But from past dealings with the brute, Asmodeus knew him to be easily influenced.

Maybe someone had been pouring poison in his ear, winding him up and finally letting him go to see what chaos he caused. I wonder who that could be? Asmodeus grew thoughtful as he tried to fathom a likely candidate.

'I also presume, Shemyaza...' The name was said with enough contempt to herald an obvious warning to one of even limited intelligence. He wasn't even limited, it seemed, '...that by the most deafening noise, you abused yourself of my guards and staff. I hope for your sake that not too many of them are injured or dead. They are proving frightfully difficult to replace, for some reason.' Something that passed for realization crossed fleetingly over Shemyaza's expression: a dawning of exactly what it was he had done. 'I also gather that other doors in my household have gone much the same way as these?'

Shemyaza nodded dumbly then, his reactions not quite catching up with the precarious moment he now stood within. Though he was about to find that out. Asmodeus looked up at the rising voice of his lord, and saw that not only was his voice rising, but he was expanding proportionately with it. Passing eye level with Shemyaza, it was the brute who now had to start looking up. But as the Adversary grew, so the temperature began to drop around him: the freezing air of menace and impending violence.

'I have as much right to be present when decisions are made as that hairy toad,' Shemyaza continued shakily now, trying to salvage some sort of lifeline. 'All plans that affect the Domain affect us all and am I not a lord of this realm as much as *him*. Even Lucifer himself knew better than to treat me this way, Zaramael.'

That did it. Few people got to use his given name since he had resurrected it. Most remembered the title at least: my lord or my liege. But to simply drop it and treat him as an equal was frankly suicidal. Then to add in the hated name of Lucifer in the same breath – it was more or less prohibited now. With the Adversary, it was do as I say not as I do. He had accumulated enough power to enforce his command, and had done so on more than one occasion already. Shemyaza had more or less signed his own death warrant by his total lack of sense and decorum.

'You dare to mention his name in my presence and utter it in the same sentence with my own?' Two massive and fantastically carved ibex-like horns pushed out of the forehead of the Adversary and swept upwards and backwards as he grew even larger. Within seconds he was double the size of Shemyaza, who now looked up at his lord like a child looks at his father. One who perhaps finally realizes he has made a mistake.

'Do you not know who you stand before?' Sparks began to leap and sizzle from the Adversary, hissing as they hit the marble floor. His huge rack of wings spread out, very nearly touching both walls. They too flashed and sparked and Asmodeus saw that they had taken on a golden, metallic sheen, glowing inwardly as they unfurled. *Such power now. Soon he will be invincible and beyond both redemption and reproach.* Now every other aspect of the Adversary was changing. His eyes had gone the black of obsidian and his fangs had grown to overshadow even some of the great carnivores. His skin deepened and toughened, looking like the hide of some prehistoric rhino. Shemyaza began to back up, now fully realizing his error. But in not turning and fleeing through a portal as fast as he could, he had made his last and most fatal mistake. With a speed that belied his now monstrous size, the Adversary snatched out and grabbed the stunned Shemyaza by the arms, talons driving into the flesh and pinning them effectively to his sides. As he screamed in both pain and outrage he saw the last sight he would behold. The expanded and gaping maw of the Adversary thundered down to envelop the head and shoulders of the brute. He bit down, sending sprays of ichor and fluids in all directions. With a wet, tearing sound, the Adversary pulled back and spat the head out to smash against the very door he had destroyed. The decapitated torso flailed its legs in its final throes as the body eventually realized it was dead. Once the legs stopped twitching, Zaramael pulled each arm from its socket and hurled the corpse away from him so hard, it seemed to flatten slightly as the body hit the wall like a side of beef. Throwing back his terrifying yet magnificent head, the Adversary roared, again. Asmodeus remained perfectly still where he was, not moving or uttering a sound. He simply sat still and quiet, lest he drew any unwanted attention to himself just in case the Adversary hadn't let off enough steam. He watched as the Adversary gathered up handfuls of the remains of Shemyaza and strode to his balcony. Kicking the doors open, the Adversary took three steps to the railing, some fifty feet from the door, and roared again. Glowing like a fallen star, the Adversary made his declaration for all to hear.

'Here is the ruin of Shemyaza, formerly known as the Strong. Now known as the Dead.' With his incredible sight and growing awareness of the realms of the Domain, he could see where the entourage of Shemyaza had camped, just outside his city walls. Body part by body part, he hurled the chunks of flesh through the sky. Enraged as he was and with his own phenomenal power, he had no trouble reaching the camp, much to the shortlived surprise of one of Shemyaza's retainers, who stood looking up just as the body of Shemyaza himself slammed down on him, squashing him dead where he stood.

'Obey me or die! Simple choices. Choose one to replace your dead lord and send him to me within one cycle of the moon's turning.' Having made his point, the Adversary turned and by the time he had crossed back to the hall, he was his original glorious self again.

'Come out from behind that door, Asmodeus. Come and tell me we are clear on all matters concerning your tasks!' Shemyaza seemingly forgotten already, Asmodeus, stepping out as though he was about to do just that, bowed deeply and flattered his lord with comments about his prowess and majesty before confirming that all was indeed, crystal clear.

'Excellent, Asmodeus. We are pleased that we understand each other so well. When you are ready to leave, come to me again and I will provide you with the crystal containing he whom I will name no more. I need not stress, nor emphasize, the consequences of failure. I believe that that little demonstration says more than I need to.'

'Indeed it does, Your Majesty. Your will is my command. Now, by your leave?' But even as he spoke, he was edging backwards towards the ruined doorway, determined to get out before his "friend" had another mood swing. He barely resembled the ambitious demon he knew a thousand years before. Power. Too much was worse than any disease, for what it consumed was morality, conscience, rationality, respect. It was an incurable thing and only ever ended one way. It was a great risk that the Adversary took. If he succeeded, well, all new beginnings. Failure, on the other hand, was nothing short of annihilation. He grew more and more unpredictable and unstable as he drew more of the Earth's living force into himself. Asmodeus was glad in a way he was going to another part of the realm, for if the Adversary did implode, he didn't want to be anywhere near him.

'Are you still here, Asmodeus?' the Adversary bellowed. With that, Asmodeus opened a portal and vanished through it. He never heard the Adversary start to laugh behind him. Softly at first as he recalled the past hour's events, then gradually it grew until he was roaring with hysterical and maniacal laughter. A very disturbing sound indeed. It was enough to turn the insane, sane. And invariably back again.

Picking up a forgotten limb of Shemyaza's, the Adversary began to chew on it, tearing off lumps of flesh and gristle to hungrily wolf them down, much like some alpha male lion feeding upon its prey. Tossing the bone aside, he headed out of the doorway. Bored with the day, he went in search of amusement, bellowing as he left the great hall, 'Somebody come and fix these doors! Do not make me have to call again.' To himself he pondered the future. *Soon, little mother, your soul will be all mine. For now, know that this pain that I cause you will be nothing to the devastating agony that's coming.*

Chapter Ten

ᴰELIVERANCE

Tomas completed several circuits of the fortress before he finally found the one thing he was searching for, the inevitable and in this instance, practically invisible escape route. No soldier, given the opportunity, would build a fortification without a means to escape should things all go horribly wrong, for not everyone was a hero who stood their ground resolutely facing their inevitable end with dignified aplomb – even if it was a valiant gesture and worthy of a mention in the history books. Standing there waiting to be slaughtered just wasn't for him. Tomas considered himself a pragmatic soldier, where common sense prevailed over bravery, or crossed that incredibly thin line into stupidity. Tomas remembered being told the distinction. Bravery was doing what needed to be done, though it might be terrifying and potentially fatal. Stupidity was doing the same thing with no idea of what was going on or what the implications were. They were the words of his father: some of the earliest advice he had imparted to his son and heir as Tomas attained an age where he could commence and forge his own military career. Simple words but effective. 'If it looks bad, don't hang around. Get out, regroup and try again. Dead heroes don't get the job done, they just get dead. Don't worry about walking away from a job, son. Things have a tendency to move in cycles – so the time will come around again to finish what you started. And always finish what you start. Most importantly though, Tom, stay alive – at all costs – and never forget to hold on to who you are. Hold on to your core principles – integrity, honor and loyalty; for little else matters that can't be replaced.' It was the most sensible recourse for any soldier, be he a contemporary warrior or a medieval Templar Knight. That said, he understood the idea of chivalry and nobility well enough. His father had spent many a night when Tomas was a child, reading him tales of Ivanhoe and Arthur and his redoubtable knights of the round table, performing deeds of incredible bravery, of standing alone against staggering odds. And even though they knew their deaths were a certainty, they stood anyway. It was the *right* thing to do. Deeds of valor and of giving their lives for a noble cause. His mind recounted many of their brave, yet invariably final words: 'Till my last breath doth leave my body and while I can stand and wield my sword – I'll ever stand against the darkness'. There were so many. He recalled how as a child, he had his stick sword, fighting many an ogre that had invaded his back garden kingdom, or some dastardly, despicable fiend of the dark void beyond the veil that barely separated the *Otherworld* from this one; valiantly dispatching enemy after enemy and saving the damsel. *Shame I couldn't save my own*, Tomas thought bitterly, his guilt at failing his family and loved ones resurfacing and casting a heavy shadow over him and sending an involuntary shiver up his spine: a shiver of destiny with the ominous touch of prescience about it which made it feel all the worse. It was followed by more memories.

His mother, bless her, had made him a tabard when he was a child, and even knitted him a grey woollen chain mail coif. Never in a million years did he think that he would actually be wearing the real thing; wielding his own version of Excalibur and fighting all manner of evil personified. It was a look reserved for heroes of old and tales of fantasy; and yet – there was a certain catharsis to standing toe to toe with your opponent and engaging in a mortal combat where the battle could go either way, dependent solely upon the skill and strength of arm of the combatants. Knowing that death most likely awaited the loser tended to focus the senses and elevate them to a state of heightened awareness, where colors seemed brighter and every smell, however minute, assailed the nostrils. That was both good and bad, depending on what you were in the proximity of. His recent opponents were a point in question of *not* having a sense of smell.

Over the subsequent years, he had reconciled dying for his profession, and death had held little fear for him. It held even less now. But he always believed that there *would* be a time and a place for such an outstanding and thoroughly futile gesture of bravery. As of yet, he hadn't found it. Nor was it here, not this day.

The secret exit he had been looking for was located in one of the seven turrets that linked the walls of the little fortress, which, in itself, was almost circular in its construction. The chapel it was built around squatted in the centre and disappeared below ground. Death told him that there was a considerable-sized catacomb below, interwoven with passageways and chambers, all spreading out beneath them, which, if things didn't go their way, would be their last line of defense. It wasn't an idea that appealed to Tomas: underground was for rabbits and ferrets, and he was neither. Few predators existed below ground and that predatory instinct was growing stronger by the moment within Tomas.

Perhaps Private Potter had sensed the imminent danger that seemed to shroud the grim looking and heavily armored warrior, and figured his own chances were greatly improved by keeping him in close proximity; for he hadn't left Tomas's side since their earlier discussion. He tried not to think of the other factor, that by being close, trouble would gravitate towards him *because* of him. Either way, the doughty soldier reasoned, he was prepared to take his chances – and if it meant going down fighting, then that would be what he would do. He was a marine after all and that still meant something.

'Clever little bastards,' Tomas breathed as he found and tentatively operated the mechanism for opening the sally port. He was surprised to discover that it moved with all the ease of a regularly and well-maintained door, not one that had stood abandoned for who knew how many centuries. Potter, who was crouched close by, overheard Tomas's mutterings.

'Who is?' Potter quizzed, assuming that Tomas was talking to him and not to himself, which he was. But Tomas responded all the same. He quite liked the affable southerner for some reason he couldn't put his finger on, and had taken him under his wing, if there was such a place. Not that Potter afforded him much alternative, shadowing his every move for the last hour or so. It was probably better than what waited for them beyond the walls; it was not the sort of enemy that these guys should have to deal with. They had been dragged into a supernatural war humanity had no way to prepare for. They were as cavemen throwing rocks at tanks. Tomas felt angry at himself for dragging them into this conflict and he found it hard to rationalize the fact that they would either be dead by now had he not, or – he thought miserably – would have eventually been caught up in the war with or without his assistance. Yet the fact remained that they were here now and he felt responsible for them. It was all so wrong. Granted, humanity had brought much of this upon itself by its own arrogance, ego and religious fanaticism; making war on each other for no other reason than a difference of opinion about something no one has ever seen. Hadn't it taken some pretty definitive persuasion after all to convince him? And look where that had gotten him. *I just hope that whatever reinforcements Death called get here in time. I don't know if I can take many more innocent and unnecessary deaths at my expense.* Tomas tried to quell the melancholy that was building within him again.

'Masons,' answering Potter's question and trying to bury his dark thoughts before they began to affect his judgment. 'The individuals who built this fortress, the same guys who slink about in secret back home. The ones with dodgy handshakes and secret winks or whatever it is they do now.'

Again, involuntarily, Tomas was transported back to his childhood and his father's tales. Stories of secret societies: Templars, Rosicrucians, Cathars, Illuminati and Masons. He could have believed his father knew everything about everything, so detailed and fanciful were the stories he recounted. So full of imagery and specifics. The acquired knowledge had stood him in good stead when he went to school, and his father's subtle teaching had given him an edge over the other children. But in hindsight, did his education diminish his innocent years and detract from his childhood? War and intrigue in any form, old or new, was no doubt the cause of his cynicism, his contempt and lack of faith in human nature; and what they had been, and no doubt still were, capable of doing to their own race. With a concerted effort, Tomas brought himself back to the present, pushing away the painful memories of yesteryear and focusing on the now.

'It wasn't always like that, though. These men knew what they were doing with stone. They had secret knowledge given to them involving the Templars and other covert organizations; *very* secret stuff. So secret, in fact, that there are barely a handful of men still alive who know the true meanings behind their organizations. Much has been lost over the years due to arrogant men. Do you know much about them?'

Potter shook his head, letting the blank expression on his face answer for him. Tomas nodded his acceptance of Potter's honest ignorance.

'I only know a little,' Tomas continued wistfully. 'My father knew shit loads. In fact, the older I got the more I came to realize just how much he did know. I mean, did you know that it was widely held that the Templars worshipped the disembodied head of someone or something called Baphomet, but later it was considered to be the mummified head of John the Baptist? I mean, you couldn't invent shit like that and why would you? My father implied that it was neither and it was all just propaganda. They held to a much deeper agenda, one that only a select few ever get to discover. Goes to show you how history and fact get all muddled up over time.'

Again the blank look, only this time it was accompanied by a solemn shake of the head and painfully obvious, 'Nope, don't know anything about any of that shit. My daddy was a Baptist.' Tomas just nodded, aware of the implications of what that meant.

'This, my young friend,' Tomas steered matters back to more immediate concerns, 'is where we slip out and hopefully back in after bloodying their noses. It's the last thing they expect and it should buy us some time while they reorganize themselves. Time for those bloody reinforcements to get here.'

Tomas was impressed by the fortress after having given it a thorough once-over in an effort to locate the secret exit. It was built by warriors with one thing in mind: to keep the enemy out whilst giving sufficient access to do as much damage to said enemy as possible. But, the flaw, Tomas discovered, and no doubt the Horsemen were aware of too, was the lack of defense against aerial assault. As far as history went and what little he knew of the Templars, they never had to deal with their enemies flying over the damn walls. When he approached Death and the other Horsemen with his plan and his concerns, all they said in response was 'Let's hope they don't'. It wasn't the most reassuring answer he could have been given.

Tomas's plan wasn't complex. Foolhardy, yes, and quite likely suicidal, but essentially sound. Before the horde arriving outside had time to formulate their plan of attack, which relied heavily upon their leader being present, apparently, and who, for that matter, currently wasn't, they would slip out under some substantial covering fire from the Horsemen and wreak as much havoc amongst them as they were capable of. Granted, most of the damage would be from Tomas, but, recovering from a direct hit from a grenade was going to slow them up somewhat. The marines weren't short of ordnance. If what Death said was true, and he had no cause to doubt him, some archangel or other was en route to squash this incursion and escort them back to Megiddo. Always assuming they weren't having troubles of their own. Tomas always had pessimistic thoughts like that. He called it realism. Sod's law had a way of doing stuff like that right when you didn't want it to, though lately, Tomas had begun to wonder if there was more to this sod person than just dumb luck. The word *fate* crept into his mind more and more.

Pestilence caught up with Tomas moments later as he was examining the inner bailey by the main gate, seeing how they could defend it once they ripped the metal sheeting off the outside. Again, Tomas assumed the worst. Potter was still edgy around the Horsemen; his upbringing was a definite handicap to facing this reality, as well as the fact that she scared the shit out of him. She was softly spoken when she did speak, and only did that infrequently, but she was a physically imposing individual. Her physical stature wasn't that much different from any other oriental woman, but the way she carried herself, and her intense gaze made her seem like a nine-foot-tall warrior queen. She bristled with weapons and Tomas had seen first-hand that she knew how to use them.

'I will accompany you, friend Tomas, when we go to meet the enemy on level terms. I believe you could use another beside you who can hurt them, not simply annoy. I think three can handle matters as well as four upon the wall.' She stated it calmly and quietly, yet at the same time left no room for argument. She was coming and that was all there was to it. Potter saw Tomas nod his acceptance and made a choice himself then. One that would have long-reaching implications. 'I'm coming too.'

Both Tomas and Pestilence swiveled their heads to fix their indomitable stares upon the marine. It had the similar effect as if they had pinned him to the wall of the bailey with iron rods. Tomas spoke first, and he realized he sounded just like his own father had when Tomas had said the same thing once. 'I don't think so, young man; it's no place for you out there.' *Young man?* Tomas echoed to himself. *Damn, he must be twenty something if he's a day. Christ, I feel old.*

But Potter was adamant and his face took on the deadpan seriousness of a marine who had made up his mind and wasn't about to have it changed by anyone or anything.

'All due respect, Tomas, Ma'am, but me and the guys aren't just going to sit in here and have some lady do our fighting for us. I know it's not going to be a walk in the park, but it's what we do. I used to be a quarterback for my college team; it's my job to get the ball into the other team's zone. This ain't no different. So – I'm coming. Okay?'

Tomas smiled at the young man's willingness and passion. Smiling to cover the sadness he felt, Tomas placed a hand on Potter's shoulders and welcomed him into the group. 'Glad to have you, son. So that's three of us. Which, if truth be told, is four too many to be out there hands on with that lot, but as they say, shit happens. Let's do it.'

Tomas closed his eyes briefly and modified his armor. It was an eclectic combination of the medieval plate and chain mail armor fused with the more modern Kevlar body armor: Kevlar padded fatigues to protect his legs, yet still afford him some movement. He expected there to be some serious running to do and too much steel wasn't going to help there. He looked formidable, and with a black Kevlar and lightweight chain mail cloak completing the ensemble, he looked like a modern day black knight. Pestilence made some slight adjustments to her own attire, and Potter could have sworn that he saw even more weapons appear.

'Right then, time to go,' Tomas stated with a dread note of finality to his voice. Then he communicated his imminent departure to Death through the mental link. Hearing the reverberating response from the archetypal Reaper that they would prepare to offer what cover they could left his mind reeling slightly. *That's still gonna take some getting used to,* Tomas thought as he shook his head as the voice faded away. 'Let's do this,' he muttered to himself as he headed out across the compound.

He was no more than halfway across the compound when three more marines came running over, weapons prepped for action, all carrying explosives and grenades.

'Wait for us, Potter!' one of them shouted as they skidded to a halt before the little group. 'We've been watching you follow this guy around and figured you were up to something.'

You're going out, aren't you?' another asked.

Potter just nodded and looked to Tomas with that same look he used earlier, as if to say 'They're coming, like it or not'.

Not, but Tomas was running out of time to argue. If they didn't go soon they would lose the element of surprise and they would be stuck in a siege situation.

'Names!' If they were coming, he needed to know who they were.

'Bowen, sir!' Tomas despaired. They were like sticks of rock. But he had no time or the heart to correct them, as he had done with Potter.

'Stevenson, sir!' snapped the other, followed by the last.

'O'Farrell, sir!'

All whipped a snappy salute, though their hands quickly found their weapons again. It was as though they were reluctant to let them go, even for an instant. He couldn't blame them really. Nor would he in their boots.

'Fair enough then, guys. The plan is simple. We slip out and edge as close as we can without being seen. Then…well, it'll be fairly obvious. Take out as many as you can; cause as much carnage as you are able. Explosives and grenades. I want the lot slung at them. When you're out, don't hang around. Get back to the fortress as quickly as you can. Understood?'

The collective response was predictably sigh inducing. 'Sir. Yes, sir!'

Grimacing, Tomas swung up the RPG transforming from the sword, and with Pestilence stringing her horn bow beside him, he jogged the remaining distance to the tower exit. Slowly pushing it open, just a crack, he checked for any unwanted loiterers. Finding none, he sent out the marines to cover, and then he and Pestilence slipped out and took point.

On the ramparts, Death, War and Famine had organized the remaining marines, stringing them out along the wall and ensuring they were all armed and briefed on what to do; and, more importantly, when they were to do it. Since entering the fortress, War had extended his own awareness to try and get a sense of who else it was after them, and who was leading this rabble along with Azaroth. His news was like his current visage. Grim.

'It's definitely Azaroth. He's making no attempt to conceal himself and he has summoned further minions now that he is aware of our current position. It appears Karcon is with him and they know exactly where we are. Precisely *this* position.'

War wasn't happy. He preferred *conducting* sieges, rather than being the recipient of one. And certainly not from this demonic upstart and his foul cohorts. After receiving this bit of news, Death wasn't exactly happy either. Not that it was easy to tell with the massive figure. His inky black cowl seemed to have a life of its own and became more agitated the more Death did. It was flowing around him as though he stood in the centre of his own maelstrom. Marines shrank back from the terrifying sight and if the demonic minions, along with Azaroth, had any clue as to how enraged the personification of Death had become – they would have turned and fled back down whatever hole they had crawled up out of. But unfortunately for all concerned they didn't; though they soon would. War changed the tack of the conversation then, more to reassure the marines and not have his associate scare them any more than they already were. 'Tomas has changed, don't you think?'

Death, rather than answer immediately, stalked over to where War stood on the battlement and looked over. His keen eyes picked out Tomas, Pestilence and the marines better than any satellite GPS. He studied the burly warrior for a few seconds and nodded his agreement, then added in his gravelike monotone: 'He has changed, though not just with our gifts – but something within him has emerged that perhaps not even he was expecting. I certainly wasn't. There was a darkness within him before, but I'm not sure he ever fully plumbed its depths or knew what he was truly capable of. I still don't think he does, though he may have an inkling now we have inadvertently unchained something within him.'

Famine had been listening and joined in. 'Do you think he can do it now, actually succeed, I mean?'

Death was silent as he watched them creep ever closer to the horde encamped only a few hundred yards away. 'I don't know. Anything is possible – but I do know that he is no longer the sacrificial lamb he imagined himself to be not many days past. I believe *he* believes in himself again. And that is worth much. For the rest? Well, let's just see if we can get out of this one in one piece first. Phanuel has encountered some difficulty and is being delayed.

We must hold this horde at bay for as long as we can. War, Tomas *has* to get through.'

'You say that now, but wasn't it you who let him go out there of all places. It's not the safest spot, in case you haven't noticed. He is out there as a lamb amongst wolves.'

Something in Death's tone changed then. It almost sounded like humor. 'This lamb has got teeth of his own, methinks, and we'll just have to give them enough covering fire so that they *do* make it back. It had merit in buying us some time and he is the one with the sword after all. Pestilence will ensure no harm befalls him.'

War looked askance at his comrade. Famine just laughed and strolled away, chortling about how unfortunate the minion would be who got between her and Tomas.

The plan for those who remained behind was just as simple as Tomas's. The marines would open fire into the front ranks of the minions. Death, War and Famine would darken the sky with their arrows behind them, driving those in front back and those behind forward. Tomas and his squad would then rip into the flanks with his RPG and their explosives. Hopefully, the resulting casualties would be high and the ensuing confusion sufficient to gain a few more hours. Vital hours in which Phanuel and his legions needed to get to them.

A last glance at the milling minions was quite enough for Death. They were still milling when the first barrage of tracer and weapon fire tore into the front ranks, hot metal tearing into their flesh and sending fragments hissing away. The wounds did regenerate, but as more and more hit them, it became a slower process. Then, the arrows of the Horsemen slammed into them from above, a few hundred yards further back.

That was Tomas's cue. He flipped the sword to Javelin mode and launched several rockets skyward, utilizing its on top attack mode. He had time to launch six of those before he flipped the sword again and swung his RPG onto his shoulder. Pestilence had fired several shafts and showed no signs of letting up. She had a greater capacity than many conventional firearms for arrows per minute. Potter and his fellow marines stood and threw for all they were worth. Tomas heard Potter shouting out 'Go deep, you bastards' as his quarterback's arm rocketed skyward grenade after grenade. Stevenson and O'Farrell had laid out many of the explosive charges they carried. The inevitable pursuit was in for a surprise. Within those few seconds, all hell broke loose, literally. The Javelin's rockets came down with devastating effect, coupled with the RPGs, wreaking havoc amongst the minions, who didn't know where to turn first. Annihilation met them whichever way they faced. Added of course to the conventional method of death, were the special effects of Famine's arrows and those of Pestilence. Famine's arrows, when they hit, turned the recipient and the area around him to a frozen wasteland. It was as though it rained liquid nitrogen. War's shafts seemed to be tipped with Greek fire or napalm. The flock of deadly ravens that were Death's arrows vaporized the unfortunate minion in a blast of black smoke. It was as though they were being negated from history. It didn't bear thinking about where they went.

Tomas's plan seemed to be working, but once the shock and chaos had subsided, the minions began to gather themselves.

'I'm out!' Stevenson shouted, quickly followed by Bowen and O'Farrell.

'Well, don't hang about, get back now,' Tomas shouted at them without looking, just as two particularly lucky, brave or stupid – he couldn't decide which – minions rushed him, snarling and brandishing their weapons. Quicker than thought, the sword was in his hands and parrying the first vicious downward stroke of one minion, whilst he ducked the swipe of the other. Standing, he punched it full in the face. Tomas's steel and Kevlar gauntlets smashed teeth, fang and bone and opened its face cruelly. A backhanded strike took care of the first as it overbalanced after Tomas's parry. The sword bit into flesh then spine. It dropped without another twitch. The sound of steel on steel caught his attention and with his peripheral vision, Tomas saw Pestilence, swords in hands, and she was leaping at four minions and engaging all of them. *Time to go*, he thought, turning, Tomas dispatched the other creature almost nonchalantly, in time to see the harried marines running for all they were worth across the clearing. All of them except Potter, who for reasons known only to him, had picked up a particularly nasty looking axe and was using it quite effectively on two minions, preventing them from chasing his companions.

'I thought I told you to run, you fool,' shouted Tomas as he leapt at the two minions who were pressing Potter hard. One turned to meet this new threat and died as the sword that slammed down on the top of its head tore out its groin. This had a distracting effect on the other, which Potter took full advantage of and separated the minion from its head.

'I'm not going to tell you again. We'll be right behind you. Now go and blow those charges.' Tomas shoved Potter on his way and turned to face another charging minion. Tomas charged it right back and at the last minute he shoulder-rolled and scythed the blade across its midriff, sending entrails spraying out to entangle its feet. Tomas rolled to his own feet and looked to Pestilence. She was a dervish of steel and deadly feet. Leaping and kicking as she sliced and diced.

'*Let's go!*' he thought to her, '*Enough is enough. I think they're on to us.*' The look she gave him mid-spin was a picture. But she turned all the same and began to run alongside Tomas.

'Why haven't those charges gone off yet?' he shouted as he drew level with the sprinting oriental woman. She merely looked at him but in his head he heard her voice say she didn't know. Tomas saw Bowen by the door. He'd re-armed and was giving them covering fire. He couldn't see Potter. *Damn! Where is the bloody man now?*

'They malfunctioned!' Tomas heard Bowen shout to him. 'They need manual activation.' Tomas swore and skidded to a halt, spraying sand and gravel as he did so. Half turning, he saw the charging horde that was hot on their heels. There were just too many to take and get to the charges. It was then he saw Potter get up from a sandy furrow where he had hidden as several minions ran by him.

'Potter! No!' Tomas shouted, but it was too late, Potter was too far away to hear over the screaming minions, and if he did, it was obvious he was going to ignore it. Tomas turned the sword into his Hochlers and let rip into the charging creatures, desperate to make his way towards Potter. He only had time to see his new friend hold up a hand in salute to him before he was buried under a dozen leaping minions. The explosion knocked them from their feet as the charges all went off. Potter had done it after all. Vaporizing himself in the process. Tomas's stomach constricted and a lump came unbidden to his throat at the thought of the heroic father his child would never see.

The red mist cleared and the sand was littered with the remains of the demon contingent which had stormed after them. The rest hesitated, unsure of what was happening, only aware that their prey had escaped them again. Potter had bravely chosen to take out as many as possible and save the lives of his companions as he did so. The only way that could be done was to let half the minions pass him and ensure he was in the middle of them.

'Damn! Damn! Damn!' Tomas kicked and punched the wall as he strode out of the turret. So angry was Tomas, that he occasionally knocked chunks of masonry free as he did so, storming in to the fortress and up to the battlements, where Death and War awaited him. Famine began conferring with Pestilence and seeing to the needs of the warriors as they diplomatically left Tomas and Death to it.

'Did you see that?' Tomas demanded of Death, Tomas's face scant inches from the Reaper's. 'That was human courage. Human sacrifice. He bought us the time to get back in as well as bloodying their noses. All this time it has been about me sacrificing myself for the good of this cause, and just as I begin to understand it, that happens. Someone I barely knew, who barely knew us and was terrified of you, I think, goes and bloody well gets himself blown up. How do I ever get *that* blood off my hands?'

'You don't, Tomas. You never will.' His voice was as calm as ever, though it still sounded like a hundred gravestones falling. 'Such is the burden of compassion, empathy and the role of a leader. Do not make our mistake and let these events become insignificant. For they most definitely are not. It is a symbol of the human spirit. It gave his life meaning and purpose. As it will all those who die willingly for this battle and for the battle to come. You cannot get emotional about this and let it affect your judgment, Tomas, or your actions; but you must never forget them. They live on as heroes in your memory and the memory of all those who knew them. Inspiration. Irrespective of where their souls travel to, they have attained immortality in your thoughts and memories. *That* is where it is meant to be. It always was. Let it make you grow stronger, Tomas, and more focused. Make his death count for something.'

They were good words, but they still rang hollow and had the consistency of grave ash in Tomas's mouth. This loss had stabbed at a part of himself he thought had died long ago. When it came to "collateral damage" he never gave it a second thought. People served his cause. Whether they lived or died was immaterial, as long as they fulfilled a role. Lately, since the explosion to be more precise, he had begun to connect more with individuals. He found that he actually had feelings for them. Potter was the embodiment of all those who had died before and been forgotten. He was the scalpel that opened the old scar tissue, and once it was open, there seemed to be no closing it. All the loss, rage and despair welled up within him and with an exultant wail of despair, Tomas launched several missiles skyward, out into the thick of the horde. What he saw next – what they all saw next – took his voice and his rage clean away. They then knew why Azaroth hadn't been present straightaway. He had been busy casting dark and powerful magicks. The evidence of that lay painfully obvious before them.

'Wha...?' Tomas was at an immediate loss for what to say. So too, it seemed, were the Horsemen. The missiles from Tomas's rocket launcher had plummeted down onto the horde. The effect should have been catastrophic. The explosions would have ripped several craters out of the ground and destroyed a large contingent of demons. Instead, the missiles seemed to impact upon an invisible shield and the fiery, concussive devastation spilt off the shield like so much flaming liquid. Falling harmlessly to Earth.

'It is as I feared,' Death stated, as flatly and emotionlessly as ever. 'This was why Azaroth wasn't here when his legions caught up with us. He must have guessed where we were heading and this was too much of a prize to give up. If we can't attack his minions, he stands a much better chance of overpowering these walls. If he does, we are in serious trouble.'

Tomas wasn't encouraged by those words, coming from one of the Four Horsemen of the Apocalypse. If they were in trouble then things weren't good.

'How much more trouble could we really be in. Surely it can't get much worse.'

Death gave Tomas one of his looks that said 'Wanna bet?'

'Can it?'

'If we can't hold them from the wall, then matters will truly get ugly. If it comes to hand-to-hand, we may be able to hold our own, for a time at least – but the marines will be slaughtered. It was a mistake to open this place, but what is done is done – so now we must stay and ensure that it doesn't fall into the hands of Azaroth. It will mean, unfortunately, that we must seek the security of the temple proper.'

'But didn't you or War say that it held as many dangers there as it does out here?' Tomas queried, fixing his gaze on Death, concern hardening his features until he looked as though he were chiseled from rock. It hadn't helped that with several weeks living on the street, he had lost any spare fat that he may have had on his already lean frame. Yet his raptor's eyes had never stopped moving, taking in all around them as though they could see something no one else could. Piercing, yet haunted by demons of his own, they weren't the eyes that anyone could easily look long into without feeling uncomfortable. These eyes now took in the marines who held their posts upon the wall, useless weapons trained upon an enemy they barely comprehended.

Tomas made another harsh choice then, weighing up what they faced and what priorities they faced.

Death continued. 'There are dangers within, certainly. It really comes down to numbers and I believe that there are fewer within than without to contend with. It improves our chances slightly. If we limit our progress into the catacombs, we may avoid them altogether. Of course that doesn't prevent them from coming to us but it should be easier to defend a passageway than these walls.'

Tomas agreed, Death merely echoed what he had been thinking. Tomas turned then and called the marines' commanding officer over and relayed his plan, which was basically to get his men off the wall now and get them inside, not to venture too far, and hold the entrance. He and the Horsemen would make as much of a stand upon the wall as they could before pulling back. The more they took out there, the fewer to lay siege to the chapel, though, truth be told, Tomas was loath to give up any ground to those fiends.

Unfortunately, the sudden absence of the marines upon the wall must have signaled something to the horde, for they immediately began to storm the walls. Tomas bolstered his armor and pulled the sword free from the backslung harness and braced himself, flicking his visor down and rolling his shoulders slightly to loosen the muscles there.

Famine moved over to stand near him and Tomas heard his shouts to the charging minions. 'Come on, you whore sons! Come – meet your doom at the blades of the Horsemen of the Apocalypse. It is only a shame that there aren't more of you: it would even the odds somewhat. Ha Hah! Ha Hah!'

Tomas looked at the warrior and wondered if he wasn't both a little crazy and partially correct. He looked formidable enough. Silvery white armor, glistening with frost, white cape billowing out behind him and with one foot up on the battlements, holding his halberd aloft and spinning it like some deadly rotor blade, he seemed impatient for the first demons to broach the fortification. Looking further along, Tomas saw War standing braced actually upon the crenulations, a foot on each, arms folded and glowering down like a crimson vulture. His helm hid all his features and the two great horns that protruded from it made him look more demonic than some of those attacking.

'Take your position, Tomas,' Death whispered. The chill in his voice made the hackles rise on the back of Tomas's neck. He spared a glance towards the Reaper and saw the monstrous scythe glinting in the fading evening light, and if he could make the skeletal visage of his face seem even more forbidding than it usually did – well, he managed it. Yet Tomas could have sworn he saw amusement on his steely features. Pestilence was not be outdone in her manner of intimidation. She, unlike War, stood balanced upon one stony rampart, twin curved swords crossed over her chest. The point upon the crown of her fur-rimmed helm seemed slightly longer too, as did the razor barbs upon her boots and elbows. He'd seen all of them used to lethal effect as she whirled into an explosive tornado of deadly spinning steel.

There they were, the five of them standing against several hundred screaming, howling demonic warriors. Clarity settled on Tomas like a mist. Time seemed to slow and every detail came into sharp focus. Like a man who has been visually impaired all his life suddenly being cured. This was what he was meant for. Like a wave of pure destiny, it came crashing over him. The cliché was incredible. He felt he had been born to stand upon this wall and defend it from the torrent of evil flooding toward him. Standing shoulder to shoulder with the four most terrifying beings in the cosmos, preparing to engage in battle. He would feel quite the hero if it wasn't such a doomed venture.

They had reached the base of the wall, and Tomas realized just how driven and stupid these minions were. They numbered in their hundreds and the defenders only five. Five could only cover so much wall. Yet these minions didn't attempt to scale where there was no defense – no, instead they converged on the warriors. Drawn like moths to a flame. And like moths, doomed to extinction when they drew too close. Like ants, the minions used each other to scale the wall and as the first head appeared level with the battlements, it was separated from its body and sent back to its comrades. Battle was joined.

So it went for the next hour. The defenders moved and flowed back and forth like wraiths. Tomas barely had time to breathe as he fought to hold his own. But he managed to catch the odd glimpse of his companions. They moved as though they were in more than one place at once. It wasn't long before the stones became slick with the sticky blood of the fallen and Tomas had to pay attention to his footing lest he slip. That one slip would be all it took. His shoulders burnt from the repetitive pounding he rained down on the heads and shoulders of those who attempted to gain a foothold. Once or twice, a cluster of minions managed to get over the wall and onto the rampart. Tomas switched the sword to his Hochlers then and blazed away at them until they thinned enough for him to drive them back, though it all too soon became apparent that they were metaphorically pissing in the wind. For every one they cut down, two more replaced them, and to make matters worse, even more could be seen cresting the horizon. They darkened the Earth with their numbers.

'*Death!*' Tomas thought, '*that doesn't look good and as much as I'm having fun here, we need to think about pulling back. We'll never stop that lot.*'

'You are right.' That was it. That was all he said. Yet Tomas heard the mental call to fall back the same time the other three did and as one, with a final devastating surge to buy them a valuable second or two, they leapt from the wall, all four landing catlike upon the ground and instantly running for the chapel entrance, their cloaks flying behind them. Tomas couldn't help but think that it looked quite impressive. He spun and let fly a blistering barrage of GPMG fire, the continuous belt of rounds rattling through the weapon and blasting the minions back off the wall for fifty paces, taking some of the wall with it as well. But as before, they just swarmed back up over their fallen, using their corpses for steps. Tomas released the general purpose machine gun and he too leapt from the wall, though his landing was less than graceful, but years of training paid off as he shoulder-rolled forward and came up running. He felt several arrows zing off his armor and more than one stick into the Kevlar padding. A pair of marines stuck their heads around the doorway and offered covering fire. The air turned warm around Tomas as hot lead flew past, slowing his pursuers. Several of the arrows changed direction and took out one of the marines. Tomas saw him dragged back in and replaced instantly by another, picking up where his comrade had left off. Tomas's legs were on fire, already weakened by the vicious mêlée upon the wall. He hadn't realized just how much strain it put on the body. He felt that horribly familiar sensation when running – when the body wants to overtake the legs and you know that to keep going you are going to overbalance and fall. He could feel the fetid breath of the minions on the back of his neck. If he did fall, that would be it: he would be dead, and they would be on him in an instant. He was feet away when that law of Sod kicked in. Trying to turn the fall into a roll as he had done earlier, Tomas dived forward. But several arrows thudding into him took him off balance and he landed badly. The two marines who stood at door duty dashed out to grab him by the shoulders and drag him the rest of the way. Pestilence stepped into the doorway and rattled off several arrows to cover the marines. Hundreds of minions filled the inner courtyard now and they were a tsunami of teeth and steel. Tomas scrambled up and leapt through the doorway, as did one marine, but the other was caught and instantly hacked to bits by the minions. His screams were terrible, but shortlived. The great stone door of the chapel slammed shut behind them and all went quiet.

Tomas closed his eyes for several seconds and took a dozen or so deep calming breaths. More marines had died because of him, and the earlier one that was shot by an arrow died a few moments later. Tomas had that sinking feeling that told him many more would meet similar fates before this was over. Resignedly, Tomas rolled over and got up. He found himself in a dank passageway, capped with an arched ceiling. It extended in both directions from the entrance way. They seemed to be in an antechamber of sorts, as the passages narrowed as they disappeared into darkness. Turning three hundred and sixty degrees to give himself a full account of where they were, he saw Famine – the tip of his halberd glowing white hot as he fused the stone doorway closed.

'Er, don't you think we might want to get out of there again in the none too distant future?'

Famine responded without turning and the answer was obvious, had he thought about it. 'If we all survive this and we need to use this door again, you can blow it up with that sword of yours. If all goes well, we'll gate out when the cavalry has disposed of the rubbish outside.'

Tomas was made aware then – and not for the first time – how he was still way out of his depth when it came to matters angelic and demonic. It was like adapting to all new rules with all new abilities. Living in four dimensions instead of three. Except he had no time to study what those rules were; he simply had to adapt as they went. Something was missing though. Tomas looked around until it occurred to him. 'Where have War and the rest of the marines gone?' Tomas looked around in case a clue proffered itself but none did. Dematerializing his war helm, Tomas scrubbed his hair and started to pluck the arrows out of his body armor.

'War and the mortals took the left-hand passageway, with a view to minimizing any surprise visits from the guardians of the catacombs.'

Tomas looked up, concerned. His gaze flicked towards the right-hand passage then back to Death. He could see Pestilence sitting cross-legged opposite the now blocked doorway; she was fussing over her bow and checking the bowstring. Famine stood behind Death, looking as bored as someone could be in the middle of a life-or-death siege.

'Anybody thought of taking the right, or do you feel confident that there's nothing likely to come that way?'

'Not at all. No one's gone yet. Why? You feel up to it?'

That sounded too contrived for Tomas's liking. As he pulled the last arrow out and discarded it in the small pile that had grown at his feet, he responded with a mixture of amusement and irritation, 'You just want me away from that doorway, don't you? in case they break through. We've run out of places to run to and if it gets down and dirty you're still trying to protect me.'

Death shrugged as though to say that was or wasn't the case, yet it wasn't a denial. But before Tomas could argue the point, Famine stepped in with a suggestion. 'Then, friend Tomas, why don't you and I take the vacant passageway and go see if we can't scare up some fusty old guardians and hone our skills some more? I find after that little scrap I've a hankering for some more.'

Tomas was amazed and he couldn't help but smile. *He still wants a bloody fight?* In the midst of death and imminent destruction he found the incongruous humor of Famine refreshing. Tomas's sense of humor had always been a little on the edge. What he found funny would horrify most people and disgust the rest, but there you had it. Tomas concluded that Famine was slightly crazy at best; downright dangerous and a complete psychopath at worst. And Famine wanted *him* to go down a dark tunnel with him? What was he thinking? But it didn't stop Tomas from agreeing to go with him. *Should be interesting and certainly better than waiting here for either those bastards to break in or some unknown nasty to come creeping up on us. Never been a big one for surprises.*

'Okay, why not!' Tomas turned to Death and all his humor vanished as he addressed the dark Reaper. You, War and Pestilence take care of those marines. Just because I'm not here to remind you of your casual indifference to us humans – '

'Try not to think of yourself as human any more, Tomas. It will be easier.'

Death's statement stopped him in his tracks and he lost the thread of his argument. 'That's just like you, isn't it?' Tomas was angry now at the cold maliciousness of Death. Even though he shouldn't have been overly surprised, it still grated. He found his temper had been a little frayed since the battle. His ability to come down from the battle-induced high that the adrenaline rush of imminent death caused, was taking longer to diminish these days. 'No matter what you do to me I'll always consider myself human. For all their failings – and they are many – I'm still proud of what I am. Just because they've lost their way, it doesn't warrant the blatant disregard you still seem to harbor about them. Just ensure they make it to safety, in spite of themselves and whatever you might think. Otherwise, Death or not, you'll see a side of me you can't even begin to imagine. You think the Adversary is bad? Believe this! You don't want me for an enemy.'

Death regarded Tomas with an impassivity that was as unnerving as any vocal retaliation. There was no way to read the expression on the Reaper's metallic, skeletal face plate. Nor was he able to fathom what was going through his mind. His thoughts too, were as silent as the grave. Long minutes passed as Tomas waited for a response. He wasn't going without one and it soon became a stand-off. Tomas refused to give ground to the intimidating tactics of Death. Too long had he gotten away with that. So the pair faced off. Tomas's eyes narrowed to viper slits as he focused his will upon the entity before him. Pestilence and Famine watched the interaction with some interest, but said nothing. If anything had inadvertently moved between Death and Tomas – it probably would have shriveled up instantaneously, so charged was the atmosphere. Tomas had faced down rulers of countries and heads of some very nasty organizations – the types where people and their entire families tended to disappear without trace on a regular basis. All of those were as trivial as looking at his own reflection by comparison to facing the Grim Reaper himself in a battle of wills. Eventually though, after Tomas realized he was holding his breath, an almost imperceptible nod issued from the Dark Lord of the Grave. And in Tomas's mind he heard the words spoken, though only barely. They were obviously intended for him alone.

'Very well, Tomas. It will be as you say. We will do our utmost to protect these mortals; we will not put them deliberately in harm's way or abandon them, but understand this, Tomas. It is a war and in war there are

casualties. You must accept this.'

'I understand that, but as long as we understand each other.' Tomas's boiling blood began to simmer down as he turned away from Death, effectively cutting off any further comment and giving Tomas the last word. It was the little victories...

'C'mon Famine. If we're going, let's go. I'm just in the bloody mood to meet something now, and heaven help it.'

Famine beamed as though he had heard the most amazing news. It was like finding a kindred spirit and Famine was enthused. 'That's the spirit.'

Tomas glanced at his companion and smiled an evil grin. It spoke volumes to the mischievous Famine. It told him that Tomas thoroughly enjoyed his face off with Death and yet he harbored no ill-will. It was all in the sport, like two alpha wolves testing the boundaries and limits; the younger conceding to the elder, but wiser for the experience. As they walked to the tunnel entrance Tomas noticed that Famine had swapped his halberd – which would be useless in the confined space – for a moody looking scimitar and an ingenious looking hand-held crossbow. One that fed up at least six quarrels, from what Tomas could make out. But as they stepped into the tunnel, all light seemed to vanish and Tomas found himself plunged into a darkness so profound, he couldn't even see his hand before his eyes.

'Bloody hell!' Tomas exclaimed, stopping abruptly, a little stunned at the swiftness of the blackout. 'Can you see, still? Because I can't see a bloody thing.'

Famine said that he could. The advantage seemed to tickle the Horseman somewhat. 'Why? Can't you? That is a pity,' the condescension evident in Famine's tone.

Tomas grunted at the poor humor and attempted to visualize his headgear night sight. It flowed out from and over his ballistic goggles and with a reassuring suddenness, the world turned an eerie luminescent green.

'That's better,' Tomas exclaimed enthusiastically. 'Just like the old days. You'll never know just how much time I spent looking at the world through this sickly green haze. I'd almost forgotten what it was like. Next thing I reckon is my old HK33, silencer and a full mag, and I'd say we're good to go.'

Famine watched as well when Tomas darkened his garb and silenced the steel and chain he wore, impressed that their protégé was getting to grips with what he had become. Smiling to himself like a proud father, he followed Tomas further into the corridor as he took point, shouldering the HK and sighting down it, Famine a few steps behind – Tomas now ready for whatever might appear in his field of vision. Hugging the walls and letting his cowled cloak obscure his profile, blending in with the darkness, Tomas set off.

After about ten minutes of cautious advancing, they had encountered nothing but the odd cobweb. Tomas wondered just what sort of spider chose or was able to live down here. *There are always bloody cobwebs hanging around. It never fails. Why is that?* Famine picked up on the stray thought and gave Tomas a factual answer, as though he were out on a biology field trip.

'Very resilient are spider webs. You know, they don't rot! Left alone and undisturbed, they could hang for centuries.'

Tomas cast a look back to Famine that said he really needed to know that. 'My concern isn't for the webs; it's what made them. If this shrine had a corrupting effect on the guardians, what effect did it have on the wildlife? Never really been big on spiders. They're not natural if you ask me.'

Again Famine had an answer. 'Funny you should say that. Though they've been here since long before the dinosaurs, they weren't supposed to be. Some of the earlier races were experimenting with various cellular life and came up with the arachnid, though not as you know them now. If you think these are bad, you should see some of the original species, still living in the Domain. In some lands they are the dominant predator and they hunt in packs. Not many escape when they hunt. Especially the arboreal variety.'

Tomas whispered back over his shoulder to his companion, trying to keep his voice low, for the slightest untoward sound echoed annoyingly in the tunnels, it seemed.

'You're a bundle of fun-filled information, aren't you? Wandering around in the bloody dark like this I feel *so* much better.' Tomas stopped and raised his fist above his head for Famine to see, assuming he knew what it meant. 'Though with that in mind, we've reached a T junction. Got any thoughts?'

Famine crept silently up alongside Tomas and had an unobtrusive peek both ways. Both looked exactly the same, dank and dark. 'If you're up for it, Tomas, I'll take one and you take the other one. Pace out five hundred and if we haven't encountered anything by then, meet back here and compare notes. If it's all clear by then, we'll hold the passage at this point – after all, we don't really want any more trouble than we already have, no matter how much fun it might be. Sound like a plan to you?'

Tomas smiled at his companion and gave him an affable clout on the arm. 'So there is a rational mind in there, not just a reckless killing machine. That gives me some comfort at least. I was beginning to worry about you.'

The glint in Famine's eye when he turned to look at Tomas before heading off down his designated passage did little to reassure him that he *didn't* have something to worry about after all.

By the time Tomas had reached a count of four hundred, he had made three turns: two left and one right; and discovered that there was a slight degradation to the floor as well as a gentle slope, as though all the passages wound inexorably downwards. Tomas wasn't sure he wanted to get so far as to find out what it was at the bottom, though he had his suspicions and they weren't pleasant. But it was at that point, just as Tomas was about to make yet another left-hand turn, when he heard a familiar sound. The telltale jangle of armor. Steel against steel. The soft swishing rasp of chain mail rubbing as it moved. It couldn't have been Famine; it was coming from the wrong direction.

Tomas dropped to his knee and pulled the HK in tight to his shoulder, the stock fitting him like a designer weapon, which in effect it was, so the weapon became an extension of the man. He gently applied pressure to the trigger, ensuring that it was a smooth movement should he need to fire, not a snatched affair. It was what set the amateurs apart from the professionals: the subtle things. Tomas, ever so slowly, slipped the barrel around the corner, followed by the merest fraction of his head. Just enough for him to see through the green haze of his night sight what it was exactly that was making the noise. He wasn't entirely prepared for what he saw.

Tomas had convinced himself that anything he found down here was going to be mutated beyond description and corrupt beyond belief. His imagination had surpassed what he had fought upon the wall. What he wasn't expecting were comparatively normal looking crusaders. Men, armored and with a familiar tabard over chain mail, brandishing a sword in one hand and sporting the iconic white shield with the red cross emblazoned upon it. There were four of them and they were definitely looking for something. They swung their heads side to side as they moved forwards, ever closer to where Tomas was secreted. It was only as they drew closer that Tomas saw their eyes, or what should have been their eyes. Instead they reflected pure white. The white of blind subterranean creatures, existing in perpetual blackness. What need have they for sight when there was nothing to see. Sound was their ally now, Tomas surmised, and so he concentrated on keeping perfectly still, watching them and waiting to see what they did next; though he knew that should they come much closer, he would have to take preventative steps.

He didn't know what it was that alerted them. He could have sworn he made no sound whatsoever – until it occurred to him. It was his heartbeat. For as one, the crusaders all stopped, turned and looked directly at him. It was a more unnerving sight with their sightless eyes and blank expressions than had they been monsters. But their faces transformed then from calm manlike features to snarling animals. Baring their teeth, the crusaders charged Tomas's location. There was nothing for it but to fire. Pfft. The five-point-six-millimeter round exited the weapon with a sound that Tomas hadn't heard in a long time. The lead warrior's glazed orbs widened instantly as the round penetrated his skull just above the bridge of his nose and took out the back of his head along with a goodly portion of his helm. His forward momentum carried his body a few more faltering steps before his body realized that there was nothing operating it any more. He collapsed face down like so much meat hitting the ground. Yet this didn't faze his comrades-in-arms one little bit. They didn't spare their fallen knight a single glance – their contorted faces were fixed on the spot where Tomas crouched. These were no rational thinking soldiers; they were driven by an imperative that would not deviate them from their chosen objective. At that moment, it was himself.

Pfft, Pfft. Twice more he delivered the same head shot to the two next charging knights – with equally similar results. Their bodies collapsed with not so much as a groan, let alone a scream. Their silent deaths were just as disturbing as their sightless and silent appearance. But the last knight was almost upon him and Tomas felt confident enough to deal with this one in a more traditional manner. The rifle immediately switched to the sword and he leapt up and to the right, which carried Tomas past the knight. He was a shadow in his black garb and flowing cloak, but the knight's head turned faultlessly. Unfortunately his sword arm didn't move with the same speed. Tomas cleaved his own weapon around as his body twisted in midair. The knight attempted a parry but the Sword of War smashed through the knight's blade and clove into his torso. By Tomas's reckoning it had severed the spine and the body joined its fellows, still and broken upon the floor. *What sort of goddamn guardians are these? They don't seem able to guard shit.* Then Tomas remembered what era they were from and realized that then all they had to worry about was probably just some wandering goat herd. Maybe they weren't expecting anything to access the chapel due to the density shifting. *Still, if the rest are like these ones then we should be safe enough for the time being.* Tomas looked down at the corpses and after a second's consideration, he brought the HK back and put several rounds into each body. *Just to be sure. What with all this weird shit, who knows what they can do. Better to be safe than sorry.* Tomas thought of the last time he'd used that particular argument. It was on the Ivory Coast, and he was accused of adopting an overkill policy. It hadn't sat well with the resident troop CO. They were to provide support for him whilst he performed an extraction. Except there were more guards than anticipated. Tomas was of the belief that dead guards were less likely to shoot you in the back or cry for help. And they weren't likely to inhibit any speedy exit. His belief was that it saved the lives of his men, which was more important than the lives of known drug dealers and terrorists or their hired thugs. All guns for hire knew the risks. It flew in the face of the conventional military's ideology which saw the reduction in caliber of their weapons – citing that a wounded man took another to look after him, thus taking out two men for the price of one. Tomas's answer was a resounding *Bollocks*. A man with a wounded leg could still activate explosives, shoot a weapon, cry out or perform any other manner of potentially lethal and destructive actions. He told the CO, 'If I'm not paying for the ammo, I'll put as many as I can spare into the bastards. And I advise you to make allowances for body armor: you're not the only ones who have it, you know. Face, groin, throat, thigh. Hit the bits that matter, for God's sake. Isn't that why you waste so much time bloody training, so that when you get to shitholes like this you can do what needs doing, when it needs doing? not pussyfooting about, shooting them in their limbs or blowing feet off. Live but maimed men tended to hold a grudge and used themselves as living propaganda as to why further violence was needed. Dead men didn't say a lot or do a lot, other than smell.'

Of course none of his beliefs were deemed politically correct, and his methods contravened more regulations of the Geneva Convention than the proverbial stick could be waved at. Tomas spat at that ridiculous bit of legisla- tion as well. 'How can you have bloody rules for war? Who ever heard of such a thing? You cannot civilize barbarism and say "We have rules. Waging war and killing innocents is all right now". Which bloody part of war is war do you not understand? There are no fucking rules in war and that is all there is to it. That is why it is war not a domestic disturbance. How can you not get that?' Tomas had fumed to his commanding officers once or twice, he couldn't remember exactly, but it was more than once. He'd seen too many die because they assumed that four shots to the chest had finished off their target, only to find that they had either missed the vital organ – highly possible now with the smaller calibers – or some basic body armor had absorbed the shot so when they drew close enough to confirm their kill, all they got was several rounds up the abdomen and groin from the wounded and very pissed off soldier. Then, the wounded enemy survived and quite likely got a medal. All you got was a pine box, an insignificant grave marker and, if you were lucky, you got to give a loved one a flag and a pathetic widow's pension. All because of some godforsaken rule about wounding. *You pays your money, you takes your choice*. If you want to play at war and soldiers, then death is a strong and high possibility. Taking prisoners costs time, money and resources. So don't take any. If people got to understand the potentially fatal and highly probable implications of war then, maybe the said people would be less inclined to start them. But then again, few souls were as single-minded and radical thinking as Tomas. It lent much to his already considerable contempt for the governments he worked with; although, not surprisingly, his outspoken and disturbing views did little to endear him to them either.

With a last look at the fallen knights, Tomas shouldered the HK and set off once more, scanning the gloom ahead for any more of the so-called guardians. He hadn't gone much more than ten feet or so before he heard an uncannily familiar sound from behind him. Tomas lowered his head, shaking it slowly in resignation. *Surely not,* he thought glumly. *Not bloody zombies! Though why not? With my luck, it'd be about right.* Sure enough, moments later, the three knights he had put down with the head shots emerged from the darkness, striding towards him with the same deadly intent as before; swords held high and poised to strike him down the moment they came within range. Their gaping wounds were blatantly obvious in the green haze that was currently his visible world. They were moving somehow faster than before, too. Their expressions – if it was at all possible – looked even more incensed than they did earlier. Their shoulders were hunched and they leant forward into the attack much like Neanderthals in Templar garb. Then they began to run. In the light of his night-vision goggles, Tomas had no way of seeing that the thick, sticky gunk that leaked from the wounds on the knights was not the deep red of mortal blood. Instead, it was a dark brown, bordering on black, slime that oozed from their wounds. Tomas reasoned that all bets were off with these guardians and that stealth meant little any more. He stood and switched to full auto and let rip an entire clip into the now charging warriors.

Their charge was slowed somewhat by the hailstorm of automatic weapon's fire, but not stopped. Most of the rounds were through-and-throughs, but those that didn't exit left gaping wounds as they impacted. Nothing should have been able to survive that. Even the demons outside had fallen to Tomas when hit, with fewer rounds than these took, from his mystically-enhanced weapons. How these creatures were able to pick themselves up like they were presently doing gave Tomas a most disconcerting feeling. But he didn't have time to dwell on the subject as the Templars – or what was left of them – were bearing down on him apace, unfazed by the hail of gunfire. Tomas might just as well have splashed water on them for all the good it did. *Well, maybe some good old-fashioned steel might prove more effective.* Tomas willed the sword back to its original form and felt it thrum with anticipation. For some reason he couldn't fathom, the sword seemed more cognizant in its original form.

The yards closed to feet and the Templars leapt the remaining distance to Tomas, attempting to cover the ground and destroy the intruder as quickly as possible. Inhuman screams ripped from them and black blood spattered from their ruined bodies as they flew through the air, swords raised. Their speed was astonishing considering their physical condition, and it was all Tomas could do to dive clear of the first attacker, who was only marginally faster than his companions. Tomas heard the knight's blade strike stone directly behind him as the knight slammed the blade down. Keeping the roll going, Tomas evaded another decapitating stroke, feeling the wind whistle past his face as he avoided the arcing blade. Coming up directly before the second knight, Tomas slammed his helmeted head into the knight's bullet-smashed chin. An audible crack told him that the neck had snapped but he doubted somehow that that would stop it for long. It staggered back a few steps, though more from the jarring impact than from any real sense of injury, but it was enough time for Tomas to put his own mighty edged weapon to use; the knight dropped to the tunnel floor in three messy pieces. Tomas, however, had no time to see if those bits were still up for a fight as his instinct alerted him to an attack from behind. The first knight had stopped and turned back. Dropping low and swinging, Tomas ducked beneath another deadly blow and simultaneously eviscerated the knight before him. What fell from the gaping abdomen of the knight almost made Tomas retch. It was the foul decomposed entrails of several hundred years' worth of rot. These were far more than he had initially given them credit for because the Templar barely acknowledged the injury; instead he carried on attacking and it was all Tomas could do, with some serious back-pedaling, to avoid being skewered. The trouble was, it simply brought him closer to the remaining two Templars, who joined in the attack. Desperate, Tomas rolled to the side to avoid being hit from behind as well as from the front, and he felt several blows glance from his armor, but not before he felt the searing pain of their swords bite across his back and shoulders. They were relentless and his armor would only protect him so much. He had to keep moving otherwise they would slice him to ribbons. Tomas bunched his leg muscles and sprang upwards, straight at the lone attacker, and bodychecked him, sending them both sprawling, as the knight wasn't expecting such an attack. As the knight staggered back and crashed to the floor under the armored weight of Tomas, Tomas drove his knee into the creature's face as he disengaged and scrambled away, thus buying himself precious moments to turn and face the trio of attackers with a fighting chance. Two ran past their comrade as it picked itself up, and they engaged Tomas, swords flashing. Tomas began the deadly dance of steel as he parried one after the other with a speed he knew he didn't possess. It was the sword bolstering him again – as it had upon the wall. He felt its strength and desire to defeat these creatures burn through him. Without it Tomas knew he would have been hard-pressed. For even though they were evidently quite dead, the Templars turned out to be excellent swordsmen. Sparks flew as the parried weapons of the knights careened off the walls, and he struck several killing blows against them, but they hardly slowed. If anything, the more he hit them, the harder and faster they got. He had to finish this and soon. The third knight joined the mêlée and Tomas found himself being slowly pressed backwards under the onslaught.

Feinting and dodging left and right, Tomas still took several hits from the lightning blades of the Templars as centuries of experience slipped through his desperate defense. Tomas was a student of human nature – it was what had made him such an efficient assassin. He could predict what someone's routine was likely to be after only a short period of study. So it was with the attacks of the Templars: he began to detect a certain style and regularity to the way they attacked him. Tomas played to this pattern in an attempt to find a way through their offense and bring this to some sort of end; at least get on the other side of them, where he could retreat back to the rendezvous point where he hoped Famine was, for a bit of an assist if these clowns insisted on following him. Though in the dark and confusion, Tomas became painfully aware that he wasn't sure exactly which way that was now, having been turned around by these creatures.

Tomas's plan was at least working in part; he was driving them back and taking fewer hits as their pattern became more pronounced. He took one down with a reverse overhand strike that saw the sword-holding arm flop uselessly to the floor. As the not so bright warrior bent to retrieve its weapon with a view to transferring it to the other hand, Tomas drove the sword down and separated its head from its body – kicking the bleeding and flailing corpse into the path of its comrades, causing them to stumble. He quickly dispatched them likewise. It seemed that dismemberment was the only way to slow them. But as he made to leave and get back to Famine, he saw that it wasn't going to be a final solution as tendrils, and what he guessed to be veins, were stringing their way across the gore covered floor to entangle with their separated parts and slowly, inexorably, draw themselves back together. He wasn't going to stand around and watch though. Enough was enough.

Tomas looked both right and left. *Which bloody way was it? Crap!Fifty-fifty chance. I suppose I'll have to leave it to the crows of fate.* Having made his decision, Tomas strode away from the fallen Templars before they got their shit together again.

As Tomas began his jog down the gloomy passageway, he began to realize that he had in fact taken the wrong way, mainly due to the walls growing rougher and less hewn than the ones he had originally gone down. These were becoming more like cave walls. *Just my bloody luck.* But before he could turn back and try to get past the guards before they were whole once more, he heard a low thrumming, a deep bass rumbling that he felt almost as much as heard. Like someone had turned on a giant subwoofer and had cranked it up. The more he concentrated upon it, the more it put his teeth on edge and caused his hackles to rise in alarm. But for all his concern, Tomas knew he would have to investigate the sound and put his mind to rest. He didn't like the idea of leaving something behind him that made that sort of sound and caused the feelings it did. *One of these days my curiosity is going to get me into more trouble than even I can handle.* Shouldering the HK and adjusting his goggles, Tomas set off once more, oblivious to the little miracles taking place upon his body. Where the Templars had struck him, the wounds were knitting and healing themselves. Tomas had just ignored them, as was his way until he had time to deal with them, so the fact they didn't hurt was a bonus, but he didn't yet know why. Hugging the walls and becoming at one with the Stygian gloom of the passageway, Tomas crept forward towards the sound.

Several turns and quite a few passageways later, Tomas brought himself to an abrupt halt. His gut instinct warned him to take this corner with more caution than the last ones. Hunkering down, Tomas peeked ever so slowly around the corner. Closing his eyes briefly, as there was nothing immediately dangerous to be seen, Tomas ranged out his senses, trying to get a clearer idea of where the sound was coming from and if he was any nearer. It was definitely louder; if louder was the word: it wasn't so much loud as more intense, and his bones veritably ached because of it now. Left. It was definitely originating from somewhere down the left-hand passageway. So that was the way he had to go. With no further hesitation, for Tomas was keen to resolve this now, he set off once more. Passing two side passageways to the right-hand side as he moved, Tomas spared them a glance as he passed, just in case something nasty was lurking there, which, fortunately for him, there wasn't.

Through the green haze of his goggles, Tomas began to see dust particles floating down before him. Looking up, he saw that small fractures were beginning to form in the roof structure and dust and small rocks were starting to fall. *Oh Shit! The whole bloody place is coming down. It's this damn vibration, I bet you. It's shaking itself apart. Time to go, Tomas, noise or no noise.* As Tomas turned to go his heart sank and his gut wrenched at the sight of the four Templars again: whole and obviously annoyed as they ran towards him. Tomas didn't wait for them to catch up. He got up and ran too, away from them and further into the catacombs – and inevitably, closer to the source of the sound.

Tomas was running and thinking furiously, when he came to the sharp right-hand corner. Almost bouncing off the wall as he rounded it, Tomas came to yet another skidding halt, for before him, standing shoulder to shoulder and filling the corridor from wall to wall, were five more Templars. Only these were different from the previous guardians he had encountered. These only resembled Templars because of their garb. Their bodies within their clothing were another matter. They were pumped up way beyond anything mortal: muscles upon muscles, and this growth must have been within the confines of their armor, because they had split the seams of their gear and ripped out. But that wasn't what made them horrendous: it was the fact that it appeared that their skin had been incinerated. It was black and charred as though they had stood before a flame-thrower for an hour or so. Where they had grown and where their muscles bulged, the charred and crispy skin had split and torn, rupturing the cooked crust of their flesh. What had spilt out of the wounds had rotted in the dank confines of the subterranean atmosphere and Tomas could

411

smell the corruption from several yards away. *Looks like they get worse the closer they get to whatever it is they are guarding. Bummer. Looks like they get bigger too. Double bummer. This is gonna get ugly, I just know it.* True to Tomas's prediction, the Templars swung their heads to fix their burnt out eye sockets on Tomas's exact location. As one, they opened their ruined mouths and screamed a sound that was like the thrumming, only much more focused and concentrated. It made his head swim and Tomas felt a trickle of blood run onto his upper lip. And what he thought were tears turned out to be blood trails from ruptured capillaries in his eyes. *I'm crying blood? Fuck!* Drawing their weapons as one, the Templars began to stride towards him like five synchronized robots. *Shit! Fuck! Shit!* Tomas backed up as fast as he could, recalling one of the side passages and hoping he could make it to one of them before those attacking him from behind cut him off. Tomas began to run back the way he came, stumbling as his head still rang.

Famine had indeed encountered his share of very persistent Templar guardians, and had enjoyed every moment of their inevitable and eventual demise. Their smoking ashes were all that remained of them. Testament to Famine's powers and their infallibility. But it wasn't the guardians that disturbed Famine and caused an uncommon frown to crease his usually jovial features. It was the absence of Tomas at the designated rendezvous point that caused him concern. That and the onset of the disturbing sound that had started up a few moments earlier. The rumbling grew louder and louder and as the first dust motes dropped down from the ceiling Famine moved with all his own supernatural speed back to the entrance where he had left Death and Pestilence. For he knew what was coming next. The rumbling escalated and just as he made it to the antechamber where they all gathered, he dived forward, shouting his warning as he did so.

'Get down! It's caving in!' Diving past Death and Pestilence, he saw them pull their cloaks up before them, just as a billowing cloud of dust and flying rubble exploded from the passageway, enveloping the three Horsemen. Yet it was as though their cloaks were made of steel. Rocks and stones hammered into the draped fabric and bounced away harmlessly. The rumbling and stony expulsion went on for several minutes before gradually abating. When it did, the three Horsemen stood alone and unharmed amid the debris and chaos, their eyes searching the ruins for something in particular.

'Where is Tomas?' was Death's eventual question.

Famine looked grim as he replied, brushing himself down to remove the grime he had just dived through. 'I don't know. We were due to meet up after checking out individual passageways. I can only guess he encountered more guardians than he could handle.'

'Yet he still lives. I can sense his life force. Though it is faint. Like he is within the confines of some sort of shielding. It dulls and diminishes the connection. I fear he is too close to the crypt proper and its dark energy is cocooning him, even perhaps drawing him towards it. If that is the case, he is now beyond our aid and on his own. We must turn our attention to other matters now. This plan has failed, it seems, and at the worst time, for it appears that the Adversary is further advanced with his plan than anticipated. Come,' Death suggested to his companion, 'let us summon War back from his own reconnoiter and see what awaits us without. I sense Phanuel is on his way to us and should be here soon.'

Famine looked long and hard at the now collapsed tunnel entrance and a series of emotions played out across his swarthy features. Eventually, resignation manifested upon his face, along with an abiding sadness, for against all his expectations, he had grown to like the irascible human; and he turned from the cave-in to join Death, who he could tell from millennia of experience, was not very happy.

Tomas heard the rumbling escalate, to the point he had to look about wildly, fully expecting the roof to come thundering down around his ears at any second, and immediately culminate in a resounding crash that would send debris and choking dust billowing down every corridor like a gaseous express train – including the one he presently occupied. Tomas hunkered down and pulled his shemagh up over his nose and draped his own cloak about himself

413

to fend off the worst and enable him to carry on breathing without ingesting half a ton of crap.

It seemed the cave-in had no effect whatsoever on the Templar guardians, for they lumbered through the settling dust cloud as though nothing had occurred. Tomas squinted into the passageway, but his visibility had dropped from negligible to impossible as the dust roiled in the darkness. He wouldn't see anything coming now until it was on top of him. *Get up, Tom, keep moving. Though where the bloody hell I'm going now is anyone's guess. Still, no such thing as lost; just temporarily misdirected. If I keep moving long enough, I'm bound to find some sort of way out of this craphole.* Tomas wasted no time. He was up and running, his hand-held Hochlers manifesting before him, cocked and ready to blast anything that sprang up before him. His night-vision goggles had a range of approximately six feet ahead of him now at best; so his pace was limited. The last thing he needed was to run headlong into some sort of trap, or more of the Templars, for the sake of a bit of caution. He had never been overly reckless. Keep a cool head when all about you are losing theirs and you stand a greater chance of surviving whatever it is that besets you. More wise words from his father; words he had kept with him since he had been told them at the age of thirteen. Though similar had oft been said over the years by others, it was his father's version that had stuck with him. It was odd, Tomas realized as he ran through the gloom, that though he hadn't spoken to the old man for twenty plus years and had rarely had a civil word for him even then, he found himself thinking of him more and more; little memories popping up, snippets of his past he thought long buried. Tomas bitterly regretted now his relationship with his father. Their last words had been in anger and there was no way to undo that. Before the explosion, Tomas had found it easy to shrug off such matters as trivial and weak, but since his life had been ripped from him and his broken body left for dead, he found that some emotional corner had been turned. As though the force of the explosion had destroyed not only the ones he loved – but some invisible dam that he had erected to hold back such crippling and handicapping emotions as guilt, remorse and regret. A conscience he thought long dead had clawed its way out of the unmarked grave that Tomas had buried it in, and now it was getting its own back. *Not a good time for warm, fuzzy trips down memory lane, old son,* Tomas muttered to himself as he shook his head and tried to clear the fog there and focus on the job at hand. *Better find a way out of this rat trap before anything else bloody well happens. Famine's gotta be wondering where I am by now and Death is probably spitting bullets at the fact his little plan has gone tits up. Hello?* Tomas came to an abrupt halt. There was a small niche in the wall, or at least Tomas took it for a niche. Only on closer inspection did he see that it was in fact another, smaller passage. It looked considerably older than the others. He reasoned that it must be one of the original tunnels for the old pagan chapel Death had spoken of. He knew also they had a tendency to be below ground – deep in the womb of the mother, or somesuch notion. He had spent some time with the navy in Malta and had been educated on the history of Gozo, albeit briefly. Fascinating stuff really, not dissimilar to what he was seeing now. A quick inspection showed markings and glyphs around the entranceway. They certainly looked old and mysterious, if not a little ominous. But Tomas had no time for archaeology; he needed to put as much ground between him and the guardians as possible whilst still trying to find an alternative exit.

Ducking into the rough hewn crevice, Tomas didn't see the runes and glyphs carved onto the lintel flare and burn briefly with a black fire as he crossed the threshold.

You gotta be kidding me? Tomas groaned to himself as he squeezed through the gap. He found himself on the top step of a flight of carved stone steps leading downwards into an even darker and more impenetrable gloom than what he had been wading through. *Just how much darker can somewhere get? Surely that defies physics.* Tomas raised a hand and watched numbly as it disappeared into the blackness beyond his elbow. Withdrawing it again. he checked it was still okay. Colder, but intact. Cautiously, he leant forward to see if the night-vision goggles had any more success. He sucked in breath and pulled back as if he had been burnt, after his bare face had touched the inky blackness. *Fuck! That's cold*, Tomas exclaimed to himself as his breath plumed before him in a frosty cloud. But before he could ponder the whys and wherefores of what was down there and why it was so hellishly cold, he heard the now familiar jingle of armor from his persistent shadows, the Templars. It was as though they had some supernatural GPS on him. They found him unerringly even through the haze of the cave-in. Tomas knew his options were limited and growing fewer by the moment. He closed his eyes for a second and reconfigured his armor to that of his Arctic gear, in the hope that it would hold the bone chilling cold at bay while he explored what waited below in the Stygian gloom. Taking a deep breath, Tomas plunged into the void and began his treacherous descent. With every step he felt the biting cold, as it penetrated his boots and began to creep insidiously up his legs, thickening and freezing the blood, slowing his movements and making every step a torturous trial. How he was going to fight as the permeating cold slowed his limbs, began to concern him. He was usually good at putting aside the effects of the elements, thanks to years of ongoing training and mental discipline, but this was something else entirely. Step by step, he made his way down. Tomas could feel the ice beneath his boots and fingertips as he kept them pressed against the wall, both for balance and to keep him on track. He didn't know how wide the stairs were for he could only see what was beneath his feet and against the wall. Tomas reached out once to feel the other side of the passageway and felt nothing but an icy draught, lazily and easily passing through his clothes to chill the skin beneath. It gave his overworked imagination the impression of a chasm, vast and gaping, so he kept himself as close to the wall as possible. Sparing one last glance behind him – to make sure that nothing had crept up on him – was a mistake. He knew it the moment he did it. There was nothing but the impenetrable blackness there, as ominous and forbidding as what lay before him; the difference being, he knew what danger lay behind him, but he had no idea what lay before him, other than what his imagination conjured conveniently for him. And based on what he had seen so far, that wasn't very pleasant.

Soon enough, his breathing had become labored under the exertion of maintaining his balance on the icy stair, and the effort of simply moving in the lung searing cold and the claustrophobic blackness. With the added mental stress of having to deal with imminent danger, he was struggling. With each step down, Tomas fully expected to come face to face with some horror. It began to feel like drowning, only worse. He didn't realize until the weapon slipped from unfeeling fingers, that his appendages were starting to lose all sensation. Tomas willed the sword away before he lost it. His body felt as though it had doubled its mass and every step was an agony-filled effort. Added to all his woes, Tomas knew that he had to resolve the growing paranoia about his pursuers. He imagined he could feel their fetid breath upon his neck, and that their blackened and charred fingers were reaching out, about to grasp him by the throat and cast him into the oblivion by his side. The trouble was now there was no going back without a fight, and forwards meant heading further into the unknown and the still plummeting temperature. *Some bloody choice*, Tomas thought bitterly.

You have to get a handle on this, Tomas, he berated himself. *For the sake of your sanity and self-preservation, think, man, think. What did you get from the Horsemen that could be of use to you?* He thought, but the marrow-freezing cold made it hard and little presented itself – except the fact that this must have unnatural origins, perhaps even demonic, or part of the defense mechanism here to stop anything getting this far. For he had felt the touch of the elements on the journey over the ocean and had been unaffected by that.

Knowing there was little for it but to face the Templars didn't do him any good either, but he had to see if he could shake them off his tail, at least for a bit. With a Herculean effort he willed the Hechler and Koch machine pistols back to his hands. Full mags with alternating tracers. He rolled his shoulders before steadying himself, facing back the way he had come. Just as he was about to squeeze the triggers, the annoying voice that speaks to you at the most inappropriate times whispered to Tomas: What if they weren't there? This would alert them to his presence, surely. *Bollocks! I'm past caring now.* Tomas opened fire. The rounds tore through the darkness, illuminating more than he would have liked. Cursing, Tomas saw the infernal guardians juddering down the icy stair after him, the automaton steps giving them a weird robotic movement which seemed out of place with their origin. But for all their lack of agility, the Templars were still making their inexorable way down and going faster than Tomas was. Unlike Tomas, they were oblivious to the fall that he had feared was off to his right. Sure enough it was there, in all its vertigo-inducing glory. Tomas quickly assessed his position as he maintained the barrage against the knights. He was only a hundred yards or so down a narrow carved stair, hewn from the face of a monumental slab of rock that must have gone down another mile at least. It gave Tomas the impression of being one of the anchor pins of the Earth, so vast and imposing did it look. Then Tomas saw dejectedly that he still had a way to go, it seemed, before he reached the bottom, for an eerie luminescence had started to seep up the rock face towards him, showing him the frozen slime and petrified mildew upon the ancient stones. The cold of the void reached out for him and Tomas felt his soul recoil at its approach, but was unable to avoid it on the precipice.

The knights staggered against the onslaught of hot metal. One toppled over the edge to fall soundlessly into the gloom. Tomas didn't even hear it hit the bottom. If in fact it did. Keeping up the barrage until they all fell back or fell off the edge, he soon ran low on enemies and eventually, Tomas left them shredded upon the steps, ripped and torn asunder from hundreds and hundreds of blistering rounds; though he knew from past experience it wouldn't really stop them; it would only delay them until they regenerated. But it would be enough, or so he hoped, to enable him to make it to the bottom unmolested by their pursuit. *Though for the love of me, I can't figure out exactly why I want to get down there. There had better be a way out other than this goddamn staircase, that's all I can say,* Tomas muttered to himself as he pressed on, talking as much to keep himself focused as it was to simply hear a voice. He feared it would be the last one he would ever hear. But for the last hour or so, he wasn't entirely sure that the voice in his head was all his own. After all, what had prompted him to take this grim route and consider it for an escape? It certainly wouldn't have been his first choice, but something had *nudged* him this way. This unsettling train of thought only managed to disturb him all the more and set his hackles rising again, hoping that whatever was down there had succumbed to falling Templars or wasn't up for a fight. *'Cos I'm bloody well not!*

Down and down he went. The cold bit deeper still as he descended and Tomas was genuinely concerned now for his appendages. He'd seen the effects of frostbite on many of his companions. Blackened and rotting fingers and toes, turning to gangrene almost before their eyes as the necrosis spread, insidiously, until whole limbs were rendered useless, and they posed a serious enough health risk that they needed amputating. Always assuming the poison hadn't infiltrated the blood system already. It was a slippery slope to inevitable death. Few got away with frostbite without losing something. For many it was their lives. The lucky merely lost limbs.

Despair began to settle on Tomas then, like a dank mist, permeating every fibre of his being. The prospect of freezing to death seemed very real to him about now. He hadn't felt his hands for some time and his feet moved automatically. To Tomas, it felt he was walking on the stumps of his legs, and lights flashed and popped around his peripheral vision as his head began to swim. Were it not for his own dogged determination and phenomenal endurance – added to the mix was sheer stubbornness and a refusal to let anything beat him – he would have fallen long ago. He couldn't even be bothered now about the Templar guardians, and whether they had risen again or not. He had passed the point of no return. Recognizing that feeling several times during his slippery descent, he had felt the need to knock his own head against the slick, ice covered wall, knocking some sense and moderate alertness in to himself, lest he fall prey to the silent killer: the weariness of giving up and letting the cold consume him, wrapping him in its frozen embrace, where he would feel nothing, ever again. No pain, no guilt, no regrets. Tomas began to hallucinate then, his mind playing cruel tricks on him as the cold pressed him. He saw his family below, beckoning to him, calling him to join them.

Tomas was relieved they were there. He reached out to them, desperate for their warm embrace – and that was when he lost his tenuous footing on the staircase. But as he began to tumble forward, with the first hit on the rough hewn steps to his head, Tomas blissfully blacked out. He never felt his body smashed and buffeted by the rock as he collapsed forwards down the hard stone steps, tumbling head over heels. It was also a fortunate thing for him that he wasn't that far from the bottom either, for after three battering forward rolls he went straight off the edge – landing on the stone flags of the bottom with a sickening, bone snapping crunch.

Tomas came to with a suddenness that had him thrashing and scrambling backwards away from whatever might be standing over him. Fortunately there was nothing there to threaten him because he didn't get very far. The broken arm hanging limply at his side collapsed when he went to put weight on it, sending lightning bolts of searing agony ripping up his shoulder and very nearly causing Tomas to black out again. He did retch though; the pain gripped him and twisted his gut viciously. He took several deep breaths, or at least tried to. With the first intake he was set off, coughing violently and spitting blood. He gave that up as a bad job, and so he settled for simply sitting up to wipe his mouth with his good hand, before giving himself a once-over. Inventorying the rest of his battered body, he discovered that he ached in places he didn't think he had and the gods had taken a cricket bat to his head, it throbbed so much. And as he tried breathing again, more gently this time, he knew he had several broken ribs. *That's not good.* Tomas knew what injuries of that severity meant to men in the field. *That's me well and truly fucked now. Broken arm and ribs. And that's just for starters, God only knows what internal injuries I've got, not to mention the bloody mother of all headaches.* Tomas sighed as another wave of pain rippled through him. But it was during a brief moment of painless lucidity, that Tomas became slowly aware that it wasn't quite so cold here, actually being at the bottom.

He knew this as the breath didn't plume quite so foggily before him and some sensation had begun to creep back into his feet and hand. He still couldn't feel the broken one, though seconds later, he wished he couldn't feel the others again either, for with sensation came pain. Yet more waves after wave of sickening, nausea-inducing pain as frozen flesh warmed slightly and nerve endings flared like little miniature suns. Through his haze of pain and misery, Tomas caught sight of the Templar guardians stepping off the bottom stair and beginning to move towards him. And stepping from the gloom came those that had fallen earlier. Tomas could have cried there and then at the futility of it all and the irony of his impending doom. He lay broken and incapacitated at the mercy of those inhuman bastards, unable to defend himself – for he was never going to be able to wield a sword or even hold a gun in his current state. He would be lucky to just be able to stand without passing out at this rate. Exercising every shred of willpower he could muster, Tomas scanned the immediate vicinity, looking for anything that might offer some hope. The best he could see was to scramble over to the large stone edifice that seemed to be the only object in the scope of his limited vision. It was about the size of a twenty-foot container, except this was made of some highly engraved stone. Tomas, however, did not have the luxury of admiring the intricate motifs that decorated this particular sarcophagus. The revelation of where he actually was crashed in on him.

Of course! That's what it is. The word sarcophagus brought it all hammering back to him. *This is the bloody crypt of that what's his name. Nakir or something. This is the heart of the chapel.* Quite frankly, if Tomas was honest with himself, it was the very last place he wanted to be. In his current befuddled state he wasn't even sure now why he chose to even come down this far. *Did I choose?* It hadn't actually done him any favors if he had. But now wasn't the time to dwell on such matters. He had more immediate concerns.

Tomas gritted his teeth and, using his good arm and almost crying out, he levered himself to his feet, where he stood and swayed slightly as his head took a few seconds longer to catch up with him. The world tilted disconcertingly as he hobbled away from the evilly grinning Templar Knights, who, seeing their prey looking helpless, drew their swords and pressed in for the kill. As Tomas edged around the crypt, he saw that the lid of the tomb had been removed at some point and was lying on its edge against its off side. Tomas didn't know what prompted the thought, but he felt that to get inside the crypt would give him a better defensive position than just running around it. All it would take for the knights to catch him would be to split up and flank him in a pincer movement. So with the last of his flagging energy, fuelled by the adrenaline of mortal danger, Tomas ran at the tilted lid, and using it as a ramp he took two leaps; one to the top of the lid, and the next propelled him over the lip. As Tomas went over, he got the fleeting impression from the momentary contact with the crypt, that it wasn't stone at all: instead it felt metallic. Iron. He tasted the tang of iron as he crashed over the lip; although that could have been his own blood as he bit his tongue with the effort of the leap.

As he sailed over the edge, he fully expected to crash into some filthy and dusty remains – the remains of the dark angel known to a select few as Nakir the Black – which in part he did. But that wasn't the end of it. Oh no. Tomas came down hard on several bones all right, but they were far from old and dusty. Instead they were viciously sharp and protruding upwards like venomous spines. Tomas felt several of them pierce his flesh as he landed hard on them. He grunted as they punctured his body and drove in deep. One gouged straight into his chest and Tomas knew then, for that split second, it was a heart shot. Blinding light drove all sense from Tomas and as his blood spurted out, he knew no more.

He knew nothing about what occurred next. That instead of landing in a broken heap, a few feet from the edge, he kept falling – and falling. His now limp body spiraled downwards in an ever increasing and spinning rush. It was impossible in the realm of human physics, but space and time were being bent out of shape within the crypt as it warped and flexed inside, and Tomas was at the heart of it. His body spun so fast in the vortex that had sprung up within the casket that he soon became a blur. Until finally, with a flare of black fire – erupting from the sarcophagi like a volcanic explosion – raw energy flowed out from the stone casket as though it were a living, blazing liquid with a sentience of its own, hunting and seeking anything to vent its wrath upon. It rose higher and higher, roaring with a malevolent fury as though it were a caged beast long held captive, and now free to wreak havoc on its tormentors. Mushrooming out, it engulfed everything in the room, including the Templar guardians, incinerating them where they stood, leaving nothing, not even ash. It splashed up walls and even got some way up the frozen staircase before it was sucked back into the crypt with a rush of air and a final scream of impotent rage that shook the cavern like an enclosed sonic boom. But in a heartbeat it was over and deathly silence prevailed once more. But with one major, fundamental difference. Tomas had disappeared.

CHAPTER ELEVEN

QUAESTA

After Jen's tearful departure, leaving Gwen and Maddy together in the grove, Gwen had started thinking about what lay before her – or not so much started, for little about recent events had been very far from her thoughts – but more so now that her makeover was complete. At first she thought about how her quest was going to start before the realization hit her – with a sinking feeling like a lead weight in her belly – that she had more than started already. The mind-blowing transformation and the revelations of the past few days had been integral to her journey; to simply cap it all – all she needed to do was to actually go somewhere. For all her pacing and nervous fidgeting around the grove, chewing her lip and fiddling with her hair, it wasn't the same as making those first steps out in the world. There would be a massive distinction between her little steps here and the first monumental steps on her journey. A part of her mind rationalized that it was a very normal and human psychological barrier. The anticipation of a thing was nearly always greater than the thing itself. Her imagination conjured no end of disastrous scenarios, each more horrific than the last. Of course, reality was a whole new ball game.

The basis of her quandary was that man, the voracious explorer that he was, had been just about everywhere in the comparatively short time he had been on the Earth. There were few places left that had not been colonized or interfered with in some way by him – so how had this tree remained hidden for so long? Quite literally, where on earth could it be? Maddy seemed to sit patiently as Gwen muttered and mumbled to herself, organizing her thoughts into something that she hoped resembled some sort of coherent and cohesive plan. She didn't think she was doing very well. The serene avatar of the Earth's mountains and minerals, fire and flame, sat upon the ground, lost in her own thoughts, her long tanned legs curled beneath her demurely, the blades of lush green grass brushing gently against her flawless skin. Maddy leant upon one hand, head tilted slightly, so her lustrous locks of flaming auburn hair cascaded over one shoulder. With her free hand she swished it through the grass as though she were draping it in a lightly flowing, if rather green river. She had issues of her own to sift through and welcomed the tranquility of the grove to do so, though for all Maddy and Gwen were both lost in their respective musings, they both knew that they didn't have the luxury of a lot of time to muse with.

When Gwen got nervous or thoughtful about an impending situation, she got hungry. That illogical sensation that said food would solve everything. Ah, but what sort of food? That was the question. Her first thought was a large tub of her favorite chocolate chip ice cream, but she didn't think she could rustle up any Ben and Jerry's out here. Plan B came without thinking. Snaking from the woods came a thick branch, laden with lush, juicy looking apples, swinging ponderously as it dangled its fruit just where it would be comfortable for her to reach it. Gwen picked one for herself and one for Maddy. Once she had what she needed, the branch receded and vanished into the woodland once more. Strolling over to her friend, she proffered the fruit, which Maddy, looking up and smiling, took graciously. Of course, it hadn't occurred to Gwen that neither of the women actually required to take sustenance this way any more. She supposed that some old habits died harder than others.

'Thank you, Gwen. This looks lovely.' Maddy took a delicate bite and her eyes widened in pleasant surprise. She took another, larger bite, chewing and swallowing before speaking again. Gwen had done much the same. She couldn't believe that what she had in her hand was simply an apple, so sweet was it, and the juice was a nectar that would have revived the dead, she was sure of it.

'Gwen, this has to be the best apple I have ever had, and I've had a few, I can tell you. This is a testament to your worthiness as the third avatar, Gwen. Well done.'

'Thanks, I think, but I didn't do it consciously. I just thought of fruit because I couldn't manage ice cream, and this branch of apples appeared. How's that for weird?'

'It's not weird, Gwen. This is your grove and unlike anywhere on the entire planet, it is more attuned to your will than you can possibly imagine. It knows what you require as your mind first thinks of the requirement. It is attuned to your every fibre as much as your arms and legs are. It responds to your will in just the same way.'

Gwen looked both happy and incredibly sad at the same time, causing Maddy to frown with increasing concern. She asked if she was all right and Gwen nodded she was, yet she still looked forlorn.

'There are moments, Maddy, much like this, when I think it's all just too much and I'm going to wake any moment and find it all a fantastic dream. It leaves me feeling like a newborn child, or a foal that is learning to walk for the first time, all wobbly and overawed by absolutely everything. I've no idea of the extent of just what I am capable of, and that frightens me just as much as the prospect of failure and all that that entails.'

Maddy just sat silently and listened, trying to understand how she felt, but it had been so long since she had been born to her own role that she now believed that she had always been this way and never had to experience what Gwen was now feeling.

'I mean, think about it. I'm a dragon and so are you. Now don't get me wrong, that's so fantastic I can't even imagine words suitable to describe the feeling. But, and there is a but, who can I tell? Where could I go as a dragon?

There aren't any conventions for enormous supernatural reptiles, are there?'
It was rhetoric and Maddy just let her get it off her chest.

'For all I am capable of that could help humanity, I have to keep it a
secret. Who could I tell? Who'd believe me anyhow? I could show them but,
mark my words, within hours I'd be hunted by the very people I'm trying to
protect; desperate to either catch me, kill me or cut me up to see just what
makes me tick. It's what they do, for some peculiar reason. Nice, eh?'

Maddy said no, not really; for she knew the truth of it. All she had to
do was remember the Roswell incident – a brief skirmish where the Celestial
Host and some scouts from the Domain had clashed. The outcome was less
than discreet and several members of the human race had to be tampered with,
for want of a better description, to muddy their memory of events. A total
wipe would have caused irreparable damage and that was unacceptable, but
the partial wipe had caused as much disruption as if they had simply removed
everyone concerned. The absence of several hundred people would be easier
to gloss over than the muddle they were left with. The resulting confusion
had only fired the humans' naturally suspicious nature all the more, making
them even more unstable. So on this matter, Maddy sympathized with Gwen.

'Looks like you know what I'm saying. It's all amazing but bloody
pointless for day-to-day stuff. In fact, I probably feel even lonelier than I
did before, in an abstract sort of way, being so different from humanity now.
Because I'm not human, am I? I'm Drakarim; I just look like a human. Damn!
Now I know how that Clark Kent feels. I used to think he whined too much
about being alien, but now I see where he's coming from. There's a lot to be
said about that trouble shared thing.'

It made Maddy thoughtful, for she realized that she had never been
without the company of Jen. Even though they had been worlds apart on
occasion, she was always there. Gwen was new to this and still felt the
solitude she had known before as a mortal. There was no easy answer; it was
something she would either learn to live with or not. Maddy hoped it would
be the former, for her sake.

Gwen ate her fruit, bathed in the pool and ran through several clothes' changes before, some hours later, finally reaching her decision.

'I think it's time I…that is,' she corrected quickly, '*we* take a little trip to town.'

Gwen had, for all her changes, finally settled on her good old favorites: tight fitting faded jeans – the ones with the torn knees – tucked into her fawn colored Ugs; topped off with her soft angora, fern green sweater – the one with the low neck and flowers embroided onto it. To complete her look, she added a necklace of moss agate with a silver ivy leaf design chain. She rarely went anywhere without one of her myriad of necklaces and pendants gracing her throat. Why should being a dragon be any exception? she thought wryly. Her change though didn't come without sensations. She got the feeling that she was visiting someone else's life now. That surreal feeling people got when they visited the sets of TV shows they followed. The transition from years of watching, to actually touching the reality of it was too much for some people. That separation from fantasy to reality and back to fantasy again, blew their minds. Gwen was about to visit a world she would never know in the same way again: for she had been on first name terms with many of the residents of Santa Fe. Now, she felt like a stranger.

It was Maddy who pointed out a relevant point to the new nature avatar.

'Are we going to walk all the way back, on two legs, I mean? I take it you remember the walk up here and how long that took, even after driving to the car park.'

How could she forget? It was the night her world had changed irrevocably.

'I hadn't really thought about it, to be honest. What did you have in mind?'

Maddy laughed her rich and throaty laugh, the one that had the boys drooling after her back in town. With a toss of her fiery hair, Maddy stood, held both arms out before her, and fell forward, as though she were about to do push-ups. Except by the time she landed on what used to be her hands, she had flowed into the sleek and russet coated form of a long-legged timber wolf. Ears pricked and tail wagging playfully, the deep brown eyes regarded Gwen with an inherent intelligence. But it was Maddy's voice issuing from its fang filled mouth that made her start.

'This might be a more suitable form for running through the forest, don't you think?' She flowed again into the form of a muscular and fine limbed deer. 'Or this, perhaps? You choose, but the exercise will do us some good, I think. A good run will work wonders for your muscles, and after all, your muffin top does need some work.'

Gwen's mouth fell open in horror and indignation at the accusation. She pulled her sweater up and investigated her midriff, paranoia insinuating that Maddy had seen something she hadn't and filling her with doubt about her own physicality. There was after considerable investigation, as she thought, no such thing. She was a petite size eight with an ideal figure. If anything, a pound or two extra still wouldn't have been noticed on her lean frame.

'You cheeky cow!' But Gwen smiled to lessen the insult and show she could take it. But Maddy was right about one thing. A good run would help her. She knew how energized she felt after one of her infrequent gym visits. Things had a way of clarifying themselves that only hours before had seemed impossible to fathom.

'You're on, but go back to the wolf look; I like that. Here, let me have a go.' Gwen concentrated, and she too shimmered and flowed, dropping to all fours. Her own honey blonde coat shone with a vitality that was reflected in her emerald eyes, her pink tongue lolling from the side of her panting mouth. Maddy gave her a once-over, scenting her a couple of times, then yipping an approval. Gwen spun a couple of times and yipped and barked back excitedly, getting the hang of her form. But Maddy had seen enough and was keen to go. The desire to run was growing stronger.

'That's enough, Gwen. Now are you up for a little race? Last one to town is a lizard!' With that, Maddy bunched her powerful hindquarters and bounded off. Gwen didn't even have the time to say that she already *was* a big lizard, as Maddy's tail vanished into the undergrowth. A second's hesitation and Gwen leapt away, bounding off, hot in pursuit of her friend, catching the odd glimpse of the rusty wolf dodging and loping with a relaxed grace. Gwen had to concentrate to just keep up, but as the miles sailed by, it became easier and she even began to catch up.

Which was fortunate, for they drew close to the wall of thorns and the deadly protective brambles. Gwen could see the lethal tendrils snaking and writhing amongst themselves as she neared. Not even a mosquito was going to get past that barrier without running afoul of her guardians. *Now that's my idea of a burglar alarm.* But she needn't have worried, for as the two loping and speeding wolves came within range of the lashing barbs, the barrier simply parted before them as though someone had drawn back a curtain. They bounded through and loped on. Not before hearing the bear trap closing of the barrier behind them. It sounded as though it were made of steel rather than wood. But putting it almost immediately from her mind, Gwen once again lost herself in the exhilaration of the run. Tongue lolling, ears back and legs stretching out, Gwen and Maddy raced on, soon arriving at and passing through the empty car park and onwards towards town. It took a little while, but Gwen began to notice the subtle shift in the weather and the temperature. Since leaving the balmy and temperate climate of her grove, the winter that should have blanketed everywhere began to reassert itself. It didn't affect her, but she was aware of it. The crisp, clean smells of the snow-covered woodland soon faded to the more disquieting aromas of the town. Her heightened wolf senses picked up as they drew closer that all was not as it should be. There was a foul stench in the air: the smell of death and corruption. Putrescence and decomposition were all around them as they reached the town limits. They stopped together, all thoughts of their race forgotten in an instant. Resuming their own forms, Gwen and Maddy stood in the middle of the street and looked about them. Silence deafened them. The absence of the usual noises of the hustle and bustle of daily activity: cars, music, people, trucks and so many other day-to-day sounds. Their absence was totally alien for the time of day it was.

'Is it just me, Maddy, or is this definitely not right? That smell – it's rank. Like something, or a lot of somethings, have died and been left out in the sun to rot.'

Maddy was looking all around her; one hand shading her eyes against the light, the other resting upon her hip. 'No, you're not wrong, Gwen, but I can't see anything from down here. Look, let's take wing and slip up to the church tower by the square: see if we can't get a better view from up there.'

Seconds later, two dark-bodied crows flapped slowly upwards, catching the weak thermals still inherent and rising smoothly, granting them a much better overview of the streets below and what was – or, as it turned out, wasn't – going on. The streets were barren, totally bereft of life. They glided high enough to avoid detection, but to still able to see clearly. But the only thing that they saw clearly was the number of fires that must be raging, for there were several plumes of black smoke roiling up from no end of buildings. Where was the damn fire department? Why wasn't anyone doing anything?

They settled upon the tower and watched for a few minutes. But there was nothing to see or hear. It was as though all the people had been evacuated and nothing was left but an empty shell, the ghost of civilization. Gwen turned to Maddy and said one word. 'Dolores.'

The meaning was not lost on Maddy as they both took wing and flapped off, heading as the crow truly flew, directly towards Earth Angel – the one place that Dolores might be if she and her grandmother hadn't fled town already like everyone else seemed to have done. The sensation that she was flying towards her shop came and went as she realized that she owned nothing any more. Not even her own life; it was the tool of the Earth now, for her to do with as she saw fit. That aside, it still grated a little. It was always harder to fully let go of something the more it meant to you. Earth Angel meant an awful lot to Gwen. It had been her salvation, giving her purpose and an identity for the first time, and she would never forget that. She alighted gently upon Old

Man Travis's roof, which was the store opposite hers – a general hardware store that had been there almost as long as the town itself. It was rumored that so had Old Man Travis himself. He looked like a walnut in dungarees and nobody knew his true age. He just always seemed to have been there.

The moment they settled upon the ridge of the roof and gazed down upon Earth Angel, they got at least one answer. Not everyone had left town. It seemed that about a hundred of them were milling around some twenty feet from the shop front. What looked odd, or odder still, considering the circumstances, was that they were all intent upon the shop, but every time someone reached out to get closer, a flash of blue sparks would flare up and the person would recoil their hand as though it had been burnt. Watching this happen every few moments, as differing people tried to get closer, sent shivers of icy dread up Gwen's spine. This wasn't right. Focusing her sharp corvid's gaze upon the scenario, Gwen noticed that there was a shimmering kind of heat haze emanating from the ground, directly before the clamoring horde. It was that which prevented the people from getting any closer, *but why? And equally, how?* What was wrong with these people, that they should be withheld from getting any nearer? Gwen got her answer before Maddy could point it out, for they both saw the same thing at the same time as several of the populace turned suddenly to stare straight at them. Then they screamed an unearthly howl of rage and agony. Gwen couldn't have been more horrified. If she had hands, she would have clasped them over her mouth to prevent herself screaming and vomiting in equal proportions. Every single one had ripped their eyes from their heads; Gwen could see the ragged tears where nails had scoured the sockets, dragging the last vestiges of the squashy orbits clear. Their faces were drawn and sunken, as though the life was being gradually sucked from them, and as their flesh pulled tighter, so it tore at the weakest points; and gaping wounds were rife. The smell of faeces and corruption was almost overwhelming as the breeze turned and sent wafts of their decay directly over Maddy and Gwen. They took off instantly: that or be overcome by the suddenness of the powerful smell. They banked around to the rear of the building and into the wind, letting the cooler, fresher air clear their heads.

Gwen spoke to Maddy, using their mind-to-mind method, for talking as a crow, flapping in the air and over the screams that had started below where the horde had seen them, was just too hard.

'What's happened, Maddy? What's wrong with them?' asked Gwen.

Maddy alighted on the flat roof of a two storey building, and before answering, she walked to the edge, leaning on the parapet. She leant over and looked down and around. Sure enough, her fears were realized as fifty of the filthy abominations that had once been the townsfolk, came scrambling into view, still pointing and screaming, their hideously disfigured faces looking upwards towards the roof and Maddy. Some began pounding on the doors and windows in an effort to get in and get to them; others were making futile leaps for the metal fire escape ladder that hung suspended several feet out of reach. Gwen came to see and asked again.

'What are they, Maddy? Talk to me! There are people down there who used to be friends of mine and yours. How could this have happened?'

Maddy leant back, but still keeping an eye on them as well as one on the roof door as she spoke. 'Gwen, there is no easy answer to this. I've seen this before, but not on this scale for millennia. They are the possessed. Demons and minions of the Domain who are not yet strong enough to take corporeal form on this world. They cannot affect their own density. They take hosts of mortalkind. A type of insulation. A skin suit, if you will. Their essence is still too powerful for the body to contain, so the body breaks down and rots. They generally tear the eyes out, for mortal vision limits them; they see more without them, if that makes any sense to you. Ramping up the pituitary gland, they utilize the third eye capability that mortals have but rarely use. It enables them to see the auras of individuals. That's how they spotted us the way they did. We tend to glow a bit brighter than most.'

'So they're dead then?' Gwen asked, her mind filling with visions of what humanity had always considered possessed. All head spinning and growling. Not this, these were far too capable. Running and howling, and in packs too. That had to be bad.

'No, not yet at least, though they soon will be. The body can't last long before it fails completely and the minion has to cast about for another before it is pulled back to the Domain – '

Maddy was cut short of her explanation by a pounding on the roof door. 'They're here! We would be a great prize for them; that's why they are so motivated in chasing us and getting to us. Any ideas?'

Gwen had one, as it turned out. 'I know it's risky, but I'm thinking that that fizzing barrier is only going to work on them, so let's drop down to the store and see what is causing it, 'cos I know it wasn't something I did.' The door slammed open with a tearing and ripping of hinges, and several possessed flooded out. 'Now might be a good time too.'

Maddy just nodded and ran for the ledge, jumping up smoothly and diving out into oblivion. Gwen was hot on her heels as Maddy transformed in midair to the crow form and flapped away. Gwen, a few seconds only behind her, did the same just as the possessed leapt at her. Or at the spot she had occupied only a heartbeat earlier. With slightly less grace, Gwen dived over the edge, falling a few feet at first before affecting her change. Then the crow she became swooped over the surprised heads of the possessed below her and she flapped away, catching up with the slowly circling Maddy. The possessed on the roof had been so close that their momentum had carried a few of them over the edge to crash into their comrades in the alley below. The sickening crunch of bones snapping from the impacts still managed to reach Gwen as she flew off, and caused her to mentally wince.

Risking Gwen's idea, Maddy spiraled down to perch on the bench that sat upon the sidewalk in front of her store. The haze didn't affect them at all, as she hoped, but their arrival sent the possessed without into a frenzy. They threw themselves against the barrier with renewed vigor, as though their perseverance would be sufficient. The two crows looked at the horde with their glossy black eyes for a few moments before hopping off the bench and returning to the human forms, still watching the possessed, for now, all they were achieving was the speedier destruction of the mortal host they occupied as each burning flash seared more and more flesh from the bodies. Maddy looked askance at Gwen and saw she was crying. In a choked voice, Gwen turned to Maddy and asked, 'Isn't there something that can be done? This is awful.'

Maddy shook her head resignedly. For the outcome was already determined. 'Unlike zombies, Gwen, these people are still alive. Their bodies have been hijacked, their own souls suppressed. The moment a minion takes over, the body is as good as dead anyway. There is no such thing as exorcism for these; it's a placebo that your kind came up with to make themselves feel better. There is only one way that a minion leaves its host: when that host eventually dies. Whilst they are in them, they are hard to kill, but not impossible. The host feels all the pain while the minion is insulated from it. To stop it, you have to kill the host. The minion escapes and all you've done is to kill an innocent. Truly diabolical. It is a sign of how advanced the Adversary is for so many possessed to be taken. If this is happening the world over, we are in more trouble than we first realized. All they need to do is infiltrate the silos where your weapons of mass destruction are held and release them. It's a miracle they haven't yet. There has to be a reason he hasn't but I can't imagine what it is.'

The smell of burning flesh began to assail Gwen's nostrils now as possessed after possessed threw themselves against the burning barrier. She saw their charred remains fall to the ground, simply to be replaced by new ones stepping on and over them to carry on where they left off. Frustration caused many to scream and howl until their throats tore from the exertion. Those that weren't screaming began to taunt and threaten. Their hideous voices bastardised the humans' vocal chords, and the result was a thousand times worse than fingernails down a chalkboard. They suggested all manner of foul practices and obscenities. Now Gwen was fairly unshockable, but these were getting very graphic and very creative, to the point where even

Gwen had to put her fingers in her ears to quell the torrent of abuse.

'Why do they have to get all nasty like that? It isn't going to do them any good, is it? Don't they think we have our own share of sexual deviants to spout this vitriol?'

'Where do you think your deviants get their ideas from?' Maddy spoke calmly but what she implied was horrendous. 'There are two types of possession. What you see here is known as greater possession, where the host is subsumed completely. Lesser possession is more like whispers in your ear, voices in your mind. Voices that will sound just like you, making you think it was your idea all along. Dreams that fill your thoughts with depravity and sickness until you accept them as reality. Humanity has never been any good at identifying these tortured souls. In one time they were banished; in another they were executed; in another, burnt at wooden poles, stoned and any other number of equally hideous torments. These simply added to their own inner torments and helped not at all. Now of course, you have all manner of long winded names for them, categorizing them as different mental illnesses – when in fact many of them truly *are* hearing voices – and then pumping them full of drugs to try to *cure* them. They can't be cured. Once they are in, that's it. They are very parasitic. Then, like a time bomb, they wait to go off.' Maddy stopped talking, her voice just fading away as she looked at the minions, killing themselves to get at them. She too had tears cascading down her cheeks as she stared, helplessly, at the people she was sworn to protect, and knowing there was nothing she could do for them. Death was just a matter of time, which would be their only release.

Standing there for the few minutes they had, drew some other attention to them. The door to the store burst open and a very relieved looking Dolores came bursting out. All bar flying into the arms of first Gwen, then Maddy. But her relief and joy soon turned to despair as she looked beyond them to see the forms of the terrifyingly determined possessed still trying to get in.

'Why do they not leave, Gwen? It has been three days now. I do not know if I can take much more of their inhuman cries. Thankfully they cannot get in, but nor can we leave. It is only by the grace of Great Spirit that Grandmother was with me when whatever this is, started. I understand what you told me, Maddy, but this…' Dolores gestured to the mob outside, '…I was not expecting.'

Maddy turned her away from the possesseds' efforts and guided both Dolores and Gwen back inside the store, closing the door on their hateful and filthy cries.

'It is as though the spirits of the dark Kachinas, such as the ogre and the more vicious aspects, have taken the souls of those poor people, and now they seek to exact their revenge. The good spirits and the powers of the Earth and harmony seem to be absent. A great darkness is coming and it suppresses the light.' Dolores spoke softly of her theory as she made tea. It wasn't that they needed tea, but it kept her hands busy and stopped them from shaking too much. They moved to the rear of the store and closed the inner door. This was much more effective in silencing them. They were able to think a little clearer – it also allowed Gwen and Maddy to see Grandmother Yellow Deer, who was reclining on the sofa that Gwen kept in the back room. More hugs and pats on the back as the old woman was just as pleased to see the girls all well, as they all were, her.

Over tea Dolores explained, with the odd word and nod from Grandmother Yellow Deer, that the townsfolk had started showing up a few days earlier, and at first, they just looked like they always did; though they all had a sort of blank look to them, vacant and distant. It wasn't until the night of the first day they appeared that their faces started to change and the first sign came that there was some sort of barrier around the store. Those that stood within the perimeter were vaporized where they stood; those on the edge were blown back with the now familiar blue flames. Dolores concluded by saying, 'Thank you for giving us this shield. I do not know what we would have done without it.'

Maddy looked confused, looking between Dolores and Grandmother Yellow Deer. Gwen was equally lost, looking between all of them. 'I'm sorry, Dolores,' Maddy started, 'but we're not responsible for this; we thought you were.'

Dolores shook her head and denied all knowledge of it. They were still looking for answers between them when the smoky spiral began to rise from the shop floor just behind them, beyond the closed door. Grandmother Yellow Deer came instantly alert and grabbed her turtleshell rattle that lay across her rug-covered lap. Her rheumy eyes fixed on the door beyond the girls, and she began to incant softly in her native tongue, gently shaking the rattle. This caught Gwen's, Maddy's and Dolores's attention. They stopped their conversation and spun to see what was bothering Grandmother. They didn't have long to wait, as the spectre ghosted through the door to hang in midair before the women. At first it was just a diaphanous cloud of gently swirling smoke, but as it coalesced, it took on another form – a form that both Maddy and Gwen immediately recognized, yet neither could believe they were seeing.

'Mrs Callaghan?' Gwen both stated and asked at the same time. She and Maddy looked at each other quickly, making sure that they were both seeing the same thing.

'Is that you, Cynthia?' Maddy asked tentatively, senses alert for some trick by the enemy. It was not unheard of sending a wraith to commit some foul deed under the guise of a familiar face. It was a peculiar image of the old lady hanging in the air before them. She was like a charcoal or pencil drawing, all outline and no color. Everything was a dull grey: grey eyes, lips, skin and clothes. Yet for all her grey amorphousness, she fixed her grey eyes on the girls and actually smiled at them. Then in a voice that sounded distant and all around them at the same time, she spoke. It was a voice Gwen wasn't likely to forget in a hurry: it was the voice of the woman who had given her the life she had.

'Yes, dear, it's me. And I must say it's good to see you both looking well. Actually, if I'm honest, it's good to see anything at all. It's been a while, but even I could do without seeing them things outside. They look pretty nasty to me.'

Gwen laughed in spite of herself, drawing an odd glance from both Maddy and Dolores. 'No really, you guys, it's fine. But isn't that just the understatement of the decade? Nasty they certainly are and I for one have to say that I'm bloody glad they're out there.'

'Yes, dearie, me too. I sure am pleased that I protected this place when I did. It wasn't easy, mind, but the result was worthwhile, don't you think?'

Gwen was stunned. 'This is your doing? That shield out there? Thank you again then, Mrs C. You're just full of surprises, aren't you?'

The wraith chuckled and wafted back and forth as the breeze from the air-con unit caught it. As her misty form broke up a little and reformed again, it made Gwen wonder about the important question that hadn't been asked yet.

'So are you dead then, Mrs C, or what?' she asked, unsure of the etiquette of talking to a spirit. 'Sorry to ask like that; just that I haven't spoken with many ghosts before and up until this moment, and to be fair, I didn't even think they existed.'

Maddy plonked herself down on the arm of the sofa, next to Dolores, who had sat next to her grandmother, shock and relief having made her legs a tad unstable.

The wraith of Mrs Cynthia Callaghan simply smiled benignly and shook her head, sending little wisps of greyness floating off to dissipate in the air.

'No dear, not yet at least. I can't remember exactly what I told you when we met; I know we didn't have long. Events were in motion and I had to move fast, but I was, I am and I expect to continue to be a practitioner of the craft, as my ancestors were before me, and, I suspect, were many of yours. But I mustn't digress. A short while after I moved here, now, when was that?' Cynthia tailed off and looked thoughtful, at least thoughtful for a smoky grey cloud with human features. 'It must have been shortly after the war. We had just dropped that dreadful thing on Japan. Boy, if those goons knew anything of karma back then. Still, I suppose economic karma will have a similar effect. Anyway, I found that there were several naturally occurring areas of vortex energy. Both here, and as far over as Arizona. Coincidentally or not, but there is one directly beneath this store. It's why I chose its location. It boosted my craft a hundredfold once I learnt how to tap into it. It's good stuff.' She smiled toothily. 'There's method to my madness, eh?'

'I'll say, Cynthia, but how is it you never told me or Jen about it? Didn't you trust us?' Maddy sounded a little hurt at that implication, for she and Jen had spent a lot of time here with the old woman, apparently. Staying on when Gwen took over.

'It's not that, dear,' Cynthia explained, 'but the fewer people who knew what I was doing the safer and more secure it would be. I've focused and concentrated the vortex energy beneath us by utilizing various relics and ancient artifacts buried and secreted all around the store. It took several years' searching to gather them all together, and even longer to get them where I needed to without rousing suspicion. After all, I couldn't just go out and dig up the street. I had to wait until there were roadworks close enough for me to slip out and plant my bits. So forgive me if it's not quite circular, but beggars can't be choosers. Of course, it's the effect that counts and that's all just theory until it actually has to work. Glad about that. In fact, it's that that summoned me.'

Gwen looked a touch confused then and scratched her head, as though trying to work it all out. 'So, if you're not dead, what are you then, and where are you, for that matter? How is it you're here at all? Sorry to sound a bit thick: it's been a trying couple of weeks.'

'Not at all, dearie. My body is lying in a hospital somewhere close to the centre of Mexico City, apparently. I'm not expected to last the night. *C'est la vie*. Or not, I suppose, but something has to give. It's the balance you see, dear: body or spirit. For one to be strong, the other has to give way. I prefer my spirit to endure, so there's the rub. Now I hope the next part of my plan works with equal effect. That'll be just wonderful.'

'What's that then, if you don't mind my asking? It might be nice to be one step ahead instead of one behind for a change.'

Cynthia wafted a little closer, still smiling. 'Not at all, dearie, I'm quite pleased about it really. Most of the artifacts I buried to boost my powers were connected to me by blood, so I was able to bind my life force to them. That's how I knew it had been activated. My body collapsed as my spirit was drawn out and pulled here. I'm guessing it was when the first of those creatures showed up. Now, however, I'll be able to boost the shield with my own essence and fuse with it, effectively becoming it. Though I guess my journey onwards will have to wait a while until I'm no longer bound to the shield, however long that might be.'

A sudden ripple swept through Cynthia and she sucked in a misty breath. Her form solidified slightly afterwards and she looked more substantial. 'Oh, dear,' Cynthia sighed with a finality that said exactly what had just happened. She moved in close to Gwen and hugged her with a tangible presence that hadn't been there before; Gwen reacted and hugged her back, whispering a thank you in her ear as she pressed in close. When she stood back, there were tears in both their eyes. Cynthia smiled and quickly moved over to stand before Maddy, who jumped up from her seat.

'Tell Jen I'm sorry I missed her, but it seems the body has passed and it's time for me to join the vortex. Never having done this before, I don't know if I'll be able to come back again, but I'll try if I can. Bless you, child. Stay safe and look after them for me!' Cynthia hugged Maddy and stepped back, looking at her hands as they began to lose color, becoming transparent, then fading from view altogether. The entire process took mere seconds before Cynthia Callaghan, craft worker extraordinaire, vanished completely, joining the mystical shield she had created around the Earth Angel store. Through all the conversation and ghostly goings on, Dolores and Grandmother Yellow Deer sat in silence, watching and listening. Dolores was a modern day Native American and she accepted more than her grandmother, who was muttering slightly about it being a bad idea having ghosts hanging around like that. Gwen smiled at the pair, glad they were here and realizing that they would be perfect to carry on the work there.

The presence of Cynthia and the power of the vortex helped Gwen overcome some of her trepidation about the milling horde outside.

'We really ought to do something about them, Maddy. It's not fair to leave them like that.' Only days ago, they had been comparatively happy and unconcerned souls, going about their business and caring for their families. Then the Adversary, for he was behind all their woes, came along and destroyed their lives, their hopes and futures. It had to stop and she was going to do all she could to make sure it did just that.

'I take it you're referring to the possessed out front. What did you have in mind?'

'Something swift and as pain free as possible. I think they've suffered enough as it is, don't you?'

Maddy agreed. Humanity didn't deserve this. Well, she amended to herself, not all of them, anyway. Not that these creatures were human any more. They were just meat – fleshy overcoats for a sinister enemy that had as much concern for the suffering of humanity as much of humanity had about stepping on a bug. Their lives were as good as over and Gwen was right: it was time to put them out of their misery.

Knowing what she had to do didn't make it any easier for Gwen; she couldn't stop the tears streaming down her cheeks as she emerged from the store and walked as calmly as she could to within a few feet of the barrier. The horde whipped itself into a frenzy at her presence, and threw itself all the more at the barrier.

Maddy came and stood next to her, placing one hand upon her shoulder for support. Gwen laid her own over it and closed her eyes, wishing she could close her ears to the sounds too, but she gritted her teeth and concentrated, putting their hideous ranting as far from her mind as possible. Visualizing and summoning to herself all the roots from all the trees in the area – and there were plenty – she massed them beneath the horde, knowing that there were more than enough beneath them to carry out their grisly task. Maddy spoke in her mind, *Do it.*

With tears still brimming in her eyes, Gwen released her deadly subterranean forest.

The possessed had no time to react. The devastation was so abrupt that it was as though the massive pincushion of razor edged and barbed spears had always been there. Each possessed was impaled on at least three barbs. Death was almost instantaneous for the wretched townsfolk. The screams of the minions went on for a bit longer as they thrashed and sought other hosts. Those that by some miracle had escaped the first wave invariably fell to the second and third. None must get away; and none did. Maddy closed her own eyes and focused briefly. The street further back split apart with a thunderous crack, the tarmac and bedrock pulling apart ponderously, revealing a deep, deep chasm.

'I think we should reacquaint these souls with their mother, don't you? Let them learn the true meaning of earth to earth and ashes to ashes.'

Gwen nodded enthusiastically. Focusing some more, she managed to manipulate the barbs to deposit their flailing and parasitic refuse into the chasm, where many fell, screaming and cursing; flames licking out of the chasm as the bodies fell, consuming their bodies and freeing their souls. Or so she hoped. When the last had been sent plummeting to the depths, Maddy and Gwen restored the area as best they could, closing the chasm as though it had never been; and Gwen retracted the roots, allowing them to return to what they were supposed to do. Maddy fixed the road to cover the carnage left behind. It made little difference, but it wouldn't remind and disturb Dolores and her grandmother too much should they come out the front again.

'We won't be able to be that respectful for all the possessed we encounter. Time and events simply won't allow it, but for now, it is the least we could do for them.'

Gwen nodded automatically. She heard the words but they simply washed over her in a buzz of fuzzy sounds. The roaring in her own ears drowned out most of it.

'I can't believe I just killed that many people. I... Maddy, did I just really do that?'

Maddy came and took Gwen by the shoulders. Turning her gently; she guided her back into the store, past the awestruck Dolores, who had watched it all; seen it with her own two eyes and was still struggling to comprehend what her two friends had just done. Maddy then led Gwen through the store to the back room, where Grandmother was still sitting, eyes closed and chanting quietly to herself and intermittently shaking the turtle rattle in time with her chant. She didn't even notice as Gwen was softly placed beside her. A flash of lucidity lit up in Gwen's eyes and she looked at Maddy, Grandmother, then at Dolores, who had followed the pair through to the back room.

Gwen smiled in a lopsided sort of way. 'I'm really sorry about this, but I've never killed that many people before and I don't know if I can... Is it hot in here or is it just me?' Gwen's eyes rolled up in her head and she fainted dead away, sliding bonelessly from the sofa and collapsing in a Gwen-shaped puddle on the floor. Maddy simply took one of the Navajo blankets that adorned the sofa, and laid it over Gwen's prone form.

'Let her sleep, for a bit. It was a bit traumatic for her I suppose, though unfortunately, I expect she'll get used to it. We, on the other hand...' Maddy spoke directly to Dolores now, '...have some serious work to do.'

Dolores looked bemused. What sort of work could *she* possibly have to do? Dolores figured that she was the least empowered one there. Even a ghost had more power than she did. Grandmother was in one of her chants, communing with who knew what. She could be like that for days, and had been on more than one occasion.

'So what are *we* going to do, exactly?' Dolores asked, trepidation evident in her voice as she wasn't entirely sure she wanted to know the answer. Sensing the Native American woman's nervousness, Maddy put her out of her misery with a smile.

'It's nothing you have to worry about, Res. Gwen has a task ahead of her that requires some research. What we need to do is scour all the books here in hope of locating something that gives us a clue to the possible whereabouts of the First Tree. That was part of what drew us here initially. It's what Gwen wanted to do first before setting off. Like a supernatural route planner, for want of a better description. You start down here and keep an eye on our girl and I'll start upstairs with her personal collection. Let's hope we find something useful here or else we'll have to head to the house. I know she's got some more books there.'

But after a couple of hours searching, they hadn't turned up much more than what Gwen had already surmised. Her route of possibilities was almost a straight line, for none of them stood out above any other. There were a few sacred sites that may offer further clues – across the Atlantic coast: in Ireland; and in mainland Britain, the obvious places like Stonehenge, Avebury, Tintagel in Cornwall, Rosslyn up in Edinburgh, the Orkneys, as well as a few others. Then it was off to France – Carnac, and Rennes le Chateau – through Spain and Italy, out across Central Europe; and eventually arriving on the shores of Syria, for there were a few options in the Middle East. After all, it was a region rife with myths and legends. It wasn't called the Holy Land for nothing as ever since humanity gained its freedom, the land has been beset with deities and legends. Beyond that though, all bets were probably going to be off. Gwen didn't have an infinite amount of time to go gallivanting across the globe. She had to be precise and focused. If she started in the Dark Continent (Africa) or the Russian land mass, she could be gone forever. Jen and Maddy would willingly help her, but in this, only Gwen would be able to recognize what it was she sought. That was why she was chosen. The more Maddy looked at the enormity of the task before Gwen, the more her own heart sank. It was doomed from the outset.

Gwen came shuffling upstairs, looking for her friend, scrubbing her hand through her slept-on hair. And annoyingly for any woman who would have seen it, it just sorted itself out into lustrous perfection with a gentle shake of her head.

'What have I missed?' Gwen asked a little groggily as the last vestiges of her shock induced sleep left her.

Maddy chuckled at her question. 'You sound just like somebody else I know. Never mind, Gwen, come and sit down and we'll go through it with you. How about some tea? I'll do it. Res will bring you up to speed.'

The Pueblo woman nodded vigorously as Maddy disappeared off to the little kitchenette, her usual easy smile back in place after the horrors of earlier. She patted a cushion next to her and Gwen plumped herself onto it, looking down to what the girls had amassed: a prodigious amount of papers and open books with all manner of bookmarks. They had scavenged the store for everything remotely useful. *Why not? Sales would be a bit down for a while anyway*, Gwen reasoned to herself. *Why not put it to some use? That's what it's for, anyway.*

'So what have we got here then?' Gwen ruffled through a few fragments before Dolores slapped her fingers away playfully, with a mock annoyed expression on her face.

'Leave it alone. You'll mix up the order!'

Gwen looked at her with surprise. '*That's* in order?' She looked at Dolores sideways and added a 'yeah, right!'

'We don't have anything definitive, Gwen, I'm sorry, but we have a sort of direction. Though I don't know how you're going to cover all these places in the time we apparently have.'

Gwen elbowed Dolores softly in the side and winked at her. 'Ah, Res, I've got one or two tricks up my sleeve now like you wouldn't believe.'

'After what I've seen today, I bet I would.' Dolores paused briefly before asking, 'Do you... I mean, do you *feel* any different? 'Cos you don't *look* all that different other than looking as well and as fit as I've ever seen you. I don't know what you're on but I wouldn't mind a basinful myself. Your skin, hair, eyes – well just about every damn thing, you cow. Seems you got something of a trade-off out of this deal.'

'It's just as well. The bloody stress of what they want me to do would have me looking like Grandmother otherwise.'

Dolores nodded and tried not to laugh at the image of Gwen looking as ancient as her grandmother, who, as it turned out, had finally stopped her chanting and had fallen into deep sleep, still propped up in the chair where she had been the last three days.

'I think, Gwen, that for my people, you may well be the personification of the White Buffalo Calf Woman. According to Jen and Maddy, you embody much of what legend says of her. That, and what your arrival heralds.'

Gwen didn't look so sure. 'Don't mind my cynicism, Res. But it's been my experience that people rarely accept something that doesn't conform to their preconceived notion of what they expect to see. I appreciate your people are closer to the land and the spirits of nature than many other cultures, especially us in the West, but humanity isn't known for its rationality when it comes to things sacred. The diversity of cultures, and each having their own notion of who they are and how they will be returning, and when, doesn't allow for much deviation. I'm not sure I'm what they had in mind.'

'Maybe this conflict will make that allowance, when what they expect to happen doesn't. They will know the disappointment that my people felt when many of the things they expected to happen didn't. It is accepted that the calf was born to us. What follows would be at the discretion of the spirits. For that is how they work. It is not for us to question Gitche Manitou, but to do what we must within the great web that Grandmother Spider weaves. I'm a little more pragmatic than our elders. I'm not saying they are wrong to hold to tradition; but to see perhaps, how tradition works in this time, allowances must be made.'

Gwen had heard much of this before from Res. For all her traditional upbringing, she had a modernistic and contemporary slant on the future of the people. She would adapt them to this world as best she could, convinced there was a happy middle ground between the two. Time had been their enemy as much as the white eyes.

'We have, like so many other peoples of the fourth world, where we exist presently, become stagnated in our ritual and belief. It has grown solid and immovable through habit. Time without change has created a complacency that has proven to be our undoing. You and your kind must make all new believers from the people and from the rest of the world. Show them what they have forgotten in their rigid ways.'

Gwen had the distinct impression that she had just had a pep talk from Dolores: the sort given to soldiers before battle, or fighters before they get into the ring. Dolores believed in her. That was the bottom line and it touched another raw nerve in Gwen, causing her to break down in tears again, clasping her friend in a tight embrace as she did so, feeling a love for the woman whose friendship had supported and guided her more than she knew.

'Ah Yeah, Gwen! If I thought you were going to react so, I would have kept quiet. But you are closer to the gods now than us mere mortals. Our future is in your hands; you know what I mean, don't you?'

Gwen snuffled and sighed in mock exasperation, before holding Dolores out at arm's reach and looking deeply into her dark eyes. 'Of course I do, you swine. But I'm a bit delicate right now, and all that sentimental gush got right to me, that's all. But I thank you for your belief, Res, I really do. It means a lot. You're the best friend a girl could have, excluding her rabbit of course.' This broke the tension and had them both hugging again and laughing.

Maddy came back in with a tray of steaming tea and hot buttered crumpets. As she placed the tray down she looked between the two women, trying to ascertain what had just passed between them, settling on the fact that whatever it was, it had been good for Gwen. There was a glint to her eyes that she hadn't seen in a while.

'Look what I found; they were lurking at the back of the Aladdin's cave of a refrigerator of yours, Gwen. You really ought to get to the back of it from time to time. I took the little blue bits off, and they seemed fine, but there are things in there that are about to evolve. I'm sure I saw legs on a vegetable. Oh, and before I forget, the printer is out of paper.'

Gwen slapped her forehead, recall flooding back. It was one of the things she was going to do after meeting Dolores on that fateful day when her life as she knew it went so far off the rails that a whole new form of transport had to be invented.

'Ass. I meant to get some before you know what all kicked off. Can't you find any more anywhere else?'

Maddy said she couldn't and it was a pain because there were a few things on what remained of the net that might have been useful, but she would just have to do without it.

'I think I've got more than enough stuff here anyway. I'm not going to be able to take half of this with me, there's just too much.'

Dolores pulled out a sheet of paper. 'That's why we knocked this up.' Dolores passed it to Gwen. 'It's a very rough track taking you eventually towards the Middle East. We were thinking that if you haven't found it by then, and if we are all still alive, maybe you can return here. I'll keep looking, though I've no idea how I'd get a message to you. Guess we'll cross that bridge should we get that far, yeah?'

Gwen was reading the extensive list avidly, mentally working out where many of the places mentioned actually were. Geography hadn't been one of her strong points.

'Bloody hell, this is going to take an age as it is. Have you seen how many search areas there are on here?' They just widened their eyes at her. 'Of course you have, duh! You put them here, but I don't know. These are just sacred sites that anyone can visit now; I don't know how a bloody great tree could hide there for so long without someone discovering it.'

But it was Maddy who pointed out that these sites may be, for her, access points to these missing realms that humanity has sought and lost. Atlantis, Lemuria, Avalon. After all, wasn't the latter known as the Isle of Apples? That was a tree. It was a long shot. But that was all they had: long shots.

Gwen was full of doubts and questions. What would it look like? How would she recognize it? How would she access these sites? What would a door look like? She could sit here for a month just running through the questions this quest brought up. But that wouldn't help her. She knew them for what they were: reasons to postpone actually leaving. A part of her knew that she would have to make some harsh choices in the field and on the spot. There was little preparation for a journey such as hers. Knowing that, however, didn't make any of it any easier. They sat back and contemplated the array of books and paperwork and research before them as they polished off the tea and crumpets, hoping that some revelation or answer would leap out and present itself. An hour later, it still hadn't. And time was ticking like some infernal bomb. She had to make a definitive choice. A plan of action needed a beginning.

'I'll be leaving first thing in the morning then. No point putting it off any more.'

Her two companions simply looked at her, both equally aware of the weight about to be shouldered by their friend, and honoring the courage it had to take to make such a monumental decision. Starting a thing was always the most difficult. It was akin to pushing an enormous rock. That initial effort took the most strength, but once it was rolling, maintaining momentum was much easier. How many developments in humanity's brief lifetime had failed, because of a lack of initial strength? Maybe if they had asked for help and those asked had actually provided it, rather than considering only their own self-absorbed lives, things might have been a little different today.

'Look, you guys, I've slept enough today, albeit on an involuntary basis. I feel as refreshed as I'm going to be with this hanging over me, so why don't you get some sleep yourselves. I'm going to sit outside for a bit and get some air. Let some of that good old Santa Fe air clear my head a bit.'

The moment Gwen mentioned sleep, Dolores's eyes drooped a little lower, the pressure of the day's events catching up with her suddenly. 'Good idea. Now that you mention it, I feel like I've been dropped down a mountain side. Grandmother seems okay. What harm can a few hours do?' Dolores stretched, stood and yawned; stretched some more, and went to find somewhere comfortable to curl up.

Maddy waited until Dolores was out of earshot before speaking. 'I'll break the news to her when she wakes up, but I'll say goodbye now. You don't get away with it that easily, you know.'

Gwen was stunned, for she had only just thought about slipping away under the cover of darkness, forgoing the emotional goodbyes she thoroughly detested, and embarking on her first steps while her friends slept. 'How did you guess that?' Gwen had to ask. 'Did you read my mind?'

Maddy shook her mane of fiery locks and smiled ruefully. 'Not really. It's just what I would have done were I you and that thing you have for goodbyes.'

Sussed. Gwen grinned at the girl who had been her assistant, mentor, lover and now sister. This girl could read her far too well and that wasn't good. Gwen liked her own air of mystery and figured that she had become far too predictable. That would have to change too. It smacked of what Dolores had said about time and repetition. It made bad practice and worse habits into permanent fixtures. Gwen embraced Maddy with an intensity that surprised them both. Breaking apart, both girls had tears streaming down their flawless cheeks, leaving red-rimmed eyes and moist salty tracks in their wake.

'I'm not going to give you any big speech about the student graduating, or the fledgling about to take her first flight or any such bollocks; I know how that would grate on you. So all I'm going to say is good luck, sister. May your journey be fruitful, literally. And stay safe. Don't do anything you're not sure of and, most importantly, and I can't stress this enough...' Gwen rolled her eyes, which said 'Get on with it, woman', '...If you get into trouble you don't think you can get yourself out of, call us. We will come if we can.'

'Are you quite finished? I wanted to avoid all this as – you – well – know!' Gwen emphasized the last words with a pointy finger, prodding Maddy in the shoulder. 'Thanks anyway, and yes, I'll call. But if I don't drag my sorry arse out of that door sooner rather than later, it's only going to be that much harder. So yes, I really was going to sit and take in some air, maybe a few memories while I'm at it – but yes, you were right, too. I was just going to slip off while it's quiet, and I can try out a few shapes as I head across country.'

Maddy nodded she understood. There were no more words that could add or change anything for her or between them. So instead, they hugged again. This time when Gwen stood back, she really stood back, taking a couple of backward steps. Maddy nodded once more, almost imperceptibly, and she hooded her eyes. It was more of a deferential bow. That done, she turned and headed back in to where Dolores went. She just heard Gwen's last words as she closed the door.

'Look after them, Maddy, look after all of them.' Then Gwen herself stepped outside into the chilly night air, not that the cold affected her, but she could see it sparkling on the glass and lying on a multitude of other surfaces. Winter was increasing its stranglehold on the town again, and it looked like it was going to be a harsh one. She looked up but there were no stars to see, just the dark roiling clouds that threatened the mother of all snowstorms. Gwen hoped and prayed that her friends out in the Pueblos and upon the Mesas were going to be safe enough and provisioned enough, for she got the feeling that when this hit, life here was going to get pretty rough. Maddy will help them, Gwen tried to convince herself, but she knew deep down that there was only so much one Drakarim, however motivated, could accomplish – especially when she had duties of her own to attend to. *Damn! Why are there so many things to think of, and why is everything spread so thinly? If it isn't one bloody thing it's another. And I've got an extended lifetime of this now. I bloody well hope that Valium still works on me – I'm gonna want shit loads of it before this is finished, I expect.* But a much deeper part of her mind replied, *No you won't.*

Gwen sat outside for about another two hours, reliving moments and pondering the variables of her future, both immediate and long term. But two hours later she still had nothing definitive and concrete to give her any peace. In fact her head was swimming with scenarios and possibilities, merged with vivid images spawned from her overactive imagination. They didn't help at all, considering what she had done earlier that day.

'Sod it. If I sit here much longer I'm going back in.' Gwen stood and stretched her muscles, feeling them pop and expand. 'Well, here goes nothing.' Gwen closed her eyes and reimagined the crow form from earlier. It was only an hour before dawn, so she wouldn't stand out. The spiraling and shimmering emerald vortex spun up around Gwen. When it dissipated, what remained was a blue-black, glossy crow, sitting perched on the back of the bench. With three good throaty caws, Gwen flew up from the bench and circled several times as she gained height. She glanced down, looking at the Earth below her. But not just with corvid's eyes, but with the eyes of the avatar of nature. She saw the flashing dragon lines that ran throughout the planet, burning bright and flaring every now and again as they criss-crossed the globe. They gave her an innate sense of direction, one she had never had before. She was notorious and could probably get lost on a straight road if left to her own devices. With a few powerful beats of her wings, she was off.

Gwen flew steadily for a while until she had passed what she knew to be the city limits. Knowing also that habitation was thinner out here and she was less likely to cause a stir, Gwen shimmered once more and the sky was momentarily full of gigantic forest green dragon. Gwen bunched her powerful muscles and with a mighty down thrust, she tore across the sky, not only breaking the sound barrier with a thunderous boom, but smashing it into thousands of tiny pieces that fell unseen and unheard upon the desert sands.

Though to say entirely unseen would be somewhat presumptuous. Unseen by human eyes she may have been, but the two deep-set and muddy yellow eyes that watched the transition of the crow to monstrous reptile were not human. At least not any more. They hadn't been human for a hundred and fifty years. Not since his lord, recently freed from his imprisonment, had ventured forth to this world at the sufferance of he who released him, to recruit as many warriors as he could in the turning of the moon. His mining camp had been decimated. None escaped. Those who did not survive the turn were doomed to become food for those that did. It was why he was here now. His rise through the ranks of Fenris's hounds had earned him the opportunity to return to this world and scout. To be a scout warranted slightly more intelligence than a mere hound. They were the infantry to his sergeant major. Brutal and relentless hunters, they killed on command and that was what they did best. It was the likes of himself who told them where to kill. He stood to get a better view of the rapidly receding creature. He was a good nine feet to the shoulder and built powerfully in the upper body, designed for strength, with the ability to tear a human or an animal clean in two with its bare hands. It narrowed at the waist and ended with long rangy legs, and meaty thighs for distance running and speed. There was nothing on Earth that could match it in a one-on-one contest. Its wiry grey fur covered its body in its entirety, topping off on its pricked ears, down over its muzzle and completing the journey on its huge, padded and taloned feet. Feet that could disembowel with a stroke. Currently it was one of a thousand werebeasts that were spread out across the land, seeking and searching for vital news for their lord, and for fresh meat for his growing army. It had not been told of such incredible beasts as what just flew over its head. It would have to report this back to his lord. But something deep in its animal brain, the bit that governed survival, told it that this wasn't going to be greeted as good news. Perhaps it should find another to pass this news on. Fenris considered these lands undefended and ripe. He wouldn't take to being told, in however roundabout a way, that he was wrong about that. But someone would tell him and he would decide what they were to do next. Whatever it was, it growled in pleasure to itself. Humanity was about to slip several notches down the food chain.

Chapter Twelve

Coalescere

SENSATION RETURNED BEFORE MEMORY, AND FOR WHAT felt like an eternity, all he knew was pain. It blazed through every nerve and fibre of his being, setting each and every molecule individually aflame, and he felt each and every one of them. The inferno pulsed through his body for what seemed an age. He didn't even know if he was screaming or not, for the infernal flames that scoured his body seared his throat also, the intense and immeasurable agony driving him to the point of madness and beyond.

Some time later, for he had no way to measure the time, and exercising the last vestiges of his ravaged willpower, he tried to open his eyes and see just what it was that was devouring him, but he couldn't be sure if they were open or not, for there was nothing but blackness. Blackness before he opened them and even more blackness after. Maybe they had been scorched out too; it certainly felt as though they had – it felt as though someone had taken iron nails, superheated them and hammered them into his skull. The impenetrable and agonizing darkness that surrounded him lent itself to that very possibility, as well of course, as the incandescent fire surrounding and filling his head simultaneously. Blissfully, he slipped beyond consciousness and more time elapsed.

Then, with the greatest sensation that can be felt, which is the release from pain, the torment began to subside. Tomas came to as it diminished.

He found, also, his memory returning. Fragmented at first, then with an increasing rush that brought the prone and gasping man more or less up to date. Then he really did scream. He heard and felt it rip from his ragged, torn and dry throat. Tomas frantically grasped at his chest. One of Tomas's last memories was of something stabbing him brutally before he fell through black flames. He could have sworn whatever it was went right in deep; deep enough to skewer him in the heart and any other number of vital organs, but apparently – as he was here – it must have missed, *thankfully*, because he was still alive. *Or at least sort of, if this is what's called life. Death's gift had some practical use after all. I bloody well told him I didn't want to try this out anytime soon as well. Lot of good that did me,* Tomas sighed. Then panic kicked in. *Templars!* With this last memory came an urgency to be up, moving and defending himself, but he found that even though the pain had lessened, he was still unable to move. *It's just one bloody problem after another. I only hope those Templar guards aren't still hanging about or maybe, if I'm really lucky, there's something else now looming over me: all teeth, claws and a pointy tail, holding a bloody great pitchfork or some shit, waiting to stab my arse, eat me or worse. Though I'm sure that whatever it wants, it can't hurt any more than the last couple of hours, or however long I was out. And as it's not doing anything and I couldn't do anything about it if it were, I might as well lie here for a bit longer. At least...* Tomas reasoned with some degree of resignation *...it feels a bit warmer now, and that can't be all bad. Can it?* Tomas's rhetorical question meant he knew what he had to do next. Hugely reluctant to do so – just in case there *was* actually something unsavory standing there waiting for him – but knowing he must, Tomas tried opening his eyes again. Thankfully, this time the darkness receded slightly, giving way to a greyness that grew slowly brighter as he waited. *So far so good. At least it doesn't look like I'm going to be blind in the hereafter – one good thing, I reckon.* Tomas scrubbed at his eyes to see if that would speed things up – it didn't – it just made his headache return with a vengeance as he pushed the hot pins back into his skull. *Argh!* It seemed he was still a little delicate from his experience. *Don't suppose there's a lot of chance of an Aspirin anywhere?* He grumbled to himself as he tried to sit up, with a groan and bit of a struggle, for he knew that wherever he was, lying flat on his back wasn't going to be a lot of help to him. Tomas managed to drag himself to his elbows – a small task that took about half an hour because it felt like he had broken glass for nerve endings.

Now, considering what he had just experienced, he wasn't entirely sure what to expect when his sight did eventually return to him, which followed a good hour later as he figured time, but it sure as hell wasn't what he saw before him. He had smelt the air already and it didn't *seem* to be the fire and brimstone that he had just experienced. In fact it smelt an awful lot like the West Country he had not long left. The smell after rainfall: fresh and vibrant. And what he felt beneath his exploratory fingers matched the image in his mind. *Nah, can't be.* What he eventually saw matched the aroma too, though it didn't make it any more believeable to see it. *You have to be kidding!* Tomas found he couldn't find words to describe what he was seeing. It wasn't just grass. It wasn't just *a lot* of grass – it had to be a world of grass. Endless swathes of green dotted occasionally with some trees. Rolling hills simply stretched away before him, right up to the very distant horizon, where it collided full on with the most startling crimson sky that Tomas had ever seen. But it was the two moons that dominated the sky before him that told him he wasn't in Kansas any more. *Now that's odd. Either I've got double vision or I'm well and truly buggered.* His mind was desperately refusing to accept the peculiar night sky before him. *Mirage, hallucination or a reflection of a distant body of water, that's got to be it!* Accepting those pathetically tenuous reasons or putting it down to the blow to the head he must have had, Tomas shook his head, sending droplets of sweat from his damp hair flying, and relegated the odd phenomena to a distant part of his mind; for worrying about that wasn't going to help him with his current predicament. Having done so, he scanned the area more thoroughly. The grasslands would have seemed hypnotically vast, rippling back and forth in the barely perceptible breeze, were it not for the small copses that broke up the lightly swaying and verdant ocean. Tomas tried to get a three hundred and sixty degree view and came face to face with a sheer wall of bark and leaf towering behind him. Obviously the copses were the precursors to the forest that must have started or finished, he estimated, a mile or two behind his current position. And even at that distance, the trees looked unnaturally huge. *Just where the bloody hell am I and how did I miss that?* Tomas just stared around him, soaking up the view as he gradually regained full movement. Seeing the two moons again and squinting suspiciously at them, Tomas stood, his legs like a newborn foal, wanting to go their own separate ways, and began stretching to loosen muscles that had cramped and bunched as he thought he was dying. Tomas shook his head again to rid himself of that particular memory. Unsuccessfully.

Keeping one eye out for any movement or the approach of anything untoward, and the other on those strange moons, he began to exercise as he walked. Tomas accepted it would be hard to differentiate friend from foe in light of recent events as well as his current circumstance. It left him one viable option. *Everyone is an enemy until proven otherwise!* Safest course, take no chances that way. Tomas continued his regime of exercise. Content that he had prepared his mind as much as it was going to be, he turned his thoughts to his aching body. If he needed to fight or defend himself he would need all his faculties working and responsive. He couldn't clog them with too many questions and assumptions. Answers would present themselves in due course. It didn't help to worry about what he couldn't change. Concentrate on what he could. With that thought, commonsense prevailed and he trudged over to the nearest copse of trees as quick as his strained and weary legs would carry him. Keeping low to minimize his silhouette against the skyline, he even managed to materialize himself a green cowled cloak, which served to both conceal him and reassure him that the sword was still with him and that he still had use of his gifts.

Once safely ensconced within the small cluster of trees, Tomas completed his stretches and exercises. Stripping off, he examined his body for any sign of injury – particularly where the bone fragments, as he recalled them, had stabbed him several times as well. *At least they've healed. I can't even see where they went in now. I suppose that's what I get for diving into a crypt full of the damn sharp sticky up things. What on earth was I thinking?* Then it occurred to Tomas that perhaps he wasn't thinking, and something else was doing that for him. So many things weren't right about that crypt business. Tomas replayed it over and over. The apathy, the biting cold. Famine's gift was supposed to inhibit the susceptibility to such extremes of temperature. How had that gotten through to him? Why would he leap into an indefensible box, to be trapped by the Templar guardians? His only conclusion was that he was compelled somehow. Death and the others had spoken of enchantments and the like. Maybe there was something about old Nakir's bones that coerced him to jump in. He had been a demon after all, and they were nefarious by nature, or so his religious instructions' tutor had informed him. Perhaps something of his evil nature had stayed with the bones. It was a theory at least. Tomas frowned at that thought. The idea that his mind was still susceptible to manipulation from a creature that had been dead for God knows how long meant there was a flaw to his gifts. *What other flaws were there?* He'd have to watch that in future, always assuming he had one. Tomas racked his foggy memory for any information on the crypt. He knew Death had spoken of the remains and the reason they had hidden it, but he couldn't recall anything in there that was conclusive or useful to help him explain where he was in the world. All Tomas could come up with was it was some sort of portal, the type the Horsemen used to get around with.

Donning his armor once again – *for the last thing I want right now, is to be caught in a strange land stark bollock naked, with my guard down and no weapon in my hand, at least not one that will do me any good* – Tomas explored his immediate locale. Examined the trees and bushes, looking for something familiar. There were some red berries hanging off something that resembled a bramble on steroids. So rapacious were the thorns, Tomas almost gave up trying to get the fruit, but he armored his arm and forged on. Sniffing them, they didn't smell dubious. So he tried one, tentatively. But they seemed fine, tasting sweet and juicy, so he gathered a few of those and some nuts from one of the trees that resembled a hazel. He didn't actually need them, but the process helped him think. Thinking wasn't always a good thing though. For the first time in a long while, he caught a whiff of himself and it made him grimace. Perhaps it was the fresher air of the environment, or maybe a little self-worth was returning to him. Either way, he concluded he needed a bath. Badly. But that would have to wait until he found some water, for there didn't seem to be any hereabouts for quite some considerable distance, judging by what he had seen already. First things first: he needed to get somewhere else so he could work out where he was; here wasn't helping at all. There had to be signs of civilization around somewhere. Maybe a ranger's station or some campers. *Anywhere there was a patch of grass not surrounded by houses, some twat with a tent always found it and planted himself there. What's the bloody matter with them? The whole point of civilization was to progress. We built houses and they still want to live like savages. If they had spent the amount of time I have roughing it outdoors, they'd soon get fed up with the whole camping idea.* But needs must. So he picked a direction. Having seen what was on this side of the copse, Tomas decided to go out the other side. Yet as he broke the treeline, Tomas instantly saw two things. One was that there was a steep drop off this side, approximately thirty feet down that slid steeply to a more level stretch of grassland; the second thing was that there was someone running towards him. Well, not him exactly, but his direction at least. *Maybe I won't have to go too far after all.* Hunkering down, Tomas watched the figure for a few seconds and with his own hunter's awareness. He saw that there was something very wrong with the way he was running. By the repeated glances over his shoulder, Tomas realized that it was less likely he was running to, more like running from. And that didn't bode well. *So what's chasing him in the middle of nowhere?* Adding to that fact, the runner stumbled several times as he tried to run and look over his shoulder at the same time. And the more Tomas watched him, the more tired and spent the runner looked. *Whatever is chasing him is going to find it damn quick and easy catching him at this rate. Poor git looks done in.* Maybe because he didn't look to have much left, it piqued Tomas's curiosity and even managed to dig out a little sympathy. Tomas whipped up the HK with the telescopic sight to get a closer look at the man. Tomas's expression hardened to that of chiseled granite as he saw the condition the man was in. He was thin, almost emaciated, dressed in rags, and bleeding from so many cuts that it was a miracle he hadn't fallen and bled out already. Hands, feet and chest looked to be the worst. *Who or what could have done this to him?* Tomas mused, but he didn't have long to wait for the answer. Seeing the man had no energy left, he wasn't about to try and climb the incline to the safety of the trees; instead he was about to circumvent it and go around. They would catch him for certain if he did that. Tomas stepped out and shouted down to the man, praying that he understood English.

'Up here, as quick as you can; it'll be safer within the trees!' A fact. For chasing him were at least a dozen riders, vicious looking armored men on horseback. Their mounts would have had great difficulty scrambling up the steep embankment. 'Come on quickly before they catch you.' Tomas waved the man up, but the look of fear that came over him told him that he wasn't buying it. Fair enough, Tomas reasoned. To someone as desperate as he obviously was, one armored stranger looked much like any other. And speaking of the other, they were rapidly gaining on him. Tomas didn't like one-sided battles. He never had, not unless he was on the winning side, which to a man of his resilience, he usually was. Tomas made a decision, rash and against any sane odds, after getting a rough head count of the approaching riders. He leapt down the grassy slope, sliding down expertly, one hand on the slope to stabilize himself as he part ran, part slid. About halfway down Tomas saw one of the riders pull out a hand-held crossbow and loose a shaft at the fleeing man, who screamed in abject terror as the missile whistled past his ear, drawing a thin line of blood. A little more to the right and it would have pierced his skull like a melon. *Now that's just not fair, shooting the guy in the back.* Tomas slid to a halt, sending stones and tufts of grass careening down the hillock and braced himself, swinging the HK to his shoulder, scope and silencer fitted. One quick look and he squeezed. Pfft. The rider with the crossbow left his saddle, spinning as his head exploded. The other riders hadn't noticed the nature of their comrade's dilemma, only seeing the body cascade off the back of his horse. Tomas saw them laugh riotously at their friend's plight. *Nice sympathetic bunch,* Tomas growled sourly as their laughter reached him. Another rider pulled up and nocked a bow, and was about to try the same thing when Tomas sighted him too. Pfft. Now this time, they did see what happened. One in particular got a real eyeful as the exploding brain matter was spattered all over him. *That'll teach him to ride too close*, Tomas laughed to himself as he watched the riders disperse, galvanized by the sudden death and realization that it was of two of their posse, not one. Putting two and two together, and guessing that their earlier joke had been from a dire event, their mood darkened immediately as they reined in. They began barking orders to each other, and Tomas shouted down to the skinny man again. Perhaps seeing his pursuers drop away may have changed his ideas about him.

'Now will you get your raggedy arse up here? If I wanted you dead, you would be by now. C'mon, I'll help you.' Tomas extended a hand – a gesture of goodwill and a useful handhold, for the skinny man wasn't going to have the strength to make it up by himself. Tomas wasn't sure if the riders had seen him yet. He hoped not, not that he cared much either way: his mood wasn't exactly love and light right now. And the one thing that fired him up more than anything else was right before him. He hated bullies. Hated them with a vengeance. Ever since school when the first bully had tried to pick on him. A big, spotty ginger thing called Sykes. Tomas remembered him clearly. Sykes and his cronies had gathered around him on his first day at Mornington Military Academy, where his father had sent him.

'New boy!' The ginger lardass sneered. Tomas hadn't gotten much more than a hundred yards up the long gravel driveway that formed the estate where the private school was situated, after his father had dropped him off moments earlier. Tomas just looked at him with a calm equanimity, tilting his head with a curiosity as though a turd had just lifted off his shoe, and started to talk to him. Tomas chose to ignore him after a moment's consideration and give him the benefit of the doubt, assuming that he was mistaken in his choice, and should be allowed to go off and find himself another boy to pick on. So, he started to move off past the gang. Ginger stepped in front of him.

'Where do you think you are going, new boy? You haven't paid the new boy tax yet. Now hand over everything you have and we'll let you in,' Ginger spoke – a whiny sort of nasal sound. He grinned to his equally sweaty friends. The halitosis wafted out and Tomas grimaced as he caught a whiff, waving a hand before his nose.

'Phew, you been eating shit?' The gang laughed and abruptly stopped again at an angry glare from shit breath. 'Now, I'd rather not talk, if you don't mind. Apart from the smell, I'm a little late. And I *hate* being late.' Again he tried to move past them. Ginger repeated his earlier move and stepped once again in front of Tomas, who looked at Ginger sadly and shook his head.

'Look, dung breath, I've tried to be nice about this, but if you don't move your smelly, fat ginger butt out of my way…well, let me put it another way. I don't know if the school nurse makes house calls, but I expect you'll find out.'

His friends looked a little bemused. Victims weren't supposed to talk like this; they were supposed to whimper and cower and hand over their stuff. They looked between Tomas and Ginger, alternating between sneers and expressions of uncertainty. Ginger, however, was livid and his eyes began to bulge out of his head and he started to spit too as he lost the power of coherent speech. A rather unpleasant combination, like a putrid pumpkin with frog eyes. 'Wha… Wha… Who do you think you are, you…you…miserable wretch?'

Tomas dodged the flying spittle easily as he grinned back at the floundering ginger volcano. 'My name is Tomas, and you would do well to remember it, that is if you haven't got the memory span of a goldfish as well as the coloration.'

That did it. Ginger lunged at him with his fat, pale and pudgy hands. Tomas neatly sidestepped, as his Aikido training by his father had taught him, and with a little help, he sent Ginger sprawling, face down in the gravel. Tomas quickly drew level to him and kicked him soundly in the jaw. Sending two teeth whirling away to mingle with the driveway. Ginger screamed and held his face as he spat blood. Tomas simply looked at the others before they could formulate a group thought.

'Before you think about trying something, make sure which one of you wants to join your friend here in the infirmary. For I promise you this, at least two of you will be the worse for wear, no matter what you do to me. Your choice.' Tomas waited for only a few seconds before calling their bluff and walking off past them, though not before delivering a sound boot to the testicles of the howling bully. It got even louder then, if not a little higher. Neither Ginger, nor his cronies ever bothered him again. *You have to nip these things in the bud before they get used to the idea.* Sage words from his father. Unfortunately, like skinny down there, there will always be victims. Some people simply don't have it in them to stand up for themselves. *I swear some people have* Loser *imprinted on their DNA.* Unfortunately, one of his colleagues at the Mornington Academy found out about this genetic anomaly the hard way. Ginger may not have bothered Tomas any more; in fact he gave him a very wide berth. But it didn't stop him taking his petty frustrations out on others. Where Tomas discovered such treatment, he quashed it. But Roberts had kept his abuse to himself, denying it and bottling things up inside until he could take no more. They found him hanging in his dorm room. A hastily scribbled note explained his misery. Tomas immediately went looking for Sykes. Tomas was furious and something had snapped in him. He wasn't sure what it was until he found the cowering fat kid. When he found him and after he beat his way through the few toadies who still hung around him, he beat a confession out of him. Sykes was hospitalized due to the severity of his wounds and he would always walk with a limp and have limited use of his left hand ever after that. Even though Sykes was expelled for his part in the suicide, Tomas was expelled also for use of excessive force. Odd, he thought at the time, considering it was a military academy where they taught people to eventually kill in all manner of interesting ways. Still, he supposed later, he was fortunate he wasn't officially charged; but Sykes's equally fat, ginger parents must have known what a malignant little bastard their son was and maintained his beating and Tomas's expulsion were punishment enough – though Tomas had the impression his own father had suggested several scenarios to the fat and ginger parents *had* they pressed charges. He was sure he overheard the words *disappear* and *deep quarry* mentioned as they passed in the car park when Tomas was picked up. His father was duly disappointed that Tomas had been booted out of such a prestigious school, but he was equally proud of his son for the reason it happened.

'You have fine values, son. Though perhaps you went a bit too far with your interrogation. A good interrogator always knows just how far to go to exact what he needs. I don't condone some of the methods employed but they are certainly more discreet than systematically breaking all the fingers on someone's hand between two bricks. I'm not even going to ask what you did to his kneecap, but I can guess it involved a power tool and a fine drill bit – imaginative but crude. I thought I taught you better than that.'

He had, but Tomas knew this was from somewhere deep in him and had little to do with what he had learnt. Something had awakened in Tomas and it scared him. But it also excited him a little. The liberation that came with inflicting such pain and retribution became the narcotic that drove him to later excel at his governmental role.

'But he made me so angry, Father. He was told time and time again. I might as well have been talking to myself for all he listened. He needed to learn.'

'Yes, he very well may have. But now, believe it or not, he'll be worse. For he will become bitter and twisted. His failings will all be somebody else's fault. You will become the embodiment of everything he abhors. Tragic as he is, he will be this way until the day he dies.' So he was. He grew into a fat, lazy, wife beater. How he ever found anyone blind and stupid enough to marry him was anyone's guess. That had always stunned Tomas; something was certainly in the eye of the beholder. Maybe she had no sense of smell, desensitized fingers and was clinically blind. Either way, she put paid to his mistreatment of her by sticking a carving knife twenty-seven times into his fat frame. She was now serving life in a women's prison. Tomas frowned as he recalled the trial. There was little justice in the world and the worthless git even caused misery both by dying and after his death. The saga of Sykes had stayed with Tomas for years and had reinforced his hatred of bullies and those who picked on the underdog. He had never reconciled it as such, but he came to realize in that moment, it was a weakness. An inherent trait that proved to himself, more than anyone else, that he was at least still moderately human. *Then again, wasn't it a constraint of the knights of old? One of their tenets? Protect the weak and those who are incapable of protecting themselves? Maybe I'm just fulfilling a genetic imperative. Either way, the poor git scrambling at the base of the hill needs my help, whether he knows it himself or not.*

The fleeing man was definitely struggling. The adrenaline that had kept him running till now was fading fast. The stranger above him offered help but it could be a trap. Trouble was, he was spent. He had nothing left to give. So with a limited choice on offer, he took the one of help, for right or wrong. But he couldn't scramble up the hill: it was just too steep and his arms felt like lead and his legs like jelly. He looked up, plaintively searching for the origin of the voice. He was startled nearly to death as the voice appeared right next to him. Tomas dropped the camouflage he had adopted to slide the rest of the way down the hill and tried to reassure the man.

'Here!' Tomas held out his hand. 'Let me help you up; it's gonna be a bit of a scramble.' Tomas gripped the wrist of the proffered hand. It would give him better purchase on the thin arm as he pulled him up, as he knew he would have to. With a quick glance behind to the riders, checking their whereabouts, Tomas draped his cloak over his charge and merged them with the grassy hill as he part pulled, part carried the depleted man to the top, where he promptly collapsed. Tomas swiftly gathered more of the berries he had found earlier and deposited them on the prone man's chest. Then, with a look of abject ferocity and a hunter's glee, Tomas checked over his shoulder back in the direction of the riders. Had the riders been able to see his expression, they would have turned and fled. Perhaps even gathered their families and left the country. It wasn't a look anyone wanted turned on them. Not if they expected to live long anyway.

'Right then, chaps,' Tomas hissed. 'Your turn. Let's see how you like it.' Tomas jogged to the edge again and looked over. They had regrouped and were picking over the remains of their fallen colleagues. *Sensible if nothing else*: the dead have no use for their gear. Tomas began to appraise them and their threat potential. There were nine of them and Tomas needed to level the playing field before he made himself known. Hunkering down, he shouldered the weapon again and coolly picked his first three targets. These still sat upon their horses, keeping a futile guard as the rest rifled the dead warriors for armor, what looked like gold coins and for weapons. Pfft. Pfft. Pfft. The three were tipped from their saddles. One, Tomas knew was dead, as part of his skull was blown away, but the slight movements diminished his accuracy as the first fell. *Shit! I'm losing my touch.* The second took a round to the chest and the third was only clipped in the shoulder, but Tomas thought the bad fall – as he landed on his neck and head – did what the shot failed to do. The rest leapt up and pulled their horses around to act as shields as they drew their own weapons. *One with a bow. Now that could be problematic, I don't like it when they shoot back.* Pfft. Another one fell. *There; that puts paid to that niggle.* Tomas heard sounds from behind him and in his heightened state of awareness, he spun and the hot, slightly smoking barrel settled a few inches from the skinny man's nose. He started to scream and Tomas jumped up and slammed his hand over his mouth. Skinny's eyes went wide with fear.

'Shush, man, I'm not going to hurt you, but you really shouldn't sneak up on people like that: it could get you killed by accident. Now, I'm going to take my hand away, I hope you understand what I'm saying, but I need you to be quiet and not scream. You do understand. don't you?'

Skinny nodded slowly and gripped Tomas's steel trap hand and slowly prized it from his mouth. 'My...my name is Niall. Why are you helping me? They'll kill us both now. Me for running and you for helping.'

Tomas laughed then at the thought of them killing him and the fear returned to Niall's eyes. The sound of Tomas's laughter was more unnerving than the riders, apparently. Tomas saw this and smiled to lessen the effect. He wasn't sure he was successful. It was a bit like having the proverbial alligator smile at you, just before...well, before. 'It's a long story and I won't bother you with it, but simply put, I didn't like the odds. Thought I'd even things up a bit. Plus,' Tomas added, 'I need information about where I am and how I can get back and I'm not going to get that if you're dead. And you looked chattier than those fellows down there. So sit tight, eat some berries and I'll be right back.' Tomas turned to go, then spun back with an afterthought. 'Try to stay quiet and still. You're no good to me dead and I don't want to have to chase you as well as them.'

Niall nodded, wide-eyed and awestruck. He just squatted down where he was and grasped his knees in both arms. Tomas stared for a second and nodded a 'good!'

Returning to the edge, he saw the riders had reached the bottom and were studying the tracks there. Tomas grinned predatorily and rolled his shoulders, loosening the muscles there, ready for action. Pulling up his cowl and blending again, he leapt down the slope, gaining speed as he slid down. The riders looked up at the commotion but didn't see anything at first. Not until Tomas had reached roughly head height with the riders, then he exploded outwards feet first, booting one of the horsemen from his mount, the jaw cracking explosively as Tomas connected squarely. The rider went barreling off the side of his horse, closely followed by Tomas, who rolled expertly away before coming to his feet again. He spun just in time to see the rest dive clear and draw their weapons. They had seen him now: of that there was little doubt. Tomas moved quickly and jumped on the throat of the prone man whom he felled, twisting his boot with a satisfactory crunch making sure he didn't get up again; and then Tomas ran off a few yards, giving the riders space to mount, which they did rapidly, watching him all the time.

'Storm!' Tomas yelled, still grinning. He pulled his Hochler out and fired off a few warning rounds, which kept the riders at bay. Within seconds, the thundercloud that had materialized beside him took on the familiar shape of his warhorse. Tomas sprang into the saddle and switched his machine pistol back to the sword and bolstered his own armor to the more forbidding black combination of plate armor and Kevlar. Storm whinnied proudly and reared as soon as Tomas was settled. It was a magnificent sight, designed to unnerve their enemies. But it seemed that they were too dense to take the hint.

In less time than it took to say charge, Storm bounded forward, naught to sixty faster than the fastest performance car. The recalcitrant riders stood little chance really as Tomas thundered into their ranks. Storm, in his steel barding, bodychecked the inferior mounts of the warriors, sending two sprawling and unhorsing one completely. Storm slammed both front hooves into the soft ground and kicked back with his rear legs. The man who had been unhorsed was a little dazed but standing still, though only for a second as the steel-shod hoof of Storm took him squarely in the face and rocketed him back off his feet to land in a broken, bleeding and crumpled heap several feet away. Seconds later Tomas swung the blade in a sweeping scythe-like motion, taking the chest and several ribs out of one horseman to his right; and slammed his fist into the face of the rider to his left, snapping his head back with an audible crack. Storm wheeled and spun for another pass, faster than the remaining warriors could spin their own now terrified horses, obviously non battle-trained mounts. Tomas slashed the blade diagonally down, opening the back to the spine of the nearest rider. Tomas got a better look then at the warriors' armor as he ran rings around them. It was a jumbled and confused mix of plate, mail and chain from all over history and time. He saw Roman greaves and breastplates with German plate armor alongside boiled leather. Greek and Persian bits as well. It was like they had raided a Gladiators' store house. But their weapons were well cared for, if ineffectual. As one or two brave riders attempted to slash at him, he felt the ring of their blades against his armor, but barely felt the blows. He was grinning maliciously from ear to ear as the adrenaline coursed through his own body, his laughter ringing out as loud as the clash of steel on steel, heart and mind focused on the fight and thoroughly enjoying it. Tomas swung the sword like a soul possessed; the blade was cutting lethal arcs all around him, lending its own prowess to Tomas's growing skill. Against such determined opposition, the battle was soon over. Those who lay groaning upon the ground but unable to move watched with dull flat eyes, like those of sharks, as Tomas stood over them. They gave the look of being unrepentant and unco-operative. But Tomas tried all the same. 'Who are you and where are you from and, more importantly, why were you chasing that man?'

Nothing, the wounded and dying were defiant until their inevitable end. One even spat up at Tomas. He died with a sword blade though the mouth, and Tomas moved on to the next, then the next with the same question. None, as he expected, gave him anything at all. Loyalty was a rare commodity these days, Tomas noted sourly, a trait that often tended to only go one way but these exhibited nothing but stupidity. Those in power expected loyalty, though many really earned it – yet when the time came for those selfsame lords and commanders to return it, they more often than not shirked their responsibility and spun it every which way possible to get out of any and all obligations to those they considered lower than them. It was partly why Tomas had such an authority issue, so for these men to exhibit such a trait was not entirely unexpected. It was, however, misguided. They did not know Tomas. Nor did they know his concept of war. Leave none alive behind you who can tell tales or take revenge. And don't leave it to chance that they *may* die. Make sure. The Regiment taught that a double tap was a foregone conclusion; it was

SOP – standard operating procedure – for many others too. Mercy was for the foolish as far as Tomas was concerned. Soldiers didn't go into the occupation of war blind to the risks. Every soldier knows nowadays, more than any other time, what can happen and how expendable they are in the grand scheme of things. Cannon fodder for the most part. It always had been and always would be, no matter how they giftwrapped it for the gullible and all too trusting. Yet oddly enough, there seemed to be a never ending supply of raw recruits who were prepared to die for the folly of others – others who weren't likely to ever go anywhere near where the dying was being done. It was yet another reason in Tomas's book to detest such people. He believed as his father had: never order someone to do something you weren't capable of or unwilling to do yourself, for it is the sign of a bad commander and of a lesser man. Men such as these are not to be trusted and certainly not respected. And Tomas never had. His father's advice had been proven to be accurate on many occasions, so Tomas had grown to put his faith in no-one but himself. If he wanted something doing, he usually did it himself. At least he knew the outcome and the success or failure lay only at his own door. So Tomas looked down at the dead warriors and wondered who they were prepared to die for.

Tomas did as the riders had, and checked amongst the dead for any clues. The gold coins were unstamped and crude; their weapons bore no markings and insignia, but did look fairly new. Tomas thought this odd; and why didn't they have guns or any other modern weaponry? This was getting stranger by the moment. It was as though he had traveled back in time: crude weapons and horses. Maybe Niall would have the answers he sought. Leaving the corpses where they lay, Tomas made his way back up the hill to the copse, struggling a little bit as the fire of battle cooled in him and the aches and pains of recent events caught up with him; and allowed Storm to dissipate and return to the brand upon his arm, albeit grudgingly. Tomas enjoyed the magnificent stallion's presence. A staunch and capable ally. *More bloody useful in a fight than many of those clowns I've had the misfortune of fighting with. I could have done with you, boy, several years ago.* Tomas patted the neck of the big stallion just as he turned incorporeal and ghosted away. Tomas was sure he heard the snort of a response from Storm just as he vanished: a pleased and self-satisfied sound. Tomas smiled to himself at the image it conjured in his mind and was glad of the friend he had there.

Niall was still faithfully cowering where he left him, looking for all he was worth just like a rabbit caught in the headlights of an oncoming truck. Tomas didn't stop to chat; instead he grabbed Niall by the arm and hoisted him off his feet. Dragging him behind him deeper into the copse and out of sight of any reinforcements the rabble he had just trounced might have had.

'Right then, Niall, time for a little Q and A.'

Niall looked as blank as Tomas half expected him to. Tomas groaned, sensing this was going to be harder than he first thought. 'I ask you questions. Q. You provide me answers. A. Got it?'

Niall nodded so vigorously, his head was in danger of snapping off.

'Calm down, son, I get it. Now sit there and tell me first off where the hell we are.'

Niall sat as he had before, squatting down, his body swinging between his bent legs. Tomas saw that he had scoffed all the berries he had left him and judging by the smears of berry juice on his face he had shoved them in like he hadn't eaten in a while. Trouble was, there was little he could do about that. Tomas had no need of food or water, due to his gifts, though this now presented him a moral dilemma. He couldn't help this obviously starving little man or anyone else for that matter. His gifts were restricted to him alone and he was unable, it seemed, to confer any of the benefits elsewhere. So powerful, yet so helpless. *Gifted but useless. Funny, that's what I recall my old tutor telling me. Gifted but useless and destined to go to Hell for my attitude, blasphemous thoughts and frequent sinning.* Tomas remembered Professor Bracken fondly, though he was old then and probably dead now. But he was a man full of virtues and attended church more regularly than the priest; Tomas was convinced of it and even imagined the man flagellating himself for stepping on a crack in the pavement, so fervent was he. But Tomas's trip down memory lane was brought to an abrupt halt by Niall's reply.

'The Domain! I thought everybody knew that.'

Tomas spun so fast and grabbed Niall by the shoulders that the skinny man squealed in fear again. 'Where did you say?' Tomas had heard but he needed to hear it again to get it clear in his mind. For he simply couldn't believe it.

'The...the Domain. We...we are currently on the edge of the lands ruled by the Great Lord Be'elzebub himself. How can you be here and not know this?'

Tomas looked sideways at Niall as he let him go and sat down on the soft grass beside him, grasping his head in his own hands and groaning. The blanks in his memory were filling up now. The crypt: it had been sealed because it was a portal to the Domain. Hell. *Bloody hell. Crap. I'm in Hell after all. Shit.* So many questions poured through Tomas. The hows and whys of his transportation. The fact he was on another planet entirely nearly blew his mind.

'Are you...okay?' Niall asked tentatively. 'Because you don't look so good.'

'Thanks for that, Niall; you don't look too good either. Care to explain why that is and how you came to be running away like you were?'

Niall looked wistful as he looked away in the direction he had come from. 'I didn't want to die, though there are those who pray for it daily here. I didn't want to become one of those. I was lucky, I suppose. I was a field worker.' Tomas looked up at him as Niall's voice grew bitter at the recollection. 'I had the privilege of working all day and most of the night for one meal and the option to sleep in a sack or simply upon the hard ground. Bastard reckoned I looked at him funny when he threw the sack at me. Looked at him funny, my eye, but that's all it takes here. So here I am, running from the only life I know, rather than die at the hands of some sadistic lunatic who was only bored and wanted to beat up on someone.'

Tomas nodded understanding; he had met plenty of those and even served with a few. Niall groaned and sat down heavily. 'I reckon they consider me as good as dead by now and have given my slot to another lucky bastard.' Niall laughed a humorless sound. 'So there goes my hope of another meal. Don't suppose you've got anything else other than those few berries, have you? It's surprising how running for your life works up an appetite.'

Tomas laughed then and slapped Niall on the back, nearly propelling him across the clearing in which they sat. 'No, I haven't, but I reckon I can rustle something up for you. Sit tight.'

Tomas was back roughly twenty minutes later with a large and dripping slice of horse rump. Tomas expertly constructed a small fire pit and soon had the horse steak sizzling over a moderate flame. While Niall devoured the meat, Tomas also fetched some clothes from the dead men who had no use for them any more – as well as a half-full wineskin, which was better than gold at that moment. Both Tomas and Niall drank deeply and Niall finally fell back, sated and feeling better than he had in a very long time.

'If this is a dream, I don't want it to ever end. I can't remember the last time I had wine, or had a belly as full as this. Clothes such as these were reserved for the Dark Lord's bounty hunters only. I could only dream of wearing such as these.' But after Niall had dressed, Tomas quizzed him some more on who they were.

'They roam these lands, hiring themselves out to the ruling classes to fetch their runaways for them. The idle lords are quick to employ these scum so they don't have to get off their own asses and sully their hands. Still, they got better than they deserved, if you ask me. Years of torture wouldn't have been good enough for them for all the poor sods they've captured and killed.'

Tomas saw a sliver of steel in this pathetic looking scarecrow of a man and it brought a smile to his usually severe features. 'It's good you hold your sense of humor and self-worth, Niall. In my world that makes you a stronger man, stronger by far than those dead fools out there. Never let any predicament get you down; never give in to defeat. I used to say that the worst that can happen to anyone is death and usually, after that, it won't hurt any more. Now, I'm a little unsure about that. This place isn't entirely what I was expecting from the Domain.' Tomas neglected to mention all he had heard came from the Four Horsemen of the Apocalypse: he didn't want to blow the poor soul's mind any more than it already was.

'Let me guess: demons? Pitchforks and fiery pits? Fire and brimstone?' Niall offered.

Tomas nodded that it was precisely what he had in mind.

Niall shrugged noncommittally. 'Well, they are all here, just not here…' Niall pointed downwards, '…if you get my meaning. This is a big place. There are entire continents devoted to those things, so I've heard. But this one has only the aptly named Desert of the Desolated. At least I think that's its name. It's a desert and it's desolate, so you figure it out. The other place is the frozen wastes of Tartaran, thankfully separated by the Tartarus Mountains. Apparently it's so cold there that the air itself turns solid in places.'

Tomas was trying to take things in. He recognized some of the names, like Tartarus. It was reputedly one of the lowest levels of Hell and generally not a nice place.

'This side of the mountains,' Niall continued, 'is primarily the demesne of Be'elzebub and the lord Lucifer himself.'

Tomas started like he'd been shot. 'Did you say Lucifer?'

Niall nodded eagerly, though he quickly became suspicious, not sure if Tomas's interest was a good or bad thing. 'Why so keen to know about him? He's not really in favor any more. Not since the Adversary took over, anyway.'

Tomas put his finger to Niall's lips, silencing him for the time being, for there were too many things whirling through Tomas's mind for him to keep up with any more information. He was in or at least close to Lucifer's realm, though he thought that the entire Domain was his. He would ponder the hierarchy another time. For now, thoughts about his currently suspended mission resurfaced. Somewhere in the back of his mind he thought he remembered something about the Megiddo fortress on Earth being connected somehow to Lucifer's palace. Because that was where the Adversary was. Now, if he could get there, maybe he could come up behind the Adversary rather than try to go head on.

'Oh dear, I don't think I like the look that's just come over your face, Lord Tomas.' It was the first time he had been called his name by Niall.

'I'm not a lord, Niall, and I appreciate you not calling me that.'

Niall nodded reluctantly, as though the idea didn't sit too well. 'It's a habit, I'm afraid. Truly, for everyone here insists on having a title. It's safer to confer lordship on everyone to avoid a beating for being inappropriate. I learnt that shortly after arriving here. Some...' Niall closed his eyes, concentrating briefly, '...best I can judge, twelve years ago. Hard to tell exactly as time seems to drag a bit here. Especially when you're in a field breaking your back for twenty hours of daylight. It may not be the fiery version you envisage, but it sure *feels* like Hell to me.'

Tomas couldn't deny that. He'd seen some of the workers in the fields of Cambodia, Mexico, Korea and numerous other parts of the world where life was cheap and the reward was to scrape together enough food to last another day so they could do it all again. It must feel like Hell to them too. It made him wonder where the older, more superstitious cultures got their idea of what hell was actually like from. Maybe, some of them had slipped through to the Domain and made it back somehow; or perhaps a demon they encountered came from the more fiery regions and painted a very graphic picture, maybe even using mind communication similar to what he shared with the Horsemen. Theories upon theories. Who knew, really? But they had got it about as wrong as they could get, judging by where they currently were. Tomas recalled Niall's words: how he had been here twelve years.

'Where were you before you came to be here, Niall? Can you remember?'

'Oh, yeah. I was on a ship. Chained in a hold and destined for some place called the new world. Australia, I think it was called. They said I was a convict. Worst thing I ever did was coming over from County Cork. I shoulda stayed put. Greener grass and all that bollocks. But I reckon it was just an excuse to rid themselves of shit loads of undesirables they couldn't feed, house or be bothered about. Not sure if I got a better deal or not.'

Tomas didn't know what to say. He hadn't been able to place the accent, but even that made sense now. Though Niall thought it was only twelve years ago, bloody hell: it was more like two hundred and twelve. At least. Poor guy has no idea whatsoever.

'Tough one, mate, though I believe you didn't miss much. It was a rough place where the rest went and plenty died. You're alive now; take some solace in that.' Tomas didn't have the heart to tell him it was over two hundred years since the day he came to end up here. He himself had trouble with that concept. Heavens only knew how Niall's limited and archaic understanding would cope with that little bombshell.

After bandaging Niall's wounds as best he could, he helped him dress in the stolen clothes and even let him sleep for a while. Tomas kept a lookout in case the corpses at the bottom of the hill had friends or even, knowing his luck, got up and wanted round two. But as luck had it, they didn't, thus providing Tomas with ample time to think about what they needed to do next. Directionwise, he figured the way Niall had come was out. He'd have kittens if he thought that Tomas was taking him back the way he had just half killed himself running from. There was little either side except more grass. That looked a bit exposed for Tomas's liking, so all his conclusions suggested the forest was their best bet.

Niall woke up suddenly and spun about as though his life were in peril, eyes wide and panic evident in his movements.

'Easy, mate, you're okay. You're safe, so you can relax. Looks like you got some sleep though. Don't get a lot of that, I take it?'

Niall shook his head vehemently, still a bit confused. Tomas tossed him the water skin he had scavenged earlier, and having to catch it or be brained by it, brought him quickly to his senses.

'But you did look tired after your run, so I hope you feel up to travel-ing this morning. We are heading for the woods there.' Tomas thumbed the direction they were going to go. 'It's a good couple of miles, so we'll use Storm to cover it quickly. You're not scared of horses are you, or anything daft like that?' Again, Niall shook his head.

'Good, because if there are any more of those hunters after you, I'm not sure we'll have the element of surprise a second time. It was lucky I caught them off guard as it was.'

Niall nearly choked. Was this stranger kidding? He had just seen this man casually slaughter roughly a dozen men on horseback, riding a magical steed that turns to smoke, wielding a mystical sword that comes and goes at his will and *he* thinks he caught them off guard? Tomas smiled at Niall's observations and admitted that it did sound fairly impressive, but that aside, he knew his limitations. Here, he was outmanned and potentially outgunned, though not if they all used those archaic weapons, but it was a risk he wasn't prepared to take until he knew more about this place. It never paid to get too cocky over small victories. They underestimated him. They wouldn't do that again and it wasn't in Tomas's nature anyway to hang around and give them another opportunity. He used to be a ghost and his enemy only ever saw him just as they died. Tomas was trained and his continued existence had been to avoid putting himself in harm's way unnecessarily, but that was what he had just done to save Niall, one man he didn't even know. Part of his mind was questioning his motives because it wasn't his *modus operandi*. This sort of reckless behavior was all King Arthurlike – knights who were outnumbered but who still leapt in to rescue the oppressed. Another quote from his father drifted in and echoed in his mind. *Evil flourishes only when good people do nothing.*

'Before we set off, Niall, I want to check those wounds of yours. They looked dirty but not particularly deep. We don't want you keeling over with some nasty infection, do we? God knows what you could catch here, though I really ought to get out of the habit of saying that, 'cos I don't reckon anyone's god has much to do with what goes on here.' Tomas made a mental note to try and rustle up a few different expletives; he was bound to need them, for the old ones were apparently a bit out of date now.

Niall looked at Tomas with an expression that made him feel uncomfortable. It was a mixture of gratitude, relief and awe reflected in his grey, haunted eyes. Tomas hoped he wouldn't end up letting him down as well. Images of his family and Potter and so, so many others sprang unbidden to his mind. Years of thinking of no one but himself and disregarding all thoughts of the consequences of his actions. They were always somebody else's problems. Problems he was responsible for creating. Tomas knew it would be lethal to try and recall all the people he could have helped but didn't. It was a dark and deadly slope, slippery with the innocent blood that coated it. Tomas shook his head vigorously, dispelling the soul-sapping images and putting the idea of failure as far away from his mind as possible; though he couldn't entirely shake the feeling that the damning and depressing thoughts weren't entirely his as he pushed them away.

Wounds dressed, Niall clambered back into the borrowed clothing while Tomas summoned Storm, who ghosted into being as though he had always stood there, one great hoof pawing the earth. *'Easy, boy. But it's good to see you, too.'*

'Once we get in the forest, we'll see if we can't rustle up some decent grub for you. There must be all sorts of things running around in there.'

Niall looked fearful, glancing between Tomas and the forest, his hands clutching to himself. 'There are, Lord Tomas...' Tomas scowled at him. '... Er, sorry, Tomas. As I was saying, there are all sorts in there, all right. Stories of the Great Forest reached us even where we were, and it's said that whole armies have gone in there and never been seen again.'

Ordinarily Tomas would have laughed off such superstitious mumbo jumbo as just that, but recent events had opened his mind to things he had previously scoffed at. Tomas too regarded the alien looking forest before them. It was not dissimilar to the thought of leaving the safety of dry land for the vast, deep and dark oceans. It was another world in there. A world of shadows, sounds and possibilities. It was bright out here, in the sun, but it would be gloomy in there even now. Night time would see it turn to impenetrable blackness. He had experienced that in the jungles of Cambodia. He had been fine until he had to fight his way out of an ambush and he had lost his night-vision goggles. It had been a close call, but the sudden use of a flare – which he expected; they didn't – blinded the bandits and allowed him to even the odds. He had spent six days in that permanent twilight world, but what lay before them looked considerably darker and undoubtedly a greater expanse by far than the Cambodian wilderness he had to navigate.

However, Tomas had to contain his own reservations and put a brave front on for the anxious Niall. The poor man had gone through enough in his… Tomas was about to say 'life' to himself, but it was more than that. By his own admission, Niall had been here since the mid-seventeen hundreds, though Niall thought it was only a score of years. How that could be was an explanation for another time, and one Tomas would find fascinating, to be sure. But for now, Tomas's imperative was to protect the one thing he could, even from urban myth. Tomas clapped Niall friendly-like on the back – gently – but still nearly sending him reeling.

'Try not to worry about it, Niall. We have tales like that back where I come from too, many of them greatly exaggerated. I've spent enough time in places like that to know how they can affect the mind. In our case, they may be of some use to us and aid our cause.'

Niall frowned at that, completely lost as to how a haunted forest could help anything, other than to kill you in all new and probably horrible ways. 'Lord Tomas, how can that dreadful place aid us? I had no intention of going anywhere near it myself. I'd rather have faced my pursuers; at least they were just men.'

'For the last time, Niall, I'm not a lord.' Tomas felt his temper rise disproportionately to the crime and for a second, all he wanted to do was to smash his fists into Niall's pathetic, simpering face; again and again and aga… What was he thinking? Tomas had to quash the thought as though he were swallowing back vomit. It went down with the same reluctance. *Bloody hell, what was that?* He couldn't remember the last time a sudden rage had flared to that intensity before. At least not so sudden and violent and over something so trivial. Niall had seen the look cross Tomas's eyes and he began to cower back from him, that flight-or-fight instinct worming its way into him. In this case it would be flight. Tomas had to reassure him fast, even as he fought the rage bubbling just below the surface within himself.

'Sorry, Niall,' Tomas began. 'It's just that I had a spell in the military and I, for some reason that I never got, had a bit of a problem with authority. I earned my rank the hard way; it wasn't given to me as a matter of course like so many of our own alleged nobility. They get given command and have no idea how to tie their shoelaces let alone make life-or-death decisions that determine whether those men live or not. I don't like them, Niall, and that is putting it mildly.' The rage was simmering again at the thought of the pompous officers he had come up against. 'I couldn't be further from owning that title than you are from flying to those two moons up there. I'm just like you…well, not just like you – I've had a bit more luck – but see where that got me. I'm here with you, after all,' Tomas sighed wearily. 'So please, Niall, enough with the lord shit, heh? Plain old Tomas will do nicely. Stick with that and we'll get along famously.' Niall nodded mutely.

'Good, now let's get our sorry arses into that wood and see if we can't find you dinner.' Tomas was unaware of the fact he had omitted himself from the food requirement. He didn't feel hungry or thirsty for that matter; but he didn't think that odd. *Bloody gifts again, no doubt.* He had more than enough to worry about without worrying about something he wasn't experiencing.

Several fraught hours later found Tomas and Niall quite a few miles into the woodland – Tomas would have continued, but Niall was nearly unconscious and falling off the saddle where he sat behind Tomas – so they stopped and Tomas hunted. Now they were huddled around a small fire, banked and contained at the edge of a sizeable clearing within the forest.

Sizeable inasmuch as a couple of football stadiums would have fitted comfortably within the open meadow space that was an ironic oasis amidst the oppressive woodland. Perhaps in another time, a small town might have been built in such a clearing – it was certainly big enough. Tomas had heard the familiar sound of moving water somewhere in the gloom, so guessed there was a water source nearby too. It had the makings of a good retreat. The land seemed fertile and there was game aplenty judging by the herd he had spotted moving silently through the trees. One shot and an hour of careful cleaning later and a small creature that closely resembled a deer – which was good enough for Tomas – rotated on a makeshift spit. Niall's previous concerns seemed to vanish with the aromatic and meaty smoke that wafted up from the juicily roasting flesh. The sun had set and the two moons were now slowly rising up over the treeline, casting their silvery and chilly light over the scene. Shadows seemed to flit in and out of the trees on the other side of the clearing and Tomas had spent a good hour with his new, sword provided, night-vision and range-finding goggles, just scanning the surrounding trees and meadow. But he saw nothing other than his own imagination-fuelled spectres. Tomas knew he needed to focus and calm his mind. Let his senses range out and guide him. But since arriving in the Domain, he found it increasingly hard to concentrate. His nerves were ragged and sensitive. Look how he had flown off the handle at Niall. That wasn't him. He was much more controlled, at least normally. Only he wasn't normal now, was he? He had been changed somehow by the Horsemen. Was this some kind of side effect? For whatever he gained he had to lose something else? Granted, he was new to all this mystically powered stuff, but it seemed unfair to have to deal with a whole bunch of so-called gifts while undergoing some other sort of change to accommodate them: like learning to scuba dive, being thrown into the ocean while forgetting how to swim and how to use the oxygen equipment. Not a good combination, added to the fact that the headache Tomas had when he went down into the crypt had started to creep back, putting slight pressure on the veins at the back of his eyes and a throb at his temples that resonated down his cheekbone, through his jaw and ended up scrunching up his neck muscles on one side. Tomas looked over at Niall and saw he had curled up into a fetal ball and was sound asleep. Belly full for the first time in who knew how long, he had all the contentment he could handle. *Lucky bastard*, Tomas thought enviously. *These bloody gifts should come with a health warning. I could use some sleep about now to shift this goddamn headache, but I don't feel like sleeping, thanks to those bloody Horsemen. I don't fancy spending the rest of my days wide-eyed and wide awake.It can't be good for you, surely.* Tomas was still muttering to himself as he did a brief recon of the little campsite, checking on anything that might be creeping about. He set a few basic traps to catch the unwary. He was limited by his resources but he had time to carve a few stake springs and other various woody but nasty surprises. A few hours more saw Tomas sitting with his back against a tree, idly contemplating his next move. Niall was still sleeping. He didn't even notice his own eyes close and his breathing regulate into the semi-restful state of a light sleep. Images of a faceless crowd gathered around him and they started to poke him with sticks. Sharp sticks too, for he looked down to find himself bleeding from more than a few jabs. One particularly forceful jab snapped him back to reality and he opened his eyes with that sudden realization that he had slept and hadn't meant to. But there before him, was a figure with a vicious looking spear, and it was stabbing at him again.

'This one sleeps like the dead. Should I just kill it and save it the trouble of waking?' The figure went to stab him again. A woman too, judging by the voice. But Tomas galvanized himself and rolled agilely to one side, manifesting the sword to his hand. He backswung as he rolled, neatly severing the tip of the spear and eliciting a growl of anger from the spear wielder. He rolled up to his feet, only to come face to face with three more razor tipped pole arms lightly touching him upon his chest.

A delicate voice instructed him to remain still if he wanted to live. Delicate, yet Tomas had the distinct feeling that they were more than capable of backing up their claim.

'Easy, ladies!' Tomas made the sword disappear – another gasp from the women at this – and Tomas raised both hands high to show his intent. *I hope they know what this means*, he thought hopefully. *Where's Niall?* Tomas looked about for the timid man. As he did so, he saw there were several women standing guard and Tomas took a few seconds to put two and two together. He had seen them before, though not in the flesh.

'Where's my companion?' Tomas hadn't moved but he weighed up his chances of breaking free from these Valkyries. For that was what they were, or at least looked like. He had seen depictions of them back when he was a boy, and they certainly lived up to their descriptions. Silvery helms with various adornments, some with horns, some with wings, and others with animal depictions on them. Dazzling armored breastplates, bracers and greaves. Battle skirts of leather and steel plate hung to mid-thigh and exposed an awful lot of leg. *That's gotta be distracting in a battle*, Tomas smiled to himself, despite his predicament. Aside from their armor, they all sported long cloaks and bows as well as a whole plethora of other weapons.

'Is this your companion?' One of the women dragged him cringing and whimpering, and deposited him in a whining heap at Tomas's feet. Tomas ignored the women's pointed weapons and knelt to check on his erstwhile comrade.

'Are you okay, Niall? Did they hurt you?' The little man shook his head, implying he was all right, if a bit terrified. Tomas looked him over for puncture wounds but found no new ones. Tomas tried to rationalize how this could have happened. They had eluded his traps and managed to get close enough to poke him with a spear. And the biggest question of all, why had he slept? He hadn't meant to, or even thought he could. It was all getting a bit too much. One problem led to two and two to four. Tomas found himself getting annoyed by the non-stop let up of things trying to kill him, stab him or just generally get in his way. Tomas stood abruptly, which surprised the women slightly, and they narrowed their gaze and watched him suspiciously. Tomas made to walk towards them and they prodded their spears at him once more, but much to their increased surprise, Tomas batted them away contemptuously with a sudden sweep of his arm. One, however, pressed forward and left an angry red line upon his neck as the blade sliced past.

'Ow!' Tomas's hand went to his neck and it came away bloody. 'That's it. Enough is enough.' Tomas grabbed the nearest spear and pulled mightily, yanking the wielder off balance. She wasn't expecting such a move. Nor was she expecting Tomas to grab her and spin her, circling his arm around her neck and pulling her further off balance and placing her between him and her companions as a shield. *After all, they are shield maidens.* Tomas was amused by his own pun and laughed out loud. This only made them think he was mad or moonstruck. The women were stunned only briefly by his actions, but that soon passed and they all drew bows and leveled arrows at him. Tomas called out angrily, putting force and disdain into his challenge.

'Who is in charge here? And what are *girls* doing out on their own and with *weapons*. Who allowed this?' Tomas was hoping to snag a nerve and he wasn't disappointed as several more women emerged from the trees, death in their eyes and bows trained upon him. Niall curled even tighter, if that was humanly possible and whimpered quietly, thinking his end imminent. Tomas mentally summoned his armor and he heard more gasps from the Valkyries. They weren't expecting this sort of response. Mayhap they thought them both mere runaways, and were after the bounty. Tomas braced for the worst as the women pulled back on their bows. He heard the creaking as they tensed.

'*Wait!* Hold your fire and lower your weapons!' The speaker stepped free of the treeline, where she had remained concealed till now. If Tomas thought the other women were impressive, he was totally unprepared for the one who walked towards him.

'This one has spirit, and judging by his accouterments, has some worthy explanation ahead of him. Tell me, slave, whose body did you rob that armor from and why do you venture into our forest?' She placed both fists upon her shapely hips and waited for Tomas to speak, but even she raised an eyebrow when Tomas merely broke out laughing. As a gesture and a calculated gamble, Tomas let his captive go and went over to pick Niall up. He could feel the irritation pulse out from them at his lack of subservience and arrogant behavior towards those who obviously thought themselves superior and in charge. Tomas stopped laughing and spoke out, not looking at them as he picked up the terrified man and propped him against a nearby tree.

'Never mind who I am. Who the hell are you? Anyone tell you it's impolite to sneak up on people? Let alone just walking into our camp and starting to poke people with spears, terrifying my friend and doling out orders like you actually owned something. I didn't see a sign when I came in...' Tomas gesticulated at an invisible sign over his head, '...saying "Valkyrie Forest. Do not enter". So why don't you all back up, take a breath and why don't we all start over, less the spears? Tell me who you are and how you avoided my traps, and I'll tell you who I am and why I'm here. Then maybe, just maybe, we'll see if we have either common ground or whether it's gonna get real messy real quick. Especially if you tell me you are something to do with those scruffy looking mercenaries who were chasing my friend here.'

Tomas turned and leveled his implacable hunter's gaze firmly on the eyes of their apparent leader. She returned the gaze with an implacable one of her own and Tomas saw a resolve there that matched his. Then the sun came out in the most unlikely of places. She smiled and Tomas was warmed by it in a way he had not anticipated, or experienced in some time. He found himself staring, concentration gone.

'That answers much and explains more than you can know,' she said coolly.

Tomas raised an eyebrow, waiting for further clarification, staying silent to prompt her to talk more and to buy himself time to get his shit together again.

'My name is Treya Thorsen and these warriors are my sisters. The dark eyed one who is staring at you with such intensity is Ingrid. It was her spear you ruined.'

True enough, she was looking at Tomas with a gaze that had him dismantled and examined from every angle, searching for treachery and a reason to kill him. Painfully too, by the looks of it. She was nowhere near as beautiful and radiant as the woman before him and she would never be considered a beauty, but she had the biggest brown eyes he had ever seen on a woman. They detracted from her manly chin and a nose that had been broken once too many times. She was still pretty but scary with it.

'Really? That's nice. Sorry about the spear but you ought to be careful where you stick it in future.' Ignoring her then, Tomas turned back to Treya and made a choice.

'My name, while we are on the subject, is Tomas. This is Niall, who has escaped oppression and is under my protection, so I'll trust you to leave him alone from here on or answer to me. For myself, well, that's something of a long story which I'll cut very short for you and, subject to where your alliances lie, could be even shorter still.'

'Treya!' Ingrid barked angrily to her leader. 'We should kill them now and be done with it. We can take no chances with spies. You know they have tried before.'

'No, Ingrid, I think not. That one is too pathetic to be a spy.' She waved a dismissive hand at Niall, and then rubbed her chin as she considered Tomas. 'There is something about this one that does not speak spy. I'm not sure quite what it does say. He dresses for battle, not sneaking around as with most spies. This one is likely to draw too much attention to himself to be a good spy. But, I will reserve judgment for now and hear what he has to say, so stay your weapon, Ingrid – for now.'

Tomas gave Ingrid a look that was equivalent to sticking his tongue out at her. She fumed quietly and looked daggers back at him, which turned to swords when he smiled back at her.

But Tomas chose his path and, containing his distraction at Treya's stunning looks and exceptional physique, he recounted his tale, omitting the bits about Michael and the Horsemen, as he kept an eye on Niall and prepared a cold breakfast for him, talking as he worked; and how he came to be in the

Domain, excluding his gifts as well. Tomas quickly went over what he had just told them and realized there was very little mystical about what he had just said. It could have been any mission he had undertaken. *That's good.* It paid to have a card up your sleeve, just in case. The Valkyries never took their eyes off him, almost expecting him to try something sudden. He told the tale with an economy of embellishment and efficiency from years of delivering straightforward reports. He had been allowed a certain autonomy in his line of work and the powers-that- be were wary of too much collateral damage, so Tomas kept those bits out and just told them, for the most part, just what they wanted to hear. He made sure though that he did his own housekeeping and there were very few cases of unsolved and messy discoveries left in his wake.

For most of his life, Tomas had been considered a moral vacuum, existing in a shade of grey that had a classification all of its own. But his lack of morals and low regard for human life wasn't to say he didn't have principles. He had firm views on many subjects and lived his life accordingly. Come between Tomas and his principles at your own peril, and few did. And those few people he was forced to interact with or through work related inconvenience quickly maintained their distance from the sombre and introverted man who exuded violence and possessed cold dark eyes like chips of dirty ice. People tried not to involve themselves with him very often, even those who gave him his orders. He was something of a pariah amongst his peers, co-workers and commanding officers. He was branded cold and emotionless, and most simply thought him a distasteful and nasty piece of work. They didn't know him – they didn't want to – but he just throbbed menace when he looked at them, and that made people form an automatic subconscious mental image: one of danger, violence and brutality. He smiled little back then and that only added to his cruel and distant reputation. He had been nicknamed behind his back, and though they thought he didn't know, he did. He never let on, because unbeknownst to them, he quite liked it; though they blanched when he adopted it for his codename. They all knew then that he had known it for a while and those who did have dealings with him found it hard to look him in the eye for fear of what he might do. Tomas was secretly amused by it all. A good reputation could do more things than the average person thought. They called him 'the Morning Star', because for one, they only ever saw him early in the morning when he came to report, but mostly because he was distant, cold, usually only seen at night, and gave off little light and no warmth.

It was a memory that hadn't surfaced for quite some time now. He had buried that particularly cheerless part of his history pretty much the moment he had been blown up along with the rest of his life and family. Apparently it wasn't as deep as he thought.

In fact, he couldn't imagine what had prompted its surfacing. In the blink of an eye, he reviewed what he had just told the Valkyries and none of it would have prompted that little gem. Tomas put it from his mind as another anomalous effect of this place. He was, after all, for all intents and purposes, in Hell, though it resembled the archaic and traditional version in no way, shape or form. But if what Niall had told him was true, there actually *were* places here that came close and they were definitely worth avoiding.

Tomas watched them as they spoke amongst themselves, no doubt considering his wild and fanciful tale. If he had heard it for the first time from one of his captives, he would have shot the man there and then for lying. *However, these women were bloody Valkyries after all. So perhaps their grasp of the fantastic is a bit better than mine.*

'Very well, I have considered your tale...' Treya spoke as she walked back, with all the grace of a hunting feline, thought Tomas, and stood before him. So close in fact, he could smell her, which did little for his concentration. It was heady and musky. He could smell her perspiration as it glistened on her sun-browned skin, her pheromones playing havoc with his focus as well as other parts of his anatomy. He began to mentally remove her armor and imagine her flesh and curves beneath. And, oh, there were curves aplenty, in all the right places. She was the sort of woman who would pick her man, chew him up and blow him out again in bubbles, then move on to the next. What man could satisfy a goddess like this? Still, Tomas thought, he would

certainly give it a go, '…much to my second's annoyance…' Treya continued, oblivious to Tomas's lascivious thoughts, as Ingrid glared at him with
undisguised malice, '…for I do believe she wants to kill you, considering you
more trouble than you appear to be worth. Are you?'

The sudden question threw him and brought him back to what passed for
reality with a crash. Then to his added chagrin, he blushed like a schoolboy
being caught out ogling the physical education mistress's breasts, which he
had done at every possible occasion – something that didn't pass unnoticed
either. Tomas was left with little option other than to play on it and bluff his
way through his embarrassment.

'That really depends on your definition of trouble. And as for my worth,'
Tomas waggled his hand and shrugged, pulling a face that implied a variety
of options.

'You see, my worth is subject to who you ask, and as opinions vary, you
may need to ask a lot.' Tomas paused, letting the silence build, for there really
wasn't much more he could say. They knew his allegiance and knew it wasn't
to the Adversary. He still didn't know theirs, but he began to guess it wasn't
to the Adversary either, based on the fact he was still breathing and standing
unfettered. All he had seen so far said that if he ever fell into the enemy's
hands, his treatment wouldn't be so generous. So he waited for her decision.

'Ingrid thinks you are lying. You are a man and that is what you do. It is
in your nature, like the scorpions or the snake.'

Tomas wasn't about to interrupt her with the fact that snakes don't bite
unless you piss one off by standing on it or yanking it by the tail. Of course,
some cobras were the exception even to that rule, but that was just because
they had attitude. Tomas respected them for that. They didn't take any shit
from anything.

'But I will allow you to live, for I believe your story. I believe it, for
many of the names you mention are known to us. Especially the Adversary.
The Four Horsemen too are known, though I have not encountered them for
quite some time now. But suffice to say, we share a common enemy. That is

enough these days. But know this, Tomas: should your mission come into conflict with ours, we will not hesitate to kill you.'

Tomas shook his head wearily. Always threats. No matter where you went, someone always wanted to threaten you, often without any concept or idea of what it was they were posturing to. It was one thing to be confident about your abilities, but it was only a fool who underestimated their opponent. Treya's eyes narrowed at his expression as Tomas spoke:

'I thought we were going to be polite about this; we started so well after all. But, for no reason that I can see, you're back to threatening again. I've been upfront with you about what it is I'm here to do. Our choices are simple: you can help me and I you. We can fight and lots will die, pointlessly I might add; or you can go your own way and be about your own business, leaving me to be about mine. But that seems a touch short-sighted as our paths lead in the same direction. To the Adversary. Anyway, I don't particularly want to fight you. Quite the opposite, actually.' Tomas looked her up then down again, making full sure she knew what he meant by that. He was pleased to see his point taken as her eyes widened and her mouth dropped a fraction at his audacity. He even heard giggling from some of her warriors and caught some muttering about thawing the ice maiden. Tomas smiled inwardly before continuing:

'I have a task to complete and Niall needs somewhere safe away from those hunters who seem to want him back pretty badly. If you're the freedom fighters you seem to be, then another body wouldn't go amiss. I don't know what he can do but I'm sure you can train him for something. I have no doubt he will not be a disappointment to you.'

Niall looked at Tomas with something akin to adoration. It was the first time in a long time that someone had stood up for him and it brought tears unbidden to his eyes. He stood as straight as he could and came to stand beside Tomas, swaggering a little, determined not to let him down. Tomas glanced at Niall and gave him an affectionate and conspiratorial wink. Niall just beamed back, feeling about as good as he ever had.

'So, if we find ourselves traveling in the same direction, well, that's all well and good. If, however, you deem our respective purposes in opposition, then I suggest you go your way and we ours and part as friends. I have little time or patience for unnecessary diversions, though for you I would make an exception.'

Damn! Where did that come from? Tomas couldn't believe what he had just said. *What the bloody hell's going on? I sure as shit didn't mean for that to come out. I hadn't even thought it, let alone spit it out like that. I've blown it now.* It was very unlike him to blurt lascivious comments out like this; he was usually much more reserved with women. They were, for the most part, a necessary evil, or were at least until he met his late and now very deceased fiancée. She had epitomized womanhood and stood for none of his nonsense about a woman's place was by the hearth. She was the equal of any man and if truth be told, he was undeserving of her. But she saw something in him that sparked her interest. She said he had potential and the way she said it, he truly wanted to believe it. Though it was more like he *did* believe it because she said it was so. Never, in all his years, had he met anyone like her. Nor did he think he would meet her like again – until now.

Throughout the journey that Tomas and Niall had taken so far to reach the vast clearing that they had eventually camped at, they had passed several smaller clearings. The last one had held a crystal pool, fed by what Tomas thought was maybe a hidden spring, or perhaps was an outpouring of some underground river. A weak spot where the pressure of the subterranean torrent had forced water out and kept the water cold and constant. A haven for all forest life and also a likely spot to find two unwary travelers. That said, Tomas had fed and watered Niall there and moved on, just far enough away that should they have need of the water, it was only a brief ride back. As it turned out, he wasn't the only one to think cautiously and logically, for it was here that the Valkyrie scouts had first seen him and Niall. They had expertly concealed themselves and their mounts there while the main body followed Tomas to their eventual meeting.

494

Treya had kept silent all the way back to their campsite where she had coldly invited them back to while she considered his suggestion, and Tomas put her silence down to her considering his proposal rather than what he had finished it with. To him, it made sense: a coalition would give him more eyes to watch his back and more weapons when the time came to use them. Their cause was similar to his inasmuch as they both wanted the Adversary gone. But they were wary and he couldn't blame them for that. This was a place of distrust, after all. It had gotten its reputation for being a disreputable and wild place. Law was only the whim of whichever lord's land you happened to be in. And that ruling was then subject to being further overruled by the now former paramount power in the Domain, who in this case used to be Lucifer, but now was the twisted – even by Hell's standards – Adversary. The balance was out everywhere and getting worse. Tomas had decided he was fed up with walking and summoned Storm, whom he mounted and pulled Niall up behind him. He was amused by their awed looks as they gazed upon the wonder that was Storm.

They entered the clearing, though not without being seen in advance, and a greeting party awaited them as they exited the cover of the trees. Tomas wasn't prepared for what he saw – a further six Valkyries – but it was their mounts that had him gaping like a mooncalf. Catching himself, he closed his mouth with an audible clack of teeth.

'Pegasi!' Tomas stated the obvious as he took in the collection of fantastic winged horses. He had only ever seen images of the white one from Earth's mythology, but these were every color. Chestnut, roan, piebald, dappled, and grey like Storm, they stood perfectly still. Calm and contained. Though a look into their intelligent eyes told another story. They were hurricanes contained within equine flesh. Pure forces of elemental strength. At one with both the Earth and the sky. Powerful wings, folded back alongside their muscled flanks, flicked only occasionally as they sniffed the air and sensed the new arrivals. A flick of caution and unknowing. Or maybe it was of prescience.

Tomas lowered Niall down off his horse, where he had clung to Tomas like his very life depended on it, so tight that Tomas even wondered if he hadn't cracked a rib. Taking a breath to confirm otherwise, he dismounted himself. Storm watched the pegasi with something akin to interest and Tomas smiled ruefully at the returned appraisal. Professional equine courtesy amongst supernatural creatures. He wondered if Storm was envious of their wings or if the pegasi wished they could fly, like Storm, without them. Another mystery, but one for another time. Tomas moved to the water's edge and splashed some cool water onto his face and neck, stretching to pop his muscles and bones back into place. He was finding himself adapting once again to his role of warrior and much of his strength and flexibility was returning to him, but he had never been a proficient rider and it still tugged uncomfortably after sitting in the saddle too long. Niall tried to be invisible as the Valkyries breezed around him, catching up and preparing the pegasi for travel. For a few brief moments Tomas found himself alone, and hunkered down on the mossy bank. He absently studied the trees opposite and was startled by a flash of white that sped across his vision. He realized he was out of focus and daydreaming slightly. Sharpening his own raptor's vision, Tomas searched for the cause of the image. It was then that his mind tried to put a shape to what he had seen.

What did I see? Did I in fact see anything? It wouldn't be the first time my mind had played tricks on me when it found itself in a stressful situation, and they don't come more stressful than being stuck in Hell with a bunch of Valkyries, one of whom wants your head on a stick. And, facing a task that would have psychologists wetting themselves. Well, Doc, it's like this. I've fallen into Hell and I've got to kill the demon who kicked Lucifer off his throne and who wants to destroy the multiverse then rebuild it to his own spec, which, by the way, probably doesn't include humanity in the refit. And I think it's odd. I'm seeing things? Tomas was about to write it off when it flashed by again, closer this time. It was a bird, or at least that was how he figured it. Maybe it was a big owl. They flew silently and had formed many of the ghost myths back on Earth. Barn owls in particular. But there were no barns in the forest he had seen so far. Maybe they had different kinds of owl here. He was in another world so it was more likely than not. Then he heard a sound that wasn't an owl. He had heard it before too. A deep caw caw sound that said exactly what it was. A raven. He had spent a lot of time up in Scotland and the North of England, where they were more prevalent. *Bloody great crows, but they don't come in white so it couldn't have been that.* Wrong. Tomas was amazed to see this huge bird swoop in low, fingerlike wing tips barely skimming the water as it banked and landed with featherlike grace upon a jutting branch that overhung the pool, and it lowered its head and cawed – several times – to make sure it had Tomas's full attention. It also got the attention of several Valkyries, who came over to stand behind Tomas. He looked back over his shoulder to see their rapt expressions, awe and reverence evident on their faces. Returning his own gaze to the huge bird, he was instantly caught in its sapphire blue eyes. Thoughts and images began to tumble through his mind. He gasped as more and more poured in. It was as though compressed ice was being pumped through his eyes straight into his brain. He gasped and collapsed, falling backwards, to land on his back with a thump. The Valkyries leapt nimbly backwards as he fell at their feet. The images ceased abruptly. Tomas only vaguely heard the gasp from above as the Valkyries leapt back from him even further. Feeling a pressure suddenly upon his chest, he looked up then down, coming face to face with the enormous razor beak of the huge raven that perched on his breastplate. It tilted its head in a very birdlike way to focus its own blue eyes fully on Tomas. It then hammered its beak a couple of times – pang pang – onto his breastplate, apparently making sure it had his attention, and then – Tomas couldn't be sure if he believed what he heard next, but there was little avoiding it – the raven spoke to him, 'Caw, Danger! Danger! Riders! Riders! Caw Caw.'

Whatever Tomas thought about the fact of a huge talking raven sitting on him, he understood danger and riders. As he attempted to sit up, the raven extended its white wings and ghosted off him, gliding with an economy of effort to perch itself once more upon the jutting branch. Tomas looked back to see if the Valkyries had heard what he had, but he didn't even need to speak as Treya looked at him.

'We heard, and we believe it. Get up and get ready, for there are riders coming; our own scout has just confirmed it. A little short of a hundred of them. Someone wants you pretty badly to send that many men in here after you. Now we need to choose our ground; it's too confined in here. I suggest we head back to the bigger clearing and make our stand there; it will give us a slight advantage with the forest at our back and the open clearing ahead of us. They will need that space for so many men and horses, and they will have no cover. It's as good as we can hope.'

Tomas approved of her tactic and ran to Storm, who stood ready. They all mounted, even Niall, once again behind Tomas, with instructions to jump clear the moment they arrived at the clearing, and to find a big tree to climb up out of the way. There was little argument from Niall about that.

There was no time for subtlety so with great reluctance from Treya and even from Tomas to a degree, they sprang upwards and flew the few miles to the designated area they chose to meet these attackers. It went against the grain to expose themselves this way, for they were clearly visible above the treeline to a whole plethora of scrying enchantments employed by many of the Adversary's agents, but needs must; which as it transpired was prudent, for as they landed and dispersed themselves along the forest edge, the first of the attackers crested the slight incline that formed the meadowy clearing, and they wasted no time in making their intentions known as several quarrels from crossbows and more than a few arrows from conventional bows thunked and hammered into the trees around them. Tomas heard a few grunts as the Valkyries took several hits but he didn't have time to see how bad they were before another wave of shafts rained in. This time the shield maidens raised their namesakes and Tomas did likewise, the great shield forming from his armor and flowing out like liquid steel.

Enough of this shit! Tomas growled as he dropped the shield again and swung up the RPG instead to his shoulder and fired. The vapor trail alerted all to what was happening, but the riders didn't know what it would do. Apparently they weren't familiar with rocket-propelled grenades. That changed after it exploded and took out six of their own. Man and horse. Tomas disliked having to hurt the beasts, for they were innocent in this, but there was no real way to separate them. Outnumbered as they were, Treya looked at Tomas and reappraised him on the spot. Tomas, however, was busy and fired a few more shots. Wiser now, the riders tried to spread out, but they were slower than the RPG. Taking quite a few more casualties, the riders wheeled around, sending some riders out to flank the little group. Treya signaled two groups to head off and deal with them as she, Ingrid, and a dozen others drew their own longbows. Nocking, they fired with a deadly accuracy the riders hadn't banked on. Fourteen shots flew and fourteen riders fell. Tomas was impressed; Treya looked at him coolly and winked once before nocking again. Fourteen more fell before the riders managed to scramble out of range. The same fate met those riders who had attempted to pincer them. Digging in hooves, they crashed into the forest rather than fall to the deadly shafts of the Valkyries.

A breathing space while the attackers regrouped gave Treya time to check on her own wounded. There were three down: two dead and one with a quarrel embedded deep in her shoulder. Tomas took a look and grimaced. Barbed. Bastards. They went in easily enough but were devils coming out. There was only one way to remove it and that was to push it straight through. It would hurt more than when it went in the first time and by its location, she wasn't going to be using a bow for a long time.

'Niall!' Tomas shouted, and with a bit of rustling and a groan as he fell the last few feet from where he had been hiding, Niall appeared, looking as eager as he could in light of their situation.

'I need you to take...' Treya gave her name, realizing Tomas wouldn't know it. '...Hildreth back into the cover and stay with her. She'll need her wound watching so that she doesn't bleed to death.'

Ingrid saw the wound and said obviously, 'But it's not bleeding. What are you talking about?'

Without answering and hopefully catching Hildreth unawares, he pushed suddenly on the quarrel. Hildreth cut off a scream as the barbed head sliced flesh and nicked bone as it rammed out of the other side of her shoulder. In a swift move, Tomas pulled her forward and yanked the offending barb free. Blood began to flow freely from the wound then.

'It is now.' Tomas grabbed a handful of moss and shoved it into the wound, both sides, and tore a strip off his cloak to tie it off.

'Now get her back there, Niall, and keep an eye out. I don't trust them to not have sent someone around from the rear earlier. Expect the unexpected, that's what I say. That way you're not disappointed or surprised by the predictability of the enemy.'

Niall nodded as though he understood – though Tomas had his doubts – and helped Hildreth back into the forest. Tomas turned back to Treya but her face was grave. She kept looking at her fallen sisters as though it was an unfamiliar sight, which by all accounts of their prowess, it probably was. He hoped she held it together for a bit longer, for as he stood to assess the enemy, he saw them regrouping for another charge. *Damn, they're tenacious.* Ingrid came to stand beside him and she too studied the riders. Studied them as she re-nocked an arrow and, after taking two paces forward, she rammed six more into the soil for speedier access. She shot Tomas a look that spoke volumes and made him glad he wasn't facing her. Tomas's expression was equally grim and he felt a rage rising within him that these faceless riders had dared attack them and, not only that, had managed to kill some of them. They would pay dearly for their insolence. Tomas never noticed the subtle crimson haze that began to cloud his vision. He swung the RPG up to his shoulder again and planned his spread of shots, trying to anticipate where they would disperse to after the first explosion. Banking on their obvious determination to get to them; them, for it had to be the Valkyries they were after – he hadn't been in the Domain long enough to make that many enemies and he had left none alive who were chasing Niall – Tomas kicked matters off by firing two shots. Ingrid spun to face him, anger overriding her surprise at the whoosh of the rocket leaving the barrel.

'What are you doing? They are still out of range.'

Tomas smiled his most chilling smile and rolled his shoulders to loosen them.

'Not from this, they're not.' As if to emphasize his words, the first reached its destination and exploded satisfactorily, followed seconds later by its twin. The attackers parted predictably and began to charge down three separate routes. Tomas mounted Storm and without any glance towards the Valkyries to see if they were following, he leapt forwards with astonishing speed. Treya barely had time to send her forces out left and right before following in Tomas's wake. Treya, Ingrid and six Valkyries arrowed after Tomas, their winged mounts soon catching the racing Storm. Tomas forewent the RPG and he willed his twin Hochlers to his hands and sprayed a hail of rounds into the vanguard heading towards him. He grinned maliciously as several fell badly to the ground. *That's evened the odds a bit.* It was now close to three to one and that suited him fine. As he rode, he bolstered his armor and started to laugh raucously. The sound carried to the Valkyries behind him as well as to the nearest riders, and he laughed all the more when he saw their concerned looks. Too late to turn away now. The Sword of War appeared flaming in Tomas's hands and he swung it loosely at his side, ensuring they got a good look at it. Then, amidst the thunder of pounding hooves and battle cries, they crashed together. It was like a wave of steel and flesh pounding over a rock. Men and horses were smashed aside as though they were nothing as the powerful Storm bodychecked them left and right. Tomas's sword was like the lightning and it struck indiscriminately. Men screamed left and right as the fiery blade tore into them. Tomas barely felt the blows that they managed to land on him. Their futile weapons were nothing compared to his and though his armor deflected many of their blows, a few got through. But Tomas was oblivious to the blood that gushed and pumped from his rib, leg and shoulder wounds. He was a dervish of manic steel. Even the sword was thrumming its enjoyment of the carnage. This is what it had been born for, after all. So engrossed was he in the mêlée, he didn't even notice the minor wounds knit and heal themselves, his body repairing itself as he fought.

All too soon, it seemed, Tomas broke through the ranks and he found himself in clear space. Wheeling Storm on a nickel, he pounded towards their retreating backs. A semblance of the controlled Tomas returned as he saw that the attackers were now in between him and the brutally efficient and equally devastating Valkyries. *Between hammer and anvil.* Tomas laughed once more at the cliché and drove Storm onwards. He slashed the first attacker across the back, laying it open to the spine. Tomas laughed at his scream as he thundered past. Two more fell much the same way. The Sword of War was light in his hands and it snaked out right to left and back again, felling another three. The charge had been stopped by the indomitable Valkyries and Tomas came up behind the rear guard, which was desperately trying to turn and flee. Storm raised himself up to his full height and took one rider out of his saddle straightaway as his hooves connected under his chin. There was a sickening crack as his boneless body hurtled through the air in almost slow motion. Storm hammered his hooves into the bodies and backs of those too slow or foolish to move out of his way. Tomas held on and laughed all the more, riding as though he were at some medieval rodeo, and by the time Storm dropped down Tomas came face to face with Treya and her bloody Valkyries. Not a rider was left standing from their encounter. Tomas looked eagerly left and right for more, but as he discovered that there were no more, sanity gradually reasserted itself. Panting as the adrenaline too faded from his body, Tomas saw the last straggler taken down by a Valkyrie's axe separating his head from his body. Tomas watched it bounce surreally across the bloody battlefield and come to rest incongruously against a tiny bunch of poppies that had survived the onslaught. The juxtaposed sight brought him fully back to his senses. Tomas surveyed the carnage as his memory repeated his own actions back to him. What was he becoming? That laughing maniac wasn't him. He had always been cold and dispassionate about killing, not this. Something within him relished the bloodshed and craved more. It disturbed him but before he could wallow in his introspection any more, Ingrid and

Treya trotted their pegasi up alongside him.

'Are you some sort of sorcerer?' Ingrid asked, with no post-battle small talk. Straight in there, all business. 'You fight well, yet you use strange weapons that come and go along with your armor. What are you, Tomas? What are you not telling us?'

'I expect there are a lot of things I'm not telling you, Ingrid, many of which are unimportant in the grand scheme of things. What I fight with and in are two such things. Do I ask you where you get your weapons, how you came about your armor, or why you seem so permanently pissed off at everything? No I don't, because it's your business and it doesn't affect the job at hand. The moment it does, you'll be the first to know. In the meantime a thanks wouldn't go amiss.'

Ingrid looked at Tomas with undisguised fury, made all the worse as Tomas turned his back on her and rode off. He was too angry to speak coherently and he needed a few moments to get himself under control. *Bloody gratitude for you. It wasn't that I wanted any thanks – I didn't bloody well do it for that – but it's the goddamn fucking principle. Argh, ungrateful cow,* Tomas muttered to himself all the way back to the treeline, where other Valkyries were bringing in their own dead and wounded. They had lost a total of seven and another four had non-fatal wounds, including Hildreth. Not bad, really, against almost a hundred men. They certainly lived up to their reputation, but that aside, for all that they were superb fighters and would have made equally good allies, he decided to leave them alone and make his own way. Just as soon as he found Niall.

'What did you say to him, Ingrid? He looked distinctly unhappy when he rode off.'

'What makes you think I said anything to him?'

Treya narrowed her gaze at her old friend, which said she knew damn well Ingrid had spoken to him. Ingrid was as incapable of keeping a thought in her head without having to voice it as the she was from breathing.

'I only asked him about his weapons. And whether he was some sort of sorcerer,' Ingrid responded, a little sheepishly.

'That was all you could think to say? Did you not see how he fought? Nor how many of our sisters he saved by his actions?'

But at this, Ingrid regained some of her fire and spat back viciously, 'Damn him, Treya. Were it not for him all our sisters would still be alive. He brings danger down upon us and you defend him?' she asked incredulously.

'What makes you so certain it was him they were after? It is well known that we frequent this forest and there are many who would see us destroyed.'

Ingrid agreed but argued all the same with her view as she saw it. 'Yes, but be that as it may, those who would see an end to us would not be so pathetic as to send human mercenaries, least not so few as them. You do yourself an injustice, Treya – '

But her friend had heard enough. She was watching Tomas ride back and knew he was leaving. She didn't know how; she just knew it. She had to stop him.

'Enough, Ingrid. I hear you, but I'm tired of listening to you. You grow harder and harder each day. Be careful you don't get too brittle and shatter, my friend. Now go help the rest tend to the fallen. We have a ceremony to conduct.'

Without waiting for a reply, Treya turned her pegasus and lifted slightly off the ground to glide the distance to where Tomas sought his friend.

Treya caught up with the dour crimson-cloaked man amongst the trees. She watched him at first, before making herself known as he tended to Hildreth. He said something and she laughed, albeit weakly. Treya smiled to herself as she watched this stranger tend to her own people as though they were his own. He didn't bear any apparent ill-will towards them despite Ingrid's best efforts. In fact the rest seemed to warm to him slightly as he smiled easily and joked with them in an effort to raise post-battle spirits. He was a warrior and had been in conflicts before – she could see that – but for all his competence and obvious battle capability, there was still something dark and dangerous about him. It both bothered her and attracted her in equal measure. It had been a very long time since any man had intrigued her. Most were only worthy of contempt and this upsurging of emotion concerned her just as much as the danger he posed. She almost let him ride off as she lost herself momentarily in her own reverie. He had found Niall, pulled him up behind him and had begun to trot his mount away from the Valkyries. Treya had to be quick; she ran to her own pegasus and leapt up with the practised agility of one used to doing so. Heeling her steed, she took off after Tomas.

'Wait!' She called to the back of the man. She saw him stiffen at her voice, but he ignored her request and continued onwards. If anything, he picked up the pace slightly.

'Tomas, please.' The plaintive note to her voice was the key in his bringing Storm to a stop. He turned to look at her quizzically, unsure as to why she was there and what caused her to sound so peculiar. She had been colder than a penguin's butt earlier and it was only curiosity that caused Tomas to stop. Niall just clung to Tomas's midriff as though were he to fall, it would be forever. Treya ignored him as she reined in next to Tomas. He watched her as she obviously struggled with what she wanted to say. Eventually she looked up at him and the eyes that met his weren't cold at all.

'I'm sorry for Ingrid, Tomas, really. She has issues that cause her to be the way she is, and habits as ingrained as hers are hard to shake.'

Tomas's look said 'Really?' And Treya knew she would have to do better than that.

'It isn't easy, Tomas. We've been here for longer than many of us can remember and we've had to fight for most of that time, against one foe or another. We will not be subject to any ruler, not even the lord of this land, whoever he may be. It is not our world and it is not our choice to be here. We have one lord and while his eyes are turned against us, alone we remain. Allies here are few and far between, even the tenuous alliance we presently find ourselves within. Of that I will tell you more later if I can convince you to stay and help us.'

Tomas was finding it hard to stay angry with her. 'Why should I? When at least one of you wants me dead or thinks I'm some sort of infiltrator at best; a harbinger of doom and death at the worst. Like a bloody albatross.'

'Ingrid, I know. Like I said, she has issues. Back where we call home is, or was at least – it's been a while – was often a dangerous place to be. Feuds and conflict were a way of life and regularly whole villages were put to the sword for an imagined slight to someone's honor. Ingrid was a victim of such an act. I was fourteen summers and she was twelve when I rode out on my first patrol as a shield maiden of the Valkyrie Host. Ingrid's village had been attacked and she had watched as her parents were butchered before her eyes. She attacked the man who did it and it took five men to prise her from his cold corpse. She fought them too, but they nigh on beat her to death and that was only after using her for several hours. It was her rage and tenaciousness that kept the attackers there long enough for us to happen upon them. We killed every last one of them and took Ingrid with us. That's the short version, and she has been with us ever since. She has never lost her hatred of men for what they did to her and her family. I have trouble blaming her for that. Were I in her shoes, I'd probably feel the same.'

She watched Tomas's reaction to the tale and saw compassion ignite within. There was a nobility inside of him that abhorred such treatment of women, even ones who could look after themselves. She thought it quaint and reminiscent of the knights of old. *Chivalry and gallantry: you don't see much of that these days*, she thought idly as she studied him 'But times such as this are particularly painful for her, and if you return with me you will see why. I have to be present shortly for the ceremony for our dead. I'd like you to be there as well. So too would many of my sisters, I think. You made an impression on them. I believe they even like you. Like a pet, I suppose. Anyway, the majority holds sway here; plus,' Treya added with humor in her melodious voice, 'I'll protect you from Ingrid.'

Tomas laughed then, rich and full of mirth. Treya too laughed and the moment lifted slightly.

'Okay, you win. I'll come back for the ceremony, then you can tell me about this alliance you are part of.'

Treya smiled then, wide and genuinely pleased. 'Done. Now shall we go? I expect they'll be wondering where I am.'

The ride back was quiet. Each had their own thoughts to contend with and some were more confused than others. But upon arrival back at the campsite, Tomas was instantly aware of two things. First was the sombre mood of the Valkyries, for they had laid out their dead, in a line, with their cloaks folded over them as their shroud. Standing over each one was their pegasus. The second thing Tomas saw was the huge white raven. It was perched on a low hanging branch at the forest edge. Its dazzling white plumage and vibrant blue eyes were a stark contrast to the dark browns and deep greens of the trees beyond it. It cawed loudly when it saw him and lifted off the branch. It flapped lazily as it ghosted across the clearing towards him. *Towards him?* The thought suddenly occurred to Tomas to hold up his arm for the bird. He did and the raven landed lightly upon it as though Tomas were a veteran falconer. The women watched him in obvious awe and wonder as the raven sidled up his arm and squatted upon his shoulder. Tomas didn't know what to do, so he just sat there in case it pecked him with that bloody great beak that clacked and wavered beside his face. Caw Caw, it barked in his ear. *Hmmm.*

'You are honored, truly, Tomas, for one of the Hraefn to bless you, especially a Lunhraefn. I for one thought they were just myth. Never did I think I would live to see one with my own eyes, but we live in strange times and they grow stranger daily, truly.'

'I'll say.' Tomas eyed the corvid upon his shoulder warily and it eyed him back in its own inimical fashion, but beyond that, it showed no signs of hostility, seemingly content to just sit there.

'What the bloody hell is a...a what did you call it?' Tomas tried to recall what she had named it but he couldn't get his tongue around the pronunciation.

'Lunhraefn. Moon Raven. For that is where my people believe the white ravens come from. Some even believed that they were not even ravens at all but another race altogether, for not even Odin could command the Lunhraefn. They came and went with their own agendas.'

At this, the bird cawed loudly, right next to Tomas's ear, making him wince. It was as though the bird knew it was being discussed.

'Time moves on, Tomas, and we must complete the ceremony, strange bird or not. I do ask this though, that no matter what you see, do not interfere, I beg you.'

Tomas agreed and he backed Storm up several feet to a more unobtrusive spot. The raven never moved but Tomas did feel its claws grip him tighter as it stabilized itself as he moved.

From his vantage point Tomas could see all the fallen and their mounts standing over them. Through all the time they had spent talking and preparing, the pegasi had been nuzzling their fallen soul mates and whickering softly. The sound began to carry to him as the Valkyries grew silent, and it brought a lump to his throat; and tears sprang unbidden to his eyes at the mournful sound. Tomas felt an incredible sadness wash over him and it occurred to him that he was to witness something very rarely seen, and he felt privileged. He watched closely, but still didn't notice at first, that steam had begun to rise from the pegasi, as though they had just had an extensive workout. But it grew and grew until with no warning, they burst into violet flame. The pegasi screamed in agony as the flames took hold. It was so fast that Tomas couldn't have reacted even if he had been able to, paralyzed as he was by the scene before him. He saw their flesh char and peel back as the flames consumed them, still screaming, eyes wide and rolling as they lowered their heads and ignited the cloaks of their riders. The pegasi dropped to their knees and soon collapsed over their blazing partners. Tomas's own heart even stopped momentarily with an overwhelming sadness as one of the pegasi looked him straight in the eye as it blazed. Hotter and hotter it grew and brighter as well, both in equal intensity, until Tomas had to avert his eyes. But no sooner had he closed them than the heat died away. He looked up to see nothing but several piles of ash, which the wind picked up and dispersed until even that was gone. Tomas had no words; it was all he could do to not scream out his sorrow. Never in his entire life had he seen anything so pitifully sad and tragic as that. It would have broken his heart were it not already shattered. *How do they stand it, knowing this is what happens?* Though he did get his voice back, eventually, after the rest of the wounded Valkyries had been helped to the backs of their mounts and the whole group was ready to move off. Treya moved up alongside.

'What just happened?' Tomas's look of horror told her how he had been affected. 'That has to be the most horrific thing I've ever seen, ever, as well as the most poignant. Does that happen every time?'

Treya nodded solemnly. Her voice echoed the sadness. 'When a Valkyrie reaches an age where she can ride, usually about four or five, she bonds with her steed. She is there at its birth and they share the first breath together. From that moment on, they are bound together by more than just mutual love. You've seen what happens when a rider dies; their steed sacrifices itself to join them.'

'What happens if the pegasus should die first?' Truth be told, after what he had just seen, he wasn't sure he really wanted to know, but the question was out there now.

'You've heard of tales of the banshee and other vengeful spirits? Well, part of that is based in fact. It's not all mischievous elementals. Something snaps within the Valkyrie and she mourns so hard that the bond within her turns poisonous and, although it eventually consumes her, she becomes a wild thing. Deadly and dangerous. She flees all reminders of her soul mate, but her grief makes her so unstable that she kills anyone who comes close to her or she happens upon. They roam the desolate lands, avoiding people where they can, for the poison within changes them physically too. They become something ugly and lethal. It's not pleasant, but such is the bond we share, we accept the risks involved. Such is the risk with all relationships, I believe.' Treya looked deadly serious and quite sincere.

'Bloody hell, woman, I think not. People don't go up in flames, writhing

in agony when someone leaves them, though it might feel like it for a while.'
Tomas instantly recalled his own recent loss, where he *actually had*, in fact,
gone up in flames as the explosion ripped his future from him. The memory
burned as hot and bright as the day it happened. 'I assure you it's not the
same. They get over it and move on. Hopefully wiser and a little stronger –
though...' Tomas looked away, his face turned blank and distant, '...who am
I to say? I've had my own shit to deal with so maybe I'm talking out of my
arse anyway.'

Treya saw something else then. It was fleeting as Tomas turned away,
but she caught a glimpse of his own sorrow and pain. And it seemed considerable. But before she could ask him about it, Ingrid rode up, looking as stern
and angry as before. Her sudden arrival and abrupt stop caused the raven to
lift off Tomas, cawing in a most annoyed fashion and flapping off to a nearby
branch to glare at her. *Good taste. Bird. I see she gets under your skin too.*

'We should go, and fast. This delay has already cost us dearly; we do
not want to risk losing any more of our number because of this man. Those
warriors may have had friends, a lot of friends, and they may be merely a
scouting party to flush us out.'

Tomas looked hard at Ingrid but she wasn't impressed. She had grown
up around Viking warriors who fazed her not at all. He stood little chance,
though she did cast a look of trepidation towards the raven that had perched
upon his shoulder until she turned up, watching events unfold with its raven's
gaze. Ingrid spoke to Tomas directly then, for the first time in a while.

'I still believe we should have killed you while you slept. For all your
skill with a sword, I would sooner have you dead than my sisters.' With that,
she turned her mount and rejoined the others, barking out orders and getting
them moving. Even Niall had a horse now. After the ceremony, one of the
Valkyries had rounded up a horse from the dead attackers and proffered it
to him. He didn't know how to ride, so Ingrid shadowed him and kept him
upright as he grew used to it. Tomas watched her for a while, just as Treya
watched him. Angry as he was at her adamant refusal to accept that he was

who he said he was and not some foul spy, Tomas knew he couldn't leave things the way they were: it would only fester and be even harder to resolve later. With one eye on the raven, still unsure of its motives and why it had taken such a shine to him, Tomas heeled Storm to catch up with Ingrid. Meantime, Treya watched closely. She valued her friend's opinion and her judge of character. For even though it may seem she had a bias considering her earlier abuse, she had good instincts, assuming she could get past her own suspicious nature. Tomas caught up with her and trotted Storm beside her as they entered the forest proper and began their journey to wherever it was they were taking him. He didn't speak straightaway, just rode beside her. He knew, perversely, that it would annoy her into talking to him, which he guessed was the last thing she really wanted to do.

'What do you want? You obviously want something because I'm sure I'm the last person you want to ride next to, and you are certainly the last person I want near me.'

'You're probably right on one of those points, but I hope to change even that. Look, I know why you hate men as much as you do...' Ingrid spun her head around so fast to cast daggers from her eyes at her so-called friend and sister – who had obviously divulged her past to this man – that she nearly snapped her own neck in the process. A heartbeat later she turned her blazing gaze back to Tomas and he was thankful looks couldn't kill, otherwise there wouldn't be enough left of him to shovel into a jiffy bag. '...but,' he continued bravely, 'I'm not them. A lot of men aren't them. And I appreciate that the saying "What doesn't kill you only makes you stronger" doesn't help with the nightmares. But if there is half the woman in there that I think there is, you'll know that I'm telling the truth. It would be easier by far if I was actually what you want me to be. Because I'm not, however, it means you have to accept that the fire that has driven you so long is lacking fuel, and that's hard. Accepting there might actually be people out there who can genuinely be who they claim, and even like you for what you are, not what you think you are or should be.' Tomas didn't know if that made any sense to her: it barely made any to him. He wasn't good with this sort of stuff as a rule. Ingrid fixed her deep, earthy brown eyes on his and he felt he was being turned inside out as she stared long and hard at him, but she still hadn't spoken any more. He evidently hadn't finished.

'You are at war, so am I. I even think we are on the same side. But in war, as it has always been, unfortunately, people die for all manner of ridiculous reasons. Your sisters didn't die in vain. They saved an innocent life and one slightly not so innocent. Niall back there, whoever he is, didn't ask for this. Nor did I. But if good people do nothing, evil wins without any resistance. What you did was valiant and brave and pointless. Such is the reasoning of war.'

Ingrid looked away from him then and turned her gaze to the forest path before them, but not before Tomas saw tears well up, which she tried to conceal from him. He said nothing about them and continued talking to her, hopeful he had broken through a wall, though there were still many more to go.

'We have all lost friends and family. I know how hard it is for you to trust someone you have only just met. We haven't had years of bonding and fellowship and on top of that, I'm a man. Not another woman like your sisters. I make you uncomfortable I know, but try to consider me like a brother. As a fellow soldier, were you in my regiment and we found ourselves in a situation much as we did earlier, know this Ingrid, I would die for you without a thought. Loyalty, trust and honor – they are watchwords for me and my kind. I'm betting they mean something to you too. All I ask, Ingrid…' At this point, Tomas gambled his safety and reached out to put a gentle hand upon her forearm as she held her reins, knowing it would reinforce his words three hundred per cent, '…is that you give Niall and myself a chance. A chance to prove to you we are true friends and on the same side. Please, Ingrid, it would mean a great deal. Not just to me but to Treya too. She has faith in you.'

Tomas knew desperate measures warranted desperate acts, so he wasn't averse to throwing in a bit of emotional leverage to help tip matters. He held her arm for a few moments longer than necessary, letting it all sink in before sitting back and shutting up. Tomas wheeled Storm around and silently trotted back to his place in the line, leaving her to mull things over. In fact, on further thought, he pulled out of the line altogether, stopping as the line of Valkyries trotted past him. A few smiles came his way from the women. Some even made him blush as they looked at him with something other than war on their minds. He felt distinctly grubby by the time they had all passed and Niall came trotting along. He was taking a gamble but the effect would be worth the trouble, and if it backfired then he was no worse off than when he arrived.

'Tell Treya I'm sorry. I tried with Ingrid but I don't hold out much hope. I'll move faster on my own anyway, and they'll be safer too if those warriors were after me. You stay with them, Niall. I'm heading back to the clearing to see what I can learn from the dead warriors before moving on,' he said, as the little man started to object and protest. 'No really, Niall, you'll be much safer with them than with me, considering where I'm going. You definitely won't want to be with me then. Good luck, my friend, and may whatever gods you look to, go with you.' Tomas reached over and clapped Niall affectionately on the shoulder and took his hand in his, shaking it warmly. Tomas winked once more conspiratorially at him, and melted back into the forest. Turning Storm, Tomas made his way back to the clearing. It wasn't easy going through the thicker forest, avoiding the path. From the corner of his eye, he could see the raven darting through the branches above him, the huge ghostly white bird keeping pace. An hour later saw him back where they had started from, at the edge of the vast clearing. As Tomas broke cover, though not without adapting his cloak to camouflage him with the background, even Storm darkened his coat to that of a deep gunmetal grey so he didn't clash with his surroundings. Tomas patted the big horse affectionately, praising him for being a good friend and more intelligent than many people he knew. Tomas looked out at the fallen warriors, who were still where they had left them, though there were signs of scavengers already sharing out their flesh. As the white raven broke cover behind him and glided out over the battlefield, a cloud of carrion birds lifted off and flapped angrily away, cawing and screeching at being disturbed.

I expect Niall's broken the news to Treya by now. Now one of two things will happen and there's nothing to do for the moment but wait and see. So Tomas gave Storm another pat down and sent him swirling, wraithlike, back to the brand upon his shoulder. Finding a good tree that afforded an equally good view of the clearing – both where the Valkyries might emerge and where the attackers had come from – Tomas clambered up and pulled his ghillie cloak around him and faded from view. Were it not for the bloody great white raven perched nearby, they would never know he was even there, let alone see him – even if one of them were to climb the same tree. As Tomas mused how useful this would have been when he was sniping, he glared at the raven. Tomas's glare washed off it like so much water off the proverbial duck's back and all the time it sat there, calmly preening. He even tried shooing it away. *Sod off, will you, you bloody great lump. Sitting there, I might as well have a big neon sign over my head.* But it just looked at him with one sapphire eye and cawed once, as if to say 'Shut up and mind your own business; can't you see I'm busy?' But strangely, as though it knew his mind, it began to slowly fade away, becoming, eventually, as translucent as a real ghost. Tomas could still make it out but he could see the trees beyond it – through it. *Nice one! Thanks for that; maybe you're not so bad after all.* Tomas was struck by the fact that it probably *was* more intelligent than it appeared so he moderated his tone and offered it the same respect he had for Storm. *After all, it hasn't done me any harm and has actually been of service. More use than many people I know.* So with a final nod to his apparent new companion, Tomas returned to his vigil. *I'll be starting my own bloody zoo at this rate. Whatever next?*

Thankfully, he didn't have as long to wait as he feared. Mentally, he had given them until the sun rose again before commencing with his journey but he barely had time to get comfortable before Treya burst into the clearing, followed by a worried looking Niall, hanging on to his horse for grim death, and he was followed by a furious looking and muttering Ingrid. The rest followed in due course until they all were back where they had started. Tomas was impressed. He couldn't hear what was being said but he could see Ingrid's mouth working vigorously and Treya was shaking her head every now and again until she too turned and barked something at Ingrid that silenced her abruptly, though it didn't stop her face looking like thunder. He guessed that even Valkyries sulk.

'Tomas!' Treya shouted in to the evening air. Somehow she was either more astute than he gave her credit for or she was simply hoping that he would be here still. *Time to make an entrance*, Tomas thought as he dropped from his vantage point and walked out into the clearing, materializing as if from thin air as he did so.

'Why not shout a bit louder. I'm sure that there are no more of these mercenary scum lurking anywhere nearby. Can you say the same, yelling out like that?'

Treya didn't look overly startled at his mysterious appearance but she did look concerned slightly at the thought of alerting further enemies to their presence. *What am I doing? He's just a man, for Odin's sake. Making me make stupid mistakes like that.* She removed her helm and ran her fingers through her damp hair, a gesture he had seen many a time from leaders who had more on their plate than they really wanted. As he walked towards them, Storm reappeared, mistlike and amorphous; coalescing into his shape and walking beside Tomas as he walked. Tomas mounted fluidly, hardly breaking stride and – just to add to the impact – the moment he was settled in the saddle, the Lunhraefn also reappeared and glided down to settle majestically upon Tomas's shoulder as though it had been doing it for years. *Now that's gotta look impressive. I don't care who sees that.* He stopped a few feet in front of Treya and waited, seeing if she had any more to say. He hoped so. It would have been a futile ride back otherwise.

'Join our cause, Tomas. There is an aura of destiny about you. One that interweaves with us in ways I do not begin to understand, but I also believe that clarity will come with time and all the questions will be answered. Ingrid has something to say to you also. Please be patient with her.' Treya glared over at her second with a look that would have frozen the very air around them. 'Haven't you, Ingrid!'

Ingrid, for her part, looked like an animal caught in a trap and resigned to the fact that there was no way out without chewing off a limb. 'Join us, Tomas. I'm... I'm... Treya, please,' Ingrid implored her friend and leader. But all she got was an unsympathetic glare that was several degrees colder than the first one.

'Tomas!' Ingrid started again, 'I'm sorry. I'll give you and Niall a chance. There, I've said it, now can we go before someone really does come spoiling for another fight?' Tomas tried to look serious and moody but failed miserably and he burst out laughing. His smile lessened the impact of his humor and he moved up alongside Ingrid and held out his hand. She took it tentatively, looking first at it then at him. Finally she gripped his wrist and he pulled her towards him. The unexpected move caught her unawares and she nearly toppled from her mount. Tomas caught her and planted a fleeting kiss upon her cheek, then prudently backed away before she drew her sword.

'Friends then,' Tomas said as he moved towards Treya to do similarly, though he figured she would be wiser to the trick and be ready for him. He held out his hand the same way. She reached out stiffly, her body braced for any foolhardy gestures like he had made to Ingrid, though she did find that amusing, imagining what she must be thinking after such a daring act. Their wrists came together and Tomas gripped her arm, feeling the sudden warmth of her skin, even through her gauntlets. Then he made a monumental mistake. He knew it was a mistake the moment he did it, but he couldn't help himself. It was like being detached from yourself and watching your mouth work without your control. A distant part of his mind said *Don't do it!* Tomas looked into her eyes. Something held him there and he was only dimly aware of the other Valkyries around him. Tomas realized something then – that this woman could never look more beautiful than she did at that moment, her hand in his and a slight sheen to her tanned skin giving her a glow that transfixed him. He would be quite happy to sit there and gaze into those eyes until he grew old and died. Something was wrong though. Treya's mouth fell open and her eyes widened in shock. She looked as though he had drawn his sword and plunged it into her. For the first time since meeting her, he saw her composure slip and color blossom in her cheeks. Thoughts assailed him and then, with the weight of a small planet, the vital realization hit him. He had just said that out loud. *Oh my God, what have I done now? What is it with my bloody great big mouth? Why won't it keep whatever might be going on in my head to its bloody self? Why do I have to keep blurting stuff out that just embarrasses us both? I'm definitely losing it. God! What will I do next? No. Shit. That doesn't bear thinking about. Put it out of your mind, Tom old son, worry about this. You're already in enough shit to drown the Bismarck.* If matters weren't bad enough, they both saw at the same time that they still held on to each other. Both looked down then up and then let go of the other as though an electric current scorched through the connection. Tomas's mouth moved but no sound emerged. What could he say? Not that he hadn't said enough already. Treya turned quickly away and began to bark orders to get the Valkyries underway. Tomas saw Niall smiling mischievously at him. That didn't help. Nor did the fact that the only other sound he could hear was the other Valkyries all laughing at their leader's expense like it was the greatest joke ever.

Chapter Thirteen

Escalation

Tomas's arrival in the Domain hadn't gone as entirely unnoticed as he would have liked, for what Tomas didn't know beyond what the Horseman had told him – which was sketchy at best – was that when any portal was opened anywhere, it left a specific energy signature, an echo of sorts. Much like a ghost or what most people perceive as ghosts. Tomas had taken metaphysics at school and found it fascinating for a short time before discovering the wonder of guns. He had read that when a person's living molecules stop vibrating and the charge or life force as such leaves them, the echo of that vibration continues for an immeasurable period of time. The magnetic wavelength or signal of that now deceased person finds itself drawn to strong electromagnetic areas with a similar wavelength or resonance to theirs. Often as not they are areas of significance. Trauma, sudden and painful death or where something has been repeated thus creating the greatest memory or at least strongest one at the point of death. An example as was cited was where perhaps a group mind such as a regiment of marching Romans patroled repeatedly or the Earth's magnetic fields are strong there and of a similar frequency. So many factors impact and are required to manifest one of these visions that scientifically predicting them or instigating them is virtually impossible. It had given Tomas pause for thought on many an occasion about how these resonating

519

spectres of their former selves are drawn to certain areas like magnets; and as time is relative, subject to where and when anything is in the multiverse, it could resonate for what humanity would call eternity irrespective of any environmental change.

However, in this case, the portal Tomas fell through left a degrading haze of similarly displaced energy which emanated at a unique frequency all of its own, much like a fingerprint or DNA, leaving a faint trace like so much radiation. And just like degrading radiation, it can be detected. Thus any being skilled in either the mystical arts or possessing the ability to track such things, would be alerted to it. Unlike radiation though, those who were expert on these things could not only identify the where and when of the portal, but the who and the how, identifying its source. For though there were few left on the Earth who were capable of such a feat – and that was few, not none – for as sure as the sun rose each day, there were individuals abroad upon the Earth who as far as mankind was concerned, had no business being there; and they are capable of many fantastic and terrifying things, things rarely spoken of except in hushed tones or in the darkest of corners. That fact, however, was more than compensated for within the Domain. The majority of the ruling lords were capable of sensing portals, and those lesser beings that were able to open them, albeit with tremendous strain and effort, could feel their presence also. But in this instance, it wasn't either of those who caught the scent of the opening of such a portal. The slight and subtle aroma of electrically charged air and burnt ozone was the only residue left hanging in the air, and one other specific element, that of *magic* – which caught another's attention. The beasts that sniffed the air now and ran unerringly to the location with the predatory speed of creatures built for such activity were something else altogether. They were the Hounds of Fenris: enormous, powerfully muscled werebeasts, as humanity would learn to call them. Averaging nine feet to the shoulder – some bigger – they were the best and the worst from both species: an unholy fusion of man and wolf, powerfully built, yet faster than anything that walked either world. Known for their endurance and ferocity, they could run for days without tiring and still fight a pitched battle upon arrival. Little escaped them if they were hunting it.

These massive coarse-haired creatures – with hair cum fur, thick and wiry, much like that of a wild boar, acting almost as a protective layer, making them hard to hold and which was thick enough to even turn the blows of many weapons – were presently loping across the grasslands with phenomenal speed, their long bony feet gripping the terrain and propelling them so fast it looked as though they almost flew from time to time, then occasionally switching between two and four legs, at which time they resumed a more bestial appearance. Their large ears laid back against their thick skulls; lupine muzzles stretched forward, nostrils flaring to catch every scent the air had to offer and lips pulled back to show row after row of razor canines, coated in saliva and fetid drool, cascading from their maws as they ran. But it was the eyes that differentiated these from mere beasts: sentient, aware and very human, giving off a subtle crimson glow. Eyes that concealed a brutal and malevolent intelligence. And much like the humans that many of these creatures were recruited from, they exhibited various levels of that intelligence.

This particular group of hounds had been drawn to the outpouring of energy that was the result of Tomas falling into the Domain. What they found, at the bottom of a small incline, which led up to a small copse of willow, hazel and beech trees, was the dead and bloating bodies of several bounty hunters. This was primarily a scouting pack and food had been scarce on their journey, so the leader of the pack allowed his group to feed. It wasn't pretty or satisfying, as they tore into the softening flesh and disgorged the cool entrails and internal organs – for they much preferred fresh, warm and preferably still living meat, pulsing with warm, energizing blood – but the hungry can't afford to be fussy. And soon enough, the grass was matted with the black congealed blood of the ravaged dead.

The leader of this pack was of marginally higher intelligence than the rest, which didn't exactly elevate it, hence its rank as pack leader, but it needed to make a choice and this one taxed its limited mind to its extremes. Their lord Fenris needed to know what they had found – that was their imperative – but they also needed to maintain the scent connection before it faded any more, which it almost had. So, with great difficulty, brow furrowed and the strain showing visibly, it made a choice. Growling its orders in a guttural language that only they understood, it sent one of the pack back with the news of the discovery and to obtain fresh orders – while the leader, and those four remaining, picked up on the scent, absorbing all they could from the tenuous and fading discharge. Ensuring the pack and the messenger all knew what they had to do; they each in turn set off to find whatever had arrived in their world and wrought such indiscriminate and bloody carnage.

Their lord would be unforgiving if a deadly enemy had arrived – one who could kill this many humans and vanish without a trace – and he wasn't told about it; and the leader felt it prudent that someone other than him deliver such news. He wasn't *that* stupid; that was *why* he was pack leader. Fenris wasn't known for his patience or mercy when he heard something he didn't like. Though had the pack *actually* known who it was who had fallen through into their territory – for though they were skilled in tracking they lacked the finely honed ability of an arch demon to identify the source and who exactly passed through the portal other than vague impressions – of course had they been able, they would have battled the entire Celestial Host to bring back the head and heart as proof of death of the hated one, Tomas Walker, a mortal the Adversary and their lord Fenris wanted dead. Both wanted him most urgently too. Such ignorance had brought Tomas a brief respite even if it was one he was oblivious to. He might have rung a gong announcing his arrival in the Domain and even signed it *Tomas was here*, but those who chased him couldn't metaphorically read, so they just knew someone dangerous and capable had arrived, not who. It is said ignorance is bliss. In this case it was life saving. It would be enough to give angels nightmares knowing the Hounds of Fenris sought their death. Brutal, violent killing machines with no compassion, conscience or compunction about ripping someone's head off and tearing their spine out for simply being in their vicinity. Whole villages and small towns had been known to fall to their rapacious attacks simply for being in their way. It was the human attribute that made them more terrifying, for like cats, humans tend to enjoy playing with their prey before killing it. The hounds enjoyed inflicting pain; it helped them to forget their own constant agonies. For the transformation left a hound in a state of constant pain. Acts of torture and cruelty were like morphine to them. The more they did it, the greater the release, yet the more they did it, the greater they needed to continue doing it. Like any narcotic, freedom from pain drove even the strongest to succumb.

The last time Fenris was free, many thousands of years before, he had begun to amass a force in preparation for a titanic battle, and before his premature incarceration by his family there were several hundred hounds, loyal to Fenris, left existing upon the Earth when he disappeared. Left to fend for themselves, they had to learn to adapt and hide themselves from those who would destroy them for who they were. Earth history made many references to the Wolf Lord, for his influence was widely felt, though cultural variations renamed and reshaped him. But there was no disguising the dark malevolence and the fear this creature extracted from its followers. Anubis for the Egyptians, the jackal headed guardian of the dead; Coyote for the Native Americans; Fenris to others; and even the Christians tried to advocate that their mortal enemy, the Antichrist, would allegedly be spawned from a jackal. However, humanity's myth and legend pales into a paltry insignificance against the sheer horror, malignant ambition and raw evil of the timeless and ultimate survivor that was the Wolf Lord himself.

Their extraordinarily long lives allowed them the time – at least those that survived – to learn the ways of man and blend themselves better into his world. Shape-shifting, an innate ability, was their only real defense from persecution. Yet initially, it was hard to maintain a human form due to their violent nature, and more than a few slipped – letting humanity learn of their dangerous existence, and who subsequently made a valiant yet futile attempt to wipe them out where and when they could – not an easy task even then. So, like all ancient tales, and these were no exception, they passed into legend as they were handed down and invariably spread out by word of mouth. This is the birth of many a myth and as it changes and twists over the centuries, some turning into books, others being irrevocably lost, the fear that originally motivated these stories becomes diluted and they simply become tall tales to scare children. For there was very little moral fibre to be had from them. Mortalkind soon succumbed to their one great weakness: the loss of that fear through complacency and their inherent arrogance. To lose such fear was a mistake that humanity was about to both regret and reacquaint itself with.

The diluted blood of Fenris still runs in many souls who live upon the Earth, for those early shape-shifters bred with mortals and a few, alive today, even know what they are. But they were no longer the savages that the newly released Fenris spawned, like those that hunted the Domain. These modern beings considered their condition a burden and fought their nature with every cell and molecule of their being. Some who struggled with this, found release in warring and many joined the military of whatever era they lived in. Excelling in battle and ferocity, they soon rose through their ranks and many became great leaders and even kings. It was somewhere they could put their special skills to a more practical use. Others accepted the call of the wild in a more passive way and the enhanced abilities their blood gave them allowed them to find an affinity for nature that few could match, but they also understood and accepted their darker side, suppressing it where they could but aware of what they were capable of if pushed too far.

As is the way with many of the myths that arose around the planet concerning these dark, misunderstood and fell creatures, most of them were pure nonsense. Silver bullets and full moon transformations are two such fallacies. Granted, the lunar cycle accentuated their awareness, heightened their senses and increased their savagery. Being partially subject to the powerful electromagnetic influences between the two giant magnets that are the moon and the core of the Earth, which between them push and pull the waters within all life forms – and the increase in this electromagnetic energy – causes surges of power to course unchecked through these individuals more so than many other creratures, and sometimes the effects are destructive and devastating.

With others it is creative and enlightening. History was rife with these *lunatics*, those believed to be subject to the moon's influence – an archaic tag but one that stuck, for humanity likes to categorize that which it fears or cannot understand, even if it has to utilize a medieval and superstitious reference to do it. But usually it was for the wrong reasons, albeit convenient on occasion.

There were those who lived and hid on the Earth who tended to be more of the loner variety, hoping they would be left in peace, but ironically that was no protection – quite the opposite in fact – for to live alone was considered dubious and suspicious, even now. The inquisitions and witch hunts that scoured the land, hunting and tormenting these poor souls and putting many more to the flame, reduced their number all the more. Fire could kill the gifted as easily as any mortal. Those that survived those dreadful years went so far underground then, that they managed to drop off the radar of humanity altogether for a time. Unfortunately, times change and an unconscious awakening was taking place throughout the entire multiverse – at a time when humanity was balanced precariously upon a knife edge of its own forging, the blade sinking in and the droplets of blood gaining momentum as they slid down the razor edge. Such an awakening was having disastrous consequences on a global scale that was unprecedented. And it was only due to get worse. Much, much worse.

Being of pure stock, spawned from the lord Fenris himself, the pack mentality amongst those in the Domain was strong, as it was intended to be, not diluted like those miserable wretches on Earth, and those that hunted the Domain were fully of that pack mind. The Hounds that discovered Tomas's entry point were a pack. There were six beasts to a pack, three packs to a hunt and one hundred hunts to a scourge. Presently, within the Domain at the command of the Wolf Lord Fenris, there was just shy of two thousand scourge. And their numbers grew daily. Soon they would be looking for more food. Interestingly enough, the ancient name of Man finds its roots in the word Manna and Moon; in recent scriptures the term manna is applied to divine food. Wrongly considered to be food *from* the gods *to* man, it was actually that *man* was the food of the gods. This is one of the many misinterpretations humanity has deluded itself with and it was only through the guardianship and protection of the Ch'drnOmThophilim, Drakarim, Unc'anharaphim and the Four Horsemen, that humanity was not wiped out in its infancy by those who would see the Covenant destroyed, and mortalkind along with it. Man had been so long under the impression he was at the top of the food chain, it was going to come as quite a shock when he dropped several rungs.

Fenris was of the reasoning that in order to take his rightful place as one of the ruling lords of the newly formed empire when the Adversary finally succeeded, he would again need an impressive army. Who knew, maybe an accident would befall the Adversary. After all, it was risky endeavor he was undertaking and it would take somebody with strength and power to step into the breach left by such a tragic occurrence. This thought rarely left the mind of the ever scheming Wolf Lord.

In order to maintain his newly found and ingratiated status, Fenris was assisting the Adversary in policing the Domain. For until the Adversary had grown in power sufficiently to rule with the divine authority Lucifer possessed, an authority that had him connected, more or less, to every part of his world, even though there were pockets within the Domain where Lucifer's awareness didn't reach, they were considered too few to worry about so he ignored them – an oversight that had been fundamental to his downfall, for it allowed his conspirators to plot and plan there. Now the Adversary grew in power daily and it wouldn't be long before he surpassed Lucifer and the rest of the Ch'drnOmThophilim altogether. But until then, he needed an eye kept on the dissenters who thought he was going about things in ways that didn't suit them. Needless to say, their opinion wasn't shared by the Adversary himself and he sought to quash any rebels before they got a leprous toehold and upset his carefully laid plans.

This was a role formerly held by Shemyaza the Strong, who had ambitions to aspire to dizzier heights but was now known as Shemyaza the Dead. His high opinion of himself had made him careless and brought him to an abrupt and messy end. Fenris, who had an equally high and elevated opinion of himself but was prudent enough to keep it to himself around the Adversary, was not slow in moving himself and his armies into the palace and lands of the former demon lord. In doing so, he inherited, or more precisely, *took* the title from him and assumed his duties for the Adversary. Fenris substantially bolstered his army by turning the majority of Shemyaza's people – those foolish enough not to have run, of course – into his servants. There were those who couldn't run and the dungeons had been well stocked. Sunk into the ground several miles deep, they were a true testimony to what Hell should look like: vast caverns that were filled with tormented souls, where natural springs of liquid flame scoured flesh and turned these chambers into huge, torturous ovens. Still, for all the choice the slaves and prisoners had – join or die – some still fought against the transformation. The more they struggled, the greater the pain they had to contend with and the longer it took to pass. If they survived their probation of agony, they would be fine if not entirely sane and stable, but that didn't matter. If not – and they fought even that – there was another service they could perform, but only the once.

Soon enough the pile of skulls and bones grew to monumental proportions and was testimony to the occupants' identity. It became, in no time at all, a place not visited lightly – not that it was visited much beforehand – but now, unless you wished to add to the ever increasing pile of bones that was accumulating and being used to expand the residence of Fenris, the wise stayed away.

Fenris this day, as had been the way of most days of late, was in a foul humor. News of the secret mission to be undertaken by Asmodeus had reached him – for there were few secrets among the upper echelons, where spies abounded – and he was not pleased. Should the fat hairy demon lord succeed, it would be *him* in great favor and *not* Fenris: a fact Fenris found totally unacceptable, for was it not he who provided the gaol that currently housed Lucifer, the former regent of this world? Fenris snarled and growled his rhetoric aloud as he paced back and forth. Was it not he who provided the muscle and support of his hounds to the Adversary? Was it not he, Fenris, who should be given the honored tasks? And definitely should it not have been him the one assigned to capture the abhorrent and elusive human, Walker? Fenris raged once more and wrecked more of the hall he currently occupied, as he chewed over the news again and again. He had gnawed over it several times already and he now found himself railing alone; especially after those who brought the news in the first place now adorned the palace walls – or at least their entrails and blood now did. Several smashed, torn and ravaged corpses lay sprawled at the base of the walls. It was very unhealthy these days delivering news to the Wolf Lord. Fenris knew little of Asmodeus, for their paths had rarely crossed even before Fenris's premature incarceration. But what he did know of him he disliked vehemently. Fenris considered the old toad to be archaic in his methods even by the Domain's standards – having to organize his army and outfit his soldiers for travel, prepare wagons for supplies and gather mounts for all of them; whereas his warriors were ready to run, fight or travel in a heartbeat. They needed no mounts, for they could outrun anything on the Domain: two, four and maybe even six legs. Any more than six might be problematic but their extraordinary endurance would simply run them to ground eventually. They needed no gear, having already been graced with all they would ever need in armor and weaponry: fur as strong as the best mail, instant healing from all bar the most fatal of wounds, and weapons in tooth and claw. What more did they need? They would simply eat whoever got in their way. So with these facts in his mind, he resolved to make this task his. Now all he had to do was find a way to depose Asmodeus.

Leaving the charnel house that was just one of the many great halls, Fenris made his way to another equally palatial hall where he held his many audiences with his visitors and returning scouts; mostly returning scouts for visitors were rare and he didn't encourage them anyway. He had sensed a lone hound returning at great speed, which meant either something disastrous had occurred or something vitally important. Fenris plumped for the latter, for had it been the former, even with the low intelligence of a pack member, given a sensible choice, it would have known that it would be better to have died than be the one delivering such dire news on its own.

Fenris arrived at the hall scant moments before his scout was shown in by two massive guards, who differentiated themselves within the castle by sporting armor scavenged from Shemyaza's armory. Somehow it made them look even more ferocious for its adornment, and each sported massive two-handed swords strapped across their broad backs. These were the elite guards of Fenris, highly intelligent and exceptionally capable. They were the biggest, fastest and strongest of their kind and there were forty *scourge* in residence guarding the castle at all times. Twenty of these would travel wherever the Wolf Lord went, for they were his personal guard. Not that he really needed protecting, but it was good to utilize an impressive show of force from time to time.

Fenris was reclining indolently upon his throne when the scout came rushing in and abased itself upon the marble flags, hitting his head so hard on the floor it gave off an audible thud as he slammed it down. But he never moved until his lord gave him leave to do so. He was well trained and knew his place within the pack. Eventually Fenris gave it permission to rise and speak, which it did instantly, for Fenris hated hesitancy; he believed it smacked of deceit. The creature transformed slightly to a more human form, affording it greater powers of communication rather than the guttural grunts and howls it would have had to use.

'I have been sent with grave news, my lord Fenris. An enemy has arrived in the Domain and massacred several human mercenaries. He was left their ruined corpses to rot. He not devour his enemy. Taste bad too.'

Fenris frowned at the lack of "graveness" about this report. 'Tell me, dog, what is so "grave" about this? Enemies come here all the time and kill each other. What has this to do with me and mine?'

The hound shook its shaggy head as it tried to organize its thoughts to best convey what it was trying to say. 'It is old magic, my lord, wild magic. We not recognize it. There was power in it that we not know, not old but different from any here. Smells of death. Whatever came very dangerous! Many men dead. Them not what came through, they from Domain. Hunters. Pack has scent and awaits our lord's command.'

Fenris was excited, but remained calm before his minion. Could this be the mortal that Asmodeus was to capture? It was simply too much to hope for, that the hated human had fallen into his claws with such providence. And his warriors had the scent.

'Why has this creature that killed so many not been brought before me? If you have the scent, why have you come back empty-handed?'

The minion was unsure of the response, because their orders were to scout and report; not to capture, kill or engage. 'We follow our orders, your orders, my lord. We scout and I report.'

The spark of rage had flared within Fenris; this scout was right about their orders. They were mere dog soldiers: find and report. But he didn't like being reminded of that fact by one of them. 'Where was this sighting, hound? Was it far?'

The hound once again shook its unkempt mane and pointed a dirty taloned finger westwards. 'It was on the edge of the Great Forest. We believe whatever it was went that way.'

Fenris was growing more and more impatient with the way this meeting was going. So near yet so far, for should the mortal actually be the one sought, and should he have made it to the forest, he would be nigh on impossible to find. Small countries could be lost within its leafy embrace and there were things that allegedly lived within its confines that even the oldest amongst them had never seen. Many before him had tried to claim the forest as their own, entering to make their point, only to vanish and never be seen or heard of again. Them and their armies. The forest was supposedly a litter with ancient strongholds and fortresses of fantastic design and proportion, built by beings far older than those who inhabited the Domain now, but no one had ever returned who went in search of them. Maybe he would be the first. Forests were for wolves, after all.

The broken and torn mess that was the scout landed in a wet heap upon the grass close to where it parted company with its fellows. It gasped from shredded lungs, and with shattered arms and hands, it tried to contain its steaming innards from spilling out. It couldn't stand, for it only had one leg at present and that was broken in several places, with muscle and tissue ripped from it. But though its wounds had already started to heal, it still lay bleeding and in agony, desperate to deliver the message Fenris had instilled in it, but unable to do so until it regenerated and healed sufficiently to pick itself up and catch up with its fellow pack members. Fortunately, that wouldn't be too long. Small consolation. It didn't recall the exact moment Fenris had pounced on it; everything was just a blur of crimson agony as its body was subjected to its lord's will. After what seemed an eternity of teeth and talon, it was sent hurtling through a portal, opened by Fenris, to land unceremoniously upon the ground where he had left a day earlier. It had taken a solid day of hard running to make it back to the Wolf Lord's new residence and only a heartbeat to return. But based upon how he felt at that present moment, he would rather have run back.

Fenris summoned one of the few remaining palace servants who had been in service to Shemyaza the Dense. He summoned it by pulling on an ornamental looking rope that hung behind the throne. At first, after he had arrived at the castle and taken over, he had caught it by accident, having swung his massive paw in outrage at something he couldn't recall now, and moments later food turned up, though to be more exact, the human slaves of Shemyaza the Moronic turned up. But it amounted to much the same thing at the time. But Fenris wasn't stupid and soon gave up eating the domestic help, for he found them harder to replace than he would have liked. He could have used his hounds to do his bidding but they were hard to train for domestic duties and he had neither the time nor the patience, as the scout had just found out, to keep repeating himself to them. He needed his slaves with a bit more intelligence and a modicum of free thought in order to best provide for him. After his lesson in discipline to the scout, he found he had worked up a hunger that required sating. However, when the slave entered and saw the blood and carnage splashed all around, it promptly defecated itself. The smell of shit and fear, especially the fear, reached the powerful nostrils of Fenris and that smell was the ultimate downfall of the minion. Fenris had only thought to summon food, but the fear simply enhanced the already excited state Fenris was in from his brief educational session. Why Shemyaza the Ignorant kept these pathetic things around was beyond him: they were weak and scared of their own shadow half the time, but, they did taste good.

THE ADVERSARY

Matters were moving apace and he needed a trophy to present to *his* Dark Lord, the Adversary. The head and heart of this meddlesome mortal would do well. His army grew steadily and would soon be ready for the next phase of the Adversary's plan. Of course, the fact that he, Fenris, and *not* Asmodeus, would present this gift to their lord was not lost on him, and he grinned cruelly as he finished his meal. Crunching upon a fleshy thigh bone, he drew out the marrow and cast the remains aside. Sitting back in his intricately carved throne – the detail and skill involved in its construction was totally lost on the Wolf Lord, as too was the finesse of the tapestries that adorned the castle walls, alongside shields and trophies and fantastic weapons arrayed all about – he pulled the cord once more. The minion had whetted his appetite and he craved more meat. Maybe this next slave would bring something to distract him with. If not, well… He sat back and awaited its arrival and picked a scrap of the last minion from his teeth subconsciously, hinting at what the *if not* entailed.

Yet while Fenris reclined and pondered his next meal upon the Domain, elsewhere in the multiverse matters were reaching a dramatic climax. Matters that had previously been attributed to mere mortal angst. Clashes of religion, opinion, race and the political machinations of short-sighted and greedy men were now elevating themselves beyond the accepted norm, and these said people were now starting to finally notice that something was going horribly wrong.

All around the populated and semi-civilized Earth, mortalkind was transfixed upon one of its more informative yet disastrous creations. Television. Most couldn't believe what they were seeing, and those that could, wept. Not since the 9/11 bombing and the recent continuation of the Middle Eastern wars had humanity borne witness to such mass destruction in the present age. So much devastation was being wrought around the world, in fact, that the news channels were having trouble keeping up with reports on them all. Sky News, CNN, Fox, ABC, the BBC, Al-Jazeera and a myriad of other stations were chasing around the globe, trying to make sense of the destruction and incalculable loss of life. This was violence on a scale that was unprecedented. Not even during two world wars had so much been carried out in such a short space of time. Technology had unfortunately expedited humans' ability to wreak monumental havoc and chaos.

At first, much of the violence was attributed to terrorists, as was to be expected, and in particular Al-Qaeda, with thoughts that Iraq, Iran or Syria or even Russia had some involvement. But mostly it was attributed to some Al-Qaeda cell whose leaders in past months had been promising an escalation to their violence. It was an easy finger point. Unfortunately the multiverse is far more complicated than that and it soon became apparent that this went far beyond the capabilities of a mere terrorist organization, even one with such alleged global networks. For as far as the outside world began to see, it appeared that they suffered as much as those they preyed upon. Security services were thoroughly baffled and all their intel amounted to squat. The CIA, FBI, and NSA in the United States; MOSAD in Israel; the MI5 and MI6 in Britain; and a host of other countries who monitored the world's affairs were just as baffled. For many of the perpetrators had no prior history or even the remotest affiliation with anything or anyone's group or organization, not even the boy scouts. But all around the world, members of the public were carrying out bizarre suicides as well as suicidal attacks on others, and further acts of unprovoked and brutal violence. News reports initially put that down to binge drinking, drugs and the stresses of a twenty-four seven society. But by the end of the week, that excuse was abandoned for the pathetic attempt it was. Some sort of airborne and biological attack was put forward next: an epidemic that was sweeping the world, causing people to commit the most outrageous acts of horror and violence. It was not restricted to just any one country and all the previous propaganda of the evil West fell away as both the East and West suffered equally. Yet in the face of a mutual dilemma of such epic and global proportions, there were still those that found time to blame the other and spend their final days hurling accusations and vitriol at each other.

Many of the world leaders went into seclusion, hoping desperately that they would be safe from the madness that was sweeping the world. All their weapons of mass destruction meant absolutely nothing in the face of the global plight that was ravaging the international community. It was like having no end of fingers when all you needed was a thumb.

Law and order started to break down: not to start with from the pressure of dealing with the increasing violence, but from within. Their own people began to succumb to whatever afflicted the human race. Likewise, in the armed forces, internal fractures caused as much turmoil as that which had turned the streets into battlegrounds – a situation made worse, of course, because they had a ready supply of weaponry and firepower.

Fighter pilots ran amok, disgorging millions of dollars' worth of ordnance on non-military targets, dropping their missiles arbitrarily. They fired them wherever they felt the urge and hundreds of innocent lives paid heavily before the pilots finally flew their aircraft kamikaze fashion into the ground in one last fatal and destructive explosion. Their Paveway and Hellfire missiles had torn up enormous areas of stone and concrete and sent molten death and lethal shrapnel flying through the air, killing all in its path. National security was beside itself. It couldn't afford to have their assets running amok with such an arsenal at their disposal. Yet for all its technological innovation, it was at a complete loss at how to stop them. Hundreds of satellites orbiting the Earth told them where these rogues and renegades were and even showed the extent of the destruction wrought by them. But they didn't know how to stop them. Who could they trust? What did they send up against them? Another of their own? Violence then begets violence in order to try and slow the devastation – a vicious and accelerating downward spiral that could only end one way.

Violence and depravity blossomed like a cancer within the domestic sector and entire swathes of countryside were reduced to burning wastelands as individuals and gangs ran amok. Rapes, assaults and murder were increasing exponentially and no one had any answers. Except world religion, of course. They bleated that the end was nigh and this was the end of days, but they had been doing that for years. How many times could a body cry wolf before it lost its meaning? Yet the law of averages worked out that one time they might actually be right. But assuming they actually were right, what solution did they have? The same one they had used over and over. Nothing. Bury their heads in the sand with a good dose of delusion – call it prayer and faith – and hope their ass was still there when they pulled it out again.

Churches, mosques and synagogues were sacked and destroyed with equal measure during these dark days. In fact, it seemed that those doing the sacking took greater pleasure from burning them than laying waste to such mundane places as supermarkets and banks. It was as if they represented something particularly abhorrent to the perpetrators.

By the end of the month – February – national and international travel had almost ground to a standstill. Airports were the first to close – the loss of so many of their aircraft played a huge factor there – rail links shut, and roads were virtually empty. Only the desperate and the dangerous traveled them now. Humanity had been contained, in its cities and towns as well as upon their own continents, which really only made matters worse, for being incapable of getting away from the afflicted, it festered and exploded outwards, like a dam that held back an unearthly destruction and was cracking. In places the damage was minimal and normality seemed unaffected, people oddly going about their daily lives as though this was just some TV show they watched or heard about on the radio; for the media, like some virulent cockroach, was the last to give up the ghost and close down, which it did by the end of February. The total global collapse now was not a matter of if, but when. There were numerous leaks in the dam and more were breaking through every day, spreading their violence and destruction wherever they landed.

Yet amidst the carnage, it was the individual suicides that appeared the most disturbing. Random souls were throwing themselves into harm's way everywhere they turned. For no rational or explainable reason, people were ripping their eyes from their sockets and flinging themselves off roofs, into the paths of the still-working vehicles, into machinery and off cliffs and bridges. Those that witnessed this atrocity swore that they heard the poor soul laughing as it died. Such bloodshed sent more than a few delicate beings forever over the edge into the uncharted realms of sanity, or lack thereof. Then they ran amok, crying, screaming and howling themselves, swearing they saw creatures and beings from other worlds wherever they looked; and, who knows, just maybe they did.

The possessed were running amok, and chaos and carnage followed in their wake. For thousands of years these creatures, who now inhabited the bodies of the unwilling, had only been able to communicate with humanity via the most tenuous means: insidious whispers in the recesses of their dreams; diaphanous voices from the dark part of their soul, subtly nudging, coercing and encouraging acts of despicable evil. The few who were susceptible to them eventually acted upon them. History was rife with serial killers and psychopaths who "heard voices" in their head, and it wasn't just the sad, depressed loner existing in his squalid basement apartment who heard them; the infernal influence reached some influential souls too. Two world wars can attest to their success. Even before that, when popes and kings governed the up-and-coming civilizations, were their lofty ears whispered into in the dead of night, sowing the seeds of paranoia and greed, desire and hunger, causing man to turn against man to satisfy this demon in his head.

Yet now, as the Earth's protective shield fell to the ravages of the Adversary and his nefarious design, the demons from the Domain were able to make the transition from their world to this with greater ease. Gone were the whispers and the voices. Now, the demons could take full possession of the unfortunate, displacing their soul and mind in favor of their direct control. Relegating the individual, whose body it was, to nothing more than being an unwilling passenger in their own body, still aware of what it was doing, and, worse still, able to still feel the pain inflicted upon it. With this sort of control, even the myth of exorcism was a pipe dream. Whereas before, it was akin to dislodging a man who hung from a cliff by a fingernail – so frail was the demon's connection – now, the spawn had the soul in a full bear hug, with arms and legs entwined around it. What added insult to extreme injury with this type of full-on possession, was that there was no recovery; for if the parasitic demon didn't kill its host just for the fun of it, then the body would rot away over the course of about a week and they would die anyway. Human flesh just couldn't take the invasion of one of these things. The surprise for many of these unsuspecting victims was how these creatures managed to possess them at all. Many were good, clean living people who had harmed no one or ever contemplated any sort of wrongdoing. Their initial and invariably last thought, was unsurprisingly, *why me?* But the answer would be as terrifying as the possession itself. Acceptance. Humanity had grown complacent about many of the things that demons found inflammatory. Death, violence and brutality were commonplace now. The press and media bombarded children at every turn with the depravities of a race through television and video games, numbing and desensitizing minds that should have been appalled and terrified by what they saw, not entertained. A line was crossed for mortalkind when it made such entertainment from bloody and lethal violence. Humanity became immune to the horror of what humans do to other humans in the name of sport, entertainment and fun, the same way rats become immune to the poisons used against them. They accepted it as a symptom of the times they were living in and adjusted their lives accordingly. In fact the more open one was to violence and savagery, the easier it was to possess them. It was that acceptance and gullibility that signed humanity's death warrant and opened the door to the horrors that were now taking full advantage of their new-found freedom. A strong mind could withstand the onslaught at this early stage, but the demons had an ample supply of weak-willed souls to possess, and it was only a matter of time before they held the majority. In the stormy and turbulent days that had befallen humanity, how long could even the strongest mind hope to withstand the invasion of mind, body and world?

Cries and pleas and went up from the world: supplications to their respective gods to save them, entreating any who would listen, and wailing about how a just God could let its people suffer this way. Though hadn't that always been the call? And hadn't humanity always suffered somewhere, somewhen? Yet when the people strained to hear an answer, they were greeted with the usual reply.

Silence.

Chapter Fourteen

Resistere

THE SOUNDS OF VALKYRIES LAUGHING ECHOED IN Tomas's mind for the next few hours as the entourage rode through the forest. But even though it had diminished somewhat, every now and again he would catch sight of one or two of the more forward shield maidens looking at him in an amused way, slight smiles playing about their features and humor sparkling in their eyes. Tomas had expected reprisals. He still couldn't believe what he had blurted out. It was as though somebody else had taken control of his mouth and voice, seriously meddling with his head. For it truly felt to him that he was experiencing those lascivious thoughts, but later, after rationalizing it, he knew *he* hadn't felt them at all. Yes, she was attractive – as fit as any woman he had encountered, and with a body any supermodel would die for, and, if Tomas was honest, he *did* appreciate that. Although he might not be entirely human any more, he was still a man and he wasn't dead yet. *Definitely a good thing*, Tomas reminded himself. But he had always controlled his thoughts and kept a tight rein on his feelings. *Which makes this cock-up all the more mysterious.* Having honed his mind and disciplined himself to take or leave women, he was at a loss to figure the mental lapse. In fact, that was what he usually *did* do with them, or used to at least. Taking them when he felt the need or if it served his purpose, and either leaving them, or in the worst-case scenarios, having to dispose of them on a more permanent basis. Not until his fiancée, had he felt any twinge of genuine emotion and commitment for a woman, excluding his mother and sister – they didn't count. Most were just good for the usual. If he was honest with himself, he was something of a misogynist, *was* being the operative word. He was belatedly learning what an ass that made him. And he was just learning what love and commitment were really all about when they were stolen from him. It was like the opening of a water lily blossom, burgeoning and full of potential, but before it could open to full bloom in the daylight of the woman he wanted to spend his life with, it was brutally cut short by – as he had recently discovered – a dark malignant force he had paid lip service to over the years. There was an old adage that said the devil's greatest trick was convincing the world he didn't exist. Wrong. He did and he was called the Adversary. An obscure demon of sheer ruthless malevolence by all accounts; and if Tomas had any say in the matter, one who was going to pay dearly for what it had done to him. As far as Tomas figured it: sod the world, *he* was first in line for some payback. The world and whoever else could just get in line.

Though for all the mystery of *why* he had opened his bloody great gob like that and made a prat of himself, there was in fact a seed of truth there. She did fascinate him and in any ordinary circumstance he would certainly want to nail that. But now she had given him the cold shoulder and put about as much space between him and her as she could manage without leaving completely, and was currently riding point at the head of their armored column. Not that he was checking up on her whereabouts. At least that's what he told himself.

Vigilance was doubly necessary when riding through a forest where visibility was limited, and none of the Valkyries had relaxed their eyes since their troop had started out – at least the ones that weren't scrutinizing him. They rarely left the dark and concealing forest to either side of them. Tomas himself studied the wall of multihued green foliage and bark and he even managed from time to time to catch the briefest of glimpses of the white raven that seemed to have adopted him as it ghosted through the trees, keeping pace with them. Tomas found himself sandwiched between the warrior women, which ordinarily wouldn't have been a bad thing, but this felt different somehow. Other than Treya, it felt like riding with his sister or any other female relative. There was a distinct lack of sexuality to the proceedings. At least on his part as, for all their short skirts and bare flesh, the air of menace they gave off dispelled any lascivious thoughts. The majority rode ahead of him, with Niall balancing upon his acquired mount riding next to Hildreth. Both looked out for each other. She kept him upright and he monitored her wound and cleaned the dressing. There were several behind him too, along with Ingrid, who brought up the rear, ensuring they weren't followed. And, Tomas mused, to better keep an eye on him. Smiling and chuckling to himself, he thought it was funny, really. *If she was to remove that poker from up her arse, we'd probably get on quite well 'cos she's a damn good fighter for a girl.*

It was during this hushed period as they rode in relative silence, each lost in their own thoughts, when Tomas sensed they weren't as alone as he would have liked and something was definitely watching them. His sixth sense had always served him well in the past as regards being tailed, watched or generally being looked at in a more than casual manner. Years of distrust had honed this skill. You didn't survive the convoluted machinations of the cold war years, when every Tom, Dick and Harry was recruited as a spy, without learning a few things. Long before the technologically-enhanced surveillance equipment became so readily available, if you needed to hear what someone was saying or watch where they went, it took a physical presence to actually do it. Now, what with the advent of bugs and satellites, GPS and cameras up the wazzoo fitted into all and sundry, spies sit in offices and vans now, watching screens and cavorting about the internet and cyberspace. *He* had even been called a *dinosaur* – the nerve of them – just because he liked the old-fashioned methods. *I got the bloody job done when their damn computers went tits up, which was more often than not. I'd like to see one of them tech heads lying face down in the desert, having crawled several miles with a laser designator, to spot the target for some air strike. Tossers. They'd probably wet themselves. I'll give them dinosaur.* His hackles were up on his neck and the little voice in his head pressed him to some urgency. So Tomas resolved to kill two birds with one metaphorical stone; glancing uneasily to the trees in case the raven had picked up on that thought. It probably wouldn't like the "killing birds" bit. Yet he knew he had to make peace with the fiery Ingrid and casually, without alerting the watchers, let her know his suspicions, as it seemed Treya wasn't talking to him.

Slowing Storm to a slow walk, so that those following him had to go round him or over him, Tomas soon found himself waiting as Ingrid rode into view. Matching Storm to her mount's pace, he slipped alongside her, earning himself the most debilitating glance he had ever had turned on him. It was designed to convey a feeling of intimidation and fury. Tomas had little doubt that a man of lesser conviction would think twice about merely being near her as she looked that way at him, let alone *talk* to her. But Tomas was made of sterner stuff. Or so he hoped. Coughing unconsciously before he spoke, there was little to do but jump straight in. He figured her for one who didn't do small talk anyway.

'Look, Ingrid,' Tomas started, immediately growing in confidence as he spoke. It was always the anticipation of doing a thing that was the worst, in his opinion. Once you got going it was all plain sailing from then on. 'I know you don't like me much.' It wasn't a huge assumption, based on the way Ingrid snorted as he stated the obvious. 'Yeah, okay, point taken, but we are traveling together. I imagine, if we're unlucky, we'll even be fighting together, watching each other's back. Now I know that professional fighters can do that without particularly liking their comrade, but it's a damn sight easier if you actually get along with the person you risk taking a round or even dying for. I don't dislike you. Why should I? I don't even know you, much the same as you don't know me.' She turned to regard him as though she cared little about what he thought. 'But I understand you, Ingrid. Really. If you had seen what I've seen, you'd know that for truth. But I'm not here to blow smoke up your arse. We'll either get on or we won't. I just hope we all live long enough to find out which. Now that might not be all that long if I'm right about something.'

Ingrid growled a reply to him, asking what he was blabbing on about.

'I have the strong sense we are being watched, and have been for at least an hour now. I can't put my finger on where they or it is. It's just a feeling, but these feelings have kept me alive in the past, so I've learnt to listen to them.'

Ingrid didn't seem to be overly concerned about his warning, yet she regarded him with a hint of curiosity. 'Do you feel danger from whatever you think is watching us?' Her cool demeanor was no indication of her explosive fighting capability. She was naught to sixty yesterday. Tomas knew – he'd seen her in action – so he answered her as honestly as he could, concentrating briefly on exactly what it was he did feel. Oddly enough, it wasn't that feeling of imminent danger he had, not yet anyway, just the discomfort of knowing that eyes were upon your every move. He wasn't used to that. So that was what he told Ingrid. But instead of laughing at him in her contemptuous manner, she seemed to reappraise him slightly, as though he had unexpectedly passed some sort of test.

'You are more perceptive than you appear, for all your fancy armor and weapons. You are quite right; we are being watched. But by nothing you need concern yourself with. We have allies who assist us with scouting and carrying messages to those who we answer to. It is those that you sense, so you can relax and resume your position in line, unless you intend to bother me further', though her tone suggested it would be unwise to do so.

She's a hard one all right, Tomas thought grimly. But he tried to remember what it was that turned her so and he couldn't blame her really. She had been angry for so long that she probably didn't know how to be anything else, and all he was doing was prodding a recently opened wound. But, like a badly broken bone, sometimes it was necessary to break it again in order to reset it properly and facilitate the healing process the way it should have healed the first time.

'All right then, if you don't think we're in any immediate peril, I'll take your word for it, but it would have been nice to have been told about them. So as you're keeping mum about them – tell me about Treya then. Have I offended her in some way?'

Ingrid gave him such a look then, but even she couldn't get her words out quickly enough, such was the perceived outrageousness of Tomas's question, so he pressed on.

'Granted, my slip of the tongue didn't help, but I didn't expect her to take it quite so hard. Surely she's a big girl now and I would have thought she'd heard much worse from your bloody Viking warriors you supposedly gathered up for Ragnarok. Not to mention the fact you're in bloody Hell, for heaven's sake. You can't tell me there aren't some foul mouths down here,' Tomas rallied on, intent on saying his bit to his comparatively captive audience. 'Look,' Tomas tried with a resigned and sympathetic tone, appealing to any hint of compassion that might be in there, if not for him, then for Treya, 'it's a long story and I'm not entirely sure I get it myself yet, but since falling into this hellhole, I haven't been entirely my normal self, whatever that might be. Maybe it's a bit of stress, an overloaded fuse or two – I've had a lot to deal with lately – but, like I say, that's another story and you know most of it already. But I didn't think you girls held a grudge. Figured you for better than that.'

Ingrid looked at Tomas, and then she looked ahead to where her friend rode. Though she couldn't see her, she knew she was there all the same. Ingrid pulled a face that spoke of uncertainty. She was keen to say something. Tomas could tell, but he kept silent, letting her work it out. He surmised she wasn't good at explanations and certainly not any where her friend was concerned. Finally she spoke, and it was in hushed tones as though she subconsciously feared she would be overheard by Treya, several hundred yards ahead.

'You have not offended her, mortal. It would take more than you – but you have confused her. For since our exile in this forsaken land, Treya has yet to meet her match in combat and spirit. Your skills impressed her. That much

544

was obvious, even to me. I believe you are a very dangerous individual, and for many reasons. But when you made your declaration, you blindsided her, and that fact alone – more than you – irritates her.'

'Like I said, Ingrid, I didn't mean to embarrass her, or myself for that matter – '

Ingrid silenced him from further explanation with a raised hand.

'Yes, yes, whatever, but know this. Words are as pebbles cast into water. They may pass beneath the surface quickly enough, but the waves they make ripple outwards and have consequences. And like the stone that remains where it was cast, they will not be forgotten. The heart and soul of a Valkyrie are dangerous things to fool with. It would be simpler and safer to attempt to pass through a stampede of enraged bison during rutting season – blindfolded.' *Nice thought.* 'When we reach the rendezvous, I expect she will converse with you again. For now, as the good and dutiful leader Treya is, she deals with her responsibilities, ensuring all matters and the journey go smoothly. Treya takes all her duties seriously, and Odin help the poor soul that comes between her and her duty. Oh yes,' Ingrid smirked cruelly, 'that'll be you, then.'

Tomas grimaced himself at her barb. 'Fair enough, I accept much of what you say and think, but there's one little fact you might have slipped past....' Ingrid raised her eyebrows in an 'oh?' '...It was *you* that came to us; we were minding our own business...' Ingrid spun her head to glare at him again. *Just for a change,* Tomas groaned to himself. *So much for making headway. We're back to glowers again. I'd say that was one step forward two back. Bloody woman.*

'You were minding it in our forest, close to where we were camped. Too close to be totally coincidental. Any sensible warrior would have done the same. Tell me you wouldn't if you were in enemy territory and there were strangers nearby who should not be there. Well?'

Tomas had to admit she was right. He would have done the same, and had done before. Not always so pleasantly either. There was many a corpse sitting propped against trees with their throats cut. Tomas even suspected, but he rarely dwelt upon it, that some of them might even have been innocent. Maybe. He should be grateful they only poked him with a stick. He decided to push for a bit more information while Ingrid was in a chatty mode and though he was pushing his luck he couldn't resist a poke back himself.

'It's a bit of a big forest to call yours, isn't it? I'm sure you can't ride around accosting everybody who wanders in here, gee…' Sarcasm began to creep into Tomas's voice, '…I guess we were just lucky. So just where is this rendezvous you all seem intent on hauling us off to, or is that another secret not to be shared with an ally? Should I be grateful I'm not blindfolded and hogtied, or do you still think us agents of the Adversary?' He almost felt the temperature drop around her. Tomas realized, guiltily, that her rigidity and aloofness brought out the antagonist in Tomas and he instantly regretted it 'cos it wasn't big and nor was it clever, as his sister so readily told him when he poked fun at her as kids. It didn't seem that way at the time, but he made her life a fair misery and he wished he could have made it up to her somehow before all this shit kicked off. What with all that was going on, would he ever get the opportunity? He just hoped she was all right, but with the family luck, he feared the worst.

'You cannot bait me, mortal. I am Valkyrie, shield maiden to Odin and tempered in the fires of Valhalla. Your words are as mere smoke, so save your breath. As far as our destination goes you will find out in due course, unless you do not trust us? The sword cuts both ways, mortal, remember this. Suffice to say we are heading to a deeper encampment, one of several, I might add. Two days of travel should see us there.'

'Two days?' Tomas repeated back to her, incredulity evident in his voice. 'Why so bloody long? Why not fly? We'll get there a damn sight quicker. You might have all the time in the world but I'm on something of a deadline, not wishing to sound overly melodramatic, but my world is at stake.'

Again Ingrid pierced him with her steely gaze and said in hushed tones that he barely heard over the natural forest noises, 'All the worlds are in peril,

Tomas. Yours, ours and this one we walk upon included. Time is a matter of perspective, depending which world you stand upon. Days here are hours on Earth and days there are weeks here.'

Tomas mulled this over in silence for a few minutes, Astronomy had never been his strong point but he supposed it was all to do with orbits and rotations around the sun. It was a big subject and opened a can of worms with the older cultures. Those wily Egyptians and the Mayans with that odd Venusian calendar they have. Why Venus, of all places? There was little doubt they knew something modern humanity definitely didn't, and they weren't sharing. There were fast becoming more questions than he could get answers for, and the more he discovered, the more he realized the depths of humanity's ignorance. Tomas conceded that there were some bright minds back in *ye olde* days, but they were still limited by their understanding and interpreted what they experienced accordingly. All the subsequent generations did was to repeat it verbatim and accept it for what those back then put forward as their explanation. If humanity deviated by just one degree from their path several thousand years ago, just how far off would they be by now? Tomas shook his head sadly and gave Storm's neck a reassuring pat, ruffling his fingers in the fine silky mane. Storm whickered appreciatively at the attention. The response put the smile back on Tomas's face and he thought he would give conversation with Ingrid one more go. He was nothing if not persistent.

'Ingrid.' His sudden exclamation caught her unawares, thinking as she did, that Tomas had given up annoying her. She scowled at his perseverance; he was like a fly that didn't know when to buzz off, and just kept flitting before your eyes.

'Ingrid,' Tomas repeated, assured he had her attention again. 'If this truly is Hell, how is it I find myself meandering through the biggest forest I've ever been in and running into living and breathing Norse myths? Valkyries and Hell were never in the same yarn that I remember. I thought you were all Asgard and Valhalla and stuff, flying around Scandinavia, plucking warriors from battle and the likes.'

Ingrid snarled again. 'Is there actually going to be a question here or are you just trying to put me to sleep with some poor bedtime story of a history I am more than familiar with?'

Tomas grinned ruefully and nodded, dragging his hand through his own unkempt hair as he gathered his thoughts, absently noticing how long his hair was and how it could use some attention. 'Yes there is, sorry. Basically I was wondering what the bloody hell you are doing here in the first place. Surely this isn't a vacation spot for you lot, is it?'

The flippant comment was lost on the dour warrior as she had no idea what a vacation was. 'You ask too many questions of matters that are no concern of yours.' But just when Tomas thought she would say no more, Ingrid spoke again. 'However, seeing as Treya feels the need to divulge privileged information about her sisters to you with little thought, why can I not do the same? What harm can it do?'

The rhetorical question wasn't lost on Tomas; he figured she was giving herself approval to tell him something that probably involved Treya and he also guessed that it was in retaliation for Treya telling him about Ingrid's youth.

'We have known of this world for millennia. Odin even had some say in its formation, but it was part of the Covenant that none should interfere with what took place here. Only certain beings were permitted to venture here: those with the power of the portals and even then, only for the most desperate of reasons. Access was closely guarded and Lucifer was empowered to be aware of all gates that opened both to here and from here. Valkyries do have that privilege. We have some power, yes, but not of portals. What you see about you is only the surface of what takes place here. It is a place of punishment and captivity; do not be fooled otherwise. Within the walls of many of the cities and deep below the rock in their labyrinthine dungeons which burrow down many leagues, there is another world of pain and torture. Fire and blood. It is a place where many go and few ever return from. But perpetual fire and brimstone does not feed the masses. Many slaves are here who need to eat: a slave is no good if it starves to death; not to mention that many here feed on slaves and they don't appreciate poor pickings. There is a basic feudal system here: slaves who grow food for other slaves to eat and lords to rule over them; some greater, some lesser. Much the same as back home where any hierarchy is established. Yet even we had little idea what to expect when we were first exiled here.'

'That's what I can't understand,' Tomas queried. 'I thought you lot were the chosen of Odin. What on earth could you have done to get yourselves sent here?'

'Treya has a temper. You may live long enough to discover this. She also has a half-sister, Athillia, spawned by Thor's second wife, who is a shallow and cruel woman: a harridan that makes keeping a harpy's company a pleasant proposition. Beautiful on the surface, but there is none uglier beneath that skin – which we're not sure is even hers. But Thor is besotted with her and she can do no wrong when she bats her lashes at him. Typical man.' Ingrid harrumphed at the thought of masculine weakness and Tomas had to agree. He had many a colleague who fell foul of some woman's wiles because they couldn't keep it in their trousers. That was why women made such good spies. They could smile at you and keep smiling as they slid the knife in, twisting it *as* they smiled.

'Athillia can do no wrong in the eyes of her mother, or Thor for that matter. She has him ensorcelled: a feeling we believe is of unnatural origins, but unfortunately cannot yet prove. It is not helped either by the fact that this trollop of a wife was once a lover of Odin himself. She has no compunction about spreading herself about to get what she wants, it seems, and Thor is apparently unaware of this fact. Nor is he likely to find out unless we can return to open his eyes. Treya is beside herself with worry about her father, for she believes that this harpy has an agenda of her own. One that will wind up with the death of her father.'

Tomas watched the play of expressions on Ingrid's face as she spoke and he noticed the barely contained fury at the mention of this harpy wife of Thor.

He wouldn't want to be her if Ingrid ever made it back. But Ingrid regained her composure and continued:

'Athillia was given command of a host of Valkyries. Bah, the word sticks in my craw. *Given*. No Valkyrie was given anything. They earned their ranks though duty and service, yet this snake in a girl's skin was given command of a host of shield maidens, with Treya as her second, and I second to Treya.' Tomas paid close attention which prompted Ingrid to carry on. 'We were caught unawares by several packs of Fenris's beasts, for Athillia refused to heed Treya's advice, and many sisters died horribly that day. Yet when it came to an accounting at the All Fathers Hall, it was Athillia who was believed over Treya. Athillia accused Treya of disobeying her orders and leading the host against her instructions into the massacre, which conveniently enough, she barely escaped from with her life after felling many beasts. The lie was that Treya ran in fear, abandoning her sisters to their fate. Truth was that were it not for Treya and her quick thinking and uncanny leadership skills, many more would have fallen that day, including the cowering and fear frozen Athillia. Treya rallied the sisters and saved their lives. But Athillia was as feared as she was hated – and many sisters were coerced to give evidence against Treya and praise Athillia for her bravery and skill; attributing the failure to Treya and the heroics to Athillia. Those who knew the truth, and there were many, stood by Treya. It is a measure of our honor that we would not lower ourselves to retaliate with further accusations, for that made us appear as though we had to justify our actions. Thor, with the support of Odin, who was equally beguiled by Thor's wife, exiled Treya and all who stood with her there and then, with no trial or hearing. It was only by Odin's good grace that we were allowed our steeds, for to be parted from them would have been too much to bear.'

Tomas could only imagine the pain that would cause, for he had been witness to the funeral ceremony, and that was terrible enough. But Ingrid hadn't quite finished her tale and he didn't want to interrupt, for this was the longest she had ever spoken that he had heard.

'It is only through mischance that we came across this petty rebellion, but it serves our purpose as well as those who instigated it. For one of the leaders has promised to help us return to Asgard if we lend our skills to their cause.' Again Ingrid shook her head sadly as though she bore a great burden – one that was still growing by the way she sighed. 'It is unfortunate that this rebellion has turned into something else entirely. Something that has far reaching implications and is far more serious than our honor. So we stay and I fear that we will all die here for this cause.' She turned her frosty gaze back to Tomas, holding his attention with her enormous, moist, brown eyes. She pierced his skull with that gaze and plumbed his soul as she spoke. 'You have already seen my sisters die. You are in part responsible for their deaths so I am holding you responsible for the lives of my remaining sisters. I expect you to do all in your power to keep them alive or you will be answerable to me, Tomas *human.*'

Tomas felt a world of despair hit him like an avalanche. *Bloody hell, that's the last thing I poxy well want. To be responsible for more lives. I'm barely responsible for my own these days. Then there's Niall. Poor sod that he is, he's still baggage I didn't want and there was I, hoping to palm him off on these girls. Now I've been saddled with them too. This is getting way out of hand but what can I do without dropping myself in it further? I'm up to my bloody neck as it is.* Tomas sighed deeply at the injustice of his life and Ingrid took the ragged sound as acceptance of her terms.

Tomas ran through his options and found them limited. He was in a world unlike anything he had ever encountered so simply making a run for it was probably out of the question. Where would he go? It was Hell after all. There were probably no end of nasty things out there he could run afoul of, and what he didn't need were any more distractions. Or life threatening fights to the death anytime soon. No, there was nothing for it but to go along with this path and see where it led and pray he didn't screw up any more, for there were more lives at stake now than just his. He needed more information. Granted, what he had just gotten from Ingrid was insightful, but not overly helpful. He would have to squeeze a bit more. It was like the thought of having to squeeze juice out of an urchin with your bare hand – after you've tried once already and know just how much it bloody hurts.

'Tell me more about this rebellion, Ingrid, while you're in a chatty mood and happily handing out responsibility. If I am to be accountable, I want to know more about what's going on, and if your illustrious leader isn't talking to me, then it's your job, so spill. Starting with where we are going and who you are answerable to.'

Ingrid's severe features screwed up as she ignored him at first, working through just what she should or could tell him without getting herself in hot water. 'I will tell you of our part in the rebellion and that is all. Treya will have to tell you the rest, and the rendezvous will provide you with further answers. You will have to wait until then. It is more than my hide is worth to share such sensitive details with the likes of you. You'll just have to learn patience.'

It was Tomas's turn to snarl. Bloody pigheaded woman, I'd rather squeeze the damn urchin. But true to her word, Ingrid told him of the rebellion and the role of the Adversary; of what he had done to the Domain since usurping Lucifer; and who he had recruited as his generals, as well as some of the scuttlebutt about potential threats and possible plans and objectives, though few had been substantiated as of yet and many others were still only theories. Tomas nodded where appropriate and listened carefully, only interrupting to ask for qualification or expanding of points Ingrid had brushed over vaguely, or to elicit a few more details. Tomas was a superb interrogator and he got a bit more from her than she probably intended, through his canny questioning. Finally, he reasoned he had all he was going to get on this subject, which wasn't a vast amount, and much of it mirrored what he had seen and had been told already.

'Thanks for that, though much sounds familiar, and echoes what Michael told me.'

Ingrid had the good grace to look genuinely surprised then as she regarded him, open eyed and innocent looking. 'Michael? Are you referring to the Archangel Michael?'

Tomas nodded. 'One and the same. Why?'

Ingrid got a grip on herself then and resumed her normal stony expression. 'I find it hard to believe you have spoken to the Archangel Michael himself,' she snorted, and took on an expression that said 'Yeah, right'.

Tomas filled her in on the meeting and was pleased to see her face change to a more incredulous look as it became obvious that he had indeed met him. He described the big warrior down to the last detail and unconsciously rubbed his jaw as he spoke.

'So there you go, Ingrid. Surely that puts me on the side of right, though I don't know what he thinks of me at the moment. Probably thinks I'm dead. I was due to meet him at Megiddo but I was separated from the Four Horsemen at Al'Mayakin, which was where I fell through Nakir's crypt and ended up here. The rest you know.'

Tomas had a brief moment where he feared that Ingrid was going to fall off her mount. So fixed on him was she, that she wasn't watching where she rode and a low hanging branch nearly had her off.

Finding her voice and her credibility as she barely dodged the limb and regained some composure, she spoke softly then. And Tomas was pleased to note a touch of awe there.

'You keep some elevated company, Tomas mortal. The fabled Horsemen and that of archangels. Why did you not divulge any of this earlier?'

'It doesn't do to brag and you would have been less likely to have believed me then, when you knew even less of me than you do now. I have to say, that if you would have asked me any of this a month ago, I'd have laughed out loud and disbelieved me too. But that was another life. So much has happened in such a short space of time that I'm getting a little numb to what normally would shock and scare me rigid. I'm not sure there's anything left that will faze me now.'

Ingrid shrugged noncommittally. 'Wait and see. There might be one or two things out there yet.'

Terrific, that's not exactly what I meant; I was kind of hoping that I really had done all that could be done on that front. I don't really want any more.

Then Ingrid sideswiped him with the question, 'Did you really mean what you said to Treya?'

Tomas blushed like a schoolboy. Crimson, root to tip, as the memory resurfaced within him like a drowning man gasping for air. The vision of Treya, radiant before him, though he wondered if his memory had taken on some poetic license and enhanced the image somewhat. He was sure there wasn't a light behind her, and nor was there a breeze blowing her hair. It took on the surreal view of one of those fake cosmetics adverts: all airbrushed and soft focus. Not that he was complaining: it was a pleasant image after all. Ingrid was still watching him intently and Tomas knew he would have to give an answer. But what to say? Did he mean it or was he under some sort of spell or hypnotic trance. He did feel a bit different since falling into the Domain, but was that just his overworked imagination or part of his gifts reacting with the transition. There was no way to tell, or no one to ask. But as he pondered this quandary, a certain clarity formed over the issue in question. He did find himself attracted to Treya, and in a way he hadn't anticipated. So really, for now at least, there was only one answer he could give Ingrid.

'Yes. Yes I did, but, believe me, I find it just as surprising as she does. It was the absolute and emphatically the last thing I was expecting to experience so forgive me if I seem a little hesitant about it all.' Tomas, though, couldn't fathom why he kept blushing when Treya's name came up: he was a forty-something-year-old man, not a spotty youth who had never had a woman before. Tomas had the metaphorical woman in every port. Fraternizing with the opposite sex was part and parcel of his work. It got him information, got him close to targets and even helped with the comedown after a job, giving him an outlet for the adrenaline overload he often found himself with. But not until his fiancée had he seen beyond their usefulness as a commodity, rather than as a companion. It was at that moment that Tomas realized the image of his fiancée was fading fast from his mind. However hard he tried to focus on her memory and her features, he couldn't. All he kept seeing was aspects of Treya. Part of Tomas's mind was distraught at what it considered was a betrayal of her memory, but another part whispered to him that it was nothing of the sort. She was the woman who broke the spell of his misogyny and the guilt-laden shell of his loneliness, but she wasn't the true one for him, not his soul mate, that individual who is the mirror image of what makes a person. It made Tomas realize that Jillian, his beautiful and sweet fiancée, was too gentle a soul for him. Her softness and kindness, ready smile and open arms were what drew him from the hard life he knew. Hers was the extreme opposite and maybe he needed that extreme to tear him away and open his eyes. But the reality was that the woman he really needed had to understand his world and his part in it. Treya was that woman. She was war and woman, sword edge and soft curves. And all he wanted to do was…

Tomas stopped, mentally shook his head and brought himself back to reality, and found himself face to face with Ingrid – eyes ablaze, looking at him with profound interest.

'What?' Tomas asked, but all Ingrid did was smile: a refreshing change, if he was honest, but a bit scary at the same time. He could tell she was unaccustomed to smiling.

'Pack it in, will you? You're unnerving me, smiling like that. I feel like a mouse in a cat's nest.'

Ingrid laughed fully then and smacked Tomas on the back. It was meant in a comradely way but it nearly unhorsed him. Tomas smiled a *thanks* weakly back. Accepting the moment of privilege at Ingrid's smile, Tomas dug a bit. 'So, bearing in mind my own surreal predicament, how exactly have I confused *her*? I thought what I said was fairly blatant and not all that open to interpretation.'

'I've known Treya pretty much all my life.' Ingrid sat back in the saddle, looking more relaxed than she had since he met her. *Maybe I'm getting somewhere, finally.* 'She is like the big sister I never had and more family to me than my own. This,' Ingrid waved in Treya's direction, 'is the first time

I've seen her behave this way with a man. For no man has ever said what you did – not and lived anyway.' Ingrid looked thoughtful and cast a sideways glance at Tomas. 'Though none of them that I know of, ever looked at her the way you did. By Odin, you actually *looked* as though you meant it.'

Tomas was mortified. *How to win friends in one easy move; just blurt out your innermost thoughts.* 'Could you tell Treya, please, that I won't – or at least I'll try – not to embarrass her like that again,' Tomas asked. 'I'll try not to put my size tens in it again and —'

Ingrid cut him off with a bark of a laugh and a mortified expression of her own. 'By Odin, no…' Tomas thought she had turned on him again. But it wasn't that at all. '…It does her good. She needs to get a grip on herself and I've seen you fight. If, and I say if, you are not a spy for the Adversary, then you may be a suitable match for my sister.'

Tomas did the blushing thing again. *She's bloody matchmaking me now?* Tomas thought incredulously, but found he couldn't find the words to argue with her.

'She needs someone her equal. Thor despaired she would ever find anyone. Even in Asgard there were few who courted her: she can be a touch intimidating when she wants.' *I can't say I've noticed,* Tomas mused to himself as Ingrid continued, 'My sisters all seem to approve of you so far, based on what they have seen, though some do question as to whether you are up to the task *beneath* that armor of yours.'

He colored again. *I've got to get a handle on that. It's starting to piss me off now.* 'Thanks for the rating, but you can't just discuss me like a hat or something. Don't you think I get some say in this?'

Ingrid laughed again. *Bloody hell, once you get her going, there's no stopping her.* 'Now what's so funny?' Tomas grumbled.

'You, you silly man. Your kind never learns, do you? Your side of the species has never had a say. The only place you go wrong is by trying to be something you are not. Women detest deceit and it is the one thing that will turn her from you forever. If men stopped lying, they would find their fortunes improving with the opposite sex, but then again, they are too stupid to understand that. So it goes.'

'Thanks for that. I feel so much better now,' Tomas muttered sourly, which only cheered Ingrid all the more. Another of those truisms, that women found entertainment in the discomfiture of men. He'd need to live for an eternity before he came close to understanding what made them tick, if then.

'Treya will sort herself out in due course, rest assured. You will be the first to know it when she does and believe me, she will, so be prepared and forewarned. Yet whatever the outcome, it does make good sport to watch. Ha!' Ingrid spurred her mount forward with a sudden leap and galloped ahead. Obviously the conversation was at an end. But it hadn't been wasted; not entirely anyway. He put aside his discomfort and considered the possible future and what he was about to get embroiled in, wondering if it would help his mission or hinder it. Wondering what plans were in store for him next at the fickle hands of Fate. *Bearing in mind who I've met so far, it wouldn't surprise me if Fate was a she and was as real as the Horsemen, with a warped sense of humor to boot.*

The next couple of hours passed uneventfully. The raven came and went, once with half of what looked like a six-legged rabbit hanging out of its beak. Tomas moved up and down the line himself, avoiding Ingrid's smirking eyes as he did so, getting to know some of the other Valkyries and spending a bit of time with Niall. It turned out that the company of women brought Niall right out of his shell and he was regaling them with tales of his home, back in County Cork, Ireland, and how he traveled to England in search of his fortune. As Tomas had ascertained, they found amusement in the tales of his subsequent misfortune and how he ended up on a convict ship bound for Australia.

They seemed to like the chatty little man and they kind of adopted him as their baby brother. It helped that he had tended Hildreth and some of the wounded as they traveled. They fed him and gave him horseriding tips, of how to minimize some of the muscle strain he was going to feel, for one who was as unaccustomed to riding as he was. His was a good horse, even if it was the only non-supernatural creature amongst them, and it seemed perky: ears up and bright-eyed. It probably appreciated the gentler master if the spur scars on its flanks were any indication. Niall whispered to Tomas that he had even had a few offers to rub out some of the stiffness in his thighs when they camped. Niall winked conspiratorially and Tomas shook his head, sighing, for he doubted Niall had any idea what he might be letting himself in for. Tomas grinned and tousled the little man's hair affectionately and told him to be careful, lest he end up as some Valkyrie's breakfast.

Tomas cantered off for a few moments of respite himself, going over everything that had happened so far, trying unsuccessfully to make any sense of it all. Dusk approached and the raven swooped in to roost upon his shoulder for a while. It was an unsettling feeling at first, but the longer it sat there, the more Tomas grew to appreciate its presence. It had a certain smell he couldn't put his finger on, but it wasn't unpleasant. It sat and preened its massive wings and chortled to itself as it did so. Tomas felt relaxed, for the first time since…

With a sudden shock – for Tomas had never had cause to think about it – he realized he didn't know the last time he wasn't sleeping with one eye open and his hand only millimeters from his Berretta. He couldn't put his finger on the last time he hadn't been on edge: tense and alert for something. When he was on a mission, he had to stay vigilant. Basically that or die. There was always somebody else out to get you before you got them. It was like four dimensional chess and you had to be a grand master of your game and be a dozen moves at least ahead of your opponent or else you died. When he managed to leave the company, his edginess increased tenfold, because not only was he still covering his tracks from the enemies he had made, but he was now hiding from those he had worked for. After the explosion matters only got worse and he doubted he would have lived much longer anyway if Michael and the Horsemen hadn't found him. A mortal body and psyche could only take so much, and his had been pushed to the edge and a touch over. Since that weird meeting in Glastonbury, his life had just been one breakneck rollercoaster ride of situation after situation. He hadn't had an awful lot of time for much of what was going on with his life to sink in and fully register – until now. Oddly, riding a mystical horse, magically bound to him, in the midst of legendary Valkyries, carrying the Sword of War and riding through a forest in Hell with a mythical white raven perched serenely upon his shoulder, he was at peace with himself for the first time probably in his entire life, and he liked it.

Without the need for sleep now thanks to his gifts, he was beginning to view that particular aspect as a pain in the ass: Tomas found it gave him far too much time to dwell on matters he couldn't affect and gave him the time to conjure far too many scenarios and possibilities which had started to give him a headache, and that, for certain was no gift. Sitting around the camp fire earlier that night he came to the conclusion he wasn't so much a guest amongst the Valkyries, but more like an unfettered prisoner. He made to walk the perimeter as he would on any camp duty – it was inbred in him to take his turn at stag – but all that happened was that the shield maidens made it quite clear he was to remain in the camp. Though they phrased it to make it seem as though they had matters well in hand, and his services were not required; they wanted him in firelight where they could keep an eye on him. The raven retired to a low hanging limb, where it, too, could watch him, though that seemed with a more possessive eye then a distrustful one. Tomas paced for an hour or so, and checked on the wounded, who were doing well. The Valkyries had remarkable healing capabilities, apparently. Another week of rest and they would all be fighting fit once more, with barely a scar to show for it.

The darkest hours came and went, and Tomas spent those with his night-vision goggles on, looking as deeply into the forest as he could, trying to catch a glimpse of those elusive watchers Ingrid mentioned. He hadn't forgotten them and it niggled him that he couldn't catch sight of them. Though he couldn't see much through the dense foliage even with the goggles, it made him feel marginally better for trying. Yet for all the tedium of being camp-bound, he did come to one conclusive decision. He would make the first move with Treya. He understood pride and felt it would be a softer approach if he were to apologize and shoulder the burden of responsibility; it was his fault after all. That decided, he helped prepare the meal to break their fast, and waited for Treya to come in from her turn of last sentry, which she had taken despite having been in and out all night, seemingly everywhere. Ingrid was right; she did take her role seriously and from what Tomas saw, was very good at it.

'Good morning, Treya,' were the first words out of his mouth when she came to the kettle pot, which was bubbling with a honey-sweetened oatmeal. She just looked at him, stony faced and expressionless as she scooped out a bowlful and began eating. Only when she had finished, did she respond to Tomas's greeting.

'And what precisely is so good about it?' she asked, placing her bowl with the others that had been discarded for cleaning and packing. Tomas was a little unsure, as she still seemed a touch frosty, but he was committed to talk to her now so he carried on.

'Seems we had an uneventful night; at least it was from where I was permitted to go, which wasn't far, I might add.'

Treya cocked her head slightly at the comment, picking up on the underlying barb but not rising to it, choosing instead to give Tomas a summarized report of the night's activities. 'Our outriders and scouts took out eleven demons who ventured too near. Perhaps they were scouts for the Adversary, but they died, however, before being put to the question. There was a surprise skirmish that resulted in one wounded sister, though not dire enough to stop her fighting. But if that is your definition of a quiet night, then yes, it was uneventful.'

Tomas gritted his teeth as he mentally berated himself for putting his foot in it again, but by the same token it got his back up that he knew none of this because they confined him to the campsite. His mouth got wind of that thought and ran with it.

'Look, Treya, there's no easy way to say it, but we can't carry on like this. Whether it was my comment about your beauty or whether you still think me a spy, I don't know, but confining me to camp isn't going to help. I could have been some use last night and it isn't polite to have to fight your allies to get them to let you help them, which is what it would have come to as your Valkyries blocked my way every time I got near the forest edge. Now, either we get over this and put that behind us, or we part company. I don't have the time to traipse about on eggshells, existing in fear of upsetting someone's delicate sensibilities. I am no one's prisoner and if I want to go into the woods, or anywhere for that matter, I'll go unless there is a damn good reason why not.' Treya stood stony faced, listening to Tomas's ultimatum. 'I'm prepared to let last night go on the grounds of security; I trust I won't be hampered again.' Tomas said it in such a way that it brooked no argument. 'Of course, I'd like us to get past my embarrassing slip, so if I say I'm sorry, can we start again? I've had the fourth, fifth and fifty-fourth degree from your maidens, who I have to say, make the Inquisition look like a gaggle of knitting grandmothers. And for all her ferocity and rigidity, you have a good friend in Ingrid; it seems she cares very much for you. She is very protective, I can assure you.'

Tomas smiled ruefully to lighten the moment. Treya had to smile in return, for she too knew just how *protective* Ingrid could be. Some people never recovered from being protected by her. It rather implied Tomas needed protecting *from* her and Treya knew that. She knew her sister well enough and that brief lapse in her guard opened the vital chink in her armor; Tomas pressed his advantage, reluctant to let the moment pass.

'Friends?' was all he said, leaving the word hanging for her to either grasp or not.

'Are you able to keep your thoughts to yourself now, or should I brace myself for any further revelations?'

Tomas chuckled at he thought and shook his head, though he did fix her with his blue eyes, making sure she felt the sincerity of what he was saying.

'Fingers crossed, but I should be able to keep my thoughts to myself from here on, but what you're saying is you don't mind me thinking it?'

It was Treya's turn to laugh then. She had been brought up around loud and lewd Vikings after all. 'Think what you will. I do. For now though – friends?'

What did she mean by that? What does she bloody well think? But even as he dwelt on her cryptic comment, he seized the moment and held out his hand. There was only the slightest of hesitations – though it felt like an age – before Treya clasped his wrist and Tomas did likewise. Nobody commented on the fact that they held the contact of arm and eyes just a touch longer than was necessary. He didn't care: she was smiling. And If Tomas or Treya actually noticed it, they too chose to say nothing.

An hour before noon they broke free of the forest and stopped at the treeline on the edge of another massive clearing. Tomas knew it was huge because he couldn't even see trees on the horizon, though they swept off to either side of the group. As he took in the vista before him, he noticed the little things that normally wouldn't register with him: the sparkling dew that remained upon the grass; the low patchy mist as the morning sun vaporized it; swarms of insects that flitted and buzzed, earnestly going about their business, which in part was avoiding the small birds that swooped in and snatched them from the air. It looked idyllic, tranquil even. The sort of place that families would gather for picnics and communal barbecues; with kids running and laughing all over the place, annoying their parents and the other adults as only kids know how to. But then reality crashed back in on him – an ocean landing on his head. This was the Domain, Hell. Centuries of indoctrination had etched the image of Hell as a fiery place of torment and belching flame, filled with pointy-tailed demons wielding pitchforks and other implements of pain. Not this: it didn't fit at all. Humanity didn't know the half of it. Tomas had an epiphany then. This is a honey trap. Maybe this is how so many folk disappear each year. Tempted to a better life in this paradise, this Eden. To those who had nothing or were trapped in the crime-filled, filthy inner city ghettoes, this and whatever else is dangled carrotlike before them, must look like a godsend. The bloody proverbial greener grass. Yet if what he was told was true, and he had no cause to doubt it, the Promised Land probably evaporated quick smart and those hapless souls found themselves caught in the spider web of all webs, and with their one-way ticket spent and cashed, the poor bastards were well and truly done for. Hah, Mother was right: if ever there was a bloody good reason to not talk to strangers, this place was it. No wonder they rarely found anyone: I expect Mars is the last place they'd think of looking.

Tomas was still staring out across the meadow when Treya appeared beside him. He was aware of her, but caught in the peculiar transfixion that occurs sometimes when you can't tear your eyes from whatever it is you're looking at, for no apparent reason. He idly saw her lift a highly carved and ornate horn to her lips. As she pursed to blow it, several thoughts flashed through Tomas's head that would have earned him a good smack if Treya had gotten wind of them. She puffed her cheeks and blew. What snapped Tomas out of his trance was the fact he heard nothing. Not a sound. He prodded his ears, thinking it might have been him, but his hearing seemed okay. Turning to Treya, he had to ask, 'Are you sure that it was supposed to do that? Doesn't a horn usually make some sort of ear-blasting sound? At least they do where I come from.'

Treya just looked at him with a calm and cool patience that adults have when a child asks an obvious yet stupid question. All Treya deigned to tell him, was to sit patiently and wait. And to remember where he was. The same rules didn't apply here as they did elsewhere.

Tomas laughed. 'I'm not likely to bloody forget where I am anytime soon. So many people condemned me to an eternity here, I reckon most of them would be spinning in their graves or kicking their heels with glee. If only they knew what Hell looks like they would be right pissed off. I mean…' Tomas looked about him, '…it kinda takes the sting out of the whole *Go To Hell* thing. Frankly, I've been in a lot worse places.'

Treya leveled a look at him that said 'Shut up and watch', though it wasn't so much watch, as listen, for Tomas saw nothing untoward, but he did start to hear a low rumbling which grew louder as he listened. It had that distinct sound he had heard close up once before. Stampede.

He had very nearly met his doom with one of those in Africa as several thousand water buffalo took a sudden diversion and almost smashed him to a pulp. But bless them anyway because they finished off what he had started. He had been doing a little off the books work for a security agency that specialized in hostage recovery. As matters transpired the captives had killed the hostage almost immediately – it seemed they had no intention of returning him – but seeing as Tomas had gone to all the trouble of flying out there, he thought he might as well finish the job and take them out. They got wind of him somehow and did a runner. They made it almost halfway across the national park before he caught up to them, but all plans went tits up when the herd turned ninety degrees. There wasn't enough left of the captives to even make it worthwhile for the vultures to bother getting off their perch. Tomas would have joined them were it not for the bloody convenience of a particularly large tree. He had never clambered so fast in his life as the buffalo thundered beneath him. The sound Tomas was hearing now put him very much in mind of those buffalo and he cast a cautionary look towards Treya – who sat undisturbed by it all as though nothing was occurring. Tomas looked to the other Valkyries, who, too, sat their mounts as though they had all the time in the world, paying no attention at all to the ground-shaking rumbling that grew louder and closer by the moment. It seemed only Niall looked as bothered as Tomas was. No surprise there though; he was scared of his own shadow. Any second now. Tomas braced himself for whatever was about to happen or appear. Due to the morning sun and the increase in temperature, a haze had formed on the crest of the rise that stretched out before them so that whatever crested it would appear to materialize out of thin air. He wasn't expecting what did appear. Not at all.

Tomas's hand dropped automatically to his side where his firearm used to be, but instead of gripping his HK, the Sword of War nestled itself into his palm, thrumming excitedly at the prospect of battle. But Treya had seen the move and hissed at him like some scorched cat.

'Put it away, Tomas, they are no threat to us.'

Tomas narrowed his gaze to better see what he was having trouble believing, even though it was right before him. 'That's easy for you to say. I take it you're seeing what I am?'

She nodded. They were monstrous creatures and Tomas's first thought, as they became clearer, was that they were centaurs. But closer inspection dispelled that notion. They were an amalgam of the Minotaur and centaur. They had massive torsos, with snorting and fantastically horned bulls' heads atop them. They were fused to the thundering body of a horse that was easily twice the size of Storm, and he was big. They carried bows that had to be made of whole trees and a quiver of shafts hung at their flanks, along with huge scimitars. *There is definitely no messing with these guys. Bloody woman better be right about them not being a threat. They look pretty hazardous even from here.* Their torsos were covered with ornate and shining breastplates, but they barely concealed the power beneath.

'So who or what are they?' Tomas had to raise his voice to be heard over the pounding of hooves as the dozen or so creatures drew closer. 'They look like bloody bulldozers on legs.'

Treya leant close to avoid shouting and Tomas was momentarily distracted by her smell. Inhaling deeply, he returned his concentration to what she said. 'They are the *Shunkari*. Bisotaur nomads from the deep wilds. It is said there are none better with a bow than their warriors.' Tomas could see why: it wasn't so much a bow, more like a bloody harpoon. No doubt it killed whatever it hit. And by the size of them, it must be like being hit with a land-to-air missile. 'They are the heralds and personal honor guard of the one we are here to meet.'

'And who might that be?' Tomas was incredulous. 'What has *these* as an honor guard?' But the question fell on deaf ears as she turned her feminine selective hearing on and ignored him. But all and further questions were put on hold as the bisotaurs skidded to a dramatic halt before them, sending a shower of turf spraying up as their gargantuan hooves dug in and brought them to an abrupt stop, scant feet from the group. No doubt it was a move designed to impress and put those they were to address on the back foot.

Tomas had to look up to meet the eye of the nearest beast. The raven, which had alighted on Tomas as the rumbling had started, took one look at the creatures, and, tilting its head in that inimical fashion ravens have, it cawed twice and summarily ignored them, picking and plucking at its feathers as though it could make them any cleaner and whiter than they already were. The bisotaur looked down upon Tomas with something akin to curiosity mixed with contempt, though Tomas imagined it held contempt for anything smaller than it was, which in his estimation was going to be most things. With hands that could crush a man's head like a ripe tomato – the biggest one, which much to Tomas's chagrin, was the one before him – drew its scimitar from where it was sheathed in an elaborate scabbard secured along its flank, with a sound of rasping steel and leveled the glinting, obviously sharp blade directly at him. It took all Tomas's willpower to restrain himself. A part of him wanted nothing more than to draw his own weapon and leap at the beast with a hatred he didn't think he could possess.

'Who is this creature, Treya Thorsen, who accompanies you and your maidens?'

Tomas couldn't attribute at first, the deep mellifluous voice with the bovine-equine hybrid before him. It was so incongruous, as the voice was smooth, sounding well educated and cultured; whereas the image was bestial, barbaric and extremely violent. He wouldn't have been surprised if their vocabulary only stretched to *kill, eat, rut*. It would probably have been enough, but this was something else. Tomas reminded himself that he shouldn't really be surprised by what he saw here, not when he recalled where *here* was, exactly again. Still fighting the almost overwhelming urge to lunge at it, Tomas clamped his teeth together, drawing a little blood where his tongue was too slow in getting out of the way – but it helped his control and he quickly had the urge to kill suppressed while he tried to listen to the conversation between Treya and the creature. Bisotaur, he corrected himself: it sounded too intelligent to be called a creature. He listened as Treya detailed their meeting and explained how Tomas's agenda matched their own and how he could be an asset to the cause. Tomas chuckled to himself; he hadn't been called an asset for some time now. That was what the brass referred to him as: an asset, much the same as a car, or a desk or toaster; anything that was of little importance and easily disposed of. All the regular troops were nothing more than assets to be deployed whenever and wherever some bloody Rupert saw fit; like some massive war game, except real people got hurt and died when they screwed up – which was quite often. Tomas was glad he was out of the game, but it only meant some other poor bastard got to replace him and the game went on. Perversely, Tomas thought, this war was precisely what humanity needed to make them sit up and smell the roses, stop bickering like children amongst themselves about inconsequential things, and come together for a common cause. *Pah! Chance would be a fine thing*. Tomas left his bitter thought hanging just as Treya finished speaking. The bisotaur sheathed his sword – a fact Tomas was slightly pleased about, for now he was calmer again. A reality check told him he didn't really want to be taking a blow from that. It would probably pound him into the ground like a hammer hitting a nail. But it didn't stop them looking at him with their scrutinizing gaze. Tomas returned it with steel of his own. They locked gazes for what seemed an eternity until eventually, the big one before him broke contact. He looked over his shoulder as if checking for something. Then he declared in a loud voice – it was clear from that why he was a herald, and Tomas wished he had some ear defenders:

'Bow before the awesome and dreadful majesty of our lord, for he does cometh!'

Simple, if a bit dramatic, thought Tomas. *Not overly fussy or pretentious, but bow? I don't think so.*

'Sorry, Trey. Who did he say was coming? 'Cos I don't do bowing.

Never have, not going to start now.'

But Treya didn't get the chance to respond as a voice exploded inside Tomas's head like he was wired up to the national grid. He wanted to scream, but clamped his teeth shut once again, forcing himself to accept the pain rather than fight against it – a trick he had learnt from an interrogator once, but it wasn't really working here. The voice ripped through his skull like so much white hot razor wire. 'Never can be a very long time, human, subject to what is happening to you. Never say never, would be my advice.'

Tomas gripped his head as though the pressure he applied would drive the voice out. But it didn't. The raven flew off with an indignant caw of disgust at being disturbed by what it saw as Tomas's erratic behavior. Oddly, it flew to Ingrid and much to her astonishment, it settled on her shoulder to watch proceedings. She sat rigid, her wide eyes turned towards it, but her head faced forward as though it would savage her in a heartbeat if she turned to face it. Seeing ravens flying and tearing at corpses on a battlefield was one thing, having one on your shoulder was something else.

Summoning whatever strength he could, from depths he never even knew he possessed, Tomas screamed back for the voice to get out of his head. Then, quite suddenly – so sudden, in fact, that Tomas nearly fell from his horse with relief – the pain and the voice, along with the pressure in his head, all vanished as though they had never been there. Tomas was furious, and this time he knew it was him that felt it. Ever since Michael had violated him – which was how Tomas saw it – he seemed to have developed an aversion for beings using the inside of his head for an intercom. The Sword of War appeared in his hand and Tomas stood in the stirrups, looking around for the source of the voice.

'Where are you?' Tomas shouted. 'Show yourself, you bastard, and I'll show you just what the inside of *your* head will feel like with my foot in it.' Tomas scanned the horizon, expecting the bisotaur's master to come in from the same direction that they had arrived from. He didn't anticipate an aerial arrival. Nor did he see it coming until the owner of the voice slammed in to the ground before them, flattening the grass around it for a hundred paces with the downdraft of its enormous wings and what passed for feet sinking into the ground several inches with the force of the impact. His mind registered what was before him fractionally slower than the urge to attack it, but just as Tomas tensed to charge the owner of the razor wire voice, Treya's arm found his, and her own voice cut a swathe through the red haze that had dropped once again before his eyes.

'*Don't, Tomas*! Please. I'm sure that once he has apologized for his thoughtless behavior and you apologize for your overreaction, we can all get along like civilized individuals. This is after all supposed to be a peaceful meeting of allies, not some ego battle for supremacy.'

Tomas turned to the woman beside him and looked at her as though he saw her for the first time. He really had to get a grip on this hair trigger of his. Flying into a rage at the drop of a hat was going to get him killed a lot sooner than was really necessary. The haze dissipated and he turned back to look at the imposing figure that had appeared before them and was presently folding wings the size of a DC10's behind its back and striding towards them purposefully. With the haze gone and his common sense returned to him, Tomas instantly thought better about tackling the being who had several bisotaurs as guards and looked as though he could stop tanks on his own anyway.

'I'm good now, Trey, honestly,' he added when she shot him an 'are you sure?' look.

Seemingly satisfied with his condition, Treya sat back up and faced their visitor, who had stopped and was staring at them, monstrous fists perched upon equally monstrous hairy hips, great multifaceted eyes taking in the strange sight before him.

'Tomas,' Treya intoned formally, 'may I present to you our commander and ally, the Dark Prince of Demons and mastermind of this rebellion, hailed as the Lord of Flies and Lucifer's paramount advisor, the lord Be'elzebub.'

Tomas almost laughed out loud at the thought of his former colleagues and teachers and what their faces would look like if they could see him now and who he was about to have a conversation with. 'Surreal to meet you. As you may or may not know after your excursion through my grey matter, my name is Tomas Walker. And before we get down to business, let me just add this: stay out of my head unless invited, and that won't be happening anytime soon, I can assure you. I'm the only one who wanders around in my head. Other than that, the pleasure is all yours, I'm sure.'

Treya looked at Tomas with something akin to horror. What was he thinking, talking to one of the ruling lords of the Domain in such an offhand manner, as though he were addressing some serf. Tomas never had much truck with titles or those who lorded it over others. Their shit stinks just like everybody else's, he always used to say. Lords, ladies, kings and queens – he had met several during the many functions he had been forced to attend during the course of his work. He could mingle and socialize with the best, discussing a myriad of topics. He knew a little about a lot – which usually turned out to be a darned sight more than that bunch of stuck up, toffee-nosed Ruperts. Tomas met the peculiar gaze of Be'elzebub with the hard-edged flinty stare he always got when he was around the ruling classes. He didn't like to think it was a chip on his shoulder; he hadn't gone without as a child. His family would have been considered upper middle class at worst, lower upper class at best. Either way, it was like some weird purgatory: looked down on by the family money and inherited haves, and despised and envied by the lower echelons and lower class have-nots.

Be'elzebub had the stereotypical look of what Tomas thought a demon should look like. He had the head of a giant fly, which kind of went without saying, him being the Lord of Flies and all; and what looked like the chest and arms of some scaly, armored looking thing. Tomas thought it resembled rhinoceros hide. His arms were the size of trees, with huge, clawed bear paw hands. But it was the hairy, hoofed goat legs that clinched it. He was disappointed that there was no forked tail waving about behind him. But Tomas did notice that the gargantuan leathery wings that he had seen him fold up seemed to have vanished. He recalled something about density and that they were still there, just out of phase for convenience of movement. They held each other's gaze for long minutes until a strange sound began to emanate from the being. It took Tomas a few minutes to realize that it was laughter – a weird gurgling rumble which tapered off, and then he spoke. It was a gentler and more moderated tone this time and fell considerably kinder on his ears than the last communication.

'Well met, Tomas Walker. And as our mutual companion admonishes...' At that, Be'elzebub looked at Treya and bowed slightly, '...I apologize for my rude intrusion to one unfamiliar with our ways and not subject to our governance. I confess, I am unused to such rebellious behavior from my own people, though I find myself leading a rebellion against another. The irony is not lost on me. Yet that aside, I find myself actually liking you, little human. You have spirit and I sense your words are not just wind. I feel a power within you and it was that which repulsed me from your thoughts. It is intriguing but I do not believe I could enter your mind again, not easily anyway. There is a void there; an impenetrable darkness that seems familiar yet alien at the same time. You are something of an enigma, Tomas human, and I welcome you to our little war.'

Tomas was unsure what to make of the odd creature. There was sincerity to his words that made Tomas uneasy. He had been distrustful of honeyed words from an early age and they still didn't sit well with him. *Too long, old son. You wouldn't know how to trust someone now if you wanted to.* Trouble was, he did want to. He'd spent so long being Billy No Mates, cavorting around the world, and the only people he ever got close to were those he had to take out. It had to have an effect on him. Now here he was, in the Domain – Hell, talking to Be'elzebub, the Lord of Flies, and he found himself wanting to believe and trust what this demon told him. *Bloody hell. There has to be something seriously wrong with me, not that it would take a lot of diagnosing.*

'Thanks, I think. Treya speaks highly of you and this *little war* of yours has spread beyond this realm to mine, infecting it like some nasty virus. I hope I've got the cure to both our problems.'

Be'elzebub did the fly thing as Tomas spoke, tilting his head jerkily from left to right as he listened, and even his proboscis flicked out once, tasting the air, Tomas supposed. It was quite disconcerting.

'Very well, Tomas human…'

Tomas interrupted him at that point. 'Either Tomas, or Tomas Walker if you must, but drop the human bit. I know what I am or was, thanks. I don't need reminding. So can we settle for just Tomas?'

'Certainly, just Tomas.'

Tomas grimaced.

'Only joking, Tomas. Just because this is the Domain, doesn't mean we are all stupid, you know. Now, my heralds tell me you have traveled far and have been wounded from recent battles. I would be remiss in my duties if I did not see you attended to. My entourage awaits an hour beyond the rise. Retire there and I will meet with you as the sun sets. Take your ease and let my physicians tend your wounded. Consider yourselves my guests.' Be'elzebub amended himself, 'Make that honored guests. I have some matters to attend to but I will return, for we have matters to discuss and little time with which to discuss them.' He shook his bug head sadly. 'Ah, there always seems to be a rush these days, unlike days gone by. Yet it does not bode well to dwell on the past when we have an uncertain future to take care of first. I bid you farewell for now. We will speak again when you are rested.'

Without any further ado, Be'elzebub manifested and spread four pairs of translucent, veiny and distinctly reptilian wings. With the one mighty down thrust, he was gone, launching himself skyward so fast, it was as though he simply vanished. The only indication that he had done otherwise was the gale force wind that whipped the cloaks and tore at the hair of those in the immediate vicinity, caused by the downdraft.

'Well, that was an experience,' Tomas said evenly after the wind had died down and the heralds had begun to canter off in the direction of the camp, indifferent to whether Tomas and the Valkyries followed them. Treya smiled thinly at him, barely concealing her own irritation at Tomas's behavior. It wasn't how one spoke to one of Be'elzebub's station. He was there on her recommendation, his behavior reflected on her, and she didn't like looking bad. There was something dangerously reckless about this human, but there was something else there too. Something she couldn't put her finger on, and that added to her irritation with him. Fascinated and irritated at the same time. A volatile combination at the best of times. And these were far from the best of times.

Tomas rubbed his face wearily, becoming aware of how his face felt and how it must have looked. His unshaven appearance must have given him a vagabond visage, though it rarely bothered him when he was on active service; where in fact a beard was a useful commodity. It hid many western features when he was seconded to the Regiment and helped with some *security* issues just prior to Kuwait kicking off. He remembered the SAS boys with affection, mainly because they were a rough bunch, hard as nails and with an attitude like his. Do what was necessary to get the job done. And they did. They were bloody good at it too, which was why the entire world envied them. But enough reminiscing: it wasn't helping. He would, however, have to do something about the shaggy growth sprouting from his face. It made him feel self-conscious around Treya for some reason he refused to acknowledge. But that was the least of his immediate concerns; he was more worried about the *void* Be'elzebub mentioned. And whether it had anything to do with his apparent lack of self-control when it came to his temper. Tomas tried not to dwell on it, but found it refused to move far from his thoughts. Temporarily shoving it into one of the mental filing cabinets he had, Tomas turned to Treya as they too began to herd the little group in the direction indicated.

'Thanks for the heads up back there. I felt I was about to do something particularly stupid. I don't know…and I mean it; I really don't know what came over me, but it's gone now.' *At least I hope so*, Tomas added to himself. 'He didn't seem as bad as all that. I think he got some really bad press back on my world.'

Treya just huffed at him and said in her cool tone – the one that Tomas remembered as her pissed off tone, 'Go fetch your bird. It sits with Ingrid and I don't think she enjoys its company as much as you do, plus she has duties to attend to, as do I. Do try to keep up; I would not like to keep Be'elzebub waiting any longer than I have to.' With that she wheeled her mount and began barking orders to get the group underway. For the first time since the meeting, Tomas wondered how Niall was. He saw the little man at the back of the group looking for all he was worth like a rabbit caught in the headlights of the biggest truck imaginable and with absolutely nowhere to go other than under its wheels. Tomas didn't even think he had stopped shaking by the time they reached the encampment, and then he just started all over again. Holding out his arm, Tomas mentally called for the raven and much to his surprise, it came, leaving Ingrid muttering unsubtle curses about her uninvited companions, both winged and mounted. He didn't have the heart to tell her about the trail of shit down her shoulder blade: she might very well have exploded.

As they rode, Tomas actually began to think that he might have a fighting chance in his previously suicidal plan, what with his new-found allies, who seemed, conveniently enough, hell-bent on the same result as he was: the Adversary dead. It was always a good thing to have several arrows for your bow, rather than the half of one he had started with.

Tomas wondered what the Horsemen would think of his chances now, assuming they thought of him at all. As it was they had little faith in him when he saw them last. They probably thought he was dead now, and had moved on to their semi non-existent back up plan – presuming they even had one. It sounded just like his old employer; they would deny his existence in a heartbeat and drag some other poor schmuck to take his place and continue the cycle of futility. He was good but he was as dispensable as a toothbrush, and he knew it.

ᚦᛗᛖᚹᛟᛗ ᚱᛋᚠᚱᛋ

Back at the clearing, the bloating dead mercenaries were entertaining several hundred crows, ravens and vultures, and no small contingent of flies; offering a feast of eyeballs and succulent internal organs. But even these delicacies weren't enough to keep the birds' attention when the first of the hounds loped into the clearing. Their great shaggy forms moved through the bodies, snuffling and sniffing, taking in every scent that still clung to them. Eventually, they were satisfied that they were on the right trail of their prey. That made the bodies superfluous, at least for trail finding. But they served another purpose and the ravening hounds fell upon the flesh with a savagery that was terrifying to behold. Yet again, there was little left after their frenzy, just a few marrow-stripped bones. Sated, for the time being anyway, they casually reconnoitered the area, ensuring they didn't miss anything before continuing the hunt. But the scent was fading fast, making it harder to determine exactly which direction their prey had gone. They would have to range out and back, like the spokes of a wheel, out and back until they could be certain which was the route to go. Time consuming but they had to be certain. Howling together, they drew the pack back into tight formation and tore off into the dark forest once more, salivating as the anticipation of the hunt drove them wild, confident they were close, and that they would soon be back on track. To them, success was inevitable.

ᚦᛗᚠᚾᛟᛗ ᚱᛌᚠᚱᛌ

'I left sisters on the battlefield, but it could have been much worse. Were it not for this mortal we would have been hard-pressed.' She refused to accept the fact they could have lost against the mercenaries, for they were Valkyries, and loss wasn't in their vocabulary. Be'elzebub listened intently as Treya recounted their meeting and journey in more detail. The demon lord asked few questions, but those he did, were specific.

'You say he admits to consorting with the Archangel Michael and the Four Horsemen?'

575

Treya nodded this was so. She was alone with Be'elzebub in his enormous pavilion. She had instructed Ingrid and the rest to keep an eye on Tomas even as they attended to their own needs. She had frowned when more than one of her sisters had smiled appreciatively at the prospect of *attending to his needs*. Treya simply turned away and strode belligerently away to give her report to the Lord of Flies. It wouldn't do to express her interest in this mortal in front of the others, but she found it disturbing that she found herself angry and jealous at the same time of her sisters, for she knew how they would *attend* him. *Rot them and rot him if he lets them!* Trying to put the image away of them all cavorting and feasting while she went about her duties, Treya focused her mind back to the matter at hand and who she was talking to. Be'elzebub himself reclined in a mountain of cushions, looking for all he was worth like some nomadic chieftain from the steppe. He had robed himself in luxurious silks and fabrics and was being attended to himself by slaves to either side. And, Treya noticed, one actually *under* the robes. She tried to put the image of what it was doing exactly, far from her mind, but the motion of the slave betrayed it. *I suppose I should be grateful and thank Odin he bothered with the robes at all.* Treya completed her initial report in as much detail as she could and Be'elzebub dismissed her to go and refresh herself and rejoin him again within the hour. He would be ready for her presently; he had 'dessert' to enjoy first. Treya refused to consider what or who that might be, and left. But she didn't go straight back to her sisters and Tomas. Firstly, she couldn't face the prospect of what they might be up to. She wasn't sure she could handle the disappointment if he had let himself be tempted by her very forward sisters. Secondly, one of the questions posed by Be'elzebub bothered her and she wanted to think on it further. But when she returned, the dessert hadn't finished. It was still bobbing beneath the voluminous robe and Treya grimaced with revulsion.

'He isn't entirely mortal, you realize,' Be'elzebub started, oblivious to her reaction, and Treya nodded that she thought as much. 'When he drove me from his mind, I caught a glimpse of something in there. Something dark and powerful. Of course, it could be something from his involvement with the Horsemen. They are enigmatic figures even by our standards and their plans and schemes are their own. Do you think he can be relied on? Can he control that temper of his, here of all places? You know how it can affect certain individuals' inhibitions.'

Treya did. She had felt the influence of the Domain herself when she had first arrived and nearly succumbed to its insidious coercion. But she and her sisters were made of sterner stuff than most and shrugged it off. 'I don't know, truth to be told. It was the first time I have seen such a flare of rage. During battle I put it down to berserker fury, but you are right. I will watch him closely.'

Be'elzebub smiled in his own inimical way, which was an eerie sight on a fly. 'I am sure you will, Treya Thorsen, I am sure you will.'

Treya had made her way to the horse pickets while the demon concluded his recreation and where the pegasi waited patiently, lazily grazing on the verdant grass, more out of boredom than any real need for food. Treya methodically checked the hobbles on the regular mounts and made small talk with several of the sentries as she made a round, all the time pondering her conversation with Be'elzebub, running it over and over in her mind.

'You are aware he is being hunted?' The Lord of Flies had said nonchalantly, in such a way as to gauge her reaction to the revelation. He was disappointed if he wanted something more dramatic.

'Aren't we all?' Treya responded coolly. 'You say this to provoke me, yes?'

'Not at all, my dear,' he lied smoothly. 'But it was part of the reason I did not greet you personally, for I was delayed by a small scouting party, which, as it happened, was out scouting for Asmodeus, gathering intelligence on the whereabouts of a renegade human who had recently arrived in the Domain. Coincidence? I think not. The struggle was brief and messy, but they did talk.'

Treya indicated he should continue, as he obviously had her on the hook now. Treya detested these little mind games, but she accommodated his whimsy.

'Asmodeus has been ordered by the Adversary to capture Tomas, I presume, at all costs. And I mean *all* costs. And...' Be'elzebub drawled as though it were a juicy piece of gossip, '...Fenris has deposed Shemyaza and strengthened his position, substantially bolstering his army of hounds with Shemyaza's followers. He has also dispatched several packs to capture and return the body of Tomas, minus his head, apparently. Fenris wants it for a trophy. How do you feel about throwing your lot in with him now? You could lose more sisters.' He sat back then and eagerly awaited Treya's response. *Such petty cruelty and juvenile mind games*, Treya thought bitterly. *He no doubt pulls the arms off humans just for fun and laughs as they scream and die horribly, in shock and bleeding out. Well he'll get no satisfaction from me this day or any other, not that it will stop him trying.* Treya sighed wearily and responded with the only answer she could give him and had intended to anyway.

'Of course we will support him. The fates have sent him from the archangels and the Horsemen. He must be of import to the war and as in all war, losses are inevitable, though ours will not come without a heavy price. We do not fall easily. We are warriors of the highest order and there are few who can stand against us.' For all his machinations, Be'elzebub knew this to be true, for he had fought alongside them before now and seen their prodigious battle skills. 'Tomas needs our support and we will stand by him. We owe him a blood debt for saving many of our sisters and we...' Treya stood a little straighter as she amended her words, '...I, intend to see that we honor it. We will not abandon him, but does this mean you will abandon us, now the risks have increased?'

Be'elzebub sat up and looked as intense as a large fly head could, rainbow hues reflecting off his multifaceted eyes, and antennae twitching spasmodically. Through all this, the slave hadn't budged from beneath his robes and Treya fought to hide her disgust.

'No, Valkyrie, you still have my allegiance as well as the promise I made you to expedite your return to Valhalla when my lord Lucifer is freed to reign once more and the usurper dealt with. But therein lies the dilemma.'

Treya paced back and forth before the demon, frowning as she did so, her hand reaching automatically for the hilt of her sword, eyes furtively scanning the huge tent for signs of betrayal.

'What dilemma do you speak of that causes you such concern? You're not having second thoughts, are you? Not now, surely? It would be a devastating blow to the rebellion.' Treya suddenly drew her blade and adopted a fighting stance. 'Or is that the plan: cripple the movement at a critical time by pulling your support?' Treya was prepared for whatever infernal trap he had prepared. He couldn't fail but to see her muscles bunching and rippling beneath her sweat-slick tanned skin as she tensed for any imminent attack. She was in full fight-or-flight mode and Be'elzebub knew he needed to pacify her fast before she exploded in violence and steel.

'Be easy, Treya. I'm not setting you up, nor am I pulling anything out of the rebellion. It is just that our cause has gotten a little more difficult and the timeframe to accomplish it considerably shorter.'

Treya relaxed a little, sheathing her blade but remaining on edge still, as if she would spring into action at a heartbeat's notice. This behavior both amused and intrigued the Lord of Flies. He watched the Valkyrie at every opportunity. They were like big cats. All slinky and lethal suppleness. Yet they had claws and teeth that could devastate the ranks of most of what the other lords could throw at them. He mused frequently that he should have had them as his heralds instead of the bisotaurs. Granted they were big and imposing, phenomenal in battle and excellent strategists. However...they were nowhere as easy on the eye as the Valkyries, and the shield maidens certainly smelt a lot better and didn't require a contingent of slaves to clean up behind them during their time in camp, though the plants benefited. Where the bisotaurs were arrogant, confident in their belief that none would be foolish enough to attack them, the Valkyries were suspicion personified, especially Treya's second – Ingmar or Inghild or whatever her name was. Ingrid, that was it. Such caution was as necessary as breathing in the Domain and he believed that Treya still felt he would turn on them at a moment's notice; her demonstration this evening had been proof of that. Be'elzebub was no stranger to deception and deceit. He wasn't the Prince of Lies and a ruling member of the High Court beside Lucifer for nothing. Or at least had been. Thus court intrigues and paranoia were part and parcel of everyday life here, but a small part of him was still put out that the Valkyrie had not fully come round to him yet. She watched him suspiciously.

'I have learnt from my spies within the Adversary's palace – those that still live anyway, for it seems the beast is systematically wiping them out, mostly by sprees of killing everything in sight. Either he is truly out of his diabolical mind or he is playing the law of averages though personally, I err to the former. However, I digress.'

A servant had appeared with goblets of wine and bowls of fruit. Placing them before Treya, the shield maiden declined and asked for water instead. The slave all bar ran from the pavilion in order to comply. Be'elzebub watched the slave go before continuing, 'The Adversary, malignant canker that he is, plans to send my incarcerated lord, Lucifer himself, imprisoned within none other than the Wolf Lord's former gaol, to the barren moon of Daemos. This, should he succeed, will be totally unassailable. It is so heavily enchanted, not helped by its mineral content: being mostly iron, it shields itself. Lucifer had only one portal to the moon and he retained its secret. It was his retreat. Apparently the Adversary has possession of it now. This is not good.'

Treya's interest had piqued at this twist of events and her tactical mind fired up once more. 'It does beg the question why the Adversary hasn't just killed him and be done with it.'

The slave returned with the water, magically chilled in a copper pitcher that glistened with rime as it replaced the wine before her. Treya poured her own and waved the slave away with a dismissive hand. She was contemptuous of the whole idea of slaves. People should only serve others if they chose to do so, not because they were ordered to. Be'elzebub let her take a pull before continuing. She drank her water like she drank ale: knocked back, and not sipped demurely like a typical female. She also drank that way, he had discovered earlier, to maximize her reaction time in case of attack. He wondered if she did everything that fast for the same reason. Grunt grunt, thanks a lot, now get off. She did fascinate the ancient demon lord; maybe once this was over he might think twice about sending her back, and keep her for his own personal amusement. He did like them feisty and she would certainly be spitting razors and fur like a wild cat at the turn in events. Be'elzebub let that thought warm him as he continued his explanation.

'It is not known yet how he managed such a feat as switching Lucifer for Fenris. It was widely believed that all transference incantations and devices were destroyed long ago in order to contain the damned dog.'

'Apparently not.' Treya had a way with words.

'No, apparently not. You are right. But it seems he doesn't want the Light Bringer dead yet in case he is still inextricably tied to the Domain or until the Adversary is strong enough to control this world himself. Should he succeed in his plan ours will become as sand in the Desert of Desolation during one of its many lethal sandstorms.'

Treya sat, deflated at this news; it put many plans in jeopardy. 'We will have to attack Asmodeus much sooner than we intended. You say there is only one portal. Do I take it that Asmodeus has to transport the Dark Lord there in person, so to speak?'

The fly nodded as it waited for Treya to figure out the implications.

'Surely they will just open a portal to this gateway and transport him from there. How will we interrupt this plan?' Fortunately, paranoia can work against those who live by it and Be'elzebub was about to clarify the loophole in their plan, but Treya stopped him. 'Wait. Before we go through it all, let us summon Tomas and Ingrid and go through it with them present. It will save me having to go over it twice because you know that whatever you tell me, I will tell them.'

Be'elzebub offered no verbal response, merely waving a hand as though to say 'Be off with you then'.

'I'll be back in a moment. See that you have finished with your body slave by the time I return. I can only take so much and your flagrant disregard for my feelings is abhorrent.' With that, Treya turned and ducked out of the tent. Be'elzebub dragged the sweating and brutalized slave from beneath his robes the moment she was gone and the flap dropped back in place. Its mouth was bleeding profusely from overuse and its jaw hung slack, no doubt broken some time ago, but it knew better than to stop or cry out. Be'elzebub healed it with a pass of his clawed hand and it almost sagged in relief.

'Go clean yourself up and await my summons. I want you back when I have finished with my meetings, and you need to perform better than this last stint or you'll truly know what pain is. Do I make myself clear?'

The slave whimpered and nodded emphatically as it bowed its way out backwards, turning only at the last minute to dash through the flap.

Tomas had been studying the camp. Well, as much as he could in between fending off amorous Valkyries. He felt something like a mouse in a cattery and got the distinct impression he was being toyed with, though another part of him felt it was more like tested. But for what, he couldn't imagine, or at least tried not to. He had picked over his food: after all, it wasn't like he was hungry or needed the sustenance. But it was polite and he kept up the pretense, and also, he had to admit, the camp spread was impressive. It was set out like a royal banquet and it seemed nothing was missing and it all looked freshly prepared. Even the round loaves of warm honey bread steamed as though they had just come out of the oven. But then again, there were hundreds of bodies with them in the camp and quite likely thousands more camped around it, both inside and outside the forest. Tomas wasn't sure what or who they all were exactly as some were humanoid; others were so alien it was all he could do to not stare at them. He assumed some were guests, nobility maybe, while others were part of some entourage or bodyguards; whatever the reason, there were a lot more of them than Tomas felt completely comfortable being around right about then. He knew he'd need eyes up his arse, down his back and anywhere else he could think of as well as on the back of his head with this lot.

He had watched as Treya had emerged from the pavilion and returned an hour or so later. She did a check of the sentries and horses, but Tomas thought she looked troubled. He was quite curious to know what was being said in there but figured that he would find out soon enough, one way or another. Extricating himself from the clutches of the Valkyries, Tomas made a casual circuit of the camp himself, checking the location of the sentries, where the horses were picketed and what would be the best route out if things went askew. He got more than a few strange looks, but no one stopped him. He was an *honored* guest after all. Unfortunately, to Tomas's dismay, the camp was well secured and left him with only one alternative if it all went pear-shaped. Up. It wasn't an option he had ever considered before and it still felt weird, but the ever-present sensation of Storm, bonded to him, reassured him that it was a good option. Even the raven cawed its agreement between mouthfuls of rabbit that it was busy tearing its way through on a low branch close to where he had sat.

Just as he sauntered back to the bench he was sharing with the shield maidens, he saw Treya emerge once more from the pavilion, looking for all intents and purposes like a falcon that wasn't sure if it should turn and fight or flee for all it was worth. Her eyes darted left and right as she crossed the camp to them in easy, fluid strides. Tomas was amazed at her elegance, convinced that the more volatile a situation became, the more graceful she got. He could see she was coiled tight though. Whatever had been said in there had put her on alert and she evidently didn't like it.

'Tomas! Ingrid!' Treya barked, looking both at him and Ingrid, who had sat as far from him as possible. Him and his bloody bird, who she kept looking daggers at. She had obviously found his gift to her on her armored shoulder plates. And it didn't help when Tomas struggled to keep a straight face whenever she glowered at him. But she leapt to her feet the moment Treya called her name. Ingrid in turn called her captains: three of them. She may have been Treya's second, but even she couldn't be everywhere at once so she too delegated.

Tomas was the last to get up and before he moved he asked, 'What is it, Trey? What does he want now?'

She looked at him, with a mixture of emotions playing across her features. The prime one was consternation. Why couldn't he just do as he was told? If she said come, why didn't he just come? Why were there always questions?

'Be'elzebub has some news to impart and it seems prudent that you all hear it first-hand, rather than repeat ourselves, though I warn you. It is not good.'

Tomas shrugged. 'So what's new? I haven't had any bloody good news for so long now, I probably wouldn't know it if it bit me on the arse. All I get these days is variations on a theme. It's either worse, worser or worserer.'

Treya looked at him as though she had no idea what he was rambling on about. As he spoke though, the raven ghosted down to land on his shoulder. It obviously wanted to hear what was said as well. Ingrid moved past him and shot a dagger look at the bird. It cocked its head back and cawed once to her. Tomas laughed and her face turned even more thunderous, if that was at all possible.

'What's up, Ingrid? I think he likes you.'

In a voice that was cold enough to freeze water, she replied as she moved past, 'I like it too. On a spit, turning slowly over a roaring flame, with a little butter and some ale. Maybe even with some spiced breadcrumbs shoved up its – '

'Ingrid!' Tomas rebuked, laughter desperate to escape him. 'That's no way to speak about a companion, is it? Shame on you.' With that, Tomas slipped though the tangle of legs and feet that were sprawled around him and caught up with Treya, who was waiting for them, patience barely contained.

'After you.' Tomas moved to the pavilion entrance and held the flap open for them. He coughed purposely as he said, 'Ladies first. There's always a place for chivalry.'

Treya and Ingrid glowered at him. Ingrid's captains just winked and smiled conspiratorially as though they knew what he was up to and were enjoying every minute of their leader's discomfort. *Some things never change, it seems.* The squaddies back home always found great pleasure in any incident that involved one of the Ruperts getting egg on their face. And generally, the more painful it was, the funnier it became. *The great us and them divide. I don't reckon it'll ever change wherever there are people. Or anything, for that matter. It seems there are always leaders and followers, even in the bloody animal kingdom. Must be one of them cosmic laws or something.* Tomas put the stray thought from his mind as he ducked into the pavilion behind the women, cautious to not knock the raven from its roost on his shoulder. At the same time, he manifested the Sword of War to his hands. Knowing it was there was all well and good, but it was the comforting sensation of having the hilt pressed firmly into his palm that he sought. It wouldn't hurt to show a bit of steel anyway. He didn't want the demon to think him incapable of protecting himself should the need arise. *Prevention is always better than cure, I say.*

He wasn't sure what he did, or how he did it, but while he thought about preventative measures Tomas thought about closing his mind, encasing it in steel shutters, making it as armored as he was. He visualized this impenetrable barrier inside his mind and put on his most businesslike face. *After all, I am about to enter the presence of the Lord of Flies, Prince of Deceivers, and all around bad guy; and after the last time, he's the last bloody thing I want traipsing through my head.* He wasn't sure it would work but it was worth a try. What added salt to his wounds was he seemed about to forge an alliance with him. *Whatever next?* Bad question, as it turned out.

His first view of the pavilion's interior didn't disappoint. It was lushly set out with rugs, throws and cushions everywhere. *Sheikh Be'elzebub. All he's missing is a bloody hookah.* Treya, Ingrid and the Valkyrie captains had refused to sit but had dropped to one knee for the sake of propriety. But it also enabled them to launch upwards in a heartbeat should the need arise. Ever battle conscious, Tomas liked that. It had been something of a surreal journey to get where he currently found himself: so fast he really hadn't had a lot of time to truly assess his own battle readiness capabilities. Since the explosion, they had been pretty much non-existent. And frankly, he couldn't have given a toss either way. But since Michael and the Horsemen had dragged his sorry ass into this nightmare, he had been given little choice but to get his shit together, though he hadn't thought about just how together it had become. Where he had been running to fat through inactivity, poor diet and sleeping under newspaper, he was now more toned and fitter than he had been in a while; what with so much happening these past days or was it weeks? *Damn!* He couldn't remember exactly when it had all started – if it was only days, it sure *felt* like weeks – and how long it had been since he was propelled into this chaos-strewn disaster. But, however long it had been, it had dragged the man Tomas was back from a very bleak and probably short future. If he had just died right there, in one of those anonymous alleyways, buried under the refuse of a society that had no idea he existed, he wouldn't have cared. No one would. No, that's not technically true; Gwen might have shed a tear, might. But then again, who would be able to tell her? There was no one alive who knew the two of them, except maybe Chambers, the family's brief. But who would put his corpse together with an upmarket legal firm of barristers? Yet fate took the piss out of him once more and gave him an opportunity to redeem himself. A whirlwind of cataclysmic events later and here he was, in Hell, about to meet the mythological Be'elzebub – a bloody demon that has been documented throughout Earth history – in the company of Valkyries, and all he could really think about at that moment was how alive he felt. The first time in far too long. His senses felt sharper than ever, his mind sifting and organizing the many tactical aspects of his mission and his current predicament. The adrenaline was surging though him again, not with the prospect of any imminent enemy engagement, but just with the whole bloody mess. This was what he was born to do. Somehow he realized that now, probably for the first time. Yeah, he had given it some thought when he was being dragged around the world by the Horsemen, but only when it really kicked off and he got his hands dirty did he fully appreciate what the stakes were and what he was up against. The prospect of a thing is no substitute for being in the thick of things and having to think on your feet; react to events as they happen; make instant decisions, ones that could affect the lives of either yourself or thousands of innocents or both. There were no rehearsals for life, his father used to say, no looking at the script in advance; but if you expect the unexpected and assume the worst-case scenario, little can sneak up and get the better of you.

The few seconds that Tomas took to experience his epiphany had him standing in the entrance way to the pavilion, and Be'elzebub took it for uncertainty as to what to do next, so he gestured for Tomas to take a seat.

'I think I'll stand, thanks.'

Be'elzebub just shrugged and turned away from him. 'Suit yourself.'

Tomas moved slightly to one side, so that should anything barrel in behind him, he wasn't in its immediate path. He stood straight, legs braced and arms folded, his hand still gripping the hilt of the sword. His black cloak hung to his ankles and made him look not dissimilar to the raven that perched upon his shoulder. Two sets of dark unblinking eyes fixed themselves on the demon lord and waited patiently for it to speak. Which it did when it realized this was as good a reception as it was going to get.

'Very well, as you will. I am not insulted by this show of distrust, even though I have sworn to uphold my promises to your Valkyries. Remember, they are only as good as long as we all survive this. It is our shared doom that brings us together. I expect that were we not bound by our common enemy, we would be enemies ourselves, though none of that is of any import when faced with the imminent destruction of all we hold dear.' The tone of Be'elzebub's voice was irritated at first, no doubt by Tomas's disdain for his

587

hospitality and the volatile behavior of the Valkyries, but as he got into his flow, it switched to the more honeyed tones of a courtier or a politician.

'But as you are all off-worlders and not denizens of the Domain, I will forgive your rudeness. Be grateful, human, that this warrior speaks so highly of you.'

Tomas just leveled his implacable gaze on the fly head and sneered, 'Is this going to be a long yarn?' Tomas had heard these tones before. It was often employed by those who wanted something from you. Most likely your life.

'No. It isn't.' The honey dropped like a lead weight and his voice became like stone. 'Time is something we now find ourselves desperately short of. Suffice to say, plans have to be changed radically: ours and maybe yours too. Perhaps you could give us the benefit of your insight, though before you do, allow me to make a small declaration. In order for you to advise and be present at a council of war involving one of the ruling lords, namely myself, you need some standing. Treya is the daughter of Thor and has a title already.' Be'elzebub rubbed his mouthparts, flicking his proboscis out thoughtfully. 'Earl, I think. That is high enough to permit you to attend and speak. We are sticklers for our rules and laws here. Should we survive this, it would be a loss of honor to have had aid from an off-world animal. A mere human.'

Be'elzebub stamped his massive hoof down on the floor and Tomas felt a small concussion blast out from the move. And just for a second, a wave of intense cold passed through him. Unnerved by this, Tomas part drew the sword and took a step toward the demon lord. 'What did you just do?'

But Be'elzebub seemed unconcerned by Tomas's action. 'Sit, Earl Tomas. It was nothing harmful, but the essence of the title needed to be affirmed with you, which was all that happened. The Domain will now recognize you, Earl Tomas Walker. So please...' Be'elzebub gestured to a large pile of cushions to his left, '...sit!'

Seeing nothing he could do that wouldn't exasperate the situation, Tomas sighed to himself in weary resignation and moved to sit, sliding the sword back into the scabbard he had materialized for it with an audible hiss of steel, a sound not lost on the demon lord. Tomas made sure it was placed in such a way that his sword was free and he could move quickly if needed. He didn't want to be caught flailing around in a mire of tangling and entrapping soft furnishings if the shit should hit the fan.

'Satisfied?' Tomas asked, restrained civility forcing itself from between his teeth.

'Barely, but it will suffice, my lord earl.'

Tomas grimaced. It was as bad as being called sir. Amend that; it was worse. He was officially a Rupert. Now he truly would have his poor dead parents and former teachers well and surely spinning in their graves, though it would quite likely have his old CO laughing himself senseless, knowing Tomas's dislike for any member of the ruling classes. Becoming a member of Hell's nobility wasn't what he had in mind on his list of aspirations and achievements. His mother had been a devout Catholic, and her son was now an earl in Hell. If she wasn't dead already, poor darling, this would kill her.

'Let's get this over with,' Tomas stated with a flat finality that raised an eyebrow in more than one Valkyrie.

'Certain relevant information has been revealed to us, primarily because of you, Earl Tomas –'

Tomas waved a hand to stop matters before they got going. 'Look, if we are going to continue this, can we drop the earl bit? You have done your formality thing. Fine, I'll live with it but don't go on. Tomas will do just fine. Tom, if you prefer, or even tosser. I don't care as long as you lose the title every time you address me.'

'As you wish, but know this – you are more popular than you think, Tomas. You are being hunted by two factions of the Adversary's supporters.'

'Good for them! I've been hunted before and I'm still here. Anyway it's always nice to feel you're wanted. It gives me a sort of fuzzy feeling, you know – right here.' Tomas balled his fist and thumped himself gently a couple of times where his heart was. Treya shook her head slightly in exasperation at his blasé attitude. *It was a wonder he hadn't got himself killed long before now. So reckless.*

Be'elzebub wasn't impressed. 'Fuzzy you might be, but you have not been hunted by what hunts you now. The Hounds of Fenris for one; and secondly, by the trackers and bounty hunters of Asmodeus. It seems the Adversary wants you dead as badly as we want him. Now, why is that?'

All eyes turned to Tomas, who just shrugged and was about to say 'How the hell should I know?' When he heard it in the back of his head he realized that sounded a bit naff considering who, what and where he was. So instead he just shrugged and said he didn't know, maintaining an expression of innocence, though he did suspect why, taking into account what the Horsemen had told him and signed him up for. *Apparently, being one of these guardians or defenders or whatever the bloody hell I'm supposed to be, draws some pretty fucking unpleasant attention. It's like being dropped into the middle of flaming Baghdad wearing a stars and stripes outfit and holding a placard saying 'George Bush for God, and Allah is from America'.* Every Tom, Dick and Ali was going to be gunning for him. So what's new? He'd spent his life so far being chased and hunted by someone or other, so why should his future – what he had of one – be any different?

'Doesn't matter really, does it?' The question was rhetorical and Be'elzebub knew it. Their task was such that running wasn't an option. There was nowhere in the multiverse to run to. The doom they faced was on such an apocalyptic scale that the mind had trouble bending itself around the idea that stars and planets we considered light years away were just as threatened by what the Adversary planned as they themselves were on the same world as the megalomaniacal demon himself. The chips were down; it was the last turn of the card. Whatever analogy or metaphor anyone wanted to apply worked right now. This was it: shit or bust, like it or not.

But Tomas was not a defeatist. Never had been and he certainly wasn't about to start now. It was when he was stuck in the corner with few options that he came into his own. And the one thing that always formed part of his plan was simple: the best form of defense is always a good offense. He'd said that a few times too.

'When the enemy thinks he's chasing you, and got you on the run, my experience has always been to put yourself where he least expects to find you. Right on his doorstep. You want my opinion?'

Be'elzebub nodded almost imperceptibly. 'That's why you're here. Treya believes you have something to offer our struggle beyond being bait. Tell me, how do you propose to complete your mission?'

Tomas immediately tensed. He'd heard the tone of this sort of question before and knew the test had begun.

'Firstly, Bub…' Treya's eyes widened so much then, Tomas feared they were going to eject themselves, '…I'll continue, with or without your help, or Treya's, for that matter. I've been up against whole bloody countries before and I'm still here to talk about it. Though here is relative, I suppose. But in many ways, the fewer people I have to depend on to do their damn job, the easier it is. Fewer screw ups that way. Plus, when the only thing I have to hide is my own arse, that becomes easier than concealing the odd army or two. I'm a one-man surgical strike and thanks to a bit of luck, if falling into Hell could be considered lucky, I'm nearer to the bastard I'm after than I was when I was on my own planet.' That still sounded strange to his ears. 'However…if you want to help, the more the merrier.' *He's not getting details – not that I have any. I'm winging it all the way so far.* Tomas cast a wary glance to the raven that gripped his shoulder and was still silently watching everything. *Winging it in more ways than one. Why don't you find something else to sit on for a minute in case I have to do something radical and energetic. We don't want you getting caught in the flap, if you pardon the expression.*

'*Very well.*' Tomas nearly fell over. It was the first time the damn bird had answered him with anything like a coherent answer. *It bloody well does understand me.*

'*Of course I do. What do you think I am? Stupid? Now pay attention to what takes place here. This alliance could be crucial and from what I have seen, your presence here is pivotal. Now be nice and try to be helpful; I'll keep an eye out for trouble and any sort of deception.'*

Tomas was aware that all assembled were looking at him in a peculiar way and that if he didn't say something soon, they would suspect him of something.

'So what do you say? Why don't we see if we can be of use to each other?' *'How's that?'*

'*Better.'*

Tomas was astounded by this turn of events. *'Why didn't you talk before?'* Tomas asked mentally, getting the hang of the telepathic link the same way he had with Death. The raven lifted off his shoulder and glided over to an ornament that stood to one side of the pavilion, landing promptly on it and shitting down the back of it. Be'elzebub didn't see that and Tomas could have sworn that the bird winked at him.

'Didn't have much to say and I was learning your frequency. I had a bit, but I needed time to merge wavelengths with you. You wouldn't want all and sundry listening in on our little chats, would you?' Tomas shook his head ruefully and turned back to the demon lord and Treya. He could see that they knew something had just happened, but didn't know what. She watched him suspiciously. Nothing new there.

'Maybe we got off on the wrong foot; I'm not the most trusting sort of guy, as you may have guessed.' Tomas smiled disarmingly. He could be charming when he wanted to be, and the effect wasn't lost on Treya or the rest of the Valkyries. She still watched him but Ingrid and the others seemed to relax a little at this turn. Or maybe it was just his imagination. 'Why don't you tell me where we are and why you feel time is any shorter than it always has been? I'll put aside my lifetime of distrust at what and who you are; after all I have had to ally myself with some right shits in the past. Adding a demon lord to the list won't kill me. Will it?'

Be'elzebub laughed himself then, an unpleasant sound at best. 'No, Tomas, it will not. Not until we have defeated the Adversary and are free to become enemies again, for I have little doubt that is the way of things. We are who we are, for good or ill.' Be'elzebub raised his goblet and made a toast. 'To our alliance. May we all live long enough to see the balance returned.'

A servant passed Tomas a goblet and he accepted, albeit reluctantly. Eyeing the contents dubiously, Tomas smiled wanly at them, perturbed at the thought of drinking, but decided to go for it anyway. *What the hell*. He held his own goblet aloft and echoed the toast. 'To victory, for there is no alternative.' He drank, giving it a few seconds to see what happened. Nothing nasty seemed to be happening to him and it tasted pleasant enough.

The next hour was spent bringing Ingrid, Tomas and the captains up to speed with what Be'elzebub knew about Asmodeus, Lucifer and Fenris. As Tomas listened, the raven filled him in on some of the backgrounds of both the Wolf Lord and Asmodeus, and how the kingdom of Asmodeus was an unpleasant place. There he was known as the Spider King. He was widely feared and his army of arboreal spiders were some of the most deadly assassins in the Domain. No doubt some had been dispatched to kill Tomas.

'Thanks. You're just full of cheery thoughts, aren't you?' The raven just added that it was better he knew what sought him than wait for it to bite him in the ass. *'But my arse is armor plated. A spider will have a tough time biting me through that and my gift from pestilence protects me from poisons and disease.'* At least he hoped so.

'That's all well and good, but they are the size of a large dog and it's not the venom you have to worry about, it's the flesh-dissolving gastric juices they will pump into you, liquefying your insides. If you can't die easily, imagine an eternity cocooned in perpetual agony as you dissolve forever; paralyzed and feeding a million spiderlings within your body cavities.'

Tomas just glared at the raven, who sat innocently preening. Eventually though, there was no more to say. They all knew where they stood and what was at stake. It wasn't very promising as so much depended on luck and speed. And how long it took Asmodeus to reach this secretive portal to one of the Martian moons. The fact he traveled overland bought them some time, but not a lot. Apparently the gateway was warded by some seriously nasty barriers. The Adversary didn't have the access commands to override them and they doubted that Lucifer had told Asmodeus about them, for Be'elzebub was only passingly familiar with them and he stood higher than Asmodeus in the hierarchy. Just – though that small differential was enough to create an eternal animosity between he Lord of Flies and the Spider King. Tomas laughed out loud then and caught everyone's attention.

'What do you find so amusing, Tomas?' Be'elzebub asked. Tomas looked around the pavilion and realized all eyes were on him, expressions serious but curious. All except Ingrid, and she just glared perpetually at him.

'It's nothing really, but a thought just occurred. I think I've got a way to get the big guy back. It's not pretty or overly complex but without sounding too much like a cliché, it just might work. But it's the irony that I find entertaining.' Their faces, if not so much Be'elzebub's flashing mutli-faceted fly eyes, urged him to go on. 'Well, it's not often that the fly sets the trap for the spider.'

Ingrid lowered her head and shook it sadly while Treya just groaned, but a tiny smile creased her features for the first time in what seemed an age to Tomas. Sensing some headway, Tomas continued, laying out his basic plan.

'How's your credibility with Asmodeus? I mean, other than him wanting to pound your arse into the ground and probably see you torn limb from limb in the most humiliating and painful way possible, which is normal for feudal enemies like you two. I've seen it hundreds of times. On Earth, we call such places governments. Where rulers of countries smile at each other whilst wishing the other ill. Forming alliances where they would sooner nuke them. Hypocrites and two faced, shallow sons of bitches. Personally I despise all of them. But unlike with them, I find I actually like you. Weird as it is, we know where we stand and make no bones about it. A spade is a spade. Were we not in this shit up to our eyeballs – well, not you so much, not having eyeballs and all, but you get me – you would happily gut me from top to tail or I'd be slicing you into pastrami; that's life and shit happens. But my point is, for all that, are you prime suspect for this rebellion or do you still have some social standing where you can get together with your fellow demons and shoot the breeze?'

Be'elzebub was silent for a moment only as his insidious mind got the gist of where Tomas was heading. Be'elzebub chuckled at the audacity. 'He suspects much, as do many of the court, but none can prove anything as yet. But suspicion and treachery are part and parcel of existence here, so not much changed really. Lucifer simply vanished one day and the next, the Adversary appeared with some tale of fancy that saw Lucifer absent for a brief period. It wasn't long before it became apparent what had happened; we all have spies and there are no shortage of those who are prepared to spill their guts to save their sorry hides or in the hope of advancement.'

'I think you know where I'm heading with this, but for the benefit of the girls, who may be a bit slow...' Ingrid actually growled and he felt the weight of furious looks of indignation from all those assembled; but Tomas smiled to take the sting out of the barb, knowing too, he was going to pay for that later, '...Easy, ladies. We're all friends here.'

'Not for much longer with smart-mouthed comments like that, you – '

'Looks like I got a bite there, Ingrid. You need to control that temper of yours.'

She nearly exploded right there on the spot. Her face went several unpleasant shades of crimson and her fingers clenched and unclenched around her sword hilt. But it was Treya who calmed her, or not so much calmed as restrained the fiery Valkyrie. Perhaps just so Treya could hit him first.

Be'elzebub continued, anticipating Tomas's idea. 'Would I be right in thinking that you are the key that will open the door to Asmodeus's camp? I have you captive and I'm giving you to Asmodeus to take the credit because I'm too untrustworthy because I was closer to Lucifer than he.'

'Spot on, but you'll need your army if you have one.'

Treya interjected that he did and it was substantial but would take a little time to gather together, for, due to conflicts on many fronts, they had been divided to deal with various problems.

'Well, we'll need as many as we can pull together to make an impression. Asmodeus needs to see your main force. Of course it would be ideal if he didn't see the rest of it. You and the main body wait in the open where he can see you, at a point of our choosing somewhere between wherever he is now and wherever this portal is. The rest have to be concealed to close the box on his forces.' Be'elzebub nodded appreciatively. 'This is a onetime deal, you understand. Once you turn on him your cover or status will be blown away like so much smoke. You have to distract him and buy as much time as you can before handing me over, because he's no doubt gonna want me straightaway. He'll be seeing power and rewards and all manner of things for being the one to capture me, so his patience won't be all that, but you need to keep him interested while me, Treya and the Valkyries, with a bit of borrowed muscle from you, track down where they've got Lucifer stashed, and get him out. I suspect the moment we do that, everything's gonna kick off and Asmodeus will know he's been set up. That's where you and yours come into their own.'

Everyone was nodding now, even Ingrid. But Tomas's expression went deadly serious and his voice as grave as he could make it. 'You realize that none of Asmodeus's forces can walk away alive. Not even Asmodeus himself. Should we succeed in freeing Lucifer, and I can't believe I'm saying that even now, his freedom must remain a secret. If wind should get back to the Adversary of his nemesis's rescue, he'll do something reactionary which we don't want. As it is, he's just doing whatever it is he's up to, which is bad enough, but at least we have a rough idea of where and what. He could panic at Lucifer's freedom and choose to wipe shit out even faster than he is. Can you do it?'

Be'elzebub stood from his makeshift dais of cushions and paced back and forth briefly, weighing up the plan, mentally going over the requirements of such an audacious stroke. Turning to Tomas, the Demon nodded. 'It is as much of a plan as we can hope for, at this point anyway. I like the prospect of taking the offensive against that piece of Karak dung. He and I have had this coming for a long time. It is only prudence that has kept us from each other's throats; that and Lucifer's wish for us to maintain as peaceful relations as we can for as long as possible. He didn't want a civil war here.'

Tomas smiled evilly back at the Lord of Flies. 'It's just as well he's not here then, isn't it, to talk sense to you? What the eye doesn't see the brain can do fuck all about. Used to be my motto when it came to the jobs I had to do. Bloody hell, my lot would have had a fit if they knew how many times I've come close to starting wars in order to get the job done. Worried myself more than once, I have to say. There was this one time in Libya…' Tomas raised his eyes skyward, '…that was a close one, but that's another story.'

Treya and the others had stood also, heralding the end of the meeting. True enough, there wasn't much more they could accomplish sitting around on cushions. Be'elzebub extended a clawed hand to Tomas, as though to help him rise. Tomas looked at it for a second before clasping it firmly. He was duly impressed by the strength he felt there as he was hauled to his feet as effortlessly as though he were one of the cushions themselves. Tomas regained his composure instantly and stood before the hulking creature before him. Tomas had momentarily forgotten just how bloody big he was. Standing looking down at Tomas, Be'elzebub towered over him, no doubt feeling safe and secure within his own pavilion. After all, what threat could one mere mortal have been? But Be'elzebub didn't know Tomas well enough to answer that confidently.

'I was just thinking,' Tomas said conversationally, moments after releasing – or being released – by the demon lord's bear paw of a hand, and turning to face Be'elzebub, 'mostly about having things done to one's person without consent, and especially to friends and allies, and I refer in part to you yomping through my head.' Tomas was holding his hands away from the Sword of War intentionally, giving the demon lord reassurance he wasn't about to draw it, which he wasn't. 'I think that we need to understand each other a bit better if this plan is going to work and I'm going to throw my lot in with you.' As he spoke, Tomas turned and casually pointed at the Lord of Flies. Instantly, as though it had always been there, the sword manifested in Tomas's hand and the razor tip was pressed lightly to Be'elzebub's neck. The sword thrummed excitedly and the quivering tip nicked the scaly skin and drew a thin line of steaming black ichor, which dripped off the blade and spat and hissed as it hit the floor, eating a small hole in the carpeting beneath their feet.

'Know this, Be'elzebub. I am not without resource. I may appear to you as just another mere mortal. What did you call us? Animals? Well, trust me when I tell you that I'm not one to cross. I am a nasty fucking animal with more teeth than you can count, and I bite. And I will continue to bite until I am satisfied that either me or whatever I'm biting is dead. I expect if you were to ask around, there's more than one discontented soul here to attest to that. For the few who know me, I make a good friend. For the rest...' Tomas paused for effect, letting the tip of the sword reinforce his words as it sliced a bit more, ever so slightly, '...I make the worst of enemies. I don't do mercy, I don't do rules, and I don't play fair. I have a long memory and I always repay any act against me in kind: good or ill. You need to choose which side of mine you want to be on, both now and in the future; in case you have any plans you haven't shared with the group. I'm sure you follow me with the utmost in crystal clarity.'

Tomas didn't even blink as he spoke; he simply stared with the two chips of sparkling ice that passed for his eyes, boring directly into the flashing and scintillating multifaceted orbs that passed for Be'elzebub's. When he stopped talking, he blinked and the sword disappeared, and Tomas felt a twinge of disappointment from it. *Soon, my friend, I'm sure even you will have had your fill of blood and death in the days to come.* Tomas held out his hand once again to shake, inviting the now trembling and apparently livid demon lord to seal their accord and confirm their new mutual understanding. *Make me a bloody earl against my will, tosser! Let's see how he likes the boot being on the other foot.* Be'elzebub though, for his part, didn't know what to do first. He stared at the human before him and the greater part of him wanted to explode in abject violence and rip the creature into more pieces than there were stars in the sky. Another part wanted to laugh and another to panic. This was a first. No one and nothing had ever drawn blood from him since he had joined the Light Bringer in setting up the Domain. He was powerful even then, growing into his role and growing in strength in equal measure. Added to that, there were only so many things powerful enough in the entire multiverse that actually *could* cut him. What power did this human wield? This animal had succeeded where both angels and demons alike had failed, and that disturbed the Lord of Flies almost as much as the Adversary did. He had succeeded in eliciting the sweet and sublime sensation that most know as fear. He had forgotten what that felt like – until now. For Be'elzebub realized that with the blade at his throat, Tomas could have easily finished him. He felt that from the touch of the blade. Indecision roiled through him and all in the pavilion were on edge. Hands had slipped to weapons,waiting for inevitable chaos that was sure to ensue. But it didn't. It seemed that time had stopped.

Be'elzebub lowered his monstrous head to gaze at the mortal with his outstretched hand and saw things for what they were. It was a show of power. One entity of power to another, and power respected power. Tomas knew he needed the respect of the Lord of Flies in order to elicit the necessary trust. Not just the lip service trust that is thrown about aimlessly at times like these. It was one thing to hear of acts but it was another thing altogether to be on the receiving end of them.

Tomas watched for some sign of Be'elzebub's reaction, but it was hard as the huge barrel chest heaved in and out with barely suppressed fury. The lack of expression on the fly's head was of no use, but Tomas knew he had to stand and face whatever he chose to do. The first to break at these fraught moments would lose. Lose respect, honor and standing. But Tomas still nearly leapt back twenty feet when the big demon suddenly threw his head back and laughed as if it was all the funniest thing ever. The tension that had become so palpable, so highly charged with the anticipation of violence, melted away and the Valkyries began to relax, though only slightly. Their eyes were still narrowed suspiciously and for a moment Tomas wasn't sure who they would have attacked if it all went pear-shaped, especially as it wasn't him who had promised to return them to their home. Then, as he pondered that possibility and before he knew what hit him, Be'elzebub had grasped his outstretched arm and pumped him up and down exuberantly, much to Tomas's shock, relief and subsequent very nearly dislocated shoulder.

'Well met, Earl Tomas Walker. Very impressive. Very dangerous and extremely risky, but it took balls to do what you did and we do have an understanding. I for my part will learn from this and not make the same mistake of underestimating you in the future. Let us consider ourselves both duly warned, and treat this day as the first of an interesting future.'

What the bloody hell did he mean by interesting? Still, there's no going back now: whatever will be will inevitably be, Tomas old son.

'For the remainder of this night until first light, we will feast and welcome you, Earl Tomas, the newest member of our ruling house, to our ranks. There will be one or two generals who will want to meet you. They will recommend warriors to assist you and I will dispatch heralds to track down Asmodeus and set up our little rendezvous.'

'Sounds like a plan to me. What say you, Treya? You've been remarkably quiet.'

'Are you implying I talk a lot, *Earl* Walker?'

Yep, if there were two ways to interpret something said and one of them was the total opposite of what you wanted it to say, then a woman found it and jumped on it with both feet. He sighed as he spoke. 'Not at all, Treya, it's just that I thought you might have had some questions or suggestions of your own to add to the plan, that's all, being legendary warriors as you are.'

He knew it sounded like total blag the moment he said it, but for some reason it seemed to work and she harrumphed as if to say 'Well, that's all right then'.

Bloody hell. As if I didn't have enough problems without having to walk on eggshells around these women. Not just regular women either; bloody capable women armed to the teeth with bloody great big swords and a will to use them. Tomas wondered idly, as they all left the pavilion and headed for the cook fire, which was the bigger danger: the Adversary or a pissed off Treya. He didn't want to wager on that. Oh no, not in the slightest.

Earlier, just before the hounds broke into the clearing and discovered the bodies of the fallen mercenaries, a vulture circled lazily over their fly covered and maggot ridden corpses. That in itself wasn't anything extraordinary, for there were several others coasting the thermals as well as crows and ravens making their way to dinner. All being more cautious than normal, for this was the Domain. And it was far more deadly and treacherous than any realm upon the Earth. Hunter could become hunted in a heartbeat, and it didn't matter how big or how many there were. There was always something bigger, faster and more numerous lurking, just waiting for an opportunity to either eat or kill you, though not necessarily both at the same time.

But this one particular vulture had no need to worry about such matters. This vulture didn't worry about anything at all. It was oblivious to everything as its tiny mind had been relegated to a dark recess in its consciousness. A mind vastly superior to the one that usually inhabited its body was in control and was using it to scan the area below. In a moment of lucidity and curiosity, the Adversary had ventured to the slave compounds, looking for something to vent his seemingly ever-present fury upon. He had thought of a hunt. It would both allow him some vent on his tortured spleen and provide an opportunity to gather many of the nobles who both supported him, and those who had reservations but were not averse to any friendly persuasion. A hunt, followed by a feast and games, would distract many of them from their perpetual plotting and scheming. But as he approached the compound he sensed that something was amiss. Dragging the slavemaster out, the Adversary quickly discovered that not only had several of his slaves managed to escape, but those who went after them had failed to return also. Furious, the Adversary had ranged his mind out, seeking a sign of their whereabouts. His mind skimmed a myriad of creatures, catching sights and sensations from their eyes and memories. It was from the disjointed images of the vulture that the Adversary now found himself staring at the ruined bodies of his catchers – torn and decimated in the midst of this abominable forest. This accursed woodland that seemingly stretched forever, covered the greater part of a quarter of the Domain's land mass and most importantly, hid far too many things from his spies and from his scrutiny. Several high ranking nobles of the Domain's ruling council governed portions of this forest where it encroached upon their realms, one of them being the hated and despised Be'elzebub. The Prince of Lies was an apt title for him, for the Adversary was convinced he was a part of, if not the instigator of the rebellion that even now, fought to undermine him. He was sure they were skulking somewhere in this bloody forest but it would take his entire army a lifetime to scour it and even then, if they came back out again, they would probably be empty-handed. No, he would wait until he had amassed enough power from the dying Earth, then, before he launched his final and all out assault upon the multiverse, he would enjoy the moment by ripping up the entire woodland by its roots and leveling it so that not even the lowliest insect had anywhere to hide. It would make the deserts look bounteous by comparison. *What was that?*

The Adversary had almost missed it, so wrapped in his revenge was he. But the glint of sunlight on silver attracted the vulture's keen eye. He swooped lower to get a better view. Arrows. Shining silver arrows. The maidens had been careless in their collecting for they had missed two of their precious arrows. He recognized them for the thorn in his side that they were. *Valkyries.* Now they *were* part of the resistance that conspired to overthrow him and they were supported by one of the ruling houses. Though he didn't know which one, he had his suspicions. *Be'elzebub; I'll have your scaly insectoid arse yet. You can't hide from me forever.* Yet for all his suspicions, the Adversary knew he couldn't act without definitive proof for fear of losing the lords he currently had. They would demand evidence and a couple of arrows were far from sufficient. He was sick of the petty squabbling and the ridiculous game he had to put up with from the nobles. He needed to end it and soon. He needed the power of the dying Earth and he needed it faster than it was providing it. It was tenacious and refused to die without a fight, but once he had secured that which he sought, her end would be assured no matter what she did, and her life force would be his. Then things would get really interesting.

The Adversary had seen enough; he had other matters to attend to. Deciding the hunt would still go ahead, he needed to plan for how the event would benefit him and who would have accidents. A hunt wasn't a good hunt without somebody suffering some sort of mishap. And it wasn't a worthy mishap if it didn't benefit him in some way. The Adversary withdrew his consciousness from the bird so fast that he departed before the suppressed mind had the time to realize it was suddenly back in control. Part of that control would have included flying, which it failed to get a grip on before its body had plummeted from the sky and smashed itself upon the ground with a sickening, bone smashing thud. After that it didn't have to worry about anything else. Its fellow carrion eaters shared a common thought, however: that of the menu now having some variation.

Be'elzebub reclined in his pavilion until the last possible moment as the rest of the camp was struck and prepared for travel. The bisotaurs bellowed orders and warriors and servants alike hustled to dismantle and pack away the tents, cooking fires and spits; fill in latrines, and no end of other routine tasks that would eradicate the majority of traces that any sort of camp had been there. By the time they had finished, which wasn't long, Tomas had watched proceedings from a short distance away, and thought his old quartermaster would have been suitably impressed by their efficiency. There was little to indicate there had been any sort of camp at all, let alone one the size that had just packed up. After leaving the feast and the dozing Valkyries just before sun up, Tomas had walked off a ways, seeking the solitude of the forest before events picked up again. Joined by the raven, he walked the perimeter of the camp, trying to get some idea of the forces and individuals that felt the urge to rebel. What he saw didn't look so different from any other military maneuver. There were men sitting and sleeping around fires. Some were gambling, others carving small animals and detail into pieces of wood. Others again were tending their weapons and armor. All manner of activities that helped settle the mind and focus their attention. Smoking, dicing, eating, sewing. The one thing Tomas saw that bound all these men together was that they all bore the look of hardened and seasoned warriors.

It was the little things that set them apart from less capable men. If they had been farmers or accountants or innkeepers before they became soldiers, it was forgotten now. They all had the look that said they had seen death up close and personal. Their eyes betrayed what their actions disguised. He had seen similar during the Gulf War and when he had crossed paths with some lads shortly after Baghdad had been taken. They had seen more than they had wanted to and it had left its mark. But those it didn't destroy, it changed. It made them stronger, yes, but it haunted them nevertheless. This haunting took on the guise of a myriad of superstitions and pre-battle ritual. It also came as insomnia, which was why so many veterans had a tough time sleeping. Faces would float before their closed eyes, accusing, demanding reason, and demanding retribution. These faces, in their varied conditions, from intact yet angry, right the way through to blown apart and decomposing, were always recognizable. Any long-serving soldier and battle-weary campaigner will tell you that it's an acquired knack sleeping wherever and whenever you can – the body needs to rest after all – but it doesn't make it an enjoyable process.

These were the faces Tomas saw as he circumnavigated the camp in the early hours just before the sun rose. He didn't want to imagine just what their eyes had seen, here of all places. Tomas envisioned battlefields in the Domain making those back on Earth look like an afternoon out in the park. He shivered involuntarily, though not with the cold, just his icy imagination doing a reel by reel with images stolen from his memory after having seen too many charnel fields of his own. Tomas had his own faces to haunt him and they did a damn good job of it too. He was thankful for Famine's gift of no longer having to need sleep: it kept the ghosts away. Tomas spoke to a few of the soldiers in passing – nothing deep, just a shared greeting from one soldier to another. That greeting that said 'I'll say hello to you now; I might be dead before I get to say anything to you again'. A soldier's life was a day-to-day affair, especially in wars like this. The odds never looked good. There was no avoiding the fact, modern day missiles saved lives. Well, at least those of the soldiers sending the missiles. The hand-to-hand carnage of days gone by was a rare thing now. Other than the odd suicide bomber or roadside bomb, enemy soldiers didn't get all up close and friendly with each other so much any more. Maybe that was where it had all gone wrong. It was too easy to wage war from a distance, look at a screen, and push a button. War was almost virtual. It was another thing to look your enemy right in the eye, face to face, knowing that this encounter could very well be your last – either alive or at least whole. It gave a whole new perspective to see those same eyes, so confident only moments before, take on the look of surprise when they are trying to hold entrails in, preventing their internal organs becoming external ones from a sliced open abdomen, watching their life blood spill through their fingers like so much air. Like the sand in an hourglass that says your time is well and truly up.

'There you are!' The hail took Tomas by surprise, though he didn't show it, merely turning to face the voice. The voice was that of Ingrid; he would recognize her dulcet tones anywhere. Seeing her though brought him back to the present with a welcome jolt. He wasn't a fan of the past, especially his. Tomas knew he was getting morose again; he did from time to time. Things just compounded sometimes and he would get all maudlin. He used to find a bar somewhere and drown those feelings until they went away, until everything went away. He'd hole up in some seedy motel and get totally shitfaced. He didn't do it often – he didn't like being so vulnerable – but it stopped him putting a round through his head when the faces became too much to handle, too many to compete with. What would he do now? Thankfully there was no time to dwell on *that*.

'Morning, Ingrid. Ready to go save the Universe?' He spoke with a light banter he really didn't feel and he guessed his own eyes betrayed him because the look she gave him was one of curiosity, and was that sympathy? Surely not, not from her.

'Be'elzebub requires your attendance. He has the additional warriors for us and during the night, while you were off and wandering like some wraith, a scout returned with some news about Asmodeus. I suspect you might be interested in hearing what he had to say. Treya and the rest of the sisters await your return.'

Tomas smiled at the severe Valkyrie, who stood fists on hips before him, legs braced and bristling with weapons as though she would spring into action at any second. With her hair blowing gently in the morning breeze and the light of the hazy half-light of the morning silhouetting her, he could see why the Vikings of a forgotten age saw these creatures as personifications of death and war – she was certainly impressive. Even a bit scary, if he was truly honest and it sent shivers tingling up his spine.

'Lead on, Milady, let's not keep our affable host waiting.' Tomas did a mock bow, trying to copy something he saw on some old Hollywood movie with Errol Flynn or the like. Leg forward and sweeping one arm round to skim the grass with his fingertips, he rose and smiled at her once more; but she glowered, turned and strode off, not waiting to see if he followed or not. He could hear her muttering as she stalked away and it cheered him up as he set off to follow her, keen to hear what this scout had to say.

By the time he and Ingrid walked back into the clearing, it was just that. A clearing. No sign of the encampment at all that had totally filled the space only hours ago – just a few stragglers and isolated groups. Tomas just caught sight of the tail end of the caravan as it crested the rise and headed away from them. A twig snapping behind him caused Tomas to look over his shoulder just as Treya, Be'elzebub and the rest of the Valkyries began gathering together, checking their own armor and weapons in anticipation of the off. Each was leading their pegasus and they stood with a grace and poise that put any warhorse to shame. *Except Storm, of course,* Tomas thought possessively.

'Looks like I've missed the coffee and doughnuts,' Tomas quipped as he moved to meet the two figures crossing towards him. The raven hopped a bit on his shoulder and Tomas held out his arm for it to sidle down and perch upon his armored forearm. He slipped it a bit of roasted rabbit that he had picked up on his circuit at one of the camp fires, and it gobbled it down wolfishly.

'Easy, old son. You'd think you'd never eaten before, and I'm quite attached to these fingers.'

The raven looked up at him, intelligence powering its black eyes. *'If you must call me anything, you may call me Bran. I am not your old son, my feathered friend, or hey bird. Are we clear?'* Tomas nodded. *'Good. Now, is there any more of that rabbit?'* Tomas couldn't help but chuckle then at the dry, self-effacing humor of the peculiar companion he had somehow inherited as he shoved more rabbit into its craw.

'It is good to see you so amused this fine morning, my lord Tomas.'

Tomas winced. He'd forgotten about that bloody title crap Be'elzebub insisted upon. The sooner they were away, the better: he could forget about that annoying aspect of their alliance. 'Isn't it. Now what do you know? Ingrid tells me you've some useful news from a scout.' Tomas left the question hanging as they met and stood together in the now open space left by the retreating rebels. Be'elzebub was resplendent this morning in an array of multicolored silken robes that fell just short of his hairy calves and cloven hoofs. They complemented the multihued, multifaceted eyes of his fly visage. And he veritably dripped in gold and precious jewels, right down to the ornate long sword that hung oddly at his hip. Tomas couldn't imagine the demon even deigning to use such a weapon.

'It is a badge of office only.' He had caught Tomas's gaze and anticipated the question regarding the insignificant looking sword. 'And this garish looking garb also.'

'You don't need to impress me, really. I get it, and you're a big shot. Now what about the scout.'

Be'elzebub shook his head sadly from side to side. 'You are just like this one, Tomas.' He indicated Treya. 'She too had little time for small talk this morning and only wished to hear of the news that my minion returned with.'

THE ADVERSARY

This time it was Treya who spoke up, adopting what must have been a Valkyrie stance of irritation: fists on hips and feet braced. 'We are at war, Be'elzebub, not one of your games of intrigue and political nonsense. If this will assist us in our purpose, then we should act with all haste to take what advantage we can from the situation before something else intervenes and creates several more problems before we can resolve this one. And this is a fairly important matter, would you not agree? Or is Lucifer's freedom not so important to you after all?'

This calculating statement had the desired effect on the Lord of Flies and he stood a little straighter, as befitting his rank, and he looked at the assembled warriors before him and at Tomas especially. His gaze lingered on the armored man and his raven for many long seconds. Much depended on him and his brazen plan. It all seemed too simple, yet the consequences of failure didn't bear thinking about either, though, truth be told, it was all he *had* thought about these past few hours: how everything they had done up to this point would be for nothing should the Adversary succeed and he exiles Lucifer beyond reach. And with this attack, everything he was would be put in jeopardy when events were set in motion. The moment he attacked Asmodeus, it would be known he was against the Adversary and everything the usurper had would be turned against him. They had to succeed. And he hated the fact that this animal was the one to accomplish it if it could be done.

'I think you know the answer to that, Treya Thorsen, so do not presume to goad me. Many lives and futures are at stake, yours included.' It was obvious to anybody there that Be'elzebub was annoyed, but it wasn't clear at what. He was taking his frustrations out on those around him and that meant he was worried. And if he was worried, Tomas considered that a very bad thing indeed. Tomas walked slowly around the little group, Treya's eyes on him as he moved. Ingrid watched him too, her hand hovering near her ever-present sword, and he was sure she didn't actually blink as she studied him. But he also knew that she watched the surrounding forest for danger, as too did the Valkyrie Host.

That was it! Tomas looked closer at the gathered women and realized there were more than there were when they first met. Spinning back to face the fly lord, he exclaimed, 'That's the extra bodies you offered: more Valkyries?'

Be'elzebub looked at him directly and clasped his hands behind him in a most bureaucratic fashion. 'I don't have the personnel to spare you for your part of what must be done. These are Treya's sisters and form part of her cohort anyway. They served with me here as liaison, but it seems they would be better off with you. All under one banner, so to speak.

Tomas was naturally distrustful of any sound reasoning, for there was usually an ulterior motive. 'Yeah, right, and should it all go pear-shaped, you rid yourself of all those you owe an obligation to, and have a convenient scapegoat to pass off the plan to, no doubt exonerating you in the process. Ah I can hear it now. "It was them, my lord, the animal and the exiles; I had nothing to do – "'

'Enough!' Be'elzebub roared his outrage and even seemed to grow a little as he did so. Tomas got a glimpse then of the other side of this creature and it wasn't one he particularly wanted to see any more of than he had to.

'No? Is that not how it is then? If it isn't, why don't you tell us what the scout reported and let us get on with things. I can't be arsed to keep bartering and fencing with you about trust and the hazards we face if this is to work and you get your precious Lucifer back. Frankly, given the choice, I'd see them, both Lucifer and the Adversary, dead and save the cosmos one whole heap of trouble 'cos where I come from they seem as bad as each other. But…' Tomas continued before Be'elzebub could object, '…there would always be some other candidate willing to step in and try and make a name for themselves, so I'm still willing to put my neck on the line for this plan, because, if you'll pardon the analogy, it's better the devil you know than the devil you don't and you seem to back this Lucifer guy and apparently put your neck on the block for him. Back home we say the friend of my friend is my friend too.' Tomas realized who he had just considered as a friend and chuckled to himself. *Now that was some name to drop into conversation as an old pal I helped out once who'd gotten himself into a spot of bother.* Eyes screwed up in concern as Tomas appeared to giggle to himself but nothing was said about it.

'So it is, Lord Tomas Walker,' Be'elzebub said, unconcerned by his behavior, 'but in this case, there is another unknown devil, if you will. The scout reported that Asmodeus has sent outriders to pathfind for him, and they have been spotted east of the Tartarus Mountains, running a parallel course with the Reaver of Souls.'

Tomas frowned at the pronunciation and corrected the demon. 'You mean river, right?'

Be'elzebub shook his head, implying the negative. 'No, I mean Reaver. For the lord of that realm is something of an enigma, even to us. The Reaver of Souls is a waterway that flows through the underground kingdom of Tartarus, plunging deep beneath the mountains and resurfacing on the edge of the forest and eventually flowing into the wastelands and the Desert of Desolation.'

Again Tomas frowned, trying to get his head around the geography of the Domain. 'It can't be much of a desert with a bloody great river running through it.'

'You've obviously never heard of the River Acheron then?'

Tomas had. Who hadn't? He quite liked the myth about the eerie ferryman, paying or not paying him and the implications of such, but mostly, as he told Be'elzebub, he was Charon, the ferryman of souls into the realm of the dead.

'Close. It is a legend he allows to survive, for it prevents any further scrutiny into his realm. He is infinitely more than that and is a very dangerous and unpredictable being. I can't even say for sure what he is. He arrived here shortly after Lucifer and has been here ever since, though I am aware of his travels to other worlds. The river acts as a portal for him to any other river or watercourse on any other world, but he is seen so infrequently that he is almost a myth here too.'

Tomas still wasn't sure what the problem was so he shrugged. 'And?'

'Charon, the Riparian, the Reaver of Souls or whatever title he opts, has so far been a neutral player in this battle. The pass the pathfinders have been seen scouting is a little-known gap through the Tartarus Mountains and one closely guarded. Few even know of its existence and it makes for a dangerous area to have two armies clash. If we allow them to leave the Stygian Valley, where the pass leaves the mountains, we risk the fact that Lucifer's portal is actually there, we don't know. But on the other hand, the semi-permanent twilight that pervades the valley would be an ideal environment for an ambush. My army would wait at the exit to the valley, effectively trapping him in there, while you execute your part of the plan and rescue my lord Lucifer.'

'So what you're saying is that you are bothered about this Reaver of Souls getting involved and you not knowing which side he'll come down on?'

'Basically, yes. It does complicate matters and once I engage Asmodeus's forces both my army and my reputation will be on the line; plus the prospect of facing two enemies does not sit well. I do not have the resources to tackle two fronts at once.'

'Hopefully you won't have to, but I suspect we should cross that particular bridge as and when, not to mention if, it comes up. I think we have enough problems already without inventing umpteen more. Maybe Lucifer has some sway with this Reaver, so the sooner we get him out, the quicker he can expedite our withdrawal without the need for any more fighting.'

But they all knew that the fighting would only then truly begin in earnest as Lucifer rallied those still loyal to him within the Domain and tried to retake his position from the Adversary. It was all a race before the Adversary found whatever it was he was after and had accumulated enough power to not bother with any of it any more, and simply annihilate everything before him, snowballing into a cosmic maelstrom of destruction and remaking it all in his own manner. Nothing wanted that.

As Tomas pondered the imponderable and images of a post-apocalyptic future floated through his unfocused mind, he caught sight of the rainbow-hued robes of Be'elzebub again and that popped another question in to his rapidly filling head.

'All that aside, why are you dressed up like a dog's dinner and not armored for war like everything else?'

Be'elzebub did a little preening at his colorful silks. 'Exquisite, aren't they, like this little sword here. They are what I am expected to be seen in at court, which is where I must go now. I still have a pretense there to maintain, at least until I blow that all to hell, if you will excuse my poor humor. Who knows, I may even be able to glean something useful from the squawking popinjays who rarely leave the palace. At least those the Adversary has left alive anyway – he is not the most stable of beings any more.'

Tomas barked so suddenly with his laughter that the raven nearly fell from his arm and Ingrid's sword was two thirds out of its scabbard. 'No shit! You sure have a way of understating things, Bub. The fruitcake is about to deconstruct the entire multiverse and you just say he's a bit unstable.' Tomas laughed a bit more even as he grimaced at the mentality of the individuals he was surrounding himself with. Bloody hell, with allies like these, I really don't need enemies. Stable or otherwise.

Treya added, as though it was an afterthought, a few details about their scouts. 'We have been given a few more scouts to assist us, Tomas, but you may not have seen them yet. They watch our backs and flanks and are as elusive as they are good at what they do.'

Tomas turned to her, pleased by the distraction, and what a distraction. 'I think I have seen them already, when I rode with Ingrid. I thought earlier that they were conspicuous by their absence.'

Treya whistled and there was an instant flurry of foliage from the forest edge. What Tomas saw as they emerged into the clearing very nearly had the Sword of War appearing in his hand. As it was he could feel it pulsing with the presence of the insectoid demons that crabbed their way across the open grass towards them. They looked like some mad scientist had taken several species of crab, beetle, lizard, wasp and locust, chucked them into a mixer and thrown in a rhino, a gorilla and a boar just for good measure; flicked a switch, and they are what came out. It amazed Tomas that something so monstrous and bulky could remain as hidden as it had.

But as they walked, as though reading his thoughts, they color shifted through several variations of the grass they crossed and all bar vanished. *Chameleons*. That explained the lizard and how they kept out of sight. They still moved towards him on the crablike legs and with astonishing speed too, but he was more than surprised when their armored and heavily shielded wing cases snapped open and four pairs of ragged looking locust wings sprung out and started buzzing, lifting them off the ground and propelling them even faster in their direction. Then, with no warning, they sped off; upwards and back towards the forest. Splitting up and resuming their duties, Tomas supposed.

'Impressive, and they've been with us since I met you?'

Treya nodded. 'Thought you might like to see them, seeing as you seemed disappointed by the extra sisters Be'elzebub released to us.'

Tomas felt a momentary pang of guilt. He had seemed ungrateful and secretly he was a bit jarred off. The lack of male muscle was making him feel a bit of an odd one out. He couldn't count Niall. 'Sorry, Trey. It's not that I was disappointed. How could I be? You girls kick arse better than a lot of guys I know. It's just…well, I don't know really. I'm not sure what I expected. My own little contingent of demons to order about? I don't know, I had no idea. I'd rather have you girls with me any time if given a choice.' Tomas smiled at her, his most charming, or so he hoped, to reinforce the compliment, which wasn't entirely hollow, but he didn't feel inside the way he was trying to show on the outside. The prospect of being responsible for their deaths was a more onerous burden to shoulder than sending demons to their deaths against other demons. He could have lived happily with that notion but he couldn't very well say that in front of Be'elzebub: they still needed his support.

Be'elzebub interjected, 'I believe our business for now is concluded, I will take my leave of you now. The scouts know the direction of the pass and

I suggest all prudent haste, for it is several days from here and as I gather you are not flying, it may be a few more. But if Asmodeus only has his pathfinders there at present, it will be at least that long before even the head of his column arrives there. Time aplenty to reorganize my own forces to intercept him at the valley entrance, containing him for your forces to hit the rear. Good.' Be'elzebub seemed content that as much as they could do now was in order. 'Farewell. I will be in touch when I know more. Oh, and do not forget the hounds that hunt you. Be vigilant.'

He said no more. Instead, he snapped out his own vast rack of wings and with the downdraft like standing behind the engine of a 747, he rocketed skyward. The grass was flattened and cloaks and hair blew all over. He looked to Treya, who was settling both of her own. She shrugged and muttered as her eyes followed the speck that was now Be'elzebub before he vanished completely.

'I hate it when he does that. I swear he does it just to annoy me.' Tomas grunted.

'You're annoyed? We can't fly in case we're spotted by who knows what, so we stay on the ground and have to contend with some bloody dogs chasing us.' Treya leveled her most serious gaze at him. She still looked lovely, even when she was serious. 'The hounds are more than dogs, Tomas. They are the spawn of Fenris himself. Savage and merciless man-beasts. Driven by the agony of the fusion and their fear of their lord, the only way they can satisfy both is by carnage. The greater pain and terror they can inflict on their victim, the greater release they benefit from. At least that is how it was when Fenris terrorized Asgard and started his conquest of Midgard. Your kind has no idea how thankful to Tyr and Odin you should be for capturing him. At the peak of his power, he was as strong as the Adversary is now, only his arrogance let him down and allowed himself to be chained. He is free now and he grows in strength again, nurtured by the Adversary. His spawn will be as terrifying as they ever were and as hard to kill if not harder. I for one would rather not have to fight them: I fear the loss of lives of my sisters would be too great. I suspect it is because of these hounds that Be'elzebub refused to provide any of his own warriors - Bastard.'

The cool façade she usually wore slipped then, ever so slightly, and Tomas caught sight of the passion beneath. *So there is some fire in there. I like that.* 'I guess we should be making tracks then, before those things get any closer. I take it the scouts have taken up positions and will let us know in good time if they get too close?'

Treya nodded as she began moving towards her mount, which was being unnecessarily held by another sister. They would have stood stock still if not held; they were superbly trained, and bonded to their rider much like he was to Storm, whom he summoned as the rest mounted.

'They are telepathic and we have learnt to understand them. It may take you a little time to get a hang of their manner of communicating. Hopefully, we'll all live long enough for that to happen. In the meantime, stick close to either Ingrid or myself as it's us they talk to.'

Tomas smiled at her receding back and just had to say it. 'Is that an invitation?'

She turned and looked at him over her shoulder with fire in her eyes but with a smile playing across her moist lips. 'You'll know an invitation when and if you ever have one, Tomas, you have my word on that. Now mount and let's go while we still have much of the day: we have far to go.'

The thundercloud colored warhorse ghosted into existence, saddled and barded for war. And Tomas was as pleased to see the beast as he could ever have been. It seemed the bond ran deeper than his shoulder brand; it fused to his spirit. One man and his horse: his friend, his companion, his brother. That was it. That was the depth of his bond to this fabulous animal. It was as though he had a brother who just happened to be a horse. A minor inconvenience but no less tangible. Storm solidified and whinnied his greeting to his rider. Tomas made a show of patting the muscular neck and running his hand across the powerful back. Storm enjoyed this and stomped the ground with one mighty forepaw, his hoof digging great clods from the soft soil. As Tomas mounted, Storm took in his surroundings and lingered on the gathering of pegasi nearby, watching as the Valkyries mounted and settled their weapons about them. Storm took in the winged mounts and Tomas was convinced that he stood a little straighter as he did so, head a little higher. It knew it was a supernatural being and had no need of wings to fly, unlike the pegasi, and unless Tomas was mistaken, relished the fact. Were horses capable of pride? If so, Storm was as proud as he could be. Tomas truly loved this horse and its character grew on him the more he saw of it. It had attitude; and that was one thing Tomas respected. One of Tomas's many pet hates was soppy people. Those limp wristed, weak willed and dispirited individuals who sapped the life out of all around them. They had the handshake of a moist dead fish and the eyes to match. They were life's followers, victims, and sheep. How they made it through the day without getting themselves killed was one of life's mysteries to him. They would be food here without a shadow of a doubt. They wouldn't be much use for anything else. The spark or absence of the spark was what set people apart. But where did it come from? Why did some people have it and others not? Tomas pondered this as he settled himself upon the saddle and adjusted his own cloak and armor, switching it to the lighter and more flexible Kevlar and Gore-Tex components. But he kept his ballistic rating up there just in case he was jumped suddenly and needed the protection.

The spark. He had encountered so few people with it that he had begun to wonder if it was an evolutionary thing. He found that those with it tended to be loners, social misfits and those types of people who for no discernible reason made others uncomfortable. It was like the way a wolf made a rabbit uncomfortable. Something deep and instinctive said that it was dangerous and would kill it. The way deer just knew they were in permanent danger from predators. It wasn't deer that killed deer. It was another species entirely. That was where humanity had gone wrong, in Tomas's opinion. They were just about the only species that killed its own for something other than food. He had heard the arguments about chimps but there would always be an exception. It wasn't distinctive enough to worry about. Tomas had noticed that prey and victims were mostly herd creatures and that predators were usually solitary, occasionally a pack. Dogs, wolves and hyenas as a rule, lionesses as a feline exception, but mostly, life's hunters were solitary. That was him. But the question that haunted him for most of his life was, how? How had he manifested this gene when both his parents were regular people? Was the hunter gene dormant until activated? If so, what activated it? Did it skip generations? He never knew his grandparents. It was too deep a subject to dwell on for too long without him getting a headache, but maybe there was something to what the Horsemen had told him. Destiny. His particular chromosomal make-up was handed down through the ages until needed. Manipulated into random people until they either died or had to step up to the plate, whichever came first.

Tomas was drawn from his philosophical meanderings by the feeling he was being watched. He turned to see Treya sitting her horse and regarding him up and down.

'What? Do you appraise everything like that?' Tomas asked playfully.

'Depends on whether it has any real use or value to begin with. It is always good to know the capability of what one has between one's legs. Does it have the strength, stamina, blood? Will it let you down when the moment arrives for it to perform? What flaws, if any, must be compensated for. Rider and ridden must always be a good fit in more ways than one. Why Tomas? Does such scrutiny make you uncomfortable?'

Tomas grinned back wolfishly, enjoying the innuendo and double-entendres.

'Not at all. In fact I agree wholly; the union should be a meeting of both mind and body. The ride would be very painful otherwise. The flesh should be sufficient to absorb repeated impacts. I mean, there's nothing worse than riding bones. Of course, a willingness to be ridden in the first place is a requirement, for all the physical looks in the world are to no avail if all it is going to do is buck and bite you. The ride beneath you should be fluid and compliant, making it all the more pleasurable. Working in harmony is much more advantageous, don't you think?'

Tomas looked directly into Treya's sparkling eyes as he delivered his last comment and for a time she gazed back and they floated, separate from their environment. They were alone in their own world; just her and him, wallowing in the gaze of the other, each absorbing something of the other. Tomas hungrily took in every impression he could: face, hair, neck, breasts, and legs; and how those legs stretched slightly over her mount, the subtle play of muscles tensing beneath her tanned thighs as they subconsciously strained to hold her in position in the saddle, even down to her shapely calves hanging loosely where the stirrups should be, encased as they were in close hugging steel, which still couldn't disguise her intense and blatant femininity. A quick flash of Lady Godiva hung tantalizingly before his inner eye briefly, before being squashed by a high pitched whine.

Ingrid's voice cut through the air like a ripsaw and both Tomas and Treya looked away, slightly guiltily. Like schoolchildren being caught doing something they shouldn't.

'When you two have finished gawping at each other like moon calves, could we get a move on? Staying so still like this in the middle of such a large clearing is making me and the others nervous. Treya, come on, get a grip.'

'Of course.' Treya and her pegasus cantered to the front of the group and began to lead the Valkyries away, though not before tossing a sly wink to Tomas, who was astounded at her brazen behavior. But he smiled back lasciviously and fell into line with the rest. He caught sight of Niall a little way ahead. He was settling in well, though Tomas would have preferred the little man to have gone with the caravan. But Hildreth had sworn to keep him safe. The raven glided ahead and Tomas caught sight of it perching high in what looked like a large Oak.

'*I too will scout our way. Watch for me,*' the raven communicated.

'*Okay, Bran,*' Tomas responded silently.

The group had barely been gone from the clearing twelve hours before the first hound burst through the treeline. Followed soon after by eight more. The remains of one pack had joined with the first, after an encounter that left several of its number massacred beyond recovery by a silken robed demon lord. After an hour of snuffling and sniffing the clearing, the pack gathered and conferred, howling their success, for they had finally picked up the scent of the hated human and knew they were close, only hours behind. The hunt was truly on now as they rose horrifically to their hind legs, and flexed talons and muscles, cracking their monstrous jaws as they howled in anticipation of blood and flesh. As one, the eight hounds bounded away and crashed into the treeline where the scent led them. Massive arms swatting foliage away as they powered through the undergrowth, eyes aglow as the gloom descended from the canopy above, they ran. Ran as though their lives depended on it. Which of course it did. But between them or their prey, they were confident of their success. And that confidence lent them speed.

CHAPTER FIFTEEN

SERENDIPITY

G WEN HUGGED THE COASTLINE OF THE EASTERN Seaboard for as much of her journey as she could. Soaring past New York, she caught a glimpse of the fabled Lady Liberty as she held her flaming brand as high as she could. *Liberty! Now that's an interesting concept,* Gwen harrumphed to herself in disgust. Was there such a thing any more? With credit referencing, DNA profiling and database compilation, heightened passport control and immigration crackdowns, just who was at liberty to do or go anywhere any more? Gwen recalled all the questions the man from the bank had asked her when she bought the shop and house; it was everything bar her blood type and inside leg measurement. To go, buy or even shop was an impossibility now. *Not without big brother watching and monitoring your every single bloody move,* Gwen thought sourly. *There are cameras just about everywhere these days; then there is the NSA, CIA and who knows who else with their spy satellites watching everyone from space.* She had flipped the bird skyward on many occasions just to see if anyone was watching and to let them know she knew they were doing it, but she never got the knock on the door by the men in black she had always half expected because of it. Gwen's sour humor vanished as she wondered what they saw now, some poor soul having a fit as the blip on his screen thundered from one side to the other. She was in no doubt that she was causing some stir on someone's radar. She was, after all, larger than any fighter aircraft and considerably faster too if she put her mind to it, but she hadn't seen many aircraft of any description for some time, not since she left Santa Fe anyway.

Based on what Jen and Maddy had told her and what she had seen herself, she suspected they had their hands full. Though the skies were usually busy with both military and commercial aircraft, it wasn't every day a superpower was invaded, and not by what was attempting it this time. This made any attempt by the Russians or Koreans or whoever else who wanted to have a go seem trivial by comparison. Gwen suspected too, that there was an awful lot of *denial* going on. *No doubt the God botherers will be flocking to their respective churches and probably dying gruesome deaths, trapped inside, while demons tear them to shreds secure in the knowledge that the house is unprotected by any deity, much like the poor saps within.* The alleged house of God proved no more of a sanctuary for the religious than did the bunkers and homes of the non-religious. There was no discrimination in what the demons were attempting. They wanted *all* humans dead. *But should we be surprised? We had been systematically wiping out species after species since we got up off four legs; why shouldn't another more aggressive species want to wipe humanity out?* It wasn't a cheery thought Gwen had, *but then again,* she mused, *I haven't had one of them in a long time.*

The home forces were faring no better than those annihilated species. Human armies protecting the populace had to be spread pretty thin as well, though Gwen could only speak for her adoptive home's soldiers, what with so many in the Middle East, and Homeland Security still being a fledgling force when compared to what it faced: a force as ancient as the Earth herself. Beings that taught humanity about war and death, and how to kill in a multitude of nasty ways. Even for all their cruelty, violence and devastation, humanity was still the pupil to these beings' mastery of all things abhorrent, brutal and malevolent, though Gwen hoped futilely that the Adversary's invasion hadn't become so widespread and destructive in such a short space of time as to create such global chaos as she witnessed in Santa Fe, as he no doubt intended; because Gwen still labored under the impression that she stood a chance and that she had been summoned *before* matters had degenerated beyond salvation – though if she was honest, judging by the state of the world as she remembered it, she couldn't see how it couldn't not be. *We let him in.*

Her moment of moderate humor passed, vanishing like snow in the desert as she considered the consequences for the hundredth time of a demonic rampage – not just on a tiny and ridiculous scale like those seen on TV, but on a scale unprecedented at any time in history. Even Alexander didn't accomplish what the Adversary was undertaking. That was nation against nation, and this didn't even come close, for it was world against world, and only that if they were lucky. It was greater still than the eradication of a single species – humanity knew all about that, having tried it several times; and some were still trying it – it was instead more like entire planets set against other planets in such a way even H G Wells might want to rethink. Races immeasurably older than humanity now faced extinction at the hands of the Adversary. But what scared Gwen more than that threat, was the fact that humans still fought amongst themselves even when faced with a common enemy. Gwen flew on, troubled and uneasy, lost in her own thoughts as she saw the imagined horrors in her mind's eye over and over, again and again.

Leaving US airspace with a sonic boom – one of many she had done as she powered across the vast open expanses of Middle America and turned up the coast – Gwen crossed over into Canadian territory and continued her coastal tracking. She didn't know exactly what she was seeing or where she was, as there were no signs that high up and geography wasn't one of her strong points, but it wasn't long before she saw less and less land, and that gave her all the clue she needed, followed by the occasional floating ice flow. Sensing the current of the Earth's magnetic field, she banked slightly and was soon skimming past what she took for Greenland. It was there she saw her first whale sign. Excitedly, this prompted her to take a change of travel plan, angling southwards to follow them. Gwen loved whales; she had always had a soft spot for them. She had no idea what it was that attracted her to them. It was as irrational as many other human emotions. They touched a place within her that blossomed like a spring flower when she listened to their song or saw them on TV, but this was just the icing to her cake: the ability to actually watch them in the flesh. Of course, she could swim with them too. The thought hit her like she had flown into a wall. In one swift move, she folded her wings back and dived. Braking at the last minute so she didn't hit the concrete-hard water's surface, she shifted form, slipping into that of the orca. The killer whale slid gracefully through the roiling ocean surface and her whole perspective took a radical turn.

She swam in circles for several long minutes as she acclimatized herself and got her head and senses around this new and alien environment. Satisfied with her new mode of travel, she shifted once more, adopting the larger and more ponderous form of the humpback whale which had drawn her attention in the first place. She figured the bigger species was going to be more suitable for powering across the ocean depths anyway. Re-aligning her senses, she drove her great tail and swept her flukes down, propelling her hulking form away at a speed that surprised even herself. She reveled in this new form and sported amongst the ice and waves like a newborn experiencing the joy of life for the first time. It was then she heard her first whale song in the ocean. She wasn't anywhere prepared for the intensely spiritual, profound and subtle change that dropped over her mind like a fine web at hearing it. Her thoughts began to slow and elongate. What before would have been a transient idea, now took on a deeper and more deliberate thought form. She began to sense currents and undercurrents to even the simplest of concepts; realising that there was little that was truly simple, and that *everything* had a purpose, implications and repercussions. Their meanings just weren't always obvious. And how so many of them were devastatingly far reaching.

Gwen began to reflect more and more upon her own life in this intense and thought provoking whale manner. Initially, it made her uncomfortable as she went over her many inadequacies – too many – but they paled into insignificance as she expanded her awareness to include the rest of her two-legged species. The results stunned her. She had never delved this deep before and it made her wonder just how superficial her life, all life, had been up till that moment – just scratching at the surface of their existence, oblivious to what lay beneath, like a stone that skimmed the surface of a lake, unaware of the vastness below. Her humanity took another pummeling – what little remained anyway.

Time too was another casualty of her transition. She began to measure it by different imperatives as her perception took yet another twist. Gwen began to imagine humanity as mayflies – it was as though her mind's eye had put her view of mortal life on fast forward – so brief and shortlived, yet they hurried through their lives, missing so much; they were fleeting in comparison to the ponderous and gentle pace of the whale. And It didn't help either that in the back of Gwen's mind she recalled the prospect of outliving everything and everyone she currently knew if what the girls had said was true, and she had little cause to doubt them. She was Drakarim now, and though she was yet to fully understand what that implied – Gwen shivered involuntarily at the thought of finding out too – she knew that unless something unpleasant happened to her, she was up for, potentially at least, a long life such that even the whales would be relatively shortlived, along with trees and mountains; but she couldn't quite get her head around that prospect yet.

Beyond the philosophical ramifications she meandered through, there was one abiding sensation that pervaded her soul above and beyond the rest of her introspections – peace. Deep below the waves and turmoil of the surface world, she felt a peace and serenity unmatched above. Total escapism. It was unlike anything she had ever experienced. The whales feared nothing down here. They were nobility here, for there was nothing to fear. It was only when they had to surface did they have cause for concern; and it was the same cause that had much of Mother Nature's creatures living in mortal dread. Humanity.

THE ADVERSARY

Gwen caught up with several of the leviathans as they ghosted majestically through the dark waters, smaller fish flashing by like shooting stars, and she began to converse, slowly at first, with these sixty-five ton plus gentle giants as she was a stranger to them and they were naturally wary. But somehow, before even Gwen could fully introduce herself – unfamiliar with whale etiquette – they recognized her, for if not who, but what she was. Reverently they began to communicate with her, politely, softly, and with a gentleness that made her heart wrench. They spoke not with words, but with a pure sound and emotion. Images flashed through her mind as she discovered their telepathic language and she was soon reduced to tears by their plight and total incomprehension of humanity's genocidal attacks on their kind and that of the many oceanic creatures, who they felt a responsibility for. Failing them with their inability to stop it and failing too to understand humanity's compulsion to kill so much and so many, and so frequently. The whales had endeavored over man's brief history to communicate with the two-leggeds land-bound, but for the most part, they were met with only fear and ignorance. There was a brief moment of communicative success with a primitive race that later became known to humanity as the Inuit. But for all their respect and reverence of the great whales, it didn't stop them killing them, though many whales willingly gave up their lives to aid the two-leggeds in the hope that they would eventually come to learn what the whales tried to instill in them. Unfortunately, it never happened.

For all their tales of death and torment, Gwen never once felt hate or vengeance from them, only sadness. That and pity, though not the condescending type humanity proffered. It was a deep and soul-destroying sorrow at failing to bridge the gulf that separated their world from that of the land walkers; for there were things that lay in the great depths and ocean beds that man would never know and what the whales had endeavored to share. It was more than just a tragic loss: it was a loss which they saw as such a waste of knowledge. For the knowledge they had was phenomenal, and yet it was lost on the petty and tiny minded humans they hoped to teach. If it couldn't be achieved with a harpoon or a sharp blade, they didn't want to know. For a time, Gwen knew only shame.

They took Gwen to some of the deep places and shared many of the wonders with her that man knew nothing of, and Gwen wept all the more, her salty tears mingling with the salt of the sea. Where the seawater containing her tears washed over rocks and touched the seabed, new plants and life bloomed and sprouted. Yet for all the new life that blossomed as she swept past, Gwen came to understand, tragically, that the whales' song, for the most part, wasn't just them communing; it was their living eulogy. They sang their own death song as they died slowly, one by one, not so much from humanity's depravities, but of broken hearts at their failure to reach an understanding. When the last note from the last whales song died and faded to silence with their extinction something fundamental would be lost, never again to be felt by any in the Multiverse. That day was fast approaching.

The question that kept repeating and echoing through her mind was, why? With all man's ingenuity and feats of engineering, scientific discovery and supposed intellect, what on earth could he want from a whale's corpse that he couldn't fabricate or reproduce otherwise? Surely we had gotten past the pathetic idea that it was okay to keep making the same mistakes and committing the same acts of heinous cruelty just because our predecessors did. That didn't make it okay at all. Habitual death. It made no sense to her whatsoever, no matter who it affected. Images of Asian whalers filled her mind and she grew angry all over again as the combined pictures from both her own mind and that of the whales filled her head with blood and terror. That would stop. If they survived this catastrophe, she would see to it personally that the barbaric practice ceased once and for all or else her rage wasn't going to be a healthy thing to be around. She swam on.

Gwen got a sense of the whales' numbers from their shared consciousness and realized that there were only a few hundred thousand left on the entire planet. Once humans had driven them to extinction, what would they do next? How many more species would suffer the same unnecessary fate?

What would replace the whale for whatever it was they wanted from them? If they would have to find a substitute at that time, why not find it now and evolve ever so slightly, leaving these beautiful and gentle creatures in peace. Sadly and shamefully, Gwen knew the answer to that all too well.

Gwen just swam then with the majestic whales for a time, once they had finished speaking, for there was only so much to say about what they couldn't change and before they all grew too morose, if such a thing was possible, for Gwen didn't think she had ever been so sad. It seemed odd to hear from a whale that life was too short to be miserable all the time, not in a world of such utter beauty and tranquility as the one they swam in. Her new-found companions began to sing again as they soared through the waters, only this was a song of joy and power and her spirits lifted slightly. It was easy to see how some artists had envisioned these huge beings gracefully propelling themselves through the timeless void of space as the fish and other denizens of the deep waters sparkled and flashed their lights and colors like a myriad of living stars, though as the world beneath the waves was far more alien to man than space was, it made sense that humanity could not comprehend them. Too busy flinging lumps of metal upwards into space, trying to understand worlds that held no connection to them; and hurling their refuse into the oceans, rather than exploring downwards, trying to understand the very world they were an intrinsic part of. Humans were mostly water in their composition, yet it was the least understood aspect of their world, good only for plundering and dumping, though Gwen knew she was being unfair to those few who did try. But they were just that – too few – and probably too late. Gwen closed her eyes and drifted serenely, carried along by the powerful ocean current.

Many years ago, long before her time at Earth Angel, Gwen had been a member of a small New Age group who had tried to teach her meditation. They bleated incessantly about *going inside*, plumbing her inner depths and discovering her own mystery. Back then, for all her need to find *something*, she doubted they ever really knew what the hell they were talking about, though it sounded good. She plumbed and plumbed, but the only thing she ever explored in any detail was the inside of her eyelids. That was, of course, when she managed to stay awake long enough. Searching for meaning in her meaningless life didn't stop her partying whenever she got the chance. Gwen used to say that it wasn't the partying that did you in, it was the recuperation. It never helped her cause when they used to insist on sitting in a gloomy semi-darkness, just a few candles to stop people treading on each other and some smelly incense to add its cloudy atmospheric dimes' worth. Sitting hour after hour as her buttocks went from one degree of numbness to another. Her carefully crossed legs would lose all sensation and she dreaded the pins and needles she would get if she ever moved again. But mostly it was like having an epidural. She lost all feeling from the waist down. She would try to forget the discomfort to come and focus on her eyelids. Her strategically placed elbows would be located just so upon her desensitized knees. Her hands would come together to form the pyramid, thumb and forefinger touching as the remainder wove themselves together, giving herself the illusion that she was an experienced meditator. It was only when one of her well-placed elbows slipped off her knee as sleep robbed her of control, that she would be dropped unceremoniously back into reality. The undignified jerk that brought her back would cause her to move more than she had that last hour, and sensation would flow back into her bloodless limbs, closely followed by pain as blood and feeling flowed back in. Eight sessions of this were all she could deal with. She rarely tried it again afterwards except when she was alone in her own bed or on her sofa with a little too much wine coursing through her system. She usually started well but invariably ended up curled up in a weird shape on her sofa. She would stumble up to bed, sometimes shedding her clothes first and sometimes not. This was her most abiding memory of her meditative experience to date. She didn't include her encounters with Grandma Yellow Deer and Dolores; they were more like mystical experiences. But here, deep in the dark and vast ocean, she felt the pull of the currents, the pulse and hum of the electromagnetic waves that resonated through the water. Much in the same way a bee sees something completely different when it looks at a flower, so too did the creatures of the oceans. They felt and followed the natural ebb and flow of the Earth's rhythms. As each frequency was conducted through the water, so too did its color field change. To the fish and ocean dwelling mammals, what was darkness to humans was a multihued color laden extravaganza. Their world was illuminated by a suffusion of every shade, hue and color imaginable and then some we hadn't. For there were frequencies that were beyond a human's perception, and they had their own color. Gwen discovered as she moved with the whales, just how limited human vision was, how much they missed. For they seemed to categorize the entire universe as they saw it and perceived it, because that was all they could see. *Limited.* Humans couldn't even see the world the way over half of the animal life they co-existed with saw it. She was more connected now to the natural flows of the world than she ever had been before, connected to something so big and vast she felt so tiny and insignificant; as though she existed on a world that was no bigger than a grain of sand and it was adrift within a desert the size of the Sahara. Gwen wished she could bottle this feeling and share it with all of humanity: things would be so different then. She'd put money on that, or at the very least, share it with her little meditation group. They'd really know what the meaning of those empty sentences that they spouted was all about afterwards.

As she floated, outside time and lost within her newly discovered world, other creatures came and went; introducing themselves to her as news of who and what she was spread far and wide. Much in the same way as the whales had, they transmitted their thoughts and feelings via images and emotion. It made Gwen well up on more than one occasion as these humble beings *spoke* to her and told her of their families and lives, each in their own way and individual styles. It made sense now to her why the Earth was seventy per cent water. At least seventy per cent of the world's intelligent life was down here. Yet the one thing she was particularly pleased about was that in her presence, nothing attacked anything else. Both prey and predator came and went with none wanting to insult her by eating each other in her vicinity.

Even the massive and greatly misunderstood sharks. Gwen wasn't so naïve as to think that they wouldn't revert back to their natural ways once they were at a sufficient distance from her, such was the nature of nature after all: as cruel and harsh as it was serene and beautiful. Harmony. Balance. The one principle spoken of by many cultures, yet rarely practised.

Gwen mused over intelligence and wondered about its measure. Granted, humanity had built machines and tools to further their progress, but on a like-for-like basis, humanity couldn't hold a candle to the creatures of the natural world. What would humanity do when in the long term, there were more unnatural objects left over, than there was *over* to spill out into? Deserts were increasing, land was falling back into the oceans at an alarming rate, water levels were rising, only partly due to global warming: the remainder from the heat of the ever increasing size of the molten core which was due to hatch from the pregnant Earth some time in the near future. Jen and Maddy had briefed her on the natural order of progression and how the planets fed the furnace that was the Sun, keeping it alive until the last planet was eventually sucked into it. Apparently, the Earth was due to shift and replace Venus, with our moon moving closer to the Sun to replace Mercury; and the ejected, white hot and bubbling core would cool and replace our moon, becoming the new moon for a new Earth, the former Mars, and so on and so forth, and its creatures progressing and moving on as they evolved, or not, as the case may be. In her heart of hearts, Gwen knew that the vast majority of humanity wouldn't be moving on. They had lost all sense of what it means to be human; of what being connected to the Earth entails; its responsibilities, not only to the other creatures that shared this world, but to each other. They had become intent on destroying each other and everything else with as much brutality as possible. There would be repercussions for that. What the Adversary was doing could be considered such a repercussion. But Gwen had been told that there was far worse out there than the Adversary. It wasn't him in himself that was so terrible; just what he was doing, misguided as it is. Oh no, there were species out there who had been exiled beyond the Covenant and prohibited from ever stepping foot on any other living world ever again. Now they *were* to be feared. Should one of those decide revenge was the order of the day, then humanity would be in really big trouble and they would scream to have the Adversary back. So what did humans do? Send out probes and tons of space garbage to draw attention to themselves. Curiosity was all well and good, but humanity wasn't mentally prepared to find anything. The moment they got any alleged visitors, all they wanted to do was shoot them down in the name of national bloody security. Surely the answer is obvious. If you don't want visitors, don't send out invites. If humanity had any inkling of what was out there, they would run for the shelter of the deepest cave, seal it up and pray nothing found them ever again.

Gwen was Drakarim. Her newly adoptive species was one of those from *out there somewhere*; Jen and Maddy had implied as much, though they had kept their exact location to themselves. For her own good, they said: until matters here were dealt with, there was no point in overburdening her with specifics. 'All in good time,' they had said. Damn, how they irritated her when they did that. But, powering through the ocean, Gwen found herself arguing with herself; though she amended that to debating. She considered the other side: that not all humans were stupid and self-destructive. Some were seekers – souls who hoped for a brighter future for their kind and for those of the animals who shared our world, and considered humans more in the role of curators., They sought enlightenment and guidance; fuelled only by a genuine need to be better, and to achieve something greater than themselves with their lives.

Poor saps. They stood out like beacons to the predators of humankind.

There were those who wrapped themselves up in the guise of teachers and gurus, spouting banalities and incomprehensible rubbish that when broken down, meant absolutely nothing; talking in riddles to disguise their own lack of substance and wisdom. But if it sounded remotely credible – the best lies have the most truth in them – and it usually did, they drew the seekers to them like moths to their parasitic, vampiric and eventually, doomed flame.

These teachers raid and plunder the ancient cultures and fuse them together, often nailing square pegs into round holes to try and find something new and exclusive to them: an ancient and forgotten wisdom that only they can impart. *Bollocks can they!* Gwen fumed to herself. Her mental debate was having its usual effect on her: she was getting annoyed again, for there was no real way to police these frauds and tricksters and she knew they knew who they were – how could they not? Sitting in their mansions and vast country houses, paid for by the gullible, and inventing some new ruse to bolster their egos and bank accounts. For all their so-called intellectualism and technological prowess, humans still hadn't managed to find or lose the *stupid* gene. Only mere hundreds of years ago, if a person said that they had heard voices from beyond, they were either revered as some sort of prophet or they were stoned as a madman. Nowadays, there were no end of individuals who allegedly spoke to the dead, or some high powered, high ranking spirit guide who had nothing better to do with their afterlife. Yet the majority of humans accepted this all in their stride. Of course, the rest just categorized them with humanity's new set of tools: illnesses, Gwen thought of next as her mind raced. They were delusional, schizophrenic with some sort of multiple personality disorder or some other sort of *ology*. Just as well they didn't have these illnesses back in biblical days otherwise the world might be an entirely different place. For as long as Gwen could remember, she was never big on religion. 'Bloody waste of time,' she used to say, earning a clip around the ear from her mother. She still thought that, if she was honest. Look what sort of trouble it had gotten the world into – there had been people all over the place hearing voices, talking to burning hedges, shafts of sunlight, and numerous other tales of disembodied voices. *Their padded cells would await them if it was nowadays.*

Take Joan of Arc. *Now there's an example*, thought Gwen, getting into her mental stride. Why did she never come up with gems like this when she argued with Jen and Maddy? Now if some young girl today was to start claiming she heard what Joan did, no army in the world would drop everything and follow her to war. She would wind up in a lovely cushioned room with all the medication she would ever want, and a lot more she didn't. Certainly the Church or other world religion would see to that it nobody else did. Absolutely no one was allowed to be in communication with the divine except them, of course. Look what happened to Joan. Apparently the divine in question had no say in that matter, of course. Its self-appointed toadies were the only ones who could dictate who could or who couldn't, which means to say no one could but them – that way their will was and still is unchallenged. Gwen thought that that attitude was up there with the epitome of arrogance. Such arrogance from an institution that claimed such humility! Then, Gwen added to her rant, there was this so-called division between the religious and the scientists. *How does that work then?* For if they abhorred science as much as they claimed, why was it that when one of their flock – Gwen had always thought that apt, for most of them followed blindly like sheep – had a spiritual experience, why did they insist on then subjecting it to every scientific experiment and test they could come up with to disprove a thing, when they believed in the biggest disprovable thing of all time. They wanted the poor soul to reproduce their experience just because they said so. Another arrogance. It was as though they could call the lightning to strike again in exactly the same place or the wind to blow on command. Really!

How humans had such an elevated opinion of themselves had been a never ending source of disappointment and concern for Gwen and she now knew that it was the same disappointment for the leviathans of the deep. But unlike them, having to surface for air every once and a while, Gwen didn't have to. Leaving the whales for some solitary time, she plumbed the bottomless trenches and chasms that split the ocean beds; and even once, she came upon a beast of mythological proportions. It regarded her as she drifted close to it. She didn't know if it was fear or excitement that coursed through her but either way, she was in awe of the giant squid that watched her. It had to be in excess of two hundred feet, tip to tentacle. And it had to have been ancient, even by their standards. It was just as well that humans couldn't get this deep, for if they came across a terrifying creature such as this – though Gwen sensed nothing hostile from it, just a sense of gentle curiosity at seeing something different in its world. It felt no fear, for what had it to fear? – all any human who saw it would probably want to do is kill it, cut it up and or eat it.

These thoughts and more resounded in Gwen's mind as she traversed the vast oceans. She lost all sense of time as she swam. So rarely had she been alone long enough to ponder the many things that irritated her, and in such depth as now. But now that she found herself in such a place, her mind opened for them to have a voice, and it seemed that with that voice, they had a lot to say. More time passed.

Something in her mind triggered a memory. It was a memory of time spent in Santa Fe, enjoying a summer's day with Dolores, who for once, wasn't working but spending the day in the store with her. Her store: Earth Angel. The one that lovely old lady had bequeathed her. As well as her two lovely shop assistants, Jen and Maddy.

Jen and Maddy! Drakarim! The quest! It all came crashing back in on her like her mind had imploded. The enormity of what she faced and the implications of her failure. Suddenly Gwen found it hard to breathe. She shifted through several forms, but it didn't help. She wasn't claustrophobic; she just needed to get to the surface. Fast. Gwen reverted to whale form and with powerful strokes of her massive tail and by sweeping her equally massive flukes downwards, she rocketed upwards like some Trident missile being shot out of one of the many non-existent nuclear submarines that she *hadn't* passed during her journey.

Gwen broke the surface with little regard until after, of what might have been up there. She managed to get her entire body, flukes and tail so far clear of the water that had there been any of those whale watchers nearby, other than wetting themselves at seeing her erupt the way she had, they might have thought she was going to sprout wings and be the first in a new species of flying whale. They might not have been far wrong, had they been watching, for before her gigantic body could slam back down into the undulating waves, Gwen morphed into a seabird and alighted upon the heaving sea. Had there been anyone in the vicinity watching a whale turn into a bird, well that would have been one fish tale that would need to have a lot of rum to have been believed. *I really ought to be more careful though, where I change: too many questions and I'm in no position yet to have to try and explain myself.* Fortunately for Gwen, though, there were no dinghy-driving anoraks up there. She was safe, for now.

Gwen had discovered that during her mental meanderings, she had drifted much further off course than she had ever intended. She had wanted to merely cross the Atlantic. Instead, she had been drawn in by the Gulf Stream and the oceanic wonders the whales had shared with her, as well as her own solo discoveries. If she was honest with herself, she could spend years down beneath the waves, just exploring. But she also knew that too much now depended on her to succeed in her quest, to dally any longer than she already had, so she had turned tail and headed back to her original destination. Gwen didn't know how many days later it was that she found herself facing yet another coastline. It seemed an age since she saw one last, and that last one would have been Greenland: a rough looking inhospitable terrain from what she saw of it from the air, bereft of any life that she could see. The one she was looking at now didn't look any more inviting. She hoped it was the one she had been aiming for originally, though she wasn't sure which bit she was looking at. Not that it mattered much to a being who could fly faster than most aircraft.

Something was tugging at Gwen's mind now she had surfaced and faced land. A more civilized and less primal urge was trying to get her attention. It was her inner voice saying to her that she could use a hot bath, a soft bed and a very large glass of Chardonnay. Agreeing with herself about all three, Gwen morphed once more, from the seabird she currently was, into a grey seal, and powered her way towards the rocky coastline. It was late afternoon by the time Gwen reached the rocks. She knew this because of the time of year and the fact it was starting to get dark. She guessed at it being about three in the afternoon. Gwen found a good solid looking flat rock and flopped herself up onto it, retaining her seal look in case of prying eyes. A petite blonde girl down here would be just *too* suspicious. Though she didn't feel the cold as such – an advantage of being what she was, because she hated the cold really, which was why she moved to the desert in the first place – Gwen shivered all the same. There was a dank and clammy fog clinging to the coastline like some gigantic amorphous parasite, leaving everything it touched wet and slimy. Everything that is that the crashing waves and ocean spray didn't reach. This fog seemed to pulse and flow along the coastline, probing and sucking at the cliffs as if its mere presence could pull the land and the rocks back into the sea. It was bad enough that the ocean seemed to have similar thoughts, but it had them about all land masses. It seemed to want to pull them back into its depths as though it begrudged them ever breaking free from its merciless grip. And no one could fault its persistence. Wave after wave crashed upon the rocks as they had done for millennia and would continue to do for eons to come, all being well, for there was little to match the patience of the oceans. They knew they would win eventually. But Gwen's contemplations on the elements and weather made her curious about this particular fog. She had felt something disconcerting when she arrived but had no idea what to ascribe it to. Now she wasn't so sure. Had her shiver been one of prescience? She had heard about the inclement weather of the Emerald Isle, but there was more to this fog than met the eye. It didn't take a meteorologist to know that, on this evening, there was no wind. But the fog was swirling like a gale was blowing. It oscillated and danced like a living thing: searching, seeking and probing. It may have been her overworked imagination struggling overtime and playing her for a fool, but she could have sworn it moved with an intent; a deliberate purpose.

Gwen resumed her seabird form and, with little effort, floated her way up the rocky escarpment, her mind still conscious of the menacing fog and her senses keen for any changes or imminent danger. Instead, all she saw were half a dozen small stone buildings, looking like large stone beehives jutting out from the rock face. *What a bloody ridiculous place to build something.* Gwen was astounded at the dwellings perched on a ledge in the middle of apparently nowhere. But it wasn't until she drifted over them, letting the odd air currents pull her where they will, did she see the great stone staircase that led away from the strange habitation. She wondered who would want to build something out there like that, let alone live in it. She saw as well, something further to dispirit her. For it was only then did she realize she hadn't actually made it to Ireland, her original goal, but instead, she had turned up on a rocky island, one of apparently three just offshore. Her bird's vision, now that she was above the fog a little, showed the other two slightly smaller islands a little way off. Her vision also showed her that both islands were covered in roosting seabirds. So too was the one she flew over. She was no ornithologist, but she did know a puffin when she saw one, and though she wasn't entirely sure, she thought the others might have been petrels. And Gwen would have been right, as she flapped her gull's wings and set off for the mainland. She had inadvertently drifted out to a collection of small islands known as the Skelligs. *I don't know how I've managed to get this far and do what I have already. I get lost in my own damn house some days. How I'm supposed to scoot all around the bloody world and find this tree when I can't even find a bloody great island without landing on the wrong bit is a fine way to carry on.* It wasn't that she was stressed – she had always been lucky that way – but there was an element of frustration that built up in her when things didn't go as smoothly as she expected them to, and that made her grouchy. She soared over the roosting birds, disturbing one or two and having to flap off a bit faster as they swooped at her, oblivious to who she was. All they saw was another bird who shouldn't have been there. She didn't have the time or the patience to explain it to them, so she just took off a bit faster and put some distance and air between her and them, flying upwards to both avoid any further harassment and to get a better view.

Gwen didn't notice at first, but the fog was suddenly conspicuous by its absence. She glanced back and saw it clinging nastily to the two islands, squatting over them like an obscene BLEVE[1]. It was an odd thought that Gwen had, as she recalled having had a gas cloud described to her once, and of how it hung in the air just waiting to explode. The gaseous reference was an appropriate choice of word to describe the fog, for though Gwen didn't know it, the word gas originated from two other words: one being the Greek Khaos and the other, the old English Chaos. This Chaos was a reference to several things that lent it credibility as a menacing entity, two of them being the Void and the Abyss. Both had infernal connotations. Yet unbeknownst to Gwen, the fog, as she flew through it, had sensed her too.

Gwen knew nothing of the region below her. As far as she was concerned, she could have been anywhere on the west coast. She needed to take stock and that meant finding someone and getting her bearings. Her bookworming back at the store had implied that Ireland was a good candidate for the First Tree. It was steeped in natural mythology and the home of the legendary druids. *Weren't they guardians of trees and groves after all?* It made sense to Gwen. Avalon was another candidate: that had a fabulous tree by all accounts, and by Gwen's thinking could have been around Ireland somewhere. After all, if Arthur sailed west from anywhere near or around the West Country of England, where might he end up? Ireland? Or one of its little isles? She knew it was tenuous, but what choice did she have? She wasn't exactly brimming over with viable alternatives. People far brighter than her had spent their entire lives looking for fabled and long-lost things and never found them. She probably had days at most to find something that no one had even looked for. *Easy, Gwen girl, never say never. Just think, this time last month you weren't a bloody big green dragon. Shit happens in the weirdest way if you let it, so breathe and see what appears; it's all you can do.* She knew she was talking to herself. She also knew she did it all the time. *Always had, always would, I suppose.* Gwen was happy with herself and who she was and had become, so therefore trusted the answers she gave herself when she was in a fix.

---

1   Boiling Liquid Expanding Vapor Explosion.

Gwen swooped down and landed on a vast stretch of beach as night fell. It wasn't the brightest of moons that night and it cast a surreal haze across the beach. The tide was out and she stood upon a vast sandy expanse. One lone seagull in the moonlight wouldn't attract too much attention, even if there was anyone to see her – but there wasn't. Not even a house light. *Bloody marvelous! I must have picked the least inhabited bit of Ireland I could find.* But for all that, it felt good beneath her gull's feet to be on solid ground once more. With another glance around her, Gwen risked a transformation back to her own form. She felt the rush of enjoyment as the cool air brushed across her skin and the salty air brought a million miniscule droplets of ocean spray and flecked her body with their touch, almost a parting farewell after cradling her in the depths for so long. Gwen didn't feel the cold and she was no longer embarrassed by her nakedness, having come to terms with who she was; but it hadn't stopped her noticing the little things about what happened to her body. Though she no longer felt the extremes of heat and cold in the same way she had, she couldn't help but notice how her breath plumed before her, like standing in a chiller. Though it wasn't *that* cold, even here, on some remote Irish beach in the early hours of the morning during mid-winter. It was too wet and salty to freeze, but the more she looked, the more she saw inconsistencies with the weather patterns. The sand beneath her bare feet wasn't just wet and hard packed, *it was frozen.* Gwen knelt down and knocked it with her knuckles. It gave a hard solid thunk, definitely *not* like sand. She stood and turned about. Her hackles had risen at this unnaturalness and she sought the cause, though there was nothing immediately obvious except for one thing: the fog. It was creeping inexorably closer, snaking its way across the water like a living thing floating a few feet above the chasing waves as if it was loath to touch them. *It doesn't seem to like salt water. Hmm.* This little revelation allowed Gwen to make a leap of assumption, for when she had first arrived at the east coast and begun to track north, a small group of minions had followed her, but wouldn't leave the land and attack her out at sea. So she had stayed offshore and they eventually gave up chasing her and swept inland. They didn't seem to want to venture over salt water either; it was an interesting little fact to store away. The fog was definitely unnatural enough to be a weapon of the Adversary. But how do you fight a fog? She knew she didn't have long as it oozed, undulated and unfurled ever closer. Placing her hands upon her hips, she set her jaw and watched it for a few moments as she organized her thoughts. Then, much to the consternation of whatever might have been behind the fog, she laughed. She had gotten a mental image of what she must look like to any observer. A tiny naked woman, standing defiant on a vast frozen beach in the middle of the night on a deserted Irish coastline, attempting to mentally halt and or prepare to fight a creeping fog. *Good girl, that's the way: keep your sense of humor.* With a reality check, she controlled herself and recalled her situation. This sobered her slightly. Gwen knew she couldn't stop a fog and it wasn't like it was moving overly fast so, turning on her heel, she strode away from the seashore, leaving it skulking behind her, and headed inland. A quick shimmer and she was a creamy pale owl, ghosting silently away. No sooner had she transformed and gained a little height, than she saw an old monastery, and hoped to see a friar or a monk, or whoever lived in such things. She would have been happy to see anyone really, at this moment in time. Any human face would have been a joy to behold about then. It wasn't that she had missed humanity particularly – quite the opposite – but when she needed information about where she was, it was typical that there wasn't a bloody soul to be seen. But she banked round and headed in the Abbey's direction. But swooping down and circling it once, Gwen dejectedly saw no signs of life; in fact, she couldn't even tell if it was inhabited at all. *Marvelous. What to do now?* Seconds later, the answer materialized out of the darkness. A road. It was the first bit of civilization she had seen that didn't look like it was out of the dark ages. *Now that's more like it.* Her owl silently winged along it for a mile or two and was rewarded with a sign, but upon closer inspection, it just read 'R566' and was no help at all. It didn't say where it went or where it had come from. Alighting upon the useless thing, she ruffled her smoky white feathers and thought about her next move. She hadn't seen any cars on her way, not coming or going, though for the life of her she couldn't imagine why anyone would be going in the direction she had just come from. There was sod all there: just a bloody huge beach and an old monastery. After an hour of sitting there, she was still alone. Not one car had passed her either way. She wondered whether it would be wise to find some tree and roost for a bit, wait till daylight and see if things got any better. *They sure as shit couldn't get any worse.* Gwen discovered almost as soon as the last resonant syllable faded from her mind, that saying those words was not dissimilar to waving a red rag at a bull whilst wearing a red jump suit, then poking it up the ass with a cattle prod before cuffing yourself to its nose ring and chewing on its ears. It was never going to end well.

Somewhere in the darkness, back in the direction of the beach, came an unearthly screech. Her every mortal fibre and Drakarim's intuition told her emphatically that it was truly unearthly. *What the bloody hell was that?* Gwen growled to herself. The owl's massive vibrant eyes fixed on the inky skyline where she sensed the sound had originated, but even with her supernatural sight, she couldn't pierce the oily blackness, and her skin had begun to crawl with a sense of dread and anticipation. It was like a thousand ants running over her flesh – an image she quashed as soon as it popped into her head. But it was followed by yet more gruesome images of her flesh being swarmed over and devoured in the most graphic and horrendous ways possible by every manner of creature from crabs, through to beetles, then worms, rats, slugs, scorpions and a plethora of equally nasty species. Was it not for the fact that Gwen was more than she was, her mortal mind would have been overwhelmed by the sheer horror of what she was experiencing. It took moments' exertion of her willpower to banish both the images and the sense of terror and dread that had accompanied it, her mind fighting the urge to brush at her skin to remove any last vestige of whatever had been crawling over her, but it was then she remembered that she was in owl form and that might have been a bit difficult anyway. In a shimmer of emerald green sparks, Gwen was herself once more and subconsciously clothed in her clinging dress of tightly woven green leaves that seemed to emerge from her very skin and flow over her body. Her hair lifted slightly from her scalp, as though a slight electrical current toyed with her and framed her face with a corona of gently waving golden hair. Power began to course exponentially through Gwen as the feeling of dread increased. It descended on her like a hailstorm, slamming into her and crashing over her like a wave over a rock. Again the screech and Gwen grimaced involuntarily, shaking her head to clear the sound. It was reminiscent of an infernal fusion of fingernails down a chalkboard and a rusty nail over glass, only ramped up through the decibel range for maximum effect. She knew then what she faced. Minions; demonic soldiers much like the ones she had run from before, only this time they were between her and the ocean, prohibiting a swift exit. Yet another howl, and this time it was accompanied by the telltale tendrils of the creeping fog. *So then, it was connected to them after all. Shoulda guessed.* But before Gwen could beat herself up about not putting two and two together, she felt another wave of the fear and terror that these creatures emanated wash over her. Grimacing at the slick oily touch of their essence, Gwen knew she had to do something; standing in the middle of the road waiting for it to come to her wasn't going to accomplish anything. At that moment, Gwen was truly glad that there were no people around. It was bad enough her confronting these creatures, but it would have been devastating for Joe Public to have to witness it. She imagined what humanity must have felt in the dark and less enlightened past when these creatures made impromptu appearances. They screwed with the mind first before destroying the body. It had to be awful beyond imagining. The total opposite, she guessed of meeting one of the Celestial Host; weren't they supposed to be all love and light? Whatever, it had to be better than what was coming from these fiends. Another screech, no two. Separate. They were closer than ever and Gwen sensed they had split up to come at her from either side. At least that was how it sounded. But instead of fear, Gwen found a spark had ignited within her, slowly smoldering as it grew into a small flame. It was the flame of righteous and indignant anger. This was *her* world now; she was responsible for its safety and wellbeing. And like the cells that protect the body from damage and infection, she felt a rising urge to swell up and eradicate this demonic infection from her body. The more she thought of it, the brighter and hotter the flame within her became until she could contain it no longer. It began to cloud her vision and with no conscious thought, Gwen threw back her head and screamed herself, venting the rage that manifested within her in the only way she knew how. Her arms were flung wide and the increased wind that had rolled in with the fog plucked at her leafy clothing and hair as if it would tear her from the ground upon which she was literally rooted. It had no chance of doing that, though it tried. She looked – again, had there been anyone to see her – like a true queen of the banshees. Clothed in flowing green, her emerald eyes aflame with iridescent veridium fire, she leant into the rising wind and screamed at the encroaching fog with such force that it balked. It actually hesitated. Where the tendrils and fronds of the fetid mist were undulating around and over everything in its path, obliterating visibility within its grey confines, at the sound of Gwen's fury, it actually retreated several yards.

Gwen's consciousness returned to her as the scream cut off. She was breathing hard, her chest rising and falling as though she had run a marathon. Anger coursed adrenaline and power through her body and she fought to both control and contain it. Reason returned to her with a jolt and she knew that she had to put an end to this abhorrence once and for all. In order to do that: rather than stand and wait for them to attack her on their terms, she would find them first and meet them on hers. Gwen grinned evilly as she turned briefly, ran a few steps and leapt into the air, arms outstretched as though she were diving; but a jade shimmer later and the hawk was powering skyward, her beating wings sending her straight into the heart of the fog. If they wanted her, they would have to catch her. She sped off, twisting and diving with all the acrobatic skills available to her. But it wasn't long before she sensed that the fiends were following her, and then another soul-wrenching screech split the night sky and confirmed it. *I really wish they would stop doing that; it's getting on my nerves and my bloody ears are bleeding.* They weren't, but she felt as though they would be if they carried on howling like they were. She needed a plan. Just being angry at them wasn't going to do it. Diving amongst a cluster of abandoned slate roofed cottages, she scored her talons along one ridge tile and banked upwards, angling sharply left to help alleviate her growing uneasiness that they were right behind her. She almost imagined their foul breath, spewing their noxious vapors on her neck. Fangs and talons just about to reach for her and rend the life from her body. *Think, Gwen, think.* She considered the dragon form but worried that seeing a bloody great big green dragon might be just as terrifying to the populace as the minions evidently were with their emanations of fear and horror. As if they weren't going to have enough nightmares to last several lifetimes as it was. Another screech. But what options did she have? She wasn't built to fight creatures such as these. Sod it; she wasn't designed to fight anything. She was a girl, not a bloody soldier. Worse still was that she didn't have any sort of weapon, or any clue as how to use one even if she did. *Probably do myself more harm than whatever I was aiming at.* Gwen ducked, dived and spun several more times but she still knew that they were gaining on her. She made a choice. *Dammit! I'm in Ireland after all and don't they have those little green people anyway and more myths and legends about fantastic creatures than you could wave a shillelagh at? So what if they saw a dragon? I am bloody green. What more do they want? Perhaps they won't be as disturbed by it as all that.* Happy with her rationale, Gwen picked up the pace and dived for a small copse of trees just ahead of her and the fog. She burst out of the damp, clinging mist and ploughed straight into the copse, weaving expertly between oak, ash and birch, taking full advantage of her lithe and muscular hawk form, until the moment when she exploded out the other side. She knew she only had seconds; they were that close. The moment her wings cleared the foliage, Gwen made the transition in a dazzling spiral shower of incandescent green sparks. Snapping her majestic draconian wings outward with an audible slap, like great sails on a galleon catching the wind, Gwen spun her reptilian self just as the minions – visible now that they were outside the concealment of their insidious mist – burst clear of the copse, sending crows and leaves in all directions, talons outstretched and overly wide mouths stretched to almost tearing as they screamed their impotent rage at their quarry. It was a scream that changed tune almost immediately, from rage to a terror of their own. For instead of finding some small feathered bird, they were met full on with a thunderous crash of bone, chiton and whatever went into these minions, as they connected with several tons of very angry, very fast and heavily spiked, scaled and armor plated green dragon tail. The effect was reminiscent of tossing a handful of melons into the path of a speeding express train. It was all over in a heartbeat. Gwen landed delicately and surveyed her handiwork, though she was slightly disappointed that the mist didn't dissipate with their demise; it merely retreated back beyond her visibility, back towards the coast. Gwen had no more time to spend on it: she had other matters to attend to and one such task was to clear the remains of the minions off her tail. She flicked her long powerful tail, whipping the mess that remained clinging stickily to it, off in a spatter of gore and slimy bits. Distracted as she was initially by her draconian hygiene, Gwen didn't hear her worst fear realized. Excited, but not in a good way, and slightly panicked voices filtered through to her as though she had sponge in her ears. They seemed distant and muffled but they became clearer as her mind focused on them, realizing them for what they were. Gwen was horrified. Whipping her massive reptilian head round on her long muscular, serpentine neck, Gwen leveled her car-sized head at them, with her sparkling and bejeweled multifaceted eyes just a few feet away from the three people who were standing there, as rigid as statues with their own fear filled eyes as wide as saucers, standing next to a beat up and dilapidated Range Rover. They were gesticulating wildly at her until her head drew even closer to them, then they stopped all movement, as if they had been frozen. The only indication that they weren't statues was the way their clothes and hair wafted gently back and forth as Gwen breathed softly in and out on them. The surreal scene was likely to be indelibly printed on their DNA for lifetimes to come as the three men, two of middle years and rough attire, unshaven, in various shades of green themselves stared back at her. Heavy, waxed waterproof coats with a brace of rabbits' feet poking out from an overly deep pocket hinted at the tale of why they were out at this unsociable hour. The third was considerably younger: no more than his mid-twenties, with the features that would ensure an interesting future. Rugged and lightly tanned from time spent out in the open, but tempered with youthful good looks; black wavy hair that he had pulled back into small ponytail; full – if quivering – lips; and startling hazel eyes. *He'll have no trouble with the girls I'll bet.* Gwen studied the three men before her, who must be so far beyond terrified they were in a whole new place. To one of the elder men's shame, Gwen saw the telltale darkening of his trousers and smelt the pungent waft of ammonia, but he paid his embarrassment no mind, refusing to take his eyes from the beast before him, fully expecting it to swallow him up any second. She saw the other older man mutter from the side of his mouth, trying to speak and not look as though he was, and making a poor show of it. He sure was no ventriloquist. 'Don't move, boys. I've heard o' these beasties. They can't see you if you don't move.'

They didn't move and it had little to do with their companion's sage advice. Encouraged by their lack of movement and the fact he hadn't been munched upon yet, he continued his life-saving advice in the face of a giant green dragon protocol. 'If we stand still long enough, maybe it will just go away. It'll be dawn soon and they don't like the sun, or so's I've heard at least. 'Twas a tale me da tol' me when I was naught but a tadpole meself.'

Without looking at him, pant wetter whispered back just as badly, 'Will you shut ya face, ya ruddy gobshite. It can probably hear you shooting ya mouth off. Mary, Mother of God, you've no got the sense yee were born with. Our Daniel has more sense than you. At least he's not blabbing like an old woman.'

Gwen was sure a full blown punch-up would have ensued before long, whether she was there or not, as they continued to berate each other about how they should behave in front of the dragon. What was she going to do with them? Of all the places to find people, right when she was in mid-transformation. They had seen it all. Gwen figured she wasn't going to get a lot of sense out of them if she spoke to them, certainly not as a dragon. Even if she resumed her own form she thought it might be hard work. Gwen snaked her head a bit closer and on an in-breath she caught the familiar smell of alcohol. Lots of alcohol. They were a trio of half-cut poachers, so who were they going to tell? And if they found anyone, who would believe them? But as Gwen moved closer, her choices were taken from her as one of them, the one they called Daniel, promptly fainted dead away at their feet. They stopped their outrageous debate and turned to look at their fallen companion, and then they looked at the dragon. She could almost see the thought going through their heads. Run or tend to their friend; run, friend, run, friend. Or even, fallen friend distract dragon. They apparently liked that one, for without a backward glance, as though they shared the same thought at the same time, the two men spun and scrambled away as fast as they could, one tossing his rabbits over his shoulder as he desperately tried to get his legs to co-ordinate with each other, possibly in the vain hope that the rabbits would distract said beastie from eating *them*. *Nice friends*, thought Gwen, with barely restrained amusement as she looked down upon the prone man sprawled in the damp grass.

Gwen wasn't quite sure what to do next as she morphed back to her own form; complete with denims, hiking boots and quilted jacket over a roll neck sweater, and adding to the ensemble one of those quaint and quirky woolen hats she saw the skiers wear as they went up the mountains back in New Mexico for the skiing there. Her quandary was either: follow the men and see where they went, for there had to be a town nearby, the men had to come from somewhere and hopefully that was where they were fleeing back to; or, tend to the fainter, seeing as she was responsible for his predicament and she couldn't leave him at the mercy of any more of those demons just in case they had friends in the area. It was a tough one as the call of civilization beckoned invitingly to her – civilization which was bound to have a public house and even a bed and breakfast with real beds. Gwen sighed and scrubbed her hand through her unkempt yet lustrous hair as she realized that in all the excitement of the quest and the series of tumultuous events that had led to her being here, she had no money. And a bed and breakfast was going to want paying. Quickly she shoved the guilty thought from her mind about seeing if the fainter had any money on him. She was just being weak and pathetic. Home comforts would have to wait. She couldn't leave him at the mercy of the oncoming night, lying unconscious in a wet field. So squashing her hat back on, Gwen picked him up, recalling the ease in which the girls moved Dolores, and found that she too had strength she didn't have before. Giggling to herself at her new-found abilities, she easily lifted the prone man and placed him in his car – at least she assumed it was his car. She assumed correctly as she did in fact rifle through his pockets and upon finding a bunch of car keys – which, to her relief, fitted – she started the car. Placing him in the passenger seat, Gwen jumped in the driver's seat and fired the car up. The dilapidated heater kicked in and after belching out some foul smelling cold air, finally started to warm up. Something that passed for music grumbled out of the stereo, which looked newer and in better condition than the entire vehicle. *What is it with boys and their car stereos? As long as they have music while they drive, they'll take any old crap out on the road and be happy. Seems our boy here is no exception.* Changing her mind about driving him away, she wondered how he would take it when he awoke and found some strange woman driving him in his car when the last thing he recalled would be staring into the jaws of imminent death in the form of a massive green dragon. No, that wouldn't be fair on him. Instead, she leant over and kissed him lightly on the cheek, which elicited a small groan signifying he was coming round. Her kiss also suffused some color back into his cheeks, as though she had kissed a tiny healing spell onto him. She was the avatar of nature after all. *Wow, I'll have to remember how to do that again. Still, good enough for now. He should be okay, or at least I hope so. I can't stay with him all night. He'll probably be too hacked off at his friends for doing a bunk and leaving him, to worry about how he got in the car.* Smiling to herself as she climbed out, she closed the door quietly and took a few backward steps away, watching to see if he woke. When he didn't immediately wake but began looking as though he was about to, Gwen sparkled into her owl form and ghosted away on silent wings, content enough he'd live.

Back to the matter at hand, which was getting herself some sort of bearing, she winged her way back towards the road and, relying on her heightened instincts, she drifted towards the right and with only a vague feeling, she headed east. After gaining a bit of height, she saw houses off in the distance. *About bloody time.* But like the few cottages she had flown over earlier, there were no lights on. *Maybe they are just being cautious, or prudent, or even guilty about their carbon footprint.* Gwen was hoping for a rational explanation but, in her gut, she just knew that wasn't going to be the case. She landed and adopted her own form again. Getting her hiker's gear back on, she stuffed her hands in her pockets and thought she would walk into town in case they had watchers monitoring the roads. Again Gwen assumed the conflict had reached even here and she behaved as though it had, as though it was a war, which of course it was. But the only war Gwen knew about was what she watched on TV. That was her only training about how to behave when entering potentially hostile territory. For all she knew it could be overrun with the Adversary's forces and everyone dead. But that didn't explain where the fainter and his companions had come from. Too many questions and too few answers. The whole thing was giving her a headache. Guessing the time at about two in the morning, she doubted there would be much open or happening anyway. *So much for my warm bed and wine.* Gwen chuckled to herself as she thought that she was whining plenty to cover that aspect. She passed a sign that, for the first time, gave her an idea of where she was going. It had two names on it and Gwen figured that one of them was the Irish for the other. It said An Snaidhm and underneath it, it had the word Sneem. *Three miles. Three bloody miles? I'm not walking that. Bugger me, I thought I was closer than that. It hadn't seemed so far away as an owl.* It was the different perspective between flying high above with the bird's eye view and pounding the tarmac on two legs, that she was going to have to get used to. But just before she resumed her owl form, she heard a sound that had been absent since she had made landfall. That of an oncoming car. Instinctively, Gwen stepped to the side of the road to avoid being hit, naturally assuming that they drove on the same side to what she was used to. But she had forgotten where she was; this wasn't America but in essence, Great Britain. The place she had left several years before. And what she didn't take into account, having gotten used to American roads, was that the Irish drove on the opposite side to them. So she virtually walked out in front of the oncoming car. All she saw was a pair of headlights, and the sound of squealing brakes with desperately gripping tyres trying to stop the forward momentum of the car on a mist-slick road, screeching on the tarmac, with a smell of burning rubber closely following the sound. She disjointedly noticed that one light was dimmer than the other, as though a bulb had blown, and with an instant recognition, she knew who this was. It was the fainter.

The car skidded into Gwen, but she bounced backwards with it as it slowed, slamming her hands onto the hood of the car to stop it going over her. She hadn't counted on her own increased strength and density. She moved only a couple of feet and the car was brought to a dead stop. She didn't notice the pair of delicate handprints she had left on the hood. Gwen squinted as the glare of the lights prevented her seeing inside, so she covered her eyes with one hand and walked around to the driver's window. As she did, Gwen heard the telltale squeal of a window being wound down. Once out of the glare of the one headlight, her vision settled itself again and she saw the familiar yet haggard face of the fainter. It wore the expression of one who had just had something happen to him but was at a total loss as how to explain it to himself, let alone anyone else.

'Hi there.' Gwen thought she should start friendly and see how it went. 'That was a close thing. Silly me, getting in the way like that. What was I thinking?'

Gwen smacked her forehead as if to say 'Duh'. Fainter looked at her as though he had seen a ghost, but couldn't work out how or where or why. Instead, he just shook his head and wiped his own moist forehead, grinning lopsidedly as he did so.

'Luckier than you know, gal.' He spoke with that cool and lilting Irish accent that gave women the world over weak knees, and even in his distraught state, his voice was still melodic if a little higher pitched than it should have been. 'The brakes on the car aren't what they were and don't always work. Especially not in the wet. Musta picked a fine time to do what they shoulda, else you would have been road kill.' The subject of killing things brought his recent memories back in a rush and the color drained from him all over again.

'You okay?' Gwen asked innocently. 'You look like you've seen a ghost.'

'You have *no idea* what I've seen, gal. It was the bi – ' He cut himself off and rethought what he was about to say. 'There's things out there that have no business being out there is all, and I have had the misfortune of seeing one o'them, but thank the Virgin Mary, Mother of God, I was spared, but I've no idea what happened to Kieran and Barry. We were altogether, then I woke up in me car on me own.' He crossed himself automatically in that time-honored good old Catholic way Gwen had seen her mother do a million times.

'Sounds scary, but maybe they just ran away. You seem all right now though, so whatever it was has gone, has it?'

He nodded. It was then that Gwen spotted the six pack of beer in the passenger foot well, as well as a few empties. 'You sure it wasn't little green men coupled with a few fermented ones and a vivid beer dream?' She inclined her head towards the cans, indicating she had seen them and put two and two together.

He saw what she was looking at and scrubbed his hands over his face and hair again, groaning as he did so. 'I don't know. I can't be sure of anything right now, but it was so real.'

Gwen nodded sagely, reaching in and putting a supportive hand on his arm. 'Of course it did; they always do. Now, I've got an idea. Why don't you do the gentlemanly thing and offer me a lift to town, where I can find a hotel and you can find your friends? I'm sure they'll put your mind to rest and you'll all have a good laugh about it.'

He frowned and seemed to be concentrating on something. Turns out, he was making a decision. He leant over and opened the passenger door from the inside. Turning back to her, he smiled weakly at her and explained that several things didn't work on the battered old car. The door was one of them. Gwen climbed up and settled herself in. Reaching across with a hand extended, Gwen introduced herself.

'Hi, I'm Gwen, and at two in the morning walking down a dark and wet country road, it's really nice to meet you.'

Daniel looked at her hand suspiciously for a few seconds before grasping it and shaking it gently, as though he were afraid he would break her. 'Daniel. Daniel Fitzgerald. Pleased to make your acquaintance, I'm sure. Now, going to town, are you? Strange time to be out and about.'

Gwen was afraid of this: how to explain her weird nocturnal roamings. Gwen shrugged, recounting the first thing that came into her head. 'My bike got a flat a couple of miles back and, would you believe it, as I was fixing it, I managed to put a hole in my tent.'

His expression said 'How the hell did you manage to do that?'

'Don't ask, but I just thought, Sod it! A night in a hotel won't do me any harm and I'll face it tomorrow in the daylight and maybe it'll be a bit drier too. So I left my bike and pack and started walking. But would you believe just how far it is to walk when you are used to riding? A long bloody way I can tell you. I thought Sneem was closer than that, but I've got blisters on my blisters now and I'm really fed up with this walking bollocks, so I really am glad you came along, my knight in rusty green armor,' Gwen quipped, describing the car's condition to a tee, smiling her most charming as she did so.

The smile and the tale weren't lost on him, but a shadow swept by and caused him to grab his rear view mirror and stare into it. He then hung out of his window and stared off into the darkness, trying to see something.

'What is it?' Gwen asked, a little panicked by his behavior. Had the minions found her again? 'We should go, Daniel. Come on. It was probably an owl.'

Gwen hoped her voice sounded calm and level. He turned back to her. The haunted look had returned and he just nodded wordlessly, winding his window up, and with one last check around and behind, he dropped the car into gear and tore off like he was in pole position at some Grand Prix. Tyres squealed as they fought for traction and soon found enough to launch them forwards. The engine screamed itself from time to time as Daniel went through the gears a little too fast. In fact, he did everything a little too fast, which included talking, but it was especially his driving that Gwen was paying the most attention to.

'You do know how to drive, I take it?' The note of panic took on a genuine tone as she reached for the seat belt and buckled herself in. Just in time too, for he took a sudden turn off the main road onto what could only be called, generously, a horse track.

'Of course I do. I've been driving these roads since I was ten. You just sit back and enjoy the ride.'

Gwen grabbed the dash with both hands as the four-wheel drive was pushed to its operating limits over the bombsite that passed for a road. She tried to see the expression of boyish glee that came over Daniel's face as he whooped and grinned as the car was thrown all over the place. Hurtling along in the dark as the car bounced up and down, suspension working at full capacity as hole after hole put it through its paces. And in between preventing her head from bouncing off the roof, Gwen tried asking where it was exactly they were going.

'Oh, we're going to my sister's place. It's just outside town.'

Gwen tried a 'why?' as the car hit another series of potholes, but the single word came out as a strangled word with several syllables: 'Wh-huh-

huh-hy'. Daniel laughed some more as he threw the vehicle into top gear and jammed his foot down on the gas as far as it would go. The vehicle picked up speed and to Gwen's consternation, began to head downhill too.

'Because, me little blonde wanderer, you have no chance whatsoever of finding a hotel open at this hour and even less of a chance since the troubles started.'

Gwen was immediately interested, even to the extent of taking her eyes off the road, to stare at Daniel. She asked what sort of troubles and he turned to look at her.

'I don't rightly know, but it's had people disappearing gradually over the last couple of months. Shops have shut and not opened again, the same with the hotels and, worst of all, the pubs have all shut. I can live without food, but not without me beer.'

'Will you watch the bloody road!' Gwen screamed at him.

Daniel casually looked forward and made a show of peering into the night, trying to see with the insipid illumination provided by the one and a half dodgy headlights.'What? Why? What have you seen?'

Gwen was gobsmacked. She couldn't believe the blasé way he was treating their breakneck journey through the Irish countryside. 'What have I seen? I've seen the bloody road you dullard and I'd really like you to keep your bloody eyes on it too.' Gwen always swore too much when she was het up, and the roller-coaster car journey she was having there and then definitely came under the category of *het up*. 'I have no intention of dying in the middle of nowhere, least of all in this death trap.' Gwen yelled right into his ear 'You know, it would actually help if you used the brakes every now and again.' But he was oblivious to her discomfort, still too involved in his own, but he still managed to take a slight offense at Gwen's description of his car.

'How can you say such things about my baby? She's a bit shy of the working parts, some of them even vital, but it keeps on going and regarding the brakes, well sure enough I would use them - if they actually worked.'

'What do you mean: *if they worked?*' Gwen stammered incredulously, taking a quick glance at the speedometer, which she wasn't entirely surprised to find was not working either, but could only guess by the way the foliage and terrain were hurtling by them in a nocturnal blur, that they were bombing by in the area of fifty to sixty miles an hour.

'Just as I say. They're fickle all right.' Daniel looked at her again as he spoke. 'But you have nothing to worry about. I know this road like the back of my hand, you see. I was born out here. Me sister is living in the house I was born in, so I grew up out here. In fact I probably put a few of these holes in this blessed road meself, so I ought to know where I'm going. The bloody car is probably on autopilot anyway.' He laughed at his own joke, but Gwen was having trouble seeing the funny side. She was in less danger from the minions than from this loon and his excuse of a car.

'We're nearly there anyway, just a few more bends and the little hill, then Bob's your uncle and Fanny's your aunt.'

Gwen's mind raced and her imagination envisioned several scenarios involving burning car wrecks. More bends and a hill? We're dead meat. She even tried closing her eyes but that made it worse. Slung around and not seeing where she was going made it worse than any fairground ride. But what made it worse for Gwen was the fact he drove one handed. The other rested nonchalantly on the gear shift. Then he had the nerve to take his hand off the wheel completely as he pointed out the dim outline of some distant building.

'There! You see that? That's me sister's house, God bless her. She'll put you up for the night and it won't be so far back to your bike. You see, she offers it out as a little bed and brekky, but off the books you understand. It's not official and all, but it helps with the bills occasionally. We get a lot of tourists round here, you see, and not all of them plan too well in advance so there's plenty to go around.'

Ignoring her wide-eyed look of horror, Daniel carried on chatting as they navigated the bends and started thundering down the hill. 'But things have been a bit quiet lately, as I said. There's been no people coming for a while; in fact, gal, the more I think of it, you're the first I've seen in months. And you *didn't* see the bloody big beastie that was out there earlier? Don't ya think that's a bit strange? 'Cos now I come to think of it, I do. You, a lone girly wandering the countryside on the selfsame night I have me experience...'

Gwen, in between hanging onto the car for grim death, was desperate for them to reach the house before he began making sense out of what shouldn't be made sense from. They hit the bottom of the hill in a spray of water as they forded a small stream that meandered across the road, thankfully slowing them considerably. At a much slower speed, the car began to rumble up the incline that was on the other side of the ford. The event distracted Daniel momentarily as he felt the need to explain what just happened. 'That was why I had to go so fast down the hill; if you don't get enough speed up, when you hit the water you don't have enough oomph to get up the other side, 'specially when both the gas *and* the brakes lock up after the water.' Gwen shot him a concerned look; one that implied that she would probably have been safer outside with whatever he thought was out there. 'So you're saying you didn't see or hear nothing?'

Gwen shook her head, but knew the gesture for the futile effort it was, so she backed it up by telling him too. 'I'm sorry, I didn't hear or see what you did, but it's a big place out there and I can't help coincidence. I'm sure you believe what you saw but can you hear yourself? Don't you know dragons don't exist? This is Ireland, I know, and you're full to the brim with mythology, but this is the twenty-first century and we don't have those sorts of things any more. They're all crocodiles and Komodo dragons now, big lizards and the like.'

Daniel, with the disconcerting habit he had of watching her instead of the road, stared at her with a mixture of expression and obvious thought going through his head, ranging from belief, agreement, confusion back to disbelief and distrust. She was even sure she saw fear flit through there somewhere. A fear in his eyes as he looked at her as though she was about to turn into something there and then and ravage him.

The car was slowing and Gwen spared a glance ahead – not entirely sure she wanted to see what they were going to plough into – but she saw, to her relief, that they had slowed to a crawl as they crested the little rise and were coasting towards a large tree about fifty feet from the house. She anticipated what was about to happen as she saw the groove in the bark a few feet from the ground. The car bounced gently off the tree and came to a whirring halt as he turned the engine off.

'There you go!'

And there she went. Climbing from the car, and placing her shaky legs and feet on the ground, Gwen pushed herself out and walked, albeit a tad wobbly, around to Daniel's side, where he had wound the window down, still watching her suspiciously. She alternated between him and the picture postcard cottage a short walk away. It was at first glance a stylized romantic looking cottage: slate roof, dry stone brick wall surrounding the building, with ivy and climbers, and with another tree forming one side of the gated entrance through the wall. There was one main door – big and green – central to the building, with a window above and two more, one either side top and bottom. But after the initial impact wore off, Gwen could see the paint was faded, peeling on the windows and doors, and some of the wood even looked rotten. Patches of render had fallen away from the wall, exposing the brick beneath. Time and weather had taken their toll without anyone keeping up repairs. *Shame. It could have been lovely if they'd bothered.* Gwen turned back to Daniel and asked if he was sure his sister wouldn't mind. It *was* still late. Or early, depending on your point of view. But he just shouted 'Yeah, yeah, it'll be fine' as he fired the engine up and began reversing round so he was pointing back the way they had come. Hanging from his window, he offered a parting comment, 'You'll be fine. Just say I said to give you the family rate; she won't mind. I've got to find me mates and see if they're hale and what they saw, 'cos I don't believe your tale. No offense gal, but it's too weird, even for me what with all that's going on and all.'

'What *is* going on then? You haven't really said,' Gwen tried as he started to pull away. But all she heard was a 'never you mind' on the wind as he tore off, bouncing and rattling until his tail lights vanished in the encroaching early morning mist. She turned a three hundred and sixty degree circle, taking in just exactly where she was. But other than the dirt road and the cottage, she could have been just about anywhere. She sensed hills and woods and mountains, but little of the people who lived amongst them. The cottage was fairly isolated, even for here, and Gwen wondered just how much business it ever got. *Guess there's only one to find out, Gwen me girl, and that's to go knock.* She was reluctant to do so, but her options were fairly limited. Plus she had had quite enough of roaming round the country for a bit. Her need for a hot bath, warm bed and glass of wine reasserted itself. That was the prompt she needed. Walking, slowly but purposefully – the theme tune to *The Twilight Zone* echoing in her head – towards the door, Gwen didn't see the big wind chime hanging from a low branch, so intent on the door was she. Suddenly, it rattled like a fire alarm, the silence of the night making it even louder to her ears. *Bloody hell, that's done it. That'll wake the entire bloody island.* Gwen had jumped to one side, one hand going to her mouth, the other to her heart where it had made her jump, and was staring at the swinging and clanging tubes as though they would still under her glare. But it was as she watched them swing slower, though no less noisily, she saw the run of string that came from it and tied off across the entrance.

What? Is that some kind of bloody trap? No, she realized, *not a trap, but an alarm, an early warning system.* But she had no time to think on it as the main door slammed open and a terrifying visage was silhouetted in the doorway, wild hair billowing about its head and tattered clothes flapping in the sudden breeze, and the most incongruous thing of all was the double-barreled shotgun that it waved in her direction. The wraith with the gun stepped out of the doorway and Gwen got a better view. It was a girl, dressed in gypsy skirt and top, a shawl over her shoulders and her mane of red hair falling unkempt way below her shoulders.

'Get away from here! I've told you before. I'll shoot!'

Gwen back-pedaled a few feet and raised her hands in a gesture of peace and defense. 'Whoa there, easy. My name is Gwen.' Gwen spoke fast in a hope she could say what she needed to before being shot. 'Daniel said I might find a room here? I'm a little lost and he found me, just gone in fact and he said something about the family rate?' Gwen took a breath then and waited. She had stopped backing up and now stood a few feet from the big tree by the gate. The woman with the gun, who Gwen took for Daniel's sister, stepped out a bit further and checked left and right, as though there might be others, lurking nearby.

'What sort of car was he driving?' she shouted out.

'A battered old Range Rover, but I wouldn't call what he does with it *driving*, more like pointing in the general direction he wants to go and hanging on. At least that's what I did.' Gwen felt a momentary relief when she heard the woman chuckle to herself at the description. *All this for a glass of wine! Jeez, I must have a bigger problem than I thought.* 'Look, if I've caught you at a bad time, I'm sorry. It wasn't my choice or my intention to upset you, but he said you wouldn't mind. He didn't, however, mention the shotgun reception, so if it's too much trouble, I'll be on my way. Sorry to have disturbed you.' Gwen backed up a little more and turned to go.

'Wait!' The lilting Irish voice wasn't so emphatic now; it had softened from its earlier warning tones. 'It's me who should be sorry. I don't usually greet everyone with this old thing, but things have been a bit hairy of late, hence the chime alarm. Long story but not one for standing out in the chill morning letting the dew settle on us.'

Gwen heard the familiar sound of a safety catch being activated on the weapon. She recalled how her dad's did the same. It was a sound from long ago, from when she was a little girl and she would sit with her father as he cleaned his weapons. He was meticulous about them. Every Friday, he would unlock his cabinet and get all seven out, and she would curl up next to him as he went about cleaning each and every one, telling her tales of his adventures as he did so. She recalled the smell of the oils and cleaners he used and it brought a lump to her throat with a rush of emotion of times past and the massive fact that he was gone and she would never see him again.

'Get yourself in here and you can tell all about why my brother is picking up waifs and strays and depositing them on me doorstep in the wee hours. I'm also guessing you could use a drink, because let me tell you, darlin', I certainly could.'

'Now you're talking my language. Make mine a double of whatever.' Gwen stepped over the string and walked up the path. Yet the moment she put her foot on the path proper, she stopped. Waves of icy coldness washed over her like repeating breakers from an ocean. Her skin tingled and she saw goose bumps rise on her arms. An electric current seemed to be coursing up her legs. Though through all this, Gwen was unharmed. She looked at the woman who had invited her in and saw an expression of curiosity mingled with fear and she took a back step, closer to the doorway. She also raised the shotgun a touch higher too. Gwen took two more steps towards her and the feeling passed. She looked back and caught a glimpse of a faint silvery light running through the stone wall, around the tree and across the threshold of the garden path. She saw it go seemingly all around the house. *A protective circle?* Gwen mused. Kneeling, she placed her hands on the ground and let her mind reach out. Fingers in the soil, she felt the barrier pulsing and it did indeed go all the way around. It was pretty strong too.

'How did you do that?' The woman with the gun asked, a tremor in her voice.

Gwen stood up and walked closer to her. As she did so, hands open and spread wide, Gwen noticed the vibrant green eyes and wild red hair, her pale complexion setting both off vividly. Her strong, yet feminine features gave her an ethereal beauty, just like one of the imagined goddesses of Irish legend.

'Do what?' Gwen asked innocently, fishing for the reason behind the question.

'Pass through the barrier, of course. Don't play me for an eediot.'

Gwen looked shocked and with mock horror she looked around, but seeing nothing, she looked back at the woman before her. 'What barrier?'

The shotgun came back up and the woman looked angry now rather than fearful. Gwen knew she was on tenuous ground and had to play this carefully.

'I think you know what damn barrier I mean. Now how did you cross it? No one has been able to yet. What are you? And I suggest you talk fast.'

Gwen slumped her shoulders in resignation. She was running out of options here. She didn't fancy getting shot. There was no point testing her new powers unnecessarily. Nor did she want to leave so soon. But this encounter had intrigued Gwen more than she knew and she wanted to find out more about the protective circle and who put it there.

Gwen folded her legs beneath her and sat on the path, cross-legged, watching the woman with the gun, who, seeing her sit, had come a little closer. Gwen watched her look up and look around. Following her gaze, Gwen noticed that the mist that had followed her and Daniel had made it as far as the threshold but not any further.

'See that?' Gwen began. 'That mist out there?' Not waiting for an answer, Gwen carried on. 'Do you feel anything from it? Any sort of unease, fear even?' The woman nodded that she did indeed feel something and she didn't like it either. 'Notice how the mist seems incapable of crossing into your garden, unlike me. Your barrier is strong enough to hold that at bay, but not me. Not because I'm stronger than that, though I might be; but because the mist is malevolent and, if I can use the word without sounding off my trolley, Evil.' Gwen paused for effect before continuing, 'I, on the other hand, am not. I'm one of the good guys, I assure you. That's how I got this far, though I did feel the energy as it tested me – strong and old, I sense. It's not something you did. Am I right?'

The woman just nodded, not yet taking her eyes from the mist beyond them.

'Thought so. I'm tempted to say your mother, but no…' Gwen screwed her face up in concentration. She was getting images and some of them made no sense: pale faces, bloody and torn, throwing themselves at the barrier and being repulsed. But they were too fast and too jumbled to make any real sense from, so Gwen just concentrated on the here and now, '…It's older than that.' Gwen spoke slowly as though she were hearing something talking to her, telling her details. 'Nah it's older than that, isn't it? A grandmother perhaps or even her mother. It's definitely feminine and I can only imagine, once, long ago, it was even stronger than it is now. Though It still seems strong enough to hold that back…' Gwen thumbed at the mist behind her, '…which right now is more than enough to make me happy. What about you? Was that answer enough to let us carry this chat indoors? I'm gagging for that drink you teased me with.'

As though waking from a dream, the woman turned to the sitting Gwen and saw her for the first time, it seemed. It was as though a spell had been dispelled from the feisty Irish woman and she found herself actually seeing Gwen for the first time, and she suppressed a little gasp as she took in her features, her own emerald eyes going wide as she took in Gwen's face and the slightly wavy hair that framed it. Then that moment too passed by and she smiled, even if it was a bit strained and crooked. As she did so, the tiny crinkles at the corner of her eyes became slightly more pronounced, making her eyes sparkle all the more; even so far as looking a bit abashed at what she had done and how she had behaved. Reaching a hand towards Gwen, she helped the slim woman to stand, whilst propping the made-safe shotgun against her midriff, butt down in order to free up both hands.

'I am *so* sorry, but there is so much I need to say to you, and I don't know where to begin; but, let me at least start over.' Taking advantage of the hand she held, Tara took it in both of hers and shook it warmly, though she didn't immediately let go. 'Hi there. My name is Tara, Tara Fitzgerald, and won't you please be welcome to my home. Come on inside and pay no attention to my mental state. I think me medication is wearing off.' Tara shrugged as though it were a normal thing. 'But, it just so happens I've got another bottle of medicinal Merlot that should just about be room temperature by now, having hopefully breathed its last. Can I tempt you?'

Gwen smiled back that she definitely could and, still hand in hand, the two women walked back down the garden path towards the cottage and went inside. As they closed the door they didn't hear the anguished and agonized screams echoing in the distance, or the tortured howls resounding in the mist, sounding as yet far off, but seemingly drawing ever closer as they left the burgeoning dawn outside.

Comfortably seated on one of the two sofas that dominated the lounge, strategically placed before the fireplace for optimum warmth, Gwen began to take in her surroundings with a touch more detail. She had dematerialized her boots when Tara wasn't looking and curled her feet up beneath her like a cat. The room was as worn and tired as the outside, with faded walls and furniture that seemed derived from the nineteen-thirties. The massive fireplace almost filled one wall and the stone that comprised it seemed older than the cottage itself. It was so big in fact, Gwen reckoned she could have stood up inside it. Oddly, Gwen thought, the more she looked at it, the more it looked like a small henge rather than a fireplace. A henge that had the cottage built around it and a wall put behind it to enclose it. The floor was old too, but unlike the stone walls and fire, it was just aged, and smooth boards with several rugs scattered over it for warmth. Yet for all its shabbiness, Gwen could feel the history in everything there. She felt that familiar familial sensation of Christmases past and gatherings of relatives at birthdays and anniversaries. This was a well used family room and it made Gwen miss her own. Just then, Tara walked back in, equally barefooted, and Gwen took another moment to assess her now genial host. She reminded her of her old art teacher; for she too frequented the baggy sweater several sizes too big, floaty skirts, and bare feet. No doubt, she thought, many a night was spent curled up with her knees tucked inside her jumper. Gwen understood this for she had a baggy fleece that had gone the same way for that very reason. Moving beyond her clothes, Gwen saw that not only did she look like her art teacher, but there was actually paint smudged on her cheek too. *Now that's too spooky.*

'Doing a bit of painting then, are you?' Gwen asked innocently. Tara's hand went automatically to her cheek after she put down the wine and glasses, touching the blue smudge. 'Or are you doing the woad thing, you know: lime in the hair, paint yourself blue, and run screaming over the hills?'

Tara laughed, probably the first genuine humor she had experienced for some time, judging by the way it exploded from her. But she calmed quickly and Gwen could see her trying to come up with a reason why she had missed the canvas and indulged in a bit of impromptu face painting.

'No, well, yes, sort of. It's hard to say and even harder now you're here. Look at me; I don't know where my brains are these days.' Tara ruffled her fiery mane with the end result that it looked no different than it did before – wild and untamed.

'I'm just glad mine are still in my head.' Gwen tilted her eyes towards the shotgun that stood propped by the door, in easy reach if the need arose: a thought that had troubled Gwen since she arrived. What need could be so dire that folk had to answer their doors armed to the teeth. That and the myriad of flashing images she had gotten from the barrier of the pale and disfigured people, screaming and howling; some mutilating themselves even as they stood at her gate. Gwen feared the worst.

'It's funny you should mention painting, though. Have your wine, warm up a little, and I'll put some toast on. Then there's something you need to see.'

Sipping her Merlot, Gwen was intrigued now. It smacked of mystery and fitted in with the ancient and myth-filled land she found herself in. Gwen had half finished her glass when Tara came back in with a plate of steaming toasted bread with what looked like fresh yellow butter slathered upon it. Gwen didn't feel hunger as such any more, but the sight and smell of the toast made her mouth water all the same and she tucked in hungrily, making cooing noises and pulling contented faces as she swallowed the slightly salty butter moistened bread; washed down with the last of her wine. She sat back eventually, sated and replete.

Tara popped her momentary bubble of contentment when she spoke, for it wasn't so much the words themselves that ensorcelled her, but an underlying feeling of power to them. They held the weight of prophecy and an ancient magic that wrapped itself around the listener; and the way Tara delivered them, they captured Gwen and held her in a grip that no amount of chain could hope to match. She was riveted, staring straight back at Tara, unable to look away even if she wanted to:

> *'White phantom, she of the ancient name,*
> *Bearer of light and the blood of kings,*
> *Mother, sister, summer's daughter,*
> *By wave and wind embraced by three rings.*
> *Take three to four heads of water,*
> *From wood she calls life, not once but twice,*
> *To his death from above, his destiny calls,*
> *She to become two as his mistletoe wife,*
> *Lifegiving spark, to her summons she calls.'*

Gwen just sat there as the words reverberated through her every molecule, echoing in her skull like she was in a concert hall. 'What was *that*?' she finally managed to ask as the words of power faded away, though not without leaving an indelible imprint on the inside of her skull. Gwen closed her eyes and saw the rhyme blazing in letters of blue fire. *What did it mean? What did any of it mean?* Gwen couldn't even begin to figure it out. She was useless at riddles at the best of times, always skipping to the back of the puzzle books that Jen left lying around, seeing what the answer was before attempting it.

'Come with me. Remember that something I said I had to show you? Well, maybe seeing it will put that rhyme into perspective. Not that it did me, but then again, I'm not you.'

Gwen was truly lost now. *Not me? What the bloody hell is she on about now?* But a part of Gwen's awareness was telling her that she was part of something much bigger than herself now, and all choices had consequences. *Was it even my choice to beach here, of all places?* Or was there an even greater power afoot? Was the Earth reaching out with what little power remained to her and influencing her direction? That was just all too big a question for the present; for she was having enough trouble clinging to what little part of reality she still had remaining. *And my bloody fingers are starting to ache.*

Again, Tara held out a hand and as soon as Gwen grasped it, she felt another jolt: this one more physical, as though she had stuck her fingers in a socket and flicked the on switch. The girls looked at each other wide-eyed, as though the other was the cause, but neither let go of the other for all that. They just chalked it up to yet another strange occurrence. Tara led Gwen up the creaky wooden stairs and along an equally groaning landing, to a small back bedroom which, Gwen could see, acted as Tara's studio. She could see canvas and paints everywhere. Sensing where Gwen was looking, Tara offered a hasty explanation: 'I do landscapes usually, and sell them, or at least I used to, up at the craft shops in Sneem, Kenmare and Killarney. One even went back to the States, apparently.' A note of pride crept into her voice at that admission. But there was no time for any well dones as they made it to the door and Tara stepped back to allow Gwen to enter first.

'To your right. You can't miss it. I didn't have a canvas big enough so I had to use the wall. You see, I was going to leave about a year ago – just pack up, take Daniel and head north; there are just too many hotels around here for a little two-room effort like this to make it, especially just out of town like we are. But that was when the dreams started, along with the voices. Then came the painting. From my art, which I had never thought of selling before – don't know why – I made just enough to keep me here. Now I see why.'

At that precise moment, so did Gwen.

It did, as Tara said, cover the entire back wall. Floor to ceiling and wall to wall. And it was so vivid and realistic, Gwen was sure that if she tried to step into it, she would feel the grass that was portrayed, beneath her feet. But it wasn't the grass or the trees and animals that abounded in the fresco; it was the figure in the centre, looking back at her with vibrant and almost living, emerald green eyes. It was so lifelike, it was like looking into a full sized mirror and looking back at herself. It was – in all its uncanny likeness – an image of Gwen.

Gwen had no words to describe the feelings that flowed through her as she gazed upon the incredible piece of art. She was no art critic, but to her, it surpassed many of the pieces she had seen, both modern and ancient. Michelangelo himself would be proud of something like that. Gwen reached out a slow, tentative finger to touch herself, to touch the leafy dress she was wearing, because it looked as though it was actually rustling in a non-existent breeze. If just to convince herself it was flat and two-dimensional. Because it looked so real, Gwen half believed that it was actually rendered in *three* dimensions. With her fingertips just centimeters from the wall, Tara coughed lightly behind her and made Gwen start, the spell broken. Withdrawing her fingers swiftly like they were burnt, she turned to look guiltily at the redhead, like a child being caught by its parent, who snaps out, almost automatically, *don't touch!* Gwen knew that there was a lengthy discourse pending about how and why and when such an undertaking had been done, but all she could manage was, 'You have got to be kidding me!'

'No, sorry, I'm not. Now you see why I looked at you gone out when we first met, and after I got an even better look at you in some light. I just couldn't believe you were there, before me, like you had just climbed off this wall and started wandering around in the garden.'

'But that's *me!*' Gwen thumbed at it, stating the obvious a bit lamely. Tara nodded her agreement, taking the revelation considerably better than Gwen. Though she supposed the artist had spent a long time with it to get used to it. Gwen was in shock. Part of the fresco included several lines of text, rendered in the same beautiful style as the rest, portrayed as an engraving on a rock at Gwen's feet, and it was the strange rhyme that Tara had come out with earlier.

Gwen looked at the detail again and it was simply amazing. She could look at it for days and still see things she had missed. There were birds and trees, fantastical creatures, a starry sky with a large, silvery moon that looked almost photographic. There were sparkling stones and crystals all over; animals and plants; several weapons including fantastically ornate swords and daggers; and amongst it all were no end of symbolic depictions: quite a few keys, astrological symbols, runes, spirals and elemental references. She was put in mind of an artist friend of hers who now lived somewhere in Cornwall, apparently, who used to do similar work. She loved that and had a few originals, but this transcended anything she had seen before. Gwen couldn't take her eyes off it.

'I thought it was me at first,' Tara spoke quietly, softly respecting the moment and not wanting to interrupt Gwen's absorption of the image. 'You see, the green eyes and ancient name bit, well, my name is Tara. Tara used to be the seat of the ancient high kings of Ireland and I've got green eyes too. There are six gems at her feet, which I took for the bracelet my mother gave me.' Tara held up and rolled the six massive moonstones that made up her jewelry around her wrist. 'And I live here in Kerry, which has three rings.'

Gwen turned to look at Tara and mouthed her question, 'What three rings?'

'There are three rings here, though not all are known about. Though they are not actually rings as such, but areas of beauty that became known as the Ring of Kerry, the Skellig Ring, and the Beara Ring. So you see why I thought it was about me, but the face was all wrong and no matter how many times I tried to change it to me, it always seemed to change back. It's been there about seven months now and I look at it every day. That's why I know the rhyme almost by heart. You're the first person I've shown it to; not even Daniel has seen it. It scares me a little.'

Gwen was stunned. 'A little? If I had done this based on dreams, seeing stuff in my head and hearing voices, you say? I reckon I would be more than a little scared. I'd need to be changing my underwear.'

Tara laughed at Gwen's admission, but added a little gem that made Gwen shiver all over again and stare once more at the fresco with new eyes. 'If only that were it, but since I've finished it, each time I come to look at it, there is something new added. The animals have changed places or the trees have moved. I even think her expression changes ever so slightly too. As though it is trying to communicate with me, somehow.'

As she was still gazing at the picture, looking for any of the changes Tara had mentioned, Gwen offered her contribution to the riddle's possible direction. 'My name is Gwendoline; it was a concession to my mother, by my father, who wanted to call me Gwenhwyfar after the Arthurian tradition. Plus, somewhere in my dad's lineage there was some Celtic in there, hence the green eyes, I guess, and I think he wanted to pay tribute to it somehow. As for the rest though, I don't know. I have a brother but I don't have any kids, thankfully; don't really want any either. It isn't like we have a shortage of them. There are plenty of happy breeders out there who are more than welcome to my share. For the love of me, I can't see what the fascination in them is. Noisy, smelly, expensive and above all time consuming. And I sure as hell don't want the rest of my life taken up with funding them, worrying what they are into and bailing them out of trouble until I'm old and toothless. Then there's all this bloody babysitting crap when they have brats of their own. No sooner have you gotten rid of your own than you have another load foisted off on you. I don't bloody think so.'

Outside, as they spoke, thunder began grumbling its presence, accentuated by the occasional flash of lightning.

'Oh, no!' Tara said, her voice nervous as she heard the thunder for the first time.

'What?' Gwen asked, concerned about the sudden change in the woman.

'Storms. It always seems to stir them up. We had better go down and make sure all the doors and windows are secure in case they get through the barrier.' Tara turned and hurried off, dragging her baggy sweater sleeves a little higher as though she meant business, only for them to fall back to the position they were in before. But it was the ritual that mattered more: doing so made her feel all businesslike. Gwen quickly followed and helped her do the rounds, checking locks and even propping a chair or two against door jambs. When Gwen finally caught back up to Tara, she was busy checking the shotgun was still loaded. Gwen was astonished at this turn of events and a touch worried.

'Who exactly does it stir up? You said them. Who are *them*?' Gwen followed Tara to the main lounge window and stood next to her as she drew the curtains and took a sly peek out, trying to see if anyone had appeared. She wasn't disappointed.

'There! Take a look, but be careful. Don't let them see you. If they think you're looking at them they scream, and trust me, it's horrible.'

Gwen teased the curtain just a fraction and took a look at what Tara was referring to. There were three people standing by the tree and one directly in front of the entrance to the garden path. She watched it try to enter but it seemed unable to do so, held back as though it were walking into a wall. But the most disturbing aspect of the scene before her was these people bore a horrific resemblance to the images she had received when she too walked into the barrier. They were pale all right, but that wasn't the half of it. All three, as far as Gwen could see, had raked their eyes out and their faces were a mess of gory scratches beneath dark, bloody, eyeless sockets. The one trying the entrance looked angry too – its mouth was open and it was mouthing obscenities as it failed time and time again to gain access. Gwen could see its mouth was all busted and half the teeth were missing. Blood had congealed down its chin and drenched its clothes at the front. Tara was right: they *were* horrific, but she had seen them before. Back in Santa Fe. These were the possessed, and they were certainly getting around.

'Does this happen every time there's a storm?' Gwen asked as she drew the curtain closed again and moved to stand near Tara, who had – if at all possible, for she was already pale of complexion – gone even paler and started to tremble slightly.

'Every time for the last few months. You'd think I'd have gotten used to it by now, but I haven't. It scares the bejesus out of me every time.' She held her hands out. 'Look at me! I'm still shaking just from knowing they are out there. What do they want, Gwen? What's the matter with them and why are they doing this?'

Gwen took Tara's hands in her own, which, Gwen was inwardly pleased about, were not shaking. And she led Tara to the sofa and guided her to sit down.

'Looks like they are still having trouble getting in, so forget them if you can for a moment at least and tell me about these dreams you're having. I'm not saying there is, but maybe there's a connection, and a fresh set of eyes and ears might help.'

While she waited for Tara to start talking, keeping her eyes on the woman, Gwen picked up and topped up the wine glasses from the half-empty bottle standing on the pine chest that doubled for a coffee table. Handing one to Tara, hoping that the alcohol would calm her nerves a bit and the glass would give her hands something to do other than tremble, Gwen waggled the bottle, signifying it was empty. She mouthed that she would just nip to the kitchen and get another one, leaving Tara sitting alone and hugging her glass, staring into its swirling crimson depths, wondering where to begin, though she had organized her thoughts as much as she was going to by the time Gwen returned. Gwen barely had time to sit and make herself as comfortable as she could before Tara launched into her tale.

'Other than you, obviously, I see fire. All sorts of fire blazing in all different colors. Sometimes the fire is spinning like a huge buggery wheel. Then there's the tree.'

Gwen felt the cold chill of prescience tingle over her flesh at the mention of the tree.

'It's the biggest damn thing I've ever seen. At its roots are things like the Eiffel tower and the pyramids and loads of other gigantic landmarks, but they are all tiny by comparison.' Tara paused, looking fretful. She took a sip of her wine, then another and then proceeded to chew on her lip for a bit before speaking again.

'What is it, Tara? There's more, isn't there?'

Tara just nodded. 'There's a man.'

Gwen wanted to sigh and say there's always a bloody man, but she held her tongue, not wanting to cheapen the woman's dream by some seedy connotation.

'He scares me though, every time I see him. I'm drawn to him and petrified of him both at the same time. I want him in ways even I'm too embarrassed to discuss, but I know that it would kill us both if I did have him. Yet danger aside, I feel driven to possess him. One half of him is golden light, so bright and dazzling that it hurts me to look at him for too long; then the other half is darkness. Thick and tangible, like how you imagine a black hole is, sucking at the light, trying to absorb it or extinguish it. Waves of cold emanate from that side so realistically that when I wake sometimes, my breath is coming from me in frosty clouds, like I'm sleeping in the fridge. The entire room is perishing. How can a dream do that? They can't affect the real world, can they?'

Gwen had no answer for her; the jury was still out on dreams. She had read a fair bit and when she did her Parapsychologist's Diploma during her first year at the store, she covered dreams and the many cultural variations on their import: from Australian natives – the Aborigines – and their dreamtime mythos, through the Aztec ideology, up to and including Freud and Jung's interpretations. There was still no real definitive answer, just lots of theories based on where you were in the world and what culture you are brought up in. Astral travel was another by-product of these dreams and she found that the body grew a small amount and lost a minor amount of weight each night when the body slept. It was widely held that this was the astral self leaving the body to venture where it would, travelling to different lands. But she hadn't heard of those different lands coming back and affecting the sleeper's world like the way Tara described.

'Then there are these rivers. Sometimes there are four, sometimes more, and they all merge into one big one. Raging and bubbling with all these people standing on both sides of the embankment. They look incredibly sad but I don't know why. Then what I thought was my own Catholic upbringing casting overtones on my dream turns out not to be, really, because I see a sky filled with angels and demons fighting. They don't look much like the Church portrayal of them but more like flying knights fighting flying animals, but their screams are terrible and there's blood everywhere. I see them falling from the sky like rain, dead and torn. Smashing into the ground and falling into the river. The screams get so loud they fill me with their pain until I can't take any more; that's when I found that I was even waking up screaming myself.'

'No wonder you've got no bloody guests,' Gwen laughed weakly, in an attempt to alleviate the mood before it got too heavy. Tara joined in just as weakly as she pictured the scene. Her eyes were moist and slightly red from the contained emotion.

'Yep, that'll do it, all right. It isn't the most socially accepted alarm call, is it? A hysterical woman screaming her lungs out first thing in the morning; or during the middle of the night either, for that matter.'

Outside, the storm had picked up and along with the intermittent thunder and the odd scream from the possessed, they could now hear packs of dogs barking and howling, adding their canine chorus to the cacophony. Tara spared her lounge window a look of anguish just for a split second. So distraught was she by what she could hear outside, she put her wine glass down too heavily, splashing a little scarlet drip over the rim like flying blood droplets to land onto the pine box. Gwen wondered if she was going to slam her hands over her ears and scream back at them all to be quiet. But she didn't. After standing and staring at the curtains for several minutes, her imagination fuelling her vision, she just sighed and sat down again. But she was at the limits of her strength. Gwen could see the strain starting to show. Tara took her seat once more.

'Who are you, Gwen? Really?' Tara turned to stare at Gwen. The intensity caught her unawares at first. Gone was the downtrodden expression of someone caught in the web of something world shattering. Gone was the look of the victim that Tara had worn when Gwen started to discuss the dream with her. Speaking of it had some sort of cathartic effect on the wary Irish woman. It seemed as though Tara had reached a point of acceptance and a great burden had been shed in doing so. She even stood a little straighter and her eyes sparkled with a curiosity that had been absent before now, though they still retained their weary seen too much look.

Gwen tried the innocent tack once more. 'What do you mean? I've told you my name and I'm here cam– '

Tara closed her eyes and shook her head sadly, holding one hand out in the halt gesture. 'No! Not the story you fed me and no doubt Daniel as well. There is more to you than you're letting on. Firstly you get through the barrier as though it wasn't there. I don't know how you did that; absolutely no one has made it through that without Daniel's or my help. Only he and I can pass through it, for some reason I am eternally grateful for. It's been that way since these troubles started. It just sprang up one day. I know because I can see it, the same way I can see the aura blazing off you, which by the way, I don't know if you can turn it down, because it's getting brighter as we speak – you must be getting excited or something. And let's not forget the bloody wall upstairs. That's you plastered all over it, remember?'

Gwen went perfectly still as she listened, all joviality gone. Tara was all business now and Gwen dropped her pleasant façade along with Tara. She tensed and prepared her mind for immediate action should matters take a turn for the worse. Had she been lulled into some trap by this person? Was this it being sprung? Her heart rate quickened as the adrenaline began to flow through her. *Shame, I quite liked her too*, Gwen thought sadly as her eyes took in the doorway and the window, searching for the nearest exit just in case.

'Since you arrived, which even you have to admit, is damn strange by any reckoning, there has been a mist or fog out there pushing against the barrier. I can feel it relentlessly driving at it; and then there's the storm. There was none forecast and yet there it is, lashing down and blowing a hoolie. But tonight it's different somehow. Those people turned up much faster than usual, shortly after you actually, and there are still more arriving; and then there are the dogs... What have you brought here, Gwen? What has followed you to my doorstep?'

Tara didn't sound so much angry at the prospect of what she may have brought, but more resigned to the inevitable and weary from the wait. It was as though she sensed the end to her perpetual nightmare was imminent. Gwen could see no real option at this moment other than to share what she knew and see how it was received. But first she needed to know Tara's affiliation and she thought she had a way to do that. Gwen recalled when she had kissed Daniel's cheek. As much as she passed something to him, she in turn got several impressions back from him. One of them had been his heart; telling her it was in the right place and there was no real malice in him, none intentional anyway. Mischief, yes, and something of the scrapper, but nothing dark and overtly violent. In essence, he was a good guy. Gwen hoped she could do the same with Tara and that the familial gene ran true. She didn't know how she had done it last time – it was an unconscious thing – but now she wanted to do it fully aware. That would be a different story, but it was worth a go. It would either spring or confirm if it really was a trap as well. Gwen took a breath and made her choice.

'Sit down, Tara. and give me your hands.' Gwen spoke with as much authority as she could muster and Tara duly sat, holding out her hands. Gwen studied them briefly. They were fine boned and long fingered. Artist's hands all right. She took them in her own and closed her eyes, concentrating on the woman before her. A deluge of images poured forth and Gwen gasped. She wasn't expecting such a bombardment. Gwen thought she would get images of her daily life, much like she had from Daniel. Oh, no. This was more like an epic movie. One that spanned centuries, or at least that was how it looked to Gwen. She saw barbarous looking men, dark clothes and painted faces. They were in the midst of fighting ferociously with armored men, and the death toll was monstrous. She saw white robed men and women, wielding wicked looking curved blades. They looked like scythes and sickles and these people knew how to use them to gruesome effect. They fought against these dark men and held them back. The images changed again, and Gwen saw packs of hounds, some with red ears, tear into the men from behind and savage them, biting through calves and legs, tearing throats. But Gwen noticed that they left the robed people alone. The images flowed once more and Gwen saw a powerful looking woman, dark of eye and pale of skin. Her shoulders were back as she moved, as though steel rods reinforced her back, and she regally walked a path that was one half moonlit and the other as radiant as a summer's day. She emanated a power that felt familiar to Gwen but she couldn't place it as the images flowed by her. There was another woman with her. She too throbbed power, but unlike the first, who clearly differentiated light from dark, hers was a foul mixture of the two – a Stygian twilight as though she were a doorway between light and dark, and Gwen sensed the bitter taste of vengeance and betrayal. Again and again the images flowed and changed. This time though, along with images, Gwen felt emotion: bitterness and resentment, verging on hatred. She didn't know the source of this outpouring of ill feeling. Was it the woman or the queenlike figure? She didn't know, but instead, she saw thousands of men, women and children, slaughtered and crucified, dying as they hung from trees and stakes and anything else that would serve. The lucky ones already lay dead at their feet. Blood flowed freely from their many wounds, staining the ground and turning it into some tiny black river as it flowed away. In it, foul things squirmed, wriggled and slithered. Above them wheeled clouds of carrion birds. Some were even brave enough to swoop down and pluck at eyes and stab at the raw and bloody wounds, tearing gobbets of flesh off before flapping away to devour their meals. Gwen heard many a scream from the tortured before the weight of their bodies ruptured their lungs and they suffocated in abject agony. Once more the images flowed and this time it was through hundreds of births, mothers and their daughters, over and over. And Gwen saw a shining silver line of light, connecting each to the last, as though the mother and infant were connected through time. And, oddly, each seemed to have to fight for its life in the first few hours. Some were even stillborn, but through immediate intervention, life was found. Some were burnt, some stabbed. Others cut, slapped or shaken. Each one had a birthmark shaped like a question mark. Wait, no. Gwen realized then it wasn't a question mark, but a sickle. Like what the robed men and women used. Druids! It came to her that that was who they were. Druids! But she didn't think that druids fought like that. Or fought at all if she thought about it. It was as though they were martially trained. Gwen had always considered them men and women of peace. Odd. But then so much of what she saw was odd. The images flew by and Gwen couldn't fathom many of them or much of what she saw. Only briefly did the vision somehow slow enough for her to see things clearly. There were knights, heavily armored and fighting other knights again; great battles with swords, axes and ballistae. Caves and deep underground chambers, rivers and doors. All this streamed by Gwen in less time than it took for the heart to beat twice. Her last image as she let go of Tara's hands was the strangest. For it was of the fireplace they sat before, only without the house surrounding it. Upon it was the woman she had seen earlier, the powerful one who was cloaked in light and dark. She lay bleeding upon the mantle. Another woman, with flowing red hair, stood with her back to Gwen so she could not see her face. She held what looked like an egg above her hands, but Gwen quickly saw that it wasn't an egg, but a smooth stone, flashing blue and silver. She saw it was in fact a huge moonstone, twice the size of the ones that Tara wore upon her wrist. The woman sprawled upon the rock held out a hand, almost beseeching the other, but to no avail. She ignored the plea and placed the stone upon her prone breast. The other woman sighed at the contact and sagged even further, as though it took her strength. The woman with the red hair then drew one of the cruel looking sickles from her hip where it had hung. There were no words or incantations or supplications. She simply raised it and swung it down upon the prone woman. Her head rolled clear and blood pumped out onto the grass. It ran in a crimson rivulet several yards, and where it pooled, a tree began to grow. It grew into a massive oak in a matter of seconds. Gwen recognized the tree as the one from the gate. The woman then plucked the stone from the corpse's chest and held it to the pommel of the sickle. There was a blinding flash and after the light diminished, Gwen saw the stone was fused to the blade and the corpse had gone. But just as the redhead was about to turn and show Gwen her face, the image faded away. Gwen sat back abruptly and let go of Tara's hands and she just stared at the woman before her. Sweat had beaded Gwen's forehead and she idly mopped her brow as she watched the stunned Irish woman for any reaction. But Tara just sat there, her hands still in her lap where Gwen had dropped them.

'What did you just do?' Tara whispered eventually. 'That was the strangest feeling. Not unpleasant, mind you, just strange. What were you trying to do?'

Gwen looked up at the woman. 'I wasn't trying, Tara. I succeeded. But I don't understand half of what I did or saw. Suffice to say I didn't feel any malice or evil from you, which was what I started out to find; 'cos there's a few things I need to tell you. You're right about one thing though.'

'Oh? What's that then?' Tara asked shakily, not sure she wanted to know after her experience, but as eager as any schoolgirl to hear what Gwen had to say all the same. She put her trepidation to one side and let Gwen talk.

Gwen sat back and poured herself a top-up of wine, twirled it in her fingers before speaking again, and, taking a sip, she moistened her throat and lips before trying to formulate the words to make what she was about to say sound even remotely credible. Flicking an errant hair from her face, she began.

'It doesn't appear to be any accident that I'm here. I had an idea where I wanted to go, but that was about it. Maybe instinct or intuition guided me; or perhaps a larger and more powerful entity influenced my choice, and trust me when I say that I don't mean God.'

Tara's expression asked who that might be, then; so Gwen, glossing over some of the more personal bits, and leaving out the other shape-changing elements, told Tara her story up to the present moment they found themselves in. Including as much of her vision as she could remember.

Now if Gwen was expecting incredulity or disbelief, she was greatly disappointed, bearing in mind her own reaction to being told what she had just divulged to this almost total stranger. Granted, it wasn't actually happening to Tara, not in the way it was to Gwen, but still; the idea that there was a giant green dragon sitting in your living room wearing a human form still took some swallowing. Yet for all that, Tara took it well, really. She just sat back, sipped her own wine and studied Gwen for what seemed to be an age. But as she waited for a reaction, she wondered that maybe it wasn't the dragon thing so much, as more the prospect of the actual existence of demons and angels – she was in the middle of Catholic and Protestant land after all, where nearly everyone is weaned on the good book in one form or another, so anything to do with God or religion wasn't to be taken lightly – and these angels were fighting for the salvation of not only humanity, but their own worlds and continued existence. In this war though, humans were mostly just going to be collateral damage. Beings of immense power were using the Earth as their battlefield and once they had devastated this world, they would be moving on to the rest. Yet the battle currently being fought on this blue planet was pivotal to the war as a whole, hence the necessity of humans having to – through the free will clause, as Gwen had come to think of it – offer themselves up to take a decisive stand, rather than just take a back seat and just hope they survived at the sacrifice of others. But it was a delicate course of action. The slightest mishap or one wrong choice could see everything lost. One such choice was being mulled over by Tara as Gwen sat silently, waiting for her reaction. Both women sipped their wine and studied the other. Gwen was impatient at the best of times and this sort of waiting did her no favors at all. So, to keep her mind from panicking, she went back over her earlier conversations with Tara, checking for irregularities or anything that might give her a clue as to how

Tara was likely to react. One thing sparked up for her. Tara admitted to seeing auras. She had said Gwen's was vibrant and too bright. *Damn, damn, and damn again.* A penny dropped suddenly in Gwen's mind, resounding with an audible chink. *That's how they found me and followed me.* It had annoyed her at the time how those demons had spotted her and kept on her tail even as she adopted her hawk form. *My bloody aura must have shone out like a supernatural beacon.* Invariably, as her power was enhanced, so too was the brightness of her field. *Makes sense if I think about it. How many other stupid mistakes am I going to have to make before I get me or someone else killed?* She'd have to figure out how to turn it down sooner rather than later. Surely it was within her capability, considering all the other stuff she could do. She would have to figure it out quickly as well, before she was caught out by any more fiends. She'd dealt with the last ones well enough, but the next ones might well be another matter. It was a matter she would rather avoid.

Suddenly, yet quietly, Tara spoke. 'Suppose I believe everything you've just told me. What then? It still doesn't explain what the fuck those bastards out there want with *me*.' Tara was primarily talking to herself as she gazed still at Gwen, so Gwen sat still and waited for her to finish. It seemed that Tara was organizing her thoughts by speaking them aloud. 'Unless it's not me they really want, but then how did they know you were coming? Maybe they didn't; maybe they were drawn by the barrier when it flared up. There are an awful lot of maybes, Gwen, so, what do you reckon?'

Gwen shrugged non-commitally. 'How the hell should I know? Didn't I just tell you that all this shit has just happened to me. I'm definitely no expert. And I'm just making this up as I go, trying not to get myself killed in the process. Trouble is, since I touched you I've got more questions now than answers. One of them would be how much do you know about that fireplace?'

'What the fuck has my fireplace got to do with anything?' Tara replied, caught off guard by the question and feeling she was being sidestepped. Gwen had told her briefly what she had seen but she went back over it with as much detail as she could recall. It had been a bit sketchy but she had gotten the gist of it. Gwen was still amazed at how calmly Tara was taking all these world-shattering revelations about her life and the world she lived in. She either knew more than she was letting on or she was going to implode later as her mind was overloaded by the enormity of it all. Inwardly, she hoped that it was neither, because any one of them could be potentially dangerous to her or anyone else. These sort of things always went south at the wrong time and she couldn't afford a meltdown at a crucial moment. Tara stared with undisguised resentment at the stone edifice that had been part of her life for so long.

'That explains why I've always hated that fucking thing. It gave me the creeps even as a girl. Now you tell me it's some sort of altar where some woman got her head cut off? Marvelous! Me mam always treated it like it was something special; now I know why. Damn! It explains so many things.'

Gwen could see Tara was upset as the flood of memories Gwen had instigated kept triggering other ones. 'I always thought my mother went a bit off when my da died. Daniel was too young to remember it, but I do. It didn't occur to me till I was about fourteen and I heard of people who cut themselves. Kids mostly. It was their way of dealing, I suppose. I thought it was just what my ma did. But she always did it here. Now I come to think about it, it was there, by the fireplace. She told me it was her favorite spot and her chair, the one you're sitting in, that was hers.' Gwen squirmed slightly in her seat and looked askance at the chair she was curled in as though she thought it might begrudge her sitting there. 'It was always placed close to the fire and I just thought she was cold. But she was blood sacrificing, wasn't she?'

Gwen thought it was likely and told her so. But just as disturbing was what she did with her daughter. It could have significant meaning to her vision. But as much as part of Gwen dreaded the answer, she knew she would have to ask. 'Did she ever cut you, Tara? Was your blood ever spilt onto this rock?'

The way the blood left Tara's face gave Gwen all the answer she needed. Perhaps the redhead in the vision was some sort of ancestor, but who was she and what did it mean for Tara; or Daniel for that matter? How was he mixed up in all this?

'I was born in this house, Gwen. But according to me ma, I wasn't breathing when I popped out; I was sorta going blue and everything. So...' As she spoke Tara stood and pulled one side of her jeans and pants down, revealing one of her butt cheeks, turning her hip so Gwen could see it. Gwen could indeed see an odd shaped burn mark. '...to kick start me, so to speak. She says the midwife grabbed a brand from the fire and pokes me on the ass with it. The shock apparently got me breathing.'

Gwen's heart felt heavy at the story, but what confirmed her suspicions more than that, was the sickle shaped burn mark glaring red at her from Tara's rump. But Gwen just smiled at the woman, in an attempt to alleviate the mood that was rapidly degenerating.

'Nice one. At least it's somewhere that should someone see it, you want them to, if you know what I mean.'

Tara pulled her jeans back up and sat again, smiling at the implication, humor warring with her own confusion and fears. But it didn't last long. 'It means something, doesn't it?'

Gwen could only nod. Though she didn't have the answer to what it actually meant, she did feel that it didn't bode too well in the grand scheme of things. But she kept her suspicions to herself; they had enough to contend with as it was without adding further mysteries to their woes. Gwen lost herself momentarily in her own thoughts and she was only barely aware of Tara rising to peek through the drawn curtains once more.

'They're still there and there are even more of them now. There's got to be at least twenty of the buggers, just standing there.'

Gwen's mind switched from the esoteric to the mundane and she asked with genuine curiosity how Tara managed to get out shopping, point in question being the wine glass she held in her hand. Tara turned from the window, and Gwen saw a look of concern there.

'Daniel has been delivering them since the barrier went up. I haven't left the house, well the grounds anyway. I did go out once to see who was standing at my gate, just after it went up, and I hadn't seen their faces up close till then. It was a man; I didn't know him and his face was hidden in the hood of his coat at first, so I couldn't see what he had done to himself. But as I drew nearer, he flung it back and screamed at me, lunging towards me as though he was going to vault the wall and attack me, but the silvery flash sent him sprawling backwards. I haven't been that close since then. That has to be near to three months ago. But I don't know how Daniel's going to get in now with that lot out there.'

Gwen tried to reassure her but didn't think it did any good. Her own heart wasn't really in it because she thought the same thing and what it meant to the continuation of her quest. She couldn't stay here for much longer, but neither could she leave Tara and Daniel to the ravages of the possessed. Were there more coming? If so, how many more would it take before they were unable to leave? Gwen was okay: she knew she could shift to bird form and just fly off; but Tara couldn't do that, and nor could Daniel. He was the next problem. Where the hell was he? Because Gwen had the distinct feeling that Tara wouldn't leave without him. *It's just one bloody problem after another these days. Why is nothing simple?*

'You know we are going to have to leave here, quite probably tonight, before that rabble gets any bigger or that barrier fails or any other number of horrible alternatives.' Tara sat down as though her legs had suddenly had the bones removed. Apparently the thought of leaving hadn't occurred to her and the prospect terrified her rigid.

'Has Daniel got a cell?'

Tara's expression said 'A what?'

'You know. A mobile?'

She shook her head glumly, explaining that he lost anything that wasn't attached to him and that even that was no guarantee. But, she continued, he usually turned up for breakfast about mid-morning if she could wait that long to see him. Gwen didn't have much choice as she saw it. So with a bit of persuasion, she sent Tara upstairs to pack a few belongings, while she kept a lookout for the possessed. If she rationalized things, she knew she could inflict considerable damage on them in her dragon form, so she had little to fear really, but it was just the idea of them that creeped her out, and the effect they had on normal people. It was odd how humans accepted evil monsters that looked like evil monsters easier than evil that looked liked them. As she watched, several more arrived. Women and children alike, torn and sundered by the unimaginable presence of some demon inhabiting and corrupting their bodies. Gwen wandered around the house, checking every window and looking out into the night to see if they had surrounded the house. To her relief, she only saw them at the front gate and wall area, though that was not to say they weren't lurking out in the darkness somewhere. A quick check told her dawn wasn't far away and she hoped the rising sun would banish them to whatever dark rock they crawled out from under.

Gwen kept watch as the sun rose and Tara busied herself with putting the house in order to leave it; flitting about, shoving objects in and out of her pack, changing her mind about what she needed or thought she needed. And yet more possessed arrived. There were nearly fifty gathered along the wall and by the gate now, eerily silent and standing still as statues, just watching, though watching was the wrong way to describe it as they all had the torn and ruined eye sockets, where nails had gouged them away, leaving bloody, empty holes. Yet they all unerringly faced the house. The fog had dissipated as the morning took shape, but the sky still held a steely menace as the thunderclouds continued to build. A light, icy, sleety rain was falling, just to add to the gloomy atmosphere, which only threatened to grow worse as the day wore on. A distant rumble of thunder emphasized Gwen's fears and she saw several bolts of fork lightning illuminate the horizon beyond the indifferent possessed, who continued to watch them.

Turning back to the fireplace, Gwen saw that the ancient markings that hadn't been too pronounced earlier were now glowing a faint blue. She moved closer as her heart rate skipped up a beat. *What now?* she wondered. Reaching out a tentative hand, Gwen felt the rock thrumming beneath her fingertips. Vibrating and resonating like a living thing. Simultaneously, all around the world, standing stones and megaliths of all shapes, sizes and proportions began to vibrate and glow their ethereal blue light. Those people who sought sanctuary within their stony circles and sheltered in their vicinity – having fled from the minions of the Adversary – found themselves reassured by the phenomena rather than scared by this sudden occurrence, but they didn't know why. Dormant for thousands of years, their purpose shrouded in the mists of time, the ancient stones had still drawn souls to them; much the same way a lodestone drew iron. Kindred spirits who felt the old world touch of magic had flocked to these ancient protectors in the same way people of other religions flocked to their temples and sanctuaries. With one fundamental difference. Where those modern day sites of reverence were abandoned by those which they were built to worship, these stones were not. It was a faith that predated known religions and it had endured. Endured where lesser, more recent ones had failed or were failing. Even the Four Horsemen, who were engaged in several conflicts across the Earth, paused briefly to wonder at the phenomena and what new sequence of events had been set in motion, or, unbeknownst to them and the world, what had been released.

Gwen had no way of knowing that her mere presence beside the altar stone would imbue it with enough energy to perform its last charge. Being a thing of the Earth, it absorbed Earth energy. Gwen was now a font of that particular power. And it drank heavily. And somewhere, veiled by time, a woman with flowing red hair turned to look over her shoulder. She felt a touch of power, subtle and distant. Smiling, she knew that the enchantment was complete and that the connection had been made. Now it was just a matter of time, literally. Returning her attention to the prone woman before her, she smiled cruelly at the beseeching hand that was stretched out towards her hoping futilely that it could touch some vestige of humanity within her. It would fail; there was none left. What little remained to her she had willingly given to the Adversary hundreds of years before when this woman, who lay weak and helpless before her, refused her supplications for more power. Hadn't she served her long and faithfully as her priestess for her entire life? Sacrificed her family for her?

Still, it mattered little now. The die was cast and she had made her choice. There was no returning or forgiving now. Mercy was no longer an option even if she wanted to extend any to the woman before her. The enchantment was too powerful and for it to achieve its goal, she needed the life essence of one of the immortals, who, as it turned out, weren't so immortal after all. It's just that humanity didn't know what it took to kill them. She did now. Lifting the iron sickle from her belt, she gripped the handle firmly in both hands and swung down.

The storm was picking up apace, booming and crashing outside. Lightning flashed its jagged signature across the sky and over the land. Trees and rocks succumbed to its awesome power, which caused timber and stone to explode with apparent ease. Gwen could feel its power tingling over her skin and she knew it was unnatural, but she knew also, she had no power over it. Maybe Jen or Maddy could have dealt with it, but they were not here – she was. Gwen felt her solitude; and their absence was like a rock in her gut. So powerful, yet so powerless at the same time. But what she didn't know about the storm was that it wasn't just targeting random trees and rocks. No, the lightning sought ancient oaks and stones of power; and the raging maelstrom was heading straight for them.

The fireplace, with its strange glow and increasing vibration, was still, for all that, a fireplace. And the fire from last night hadn't quite yet gone out. As she watched, as though it did it on purpose to taunt her, a burning ember leapt out and flew unerringly to Tara's mother's chair, which stood close by. To Gwen's astonishment, the chair instantly went up in flames and she screamed. Panic overrode her mind just for an instant, before she ran to get water and wet towels from the kitchen. Tara, upon hearing the scream, rushed downstairs and into the lounge to see what had happened. She skidded to a halt before the blaze, flinging her arms up to protect her face from the searing heat. Gwen came hurtling back in with a bowl of water and threw it over the flames. They hissed and spat, sending clouds of black smoke roiling up. The flames diminished only ever so slightly before flaring up once more with renewed vigor, the crackling and snapping sounding to Gwen too much like diabolical laughter. Angry that her efforts were so pathetic, Gwen found herself walking towards the burning chair, initially with the intent of kicking it into the fireplace where it could do less harm, but instead, she found herself wanting to actually extinguish it. From where her clothes formed about her arms, Gwen grew a cloak of thick dark leaves and she swept it up and over the flames, smothering the fire and containing the thick choking smoke. She felt a tingle on the underside of her arm but that was it. Withdrawing the cloak and standing up, she saw that the flames were gone and the smoldering remains of the chair could be seen clearly now. All that was left was the basic frame and a few springs. And something else. Something that wasn't part of the chair's design. It looked like a stone tube with several crystalline rocks attached to it and bound around with gold wire. For the entire inferno it had to have been in, it appeared unscathed. Both Tara and Gwen exchanged puzzled glances at seeing the object. But it was Tara who moved towards it first.

'Not gonna find out what the hell it is by staring at it, are we?' She reached in and plucked it from the chair's wreckage. Surprisingly, it was cool to the touch – another shock to add to Tara's growing collection. She looked it over, turning it this way and that. 'Don't know. I mean, take a look yourself.' She proffered the tube to Gwen and turned it for her to see. 'There's nothing special about these gems that I can see; they just look like regular quartz and amethyst fragments. Okay, that one's smoky quartz and that other one is rutile, but for all that, I don't know what they do.'

'Well, at a glance, I'd say they protect it from fire, for a start,' Gwen said, and Tara gave her a look that said 'Smartass'. 'You see, the thing with quartz is that it is good for receiving and transmitting frequencies. All sorts of frequencies. Radio is the most widely known, but when the New Age movement finally got their hands on the crystals, they found out, or someone did, that quartz had an effect on humans, and why wouldn't it? Much more of a subtle effect though, not the wonders that they profess now. But as you see auras, what you're seeing is the color of the myriad of frequencies all living things generate whilst alive. Magic, though not as we know it now, but the great enchantments of the past, were probably amplified and maybe even contained in quartz. That type of magic wasn't what we think of magic now, but instead was the mystical connection between all living things, and the ability to manipulate it is an ability all humanity once possessed but has lost over the centuries, or at least the majority of people have lost it. I suspect your family still has a connection. Your mother certainly had one, if this is anything to go by. Her mother too, no doubt, and so on and so forth. I expect, for better or worse, that you have it too.'

Tara rolled the tube around in her hands some more, examining it with new eyes based on what Gwen had said. It was during a twisting wringing motion in Tara's hands that the tube suddenly came apart, neatly separating into two equal sized halves. A cleverly designed screw thread could be seen at the join – a masterful piece of work because when it was together it was impossible to see the seam. Rolled inside it was a piece of parchment, equally untouched by heat or fire.

'What's that?' Tara asked, looking at the protruding scrap of paper with a mixed look of fear and curiosity .

'Well, why don't you take it out and look at it? That way you'll know what it is, won't you?' Gwen said pragmatically.

Tara raised her eyebrows at the obviousness of the statement and the stupidity of her question, and then took the scroll out. Placing the two stone tube halves down, she went to untie the scroll; then she gasped.

'What is it?' Gwen asked, instantly concerned, fearing the worst that maybe with their haste they had tripped some sort of mystical trap. Gwen was at her side in a shot.

'It's my mother's hair ribbon.'

Gwen heaved a sigh of relief, but not before punching Tara on the arm for putting her through things like that.

'Ow! Easy, gal. Sorry to have scared you though, but it was a shock, that's all.' Tara rubbed her bruised arm and undid the scroll, sniffing the ribbon, in the hope she could get some essence of her dead mother. Then, tucking the ribbon in her jeans pocket, she undid the scroll fully and began to read.

'C'mon. Out loud,' Gwen whined, disappointed at missing out on the discovery.

Tara had by then scanned the contents and she looked over at Gwen, her expression unreadable. But she began to read out loud as Gwen had asked:

> 'Dearest Daughter,
>
> I was hoping to be able to tell you all you need to know in person when you were old enough, but if you are reading this then it means I wasn't able to do that and I am probably dead. We spoke of many things when you were young. I don't know how much you can remember but whatever it is, it isn't nearly enough to help you with what you must face. I fought against our destiny in the vain hope of preventing you succumbing to the same fate as the rest of our line. It seems I failed and have paid for that failure with my death. If the fireplace ever glows blue, you need to place both hands upon it and repeat these words: *Hecate, guide me. Hecate, protect me. Hecate, grant me the sight to walk the world between worlds. Hecate, mother, sister, daughter, threefold guardian, I am your servant. Grant me what is mine by blood.* This is a double-edged sword and may cause you more harm than good, but you will need the power it grants to survive. I hope that you are strong enough to bear it, my daughter. Seek safety in the stone circles, for they are the crossroads of the Earth. Walk in the light but respect the darkness and only do what is right. I must leave you now for there is no more time. Grace be with you, my child.
>
> Eternally your loving mother,
> Riganmor Fitzgerald.'

With a desperate look, both women turned to see the fireplace was indeed still glowing. Tara took a step towards it, wringing her hands and chewing her lip as she did so.

'I'm terrified, Gwen, but this is from my mother. What harm can it do?'

'I'm as scared as you and I hate to say it but it could do a lot of harm, based on what I know of Hecate. I know it was your mother and you miss her. You are hoping this will connect you to her, and I understand that, but think about what I saw in my vision. Sacrifice, beheading and the blood. Crap, I don't know, Tara. I wouldn't. But it's your call.'

Tara nodded once then placed the scroll on the mantle. The moment she did it caught light. Panicked now, she slapped both hands on the rock and quickly read the words before it all went up in flames.

Distracted by the blaze, they hadn't noticed the storm creep up on them. Thunder crashed right on cue as Tara spoke and lightning raged outside in the most awesome pyrotechnic display Gwen had ever beheld. Even the desert storms would have been hard-pressed to compete with this one. Tara was oblivious to it as the blue light began to envelop her and suffuse her entire body with it. It blazed from her eyes like car headlights and she mouthed a silent scream, light pouring from her open mouth. Gwen couldn't have heard her anyway. The storm took all sound and annihilated it. Gwen ducked involuntarily every time a concussive lightning bolt struck something. She wondered in between explosions that this must be what it was like in Baghdad when they rained missiles down on them. But just as Gwen was about to check on the storm through the window, a mighty thunderclap, followed immediately by a lightning bolt of such magnitude, struck and blew out the lounge window and half the wall along with it, sending shards of glass and chunks of masonry hurtling into the room. Was it anyone else in there but Tara and Gwen at that moment, they would have been pulverized and shredded in equal measure. As it was, the shrapnel and debris simply vaporized as it hit the blue aura that surrounded the oblivious Tara; and for Gwen, all she had time to do was throw her arm up to protect her face as best she could. What she didn't expect was that as her arm came up, so did a wall of root, bursting from the floor and cocooning her in its protective embrace. Again, she realized, something else done on instinct and without thought had come to her aid. If only she knew what she was capable of, life might be that much easier, she thought, piqued at her trial-and-error learning curve.

The storm continued unabated and the rain now saturated the lounge as it hammered into the room, effectively amplifying the sound, which was even louder now, as Gwen emerged from her root-built shelter. Tara was slumped now against the fireplace, which had reverted to its original stone look once more, the light gone. Whatever coursed through it had either simply gone, or it now coursed through Tara instead. Only time would tell on that one. Gwen picked her up and carried her to the protective barrier and placed her gently behind it. Then she went to see what was happening outside.

Stepping out into the rain, Gwen felt its touch as something to be welcomed even for all its unnatural origins. She embraced all the elements now and headed towards the smoking ruins of the oak tree. It had taken several hits and was nothing more than a charred stump now. Of the possessed, there was little remaining either. Their blasted bodies were strewn everywhere, twisted and burnt almost beyond human recognition. *Even a demon can't inhabit a body that's destroyed to this extent, surely.* Gwen hoped that was the case at least. Several more lightning bolts slammed into the ground and she felt each one resonate through her bare feet as she trod the wet grass near the tree. Another hit the house behind her, making her duck again. Turning on her heel, she ran back in, concerned for Tara. Gwen checked Tara first, and she was fine: protected by the roots. Only then did she notice the fireplace had been sundered in two by the last strike.

Too late. Whatever you tried to prevent happening has already happened. Tara has her heritage – for good or ill, it is yet to be seen – but at least she'll have the choice. As if sensing that very fact, the storm blew past and even lessened somewhat as it moved beyond the smashed and wrecked house, expending the last of its energy out over the mountains. *At least it got rid of the possessed. One good thing to come from it, I suppose*, thought Gwen as she sank down on the soggy carpet, beneath the root shelter. She sat beside Tara and gathered the unconscious woman into her arms, affording her some rest and protection until she awoke from whatever held her unconscious mind in its thrall. Light still seeped from her closed lids, but the eyes that flicked beneath the skin showed her to be deep in rem state. She slept and Gwen would be there when she woke.

Daniel had seen the storm from town. Since most of the people had vanished, leaving shops and businesses abandoned, Daniel had taken to acting like some impromptu caretaker. Of course he took what he needed, but he made a note of it, with the full intention of paying the shop owners back if they ever returned. One of the last bastions of the townsfolk had been the pub, but even that was gone now, smashed by the lightning storm, the desolated populace fleeing in all directions in an attempt to escape the carnage wrought by the storm. Daniel had seen several not make it, or what was left of them at least. He still hadn't found his companions from the night's earlier adventures, but he was gratified that he hadn't found their bodies either. It was all like some horrible nightmare he couldn't escape. He had leapt into his car and made the best effort to get back to Tara's but he was thwarted, as there were so many fallen trees blocking the majority of the roads. Off road in the dark and the storm would be tantamount to suicide, but he knew he had few options remaining open to him. Resigned, Daniel hauled on the steering wheel.

Setting off across Gilley's field saw him vanish into the night. One tail light was all that gave him away, then that too was gone. He'd had to abandon his car six miles from home, as a bolt of lightning tore up the ground in front of him, leaving an enormous crater which he promptly drove into, not having the most reliable brakes. Stuck head first, he clambered out into the smoking mud and clawed his way back to the surface. It had been a wet and terrifying trudge, dodging lightning and several of the running possessed as he went. They seemed too focused on something else other than him, a fact he was immensely grateful for, though to be fair, Daniel didn't know they were possessed at the time: he just considered them mad. Mentally ill. Something in the water, perhaps? He had no idea what had turned the people weird, as he considered them. All he knew was that several had become violent and totally unhinged. What did it for him was watching Sean the grocer grab his dog and savage it with his teeth. It screamed and howled as he ripped its throat out with his own mouth. There was blood everywhere and he held the twitching corpse for long minutes as he swallowed the pumping claret. That was more than enough for him. Swallowing back vomit, Daniel had run far and fast away from the sight before he couldn't take it any more, and he stopped to spew his guts behind some bins. Something had definitely happened to the gentle townsfolk and he didn't like it.

By the time he reached the cottage, the storm was then leaving. He had come up the back way, as he usually did. There was an old track that few knew about. It meandered through some rough ground that at first glance was totally impassable unless, of course, you knew about the path, which he did. He had used it to great effect these past months, slipping past the freaks at the gate that stood and watched the house day in day out, for some reason that was lost on him. All he knew was he intended to avoid them at all costs. Whatever they had, he wasn't catching if he could avoid it. But as he drew close, he saw that something was wrong. He could see the front through the kitchen window. Creeping in the back he worked his way to the hallway and down towards the lounge door. Peering in carefully, making sure he wasn't seen, his mouth dropped open at what he saw; and all thoughts of stealth left him. He strode in and looked left and right, taking in the destruction of what used to be his home.

'What the bloody hell happened here? And what happened to the wall?' He was gazing at the ruins of the front, where the garden had become one with the front room, complete with newly built rockery. The man's voice had startled Gwen and she eased out from under the still comatose Tara and grabbed a piece of the exploded window frame. He hadn't seen the women behind the screen yet so she took advantage of the surprise and moved to intercept him as he crunched through the broken glass towards her. Timing her leap, she jumped out in front of him and brandished her timber, swinging it for all she was worth. It was only his own defensive instincts that saved him from losing his head as he fell backwards as the piece of frame flashed before his eyes.

'Whoa there, friend! Peace! It's me, Daniel.' He all bar screamed as he back-pedaled towards the doorway and safety. The lump of frame bounced harmlessly off the root screen as the momentum swung Gwen round. Realizing who it was and glad she hadn't decapitated him, she dropped her makeshift weapon and brushed her hands together, looking at the filthy man, who stared at her wide-eyed and obviously terrified.

'Sorry about that. Just that it's been something of a strange night and you took me by surprise, that's all. Tara did say you were coming but I must have lost track of time.'

'You! What are you doing here? Is this your doing? And where's my sister, you…you…'

Gwen held up both hands in supplication, sensing where this was going. He held her responsible for this carnage based on his last discussion with her as he sped off, thinking she was some creature of the night. Of course he hadn't thought that at the time that he was leaving her on his sister's doorstep.

'Easy, Daniel. Your sister's fine, I think. She's sleeping anyway, just there.' Gwen pointed to the shelter. 'Look for yourself. This, though, is nothing to do with me; well, not directly anyway.' Gwen gestured at the ruins. 'I think something wanted your sister and your fireplace just as bad. I'm sorry to say that I might have triggered it but other than that, all I can say is: sorry about the mess.'

He didn't know what to look at first: his sister or the little blonde woman standing barefoot and uncut amidst the array of broken glass and smashed brickwork. Fortunately for him, his choice was made for him as he heard his sister groan from behind the screen. That swayed him, and he ran towards her, though without taking his eyes from Gwen, in case she did something to him. It made for an amusing spectacle as he navigated the ruined room to get to her. He was like a puppet with his strings tangled as he lurched and skidded his way to his prone sister, who was now sitting up and rubbing her head, groaning much the same way Gwen remembered groaning after a heavy night out on the tiles. She watched as he hunkered down beside her and checked her all over for wounds, fussing like some mother hen until she swatted him away and said she was fine, just a headache. But they hugged anyway and he helped her up. Gwen just stood and watched, her arms folded across her chest and her finger absently tapping her bicep. Supporting Tara, Daniel tried to edge them both around Gwen but Tara saw what he was doing and gave him an elbow in his ribs.

'What the bloody hell are you doing, Dan? Gwen's no threat to us, quite the opposite actually. Were it not for her I might not be standing here now to talk to anyone, though I am still a bit hazy on what we did at the fireplace.' Tara turned to Gwen for some help and was about to ask her to fill in some blanks, when all thought of conversation washed from her head. Instead, her eyes were drawn beyond Gwen to the gaping wreckage that was her front wall and window. For heading towards the house was a mob of people, and they weren't walking casually. They were running and Tara could see that their eyes had been ripped from their heads, and mouths were drawn up into snarls, with hands reaching ahead of them as though they could get them there any faster than the rest of them. Tara just pointed. Fear locked her vocal chords, freezing them in terror at the sight of the charging horde of possessed. Gwen turned to see what had affected her so and she too gasped at the sight. Though that quickly turned to anger, for enough was enough. Gwen closed her eyes and concentrated for a second, remembering the bramble wall that protected her grove back home. With a ferocity and a speed that amazed even her – and she was doing it – bursting from the ground before and around the horde sprang a thick and entwining wall of thorny bramble. Like organic razor wire, it ensnared and tangled the charging horde, tripping and binding them within its barbed embrace. Yet still they fought against it, tearing and slicing their bodies beyond human endurance in their desperation to break free and get to their quarry. Flesh was shredded and ripped hideously, and their blood flowed freely from wounds that would have been fatal to normal people. But these were not normal people any more: they were demon driven and they cared nothing for the damage inflicted on their mortal transport. The trapped soul of the innocent felt everything that happened to the body that it no longer had any control over, screaming in impotent agony until it eventually died. The demon then sought another host and continued its diabolical mission.

'That should hold them for now but I don't how many more there are out there.'

Daniel was stunned. He couldn't take his eyes off the entangling wall of thorn and its struggling occupants. 'Did you just do that?'

Gwen rolled her eyes in exasperation. Now wasn't the time to explain things to him, and Tara knew that too. She poked him in the ribs again, getting his attention. 'Daniel, we have to go. Now. Before any more come. Now how did you get here without being seen? I don't see the car.'

This brought him back to the surreal world. 'Ah, well, I had a little accident with that. It's in a hole in a field somewhere. There was this bright flash and then there was this hole. You know how temperamental the brakes are…well, long story short, the car's out of the question.'

Tara scowled her disapproval at his recklessness. 'We're never going to outrun them. We need another car.'

Daniel looked thoughtful for a moment before speaking. Gwen thought that might have been a first.

'There are plenty of abandoned cars in Sneem, but it's a good six-mile hike on the best of days. This sure as shit doesn't qualify as one of them. We'll have to take the scenic route to avoid that bunch of nutters and any of their friends out a wandering. You say they are probably looking for us?'

Gwen nodded, frowning herself. *How the hell am I going to get them out of this? I need to think and there's no time for breathing, hardly, let alone thinking. First things first: get away from here. It must be like a beacon to the possessed after last night's events.* 'Okay, out the back. Daniel, you lead. You obviously got here unhindered and I know you know your way around without being spotted, so let's go. Tara, can you run?'

'Like a gazelle normally, but at this precise moment I feel like a newborn. But I'll do my best. Dan'll prop me up till I get me feet. Won't you, Daniel Haden Fitzgerald?'

Like most people, they knew they were in trouble when their full name was used. Usually it was from one irate parent or another, but in this case, he knew better than to cross his sister. She had a fiery temper, much like her mother, and though it was a dim memory for him, he had heard enough stories and seen Tara in action himself more than once to even consider crossing her when she used his name like that.

'But of course, sister dearest. I wouldn't even think about leaving you to struggle. I'd sooner stick sharp sticks in me testicles than abandon ye.'

She glowered at him and he smiled his ingratiating and even somewhat charming smile at her as he spoke.

'Take the piss like that, Daniel, and I'll do it for you. Now let's move. The nearest stone circle is in Kenmare. That's where we have to get to.'

Gwen smirked to herself despite the seriousness of the situation. Such humor and banter was important considering the severity of what they faced. The old adage of smiling in the face of adversity was never more apt. Gwen took a last look out at the possessed and sent her awareness a little further, utilising the eyes of the carrion birds that circled the possessed, scenting the blood. What she saw made her heart sink, and a cold knot of fear lodged itself in her gut. There had to be hundreds more running towards them, intent on one thing. Their deaths.

'Out the back. Go now!' There was no more banter as she propelled them out, arms wide, like a mother herding her recalcitrant children out. Gwen grabbed the stone tube on her way out, picking it up from the ruins of the fireplace where Tara had dropped it when the light overcame her, figuring it might be useful to her later. With that, she took off behind them, through the house and out the kitchen. Gwen caught up with them at the head of the concealed path at the end of their garden, leading out into the wilds beyond. She saw that Tara still had enough foresight to have grabbed her shotgun and her coat as they made good their escape, slipping into the undergrowth behind them, which Gwen turned back to and thickened the foliage with a thought; filling it with yet more briar, bramble and thorny vine she could recall, effectively concealing their direction and hopefully slowing any pursuit. They ran on; but they couldn't outrun the screams of the possessed as they howled their frustration, and the cries of those who ran to join the hunt. It was a chilling sound and Gwen could tell it was drawing closer by the second; and she knew also, they wouldn't give up till they caught them. Six miles soon began to feel like six hundred and that was just after *six hundred yards*.

CHAPTER SIXTEEN

SOLIDARIUS

THE BEAST LOWERED ITS MUZZLE TO THE ground and inhaled deeply, absorbing the multitude of images and scents from the forest floor. Taking in and assimilating every scent of every creature that had crossed the trail within the last several days. It disregarded most of them as of no consequence, though its jaws dripped glistening saliva involuntarily at the thought of their succulent flesh. However, difficult as it was, it drove those distractions from its mind. It sought one scent in particular and that demanded all of its skill. For it was no ordinary prey it hunted, that much it knew. The beast's lord had told them it was simply a man they sought, a mere mortal from off world, no more than that. Yet Fenris had not seen the carnage wrought by this *man*. The bodies left to feed the crows, strewn in the wake of this human told another story. And it wasn't very likely that it was going to have a good ending.

Standing to its full nine and a half feet, the beast swiveled around on its lithe and muscular hips, searching left and right, its golden eyes narrowing above its furred muzzle as it scanned the area for its brethren. He had ranged far ahead to ensure there were no false trails, switchbacks or evidence that the prey knew they were being hunted and were taking evasive action. He ensured that the trail they followed was true. It was. In fact, it was almost too easy and, considering the carnage he was following – a concern that was not lost on the beast – they should be catching up soon enough too, for their quarry had, by the way the imprints barely left by their mounts were evenly spaced and not too deep, made no apparent effort to conceal their travel, relying, Savad guessed, on their speed and ability to leave little by way of such tracks. He learnt more about them that way by what they *didn't* leave than what they did. It bothered him that there was more to his quarry than was earlier thought, and this disturbed the big grey beast, Something in his gut churned in a way he had not known for several hundred years.

Savad would have preferred to hunt alone, a residual desire from before his rebirth. The solitude and the challenge were a narcotic to those of his uncanny ability, but instead, he found himself leading an ever expanding pack, gathering beasts along the way, remnants of other packs and hunts of hounds they had encountered who had also made it this far, apparently following the mortal human. Fenris was obviously taking no chances by sending so many. Judging by the odd numbers arriving, many had been lost and they were grateful of the leadership he provided, but such losses were considered irrelevant here where life was cheap. Now, because of Lucifer's disappearance, there were many more unexpected perils. And even more so since the Adversary took command. For though their kind occasionally fell victim to creatures infinitely more ancient and powerful than they, the hounds were seldom bothered. But they found themselves harassed less and less these days as the internal fighting and bickering kept the greater demons and ruling lords busy protecting their own palaces, interests and places in their infernal pecking order. He laughed at their fears, unconcerned by their petty plutocracy and political wrangling. He was above such things now.

Savad. The agonized and tortured greyness that was the beast's memory recalled his name before the time of the beast. He remembered tracking in infinitely more inhospitable lands than these. He remembered sand and air so dry it almost crackled to move through it and where – unlike this endless woodland of twilight and musky dampness – tracking could be impeded by several tons of sand shifting to bury scent, spoor and sign in a heartbeat, or destroyed totally by any one of the innumerable sandstorms that savaged the landscape, shaping rock and eradicating from history the unwary traveler unfortunate and stupid enough to be caught out in such weather without the expertise to deal with such hostile climates. The deserts of his home were no place for the inexperienced. Rarely were even their bleached and sandblasted bones ever discovered. The cruel and hungry deserts of Savad's home could be merciless when they chose, devouring and destroying indiscriminately.

Savad recalled his family then, though not with any fondness for they had treated him badly. He was the third son of a merchant who plied his trade during the time of the great Saladin, when the white round eyed infidel had overrun his homeland and laid claim to his people's cities. It was not Savad's fault he had been born deformed, twisted of back and limb, yet he bore his ailments stoically. His mother had died in childbirth and his father had laid the blame for his broken son at her door, citing that she should never have borne any more children after his two perfect ones. The deformed spawn must have been from her unfaithfulness to him, with Savad the useless and deficient being the get of another man. He even went as far as to claim him a changeling or foundling and it was only through his own beneficence that he kept the mewling infant at all. The years had been difficult during his childhood. His brothers had called him their little pet demon due to his ever worsening deformities. They had made movement difficult and he was unable to carry the bolts of silk and cloth his father traded in. Nor, due to his defects' severity, was he acceptable company for his father's clients. But for all his commercial inadequacies, he had a good eye and a remarkable sense of smell. His redeeming attribute was he could hunt and track the great beasts that roamed his country's wild lands and this alone endeared him to his brothers.

As the years painstakingly crawled past, he grew into a young man with an almost mythical reputation. It was said that he could track a flying bird just by sniffing the air, telling you not only where it was going, but where it had been and what color its feathers were. Yet his father thought no more of him even then than he did when he was a useless child. All his father's amassed fortune was lavished upon Savad's indolent brothers, who relished their status amongst the merchant's community. But it was the double-edged curse of Savad's uncanny gift, the one thing that gave him any joy and attention from his peers, that brought about his undoing. For it was during one of the late winter hunts that saw him range ahead, climbing high up into the mountains and where it was when he came face to face with the beast that would forever change his world. Savad had thought the full moon would aid him in his climb up the treacherous rocks. Instead, it led him to the beast that humanity would come to know as the werewolf.

The thing that leapt from the cave mouth – all golden eyed and razor teeth – tore into his flesh, ripping and biting through muscle and bone. Savad screamed in pain and terror as the creature smashed into him and drove him backwards. Unable to retain his already tenuous grip on the rock face with his malformed hands under the incredible weight of the monster, Savad saw his death as he became airborne. What saved him, if such a thing could be called saved, was their proximity to a ledge when he appeared at the cave mouth. Both man and beast went sailing off the precipice and out into the open air. Savad recalled oddly just how cool it was as he flew through the night sky. Then came the fall, plunging hundreds of feet down the mountainside. It was sheer dumb luck that one of Savad's torn limbs became wedged in a crevasse, arresting his would-be fatal descent and snapping his leg viciously in the process. The beast that attacked him fell past unabated, raking his flesh with its talons as it sought purchase and finding none. It landed heavily on several rocky spires, brutally impaling it in enough places to end its tragic and bestial life. The day broke and passed again, leaving the unconscious and bleeding Savad suspended up the mountain through the incinerating heat of the day right around to the freezing, moonlit night once more. He passed out several times, his mind filled with visions and terrifying scenes of blood and death, though strangely, none of them were about his pending death. He just put them down to delirium, dehydration and loss of blood. But it was as the bloated silver moon reached its zenith that he became aware of how his life had irrevocably changed.

What flowed through his veins now was no longer human blood, for most of that had dribbled away throughout the searing day. His body too had been changed, altered and reformed beyond human recognition by the legacy of Fenris the Wolf Lord. For the creature that attacked him had been one of the lost offspring from the dark days when the Wolf Lord roamed the world. Dreams, nightmares and a host of impressions had flooded Savad's mind as he lay out in the rocks throughout the day as he thought he was dying. He was in fact doing the opposite. The saliva of the bite worked its way into his broken and deformed body, repairing and forever altering its structure. He awoke in the monochrome darkness of night, his golden eyes drawn to the silvery orb that hung in the blue-black night sky, and he felt a new man. Not questioning his good fortune for surviving the fall, Savad disentangled himself from the rocks and with an agility that had him leaping and laughing for joy, he leapt and sprang back up the rocks to the cave he had left so abruptly earlier. Then the change came upon him and he screamed in unimaginable agony. Ripping throat muscles and severing vocal chords, Savad screamed as he had never screamed before.

His family had paid the price in blood for their years of abuse to him. Their rent corpses were found the following day, barely identifiable, so savagely had their bodies been mutilated. Yet as there was no evidence of the body of Savad, a warrant was sent out for his arrest. Accused of the heinous crime, Savad couldn't have cared less. He relished his new-found powers and even accepted the pain that accompanied it. He was no stranger to pain, having had to live with it all his life. He left the city and roamed the wilds, adapting swiftly to the change, and slaughtering at will whilst traveling deep into the desert. It was there that he encountered the withered and ancient nomadic shaman, who immediately recognized him for what he was. And it was he who explained that the full moon was only the catalyst for the first transformation. For it was then that the fluids were moved more swiftly around the body under her influence. Savad would be able to change at will from then on. Pleased at this new ability, Savad was about to test it on the wrinkled little shaman, but instead the shaman made Savad an offer. It was in exchange for his life that the shaman offered to send Savad to a place where he could live free from mortal authority. It seemed a good offer at the time. It did not do to play semantics with a shaman, Savad was simply happy to be away from the perpetual hunters who sought him for his family's murder. From one of the many sacred sites hidden in the wilds, Savad was transported to a place that was truly free of mortal jurisdiction. But when he learnt who ruled there instead, he would have given his soul to return to the desert of his birth.

Now, what must have been many hundreds of years later – for time moved differently in the Domain, coupled with the fact that the beast that Savad had become had a greatly extended life span – Savad found himself considering his future. After rising through the ranks of the hounds – thanks to his utter ruthlessness – he had been offered an interesting prospect. Find the human and return him to his lord Fenris and he could join the force that he was building to invade Savad's former home world. He could feed on those descendants of his would-be captors, knowing he lived strong and powerful while they were just dust and meat.

Momentarily lost in these half-forgotten memories, Savad had barely noticed the rest of the pack he now commanded, catching up with him. He was distantly aware of their growls and snarls as they converged on the area, snapping at each other in the way of dogs vying for position. Savad was enjoying the unexpected distraction of his near forgotten youth but the constant bickering of his subordinates brought his attention immediately back to matters of the present. Turning to the group, he howled a command of silence, and the yapping dogs instantly cowed. His vivid golden eyes raked the ferocious creatures before him and he maintained the fang-baring snarl of contempt as he continued to growl deep in his throat, until finally, after several long minutes, they fell totally silent and obedient, their own sparkling eyes fixed on their leader.

There were three phases to their transformational abilities, Savad had learnt. Fully human, which was limited only to the more ancient hounds – of which he was now one amongst – for it required an amassing of power and that only came with age and experience. Then there was the man-wolf stage, the one they presently utilized. This was the most commonly associated form, where the primal beast was upright on two legs with the majority of animalistic attributes: fur, talons, snout, fangs and ears. In this form they were virtually unstoppable, for the legacy of Fenris flowered the strongest and they healed almost instantly from all but the most grievous of wounds. When their kind had run amok upon the Earth during the days of Fenris, mortals were as insects to them – good only for food and sport. They would have ruled that world as gods had not the kin of their lord intervened and incarcerated him. Many of their brethren fell to the hunters that tried – albeit unsuccess-fully – to eradicate their kind. Many – the elder and first of their ilk – went to ground, forced into utilizing their canny hunting abilities to emulate the prey they had up until recently chased and terrorized themselves. Now, they were the hunted and it would take all their skills just to survive. They had, but their numbers had dwindled frighteningly and they grew cautious in their ways, hunting sparingly and being constantly on the move. Worst of all, was that during their mortal guise, they had mated with the humans, ingratiating themselves into the very society that feared them and sought their deaths; spawning lesser and, to Savad's mind, pathetic half-breeds that diminished the gene pool. They were still superior to mortals in many ways and still lived longer lives – hundreds of years by comparison – but even so, he despised them as a dilution of something perfect.

Savad was infuriated by what he saw as craven behavior, for the memory of the pack had been passed to him when he joined their ranks and it ate away at him to this day. He was determined to return to the world of men and exact his revenge upon them for what they had turned his kind into. Even the insidious and vampiric snake men of the Immortal Kalith despised and hunted them. It was the problem when two apex hunters co-existed: there was always animosity as they wrangled for superiority. Though like his kind, they had all bar vanished from the worlds since their Queen, Kalith, had been exiled beyond the Covenant. And there was, or so he was told, no coming back from that. Ever.

Savad organized his pack into three groups. One he would lead onwards, following the trail he had settled on as the truest of all they had discovered. The other two groups would range out to the sides and pace them; for when they eventually came upon their prey these two groups would swing in, flanking the quarry and driving it back into Savad's waiting talons. It was a good plan and he felt buoyed by the imminence of the kill. It would be a good hard and fast run, and he estimated they would fall upon their quarry just before nightfall, when they would feast and celebrate through the glorious night. 'All hail the glory of Fenris,' Savad roared the mantra; and the creatures howled their response, 'Fenris! Fenris! Fenris!' Savad was pleased at their fervor.

Soon, he would walk the Earth once more and sweet revenge would be his. Salivating at the thought, he ordered the change. There was nothing for it, and though he feared their cries would carry to the quarry and alert them of their presence, it mattered little now, for there would be nothing they could do about their fate. The change was an even more painful affair than just being, for to be a hound was to live in perpetual pain. Only killing and feasting lessened it; that, and the accumulation of power. The change used vast amounts of their innate powers and the transformation seared every single nerve ending as though it were immersed in liquid fire. Initially, the very first transformation would either kill or temper the newly bitten recruit: natural selection, for only the strongest survived the change. Savad had just ordered the hounds to change from wolf men to full hounds. Dropping to all fours to increase the speed of the run. They would change back to wolf men when the quarry was in sight. Muscles rippled and flowed beneath fur and bones snapped, twisted and reshaped themselves. Spines that stood upright and held their massive frames in man form whipped and elongated into the long flexible spine of the wolf, granting it greater mobility for the long, loping and ground eating strides of the hunter. But as Savad had anticipated, the noise was terrifying to hear as they screamed and howled their way through the change. His only hope was that the sound, should the man hear it, fill him with fear and dread; remaining with him until Savad ripped his life from him along with his head. He wanted that sound and Savad's face to be the last things he saw and heard.

Tomas had heard it. So too had the Valkyries. Even his raven seemed on edge at the eerie sound as it ghosted through the trees to them. The Valkyries seemed oblivious to the ominous sound, even after he reminded them that he was hunted by things that made that noise. Ingrid reassured him that it would take more than a few hounds to impede the progress of a band of Valkyries. Tomas argued, or tried to, that it sounded like more than a few and it was getting closer. But Ingrid insisted that it was only wild wolves, for were it hounds, they would never betray their presence in such in a way. Tomas wasn't so sure. If there were wolves here like there were back home and they existed in a similar manner with similar hunting traits, then they would be *avoiding* large groups of people, not drawing closer to them. Wolves rarely went anywhere near people, and their reputation for killing people was so overly exaggerated that it bordered on the ridiculous. It was down to scared and pathetic humans looking for a scapegoat – a way they could make themselves feel better about killing something – and anything invariably would do. Wolves, along with sharks and tigers, to name but two, got the rep as man-eaters and were hunted to near extinction by the ignorant. Tomas didn't think these were just ordinary wolves. A sinking feeling in the pit of his stomach told him otherwise and Tomas always paid attention to his instincts. He willed his Kevlar armor for arms, legs and body; completing the ensemble with his ballistic helmet, goggles and gloves. All under a coat of black chain mail. The sword was ever present in his mind and he sensed it thrumming with barely concealed excitement at the prospect of battle. *Easy, old chap,* Tomas mumbled to himself, *Let's hope it doesn't come down to that.* But he felt that the sword wasn't convinced by his plea. If Tomas was honest with himself, he knew there was a part of his psyche that was eager for the confrontation. He visualized himself in the throes of battle, wielding his sword with blistering speed and prowess, dispatching enemies in sprays of viscera and blood, laughing and snarling as he attacked. Tomas barely recognized himself. He saw himself with eyes like two obsidian spheres and a mouthful of vicious looking canines. Shuddering, Tomas forced the image away and tried to clear his mind of any other distraction, and focus on the howling in the here and now. Storm took care of the riding, unerringly moving through the oppressive woodland trail. Tomas sought the raven, which at present was gliding alongside him. Flapping from branch to branch and tree to tree, Bran slipped through the forest like a wraith, yet was never more than a few feet from Tomas.

'*Bran, my friend, can you rise above the trees and see what it is that's chasing us? I'm not convinced it's regular wolves. That said, keep yourself safe and out of reach.*' The massive bird cawed twice that it understood, and within seconds had vanished from sight. Still unsettled, Tomas rode forward, passing Niall and Hildreth along with the rest of the battle group, and ignoring Ingrid's scowl, for he knew she knew he wasn't convinced by her explanation and she just hated being second-guessed. Especially by a man. And even more than that, by one man in particular – him.

'For someone not long in the Domain, you attract enemies well, Tomas,' were the first words that Treya spoke as he reined in alongside her.

'I know. It's nice to be popular but I can really do without them, if you know what I mean. It isn't like I haven't got enough upon my plate already without making friends like these.'

She nodded her agreement as they rode. She still seemed distant and slightly distracted, lost or at least temporarily diverted by thoughts Tomas could only wonder at.

'Ingrid doesn't think they are any threat, but I can't help but disagree with her. Regular wolves wouldn't advertise themselves like that, least not where I come from.'

'You are quite right, Tomas, they are no regular wolves. They are hounds and they will catch us by nightfall at the rate they are gaining. Yet panicking will do no good and they are at our backs, which is good for them and bad for us. So, we must continue ahead of them until we can find a more defensible position to defend against them. We have no room to swing swords in here and we will be at the mercy of their teeth and claws in such confined spaces. No, we need another clearing and there is one ahead, according to the scouts. They are too far ahead though to get back in time to be of much help to us, unfortunately, so we will need to be focused when they come. Are you focused, Tomas?'

'Of course I am. What sort of question is that?'

But Treya just tilted her helmed head and regarded him briefly before turning back to the way ahead. What did she mean by that? Tomas felt his anger flare at the way this woman treated him like an infant, always putting him down and belittling him with her damn riddles. Why didn't she just say whatever inane thing it was she wanted to say, and be done with it? He suppressed the urge to backhand her from her saddle, but it was an incredibly powerful urge and Tomas had to exert all his willpower to dampen it. *What the hell was that?* A wave of fear rippled through him. And he sensed the crimson haze begin to creep into the periphery of his vision as the rage built within him. Something wanted to explode out of him, and Tomas was almost drowned within himself as the desire to pummel his fists into something surged up within him. It was as though he could no longer contain himself within the meagre shell of flesh he found himself in. He wanted to burst free like some corrupt and explosive butterfly tearing free from the prohibitive carcass of the grub, and spread his mighty wings of destruction, annihilating everything within his immediate vicinity. The prospect of such an outpouring of devastation brought him to a state of arousal that made riding his horse an uncomfortable affair. Tomas was really scared now. This feeling had gone from one of emotions that he didn't think were his to one of physical manifestations. That couldn't be good. He found himself gripping the pommel of his horse so tightly he felt his knuckles cracking under the pressure. But he was loath to let go in case he fell beyond recall. But it was the raven that brought the Tomas he knew himself to be, back from the dark brink he didn't even imagine could be within him, just before he crashed over the edge into a red-tinged and rage-filled blackness.

'*Hounds! Tomas! Hounds!*' The raven swooped in and with claws that had no respect for his armor, clamped onto his shoulder and dug in deep; though it wasn't the grip that brought clarity flooding back into Tomas's mind like liquid sunlight. It was simply the presence of the bird that was enough to dispel the blind and irrational fury that had swamped him. Like a pin bursting an oily and filthy soap bubble, the malignant feelings just disappeared and Tomas blinked. It felt to him, as the sway of the horse and the smells of the surrounding forest reasserted themselves, that he had just missed the last few minutes. He had moved forward in time, it seemed, and his mind had no recollection of the journey. His body had been on autopilot while his mind fought for control. He knew this wasn't the first time either. Since his time at the Al'Mayakin fortress he had experienced a few of these episodes. He hadn't really noticed at the time, but each one seemed to be getting a little stronger and harder to shake. He had put it down to fatigue and the weird metamorphosis the Horsemen had imposed on him – his body adjusting to the physical and metaphysical alterations they had wrought upon mortal DNA. But now he wasn't so sure. It felt too detached. Almost like it wasn't him at all and he was just an observer in his own body as his spirit darkened and shriveled with hate-filled fury. Just the thought of striking Treya in any sort of anger filled him with a guilty remorse that made his face burn with shame.

Again the raven cawed its ominous warning to him, '*Hounds! Heed me, Tomas! Hounds!*' True enough, for just as the snow white corvid rebuked him, the ominous howling rent the forest's constant rustle. Treya turned to him and her eyes scrunched up as she concentrated on the sound whilst looking at him. He knew he shouldn't be distracted by the little wrinkle that formed at the bridge of her nose, or the way her mouth twisted ever so slightly as she thought, and how one eye closed a fraction; but he was, and he knew in that moment she could be the death of him. So rapt was he by everything about her, he might find himself watching the sway of her hip just when he should be parrying a swordthrust from some enemy that had come up upon him while he was mentally elsewhere. Tomas shook his head in a desperate attempt to clear the cobwebs that threatened to confuse him and fog his thoughts. One second he was raging uncontrollably and almost in the next breath was he having lascivious thoughts about the woman who rode beside him. His mind went from kill to kiss in less time than it took for his heart to beat, and it made his head spin.

'They are closer than I feared. We must pick up the pace.'

He knew she had spoken but all he heard was a series of incomprehensible garbles. 'Huh? What was that?'

She scowled at him and Tomas knew that it wasn't just Ingrid who objected to repeating herself. Treya was born to command and she, not unlike Tomas on a good day, expected those she ordered or spoke with to pay attention. Lives invariably depended upon instant reaction to orders. You could hardly expect in the middle of a fire fight to say 'Could you just hold up a minute while I repeat that to some cloth-eared git whose mind is currently elsewhere'. Yeah, right. Tomas mentally slapped himself and concentrated his fraught willpower on the here and now.

'Yeah, sorry about that. I'm a little distracted right now, but you did say they're closer, didn't you? And we need to get our arses in gear. Okay, let's go.'

Treya frowned at him once more before issuing the order back down the little column. Moments later, the battle group, even including Niall, who hung on for grim death, was galloping through the forest at a frightening speed. Any slip now could be disastrous. But they needn't have worried. The pegasi were as fleet footed as Storm, who wove through the trees like an equine guided missile, testing the entirety of Tomas's riding skills as he leant in and wove along with his companion. Bran had lifted off and beat his powerful wings above Tomas's head. Keeping pace with little difficulty, the raven cawed its excitement as it too swerved and banked as it dodged branches and overhangs.

What should have taken a good hour, saw the group a mere ten minutes later break through the treeline and spill out into another of the huge clearings that seemed to dot this country-sized and mind-numbingly huge forest. Running out into the open ground for several hundred yards, they slowed swiftly, banked and turned to face the direction they had just run from. They faced the trees like some mythical cavalry. Tomas had a moment's thought for General Custer and how he must have felt when he found himself in the middle of nowhere at the Little Big Horn – open ground all around and nowhere to run to, enemies on all sides and the sickening anticipation of the attack he just knew was coming – though Tomas doubted the infamous General had enough of a lucid moment to realize the arrogance and sheer stupidity of his actions and the consequences of them. He would probably never know how brutally the lives of his men were ripped from them by the righteously indignant wrath of the Native Americans. After all, it was the whites who taught them how to scalp and commit the atrocities they merely visited back upon their oppressors. Unfortunately their actions were too little too late and their innocent naivety gave the infection that was the white man, time to fester and spread.

Looking up, Tomas saw Bran circling overhead. *At least he'll be safe enough up there*, Tomas thought to himself as he willed the sword to hand in the shape of his HK33 with the forty-round mags and underslung grenade launcher. Niall and the worst of the wounded moved to the back of the group and the women with him all drew bows and nocked their silver arrows. Swinging their quivers to rest on their thighs for easy drawing, they all sat ahorse and waited. The front row, which included Treya, Ingrid, and four others all had, from somewhere Tomas couldn't fathom, manifested enormous pole arms, as well as their bows. They each held a halberd not dissimilar to the type used by Famine. Dark rune carved staves with blades the size of small scimitars perched atop them. *Bloody hell! Surely they aren't going to charge them? This sure as shit isn't Agincourt and I don't imagine the hounds will play by the rules when it comes to standing still and letting themselves be hit. Not only that, I don't have one.* But Tomas did know the speed with which they had covered the open ground. Now if the hounds were as fast as they were, they would only have seconds to get off what missile weapons they were going to before they were engaged. *Better make every shot count then, Tomas old son.* He sat in silence and watched the treeline as he went through his firing checks as automatically as breathing.

An eerie silence descended on the group, like the calm that falls just before the hurricane hits. Tomas had been here before. Same situation, different antagonists. He felt the familiar nausea rise and gurgle in his stomach and throat as he waited for the enemy to appear. This was open warfare and he didn't like it, never had. His father had told him the tales of his father during the First World War and the horror of the trenches. Those moments of running across the blasted and corpse-strewn no man's land to see the screaming and seemingly fanatical faces of the enemy, bayonets lowered the same, thundering towards you. But that seemingly fanatical expression invariably hid the same as those they saw: fear. Fear and imminent death in the worst possible place on the planet at that time, certainly as they understood it. Tomas thought then that Hell doesn't look half as bad as the images of the shell-blasted muddy expanse of la Somme. Tomas was snapped from his maudlin reverie by more soul chilling howling from the forest. They were really close now and would be breaking cover any second. He spared a last look at the women around him and he was suitably impressed by their iron discipline and steely expressions as all of them had their gaze fixed on the treeline. They were unswerving and all had arrows nocked and ready. They sat perfectly still upon their equally unfazed mounts. But he shouldn't have been so amazed at their behavior, for this is what they did best. Fight.

I hope I don't embarrass myself in front of these girls; I'll never live it down. Tomas checked his weapon again. Storm whickered suddenly and everyone tensed. Moments later, Tomas felt what had disturbed Storm. An invisible tsunami of fear came rolling out from the trees and washed over the group. The Valkyries didn't bat an eyelid; nor did Tomas. He had encountered this before and the gifts of the Horsemen helped him overcome it but poor old Niall had started to whimper at the rear of the group. He wasn't immune to the horror these creatures generated and he was scared witless. But Tomas had only moments to feel sympathy for the little man before the first of the hounds broke cover. He raised his weapon and sighted the beast, amazed at the speed it was moving but more amazed still at the way it seemed to ripple and flow as it ran, going from four legs to two. Howling filled the air as more broke cover and began the same disturbing transformation mid-run. *Bloody hell, they're huge!* Tomas fired. Rattling off several rounds and pumping out a half a dozen grenades from the launcher. But the hounds simply changed direction at the last minute and the explosions just left gaping foxholes. There was a huge grey one at the front, that had been the first to charge and it dodged the shots and arrows that tore into those that followed it. A few went down as a hail of hot metal ripped into their flesh. tearing great chunks away in a spray of fur and gore. Tomas knew that to go for head shots at the speed he had to fire would lose valuable time, so he just peppered the largest part, which was their huge torsos, but they didn't even slow. *Shit, this is going to hurt*, was the last thought that Tomas had time for before the first few hounds reached the line and leapt.

There was no time for guns or bows now and with an equally phenomenal speed, the Valkyries grabbed their pole arms and angled them forward, impaling those that leapt at them and sending them careening past, directly into the path of the slashing blades of the next rank. One landed and avoided the first two sword stokes of the Valkyrie who waited there, but just as it opened its unnaturally wide and salivating, fang filled maw, roaring its challenge and death howl, it abruptly changed to one of choking surprise as the pegasus back-kicked with its iron hard hooves and with an audible crack, shattered its spine. Momentarily stunned by this development, it didn't even see the twin swords that took its head. This had the desired effect and it flopped to the grass, twitching in its death throes. The HK was immediately replaced by the sword as Tomas narrowly avoided being unhorsed by the big grey's leap. Talons raked his shoulder and Tomas felt the fire as the dagger length nails gouged ragged tracks through his Kevlar like it was paper. *Shit! That's not good.* Storm responded to his thoughts instantly and turned and spun all ways, both avoiding the fangs and claws of the hounds whilst giving Tomas angle and room to wield his blade.

Everything became a haze then of life-and-death struggles. These were big creatures and powerful too. He swung the sword for all he was worth, ducking and rolling beneath sweeping blows that might have taken his head from his shoulders, or at the least eviscerated him. He saw silver arrows speed past him irregularly, taking one beast or another in the head or throat. These were the best places to strike them; they were also the hardest to hit.

The minutes that the battle actually took to be over felt like long, painfully drawn out hours. It was a frenzy of steel, punctuated by the screams of the dying. Tomas knew that Valkyries were dying but he couldn't spare the vital seconds needed to see who had fallen, busy desperately defending his own neck against these relentless beasts. But just when he thought they had the upper hand, two more groups emerged from the trees to their flanks and bounded in, howling what they must have considered a victory scream. *Damn. How many more of them are there?* It wasn't really a question he wanted an answer to for at least fifteen per group were loping towards them. With a combination of dazzling strokes, Tomas dispatched the hound that was pressing him and ran towards the nearest beastly morass. Dropping to a knee and swinging the sword to his shoulder, Tomas let rip with the RPG and was satisfied with the carnage that he caused within the ranks of unsuspecting hounds. *That'll teach you to run too close together, you stupid fucking dogs!* Tomas saw bits of furry limb rain down and thrash about on the bloody grass. Spinning, he let loose a couple of shots with the RPG into the other group, but they were much closer and about to engage

Ingrid and her few surviving warriors. The missiles screamed past their heads as the vapor trail cut a surreal line through the mêlée. There were several down but just as many still came on. Tomas jumped up and ran in, and ran full on into a hound that jumped into his path. He slammed into its huge chest like he had hit a wall. The creature grabbed him and drove its talons into his shoulder blades. Tomas screamed as white hot agony ripped his senses away from him. A white blur filled his vision and the pain went away suddenly. He dropped to his knees and drew a swift and ragged breath. Tomas looked up to see Bran, claws and beak savagely ripping into the hound's eyes and face. It swatted at Bran in an attempt to shake him off but the bird flapped about like a dervish, ripping and stabbing. Tomas saw at least one eye savagely torn out by the spearlike beak and flung aside. That was all the time he needed; ignoring the slowly dissipating agony in his shoulders, Tomas swung the mighty Sword of War clean through the midriff of the flailing hound and two halves fell wetly to the ground. Bran flapped away, but not before Tomas saw blood upon its white body. *'Is any of that yours?'* Tomas thought to the bird as he spun away ready for the next foe. He got a gleeful and defiant No as the battle raven flew off in search of another fight. But there was no time for thought as more hounds leapt at them. Tomas ducked suddenly as the sword warned him of an attacker from behind. Dropping to a knee, Tomas raised the sword in a lethal backwards swipe. He was rewarded with a howl of agony as he was drenched in the entrails of the sailing beast as its predatory lunge turned into a sprawling collapse. Driving his exhausted frame to its feet, he saw Ingrid in trouble and surged forward just in time to block what would have been a disembow-eling swipe intent on removing Ingrid's internal organs. The beast's blow met the Sword of War and before it could pull its swipe, it became one arm shorter. Ingrid spun seconds later, which would have been too late, nearly decapitating Tomas, who had to parry her swing on the sword. Steel met steel, but all she saw was his grinning mouth, the rest hidden behind his ballistic helmet and goggles.

'You'll have to pay more attention than that, my girl. I can't cover your arse all the time and look out for myself too, I'm good but even *I'm* not *that* good.'

Ingrid snarled at him as though she resented him saving her, but she nodded all the same. A warrior's gratitude didn't mean you had to like who was doing the saving. Ingrid leapt away with a battle-cry and finished the one-armed hound in a spray of blood, as with axe in one hand and sword in the other she made short work of the handicapped creature. Then he spun away himself to deal with yet another hound and came face to face with Treya, covered in blood and fending off two hounds herself with the most awesome display of swordwork he had ever seen. She spun and twirled her two swords with surgical precision. Removing first the limbs then the head. Spinning agilely to a halt like a dancer completing a routine, she saw Tomas and grinned evilly. Was this woman actually enjoying herself? No, he saw her eyes then and within the twin storms that raged there, he saw the intensity and the depth of the pain there at the loss of her sisters and it washed out over him as she looked at him. Her misery only hardened Tomas's resolve and added to the rotting, cancerous tumor that was his increasingly burdensome guilt. Tomas shrugged it to the back of his mind for a later reckoning. Something was going to pay heavily for every life lost, that much he promised.

He focused instead on the blood covering Treya, his eyes flicking over her body, looking for wounds, but he saw nothing obvious.

'How much of that is yours?' Tomas asked again, recalling Bran. He was a little breathless still, sucking in air as fast as he could. Treya, equally pressed, replied that most of it was from the beasts. Tomas nodded quickly that he was relieved about that and turned to seek another opponent, only wondering what she meant by most, but there were no more hounds immediately to be had. It took Tomas a few seconds to register that the beasts had moved off and were snarling and snapping at them like rabid dogs, circling them like the Indians at the Little Big Horn. *Now I know how Custer felt*, Tomas thought humorlessly. The only difference was that these dogs were up on two legs and were infinitely more dangerous. Tomas was stunned to see they had taken down only about two thirds of them. It didn't feel that many, not by a long shot, but he had hoped it was more. Sadly though, Tomas saw that their own casualties had been just as horrific, if not worse, for unlike the hounds the Valkyries had no ability to regenerate. A few hounds were still struggling to crawl away and their wounds healed before Tomas's eyes. They were desperate to put as much ground between them and the few remaining yet still deadly Valkyries as possible as their wounds knitted and strength returned. They weren't going to get that chance now that the warrior women had breathing time. As Tomas watched, he saw several silver arrows lance into the skulls of the scrambling creatures, and they finally lay still.

Apparently, after their initial surge had failed to get him, they had, unlike the animals they were fused to, utilized a very human tactic of retreat and regroup. Tomas took these few seconds' reprieve to take stock of the damage wrought by the creatures and his heart sank through the blood sodden ground he stood upon. There were more Valkyries down than he initially thought and added to the body count was poor Niall. Hildreth's torn and savaged body was draped over his corpse in a last desperate attempt to shield him from the creatures but she only succeeded in delaying the inevitable, dying herself in the process. He had failed again.

Tomas snapped. Yet another aspect of his tortured psyche rose up and he turned his iron gaze upon the circling and pacing werebeasts as he rolled his shoulders, loosening the muscles there. Had those beasts seen the intent within that piercing raptor's gaze, and had they the sense they were born with, they would have turned and fled with their tails between their legs. As it was, the creatures couldn't have anticipated Tomas's varied armory and they were unprepared for the sudden hail of bullets that tore into their flesh and scattered them as Tomas began running directly at the greatest concentration of hounds, screaming out Niall's name as a battle-cry. His twin Hochlers outstretched before him decimated their ranks, but the big grey, who had several silver arrows already protruding from his body – left there contemptuously – dived away from the devastating burst of white hot death. As Tomas ran, with the fully automatic weapons spitting their metallic venom before him, the big grey dodged the worst of it and dived clear, rolling with superhuman speed and agility, then suddenly lunged up at Tomas. Up, then completely over Tomas. Fire scored up his back, dropping him to his knees as the creature raked him on its way over. Rolling several times, dislodging the broken arrows as it landed, it found itself face to face with the remaining Valkyries, who, following Tomas's sudden lead, were finishing off the mortally wounded hounds with their silver arrows in well-placed head shots. Savad leapt at the nearest shield maiden, who was just a fraction too slow. She was still weary after the earlier brutal fight and she tried to suck in her stomach away from the slashing claws, but she didn't quite make it. Her dead body slowly crumpled to the ground as her ribs and lungs were smashed into the breeze, ripped from her body in a crimson spray. She was dead before she hit the ground.

Tomas, eyes wide, with spittle flying from his open screaming mouth, rationality momentarily evading him, picked himself up, and with the fire abating across his shoulders, he grasped the Sword of War, which he rematerialized, and attacked the hounds while they too staggered to their feet after his and the Valkyries' sudden and brutal assault, their wounds healing considerably slower due to the mystical nature of Tomas's weapon, but healing they were. They split off in different directions as Tomas sprang amongst them, his sword moving with astonishing speed as he took hound after hound. But still three slipped past him and with roars of anger and frustrated fury they hurled themselves, with talons outstretched, at the remaining Valkyries. They would take out their fury upon the women before facing the man again. Tomas looked quickly to the sky. *Where are those bloody scouts?* Tomas thought they should have been there by now, but with the speed and ferocity of the battle, he didn't realize just how little time had elapsed. Seconds felt like minutes and minutes like hours.

Treya and Ingrid were back to back. So too were the only other two remaining shield maidens and both pairs were battling desperately to hold off the hounds' onslaught. The sound of steel against talon was ringing continuously as the hounds frenzied against the women. Tomas had turned and was running back to rejoin the fight, praying he would get there in time to help. He could see the women fighting but it looked to him to be almost slow motion and his legs felt as though he were moving through water. He knew he just wasn't going to get there in time to help them. He threatened to explode with the impotent rage and frustration that surged through him and he could also see the big grey pacing on the other side of the warriors, watching him. Tomas was amazed that the bestial creature was watching the outcome of the battle as well as the whereabouts of Tomas. His feral golden eyed gaze kept switching between the two. Tomas was obviously still far enough away to be considered harmless by the beast, because the grey finally roared his defiance and threw his massive frame into the battle. His extra leverage swayed it sufficiently for the two hounds to shred the Valkyries from neck to navel, rending their flesh like so much raw meat. One couldn't resist the mass of fresh blood and stuck its muzzle into the steaming abdominal wound of one of the Valkyries, its filthy teeth clamping on the warm, pulsing liver. But its mistake was to think that the Valkyrie was incapacitated by the severity of the wound. It thought wrong, for with a scream of indomitable willpower, she grasped her sword in both hands and raised it above her head, very nearly dropping it again as the wire wrapped hilt slipped through her sweat- and blood-caked fingers, but with a final act of defiance, trembling with the unimaginable agony of her wounds, she drove the blade down through the beast's neck, severing the spine first off; then with a scream torn from the depths of her very soul, she wrenched it from side to side, effectively severing the head all bar a flap of furred skin on its neck. It fell back as dead as she was, with its head hanging garishly off its shoulder before crumpling into a heap alongside the now smiling Valkyrie.

Tomas could only watch in horror as the other beast began to feed, oblivious of its companion's plight. But the grey had other plans. It turned its bloody muzzle towards the two remaining Valkyries and Tomas saw its leg muscles bunch for the leap. Treya and Ingrid saw it too and braced themselves for the devastating impact they knew was coming.

'Noooo!' Tomas screamed. With a Herculean effort, in part aided by the sword, Tomas sprinted two steps and leapt himself, just as Savad sprang. The two collided, man and beast, in a crashing tangle of limbs, fur and slashing talons. Tomas got a hand free and punched out at the lupine face, his armored fist smashing into Savad's mouth, snapping his head back viciously and keeping the fangs from his throat. The two rolled a few feet before disentangling themselves from each other. Savad was the first to come to his feet and he drove straight in at Tomas, talons extended. But Tomas was only a second behind him and he met the charge with an awesome right hook born from pure survival instinct. He swatted one talon away like a champion boxer and swayed to the left as he delivered the blow. It took Savad by surprise that this human should stand up to him so. And he wasn't prepared for the power of the blow, for it sent the big wolf sprawling. Clods of earth were ripped up as he crashed to the ground. Tomas didn't wait for it to get up before following through with several steel encased kicks to its ribs. It howled as it rolled away and within seconds it was on its feet again, eyes afire with a hatred that drove what little sanity that remained, far from its mind. Tomas swung the Sword of War at it, causing it to duck below the flashing blade, but it came up fast, powerful haunches propelling it straight at him like wolf guided missile. Tomas wasn't fast enough to stop its salivating maw from clamping hard on the shoulder as he was barreled over backwards by the impact, blood spraying as the teeth bit deep into Tomas's flesh.

'Argh Fuck!' was about all Tomas managed to get out before he was buried under a mountain of teeth, fur and pain. While the beast still kept its fangs in Tomas's shoulder, Tomas felt the talons slam into his ribs and begin to tear him apart. Moments later Tomas's world exploded in a miasma of debilitating agony as Savad's hindquarters pulled up and he back-pedaled razor claws into Tomas's abdomen, eviscerating him with every stroke, gouging through his armor like so much tissue paper and tearing muscles from his thighs and groin. So enraged and elated was he by the fury and blood coursing through his veins as well as down his throat, that Savad didn't even feel the puny arrows of the Valkyries thud into it. All it knew was the taste of the hot coppery blood of his lord's quarry pumping down its gullet, and the visions of the rewards it would receive when he delivered the man's head. Savad was too enraptured to hear the sound of flapping growing louder above him. It would have alerted him to what was coming, but he was beyond recall at that point so when the first of the demonic scouts slammed into him he was still lost in his own delusion of victory. It was Savad's last thought.

'Leave him, Treya. You can do no more.'

Treya looked up icily at her friend as though it were her fault that Tomas lay dying before her some hours after the battle. 'That's where you are wrong *yet again*, Ingrid.' Treya knew she shouldn't take out her feelings on her friend, but her continued thorniness towards Tomas had finally found a weak exit point in Treya's armor and her contained annoyance slipped out before she could rein it in. 'There are several things I can do. Firstly I will sit with him until he either dies or succumbs to the change. If the former, I will burn his remains and send him to Valhalla, as befitting a warrior who I believe saved your life during the fight.'

Ingrid had the grace to look at her boots briefly, silently acknowledging that fact.

'If the latter,' Treya continued, 'I will kill him swiftly, saving him that degradation and agonized existence.' Treya then, for the first time since she had dropped to her knees beside Tomas, looked up at Ingrid. Her blue eyes, moist like two liquid sapphires, instantly froze the heated response that was Ingrid's natural reaction to the rebuke.

'I don't understand your feelings, Treya; you barely know this man, and all he has brought us since joining with us is pain and death. He is better off dead, as would we be.'

'How dare you?' Treya burst out, indignation and hurt welling up in her voice, but Ingrid was not about to be chastised again.

'I dare, Treya Thorsen, because It was *I* who had to slice the throats of my own sisters and listen to their pegasi cry their death knell as they went up in flames before my eyes – rather that than suffer the indignity of the change, as you so succinctly put it. We have had very few run-ins with the hounds in all this bloody war since we allied ourselves with Be'elzebub. Now...' Ingrid stabbed an accusatory finger at her friend as though she could drive her words into her soul, '...now, we have lost more sisters in the few days we have been with this *human*, than I care to count.' Her use of the word human held so much contempt in it that Treya flinched as she spoke. 'And I hold *you* responsible, Treya, you and you alone. There is a reason warriors of the sisterhood bury their feelings against the temptations of the flesh. It is against distractions like this that get them killed.'

Treya's expression burned with the conflicting anger and shame of her friend's words, but it only drove her to vent more of her own bottled up emotions. 'You have grown colder than the frozen hearts of the ice giants,' Treya spoke heatedly. 'The Fimbul Winter would be warmer than your soul by comparison, Ingrid. Just because you have never known love, how dare you accuse and condemn another for experiencing something you seem incapable of.'

Treya knew as soon as the words had left her lips that she had overstepped herself, and instantly regretted her outburst. But the sudden hurt in Ingrid's eyes told her it was too late to retract them, and something between them died that moment, forever lost and separating them by a chasm that could never be crossed or healed.

'It was never coldness, Treya, and as for love, well, I love you like a sister,' Ingrid replied, her words forced through pressed lips, her muscles tight with the contained hurt. 'Duty, devotion and love for the only family I had left. But now I see how it is, how you truly felt. I always thought you believed in me, understood me, but now I see you merely thought me an emotional cripple, forever stunted and handicapped by my past, though it was perpetrated *against me*, against my will by the very *species* you now simper over.'

THE ADVERSARY

Treya had lost her will to argue so instead she simply glowered at her friend, if indeed friend she still was. How a few words could inflict more damage than a hundred swords.

'There was a time, Treya, when the world would have trembled in fear to hear your battle-cry across the fields of war as you swooped down from the storm-driven sky to harvest warriors for the glory of your lord and that of Valhalla. Even the cold and distant Morrigan respected our prowess. Would they tremble now, I wonder?' Ingrid, however, didn't wait for any response from Treya; instead she turned on her heel and spoke softly over her shoulder so Treya had to struggle to hear her words as she walked away. 'Do what you will, just don't expect me to help. But whatever you choose to do, do it quickly. I have no desire to fight anything else today, and wasting the daylight for a dead man is not my idea of how to avoid such a thing. When you are ready to go, I'll be here with your pegasus.' With that, Ingrid strode away across the burnt and scorched grass, where she had already watched her sisters' funeral pyres with a broken heart and tear-filled eyes.

Treya knew she was right – *Damn her* – but she didn't want to admit it to herself. Had she not allied them to Tomas and his cause, then maybe her sisters would still live. Then again, maybe not. They were in a war after all, and one of mindbending proportions where even mighty Valhalla was under threat. This went beyond even the Ragnarok Odin spoke of, and that which the ancients prophesied, but Tomas had convinced her that his mission could avert the entire war by taking out the Adversary directly. She dared to believe such a thing was possible and had embroiled everyone she could into the plan. Even Be'elzebub had been swayed enough to commit all to the battle plan. But somewhere in all this blood and death, emotions she didn't even think she had had asserted themselves and handicapped her better judgment. This travesty was the outcome. Yet for the heart-wrenching sorrow that blazed through her soul at the loss of her sisters, she knew they fought as valiantly as they could and all had died glorious deaths. They would have asked for no more. Something deep within her told her that Tomas was important. She had felt it like lightning dancing along her nerves when she had first encountered him – the feeling of destiny. Her mother had always been vague about her gifts but her father, Thor, had greatly respected them and consulted with her regularly regarding her visions. Treya never believed she had inherited any of her mother's prophetic capabilities; she wasn't even sure for that matter what they were exactly. She had rarely dreamt as a girl and when she did, it was of battle. Often as not, it was of battles she found herself fighting some days, weeks, even years later. It was this foresight that elevated her to battle captain in such short order. She had a sense of the way the fight would go and it enabled her to utilize her warriors in the most beneficial way. This ability meant that fewer of her warriors fell, and cultivated a sense of invincibility in them. *So much for that*, Treya thought bitterly. Treya sighed deeply and looked down once more at the apparently sleeping man who was the cause of her dilemma. At least he was still breathing, though for how much longer was anybody's guess. The cloak she had draped over his horrific wounds hid the sight from her eyes but not from her memory, and more tears filled her eyes as she wondered for the hundredth time how much longer he would survive.

Treya still couldn't think clearly. She hadn't been able to shed the confusion and fear that had threatened to overwhelm her from the moment she had seen Tomas fall beneath the teeth, claws and savagery of the biggest hound she had ever seen. She had done too little too late to save him and were it not for the arrival of the scouts – timely, if not, sadly, too late as well – he would be in a far worse condition than the one he now still fought against. And it was this tenacious yet tenuous grip on life that kept Treya by his side, rather than just leave him as she knew she should and would have done once, not long ago either, in favor of the mission and safety of her sisters. Her head ached. There were so many strands to the web that clogged her mind and shrouded her vision of what she should do next. Ingrid was right, but Treya knew *she* was right too. *I have to be.* The whys and wherefores were just too numerous to count. She would go mad with the recriminations of what she could have done, would have done and should have done. If only… Those words were poison and they could render the strongest incapable of function, especially if they were allowed to worm their insidious way into the spirit. No, her future was tied now, inextricably, to this human in ways she was yet to discover. Of that Treya was sure. It was about the only thing she *was* sure about right then. He just had to live long enough for her to actually discover them. Treya spared a swift guilty look towards her friend, who was sitting up, immobile upon her steed, sword ready across her lap and bow with arrow nocked in her grasp, gaze fixed on the treeline. A penetrating and sweeping gaze that Treya noted sadly, purposefully took in *all* before them *except* her. The eyes just didn't make it her way, avoiding her with a deliberateness that speared her soul. Ingrid was watching for the slightest movement that meant more trouble. Treya's heart lurched at the sight of her friend performing her duty as she saw it in spite of the hurt Treya had dealt her with her cruel, harsh and thoughtless words.

'I don't suppose you've got any water handy? Or even a beer? I seem to have something of a thirst on me.'

Treya spun to see that the source of the voice was real and not some enchantment conjured up by a hopeful and distraught mind. It was real; for she could plainly see Tomas lying there, miraculously propped up on his elbows and looking at her with a mixture of relief and curiosity, eyeing her as though he had just risen from an afternoon nap, not the near-death experience he had just suffered. Emotions exploded within her breast and threatened to overwhelm her all over again. Joy, relief, wonder, anger and confusion. All warred within her for dominance and she must have looked a sight to the prone Tomas. Maybe that was why he seemed so intrigued by her face. Then he spoke again and she found out why he scrutinized her with such annoying intensity.

'Are you...crying?' Tomas asked tentatively, quite unsure how the fiery and volatile Valkyrie would take such a discovery of her apparent emotional weakness. He didn't really want a clout around the head right at that moment: he still felt like he had been run over by a truck. Several times; and one with spiked wheels too. But she didn't hit him. Instead she simply rubbed the back of her hand across her cheeks and smiled, laughing a little weakly at the discovery, glancing quickly at the moisture she had collected as though she had never seen tears before. *Maybe she's never seen her own*, Tomas thought. But then he remembered the pegasi and their tragic deaths when their riders died, and then wondered how could she not. A sudden rush of memories took away Treya's comment as images of teeth and the snarling slavering face of the hound came thundering back to him, followed by the screams of more pegasi passing. The sudden surge caused him to fall back groaning, eliciting a squeal of panic from Treya, who fell forward and grasped Tomas, rearranging herself to be able to cradle his head in her lap.

'Tomas? Tomas? Speak to me. Are you okay?' Treya knew the stupidity of her words as she said them, recalling the severity of his wounds. *Of course he's not okay. What am I saying?* But she could think of nothing else as he closed his eyes and groaned in pain. But as he writhed with inner torment, the cloak she had cast over him – to both cover the terrible and gaping wounds and exposed internal organs, and take the sight of the wreckage from her eyes – fell away. It wasn't that she hadn't seen such mortal damage before – in fact she had inflicted similar atrocities herself upon her enemies – but this time they were upon someone she found she cared for. Treya wasn't prepared for what she saw though.

Tomas's exposed chest and groin lay in full view of her astounded eyes. His clothing and armor still bore the evidence that he had been rent from thigh to shoulder by a beast with one thing on its mind: to tear, shred and eviscerate. His bloody torn clothing was hanging in tatters around his now intact ribs. Muscles, that only a short time ago were hanging limp and wetly on the outside of his body, torn from his violated skeleton, were now flexing and twitching as Tomas moved perfectly beneath unmarred skin. Treya stared with eyes that found it hard to believe what they were seeing. Other than a small scar just to the left of his navel, there was no evidence at all that Tomas had been attacked by anything. In fact, were it not for the ruined and bloody clothes he still wore, Tomas could simply be in the throes of some awful nightmare.

Suddenly, with no warning, Tomas's eyes snapped open and he sat upright, drawing in a massive yet ragged breath as though he had been under water and fighting for the surface long after his air had run out. Treya sat back on her heels and released his head where she had been soothing it, and waited to see what he would do next. She half expected him to fall back dead upon her lap, the wounds returned and the image of him healed dispelled as fantasy from her hope-filled mind. Instead, she watched him look around, taking in all about him. His gaze rested briefly on Ingrid, who as it turned out, was busy looking the other way. She hadn't yet seen his apparent recovery.

'I remember more bodies than I'm seeing out there, Trey. What happened?' Tomas turned to look at her, his expression expectant, waiting for the answer. But she couldn't quite get her words out.

'I...Er...the scouts. I mean they came back and cleared up.' That was about all she could get out to begin with until her composure reasserted itself.

'What do you mean: cleared up?' Tomas looked about one more time but nothing had changed. He screwed up his face in concentration and grimaced at the same time, clutching his chest. 'Where did the bastard go that attacked me? I remember something huge and grey hitting me, then pain, then nothing until a few minutes ago. Though I am sure that I didn't kill it; in fact I think I was losing if the phantom pain I'm still feeling is anything to go by.' It was the only way Tomas could describe the searing pain that still gripped him. Like the lingering pain that often remained after a limb had been removed, either by surgery or by accident. During the course of Tomas's work, he had – partly through necessity and part through occupational hazard – spent time with various doctors. One had once described to him a plausible theory about phantom pain. What he could remember was that the whole body vibrated at a certain frequency, every single molecule. And that vibration, powered by the electromagnetic field, left a resonating echo when the limb was removed. And because it resonated at the same frequency as the body, the body picked it up like a radio signal and transmitted whatever the limb was feeling before it was removed. Most of the technical details had sailed right over Tomas's head when he heard this reasoning, but the principle stuck. He had grasped basic scientific principles back then but when it came to the *weird shit* – as part of him still referred to his *change* – that had happened to him over the past couple of weeks, he felt like a child that had a gadget and only found out what it could do some time later, and then by accident rather than design. Apparently his mind wasn't quite ready yet for the healing part of his gifts and it still thought his body ought to be shredded and gutted. And boy, that was *just* what it felt like.

'The scouts came back as you were being attacked.' Treya tried, unsuccessfully, to put the image of Tomas being gutted aside as she recounted events. 'They ate the bodies, or most of them anyway; they think one maybe two escaped.' Treya shrugged at Tomas's raised eyebrow of surprise. 'There's no coming back from that,' she explained easily, 'and it is what you could call a permanent solution to the hounds' nigh on invulnerability.'

Tomas gaped as the image and the vague memory coalesced before his inner eye. Part of his consciousness must have been watching the event to provide such pleasant Technicolor detail. Tomas grimaced again at the sight. 'They ate them?' incredulity still evident in his voice. 'But there had to be at least a dozen, if not more. How?'

Treya was nodding as he spoke. 'True enough, but they are like snakes in that respect.'

Treya then kindly described how they managed such a feat. Tomas shuddered; another image he didn't want. He wasn't a big fan of snakes since during an early solo mission which meant he had to hole up in a smallish cave several miles outside Las Vegas, where he was to silence a particularly loudmouthed senator who was busy talking to all the wrong people. As it turned out, this cave was full of sleeping and chilly rattlesnakes, which he only discovered shortly after his body heat roused a few curious individuals, wriggling over him and scenting him as a potential threat. He never felt less threatening, ever, than he did that day. It taught him many things too. Other than how to lie so still whilst trying to lower a heart rate that was so loud in his ears it threatened to deafen him permanently; he learnt to check his damn caves a far sight better in the future. It also helped to carry anti-venom of the indigenous poisonous things if he was going into their world. Bloody spiders were another problem altogether. And he didn't like them much either.

'They will probably not eat now for several months,' Treya continued. 'Once they have digested what they want from the bodies, they will regurgitate what they don't need. I've only seen them do it once and that was enough for me, let me tell you. It smelt unbearable, and it was disgusting to watch the acids dissolve the remains until only a smear on the ground remained.'

Tomas tried sitting up a little more and the cloak fell away completely, causing Treya to look away suddenly as he did so. Too fast and too contrived and it caught Tomas's attention as to why she was behaving oddly like that, but before he could say anything, the light breeze playing over his bare flesh told him all he needed to know. Looking down at himself he saw his nakedness down to mid-thigh and with a flush of embarrassment himself, he willed his clothes and armor to repair themselves – something it seemed they didn't do when he was unconscious. He coughed to indicate that he was decent again.

'Sorry about that. You should have said. Though I wouldn't have thought you Valkyries were all bashful like that.'

Treya harrumphed and quickly covered her action by resorting to her usual gruff demeanor. 'Yes, very well. If you're okay then I suggest you get up; and let's get going. We've wasted enough time waiting for you as it is. Ingrid is furious with us both and wanted to kill you while you slept.'

At the mention of her name, the surly Valkyrie spoke up. She had cantered over when she saw Tomas sitting up. 'Back away, Treya, and I will dispatch it for you if you cannot bring yourself to do it.'

Both Tomas and Treya looked at Ingrid like she had grown a set of extra limbs and two more heads. 'What the bloody hell are you on about, Ingrid? Dispatch what? There's nothing here but us now.'

Ingrid had raised her bow and drew a bead on Tomas, momentarily confusing him all the more. He scrambled back as best he could to put distance between him and the crazed woman with the large bow. 'Whoa there. Easy with that. What are you doing? Why are you pointing that at me?'

Then it clicked. But Treya still looked confused.

'Treya, I'm only going to say it one more time: back away before he changes. Either back away or kill it yourself.'

Treya was looking between Tomas and Ingrid when her penny finally dropped. Instinct made her reach for her blade and it was half drawn before she stopped herself and stepped between the two. 'Put it down, Ingrid. If he was going to change he would have done it by now, not heal himself then hold a conversation. It doesn't work that way and you know it.'

'But by his own admission, Trey, he's different.' Ingrid moved past Treya to get her shot back. 'Maybe those gifts from the Horsemen affect him in more subtle ways. Maybe it slows the transformation or gives him control over it. Either way, he's been bitten. More than bitten by what I saw and nothing survives a bite from a hound, Trey. Nothing.'

Tomas tried to placate Ingrid before she fired that monstrous bow of hers. 'I'm all right, Ingrid, really. Please put that down before you do someone, namely me, a mischief. I'm not infected, nor am I going to sprout teeth hair and run around with the urge to bite people. Pestilence saw to that. At least I hope she did. All things being well, I'm immune to their infection; and Death, bless his miserable and dour arse, said I was hard to kill, thanks to his gift. Though it's a hard thing to verify until, you know, something like this happens. Trust me; it's not something I want to repeat anytime soon neither. So please put it down, will you?'

As if to emphasize his explanation, Bran swooped out of the trees and alighted on Tomas's shoulder. Fixing Ingrid with its obsidian eye and cawing out to her, 'Healed! Healed!'

Tomas smiled. '*Good to see you, Bran. Glad you're Okay.*' He was growing quite fond of the strange white raven that had appeared and even more strange – though Tomas was not ungrateful – befriended him.

'There you go. An independent source.' Tomas looked at Treya and saw her appraising him. She caught his eye and he winked at her. Tomas smiled at the sight of her blushing, caught in the act of doing something she shouldn't. Though she had no idea that Tomas didn't know what was going through her mind, she felt guilty all the same and mentally dispelled the image of Tomas lying naked under her cloak. But she still felt her cheeks warm at the gesture and she swore under her breath and strode off to fetch her mount, leaving him to sort out his own problem with Ingrid. He was big enough and ugly enough to deal with her, so she left them to it. Tomas summoned Storm and the ghostly steeldust stallion solidified beside Tomas, saddled and keen to go. He pawed at the earth, iron-shod hooves gouging furrows in the soil, wound tight with barely contained anticipation. But when Tomas stepped close and whispered to the intelligence he knew existed within that form, their eyes met and Storm lowered his head passively for Tomas to make a fuss of him. Which he dutifully did. Because for all his aloofness and equine pride, he did like his head scratched.

'If I was one of those hounds, Ingrid, don't you think Storm or even your own pegasus would behave a little different?' To drive Tomas's point home before Ingrid drove hers, he walked, palms out towards her and her own mount. Bran flapped away and settled on a branch to watch. She pulled back further on the string and Tomas heard it creak ominously, but he had to get her past this foolish notion. *Understandable reaction, I suppose, given what these hounds' reputation suggests, but I really don't have the time for these sort of games. It's enough I have to worry about every other bastard trying to kill me, or worse, without worrying that one of my own companions wants to fill me full of holes. Though truth be told, she probably wants to do that just for the hell of it anyway. Even so...*

'There, see? Nothing.' As Tomas reached a hand out to touch the velvety soft nose of the magnificent beast. Ingrid's eyes went wide in mortification at the prospect of what Tomas intended. He thought she was going to shoot him just for doing that. Yet the pegasus allowed the contact and even sniffed his fingers, dark sensitive nostrils flaring, wary but curious hazel eyes fixed on the man before it, and wings flicking in a distinctly birdlike way as it drew in Tomas's scent. Even a battle-trained mount would shy at something as potentially dangerous as she was making him out to be, standing *that* close *and* rubbing its nose.

'Look, Ingrid, here we go again.' Tomas recalled earlier conversations that went along a similar thread. 'I get you don't like me; I get that you see me as some sort of threat to you and Treya, on several levels too, I might add, not just a physical one. I even get the anger you've carried for so long. Believe me, I've got my own share of baggage and anger management issues to get a handle on, but I am at least trying. As I recall, I saved your life out there. Not because it was you and I was trying to score some brownie points with you.' He ignored her bemused look at his choice of words. 'There really wasn't time for that. I just did what I did because that's what warriors do. They save each other's lives when the time comes to do so. At least back where I come from they do. There's a code that binds them together stronger than any steel forged chains and I can't even conceive of them willingly or knowingly breaking them. You watch your back, the backs of your comrades, and they yours. Plus, you never leave a man...or a woman behind.' Tomas knew in the dark portion of his soul he had done just the opposite on several occasions as his role demanded more of him than merely his integrity and honor. He hated that sacrifice of himself, but the years had hardened him to the reality of what he did. But now, however, wasn't the time for that degree of honesty. *Coward.*

'We've both lost friends today. I feel for you, really I do. You lost sisters and I lost Niall. Granted I didn't know him for long, but he was my responsibility, do you understand? *Mine.*' Tomas hissed the last word out with a vehemence that startled both of them as his guilt surfaced, tempered with the anger he felt at himself for failing the man. 'I feel his loss as deeply as any, more so because he was an innocent. You and I are warriors; we expect death.' Tomas pictured the stoic Horseman's face as he spoke and shivered. 'We confront that spectre every time we draw a weapon and engage the enemy. We know that that fight could be our last, yet still we go forward into the unknown; we do what we were trained for or bred for. We kill to the best of our ability. I don't know about you, but I've no desire to end my life any sooner than I really have to. I don't want to die, nor do I want those associated to me to die, and that includes you, Ingrid, and you can choose to believe me or not. Either way, you need to put that bow down and accept we are alone now. Just we three, and that, Ingrid, puts us at a very real disadvantage if we need to fight anything else. Look what happened last time. Where are your sisters now?'

'We have the scouts. That make's us nine,' Ingrid retorted hotly, emotion choking her thought process from any real argument yet still trying to save some face. But Tomas wasn't hearing any excuses from her, not now. She needed a reality check and Tomas was in no mood to pull his punches.

'Really? Fat lot of good they were last time, ranging too far ahead as they were. It was all bloody over by the time they got back. If it wasn't for my gifts I'd have been royally fucked. So, we either keep the scouts closer and lose our advantage of surprise of having them as a concealed ally from anything else chasing us, or let them carry on doing what they do. That said, then we are only three and likely to be screwed if we get attacked again. Truly buggered unless we get our shit sorted and start working together as well as trusting each other. And pointing that bloody bow at me isn't a great way to start. So I'm going to mount my horse and ride away; you may have a choice but I've still got a job to do and I fully intend to do it. If you want to shoot me, you'll have to shoot me in the back. It's your honor. So fill your boots.'

Tomas turned angrily away then and strode to where Storm stood patiently, eyeing proceedings with a suspiciously dark orb. Every step Tomas took, he fully expected to feel the impact of three foot of arrow punching through his back, but he made it to Storm unmolested. Mounting and holding out an arm for Bran, encouraging the raven to alight and roost upon his shoulder as he rode, and keeping his back to Ingrid, Tomas cantered across the short distance to where Treya sat on her own mount, watching the whole thing, her own gaze alternating between Tomas and Ingrid, her own thoughts in turmoil at the prospect of what she would do should Ingrid let fly. Would she alienate her friend all the more by going to Tomas's side, or support her friend for the real fear she thought justified? It wasn't something she wanted to have to choose. Treya hoped and prayed to Odin the All Father, that Ingrid saw sense and put the bow away, trusting to faith and the trust Treya herself put in this human; in his association to the Four Horsemen of the Apocalypse.

ᚦᛗᚠᚾᛟᛗ ᚱᛋᚠᚱᛋ

It was this very association to the Absolutes that was currently being questioned back on Earth. Death had stopped abruptly mid-conversation. An alien sensation ripped through him and it took him a few seconds to fathom its origins. They had just arrived back in Britain, close to the original meeting place of Tomas and Michael, atop the enigmatic Silbury Hill. It was the first time in several days that they had come together, each having had missions of their own to attend to, battles to fight, and minions of the Adversary to send howling into oblivion. They were battle weary and showing signs of having a hard time of it. The fighting had been fierce and many of the Celestial Host had fallen. Matters weren't improving across the globe either. If anything they were deteriorating, as city after city fell to the increasing might and ever expanding numbers of demon incursions. Humans fought valiantly. Their armies rallied and threw their collective might at the invading hordes, but with little lasting effect. Iron was what hurt these creatures and there was too little of it in the ordnance of mortals. The Horsemen and the warriors of the Celestial Hosts did their best to educate the human soldiers but it was slow work incorporating the deadly element into their weapons, not to mention convincing them of what and who it was exactly that they were fighting. It took several demonstrations to convince the skeptical mortals who it was

– with commendable patience it might be added – that was trying desperately to help them. But once Death, War, Pestilence and Famine turned their mind and phenomenal abilities to convincing someone, there would be no mistaking their convincing. It became indelibly imprinted on the poor souls' DNA; stamped eternally in them much like a stick of rock candy. Belief would now be found in every single cell of their bodies. But it didn't help with the ever increasing numbers of possessed corrupting the process and hindering matters wherever possible. It was whilst they discussed their most recent findings that Death felt the searing pain of Tomas's demise at the claws of Savad, the Hound of Fenris. Momentarily he felt a surge of power through the connection, that both excited then almost instantly deflated the dark garbed Reaper. For it confirmed that firstly Tomas *had* survived the transition to the Domain through the Al'Mayakin gate, but had, after only a short time of that survival, subsequently died there. It was a double blow to the grim Horseman, but there was little to do other than mourn the mortal, again, for his effort, and press on with the war, at least for however long they had left before the Adversary managed to complete his infernal scheme. A scheme that, much to the continued consternation of the Horsemen, they had been unable to fathom entirely. All they knew was that it entailed reaching the core of the Earth; or at least as close to it as he should have been able to get.

Beyond the density range of mortals and between that of Mars and Venus, lay the Earth's final protection from external influence and invasion. It was *the* Labyrinth: the influence for all others that humanity grew aware of, from the Neolithic cave drawings to the Sumerian cults and the Minoan Bull legend. It was a vast ring that surrounded the heart of the Earth; accessed by seven fantastic gates that only her avatars, the Horsemen – for all was within their sphere of influence and law, even the sentient planets – and those with sufficient power could penetrate. It was power so great that not even the Drakarim or the Unc'anharaphim combined possessed it. Needless to say, there were few entities in the entire multiverse with that sort of capability – none the Horsemen were aware of anyway. But they were grumbling a lot these days about matters they were finding they were *not* aware of. Their carefully constructed system was collapsing around their ears more and more each day. To say they were not happy was the understatement to end them all.

But they knew that even should the Adversary gain access to the deep maze, he would need the seven keys to pass all the way through to the core and the Earth's heart. These *keys* were not keys as such, but receptacles of power that even in their altered form were in fact the missing keystones for each portal. They had been scattered shortly after the formation of the Labyrinth and not even the Four Horsemen knew of the whereabouts of all of them – a fact that rankled them, particularly War. He was fastidious over such matters and the continued absence of the keys vexed him. *How can you defend something when you have no idea where in the entire multiverse it is?* Though in reality, he knew they had to be on the Earth somewhere; it was just the *where* that got to him. It was one of many liturgies he muttered when the subject of the keys came up. It came up a lot these days, for they knew that the Adversary had at least four already. History spoke of certain items of power repeatedly through many cultures. The stories varied, as did the nature of the keys, but the central theme was wholly accurate. For the keystones, as they really were, through dark enchantments of the Nephillim, became altered or re-forged, if you will. Such transgressions were part of the reasoning for their exile, for they had committed many more heinous acts to warrant such an exile; but over centuries and centuries of searching, and at great cost to their number, a few of the more powerful managed to obtain many of these keystones. They utilized their awesome and innate powers to bolster their own dark magics, then reshaped them from the raw mineral form they were originally cast in, and turned at least three of them into weapons. The world became aware shortly thereafter of a sword, a spear and a bow – all bearing exceptional properties. The fourth they were aware of was turned into a vast cauldron, imbued with both incredible regenerative and degenerative powers.

Upon the capture of the Nephillim shortly after the transformation of the keys, the keys were dispersed among the Ch'drnOmThophilim for safekeeping. It was, and still is, the curse of their shame that now motivated the Children of Thought to fight so hard alongside humanity and willingly sacrifice themselves in this cataclysmic war. For it was the Ch'drnOmThophilim who eventually lost the four keys to the Adversary's agents. There were still three more loose in the ether, and no one living had ever seen them. Not even before the Ch'drnOmThophilim left the Earth for the last time, selfishly leaving humanity to fend for itself as they slunk off to lick their wounds and bemoan their lot. The Horsemen, who had become equally distanced from mortalkind, hoped the keys were sufficiently well hidden to stay that way. The Ch'drnOmThophilim left in the belief that if they, humanity's gods, couldn't find the lost keys, no one could, and then matters would remain in balance if nothing else. How wrong they were, for the Adversary had bent all his immense will to finding the first four and in doing so, every clue he could that would steer him towards the last three.

Now, the more the Horsemen learnt about the Adversary, and the more battles they fought, they could only – and with a heavy soul – accept that he now either had the last three or knew of their whereabouts, and was forging his way towards the portal that would take him to the Labyrinth. Why else would he launch an all out assault upon the peoples of the Earth now? Why pick this time to manifest and expose not only himself – as the subtle power behind the throne of Hell and as being Lucifer's hand – but that of his recently gathered armies, and unleash their fury upon the Earth's plane? It drew the Horsemen to that one depressing conclusion: his goal was in his sights. And that they, in their arrogance and misguided self-belief in their ability to stop such things, were too late.

The Adversary had chosen the portal that through his sublimely dark influence, under the guise of benevolence, he had Solomon build below the ancient fortress of Megiddo. Partly due to its isolation from prying eyes, the convergence of the dragon lines, and also in part due to the imprinted history of the land that made it the perfect location for the ceremonial temple. There had been many conflicts and battles fought upon that soil, both prior to and since, with too many of them involving those guardians of the Celestial Host and demonic the agents of the Adversary – with so much spilt blood, laden with arcane energy, that it flowed into the soil and empowered the land, fuelling the great dark enchantments laid there, and it was those that enabled the Adversary to thwart the Covenant and take form there himself, albeit only for short periods of time to begin with. But it was enough for him to complete the process he had set in motion. Then it had taken the deaths of the Earth's guardians, executed over centuries, to finally gain access to this portal's entrance, as its protection and location was one of the closely guarded secrets they held; for even though Solomon had built and designed the structure under the guidance and influence of the Adversary, he had still managed to wield enough of his own free will and underestimated intellect to shield and secure the most important aspects of the temple, initially from his enemies and those not initiated into the mystical practices. But it was good enough to thwart the Adversary too. Soloman was thus a thorn in the Adversary's side and a great hindrance to his grand scheme, but the Adversary was nothing if not patient. He swore retribution on Solomon, all who were born to his bloodline, and every single guardian who defied what he saw as his right. The guardians had fought for centuries to hold the agents of the Adversary at bay, prohibiting him the access he needed. But as each guardian was found and slaughtered, he moved inexorably closer to achieving his goal.

A side effect of the Adversary's malevolent sorcery had been to draw violence and discord like a malignant black magnet. His magical machinations were even strong enough to attract several of the dark meteors or void stones, as they were known to the higher beings, which were either current or former gaols of exiled beings. These were beyond malevolent and they corrupted all they encountered, allowing vast amounts of negative energy to pour into the land around wherever they crashed to Earth, subtly twisting the views and perceptions of the people who lived there. These void stones were immensely powerful and were highly sought by magicians and sorcerers, who endeavored to utilize their power. Unable to contain their evil, they created such turmoil and conflict that the wars and deaths that followed began to soak the land in even more blood, which just perpetuated the Adversary's accursed evil all the more, and fuelled further the great spells he cast there. It is believed by the more powerful sorcerers still at large on the earth that what humanity calls plutonium is nothing more than distilled and ancient void rock.

It was during the many crusades that swept across the Middle East in particular, and the unimaginable numbers of deaths that occurred then, that the corruption of so many innocent souls was caused; and that had swollen the Adversary's power a hundredfold, spreading his foulness across the world all the more. There have been events since then that added to the soul rot under the influence of the void stones. The Third Reich were the most recently influenced by their darkness, as can be seen by their use of mystical symbology and imagery throughout their ranks. But it was during those dark days of the Crusades that the Adversary's infernal influence had been felt the strongest, and even the leaders of the world's religions had no defense from his insidious influence. The jealousy-driven and irrational slaughter of the Knights Templar was a fine example, for their order, accused of heretic practices and of being in league with the Adversary, were in fact devoted to *defending* the Temple from the great enemy. It was a great victory for the Adversary to rid himself of so many earthly guardians in one vile coup. They knew far too much and would have posed a considerable threat to his demonic ambitions. It was even from them that he managed to acquire the fourth key: the Spear, entrusted to their keeping by the Ch'drnOmThophilim during their time at the Great Temple of Solomon. Due to their persecution and disastrous propaganda, much of which continues to this day, the order crumbled, and after that, those few who survived the carnage of their eradication were driven deep underground and lost to history and the eternal war as they went into hiding. Though that was due to change.

The Horsemen knew that wherever the Adversary had been and plied his dark arts, human war and inhuman atrocities soon followed in their wake. It was a vicious circle that was almost indestructible. Any other pertinent knowledge the guardians had was now either lost or in the nefarious hands of the Adversary, none of which boded well for the Horsemen and the warriors of the Celestial Host, let alone the vulnerable and potentially doomed humanity. If only they hadn't lost Tomas so soon. For now too much depended on the untried and newly awakened avatar of the earth: Tomas's sister, Gwen. The only trouble with that was, that should she succeed in finding the First Tree, granted she would be able to restore many of the Celestial Host and empower them to hopefully defeat the Adversary, but it would signal the beginning of a prophesy Death had hoped would never see the light of day. It would be the catalyst for yet another sequence of events that stood to annihilate humanity. Death sighed at the futility of it all. Doomed if they lost and doomed if they succeeded, it simply fell to which path they took. The Adversary's was plain; it was laid out before them already. The path of the Tree was enshrouded in darkness and uncertainty. It was the one view of his future that Death was blind to and if his associates knew anything of it, they had never mentioned it. Death was convinced that the spirit of Fate was a malicious and mischievous joker, taking great pleasure in thwarting his orderly design for the worlds within his governance. It was only then that Death realized, for the first time in his multiversally long life, just how weary he was. He expected to feel considerably worse too before the war was over.

ᚦᛗᚠᚾ◇ᛗ ᚱᛋᚠᚱᛋ

Tomas was still weary too. He still felt pain from the wounds he had suffered juddering through his flesh and bones as Storm – as gentle and smooth a mover as any mode of transport Tomas had ridden on or in – made his way across to Treya and caused him to grit his teeth against the waves of pain. Those few seconds seemed to take an age while he waited for Ingrid to make her choice, but it allowed Tomas to make one of his own. It had just come to him, flashing in his mind like lightning. *Maybe that was what an epiphany felt like,* he mused as he reined in. But as he pulled up before Treya he formulated the words in his mind that would convey his plan whilst waiting for Ingrid. He knew she wouldn't shoot him as he sat beside Treya, because that would only drive the wedge he noticed had formed between the two women, even deeper.

He spared a glance behind him, relieved all the same to see her putting her weapons away and shaking her head. He could see her mouth moving as she did so and Tomas winced at the very unladylike curses and promises of vengeance she was no doubt muttering, thanks to him. *Ah well, what's a few more to add to the long list I've already got stacked up against me. Hung for a sheep as hung for a lamb, they say. Well, I must have a whole bloody flock by now.* Tomas laughed a brief and strained laugh at his predicament, soliciting further scrutiny from Treya. Ingrid silently cantered up and reined her own mount in on the other side of Treya, putting as much distance between herself and Tomas as feasibly possible whilst still remaining in close proximity to Treya.

'Fair enough,' Tomas directed his comment to Ingrid whilst looking at Treya. 'Good choice though, Ingrid, and one I thank you for.'

She just snorted and waited for him to continue. He plunged himself into Treya's eyes for a second or two, having a similar effect on him like a plunge pool after a good sauna. It refreshed him a little.

'I've given it some thought, and if you choose to come with me, I'm making a diversion. I know what we spoke of with Be'elzebub but things have changed. That frantic fight for our lives with those hounds changed it. I'm heading directly to the valley entrance Be'elzebub spoke of in whatever that mountain was called again.'

'The Tartarus Mountains,' Treya offered. Tomas nodded, still uncomfortable with the hellish names of places here. 'But why? That is not part of the plan. You are to wait until he arrives there and we are due to attack from the rear, freeing the lord Lucifer. I will have a scout inform him of the change of plan.'

Tomas was furious and snapped at Treya a little more harshly than he intended. 'No you bloody well won't,' he barked. In a voice only slightly less harsh he carried on, 'That is the whole point of the deviation. I don't want him knowing where we go. In case you've forgotten, we have only just survived an attack by creatures of this realm. Who is to say our destination wasn't compromised. And how many beings knew where we went?' Tomas let the implication sink in. 'No, I want to be on the *other* side of the valley when Be'elzebub arrives. Considering that we now have fewer forces to attack with, we need a change of plan. As far as he is concerned, he'll either do what we intended or he'll be looking for me in altogether the wrong places. I won't be a sitting target, Trey. Now you two, as I said before, can either come with me or do your own thing. I won't hold it against you if you choose to leave. You have lost a lot after all, and I hold myself responsible for that.'

'So do I,' Ingrid added caustically. Tomas just glared at her and shook his head. But before he could speak, Treya interrupted them both.

'I'm coming with you, and so is Ingrid. We owe our sisters vengeance and we do them no honor by walking away from a fight. We are with you until our last breath and will go with you wherever you choose to go.' Treya turned to her friend and added for her benefit, 'Won't we, Ingrid?'

Ingrid in turn glared back at her friend with undisguised disgust at the way she lessened herself, in Ingrid's eyes anyway, before this man. But to her credit, though her eyes betrayed her, she acquiesced and nodded her agreement that she too would remain with his cause.

Tomas read the looks and huffs between them as agreement and inwardly he was pleased they were staying with him. There was something beyond fascinating about Treya that he couldn't put his finger on but he knew it would leave a void within him if she was not near him. That disturbed him and pleased him in equal measure, and even Ingrid, for all her bluster and daggerlike stares, was a solid companion. He had known soldiers like her back on Earth and once they got their frustrations out of their system and you proved yourself to them, they became invaluable and stoic friends.

He hoped she would become one of them; the alternative wasn't worth contemplating: Ingrid as an enemy. He shuddered at the thought and put that vision away.

'So how do we do this? I have been relying to an extent on you girls and the scouts to pathfind, but now we need to deviate you'll need to let the scouts know, and we'll need a direction. I want to get there by the shortest possible route, taking the least time. I want to see this valley before everybody else gets there and recon all my options before I run out of them. The fewer individuals who know my movements…' Tomas caught the flinty looks from Treya and Ingrid and amended his sentence, '…*our* movements, the happier I'm going to be.'

Ingrid closed her eyes and Tomas felt a chill slide down his spine like iced water pouring down it. Something in him felt the connection between the Valkyrie and the scouts. How could that be? His gifts didn't extend to others yet that was exactly what it was. Tomas knew something was wrong with him, something fundamental. The black moods; the ever-present anger just simmering below the surface, waiting for the opportunity to erupt; spontaneous violence and the desire to see copious amounts of blood flowing just wasn't him, but he had no idea what to do about it or what could be causing it. When it struck, it took all of Tomas's will to fight it lest it consume him. When it did, it felt like drowning in black freezing water and he had to fight like crazy to keep his head above the thick, viscous and choking water. He knew if he let it drag him under, he would never surface again. That thought filled him with dread but all Tomas could think of was he was suffering some kind of side effect of the Horsemen's gifts. Even they didn't know exactly how they would affect him. Moments later Ingrid confirmed what he had felt, that she had relayed the new course to the scouts and they had shown her the way and were now adjusting their search parameters. She pointed to the trees and it just so happened to be the darkest and densest section of the forest that they were in. Tomas's shoulders slumped in resignation.

'Isn't that just typical. You couldn't point out the sunny and easiest to traverse route could you, oh no. Why is that? In a three hundred and sixty degree circumference, the other three hundred and fifty-nine look fine and passable, yet the way we have to go looks a bastard. How are we supposed to get the horses through there?' It did indeed look darker and more forbidding than the rest. The trees seemed gnarled and twisting inwards to block the way, and the ground was choked with barbed and tangled briars.

'We don't,' said Ingrid. 'We walk. The pegasi will meet us on the other side and you can do whatever it is you do with your mount, can't you?'

Tomas wasn't pleased, but he tried not to let his disappointment show. Time was his enemy but everything conspired to thwart him, making him take longer to do what he needed to do. 'It seems convenient that the way we need to go looks the hardest. Do you reckon there's a reason for that? I mean, this is Hell, or the Domain or whatever. Does something know something we don't? Not that I'm a suspicious and cynical git, you understand, however…'

Treya adjusted her weaponry and dismounted before speaking. Ingrid did likewise. Both stood silently, looking towards the forest for several minutes before Treya spoke. 'That way, towards the Tartarus Mountains as you know, is the realm of Charon. I imagine it is his way of deterring visitors. The Reaver is a secretive being and few have ever had dealings with him. We certainly haven't since we've been here. And all those we have been in contact with recommend strongly and in no uncertain terms to avoid his realm wherever possible. I imagine it is only a mark of the severity of what we face that Be'elzebub even agreed to set foot upon his lands, though he should be safe enough, being a demon lord of the upper echelon. Charon and Asmodeus hold similar status but where Be'elzebub and Asmodeus are active in the council of lords, Charon has rarely attended and keeps to his lands, or so I hear anyway. It is supposedly why he retained his neutrality to date and abstained from choosing sides. Though I suspect what we are planning may force his hand.'

'Won't he try to stop Asmodeus from crossing the pass in the first place? If he's moving an army through his lands without his permission, wouldn't that be seen as provocative?'

Treya shrugged uncertainly. 'As we discussed back at camp, we don't know that Asmodeus *doesn't* have permission. That's what makes this so risky: we could end up with a fight on two fronts, and of the two, and I'd rather tackle Asmodeus than the Reaver.'

Tomas groaned and scrubbed his hands through his hair, then across his face, and ended up rubbing fingers over the bristly growth on his chin as he looked thoughtful, his gaze taking on that distant look as though he could see what was happening in the valley already. 'We'll have to risk it. I have little choice right about now. If I can get Lucifer free...' Again Tomas laughed abruptly at the irony of what he was saying, eliciting more concerned looks from the Valkyrie, '...then he might be grateful enough to help me get to the Adversary. If anyone knows the way into the palatial fortress he's holed up in it ought to be him. There are so many variables to this plan, so many things that can go wrong and send it all pear-shaped, that if we had any sense we'd just pack up and go home, but we don't have that luxury so we'll just have to play it by ear and ad lib when we have to. If this Reaver interferes, then we'll just have to cross that river when we come to it.' Tomas giggled inanely at his own jest but the two women just looked at him blankly. 'Get it? Cross that river? Ferryman? Oh, never mind. It's never the same if you have to explain it and I never was really any good at jokes.'

Treya said 'Ah' as though she finally caught on to what he was saying. 'So that was jest? Were I you though, I would stick to fighting and be grateful you don't fight as badly as you jest, otherwise we would all be doomed before we start.'

It took the rest of the day and most of the next for the pain that hampered Tomas to pass. Having to use the Sword of War to hack the way clear seemed a bit ignoble for the blade, but the work loosed and strengthened muscles previously shredded and pummeled by the fight. As evening drew in on the third day, he felt much like his old self again.

Bran and Ingrid had hunted briefly, for though Tomas might not need sustenance, it seemed the Valkyries still did, though like camels, it appeared they could go long periods without. Tomas, however, kept his comparison to himself: he didn't think it would go down too well.

While they cooked and ate, he moved away from the women and went through some shadow fighting with the sword, rolling his shoulders and loosening his neck by tilting his head to either side. A couple of hours later he was winding down after chopping several logs to matchwood, which served a useful purpose for fuelling the fire for the night. It had been a double-edged choice: to build a fire to keep undesirables away, or not build it for fear of attracting said undesirables. But the light and warmth were welcome in the inky dark, dank, and at night, ice cold forest. But it was while he was scooping up the wood fragments to carry through to the fire that he saw something he couldn't believe at first he was seeing.

Back on Earth, many, many years before, Tomas had spent some time in Michigan with a group of militia men there. Patriots who had formed their own military organization and who were well provisioned and exceedingly well trained. Many of them were experts in forest lore, some through being ex-military and others through generations of woodland hunting; Tomas learnt much about the various signs and how to convey information and mark trails so that only those conversant in the forest language could read them. It told those who knew how to read it, which path to take to avoid traps, what traps were there and how many men to expect. What Tomas was looking at on the bark fragment, was a sign as clear as day that said there were men here: trained men and a lot of them. Tomas stood abruptly, his mind racing, and spent the next couple of hours scouring the woods in the failing light looking for more signs. When the light failed, he summoned his night-vision headgear and carried on. He found three more markers as well as several footprints left in the loamy soil, and what they implied didn't encourage him at all.

'Call the scouts back in' were Tomas's first words the moment he stepped back into the firelight. Treya and Ingrid were sitting cross-legged upon the ground and were both systematically cleaning and oiling their weapons.

Treya looked up, concerned, while Ingrid just carried on, paying him no heed.

'Why?' was all Treya said, though the word was tinged with more than a hint of concern. Tomas rolled his eyes in frustration.

'Am I going to have to explain *every* single thing *every* single time something needs doing? 'Cos if so, this is gonna take a painfully long time and it's time we don't have. So if you don't mind...' Tomas's voice was rising as his temper flared, '...order the bloody scouts back here or teach me how to do it and I'll do it myself.'

Both Treya and Ingrid immediately got to their feet, their faces like thunder at this unexpected rebuke. Tomas felt only a hint of shame at the way he spoke to the two women, but his anger overrode it. 'So now you're up, tell me: how's your woodcraft? Seeing as you're both sitting there minding your own business, I don't suppose you've noticed anything out of the ordinary?'

They looked at each other and Ingrid closed her eyes, telling Tomas she was in communication with the scouts. When she opened them again her expression changed dramatically; from hostile and spoiling for a fight, to curious and instantly wary.

'The scouts are returning, but how did you know what they have seen?'

Tomas shook his head and handed her a fragment of bark. 'I didn't, but I'm betting they've just told you that there's sign of a large body of men not too far from our present location.'

Ingrid nodded that he was correct and added a bit more he didn't know. 'There is also a large structure roughly a day's walk from here. It appears to be some kind of fortification.' Ingrid frowned as she spoke. 'Though there is no demon lord we know of who lives *within* these forests, and especially not as close to the Reaver's realm as it would be.'

Tomas looked thoughtful himself for a moment or two, trying to ascertain the who or why. Again, there were too many variables to make him completely comfortable. 'We can only assume loose facts. That the fortress is either still under the rule of this Reaver; and whoever might still be in it, assuming it's inhabited, is working for him. Or, it was some abandoned fortress that the forest has grown around and these men are using it for their base. Which means that they could be doing any number of things.'

Treya asked, 'Such as?'

'They could be brigands, mercenaries, or those bastards who hunted Niall might be using it for a base. Those as well as countless other variations on a theme. I have to consider those options as possibilities, but based on what I found out there, I'm not so sure.'

Tomas looked thoughtful and this time it was Treya's turn to give an exasperated sigh as she waited for him to explain further. When he didn't she snapped at him. 'Well, spit it out, man. What have you found that draws you to such enigmatic conclusions? No secrets. To trust each other implicitly, we Valkyries hold no secrets from each other – that now includes you – so say what is on your mind.'

Tomas took the bark fragment back from Ingrid and paced back and forth before the smoldering embers of the night's fire. Tomas looked briefly at the dying flames and gave them a stir with his booted foot and tossed the bark into it, eliciting a shower of sparks and some vicious crackling as the flames hungrily devoured the small snack he had thrown it.

'It was in the footprints I found. You see, military people tend to be fussy about their footwear. Having to spend long periods of time in them and subject them to all manner of weather conditions, they become something of a vital bit of kit. But even though a good soldier will spare no expense on his boots, they tend to use only certain brands.' The two Valkyries started to look a little lost. 'Bear with me. Now, I'm not bad at hunting, but it is people that I usually hunt and, like tracking any other animal, you learn to read their signs. What I found out in the woods tells me that there are men out there who are wearing specialist boots that are only available in a few places. I can even tell by the tread patterns in the soil what sort of boot they are.' They still looked uncertain, so Tomas demonstrated by clearing a patch of soil and imprinting his own boot into it. 'There! You see. It leaves a distinctive pattern. Now based on the depth of the imprint, I figure they are either big heavy men or they are loaded up. Either packs or weapons or both.' Tomas knelt down beside his print and poked at it with his finger, highlighting depression and depth. 'Judging by the angle of depth and that some of them were well spaced, it meant that some were running at one point; Adding to that, the tracks went both ways: the depressions were close together coming this way and wide spaced leaving. It suggests they know we are here and they've hightailed it back to report. Finally, there is moisture in the prints, indicating they are reasonably fresh.'

Ingrid immediately drew her weapons and began scanning the thick forest for anything suspicious, which, based on the fact it was pitch black beyond the firelight, was just about everything. Tomas held up a placating hand.

'Easy, Ingrid. If…and it's a big if, they are the sort of guys they imply they are by their gear and woodcraft, then we have little chance of seeing them by day, let alone in this darkness. Even when I used my own ability to penetrate the night, I didn't see any close by.' He used the ambiguous description of his tri-nocular night-vision goggles so as to not confuse the medievally minded Valkyries. Tomas doubted the women would see them even in daylight. When he trained with the militia he actually stood on two of their snipers. So well concealed were they in their custom fitted gillie suits, and loose net overclothes that were so filled and tied up with foliage and color blended strips of fabric, that they were almost invisible in the wilderness. The true experts even knew how to disguise their scent if they were caught upwind. Tomas sat down himself and stretched his legs out in relaxed position.

'You may as well sit down and wait for the sun to come up.' As he spoke, the six demonic scouts scuttled back into camp and settled themselves in a protective ring around the group. Tomas watched them carefully, still a little unsure of their motives.

'We'll be at a distinct disadvantage wandering around in the woods in the dark trying to find them. My guess is they already know where we are and if they want to find us they will; if not, we'll go find them tomorrow in the daylight.' Tomas added under his breath about what passed for daylight anyway in that twilight world within the woods.

Tomas felt no desire for sleep, and found it hard to close his eyes even feigning it, but he wanted to give the impression he was resting. It wouldn't do for any nocturnal observer to see him walk all day, remain awake all night, then walk all the next day. It would arouse suspicions about him and he wanted as few things known about him as possible. These were, he hoped, soldiers not unlike those he fought with back home, even as recently as Potter and the marines at Al'Mayakin. They expected the world to be black and white, right and wrong, good and evil. They liked their people straightforward too. If they shot one, they expected them to die. If they saw Tomas's wounds from his encounter with the hound, even they would probably burn him for witchcraft for getting up unmarked from that. So if he was to appeal to their sense of honor or whatever soldiers' code they adhered to, he didn't want them thinking there was something not right about him. What they didn't count on though was Bran.

'*Are you there, my friend?*' Tomas sent the thought out to the battle raven, unsure if the huge bird slept at night or was nocturnal like owls or the like.

'*Yes, I am here, Tomas, though I am sleepy. There is a small type of wild rabbit in this forest that is quite tasty and I have fed well.*'

Tomas pulled a face at the image Bran sent of him feeding. One foot on the carcass and pulling ribbons of flesh from its bones. '*Thanks for that. Did you have to be so graphic? I was with you at the "I've fed well" bit. Now I need you to do a bit of night flying for me. Are you up to it?*'

Bran grunted reluctantly that he was, though he would rather not on a full belly. Tomas sympathized, but only so far. He expressed how important this was and tried showing an image of what was out there. Bran chortled at the sight of men looking like bushes.

'*Be careful though; these bushes are dangerous and may have weapons like mine. Weapons that fire hot metal faster than you can fly, and many more than a bow can send.'* Tomas felt the seriousness of the threat register with the raven and he felt a confidence from it that it would take more precautions now than perhaps it would have done before.

'*I take it you want me to see how many of these walking bushes are in the area and tell you where they are?'*

Tomas mentally nodded, then wondered how that worked precisely, so added that was exactly what he wanted.

'*Very well. It may take a little time, so await my call. I will show you what I see when I see it.'* Bran broke the contact and Tomas got the impression at that fleeting moment of the spectral white raven taking flight on silent wings.

It was just as the sun was rising, a couple of hours later, when Bran called to Tomas, who responded he was ready. Fact was, Tomas was more than ready. His usual patience was wearing thinner here than any other time and Tomas was at a loss as to why, which only frustrated him all the more. Not so long ago he recalled that he could sit immobile for hours, even days, as he stalked his quarry or hid from pursuit. Now he was champing at the bit after only a few hours. Tomas endeavored to keep the impatience from his thoughts as he asked whether Bran had found anything.

'*Several things, as it turns out. Your camp seems quite popular.'* Tomas grimaced and prepared himself for the images of their whereabouts. '*There are a few close by, but the majority are gathered about half a day's walk for you slow two-leggeds. I will stay ahead of you and point them out to you as you draw close to them. And be aware, for you were right: they do have weapons like yours, only bigger, certainly longer. Try not to get weapon envy, I know how it is with you human males; you gauge effectiveness on how big or long something is, as though it is a direct reflection upon your masculinity. Though I don't suspect you are that insecure, are you, Tomas?'*

Tomas sensed Bran's caustic bird humor overlaying its words and he just pulled a face of disdain and sent that image to Bran, who laughed raucously. Tomas heard the cawing from where he sat.

'You're talking to your bird, aren't you?' Treya's husky voice wafted over to him from where she lay upon her side, watching him. Tomas hadn't seen her move. In fact he had tried not to look at her all night as she reclined back and stretched her own long, muscular legs out: a move that only caused her battledress to ride even higher up her thighs. It was a sight Tomas only looked at the once, for it caused all manner of thoughts to unleash themselves within his fertile mind and run rampant. Urges and sensations coursed through him suddenly, and the desire to take her roughly swept through him with such intensity that he groaned outwardly and rolled away from them. It was only by gripping the red hot end of one of the brands protruding from the fireplace, pain breaking the flow of images, did he manage to avert his gaze at all and move to the other side of the fire, putting both Treya and Ingrid in shadow and removing the temptation to look further; thus allowing areas of engorged anatomy to settle to a more comfortable position. It had panicked Tomas for a while back then, because as before, he knew – he didn't know *how* he knew but he did – that those feelings weren't entirely his. *Where the bloody hell is that shit coming from?* He had never been like that before. Tomas knew the depths of his own depravities and even admitted to many of his sexual fantasies, but the urges that flowed uncontrollably through him now were not his. Sexual violence had never been one of his kinks but it pervaded his thoughts with increasing regularity. The desire to throttle and punch even as he rutted, filled his mouth with a coppery metallic tang that made him spit. When he did, he found he had been biting his own inner cheek, lip and tongue, for apparently the taste of blood excited him all the more. No doubt if he ever succumbed to one of these terrifying urges, and lost control of himself, he got the impression that he would bite whoever was unfortunate to be under him, severely too. These fears and worse pervaded Tomas's thoughts as Treya lay there waiting for him to answer her.

'Sorry about that. Daydreaming for a while there.' *Nightmare, more like it.* 'But yes I was. Bran has been quite revelatory. I'll fill you in as we go. Let's bury the fire and be on our way.'

Within moments they were back on the forest trail. This time, however, Tomas had kept the scouts behind them; he didn't want whoever was out there to see those creatures first, though if they hadn't already, Tomas wondered just what they would make of them. And he very much doubted it would be friendly. From somewhere, though, they had withdrawn hooded cloaks and had bundled themselves up, and hid many of their potentially terrifying features away. So at a distance they more resembled large bulky people rather than the murderously lethal demonic minions they were.

Every now and again Tomas would either get an image from Bran regarding a watching soldier, expertly concealed from human eyes, but not from the extraordinary vision of the ghostly raven as it glided through the trees above them. Or, Tomas would spot some sign, etched into a tree or by the way some low foliage had been broken, that told him as much as Bran showed him.

The small group of nine changed direction several times as they stumped their way through the woods and dense foliage, occasionally having to hack away at some stubborn briars that had impeded their path. But for the most part, the forest sign left by the soldiers or by Bran's direction was enough to keep them on a clear path.

'*There is a large concentration of the walking hedges a little way ahead of you. The first is by that mossy log fall, just to the left, at the height where your leg bends.*'

Tomas stopped the group and concentrated ahead of him, trying not to look directly at the spot Bran pointed out. It took a few moments of close scrutiny, but at last he saw what he was looking for: the distinctive shape of the rifle barrel poking out at him, draped in camo tape and strips of Hessian, and plant dangling from the barrel to break up its shape.

'Just to be on the safe side, Ingrid, is this the right direction for that old fortress?'

Ingrid consulted with the scouts, who said that it was. Then Bran added his own information: '*I have seen the fortress from a distance; it is big with a wide killing strip before it. It will not be easy to approach undetected.*'

Tomas smiled evilly then and looked around him. 'I don't intend to approach undetected. I expect these fellows lying in the grass here to take us in as guests.' Tomas spoke loudly, ensuring that the nearest of the snipers heard him. But nobody moved, as he expected. They were trained to lie perfectly still even if someone, like he had, walked clean over them. Bran started slipping images into Tomas's mind of the whereabouts of the rest, and his eyes nearly dried up as he relayed the mental images to his optic nerves and he sought them out. He had to remind himself to blink on more than one occasion.

'Okay now, enough fun and games. You know I'm here and I know you're there. The fact that I am here means that I've avoided enough of your traps for you to know I can read your basic woodcraft. There are at least eleven of you lying on your bellies out there and two up the trees to my left and one up the tree to my right, not forgetting the three behind me.' Tomas thought he heard an urgent mutter from deep in the foliage, but he carried on anyway. 'Now, unless you are too scared to come out and talk, preferring rather to skulk in the bushes, I can go with that. I'll just take my people here and go and knock on the gates of where you are no doubt calling home, but I assure you of this: if I have to do that, you'll need new gates. I'll give you a minute.'

Tomas turned immediately to Ingrid, feeling that of the group she was the most volatile. Even the scouts wouldn't act without permission unless matters were as dire as before, but by then, with their diminished numbers it probably wouldn't make any difference.

'No matter what happens in the next few minutes, I want you to remain calm. No pulling weapons and shooting people; no brandishing swords, axes or knives or anything else you've got secreted about yourself. Do you understand me, Ingrid?'

She nodded, with barely restrained violence and anger at Tomas for telling her what to do like some child. *That bloody woman is more hazardous than walking around with half a dozen bottles of nitro stuffed in your pocket. I swear she would fight with her own shadow, given the chance.*

'What's your name?' came a shout from somewhere within the trees. Tomas smiled. They had cracked first. *Bet they were surprised I knew their locations. Ha!*

'Tomas. Tomas Walker, and that's as much as you get until I see a face.'

'State your business!'

This time, Tomas detected a hint of an accent, Welsh, if he wasn't mistaken. 'I'm sure you're not as stupid as you seem. That was another question, when I asked for a face. I do not hold long conversations with any old disembodied voice. Now show yourself or you won't like what happens next.' *That ought to stir them up a bit*, Tomas thought mischievously. He actually hoped they played stubborn and remained silent and still. Which was exactly what they did do. Tomas knelt down and picked up a handful of fist sized rocks, and then, with accuracy born of years of knife throwing, he proceeded to toss them at the concealed snipers. They were big enough to leave a bruise if they landed. By the time Tomas had bounced rocks off nine of the snipers, the voice piped up once more. This time the Welsh accent was distinctly evident. 'Righto, fella, you're starting to piss me off now, so why – '

His threat was cut off as Tomas finally got a bead on his location and he lobbed a coconut sized rock at him. Tomas had been privy to enough baseball matches on various bases to have a reasonable pitching arm and, much to his satisfaction, he was rewarded with a resounding ding, as the rock careened off his helmet. 'Ooowww, shit. That bloody hurt, you bastard.'

Tomas smiled maliciously at the reaction. He had assessed their dedication and resilience amidst the rock barrage and even though he knew they knew he knew where each and every one was even though he shouldn't, they remained at their posts, and that showed discipline. He guessed they were pretty damn good at what they did. It was just that he had an unfair advantage over them. But now for his trump card, and that required no special ability.

'I'm sure that no matter what army you're in, that is no way to talk to a commanding officer. For your part, seeing as you're the one doing the talking, let me guess. Corporal? Certainly no higher than a sergeant otherwise you wouldn't be out here, you'd be tucked up all warm and cozy back at base with the other Ruperts.'

'Lance corporal, if you must know.' There was an edge of defiance still evident in the response, but it was now more colored by uncertainty. The prospect of a higher ranking officer was always something to be taken seriously. At least more seriously than he originally took Tomas's presence. 'So if you're a CO, why are you wandering around out here with a couple of women and that group of the ugliest looking monks I've ever seen, and where have you come from?' There was a heartbeat's pause before a 'sir' was added. Tomas mentally said an elated 'Yes!' He had them now; all he needed to do was maintain his composure and play out the role, as he had done on many occasions previous.

'That, my cautious Welsh friend, is for your CO to know and for you to speculate about. Needless to say, I outrank you and suggest that you and your men get up off the damp ground and step forward, that is unless the rank of major no longer holds the import here that it used to.' Tomas waited for the implications of disobeying a major to sink in, then he added, 'Now that you've ingested that little gem, call your men up and present yourselves front and centre. Do that and I promise we won't hurt you. You have a count of five.' Laughter drifted to Tomas from several locations as though they were amused by his bravado, but it only confirmed the locations he had earmarked earlier.

'You've certainly got stones for a man in your position, major or not. You're outnumbered badly and I'm sorry to say that you wouldn't be the first major I've had to kill in the line of my duty. I'm under orders to let nobody through. And even to one of my lowly rank, nobody still means nobody. So I suggest you turn around and sod off back from wherever the hell you came from...sir.'

Tomas smiled at the irony, but by now he had located the exact spot where Lancejack Welsh was speaking from. 'Fair enough, but that might be a little difficult about now.' Tomas started to walk towards the voice's location. 'Now you and I are going to talk; rather I'm going to talk and you are going to listen. You have to decide, however, how many men you want to lose before we get past this duty bollocks and we move on to more comfortable surroundings where the man who is paid to make the tricky decisions can actually make one.' Tomas had taken no more than three steps before half a dozen bushes stood up and trained their weapons on him. At least three red dots appeared on his chest, which Tomas duly noted and silently increased the Kevlar levels there, discreetly beneath his existing armor. They weren't, however, expecting the sudden and raucous laughter that erupted from Treya and Ingrid as they beheld walking and talking bushes. Tomas saw the almost imperceptible nod from lancejack and he braced himself for the impact. One round slammed into his chest, taking him back a step. Treya and Ingrid immediately stopped laughing and their weapons were in their hands faster than the eye could follow. But Tomas held up a hand to stop them, aware as well of the reactions from the gunmen to the fact that he hadn't fallen dead with the heart shot. Tomas turned deliberately and spoke calmly. 'Wait! Don't kill them.'

Matters were escalating rapidly and could turn very ugly very quickly unless he did something. Tomas knew he needed to diffuse the situation quickly. 'By the way, Welsh, did I forget to mention I'm hard to kill?' Tomas drawled as he continued towards him. 'But that's not to say I want any more of your goons taking potshots. You get that one for free because you know no better, but should any of you try that again, I promise you that most of you won't live to see the shot hit.' As he spoke Tomas kept walking until he was only a dozen paces from Welsh. The lance corporal stepped out fully from behind the tree that concealed him and leveled his weapon at Tomas, who immediately noticed it was the latest issue SA80 assault rifle. At least it was the last time he saw one. It was either black market or these boys were British forces.

'That's quite close enough, boyo. I'm sure that however hard you are to drop, my chances from here are fairly good, wouldn't you say?' Welsh grinned. It was a skewed sight as he was covered in camo cream and dirt. The sight of pearly teeth beaming at him from a bush was a little incongruous, but Tomas held his hands open in the gesture of peace and smiled back, except there was no humor in Tomas's response. He was, unbeknownst to both groups, fighting the rising urge to manifest the sword and wade into the soldiers, hacking them to pieces for their lack of immediate obedience. It was Tomas's will against whatever it was that tried to force the berserk rage upon him. The soldier before Tomas only saw the grim visage of the man, not the intent behind the eyes. He sensed it was akin to standing nose to nose with an alligator as it smiled at you.

'You are right, Welsh, but what is the point? I would be dead and so would you, with most of your men following you, and that would achieve nothing. Instead, why don't you and several of your men escort us to the fortress, where I can meet with your CO and let him determine what happens next. You are only respecting the chain of command, after all. Now I've been very patient up until now, but there is only so much of that to go around and I'm starting to run a little low, so consider this the last time I am going to ask you. Refuse me once more and we will be going through you and your men, which I have to say is a terrible shame because even though you're behaving like an arse, I quite like you. Don't figure.'

Welsh had the look of someone who really wished it was another standing where he was instead of him; indecision was written all over his face. 'You say it will get really messy if I don't?'

Tomas just nodded slowly. He imagined Ingrid and Treya were fit to burst by now with the other soldiers all pointing their rifles at them but he hoped they held for a few seconds more. Tomas sensed Welsh was close to coming to his senses. 'You say that I'll be as dead as you if I squeeze the trigger and put an end to you?'

Again Tomas nodded slowly and this time, as he did so, he raised one empty hand slowly as if he was going to place it on the soldier's shoulder. Instead, the Sword of War materialized and three feet of shining steel hissed into being, with the razor sharp tip resting against the cheek of Welsh. 'Squeeze that trigger and your head will hit the floor the same time as I do, if not a little sooner.'

Welsh started at the sudden appearance of the weapon but his jerky movement only caused the slightly thrumming sword to flick sideways of its own accord and slice open his cheek sufficiently for the blood to flow readily down his neck and satisfyingly, along the sword.

'That, son, is just a gentle reminder for you to remove your finger slowly from the trigger and pay attention to what I'm telling you. I've plenty more tricks up my sleeve if you'd like to test them. Now, I'd like to be your friend and believe me, that's a better place to be than where you're heading with this indecision. *Now choose!*' Tomas's voice rose sufficiently to get the attention of the rest of the group. Several took their eyes off the two Valkyries and watched Welsh to see what he would do. Long seconds passed as the blood trickled down his cheek, the sword not once wavering from the flap of skin it had sliced open. Tomas's eyes were locked onto Welsh's and Welsh saw something there that made his mind up for him. If he feared anything in his life, it paled to insignificance compared to what he saw in Tomas's eyes in that moment. Slowly and sensibly he raised his weapon and flicked the safety on. He held the other hand out to his side to show it empty and away from his sidearm.

'Stand...down, guys!' The order was a bit quivery as it was hard to talk with a sword jammed against your face, but that was infinitely better than the alternative.

'Very good choice. Why couldn't you make that sort of sensible decision earlier, without having to make us resort to threats?' In less time than it took for eye to blink, the sword changed once more to Tomas's Heckler and Koch snubnosed MP5K and a red laser dot appeared on the bridge of Welsh's nose. 'Be grateful I didn't just put a round between your eyes and move on to the next in command. I urge you to not underestimate me again. Now on a friendlier note, do you have a name or do I call you Welsh all the way to the fortress?' Tomas even heard one or two sharp intakes of breath at his display. *Good! It'll pay to keep them unsure of just who they are dealing with until I know a little more about who they are and how the bloody hell they ended up here, 'cos they sure aren't behaving like a bunch of guys who know they are in Hell. I'm betting they have no clue as to where they are, which makes meeting their CO even more of an interesting prospect. Either he knows and he's not letting on, which makes him dangerous, or he doesn't know and hopefully he'll appreciate the heads up. Though neither option really answers why they are here, in the middle of nowhere, relatively speaking. This really is going to be an interesting meeting. Meeting a demon like Be'elzebub kind of speaks for itself: you know where you are with that, but people...now they are infinitely more untrustworthy. Like serial killers, I suppose, they just look like everyone else until they stab you in the back.*

'Toby Stevens. Lance Corporal Toby Stevens, former Royal Fusiliers... sir.' There was that pause again, just before the sir was added. It was as though he was uncomfortable using it. Then the word *former* flagged up in Tomas's mind. He hadn't heard it at first, just accepting the name and rank. Then the penny dropped.

'Thanks for that, Stevens, but what do you mean: *former*?'

Toby looked a tad sheepish at the admission, as though he should have mentioned it earlier. He shrugged and grimaced slightly at the prospect of explaining himself. 'Long story really, sir, but in a nutshell, we're all formers. Some honorably discharged, others dishonorably, some simply disillusioned with the way things were being run, and one or two vets who took their retirement but missed the rush too much.'

'Go on!' Tomas prompted. 'None of that explains why you're all skulking around out in the woods as though you are on some sort of training maneuvers, kitted up as though you still work for Her Majesty's goon squad.'

Toby shouldered his weapon so it sat more comfortably as he waved to the rest of the men to do likewise and gather around them. 'We all work for private security firms now; you know: hostage recapture, anti-terrorist protection and all that kinda stuff. In fact there are three companies here. As you figured, they're back at the fortress. The colonel recruited us all to hunt down some big time terrorist leader, real loose cannon, apparently.'

Tomas's eyebrows lifted with disbelieving curiosity. 'A terrorist? Just one? Three firms for one man? Who on earth is that dangerous? Even Bin Laden didn't get that many mercs after him, and who would front the cash to pay for three whole firms? That's a lot of resource.'

Toby nodded his agreement. 'You don't have to tell us, but we're not complaining: we've seen half the fee banked already. We're promised the rest on completion. Easy money so far.' As he spoke, the wound on Toby's cheek started to bleed again. His talking kept the wound open, defying all attempts to staunch the flow. Toby eventually called another of the soldiers over, who pulled out his med kit and began work on closing the flap and mopping up the blood.

'Good call. That much blood can attract things here much in the same way it attracts sharks out in the open water.'

Toby asked what sort of things, between stitches.

'Let me put it this way, Dorothy, you're not in Kansas any more and there are things here that will make your darkest nightmares look like a picnic on a sunny day.'

Toby didn't look too happy at that and Tomas sympathized with him, because there wasn't really an awful lot to be happy about. The way things were back on Earth when he left it were bad enough, but what he found himself embroiled in now, and where he found himself presently, topped that by a long shot. All in all, Tomas reasoned, life sucked big time. He tried to remember what actual *normal* life was like when he was a newbie in the corp. His whole existence was governed by what he was told to do next. Run, stop, shoot, eat, shit and even breath. He was kept in the dark about so much and the big picture was an elusive concept, the sole possession of the Ruperts. It was for them to know and for him to do as he was told. But the more he learnt, the more jaded he became with not knowing the facts that dictated his future. He looked at Toby and the men now gathered around him, and saw the same look on their faces. Wary, skeptical, and as Toby had said before, disillusioned. They were looking lasciviously at the two Valkyries and suspiciously at the hooded minions. Treya and Ingrid, along with the demons, hadn't come forward to join the group yet and still held a way off, glowering at Tomas, no doubt. Probably not a bad thing as yet, Tomas thought, keeping them back – they had a habit of complicating things without saying anything – but he changed his mind about one part of his burgeoning plan: he hadn't intended to tell these guys anything about their situation until he had spoken to their CO, but on finding out that they were privateers, he reassessed them. Their CO should have really confided in them more than he obviously had. Soldiers of the private sector needed to communicate even more than regulars, and trust each other a lot deeper than the average squaddie, though he doubted any of these guys were average – because the only people you had to rely on when the shit hit the proverbial fan was each other. There weren't battalions of reserves and air support and all the rest that went along with being a regular, waiting for these guys. The chain of command was much shorter when you fought for money like these boys did, and it galled Tomas that they were being kept so very much in the dark, for he doubted they would be so blasé if they truly knew where they were.

'When you've finished being stitched up by your man there, I'll show you something that might determine if you're not being stitched up by your

CO.' This comment got the attention of several of the soldiers and drew a few 'what do you mean by that remark?' comments.

Toby batted away the medic just before he had finished, Tomas's statement demanding his full attention. 'Yeah! What *do* you mean by that? Accusing the colonel of fitting us up is a bit risky when you haven't even met him and don't know shit about why we are here. What makes you such a fucking expert?'

Tomas sensed the anger Toby was exhibiting masked another emotion – one that said that he had reservations of his own and that he felt guilty for having them – but to hear someone else validate them roused his buried suspicion again. 'Easy, Taff...' Toby stiffened visibly and Tomas saw his knuckles go white as he clenched his fists; obviously he didn't like the nomenclature. '...Remember, I'm on your side here and I'm here to help if you'll let me. Sorry about the Taff bit. I see that's a sore point but you shouldn't be so sensitive; it'll get you killed sooner rather than later if you let it get the better of you. Anyway, now I have your attention again; it's just a thought, but while I keep mentioning the vague *here*, do you know exactly where *here* is?'

Toby looked puzzled at the question; somehow it wasn't what he was expecting.

'What do you mean "here"? The woods or Canada?'

Tomas burst out with sudden laughter. So abrupt was his outburst that more than one of the soldiers whipped up the guns and looked about them jerkily, as though his bark had been a signal for a surprise attack. 'Canada? Shit! I know it's dull up there sometimes and the weather sucks, but it isn't that bad. Jeez! Is that where you think you are? Ha ha ha.' Tomas couldn't contain his ironic laughter any longer and his outburst drew anxious looks from all around. 'You poor sods, you're a bit further afield than that. Is that what he told you?'

Toby's face reddened in suppressed anger and a smattering of humili-ation, feeling himself the butt of someone else's joke. One he shouldn't have fallen for but had. Through gritted teeth he asked what was so funny. He wished afterwards that he had never asked that particular question. Not when Tomas explained it to them, and definitely not when Tomas introduced them to the demonic scouts by way of a *demon*stration.

It was several fraught hours later by the time that Toby and his band of soldiers for hire had calmed sufficiently for reasonable conversation to resume. Tomas had been bombarded with questions about how this could have happened and how true all he had told them really was. He had gone over it several times in as many different ways to convince them. By then Treya and Ingrid had joined the group. Tomas introduced them as Valkyries, which got a mixed reception from a few. However, a brief display of the Valkyries' martial prowess, which left several of the men flat on their backs with various bladed weapons pinning them to the ground, coupled with the Valkyries' version of recent events, caused the men's eyes to widen like saucers. They looked less like rugged warriors then and more like rabbits trapped in the headlights of an oncoming truck. Which in a sense, they were. These men were just being used by someone considerably higher up. The sixty-four million dollar question was now just how high did the ignorance go. Did their CO truly know what was happening or was he as much a gullible victim as these men? That was what Tomas had to find out, and fast. These men could either help or hamper him now, always assuming they really were after a terrorist and not on some wild goose chase. Tomas wasn't so arrogant as to think of himself as the wild goose, but stranger things had been happening to him than this idea, though it would be somewhere beyond coincidental to actually run into the people who sought him. Ironic didn't touch it.

There was only one way for him to resolve this mystery and that was to walk into the lion's den himself and confront their CO face to face. Toby had told him that the three companies consisted of some sixty-three men in all, including the colonel. Tomas had to ask, but like Toby before him, Tomas found he had a habit of asking very stupid questions. Questions that had answers that left a bad taste for a long time afterwards.

'Colonel who, by the way? Who's running this outfit?' Toby supplied the answer and Tomas's heart sank. He was convinced that matters couldn't actually get any worse than they already were, but upon hearing the colonel's name, he was proved wrong – again.

'Colonel Alan Carmichael. Why? Do you know him?' Toby saw the look of dismay on Tomas's face and had his own answer. 'You do, don't you?' Allowing for all they had spoken of and all he had been through, Tomas should have said 'No, never heard of him', but that wasn't the case at all. Tomas *had* heard of him. He had even served with him, though only once, but that once was quite enough. Worst of all, Tomas had even been there when Carmichael's world had irrevocably changed. It had changed the man's soul as well, and not for the better, as anyone who had dealings with him thereafter soon discovered. It was his new-found attitude that had finally gotten him thrown – about as dishonorably as you can get – right out of the service, where, without the modicum of regulation and discipline that the military had provided, and the subsequent removal of ethical and moral constraint, he just got worse. A highly trained law unto himself.

'Unfortunately, and though it pains me to admit it, yes I do. Just how far has a body got to go to get away from the people who you really don't want to see. I'm on another fucking planet and this bastard still haunts me!' Tomas growled. He wasn't happy and it came off him in waves. Images sped through his mind of the numerous encounters he had had with the infamous colonel as their paths crossed over the ensuing years and Tomas grimaced at the sight, his anger rising at the despicable things the colonel was known to have done. Just then Toby caught sight of something flit across Tomas's eyes and he recoiled suddenly in horror. Tomas looked curiously at the wiry Welsh soldier, cocking his head birdlike to one side in a distinctly *un*Tomas like way as he watched the strange reaction. Tomas took in the pale features of the soldier, his cornflower blue eyes and sandy colored hair. Now that he had removed his ballistic helmet and goggles the Welshman's features were more evident. A smattering of freckles dotted his nose, giving him a boyish look, though his killer's eyes removed that notion almost instantly. But the impression of boyishness clashed now as well with the angry red scar on his cheek, the field stitches puckering the wound, but even though it was expertly done, it would still leave a fine scar. A permanent reminder of his encounter with Tomas.

Physically, Toby was deceptive: he wasn't big, and nor was he tall, but Tomas sensed a strength within him, steel wire for an inner core. When he pulled his sleeves up, Tomas saw the corded muscles flexing beneath his pale flesh. Tomas was put in mind of a mink or weasel, for they too were small, lean and wiry but were ferocious when they chose to be. Keen killers and canny hunters with a sharp mind and equally sharp teeth. That was the impression Tomas drew from the youth as he scrutinized him, because for all his evident battle experience, Toby could only have been in his mid to late twenties, which to Tomas's early forties made him little more than a boy. In fact, for all he knew, he could have had a son his age, had he been inclined or bothered to keep track of any of the women he had used in the past. But Tomas didn't do kids so he paid the past no heed. But for all his swift appraisal of Toby, it was this last reaction that piqued Tomas's curiosity. It seemed the first genuine look of horror to cross his features since they met. Even the scouts didn't elicit such a reaction from the confident young man.

'What's up, Toby?' Tomas asked. 'You look as though you've seen a ghost. Something I said?'

But Toby was concentrating on Tomas's eyes, looking for something within them, it seemed. 'Nah, it wasn't what you said but what you did. Neat trick, 'cos it sure as shit scared the crap outta me. Just don't do that again without warning, will ya. It wasn't nice.'

Tomas's brow furrowed in confusion. *What did he see that scared him like that?*

'Sorry, son, I've no idea what you're on about.'

Toby looked around him for a sign that anyone else sitting close by had seen it too. None of his own did but Treya watched him intently with her own cool evaluating gaze. But even with her, it was a toss up whether she was going to speak or not. Tomas could see the indecision warring across her pretty features, as though by speaking she would be setting something free that she couldn't decide whether or not it should be. But she made her mind up and asked.

'What did you see, Toby Stevens?' She spoke to him softly, not wanting to spook him any further by blurting her question out at him, for she was keen to hear of someone else seeing what she thought only she had. Toby turned to regard her and saw from her earnest expression that she had indeed seen it too. Though not this time, he guessed, looking at her, but before, and she wanted to know if it was the same.

'You know, don't you? You've seen him do that before,' Toby answered a little shakily.

Tomas was getting annoyed now. Why the bloody hell were these two talking about him when he was sitting right before them like he didn't exist.

'He's done the eye thing in front of you too?'

That was it. Tomas stood up and glared at the two of them in turn. *Eye thing? What have they seen that has bothered them so much? It doesn't make sense.* 'What are you both blabbing on about? Treya? Talk to me.'

She didn't move during Tomas's outburst, but merely looked up at him calmly, and in a voice that belied her violent nature she asked him to sit back down again and stop behaving like a petulant child. But she explained anyway, just like she was talking to a child. 'When you get angry, Tomas, something dark moves through you and it manifests in your eyes. If you are unlucky enough to see it, which I have once and it appears Toby here just did, it is quite disconcerting. They change, Tomas, only briefly, but the change is profound and with it comes a feeling of dread. Am I right, Toby? Did you feel it?'

The Welshman nodded his head vigorously. 'Oh yeah! Too bloody right

I did. Thought he was going to take me out right there and then. Bloody eyes looked like some rabid crocodile, all sickly yellow with vertically slashed pupils, creepy as fuck. Never seen the like, nor, by the way, do I want to see it again, thanks. Jeez. I'm gonna see those bloody things in my sleep for ages now'

'Maybe it is a side effect of your gifts, Tomas.' Treya offered, skeptically looking at Toby pulling faces. 'Then again,' as she turned to look at Tomas once more, 'maybe it isn't. It seems too malevolent to be associated to something that was intended to be so benign. And Tomas, while we broach the subject, it seems valid to point out that you do this when you appear to be losing your temper or become angry. As though rage awakens something within you, your loss of control giving it an opportunity to express itself. Does any of this make sense to you, Tomas?'

Tomas for his part just stared at Treya with a growing sense of the dread she had mentioned. 'No not really, Trey. I know I've always had a bit of a temper but since being here it's been on something of a hair trigger. I just put it down to the influence of this place.'

'Ingrid thought you were berserk when she first saw you fight, but now I'm not so sure. You are too controlled in all other aspects to be a true berserk. It has to be something else that drives you, or through you.'

Tomas couldn't believe it. Someone else had *seen* and perhaps even recognized what he had only *felt* growing within him. This couldn't be good. Feeling ill was one thing but having physically manifested symptoms was another thing altogether. It was like confirmation of having some foul disease that previously you only worried about. Knowing it, however, hit home, like standing between two speeding trains as they collided. What he had secretly feared and tried to ignore was now a reality and that put a whole new slant on things. Not only did he have to worry about saving the bloody multiverse from some tyrannical and totally megalomaniacal demon lord, but he had to do it soon before whatever was affecting him did something irreversible to him and he couldn't do anything at all. Not for the first time, nor was it likely to be the last, but a litany of 'Why me' slid futilely through Tomas's mind. 'Why me?'

Night came suddenly and the men, along with Tomas's grudging consent, made a hasty camp, breaking out what few rations they had and building a couple of small cook fires to heat water and, as it turned out, to spit the few rabbits that Bran flew in with. Having seen the scouts and been told where they were, the soldiers, ever pragmatic, just watched, albeit suspiciously, hands never far from their weapons as the huge white battle raven swooped in and deposited its prey beside Tomas. The scouts – more to alleviate the soldiers' already heightened anxiety and tensions – remained on the outside of the camp, out of immediate view, and performing the duty they did best: watching, allowing all the men to come in from their numerous and varied hiding places and have some hot food. It also gave Tomas the chance to see all of them face to face – a habit he had developed, another lesson passed on from his father. He had always told the young Tomas that 'when a man leads another man, he should always remember that he is in fact a man, not just an asset or tool to be utilized and disposed of. For all you can, get to know these people who will serve with you, save you and defend you. For should they fall due to an order you give, they need to be remembered for who and what they were. It is your honor and responsibility to do this, Tomas. Their memory and their valor must live on with you, so always make that effort. It is the failing of so many command-ers who just reduce them to numbers, or worse: cannon fodder. Some do it in ignorance, but watch out for those who do it knowingly'.

Tomas always remembered his words but what his father failed to mention was how much of a burden that became. Every death he was responsible for became another weight tied to him. He already had trouble putting one foot in front of the other with the daily recurring faces of those he had either sent to their deaths or who had died because of him, screaming their accusations at him. *Where will it all end?* Tomas despaired silently, for the Horsemen had implied that should he live through this disaster, his life would extend beyond those of regular men. *Fuck! An eternity looking at those bloody faces doesn't bear thinking about. As it is they'll probably drive me insane long before that. Just as well I don't stand a snowball's chance in H...shit, here...of actually succeeding. I don't know about hero, I feel more like bloody Pac Man. I've even lost one life already if what Treya says is true about that damn hound.* Tomas descended into a silence all of his own and sat apart from the group for the remainder of the night, drawing concerned glances from Treya, annoyed ones from Ingrid and suspicious ones from the soldiers. Tomas's only saving comfort was Bran, who roosted upon his shoulder. The battle raven was proving to be an uncannily and unexpectedly welcome presence, suffusing Tomas with a warmth and feeling of tranquility he never thought to feel again, which although being extremely welcome, was at odds with the images of Carmichael and his atrocities that came and went through Tomas's head throughout the remainder of the night.

The long, depressing and melancholic night finally gave way to the renewed optimism of the new day. As the sun rose, so too did Tomas's spirits – a fact that both Treya and Toby were pleased to note when he sauntered back into camp and asked what was for breakfast. Not that he was hungry, but it was good to show the habit of every fighting man he had ever met. Start the day if you can with a good meal, because it just might be your last. Treya appraised him for a few seconds, and then smiled her own radiant smile whilst passing him a couple of dry biscuits and some greasy rabbit scraps atop them.

'Hmm,' Tomas said dryly, 'they look delicious. My compliments to the chef.'

Toby clapped him on the shoulder by way of greeting, easing the tension of the previous evening. 'Welcome back, chief, you look a bit perkier this morning. Get some sleep, did ya?'

Tomas just said, 'Something like that,' smiled weakly, and broke his fast, washing it down with a glug of water from Treya's canteen.

'Lovely,' Tomas said croakily as he passed the canteen back to Treya. 'Now we've got a long day ahead of us, so, Toby...'

Toby snapped a rough salute and grinned mischievously. 'Yes, chief?'

Tomas rolled his eyes in vague resignation. There was always one. It was just that somehow, Tomas always seemed to attract that particular one. He opted to nip this errant behavior in the bud though. He was never comfortable with his rank.

'We'll have less of that, if you don't mind. I might be a major, but a Rupert I am not, so lose the salute.'

Toby nodded solemnly, but though his face smiled, his eyes were grave and serious.

'I want you to bring all your lads back with you as you take us to the fortress. Our guys will stand stag for you.'

Treya interrupted, stating that there were no deer in the vicinity. If there were, they would not have fed on rabbit. Suppressing a chuckle, Tomas very quickly explained that it meant to stand guard duty and had nothing to do with venison, but it was better if the scouts remained outside for the time being and they would be more adept anyway at watching out for the more *dubious* things that might be following them. They had intentionally kept the details of the hounds from the soldiers. They didn't want to scare them too much too soon, not until they had at least gotten used to the fact they were in Hell, not Canada. Treya caught his gist and kept silent for the remainder of Tomas's initial plan, which, as it transpired, wasn't much more than getting inside the fortress walls for now. Tomas knew he was winging it, but until he could gauge the mood of the rest of the men, and just what Carmichael was up to, he would simply go with the flow. Tomas knew he had little to worry about at the thought of having to fight his way out if things turned ugly. Between his own arsenal and the added benefit of flying mounts, walls posed no barrier, but it would be a shame to have to kill innocent men to perpetuate what he hoped would be an unnecessary escape.

It was as they walked through the forest, several hours later, that Tomas picked up his pace and moved up alongside Toby and asked him how much further and just how he and the rest of his men came to be in *Canada*. It still made Tomas smile at that thought. Because you didn't just move sixty-three men several hundred thousand light years away from their home and their planet without them noticing. At least he hoped not. Though it did explain some things. Things like the Bermuda Triangle, for example. Tomas knew of other places in the world where people had vanished. Maybe this is what happens to them. The thought made Tomas cringe inside. *Shit! That's worse than* Deliverance, *but at least that little banjo playing fucker was human. Being kidnapped by the things that call Hell home would make you do more than squeal like a pig, I'm sure. Damn, where's Burt Reynolds when you need him?*

'Not much further, chief. Should be there by dark.'

Tomas nodded acceptance of the fact as he formulated the words of how to ask the question that had concerned him moments earlier. 'How exactly *did* you all get here?' was all that he ended up with. 'I mean, how did the colonel get sixty-three of you to Canada in the first place without you noticing something was amiss?'

Toby looked at the ground and scuffed the leafy mulch that passed for soil as he walked. It appeared to be a subject that bothered Toby too. 'Funny one that, though not funny ha ha, if you take my meaning.'

Tomas nodded again and encouraged Toby to continue.

'It was asking that very question that got me sent out here, I reckon, 'cos the colonel didn't seem all that happy when we first turned up here. It was as though we were somewhere he wasn't expecting us to be. Which I thought was funny like, considering how sorted he'd been up till that point.'

'Organized? How's that then?' Tomas asked calmly, gently probing for more details.

'You see all this gear?'

Tomas nodded patiently again.

'Well, it was all stacked up in this fucking great warehouse. The bastard could have started a war with a small country with what he had in there. You name it, he had at least one, probably three; though knowing him, that was just weapons and DPM. He even had that for all countries and all terrains. From snow to deserts. You can't say he wasn't prepared for any eventuality.' Toby seemed impressed by that much of Carmichael at least, which didn't surprise Tomas in the slightest. He might have turned into a psychopathic murdering bastard, but he was charismatic and a respected leader. And he was a natural organizor. It was this self-confidence he exuded that caused men to follow him.

'Where was this warehouse of his?' It wasn't really relevant, but the Feds had been after him for some time and Tomas was curious as to where he holed up.

'Well, this is why me and the boys thought we were in Canada. The colonel's stash was in a disused industrial square just outside Halifax, you know, the one actually up in bloody Canada?'

Tomas smiled at his assumption. 'Fair enough then, I suppose', Tomas conceded.

'Well, it was bad enough it was the back of bloody beyond, but out the back of this warehouse was a river and a jetty, where the colonel had three little cruisers tied up, all covered with camo netting to avert prying eyes.' Toby pointed upwards, implying satellites. 'So I figured we was up for a little river boat trip up country. Why wouldn't I?' Toby was getting into the tale now, Tomas could tell. *Bloody Welsh: natural storytellers. No doubt it came from their Celtic roots or somesuch.* Tomas enjoyed it all the same.

'Why wouldn't you indeed?' Tomas agreed. 'So what happened next?'

'That was the funny part, or not really. Depends on how you look at it. We all geared up and got in. Bug out was at 0600 and were all set up for a long jaunt. Well we couldn'ta been more than a couple of hours in. Griff was already snoring and we was ready to throw Jenkins overboard. Bad guts, if you catch my drift.'

A voice wafted from behind them; no doubt the fragrant Jenkins had been earwigging.

'I told you it wasn't me. Mine don't smell. It was probably that scouse tosser Cartwright; he talks shit all the time. It's no wonder his breath stinks like a latrine.'

There was a thwack sound like something hard hitting a ballistic helmet, followed by an exclamation of pain from Jenkins. Then brief laughter followed. keeping the mood light.

'Easy, boys,' Toby called over his shoulder, 'Keep the high jinks down. We're supposed to be setting a good example to our guests here. We don't want them thinking we're a bunch of comedians.'

'Call me a scouse tosser again and I'll give you something to laugh about, you cockless Geordie dock rat.' A distinct Liverpudlian accent reached Tomas's ear next, followed by more good-natured laughter. But he heard Jenkins mutter a response all the same. It was only Tomas's perceptive hearing that allowed him to pick it up amidst the laughter and general hilarity.

'That's not a denial that ya breath don't stink though, is it.'

Tomas shook his head.

'So, Toby…' Tomas prompted the Welshman to continue his story as the banter tailed off, with a quick glance back to ensure that Treya and Ingrid were okay and hadn't beaten anyone up for saying something they shouldn't or – heaven forbid – touching. Tomas expected that that was punishable by a grisly death in Ingrid's book, though of course touching Treya was punishable by similar in Tomas's. But they were fine. Treya walked alone in the middle and Ingrid, as ever, brought up the rear, with bow in hand and nocked in readiness. But Tomas was confident they were free from pursuers for now, what with the scouts on alert and Bran doing sweeps above them, keeping watch. For the first time since coming back from the brink of death at the talons of the hounds, Tomas felt relaxed. '… What happened on your river trip?'

Toby gave a look of mentally catching himself up and once he had got it straight he carried on like he hadn't been interrupted. 'Needless to say, we didn't throw him overboard. Pity though: his guts ain't improved any. But that aside, none of us noticed the fog creeping up river at first, fog being quite natural on the waterways and all. Basically it had been a clear day when we left. Cold but clear. Shouldn't really have been any fog, not even a mist. But it was Cartwright who was the first to notice the pea-souper and I call it that not just 'cos it was thick like them old London fogs you read about, but because it was *bloody green*! Would you believe it? Anyway...' Toby continued as if it was a trivial matter compared to finishing the story, '...him being trunky and all that, he was bugling out the porthole at the time when it fell upon us.' Toby waggled his finger on the end of his nose for clarification. 'That snout of his will get him into trouble one day.'

'Fell, you say? Strange way to describe fog.' Tomas dug for a bit of clarification.

'That's what it felt like. Carty said it wasn't there one minute, and thick as a stone wall the next. I even went up on deck to have a word with the colonel but I could hardly find my way from one end of the boat to the other. I had to go hand over hand. I never did find him though, 'cos I must have got about halfway when I heard him talking to someone else. That was odd for a start 'cos other than us, there was only the guy at the wheel and he was the other end of the boat. I didn't want to interrupt him, mind, 'cos whoever was answering him had a voice like so much broken glass being stuffed down someone's throat. Like your freakin' eyes, it spooked me enough to keep my gob shut and go back below to wait it out with the rest. The colonel's business is the colonel's business, if you get me.'

Tomas did, but he frowned as he tried to make sense of what he was hearing, but it still didn't make any to him, not yet at least. So Tomas pressed Toby for yet more details of the journey after the fog lifted.

'As I said earlier, that's where things went tits up. We came out of the fog no more than an hour after we went into it, but when it lifted it was pitch black outside. Night had fallen when it shouldn't have been much past eleven in the morning. Now how feckin' weird is that? We all swore that none of us other than Griff – who could sleep through a bloody hurricane, and had apparently – had slept. But when I asked the colonel what was happening, he nearly bit my head off. He was furious. I had never seen him like that before; he was always so controlled on the few occasions I had dealings directly with him. He kept swearing about how wrong it all was. There wasn't supposed to be a forest. He was adamant that we weren't in the right place. I tell you, I didn't want to be that guy driving.'

Tomas grimaced at what he imagined the conversation went like. Short and abrupt. Invariably not ending well for the poor chap on the receiving end.

'So there you have it, more or less. The abridged version. I won't bore you with all the shouting and arguing that ensued as the colonel came and went out of the forest. It was dawn by the time he calmed down and told us to march here. The river...' Toby paused as he looked about, taking a bearing, '...is about three days that way.' Toby pointed off to their right. Tomas looked back to Treya for confirmation and she nodded that he was correct. A river was always worth remembering.

'And here we've been for the past fortnight now. The colonel sent me out with these guys to keep me out of his hair, I reckon.' Toby ticked off on his fingers as he recounted his time in the forest. 'Four days ago now. Shit, seems longer somehow.'

Tomas was making mental notes, pleased in a mercenary sort of way that there was some discord amongst them; it might make his task easier after all. 'What of the colonel?' He was still the fly in his proverbial ointment.

'No idea. He swanned off up one of the towers shortly after we got there, and no one's seen him since. His little mouthpiece acts as go-between for him. Collins. He's the obligatory bean counter. Follows the colonel everywhere. Snivelly little git if you ask me, but that aside, he's the best damn quartermaster I've ever come across.'

Tomas stopped, and the rest of the group did likewise as Toby raised his fist above his head.

'So if you're out here, the colonel is up his tower, and Collins is just the QM, who's in charge of day-to-day discipline?'

Toby grinned that mischievous grin of his. 'Ah! That'll be Dutch. You'll like him. Can't say he'll reciprocate though. Got some strange ideas, that one. Can't for the love of me work out why the colonel hired his merry band of psychos. Handy in a scrap, I suppose, but as they spend most of their time fighting amongst themselves I haven't bothered to get too close to ask for the finer details. I just leave 'em to it. Safer that way. I imagine that when the time comes to do whatever it is we have to do, they'll pull their weight. They're not here for nothing, are they?'

Tomas was more curious now than ever before. Why was there more than one *off the books* fighting group here? And why were they all recruited by Carmichael? What was he up to? *Guess I'll find out soon enough.*

Tomas got them all moving again. Or at least he got Toby to get them moving. He had more questions than he could expect sensible answers for, but he wasn't going to get any satisfaction out here in the woods picking bits and pieces out of Toby.

'Be aware, Tomas, we are within the Reaver's borders and these men are unaware of just what he is capable of,' Treya whispered to Tomas as she drew alongside him.

'How do *you* know what he is capable of?' Tomas asked in hushed response. 'And why are we whispering?'

Tomas smiled at how it must look. Her, a battle hardened and ferocious warrior woman; him, a trained killer and seasoned veteran of hundreds of covert and off the books missions himself, whispering like teenagers in some slashy horror flick as they wandered through the spooky woods. But Treya was oblivious to the analogy and looked at Tomas blankly when he tried to explain it. He soon gave up.

'I don't, personally,' Treya continued, 'but there are rumors and stories of his activities that make Loki's antics look like those of some mischievous child.'

Tomas pressed her for more. *Sometimes it's like getting blood out a bastard stone with these Valkyries*, Tomas grumbled to himself.

'And you believe them?'

She shrugged as though she could have gone either way. 'Prudence when something is an unknown isn't a bad thing. Not here, at least.'

'True enough,' Tomas conceded as he recalled what he had already seen. 'But I reckon that if this Reaver was overly bothered by our presence, he would have shown himself by now. As it is, as long as we don't appear as any threat to him and his, he'll leave us alone. That's what I'm banking on anyway. We don't need any more enemies; we've enough as it is.'

Treya looked oddly at Tomas, her brows drawing together questioningly. 'We? Surely you mean you. Ours is a cause to return myself and the Valkyries back to our rightful home and clear my name before Odin, besmirched by that treacherous witch. It is you that the Adversary wants dead and...' Treya added for effect, '...so too now, it appears, does Fenris. You certainly pick good enemies.'

'Nice!' Tomas replied bitterly 'It's all *we* when the shit hits the fan, but when it comes to who's after who, all the enemies are mine?'

Treya nodded, smiling cruelly as she did so.

'Well, it seems that someone forgot to tell the hounds that attacked us that little fact. I reckon that you got tarred with my brush when you chucked your lot in with me. You and Be'elzebub. So these enemies are *ours* and you'd better get your pretty little head around that idea sooner rather than later, before something bites it off, mistaking you for me.'

Treya scowled at Tomas's reasoning though she didn't, he noticed, refute his logic.

'You know though, Trey, I can't help but shake the feeling that this Reaver character has something to do with these guys being here. I mean...' Tomas told Treya his suspicions based on what Toby had told him, '...

Carmichael wasn't happy about being washed up here, so... why here at all? How or who thought to redirect the group here? With this Reaver's reputation and all, were they hoping he would eradicate them? Someone's plans have gone tits up. The question is, whose, and who is Carmichael working for...' Treya looked dubious and Tomas had to agree, '...the good guys or the Adversary? There is no way to tell as of yet but if I had to guess I know which bad guy I would pick.' Tomas stared at the back of Toby's head as he spoke. 'Toby doesn't know. All he knows is that they are here and they are waiting for orders. We need to be on our guard, Trey. Watch for anything even remotely suspicious, but don't let on you've seen it. Just tell me.' The fiery shield maiden looked at Tomas as though he had just told her to get in the kitchen and prepare his meal before readying herself in the bedroom. Tomas knew that look and quickly clarified things. 'It's just that I know how to talk to these people and I don't want to let on that we know anything. You know how blunt and to the point you and Ingrid can be.' Tomas hoped that would do it and thankfully, the fire banked in her eyes to a dull smolder. He liked that look though.

'Sorry, Trey, didn't mean to sound condescending. It's just that this could be a bit delicate. Their leader Carmichael and I have a little bit of history, and it's not the best of relationships.' Treya asked what he meant by that. 'We hate each other's guts, basically.'

It was the first time Tomas could recall in the short time he had known the Valkyrie woman that he had seen such a look of incredulity emblazoned upon her icily beautiful features. He had witnessed a myriad of other expressions, all of which were fully expected, but this was, it seemed, a look of genuine surprise.

'What? Is it the fact I hate someone or that I owned up to it so easily?'

Treya tossed her mane of flowing locks as she shook her head to the contrary. 'No, Tomas, it is neither of those. It is simply the fact that you are here, in the Domain, very far from your own world. But not only against all odds do you run into your own kind, but you have actual history with their leader and a potentially dangerous one too. Do you not find this just too contrived? You already have enemies aplenty, yet we find ourselves walking into the lair of another one of those who would not grieve to see you dead. Is this wise?'

'Probably not, but whoever said I made wise choices?' Tomas smiled ruefully and shrugged non-committally, looking away from Treya's seeking eyes. Instead he stared at a random spot somewhere off in the distance. She could see torment and pain warring with his own self-control as Tomas tried not to let his wayward memory revisit the events that led up to his and Carmichael's enmity, but to no avail. It seemed that something within him wanted him to know more than he wanted to forget.

Alan Carmichael, a man of iron discipline, had risen swiftly through the ranks after distinguishing himself as a cool head during many of the African revolts he had been called upon to involve himself in. He had been a sniper. A damn good one too, holding many records for accuracy over distance, and he had, at one time, even held the record for the greatest kill shot over distance.

Back then, he had rarely smiled or showed any kind of emotional expression and it earned him the nickname "Stone Cold". Tomas understood the solitude of the work and sympathized at the time with him, for Alan "Stone Cold" Carmichael had few friends, but his reputation and increasing number of commendations got him quite a few invites to social events all the same. In a warped and misplaced sense of valor, he was considered something of a war hero, his deadly aim removing many of the individuals who were responsible for the various governments' many troubles. Tomas knew there were several ways to skin a cat politically, so to speak. He had been called upon himself to extract many a thorn from the proverbial side of his employers, but unlike Carmichael, Tomas had remained off the books and out of the limelight. It amused Tomas to think that even now, he scared his employers, the memory bringing a grim smile to Tomas's lips and a spark of wry humor to his eye. The fact they couldn't find him after the explosion must have driven them crazy just wondering what he would do next. It mattered little to Tomas now and the idea of vengeance or retribution would do nothing to bring his family and fiancée back. He knew all too well now that dead was dead. At least to the world they left behind. But his employers didn't. They thought of retaliation the way people thought of breathing; therefore, so did everyone else and Tomas was one individual that you didn't want coming after you, and they knew it. But Carmichael was different; he was groomed as a political creature. He was coldly good looking with his perpetually pale skin and immaculate sandy brown hair cut marine short and without a hair out of place; but when he turned his will to it he was charming, charismatic and decisive. A natural leader, he probably could have gone all the way to the White House. Maybe that had been the plan. Clean record and no discernible skeletons in his closets, not even a speeding ticket. So, the Washington royalty had him attend all their fancy and superficial functions, shaking hands and meeting influential people. It was during one of these banal events that he first met Abigail.

Elevated swiftly to the rank of colonel in uncommonly short time, Carmichael was given a command back in a high profile region of Africa that he was so familiar with. He and his troops were there essentially on a peacekeeping mission. It would be excellent PR for his forthcoming career, and the media were all over the area like a rash. Though behind the peacekeeping was another, more subversive agenda. He was also there to gather intelligence on several known insurgents who were making trouble for the current administration. They didn't like troublemakers and dealt with them accordingly.

Abigail Porter, the daughter of a powerful senator, had agreed to marry Carmichael six months earlier and after a whirlwind wedding that made it to all the glossy magazines and media outlets, both television and press, fell pregnant just as he was shipping out. Now it transpired that Abigail turned out to be the only person who made the usually stoic Carmichael show any kind of emotion on a regular and necessary basis, so it was considered prudent that she accompany him. Seeing as he was moving in and out of a particularly volatile political arena, the suits wanted him as amenable and press friendly as possible and, if Abigail was the person to do that, along she went.

Much of what was intended went according to plan but like all things that seem to be running too smoothly, they took a turn quite suddenly, and that's when everything went sideways. After about a year, a local woman from a nearby village began to pay regular visits to the compound where Abigail resided, trading fruit and beaded jewelry at first, but when she found that the delicate and frail looking senator's daughter was pregnant, she began offering tentative snippets of advice and things to look for to help the baby and make the birthing easier. This was useful, considering it was likely that Abigail was going to give birth there – another political twist that would reap dividends later when Howard reached the dizzy heights of political power. He would show his child – the symbol of his empathy – connected by blood to the dark land he had once served in. That could be spun to his advantage.

The visits to Abigail gradually extended to the local lady supplying herbal tinctures to ease the increased vomiting and cramps the expectant mother found herself suffering. The two women grew close and within those early months Motusi became quite the companion. She also turned out to be the village wise woman and wife of the chief – a small fact she kept to herself – firstly visiting Abigail, with Abigail in turn starting to visit Motusi at her dwelling within the village, albeit with a six-man armed escort. Two stood guard outside the door while the other four positioned themselves around the village perimeter. No chances were taken with the commander's wife, for fear of reprisal from the commander himself for one, and the fact that everyone loved the ever smiling and benevolent Abigail for another. And it was this latter reason that motivated the men more than the fear. Many of the soldiers knew they had suffered lighter than they would have at the hands of the commander, her husband, when one or more stepped out of line, were it not for her intervention and gentle request that he, Stone Cold Carmichael, remember that they were only human and had families who depended on them. He was to be a father soon and he should start practising now: the experience would do him good. So the men treated the heavily pregnant Abigail like she was the most valuable thing in the entire world. But fragile things in hostile environments attracted danger like magnets.

What no one knew, not even Motusi, unfortunately – for her husband's duty as chief entailed him traveling a lot and attending a good many meetings with the other chiefs and elders of the region as they sought to hold together the warring factions that wanted blood and violence – was that he had been subverting many of the other chiefs to his way of thinking and had become the reluctant yet dedicated leader of the very insurgents that Carmichael was there to root out. But the medieval feuding of the tribal warlords meant that everything existed in a permanent state of flux and it so happened that another sought the mantle of leader and saw Motusi's husband as an obstacle to that challenge – a threat that had to be eradicated. In a land where life was cheap, it could be all too easily accomplished.

Nobody saw the RPGs that tore into Motusi's hut moments after she and Abigail had entered and closed the rickety and loosely hinged door behind them. The entire building became an exploding fireball that blossomed out seconds later and incinerated the two guards before they knew what had hit them, and flung their shrapnel pierced and broken bodies forty feet into the air as the superheated explosion blasted them from their posts. Nothing remained of the dwelling or those within it. The ensuing fire fight as the rebels swarmed into the village saw the four soldiers, suddenly badly outnumbered and outgunned, defend themselves valiantly but they eventually succumbed to the rebels' superior numbers. The guards' severed heads were sent back to the compound with a fistful of photographs which showed the barely recognizable and severely charred remains of two bodies strewn amidst the smoldering ashes, along with a hastily scrawled demand that the soldiers leave the area or meet a similar fate.

Now if they thought the colonel was stone cold before, they hadn't seen anything of the man who appeared before them shortly after receiving his world-shattering mail. He ordered every soldier on duty and all those off duty too, to weapon up, load every vehicle at their disposal with as much ordnance as it would carry, and be prepared to move out within the hour. One soldier had the temerity to ask what they hoped to achieve as the rebels were no doubt long gone by then. No one said another word after his dead body hit the ground, a tiny swirl of smoke still wafting from the bullet hole in his forehead.

'Any more questions?' Carmichael had asked, with ice dripping from every word. There were none. Shocked and stunned, but as ordered, the entire regiment moved out well within the timeframe Carmichael allotted, and by the end of the week he had systematically eradicated all bar one of the rebel chieftains and the majority of their villages. It was a slaughter. Men, women and children fell before the machine that Carmichael set against them. He himself had one or two desertions. The prospect of a bullet in the head couldn't deter some of the men from escaping the monster he had become and was turning his men into. But even these were eventually hunted down and killed for their 'traitorous behavior and disloyalty'. That was how Carmichael saw it. His remaining men took to their new role with the enthusiasm of a pit bull having its muzzle removed and told to attack. They relished their new-found freedom, no longer hampered by the *ROE* that bound their hands tighter than if they were cable tied together. The rules of engagement no longer applied to them, Carmichael had seen to that.

Of course, the media had seen it too. There was virtually no escape from at least one of usually a dozen or so newshounds or their infernal cameras that managed to follow them just about everywhere getting some sort of idea what he was up to. Not even in the dark hinterlands of deepest Africa could a secret remain so. Initially, Carmichael was free from interference from his superiors back home, which was just as well. But once news of his irrational behavior, with pictures and details of the aftermath of his atrocities, reached

Washington, the shit really hit the fan. One of those really, really big fans. Though Carmichael knew that a response would still not be in time to stop him completing his mission. It was a veritable bloodbath. Very little else came close to describing it. He moved freely through the country, either killing or bribing his way around any bureaucratic interference. His trail of carnage eventually wound up in Somalia – a volatile area where Carmichael felt right at home.

In those bloody weeks, he had elevated himself to the top of the FBI's most wanted list. The NSA, DoD and even Homeland Security were up in arms as alleged allies of the decimated African leaders and many incidental casualties threatened and postured their own retaliation to the horrors they saw only as American-sanctioned. Washington was desperately fending off the circling buzzards of the media, for no amount of spin could remove the images sent back from the few surviving reporters on the ground. Tomas remembered that shit storm well. It made Watergate look like a mere clerical error. And it was shortly after that when Carmichael dropped off the radar; after leaving Somalia and moving to the Democratic Republic of Congo, where he showed up to recruit more disillusioned soldiers, both regular and mercenary, who were tired of the never ending spiral of bullshit that kept them running in circles and achieving very little. But he quickly moved on again, constantly moving to avoid detection. Even Tomas found he agreed with much of the rhetoric Carmichael spouted when their paths inevitably crossed, but they had butted heads before and Tomas disliked the man intensely so he turned him down him point-blank – refusing to associate himself with what Carmichael termed his crusade against the pathetic rulers of the world. Tomas considered him a right out there, top of his class loon. A megalomaniac with serious delusions of grandeur and to be avoided at all costs. The man was dangerous all right, but what Tomas *didn't* know was that his father – still in active service at the time – actually went along with the rhetoric, even to seemingly join his growing movement. But after a lengthy and bloody coup, Tomas's father was instrumental in bringing the renegade Carmichael finally, and almost disastrously, to justice.

But nothing is ever simple and as soon as more than one person gets involved in a process, it is bound to go wrong. After a media circus trial, where the entire world tuned in, eager for an outcome that would satisfy everyone, preferably ending with Carmichael's death, there were more senators, lawyers and hand wringing politicians than you could wave a stick at, all trying to have their input and glean what publicity there was to be had from the trial. The world had never been so publicly close to open, global war before and not since the travesty that surrounded the fumbled execution of Saddam Hussein many years earlier had one man wrought such chaos. Nor since the Cuban missile crisis – which was severely downplayed – had tempers been so frayed; volatile to the point of tearing, and more fingers hovering dangerously close over buttons that no one really wanted pressing and many shouldn't have even had. It was during this trial that Carmichael performed his last act of anti-establishment publicity and spat in the faces of his gaolers. In the most spectacular, internationally witnessed and bloody escape in history, several hundred innocents died from the numerous and preplanned explosions which sundered the court house where he was being held, coupled with decimating gunfire that erupted seemingly from everywhere at once. Carmichael's people extricated him from his incarceration and whisked him away with such speed it would have even had David Copperfield applauding. Carmichael seemingly vanished from the world almost immediately after that, though not before promising retribution to those who had betrayed him and those who were the authors of his downfall. He swore painful deaths to those who were responsible and similar for their families and their families' families. He burned with a hatred that was awesome to behold and chilling to be the recipient of. Tomas's father was close to the top of Carmichael's list apparently, as Tomas figured he would be, but his father considered the man more insane than really dangerous now that he was an international fugitive, wanted in almost every civilized and even uncivilized country. He figured it was only a matter of time before he got his comeuppance. But the colonel, ever elusive, had defied all attempts to track him down, even by Tomas, much to his surprise and increasing annoyance. Tomas hated to admit it, but Carmichael was almost as good as he was. Almost. Yet as much as Tomas would have tracked him down even if it took the rest of his life, Tomas's employers weren't so understanding and recalled him.

Years past and Carmichael became just another forgotten psycho, but Tomas, still active in the field of espionage, counter-terrorism and other black ops missions, heard whispers, making him painfully aware that Carmichael was in fact, still very active. Various factions led to other factions who had heard of him and even had dealings – weapons transactions, mostly. A lot of weapons. Though he was very careful these days and left few witnesses to identify him, some rumors still managed to slip out. And ironically, Carmichael had in turn heard about Tomas's growing reputation. He even tentatively contacted him, right out of the blue, offering a final opportunity to join him. He wanted the hunter to join his ranks. Stunned almost into apoplexy at the audacity of the man, Tomas refused again, though he did try for a meeting to discuss it further in the vain hope he could get close enough to take him out, but Carmichael wouldn't play ball. He was too cagey now. Tomas was amazed at the temerity of the man for even thinking he would work for and with him. After all, this was the man who threatened to wipe out his father and his father's family, which actually included *him*.

Tomas was a surgical instrument to Carmichael's battering ram. But you didn't just say no to the colonel and think that was an end to it. Which Tomas did. He figured it was just to prove *Carmichael* could find *him* whenever *he* wanted to and not to offer him any sort of job at all.

Carmichael, however, had other plans all of his own for his nemesis, and cleverly set Tomas up. Though Tomas was never able to connect it to Carmichael, he had his suspicions. The outcome was the same though and he kicked himself daily for not seeing it coming. In reality, it could have been any one of the many enemies Tomas had fostered over the years but few had the military access to pull off such a stunt. Carmichael created a false mission where Tomas was exposed publicly as a double agent as well as a ruthless killer himself. The unnecessary deaths of innocents and the treachery behind them was one thing, but the accusation of cold blooded murder by the very people he worked for and their reluctance to fully believe in him was another altogether. They knew what he did and how he did it; *it was them who actually paid him for doing it*. What he was accused of was so far out of character there was no way they should have fallen for the ruse. But like all governments, they were so busy covering their lily white ass that a little thing like the facts went totally by the wayside. *Plausible deniability*, he was told with an indifferent shrug when he asked what the fuck was going on. It was this last show of two-faced treachery that drove Tomas to finally throw in the towel and retire. Of course, his exposure had negated much of his usefulness to the men who employed him anyway. With his sordid dealings dragged out for the world to see, he was no longer a shadow. After narrowly escaping an Algerian prison sentence and a court martial, it was just left to figure out just how his *retirement* was going to happen exactly, that caused Tomas numerous concerns. One didn't just walk away from the people he worked for, not without enough on them to ensure *they* kept *you* alive. Fortunately for him and unfortunately for them, Tomas had plenty of dirt, only before he could finalize his *pension* with his employers, his own world got turned on its head again – as these things do. At totally the wrong time, and the last thing he expected to do – he got engaged.

Painful memories then of his fiancée and parents began to flood over the sour recollections of Carmichael, drowning the bitter feelings of his dark past with a warmth that only those last few months could generate. He truly thought he could have been happy, and his parents adored her. Four months of serenity where even he came to believe he could actually have a future away from the grim world he had spent the majority of his adult life skulking in. Four months of bliss that ended abruptly with the catastrophic explosion, blamed upon some anonymous suicide bomber, that tore every remaining shred of humanity away from him as his family and future bride were blown to vapor, caught in the heart of the devastation. They were dead and he was left for the same. Tomas shut off the memories with a decisive act of willpower, for they were still surprisingly painful and it was something Tomas had considered a while ago that he was over. Apparently he wasn't as over it as he thought, but he had no time now to indulge his sorrow. He stemmed the flow of images in his head like he was turning off a tap, and he wasn't sure, but he thought he sensed an internal yet detached feeling of disappointment at the cessation.

Tomas frowned, looking around him at the eyes trained on him, and tried to focus his mind on what was going on around him now, not on his painful and traumatic past. Treya gave him a sideways look, as though she wanted to ask him questions, but prudently kept silent. She figured he would talk when he wanted to; she could wait. Always assuming of course they lived long enough.

'Sorry about that. Seemed to have got caught up in a bit of daydreaming for some godforsaken reason.' Tomas scrubbed his face and adjusted himself in the saddle. 'Though, to be fair, it was more of a bloody nightmare than any dream I'd like.' He shrugged and rolled his eyes skyward as if to say he was back on track again and he was ready to carry on.

Treya called Ingrid forward and she came up alongside the pair. 'Ingrid! Stop scaring them. They don't need to know what's here just yet.'

She had been regaling the men with tales of Asmodeus and his battalions of giant arboreal hunting spiders; who made their homes in 'forests just like this one', she had told them, and how their raiding parties had been known to strip a small town in less than a day.

Hopefully...' Treya scowled at her friend as she smiled back gleefully, pleased with herself at the misery she had imposed on the hapless men, '... with their help and the success of the plan we are committed to, the lord Lucifer will be able to return them to their own world as he returns us to ours.'

Ingrid looked only slightly put out at the reprimand: she had been enjoying herself too much, watching the incredulous looks from the soldiers as she terrorized them, causing them to worry overly about where they went. She just shrugged and looked about as unrepentant as she was.

'What have the scouts seen, Ingrid?' Tomas asked quickly, changing the subject and giving her something to focus on other than Toby's men. Ingrid looked faraway for a second or two before speaking, as she communed with the scouts and they responded.

'We are close. Maybe no more than an hour, two at the outside if this accursed forest doesn't let up and hinder our progress any more than it has already.' They had been forced to navigate several sizeable dead falls, turning their straight line progress into something of a meandering journey. Tomas held out his arm and Bran swooped down through the trees – making several of the soldiers duck nervously – cawing as it back winged to alight on the offered perch, claws gripping into Tomas's armored forearm as it shook out its snow white plumage and settled down.

'*Have you seen anything they might have missed?*' Tomas thought to the bird. It wasn't that he didn't distrust the demonic scouts, but he liked his intel a little more direct than third-hand via someone who cared little for him.

'*I have seen much, Tomas, but I concur with the Valkyries. We are close and there are more men ahead waiting for us at the fortress. We have no way of concealing ourselves from them when we clear the trees, for there is a vast open expanse before the gates.*' Killing ground. Tomas knew the importance of such an area. Many modern towns had sprung up when the common folk camped out around the walls and base of the fortifications, expanding outwards and around. It was socially and commercially benefi-cial, but tactically it was a pain in the ass. It gave any invader cover and then there were the inhabitants of said town. They either had to be brought within the walls or left to die. Brought in, they became a drain on resources and an increased risk of disease with so many people at close quarters.

Outside dead was little better; they would rot there and still be a problem. It was early germ warfare at its messiest. No, Tomas liked his fortresses to be isolated like this, ideally atop a vast hill where nothing could be built outside, making it easily defensible and preventing some poor sod having to make the moral choice about letting people outside die. Though he had seen little evidence of any hills in this region – there had been plenty off in the distance, though they more resembled mountains than any mere hill, and forested all the way up by the looks of it – it didn't matter so much as far as this fortress was concerned. He couldn't see any army bothering to make its way through this forest to lay siege to any fortress within its leafy boundaries. It would be a logistical nightmare. So it had that in its favor in lieu of a hill.

'*No other surprises?*' Tomas didn't like surprises, even though he had had more than enough of them of late.

'*Nothing visibly out of the ordinary.*'

Tomas barked a small laugh at the casual irony of Bran's comment.

'*How have I amused you, Tomas? I see nothing funny about simply relaying facts.*'

Tomas got the impression that Bran was taking his laughter personally. '*Ordinary, Bran, is a word, it seems, open to considerable interpretation depending on one's point of view. There has been little of late that comes under the "ordinary" banner, as far as my life goes. I'm not even sure "extraordinary" covers what is taking place right now, though it sure is a damn good place to start.*'

Bran hopped off Tomas's arm and settled down on his shoulder. Having tired of flying, the battle raven chose to ride for a bit and this amused Tomas all the more, causing further laughter from the usually stoic Tomas. Bran cawed twice at Tomas's sudden sound and this only elicited more laughter.

Reproving looks cast, the group moved off again, determined to make the fortress before the fast approaching night and images of tree climbing spiders the size of small cars filled the fertile imaginations of the soldiers.

Ingrid smirked and giggled to herself constantly as she caught sight of their furtive glances upwards into the dark and shadowy tree tops every now and again.

'She has a definite cruel streak, that one,' Tomas whispered to Treya, figuring there was no point in antagonizing her and drawing her attention down on him any more than it already was. Though he did pity the soldiers somewhat.

'You haven't seen anything, Tomas. This is like breathing for her. You wouldn't even want to be on the same plane of existence as Ingrid when she really gets going. A frost giant made that mistake once. Once.'

Tomas didn't even know where to start with that one. 'A frost giant? That's what you said, right? I don't even want to know what a bloody frost giant is, thank you very much.'

Treya was about to elaborate, but Tomas stopped her, shaking his head in dismay, for in the back of his mind he knew it sounded big, ugly, mean and dangerous.

It was almost dark when Toby called a halt to the group, and Tomas moved up alongside him. Toby pointed through the last couple of remaining trees towards the dark structure that squatted off in the distance.

'How far?' Tomas asked.

Toby answered that it was about three miles across the scrubby and flattened grass, though it wasn't a straight line to the gate. They had dotted the terrain with claymores and other nasty surprises in order to deter any unwanted visitors until they knew where they were exactly, and what the next step was to be. Though they didn't realize they were quite so far off the map.

It was a large and typical structure with crenulated battlements and towers, which even at the distance he was seeing them from were impressive. Its size made it seem closer than it was. *What lived here before?* Tomas mused, not for the first time since hearing about the fortress.

'*Would you be surprised to know that this used to be the Reaver's home once?'* Bran answered to the unspoken question in Tomas's mind.

'*Once, but not now, I take it?'*

Bran told Tomas that it had been abandoned for thousands of years. Few chose to step inside even if they ever came across the fortress. The Reaver's reputation throughout the Domain was widely known and those who crossed him did so at their peril. So only those who knew nothing of the dark ferryman dared venture near, and they were few and far between. Even the most distant of souls had heard something about the Reaver. There was a little of his legend in virtually all cultures in one form or another. To Tomas, he was Charon, the ferryman who took the souls of the dead across the River Styx, though even he knew it was the Acheron River and not the oft-thought Styx. Of course, the soldiers would be oblivious to the danger they courted. They thought they were in Canada, after all, though Tomas had to concede that it was uncannily similar, and thankfully, about as exciting. *Let's hope it stays that way,* Tomas muttered to himself as his eyes, like those of the soldiers, scanned the trees.

Like many ancient structures on both the Domain and Earth, they were built on nexus points, their sites purposely chosen as conduits of the natural energy that all planets give out. Stonehenge and Glastonbury to Machu Pichu and the Nazca lines, up to the Chapel of the Holy Cross in Sedona, to name just a few. So too was the fortress that Tomas gazed at in the velvety darkness. The Reaver chose the site with care, and every single stone and lintel was now suffused with the raw energy given off by the planet Mars. To those sensitive to the subtle energies of the planets, the fortress acted like a chalice of nourishment. To be within its walls was to be refreshed and revitalized by the inherent power there. A dark sentience had been sensing the ever growing presence of the fortress with an eagerness that was hard to conceal. Once within its pulsing embrace, it would grow in strength a hundredfold and would be finally able to exert more of its malignant influence with power of its own, without having to leach it from its host first. The shard that had pierced the side of Tomas throbbed with anticipation, and the evil cancer that was Nakir the Black grew fractionally, working its way deeper inside and fusing itself to the bone and flesh that surrounded it. Already its emotions were able to surge forth, though only under stressful situations; but that should change after being immersed in the spiraling vortex of the fortress's nexus points. Once the domination of the mind had taken place, then Nakir could concentrate on the body. Using the host much like a chrysalis, Nakir would absorb the flesh and bone around him, manipulating it to his own ends until he had a body he was satisfied with. Then no force upon the Domain would stop him wreaking his vengeance on those who brought him to his present condition. Feeling their insidious touch inside the mortal host he currently dwelt within, he would start on them. The Four Horsemen of the Apocalypse would be his first, but by no means would they be the last to suffer. Unable to express himself physically yet, but overjoyed by the prospect of revenge, the spirit of Nakir the Black laughed and laughed and laughed.

CHAPTER SEVENTEEN

ELEMENTUM

'HOW LONG?' DANIEL ASKED THE QUESTION OF the now strangely distanced doctor – who himself had adopted a sad expression of helpless sympathy – one that must have been ingrained into them during their medical training. Daniel grimaced inwardly at the insipid, pale and pasty face before him as though he had never seen it before. It was the question Daniel figured that just about everyone in his predicament must have asked when their mortality was handed to them with an expiry date. And like them, no doubt, whose voices invariably came out dull and flat, devoid of the life they had just been robbed of, his too came out completely emotionless. The unfairness of it stripped his rationality and colored the world in shades never before imagined. He was going to die. And not even because of anything he had actually done; a serial killer on death row must find it easier to come to terms with their impending doom because at least they knew why. Or at least Daniel assumed they did. His mind was too busy scrambling with the implications of what he had just been told, to bother with such trivial things as details and the overall moral viewpoint of perspective.

The actual voice, however, that spilt from his head, which, Daniel distractedly noticed, was at least coherent and steady, and seemed to be acting on autopilot for him, speaking the words and asking the questions that he needed answers for instead of the high pitched scream of abject disbelief that he wanted so badly to set free, whilst simultaneously absorbing the cataclysmic fact that, all bar the shouting, his life – as he knew it – was essentially over.

'Two years at the absolute most, Mr Fitzgerald; more likely eighteen months if we are honest with ourselves.' *We? What the fuck is this "we" shit?* Daniel wanted to throttle the superficial look of pity off the face of the man before him; the same man, he recalled bitterly, who had given him the only hope he had to begin with, some thirteen months earlier, but then cruelly yanked the rug from beneath his flailing feet by explaining – as though he were talking to a child – that the tumor in his head, nestled cozily in his grey matter, was now totally inoperable.

'But you said there was a chance. That there was a new experimental procedure that might be able to reach it. What the fuck happened to that?' Daniel stopped talking abruptly, conscious of his rising voice. If he continued talking, he would degenerate into a screaming hysteric. Not yet. He needed to remain calm for now; to get all the facts before he figured out what he was to become next.

'Now, Daniel. If you remember, we said that it was only a slim chance and we shouldn't get our hopes up, we – '

Not known for his patience at the best of times, which these really weren't, Daniel couldn't take it any more. A tiny part of his mind knew it was the frustration getting the better of him and he should be more understanding, but the greater part: the part that had just been told he was going to die, overrode that.

'Will you stop saying "we",' Daniel shouted suddenly, causing the doctor to flinch involuntarily. Daniel instantly calmed again. 'It's not you who's got a fucking lump in his head which is going to snuff him out like a fucking candle without a moment's notice anytime soon, is it?' He didn't wait for the now pale man before him to answer. 'No, it's not. So quit the fucking empathy, will you? It's not working. You can't just blurt out that I'm going to die within eighteen to twenty-four months and expect me to act rationally, can you? For the love of God, it's not we; it's me. Got that? Me! All right? *Me, me, me, fucking me!'*

The doctor blanched a little more in the face of Daniel's outburst and Daniel secretly took a little guilty pleasure from his fear and trepidation. Though it couldn't be easy, Daniel mused disjointedly – as though he was having a lesser conversation with himself inside his head while the rest of him went into meltdown – having to be the one who broke the news to people that they were going to die. Though it had to be an integral and fundamental part of their job, they were mainly onto a loser to begin with. Death came to the greater majority of his customers. Though it comes to us all anyway, he reasoned logically, sometimes it came prematurely and often painfully, with little dignity. Others, like his case, where the tumor was just going to switch him off one day, much like a walking organic light bulb, were unobtrusive and comparatively pain free; though the headaches when they came totally poleaxed him and sent him crawling for his bed in a very dark and quiet room, with more pills chundering down his throat than were really good for him. That tiny part of his consciousness that kept him going through it all and not hurling himself off some bridge tried to keep him sane, and that same small part of Daniel that still had its diaphanous grip on reality, actually felt sorry for the man. But then again, he argued with himself, it was that selfsame man who was going to go home to his life after ruining Daniel's and relegating his ailment to just another case file; to be forgotten and filed after he left the office. Relegated to the status of just one more distraught victim of the dreaded ever-present spectre of cancer. It was a terrible job really, but it was one he chose and got paid very well for, no doubt. But at the end of the day, however much of a shitty job it was, somebody had to do it, so why shouldn't he earn his bag of thirty silver pieces.

The rest of the conversation didn't go too well after that and Daniel stormed out of the doctor's office, slamming several doors on his way out, even rattling many of the ridiculously thin panes of glass in their frames, almost daring them to smash and shatter onto the thin, well-worn carpet. Catching sight of the receptionist as he stomped past, Daniel caught sight of her watching him in turn with a mixture of pity and wariness before going back to her nails and typing, whichever she thought the more important. Daniel had turned away, hoping she hadn't seen, but he knew she had spotted the tears that flowed down his ruddy cheeks. And knowing she knew just made it worse. He resented her the life that should have been his. In fact, by the time Daniel had made it outside to the suddenly chill air of the street, after the claustrophobic and slightly warm antiseptic air of the doctor's consultation room, he resented just about everyone their life.

He hadn't told Tara about the increasing headaches that escalated over the last couple of years, nor about the equally increasing number of visits to the doctor, which culminated in the MRI scan and capped it off with the eventual diagnosis of his cerebral cancer. They had been optimistic during those early days, but quite suddenly the little bastard had begun to grow at an alarming rate: a rate that was unconcerned with NHS waiting times and the availability of consultants, who were probably too busy on the golf course to bother themselves with no-hopers like him. Daniel's cynicism painted a very harsh reality – one that where people he despised were cruel, cold and complete wastes of the polluted and disease filled air they breathed. But they said it didn't look good.

That was what he had been told anyway, and he was to prepare himself for the worst-case scenario. He had; or at least he had tried. But how do you ever prepare for news like that? Numbly, Daniel went about his life, what he considered was left of it. He seemed to those who knew him, to adopt a certain recklessness that came across as irresponsible and deplorable. Daniel cared less and less but it wasn't until after a blazing row with his two best friends, Kieran Doyle and his cousin Barry, that Daniel realized how much of a prat he had been.

As they had after his every visit to his oncologist, they both found him and eventually left him draped over the bar, where they had propped him to continue to wallow in the misery of his own making, while they went off to plan their regular fishing cum business trip. Though it was always more business than fishing. The only thing they caught were the two dozen watertight drums filled with some two hundred and fifty thousand cigarettes which the helicopter had dropped off on the west side of the Ballinskelligs. All the cousins had to do was snag onto the weighted drums by the hook with the flashing light attached, and pull them aboard. A bit like a larger scale version of the fairground attraction, only this time the prize wasn't a goldfish, but an easy few grand on the not so much black, but more of a nicotine colored market.

The morning of his last consultation, where he got his final timetable, had been the day he really blew up at his friends. They had left and Daniel had stumbled out of the bar, barely able to walk let alone drive, and had fallen into his death trap of a vehicle. After ten minutes of rummaging through every pocket at least six times, he finally found the keys and fired the battered old Range Rover up. Gunning the muddy green and slightly rusty four by four away from the kerb and nearly running over a couple of errant shoppers in the process, he swerved off to a hail of abuse from the lucky-to-be-alive pedestrians behind him. Daniel waved the middle finger of his right hand out of the window at them to tell them he couldn't have cared less, and proceeded to grumble out of town. He found the N70 almost by accident rather than by design, and set off southwards. He originally intended to stop at Tara's and spend some time there – it always calmed him somehow – but he was too full of drink this day and he had plenty of supplies on the back seat to ensure he stayed in his cups for at least a week.

Daniel vaguely remembered it was a Wednesday; and it was Friday when he was due to be going with the cousins on their fishing excursion, which gave him – to his alcohol befuddled mind – two days to decide whether he was going to throw himself overboard and beat death to the punchline before he got him. Or, take out the biggest loan he could find and blow it all on all the things he knew to be bad for him, but fun. It wasn't like he was going to have to pay it back, was he? Passing Sneem at something close to ninety miles an hour, he navigated the roads with an almost inhuman ability, with the car occasionally cornering on two wheels and squealing its displeasure at such treatment – protests that this day, fell on very deaf and totally intoxicated ears as Daniel exhorted it to greater feats of mechanical acrobatics.

He didn't know how long he drove for, not that he cared much anyway, but it was getting dark and his tear-filled and booze-swamped eyes were struggling to see more than a few feet past the dent-filled and cable tie supported bonnet. So he pulled off the road at the first muddy track he saw and parked the thankful and – if it could have – sweating car close to a small copse of oak and ash trees, about three quarters of a mile off the main highway, and summarily passed out.

Daniel woke slowly. A sickly grey light filtered its way into the dim interior of the car, and it was this that told Daniel's tender brain that it was at least daytime. But the light was so nondescript that the actual time eluded him. It could have been anything from early morning to just before sunset. Daniel took in his position within the car before moving his limbs. Simply moving his eyes was painful enough for now. He was sprawled across the back seat with one leg hanging over the passenger seat, the other propped up on the rear door with the base of his boot pressed firmly to the glass. Daniel absently realized his right leg, where it was draped, had gone to sleep too and stayed that way. He knew that when he dragged himself together, his foot was going to give him merry hell as sensation came flooding back into it. The stench of vomit assailed his nostrils and he almost gagged before he realized that it had been him that had done it. Some point during the night he had rolled over and thrown up all over himself. Then he caught a whiff of his own breath and decided the vomit was preferable. It was as though the entire population of Kerry's seagulls had taken turns in shitting in his mouth. Painfully, as his neck had constricted due to the awkward angle he had found himself lying in, he turned to survey his handiwork of the previous night. There were several empty bottles and cans along with what looked like ancient discarded pizza boxes. In disgust, Daniel realized that at some stage during the night, as he poured unhealthy amounts of booze into himself, he had gotten a nasty case of the munchies. Apparently, as the evidence before him substantiated, he had discovered some weeks-old abandoned pizza and a few old cartons of Chinese noodles that had been carelessly tossed and subsequently forgotten a week or two earlier. In his haze, Daniel had ignored the patches of soft, velvety blue fur that had cultivated itself on the material formerly known as food, along with the fag ash and mud from the rear foot well where he had retrieved it from, and shoveled it down his neck. Like all things alcohol glazed, it had seemed a sound idea at the time and had even tasted pretty good too. At least that was what his fogged memory told him. But in the cold light of day, or something that loosely resembled it, he realized that even the damn seagulls would have wisely left it alone.

Daniel was a big believer in not remembering things when he had gadgets that would do it for him. So with a Herculean effort and no small amount of contorting, he managed to extricate his phone from his coat pocket, amazed that he had managed to hang on to this one for as long as he had, for he was notorious for losing them. Flipping the thing open, he struggled to focus his bleary eyes on what it was telling him. When he did, he couldn't believe what he was seeing for several minutes afterwards.

Feckin Saturday? He looked at it again as if it was going to say something different the second time around, but it didn't. The little word kept glaring at him as if defying him to disprove it.

'How the hell did that happen? What did you drink, Daniel? That's two feckin days you've lost, you complete, utter and total imbecile.' As he was berating himself, he tried desperately to haul himself upright, eventually doing so, and then with more effort than should have been required, he opened the rear door, fully intending to stumble out and park himself back in the driver's seat. The door crunched open and he gazed upon an alien world. It was only after several very confused seconds that he cottoned on as to why the light was so diffused through the glass of the car; it was frosted over as though it had been etched opaque. The copse, the surrounding fields and just about everything else he could see, was a dazzling, stark and icy white. Words failed him as he slowly got out and turned in a deliberate three hundred and sixty degree circle, taking in the fantastic vista he found himself in. Daniel inadvertently put a casual hand on the roof of his car and had to snatch it back suddenly as though it had been burnt. He looked confusedly at the red patch of skin on his palm, and then at the icy spot on his car where the intense cold had seared him. He drew a deep breath and almost choked as the biting cold tore into his unprepared lungs. He had been temporarily protected from the extreme climate change when he first emerged from his cocoon by the two-day-old bubble of warm fetid air that clung to his clothes and skin. That soon evaporated under the frigid wind that howled across the land, ripping and tearing at everything, including him, with icy fingers of razor wire. He tried to breathe again but only ended up coughing as the chill air was too much for his body to take.

'What happened?' he asked himself lamely, as he could see exactly what had happened, but the why and the how were lost on him completely. Kerry, or certainly the part he was in, had turned into a winter nightmare land and he had been asleep in a drunken stupor the entire time and missed it. *This isn't good and it's certainly not feckin good for me.* Daniel started to shiver as the dank sweat that had cloyingly covered his body beneath his vomit-stained clothes began to freeze on his skin. *Sod this shit, I'm not freezing to death out here with that hyperthermawhotsit and wastin' me life in the damn middle of nowhere.* Galvanized into some sort of action plan, Daniel staggered about like he was still blind drunk, trying to get himself into the driver's seat. With a prayer and promise to go to church more often, which was the same one he uttered every time he tried to start his car and was the same one he knew he would never keep, Daniel turned the key. Much to Daniel's intense joy, great relief and total surprise, it roared into life first time. He wasted no time in wheel spinning the vehicle out of the field and back onto the road; and gunning the engine as hard as he dared, Daniel headed back to town.

The next couple of weeks were as surreal for Daniel as any movie or novel could have portrayed them. He had arrived at first to find the town deserted. It was picture postcard beautiful – all white and frost coated – but at the same time it was creepy beyond belief. Over the following days he had found more and more equally confused people, but one thing came to light as they each recounted their tales in the bar Daniel usually frequented before it had become deserted. They had chosen it as a meeting place and rallying point for any other survivors they found. The thing that bound them together in a common goal was the fact they all had been out of town at the time of the big freeze. Well out of town. For it seemed that the worst of the weather had centered on the areas of civilization. Oddly, the towns were affected more than the outlying countryside – a fact that no one had any explanation for. But it was a situation Daniel was grateful for, seeing as Tara lived out on the periphery. He had visited her often after that and she was fine, if a little confused by it all. She tried to calm her younger brother initially and reassure him that it was all just a coincidence, at first blaming it all on global warming. But she soon gave that up for the obvious reasons. One: it sure as hell wasn't warm. Two: it didn't account for the missing populace. And three: Why wasn't it mentioned anywhere on the TV about any freak weather phenomena or missing people in and around the Southern Ireland region? The news was filled with the usual stuff about terrorists and how badly off the rich people were because they had lost a few million quid in a stock market glitch. Poor them, Daniel thought bitterly as he drove away from Tara's that last time, leaving her with plenty to think about but safely out of the way all the same. Her cottage, formerly their mother's cottage, was always a safe haven from trouble. Somehow, misfortune seemed to slough off it as though it was Teflon coated. Daniel crossed everything he had that it stayed that way too.

The Adversary

The day he had found his two friends again – after their fishing trip had run into a few problems and they had been forced to take shelter on the Skellig Islands for a while – was the day that Gwen had arrived. Not that he knew it was Gwen of course, but a massive green dragon was something of a memorable sight all the same. Kieran and Barry had fled, sensibly really, while he had stupidly passed out. Shock and a little too much vodka had overwhelmed his stressed synapse. Matters had just gone downhill from there. As if they weren't bad enough before, the shit had really hit the fan the moment Gwen had arrived at Tara's. Within what seemed like just a few hours, the populace had returned. But on seeing them, Daniel wished with all his might that they would just fuck off again. Gwen had explained as best she could that they were possessed. *Fucking possessed?* Daniel had a tough time getting his head around that one. At least until he saw them up close. That did it. He put two and two together and came up with *The Exorcist*. He never did like that film; now he knew why. These people were a mess all right and it was a miracle that they could even stay upright let alone run and scream the way they eventually did. But it was when they started turning up at the house shortly after the troubles, as he called them, all started, that Daniel knew something was truly not right. It was just ones and twos at first and Daniel could slip past them easily enough over the ensuing weeks as he brought Tara's supplies to her. For some reason, they couldn't get past the front gate. It was as though some invisible hand held them back – a fact that got no complaints from Daniel; nor Tara, for that matter. It was that fact that kept her inside and Daniel was glad about that – at least she was safe for now – but it still gave him the creeps.

Now, as he ran for his life, they gave him more than the creeps. He had seen them in action and they scared him witless now. It was pure adrenaline that powered his limbs as his mind came to terms with the fact that the world he once thought he knew no longer existed. He was living some fantastic nightmare, ripped from the pages of some far too graphic novel, like the sort that Kieran used to read and Daniel used to scoff at. Seems Keiran had the last laugh after all, *bastard*! Daniel knew they were never going to make it to Sneem, not in a million years, not running anyway. His mind raced as his legs pumped. Sparing a glance behind him, he saw that the undergrowth they had just run through had thickened considerably, hampering their pursuers. *How the bloody hell did that happen?* Then he remembered Gwen.

'Can't you do anything else?' he panted as he ran. Talking *and* running took more out of him than he would have liked. He wasn't the most energetic of sorts at best. Multitasking like he was doing took more out of him than he had to spare. Gwen seemed to see this and she slowed the fleeing group, with several concerned looks behind her. The screams hadn't stopped but the pursuit had, at least temporarily. They were tangled and out of sight in a crunching and contorting morass of thorny bramble and briar. Daniel envisioned the barbs shredding the flesh of the possessed but knew it wouldn't hold them long. He looked to Gwen and Tara, hoping that one of them would have a suggestion that got them out of their current predicament. He wasn't expecting the one Gwen came up with though. Able to concentrate now without distractions, Gwen asked them if they knew how to ride.

'Ride what?' Daniel asked, a look of trepidation creasing his face, knowing as he asked it that he didn't really want to know. He had seen enough weird shit in the last few hours to last him several lifetimes and he knew also that innocent questions like his last one were likely to have answers he didn't want to hear.

'Horses, silly,' Gwen responded as though it were the most obvious thing in the world. 'What else is there out here to ride? I can't see anything, can you?'

Daniel scowled and looked purposely to either side as he answered her, 'No I don't, but I don't see any bloody horses either, so easy with the smart answers, me gal. I'm a little fraught about now, as you might have guessed.'

'Well? Can you?' Gwen ignored the veiled threat in his answer, putting it down to stress.

'Can I what?'

'Ride a horse, Daniel, ride a horse.'

It was Tara who answered for them both. 'Yes, Gwen, we can. Though not well, we aren't likely to fall off easily either.'

'Good. Now that I've got a few seconds to get my breath back and get my thoughts in order, I'm going to get us a horse. That should make the trip to Sneem a little easier.'

Again Daniel looked around him, only this time instead of wariness, scorn colored his words. 'Oh yeah, there they are! There's that herd of horses that always appears when there's trouble. How silly of me not to have noticed.'

Tara smacked her brother smartly across the back of the head, shutting him up abruptly. He yelped and his head flopped forward, as much in surprise as in any sort of pain.

'Less of your lip, my lad. Gwen is trying to save your sorry excuse of a life. Try having a bit of faith. Just look behind you. You have no idea…in fact *we* have no idea, what she is capable of, so unless you have any better ideas?' Daniel shook his head sulkily but silently. 'I thought not, so let's hear the gal out.'

Tara turned to Gwen expectantly, as did Daniel after a few seconds of rubbing his smarting head, his thoughts ajumble with their current predicament, but he couldn't help but wonder what sort of effect Tara's smack had on his brain's unwanted passenger.

'There are a few things I haven't told you…' Gwen started warily, looking straight at Daniel, '…and I'm not sure how much you can remember, Tara, about our little chat last night, but there are one or two things I can do that might test your sanity more than you really need right now. But needs must, so please, don't be scared or do anything stupid.'

'I'm way past doing something stupid now,' Daniel grumbled. 'I should have done that ages ago; I wouldn't be in the middle of this shit right now.'

Tara frowned at the cryptic comment but didn't press it, though her gaze did linger on his face for a while longer, searching for something, anything that would provide her with a clue as to what her little brother was keeping from her. She knew he had a secret, but he had been uncharacteristically good at hiding it from her. Normally she could ferret out anything he tried to keep secret, but this was something else. Her thoughts were interrupted when Gwen spoke next. Not by the fact she spoke, but by what she said.

'Okay, right then, there's no easy way to say this. I'm going to turn into a horse.'

Daniel burst out laughing. It was an explosive release of sound that startled Tara at first and made Gwen scowl. Tara turned to rebuke him for scaring her, but as she turned, the air shimmered before her and Daniel. On seeing what was before his disbelieving eyes, Daniel shut up as abruptly as he had started. Both brother and sister stood dumbly staring at the massive golden mare that stood before them. At sixteen hands to the shoulder, Gwen made quite an imposing sight. Rhiannon herself would be impressed by the form Gwen had assumed. She was easily as big as the Clydesdale horses that pulled the Budweiser wagons she had seen at Sea World on one of her earlier trips before settling in Santa Fe.

'We don't have all day. Get on!' the horse said as she bent a foreleg so they could mount more easily. That did it. A talking horse broke the spell that transfixed the pair and they shared a glance with each other, just briefly, before clambering up onto Gwen's back. Daniel straddled Gwen's wide back first, followed by Tara, who encircled Daniel's waist with her arms. Daniel entangled his hands into Gwen's mane as she stood, and he gripped her ribs with his thighs to hold himself in place.

'Are we sitting comfortably?' Gwen's voice issued from the horse's mouth and she turned to look at them, flicking her ears slightly as she did so. They just nodded, but that was good enough for Gwen. Her equine eyes took in the possessed beyond them, still trying to get through the briar barrier. They were tearing furiously and several were close to breaking free. *Time to go*, she thought, and bunching her powerful hindquarters, Gwen leapt away. Muscular legs began to pump as she built up speed, her hooves pounding on the hard frozen landscape as the scenery began to blur by for her riders. Icy wind made Tara's and Daniel's eyes water, so their view of the world became somewhat distorted and surreal. They leant forward into the shelter of Gwen's mane and powerful neck as she thundered on.

Daniel gave directions as best he could and soon enough Gwen was galloping through the fields that ran parallel to the road. But even as they ran, they could see possessed running towards them across the barren landscape. Like some uncanny and unwanted GPS signal, the creatures seemed to home in on them no matter where they were. Had they remained on foot, they would have been overrun by now, Gwen was sure of it. She desperately wanted to glance back at their pursuers but at the speed she was running at, she didn't dare. It was going to be touch and go even now, she thought worriedly, to make it to Sneem, let alone Kenmare where the stone circle was. Gwen didn't fancy her chances running that far, laden down as she was, not that she knew exactly how far that was. It wasn't that they were particularly heavy to her supernaturally powered body; but in an unfamiliar form, it took more effort than she would have liked. Flight like this wasn't conducive to thinking and she needed to think about what they were going to do next. They couldn't just keep running. Sooner or later they would have to stop; then what?

The sign that said they were now in Sneem, or at least the edge of it, came and went as Gwen slowed, satisfied that, for the moment at least, there were no possessed in the immediate vicinity.

'Where to now?' Gwen asked over her shoulder. Daniel was scanning both left and right as though he were looking for something in particular. 'And you can let go of my mane a little – we've slowed down now – otherwise I'm going to have the mother of all facelifts with you pulling like that.'

Daniel grimaced slightly but released his grip all the same, the color flowing back into his white knuckles. 'Over there!' he said croakily, the chill air drying his throat as he sucked in terrified lungfuls. 'There's a house that's tucked away that I used a few times. I know it's empty 'cos the owners have buggered off to Australia, and it's been up for sale for ages. I found some old letters in a cupboard. That's how I know.' Daniel added quickly to Tara's questioning look of how he knew so much. 'It made a useful crash pad when I'd had a few too many. I saw where they left the key once and when I looked, well, imagine my surprise when it was still there. So – ' Tara dug him in the ribs. 'Ow! What was that for? It isn't like I broke in or somesuch.' Daniel's voice had taken on a whiny, sulky tone. 'I had a key and they weren't using it. No harm, no foul, I say.' He didn't like being told off. Much like a big child that had refused to grow up.

'You would,' Tara harrumphed behind him. Gwen stopped and let her passengers off. Reverting back to her own form; she stretched and took a second or two to get used to two legs rather than four before heading across the street from their present position. Tara and Daniel did likewise, their abused bodies unused to the rigors of high speed bareback riding. They were going to be sore later. Gwen, though, strode over the empty pavement and desolate road like a queen, confident and assured. Filled with her own power as she was from the transformation, her psyche adopted a form that her subconscious felt was more appropriate for one of her position and current predicament. Green was the color of the day and it took the form of a close-fitting and figure hugging dress made from every type of leaf imaginable; overlapping so cleverly, they looked like the scales of the dragon that she was or like an expertly crafted metallic green mail shift. The dress fell to just below her knee, where she manifested high, sage colored boots, tooled with intricate designs of vines and roses. Ivy wound its way down her arms and ended at her wrists, flowing around her and into her. At her throat hung a multifaceted green tourmaline of such lustre and clarity that it veritably shone with an inner fire, as though it held its own star deep inside. But what made Daniel's throat catch was Gwen's face, especially her eyes. For they shone like twin emerald stars; blazing in a field of hazy green moss that airbrushed itself across her eyes from temple to temple. The tiny blue spirals had rematerialized too, swirling and subtly covering any exposed skin.

Several danced across her forehead and across each cheek. Daniel thought that Gwen looked more like a goddess now than any picture he had ever seen of one. Long delicate fingers with equally long, deep, forest green fingernails at their tips pushed their way into her hair, which was alive with tendrils of ivy and small dark leaves.

'Wow!' was about all Daniel could manage as he took in the beauty beside him.

'What?' Gwen didn't notice at first how she must have looked to the others, but Daniel's comment made her do a quick inventory. 'Oh, I see, well... Yes... Um, well it has a tendency to do that sometimes when I'm not concentrating. Even I forget who I am now, though it seems by this not so subtle hint someone doesn't like to let me do that.'

'Someone? Like who?' Daniel asked one of those questions again and regretted it.

'The Earth. She's who I answer to now, you know. Long story. I'll tell you about it one day. For now though, let's get inside, shall we? You mentioned something about a key?' Gwen looked wide-eyed and expectantly at Daniel, her face and body language conveying more than words that he should get a move on and fetch it; getting the door open as soon as he was able, if not sooner.

They hadn't been inside for much more than a quarter of an hour. Tara had rechecked their packs and even scavenged a few extra things from the semi-empty house. Daniel had disappeared into the lavatory, complaining about the cold and his sore nuts. He was going to check they were still intact, and evacuate his bowels at the same time.

'Nice!' Gwen had commented. 'You're all class, you know.'

Tara had grimaced distastefully and added her own gripe. 'Thanks for sharing that, Daniel. I'm sure we really wanted to know that, but seeing as you're full of shit most of the time anyhow, it's no big surprise.'

But the moment he got the door shut and had thrown the lock across, he whipped out the flask that he perpetually kept tucked in his jacket, and pulled

814

several swallows of rough brandy that he kept in it, convincing himself that it was for medicinal purposes, to calm his shattered nerves. He was still repeating those reasons when the last drop slipped down his throat. He emerged a little happier than when he went in. The lopsided grin on his face gave testimony to that, but it also gave him away to his astute sister, who had seen it before. Too many times before apparently, as one look at her and he knew she wasn't happy.

'You've been drinking?' she rounded on him like a fiery tempest. Daniel wanted to say something clever, but all he could manage was a stupid expression and a shrug.

'How could you, at a time like this? Are you completely witless or is today an exception?'

How could he answer that? Daniel wanted to, desperately, but he didn't know the words. He wanted to tell her about his cancer, about how short his life was; about how it felt infinitely shorter still with those possessed baying for their blood. He wanted to spill his guts about the dragon and the horrors that would haunt him until his rapidly approaching dying day, and how he was struggling to handle any of it. But how could he explain any of that to his sister and make her understand that the alcohol dulled the ache and quelled the voices of regret and recrimination in his head. How it enabled him to continue putting one foot in front of the other day after day, for however many he had left. He had always maintained that it was for her sake that he never spoke of it, but it probably wasn't, if he was honest with himself. It was because he didn't know how to and if he did, that would make it even more real than it already was. He would never be able to take the pity and hurt in Tara's face once she knew. It would be all he would ever see again. Every time he looked at her, he would see his death there. And it scared him far more than he could ever admit, even to himself. So he drank.

Gwen had overheard the conversation and had come back into the room from tentatively exploring the ramshackle house. She had peeked in the odd cupboard and opened the odd drawer, more for idle curiosity than in the hope of finding anything. But even these sly observations made her feel slightly uncomfortable at the idea of invading someone else's life. Her conscience had obviously grown along with her power. *Bummer!* she thought, lightly. She interspersed her investigations with brief looks out of the various windows, paranoia ever present in her mind now that there were, or at least could be, enemies at every turn. But thankfully, they were still undiscovered though she knew in her heart of hearts that it couldn't and wouldn't stay that way for long. But she was interrupted by Tara's outburst and she sauntered back to see her ripping into her brother, who just stood before her grinning: a sort of guilty, lopsided grin of the partially inebriated. She had seen that look before too. Her own anger flared. They didn't have the luxury of supporting a half-cut Daniel when death could descend on them any moment. Everyone needed their wits – what ones they had left – firing on all cylinders. Gwen accelerated and stalked right up to Daniel, almost barging Tara out of the way. With the sound of flesh smacking resoundingly against flesh, Gwen slammed both hands onto either side of Daniel's face, her tiny hands gripping his reddening cheeks and ears in a vice like grip; and then she spoke to him. But it wasn't the kind words of Gwen the woman that issued forth. Instead, with the power of the position she now held, her voice took on a physical presence all of its own. When she spoke, it vibrated through every molecule in his body and he heard her words on more levels than he knew existed.

'You will not drink alcohol ever again, you foolish man! Do you know what it does to you?'

Daniel just gazed blankly back at her, too rapt by the power coursing through him, emanating from her rapidly heating hands. Her voice fizzed and snapped like it should have been throwing off white hot sparks, and blue vapor began to issue from Daniel's exposed skin, as though his flesh steamed as the alcohol was evaporated. Every pore was evacuating the accumulated booze from his system. Gwen unconsciously purged his body of all traces and effects of the brandy, along with the remains of any excess that already permeated his body. But as he began to shake, her hands gripped him tighter and a low moan trembled from his slackening mouth. Gwen pinned his eyes with hers as though she could see into his very soul, drumming her message home into him as she concentrated on scouring him from the inside out, removing all trace and desire for anything remotely alcoholic. But quite suddenly, she encountered something she hadn't expected. It took her so much by surprise that she abruptly let go and took a step back, looking at Daniel with a wholly different expression, mostly one of concern. Daniel just juddered and dropped to his knees as though someone had turned off the current that he was plugged into. Collapsing to his haunches as though his bones had turned to putty, Daniel put his hands on his knees and sucked in several deep recuperating breaths. Finally, after several silent and tense minutes, he looked up, first at Gwen, then Tara.

'I don't know what to say.' His own voice was quiet, but clear and more importantly, sober. 'I don't know the last time I felt like this; I can't remember that far back. But wow, Gwen!' She looked at him questioningly as he said her name. 'You could make a fortune with a detox regime like that. I don't even want a drink now. How about that?' But Daniel lost his joyful expression and his voice held no trace of the humor that his words should have held.

Then Gwen asked him her question. 'What's that in your head?'

In fact, any vestige of expression he might have had but had been unaware of left him then and his eyes narrowed suspiciously, anxiously flicking between Gwen and Tara.

'What are you talking about, Gwen?' he asked steadily, as though testing where she was going with this but dreading the answer he knew was coming.

'That thing nestled in your brain. Did you not know?' Gwen was concerned now; conscious that she had unearthed something he didn't know about and after saving him from one poison, only to draw his attention to another, much worse condition. Again, long moments passed before Daniel moved, only to slump even lower. As though all the will to live had drained completely from his person, along with the alcohol. Tara moved faster than Gwen could have thought as she dropped beside her brother and threw her arms around him. Gwen watched silently as the brother and sister held each other. She saw Daniel's shoulders shudder and she knew he was crying.

'I'm so sorry, Daniel, I didn't mean...'

But Daniel held up a forestalling hand whilst still looking down. Eventually though, looking up at her with startling red-rimmed eyes, he sat up ever so slightly, a little straighter than he had been, and when he spoke his own voice had lost the remaining spark that he had exhibited only moments earlier.

'I never wanted anyone to know; I just wanted a life. Until that is, it ended.'

Tara sat back and looked at him curiously. Curious but with a shadow of the hurt she was now feeling at being excluded from a fundamental part of her brother's life. 'You don't have to say anything you don't want to, Dan,' Tara started, but again Daniel shook his head and stopped the two girls from drowning him in consideration and sympathy. It was the one thing he dreaded almost as much as dying. Those looks, that tone of voice that said 'How sad, what a waste, isn't it a shame, and he's such a nice boy'. They had no idea. One day soon, he would be gone and they would all say the same thing except in the past tense. How meaningless was that but Daniel told them both his story anyway. By the end of it, both Gwen and Tara had tears in their eyes.

'That's why I kept it to myself, Taz,' using the nickname for his sister for the first time in Gwen's hearing. 'I didn't and still don't want all the worried looks and pitiful glances, nor the whispers behind my back. There's nothing to be done about it, apparently. It's inoperable and has been for some time, it seems. I thought it was a big deal until this shit hit the fan; now it seems fairly unimportant by comparison. Judging by the faces of some of them people back there chasing us, there's those worse off than me.'

Tara spun to Gwen, a look of hope blossoming in her face as she recalled his detox. 'Can't you fix it? You can do incredible things. You can, can't you?'

Gwen's heart broke at the desperation in her pleading voice and the glimmer of life in Daniel's eyes. She recalled her feelings when she had first discovered the mass there in his brain. 'No.' The word couldn't have had a more devastating effect if she had taken a Louisville Slugger to the pair.

'What do you mean, no? I've just seen what you are capable of. Surely a simple thing like removing a tumor should be child's play to one like you, should it not?'

'No it isn't, Tara. You must remember, I'm new to this and I simply don't know how to do such a thing. What I saw is so entwined and threaded through his brain that, firstly, it's a miracle he's even walking and talking as it is. Secondly, if I touch it, I'm more likely to kill him rather than cure him. And I'd rather he live with whatever's keeping him going now than see him dead at my feet because I screwed up. Wouldn't you?'

But Gwen knew her reasoning had fallen on deaf ears. All Tara had heard was the 'no', not the sense behind it. She saw it in her eyes. They had all the warmth of a shark for the briefest second, and Gwen knew beyond any shadow of a doubt, that whatever might have been between them had perished there and then with her refusal to help her dying brother. Tara took a long lingering look at Daniel, kissed his cheek and stood, then promptly stormed off upstairs. Gwen heard a door slamming several times, then silence.

'She'll be fine when she calms a bit,' Daniel croaked, his throat constricted by emotion. 'She's always had a fiery temper on her and she doesn't see the shades of grey that life really is; only the black and white of how she wants it to be.'

Gwen stared at the young man before her and she couldn't speak for the understanding in his eyes. If she did, she knew she would break down and cry too.

'It's okay, Gwen. Don't feel bad. You've done one good thing and I've already been told I'm a goner once, and I've accepted that, even if I don't like it. Now I know what they mean when they say ignorance is bliss.'

He stood, a little shakily at first, then gradually, straighter even than he was before. 'I might be a dead man walking, but I bet most of those who've got what I have don't feel this good about it. I haven't felt this invigorated for years. Thanks.'

That did it for Gwen. She swiftly drew him into a rib crushing embrace as she broke down and cried on his shoulder. Her emotions were jumbled beyond her ability to control them, so she just let them sort themselves out. Daniel just smiled and held her back until she was finished.

'You want a cup of tea?' he asked after about ten minutes, when he felt her body begin to relax and the tears slow to a soft snuffle. She leant back, still holding him, and nodded weakly. Daniel then gently disentangled himself from her and slipped into the kitchen, leaving Gwen to watch his back and rub her eyes with the back of her hand.

But just as Daniel came back with a tray of steaming tea in a hotch potch collection of mugs and cups, Tara came thundering down the stairs.

'They've found us!' She looked at both Gwen and Daniel as she spoke and Gwen got the distinct impression she was looking at a wholly differ-ent woman to the one who had gone upstairs only minutes before. 'They're coming up the damned street as we speak. What do we do: stay here or make a run for it? There's hundreds of them.'

Daniel threw the tray to one side, knowing that tea was off the menu now. They had more important issues to worry about and he offered a solution to them.

'I found some car keys here when I last dropped in. Never used them though. I had me own car and it didn't seem right somehow.'

'But using their house was okay? You have a strange view of priorities, Daniel.' Gwen responded with a smile, trying to regain some levity in the face of the horror outside that was, by all accounts, hurtling towards them as they spoke

He just shrugged and gave his disarming lopsided grin he gave when she first encountered him.

'Do you know which one it is?' Tara sensibly asked. 'We don't want to be fannying around trying to find which car your key fits with that lot bearing down on us: we've only got minutes as it is.'

Tara was gathering her belongings together as she spoke and shouldering them for the off. Daniel just winked and plucked a bunch of keys out of a jar that stood on the discarded dresser in the dining room where they stood. He held it up and at a glance, Gwen saw it was black and tablet shaped, with four interconnected rings on it.

Tara looked as blank as she had before he pulled his automotive rabbit out of his ceramic hat. 'And? Is that supposed to mean something?'

Daniel just rolled his eyes. 'Girls! What is it with you and cars? It's an Audi.' Still nothing. 'It's got infrared central locking. That means: when I push this, it'll bleep, flash its lights and unlock the doors. Then we'll know which one to run to, won't we. Bloody hell, and you thought I was the addled one.'

The girls scowled at him and Gwen pushed him towards the door. 'Let's go then. Stop being a smartass and find the car.'

They opened the door cautiously and Gwen instantly heard the screams of the approaching horde. They dived out and headed towards the parked cars, veering off as Daniel spotted the A4 estate several yards back. He held out the key fob and pushed the button. True to his description, it flashed its lights and they heard an audible click.

'Now I just hope it starts.'

The trio skidded to a halt by the silver vehicle just as the first possessed hove into view. Gwen rounded on Daniel as she threw open one of the doors. 'What do you mean: you hope it starts?'

'Like I said, it hasn't been used in some time. Maybe it was part of the deal with the house. Can't be easy taking a car to Oz. Guess they musta bought a new one out there, and like I said, I never bothered with it. So who knows?'

A shot rang out and Gwen spun to see Tara, with a look of horror and disgust on her usually pretty features, and the smoking shotgun held out before her. One of the possessed staggered slightly from the impact, bits of it spattering to the ground, but other than that it kept coming.

'Get in the car, Tara,' Gwen shouted at her. 'I'm not sure that's going to be a lot of use unless it's up close and personal.'

Having little choice but to agree as her target kept howling towards her, dripping and bleeding, Tara dived in and slammed the door behind her; and the moment she did, she smacked Daniel smartly on the back of the head. 'Will you get this thing moving, for God's sake? Can't you see that lot heading straight for us?'

Daniel took the slap the way a younger brother accepts such things from his big sister – that familial banter born over years of closeness, for there was no malice to their casual abuse of each other, just sibling rough-housing.

The Audi fired up as Gwen dived in herself, and with a dramatic wheel spin where the tyres sought purchase on the icy road, the car slewed out into the road proper, slamming Gwen's door for her and nearly taking a foot off in the process. Unfortunately, all they achieved was to allow the gap to close between the rampaging possessed and themselves as Daniel fought to regain control of the slipping and sliding car; as he did so, allowing what they were trying to get away from to get closer by the second. Time slowed as the possessed swarmed around the vehicle, screaming and howling as they tore at the car with ragged fingernails in their desperation to extricate its passengers. Tara screamed too as she saw the faces of people she knew, ripped and tortured by the demon possessing their bodies – this being the first time she had been this close. Gwen too screamed, but not in panic or fear, but anger; and directed it at Daniel.

'What the bloody hell are you trying to do? Are you actually trying to kill us?'

'I'm doing the best I can,' he wailed back. 'You said drive, so I'm driving.'

822

'But you're going the wrong bloody way!' Tara added her holler to the escalating din both in and outside. Daniel looked on the verge of snapping as he scanned left and right with eyes that seemed to have trouble keeping up with the movement.

'How should I know where we're going? You didn't say and the damn car was facing this way anyhow. So this is the way we went.' There were concussive thumps which almost punctuated Daniel's comment. Glancing back, he saw Gwen closing the door again after slamming the metallic shield into a couple of possessed who refused to give up.

'Turn us around now and get us out of these creatures' way before one actually succeeds in getting in here. Christ, that doesn't bear thinking about,' Gwen added, more to herself than anyone else. Bodies were bouncing and falling over and under the car as Daniel continued to plough into them. Conducting a flawless three point turn whilst barreling possessed out of the way at the same time, he spun them about until they were facing the way they had just come from. Gwen continued to use her door as a battering ram wherever possible, without putting herself or the others in jeopardy, as Daniel put his foot down. Again, the car fought for traction, found it, and leapt forward, smashing and scattering possessed left, right and centre. But it was going to be a harder fight now, for the press of bodies impeded the forward momentum of the car, and the engine screamed back in protest. Gwen watched in horror as more and more began to beat on the sorely abused car.

'This is getting us nowhere fast.' Gwen stated the obvious, more for her own benefit than to voice the unnecessary. 'We need to clear a path.' Again, it was an obvious statement but it helped galvanize her thoughts and those of Tara too, it seemed, who had seen the imminent danger of being overwhelmed. She hit the electric window button and it dropped a few inches. She shoved the barrel of the shotgun out and fired.

'You were right, Gwen; up close and personal is much more effective.' Several ruined bodies and heads were flung back as the weapon discharged. Tara quickly reloaded and fired twice more. Loading again, Tara risked opening the window fully before they recovered and she leant out, Hollywood style, giving both barrels to the press of bodies impeding their way. It had the desired effect and the car lurched forward, gaining momentum. Daniel flicked on the wipers to clear the gore that had spattered there, and gunned the Audi away. But just as they pulled away from the snarling horde and thought they were home free, another group of possessed came sprawling out of a side road. By rights, this should have posed little to no threat to the rapidly accelerating car, but Daniel suddenly leapt onto the brakes and brought the car to a screeching and swerving halt. His gaze was fixed dead ahead on the lead figure, who, seeing who was behind the wheel of the car, grinned a flesh splitting grimace and leapt to the top of a nearby parked car and squatted down upon its roof, doing a macabre impersonation of a wild and feral frog poised to leap from a metallic blue BMW lily pad. Daniel looked directly at his best friend Kieran, who now resembled something freshly dug up and hacked at with various edged weapons. His clothes were shredded and gaping wounds bled a dark viscous fluid from numerous parts of his emaciated body.

'Ddddaaannniiieeellll!' A voice like broken frozen glass grazed its way across the wintry and glacial air. 'Cooommme to ussssss, Daanniieelll. Giiivve yoursssselffff to the daarrkkknesss you seeekkk in yourrr hearttt. Commme to meeeee!'

There was almost a compulsion in the hideous screech that passed for his voice, and Daniel looked drawn towards leaping out of the car and running to his friend. But it was Gwen's whispered voice in his ear that snapped him out of the daze he found himself in.

'That's not your friend, Daniel. Your friend is dead.' Her melodious voice wove its way through Daniel's mind, severing the sticky, tenuous webs of enchantment that were carried insidiously in the demon's voice. 'What occupies his corpse now has no right to be here on this world, certainly not in the body of your friend. Fight it, Daniel; for the love of God and your sister, fight it. If those behind us catch us, we're dead.' Gwen had recognized Kieran from his moment of draconian advice the night she arrived. Fragments of an idea came to her as she spoke words of encouragement to Daniel. Why wasn't he petrified of her? Why was he out when the minions had been abroad and chasing her? In light of recent events, that was two too many coincidences for her liking.

'Daniel! Do something! Now!' Gwen's tone changed abruptly to forceful dominance to spur him into action. But in truth, she was only hoping he would drive away, not reach back and grab Tara's shotgun from her hand, where she was loading the last shell into the weapon. Daniel leapt from the car and ran to his friend, who watched him curiously. Still smiling, he cocked his head sideways, birdlike. Even when Daniel leveled the weapon at his friend's head, the Demon continued with its silent mocking expression. Perhaps it held the belief that Daniel had joined its cause and the web of coercion it had laid upon him had been sufficient, rendering the man before him helpless.

The demon that was Kieran had barely a microsecond to register its error as the head it wore exploded in a spray of blood, brain and bone matter.

Daniel wept as he jumped back into the car and hit the gas. Both girls were thrust back into their seats as Daniel purged his devastated emotions in an outpouring of deadly and nigh on suicidal speed. He had bounced off several other cars, cracked the windshield and virtually destroyed the hood as he ploughed through body after body of the possessed as they spilled out into the street, leaping at the car in some futile effort to halt its flight, before he slowed his semi-suicidal rally. But even as the emotional adrenaline rush subsided within him, they hadn't gone more than a mile out the other side of Sneem before their collective hearts sank. The deepest pit of despair still wouldn't have accommodated their depleted spirits when they rounded a corner and came skidding to a halt; for before them had to be close to a thousand screaming possessed, pouring across the open countryside like a plague of humanoid, cannibalistic ants. If Gwen had foolishly thought the plague that infected these poor people was restricted to Sneem or the villages and locals in that vicinity, she was poorly mistaken. What was howling towards them had to be from somewhere much larger and invariably further away. *So it's spread!* Gwen thought forlornly, wondering what to do next. Tara prompted her train of thought.

'This isn't good, Gwen. As the crow flies, that's the direction of the Kenmare stone circle, which, I needn't remind you, is where we need to be.'

Gwen briefly considered calling out for help. Back in Santa Fe, when the Ogre Kachinas attacked, she called for the animals to help, but she didn't really want them to get hurt here by engaging these unfeeling creatures. There had to be another way to get through them. Then it occurred to her. Not through them, but as Tara said – as the crow flies. *We'll just have to go over them. This should be interesting.* Gwen got out of the car and closed the door behind her. As she did, the sounds of those possessed ahead and the distant cries of those behind reached her ears. It was an infernal, unnatural sound and she found herself inwardly raging at their temerity for even being here, let alone corrupting and desecrating those that called the Earth home. Someone would pay dearly for this, that much she promised, but to keep that particular promise, all she had to do was find the one who was responsible; and that was a far more daunting prospect than facing its minions.

Putting thoughts of retribution and vengeance behind her for now, Gwen tapped on the glass for Tara to wind her window down. Leaning in after, Gwen spoke swiftly. She didn't want this to become a lengthy convoluted discussion or give them too long to think about what she proposed. They were going to have enough trouble with this as it was without adding to their woes. The horse had been bad enough, and Gwen still felt their eyes on her when they thought she wasn't looking. Seeing a person actually change into another creature and knowing it wasn't some computer generated wizardry just had to do something to their sanity retention capacity. But that had only been a mere horse – a creature they were familiar with. Gwen hadn't used the word, but the implication hung heavy and Daniel had already been privy to a close encounter of the draconian kind, and that had been enough to drive conscious thought from him. *Let's hope he fares a little better this time,* Gwen thought wryly as she backed up a few paces.

'Oh, by the way,' Gwen shouted to the car, 'you might want to put your seat belts on; this won't exactly be a regular take-off.'

Daniel spun and spoke to Tara, and with Gwen's exceptional hearing now, she picked up what he said and she sighed. Apparently he hadn't been listening, or had simply blocked it out as some sort of mental defense.

'What does she mean, Taz? What's taking off?'

Even Tara rolled her eyes. 'We are. Buckle up and hang on.'

Watching his sister hastily pull the strap over her chest and click it firmly in the belt device at her side, Daniel swiftly followed suit, concentrating so much on securing his own belt, he didn't see the crystalline emerald sparkles that marked Gwen's transition to the small hawk form she assumed. Powering upwards in almost vertical trajectory, she knew she needed room for the larger transformation and she could use a bit of gliding momentum.

Daniel's last look stayed with Gwen for some time as she saw his mortified face peering up through the sun roof at the malachite underbelly of the jumbo jet sized dragon that swooped down over them. His gaze had been drawn upwards as Gwen had cast a shadow over the tiny car and he looked up to see the cause, immediately wishing he hadn't. Again. Gwen's JCB-like forepaws gripped the car on both sides, causing a disconcerting crunching sound within as her scimitar sized talons found purchase in the fragile chassis, but she couldn't hear their screams of panic as the Audi was lifted off the ground faster than if it had been catapulted off the flight deck of a navy carrier. Though she did hear the frustrated and malevolent howls of the swarming possessed beneath her, impotently waving their arms in a pathetic defiance as her sail-like wings beat at the air and sent her soaring skyward.

Hah! You ugly demonic bastards. You didn't see that coming, did you? But, feeling the amassed power of her dragon form flowing through her, she wanted nothing more than to drop the inconvenience she held in her forepaws and turn back to strafe the swarm with fire. Over and over she would raze the soil clean until she had eradicated them all. To purify the Earth from their foul presence. But she couldn't. She had a mission. But even so, Gwen thought angrily, even with her hands full, so to speak, she would give them something to remember her by. Swooping lower, she only intended to bellow a battle-cry at them, but her own fury overspilt into something else and she belched forth a cone of fire so blisteringly hot, she not only took out a corridor of possessed and left a four-foot molten trench in her wake, but the heat she generated peeled the paint off the car she held.

Daniel watched in wide-eyed terror as the bonnet before him rippled and silver paint began to peel away as though the engine had caught fire. Then both he and Tara felt the heat. It was worse than being left in the midday sun for hours with all the windows shut. They were basically cooking within the car like an impromptu microwave. Before it got the better of them and they passed out from the soaring temperature, Daniel grabbed the butt of the shotgun and smashed a window open. They both sighed as gales of cold, relieving air blasted through the car; though their pleasure was shortlived as they both started to shiver then. Tara just looked blankly at Daniel, who just shrugged before they both ducked down into their respective foot wells to get out of the draught.

Gwen inhaled as she passed the now floundering possessed and felt good in herself that she had at least struck a blow against the darkness. That was until she looked up. Gwen had thought the swarm of possessed to be impressive albeit in a diabolical kind of way, but that paled into real insignificance against the monstrous demon army that was filling the horizon before her. It was as though an inky cloud was rolling across the landscape, annihilating everything in its path. What it passed over ceased to exist behind. There were no prisoners, no mercy, and no nothing. Every animal, plant and human in the demon army's path was extinguished. And their numbers had to top several hundred thousand to create such an unholy spectacle. Her supernatural vision showed her far more than she really wanted to see, and Gwen felt true fear touch her soul with fingers of barbed steel, for she knew that they had seen her too.

Oh Shit! was about all she could think of to say. Gwen recalled her recent encounter with just a few minions and now there were just so many. Gwen could do nothing but fly on and wonder if her passengers had seen them too. The only thankful thing was the fact Gwen could see the stone circle and she knew she would be there long before the approaching army got anywhere near their position. But Gwen was no military tactician and she knew nothing of scouts who ranged ahead of the main body, gathering intel for the commanders. Not yet anyway.

Gwen swooped lower and deposited the car just outside the circle in an adjacent field, she watched it roll a few feet and come to a juddering halt as it squelched in a muddy patch. The heat from the cooling vehicle and Gwen's body briefly melted the frozen earth. She banked round and landed, neater than she had before, some way behind the car so as not to flatten it. *At least I'm getting better at something,* Gwen mused as she resumed her own form, adopting the natural armored foliage look she had used earlier. Gwen caught up to the car just as Daniel and Tara were literally falling out of the abused vehicle, through doors that would barely open and definitely no longer close. They both saw her and, as one, took an involuntary step back before they knew what they were doing. It was a small thing, but Gwen saw it. With that tiny gesture, another of the diaphanous threads that supported her heart tore irreparably. One more reminder that she was different now, more alone than she ever thought she would or could be.

'That was you, wasn't it?' Daniel blurted.

There was no need to explain the obvious of what *that* was. Gwen just nodded and looked at them both with sad eyes, assessing them for injury. They seemed fine, externally anyway.

'I wanted to believe so badly, Gwen, honestly I did, but even with all that was going on, it was still hard. It's the twenty-first century, isn't it?

Nobody believes in anything any more. I don't count religion: that's just blind faith in the teachings of men. What I mean is the belief in the wonders of the world, the Universe – '

'Multiverse,' Gwen interrupted calmly, yet her voice carried such authority that Tara immediately stopped speaking. 'There are more *verses* out there than just this one, Tara. I had it likened to grains of sand in a desert, except...' Gwen pointed upwards, '...the desert is up there. And I don't mean to stop you, Tara. I get where you're coming from. Believe me, I had the same thoughts; it's just that it's not all wonderful and if you saw what I just did as we flew, you'll know it's about to get a lot worse. We are ants that have only just glimpsed what's beyond our cozy little environment. There is far more out there than can be imagined on Heaven and Earth, or something like that, and trust me when I say you don't want to meet the majority of it. In fact, it looks like the majority of it is actually heading this way. I'd say by this time tomorrow, where we're standing will be nothing but black, dead ash. Us too, unless we get our collective asses in gear.'

'Bloody hell, you lost your happy thoughts on the journey here?' Daniel asked. 'What have you done with the other Gwen? She at least had a little optimism. I liked that idea. You know: positive, upbeat and all that. But you're scaring and depressing me in equal measure and I assure you, gal, *that,* I really don't need. I've got enough worries already, thanks, without you adding to them with your cheerful philosophizing. And what happened up there anyway? We nearly fried! You didn't pissing well warn us about *that.*'

Gwen looked apologetic but said nothing. Instead, she turned away from the siblings and began walking around the stone circle, studying small rocks that protruded from the soil, finishing her lap at the dolmen in the middle. The entire time Gwen was doing this, Tara was watching Daniel thoughtfully, as though she was seeing him for the first time. Usually, when faced with insurmountable odds and things beyond his comprehension, Daniel had a tendency to glaze over, resembling the proverbial rabbit caught in the headlights of the oncoming and very imminent future. But here he was; taking in the prospect of a giant green dragon, an invading army of nothing short of monsters and, after having blown his best friend's head into vapor, holding what was almost a sensible and coherent conversation. Her brother had done more than just sober up; he had grown up and she hadn't noticed. Tara felt an overwhelming urge to smother him and protect the little brother she had taken for granted for so long. A wave of guilt washed over her like so much Arctic water. He had been going through such torment with his illness and he had not felt he could share it with her. What had she done to engender such secrecy from her own brother? Tara wanted nothing more now than to shield him from the horrors they faced, but, most of all, to rid him of the terrible disease that promised to steal him away from her without a moment's notice. This was *her* brother, *her* flesh and blood, the only living family she had left in the entire world; and Tara vowed there and then to do everything in her power. Wait, Tara amended, her newly inherited powers – however that may turn out – and, Gwen or no Gwen, to save Daniel from his fate.

Gwen stood at the dolmen, eyes closed and one delicate hand placed reverently upon its rough, weathered cold stone surface. She was momentarily lost in the pulse and flow of power that permeated the rock, fed from deep within the Earth much like a natural spring; only in this case, it wasn't water that gushed forth, but power. The unnatural storm that had blown out Tara's home had failed in its mission to destroy all the sacred circles. She didn't know how, nor did she particularly care at this point. She was just thankful that it had survived at all. Perhaps those behind the dark storm considered it too inconsequential. Those in power have a tendency to be arrogant that way, when in reality, nothing at all is inconsequential. Everything had a purpose. That was why it was there in the first place. Even in the largest machine man had ever made, the tiny sprung washer, or miniscule screw was there, serving its purpose. But unfortunately, such is the way with those who rise to power, they become blinkered and blinded to small things and all they see are the massive cogs and main moving parts. One day maybe, Gwen meditated to herself as she absorbed the power of the dolmen, humanity will learn to appreciate the smaller details and those they considered lesser in their world, and maybe it will be richer for it. Getting back to the reason they were there though, Gwen focused on bringing the power of the circle up where Tara could access it, but she hit a wall. Not in the power, but in her own mind. How did she do it and what was it precisely she wanted to do? She needed to talk to Tara. Gwen lifted her hand off the stone and immediately felt the difference. It was akin to taking a bare hand out of warm water when you were standing naked in the snow, freezing. A part of Gwen instantly missed that connection like a child misses the connection to its mother. The sense of safety, security and invulnerability bestowed by that bond left Gwen bereft and sad as she severed the connection and turned towards Tara and Daniel. But before she could utter a word, her eyes were instantly drawn to the sky, where the siblings were now staring in horror. Something or some things were plummeting out of the clouds at a phenomenal speed. And just to add insult to their already injurious predicament, it looked as though it was aimed directly at the spot they currently occupied. Each of the trio thought of their own variation on their end. Tara thought aeroplane, Daniel considered a missile and Gwen instantly plumped for minions. But as the rapidly descending shape drew ever closer, four individual shapes could be distinguished. Closer still and Gwen could see they were humanoids on horseback – a fact Gwen could appreciate a little better than her companions were likely to. And there was only one group of individuals that came to her mind who fitted that description. Moments later, her suspicions were realized as the riders alighted expertly in the adjacent field and ghosted their way across to the periphery of the circle, where one of the riders – a large, heavily built and cowled figure, clad in midnight hued plate armor, complete with steel, full faced helm with the face plate carved into the visage of a grinning skull; a shield of what appeared to be a conglomeration of interlocking metallic and viciously spiked bones on the arm holding the reins; and an impressively huge, ebony-and-silver scythe with a fantastically carved and what looked to be razor sharp blade at its tip in the other hand – bowed his head in acknowledgement, the way a king would to another ruler. Then in a voice that made Daniel moan and drop to the ground and Tara slam her hands over her ears, he greeted Gwen in almost courteous fashion.

'Well met, Avatar. The Four Horsemen of the Apocalypse offer you and your companions whatever assistance we may be of in your time of need. For as I suspect you have, we too have seen the wrath of the Adversary in the form of his legions descending on this location with all possible haste. It seems you have upset the Dread Lord somehow.' Death paused briefly and before Gwen could formulate any sort of response, he added, with almost a tinge of satisfaction to his concussive voice, a pleased full stop.

'Well done.'

'For what?' Gwen asked, genuinely surprised by the compliment. 'I don't have the tree; I still don't even know where it is, let alone be any closer to finding it.'

'No, that seems true enough, but you do seem to have found something.'

Daniel moaned some more, a little louder this time. This caught the Reaper's attention and he looked straight at Daniel. His indomitable gaze lingered on the fetal-positioned human before moving to Tara. It was impossible to gauge what he thought, if anything, beyond the steel mask that hid him within the inky cowl, but he did seem to be taking a disturbing amount of interest in the siblings. When Death next spoke, his voice began softening to that of mortal tolerance, and firstly he addressed Daniel:

'Get up, Daniel. I am sorry for any distress I may have caused you by my demeanor. We have been in battle almost solidly these past few weeks and I have become accustomed to having to utilize more power than I would like to, to overwhelm the lesser creatures. I forget that you mortals also suffer from the effects of too powerful an aura. This should be more acceptable.'

Daniel expressed his gratitude by rolling over and groaning some more and clutching his head. Death looked closer. 'Ah, I see the cause of your concern now. Allow me.'

Death waved a hand and Daniel immediately stopped groaning and sat up. A look of wonder and relief fleetingly crossed his features until his eyes focused on the cause of his problem. He back-pedaled away from the figure so fast he slammed back first into one of the standing stones; driving the wind from his lungs with an ooof that made Gwen flinch, and causing him to topple once more.

'Famine!' Death called to his own companions. 'Help the poor fellow, will you, before he hurts himself. I need to speak with the avatar.'

Famine, for his part, tossed his head and harrumphed, muttering to himself as he dismounted. 'Just what did your last slave die from?'

'Disobeying an instruction, I believe. Now will you stop sulking and help the mortal. You know very well why we had to leave the battle when we did. You'll get another chance, I have no doubt.'

For all Famine's petulance at being ordered like a mere squire, he was smiling as he arrived at Daniel's side and helped him to sit up. 'Are you well, young sir?'

His clipped accent reached Gwen and she detected a hint of the Spanish about it. Musical and cultured. She got the impression that if he walked into a room and started talking, the atmosphere would turn jovial and he would be the centre of attention. Daniel's eyes were still out on crab stalks as he looked at the four armored figures. Realization of who they were fought toe to toe with his religious upbringing. Possessed was one thing – that could be passed off as some infection – but these were straight out of the Book of Revelation and that drove things home to Daniel in ways Gwen sympathized with, recalling her mother's devout faith. 'Th... Th... That's... That's...'

Famine smiled and helped him out. 'Yes, that's Death. But don't go on like that; it'll just go to his head and he's enough of a handful already, dishing out orders left, right and centre like he's some big cheese. Honestly, I've lost count of the number of helmets we have had to have made for him as he keeps outgrowing them.'

Death shot Famine such a look it would have stopped a stampeding rhino in its tracks. But Famine just smiled back the easy smile of one who's been through this many, many times before. Ignoring Death, he returned his attention back to Daniel. As he did so, the coldly beautiful oriental woman, who the other three knew as Pestilence, also dismounted and came over to join Famine. Only one rider remained in his saddle. Gwen deduced that it was War, as much by his vast array of armamentaria distributed all over him and his equally massive warhorse than by any other reasoning. He kept vigil, it seemed.

Tara, for all the initial conversation and byplay, simply stood and watched after Death modified his voice, though her head was still ringing. Her eyes darted between the mystical figures, watching every movement, expecting them to vanish any second. But as soon as two of the Horsemen converged on Daniel, she steeled herself and went to him also, kneeling the other side of him to Famine, with Pestilence standing, legs braced before him, looking down on the trio coolly.

'There is nothing to be done, Famine,' she almost whispered, so quiet was her voice in comparison to Death's booming baritone. 'It is a miracle he still lives at all. He is too far beyond the balance to recall him now. The *coup de grace* would be the kindest thing for him now. I will administer it if you do not have the stomach Famine.'

Tara leapt up and planted herself squarely before the small, wiry oriental just as she pulled one of her wickedly curved swords up from over one shoulder with a ring of steel sounding from where they were secured.

'Don't you dare!' Tara hissed in a voice that was colder than the surrounding countryside. One of the Horsemen of the Apocalypse she may be, but that wouldn't be enough to get her through Tara to lay even a finger on Daniel. Tara could be fiery and intimidating when she put her mind to it and was duly motivated. She was motivated now. The prospect of them even *suggesting* they put her brother down like he was a sick dog incensed her almost beyond reason. An unseen and unfelt wind lifted Tara's hair and it flowed about her like a living thing. Having no weapon didn't deter her either. Tara's hands bunched into claws and she would have tackled the heavily armed woman bare handed if that was what it took. Gwen glanced back at the scene, alerted by a subtle shift in the power of the circle, to see the two women standing off from one another. Pestilence hadn't sheathed her blade yet and imminent violence hung in the air. Their gazes locked and Gwen was convinced that nothing could have lived had it stepped between them into that void. But Gwen could see that Tara was livid and on the verge of doing something really stupid.

'Excuse me a moment, my lord Death.' Gwen felt it was the right thing to say as she excused herself and stepped back to see what was occurring with her companions. 'What the bloody hell is going on here? We are supposed to be on the same side!' Gwen demanded of anyone who would answer her; she didn't care who at that point.

Daniel was nearly apoplectic now. What with all he had been through, now his sister wanted to fight one of the fabled Horsemen to stop her from putting him out of his misery. It was all too much for him and his overtaxed brain, complete with its cerebellum cuckoo, so it sought a dark place where it could hide, blissfully dragging Daniel into oblivion with it. He groaned and slid bonelessly down the rock, ignobly falling against Famine, who seeing the whole thing as one big joke, just smiled and gently propped him back up.

'I would have thought you, Lady Gwendoline, being the avatar of nature, of all beings on this world understood the natural order of things.'

Gwen just arched an eyebrow and folded her arms over her chest, index finger tapping against her bicep. 'I'm new. Enlighten me!'

'I trust you know what this human has inside his head?' Pestilence asked.

'This human has a name, I'll have you know. It's Daniel, you cold hearted bi– '

Gwen stopped Tara before she put her other foot in the place currently occupied by her teeth. 'Enough, Tara. No one will be harming Daniel; you have my word.'

Tara turned to glare at Gwen, then back to Pestilence, as though she couldn't believe what she was hearing.

'That's all very well and bloody good. But not one of you has offered to heal him, have you! Why not? I've heard your feeble excuse, Gwen and I can't believe that. You're Nature, for God's sake. Cancer surely works against nature. Why wouldn't you want to free people from its insidious poison? I don't understand – I'm just a *mere mortal*.'

The contempt in her words made Gwen flinch inwardly. She had a point but what could Gwen say? How could she make Tara see that even cancer had its place in the natural order. It was a great equalizer that was all the more fearsome for humanity's lack of understanding about its nature. Like any riddle, once humans had learnt all the lessons it had to impart, as in the case with bubonic plague, maybe it wouldn't be so terrible. True, Gwen had never lost anyone close to the filthy disease, but she believed it had a place in the world. Man was top of his alleged food chain and had no predator to cull his ever expanding numbers. Yes, it was a terrible ailment and it caused great pain and suffering to those it left behind, but so did being run over by a bus. Humanity didn't abolish public transport. She had gone through this very argument several times with her friends back home: Dolores, Jen and Maddy. It was a complex and emotive subject and certainly not a suitable exercise to be entertaining considering their dire circumstance and the horde of minions just over the horizon.

'There is far too much to even try to understand right now, Tara, and I'm in no way condoning the blasé attitude of Pestilence…' Gwen turned her own indomitable gaze upon the still expressionless face of Pestilence, who in turn locked her unblinking eyes with Gwen's, '…however, euthanasia is not an option here, call it whatever you will. Nor is this a battlefield – '

'Not yet, anyway,' Famine interjected serenely, eliciting further scowls from everyone.

'As I was saying,' Gwen reiterated, 'nor is this a battlefield where the sick and wounded are just a burden. Should I find the fabled First Tree, then maybe the fruit from that will decide who lives and who dies and of what. Until then, he is in my care and no one is to lay a hostile finger on him. If you can't or won't help, back off.'

Pestilence moved her cherry shaped lips in order to say something but Gwen forestalled her. 'No, don't even bother. I don't need to be the avatar of nature to understand the natural order, nor the balance between who dies and why, and who lives. But answer me this. You're Pestilence. To my mind that makes you responsible for all disease and associated ailments. Why can't you of all people heal him?'

Pestilence looked at the group assembled around her, and then she glanced at Death, who nodded almost imperceptibly. 'I can't. It is as simple as that. There is a point where any ailment or disease or poison progresses too far in the organism, in this case, human. Since the Adversary rose to power, we have become weaker. At least here on this world. Our powers are restricted in the Domain and upon the home worlds of the Drakarim and the Children of Thought; though we are not without power, I hasten to add. As is said before, it is a miracle he even breathes with the amount of cellular degeneration and sheer size of the tumor within his brain. He could die at any moment.'

Gwen glared harder, if that was at all possible, though apparently it was; for even Pestilence blanched ever so slightly under her steely gaze. Pestilence finally released her sword and let it slip back into its scabbard, and lowered her own almond shaped eyes and cast an unreadable expression over the unconscious Daniel. 'Very well. As the human...' Pestilence turned to Tara, '...Daniel, means so much to you, I will slow the growth and shield the remainder of his brain from the disease. He will feel no pain at least. It is as much as I can do. It will only delay the inevitable, but as you say, Lady Gwendoline, perhaps you will find the Tree in time to save us all.'

With that, faster than Gwen could have thought possible, Pestilence sidestepped her and with a squeal from Tara as she watched helplessly, plunged all four fingers straight into Daniel's forehead, right up to the knuckles. In the time it took for her to blink, she withdrew them again, turned and strode back to her horse. Over her shoulder Gwen heard: 'It is done.' But Tara wasn't. She rounded on the gathering of impossible entities and, planting her hands on her hips, addressed them all, irrespective of rank or stature.

'Is that your lot? There are supposedly five of the most powerful entities I've ever bloody heard of standing before me and not one of you can do anything helpful about my brother's ailment? I can't believe it. Exactly how fucking useless are you?'

Death stepped forward, though nothing about his manner said placating. He merely stepped before the furious redhead and looked down at her. To Tara's credit, she simply looked up and locked her own steely, emerald green gaze onto the two sparkling, sapphire blue lights that shone within Death's armored helm which passed for his eyes, waiting for him to say whatever it was he wanted to say.

'My Lady Tara, why can you not accept that all things must die eventually? Even us, who may seem beyond immortal to you, yet it only means that we measure time differently. Daniel will die in due course, for that is his destiny to do so. Much the same way it was the fate of your mother and father to die when they did.'

'What do you know of my parents?' Tara was too angry to realize the irony of her question considering who she was talking to. 'What have their deaths got to do with why you can't save Daniel? They didn't die of cancer. There was no curing what killed them.'

Death stood impassive against her wrath and responded coolly, 'What do you know of their deaths?' It was a simple question but it seemed to deflate Tara considerably. It forced her to dredge up memories long buried, and the doing so obviously pained her, that pain taking the heat from her fury and the color from her face.

'I don't know much. I was too young, only eleven, and Daniel was just a toddler when my ma died. My da told us it was a drowning accident but the body was never recovered. And his death was just as empty. We had no body to mourn over 'cos the authorities wouldn't tell me much and my da's brother, who came to take care of us, never spoke of it neither.'

Death watched the redhead as she cast her mind back into the soul wrenching part of her past that set her on her present path. 'Do you know what happened to your father, exactly?'

Tara nodded slowly. 'He didn't want to tell us, but when our uncle eventually left – his work finally took him to Europe somewhere, and he just never came back, dirty, pervy, miserable old fucker. I hope he's dead in a ditch somewhere, riddled with some foul sexual disease that has rotted his scrawny bollocks – anyway...' Tara had fired up again as the thoughts of her child molesting uncle coalesced, '...he told us that da had died when his boat blew up. I've hated the water ever since. Can't imagine why, hey?' Tara spat bitterly.

'It is understandable, Tara; the sea doesn't appear to have been too kind to you and your family. Your father wasn't a well man. Early stage prostate cancer. His illness could have been treated, but he chose to ignore it. Instead, he took up a career that ended his life even sooner. He supplied weapons for some very unpleasant people. Weapons that were used against the wrong people. He was caught in the backlash of retaliation and his vessel, along with his cargo and its crew, were destroyed. It was not in the nature of those who carried this out to publicize their activities, so it was glossed over. It...' Death stopped suddenly and took a step back from Tara, still watching her intently though.

'What is it? What's wrong?' Tara was so caught up in the recount of her father's death, hearing for the first time the facts surrounding his demise, that Death's sudden halt left her hanging in midair, momentarily forgetting her earlier outburst. Death continued to stare at Tara, and then he turned his cowled head to run his cobalt gaze over Gwen. Gwen saw it lower slightly and she saw him shake his head ever so slightly from side to side as though he suddenly knew something he wished he hadn't.

'What on earth could he have seen to make *Death* react so?' asked Gwen, to nobody in particular. The icy fingers of prescience all bar throttled her spine as she got the very distinct feeling that whatever it was boded ill.

'What?' Tara shouted a little louder when nobody responded to her the first time.

Death answered her finally, but his tone had changed, subtly. It was as though he no longer wanted to explain anything and even wished he hadn't started talking in the first place. 'It is not that I am omnipotent, Tara, and know all there is to know about everyone who has died, but the bloodlines allow me to connect to the past and those who lived within it. Through you I can connect to your entire ancestry, and at this moment I can honestly say it is not an ability that has proved useful. You have some very colorful individuals in your bloodline, Tara, and I can only hope you do not live up to their expectations, though it seems recent events have conspired to challenge you on that front.'

Something had changed. The energy of the group had shifted away from their inability to cure Daniel to something infinitely more dangerous. Gwen, who had been present at Tara's initiation, for there was little else to describe the ritual she had performed on the altar stone of her mantelpiece, made the assumption that Death had seen it too now and recognized it. Maybe he had seen the dark woman with the sickle from her vision or even knew who she was. That and more, maybe. The skein was tangling rapidly since Gwen had left the relative tranquility of her life in Santa Fe. A life that seemed suddenly so distant, almost dreamlike. Did she really do that? Gwen thought of the painting in Tara's back bedroom almost prophesying her arrival. How was that even possible? It was fast becoming a paranormal dot to dot, with some cosmic pencil slowly connecting people and events together in ways she didn't even begin to understand. Though at this moment in time, Gwen was blissfully unaware of just how relevant and potentially devastating her observation would be.

'There is no more time for this, Tara. Just accept that this is how it must be. Daniel has. Perhaps you should ask him before you say and do something you or the rest of us may regret! We are in a war where the rules of the cosmos are in flux; powers are waxing and waning while the balance shifts. We all could die at any time, Tara. Be grateful for the time you do have with your brother and do not think dark thoughts I sense are building within you about the futility of saving him, nor the lengths you feel you will go to. It simply cannot be done the way matters stand presently. Gwen is quite possibly our only hope – certainly she is Daniel's. I suggest you channel your energies into helping her rather than harboring resentment to those who would aid you but are unable to do so.'

Tara blanched and what color she had left in her already pale skin, fled. Gwen thought that it was a look of guilt that flitted over her companion's features, but it was gone before she could be sure. Either way, it seemed the fight had gone out of Tara at Death's pertinent and somewhat on the money observation. Death then stalked away from Tara before she could say anything else, but it didn't look as though she even wanted to – she simply and silently moved to kneel by Daniel's still unconscious form. As she did so, Famine stood and backed away respectably, only stopping to lean against the dolmen in the circle's centre. He glanced at War, who held up three fingers. Famine nodded and looked to Death. Death in turn glanced back and Gwen realized they were communicating mentally.

'Hey! That's a bit rude, you know,' Gwen said simply, guessing they would figure out what she was referring to.

Famine did and winked at Gwen almost cheekily. 'Good to see you're sharp, Avatar, but you are right; it was rude and we apologize. You have a right to know but it wasn't anything personal, only War letting us know the enemy is a mere three miles away and approaching fast. And it is with some regret that they are going to be here before Ezekiel and his Celestial Host arrive. And that means we will have to hold them ourselves until they turn up. Oh well.'

He sounded jovially resigned to the fact that he would be outnumbered roughly a few hundred thousand to one. Gwen was staggered how he could be so offhand about it. Even though he was a principal power in the multiverse, even he could die, it seemed, if what Death was saying had any bearing on them. Beings considered previously immortal were now vulnerable and in danger of annihilation. Maybe even the Four Horsemen, who had the supreme power of humanity, creating plague and starvation on scales unimaginable, setting brother against brother in senseless conflict, were no longer the all-powerful beings they started out as. They were still powerful, but against an enemy such as the Adversary, his generals and the other demonic creatures set against this world, they had their work cut out, especially when they were losing power as the Adversary gained it...

Famine watched Gwen and knew she knew that much of what he said was bravado, to maintain some sort of morale. It wouldn't do for lesser creatures to see the fabled Apocalyptic Horsemen waver in the face of seemingly insurmountable odds. They needed to appear as invincible and indomitable as ever. Gwen looked back at Famine and thought he was doing a pretty good job of it too. Leaving Tara to take care of Daniel, Pestilence rejoined War and they both drew weapons. Turning their steeds, they cantered away in the direction of the encroaching horde.

'They go to dispose of any scouts that may have ventured too close. Being so few, we need the element of surprise.'

Gwen laughed at the idea. 'There only being four of you, I think they'll be surprised all right.'

Famine saw her point and he too laughed out loud – a rich and achingly infectious sound. 'You are full of observations, my Lady Gwendoline,' Famine remarked, when his mirth had subsided. 'But that surprise will lead them to arrogance, believing us to be merely four. Arrogance, as you surely know, then slips smartly into the realm of stupidity, and stupid enemies are much easier to dispatch. Weaker we may be, but we are not without a few surprises of our own.'

'True enough, though I am loath to employ them on this rabble,' Death commented as he moved across the circle to end up next to Famine and Gwen.

'You wanted to talk to me earlier?' Gwen prompted, and the Reaper nodded.

'I did. We came because we sensed an extraordinary channeling of energy towards this island. It had to hold some significance. We arrived to find yourself and these humans fleeing more possessed than we have seen together in a long time, and added to that, an army of the Adversary's minions large enough to raze this entire island. There is something here that he wants badly. Either to possess or to stop – we don't know which – but we can't allow either to happen. What did you intend, Avatar?'

The question threw Gwen because she didn't actually have an answer. Their imperative had been to get to the circle, based on the letter from Tara's mother. And Tara's insistence that they get to a stone circle, this being the closest of any significance. But beyond that, she had no idea. How much protection was it going to be? Was it going to keep out a hundred thousand slavering demons? There were again more questions arising from her actions than she could fathom answers for, and it set her head spinning again.

'Honestly, I've no idea. Our plan, which was a hasty one at best, mainly due to hundreds of bloody possessed screaming after our blood, only got us this far. I was hoping for some respite or at least a clue as to our next move. Let's face it: fate hasn't been slow in presenting situations. I feel like a bloody pinball, bounced from pillar to post. I was hoping that something would manifest itself once we got here, but other than you, nothing has yet.' Gwen frowned, as an errant thought popped into her head. 'Unless it is you, you know, you're what's supposed to happen next.'

Death paced back and forth, obviously agitated about something. His scythe had mysteriously vanished and he had clasped both heavily gauntleted hands behind his back as he did so; looking so much like a military general and less like the iconic Grim Reaper, that it seemed to humanize him slightly in Gwen's eyes. More of a powerful ally than a principal power to be revered and feared.

'Tell me what you have learnt so far then, Gwendoline, and we shall see if we are indeed a part of your puzzle. But I suggest you be quick about it: I fear our time is short.'

Gwen took a second to reorganize her thoughts, and then she told Death and Famine all she had experienced since arriving upon the Emerald Isle. She omitted nothing and waited with bated breath after she had finished, as both Famine and Death weighed up her account and sifted through it for anything pertinent. Long minutes seemed to stretch by.

'Dilmun,' Famine said suddenly.

'What?'

'That's so unladylike, Gwen. You should say pardon me or I'm sorry, could you repeat that. Not "What?". Remember your station, my lady.' Famine clucked at her.

'What? We're about to overrun by an army of demons who are baying for blood and all you are concerned about is my bloody etiquette? I'm really beginning to worry about you, you know.'

Famine just smiled his ingratiating smile: one that he no doubt employed against the senoritas of history, and simply replied, 'Just because all about you is losing its way, there's no need to lower oneself to their level, but in response to your eloquent request that I repeat myself: Dilmun, or that is what it used to be called. As I recall, the one place that sticks out geographically where four heads of water meet – which is the merging of four mighty rivers – was at the area you now know as the Persian Gulf. It never used to be the size it is now, you know. It wasn't much bigger than a large river itself, and the land of Dilmun existed on its banks. Prior to that even, it was a lush and fertile land, a true garden of paradise.'

Gwen and Death both looked at Famine as though he had sprouted a second head.

'What?' he asked, innocently looking back, alternating his gaze between the two.

'Don't "what" me either,' Gwen snapped. 'Is there anything connecting the bits inside your head or do they all freefloat around each other like orbiting planets?'

'I'm sure I don't understand what you are implying, Lady Gwendoline. I have a very complex mental process, I'll have you know.'

Gwen just raised her eyebrows as though she had serious misgivings about that statement. 'I've been beating myself senseless trying to figure out the possible locations and likely countries where this tree could be. I've even entertained mythical countries like Atlantis or Avalon, not that I have any idea where they are either, but it bore consideration. Of course, the Garden of Eden was my first choice, but like the other two, where the hell do you start looking for that? Then along you come, like it's a matter of inconsequence, and just blurt it out like it's just occurred to you. Do you realize how much time you might have saved me if you had given someone that little bit of news just a tad sooner?'

Famine stood from where he leant, and raised a knowing finger and winked annoyingly again at her. 'Aha, but if you knew that from the get-go, you would have gone straight there and not arrived here. From what you said, you were expected, so maybe it is just as well you detoured. For even after the millennia I've been around, it still amazes me how the Fates weave their threads of destiny, and there are days when I really wonder if they know what they are doing. If they did, I mean, would we be in the dire straits we currently find ourselves?'

Death interrupted any further conjecture on the state of the cosmos. 'Now is not the time for philosophizing, Famine. War and Pestilence have already taken out six scouts and they have seen evidence of more in the vicinity.'

A groan from behind them made them all turn. Daniel had come to and was sitting up and rubbing his head, with a curious expression on his face.

Tara was fussing over him as though he were ten and had just had a close call.

'My headache's gone,' they heard him say. 'Jeez, I didn't even realize I had one until…well, until I haven't. I must have gotten so used to it being there that I shut it out.' It was at that moment that it all came flooding back as to where he was and in whose company he found himself. He locked his gaze on the Grim Reaper, as though seeing him for the first time. 'You're real, aren't you? I mean you're actually Death.' They weren't so much questions as much as they were affirmations for the sake of his own sanity.

'I am.'

'I can't say I'm pleased to meet you, though I guessed I would sooner rather than later. Presumably you know why.'

Death nodded.

'I don't want to die, not so young anyway. It's not fair! Do I have to?' He didn't need to say what he would have to do: it was blatantly apparent.

'In answer to all those, Daniel: no, it probably isn't fair, though fairness is entirely a matter of perspective, for whether it is fair or not, it is necessary; though it is truly nothing to be as fearful of as your species seems to be. In all the time you have lived as a race, you still cannot accept death as a spiritual and natural process, to be embraced and celebrated. Consider it graduation. Your soul has learnt enough in this life to move on.'

Daniel looked unconvinced. Death saw this one as a hard sell, but still gave it a go.

'If you believe nothing else, Daniel Haden Fitzgerald, believe me, for I can offer you assurances that no mortal religious organization can even begin to match, if you catch my drift.' Daniel nodded. 'They have built an empire based on what they *believe* exists. Unfortunately, it is based on what *they* think and have come to believe exists, not what *really* exists. You have a phrase which says that they have built a mountain from a termite mound. The truth is not for them to know; it never was. Were they secure in the knowledge of what awaited them, they would not strive in this life, which is what they need to do. Would a student strive to gain knowledge if it knew it would pass, whatever it did? Probably not.'

Daniel was trying desperately to hear what he was being told, but the expression on his face said he was struggling. Death continued all the same. 'But the one constant is that every human will die; at some point. What the Adversary is proposing will bring that about far too soon. He will eradicate both the present and the future, even to eradicating us.' Death gestured to himself and his comrades. 'That is a prospect that must *not* be considered. However appealing it may sound to shortlived creatures such as yourselves, the implications would simply be catastrophic.'

Death was trying, he really was, but Daniel's mental sponge had absorbed all it could and the excess was dribbling away as fast as Death was pouring words in. But Tara had picked up on a few vital bits though she remained silent as Death continued, merely chewing her lip as what she had heard wormed its way through her battered mind.

'That's all well and good,' Daniel said, as though Death had not spoken at all, 'but you must have missed the bit where I said I didn't want to die!'

Death just shook his massive armored and cowled head at the futility of what he was attempting. And Gwen noted a hint of annoyance in his voice as he spoke.

'You won't. Not just yet, anyway. You have as much of a chance at life as your sister. Pestilence has stilled your disease for now and removed any pain you may have felt. I suggest you make something of what life remains to you, for if the enemy wins, you'll be praying for me with a fervor you never knew even existed.'

Death turned away from Daniel and endeavored to talk to Gwen once more. There was obviously something he wanted to tell her, but again, he had no opportunity as Tara rose and strode across the clearing to join them. Death had time for two words only before Tara joined them.

'Watch her.'

'I can feel it, Gwen, the power in these stones.' Tara seemed excited for the first time since Gwen had declined to heal Daniel, though she couldn't get it through to Tara that it wasn't a declination to heal him; it was simply that she knew that in her present neophytic state, she'd probably kill him before curing him. Tara took that admission badly, as though Gwen was doing it on purpose, She had seemed sombre ever since and her eyes had lost the earlier sparkle, to be replaced with something more hooded and sultry, like a pair of embers, smoldering white hot below an ashen surface, just waiting to ignite into a conflagration. It hadn't helped either when Pestilence and the Horsemen abstained from healing her little brother. That just poured more fuel on her already barely contained incendiary. Gwen was worried about just what might be burnt should she actually explode, what with her newly inherited powers and all. Her mother had implied they were a double-edged sword and Death was right about one thing: she did indeed need careful watching.

'What do you feel, Tara?' Gwen asked carefully, for she too had felt the resonant thrum of the stones and she didn't want to give away what that felt like before hearing it from Tara. *Good grief. I'm turning into a suspicious and cynical old cow. Is this how I'm going to see everyone from here on? That they all have some ulterior motive? I don't know if I like the sound of myself having to be like that; gotta watch that. I don't want it getting the better of me. Last thing I want is to be some bitter and twisted old mare.*

'It's hard to describe, but it's a little like standing on something with its engine running, only it seems to be running to some sort of melody. I know it sounds strange, but that's how it feels.'

It didn't, not to Gwen anyway. She sensed a harmony to the resonance too but it felt more like a band tuning and warming up than actually playing a song. The music was there, but not quite. 'You're right; it's there, but it seems to be discordant at present. I get the impression that it has just awoken from a long sleep and isn't quite in tune with itself yet. The storm may have done that, or it might have been us.'

Tara gave this some thought. 'You might have something there, Gwen.

This is known as the Druids' Circle. I seem to have some affinity to that particular branch, if you pardon the pun, of magical practice. Daniel used to rib me about my witchiness, but I don't feel as strongly about that side of the craft as I do about the druidic aspect.'

Gwen agreed. From what she had seen so far, that made sense. 'And you with a brand of a sickle on your ass: that goes some way to validating your thought.' Gwen smiled at her own remark, trying to resurrect the humor that Tara seemed to have lost. She got a strained smile back, as though it fought against her annoyance. Neither seemed to have dominance at the moment and Tara was currently lost in between. Gwen hoped she had the strength to fight against the dark thoughts that could creep up on a person if they weren't careful. Anger and resentment could fester and turn into something destructive if left unchecked, and in the current climate, that was likely to leave that person open and vulnerable to malignant influence. It looked for doorways just like that; ways to permeate and insidiously corrupt bright souls.

'Yeah, that does seem to give it away, doesn't it, but you might be right too: it wasn't this strong when we first got here, I'm sure of it, and it's getting stronger as we speak.'

Tara glanced around; half convinced the stones would start glowing like her mantle any second now. Gwen looked thoughtful as she too studied the phenomenon.

'We seem to be a nexus for a myriad of forces,' Death stated, as he too began to look around warily. 'I imagine this site hasn't had a gathering of powerful forces such as we represent for some considerable time. And, War says the demon army is closing in, from our opposite side. There seems to be a crowd of possessed heading this way too; and from the west there is an energy I haven't felt for a long time. Though it is not evil in its intent, I caution you to be prepared all the same. You should be safe from direct diabolical influence here, but I suggest you complete whatever it is you need to do here before both the army and the possessed arrive. I will take my leave of you now, Avatar, for we must hold the rabble back to buy time for Ezekiel to arrive. He comes with haste, but will not be here before the enemy. Farewell, Avatar, Lady Tara, and you too Master Daniel. On behalf of the multiverse, I pray you succeed in this quest. Sooner rather than later would be preferable if you could manage it.'

With no other word or gesture, Death turned and ran the few steps to his magnificent ghostly, translucent stallion, and with a swift move that saw him almost fly, he vaulted to his saddle, spun his mount and was galloping away before Gwen had drawn her next breath. During the conversation, Famine had mounted and was galloping away with Death and, Gwen wasn't entirely sure, for it could have been the wind, but she thought she heard laughter from the outrageous and oddly exuberant Horseman.

Gwen turned to face Tara and for a few seconds before speaking, she looked directly at the fiery redhead. She wasn't sure what she was looking for and expected to see, but the woman before her had somehow transformed in the brief time she had known her. Of course, her own arrival in the Irish woman's life hadn't exactly been uneventful. Her shoulders sagged almost imperceptibly as she accepted the fact that she was responsible for yet another life having its world inverted in ways they didn't exactly expect or invariably want. The same went for Daniel. How many more lives was she going to ruin as she *saved* the rest of humanity? But her self-pity wasn't going to help them right now; Gwen sloughed her sombre mood like a discarded coat and addressed the other woman. 'So, Tara, what is it exactly we need to do here? Death implied we were here for a reason other than safety. And what is it with that sound? I take it that it has as much to do with you as it does with me?'

Gwen left the question hanging and folded her arms. For some reason that escaped her, when she adopted that stance she seemed to become more imposing to those before her, more authoritative. Jen had told her once that it was her electromagnetic field. Her mind demanded a response, one that she thought she should get, and her own body's generated field expanded accordingly to swamp those before her, encouraging them to answer her and show due respect. Apparently this was the same practice unconsciously applied to those people termed *born leaders* and *charismatic*. Few people had it and even fewer actually knew what it was they had. Gwen believed these people would be very dangerous indeed if they understood what it was they did and how they did it.

'Whatever it is, Gwen, a part of me is saying that we can't do it until the wee hours. Between two and four in the morning. I'm at my strongest then, I sense.'

Gwen raised an eyebrow provocatively, as if she expected further information.

'Since that…that thing back at the house and I blacked out, well, I've been seeing stuff in my head every now and again.'

'Stuff?'

'Yeah, images and people and animals and all manner of weird shit just flying through my head like a DVD on fast forward. Some keep repeating themselves but since we got here, I've managed to slow a few of them down and get a handle on one or two. There is another woman there. She looks a bit like me, but I know it isn't me, and it's her I can hear talking.' Tara nodded knowingly and smiled a crooked smile: one that would have had men dribbling at her feet. It spoke of mischievousness and recklessness, and was firmly embedded in a morass of sultry earthiness. She ran her hands into her thick mane of flaming hair and tossed it casually over one shoulder as she spoke, where it fell into place in such a way that it only enhanced her beauty.

'Sounds crazy, doesn't it?' Tara continued, starting to pace back and forth as she did so, fiddling with her clothes; straightening her skirt and adjusting her top and coat. 'But it seems to be making sense. It is as though she is reminding me of things I already knew but had forgotten; and one of them, Gwen, is how to use these rings to travel great distances.'

Tara let that bit of information sink in before carrying on. She saw the reaction on Gwen's face: one of barely contained surprise and even a little awe. 'I know. Incredible, isn't it? It has something to do with this tone, this harmonic that the stones generate. There is a way to harness it and, something like tuning a radio in, channel it to create a link with other circles. Sounds fantastic, doesn't it?'

'It does,' Gwen said warily. 'Is this all from the woman in your mind?' Gwen asked this as the image she had seen of the woman with the sickle came to hers. The woman who had beheaded the other on the altar. There was something about her that pricked at Gwen's consciousness, even her newly expanded consciousness. There was a feeling of cruelty and selfishness. A sense of treachery and murder that emanated from her like maggots crawling from a corpse. It made Gwen's flesh creep at the mere memory of her. She couldn't comprehend how she might have felt should she have found herself before the woman in the flesh. But she kept her features impassive and waited for Tara to explain further, if she would. Turns out she didn't, for at that moment Daniel decided to get himself up off the damp grass and, complaining about soggy pants as he did so, he walked over to Tara and Gwen, moving with the distinctive walk of one who has wet underwear. He stopped and tried to crane his head round to see and at the same time pull his jeans around so he could see the extent of the wet patch.

'Will you feckin look at that! It looks like I've wet meself. Who thought it would be a good idea to park me on the wet grass? Thanks a feckin' bunch.'

Daniel stopped abruptly as he felt the gaze of the two women upon him. He was oblivious to the fact he had interrupted their conversation with abject trivia. He was also unaware of the annoyance leveled at him by Gwen for cutting short her questioning of Tara.

'What? Where did Dea– You know who I mean. Where did they go?' He couldn't bring himself to say the names of the beings that had appeared before him. His mind had slipped into defensive denial mode. A natural safety zone for the majority of humanity.

'They've gone, Daniel; you can relax now,' Tara tried to reassure him. Gwen thought she was pleased at the interruption and was happy to change the subject.

'Relax?' Daniel blurted, teetering on the edge of hysteria again. 'Relax? I don't think I'm ever going to relax again. Speaking of ever again, what do we do now? I take it going home isn't an option, seeing as there is little left of it thanks to…thanks to…' He fought for the words, and failed. 'Thanks to, you know who I mean.'

'We have to wait, Dan,' Tara said calmly and coercively, using her past techniques to help put her brother's mind at rest. 'We will be leaving here, but we can't do anything until much later.' Tara put an encouraging hand on his forearm, reinforcing her calming words.

'How much later? Other than a wet ass, I'm starting to feel a bit exposed here. The town is just over there. What is to stop any more of those damned possessed from getting us here? It's just a stone circle; it's not a bloody fortress.'

'Death and the other horsemen are taking care of those, Daniel…' Gwen saw the boy flinch as Tara mentioned the Horsemen, '…and the demon army.'

He grimaced. 'Thanks! Did you really have to mention *all* of that? Couldn't you have just said "Don't worry, we'll be all right"?'

They all wondered then, in the privacy of their own minds, whether they would actually be all right ever again. It seemed doubtful.

Their momentary reverie was brought to an abrupt halt as Daniel asked a very pertinent question. One they had all seemingly avoided thinking about until now.

'So what are we going to do until two in the morning then? It isn't exactly a social hot spot, in case you hadn't noticed. Nor is there a bar…'

Gwen shot him a look so venomous, Daniel stalled and sputtered to a semi-silence. 'Old habits and all that. I was just saying. No need to get tetchy,' he added submissively.

The three of them moved about the circle for about fifteen minutes, each avoiding the other and only regarding their companions in a sullen silence. No one had any answer. Gwen didn't want to leave the protection of the circle, but she was curious as to how the Horsemen were faring.

Her hearing could pick up the distant sounds of combat and it was slowly shredding her already taut and frayed nerves. Tara was lost in her own thoughts, alternating between her visions and the awakening of her newly found powers. Blossoming between the two was the beginnings of a plan to save her brother, along with the realization that when she had said she would do whatever it takes to save Daniel, she meant it on levels so profound, her desire had transcended time, gaining momentum with every refusal to help him she received; and another had not only heard, but responded, setting events in motion that would reverberate throughout history.

Daniel, however, was simply misery incarnate. For although the interior of the circle seemed immune to the winter that was building on the outside, he still shivered – a feeling not helped by his moist bottom and the lack of centrally heating spirits that his bloodstream was usually full of by now. His shivers were part weather, part fear and part shock. Though he didn't like to admit it, he was terrified and his drinking had increased proportionally to his diagnosis and ever depressing situation. The thing was, he probably had more concerns with his liver's health than that of his tender brain, with the sudden and vast quantities of alcohol being poured into it, but neither organ concerned him now. The Grim Reaper had intimated that his future was somehow connected to Gwen's quest, and not only his immediate future, but his long-term one too. Whatever it was she was up to could cure him. Pure and simple. That fact alone had endeared her to him in ways he hadn't considered before, along with the monumental events that were going on around him too. He felt small and insignificant in the face of what he was witnessing, but amidst his personal maelstrom, he now had the one thing that had eluded him before. Hope.

Gwen's thoughts drifted without direction. There were so many things flitting through her mind, she couldn't focus on any one of them with the intensity they deserved. One of her errant thoughts touched upon the music that was still emanating from the stones and she wondered if anyone other than herself and Tara and Daniel could hear it, or whether it was restricted to their immediate proximity.

'We hear it, Avatar!' came a thousand voices that resounded in Gwen's mind like the rumble of orchestrated thunder. A pure sound that she felt through to her bones, and it resonated the marrow within. The nearest Gwen had felt to the stunning sound was the day she had put her headphones on and switched on the power, totally forgetting she had used her stereo the previous day and had the volume up on high as she listened to Carmina Burana. The Carl Orff opera was one of her favorites, and she hadn't noticed the volume at first as the first part of the track had been quiet, until the choir had kicked in full pelt. Gwen was half convinced her ears were bleeding when she whipped the headphones off. Certainly her head was ringing slightly and her nerve endings were jangling. But even that didn't compare to the voices as they bounced off the inside of her skull like her head was inside of the Albert Hall.

'We hear them, Avatar, as we hear you, and see you. We come!'

Gwen was rapidly becoming accustomed to the voice cum voices and, true enough, they did seem to be drawing closer. They were more distinct and clearer than the first hail. That or her head had stopped tingling.

'Who are you?' Gwen spoke in her mind, so as not to alarm Tara and Daniel, though when she looked at them they had a bemused expression and they were looking about them as though they had heard something, but couldn't fathom its source.

'What's going on, Gwen?' Tara asked, but Gwen hushed her with a finger to her lips. Tara and Daniel moved to the centre of the circle, and stood by the dolmen.

'That's what I'm trying to figure out,' Gwen whispered. 'I think it's the other power Death mentioned was heading this way, and they seem to know me.'

'Who are you? Answer me!' Gwen demanded in her thoughts as she switched back her mind's attention.

'One amongst us comes, Avatar. She speaks for us all.'

856

Gwen waited, though not as patiently as she would have liked. She felt her body tense and fidget with nervous energy as she awaited the arrival of the voice's spokesperson. Something in her mind's newly wired capability engaged and with a thought, Gwen parted a translucent curtain of reality. It was as though the terrain and view that surrounded them was painted onto canvas and she pulled it back like a curtain. Beyond the veil was a panorama that resembled the one before it, only it was brighter – the colors more vivid and alive. But what made her gasp was the profusion of figures capering and dancing around them, cavorting off the stones that encircled them and frolicking in the fields beyond, as though they were young colts finding their legs – spinning and cartwheeling. Some even flitted through the air like massive darting dragonflies, sparkling and diaphanous wings buzzing and thrumming as they dived and soared. At first glance, it resembled a hazy dream of fairies and sprites from some Pre-Raphaelite canvas. But as her own supernatural sight began to assert itself, she saw the reality of that dream. She saw thousands of faces and bodies, in as many colors and anatomical configurations. To the ignorant, many of these creatures would be considered ugly, and others aesthetically beautiful. But to Gwen, she saw fear and horror. There was pain etched on every one of their otherworldly faces. They had experienced some terrifying ordeal and they were fleeing, much like animals will flee a wild fire. These were refugees from the elementals. *My God! What has happened to set these beings on the run?* The thought hammered through Gwen with the horror of what such an event implied. In her response – her need to protect these spirits of the wild – Gwen pushed the energy that was pulsing from the stones, and expanded its sphere of influence. She saw it grow and shimmer as it encapsulated the elementals, and still it expanded. Those suddenly finding themselves within seemed to deflate almost. The tension of fear and what passed for adrenaline within them fled like bad air out of a balloon. Those finding themselves now within the incandescent bubble settled on the rocks and on the ground, calmer and visibly relaxed. They sat silently now and watched Gwen with an almost animal intensity, vivid multihued eyes swirling and dilating as they focused on the small blonde woman before them. Then they started singing. Their song fused with the shield Gwen was expanding and if she thought about what she had done, rather than act on instinct again, she would have known how little effort it took to do what her will instructed. But even that tiny exertion evaporated like morning dew when the music started. At that moment Gwen knew that what she was hearing was none other than the song of life – the song that pervades every living thing. In the case of what she was hearing at that moment, it was solely for life on this planet, but songs such as she was now a part of were sung throughout the multiverse, each symbiotically attuned to its own planet or star and the life forms that dwelt therein. What Earth scientists called cosmic energy was nothing in fact but music. A harmonizing galactic and multiversal orchestra made up the interwoven songs of all worlds spanning the vast tracts of space. And all humanity sees in its limited capacity is just so many waves, frequencies, miscellaneous and unidentifiable signals – not the music. And from macrocosm to microcosm, Gwen saw that every spark of life, from every solitary blade of grass, every individual ant and insect and even down to a solitary pebble on a beach: all that and more contributed to the song. As she felt this, Gwen was humbled, even shamed, for her prior ignorance of her place in the weave. It affected her in such a manner that she had no way to express herself other than to simply cry. It was all she could do, so Gwen wept where she stood, caught up in the rapturous expansion of her awareness and the acceptance of her place within the cosmic harmonic, and flowers sprang up at her feet, born from her tears.

'Well met, Avatar. You have our thanks and our gratitude for your shelter. Too long has it been since your kind and ours sang the songs of power together, though I am saddened by the reasons they are being sung this day. We do, however, need to talk. And with some urgency, if I may enter into your presence?'

Gwen couldn't argue with their need to talk. Something had driven these beings from their homes and she wanted to know what or who it was that was capable of such a thing, and how they had the audacity to do it in *her world*. Someone, Gwen promised coldly, was going to pay dearly for this.

The more rational and clear thinking part of Gwen responded to the silky and honey coated voice that requested her permission, as though she were some sort of royalty, to grant an audience to anyone.

'Of course you can, you silly thing; you don't need my permission for that. Get yourself within the barrier as fast as you can. I don't want to push this out too far in case I'm giving too much away to the enemy about the level of power here, and draw any more danger to us.'

Gwen could see shapes flitting so fast across the countryside that no mortal eye would have been able to track them. And even if they could, Gwen knew these beings existed in a realm so close, but so infinitely far from ours, that they could stand on and around a mortal, and the mortal would never even know they were there. They lived in a world just beyond our capabilities to perceive, like the light beyond infrared or ultraviolet – we know it's there but can't interact with it without special equipment. Humans didn't possess the knowledge to devise such equipment that would expose this realm, yet. Firstly they had to accept it was even there in order to go looking and, with the memories of past encounters with closed minded scientists, she knew they were safe enough for now. Though obviously, something *had* found them.

Like a harpist, Gwen touched every strand of the musical tapestry, feeling its origins and filling with wonder as she felt the myriad of contributions from plants and animals, each offering a tiny aspect of itself to the song, each reinforcing the sphere of energy. As Gwen strummed the amorphous strings, one suddenly stood out, brighter, stronger and clearer than the rest. Gwen withdrew her awareness and focused on this new thread. Materializing out of thin air and cloaked in starburst radiance, was a lithe and willowy figure who proceeded to walk across the field, crossing the fence and entering the Druids' Circle, stopping several feet shy of Gwen. The figure then promptly knelt and lowered what Gwen took for its head.

'Stand up, please. There's no need for that.' Gwen blushed with the embarrassment of it. It had even taken her several months to get used to being called ma'am by the overly polite Americans she had first encountered upon arriving on their shores. She had never been comfortable with formality and recent events had only made her more self-conscious about it. What was expected of her now? She was Drakarim but she still didn't really know what that meant. Nor, she doubted, would she until this war was won. And always assuming she survived it.

The being of light stood and nodded acquiescence to Gwen, then turned her dazzling gaze upon the other two souls who inhabited the circle. To Tara and Daniel, who hadn't moved from their earlier positions, it seemed as though Gwen was talking to herself. She had to their minds forgotten about them as her eyes had glazed over and a faraway expression had molded itself to her delicate features. She stared off into an unknown distance. As Tara watched, her skin began to tingle and gooseflesh. Daniel's did the same, and what looked to them like a heat haze began to lift up from the rocks and gradually move away from them. Tiny motes of light started to dance in the air then, as though some invisible fire was sending smoldering embers to skip and chase in the charged air above them. They both thought little of them, rendering them a side effect of the highly charged stones of the Druids' Circle. But it was only after several minutes of Gwen muttering to herself that Tara saw one of the sparkling embers hanging immobile before her, perfectly still, like a hovering kestrel in midair.

'Wait here, Dan; I'll be back in a moment.' Not waiting for any kind of response, positive or negative or other, she walked steadily over to where Gwen stood and positioned herself beside her, fixing her own emerald gaze upon the gravity defying sparkle.

'What is it?' Tara asked Gwen in a conspiratorial tone, inclining her head and letting the words trail from the corner of her mouth.

'Why are you whispering?' Gwen answered, in the same melodramatic manner.

'I don't know. Can it hear us?' Tara nodded ever so slightly towards the phenomenon, to indicate she meant the gently bobbing light.

Gwen smiled. Though she knew the being before her could see and hear all that transpired, she played along with Tara, half hoping that that it would allay some of the shock she was due to experience when she discovered the truth.

'I believe so, Tara. Tell me, what exactly can you see?'

Tara told her.

'I see. I suppose that's something. Try tapping into your new abilities, or letting your mind unfocus from the logical, if that makes any sense. Let your intuition and instincts take over.' Gwen reviewed what she had just said and grimaced. 'Bloody hell, I sound like one of those freakin' New Age yo-yos. You know what I mean anyway. Trust me when I tell you there's more here than just a floating ball of light.' Gwen sensed the entity smiling back as it seemed to enjoy the charade.

'Allow me to assist,' the entity said, and Tara almost leapt out of her skin when a glowing finger of light prodded her on the forehead. Tara's sight was opened to the realm before her and if her eye's lids had gone any wider, they would have slipped over the back of her eyes and vanished altogether.

'*Oh – my – good – God!*' was about all Tara could manage. Her exclamation all bar fell from her wide open and stunned mouth as she gawped at the glowing figure before her. Apparently there was nothing like a truly enigmatic, magical and internally illuminated – to the point of absolute incandescence – being to overawe the rational mind. But Tara was never one to be slow coming forward and she regained her composure fast, though Gwen did slip one finger beneath her jaw to close her mouth.

'Do close your mouth. It's rude to drool, I imagine, in any realm, Tara my dear.' But before either of them could do or say anything further, the being had skipped past them and danced around Daniel, who was bemused at first by the little light. But when she reached out and smacked him on the forehead, much the same way Tara did, Gwen noticed ironically, he yelped and let out a strangled cry as his eyes suddenly focused upon the ghostly apparition capering in front of him.

'Argh! Don't hurt me. I'm with them.'

Her laugh was musical and reminded Gwen of a thousand tiny bells as rainfall cascaded over them.

'I have no intention of hurting you, mortal. Quite the opposite, in fact. Do you not find me appealing?'

Daniel's gaze was drawn almost against his will to fall upon the glowing elemental. But apparently he saw something that neither Gwen nor Tara saw and he screamed, collapsing to the ground yet again, his hands flying to his groin as though he had just been horsekicked there. Gwen and Tara raced to his side and Gwen shot a disapproving stare at the entity.

'What did you do to him?' The rage in Gwen's voice reverberated and the entity recoiled in fear, sensing the power inherent beneath it.

'I am sorry, Avatar. Long has it been since I have been before a mortal man, I merely gave him a glimpse of my true self.'

Gwen knew little about the elementals, but some of the folklore she did know was that many varieties of nymph, from whence the word nymphomaniac arises, used to lure men astray, promising carnal pleasures the likes of which they could only imagine. These unlucky souls would follow these mischievous sprites until they either died of starvation and thirst, so enraptured would they be by the nymph; or, they would be spirited away to forever roam the other realms, lost and alone, unable to die but beset by the agonies of desire for the nymph that led them there, and forever unquenched. Daniel brought Gwen's thoughts back to the present as he moaned and writhed on the ground.

'Stop it now! Whatever you are doing to him, stop it this instant.' As though a dimmer switch had been turned, the being faded noticeably, her inner illumination giving rise to a silvery green toned skin and the biggest, darkest orange eyes she had ever seen. She had only ever seen eyes similar to those once before, and that was on deer, though they weren't orange. Huge watery amber pools with enormous lashes. On a deer they would be amazing enough, but on this creature, well, Gwen saw how easy it would be to drown in them and be lost forever, and she was nature's avatar. Poor old Daniel stood no chance whatsoever.

Gwen watched Daniel try and pull himself together, shrugging off all offers of help as he recovered gradually after taking both barrels of the elemental's sexual energy. It was the same power sirens and nymphs used in the legends, except this one had been out of practice and turned it on full for Daniel. The effect was embarrassingly obvious for those watching, and sheer agony for him. So now he sat apart from the rest of them, having cleaned himself up from the spontaneous orgasmic effect the elemental had manifested in him. Feeling decidedly outnumbered by three females to one relentlessly battered male, he sat outstretched and glowered at them from time to time as the three of them got to know each other. He watched as the elemental made a few physical adjustments on Gwen's advisement, and groaned just loud enough for the women to hear him as he saw what she did. She didn't look any better in his eyes, though *better* wasn't the right term, he knew. But she had just gone from the ultimate supernatural love honey who could sexually vaporize a man with a glance, and by trying to emulate her two companions, had toned herself down to a five foot nothing super, super model lookalike that would stop traffic and be the death of countless men as they crashed cars while gawping like idiots at her. Diminutive she may be, but there were no doubts whatsoever that she wasn't perfectly formed. Gwen had given her some things from Tara's pack, which caused Tara to scowl. What was it with women and sharing their clothes? Though Daniel had his answer soon enough, because the way she wrapped the old shirt around her chest, leaving her midriff exposed, and the way the skirt, which she tore several ragged inches off the bottom – which only enhanced its look – hung on her hips perfectly, just leaving her bare feet poking out, she made the other two look positively dowdy. To all intents and purposes, she looked like a regular girl of about nineteen to twenty-five, that is except the eyes. She turned once in his direction, as though she sought some kind of approval from her unwilling victim. She smiled and did a little turn, but Daniel just scowled all the more and turned away, though not before catching sight of her strikingly orange eyes, not helped by the vertical pupils that slashed downwards through the middles. He was instantly put in mind of some feline hybrid: that she was what cats would look like if they could adopt human form.

'Finally, now that we've made you something close to presentable, mainly so you don't inadvertently do any more harm to Tara's brother there, I think it would be nice if we knew your name. Mine isn't Avatar...' Gwen smiled to lessen the reproach, '...it's Gwen and this is; well as you might have heard me say, Tara; and that there is Daniel, her brother. And you are...?'

What came out, no human was going to pronounce.

'I see! Well I'm not even going to try saying that; I'd have my lips and teeth tied into so many knots, not even my dentist would be able to unravel them. Try it again, please, and see if you can simplify it or at least say it a little slower.'

'AmberBiethsalamVasCorinamber. How's that? I've taken the linguistic nuances out and translated it as best I can.'

Gwen tried it and so did Tara. Both managed it fairly well, though it was still something of a mouthful.

'Nice. It's got a lovely ring to it, almost musical. Does it mean anything?' Gwen asked, while at the same time shooting a reproachful glance at Daniel, who muttered, not quite under his breath: 'Yeah. It means Hello, I'm a vicious, spiteful orange eyed thing.'

The elemental heard him and turned swiftly in his direction, hissing and spitting, her amber eyes flaring, and revealing at the same time, a mouthful of translucent, razor sharp, needlelike teeth that any piranha would have gladly swapped its own for. Wicked talons extended from her hands just like cat's claws, which she brandished at him, and Daniel recoiled fearfully, but only as far as one of the stones. Slamming into it brought him up short and knocked the wind from him. The elemental was all for leaping at him and inflicting even more horrible things on his tortured frame, but Gwen's icy voice chilled the flame of the elemental's response and made Daniel turn away guiltily, desperately sucking in air. Tara mumbled something about how Gwen now knew how *she* felt: just wait until she had twenty-four years of it like she had.

'Simmer down, children, or you're going to make Mommy cross. And Mommy doesn't like pulling rank...' Gwen waggled her finger at them threateningly and several roots popped out of the ground and began waving menacingly in sync with Gwen. '...But in case it has escaped the attention of either of you, I am the avatar of nature. Believe me when I tell you that should I be pushed too far, and unless you both behave and play nice, you will spend the rest of your lives as dung beetles; and I assure you, there will be plenty of filthy, putrid, smelly dung for you to play in until you learn to get along. *Do I make myself clear?*'

Gwen only raised her voice at the end, but the Drakarim in it had the desired effect. Their tenuous peace resumed as the elemental smartly turned her back on Daniel and smiled winsomely at Gwen, teeth and claws vanishing as though they were never there. Daniel just glowered, drew in several further ragged breaths where he had knocked his own out, and muttered incomprehensible curses about women and demons.

'That's better,' Gwen continued in that same mommylike patronizing voice that makes any rational person want to heave repeatedly as though overdosing on verbal sugar. Gwen was good at it too. She made a Stepford wife look like a howling barbarian.

'Now, you were about to tell us what your name means,' Gwen reiterated sweetly, as though nothing untoward had just occurred. Daniel obediently stayed silent, though his expression was petulant. The elemental ignored him, much the way a big cat would ignore a maggot. Or, as the little group discovered, the way royalty ignore those beneath them.

'It means, in a roundabout sort of way, the royal living flame of the ancient and noble Birch, daughter of Silvaraphim Corinamber and Guardian of the Crescent. Or something like that; it is very long winded and somewhat pretentious and I never really had to use it before, let alone explain it. You, however, may simply call me Amber.'

Gwen's eyes widened slightly in surprise at the revelation that Amber was elemental nobility, though she found that she was getting a little numb to these mind-staggering discoveries she kept coming across. After all, just how much more fantastic could her life get? So! She was talking to a being that no one had seen for centuries and was only documented in myth and legend. Not what she was expecting, she had to admit, though if she gave it any real thought, she would have had to admit that she had no idea what to expect from one of the fey folk. They were apparently, considering the multitude she had witnessed arriving at the circle, as diverse and anomalous as birds in the sky and fish in the sea. And that wasn't including the earthy woodland and fire elementals. They were as individual as humans and their various cultural nuances. She sighed wearily and this drew concerned looks from everyone, even the sulking Daniel. Gwen felt suddenly burdened all over again by how much she had to learn about the new world around her, and the ancient world that had remained hidden from view for so long.

'You are a dryade, yes?' Amber asked Tara, quite out of the blue, catching the Irish woman on the back foot, not expecting to be embroiled in Gwen's conversation with the sidhe woman. For Tara had no allusion as to what Amber was. One of the fey folk, faery, a wood nymph, though apparently not of the malevolent banshee type. But they were all tricksy right enough. Just not as evil and spiteful as some, but still more so than others; and Tara's instinct was to be wary of talking to her kind, lest she become trapped in some dangerous word game with her. They were renowned for having silver tongues and could talk a person right out of their skin if they had a will to. Now as for Gwen, Tara expected she could handle herself in a confrontation with these beasties, as she was proving with this one. But Tara wasn't so sure about getting involved herself: she had enough to worry about with the other stuff swirling in her mind without having to contend with this.

'No, good grief, no,' Tara said indignantly. 'I'm not one of you, I'm a human.'

Amber laughed. A rich throaty sound, one that made Tara blush and Daniel squirm with the recollection of recent events. But she shook her mane of flowing locks and leapt up onto the dolmen and with one swift move, spun and folded her legs beneath her to sit cross-legged on the rock. She propped her head into her hands and her fingers tapped lightly on her cheeks to some invisible tune that only she could hear. Daniel tried not to look as her skirt was pulled up over her now bare knees, exposing too much flesh for his liking. He was comedic to watch as he tried to stare at everything else *except* her.

'Not any more, you're not. Not entirely anyway. You have the color and the frequency of the priestesses. Those that sought harmony with the elemental realms and the mundane world you live in, and defended the forests and the wild places, the holy wells and sacred groves and rings, like this one. I believe you called them *druids*?'

'Druids? Yes I know what they are,' Tara responded, somewhat relieved about the direction of conversation, though still cautious as to where it might be heading. 'But I'm not one of them: they're a bunch of white robed and bearded old men, aren't they?'

This time both Gwen and Amber laughed and Tara scowled in response to their joviality at her expense. She didn't like being laughed at.

'What's so funny?' Tara asked hotly. 'Well the ones I've seen are anyway. What's wrong with that?'

Gwen found it ironic that a woman brought up in the land that probably had more famous druidic characters than anywhere else, should know so little about them. She wondered in light of her recent discovery whether or not her mother intentionally kept her in the dark about druids. Gwen quickly filled in some blanks for her with what she had learnt herself. There were some advantages to running a New Age store: she got to read all the books for free. *Well, not entirely free, I suppose. I did have to buy the damn things in the first place. And speaking of the store, I wonder how Dolores is getting on.* Gwen mentally digressed as Tara absorbed what she had just heard.

'But you called me a dryade? Isn't that one of your kind?'

'It's an old word and often misused, but don't you see the similarity? We are both forces of nature who contend to see that the natural order remains the way it should. Some of us, rather than just remain passive, choose to defend that balance, though in varying ways. Amongst our kind, much the same as in yours, there are those who perpetually extol the merits of peaceful resolution and the avoidance of conflict even in the face of certain destruction, choosing rather to run and hide than stand and fight for our right to exist.'

Tara was nodding as the undercurrent of what Amber was saying resonated through much of humanity's troubles, both recent and past. She recalled her father's tales and much of the bitter infighting of the days of the IRA, long before Al-Qaeda and the bloody Taliban and all those other religion based zealots.

'It is a shame we no longer have the wolves: they would be an invaluable asset right about now,' Amber said and looked away, thoughtful for a moment before continuing as though recalling something lost, and Tara turned a confused glance her way, slowly walking towards her as she didn't want to raise her voice too much as the night crept slowly upon them and the darkness descended. She pulled her sweater and coat tighter around her, hugging herself as the bitter chill beyond the ring still managed to permeate her too few layers, and she shivered involuntarily.

'How can a pack of wolves be of any use? They're just animals. To be fair though, bloody big animals with serious teeth, but from what I've seen so far, they'd be ripped to bits. We had a tough enough job with Gwen, a shotgun and a car.'

But Amber was shaking her head as Tara spoke. 'No ,Tara, the wolves were dryades, like you and like me. More like me in any case if you get my drift, but they were a special caste of dryade. These were warriors. Peace only went so far and when it failed, there were the wolves. Their purpose was not offensive, mind, but defensive. Our kind never had any reason to attack another, not ourselves nor the world of men. Peaceful co-existence is much more preferable but even our history tells of skirmishes, minor arguments that got out of hand. Then again, whose don't? Your realm and ours clashed several hundred years ago and a fraction of it has been transcribed into your legends, though much of it is incomplete and inaccurate. Your druids, as you came to call them, were terrible at writing anything down and they were supposed to be the intelligent ones?' Amber chuckled at the thought, though not in a maligning, detrimental way; but it was more of a pitying, regretful sound. 'The wolves, Tara, were a fighting force to be reckoned with. They combined magic with martial prowess as well as being shape shifters. They were experts with bow, knife and sword, but their weapon of preference was their Scarta – sickle swords, for want of a better translation. It was from their mystical curved blades that humanity drew many of their designs, in this case, the druid sickle. It is prevalent throughout your history.'

'I'm sorry, Amber, but I really have no idea what you are talking about, though it sounds wonderful and all. It's not me, I'm afraid. I can manage to cut myself peeling vegetables, let alone swinging some bloody curved sword; I'd do meself a mischief.'

'No one is asking you to, Tara. I'm just saying that was what they did, and though you are a dryade, I sense your power is more sorceress than warrioress.'

Amber looked at Gwen, as though seeking some sort of confirmation. Gwen joined the duo and with a nod from Tara – a subtle permission giving – Gwen went through the tale again. Amber was a good listener and sat stock still until Gwen finished. Finally, when she was sure Gwen had finished speaking, Amber sat and absorbed her words for a few moments before speaking again herself.

'So it begins again.' Amber's softly glowing eyes settled on Tara with a mixture of pity and reluctance. 'You bear the mark, I presume?'

The question could have related to anything, but Tara knew in her bones that the mark in question was the sickle brand, the scar that tied her by blood ritual to the legacy her mother had bequeathed her, albeit reluctantly. Tara nodded.

'You don't seem too happy about it? Perhaps that is a good thing. You will not be seduced by the power as many before you were. It colors perceptions until the worst deed seems rational and justified. We have seen the remains of cities and cultures; the smoking ruins and debris of peoples whose thirst for power blinded them to the consequences of their actions.'

'My ma didn't want me to have this, but as Gwen said, my choices were limited at the time and my hand was forced. What was I to do? I didn't have a scooby as to what was going on; all I saw was thunder and lightning and my fucking world collapsing around my ears. After twenty odd years, I find a letter from my ma almost *predicting* what was taking place and she implied that I wasn't going to survive without embracing the legacy she sought to deny me. What would you have done?' Tara's voice had risen as the emotional level rose; elevated by the fact that her memories were still fresh and poignant.

Amber nodded sagely and reached out a delicate hand to place on Tara's shoulder. Tara didn't flinch, though her mind wanted to under the elemental's touch.

'True enough, you did what you had to. It is all any of us can do. It seems your rite of passage is turning into a baptism of fire.'

Tara started. 'My what?'

'Rite of passage.'

Tara blinked and even Gwen was curious as to the context.

'But isn't that some kind of initiation, sort of girl to woman and boy to man kind of stuff. I'm a little old for all that shit now, though not probably by your standards.' Tara recalled how old these creatures got to be.

'No, no, it's not like that at all. It's another example of how you humans change the meanings of many words to suit your own ends, and the original is lost to time. Rite of passage was for the Dryades and the priests and priestesses who connected to the natural order. They existed all over this world. Some still do, but we have not seen or heard from them for a long time now.'

'So what is it then, if it's not what we think?' Tara was getting irritated. Gwen could sense it in her manner and the discordant tones of her voice. A look at her aura told Gwen that she was in conflict with herself, and the colors oscillated around her like a cuttlefish on speed. What Gwen didn't know was that Tara was being bombarded with images and words, chants and songs, faces and names; all coming at her in a tsunami of voices. They swamped her and surrounded her, filling her and carrying her along. It was all she could do to hang on to her identity amidst the cacophony and deluge in her mind. It was why Tara was quizzing Amber, in a futile attempt to retain herself. It was an exercise in concentration. Whether Amber knew this was another matter; she gave no outward sign that she was aware of the inner struggle taking place before her, even though her senses were acute to the power flows and lines of energy given off by living matter. She carried on her explanation regardless.

'When humanity was closer to us and the natural order of the world, they sought the assistance and approval of those powers who were elevated beyond this realm. Like students and supplicants, they endeavored to honor those powers and sang songs of power, gave offerings and gifts, and the greatest of all, displayed a selflessness and devotion to others that opened their hearts and minds. When they sang the songs and completed the ceremony, they would be able to cross over to the adjacent realms, ours being the closest. By crossing over, they could traverse the dragon lines of the world and cover vast distances in the blink of an eye. Some could even slip through the holes in time and see possible futures. They learnt many great things from us and the Ch'drnOmThophilim, who also visited our realm. What we granted to these seekers, was what was known then as the Rite of Passage. Some of your shamans call it Vision Quest now, or Dreamtime. There are more names but it equates to the same thing.'

Tara frowned at the unfamiliar name and Gwen realized she hadn't mentioned them, though Jen and Maddy had explained to her who they were and who they embodied.

'The chdn...topilim... What? Who are they or what are they? I've never heard that word before and I sure as hell can't say it.'

'Simply, Tara, they are the Children of Thought. Your kind came to know them as angels, but before that they were the old gods. They assumed whatever form was necessary to guide and steer humanity. But you all lost your way and the Children of Thought slipped away too, arrogantly believing that you as a race had failed and were doomed to self-destruct. But you didn't fade away as they thought, and their absence let the rot take hold. We tried to encourage them to return but they paid us no heed, for we are not as powerful as they and we are tied to this world, unlike them, who exist on a world of their own. So we too drifted away from this realm, taking refuge in ours and the wild places where humanity could no longer find us. But something else found us instead. That is part of the reason I am here, Avatar.'

Gwen knew by the serious use of her new title, Amber had something important to say.

'Avatar, we need your help. As the demon army pushes across this land, more and more of my kin are driven from their trees and rivers. Even the rocks tremble before the onslaught. It seems the Adversary is hell-bent on wiping out all life before him. We suffer, Avatar, and unless these elementals find new homes soon, they will wither and die.' Amber gestured around them and a thousand faces appeared. Gwen heard Tara and even Daniel gasp as they saw what they were surrounded by. 'Was it not for the beacon you sent up by activating this ancient Dryade circle, we would be lost, doomed to extinction; for although we exist in an adjacent realm, without this one and its trees and wildlife, ours – along with my people – faces annihilation.'

'Sorry to throw a wet squib on your girly chat, but is it my ears or is that sound getting nearer?'

Gwen suddenly perked up. So enraptured had she been in the brief lesson and conversation with Tara and Amber, that she had somehow forgotten the battles taking place just outside. She didn't even know if Ezekiel had arrived to support the Horsemen. But now with Daniel's comment, she heard by the horrible screams and the clash of a vast number of weapons, though sounding more like the crash of thunder or waves against rocks than steel against steel, that someone had arrived and engaged the enemy. The disturbing thing though, was that Daniel was right: it was closer now. Much closer.

'What time is it, Dan?'

Dan rolled his wrist and squinted at his timepiece. 'Two thirty-five. Well, I think it is anyway, always assuming my watch hasn't stopped again.' He shrugged and looked guiltily embarrassed.

'Doesn't anything of yours work?' Gwen asked, exasperation evident in her voice, though the moment she said the words, she saw the potential for a double entendre and a smartass remark from Daniel.

But to his credit, as he was still out of sorts from Amber's arrival and having his body pushed to limits he didn't even know he had, he answered simply, 'Not all of the time, but it isn't my fault. It's just stuff, and stuff has always gone on the fritz around me. Don't know why. It just does. Sorry.'

'No problem, Daniel, it can't be helped now. Tara?' Gwen turned to the other woman and asked if she was good to try out her new ability. Tara just pulled a face that said any time was as good as any other.

'I can help, Avatar,' Amber offered. 'I know the rite of travel if you know the destination. Tara will supply the power and the incantation as she is the dryade. Can we take everyone?'

'I don't see that we have much choice in the matter,' Gwen replied. 'If we can get everyone in the sphere, or even better, in the circle, we'll do our best. I think the most suitable place would be my grove back home. It is in the heart of a national park and considering my new role, I'm guessing it'll constitute as a sacred grove, and there should be enough trees and wildlife there to transplant the entirety of this island if needs be.'

Amber looked pleased and Tara looked reticent.

'What is it, Tara? You can do it, can't you?' Tara blanched and the color left her face. She was pale already and her skin looked almost translucent, putting her red lips and green eyes in stark relief. She looked worried. 'Tara, you're starting to scare me. Talk to me. What's up?'

'The images; the ones in my head. They have started to slow down and organize themselves. As you've been talking about subjects, images and words relating to them have slowed and appeared to me.' Tara wrung her hands and looked between the elemental and Gwen.

'Go on, Tara. For the love of God, say what's bothering you. We don't have all day. Really!'

Tara flinched at Gwen's words, as though the limited time they had just added salt to her wounds. 'This rite of travel you spoke of: for me to use it, I need the Athame.'

Gwen knew the word: it was a ceremonial tool used by contemporary witches, wiccans and pagans as part of their magical practices, and it was more often than not represented by a small dagger. Gwen reiterated her thoughts aloud for Tara, who shook her head.

'No it's not that, Gwen; this is special. It has been handed down through the ages and my ma had it last. But I've never seen it. I hope it's not still back at the house.'

Gwen's frustration was getting the better of her and she snapped back at the pale woman. 'Well give us a bloody clue, will you? What does it look like? We've got no more than one and a bit hours before your window closes and God only knows how much time before the demon army break through or the possessed descend on us. If I have to, I'll fly back and search the house for it, but I need to know what I'd be looking for.'

'It's a sickle, Gwen, but unlike any other.' Gwen's mind instantly replayed the woman from the reading she got from Tara. The woman with her back to them, wielding the sickle that decapitated the helpless woman on the altar.

'Describe it!' demanded both Amber and Gwen simultaneously. They looked at each other, questions in both their eyes. Seconds passed and they turned back to Tara.

'It is longer than most, and the handle is jet black; ebony perhaps, or jet. It is warm.' Tara closed her eyes and drifted in the memory. 'The blade is a dull silver and sharper than any man-made metal. It was forged from the ore from space, that which falls to Earth. The blade was made molten by the breath of dragons, and shaped by a dryade. Grave runes and sigils adorn its blade; and in the hilt, there is a moonstone the size of a heart. It bears a name that should never be spoken, and its soul is vengeance.'

This time it was Amber's turn to pale. And Gwen was really concerned now. It didn't sound like the type of object that she even wanted to see, let alone find. And she sure as hell didn't want it in the hands of Tara, another dryade, who, now she thought about it, bore a striking resemblance to the woman from the vision. Especially not when she said that a dryade had been a part of the forging of this Athame, sickle or whatever it really was. It seemed prudent to keep her away from it. In fact to keep everyone away from it. But as Gwen was distracted by the memory, Amber had turned and was reaching a hand through a glowing tear in the veil between this reality and hers, and was speaking rapidly to something beyond. Before Gwen could ask what she was up to, her eyes locked on to the object that Amber was pulling through the tear. Gwen was thunderstruck. So much so, she found herself unable to move, to think or to make a cohesive decision. It was only a second or two, no more, but it was all the time needed for Amber to pass the object to Tara and for Tara's eager hand to snake out and grasp it, gripping with the same determination of a drowning man reaching for a life ring. As though her very existence depended on her possessing the object, Tara's face lit up with joy and exultation as she cradled the sickle to her breast. Gwen was sure that even a mother reunited with a lost child wouldn't have looked as joyous.

'Amber?...' Gwen asked the elemental in a strained and subdued voice. Gwen felt the very air change within the circle with the arrival of the artifact.

Amber turned her lightly glowing, dull orange eyes on Gwen and they held the question of 'What did I do wrong?' It was the look of an innocent, or one fulfilling a charge. '…What have you done?'

'It is hers. I have carried it with me since it was left to my care by the woman I now know to be Tara's mother. I was told to not speak of it unless it was spoken of to me. Nor was I to show it unless it was described to me. But Tara described it perfectly and when she said she needed it for the rite, I was honor-bound to return to her what was rightfully hers by birth. She is her mother's daughter. Whether her mother wished it or not, destiny and events transpire to send us in whatever direction it sees fit, and we are but flotsam upon its river.'

Gwen watched Tara cuddle and coo to the artifact, talking to it as though it actually were a long-lost child. A dull moist sheen had formed upon her brow as though she was suddenly feverish; and her eyes, when they opened, were distant and a little glazed. Having dropped to her knees with the blade, Tara was rocking gently back and forth and muttering incomprehensible words to the sickle, or so Gwen presumed. Gwen was reluctant to disturb her for the moment, likening her predicament to that of waking a sleepwalker – not a recommended course. But she kept an eye on her.

'Amber! How is it you had *that*!' Gwen thumbed at the artifact, as she realized she had a distinct repulsion to the item. It wasn't something she could define but it made her flesh creep just talking about it. Heaven forbid she had to touch it: she felt that would tip her over to full blown vomiting.

'My father, the King Corinamber, ruler of the woodland elementals, entrusted me with it, and who am I to gainsay the word of my father and my king?' Amber seemed a little testy at being questioned about her charge, and Gwen grimaced. She had to move cautiously here, tread softly. The last thing she wanted to do was in one fell swoop alienate everyone around her and set them against each other. This was something that would just have to play itself out. Her main priority, in fact her only priority, was the First Tree. All other matters had to be secondary, but that didn't mean they weren't worth watching and being aware of.

'I'm not saying that, Amber, but all I am asking is how your people came to have it in the first place if it was in the hands of Tara's mother, who I hasten to add, left a note saying that if Tara was reading it, she was dead. Do you know how she died?'

This last question snapped Tara back to her senses and she bounded to her feet and rushed forward to where Gwen and Amber stood. She almost bowled them over with her eagerness to get to them and hear what Amber had to say.

'Easy, girl.' Gwen put her arm out as a barrier and Tara all bar bounced off it, inches from Amber.

'Tell me, Amber, tell me how she died.' Tara's voice seemed calm as she asked the question, but Gwen sensed the barely restrained emotion roiling beneath her cool exterior. But Daniel, who had watched events unfold before him, wide-eyed and stunned as though he was watching something on some trashy television show, seemed to be the only one who had any sort of grasp on the perils of the immediate.

'As much as I would love to know how my dear ma died, she at this moment in time is already dead and nothing we say will change that. We, however, are not, and if we don't get our collective asses out of here, and now me sis has her thingamabob, as I understand it, we can do just that. Move first, chat later. Does that sound like a sensible plan to anyone but me?'

All eyes turned to him. Three varying, but equally intense stares couldn't have pinned him to the spot any better than had three spears nailed him to the ground. Gwen's emerald gaze, beneficent and cool; Amber's fiery orange stare, all alien and dangerous, yet so full of invitation he felt like a moth before a flame; and his sister's. That one scared him the most now, for it had a faraway look to it and he felt akin to a mouse, trapped and held before a very wild cat, as he caught sight of Tara's feral and terrifying expression scrutinizing him, disassembling him where he stood as though she was seeing him for the first time. What he didn't know was that a part of Tara, a part she was unaware of, *was* actually seeing for the first time in several hundred years through eyes that weren't her own.

Daniel held up his hands in supplication and tried to take a step back. It took a concerted effort of will to do just that, but he did. And he felt better for it.

'Easy, ladies, it was only a thought. I didn't want to interrupt anything or such but that sound is getting closer and I can make out voices now. Sorry to say, but they are shredding my nerves a bit. It's like fingernails on a chalkboard, or tinfoil on your teeth. I'd really like to get out of here if it's all right with you. Just don't hurt me anymore, please?'

Daniel's pleading dispelled the moment and Gwen nodded as the imperative returned along with her sense. Even Tara seemed to return to herself as she glanced away and muttered her agreement, though it didn't stop a brief arrow-shot glance at Amber that said she wasn't finished with the elemental yet.

'Gather everything that's coming,' Tara spoke loudly and with a force that hadn't been there before. Gwen narrowed her vision to study Tara as she mentally summoned the elementals closer. Amber did the same and soon enough, the circle was full to almost spilling out with the wispy and wild eyed creatures. Daniel came to stand beside Gwen and he gripped her hand – hard enough to earn a curious glance from Gwen. It was then she saw the fear in his eyes, but not what he was fearful of. She put it down to everything that was happening to him, and she smiled a smile of reassurance, gripping his hand in return to emphasize her smile.

'Let's do this, Tara.'

'Very well. Elemental?' Tara turned to the elemental. 'Begin your song.'

As they did, Tara began to chant. The music that sprang up would have moved riots to peace, stampedes to a standstill and storms to calm. It rose in a spiraling vortex, twisting up into the night sky and unfolding above them like an umbrella of light and sound, cascading back down onto them to recirculate and rise again. Faster and faster it spun and twisted, rising and falling. With everyone at its centre within the Druids' Circle, the sound escalated to a crescendo of unimaginable sound and sensation that, with a concussive boom that sent a shock wave rolling out across the land for a hundred yards in every direction, the power imploded on the group in a shower of incandescent lights.

When darkness finally regained control of the night, the grove was silent and eerily still. But of the activity that had ripped through the air only moments before, there now was none. When the eyes could settle without strain and should they cast about, all they would see was that only the stones remained. Of Tara, Gwen, Amber, Daniel and the elementals, there was no sign.

Chapter Eighteen

Commandare

THE GROUP CLEARED THE FOREST EDGE JUST as darkness settled. Like coal black silk, it draped out and spread across the land; and like a living thing, it fell upon the terrain as a predator falls upon its prey, enveloping and smothering everything in its cloaking embrace. Its touch solidified the shadows and cast a malignant perspective on their surroundings, causing terrifying shapes and fell creatures to steal through the abyss like night and haunt the imaginations of the soldiers. Though they had been in the forest for some considerable time now, for the moment they were free of its clinging, oppressive grip – looking back upon it now filled the observer with a soul deep dread. It was the sort of place that any rational and sane person would swear on the life of their nearest and dearest that were even the entire hoary legions of Hell chasing them, they couldn't make them even *want* to go back in. It was such a primordial place, and it touched the deep rooted fears of the mortals amongst them, dragging out the ancient terrors of their ancestors, which are to this day still firmly embedded in most sensible humans' brains. Of course there were always the few really dense ones; ones that had no right even claiming homo sapien status. No sense, no feeling. Everyone knew at least one person like that. Some knew plenty more. Apparently fearless, but in reality, just too stupid to know the difference. Now they were the really dangerous ones.

Passing from the shadow of the possessive forest, its last tenuous hold reluctantly falling away as the moons that orbited above cast their wan light down upon the group who, with space now to move, reorganized their column into a more suitable formation, Toby and several of his men took point and Tomas, Treya and Ingrid were brought together in the centre, with the remaining men guarding the rear and flanks. The column moved out into the killing ground, the column itself no wider than two men abreast. Tomas kept swiveling his head round, studying each man and Valkyrie, ensuring everyone was doing what they were supposed to, his own predator's gaze missing nothing. It wasn't that he was particularly distrustful of the soldiers, mainly because he knew just how out of their depth they were, but it was his nature to be cautious, so he watched. When they moved out, he began studying as best he could the winding and circuitous route across the killing ground that they adopted.

'Stick close,' Toby called back, basically for the benefit of Tomas and his entourage. 'Walk where we walk, and for God's sake don't deviate from the path we're taking, not if you value your limbs anyway.' With a hand gesture to the soldiers at the rear, Toby set off and the group – with good caterpillar motion, like the way cars move in traffic snarl ups – followed close behind. Tomas watched how relaxed the men became the further from the forest they got. *If only they knew who I was talking to just a short while ago. Seeing Be'elzebub would convince them of where they were, all right.* Though they were only a few hundred yards from the edge, they seemed to be less wired. Their shoulders were dropped more and their weapons were web slung off their body armor casually now instead of held up alert and fingers on triggers. That sort of tension can take a lot out of a person. That forced, maintained adrenaline threshold wasn't supposed to last as long as they had held it. It tired you out faster than a route march with a full forty-pound Bergen, and Tomas could see the dark shadows below many of the soldiers' eyes, and drawn cheeks and sallow complexions that told the story of their fatigue. They had been under considerable pressure too long now, but the sight of their ad hoc home lessened some of that anxiety. Tomas did wince a bit though, especially as he had added to that tension by being up front with them about where they were. *Still, shit happens everywhere and you have to deal with it.* Character building, his father had called it. *Yeah, right, thanks, Dad, but a body only needs so much bloody character.* It wasn't character that these guys needed; they needed a damn good rest and some serious R and R. Any element kept under the tension they were under would eventually snap. Tomas knew. He'd seen it. *Damn messy business and a lot of good people, innocent people, had died because of it.*

Because of him. He thought he knew his people well enough, but the small team he had been forced to work with once weren't made of the same stuff as him. They thought they were and Tomas had believed them, ignoring his own instincts that told him otherwise. Having infiltrated the 'Patriots' Army of The Lord' as they called themselves – a bunch of self-funded and self-armed militia men basically with delusions of grandeur – Tomas and his three-man team had to gather as much intel as possible and feed it out to their contact. Apparently this army had several agendas in place and high security targets were a part of it. There was also the matter of a recent cache of explosives going conveniently missing. The trail led to the PAOTL. It wasn't hard to enlist. Tomas fitted right in from the get-go. He was as much of an outsider as the rest of them and he had personal views that paralleled theirs anyway. But his associates soon grew nervous when they saw how dedicated and fanatical they were. They trained as though it were the end of days and Tomas saw the signs, those early fractures, but chose to ignore them, hoping their own training and experience would get them over it. It didn't. They began to make the militia men just as edgy, and after several run-ins and a few dust-ups, it seemed to start to rub off on them like a contagion. Before Tomas could contain it, they had brought one of their plans forward to devastating effect. Tomas couldn't even get word out in time, because several groups had mobilized and the hospital where the senator, in six weeks' time was due to visit, prematurely exploded in a fireball that would have made any terrorist smile. Tomas wasn't there to hear the screams and see the damage wrought first hand. He had been back at the compound at the time and only saw the carnage on the evening news. Apparently, his fellow operatives were still inside the ER department when the detonation took place. His fellow operatives' irrational behavior had tipped off the militia men and it had been their way of disposing of them. Tomas swore and cursed himself for ignoring what he saw as obvious. The question now, of course, was, what did they think of him. He and his now dead team had been with the group for five long months. It was nothing to Tomas, but the constant day-in-day-out pressure of maintaining a fiction had been too much for the others. It took a certain something to remain as detached as Tomas. Few had that capability and that was why he was chosen for the distasteful missions that required his certain talents. The collateral damage, as his superiors liked to call it; the death and ruin of hundreds of innocents at the hospital as Tomas viewed it, was the outcome of *not* having what it takes. He had stayed with the group for a further three months after the Mercy Hospital incident, shrugging it off and putting it behind him, as though there was anything he could do about it now. They watched him for about a month afterwards but he rode the storm immediately after the carnage and carried on his training with them. Tomas provided intel on twenty-three further planned missions before leaving quietly one night. Though not before removing their chain of command: cutting their throats and double-tapping them to make sure, silencing the nine primary leaders there, and planting enough explosives throughout the compound and weapons cache that the resulting scorch mark would be seen from space. Ever the opportunist, however, Tomas had kept flash drive copies of all their files for future reference, just in case the Government used one of their plans to further their own aims and blame the PAOTL. Plausible deniability again. Tomas always liked to keep an ace or two up his sleeve just in case they ever turned on him, a fact that wasn't such an out there possibility when they eventually did. He was dangerous to them, and he knew way too much for his own good. One day their paranoia would get the better of them and Tomas wanted to be as prepared for it as he could be. *Boy, if they knew then what I know now, a few scrappy files and a handful of dodgy photos might have been the least of their problems. Though when your head is stuck so far up your own arse like theirs is, the world takes on a skewed view and with too many years' worrying about what everyone else was up to, they missed the rot in their own apple barrel. Everyone bloody did, everywhere.*

Tomas, not for the first time, wondered why he was so detached, so devoid of conscience, when it came to humanity. It wasn't bravado or bullshit, or machismo or testosterone. It wasn't something a soul *needed* to have; it was what the soul *didn't* have. That was the trick. Tomas knew there was a void in him. A dark abyss that he could retreat into when things needed to get messy. He didn't think about it, he just did it. Cool and collected as though it were another day in the office. Except these days, the faces of those who died because of him were starting to surface, bobbing up from the dark and concealing ocean of his psyche like foul air filled and bloated corpses. Their pale, sickly, slick faces staring at him accusingly. But what he found really scary, was that these were clearly defined faces of people he had never actually seen before or didn't remember seeing, at least. But it seemed that they had seen him, and since the explosion, where he had almost joined them, they had begun to surface with horrifying speed and numbers. Tomas closed his mind's eye and willed them to go away for now, promising them their day of retribution, but to just allow him time to complete this mission for the rest of the living. Not that he suspected they cared much for them – he didn't himself – but they were too caught up in their own vengeance to notice such mundane matters.

Making a mental note of the markers the soldiers had used to expose the safe trail, Tomas brought himself back to the present. They had been walking for about half an hour and hadn't really gotten as far as he would have liked or expected. It was still a considerable distance to the fortress and the weaving path they were taking would take them the entire day at least. Of course, this being Hell and them not knowing what to expect here – at least they didn't when they set out their claymores and other IEDs (or improvised explosive devices) as he had explained to Treya earlier when she had asked about the strange path they were taking – it had to be hoped that nothing mischievous had slipped out and reorganized things for them. It would be messy finding out. But soon enough Tomas grew tired of watching rocks and sticks. He was also getting fed up with the back and forth path they were taking. It was like the cattle grid queues at Disney World, where they make you go backwards and forwards countless times getting nowhere fast, though you have actually walked half a mile to move only a few feet. Tomas knew it was so they could cram more punters in but that didn't make it any less annoying. He watched as the fortress loomed closer, then fell away again.

'Taking no chances, were you!' Tomas grumbled caustically to the soldier in front of him, who like most soldiers and mercs he knew, were Teflon coated to sarcasm.

'No, sir!' came the deadpan reply and Tomas rolled his eyes, giving up with that tack. It was akin to throwing tennis balls against a wall and hoping one would stick. However, after a few more minutes' trudging he couldn't resist the obvious question, 'Are we planning to get there anytime soon or are we just going to wander backwards and forwards out here all day? I mean, just how many mines have you got buried?'

The soldier didn't look back at Tomas – he was busy concentrating on where he put his feet – but he answered all the same in that flat monotone often used when people had trouble doing more than one thing at once. Polite but disinterested. 'We'll be there soon enough, sir, but I can't rightly say how many we planted. As soon as we found this place, the colonel said he wanted to ensure privacy. He gave us a whole crateful of the little suckers and told us to use them up, and when we had, he gave us another one. So I'd be more mindful of where I was walking than talking, if you get my meaning… sir.' The last word was added after a pause for effect, which wasn't lost on

Tomas. He'd used the same tone himself on numerous occasions when he had one of his many run-ins with the brass. Now they were individuals Tomas instantly consigned into his *very dangerous* category, primarily because Tomas considered them blissfully ignorant of the really real world and the only reason they held their office at all was because someone knew someone, or went to school with someone and was rogered repeatedly by said someone at some expensive public school, or was married to their sister or brother, or both, for that matter. Tomas had a low opinion of most of the Ruperts he had ever encountered and in true self-preservation style, had dossiers on many of their incestuous and depraved lives. Ensuring they knew he had such intel generally ensured an autonomous existence, though he had to sleep with one eye open and watch who might be following him in order to get that info back. He never said it was an ideal solution. With this in mind, Tomas smiled ruefully at what the grunt in front of him must be thinking about him, Tomas having owned up to his Major's rank, albeit honorary.

'*Does your kind have no respect for their war leaders?*' Bran asked in Tomas's mind, as he rode casually along upon Tomas's shoulder.

' *No, not a lot,*' Tomas replied. '*Respect is earned and not simply given, as far as I'm concerned, and our leaders should be measured by their actions and not by who they've slept with. I guess I'm a bit of a dinosaur like that; I'd like my commanders to lead from the front like the kings of old. Riding at the head of their army and as willing to die for his people as much as he is willing to send those selfsame people to their deaths.*'

Bran considered Tomas's words and with a mental nod, and offered approval before lapsing into silence once more. Tomas tilted his head and saw that the raven had a black, glistening eye out on the surroundings still.

'*Ever vigilant?*' Tomas asked teasingly, his mental voice light.

'*Always,*' came the raven's reply.

The day wore on. Ingrid moaned on and off about the futility of this and they should just leave the men to it and fly the rest of the way. Their mounts would arrive soon enough from a summons and Tomas had Storm.

Tomas just shook his head and asked Treya to explain it to her, again. They stopped around the midday mark to refresh themselves. As the mortal soldiers relieved themselves, Treya and Ingrid watched intently, laughing and pointing occasionally. Bloody Valkyries! Tomas knew they were cruel sometimes, otherwise the Vikings wouldn't have written about them in such a way. But there was cruel and there was really cruel. Even the toughest and manliest of men didn't enjoy being ridiculed when he had to take a piss in front of two women, for there was no cover whatsoever where they walked, just patches of burnt scrubby grass. Tomas smiled and left them to it. Instead he turned his attention on the fortress ahead of them. Still several miles off, it was an impressive structure. Tomas willed his rifle with the range finder telescopic lens attached and took a closer look. It was amazing that something so evidently massive could hide away in the middle of this forest and still maintain open ground of several miles around it. It wasn't exactly hidden, but Tomas remembered Al'Mayakin. That hid in the desert for millennia, Famine had said. Maybe this had similar attributes. Tomas looked at the walls and saw that they were reassuringly solid looking enough. He couldn't see details all that clearly but it looked to him that the stones that comprised the walls were fitted together better than could be evidenced back on Earth. This was craftsmanship to match the pyramids. *Who knows, maybe it was the same guys who built them who built this. The way things are shaping up it wouldn't surprise me. I mean, where did they go after they built them? You can't tell me experience like that just died and was lost. Probably got recruited to come build this or some other structure. Didn't they say humans vanished from Earth to come here?* Tomas ranged his gaze from left to right, taking in the entire wall he could see, and the pair of gigantic gates that stood defiantly in the centre. Though not prominent, they were set back into a recess, which meant that it bottlenecked any invading force trying to get in through them. *Wouldn't want to be the one who had to storm it though. Looks damned impregnable from here.* Tomas could see killing slots at varying heights, and the lip of the wall, just below the crenulations, cantilevered some ten or twelve feet out from the wall itself. So unless your scaling ladder made it to the top, which had to be a good hundred feet, maybe more, there would be no climbing up. Then, to stop even that, there were huge iron spikes that thrust out horizontally, Tomas reckoned every four feet. At a distance, it looked as though the fortress wore a crown of thorns. Except these thorns still had bodies and bones from creatures that had no business on any world, draped from them.

'The colonel liked them hanging there and figured it was good enough for whoever owned it first, acting as a deterrent for any unwelcome visitors. Bit macabre if you ask me, but then again, no one did, so they stayed.' Toby had come up on Tomas and followed the direction of the rifle scope and guessed what he was looking at. Tomas lowered the weapon and glanced up at the corporal.

'Didn't you wonder then what those bodies were? Surely you didn't think things like that existed in Canada, and just how many castles like that one do you think got built out in the woods?' Tomas knew he would have questions by the boat load about somewhere like this. At least he would have were he in Toby's shoes. Tomas knew better about a lot of things he wished he didn't now, and this slotted somewhere in that category.

'Why are you lying down and aiming at that fortress, Tomas? Even a blind man could hit that sitting out there like it is,' asked Treya inquisitively as she too wandered over, tired of baiting the soldiers, and joined him and Toby.

Tomas smiled at her archaically based observation but didn't look up. 'I'm not aiming at it; I'm having a closer look. This device on my weapon allows me to see closer, as though I stood before its walls. Call me cautious but I like to see what and where I'm going wherever possible, and of course, what I need to consider if I need to leave in a hurry.'

Toby shot him a concerned look, understanding the implications all too well of what that could mean. Tomas caught the scent of his concern and appeased him a little by adding that any meeting with him and the colonel might not go as planned or as he hoped, and he didn't want some hot-headed argument about his leaving if that is what it came to.

'I'm sure you understand the tactical need for forward planning, Toby. Never go in somewhere that you don't know how to get out of.' But before either could carry on that conversation Treya made a remark that stopped them cold and caused them to trade glances.

'It's a bit small for my tastes. I take it neither of you two have ever seen Valhalla?'

There was little in the way of sensible response to a question like that. 'Er, no, Trey, it would be fair to say that neither of us has ever seen Valhalla. In fact, I'd go as far as to say that the vast majority of the population of both Earth and the Domain has never seen Valhalla. The aforementioned majority, me included, wouldn't have thought up until recently that such a place even existed outside the realms of myth and legend. So do stop the one-upmanship comments before you blow these guys' minds any more than they already are. Now if you and Ingrid have finished scaring the crap out of the men, can we get a move on? I'm feeling a little exposed out here. This trip has already taken far too long; longer than I anticipated to cover such a short distance, and I'd like to get there before nightfall. Wandering about in a minefield in the dark is no fun, I can tell you. And these guys might know the route but they are tired and stressed and all it takes is one misstep and Kaboom. One leg less – if you're lucky.'

Treya glowered at him but acquiesced. Another hour elapsed and Tomas's patience was wearing thin. Ingrid wouldn't shut up tormenting the nearest soldiers to her. In fact, she had upped the level of description just to piss Tomas off. At least that was Tomas's assessment. If he said don't, she did it all the more. She knew he knew it wouldn't be good to fall out before the mortals he hoped to win over. Showing division amongst themselves would be catastrophic, so Tomas gritted his teeth and tried to blot out her cruel laughter as some poor grunt swore in shock behind him.

'Look, shouldn't we signal them or something? Give them some sort of indication as to why you are returning prematurely and with guests?' Tomas's voice carried to Toby, who was second from the front. Without turning, Toby answered, boredom coloring his voice.

'They've seen us already. They are under standing orders to keep an eye on the forest edge at all times. There are sentries at each corner tower and one for the centre of each wall, of which there are four, in case you wondered. It's a big square and before you ask, that is the only gate we've found so far. If there are any more, they're damned well hidden I can tell you. So relax, boyo, and enjoy the walk. We'll be picking up the pace shortly. The majority of the IEDs are further out, giving us breathing space out front if we needed it.'

'Fair enough, and there was I looking forward to ringing the doorbell.'

True to Toby's word, another hour saw them standing before the gates. Tomas was increasingly impressed by the size and scale of the fortress the closer they got. The giant wood and steel banded gates looked big enough to roll siege engines in and out without dismantling them, should someone be inclined to, that is. The last time he had seen doors this size was during a visit to the NASA space centre in Florida. The hangar where they kept the shuttle had doors like this, but, Tomas had to admit, they didn't look half as impressive as these did. Tomas took in all the dents, chips and impact marks that covered the wood as though they had withstood their fair share of siege attempts and laughed them off.

Standing before the gates themselves meant that the group had to enter the bottlenecked access passage that funneled them in. For sixty feet they felt the claustrophobic presence of the walls as they wrapped themselves around the group. Tomas caught quick glances of men moving behind arrow slits, watching their progress. He even spotted a barrel or two from some unidentifiable weapon following them. The moment they entered the passage they had left the scorched ground behind them and they found themselves walking over monstrous timbers laid horizontally into the ground, almost as though they were gates in the floor. The moment that comparison popped into Tomas's head, he knew what it was they walked over.

'I hope you trust your people, Toby. I don't fancy dropping through into who knows what if they decide to open this trap, and I know I said I was done with threats, but in this case I can feel a necessity. Any tricks or secret signals and I can assure you things will get real messy real quick, and it won't be we three who'll be doing the dying. Do I make myself clear, Toby?'

Toby nodded resignedly, as though he expected such a reaction. 'I thought we were past all this shit, Tomas, sir.' Toby added the sir bit as though it was a dirty word and Tomas noticed. 'I gave you my word that I would deliver you here alive and well and in good faith with no tricks, and here we are.'

'Not yet, we're not,' Tomas replied coldly. 'Not until we are all safely on the other side with our feet on terra firma, and yes, I know that relates to Earth but I don't know what Martian firma is.'

Toby laughed then. A grim and humorless sound and he shook his head sadly, but when he looked up and caught Tomas's gaze, Tomas saw there was no trickery there, just a sad acceptance of the way things were.

'You can't threaten me and make bad jokes at the same time, Tomas; it loses a little something, if you get me. A bit like a lion roaring with no teeth.' Toby stopped any protest from Tomas about teeth with a hand up, signifying peace. 'Easy, big fella, I know you got some natty canines, but bear with me, there's no tricks or the like and we won't be opening the moat gate, just this big sucker here.'

Toby slammed the butt of his rifle against the door and it thundered in the confined space, matching Tomas's expectations of what it would sound like. He listened as the timbers and locks on the other side were moved, unbolted and undone. It sounded a lot like a gigantic bank vault being unlocked. Then, with well-oiled hinges, one of the oaken barriers swung ponderously and silently inwards, revealing yet another passageway, or Tomas figured, the continuance of the one they were in. There was yet another moat gate in the floor and Tomas gestured for Toby and his men to go first. Toby just smiled as if he was expecting just that.

'Distrustful bastard, aren't you.'

Tomas smiled, all teeth and no humor. 'And then some. If you knew what I know, so would you be. It's kept me alive thus far and I'm too long in the tooth to change my habits now. Nor would I even if I wanted to. So please…' Tomas gestured for Toby to lead the way, '…after you.'

Toby looked at his men. They had been watching the exchange with interest. He knew that several of the men looked at Tomas with something close to awe, and others still had a look of uncertainty in their eyes. Toby knew that subject to what he did next, things could go either way and he wasn't a hundred per cent sure any more of which side his men would fall. Carmichael hadn't done a lot to endear himself to many of the company, and since he had ensconced himself up the keep tower they had been left to fend for themselves, just maintaining things until they got new orders; from whoever.

'In that case, as you put it so eloquently, would you ladies and sir care to follow me?' Toby indicated his men should go ahead and he, along with two others, flanked Tomas and the Valkyries, and walked in side by side.

Tomas heard one of the sentries ask for a series of random words from the first soldier to cross the threshold, and after giving them, they were let in, though Tomas noticed that weapons weren't lowered as they emerged from the passage, and the giant gate swung silently back into place, only alerting anyone that it had moved at all by the resounding boom of its closure. Tomas, knowing what he did about where he was, didn't like to disappoint those on guard by telling them their security was terrible. There were creatures out there that could probably scoop out the contents of a man's mind, gaining all the information they needed for infiltration as easily as they scooped the contents of a melon from its skin. Not only that, but Be'elzebub had hinted at beings that could shape change, transforming themselves into the likeness of anyone they chose, and that was without the possessed. Like the poor sod he had dealt with in the alley, prior to his troubles really taking off. Getting in here was just too easy. He would have to have serious words with someone if they weren't compromised already.

That, of course, meant talking to Carmichael. Tomas shuddered inwardly. There was no way any meeting with that man was going to go well. Too much sludge had passed beneath their bridges for any clear water to flow now. Having Tomas point out security issues to the man who should have implemented them was the easy way to put his back up, assuming he even deigned to talk to him in the first place. That was still a fifty-fifty option. Tomas saw one of the guards scamper off after a brief discourse with Toby. He nodded several times as Toby spoke and the sentry snapped off a shabby salute and double timed it away from them. Tomas saw he was heading for the main keep building.

'Bran, can you get to the towers and keep your eyes open? I need an aerial perspective of troop movements down here. You know, who's going where and with whom etc. Can you do that?' Bran replied with an image of contempt, making Tomas wince that he had explained it at all. *'Sorry. Used to having to justify what I need doing.'*

Bran turned an obsidian eye on Tomas and he could have sworn it winked at him deliberately before Bran flapped off and soared to the battlements, drawing bemused looks from the sentries as it banked and flapped a bit more, spiraling up until it reached the highest of the crenulations on the tallest tower, where it alighted, ruffled its feathers as it settled, and turned to watch events below. The tower where Bran now roosted happened to be situated above the central keep and rose a further hundred feet above the four corner towers, and Tomas considered it odd he hadn't seen it from a distance, nor as they drew closer. It was only visible from within the fortress, it seemed. *Now that's interesting. I wonder how many of these guys have noticed that.* Tomas pondered the hows for a few seconds before his own brain started to object, so he just filed that useful snippet away for future consideration as they were led into the central courtyard.

Tomas hadn't realized just how dingy the passage was until he was reacquainted with the sunlight. The contrasting light had him squinting and shading his eyes as he emerged into the courtyard proper. He slipped on a pair of borrowed sunglasses which he had taken from one of the marines, stuffed into an inner pocket and forgotten about, considering there was a lack of sun in the woods and he had been unable to return them when he was back at Al'Mayakin. They were good ones too: Wiley X SG-1 ballistic shades. Tomas wasn't a snob but he did believe in the fact that you got what you paid for. More importantly than that, they kept the sun out and that was what he wanted right then. Of course, the tactical advantage of having the people you are watching not being able to see your eyes watching them was a plus. Tomas cast his gaze around the yard as discreetly as possible, taking in the placements around the battlements and the cautious expressions of the men working out in the yard itself. The way some were being put through their paces and others were just working out gave the distinct impression they had just walked into a prison compound. And as he saw them, his own entrance hadn't gone unnoticed and the same steely and uncompromising faces were weighing him up too. Their grim faces showed that they had seen more than their fare share of action and were fully expecting to see more before too long. Tomas could see that straightaway by their bearing. There was a distinct lack of posturing, humor and overly relaxed behavior. Throughout the world over, at the many camps Tomas had been in or passed through, he was used to seeing this many soldiers together, regular or freelance, much more at ease in the relative security of their compound, blowing off steam; partly to relieve the adrenaline surges and testosterone rushes of being out in a theatre of combat as much as it was to alleviate any fear of imminent death; but there was no football here, cards, joviality, music or any other recreational activities. It was all business. The business of war and death and being prepared for immediate action should the need arise. It was as vital to be mentally prepared as well as physically in order to engage and accept whatever fate was dealing you at a moment's notice. But Tomas also saw the strain on their scarred, battered and weathered faces.

It was the same tired visage his own escort wore. There were tensions here that went beyond waiting for a fight. There was a tightness in the air that threatened to snap anytime soon like so much steel cable with its threads unraveling. But mutinies involving paid soldiers with too many guns to hand rarely ended well. Tomas had seen that too. *I've seen far too bloody much. I think it's a wonder I held it together this long*, Tomas realized as he continued his snapshot assessment of the soldiers. It was apparent that there was something fundamentally amiss here – something that had these men on edge, nervy, and by the expressions on many of their faces, especially his escort, who he had been up close and personal to, he could see that they were more than any thing else, simply tired. Being on edge like they seemed for any prolonged period will have serious effects like that, and that's when things get dangerous.

They hadn't walked more than a few steps into the compound proper, and Tomas had slipped into mental autopilot as he assessed and was assessed in return by the men around him. He felt long-dormant emotions and feelings resurface within him as not only the sight of a military training camp brought back memories, but the smell of sweat and gun oil assailed his senses. Plus, which wasn't so sweet: the all too familiar fragrance of a latrine that needed backfilling and a fresh one digging. It told a story in one eye-watering lungful, of men who had been in one place too long.

Yet for all the thousand-yard stares and contemptuous snarls of the men working out in the yard regarding Tomas, the moment they clapped eyes on Treya and Ingrid the gorilla-like posturing shifted from intimidating him to displaying prowess for the women.

Tomas saw weights that were lying discarded on the floor when he had first walked in, hastily added to bars and the sounds and strains of men grunting as they tried to lift something impressive, wafted over to him. Tomas just smiled and shook his head, diverting his attention to the group furthest away, who were practising archery. The grunting musclemen would soon learn the error of their ways when the Valkyries started on them. An image of Ingrid grinding them beneath her steel-clad booted foot sprang unbidden to him and it was all Tomas could do to not warn the men of their folly. *Bollocks to it. A little humility will do 'em good, I reckon. Not only that, it'll help secure their position as figures of authority to be respected. Shame they'll have to learn that the hard way,* Tomas chuckled cruelly to himself as he casually and unobtrusively steered his escort away from where they wanted to go to where *he* wanted to go, which was closer to the archers. There was something interesting about the way the big bald fellow exhorted the obviously weary archers to further efforts.

'Come on, you useless scum. Put some arm into it! My bloody grandmother has got more pull in her arm and she's fucking ninety-four!'

The man doing the shouting moved behind one of the soldiers and lowered his mouth to the soldier's ear before shouting in it loud enough to disturb the hair on the other side of his head. 'Pull, you sack of shit! Put some bloody arm into it, or are you going to wait until your enemy is standing in front of you?'

In response, the soldier gritted his teeth until Tomas was sure he heard one crack and managed another foot of pull on the bow he held, releasing almost instantly. Tomas followed the flight of the arrow but it sailed over the target instead of hitting it, though it did embed itself into the tower door some forty feet beyond it. Seconds later, while the shaft was still quivering, the door opened and a very unhappy face peered round cautiously. His caution evaporated when he saw the cloth yardshaft twanging gently in the woodwork.

'Are you *trying* to kill me, you fucking great Scandinavian moron?'

But instead of any heated reply, the huge bald trainer just laughed. A deep belly laugh of genuine mirth that carried across the yard to everyone in range, drawing a few inquisitive looks; as though to say 'What has he done this time?'

'Collins, you little tunnel rat. If you didn't keep sticking your ugly little head out at the most inappropriate moments my men wouldn't find themselves drawn to shooting at it. It makes such a lovely target and you apparently seem to have such a knack for being one.'

Color infused the man called Collins's face at the jibe. This was obviously an ongoing scenario. 'You know full well I have to maintain an inventory of what little food we have left in order to keep your big mouths and even bigger bellies full without depleting our supplies before we bug out of this shithole, and...' Collins's voice rose in a nasal sort of way, the kind of irritating voice that you imagined accountants and weasely bankers used when they were justifying their obsequious positions, '...you and I both know that you put your targets that way round just so you could piss me off all the more. Well it won't work, do you hear me?' The way his voice rose, dogs a hundred miles all around heard him.

'Ah, Collins, I see that small man syndrome hasn't made you bitter and twisted. At least your voice has some height. Or that might just be your lack of balls.'

The men took the opportunity for a quick slug of water and a fag while their CO took the rise out of someone else instead of them. Collins, however, didn't see the funny side. 'It was just one, you Neanderthal, and it was shot off while I was in combat.'

Baldy shrugged as if it meant nothing to him anyway. 'So you say, Collins, but running away from a fight isn't combat and being shot in the ass doesn't count to me as a battle wound. These are battle wounds.'

With this, Baldy yanked his grimy and sweaty shirt off over his head, revealing a torso that had seen better days by a long stretch. In fact, Tomas had seen autopsy cadavers with fewer scars and wounds on them. 'I've been shot, stabbed, burnt, blown up and smashed in the course of my work, Collins, and I've still completed every mission I've ever been sent on. Can you say the same, you sniveling little pack rat?' Somewhere in the banter, the humor had slipped out of Baldy's voice and his true feelings of distaste for the man before him were starting to slip through.

'Don't call me a pack rat, you barbarian! I'm a quartermaster and have the papers to prove it. Plus, I was appointed by Colonel Carmich– '

Baldy let out a roar that silenced Collins and made his eyes go wide. Especially when Baldy grabbed the nearest bow along with the arrow that was part nocked, from one of the gawping soldiers.

'Don't mention that slimy, two faced backstabbing son of a whore to me. When he bothers to get his sorry ass out of that tower and makes some effort to sort this cluster fuck out, I'll hear his name. Then, and only then. Certainly not before and not by you.'

Baldy drew the bowstring back until Tomas heard it creak from across the compound. He sighted the arrow along its fletching and there was no doubt as to its target. Collins squealed and began running as fast as his stumpy legs would carry him from the abandoned tower doorway towards the keep. Baldy quickly followed his direction and let fly. The arrow sped off faster than any mortal eye could follow; its sound followed a few nanoseconds later. But to Tomas's amazement, he found he could follow its trajectory and quickly assessed that it wasn't going to actually hit Collins, but still come close. It thunked into a window frame just above Collins's head. The diminutive quartermaster squealed again and his hands flew to his head as he staggered, losing the rhythm of his flight. He saw the newly quivering arrow above him and saw that there were strands of hair attached to the arrow. His hair! Collins glowered with the full force of his ire and if hate could have been made solid, a million arrows of steel would have flown across the yard and pinned Baldy like a bug to the wall beyond. Collins, knowing he had lost this encounter, said no more. Instead he turned and walked, not running this time. The need for that had passed. He summoned all the dignity a man no more than four foot eleven could muster, and walked the rest of the way to the keep, and disappeared inside without another word or glance in Baldy's direction.

Like somebody lobbing a grenade, laughter erupted from the archery group at Baldy's display and Tomas turned to see how he dealt with this. Instead though, Baldy's gaze, as it swept around the compound with the intent of returning to his own business, caught sight of Toby and Tomas watching their antics. He took a few seconds to register what he was seeing before speaking again in that deep voice that was used to carrying over gunfire and distance.

'Finally found something out there, have you, Toby? Well be a good boy and put it to use, will you. Send it to fetch my arrows and bring them over here!'

Tomas wasn't sure what he had heard for a few seconds, and then Toby looked at him, and the full meaning hit.

'Do us a favor, Tomas. Keep him quiet and fetch his arrows, will you? Otherwise he'll get the bit between his teeth and he'll annoy the crap out of us… Well, you actually, until I can get you in to see Carmichael. It won't take a second, will it, boyo? There's a good man.' Poor Toby. It was a tough choice as to whose back he was going to end up putting out. Caught between the proverbial bald rock and Tomas's hard gaze, Toby squirmed and grinned a little lopsidedly, shrugging as he did so, then backing up a step and holding up both hands in a gesture of supplication.

'Hey, don't shoot the messenger, I'm just relaying what he said and forewarning you of what might happen if you ignore my advice. Which I get the feeling you're gonna. Just let me get out of the way first.' Toby scuttled back to the ranks and Tomas switched his raptor's stare between Toby and Baldy, and then smiled evilly himself, though there was no humor in it and the temperature dropped a few degrees when he did it. Tomas rolled his shoulders and sauntered over to where the first arrow was protruding from the frame. He pulled it free and moved on to the next. Other than the one in the door there were several others lying in the sand that covered Baldy's half of the compound.

'Don't do anything rash, Tomas. We have just arrived and I have not eaten yet. I do not wish to fight my way out so soon after only just getting in.' The sensible words and pragmatic advice of Treya drifted over and hovered around Tomas's head. His ears heard them but refused them entry to his consciousness. Here was an opportunity to get to know a few people, and Tomas just loved making friends.

As Tomas bent to retrieve the handful of spent arrows embedded in the sand he felt as much as heard the whoosh and thunk of an arrow passing by him within millimeters of his back. Without standing, Tomas just turned his head to see it quivering in the door, much the same as the last one that nearly impaled Collins the quartermaster. Tomas merely stood, and pulled it from the woodwork. But just as he turned to the protruding shaft and laid his hand upon it, there was a thunk thunk either side of his head, where two more arrows slammed home inches from his face. Tomas spun to see what was happening, a feigned look of shock etched upon his own features. He would play up to their sport for a bit. Baldy simply shrugged and hollered in a voice that would have been heard back in the forest, 'Sorry! Accident. Won't happen again.' Tomas raised a hand to say that was fine then, and resumed plucking fallen arrows from the surroundings. Tomas was a bit perturbed that there were so many. Surely they couldn't all have been that bad a shot?

'You don't fancy grabbing those few that *did* actually manage to hit the targets while you're at it, old chum? Seeing as you're doing such a bang up job of it.' Baldy's voice boomed down towards Tomas and Tomas simply raised an acknowledging hand and went about his new instruction.

Tomas must have had a handful of about fifteen arrows before the next one slammed into the target beside him. Again he looked up, alarmed, and received the same non-committal shrug and toothy grin from Baldy, who was by now the only one holding a bow. Tomas knew this game: Baldy was the training example for the rest, the demonstration of his prowess to encourage the others to pull their proverbial fingers out. But Tomas was nobody's scapegoat and he planned to only let this little farce carry on so long. Taking his eye off Baldy to pluck the last few remaining arrows from the straw stuffed mannequins, he was suddenly spun around as one arrow nicked his shoulder armor and another ricocheted off his hip, both embedding themselves in the target. A third pinned him to the target itself by the collar of his cloak. This time though, Baldy ignored Tomas and he continued his lecture of the soldiers he was training: explaining what he had just done. But it was interspersed with much laughter and a few fingers pointed in Tomas' direction. Righto, pal, enough is enough. Time for a deviation to the curriculum. Tomas fully intended to extricate himself and go put Baldy in his place on a face-to-face basis but that option was taken from him as he pulled the last arrow free that held him. Tomas turned to the archers just in time to see two more shafts winging their way towards him, but they moved as though they flew through treacle. It seemed that the sword was intervening this time. It apparently had taken all the humiliation it was going to and with obvious martial pride, it planned to bring a halt to proceedings. Tomas happily agreed this time and needed little prompting. He sidestepped the trajectory and calmly plucked the arrows from the viscous air as they drew level with him. The sword materialized in Tomas's hand in its longbow form; an impressive weapon of some type of black animal horn and bound with rune-etched silver and steel, recurved to add power to what already looked powerful enough to hunt dragons with. Tomas nocked the first arrow and let fly. Before it reached halfway to its destination, Tomas had nocked and let fly the second shaft. Shoving the rest of the arrows in his belt, Tomas began to stride up the range towards Baldy, pulling one arrow out at a time and firing at him as he walked. By now the first arrow had arrived. It caught Baldy's jacket and dragged him several feet backwards with the strength of the shot. The second did the same on the other side and almost hauled Baldy off his feet; it didn't quite manage it but it had him back-pedaling like crazy just to remain upright. By the time the third, fourth and fifth shots reached him; Baldy was almost back against the keep wall. The fourth and fifth shots followed the first and second, with the arrow heads scoring a groove down the shafts of the originals as they propelled Baldy finally off his feet and pinned him to the wall proper. The fifth shot hammered into the wall in between Baldy's legs. The feathered shaft vibrating against his inner thigh with a stunning impact as the five arrows drilled themselves into the actual stonework of the keep. Tomas wasn't finished with him though, and he let fly three more with blistering speed. They too hammered into the keep wall, sending tiny fragments of stonework spinning off, one tiny shard drawing a line of blood on Baldy's cheek as the arrows drove in either side of his face, with the last scoring a groove across the top of his fleshy head. Silence unlike any other descended on the soldiers gathered around and within the yard. Tomas stopped, looked down and smiled to see several tiny red dots dancing upon his chest. Ignoring them, Tomas walked up to stand before Baldy, who now wore a look of incredulity himself. His students backed up several feet from the big – and Tomas could now see – very ugly man. Tomas figured he had a reputation and judging by the way his men gave him room, coupled with the scars, lumps, bumps and bruises on his misshapen and battered head, it wasn't one he was slow forthcoming with. But Tomas had seen bigger men fall, having put many of them down himself. He stood within arm's reach of Baldy, just to prove he wasn't intimidated, and slowly looked him up and down, noting how his feet were barely touching the ground. Tiptoes were all he could manage as the arrows held him fast. But they were just wood. Tomas suspected the sword had enhanced them slightly to penetrate stone, but other than that, Baldy should have no problem wrestling himself free. But he didn't. He just stared at Tomas with an unreadable expression. His trainees seemed to be holding their breath, as too did the rest of the fortress. Tomas didn't see Treya shake her head wearily and look down at her feet with the resignation that all hell was about to break loose. But it didn't. Baldy's eyes drilled in to Tomas's and Tomas got the distinct impression that there was a lot going on for those prolonged minutes. Tomas met his scrutiny with steel of his own and an implacability that would see trees uproot of their own volition and move out of the way before Tomas backed down.

Tomas studied the big man before him during those seconds and guessed him to be a formidable opponent or an invaluable ally. He stood a good six feet six and was built like he should haul rocks around by hand for a living. There was corded muscle upon muscle, little fat though. But it wasn't his physique that caught anyone's attention: it was the fact he was butt ugly. If he hauled rocks, he smashed them loose from the mountain with his head. His nose had been broken so many times it had given up trying to reconfigure itself and just lay flat. Several smaller scars dotted the plateau of his face but it was the one large, angry looking one that ran from his forehead to his top lip that dominated his visage. Where it had healed badly and puckered, it had pulled his lip up into an almost permanent snarl. But whereas he had fallen from high out of the ugly tree and hit most branches on the way down, his cobalt blue eyes missed nothing and they exuded an intelligence that belied the brutality he exhibited outwardly. Tomas rolled his shoulders and waited for the inevitable explosion of flesh and fists but it never came. Instead, while still hanging like a rag doll from the wall, Baldy smiled. It didn't help Baldy's cause and if anything made him look even more disturbing. Tomas noted there were a few teeth missing then as well. Grimacing, he waited for a mouthful of abuse. That didn't come either. What did, though, made Tomas relax as well as Treya and the rest of the group.

'That was fucking incredible! I don't know how you did it or how you moved so fucking fast but I have to say, that was truly impressive shooting.'

That was for Tomas's benefit. For his trainees, Baldy had a lot of other words. The majority of them weren't polite and likened their capabilities to those of disabled and invalided primates who had spent too long cavorting in unhealthy ways with their mothers, but that aside, they should take good note of Tomas's shooting and try and learn something from it because if they weren't shooting close to that capacity by the end of the day, heads were going to do more than roll. Again, Tomas didn't notice behind him, but the only one smiling through Baldy's tirade was Ingrid. It seemed a kindred spirit had been found when it came to gutter vocabulary and expectation of only the highest standard.

'You going to get me off this bloody wall or what?' Baldy spoke softer now for Tomas's ear alone as his trainees scurried like rats with their tails on fire in an attempt to up their game on the archery front before Baldy noticed. Tomas stepped forward and pulled the arrows free, smiling as he pulled the shoulder ones free first and watching Baldy's eyes as he dropped onto the groin shot, realizing then just how close he had come to changing sex. The moment he was free he grabbed Tomas's hand and pumped his arm vigorously.

'Damned pleased to meet you. My name is Owen Van Da Geer. Dutch to everyone who knows me and I can tell you, I was starting to give up hope that anyone here could ever shoot worth a snot. I don't know where Toby found you but I'm glad you're shooting *with* us and not *at* us.'

Tomas dimly noted that Dutch didn't proffer any rank and Tomas pegged him for a professional merc, rather than just simply ex-military or a company man. Most ex-military that go private dislike the term mercenary. It implies a seedy, dishonorable attitude: money and their own skin driven. The guys from the regiments he knew of old who went private were as patriotic as ever, if not a tad more so, and made sure those that needed them knew it. Dutch didn't look the sort to lose a lot of sleep about who or where his orders and money came from, just so long as they did come. That aside, Tomas thought he just might like the big Dutchman.

Eventually, Dutch finished pumping his arm. Any longer, and water was going to spout from Tomas's mouth.

'Well I'm pleased to meet you too, Dutch. I'm Tomas, which I prefer rather than Major Walker, but something tells me you don't much care for traditional rank. My two companions are Treya Thorsen and her second in charge, Ingrid. Not sure of her surname yet. Can't pluck up the courage to ask her, if I'm honest. Oh, by the way, before you hear it elsewhere, they're Valkyries.' On hearing Dutch's name, Tomas thought it seemed a good bet that he would have some more intimate knowledge of Norse mythology, and he was curious to see how the big man reacted to such a claim.

'No shit? What? Real Valkyries?'

His bright blue hawk's vision took the pair in and weighed them up from top to bottom. Sure enough, they did fit the bill to look at. Then he turned his amused expression on Tomas, waiting for the punchline. Tomas wasn't smiling though. His own gaze was fixed on Dutch and was as serious as a heart attack.

'You're serious, aren't you?'

Tomas nodded and could see the big man's trouble in formulating his next question. It squirmed over his face until he finally gave up and asked, 'All right, let's assume for one second that you are telling me the truth and they are Valkyries and not a pair of co-eds out on some fancy dress frat party in the back of beyond, where we seem to be. How and where did you find them and what are they doing with you?'

Tomas gave him a pained expression and patted Dutch on the shoulder in a show of sympathy. 'You know what? I'm going to let you ask them personally, and should you come through that in one piece, then you can get the rest of the very unpleasant tale from Toby. I suspect he'll carry a bit more credibility than simply hearing it from me, but just to be on the safe side, in case you already know, tell me, what country do you think you're in?'

Dutch told him and Tomas blanched. It wasn't going to be a very pleasant conversation

'Nice,' Tomas drawled, implying that it was far from anything even resembling nice. 'Though before you go about that, mind telling me why trained soldiers are practising with such archaic weapons as bows and arrows? I'm under the impression there's no shortage of ordnance here.' Tomas did a once round around the battlements and the cluster of red dots vanished one by one from his chest. Dutch was still reeling from Tomas's Valkyrie revelation and implication that things weren't the way he had been led to believe. Dutch seemed to be caught momentarily in his own thoughts when Tomas prompted him. 'Well?'

He snapped back to the moment and responded in an offhanded way. 'Found them in a back room and it seemed a useful exercise to focus their minds while they're hanging around. They are a useful weapon anyway: silent and effective and at some point the bullets will invariably run out. Pays to be proficient in some other missile weapon. Other than a few of the lads who take an unhealthy pleasure from getting up close and personal with their knives, I don't recommend grappling with your enemy unless it's completely unavoidable.'

Tomas nodded his agreement while he watched the trainees persevere with their archery, and at the same time, take in as many details as he could about the guards and anything else he could see that might prove useful. But nothing out of the ordinary presented itself, other than a group of mercenaries unwittingly spending time in a fortress in Hell. Tomas found he was accepting the extraordinary as commonplace and he dreaded to think just what he might actually consider extraordinary now. He shuddered at the thought. He wasn't entirely sure he wanted to know just yet.

'Look, Dutch,' Tomas started, his tone of voice conveying as much as the words. 'As much as it's been real and all, playtime is over for the moment. I need to get back to my friends there because if I'm any judge of character, the little fellow you nearly nailed earlier, what did you call him? Collins? Well he smacks of a Rupert's puppet and I'm betting he's spilling his little old guts out, as we speak, to your CO, who I imagine is going to want to speak to me when Toby gets word to him of who I am and the fact I'm here along with you guys.'

Dutch gave that look that asked 'Where is here, exactly?'

'Not yet. You go talk to Toby while I'm gone. I've heard this enough for now and I've seen enough blood these last few days to see me out for a bit.'

'Blood?' Dutch queried, looking back at the Valkyries, Toby and the remainder of his escort.

'Oh yeah. I expect you'll ask the girls pretty much the same questions I did and after the constant badgering by your men, I'm not sure they have a lot of patience left. Certainly not Ingrid anyway. Forewarned is forearmed, though I'm not sure that will help you anyway, but hey! It's worth a shot.' Tomas laughed then, knowing he had baited Dutch enough to get his curiosity juices flowing. It was cruel really, but why should he be the only one to suffer. Shame he wouldn't get to see it. Tomas let his gaze wander up the keep tower towards where he figured Carmichael had entrenched himself. There was no point in putting off the inevitable any longer. With a comradely swat to Dutch's shoulder, Tomas turned and walked over to rejoin his friends.

'Fun over, Toby. I guess it's time you took me to your leader. Treya?'

The Valkyrie regarded him with her big moist brown eyes and tilted her head expectantly.

'Try not to let Ingrid hurt him. Not too much anyway. I think he might enjoy a bit of pain, though.' Tomas inclined his head towards Dutch, who was now heading their way. 'But I need you both to wait here. If things go badly, get the hell out; don't wait for me or kill too many of these guys if you can avoid it. Remember, it's not their fault.'

Toby scowled at Tomas again. He didn't like the continued reference to killing them as though they weren't there or were nothing more than animals. Tomas felt bad about it too, though not that much. They needed to understand the brutal reality of what they faced and what the result was of doing anything less than what was absolutely necessary in order to achieve that. And if it meant their deaths, then unfortunately, so be it. Toby was too nice to be a true mercenary, or so Tomas thought. He had morals, ethics and that greatest of handicaps; a conscience. It's a wonder it hadn't gotten him killed already, especially hanging around with that asswipe Carmichael. Still, Tomas mused, *I've known weirder bedfellows. Why should these ones be any different?*

'Very well, Tomas,' Treya answered, 'but I wonder, did you happen to notice those earthen mounds as we came in? Just beside the gate passage?'

Tomas frowned and his face said he hadn't.

'Well I at first thought they were refuse mounds; then I saw digging implements by the entrance, along with several of those weapons the humans use. It made no sense for there to be several of them unclaimed until I realized there were the same number of weapons as there were mounds. They were graves, Tomas. Fresh ones. What has happened here for there to be deaths already and without engaging the enemy? There is something wrong here, Tomas. Be wary!'

Treya left the implication hanging and Tomas narrowed his gaze thoughtfully. He absently scrubbed his hand through his unruly hair and rubbed his stubble encrusted chin as though the gesture would revive him a little and remove the claustrophobic and dragging fatigue from his bones as though it were some ancient and mystical incantation. However, Tomas wasn't afforded the luxury of thinking about it for long, as the tower door to the keep opened: the very one Collins had shot into like a rabbit down a bolthole earlier. It didn't surprise Tomas to see that it was Collins again who re-emerged. He swaggered across the yard with all the authority of someone considerably taller, and as though the events leading to him dashing in had never happened. It was quite comedic and Tomas would have laughed if he wasn't about to follow this little man into the lions' den, and for that little ray of sunshine, he needed to have his game head on. So instead, he waited patiently for Collins to march right up to him.

Collins stopped before Tomas only moments before Dutch came alongside, and Tomas felt the icy daggers that flew between the two. Neither liked the other, that much was obvious, and Tomas got the impression that left alone, Dutch would happily strangle Collins and leave his corpse out for the crows and think nothing of it.

'Why didn't you report directly to the keep when the corporal brought you in?' Collins wheezed nasally at Tomas, the assertive stride driving the wind from him more than he liked to let on, and before Tomas could answer, if indeed he chose to, Collins turned to Toby and asked him a similar version about why he didn't bring their guests directly to him. 'The colonel needs to be informed about all irregularities, as you well know, Corporal.'

Shit, thought Tomas, *this is going to be a longer meeting than I antici-pated if that's the case.*

Collins continued unabated, as though he had so many things to say and he had to get them all out before he was stopped. Tomas got the impression

909

that it happened a lot. 'You don't just send a sentry away from his duty then wander off. I've only just been informed of this. How am I to inform the colonel of matters if you neglect to keep me abreast of things, hmm?'

Toby and Tomas both knew that the diminutive self-appointed adjutant was in a different tower when they arrived, but he obviously didn't see that fact as important. The sentry obviously had to wait until Collins had collected himself from his near-death experience at the hands of Dutch and his arrows before being able to deliver his report.

'If you will kindly accompany me, sir, I will inform the colonel you are here. He may wish to speak to you.' Collins thought that was sufficient and was about to turn away and head back, fully expecting Tomas to follow timidly behind, considering himself told. Only Tomas didn't. He clamped a hand on Collins's shoulder and brought him up short. He could have sworn that Collins squealed, but he wasn't sure.

'Before you trot off like a good little doggy. I want refreshments brought out for my friends and for Toby and his men.' Tomas turned on his best Rupert's tone, and delivered it with such aplomb, he should have been granted his Equity card. 'It has been a long, hot and shitty trek to get here so there's a good boy. And just for your reference, I am a major. Speak to me or any of mine that way again and I'll see you horsewhipped, you horrid little man. Do I make myself abundantly clear?'

The color couldn't have fled from Collins' face any faster even if he had a faucet attached, as it registered with him what Tomas had just told him. 'Of course, sir. Sorry, sir. I wasn't informed, sir.' Collins shot a scathing and accusatory glance at Toby for withholding that vital bit of information; who, with total innocence, just looked skyward at a passing non-existent bird and promptly started whistling. 'Leave it with me, sir. I'll see to it myself, but if you don't mind following me for the moment, sir. The colonel, I am sure when he hears there is another officer present, will be more than pleased to greet you as a fellow gentleman.'

Bollocks, thought Tomas, picturing the colonel's face when he learnt just which major waited to speak with him. *He'll probably shoot Collins for not telling him it was me. He's an obsequious little shit, but he doesn't deserve Carmichael. Fuck me, not even Carmichael deserves Carmichael.*

'Who can I say awaits the colonel's pleasure? Major...?'

Tomas shook his head. 'No, no, no.' Tomas waggled a finger at Collins, who followed the finger diligently. 'That won't do at all. How on earth could I surprise my old chum if he knew I was here? Just say that an old friend who very nearly didn't have the chance to see him again would like a few words with him if he has the time, which I feel compelled to add, is of the essence.' *That should interest him sufficiently.* 'Any more than that is no concern of yours. Now run along and tell him what I just told you, and be quick about it.'

Collins snapped off a more perfunctory salute than the sentry earlier, and spun smartly on his heel and stalked off. If it had been concrete instead of sand beneath Collins's glaringly polished boots, they would have sounded out with every step. Tomas rolled his eyes at the amused expressions he was getting at his little charade, but what could he say?

'I know, but he's a petty pencil neck and they need telling in a certain way. Once they hear things the way they expect to hear them, even if it's not what they want to hear, they react in the way they are expected to. Simple psychology really.' Tomas was met with more blank stares than he had seen for a while and decided it was prudent to give up trying to explain things.

'Toby, tell Dutch what we told you, 'cos I think he needs to know. Oh, and Treya?'

'Yes, Tomas?'

'Be gentle with him.' Tomas turned to Ingrid, who was studying the big Dutchman as though he were some horse she had to assess. *Give her long enough and she'll be checking his teeth and withers.* 'The same goes for you, Ingrid. None of your antics.'

'Antics?' That got her attention. 'I do not understand what you mean, human.'

Tomas sighed; it was useless trying.

'That for a start, you obstreperous mare. Stop with the *human* thing, will you? It freaks people out and yes, I know that is your intention, but I need you to play nice for a short while otherwise I'll be forced to put you over my knee and discipline you in front of all these men – like last time.' *That should get a rise*, he thought, sufficient to distract her while she thought about the fact that he may or may not be bluffing. She had seen him in action after all. Ingrid suddenly burst out laughing: the first time he had seen such a genuine outburst, he was sure.

'Very good, Tomas, I see what you intend.' Then all humor vanished as though it had plunged down a bottomless pit at terminal velocity. The temperature dropped with it. 'I would, however, like to see you try.' Her hand had dropped absently to her sword as she spoke, as though a part of her feared that Tomas might actually come good on his threat. Tomas thought that it might be fun, but he caught Treya's warning glance and instantly relegated the thought as a very, *very* bad idea indeed. However...

'But as I am busy right now, Ingrid, this is your lucky day. Maybe I'll let Dutch do it.' Allowing no further discussion, Tomas turned and strode off towards the hall. Behind him he heard all hell break loose. Treya would probably never forgive him for leaving her to deal with a fired up Ingrid and he wasn't sure if Dutch would survive such an encounter, but dealing with the matter would occupy them for a while and give them reason to communicate and get to know each other. Maybe. *Ingrid likes hitting things and Dutch obviously likes being hit. Seems like a good match to me.* Tomas's long strides soon caught up to Collins, and he fell in behind the muttering quartermaster just as he opened the vaulted and steel banded door leading into the darkness beyond.

Like the main gates, these had been well oiled and swung in soundlessly, closing again with equal silence. Tomas slipped off his shades and tried to adjust his eyes to the Stygian gloom of the inner hall. He passed through a small chamber, which is to say it was still larger than most small hotel lobbies, but even that paled when he passed through another extensively decorated and ornate double archway into the hall proper. Tomas had seen smaller cathedrals. It was deceptive when viewed from the outside because he could have sworn blind that the vaulted and buttressed ceiling, with its flying arches and massive timbers, didn't rise so high when viewed from the courtyard. It was either a testament to some magnificent architecture and incredibly talented builders, or there was more to this chamber than met the eye. As his gaze moved around the hallway, Tomas saw several passageways lead off each side, no doubt, he thought, for the myriad of servants it must have taken to service the biggest and longest table he had ever seen in his entire life, which ran lengthways from a raised dais at the far end, to finish some two thirds the way down the hall. But that wasn't the half of it; though in a way it was exactly that – just one half – because the table was built like a giant wooden horseshoe. The gap was left for the guests who sat in the inner ring to be able to disperse and for the servants to have access to them. Invariably the fact it didn't fill the entire hall meant it still left room for whatever entertainment, or what passed for it, to take place at the entrance end. It had to have been a small forest to make the monstrous table and the hundreds of chairs and benches that ran along both sides. Then he realized they weren't exactly short of wood outside. Probably used what they cleared for the foundations and the killing ground. Tomas noted with interest that there was only one chair cum throne upon the dais and it sat behind another smaller version of the larger table. Whoever ruled here ruled alone and kept his or her own entourage – the privileged few who dined with the king or whatever he or she chose to be called. Bran had implied that the Reaver, Charon as he knew him, resided here once. But was he the only resident of this thorny castle? *Thorny castle? Hmmm, that's got a ring to it. Blackthorn Castle, even better. Nice. That's what I'd call this place if I lived here. With all those bloody spikes on the outside, it's quite fitting.* Tomas folded his hands behind him in the *at ease* position he found came as second nature still, and had for the last twenty-five years. To the untrained eye, Tomas moved and behaved like the epitome of what made an officer. It was just his eclectic garb and unshaven features that betrayed that charade. Collins had saluted quickly and asked Tomas to wait in the hall while he informed the colonel. So Tomas paced slowly, hands clasped behind him at ease, and took in the décor. However, he paid deliberate notice to where Collins went until the little man disappeared through a doorway. If Collins did in fact head straight towards Carmichael as he had told Tomas, the detail of the directions to Carmichael could be a useful bit of intel which Tomas filed away for future use, always assuming he actually had a future to use it in, that is. A young looking private slipped into the hall from another doorway with a tray of chilled juice and some bread, so fresh it still steamed; fruit; and some cheese, then slipped out again unobtrusively after depositing it on the end of the table. Tomas spared him one cursory glance before continuing his study of the shields, tapestries and vast array of archaic and lethal looking weapons that adorned the walls on all sides, strolling the length of the hall as though he were there on some sightseeing trip. In the middle of the horseshoe table, rising out of the centre of the floor and large enough to have a truck driven through it, was an impressive stone-hewn fireplace. A cleverly constructed stack rose skyward and vanished out through the roof. Flying buttresses spanned the hall and connected the stack to the walls, reinforcing it and giving it a stony cobweb look throughout the roof space. Tomas regarded this engineering feat with a calculating eye. For hanging from these stonework strands were ornate and seriously heavy looking candelabras, wrought from, or so it appeared from where Tomas could see them, a very dark and substantial looking iron. Each one held upon its six concentric rings each gradually reducing in diameter – and counting the candles,Tomas only guessed at the figure – in excess of two hundred thick, creamy looking columns. *I don't fancy the damn job of lighting all those buggers*, Tomas thought to himself. Within the shadows of the sweeping stonework and timbers, he could see the small holes high in the wall, where he could only assume that some poor sod did in fact have the unenviable task of clambering out and lighting, replacing and maintaining the hundreds of candles each night. Tomas shuddered; he'd always had an aversion to unnecessary manual labor, especially his. for although he could see that they were supported by chains, which also vanished into holes in the roof much like the candelabras back home, Tomas figured these were lowered and raised for major maintenance only, because it would have been a time-consuming task to drop every one and to haul these monstrosities up and down every night, and not to mention that it would have taken up valuable table space when they were lowered. It was probably easier to do the day-to-day stuff in situ. Again Tomas assessed just how high up that was and wondered if anyone had ever fallen. *That'd leave a bruise as well as make one helluva mess.* Tomas envisioned some little servant screaming as they slipped off, and landing in someone's soup. *Though this being Hell, after all, they would no doubt just laugh and chuck the corpse to the dogs. Assuming it died. Maybe even if it was just broken they'd still toss it to them just for a laugh. Sick fuckers.* Tomas filed away the little boltholes and the weighty candelabras for future reference. They'd make a handy diversion if one of them should just happen to fall behind someone if they were being chased. *Who knows,* Tomas wondered as his tactical mind ran through several options. *Maybe they do that anyway. After all, this place is probably riddled with nasty traps and the likes to both stop an invading force getting in, and fuck up one that had already gotten in.* Tomas made a mental note to be careful what he touched and where he walked. *Don't want to be setting anything off prematurely, and with that psycho Carmichael in residence, the mental fuckcase could have rigged all sorts of shit to pacify his paranoia.* Tomas continued his stroll up towards the dais with a touch more caution, looking down from time to time at the massive stone flags that were fitted together so expertly upon the floor that not even dust could have gotten between them. He forgot the ceiling for now, though his eyes were drawn to the enormous fireplace again. It was hard not to, it being such a dominating feature of the hall. Tomas peered into the cavelike structure where several spits awaited some poor creature, or creatures, to be skewered upon them. Pots and kettles aplenty surrounded the spits, waiting eagerly for the entrails and internal organs to be tossed in. Along with a few veg, they would certainly make quite a few portions of stew. Like a huge indoor barbeque. *It sure ain't no place for a veggie. They'd shit right out in here, having to sit there and suck on bread and fruit, I reckon.* The reference to veggies instantly cast Tomas's mind out and an image of his sister popped unbidden before his inner eye. The sudden thought sent waves of emotions coursing through him. Guilt, panic, and an almost overwhelming curiosity to know about her whereabouts and safety. What would she think about what he was up to? Or where he was. Did she even care? It had been quite a few years since he had seen her last and to be fair, he didn't even know where in the States she was, if indeed she was even still there. That was the last place he had heard of her living, but it was a big place and she could be anywhere. Even if she still lived in England he would have trouble enough finding her; it wasn't as small as the rest of the world invariably thought. Guaranteed, nearly every American he came across would say to him: *You're from England? Wow, I have a friend who lives there. Let me think now, it's in a little place called Lie-cester-shire,* or some other such equally unpronounceable place – each syllable of the county dragged out with painful separation and then drawled to twice its length like only an American could. *Her name is Patricia,* or Bob or something just as banal, and it would nearly always end with, *do you know her?* Tomas eventually learnt to just shake his head and deny knowledge. It was easier than trying to explain to them the relative size, and that there were some sixty million people living on the small island known as Great Britain and, strangely enough, Tomas *didn't* know them all. Then, if you were really lucky and they were particularly dense and missed your British sarcasm – as the majority of the world does – about proportionate size and some offhand reference to asylums and jails, they would then regale you about their ancestry and how they were distantly related to either some Irish family or some Scottish one, way, way back in days gone by and how they longed to visit one day. Tomas would smile vacantly and wonder just how long aircraft had been flying people back and forth and why they didn't get their stupid ass on one and go and see for themselves the fairytale land they thought Britain was. Tomas chuckled at the memory. To be fair, it wasn't all of them. He had many good friends out there, but boy, were some of them dumber than a stump. He hoped Gwen hadn't shacked up with one of them six-fingered ones with two teeth – and it was two if they were lucky and *raley perty* – and found herself living in some squalid trailer in some godforsaken hick backwater with a half a dozen mewling rugrats clamoring for her tits, while he was out in his nineteen-forties pick-up, out shooting dinner or scraping up road kill and tying it to his roof the way they seemed to, for some reason. Tomas was a hunter of men, not animals. Where was the challenge in shooting Bambi? Any imbecile could do it, and invariably most imbeciles did. Animals couldn't shoot back and rarely understood what was happening until it was too late. Tomas always maintained that if animals could watch movies, they'd watch *Deliverance* and laugh their rocks off, though Tomas had to admit that he quite liked it too: man needed something to hunt them. That thought brought Tomas back to his mission, and the memory of Gwen vanished in a puff of acrid smoke. *Shit. That's what I get for not being careful what I wish for.* The Adversary had obviously heard his plea and answered with a vengeance. Man was not only facing extinction from his own folly, but now he had a natural predator, or worse still, a supernatural predator and not one who just wanted a bit of sport. These hunters would settle for nothing less than total annihilation and eradication of all humans, everywhere. Unfortunately, that wasn't a good thing. Tomas conceded that he had a list of scum he would like to see wiped out but didn't think it was likely he could get it restricted to that. Besides, there were probably powers-that-be who wouldn't be overly pleased with his choices and, if he was honest with himself, he was just a touch biased. *There's just no winning sometimes!* Tomas grumbled to himself as he resumed his tour and tried to focus on what he might say to Carmichael, but it didn't work in his head; it rarely did. He would just have to gauge the man's mood and try to play off it. Risky, but he had little option in his current state.

By the time Tomas reached the dais, he found his patience was starting to wear thin. And by the time he had walked back to where he began, only on the other side of the hall, he was ready to kill someone. Unfortunately for Collins, he was the first person Tomas saw when he reappeared through one of the servants' entrances. He looked sweaty and nervous, wringing his hands over and over, and his eyes darted everywhere except Tomas.

'Stand still, man, and look at me!' Tomas barked at the oily little adjutant, though Tomas did notice that he didn't look quite so cocksure of himself now. *I bet he's been talking to Carmichael, who's probably ripped into him with his usual tact and diplomacy.* He had seen the way Collins had faced down Dutch, so he reasoned it wasn't any of the men who bothered him. If he was incapable of looking after himself, he wouldn't have been here in the first place. 'What is it, Collins? Out with it, man. Does your colonel intend to keep me waiting *all* day?'

Collins flinched. Tomas guessed that it was a large part of it.

'S...sorry, sir. The colonel asked me to ask you to bear with him a while longer. He is currently...indisposed.'

Tomas saw something flash across Collins's eyes that said he wished he didn't know what the colonel was doing, but had found himself privy to something that scared the living shit out of him. Collins's eyes started roving again, flicking glances behind him as though something terrible was stalking him or about to leap upon him. Then he recalled protocol and jerked up a rough salute, not his previous text book standard effort, and spoke in a shaky voice that broke up at first. He swallowed and tried again, but though it was still high pitched and grating on the ear, it was at least steady this time. 'If that'll be all, sir, I have duties to attend and I'd really like to be about them if it's all the same with yourself, Major.'

Tomas got the distinct impression that the man was terrified and desperately wanted to be anywhere at that moment other than where he currently stood. What had he seen to have shaken him up so badly? He was pompous earlier and filled with his own self-importance, seeing himself as the grease within the wheels that kept things running smoothly. Within the hour, he'd turned into a petrified little man, nervous and timid. That doesn't fit with the small man syndrome he exhibited earlier. These small men were like chihuahuas. Small and yappy ankle biters that thought they could take on anything bigger than them. Granted some could, but some, well most really, definitely couldn't, though it didn't stop them trying. That spark had gone out in Collins and that would take some doing. Tomas's hackles were up now and curiosity burned within him all the brighter because even if Collins was a pain in the proverbial, he didn't deserve to be treated this way and Tomas was ever a champion for the underdog. It just got under his skin in a way he couldn't explain. If ten people sided against one, Tomas would side with the one, even if the one was in the wrong. Things had to be fair. Tomas advocated picking on someone your own size or at least one on one. The meeting with Carmichael just took on another meaning, and Tomas *really* didn't like bullies.

'Of course, Collins. In fact, why don't you head off back to the tower you were in earlier and check on those bits and pieces you keep in there, and if you see Dutch out there and my associates, have them send a few men with you to help. Oh, and make sure they're armed. I'm sure Toby or Dutch will heed my *suggestion*, for heaven forbid I undermine your CO and issue an order.' Tomas winked at Collins and a semi-relieved smile slid across the adjutant's face and he nodded a brief thank you before scampering out in an almost undignified run.

The moment Collins was gone Tomas made up his mind. He wasn't waiting any longer. It was time to explore and, if he found Carmichael's office in the process, *well, that would be just damned inconvenient for him and bollocks to his indisposition.*

Tomas made for the passageway that Collins had appeared from, and suddenly realized just how much light the stained-glass windows that helped illuminate the hall actually let in when he plunged into the relative darkness of the passage. *Never shows this on those bloody medieval films. Too many poxy camera lights so you can see their hammy overacting faces. Oh no, it doesn't show you how these passages are like bloody caves.* In fact, were it not for a few flaming sconces interspersed at regular intervals along the passage wall, casting a dull and dancing light on proceedings as the flames flickered with every miniscule draught – and there were several of them – he would have been unable to see his hand in front of his face. *Jeez! People actually lived like this. Amazing.* Tomas moved carefully, his ears straining for the slightest sound that might either give away someone moving his way, or of the elusive Carmichael. Sliding along the wall, Tomas felt some of his old mission stealth settle over him and he realized that it actually felt quite good. He didn't realize just how much he had missed it. Tomas had tried to force away those memories and the things he had done, consigning them to the long dead past, but like some trashy B movie, the past refused to stay dead.

Tomas kept to the pools of shadow, like mini voids of darkness between the sconces, and moved swiftly along the wall. He suddenly heard raised voices coming from ahead of him and Tomas carefully moved to get a closer look. He peered through a crack in another of the oaken doors that was partially ajar, and saw that it was a vast kitchen with at least half a dozen men busying themselves inside, too embroiled in what they were about to pay any attention to who might be watching them. With so many men to feed, there had to be a few men on kitchen duty and by the glum looks on their faces, these had drawn the short straw this time around. Tomas tried to see if they had any weapons in the kitchen other than knives and kitchen implements, but he couldn't see through steam and huge bowls and racks of breads. There were two loaves missing from the tray and Tomas assumed one was his and the other one was for the girls still outside waiting patiently. Or so he hoped.

Six doors later and thankfully no further soldiers, though he did find one room full of weapons: SA80s, AK47s, a couple of Barretts, four GPMGs; and in front of all the weapons were boxes of claymores, several RPGs, and amongst them, Tomas saw at least six boxes of grenades. There was the respective ammo and mags for all of the weapons and assault rifles as well as slings, Molle webbing, body armor and several cases of small arms: Glocks, Berettas and other miscellaneous nine-millimeters. *Looks like Carmichael plans to take over a small country. They weren't kidding when they said he had plenty of kit, and this is just one room. I'd really like to see just what else he's got stashed away. It's like bloody Aladdin's cave here.* The end of the passage terminated in the bottom of a wide but steeply winding spiral staircase. Tomas looked up into the gloom speculatively. *So that's where the bastard is hiding. Here I come, Carmichael, ready or not.* Tomas studied the cavernous stairwell for just a moment longer before making his decision, then with a deep sigh of resignation and a muttered *Here goes nothing,* Tomas started the long and dark ascension.

Another habit Tomas had forgotten he possessed was counting his steps. He used to have a set of ranger beads for when he went cross country but he had lost those long ago. However, they were more useful for pacing distance and gauging how far you had traveled. Here the steps themselves would suffice, for when moving in the dark all sneaky beaky, it could occasionally become disorientating. Tomas had saved his life many times by knowing how many steps he was away from his extraction point, cover or from his nearest exit, and it had made all the difference between life or death: invariably his life, and the death of his target. There were those people who took the piss out of sufferers of OCD – obsessive compulsive disorder. Tomas didn't, because those people, in their ignorance, didn't realize it was exactly the same as what he did. In a strange sense, there was little difference in the habits of a highly trained government assassin who has had hundreds of thousands of dollars invested in him, and someone whose brain has a wire connected in a slightly different way. They did naturally what ordinary people had to learn. Some didn't manage to learn it at all, and subsequently they had shortlived careers, but it was always the way of people to ridicule that which they couldn't understand. Tomas had once read a bumper sticker which he really liked and considered apt; it was along the lines of 'You laugh at me because I'm different; I laugh at you because you're all the same'. Trouble was: for the average mortal, being different was far too scary for them. To break away from the protection of the herd, the flock, the pack was far too terrifying a prospect. It meant standing out from the crowd and being proud to do so. But Tomas was of the mind that when the creator was handing out backbones, he ran out fairly early on and couldn't be assed to make any more. All humanity got was a gelatinous substance that was meant to act like real vertebrae. But it was floppy, weak and invariably a sickly yellow color. Tomas focused on his count – forty-three – and moved on, trying not to think of the sorry humans he had been seconded by the Four Horsemen of the Apocalypse to help, and he truly wondered if it was all really worth it. Step sixty-four.

As he moved inexorably upwards, his mind ran through several scenarios of what he would like to do to those pathetic humans if he was in the Adversary's position. *Pah! So much for normality anyway: far too fucking overrated.* Tomas pondered the idea that if he could get close enough to the Adversary, maybe they could make a deal. Perhaps, rather than total extinction, they could settle for a mere cull. After all, they didn't think anything of culling several hundred seals every now and again. How would this be any different? There was an awful lot of dead wood drifting through their dreary and miserable lives that was just taking up valuable oxygen and cubic space. They would go through life sponging and mewling like pathetic bipedal parasites, taking everything they could and giving nothing back except carbon monoxide and shit. Then they would die and take up space as rotting meat. Tomas felt anger within burst into life, like someone poking the embers of a fire. The flames had died down after his earlier outbursts but the potential to ignite again in a heartbeat was still there. The subject matter of humanity's worth had been sufficient to rekindle his barely contained rage.

Tomas felt its warmth suffuse his arms and legs as his blood rose in temperature, responding to the powerful emotion. Tomas stopped. Step one hundred and thirty-eight. He took several deep calming breaths and fought against the rising tide of anger. A hint of panic allowed Tomas the control he sought because he knew, with a chill of fear, that like before, this wasn't of his doing. And unlike that last time, Tomas was learning to sense the difference and this felt distinctly detached from *his* feelings and thoughts. It felt like one of those TV hypnotists whispering in his ear, convincing him it was *his* doing, that it was *his* anger, *his* rage, *his* desire alone to do all those terrible things to people. Graphic images flashed through his mind to reinforce that thought. Images of gas chambers; flayed bodies; and deep, lime filled mass graves full of contorted and partially dissolved bodies, many with gunshot wounds to the back of their heads, others with fatal and occasionally dismembering hack marks on their mutilated bodies. Scenes of the atrocities perpetrated by the Khmer Rouge sought safe harbor in his psyche; along with other equally visceral images; along with scenes of seafaring vessels, holds filled with screaming and clamoring bodies treading the already dead beneath their bloody feet in futile efforts to escape the fate that awaited them – their eyes rolling in their heads with fear the same as cows going to slaughter, fully aware they face their deaths. In this case it was that fate which happens when they are far enough out to sea and the crew disembarks, climbing into smaller escape vessels and then waiting until they are safely away from the ship before detonating the charges that will send it sinking like a rock to the ocean floor, along with all its passengers. Image after image, each more graphic than the one before it, raced through Tomas's mind, seeking purchase, tempting, offering opportunities to re-enact many of the scenes he was seeing, if he so chose. And as they did and he was unable to squash them, the rage grew within him, feeding off his growing weakness. Tomas felt panic reach out for him with icy fingers, insidiously coiling around his soul and squeezing. This was stronger than before and here he was, stuck up a dark stairwell, with a psychopath above him and an uncertain reception below him, trapped in the middle of Hell and surrounded by heavily armed soldiers. Not the time to get a case of the jitters and have some kind of psychotic breakdown, if that was what it was. He didn't dare think of the alternative, that a bona fide *external influence* was doing a number on him. Some demon screwing with his head. *The Horsemen didn't give me anything for that and the sneaky bastards kept that little gem to themselves too. Shit.* Another wave of panic washed over him and Tomas knew he was sweating as though he was feverish. He could feel rivulets forming and running down his back. He hunkered down where he was, absently acknowledging step one hundred and ninety-seven and squatting down on his haunches, leaning with his back to the wall – just in time, as he suffered a series of juddering convulsions, and pain exploded in his side as though his ribs were being slowly snapped, one by one. The pain moved swiftly through him, culminating in his head, which couldn't have hurt any more if that frost giant Treya had mentioned had slipped up and slammed two rocks into either side of it, squashing his head like a melon in between. He so wanted to scream. Lights exploded behind his now closed eyelids as he fought against wave after wave of nausea. More pain wracked his torso, causing his insides to feel like they were trying to be outsides; Tomas truly thought he was going to black out there and then; which, from somewhere deep within him, he saw as a blessing. The world began to fade away in a crimson haze and Tomas saw oblivion hurtling towards him like the mother of armored express trains, with its headlight growing ever brighter, just as the rushing of his own blood thundering in his ears grew louder. Then, with no warning, it all just stopped and a familiar voice entered his mind like a cool soothing wall against the onrush of searing white hot pain. Tomas nearly collapsed there and then with the relief. The removal of pain is one of the sweetest sensations known to humankind, and those who've experienced it will attest that it's better even than sex. Right at that moment, Tomas would have agreed wholeheartedly with them. Then the voice spoke again.

Nakir felt the strength flowing through his consciousness. It had been growing steadily since Tomas first stepped through the gateway into the compound. Whatever power was inherent within the fortress fed the essence of the fallen angel with more energy than he had tasted in an age. But he hadn't considered the insulating capacity of the Horsemen's involvement. It shielded Nakir from much of the beneficial energy given off by the fortress, but, to his relief, not enough to prevent him from exerting his influence and wherever the mortal was going seemed to increase the insidious energy flowing into him with every step. Nakir extended his senses into Tomas's flesh and he felt the muscle and tissue of his host respond slowly at first. Nakir entwined his mind into the molecules, subtly changing them and altering them to his own design. The pain he knew he was inflicting only drove Nakir on but he was still limited in what he could manipulate in the physical. But the mental was another area completely and he flooded Tomas with visions of blood and carnage. The intent was to unhinge his mortal mind with the sheer horror and drive him into the abyss from which Nakir would resurface the victor and drown forever the mind of his involuntary gaoler. He could almost taste the freedom when the first shards of light arrowed into his thoughts and suffused his questing, preoccupied mind. Nakir screamed like he had never screamed before, in part searing agony and the rest in frustration as he felt his hold on Tomas slip and tear away from his already tenuous grasp.

'Breathe, Tomas. Deeply and slowly.' The voice was calming and strangely familiar yet as the last vestiges of human desecration slipped from his mind, he sought the voice and tried with all his might to follow the advice. It seemed good advice for as soon as he concurred, the pain began to subside and he remembered where he was: collapsed upon a darkened stairwell on the way to confront his nemesis, or one of them anyway.

What the fuck just happened there? Tomas thought he asked himself, still bewildered as to how he found himself crouched upon the step, barely upright, and he wasn't actually expecting an answer, still believing he was talking to himself, as he often did. But when the same smooth voice spoke again and, in those tones that calmed his mind, told him just what had transpired, Tomas took several more deep breaths, visibly relaxing, and these ones were of relief as he recognized who was talking to him.

'Bran. Thank God!'

A brief raspy chortle echoed in Tomas's mind at his reaction. *'I assure you, Tomas, God has nothing to do with anything here today and if your kind still believes in that particular myth about such an entity, it seems your race may find themselves to be in greater trouble than I thought you were already in. Are you good to continue?'*

Tomas nodded to himself and dragged himself to his feet, sliding his back up the stone wall. Tomas flinched as though afflicted by a nervous tic as residual images of the charnel houses that suffused his mind petered out. Tomas pulled his shirt and armor up to look at his abdomen because his mind told him that he had taken some serious bruising there. *Well it sure as shit hurts enough.* Tomas craned his neck over to get as close a look as he could get, given the poor light shed by the intermittent and dancing flames of the wall sconces. Tomas was stunned, for sure enough there were bruises, but under them he could see his ribs. Now, after forty plus years of living with his own body and having to sew it up from time to time, Tomas felt he was more than qualified to notice any fundamental differences in his physique; and two extra ribs *definitely* registered as a fundamental difference. But even that wasn't the worst of it. Glistening down his sides where his ribs were, he saw scales. Black, iridescent scales that caught whatever light was to be had in the winding stairwell and flashed it back to him like the feathers of a crow or a raven. Blue-black with a hint of violet. These were what he took for bruises and Tomas couldn't tear his eyes from them. His mouth moved slowly, but no words came out. Tomas looked up and around as though someone would appear to shed some light on his predicament but he was still, as he started, alone. He looked back down at the scales rippling across his ribs in abject disbelief.

'We have no more time to linger, Tomas, but let me assure you that now

the hold is broken, at least for now, the scaling will fade as your own psyche reasserts itself.'

Tomas couldn't tear his eyes away from the freakish snakeskin that covered his ribs. *What the fuck just happened to me?* Tomas felt his own annoyance rise with the mounting realization that there was something truly, truly wrong with him and it had nothing to do with the Horsemen. His mind frantically sought some kind of rationale but it eluded him at every turn.

'I don't know how exactly, but I sensed it the moment you arrived in the Domain and I immediately set off to find it, or you, as it turns out. It is the essence of an ancient fallen one, a being who predates even the Adversary. His name is Nakir the Black and he scoured your world thousands of years ago, almost driving your kind to extinction. Were it not for my kin and the intervention of the Four Horsemen, who imprisoned his immortal bones, he would have succeeded too.'

Tomas's mind raced to keep up and assimilate what Bran was telling him, and no matter how many times he ran it through his equally bruised synapse, he couldn't reconcile what he was hearing. How had this happened? When?

'I had hoped to never feel that creature again; I believed him banished for all time. It seems I was wrong.' Sadness and some sense of dread inevitability colored the thoughts from the battle raven and this scared Tomas almost as much as the prospect of Nakir roaming free once more. What's more, it planned to roam *in him.*

'Are you telling me I've got a fucking fallen angel inside of me?' The implication of what he was saying even as he spoke the words shook his foundation to its core.

'In a nutshell, yes.'

'Fuck!' Tomas ran out of coherent words and resorted to the old favorite. Then it hit him. Al'Mayakin. When he fell through the crypt something stabbed him right where those infernal scales had appeared. He assumed it was just a scratch that his new gifts would heal. *Boy, you couldn't*

have gotten that any more wrong if you tried, you stupid bastard, Tomas bemoaned to himself. He wasn't weak, not by anybody's standards, but the sudden gravity of what he faced crashed in on him like someone had dropped a mountain on him; and he was that close to weeping, his eyes filled up with salty water, so much so his vision grew distorted. How could he even hope to succeed? He couldn't be any further out of his depth; he wasn't even on his own planet. Not even in his wildest imaginings could he have dreamt that *that* would ever happen. Despair began then to settle on him, cocooning him in its leaching embrace, sapping his will to continue as surely as if he had opened a vein there and then, and let his life's blood flow away. '*It's hopeless. I'm royally screwed.*'

'*That might be one way to put it, Tomas, but at this moment in time it has become another battle for another day. I have blocked any further progress from Nakir for now, but you have to leave this fortress as soon as possible, for it lends him strength. I am not without resource but it will not hold him forever. If he grows in strength much more, he will be able to shatter the binding I have cast on him.*'

Tomas snapped up at that last bit. '*Are you telling me it's bound for now? Do I have the time to ask just how you, a talking bird, managed this amount of mystical spellbinding mumbo jumbo, or should I just shut up and be grateful?*' Tomas felt, rather than heard the retort from Bran, that implied, in a way that sounded stung by Tomas's offhand comment, that he should accept the latter option. '*I don't have to worry about being fucking taken over by this thing for a little while at least.*' Pragmatic as ever, Tomas grasped at what little hope was offered to him. He knew it wasn't much, but it would do, for now at least, while he completed his desperate mission without immediate distraction. And what a distraction it was. As if he didn't have enough woes without having to concern himself about further trouble brewing from within.

'*Only a short time, but I don't know how much longer he'll stay under. As I said, the sooner we get out of here the better.*'

Tomas couldn't have agreed more, but some things just couldn't be rushed. This encounter for one. He was stuck in the middle of a garrison of mercenaries whose actual purpose in coming together was still uncertain. But he didn't want to unduly piss them off and have them chasing him as he tried to get on with his already half-assed plan. He had seen them, knew them inasmuch as their capability, had seen their base of operations and a proportion of their ordnance as well as their security layout. Tomas was a liability to them if he was on the loose; adversely, Tomas didn't actually *want* to be on the loose just yet. Not if there was a chance of recruiting a private army to help him out. And he themselves, if they but knew it. He figured Toby was a believer now, and so were those of his escort, with the assistance of two very capable Valkyries. Dutch probably was too; especially if Ingrid had anything to do with it. A flutter of amusement at the picture which screamed through Tomas's mind momentarily lightened his sombre mood, imagining the chaos that likely ensued when those two met, but it lasted no longer than a nanosecond, before what passed for reality crashed back down around him along with the reminder that he was creeping up a darkened stairwell to interrupt the rude and ignorant Carmichael, who was no doubt getting his jollies off making him wait. Tomas didn't like waiting, hence his current predicament.

Tomas straightened and adjusted his armor with a thought, covering his scaly ribs. *Out of sight really isn't out of bloody mind though.* He manifested his earlier accouterments, what he had traveled in when he was with Death and the other Horsemen, toning down the black on black and replacing it with the more day-to-day eclectic combination he preferred: Kevlar body armor with chain mail over, and steel shoulder guards, all concealed under his Kevlar-lined cloak; his forest green DPM trousers with protective Kevlar thigh pads and knee pads; and drop holster, containing his Glock 9mm, tucked into more medieval looking shin-protecting, steel plated boots. His chest protecting steel cuirass sported a belt of throwing daggers running diagonally across his torso from shoulder to hip. Tomas's favorite olive-and-black shemagh coiled about his neck and he forewent any helm but did include a cowled hood on his deep forest green cloak, which he raised. Thus only by looking directly at Tomas would his features be prominent. Which was what he wanted Carmichael to do. For the sake of impact Tomas allowed the sword to manifest and sling itself across his shoulders, with the hilt protruding ominously above them where he could grab the sword easily if need be. Concealed beneath his cloak in a further pair of slung holsters, where Tomas could keep one hand upon them and draw swiftly if necessary, were the two *borrowed* Hochlers he had picked up on his journey, both fitted with full thirty-round mags with an extra one taped to each for easy changeover. Remembering the dead men he had taken them from steeled his resolve all the more. Tomas was a believer in never having enough firepower at hand and even though the sword could manifest into any hand-held weapon he could imagine, and possibly a few he couldn't, having a few extra bits about his person just settled his mind somewhat. *Old habits and all that*, he told himself.

'*So much for stealth then?*' Bran asked, knowing the answer readily enough, sensing the determination and resolve in Tomas's mind.

'Sod that Bran, I've had just about all I'm taking. Like you said, we need to get out of here sooner rather than later. To do that we need to get this meeting over with. There is no point putting it off. He knows I'm here and I know he's there. The time for pussyfooting around and playing games has come and gone. That went kicking my heels downstairs, so you ready for this while I was?' Tomas had stopped thinking to the battle raven and was talking out loud, not caring whether the colonel heard him or not.

'*I'll be right outside if you need me. But be careful, Tomas, for although I can sense you and the fallen one within you, I can sense something equally foul within the tower chamber that you head towards. And like you, it has been shielded but not well enough to escape my senses. If you ask me, there is something more than this Carmichael up there, but as to what, I have no idea at this point except it's probably dangerous.*'

Tomas smiled a chilling smile as he looked upwards into the uninviting darkness of the tower stairwell.

'Well, it's not the only thing that's dangerous, Bran. I've been known to have my moments too, you know.' Tomas rolled his shoulders, flexed his blackened steel armored gauntlets and started his ascension once more.

'Well and good, Tomas, but remember, you are in the Domain now. Here, just about everything is dangerous and in ways you can't even begin to imagine.' Bran paused for a second as he scrutinized the soldiers in the yard and on the battlements before adding his observations for Tomas's benefit. *'All is calm out here anyway, so it appears you are still undiscovered. Just don't do anything foolish.'*

Tomas nodded he understood and pressed on, determined to reach his goal and get to the heart of things. Three hundred and sixteen steps was the last count when Tomas found himself on a small landing, facing the only door in a very solid looking stone surround. There had been no windows at all in this tower, which added to its murkiness; and the last flaming sconce, attached to the wall in the stairwell, which cast its smoky and diffused light as far as it could, was unfortunately still several steps down, leaving it almost pitch black where he stood. At the foot of the door were a few trays of untouched food. One had even begun to go off, having been ignored for too long, and the sweet sickly aroma of putrid flesh and rotting fruit assailed Tomas's senses. He crinkled his nose in disgust at both the smell and the laziness in not clearing it away. It was constantly instilled in him from an early age – first his father, then the military – don't shit where you sleep and eat. On Earth, in the present, disease was a constant and ever increasing threat. It waited like a hungry wraith hovering upon every person's doorstep, just waiting for the moment they slipped and let it in; and that was in a world of paranoia and disinfectant. Here, in this pseudo-medieval world it could be catastrophic. Just take the bubonic plague for one. Look how that spread, wiping out hundreds of thousands during Europe's dark ages. *Sure as shit didn't do London any favors. Couldn't give a rat's arse about the rest of Europe, mind. That's why the powers-that-be made Britain an island. Just as bloody well too that we didn't have that poxy tunnel when Hitler wanted a piece of the action; we'd all be speaking bloody German now. What a stupid bloody idea.* Tomas grumbled to himself some more about defensibility as his mind settled on how he was to approach Carmichael. On the flip side though, at the opposing end of the spectrum, Tomas looked at his own grubby hands and concluded that it was likely that humanity suffered from so many disabling ailments primarily due to its excessive use of antibacterials, and having an overly disinfected populace. Tomas snorted in disgust at the thought of the pampered and neurotic humans who now not only wouldn't, but couldn't, even if they chose to, get their hands dirty without coming down with something incapacitating. When he was a kid he was forever covered in various combinations of mud, pondweed and manure from when he was up at the farms near where he grew up, and not a lot had changed in his life to affect that. The scourge of his poor mother he was, permanently filthy and in need of a good bath, or so she thought. That sort of interaction was, and to Tomas's mind, still was necessary to build up a good immunity system. The body needs a certain amount of bugs in it and around it to keep it healthy. It's like being bitten by a snake or spider, what cures you is more of the same. Influenza jabs to inoculate humans come from the very virus they are protecting themselves against.

Tomas wondered at first about the sloppy housekeeping, because as a rule that was just idleness and asking for trouble; but then realized that it was probably only Collins who brought the food up anyway and he obviously didn't hang around long enough to take any of the others away again, or had his hands full of other things. Always presuming of course he could actually see any of the other things. It was cold, dark and ominous up here and nobody in their right mind would want to hang around long after trudging up three hundred-and-some cold stone stairs morning, noon and night. Another thought suddenly occurred to Tomas then – a small observation, but one he used to pay attention to. He hadn't seen any rats. At all. Nor any sign of their presence. It never took the little buggers long normally to get a toehold in an encampment, especially one this size. There had to be a million hidey holes for them to swarm and breed in within a place as big and sprawling as the fortress appeared to be. *Even vermin don't want to be around you, Carmichael. Says a lot, if you ask me. I always said rats had impeccable taste.*

As Tomas's eyes adjusted to the gloom the longer he stood there, he noticed, as he slid the trays aside with the toe of his boot, that light seeped out from beneath the door, and there was movement beyond it that disturbed that light.

So, you are in there, you bastard. What are you up to? Locked away in your tower room like some Grimm's fairy tale creature or brooding wizard out of some second rate fantasy book, though the only fantasy is the one in your head, you psycho. And if you insist on playing hide-and-seek up here, consider yourself caught, and here I come, ready or not.

Tomas was about to hammer on the door when he heard a noise from behind him, coming up the stairs hastily, making no attempt to conceal itself. Boots pounded against stone and Tomas pulled out one of the Hochlers, both fitted with suppressors, and slipped deeper into the shadows to wait and see who or what it was. Pulling his cloak around him until he was virtually invisible, even in the confines of the small landing, Tomas prepared himself. He didn't have long to wait though, before a sweating and panting Collins appeared before him, looking around furtively, hand on the wall for support and a feeling of security, obviously searching for something or someone.

'You wouldn't be looking for me, would you, by any chance?' Tomas stepped out of the shadows to see the little adjutant squeak in surprise and nearly throw himself back down the stairs with the shock at seeing Tomas emerge from apparent thin air; at least it was thin air as far as Collins was concerned, with his limited visibility.

'How...? Where...? Oh never mind... Oh crap.' Collins leant forward and braced his hands on his knees as he drew in gulpful after gulpful of air, his chest inflating and deflating with a decreasingly erratic rhythm as he got his wind back. 'Phew, That's better. Sorry about that, sir, but I've never run up them blasted stairs as quick before. I came back to get you and you weren't there.' Collins shot Tomas a swift accusatory glare. 'Imagine my consternation, if you will. Having informed the colonel you were still waiting and then to have you disappear. I had to inform the colonel you had vanished, you understand, and after all that, here you are already. Really! You could have waited, you know.' As Collins got his wind back, his confidence crept back alongside it but Tomas wasn't about to have this ferret of a man rebuke him like this, especially after making him wait as long as he had. Although it wasn't Collins's fault directly, he had to respect the chain of command and he wasn't as far up it as Tomas was, so he didn't have the privilege of telling Tomas off in this way without consequence.

'Whoa there, petunia, don't you go getting all holier than thou with me. Who the hell do you think you are talking to?' Collins blanched visibly even in the diminished light. 'I've waited long enough down there, don't you think? Or are you accustomed to making *all* your visitors wait half the day for your pleasure?' Not that Tomas suspected they had many. If he wasn't the first and only he would be surprised, but it was a moot point. 'So, as no one seemed overly bothered, I thought I would just go ahead and introduce myself. My time is just as valuable as yours and his.' Tomas inclined his head towards the door. 'And I don't have a lot of it, certainly not to waste on such ill-mannered displays as this –'

Tomas was cut off from his reprimanding of Collins by the oak door swinging inwards suddenly. Only this one didn't move on well oiled hinges: it squealed and screamed like you would expect from any true haunted castle. Both Tomas and Collins turned to regard the now illuminated doorway and Tomas saw Collins flinch as though he expected some kind of horror to come rushing out and savage him. Tomas scowled and frowned at such behavior from an officer, even one as puerile as Collins. What is it with this man that he seems so terrified of Carmichael? At that moment, a voice issued from within, and Tomas felt his hackles rise involuntarily and he saw Collins back slowly towards the stairs.

'Don't just stand there all day. If you are coming in, come in, and shut the door.'

Tomas reached out and took Collins by the shoulders, turning him and gently steering him towards the stairs before he fell backwards down them. That would definitely leave a bruise.

'I'll take it from here, Collins. Just remember what I said for the future and get yourself off. Have some of that chilled wine I left down there and don't come back up here until I come down to get you. You understand me?'

Collins nodded blankly, happy to be exonerated from a duty he abhorred anyway. Without any resistance, he scampered away into the abyss and within seconds had vanished from sight. The sounds of his boots on the flags vanished shortly after. Confident that he was gone, Tomas turned and stepped into the room.

Keeping his back to the man who he glimpsed as sitting behind a massive desk, Tomas made a show of closing the heavy oaken door, slowly and with deliberate intent, before turning to face the man he had hoped to never see, alive at least, ever again. As their eyes locked and sudden, horrifying reality of recognition crackled back and forth between them, the temperature in the room seemed to noticeably drop.

'Yoouuu?' Carmichael hissed. His shocked voice was filled with more venom than a hundred snakes as he fully comprehended just who stood before him. Like Tomas, he must have had an idea of who awaited him, but the cold stark reality of physically beholding that person was another matter and Tomas was intently watching the myriad of emotions and expressions that warred for dominance on the ravaged face of the man before him. Shock, hate, calculation, scrutiny and disbelief for just a few. Carmichael was once considered handsome, groomed for government and a very public life, although things didn't go the way he or his masters intended. Tomas tried to reconcile the creature before him with the man he remembered and couldn't believe what he was seeing. The man before him looked gaunt to the point of emaciation. Sallow and yellowy skin, stretched almost to the point of ripping, seemed pulled over his skeleton as though it was all gathered behind him and stapled back there. Previously perfect teeth, all wire braced and Hollywood sparkle that formerly hid behind full, almost womanish, if somewhat cruel lips, were now as grey as gravestones, with more than one broken, and they protruded out from his face like some skeletal primate. The flesh of his face, that which filled and rounded his features to the man he was before, was virtually gone. He was now just parchment skin over bone, leaving him with a grim visage. But as hideous and disturbing as it was, it did little to disguise his predator's gaze, still emanating from within grey and sunken sockets. The two chips of flint that passed for his eyes still flared with an unhealthy energy and vitality, missing nothing as he studied Tomas.

'Aren't you supposed to be dead?' Carmichael asked after a few moments, having regained his temporarily slipped composure. He sat back and steepled his fingers, gently tapping the two forefingers together as he interlaced the remainder. Tomas smiled but there was no mirth or warmth in it. Much like a crocodile's at mealtime.

'The same could be said for you; so much for living in hope then.'

Carmichael nodded slowly, as though the response was what he expected; almost as confirmation that it actually was the man he believed it to be standing before him, not some impostor. 'I heard that you and your family were blown up by some fanatics or somesuch. You were even given a military funeral. Did you know that?' This time, it was Tomas's turn for his façade to crack. He hadn't known. After dropping off the radar the day he slipped out of the hospital, discharging himself on his own recognizance, Tomas just ran; about as far and as fast as he could to escape the long reach of his employer, winding up in East Anglia in the Salvation Army shelter by the docks in a market town called Ipswich. 'I even attended. Well, after everyone had gone, of course. It wouldn't be politic to be seen spitting on the grave of a bona fide hero now, would it?' Tomas knew the question was just to bait him and Tomas had played this game so many times. 'You were given a full military burial with full honors, the works.' Carmichael looked thoughtful for a second, his eyes drifting off Tomas, to look vaguely through him and beyond. 'Don't know where your flag went though. As I recall you had a sister...' Carmichael paused to see if this provoked any sort of reaction from Tomas. When it didn't he carried on. 'She wasn't there though. Shame. But she was there for your parents' ceremony. Strange that, don't you think? What have you done to upset your own family so, Tomas? Hmmm?'

'Thanks for that. My family is my business and when last I checked, none of yours, so do be a good fellow and keep what remains of your nose out of it. Yet still, for the dead and buried, I know I don't look too bad nor feel that rough either. You on the other hand, seem to have had better days. Did they bury you too and you just crawled back out? Or are you just too damned stubborn to actually drop dead and make a lot of people really happy?'

Tomas flinched inwardly: this wasn't going well. He had hoped to remain civil and professional with this scum sucking despot wannabe, but it seemed that that idea had gone right out of the window from the get-go. Carmichael just brought the best right out of him. The colonel didn't answer. Instead he just smiled, and Tomas really wished he hadn't. It was beyond cadaverous and if some worm or cockroach was to fall out of his mouth at that point, he wouldn't have been surprised.

'You haven't seen my assistant Collins, have you, by any chance?' Carmichael changed the subject so swiftly that Tomas was left wondering where the hidden insult was until he realized that there wasn't one: just a random conversational twist. When Tomas didn't immediately answer, Carmichael just took it as a no. 'No? Shame. He is supposed to announce any unexpected visitors to me before they barge in and start insulting me in my own office.' Carmichael seemed to be talking to himself as much as he was to Tomas. 'Never mind, I'll discipline him later for his breach of protocol. Regulations and orders must be followed, don't you know? It doesn't set a good example to the men when they are so flagrantly disregarded, don't you agree, Major?'

Tomas realized that as he studied the thing before him, the husk that used to be Colonel Carmichael, he concluded that he was in fact, quite mad. Trouble was, that wasn't the half of it.

Having stood before officers before, Tomas was used to their little mind games and Carmichael wasn't immune to playing them even here. There was no chair on Tomas's side of the desk, so any visitor would be forced to stand while Carmichael reclined in comparative comfort. Tomas fought for some self-control and attempted to steer matters back to less personal issues. Fire fighting a little against Carmichael's dictatorial mindset and protecting those that would suffer at his hands.

'Whatever you say, Colonel, this is your show. But you ought to know that I sent Collins away. I asked him to do me a very important favor. I'm sure you don't mind, do you?'

The colonel stared at him with a deadpan expression, giving away nothing of the inner fury at being undermined. Tomas knew that would stick in his craw. And they could have gone on like that for hours, both knowing it. But it was Carmichael who finally cut to the chase with the first really relevant question.

'What do you actually want, Walker? And even though I'm sure it would be a fascinating story of how you even came to be here, I'm not interested in your ramblings. I am interested, however, in what you are filling the heads of my men with. Distracting them from their concentration with children's tales as they await further orders from me regarding their mission. It was I after all who hired them in the first damn place.'

This was the bit that was going to hurt the most and cost Tomas probably the last shred of personal pride that he had left. Through gritted teeth he answered, 'I could use your help; that is if it doesn't interfere with whatever mission you may or may not be on. Because I wonder if you are aware of some of the finer details of your current predicament.'

Virtually non-existent eyebrows slid upwards on Carmichael's face as he wordlessly questioned Tomas's statement. A nonchalant wave of his bony hand suggested Tomas should continue with his *sitrep*. Tomas bit back an angry response and pressed on, omitting vast chunks of personal, and as far as Tomas saw it, irrelevant – as far as Carmichael was concerned – detail. He told him of the Domain, what it really was; and about the Adversary, along with his plan for humanity. Then, leaving out Be'elzebub and his army, Tomas hinted at a rebellion, his place in it and their plan to rescue the rightful ruler of this realm and squash the usurper's plan in one fell swoop. Hopefully. Which was where Carmichael and his band of merry men came in. Their firepower and skills could well allow him to succeed where before, it was a nigh on impossible task. Surely, what mission could be more important than saving the multiverse? Tomas finished his report of the situation, even outlining two possible theatre scenarios he had been forming since meeting Toby and the men, ready for when he or they finally engaged Asmodeus, who even Tomas had grimaced at having to mention, as well as in all likelihood, the army he would have at his back. Tomas kept the source of his intel to himself as well as how he knew about land layouts; and how he knew when and where the enemy was likely to be as well as how it was likely to react when he made his move. It was still far too soon to trust this known snake in the grass with too many pertinent details. What he had told him though regarding the Adversary was already happening on Earth, albeit on a more low key basis but was due to escalate rapidly and would soon be common knowledge everywhere judging by what Tomas had seen so far and if Michael was to be believed. Tomas did and had only really brought the isolated colonel up to date on matters he should and would find out about soon enough. Tomas wound up his request with what he saw as simple reason and just plain common sense.

'You don't like me and I don't like you; let's leave it at that. But this isn't a personal matter any more. Bigger things are at stake which make you and me unimportant. I was hoping that we could act professionally and put aside our differences for just this once, and do what needs doing. If we survive it, then we can see about putting matters to rest once and for all, just you and me.' *Though looking at you, you scrawny little bastard, it doesn't look like much of a fight. I've seen more meat on a supermodel's dinner plate than on this chicken-necked stick insect. He makes those size zero models look morbidly obese.* 'What do you say, Colonel? Soldier to soldier? One last fight?'

Carmichael, still in the reclined posture he had adopted earlier, regarded Tomas silently. For his part, Tomas wondered just what was crawling through Carmichael's mind at that moment as the two men studied each other. What thoughts and feelings was he experiencing at what he had heard? Disbelief? Indifference? It was impossible to tell with this corpse like man-thing.

There were several things in fact crawling through Carmichael's mind all right, and they weren't all thoughts; though what regarded Tomas did have a few of its own and they were thoughts that would have had Tomas fleeing for his life had he known exactly *what* was now observing him *through* Carmichael's eyes at that very moment. Oh, the colonel had heard every word Tomas had said, but so too had the other occupant of Carmichael's consciousness. The entity that had become so much a part of the colonel's world and psyche that he could no longer differentiate between the two. His own persona flowed and merged with its parasitic guest so fluidly and seamlessly that it made someone with the unfortunate illness of schizo-phrenic multiple personality disorder – as we like to call it anyway – seem like perfectly distinguishable and identifiable characters. The truth is – if humans in their arrogance were brave enough to admit it – that no one but the recipient of that state of mind truly understands what those poor unfortu-nates see or hear. Like so much of humanity's history, if another person can't see or experience what another can, they cast doubt, disbelief and even heinous accusations about them. The Inquisition and the infamous witch trials were perfect examples to name but two. Nowadays, we just call them ill or delusional, and we invent psychiatry as the all encompassing carpet to sweep those illnesses under because it is much easier, as well as lucrative, coldly taking the hard earned money from those poor troubled souls who had nowhere comforting to turn, rather than trying to understand what is really going on in their minds. Humanity has always feared what it can't understand and in order to overcome that fear, it categorizes it, shoving it into smaller, more harmless boxes in order to lessen its strangulating grip of fear. Trouble is, we can't see inside people's minds, however much we like to think we can, and that is where creatures such as what currently resided within Carmichael, had, and would always have, the last laugh.

Unbeknownst to Carmichael, during his time in Africa's heartland, where he had his breakdown upon Abigail's death, his fractured psyche had opened sufficiently to let this creature in. Long had it sought a means to return to the world of men and to find a suitable host after it had been consigned to an eternity of empty and impotent ethereal voyeurism. The witch doctors, wise men and women, and shamans of both civilized and the pulsing, beating, yet slowly dying heart of ancient Africa knew of its existence, though some more than others respected this entity; and it was they who warded heavily against its influence. But as the Dark Continent grew ever more westernized, that protection gradually faltered as its people, like many others in the old cultures, forgot what surrounded them in favor of the science and miracles of the west. They grew careless and disrespectful, until finally, after succumbing to the all too mortal petty squabbles of false power, it failed them once and for all. Centuries of guarding and warding were destroyed on the day that the RPGs destroyed the hut where Abigail met with Motusi. Inside were sacred artifacts: objects that were more keys than anything else. Sacred keys to the series of safeguards spread and hidden across the land. Keys that bound this ancient spirit so tight that it remained in a secure limbo where neither the Horsemen could harm it nor the Adversary retrieve it, though both sides knew of its existence and wanted it for themselves. One to destroy, the other to utilize its malignance for means nefarious.

The Adversary had been the one who finally reined in the creature that initially, after an age of frustrated impotence, had led Carmichael, his new host, on a rampage of death and destruction. Sating centuries of helplessness in rivers of blood. Harnessing Carmichael's potential, he had the heroic soldier-turned-mercenary go out and recruit an elite force, one beyond those who he already commanded. These were to be a formidable group of war dogs who, under his personal command, would seek out individuals of the Adversary's choosing who lived their lives in the proverbial four corners of the world, and deal with them as instructed. One of those latter instructions to Carmichael, through the entity within him and originating in the dark mind of the Adversary, was to dispose of a particular family; containing one mother, one father, one son and one daughter. The family's name was Walker. It suited Carmichael well enough, for it was this particular Walker's father who had been instrumental in his eventual capture and temporary imprisonment. Perhaps more than fate was at work here to arrange the unholy marriage of hate between the colonel and the entity inside Carmichael; known as Gaunub to those who not so much worshipped, but feared and respected it as a primordial and evil power of death and destruction; and bringing them together on a parallel path of carnage. But for all their differing origins and backgrounds, there was no objection from either party when it came to wreaking havoc and carnage across the globe wherever their master decreed. Slaughtering Tomas's family had been a bonus for Carmichael and one he had relished, taking extreme pleasure in their not so much spilt, as vaporized blood.

But there had been a glitch, a wrinkle in the plan and something had gone wrong. Not only had it been the wrong daughter – the real one being absent and only discovered much later on another continent – but the one killed turned out to be some common floozy, a mere plaything of the son and of no worth to the cause whatsoever. Then there was the son himself. Naively, as it transpired, presumed dead from the explosion. He had apparently not only survived the blast – a miracle in itself – but had escaped further capture by the minions of the Adversary and was now standing larger than life before him. Before the man and creature hired by agents whilst still on earth to find him and kill him. The irony and actual odds of their mark brazenly walking into the very room he occupied of his own free will defied comprehension; but Carmichael was never one to look a gift horse in the mouth, even one as surprising as this was.

Yet it was to Carmichael's utter disgust that Tomas was very much alive and looking far too healthy for his own good. The Colonel hadn't wanted to believe it was the same man he had despised since meeting him for the first time until he had unceremoniously barged into his presence and begun his fantastic if unbelievable tale. It was almost too much to bear for the outraged colonel. Deep within Carmichael, in a place that had been buried so far and so deep that it had almost been forgotten entirely, there remained a tiny crystalline light and within it, pulsing gently like a miniscule oasis in an ocean of black and the foulest evil, lived the last vestiges of Carmichael's humanity: the only part of him that was allowed to use the sobriquet of *human*. Upon seeing Tomas standing before him, as abhorrent as he remembered, the faintly glowing crystal light sphere finally fractured under the oppressive weight of evil that surrounded it, drowning it; and it began to wither. It listened to Tomas's plea as it died until finally, as he finished, it too, with nothing or no one to mourn it, silently passed forever from existence.

The eyes that regarded Tomas now were even harder, darker and infinitely more feral than those that had greeted the despised warrior upon their initial meeting less than an hour previously. Trouble was though, with the one and only window, large and ornate – a stained-glass effort depicting a lone warrior beset with fiends and brandishing a flaming sword beneath a starry constellation – placed directly behind the seated figure of Carmichael and the struggling yet determined light of the waning sun beaming through, it caused Tomas to have to squint against those final multihued rays of the afternoon, and Tomas didn't seem to notice the subtle difference in the creature sat behind the desk, nor the subtle transformation that had occurred as Gaunub, plague of the Dark Continent, at last and with a malignant zeal, assumed full and total control.

Tomas tried to study the man before him, and gauge some sort of reaction to what he had just told him. Carmichael hadn't interrupted at all throughout Tomas's plea; not asked one question, nor offered any opinion. All the time, his eyes never left Tomas's face, as though he was trying to bore a hole through it or gain entry to his mind somehow. It hadn't fazed the grizzled warrior one bit. Tomas had grown up and cut his teeth on such behavior. Reading and adopting many aspects of *The Art of War*, *The Five Rings* and *The Tao of Lau Tzu*. When it came to visual intimidation, it would take someone with more presence than the piece of human detritus sat behind his desk to do it. It had helped Tomas master and eventually put to extensive use his interviewing and interrogation techniques. But as it stood, Tomas couldn't read Carmichael's reaction at all. His only clue that something was adrift with him at all was when he eventually spoke again. It was deeper, more guttural. It reminded Tomas of how crocodiles vibrated their body internally to communicate. He'd seen it once and been amazed at their power, creating a sound almost beyond human hearing, a primordial growl that wells up from so deep within them that it makes the water leap and vibrate around them. Tomas's frown deepened as he listened to the colonel, hearing a range, inflection and timbre that hadn't been there before, he was sure of it.

'Well that is a…how shall we say it, singularly unique request and supported by a story that if I recall correctly, I asked you not to bore me with, and yet I'm afraid to say that upon actually hearing it, I find that it does your reputation no justice whatsoever. I can say in all honesty that I've never heard such complete and utter drivel in all my years as a soldier. Were our surgeon not busy at present I would recommend you pay him a visit and ask him to assess you for head wounds.'

Carmichael, if at all possible, managed to look even more bored than he usually did when he wasn't interested in something, and with a dismissive gesture he waved Tomas away, his parting comment leaving no room for misinterpretation as far as Tomas's wellbeing was concerned. 'But as I have no interest any more in whether you live or die, though in preference I would opt for the latter, I suggest you leave my presence voluntarily before I have to call the guards to have you thrown out.'

Tomas was stunned by this casually delivered denouncement. He knew the man to be egocentric, domineering bordering on tyrannical, and fastidious about the reports given to him, but this was so *unlike* the man Tomas knew. It was as though he was some indifferent doppelganger. The colonel was usually a man who absorbed information with an almost osmosis-like ability, leaving no detail bereft of exploration. He was a man of details and that was why he had risen so far so fast. But what Tomas had, or hadn't told him should have had him grilling him for hours about all the detail that Tomas had intentionally left out. Instead, he was being dismissed as an idiot. The fact Carmichael wished him dead was no big surprise though, but if there was any surprise to be had from the encounter so far, it was that Carmichael hadn't made those particular feelings known somewhat sooner, like for example, the moment he had clapped eyes on him. Still, Tomas hadn't cared one way or the other as long as he had gone along with his suggestion – which he hadn't. So much for the friendly, amenable tack then. His parents had instilled in the young Tomas the pearl of wisdom that if you don't ask, you don't get. He had asked and he hadn't gotten. Plan B then. What he hadn't mentioned to his parents was that if he asked and didn't get, he always found another way to obtain what he wanted. Of course there were consequences, there always were, but as long as he knew what they were, he could take preventative steps to minimize them. There was always a way: you just had to look hard enough and be prepared to get your hands dirty.

Tomas hadn't come all this way, surviving all manner of horrors, to just roll over and pass up an opportunity like this. Facing insurmountable odds, he needed all the firepower he could get and these lads looked ripe for the task. The trick now would be how to get them away from Carmichael without a bloodbath. Or at least without a very big one. It would be unfortunate to lose too many, though a few would be inevitable. Tomas snarled inwardly and like so many times in the past, wished terrible things on the head of the colonel who used people like chess pieces. More unnecessary deaths because of the colonel's raging ego, ignorance, arrogance and just sheer stupidity. He had been a man to follow once and had proven he could lead, but on the reverse side of that coin, he had also proven that he could get men killed just as easily. If not easier.

When Tomas didn't immediately obey, a look of annoyance creased Carmichael's haggard features and his eyes flared briefly with barely restrained fury, as though the skeletal figure was about to explode out from behind the desk and dive for Tomas's throat. But Gaunub relaxed, albeit with a little difficulty, and both Tomas and Carmichael saw that they both watched Carmichael's hands as the colonel released his grip on the desk, where in his sudden anger, his fingers had crunched *into* the woodwork and left indentations; the primordial entity had spent many years inhabiting Carmichael's flesh and he had learnt the language and mannerisms of the man, learning how to carry himself as befitting one of his station. He was a warrior first and foremost and that Gaunub understood. The rest followed in due course.

'I suggest you leave now while I still retain my capacity for forgiveness and patience, though I don't recommend you try to leave the grounds until I give you permission, assuming I deem it fit to do so. I haven't yet decided what to do with you all and at the same time I'm not sure I can afford to have you roaming the countryside spreading your quite *fantastic* tale and causing unnecessary dissension amongst the populace. Though the two whores you travel with may offer some amusement to the men. Now if you will, *Major...*' His rank was spoken with obvious contempt, and in Carmichael's mouth, made to sound like 'leper', '...close the door on your way out.'

Tomas spared him one last look before going. *The man is totally bark at the moon round the fucking bend. He is most definitely* not *operating with a full mag.* Tomas knew too that any further argument would be futile. He had tried reason with him and that hadn't worked. Time to move on, but a smile creased the corners of his mouth as he closed the door behind him, lending his strength and weight to the movement, slamming the wood into the hole with an audible, frame rattling thud, giving it just that little bit extra to cause the colonel further irritation. But it was then that the image of Carmichael calling Treya and Ingrid whores to their faces came to mind. *I want to be a fly on the wall when that one gets going.* Tomas winced at the prospect. *It would almost be worth giving up the option of throttling the little shit myself to see that.* Quite a few different scenarios played out before his mind's eye, and each one more satisfyingly nasty than the one preceding it, before Tomas cut them off as a moment's wishful thinking before reality returned with all the subtlety of an avalanche of wet, icy snow. Facing the prospect of the stairwell again, Tomas sighed and began the long descent, contemplating his next move as he recounted his steps back down to an even more uncertain future.

'Tomorrow?' Treya wasn't happy, not by a long stretch. Tomas had brought the two Valkyries up to speed with his fruitless conversation with Carmichael, omitting for now at least, his suicidal remarks about their occupations and possible future. He actually thought for one disastrous moment that Ingrid was going to storm past him and go give the colonel a piece of her mind right there and then, so incensed was she about how this *human* could be so blasé about their future, but Treya held her back with a few chosen words, though they did little to quench the storm that built within the fiery shield maiden. And that was just for being foolish. Heaven help him if she ever heard what he called her. Tomas doubted even Odin himself would be able to stop her.

'You want us to wait until tomorrow to discover what we already know now? He will not help us!'

Tomas nodded a sad agreement and looked across to where they had left Dutch and Toby, still deep in a fairly animated conversation of their own after their extraordinary revelation. The trio had excused themselves and now stood around one of the three wells that Treya had discovered were strategically placed within the multiple baileys. The castle was indeed much larger within the walls than its appearance without portrayed. Tomas would dearly have loved to have had the time to explore such a place. Castles had fascinated him as a boy, and if Tomas was honest with himself, they still did.

'Not only will he *not* help us,' stormed Ingrid, 'I suspect that he will now seek to have our lives. Especially if what you say is true about your history with this spineless ale-wife, and you have only driven that wedge in further by antagonizing him like this. This was an ill-advised scheme of yours, human. You have only brought more trouble down on our heads.'

'I never antagonized him at all.' Tomas put on his most innocent, butter-wouldn't-melt face, all wide-eyed and mortified. 'In fact I was quite pleased with how I contained the homicidal urges the little twat brings out in me, though in hindsight, perhaps I should have just done him there and then and gotten it over with.' His expression turned grim and sullen then. 'You're partly right, Ingrid. I didn't think it through as well as I perhaps could have done, time being against us and all, but perhaps I was a bit over optimistic that Carmichael might see the bigger picture.' Ingrid merely glowered all the more at Tomas's admission. 'It's going to get messy now, I just know it. For heaven's sake watch your backs too; he's a slippery little shit and I wouldn't put it past him to renege on anything he says, and try to off us as soon as possible.'

Treya paced back and forth, her fists on her hips and thunder in her eyes, and mouth pursed. Tomas spoke as much to himself as to anyone listening, vexed as much as Treya. 'He's hiding something and for the hell of it I can't work it out.' Tomas knew *he* was hiding something too but he didn't want to let on about Bran's revelation about his own problem just yet, and a part of him felt that he was betraying the Valkyries in keeping it from them, but he didn't need any more complications right now. Tomas figured that it was by far complicated enough and he would just play that one by ear and hope it didn't backfire on them when they least expected it. Just for a second Tomas thought about offering up a quick prayer, but no sooner had the thought taken form, it was drenched like a match being put out with a fire hose by the fact that there was little hope of anything hearing his supplication, and a slight chance of the wrong being paying attention where it shouldn't.

'Bran says that there is something *wrong* with him, something fundamental, and after seeing him, I have to agree,' Tomas said and pushed his guilty thoughts as far from his mind as he was able, and changed the subject to something more positive. 'But I want his army more than he does. He just doesn't seem to know that yet and when he finds out, that's when we'll see his true colors.'

'Loki would have liked this man,' Treya whispered, like she loathed saying the name of the Norse deity, just in case he was listening for it. 'Wherever there is discord, mischief and malice, he is there. Often he is the instigator, and wherever deceit, deception and betrayal are employed, he is in his element.'

Ingrid shot her a sharp look at the mention of the name too, and she muttered an oath at the folly.

'Sounds a charming sort of bloke,' Tomas remarked cordially, 'but you say *is* like he's still about. He's not...is he?' The thought of any more of the old gods such as Loki joining in this battle was almost more than he could handle. He was having enough trouble with just one of them and he hadn't even found that one yet. Things were rapidly going from bad to worse and the more he thought about it, the more he discovered, and what he had discovered so far hadn't proved to be anything worth shouting about. Tomas again wondered just how much shit he had gotten himself involved in. Things weren't going his way at all. And Treya's answer did little to bolster his confidence in any way.

'I don't know about now, but he was very much at large the last time we were in Valhalla, and why Odin lets him roam loose is anyone's guess. Asgard would be a much safer place were he not in it.' Treya's neutral expression turned suddenly very frosty. 'Were it down to me, he would be cast into the deepest and darkest hole I could find, and I would then backfill it with sharp rocks.'

Was Tomas seeing another side of Treya?

'I'd heard about his reputation back on Earth and there aren't many stories that sing his praises about anything other than being a right royal pain in the arse to all concerned.' Tomas rubbed his chin thoughtfully, imagining the two side by side. 'Does sound a bit like Carmichael though, I must admit. And you say Loki is still around somewhere?' Then it occurred to Tomas with a start. 'He's not part of all this, is he? Involved somehow and off about who knows what, while we all chase our tails with the Adversary? I mean, isn't he something to do with Fenris as well? Damn, the last thing we need is some deranged Norse deity stirring things even more than they already are.'

'He is the father of Fenris.'

Tomas lowered and shook his head in consternation, muttering under his breath about just how *not good* this was getting.

'But I don't think so. I hadn't...' Treya added hesitantly as though reluctant to embellish, '...seen much of him before our...departure here.'

Tomas knew her exile was a sore point and she still had trouble talking about it. She continued: 'Well, I've been away now for too long, and much could have happened, but if he were here I am sure we would know about it.' Treya started to look a trifle worried herself now, but she shook it off with a quick shake of her head. 'No, I'm sure that Thor, my father and the All Father himself, would have something to say about that. They used to keep a weather eye out on him and as a brother, my father always found him something of an embarrassment.'

At that point the familial connection registered with Tomas. 'That's just fantastic. You have a raging psychotic uncle who has delusions of world domination at the very least, and here we are talking about him like he's good ol' uncle Bob who pops round for occasional visits, birthdays and Christmas. It never ends, does it?'

Treya knew by now that the question was rhetorical and just gave Tomas a look of sympathy and a little shake of her head to imply the *no* he already knew.

'So what do we do now?' Treya asked, changing the subject and deferring to Tomas's knowledge of the soldiers who they found themselves surrounded by. She had been silently impressed with how he handled the small group who escorted them here, and was keen to see how he dealt with a larger force. From her conversations with Dutch and Toby, while Tomas was enjoying Carmichael's company, she had them both pegged as competent too; potential leaders – and if they followed Tomas and men followed them, well…then they were halfway there already. It was just the other half that worried Treya.

Collins came scampering out of the keep just as Tomas, Treya and Ingrid began walking back towards where Toby, who had since slipped off about duties of his own, and Dutch, who also by now had – with a bit of gentle persuasion such as his boot up the occasional ass and much shouting – recommenced the men's archery and improvised weapons practice in the middle bailey, which as it turned out was where they were. There was a further upper and lower bailey. Now that Tomas bothered to look a little closer, he could see the gates in the partition walls, what he originally took for the curtain wall, where guards patrolled back and forth. He could see them moving behind the merlons, crenels and embrasures that protected them and separated the three sections. It became apparent to Tomas that the mercenaries Carmichael had hired were divided into two very distinct types. There was the regimented and uniformed variety that Toby and his men belonged to, as well as several other combinations he could see, for although they were uniformed, they wore different styles and it was apparent they were from different countries. Dogs of war drawn together for a common purpose, and their uniforms intimated that some habits were harder than others to break, finding comfort in years of familiarity and ingrained discipline, just not shackled by the confines of their respective governments' rules. And then there was Dutch, along with his rough and ready bunch, who at first glance looked as though they were an eclectic mix of semi-organized street gang and, at worst, the soldiers of organized criminals like the Mafia of old or the newly risen Russian and Eastern European crime lords who were taking advantage of the fact that the Balkans and the Eastern Bloc countries as such were in almost complete turmoil. They looked dangerous and as hard as nails – slit your throat as good as look at you types. That was not to say the uniformed boys didn't look equally capable; but it was more like domesticated wolves that were trained to kill, living and fighting alongside wild wolves that killed instinctively, indiscriminately and with brutal necessity. You wouldn't want either coming after you.

Except Collins. Now there was an enigma. The way he huffed and puffed his way across the open ground towards them, he was more like a spaniel amongst those wolves, and one that needed to miss a meal or two, it seemed. Tomas watched the man until he juddered to a halt in front of the trio and managed a half-respectable salute, standing as straight as his heaving chest would allow as he drew in deep, oxygen replenishing breaths.

'Take a minute, Collins; you look like you need it.'

Collins looked appreciative even as Tomas studied the breathless man, looking him up and down with brutal assessment. 'Do we need to do anything about your basic fitness capability? You don't look like any sort of extended forced march would do you much good.'

Collins shook his head as he composed himself, reoxygenated finally. 'It's not that, sir, though right now, you're probably right, but it's the constantly running up the colonel's tower to take him news and receive the day's orders. Trouble is, those orders change almost by the hour and most of them are insignificant things that are already being taken care of. I don't mean to complain, sir, but it is getting a bit tedious and I'm not sure how much longer I can keep this up. It's making me forget things. Things that I wouldn't dream of normally and things that just get me shouted at by the colonel, forgetting his untouched food tray, for example.'

Tomas remembered the rotting food and thought it unlike the fastidious little man.

'I'm a quartermaster, sir. I'm very good at organizing stuff. Clothing, food, ordnance and the like, but I usually have junior staff to do all this running around shit. I'm more of a vehicular sort of chap.'

Collins looked up at Tomas, then a little ashamed of his outburst, but continued his justification nonetheless. 'The colonel knew I had taken...' Collins paused as though seeking the right words, '...early retirement, and that was why he sought me out. He needed the best and I was well... available.'

Tomas listened attentively to the adjutant's complaints, which matched Tomas's low opinion of the colonel, and guessed there was more to Collins's story than he was letting on. But he didn't pursue it; now wasn't the time.

'Understandable. However, you didn't jog your socks off out here to tell me that, insightful as it was. What was it that is so important to have you running, again?'

'Just for a change...' Tomas smiled at the sarcasm, '...the colonel summoned me the moment you left and instructed me to have rooms prepared for you and your...erm, well, your...companions.' Collins still looked nervous around the two Valkyries. He looked at them as though he were a shrew and they were hawks, eyeing him up as a snack in between meals. 'The colonel has expressed strict orders that he is not to be disturbed at all this evening and that he has, on further consideration, taken what you had to say a little more seriously than he apparently implied to yourself and, that said, he asks you to make yourself at home, at least for this evening, and I have taken the liberty of preparing rooms for you at the colonel's request, in the west tower.' Collins's eyes drifted briefly in the tower's direction and Tomas turned his own gaze to follow. It was the massive structure that Collins had emerged from earlier when he was nearly skewered by the archers. It was one of the two main towers that strung the curtain wall between them and fronted the killing ground they had crossed earlier.

'I assumed they were guest rooms for the servants of visiting dignitaries,' Collins continued. 'They are not as grand as the rooms within the keep but the colonel has forbidden any but himself to go near those.'

Tomas desperately wanted to know why that was, but held the question back for now. Answers would present themselves in due course. For now, he took this turnaround by the colonel as confirmation of his suspicions. There was something afoot and he didn't want Tomas to find out what, hence putting him in the tower the furthest from where he was and acting as placatingly as possible. And with an entire army likely to be between him and Carmichael, it was assumed that Tomas would either remain where he was put, or be spotted long before he could get too close to Carmichael again until the colonel wanted him to. Instantly Tomas's strategic mind was running through options for his planned and inevitable nocturnal recon.

'I'm sure those will do very nicely, Collins.' Tomas smiled ingratiatingly and drew surprised glances from all concerned, especially the Valkyries. They hadn't seen much of the charismatic and charming side of Tomas since their unconventional meeting. Not the leader of men and gracious officer he was required to be when the mission parameters required it. Tomas had been known to move in lofty circles himself from time to time. Embassy functions and even royal banquets had necessitated his attendance and with it, his fitting in as though he belonged there.

Treya was again watching this other side to the man before her. So far he seemed multifaceted and as random as the weather. He fought like a berserker, exhibited terrifying rages and killed with the indiscriminate capability of one who knew how to in more ways than was really necessary. Yet on the flip side of his martial prowess and somewhat unstable temper, he displayed a gentle and considerate side – a side that men related to and responded to with little to no question. Tomas issued an order and men jumped to carry it out before they realized it wasn't even him they answered to. Now, seeing him talking to Collins, she saw another facet, and it was one that caused her some distress. Tomas smiled, and her stomach knotted with an unfamiliar sensation. Gone was the grim warrior suddenly, and he was instantly replaced by a man who, had she not known better, could have had royal blood within him, so beneficent did he appear. He reminded her that he was frighteningly like her father, and the combined effect of Tomas's allure and the empty void of missing her father caused surging emotions to course through her, and it was all she could do to hold a calm external façade. But Ingrid was Treya's lifelong friend and she knew the doughty Valkyrie better than she knew herself. She saw the signs of her friend's consternation in the tightening of her jaw, the confusion and pain evident behind her eyes, and the subtle way her cheeks colored. Looking down, Ingrid saw Treya's fist clench and unclench unconsciously. The last time she had seen her this way was when they were exiled. Blood had flowed from her hands that day as she fought against the turmoil of betrayal and fury warring within her, against the fear and loss of leaving her father and family.

Ingrid too saw what Treya saw in Tomas, though she would never admit such to the arrogant little mortal who had brought them to this predicament, and knowing too that Thor himself would approve of this union. Tomas was very much like the son he should have had, not that he loved his daughter any less; and should they survive this cataclysm, and such a meeting of the two ever came about, it would be an interesting day in Valhalla, to say the least. But for now, Ingrid was simply worried what adverse effect Tomas would have on her friend's, her commander's, and her sister's judgment. Again Treya had deferred to Tomas rather than take the lead and order them accordingly, and Ingrid railed at how easily she did it. After all, they were Valkyries; these men should be cowering in fear at what portended for them. They were the daughters of gods, and primal powers in themselves. Why should they defer to anyone? But Ingrid kept her feelings to herself this one time: her opinion would not be welcome at this moment and would only distance her friend from her all the more, driving her closer to Tomas, who needed little cause to inflate his ego. He seemed to be doing that well enough himself, the way these human soldiers fawned around him.

'I've laid fires in the hearths but not lit them yet, though it doesn't really get too cold here, I've noticed, not even at night. I hadn't been to Canada before but I had this idea that it was much chillier up here than it

seems to be. Still, I take it you've the ability to light it, should you require?'
Tomas just tilted his head indicatively. 'Of course you do,' Collins continued
smoothly. 'Food will be served in the hall very shortly and you and the ...
ladies are very welcome to join the men.'

Tomas nodded his thanks but looked sideways at the two Valkyries and
thought better about that just yet, as matters were still a bit volatile.

'Thanks all the same, Collins, but we must decline. If, however, you
could arrange for some food to be sent up to our rooms, that will suffice.
Maybe tomorrow.' A sudden thought popped unbidden into Tomas's mind
and it made him smile warmly. 'Oh by the way, I don't suppose you have any
raw meat available, do you? Rabbit or somesuch?'

Collins looked momentarily confused by the request until Tomas held
out his arm suddenly and a white blur of talons and razor beak swooped
down to alight on his outstretched and thankfully armored arm.

Bran cawed loudly three times, ruffled his feathers as he shook himself,
and then settled them down smoothly as he regarded the man before him
with eyes that glistened with an intelligence that made Collins back up a
step.

'I say! Well, I never did. That was most impressive, sir. I can't say
I've ever seen...what is it, sir – a crow? – quite that big, nor that color.
Presumably that's what you want the meat for?'

Tomas laughed casually as he regarded the battle raven and thought to
it: *Show-off*, but he answered Collins as he ran a hand over the raven's head
affectionately. The raven closed its eyes then and enjoyed the attention.

'It's a raven, Collins, and yes, that is who the meat is for, so nothing you
wouldn't serve anyone else, if you don't mind.'

Collins shook his head vigorously. 'No, sir, of course not. Though on
the subject of food, I must be about my duties, if you don't mind. I need
to supervise the night's rations and see that the colonel's are prepared.'
Something seemed to leave the little man at the colonel's mention, draining
the vitality from him as though he had gotten something of himself back in

Tomas's presence, only to lose it again to the colonel's.

'Of course, Collins. We'll take it ourselves from here. Dismissed.'

Collins saluted and turned smartly, striding off this time instead of running as though reluctant to return.

'Well, I guess it answers that question, Trey. We go and see what our new accommodation looks like and try to keep out of trouble for a few hours, at least until it gets dark.' Tomas looked up and guessed it was not long before sunset, an hour or two at the most. 'Let the men get themselves settled, fed and retired. I want as few out and about as possible for what I've got in mind. Let's go find Dutch and Toby as we go, making it look as casual as possible. I'll fill you in as we walk, but basically it would be handy if the guards out tonight were ones that either Toby or Dutch chose, for reasons that will become apparent.'

Ingrid scowled on cue and Treya nodded that she understood where Tomas was going with his plan.

'You've been very quiet, Ingrid, not that I'm complaining. It's nice not having my ears roasted occasionally, but what do you think of Dutch?'

She stopped so suddenly that both Treya and Tomas took two more steps before noticing. Her rising voice gave away her sudden discomfiture at the question. 'What do you mean? What am I supposed to think of him? He is a man. What else are you implying?'

Color suffused her cheeks in a way that made Tomas laugh, or want to. He suppressed it – badly – but tried to explain without chuckling. 'I don't mean anything, Ingrid,' Tomas started smoothly, trying to diffuse her look of pending violence. 'I'm not matchmaking, if that's what you're worried about.'

She turned several shades of crimson, implying that was *exactly* what she was worried about and Tomas was afraid she was going to explode. 'But as a soldier, do you think he is trustworthy and capable? What is your military assessment of him and his men?'

She still didn't look entirely convinced as she sought an appropriate answer – one that would provide Tomas with what he wanted without betraying anything of what she personally thought. *Not that I'm thinking anything personally about the human – nothing. He means nothing to me and I've paid him no more attention than I have any other man here.* Ingrid furiously tried to convince herself of the truth of her thoughts, but images of the heavily muscled Scandinavian kept materializing, and even as she pushed each one away, another duly appeared. Ingrid snarled and shook her head, letting several oaths slip that would have made a navvy blush.

'He seems quite capable, militarily speaking. His men pay attention when he speaks, and act without hesitation. That is a good sign. They do not fear him as much as they respect him. That too, is a good prerequisite for a leader. A man that beats his dogs into submission does not benefit from the loyalty of the dog that does because it wants to.'

Tomas was still smiling as he listened to Ingrid's somewhat cryptic assessment. 'So if he was under you, militarily speaking…' Tomas exerted as much willpower as he could muster to not break into the giggles at Ingrid's chameleon impression born of the innuendo, '…you'd be more than happy with him as someone to carry out your orders?' Through this seemingly harmless question, Treya saw her friend's sudden anxiety and frowned, mainly because Tomas had found a nerve to exploit and obviously reveled in baiting her about such a tender subject. It had been far too long since Ingrid had met her match in a male, and Dutch certainly fitted the bill and type of those Ingrid used to favor. It wasn't about looks with her, but prowess; which was just as well, as Dutch didn't have a lot going for him on the looks front, having taken one too many beatings with the ugly club. But, much stock was put in the scars of battle amongst the Valkyrie, and her personal thoughts were that arrogant and self-conscious leaders rarely did what was needed to win, for fear of injury or maiming. They ignored chances and sought reasons to not, rather than to do, and both Treya and Ingrid despised that sort.

'Good!' Tomas said no more, just took one last lingering look at Ingrid and turned away chuckling before he got either a punch in the head from the blushing Valkyrie or he said something else and tipped her over the edge, where she spent much of her time anyway, and he suffered considerably more. That really wouldn't be prudent, *nor particularly nice*, thought Tomas, and he wanted her on his side rather than on his back. So he kept his harmless baiting light and friendly, though he did mentally file away the nerve that Ingrid now had exposed, just in case.

Tomas, Treya and Ingrid circulated for a while; watching the archery for a short time and even offering several tips to the men. The Valkyries demonstrated their uncanny ability with breathtaking precision and drew many looks and comments of admiration from the men. Dutch and Tomas watched passively from one side as the women drew the men to them like moths to a flame for the chance of some one-to-one tuition. After an hour of rapped knuckles, thick ears and more bruises than they could count for not performing up to the Valkyries' standards when instructed to do so, the men would have sold their grannies to have Dutch back instructing them. But for all that, one hour of instruction by Treya and Ingrid upped the soldier's game from amateur to semi-pro status. Given a few more sessions with them and the men would be shooting to Olympic standard before they knew it. Tomas watched Dutch watch Ingrid, eyeing her up and down lasciviously and Ingrid, in turn, who completely avoided watching Dutch, looked at everything but. Tomas smiled benignly as though he were watching two kids in a playground, and thought it would actually be nice for the Valkyrie to find a little bit of happiness in all this, for no matter how short a time, as he recalled her tragic past and the pain it contained.

Before leaving Dutch to wrap up for the day with some quarterstaff and mock swordwork, Tomas hinted at the fact that it would be *handy* if the night's stag duty was carried out by men loyal to Dutch, if at all possible that is, leaving the intelligent Dutchman to figure out what Tomas had in mind. He also mentioned that he would be asking the same *suggestion* of Toby. Dutch said he would see what he could do and winked understanding.

Tomas and co did a brief recce of the three baileys and the position of the gates, sentries and any other potential hindrances or hazards; navigating stables and animal pens, derelict stalls where vendors would have hawked their wares, such as vegetables, fruits, sweetmeats and, if they were lucky, cloth and utensils. They passed an abandoned smithy, coopers and several massive stone cylinders which Tomas took for silos designed for storing grain and keeping it dry as well as comparatively rat free. They also passed several two storey but equally empty barrack blocks – the soldiers were apparently quartering in two other barrack blocks in the second bailey, which were more lavishly appointed than the others. He assumed these were for the household guard, where the more scant ones were for visitors. It was over an hour later before Tomas finally found Toby as they were coming back past the keep and the massive doorway into the great hall. Toby was just coming out and Tomas thought he looked troubled. But whatever was on his mind or had been bothering him vanished like morning mist when he all but walked into the trio, his preoccupation forgotten as he smiled at the Valkyries and greeted them courteously before speaking with Tomas. The two Valkyries regarded him coolly, as though they expected such deference. Toby began asking Tomas about trivial matters as they walked away from the doorway. How was he finding the fortress? What did he think about its size? The fact it differed from out front, and was he staying with them for long? Apparently chef had something of a surprise for them that night. The colonel was known to have considered it a celebration of sorts; at least that was what Collins said, him being the only one other than Tomas to see the colonel of late, of course. But it was as though Toby didn't want to discuss anything important anywhere near where ears that shouldn't be listening might hear.

After the initial disappointment of discovering that they would not be seeing the two women that evening for dinner, Toby agreed, much like Dutch, to do what he could about putting some of his boys on duty. There was usually a rotation to keep things fair and many of the men didn't like their roster being tampered with and got crabby about it when it was, spitting their dummies out like kids But with no promises from Toby, it was the best

Tomas could hope for. All he had to do now was wait for darkness.

From the tower, with sunken eyes burning bright within their sockets, the face of Carmichael stared down into the ward beneath his window. He saw the little humans going about their routines, blissfully unaware of the fate that waited them. Hate seeped from every pore of Gaunub as he saw his nemesis moving from group to group, attempting to poison the minds of the men that he too was unaware had been recruited initially to find and eliminate *him*. Gaunub laughed a horrendous sound like gravel in a cement mixer. It was a sound no human throat should have been able to make and as such, the thing that was once Carmichael was forced to spit blood from the ruined oesophagus. The body was failing much faster now and Gaunub would, before too long, need to find a new host, though hopefully this ravaged shell would last long enough for his nefarious purpose – a purpose that, if all went well, in just a few hours would become painfully apparent to all within the fortress walls. By fulfilling his master's wishes he would be elevated in status, and power unimaginable was promised him upon his success. Of course, even the Adversary had little conception of just how much power Gaunub could imagine. It was as vast as the abyss itself and just as cold, though no more so than his revenge. That would chill blazing suns, solidifying them into lumps of frozen gas.

When the twin moons rose this night, in answer to his summons, the Adversary's messenger would come to him and grant him the power and the means to fulfill his goals.

Breath your last, Walker, for tonight, in just a few hours, your still bleeding heart shall fill my belly and your flesh will feed my minions while your skull, spine and bones will be presented as a trophy to my lord Adversary. Feast well and savor your last meal before you become one yourself. More laughter and blood followed as Gaunub relished the prospect of the forthcoming night's entertainment.

Chapter Nineteen

Eschec Mat

To Tomas's increasingly impatient mind, darkness was way too slow coming. Back when he was on the job, he would spend much of his time before any *appointment*, meticulously going over his plan; the various routines of his target; checking and double checking his escape routes, ensuring nothing had occurred since he set them up to hinder or jeopardize his various exit options; committing to memory all he could during daylight in anticipation of limited visibility and probably the need to be moving at speed in the dark. Patience was the watchword of any successful operation as far as he was concerned. Hasty actions led to fuck ups and probably got the wrong people killed, most likely himself, which wasn't something high on his priority list. But lately he found his temper bubbling just beyond exploding, and patience seemed elusive – situations which caused Tomas some internal anxiety. It bothered him but he wasn't yet ready to talk about it to anyone; not that there were many understanding individuals handy that he actually *could* talk to. *Famine would have been bloody handy about now.* Tomas recalled the odd Horseman fondly. He seemed so incongruous as one of the fabled riders of the Apocalypse – affable, helpful and friendly; though Tomas had seen the other side of the Horseman: the one that fought like he was a one-man army, and emanated power like one of the gods of old, awesome to behold in his full glory. Yet for all that, Tomas missed his company and light conversation. *No doubt he would have had something to say about me losing my marbles.* Tomas smiled at the memory. Some insight into Tomas's fluctuating and seemingly volatile mental state might be useful, but Tomas then realized the flip side to that and his thoughts turned sour again; he realized that it might just highlight something he didn't want to know about, and he had had enough of those kind of revelations of late.

Along with the fundamentals, patience and careful planning, Tomas would spend an equal amount of time with his weapons. A misfire or breakage at any crucial moment could be fatal and Tomas had, back then at least, treated his life much the same as his weapons, for all it was worth. He considered it much like any other tool of the trade. He didn't actually care if it broke, but it would be mightily inconvenient if it broke before its time through carelessness on his behalf. Tomas was then, if nothing else, pragmatic and methodical.

Things had changed a bit since then. *Ha! I'll say they've changed,* Tomas barked mentally, containing his exasperation to the confines of his own mind. *'Not that even that has been entirely mine much lately either, has it, Bran?'* Tomas used the question to check in on the battle raven, for he found himself more and more concerned about the mysterious bird when it wasn't either with him or in his sight at least.

'No, Tomas, it hasn't, and nor may it ever be again,' Bran replied.

Tomas sighed, *'Thanks for that'* but the enigmatic bird was still with him and seemingly fine. Tomas's world was undergoing a radical change and he wasn't sure if he could keep up with it, or take any pleasure from some of the imposed side effects. He liked the privacy of his mind and it niggled him to lose it, though he accepted that right now wasn't the time to worry about it. That would come later *if* they survived.

As they wound their way up the tower towards their appointed rooms, Tomas ran his thoughts over the makeshift plan he had settled on. *Though I'll wager no amount of planning could prepare the mind for the type of mission I'm on. Shit, I don't even know why I keep calling it a mission; it isn't like I'm going to be returning from it and it's likely that nobody is going to be thanking me for it, not that I got a lot of that before.* Tomas smiled wryly to himself. *Plausible deniability, my arse. I didn't exist then and I sure as shit don't exist now. I'm not on my own planet and I don't even think I'm entirely fucking human any more.* Tomas recalled the last battle with the Hounds of Fenris and shivered at the thought of his own wounds; wounds that would have – *should have* – he amended, killed anyone. *I'd have thought being human and from Earth were two things that would be right at the top of the prime considerations of what the people of Earth look for in those that save them.* But the more Tomas thought bitterly about that, he realized how wrong that assumption was. For what exactly they *did* put their faith in was information actually from creatures from *another* world. Angels weren't indigenous to Earth – after all, they hailed from another sphere of existence entirely – and they put everything imagin-able behind and absolved by a man who had to have originated *elsewhere. A two thousand-year-old alien conspiracy theory.* Tomas couldn't contain the ironic laughter and drew concerned glances from Treya and Ingrid as they paused and looked back at the chuckling idiot behind them as they ascended the tower. Tomas just waved it off and said it was nothing really, just some random thoughts he found funny and they should pay him no heed. Which, after exchanging curious glances between them, they duly did and turned back to the climb up the gloomy stairwell.

But it was as they started climbing again that Tomas realized why he was occupying his thoughts with plans and random thoughts. It was to take his mind off the vision of Treya's and even Ingrid's long, tanned and lithe legs as they moved ahead of him. For all his *changes*, he was still a man and the sight of their succulent flesh aroused thoughts in him that he usually kept buried, or at least under his control. The way their hips swayed as they climbed, and just how short their battle skirts really were – though he tried not to, he couldn't help himself and he tilted his head slightly to just catch sight of the ripe flesh of their buttocks as their legs rose to meet them.

'*Focus, Tomas!*' The voice of Bran snapped him guiltily back to attention and he did a quick double take to ensure that no one else had caught him peeping. Fortunately too, the gloom hid his blushes. But Tomas still smiled at the rebuke and savored the memory.

'*I was focusing, Bran, or trying to at least.*'

'*Yes, I could see that,*' the reply came back, dryly and slightly amused.

They found the rooms Collins had prepared for all of them. *All* of the rooms. Collins had been busy and opened up a whole floor for them, apparently, giving them the choice of several suites. For they were more than just rooms. By hotel standards back home, they were presidential suites. His mind boggled at what the more richly appointed rooms Collins hinted at that were situated over in the keep were like if these were for the visiting dignitary's servants and entourage. Each room sported intricately carved and opulently draped four-poster beds. So massive were they, it appeared the four posts were carved from whole tree trunks and they rose above the bed itself easily ten feet or more, and were draped more luxuriously than a sultan's pavilion. Furs, richly embroidered throws, and more scatter cushions than the proverbial stick could be waved at softened every other hard surface. Rugs and tapestries decorated the floors and walls, and each wall hanging depicted images of what Tomas considered and took to be different areas of the Domain: vistas of misty mountains, enchanting forests, and stark uninviting deserts, though each had a common factor: a man – at least Tomas assumed it was a man, it was at any count roughly man shaped. He appeared in all of them, engaged in various activities. Alone upon a horse in one, leading an army in another, and fighting mythical beasts in yet another. Tomas was put in mind of the window in Carmichael's room. There was a lone man, like these depicted here, too. Who was this person? And why was he in so many of the artists' works? Tomas filed that question away for another time. Maybe if he ever found anyone who knew anything about this fortress, he would ask them, though he doubted he would live long enough to concern himself over such mundane matters.

There was even a garderobe in every room and Tomas pulled a face as he peeked down the hole in the stone that led to a chute which exited on the outside of the curtain wall. Tomas pitied the poor sods who, when these places were laid to siege, were ordered to try climbing up these shit chutes in order to infiltrate the castle. Even if they succeeded it was a shit job, literally. But many died, he imagined, wedged stuck, unable to move forward or back. Tomas shuddered. That was no kind of death for anyone. They probably wouldn't even be found until it was noticed that the chute had backed up or smelt so bad that something had to be done about it. Clearing it couldn't be much fun either, certainly not if you were the one at the base of the chute as it all came flooding out. *Nice!*

Tomas took a little time and investigated all the rooms, leaving no stone metaphorically unturned. He wanted to ensure that they were in fact the only occupants of the floor and that there weren't any hidden nasty surprises that were likely to emerge later as darkness fell. Treya and Ingrid joined him on his search when he explained to their bewildered stares what he was doing looking under beds and behind tapestries, and knocking on random sections of wall for hidden doors, not that they stood a great chance of finding any, certainly not if the rooms matched the caliber of stonework they had witnessed everywhere else. An interesting hour later, and after lighting all the sconces and fireplaces, they still found themselves alone and only the stairwell that led both up to the higher floors and back down remained in darkness. There was only one more floor above them and that led to the tower roof. Tomas checked and double checked it and finally, when he was satisfied that it was secure and bolted, he devised a contraption from the numerous fire pokers and utensils to both further secure the door, making it nigh on impossible to gain entry from the outside; and at the worst, assuming they did, it would give warning to Tomas. Judging by the thickness of the doors in the fortress, he figured he was being overcautious but he didn't care: it made him feel better all the same.

Collins had told Tomas that the lower floors were where much of the unit's dry rations and incidental equipment were kept. He wasn't wrong. Tomas had peeked as they climbed the stairs and he saw sleeping bags, Bergens, coils of rope and other miscellaneous items strewn throughout, all of varying sizes, colors and thicknesses. There were bolts of some sort of fabric that stood statuelike and immobile against the far walls, along with what looked like the contents of the rest of the keep. Tomas was sure that the soldiers hadn't brought all that with them and so he assumed that these tower rooms had also contained the random supplies of the former residents of the castle, and Collins, being the pack rat he was, took it as the logical place to stock their own provisions, invariably acquiring anything useful that the former residents may have left behind; it wasn't like they had any use for them any more. There had to be enough furniture there and ornamentation, at least judging by Tomas's cursory glance, to outfit another entire country house. *It's no wonder we got the top floor; it's probably the only free space left.*

After their search for trap doors and spy holes bore no fruit, Tomas wandered the floor like a man under house arrest, which was unofficially what this was. He knew it, Carmichael knew it and he even suspected the Valkyries knew it, though they didn't act as if their liberty was under threat; they just reclined in one of the slightly more opulent suites and took advantage of the chilled wine and fruit that had been thoughtfully left, no doubt by Collins. Tomas idly wondered what it would be that did Collins in finally. He doubted it would be combat or even any of the numerous hazards the Domain had to offer. No, he reckoned it would be running around after Carmichael. The little adjutant was too conscientious for his own good. And though he was an oily little obsequious fellow, his failings on a personal front could be overlooked on the fact he was bloody good at what he did. Tomas respected that more than his social graces and was forming in his own mind several tasks that he could put him to good use for.

Tomas took a half-glass of wine distractedly and went to stand at one of the balcony windows as he criss-crossed in his mind what he would do next, and more importantly, when. Should he wait and react to Carmichael's decision, or pre-empt whatever he came up with, fully expecting it to be something decidedly unsavory, and call his bluff? But what if Carmichael did the unexpected and conceded to Tomas's request? He would have alienated the man even more and definitely ruined any chance of an alliance, however strained and tenuous. He needed more information: that much was certain. It was just how to go about getting it that was left needing an answer.

Collins came and went once more, just to say that dinner would be delayed as Carmichael wanted to arrange something *special* for his guests. In the meantime they were to relax and take their ease. Collins brought some more of the chilled wine and some fruit, fresh and warm bread, along with a variety of cheeses for them to stave off their hunger. *Hmmm! Special, my arse*, thought Tomas as Collins vanished down the now dark stairwell as though he was vanishing down the throat of some stony creature. *Still, the delay does buy me a bit of time and provides an answer to one of my many questions, namely: Go now and sod his feelings.* Tomas wouldn't lose any sleep over what Carmichael might think of him if he was caught skulking around the fortress; he was sure he could bluff out some old excuse. Trouble was, how to leave the Valkyries here without hurting their feelings? He wanted to go it alone mainly because he was sure the Valkyries' idea of a stealthy reconnoiter was nothing like his, plus, they would be able to cover for him should anyone come a knocking unexpectedly. Tomas took a deep breath and went in search of Treya to share his rough plan, anticipating the argument he might face, especially from Ingrid, who was argumentation personified.

Tomas needn't have worried at all, for they were more than happy for him to amuse himself for an hour or two, possibly three. They had found the massive baths and, to their minds, the fantastic and magical faucet that when turned, provided a never ending supply of hot water. It was in fact, part of a complex series of internal pipes stemming from the naturally heated underground spring, which had they known about it, would have explained the odd location of the fortress in the first place. It bore a close resemblance to the plumbing employed by the Romans to heat their bath houses and provide basic underfloor heating. But Tomas was unaware of the mechanics or origins of the hot water. In fact because he so took it for granted, he momentarily forgot where he was and how impossible it should be here. He was simply pleased he had dodged a bullet with the Valkyries. 'I'll be back as soon as I can; wouldn't want to miss dinner now, would I?'

But Treya and Ingrid just agreed and began pouring salts and anything else they could find in the massive wet room into the steaming bath. Tomas knew it was his cue to go when Treya suddenly began stripping off heedless of his presence. Tomas spun away so fast he nearly slammed into the door frame. *Shit! That's all I need,* Tomas muttered as he turned his back and closed the door behind him, muting the sounds of the pair of giggling shield maidens. *How the hell am I going to concentrate now with that image in my head and bloody wood in my pants?* Tomas found the bowl and jug of cold water on a dresser and stuck his head over the bowl and poured the water over his head. *Urrgh,* as he stood and shook his tangled mane like some wet dog. *Women.* But try as he might, the sight of Treya's back, naked to the waist, and devoid of her normally calf-encasing steel boots, wouldn't leave him.

He tried to pull the face of his dead fiancée to his mind, to replace the image of Treya with one who should be beside him, who shouldn't be dead and who had rescued him from his life of authorized murder. But she wouldn't appear. Tomas was startled and closed his eyes tight, concentrating on her features; but all he saw was Treya, in various poses since their meeting back at the clearing when he had abruptly arrived in the Domain. *Dammit.* Tomas lashed out and struck one of the bedposts in frustration. *Argh! Damn!* It absorbed the impact as though a fly had struck it. *What the fuck is happening to me?*

'Why can't I remember you?' Tomas spoke his frustration aloud as though it could provide him with an answer, but nothing came back to him. Nothing reassuring, anyway. The one nagging thought that did take seed in response to his question, Tomas didn't want to consider, and shrugged at the thought of her being merely an excuse to get out of the game, and that she was a manifestation of his guilt at not only killing so many before, but him being the one responsible for taking her husband from her in the first place was unthinkable. Only it wasn't. As Tomas willed his black lightweight Kevlar armor, soft boots and gloves into existence, he considered his sudden revelation. The fact it *was* true didn't make it hurt any less. He had used her as an excuse and she had died because of him. Another notch to his headstone. It hadn't been love that guided him, but desperation, need and even, if he was truthful, loneliness. She seemed so vulnerable and delicate at the time. Broken and bereft, and it had all been his fault. Was this the reason he could no longer recall her face clearly? After all was said and done, was she just another means to an end, much like he had used many women before her? They had been used to get him in; his fiancée had been used to get him out. This explained why he only saw Treya now, but did he view her in a similar way? Was she a means to an end, or was there some false desire there? She was a woman and he was a man, the usual chemistry was there, and she did make him uncomfortable in the way good looking women did, especially ones who wore as little as she did. But now wasn't the time for those sorts of thoughts; they'd have to wait. But Tomas doubted there would ever be a *good* time to scrutinize his confliction.

Pulling on his balaclava and willing his tactical helmet into place, Tomas finished his ensemble with a set of state-of-the-art night sight goggles. *Good to go!* Tomas knew he had no need to do his regular weapons check as the Sword of War would provide anything he needed when he needed it. *That is one damn handy bit of kit. Thanks, War. But where were you when I really needed this.* Visions of his many past missions where the sword could have made his life much easier flashed by at quantum speed. *Too late for regrets and 'what ifs' now, old son. Get a grip and get on with it.* After his mental rebuke, Tomas took a deep breath, rolled his shoulders and neck, and slipped from the apartment to the sounds of more giggling and splashing. He shook his head resignedly and stepped into the corridor, putting all images of naked women from his mind and trying to focus on his task at hand.

Firstly, Tomas knew, he had to get out of the tower unseen and across the bailey before he even thought about how he was going to get into the keep unnoticed. Adding a shape-blurring cloak to his outfit, Tomas pulled the cowl up and activated his goggles. They gave a slight hum as they powered up and

Tomas was inwardly impressed at the attention to detail the sword provided, for surely there was no power supply actually running it. Still, a minor matter. The world took on a vibrant orange glow as the goggles did their work. Tomas snuffed the sconces as he moved past each one, until he reached the top step of the staircase. He hunkered down by one wall and listened. The stone dulled the sound of the Valkyries, and in the hallway, they became nothing but a memory. Other than a low whistle from an errant breeze as it slipped through one of the arrow slots placed in the stairwell, all was silent. *Good, that's just the way I like it.* Keeping low and to the left-hand side, purposely placing himself on the side of the generally accepted off hand, as the majority of the world were right-handed, it gave him a slight edge when it came to avoiding that initial reaction. Chances were, any first shot would go wide, though he was hoping it didn't come to that. Tomas wanted this to be a bloodless excursion. It was why he hoped Dutch and Toby had placed *friendly* guards on duty, ones that should he be so careless as to attract their attention, he wouldn't have to kill them. It didn't do anything for morale if you wound up killing the men you hoped to fight alongside.

Ten minutes later and Tomas found himself at the bottom of the staircase and in the huge and echoey hallway that dominated the base of the tower. There were only two rooms off the hallway. Both would be communal reception rooms where the visitors in residence at the tower would meet and take their ease before being summoned to their masters' or mistresses' pleasure. Tomas slowly investigated each one carefully, but they were empty. *Looks like we're the only guests tonight. Well, that sure works for me.* Moving to the great oaken door – the one that outside poor old Collins had nearly been skewered on as he walked through it in what seemed ages ago now – Tomas grew cautious once more, listening for telltale signs of guards posted outside; hushed conversation; the movement of weapons being settled and readjusted to make carrying them for hours on end more endurable if not comfortable; the squeak of boots or careless jingle of webbing. Anything. But there was nothing. Either Carmichael didn't care about guarding him or he considered him beneath his attention. *Probably both, the bastard. Either way, that's good for me. Who knows, perhaps it's Dutch and Toby's doing that there are no guards there. Be grateful for small mercies, Tomas.* Just as he was about to push the door open, a voice piped up in his head that made him start.

'*You are making something of a meal out of this, you know. Why didn't you just ask me? I could have told you where every single guard is who is out here.*'

Tomas mentally slapped himself. Of course! Bran. '*Don't do that, will you? You nearly gave me a heart attack. Cough or something first, will you?*' Tomas got puzzled images back of what a raven coughing might look like. That made him smile beneath his concealment. '*Never mind. Where are you, exactly?*'

Bran provided a less humorous image of one of the embrasures along the dividing wall between the main bailey and the second. He moved his corvid's head from side to side and furnished Tomas with a view of the nearest guards and the bailey below; from the door that Tomas currently stood behind and out across the yard to the keep itself. '*Good. That's gonna make life much easier.*'

Bran agreed with a huff. Tomas smiled and tried to reassure the battle raven that it wasn't intentional that he hadn't asked, but that it was all new to him to have such a valuable and useful companion attached to him, that was all. Bran seemed to be mollified by this and settled down to keep a beady eye out.

Tomas slipped out of the tower and, keeping to the shadows, he crept around the bailey wall and finally wound up at the massive Keep door, where he and Collins had entered when he took him to meet Carmichael. He cast an inquisitive eye upwards, trying to spot Bran, but the raven remained elusive. '*All clear?*' Tomas asked silently.

'*Nobody has shown that they are aware of your presence, Tomas, so I would say yes, you are all clear.*' But just as Tomas was about to crack the door open Bran added a few disturbing words to his report. '*Of course, that may be a ruse to allow you to feel a security that doesn't exist and you are in fact heading for a trap.'*

Tomas stopped short and winced. *'Thanks for that. You're such a comfort sometimes, you know.'*

'Just being practical. We are a suspicious race and trust few. We haven't survived as long as we have without being overly cautious, and being correct more often than not.'

What Bran had said was true enough, for although Tomas had hinted to Dutch and Toby what he was planning, and to try to stand guards that would likely turn a blind eye to him, he didn't know them that well and wondered at the element of trust he was allowing them. He would give them the benefit of the doubt, he decided. However, he would take their possible defection into account and look out for the double-cross all the same. *'You're right: it's still early days as yet and it's better to be safe than sorry. Good call.'* With no further hesitation, Tomas cracked the door a few millimeters. He scrutinized the frame and lock area, running his gaze down the seam, looking for any sort of internal trap or early warning arrangement. Just one hair-thin wire was all it took to rig an IED (improvised explosive device) to the door and that would be a nasty surprise for any uninvited guests, but he found nothing. He had set enough of his own improvised explosive devices to know just how canny they could be, and he liked his limbs all where they were. Eventually, confident there was nothing about to go bang, Tomas cracked open the door some more, just sufficient for him to slip in, and he quietly pulled it closed behind him.

The entrance way was silent and free of guards, and if Tomas thought it odd, he remembered who it was exactly, squatting upstairs like some foul spider in its lair. Odds were, nobody volunteered for guard duty here and the matter wasn't pressed. No doubt Carmichael cared little one way or the other. Not any more. Tomas recalled his meeting with the colonel. He wasn't the same man he remembered. Something indefinable had happened to him, changed him somehow, and not just Abigail's death, but something much more profound, darker and, though Tomas loathed to use the word for what it implied, he had to say it anyway, for nothing else really nailed it: evil. Carmichael had turned into an evil thing and that didn't bode well for anyone: him, the Valkyries and the soldiers under his command. Tomas moved across the great hallway and sidled up to the corridors he had seen Collins use earlier. *Time for a more detailed investigation, I think. I'm curious as to this special dinner, for a start.* Remembering where he saw the kitchen area, Tomas slipped unobtrusively into the corridor and began making his way towards the dim light emanating from the end of the passage.

Tomas wasn't entirely sure what to expect when he got his first view of the cooks and the activity in the kitchen area, but a part of it was sure to have been men: cooks going about their business of feeding sixty-odd men. That had to be almost a full time job with that many mouths to feed. He would have thought it would be a hive of activity in there. Not so. There were four men and they moved slowly, almost ungainly, as they walked into work surfaces and bounced off them, correcting their course, and continuing. Tomas thought they were like sleepwalkers and that set alarm bells off in his head. Not for the first time, he sensed that something was wrong here. It was confirmed when one of them turned his way. Tomas fought the urge to gasp and kept perfectly still, feeling more than knowing that any movement would give him away, for the thing that used to be a man wasn't looking at him directly but something just off to his left. The man that used to be the cook looked as though something had sucked much of the moisture from him. He looked dried out, dessicated. His eyes resembled shriveled raisins, much like a grape when the juice is sucked out; his skin resembled dried parchment that had been left out in the baking sun far too long; and his mouth hung open, slack and devoid of will. They were like the zombies he had heard so many tales of. These shells were no longer occupied by the souls of the men; they were just animated corpses, hollow and abandoned, driven by a will greater than their own. Carmichael. That name leapt unbidden to Tomas as though it was the answer to all the wrongs here. *And it probably is*, Tomas thought sourly.

That man is corruption personified. And, not for the first time, Tomas regretted not killing him long ago when he had the chance. *Still, let's see if I can't rectify my mistake.* The thing that had been the cook trudged across the kitchen, oblivious to Tomas hunkered down by the entranceway, and fetched something from just out of Tomas's view. But he wished it had stayed that way when it came back into his field of vision. The cook thing was carrying the corpse of one of the soldiers across its shoulders. And judging by the decay he could see upon the dangling hands and the overwhelming stench that almost had him gagging, it had been dead and left to rot for some time. Tomas had a flash then of the graves outside the fortress and with a wave of horror, realized they were empty and the bodies were here. *In the kitchen.* The implication of just what that meant hit him so hard he nearly retched where he sat and the urge to retreat swept over him like a tidal wave. Too many questions assailed him then for coherent thought. How long? How many? Have they actually been feeding these corpses to the men? Why? And many more that Tomas just couldn't get his head around. He did a quick recall of all he had eaten since arriving at the fortress and was relieved to think that he had only partaken of fruit and bread so far. The gift from Famine had taken away his need for sustenance; it was just habit that had him nibbling occasionally, even so.

So that was what he meant by special plans. He watched as one of the cooks vanished into what he took for a cellar and returned moments later with yet another body, which he immediately started to butcher, slamming it down onto the work surface and hacking at it with a vicious looking cleaver while another was slicing muscle and sinew from a leg with a visibly sharp filleting knife. *What or who else is in that cellar?* Tomas knew he didn't really want to know, but he also accepted the fact he had to discover what was taking place here in order to put a stop to it. He knew then he would have to go down to that cellar and it wasn't a thought that filled him with any kind of enthusiasm at all.

'*This isn't wise, Tomas!*' the voice in his head told him, and Tomas's own voice echoed the sentiment.

'*You're telling me, Bran, but I have to know what happened to these men and how many more there are down there.*' Fortunately the kitchen wasn't brightly lit, and it allowed Tomas to take advantage of the moment and slip into the gloomy chamber and make his way over to a nearby stack of crates conveniently located by the very door he needed to investigate. The creatures that were once human men ignored him totally. They were programmed, it seemed, to do a task and do it they did, thankfully to the exclusion of other distractions, and Tomas took full advantage. The moment they turned their gaze from the cellar, Tomas was off. Like a shadow, he vanished down the dark and damp staircase. It was steeper than many of the others and slick with moisture. Tomas wasn't insensitive to temperature change even though he was somewhat immune now to its effects, and as he descended he felt the temperature drop considerably. A built-in and naturally formed refrigerator. Meat had to be kept fresh somehow and the ice he had noticed earlier that chilled their drinks had to come from somewhere too. Looked like he had found that somewhere.

Sixty-five steps later, Tomas found the bottom and his enhanced vision swept the room for immediate danger. He had willed an SA80 to his hands as he made his way down and it was now braced at shoulder height, with Tomas's finger poised upon the trigger for the slightest movement as he crept in further. It was a vast chamber and he made out several dozen massive barrels and crates of provisions. Tomas edged slowly over to them, alert for danger with every step, until he finally reached his intended destination. The barrels were wine and the crates held the fruits and vegetables he had seen and partaken of earlier. It was remarkable how they remained so fresh, even in the chilly atmosphere of the cellar. Clearly there was more at work here than just simple thermodynamics. He recalled how Death and the others had hinted at enchantments and the reality of magic, although they gave it another name: density manipulation or somesuch. Tomas wasn't too concerned with that or how it worked, only that its effects were evident more so here in the Domain than back on Earth, though that's not to say they weren't being employed. The Horsemen had intimated that there were still powerful entities at large upon the Earth and there was every chance they were using their arcane capabilities to further their gains, whatever they might be. Tomas shivered at the thought of what might be going on under the radar back on Earth and how long they had been allowed to get away with it. Truly it didn't bear thinking about. But he had other fish to fry right now and he couldn't spare the time to speculate on what he couldn't affect. Tomas kept moving, checking all around him and as much of the cellar as he could without becoming too disoriented. Then he rounded a massive column and found what he had hoped he wouldn't. Hanging from several gigantic and wickedly sharp looking hooks were the rest of the dead soldiers. The hooks had punched through their rib cages and they hung there like so much dead meat in any other abattoir. Five of them. Added to the two that were currently being butchered upstairs, it matched the number of graves he had seen. The empty graves. But why? That was the burning question for now. What did Carmichael want with the flesh of these dead men? Though the answer seemed all too obvious and didn't take a huge leap of deduction. The question was, what purpose did he have in feeding the flesh of the dead to those still living. Whatever it was, it didn't bode well. Tomas shook his head sadly. *Still, looks like dinner is a bust.*

Tomas was feet away from the base of the stairwell, having decided there was little more he could do in a cellar, when he heard footsteps coming down. He ducked down beside the banister and with his cloak enveloping him, he became less than a shadow. A spectre with glowing orange eyes and death ready to fire from him. The zombie entered the cellar and shambled over to the hanging bodies. With an ease that disturbed Tomas, it unhooked another and flung it casually over its shoulder as though it weighed nothing. Then it turned to make its way back the way it had come. Tomas held his breath and waited for it to pass. One foot on the step and it stopped. Suddenly. It turned its head left and right and sniffed the air. Three times it inhaled and slowly it rotated its leathery neck almost three hundred degrees as it sought the source of the aroma of whatever had caught its attention. But it was just when Tomas thought it was about to give up its search, hopefully satisfied that it was nothing but a false alarm, that it spun its head and screamed a horrific and ravaged sound. Dead eyes locked unswervingly on the spot where Tomas knelt; it tossed the dead man off its shoulder with a terrifying ease and leapt directly at Tomas, screaming all the time. Tomas fired.

Chaos ensued then. As Tomas let rip with a controlled burst of gunfire, he watched it tear through the cook, shredding his flesh and diverting his leap. He landed on the cold stone a few feet from Tomas and twitched and thrashed as though an electric current was coursing through it. All the time it screamed and it was apparent that it had summoned the others, as Tomas heard more footsteps pounding down the stairs.

Fucking fantastic. That's all I need. The whole fucking bunch of zombie cooks from Hell butting in and blocking the way out. Well, I've got no time for niceties. Tomas jumped up and stood at the bottom of the staircase as the other cooks came screaming down. Tomas let rip into them, and the cellar lit up with the muzzle flash of his weapon as he sent white hot death tearing into their flesh. They crashed to his feet and they too thrashed uncontrollably as their ripped and broken bodies tried to continue what they had been programmed to do. Would they ever stop? Tomas riddled them again with over a hundred rounds, blasting them to mush, but still their limbs struggled, albeit more weakly than before.

'Sod that! *But at least they won't be getting up anytime soon and following, though I've probably made enough noise here to wake the fucking dead anyway. So much for a quiet look around,*' he grumbled to no one in particular, but Tomas needn't have worried, for the dense stone had deadened the sound and by the time he had reached the kitchen once more, things were as quiet and still as they were prior to his misadventure.

Creeping back into the great hall, where he had waited only a few hours ago, though it seemed an eternity had passed since that meeting with the colonel, Tomas made his way back outside, determining that there was nothing more useful to be found inside, not after his last discovery. *Anything else I might find is going to be moot anyway because it's apparent by those mothers down there that the colonel is out of his fucking tree already and needs stopping before he does something else; though I can't imagine what he could bloody well do to top that shit.* Tomas was disturbed beyond belief and he didn't think he could be shocked any more. *Wrong again, Tom old son. Just when you think it's safe to go back in the water, there's another fucking shark. Live and learn though, live and learn.*

'*What are you going to do now?*' Bran asked, concerned by the mental tone Tomas had exhibited.

Tomas looked around from where he stood outside the keep doors. He looked upwards and saw the balcony and flickering window that signified a light was on in the chamber Carmichael occupied. '*I want a closer look and to listen to what is going on in there.*' Tomas gestured upwards. '*He is up to something – that much is apparent by the goon squad in the kitchen – but I'm not going up that stairwell to find out. I can't believe it's as unprotected as it seems, and if he can do that to those men, then who knows what he is capable of. Looks like the outside is the way forwards, or upwards, if you get my drift.*'

Bran did, but he sent back an image of Tomas with wings, then without. Bran had a valid point: he couldn't fly, so it was just how to get up there that eluded him for the moment. He could see the stonework was seamless and he doubted even the best mountaineer would have much success scaling it, certainly not without a shit load of equipment Tomas didn't have. He was good, but not that good. Then it came to him. Bran was right inasmuch as *he* couldn't fly, but he knew someone who could.

Storm! The fantastic mount that Death had bonded to him coalesced in a smoky grey cloud, solidifying beside him with a flick of its ears and a twitch of its tail. It turned to cast an intelligent eye over Tomas, as if to say 'Why have you disturbed me at this hour, and in the dark?' Tomas could see its tail twitch in that slightly irritated way animals have, and he moved up close to the powerful beast and ran his hand reassuringly over its haunches, culminating at its head, and he spoke soothingly to the mystical horse, in a voice that was filled with compassion and warmth.

'Hi, boy, good to see you again. Now look. Sorry to have disturbed you but I need your help. We need to get up there.' Tomas inclined his head in the direction of Carmichael's tower room and Storm raised his equine head to look also, up at a room that was several hundred feet up at the top of a tower that thrust itself skyward, almost in defiance of the gods themselves. Storm whinnied softly and an amused glint sparkled in its liquid brown eyes, again as if to say 'Easy enough. I thought you were going to ask for something difficult'.

Tomas swung himself agilely up into the saddle and no sooner was he settled than Storm reared up and pawed the air with his powerful hooves, but instead of landing back on the soil, his haunches propelled him upwards and he began climbing the night sky as if he was powering up a steep hill. Tomas leant into Storm's mane and hung on, though he needn't have concerned himself about falling off, for once he was with Storm, he could have stood on one leg at tiptoe upon the saddle as Storm galloped, and he would have been just as stable. It was something to do with the bonding. Death had explained it briefly as they flew that first time over the oceans and countries before arriving in Syria. He didn't really understand much of what he was on about back then but he was grateful for the effect.

As Storm powered higher and higher, Tomas mused on the fact of why he explained himself to Storm, discussing his plan with a horse. But the more he thought about it, he realized it was the right thing to do. Storm was a battle companion and had a right to know what he was letting himself in for. And, although he was a horse, he was far more intelligent than many people he knew, and Tomas liked him a lot more than many of the people he knew too. Higher and higher they climbed and Tomas could see several sentries now, situated on the curtain wall and on the internal bailey walls. They paid his silent ascension no heed whatsoever, which was just as well really. It would be hard to explain how and why he was flying around on a gravity-defying horse in the dark, and so close to their colonel's chamber. He hoped he wouldn't have to.

Seconds that felt a lot longer passed, and before Tomas knew it, he was drawing level to the balcony. Storm settled next to it, as stationary in midair as he would have been on solid ground. Tomas dismounted and slid over the rail to land silently on the enormous projecting stones that made up the balcony. Tomas took in the giant window that led to the chamber proper and noted what he hadn't picked up when he was on the inside, though to be fair he was a bit distracted then that the huge window was flanked either side by a pair of French doors, shaped to make the entire window appear as one large arch. It was a magnificent piece and the detail was truly astonishing. The grass on the stained-glass window almost seemed to move, so realistic was it, and the scenery felt almost alive. The man who he had seen earlier in the depiction seemed also, from this side anyway, to be staring directly at Tomas. *Now that is disconcerting*, he muttered to himself. *It's like those bloody pictures that have them eyes that follow you around wherever you look at it from; they give me the creeps too.* Tomas manifested his SA80 again and crept up to the nearest set of doors so he could hear better if anything was being said inside. It also allowed him a limited view of the room as there were one or two clear panes in that part of the enormous image. Tomas glanced back to see Storm waiting patiently in thin air and he grimaced. It wouldn't do for one of the sentries below to casually look up and see a horse floating in midair; it might cause something of a stir. So he willed Storm back to the brand for now, even though he would have liked to have kept the horse out in case an emergency exit was required. But he had to be practical. Tomas put away thoughts of fleeing; he hadn't even gotten close enough to have cause to flee yet, so there was little point getting ahead of himself. He settled in as close as he could and, dematerializing his helmet whilst leaving his cowled cloak in place, he put his ear to the glass and listened. Tomas was not happy about what he heard.

'I know, lord. I can barely believe it myself. The chances were beyond astronomical. Though the master cannot be other than pleased with the way things have worked out, can he? Right at our own gate even after the... disturbance.'

What disturbance did he mean? He sounded uncertain as to what to call it. Perhaps he was referring to a failure on someone's behalf and was being diplomatic. Tomas found that hard to believe of Carmichael. He doubted he even knew the meaning of the word any more. Then it came to him: he was referring to their arrival in the Domain. Toby had hinted at the fact that they thought they were in Canada, so it made sense that a force had relocated them against their wishes, redirecting them against their original plan and sending them here. It was to that which Carmichael referred as the disturbance – it had to be. Tomas pressed closer, hoping for more. He wondered who it was exactly that Carmichael was even talking to. Who was his co-conspirator? The voice that responded slowly to the colonel sent chills up and down Tomas's spine and he wished he hadn't heard it after all. It was part human, part animal, and part something else. It growled and hissed its words with some level of difficulty, as though the formulation of human sentences and phrases was almost beyond its capability, but they resonated with a depth that made Tomas's teeth ache to hear it.

'The Adversary will only be pleased with you, Gaunub, when his head adorns a spike and the corpses of those meddling bitches he has allied himself with are crow food, but why am I not feeding on his entrails as we speak? What delays you, O wretched one?'

Tomas couldn't tell, but Gaunub, the African deity inhabiting Carmichael's wasted carcass, was furious. It loathed with a depth that defied description the fact it had to toady itself before this messenger of the Adversary in order to achieve its goal, and patience wasn't a strong point at the best of times for the beast. But Tomas heard an inflection in the voice of Carmichael that the creature used, which gave him a clue to its state of mind. It wasn't happy to say the least. It seemed an uneasy alliance was at play here and Carmichael was on the butt end of it.

'It is not as easy as you make it seem, Mahniel. Even though we no longer have to track him across his doomed world, events have moved ahead of us. By his own admission he is no longer a mere mortal. He has been granted certain gifts. Gifts he feels will assist him in his quest.'

The other voice interrupted like so much grated glass. 'What quest? What could he possibly have to achieve here in the Domain?'

'He is planning to free Lucifer,' the former voice roared in fury, with such vehemence that the windows rattled, and Tomas flinched in pain and pulled his head back suddenly.

'Say not that offensive title lest I destroy you where you stand! Never mention that vile name again, for he is unworthy of even being spoken of in the same breath with our lord Adversary.' The roar from the hooded spectre was deafening and energy pulsed with every word.

Tomas felt warmth by his cheek and reached up to see what it was. He looked at the sticky crimson smear on his fingertip. *Blood*! His ears were bleeding and there was a ringing in his head from the sudden explosive roar. *Argh, fuck me. It would have been quieter standing behind a bastard jet engine firing up. Some fucking warning would have been nice, Damn, that hurt.* Tomas was spitting bullets as his head rang unabated. *Shit! It feels like he's burst my bloody ear drum.* It was all Tomas could do not to scream out loud as the roar deafened him, but he took several deep calming breaths to settle himself once more, a rage of his own springing into being and dulling the pain in his head. Tomas notched it up as yet another one he owed Carmichael should the time of accounting come around, as he sat back and massaged his ringing head and sore ear. Thankfully, it wore off quickly – a side effect of Death's gift, he assumed, never thinking that Nakir might be having a hand in his physiognomy. He healed quickly, it seemed, and that was good enough for now. Tomas shook his head gently to ensure all was well again, and recommenced his surveillance. *Do that again and I'll shoot you myself and to hell with the consequences,* Tomas muttered to himself as he pressed close once more. Just in time as well to hear Carmichael's testy response. He seemed as unimpressed with this Mahniel as Tomas was. *Cut from the same cloth somewhere down the line, it seems,* Tomas mused as he eavesdropped some more.

'Yes, well, whatever. That's your problem, not mine. You lot get up to whatever you want, but the reason I summoned you here, Mahniel, was for you to fulfill your promise to me. Grant me the power I seek to dominate my enemies once and for all.'

Carmichael was truly an evil bastard, Tomas thought angrily, as he listened to him pleading to this Mahniel character for his payment. He had sold out his own race for power and God knows what else. Whatever it was, it wouldn't be enough to save him if Tomas had anything to say about it. He already considered Carmichael a low life but he had sunk to all new and previously unimaginable depths in Tomas's mind now. *It ends tonight, you worthless sack of shit*, Tomas growled beneath his breath as he tried to see more of what was occurring in the chamber. And fortunately for Tomas, for the distraction may have proven too much for him right then, the light was insufficient for him to catch sight of his reflection in the colored and slightly distorted glass, but had he, he would have seen his eyes had changed from the regular blue mortal look to a sickly ochre shade with vertical slit pupils resembling more some rabid goat or enraged snake than the man he was. Controlling his breathing to hold the bubbling and simmering rage at bay, Tomas watched what happened next.

The other speaker in the chamber had been obscured from view for most of what had taken place already and Tomas was keen to catch sight of this Mahniel, but just when he thought that wasn't likely to happen, the shadow moved into focus. At first Tomas thought it was just a waft of rancid smoke hanging in the air, perhaps from some brazier or burning coals, but as it moved, it thickened, much in the same way Storm manifested and solidified. It coalesced into a manlike torso, for where there should have been legs, there was nothing but vapor and shadow. And like Tomas, it was accoutered in a voluminous black cowl, though unlike Tomas's, Mahniel's was torn at the shoulders, exposing monstrous arms the size of small trees, scaled and rippling muscle like the legs of a T-Rex instead of arms, and they were folded impatiently across an equally substantial chest. It was odd. Tomas knew it was irritated, for it exhibited a very human characteristic of tapping a vicious looking and what he took for a venom dripping claw upon the meaty bicep as it studied the thing that was once Carmichael. As it floated before the colonel it turned slightly, and Tomas saw the ridges and bony protrusions that split out the back of the cowl, where its spine should have been. A flash of the conversation with Michael came flooding back to him about how some of these ancient creatures were very dinosaur-like and had been confused with the archaic reptiles. This confusion was partly due to why humanity and all its combined scientists still couldn't fathom a continual fossil record. It was broken and interrupted constantly. Nor did it explain why, considering there were so many of these massive creatures, we can only find a few of them. It was almost as if they didn't want to be found. The scary bit was that if these things were truly as evil as this son of a bitch looked, then just what emanated from those selfsame bones that archaeologists parade for the entire world to see, as though they are so proud of them? What dark influence have they given off so far? Sometimes history was buried for a reason. Tomas sloughed his gloomy musings and filed the thoughts away for later consideration, concentrating for now on the creatures before him. Tomas finished his scrutiny of Mahniel as he saw the array of spines and horns punching through the hood of the cowl, giving the impression of a spiny crown, and even from the distance Tomas was away from the fiend, he could almost feel the tangibility of its malevolence like a solid, living thing. *If the Adversary is anything like this SOB, then I'm in deep, deep shit.* The prospect didn't make Tomas feel any better at all.

'Very well, human, I shall do as you request, for this will be your only opportunity to fulfill your end of our bargain. I want every last one of them dead. The guardian and his bitches laid out at my feet, and the rest of the humans sacrificed for the greatness of our lord Adversary.'

Tomas saw Carmichael grin evilly. Not a pretty sight as his drawn and dessicated flesh tore as he did so, exposing more teeth and sinew than should have been humanly possible. But Carmichael was past caring and Mahniel obviously had no conception of just who inhabited the shell of the colonel now. It still saw the insect-like human who had made the original agreement, not Gaunub of the Dark Continent, ancient and evil in its own right, and Mahniel was about to unwittingly empower it further. Tomas knew something had to be done but he had no idea what he could do right at that moment, other than watch and see how this played out, praying an opportunity arose, for as it stood, he didn't hold out much hope he could take both of these creatures without getting himself killed in the process, and even then he had doubts about surviving long enough to know he had succeeded.

'Good enough. Now get on with it. I grow weary of this banter and I yearn to rend flesh and taste the blood of my enemy.' Mahniel drifted closer to Carmichael until there were scant inches between them. 'Expect pain and know that your soul belongs to me until the suns die and the multiverse is plunged into eternal darkness.'

Tomas sighed. Why were these creatures so melodramatic? Even he wished they would just get on with it.

'Yes, yes whatever. Haven't I been your servant up until now? Why should after be any different? Now do what you must! Do it! Do it! Doooo iiiiiittttt!' Carmichael's voice rose to an almost maniacal pitch as he screamed into the cowl of Mahniel, entreating him to exercise his will.

Tomas sat back involuntarily. His instincts told him caution was needed at this moment. Something was going to happen and he didn't think it was going to go off with a whimper, and sitting next to so much glass probably wasn't the safest place to be. Tomas stood and moved to one side, with his back to the stonework, sneaking quick glances every second or two to keep track of events.

As Tomas watched, a green mist flowed from the cowl where Mahniel's face should have been, and it enveloped Carmichael, flowing over him and around him, finally snaking its way up his nose and down his throat. As soon as it did this, Carmichael screamed a scream to wake the dead back on Earth. There was no way anyone inside the keep hadn't heard that, and Tomas jammed his hands over his already fragile ears as the colonel howled his heart out. But Tomas couldn't take his eyes off the spectacle and as he continued to watch, a monstrous clawed hand shot out and grabbed Carmichael by the throat while the other engraved something onto the colonel's chest. This only made him scream more, the decibel level increasing beyond his human throat's capability, and it finally shredded under the effort in a spray of blood and cartilage. But that didn't seem to matter as his body began to snap, twist and warp. Like Mahniel, bones began to shift beneath his skin and crunch in and out of his flesh as they altered position and grew larger and sharper. His flesh began to simmer and bubble like molten rubber even as it tore, thickening and becoming more hidelike, with plates of some bony substance overlapping itself, not dissimilar to rhino hide. It cracked and took on the texture of an ancient, dry desert floor. Arms and legs thickened and extended with more bone cracking and snapping, elongating into some hideous reptilian configuration more resembling the legs of velociraptor than of the man he once was. But it was his face that disturbed Tomas the most. The skull flexed and cracked beneath the skin and began to grow. The eye sockets doubled in size as his once human eyes vanished into the darkness, to be immediately replaced by larger orbs, the size of tennis balls, red with vertically slit pupils. The nose and mouth area pushed out and the nostrils ripped as they became more batlike, while the lower jaw kept cracking and protruding outwards, out and out, until it was double the top jaw; and teeth and tusks erupted from the sundered flesh, coiling back on themselves until they arced above his head. Tomas realized he had held his breath all through the transformation and he let it out with a rasp as he pulled back out of sight, letting the stone of the tower steady his shattered nerves. Distractedly, he could hear the keep coming to life, booted feet pounding the stone and orders being shouted. *What the fuck has he done? I've never seen the likes of that before and I really don't want to see that again. That was just so fucking horrible.* Tomas shivered at the memory. But he knew he had to take another look, to see what was happening in there.

'Fuck!' Tomas yelled in shock and horror, for the moment he turned back to the glass, the cowled and spiny head of Mahniel was scant inches from the glass on the other side. Almost face to face except for a sliver of glass, Tomas threw himself backwards away from the abyss that stared at him from the cowl. His exclamation had been sudden and abrupt, but it had not gone unnoticed. Carmichael or Gaunub or the thing it had become spun so fast and leapt at the window with such speed that Tomas wasn't sure it had even moved at first until its own fetid breath was misting the glass inches from his face. Both creatures roared their fury and outrage at the presence of the enemy and Tomas thought of nothing but blotting the sound out and seeking self-preservation. He threw himself backwards so hard, desperate to put as much distance between himself and these things as possible, he momentarily forgot where he was exactly, though it all came rushing back as he sailed over the railing of the balcony and suddenly though belatedly remembered he was a few hundred feet up in the air. *Shit!* It was the only thought Tomas had time for as his options ran out. He knew there was nothing but a long drop and short stop waiting for him. *This is gonna hurt.* Fresh air flew past him and abruptly stopped. *Oomph.* The air was driven from his lungs as he landed back first on something, though nowhere near as hard as he expected. A panicked glance to one side told him he wasn't even on the ground. *Storm.* Nanoseconds later, Tomas realized he was draped across the saddle of the shadowy warhorse. He laughed out loud, sounding as insane to the casual observer as the two creatures he was fleeing from. 'You are one goddamn fucking intelligent horse and I love you.' Tomas shouted a jubilant 'Yes!' He would have whooped and punched the air in delight was he not stuck in the ignoble position he was in. That didn't last long though as Storm arrowed to the ground and deposited its rider safe and sound with a nicker of satisfaction, tossing its mane and head proudly.

'Yes, boy, you done good. Well done and my thanks.' Tomas made as much of a fuss of the horse as he could before reality caught up with them. Treya and Ingrid – weapons drawn – were pounding across the bailey along with Dutch, Toby and a half a dozen armed men.

'Tomas!' Treya shouted before she reached him. 'What has happened? Are you well? We heard the howls, saw your fall and were it not for the timely rescue by your mount we would be looking at your broken remains right about now. What happened up there?'

But there was no time for explanations as the night shook with another combined roar of fury and the explosion of broken glass as though something huge and volatile had gone off in Carmichael's chamber. 'Cover!' Tomas shouted as a hail of broken glass, fragments of stone and railing showered down on the gathered crowd in the bailey. One man went down as a glancing blow with the railing smashed his shoulder and another took a hit from a stray piece of masonry. 'Get those men to cover!' Two more instantly obeyed and pulled them groaning back from the carnage. But that wasn't the end of it by far. Tomas looked up and saw Carmichael leering down at them, one massive clawed hand gripping the ruined window frame so tightly his talons had pierced the stone like anchor bolts. Tomas knew the confrontation he had expected was about to occur whether he was ready for it or not and he had to get his shit together, fast.

'Get everyone out of the bailey, now!' Tomas yelled to whoever felt they were in charge. 'Treya! Move everyone inside and keep them there. They'll stand no chance against that and I'm not even sure I will, but we are about to find out. Now go, please.'

Tomas looked up just in time to see the creature that used to be Carmichael throw itself off the shattered balcony and plummet down towards him, arms and feet spread as if it planned to smother him on impact. A scream unlike anything animal, vegetable or mineral resonated through the air like flying razor blades. 'Arrrrrgggghhhhh DDDiiiiieeee TTTTooommaaassss,' it gurgled and howled its inhuman and marrow chilling war cry as it screamed its way down. Storm vanished in a swirl of steel grey vapor and Tomas dived to one side with a timely expletive as the creature landed with all the finesse of a train having been dropped beside him. The concussion wave from its impact sent several soldiers toppling from their feet and the ground cracked and split from the force and apparent weight of the thing. Gaunub cum Carmichael stepped from the twin craters it had produced and roared again as it sought its enemy, its monstrous head swiveling from side to side as it took in its surroundings and the number of eyes riveted on it. Eyes that were having trouble actually believing what they were seeing. Dutch spoke first, as it seemed the big mercenary was difficult to shock for too long.

'Is that…?' Dutch didn't need to finish his question as Tomas knew who was implied, and he answered him as he rolled to his feet and scrambled well out of immediate reach of the creature.

'Oh yeah. Pretty looking fella, isn't he? Get those men out of here, Dutch. There's nothing they can do against him now. He's sold himself out to things that have no right existing let alone making bargains like this, and for fuck's sake don't let any of them men eat anything in that hall.' Tomas jogged around the bailey with Gaunub following his every movement, like two fighters in a ring, sizing the other up before making a move.

'This fucker was going to feed you all dead men's flesh, those you buried out the front, and don't ask me why.' Tomas added as he saw Dutch's face betray the question. 'I reckon it has something to do with his deal with a thing called Mahniel.'

Gaunub roared and grabbed a chunk of masonry, flinging it at Tomas with unnatural speed and strength. Tomas dived again as the fragment sailed over his head. He felt the windrush of its passing before he heard it career off a wall. *Bastard*, Tomas snarled to himself. Looking up and spitting sand, he saw Treya and Ingrid both nocking their longbows and drawing back a pair of goose feather shafts. With a thung, both let fly, and fly true they did, both slamming into the creature's spine, right between the shoulder blades, with the fletching still quivering with the impact. It screamed aloud and flailed wildly around its head, reaching, searching for the barbs that had pricked it. The other soldiers took this as their cue and twenty-four various weapons opened fire on the preoccupied creature. It was the sound of death as hundreds of rounds blistered the creature like lethal hail. Sparks flew and the ground around it was torn up as the barrage continued. Each man had unloaded a whole clip into Carmichael, as Tomas still assumed it was. Some seven hundred rounds and several seconds later as the dust cleared, Tomas was dismayed to see the beast still standing, salivating maw agape and clutching two broken arrows in its claw. It made a noise then that Tomas took for laughter, and the blood in his veins ran cold at the sound. Tomas, or the sword – he wasn't entirely sure who took the initiative, nor did he care – but he instantly bolstered his armor. Within seconds he was encased in a combination of Kevlar, high impact polymer resin body armor, and steel plates; encasing his arms, chest, groin area and legs. The black knight of old would have sold his grandmother for the get up Tomas now stood in. His helm was reconfigured more to the ancient steel helms of the past – rounded to deflect blows and full face to protect his eyes. Steel boots and gauntlets completed the ensemble and the Sword of War appeared in his hands as though it had always been there.

Gaunub stared with undisguised malevolence at Tomas for seconds that felt like minutes, before charging him, teeth and claws ready to rend his flesh; and as the creature ate the ground between them, Tomas had just enough time to brace his feet and extend the sword before him in a defensive posture. The clash nearly sent him reeling but he sidestepped at the last and the sword reacted with a dizzying speed. The sound of steel and talon rang like a smith's anvil a dozen times before Gaunub's momentum carried him past. With a parting slash across Gaunub's shoulders that sent more sparks than flesh flying, Tomas back-pedaled as fast as he could to buy himself time and space as the creature skidded to a halt and spun for another attack.

'Get those men up to the ramparts; out of his fucking way, otherwise they're dead meat.'

Dutch, Treya and Ingrid, who had put her more obnoxious self away when matters turned to combat, spun to comply, herding the men, who needed little encouragement after their weapons had no effect. Toby, however, had other plans and had gotten his hands on an RPG and was setting it to his shoulder as Tomas hollered his orders in a metallic and echoey voice as it fought to escape his helm. He didn't see what Toby planned as the doughty soldier was just out of his line of sight. The first he knew was the familiar whooshing sound and the sight of the vapor trail that cut across his field of vision. Instinct had him diving backwards not a second too soon as the blast carried him several feet further. He hadn't realized how close Carmichael was to him. *Damn thing moves way too fast.* Tomas wasn't panting for breath just yet, but he did wonder just how long he would be able to keep up this frantic pace.

Coming to his feet, he turned to consider the explosive carnage left by Toby's shot. He couldn't see the beast, nor could he see one of the barrack buildings. It was a mass of shattered timbers and smoking ruins.

'Got the bastard!' Toby came whooping over, followed by eight other soldiers, armed with an eclectic mix of weapons from AK47s, SA80s, a few Hechler and Koch combinations and one or two Tomas didn't immediately recognize. 'You all right, sir?' Toby asked him, even as he directed the men to investigate the rubble. 'Don't worry, Major, we'll take it from here.'

But Tomas's ears were still ringing slightly from the blast and this slowed his reactions down just enough for the men to reach the smoking ruins before he knew what they were doing. Tomas screamed at them not to go in, but it was too late. They were there already and stepping into the swirling dust, weapons shouldered and about as prepared as they were going to get, but nothing could prepare them for what they found; not expecting anything to have survived the blast, anyway not at that close a range, they piled inside. They were so wrong and they paid for it with their lives. Their screams would haunt Tomas for however long he had left to live and he had just enough time to raise his arm in front of his face as the barracks exploded once more. With a blast that was almost as devastating as that which put him in there, the ruins erupted in a spray of debris and blood as pieces of the soldiers were strewn about along with bits of building, followed almost instantly by Carmichael himself, striding through the chaos, covered with blood that wasn't his own, and human flesh hanging from his savage maw. Some of the soldiers' limbs were clasped in each claw and he waved them like trophies of war as he howled his defiance.

'Oh shit!' was about all Toby had time for as Tomas propelled him away.

'The next time I ask you all to do something, you fucking well listen. Do I make myself clear?' Tomas was furious now. Less so with Carmichael than he was at himself for letting those men die because of him. 'Now get the fuck up there with everyone else before I shoot you myself. There's nothing you can do down here. It's me it's after but it'll go through you all to do it if it has to. You simply don't have the weapons that can hurt it. I do. Trust me Toby. I'll explain if I live. Now go.'

Toby, duly chastised, turned and ran. He knew he had fucked up and, like Tomas, he would carry that burden for the rest of his days, for although death was a way of life for him and his brethren, it didn't make it any easier to accept when it happened in vain, because of sheer stupidity. As he ran, it was then that he truly realized just how out of his depth he was in this strange land filled with monsters and stuff he didn't even want to know about, let alone understand.

Tomas watched him run for a few seconds before turning to face the fast approaching Carmichael. Swapping the sword for his twin Hochlers, Tomas leveled them at Carmichael and let rip. Now where before the soldiers' mundane rounds bounced off Carmichael like pebbles off a crab's shell, it was unprepared for the effect of Tomas's supernatural ordnance. Perpetually filled mags spewed flying death at Carmichael like a plague of carnivorous locusts. Each hit ripped into his flesh and sent waves of agony coursing through his metamorphosed body. He wasn't expecting that and Gaunub screamed in genuine pain for the first time in a millennium. Tomas ran directly at the creature, arms extended and weapons ablazing, knowing he had only a moment's advantage while it cottoned onto the fact he could hurt it. Arms flailing as though it tried to swat away a scourge of angry insects, the thing that was Colonel Alan Carmichael didn't see the rapidly approaching Tomas, busy as it was defending itself, but for every one round it deflected off its carapace-like skin, a dozen scored true. Within a few feet of the thing, Tomas reverted from guns to sword, and with a leap and a mighty swing, he dived to one side as he arced the glinting blade round in a powerful haymaker, determined to take the damned thing's head off with the blow if he could. And he probably would have had the creature not reacted just as fast with lightning quick reflexes and thrown its arm up to deflect that blow too. But it underestimated the origins of the blade Tomas wielded and the mighty weapon cleaved through chiton, bone, sinew and whatever else comprised the creature's arm. Carmichael screamed and ducked beneath the swinging blade as the limb hit the ground with a dull thud and spasmed violently, thrashing and spraying ichor in black globules that hissed and spat as they hit the sand and anything else they touched.

If Tomas thought he had incapacitated the creature, he was to be sorely disappointed, for instead of a prolonged and agonized howl with even a possible tactical retreat by the thing, it stopped screaming and stood and stared at the wound as Tomas rolled away to safety and came up in fighting stance a good twenty feet away, facing the beast. Holding the stump out, Gaunub examined the wound and began to laugh – a sound that was the antithesis of anything remotely resembling humor – and to Tomas's horror, as everyone watched, the limb began to sprout anew.

'You cannot kill me, Walker. Your sorry attempts only irritate me like annoying flies that buzz and sting. See!' It waved the nearly whole limb as if in evidence. 'Cut me. Do I not bleed? But in my case, do I not regenerate? Is not my master truly powerful – *human*?'

Tomas heard the contempt in his animalistic sounding voice as though being human were something to be ashamed of. Once perhaps, Tomas had been ashamed, but that was slowly changing now that he was faced with a foe that sought humanity's eradication. Humans were a bunch of arrogant, petty minded warmongers who had the definition of power crazed and selfish down to a fine art, but they were mistakes of character that humanity should be able to grow out of. They didn't deserve to be made extinct for their stupidity, least of all not by this bunch of delusional demons. To hear them gloat and brag, they came over like some poorly scripted horror movie, and Tomas had heard it all before anyway. *The faces change but the game remains the same. Same shit, different planet, or something like that.* Tomas smiled a chilling smile back at Carmichael's boast and as he watched the last of the regeneration of the severed arm, Tomas rolled his shoulders and neck gently, round and round and side to side. Loosening the muscles there. Tomas took a second to glance around the bailey, locating the positions of the men and the Valkyries. To their credit, none of them had gone far and they had taken up defensive positions behind various barriers and had a plethora of weapons trained on the creature. As Tomas turned, smiling back towards the beast, he saw several small red dots dancing and flickering on its torso. *They may not stop it, but I'm betting they'll do more than just sting.* Abruptly an image popped into Tomas's head. It came from Bran, who was observing the proceedings from on high. What he saw made Tomas smile all the more, not that anyone could see his expression behind the steel helm, but it didn't stop him. He saw Dutch, leaning on one of the embrasures with a Barrett fifty-millimeter tank stopper. These things packed a punch and Dutch obviously wanted to see just how much. Tomas raised an arm as the thing took its first step towards him, hoping the men recognized his gesture, and then he suddenly dropped it. The air around him sang as each and every man and woman let rip. Tomas picked out certain sounds amidst the cacophony of death. The Barrett, the Valkyries' bows, the Kalashnikovs. Each had a voice Tomas would have recognized in the dark and in a heartbeat. They spoke a language he truly understood. Carmichael was peppered with scorching metal and even made to stagger several steps back as the Barrett rounds slammed into him. Tomas raised an arm to cease fire and they did. Carmichael was twenty yards away now and on his knees, body smoking from the barrage it had just withstood. As it slowly regained its feet, Tomas saw its chest heaving with exertion. *Indestructible my arse. It's taking longer to heal each time and even the regular weapons are stinging it more now. Mine should really fucking hurt.* Tomas dropped to his knee and swung the sword to his shoulder, where the Javelin missile launcher appeared.

'Eat this, motherfucker!' Tomas held his breath and sighted. In less time than it took for a heart to beat, he squeezed the firing mechanism. With a whoosh, the missile covered the distance before his breath could even be released. The explosion took Tomas by surprise, never having been that close to a Javelin strike before, and a wall of flame and debris washed over him before he even had time to move. All he could do was close his eyes and hope his armor could withstand the battering. He felt himself lifted off his feet and flung backwards, with chunks of wood and masonry ricocheting off his steel plates. Tomas groaned as he hit the ground, sliding through the sand, leaving a deep furrow in his wake. Seconds passed and he opened his eyes. A good sign he wasn't dead, at least. A quick mental inventory told him he was still all in one piece and nothing hurt too much. Ribs a bit sore and ears ringing still, other than that...*well, can't complain too much.* Tomas scrambled to his feet as fast as his battered body would allow, the remnants of his smoldering cloak hanging in tatters about his shoulders, and Tomas saw the rest of him was smoking too. *After that little chargrilling, I'm fucking lucky to even still be here. I can live with being a bit singed around the edges.* Then the next thing he did was check on the remains of Carmichael. He saw movement in the rubble and hoped it was just the dust settling. *Crap, I hope that did it.* But as the thought faded in his mind, he saw the same rubble begin to heave and move with increasing intensity. Tomas had walked to within a few feet of the smoking ruin when Carmichael burst forth – again. *Doesn't this fucker ever die?* Tomas heard the collective groan from above as his people thought exactly the same thing.

'My turn now, Walker!' Carmichael roared and with that threat still hanging in the air, Carmichael cum Gaunub dived at Tomas and tackled him across the torso. Arms like industrial clamps crushed him and Tomas groaned in agony as his battered ribs underwent more punishment. He would have screamed but the air was forced from his lungs both by the grip of Gaunub and the impact with the ground as they landed. He felt as well as smelt the rancid breath of the crocodilian mouth as it clamped onto his shoulder and began to exert a bite pressure that should have taken his arm off at the scapula. Tomas thanked everything for the armor the sword provided as he gritted his teeth against the growing pressure and pain. Gaunub copied the crocodile in more ways than just looks, as he then began to roll them over and over across the bailey floor, crushing and biting as he went. The talons of his feet raked at Tomas's legs and body armor, determined to tear it from his body. Tomas was reminded of the hounds who had tried a similar tack and very nearly succeeded in eviscerating him. He had to do something, and quick. Tomas suddenly thought of the humble urchin, or the thought was sent to him, it didn't matter, but it gave him an idea. Spikes suddenly burst from Tomas's armor, which had a twofold effect. Gaunub released him with a muted howl of frustration and pain as he maintained the bite but the spikes dug into both the beast and the soft sand, bringing their rolling flight to an abrupt halt. With a swift head-butt, Tomas cracked his helm into the face of Gaunub again and again, forcing him to release his bite. On the fifth butt it worked and Tomas scrambled clear, rising with difficulty and putting some distance between him and Carmichael. Sweat dripped into his eyes from the strain of standing and Tomas was forced to dematerialize the helm in order to clear his vision. The sudden clear view of the smoldering Gaunub didn't do much to cheer him, for he still looked formidable. But it appeared that several of the wounds inflicted had still to heal and they wept black pus and ichor. Tomas smiled cruelly at the prospect and he felt a calm descend on him that, when last he felt it, he was running at a hundred enemies at Al'Mayakin.

'Right then, you bastard, time to see who'll have the last word here. Hope you got something left 'cos you are going to need it, old son.' Tomas held the sword once more and he swung it around his wrist a few times as he strode towards the still hunched creature, though it did raise its head to regard him, and its eyes burned with malevolence and a hatred that would burn rock.

'You are growing tiresome, Walker. Why do you not desist your feeble efforts and die like a good little mortal? You merely delay the inevitable.' As it spoke it grew straighter and many of the wounds Tomas's spiked attack had inflicted closed, though he noted that many hadn't and even some that did close just reopened again, as though the effort was too much to sustain. But the creature continued its baiting as it flexed its arms and cracked its talons in anticipation. 'Why did you not die like the rest of your insignificant family? I admit that I should have handled your family personally, not left it to subordinates. It's true what they say, Walker: if you want something done properly, you should do it yourself.'

The enormity of what he was hearing hit Tomas harder than Carmichael had. *This bastard was responsible for my family's death?* He couldn't get his head around it. He was hearing it but it all seemed so distant and incredible.

'You? It was you who rigged the explosion?' Tomas knew he had to ask, to hear it again.

'Not personally, no, but yes, I did order it. Mahniel found you and sent me to deal with you and your miserable kin. How was I to know it wasn't your skank of a sister with you but the whore of your last mission instead? A poor prize, if you ask me. I take it she never told you about her past life then? About how many men she had had?' A lack of expression on Tomas's face told Gaunub more than it concealed. 'I take that as a no then. Shame. She wasn't the best, nor the most expensive, but she was willing and, oh so accommodating. How do you think we got her piss poor husband to do what we wanted him to do? She was very good with the big moist cow eyes, and her ability to manipulate emotions made her invaluable in the right environment. Looks like she got you too, you stupid, pathetic animal, driven by your base needs. Once you stuck your cock in her you were hers. Then there was your spineless invertebrate of a father.'

Tomas was dumbstruck as the creature grew ever closer, though he was so wrapped up in what he was hearing he barely noticed. Carmichael was responsible for the death of his family and very nearly his own demise.

'The man hunted me for years and it was his testimony that put me behind bars. You should know me better than that, Tomas, as being one who might forget let alone forgive. I do neither. Imagine my glee when I was given the permission to do exactly what I was planning to do anyway. You have no conception just how much my masters and I hate your family.'

Tomas hadn't but he was quickly getting the idea. Enough to sell out his own soul and species for the chance for a little revenge. That took some serious hate and Tomas regarded the creature that was suddenly before him with all new eyes. But they were eyes that were now, suddenly, without warning, too close by far.

With a resounding backhand, Carmichael delivered a blow to Tomas that nearly took his head from his shoulders and launched him several feet backwards. His armor absorbed the impact from the wall he bounced off and, spitting blood, Tomas landed, albeit shakily, on his feet. Wiping the blood on the back of his hand, Tomas stood up and roared, just as Carmichael did the same, and the two antagonists charged each other. At the last second, Tomas feinted left and swung one of the hand axes he kept on his belt, into the midriff of Carmichael. With the other hand, he drove the other down onto his head but it had little effect and sparked off to one side. Carmichael roared and spun, swatting at Tomas with a claw that now sported talons the size of daggers. The hand axe was knocked from stunned fingers and Tomas only had a split second to get the sword up as more sparks rained off its blade as the two met in a metallic clash. Then began the dance of death as Carmichael swung and swung at Tomas, talons against sword, and Tomas defended for all he was worth. Two claws against one sword was always going to end badly and Tomas fought with a frenzy he barely knew he possessed. Nothing existed then but the creature before him. His eyes were wide and streaming as he concentrated on the beast and each attack. He didn't dare blink, as the ferocity of Carmichael's attacks would rend his flesh in the time it took to do it. In what could have only have been minutes, though they felt like hours to Tomas, he felt himself weakening. More than a few of Carmichael's attacks had slipped past his desperate defense, and the deadly claws had torn through his armor like so much tissue paper. There it was. Tomas was growing weaker as Carmichael grew stronger again. Maybe he was right, maybe he couldn't win. Perhaps he should just lay down his sword and give up, join his family and...

Carmichael screamed and Tomas came out of the daze he found himself slipping into. Shaking his head to clear the sticky webs of enchantment that had befallen him, Tomas saw four shafts sticking out of the back of Carmichael like a seriously ugly porcupine. Thunk, thunk and two more hit home. Carmichael screamed again and Tomas took full advantage of the respite. *The bastard has something on his fucking claws; some kind of poison that screws with the mind, my mind. Well I don't think so. You had your chance and thanks again,*

Pestilence. Now it's time to get this done. No more fannying around while he tries to rip my fucking head off. Time to put him down.

Acknowledging the Valkyries with a quick nod and a wink, Tomas then grinned insanely and with a samurai scream of battle, he leapt at the howling Carmichael, swinging the sword with an expertise that was beyond him, the blade darting and feinting left and right, its deadly edge licking out and scoring wounds on the carapace of Carmichael wherever it touched. In and out, back and forth. Tomas danced and leapt about the creature like a dervish, the sword ringing out with every impact, so much so it was almost singing a tune on the beleaguered Carmichael. Forgetting the arrows protruding from its back, it concentrated once more on Tomas, for he was inflicting more pain on it than the twigs sticking out of his spine, though that was not to say they didn't hurt, because they did. Carmichael's howls of agony were testimony to that. Being of supernatural origin too, the Valkyries' shafts took their toll on Carmichael, and ichor poured in rivulets down the thing's back.

Across the bailey once more the two fought back and forth and another rhythm settled in, but Tomas was tiring fast; faster than Carmichael and again the creature opened wounds on Tomas's battered body. With a scream of rage, the thing that was Carmichael made a decisive move and leapt directly at Tomas, who, seeing his chance, raised the sword and drove it home through the chest of Carmichael, where it erupted from the shattered spine where the arrows of the Valkyries had weakened it. But to Tomas's dismay, it was still far from dead as it dragged itself down the blade, drawing closer to Tomas, and roaring into Tomas's face from mere inches away. Tomas was deafened by the inhuman howl, and fetid saliva spattered his already scratched and beaten features. Tomas knew this was the end and he saw how. But it was with a force of will, one that he thought was already spent, that he rematerialized his steel helm; in the nick of time as the jaws clamped down on his head. Fangs crunched on supernatural steel and he heard the grinding of fang on metal almost absently. Carmichael released his bite and grabbed Tomas by the shoulders and bit him hard there. This time the rancid fangs penetrated and

Tomas screamed as he felt bone sunder beneath the bite and his now numb hand relinquished his grip on the blade. Carmichael stood back and screamed in victory, the sword sticking out of him as though it meant nothing. Claws raked Tomas once more and he felt his armor give and fire rip across his chest. He didn't feel the ribs shatter and the flesh part about his sternum as a questing claw sought to deprive him of his heart and vital organs; and consciousness was fast becoming a tenuous thing. Desperation and a moment of agonized lucidity caused Tomas to raise a fist and smash it into Carmichael's face just as he lowered his muzzle to bite and tear him once more. Tomas connected, more by luck than judgment, with one of Carmichael's eyes and it caused him a momentary burst of pain, and in that moment of blinding rage, Carmichael threw Tomas across the bailey, where he landed amidst the rubble of the ruined barrack block. Landed badly. Tomas felt one of his legs buckle and snap beneath him. He screamed as bone ripped out of his flesh, femur and tibia both shattered and sending shards of bloody bone through muscle and skin. He landed like a rag doll that had been tossed aside. Then, as he lay still, waves of pain washed over him like breakers against rocks during a stormy night.

Somewhere in the haze of his searing, agony filled mind, he heard Bran scream and the Valkyries cry a denial to the gods, but he felt little himself except he was still alive. Dimly, Tomas remembered Death's promise not to take him. *Small fucking consolation. I don't get to die, I just lie here in permanent agony.* But that was assuming Death himself still lived. Things hadn't looked too promising when he last saw the indomitable Reaper. *Times change, I suppose, and he could be dead himself by now. That said then, I'm really screwed.* Tomas coughed blood and through his one remaining eye, the other having been closed by a chunk of timber his head had bounced off when he landed, he looked down to inspect his ruined chest. He was no doctor but he knew that what he was looking at was a fatal wound. No amount of surgery was going to put that together again and the sight of his own lungs rising and falling through shattered ribs came over all too surreal. Tomas licked dry lips and looked to where the creature was. It was striding towards him, the

Sword of War sticking out from its own chest and, he wasn't sure if it was his imagination or not, but when Carmichael tried to pull it free, it seared his claw, and smoke and flames erupted from his talons. Tomas gurgled a broken laugh at the sight and spat out more blood than should be in his mouth, ever.

Then it hit him. *The sword*. It was his now. Bonded to him like Storm, and a gem of information filtered its way back into his foggy consciousness as he lay broken, awaiting the final stroke from the creature who was still striding towards him, now under a barrage of retaliatory gunfire again as Dutch and the soldiers thought him done for.

'*Come to me!*' Tomas sent the thought out and he saw Carmichael stop suddenly and look down, regarding the steel protruding from his chest. '*Come to me, now!*' It quivered within Carmichael's chest with such violence that Carmichael screamed in pain and once more dropped to one knee. It tried desperately to pull it free but all it got was more fire and scorched hands. '*Come to me, my friend!*' With a last shudder and a wet sucking sound, the sword tore itself free, taking flesh and bone with it as it ripped clear of Carmichael's chest and flew across the bailey. End over end it flew, unerringly towards its goal. Tomas raised a welcome hand and the hilt slammed into it as though it had never left. Tomas felt strength surge into him and with his own scream of defiance, he dragged himself clear of the rubble and using the sword, pulled himself upright. He thought he was under attack again and turned to see the source of the roar behind him. But it was the men, not some other fiend. They were raucously cheering at the sight of the man they considered dead, whooping and chanting his name.

Tomas! Tomas! Tomas! The sound washed over him and gave him strength where no magic could. It swelled his heart and he spun to regard the staggering beast before him. Using the sword as a crutch, Tomas hopped his way forward, a trail of blood and fluids in his wake. He knew he didn't have long, seconds at the most. The power of the sword was only good for so long and his wounds were severe. Alarmingly, Tomas noticed they weren't healing like in the encounter with the hounds. Maybe this time he was truly done for.

Gotta go sometime, I suppose. But he wasn't going out without taking his nemesis with him once and for all.

'You'll never win, you slimy piece of shit,' Tomas grated, 'never. You may have taken my family, but I'm still here to redress the balance, to give them the justice they deserve. You're a loser, Carmichael. You always were, you are now and for the next few seconds of your miserable life you still will be.' Tomas stood unaided and held the sword poised, battle ready. Carmichael stood straighter too, even though it cost him to do so, and opened its gaping fang filled maw to howl its defiance at the tiny mortal before it. But before any sound could manifest, Tomas stepped in and swung.

Carmichael raised an arm in defense, much like he had before, but this time, he hadn't counted on the fury and righteous anger behind the stroke. It hit the extended arm and went clean through, the arc carrying on to slice through the bony neck of Carmichael, and the still evilly grinning and monstrous head lifted off its shoulders, a stunned expression etched onto it before it even knew what had happened to it. Tomas allowed the momentum to carry him round in a tight circle and the backswing of the sword tore down through the spurting stump of a neck to carry on through its ribs to exit just above the hip. The three pieces of Carmichael cum Gaunub hit the bloody sand like so much dead meat. Not even a twitch came from them. It was as though in defeat, all energy and life had been extinguished and the master, this Mahniel, who controlled and fed the beast its power, simply gave up on it as a failure and left it to its fate. Tomas didn't give a toss one way or the other. He simply stared at the corpse, almost daring it to move again.

When it remained still, the last vestiges of Tomas's strength fled him and he too crumpled to the sand. He lay there, unable to move his limbs but he did manage to turn his head so that his face was looking skyward. But even that filled him with sadness as darkness encroached on his view. All around the edges of his vision, blackness crept slowly to blot out the sky. *I'm dying?* Tomas knew it would happen one day, but he wasn't entirely sure how. He hadn't expected it to be like this though. 'Who'll tell Gwen?' Tomas asked the question of no one in particular, but Bran answered all the same.

'I'll find her, Tomas, and tell her the tale of a hero. How her brother died protecting his men and his race from evil.'

Tomas smiled. It sounded good. Seconds later, as he relished that comforting thought, Treya was at his side and picking his head up, cradling it in her lap. Tomas saw her through the tunnel his vision was forming. She seemed small and far away now and her voice was distant, almost plaintive.

'Don't you dare die, Tomas Walker!'

The command was clear and Tomas fought to obey, but his body had other ideas and it began to fail him. 'I tried, Trey, I did my best.' That was how it sounded to him in his mind but his voice betrayed him and all the teary Valkyrie heard were garbled whispers. Tomas didn't see the rest of the men surround him and the grave expressions on their rugged and stoic faces. These were hard men, used to death and bloody battle, but they looked at Tomas with softer eyes, with a sadness that exposed the compassion and humanity within each of them. Many had tears in their eyes at the sight of the broken warrior dying before them, who had fought to protect them without even knowing the majority of them, who fought single handedly against something that had no right existing. It was a battle that would forever ingrain itself into their memories, and from these collective memories, so legends were born. Dutch in the meantime had picked up a weighty wood chopping axe and was heading determinedly for the monstrous but still gaping head of Carmichael. He placed a well-worn boot firmly upon it and swung the axe round. Putting his entire weight behind the blow, he grunted as the forged steel whistled overhead and struck the skull. No supernatural force drove it now and the man-made axe smashed through bone and brain matter. Again and again Dutch swung the axe until all that remained beneath his boot was mush. 'Regenerate from that if you will, you fiend,' Dutch muttered satisfactorily to himself. As he shook the gore from his footwear, Ingrid spoke softly, but blatantly to her sister:

'He is dying, Treya. Have the men prepare his grave. We must depart this keep as soon as possible. For whatever empowered that thing may still be here or calling for reinforcements even as we dally.'

Ingrid still had her bow drawn as she stood over her friend and sister. And even though something had changed between them, practicality had not altered her motives. People died but events still continued irrespective, and Ingrid held true to that ideology, however harsh. Treya looked up at her second with tears brimming in her eyes, as though she held them back from flowing by sheer force of will.

'He's not dead yet, Ingrid, and I will not leave him until that is beyond contestation. You can do as you will…' Treya took a calming breath as Ingrid had a knack of saying the wrong thing even though it was the right time, and Treya fought to control her emotive response, '…though I would suggest you summon the scouts and have them scour and track the area for any imminent invaders, secure the gates and set up a perimeter. These men will assist you, I'm sure.' Treya looked up at Dutch and Toby, her eyes giving the order her voice was unable to give as emotion grasped it too firmly. Had she been able to speak then it would have cracked and broken as her heart beat too erratically to maintain a controlled timbre.

'We'll get him inside, lady. Leave the rest to us.' Knowing what was to be done, Dutch whistled and two soldiers ran over with a makeshift stretcher and gently, they lifted the almost unconscious Tomas onto it. Others ran to set up their guard. The fact Tomas groaned as they moved him was the only indication he still lived at all, but for how much longer was anyone's guess due to the severity of his injuries and the amount of blood he had lost.

'Judging by his condition, Trey, I would say the Horsemen aren't faring too well with their end of the conflict, presuming he is as tied to them as he says.'

Treya stood beside her sister, arms folded across her chest, one finger tapping nervously against her arm, and watched the men carry Tomas into the tower, where they knew his room to be. 'Perhaps, but he recovered once from the hound's savage attack. Maybe he can again. As I understand it, Ingrid, the Horsemen aren't here. Maybe their influence is weakened because of the distance and the interference from the Adversary.'

Ingrid just shrugged in a non-committal gesture, as though she cared neither way. But what neither Treya nor anyone else watching the feisty and normally dour Valkyrie could discern, was that Ingrid actually *did* care. And that confused her more than the crisis they faced. She had watched this human win the respect and admiration of strangers, fight for them and protect them with his life. They rallied to him even though they barely knew him, and chanted his name like for the kings and heroes of her time. That sort of loyalty and respect found her weak point. Ingrid herself was a shield maiden of Odin and a Valkyrie warrior born and bred, and to see such valor in a human, so far from his own world, stirred emotions in her she thought long dead and buried. It took her back to the battlefields of her homeland and the bloody wars of old when she would swoop down and gather the heroes to return them to Valhalla. She only chose the most courageous and capable. Ingrid watched them carry Tomas away and as they disappeared into the tower, she would have chosen him. Ingrid then turned her attention to the rest of the men still present, who stood somewhat at a loss as to what to do next. Tomas had seemed the natural choice to lead them, but he was as good as dead now. That left the oddly misplaced Toby who had brought them here in the first place. Ingrid wasn't sure about him as leadership material, but the other one had it aplenty. Dutch. The name fitted him, for as far as Ingrid was concerned he more than resembled the ancient Viking warriors of her past and youth – walking testosterone and barely bridled carnage. Yet she saw the way he too watched Tomas – and her – though she tried not to think about *that*. There was a respect there that no amount of coin could buy, and Ingrid saw then that these men, paid soldiers as they were, would have followed Tomas for no payment at all, and it was in that second, that moment of clarity and poignant insight, that the arrow that pierced Ingrid's frozen core was the realization that she too would have followed him, wherever he had led them.

'Perhaps, Treya, but we shall never know, shall we?' Ingrid spoke as much to hide her own feelings as for the actual need to say anything at all. Treya stayed silent and thoughtful; as she too watched the men carrying Tomas enter the tower. Collins had appeared, pale and ashen after witnessing the fight, and he took charge of organization. Watching almost detachedly, she knew she was conflicted. She knew it and it disturbed her. What to do next? Follow the men and wait impatiently beside Tomas's bed for him to die? Or leave and try to put the experience and the memory of him far behind her: after all she still had a mission and a purpose of her own to fulfill. But what about these humans? Trapped and lost in a brutal world that wasn't their own, relatively leaderless, at least by someone who had any conception of what they faced beyond the confines of the protective and encircling walls. Could they help her and her sisters? Would Be'elzebub accept them into the rebellion? The implications of that sent her mind reeling. How had things gotten so complicated in such a short space of time? She needed to be decisive. Too much depended on her, for she still had to attempt the rescue of Lucifer if she was ever to see her sisters returned to Valhalla and her reunited with her home, and the chance for the retribution she swore she would take upon those who had her sent here in the first place.

'Prepare a pyre. He will have a king's send off as best we can manage this far from the ocean. Take some men and gather timbers from the ruins while I check on his condition.' It was expected of her to be pragmatic and the building of the pyre might buy Tomas some recovery time, or so she fooled herself. 'When the scouts arrive, have them appraise Be'elzebub of the situation and assure him we are still intent on carrying out the plan, and that we may have some unexpected assistance.'

Ingrid knew then that Treya intended to use the soldiers in whatever capacity they were able to be used in order to complete the job at hand, and nodded her assent. Spinning impressively, she strode off to carry out her task.

Treya was only a quarter of the way up the winding tower staircase when Tomas suddenly coughed, spasmed once and fell back upon his bed, his last breath escaping from his body in a barely audible hiss. By the time she arrived at the room, Toby, who had accompanied Tomas, had pulled the sheet up over him, and stood staring down at the prone figure silhouetted in profile beneath the shroud. Collins was almost in tears as he stood trembling, looking down at Tomas, with his hands clutched and wringing before him. Toby was silently mouthing a prayer for his safe conduct, the first he had uttered in years, and he was a little surprised at himself for doing so for a man he barely knew, yet he hadn't brought himself to do so for men he had fought alongside for years. What had this man evoked in him? He would never know but was thankful that he had gotten the chance to meet him, even for only a short time.

Toby had finished, turned and made it to the door just as Treya arrived. She stopped abruptly and looked Toby in the eye. There were tears there and all he did was shake his head sadly. It was enough. Treya's hand flew to her mouth to stifle a sob but she disguised it so as not to lose face before these men, which would never do.

'Please leave. I'd like a few moments with him, if you don't mind.' Treya was calm and level voiced – a fact that surprised her considering how she felt inside.

'Certainly, my lady. My men and I will be just downstairs if you need us.'

'Thank you, Toby, for everything.'

Toby seemed a little taken aback by the compliment, unsure quite what it referred to, but he nodded nonetheless and saluted Treya, as he did Tomas. It was his way of showing her the same respect he had for the man lying dead in the adjacent room.

'No. Thank *you*, my lady. It has been a privilege.' With that, he turned smartly and ordered the others ahead of him. Waiting until she was certain they were gone and out of earshot, Treya turned; facing the door and with tears finally brimming over and running down her cheeks, she stepped into the dimly lit room to say farewell.

CHAPTER TWENTY

EPILOGOS

FURY WAS BEING REDEFINED BEYOND THE POWER to describe it. Vast sections of Shemyaza's former palace were now in total ruins, with bodies of those foolish enough to be in the vicinity when the calamity occurred, strewn about the rubble. A few unlucky souls were still groaning in broken agony as they lay smashed amidst the debris, but no one was going to come to their aid and they were left to die slow and insufferably painful deaths.

Fenris, already several steps beyond the line where sanity and reason met, could hear nothing and see nothing beyond the roar in his ears and the scarlet haze before his wildly staring and obviously insane looking eyes. He saw neither brick nor stone of his newly adopted and now not so palatial demesne, nor those who dwelt within it. His rage prohibited him to differentiate between the two and so he destroyed whatever he got his monstrous paws on, be it one or the other. Of late it had been both, and those sensible enough to see their new master coming their way ran, flew, slithered and scuttled away as fast as they were able, oblivious to the fates of any left behind them as they fled.

Fortunately, this was the Domain; so humanity had no need to find words to describe Fenris's tantrum, for they would have been hard-pressed.

Perhaps the closest thing to the rage of the Wolf Lord would be a category five hurricane in wolf's clothing. Condensed and concentrated within his flesh and fur, his terrifying maw and destructive talons giving testimony to his strength and power; though at the rate he was going, he wasn't going to have much palace left to destroy, nor minions to savage and vent his spleen upon if he didn't desist sooner rather than later.

There was no pattern, or rhyme or reason to the meandering path taken by the Wolf Lord. He merely howled and roared and strode, his direction only changing when his path was blocked by the carnage wrought by his own actions; or some other contingent of minions who had been sent to try and pacify their lord, many of whom now decorated the walls of the palace in various states of dismemberment. Fenris didn't take bad news well, especially when it reflected so poorly on him; and the abject failure of his minions to carry out his simplest of orders was indeed a very poor reflection on him. But it wasn't just that his hounds had failed so miserably to stop one human, it was the embarrassment and likely repercussions he stood to face before the Adversary, that caused him such consternation. Any sign of failure within the Domain was seen as weakness and he couldn't afford to be seen as weak at this vital juncture in the conflict; not if he wanted his plans to succeed.

Long, cold and dark centuries in his gaol, with nothing but the memory of causing Tyr pain, biting off his hand as a last gesture of defiance to keep him warm, had warped, twisted and eventually snapped the cunning mind of the Dread Wolf. But not with the explosive fracture that sundered cognitive thought completely, usually to leave the recipient a drooling idiot. No, this was a much more subtle affair and one that allowed repairs to be made to his crippled synapse. Even as old connections withered and failed, new ones formed within his labyrinthine mind. But they were not straight and well-healed fusions: these were distorted and scarred connections that skewed his perceptions and even removed what few obstacles remained within his psyche that fettered and reined in his raw power in the first place. Neither his gaolers, nor those who freed him, had any way of knowing what it was now that they had released. But then again, neither did his gaolers expect him to be free again, ever, and the Adversary was too full of himself to ever consider Fenris a threat. That was due to change, but not yet. For now he would bide his time and let them think he was as he was before. But in truth, he was now, thanks to their fear and loathing of him, infinitely more dangerous than he was *before* his imprisoning, and it was a fact that he planned to visit upon all of their sorry and self-righteous carcasses before this war was over. One such coup that would have caused Odin and his kin some measure of pain would have been to eradicate the Valkyries. They were the daughters and family of the elders and several were accompanying the human. Fenris had hoped to offer their paltry deaths up as a way to inflict mental wounds upon Odin, Thor and his ilk. To let them see what was coming for them. But even that had failed and Fenris exploded again, launching into yet another frenzy as the memory of his recent report and his own pent up frustration came crashing back in on him.

Howling his anguish, Fenris rampaged, knowing there were few in the multiverse who could stand toe to toe with him and hope to live, but little did he know that one such entity, who could not only stand before the Wolf Lord but snuff him out of existence with little effort, was hurtling towards him right at that very moment.

Fenris began to calm almost as fast as he had enraged, as his initial tirade quelled and he eventually began to make his way back towards his throne room. It was a symptom of his unstable mind that he was so volatile and his mood swings were more sudden and infinitely more violent than even the harsh weather conditions of the Domain. His throne room when he arrived was empty but, as a bonus, it was at that moment still relatively intact, unlike several connected areas. Other than gouge marks in the marble walls and shattered furniture, it looked comparatively sound. Certainly compared to other parts of the city sized structure that hadn't fared so well. As he calmed, he backtracked on what he was told for the hundredth time and even now, he couldn't believe what he had been told. That not only was the human still alive, along with several of the hated Valkyries, but he wasn't even hurt. No mortal should be able to survive an attack by one of his hounds – it was unheard of. At the very least he should have taken a wound and been turned, transformed into one of the tortured souls that made up his ever growing army of hounds. It was his curse, his gift and his legacy to pass on his foul and corrupt form to those infected or, according to Fenris, blessed by him or his. To Fenris it was a divine blessing; to those on the receiving end it was way beyond the worst curse imaginable and it would last an eternity or until they died, whichever happened first. Though being nearly impossible to kill, a hound's tortured existence was expected to last a very long time indeed.

Fenris was oblivious to time and external distractions when he was thinking and plotting, so it was with some serious trepidation that a minion fearfully poked its head into the throne room. Having drawn the short straw as being the poor sap to deliver the message and not expected to return from delivering its news, the minion coughed warily, knowing it wanted its lord's attention but almost too scared for its own life to actually attract it. It needn't have worried though. Fenris had smelt its fear long before its scaled head had appeared around the scratched and scarred door.

'You are brave indeed, Zoth, to disturb my cogitations,' Fenris growled beneath his breath. 'What brings you to death's door when your brethren run like scared rabbits from my wrath?' Fenris may have been beyond insane, emotionally volatile and more dangerous to be around than almost any other living thing upon the Domain, but he wasn't stupid. He had learnt within days every soul that served within his walls and who dwelt within his newly acquired demesne, knowing them both by name and by scent. The fear he sensed now sent shivers of delight coursing through his body. He thrived upon the heady, musky smell of sheer terror. It invigorated him and made him salivate – a sight that almost made the minion die of sheer terror right there on the spot, believing itself to be its lord's next meal. Fenris locked his scowling and crimson blazing eyes upon the minion with the same intensity as though he had actually speared it to the ground.

'*Well?*' Fenris boomed when all the sorry creature did was tremble and whimper. Of course that approach didn't help either and the minion flung itself face down on the floor, prostrate before its lord, mewling for mercy in its thick guttural language. Begging not to be killed or eaten or even eaten *then* killed. Fenris was a little short of patience these days and had been to some extent for the last several thousand years. Imprisonment had done little for that trait. The Dread Wolf Lord leapt the hall in three mighty bounds and yanked the minion to its feet with one mighty swoop. It squealed and howled as though it was on fire, thinking its end imminent. Instead, Fenris held it out at arm's length and watched it wriggle for a few seconds before tiring of the sport.

'Out with it, Zoth. What brings you here? You have news?' That had been the fateful question all and sundry had learnt to fear. For it was in the wake of that question that Fenris had commenced his most recent uproarious devastation. Zoth nodded as best he could, being held by the scruff of the neck and several feet off the ground. Zoth wasn't the best of lookers at the best of times, resembling something between a hairless cat, a snake and a wart hog. He hung pathetically from the merciless grip of Fenris's talons, which gripped his nape so tightly it drew a blood of sorts. But Zoth nodded and pointed weakly upwards.

'A...a...a bright light iz coming mazter. It grow larger and larger. Heading thiz way. Here zoon.' This caught the curiosity of Fenris and with no regard for Zoth, he tossed the minion aside as though he were a soiled rag. The minion screamed for a second before slamming into the wall and sliding down, unconscious or possibly even dead. He hit the marble wall with a definitive smack and slid to the floor as though all his bones had been removed or at the very least broken. Fenris, who had already forgotten the minion, strode with urgency towards his massive balcony. Pounding out and gripping the rails as his only way of stopping himself, he scoured the sky, looking for some sign of this light. Growling, he turned and looked back the way he came, and there it was, out over his city and without a shadow of a doubt, hurtling towards the palace. Towards him! The thought hit harder than any weapon ever could. The direction the light was taking towards him was paramount. It came from the direction of the Adversary and that was not good at all.

Damn his balls. He is sending some kind of herald or accursed emissary to check up on me. Well, he is in for a surprise. Fenris snarled a harsh laugh and went back inside to await his visitor.

At the front of the palace, a grand plaza filled with fantastic statuary and stone benches, fountains of some viscous golden liquid, and well-tended shrubbery and plants, was filled with minions and servants, many of whom had vacated the palace when Fenris went on his rampage. They figured to wait outside until he calmed, making the most of their momentary respite and relative peace. They all stood transfixed by the aerial display. The fiery sphere, as they could now make out, was definitely heading their way, but they had seen so much arcane phenomena in their time in the Domain that they considered it a harmless spectacle and invariably, some minor lord or the other would manifest in their midst. There were a few, however, who had their reservations about the intent of the blazing sunlike object. Thinking its speed of approach just too threatening to stay close to, so they prudently turned tails and ran. A few others saw this hasty departure and pondered the reason behind it. They didn't have long to ponder. The closer the cometlike micro sun grew, the more wisdom several more minions obtained, and they too ran. Fast. For the pulsing and radiating heat was evident now, throbbing from the hurtling fireball with such intensity that the plants shriveled and scorched before their very eyes, initially browning as though windburnt, then blackening, finally turning to ash, and then blowing away in the searing wind that preceded the spectacle. As the heat increased exponentially, those minions who were too slow or too dim to run sooner were immolated on the spot.

Seconds later, the massive sphere of molten liquid fire slammed into the plaza, instantly dissolving rock and marble and turning the area into a white hot pool of liquid stone which splashed and rippled outwards, setting quite a few things on fire in its immediate vicinity. Tongues of flame rolled out and devoured all they touched: minions, buildings, statues, everything. Then, just when an all-out firestorm seemed imminent, and the city about to succumb to its ravages, it stopped. Like a deep breath inhaling, the fire stopped in its tracks and was sucked back into the crater like it was on rewind. With the ease of snuffing a candle between thumb and forefinger, the flames all went out. A cool breeze, as chill as the breath from the monstrous glacier trolls of the far north, immediately followed, and the glowing liquid stone rapidly cooled from incandescent white through yellow, red; then, with a cracking of fractured rock, it cooled solid. All that was left was a distinctly malevolent looking, swirling, twisting column of black, smoldering and slightly sparking smoke at the heart of the crater, where the conflagration had been sucked back into. Then with a whoosh, that too suddenly vanished into the ground.

Had anything been left alive in sight of the crater, it would have seen a figure standing there, slowly appraising its surroundings. Seconds later, with a crooked smile of amusement, the Adversary stepped up from the centre of the impact and began to walk slowly towards the palace. Yet even though the previously liquid stone had cooled and now solidified, each step the Adversary took left molten puddles of liquid footprints behind him. Each pool of molten rock bubbled like the burning heart of a series of tiny volcanoes, shimmering the light above them as it scorched the already burnt air. It crackled with ozone and phosphorous. The decaying aroma of sulphur followed in the Adversary's wake. It was a scent that was at odds with the image the Adversary wore this day. He strode across the ruined plaza like a god from Greek mythology. A toga barely covered his Herculean physique, where bronzed and sun seared muscles rippled and flowed beneath flawless skin. An enormous and wickedly curved sword was slung across his back from shoulder to hip and it seemed to absorb the very light from around the bestriding entity, casting him into an almost perpetual shadow that gave him a malign and menacing visage. Hooded eyes that glinted darkly beneath full brows missed nothing and they swept the way before him with an almost tangible presence. Moving with the economy of grace that gifts dancers and master swordsmen, the Adversary began the climb up the seventy-seven intricately carved steps that led up to the palatial doors of Shemyaza's palace. The front of the palace closely resembled the archaic pyramids of the ancient Aztecs. Each step was fractionally higher than three feet, and swept back seven feet to the next. It was an arduous climb for anyone not capable of more arcane methods of transport, and served to intimidate would-be guests as well as the mundane populace of Shemyaza's palace city. The Adversary took each step in his stride, growing in stature to accommodate the architecture.

To the casual observer, the Adversary looked angelically beautiful, perfectly toned and well muscled. But it was the more subtle aspects that betrayed his true nature, not that anything could get, or want to get, close enough to point them out. But within the fine featured face, where high cheekbones and an aquiline nose gave him a heroic profile, it was sundered by the viciously pointed canines that protruded out over his lower lip, clashing bone white against the full, lush red lips that would have been the envy of women throughout the multiverse. His eyes, like a corvid's, glistened blackly beneath perfectly rendered eyebrows, with long lashes that surrounded the almond shaped orbs. But to look into those obsidian pools was to drown in sheer terror as they sucked your soul screaming from your very atoms. Moving down those mighty arms to hands and fingers that flexed gently as he walked, as though they limbered lightly in anticipation of imminent activity, they could have been the fine boned hands of a surgeon or a concert pianist, so delicately did they move. But the thick, dirty yellow talons atip each digit spoke instead of pain and death; of ripping into flesh, tearing muscle and snapping bone. They were the hands of a paramount killer, a fusion of man and lion. In fact there was much in the way of feline grace to the Adversary's demeanor, look, movement and cruel nature, and had he been an animal it would have been a big cat. A big, nasty, evil motherfucker of a cat that would have eaten sabertooths for breakfast. Along with anything else it chose. Today he was a human personification of a big cat and he had come to pay a big, nasty and very disobedient dog a visit.

The Adversary wasn't overly surprised that he had received no greeting from the palace, official or otherwise, for this was a random visit, and he had sent no advance warning. Of course, he had just obliterated a few hundred minions with his arrival and perhaps his herald had been amidst the conflagration. No matter – he was more than capable of introducing himself. Millennia of anonymity had given him a myriad of skills in that department. He had come and gone at will throughout the multiverse as Lucifer's voice, Lucifer's will and Lucifer's assassin, orchestrating wars, deaths and changes of sovereignty as his former master dictated. But that was a past life. He was his own master now and soon to be the master of all. Starting with the multiverse. As vast as it was and as ancient as it had become, the Adversary snarled at the thought of how complacent the process had grown. In particular he considered the Absolutes and their stringent adherence to the rules. How they dictated the how, why and when of this defunct process. He would change all that soon enough, and then they would pay dearly for their interference and lack of respect for him and his role in much of what had transpired to date.

The Adversary arrived at the outer doors to the palace still without laying eyes on another soul, and he scowled in annoyance. *Now they are just being rude*, the Adversary thought as he surveyed the carnage before him. Taking in the devastation within as well as without, he entered the vaulted hallway and then the smell hit him. He wrinkled his perfect nose and strode on. *Dog.* Zaramael had made many visits to Shemyaza's palace in the past so he knew the way to the throne room well enough. It was where he guessed Fenris would be, waiting for whoever he thought had arrived, and humor of sorts crossed the Adversary's features, displacing the annoyance like the sun coming out from behind a dark cloud, as he pictured the Wolf Lord's face when he saw who it was who had actually come to see him.

Fenris, already impatient and tired of waiting for whoever it was who had arrived to come to him, stood and began to lope across the hall, intent on meeting this interloper outside. But he hadn't gotten more than halfway across the hall before the massive gold and oaken doors flexed, buckled, then exploded inwards towards him. Torn brutally off their hinges and out of their frames, they were sent hurtling across the hall at lethal speed. Fenris had barely the wit to duck the first one as it whistled overhead and flew out of the gallery doors that led to his balcony, taking most of them with it and a goodly chunk of balustrade as it spun out in to open space, to crash amidst the palace grounds somewhere. Fenris batted the other one aside in a thoughtless gesture of self-defense, for he was not without power of his own, and it whizzed across the hall, to embed itself into the wall, scant inches above the slowly consciousness-regaining Zoth, who promptly passed out again with shock.

The Wolf Lord would have been furious at the intrusion and wanton destruction of his property were it not for the fact of who it was who had perpetrated such a deed. The rage died within his breast as his feral eyes locked onto the figure striding like a behemoth into the hall. 'Your housekeeping is atrocious, Fenris, though I should expect no better from a dog.'

Fenris was stunned into almost rigidity as his lord and master swept past him to seat himself upon the one remaining item of furniture left intact in the cavernous room: the throne itself. That would have been hard to ruin as it was hewn from one sizeable chunk of labradorite and it had stood immutable since the palace itself had been raised. Rife with enchantment and runic sigils, it held more arcane power within its secretive heart than many of the demon lords put together, though none knew its true purpose any more or what it was capable of. None save Lucifer perhaps or the late Shemyaza himself. With both gone it now put its secret far from knowing, but it did start to glow ever so slightly as the Adversary seated himself upon it. The myriad of colors that coruscated through it grew brighter and the whole throne became more translucent and fabulous to behold.

Fenris paid the seat itself no mind however. So focused was he upon the figure currently sat upon it, his mind spun end over end with shock, horror and implication.

'My lord?' was about all Fenris could muster as he stared unreservedly at the Adversary, fully expecting him to vanish any moment as a figment of his imagination. But he didn't move. Nor did Fenris really think his imagination would be so cruel to him as to manifest this particular entity, and certainly not looking so enraged as he did. Fenris didn't even realize his panic had overridden any propriety he should have observed, and he just stood staring. The roar of the Adversary duly reminded him of his place as it shook the very foundations of the palace, doing almost as much damage in that one blast as Fenris had managed that day.

'Bow before me, you insolent dog! Do you not show your true master the due respect he deserves when he attends your realm? You whelp, I should have you beaten where you stand, and your mangy carcass banished to Asmodeus's realm to be flayed and confined to the searing bowels of his desolate lands. Bow low, hound, and pray your supplication pleases me!'

Fenris fell flat on his face so fast he nearly rendered himself unconscious as he hit the marble flags. If he had pressed himself and abased himself any further, he would have squeezed down the cracks between stones. Words failed the Wolf Lord and he whimpered like a kicked pup until, eventually satisfied his point had been made, the Adversary bade him to finally sit up.

'That's more like it, you cur. Now come sit by me, I have a task for you.'

Fenris slunk on his belly and ears back like a cowed dog until he was at heel to his lord. The Adversary paid him no heed and looked into the distance, as though lost in thought, and distractedly placed a taloned hand proprietarily on the head on Fenris, patting it gently like a faithful hound. With a nonchalant wave of the other hand, a trestle table appeared, laden with steaming meat and fruit, bread, cheeses and decanters full of some golden hued mercurial liquid, along with several elaborately chased and bejeweled drinking horns.

'Fenris! Get a grasp on your wits and go pour us some drink. This dust makes my throat dry.'

The Wolf Lord hastened to obey and swiftly returned, passing one to his lordship first, keeping his eyes downcast as he did so. Many had made the fateful mistake of thinking they could match the indomitable gaze of the Adversary, only to learn differently as they died. Fenris intended not to make the same mistake as many before him, though curiosity was burning him up to know what such a visit portended. 'My lord, what brings you to my humble den, and why was I not informed of your gracious visit?' Fenris was suddenly aware of how that sounded so he quickly added, 'So I could have better prepared for your arrival, of course, sire.'

The Adversary sipped his beverage and smiled to himself as he did so. The sense of power and fear he emanated, along with the fear and reverence he experienced now, was more of a heady rush to him than even the potent liquid he sipped casually. 'Drink first, Fenris, then I will answer you.'

Fenris looked at his goblet, then at the Adversary. What was in it? He wondered why he was so insistent he drink. Was it poison? Or worse? But what choice did he have, with the Adversary's penetrating gaze locked on him, awaiting his compliance to the request that was not really a request at all but an order. One to be obeyed instantly, he suspected, or face dire consequences. Fenris threw back the liquid in one gulp and waited for the agony. It never came. In fact, quite the opposite began to take place – a warm suffusion that spread throughout his body, invigorating him in a way he had not experienced for some time. 'My lord?'

The Adversary just smiled and downed his own goblet, tossing it to Fenris to refill, which he duly did, as well as his own.

'I am fully aware of your scheming and plotting, Fenris. Do not presume me lacking in the details of what transpires within my realm. You forget yourself, though I do admire ambition in my generals; and your desire to supplant Asmodeus and the rest to elevate yourself to my second is indeed admirable. However...' Fenris knew this was the bit that would either see him dead or rescued. He held his breath, '...bickering aside, I find your tenacity refreshing, but not your failure.' Fenris gulped. He knew. 'Matters have moved in ways that were unforeseen and like all good plans, dog, I am forced to change mine to accommodate these...' The Adversary sought the

correct phrase and looked thoughtful for a moment before continuing, '…
inconveniences.'

'My lord. What could inconvenience one such as yourself sufficiently
that one so lowly as I could ever possibly assist one as great as you?'

The Adversary laughed, rich, warm and musical, which complemented
the rapturous feeling the amber liquid generated within him. 'You are such
a toady, Fenris, and so full of shit I can smell it. Stand up straight, will you?
You are not some suck up lackey. You are a lord in your own right now – one
that may have stepped up a bit too fast for his own good, but a power in your
own right all the same. Behave like one, will you? Accept your reprimand and
move on. Now where was I?'

'Inconvenience?' Fenris proffered.

The Adversary drained his goblet once more and tossed it aside, forgotten. He leant forward and rested his heroic chin upon his fist and looked at
Fenris with a contemplative gleam in his eye. 'Allow me to bring you up
to speed, my faithful hound. Matters have slowed on the Earth. I do not yet
possess enough power to open the requisite number of gates to fully overrun
the mortals, for although we have destroyed many significant strongholds,
they still withstand us. Of course the accursed armies of the Celestial Host
support them at every turn and are seemingly everywhere. An impasse has
occurred in that area but that is not the inconvenience, for we will outnumber
them eventually and the tide of battle will turn in our favor.'

The Adversary looked concerned for a split second then and Fenris
spotted it. That bothered him more than anything. If something bothered the
Adversary, then it must be truly dire. His tongue lolled from his maw as he
waited for his lord to continue.

'For although I find it shocking that the mortals even have the audacity
to fight back, there are factors at play I had not anticipated, and thought long
gone.' Fenris's eyes gleamed with anticipation, eager to hear more. 'There
are Drakarim loose upon the world and they have found yet another of the
damnable guardians that I believed were all disposed of. Can you explain to

me how this could have happened? Did I not spend millennia hunting them all down to rid myself of problems just like this?'

Fenris looked confused, unsure of the rhetorical basis of his master's comment. Did he actually want an answer? It was a potentially dangerous choice. 'The one that is loose here upon the Domain, lord?' Fenris interjected the question hopefully, waiting for the explosion that never came. Instead the Adversary opted for an icy calm. The Wolf Lord wasn't sure which was more disconcerting.

'No, dog. Another. Can you believe there is another loose? And a mere woman for all that. She has awoken a power within the Earth that could have potentially disastrous consequences and put an abrupt end to our grand design. For this, she must be stopped at all costs.'

Fenris looked confused. 'My lord? A mortal woman? What harm can she possibly do?'

The Adversary rose and began to pace the hall, hands clasped behind him and one nail flicking a steely meter out on the sword as he walked. 'She seeks the One Tree. The First. The tree that sired even mighty Yggdrasil, the ancient ash from your time. The First Tree that seeded and gave power to the trees of both knowledge and life. The first tree that existed at the axis of the Earth and breathed the first breath of life into the world. It is that which has been lost even before the earliest Drakarim arrived, and whose lore seems to have been forgotten or misplaced by the Absolutes themselves, so craftily hidden has it been.'

Fenris scowled, as if not understanding. 'If it is so well hidden, then how can a mere mortal woman find it where greater powers have failed? Surely she is of no consequence.'

The Adversary stopped and looked with drawn brows upon the Dread Wolf Lord, as though seeing him for the first time. 'Has your time in your gaol made you so dense, Fenris? Have you become too arrogant in your freedom to not see beyond the immediate and the obvious to the possibility of what might be? Could be? The very fact you are free at all gives credence to the unprecedented. Powers are afoot that have not been witnessed in time longer than the very suns themselves have lived. I gather you are aware of what I am intending, what it entails, and that none before me have ever attempted such a feat?'

Fenris nodded slowly, unsure of the new direction the Adversary was heading with the conversation.

'If I can attempt something unprecedented,' the Adversary continued, 'then my enemy can also attempt the impossible. Ergo, if I stand a chance of success, so must they. Therefore I have altered my plan to suit, and you are to be the first to act upon the new changes. You are up to it, aren't you, hound?'

'Your every wish is mine to obey, mighty Star of the Twilight, Bringer of Darkness and Herald of a New World. I am indeed your faithful hound, majesty. What would you have of me?'

The Adversary smiled at Fenris and it held all the warmth of a black hole. 'Simply this, dog. I want you to take as many of your infernal hounds as you have gathered and make a war upon the Earth, the likes she has never seen. Tear, rend and savage everything before you. I want you to be the vanguard for my legions, and as well as that honor, I want you to find this mortal woman and devour her utterly. I want absolutely nothing of her DNA to remain. Do I make myself clear?'

Fenris nodded eagerly. His lolling tongue flopped up and down, sending streams of saliva flying all over the place, though none ever reached the Adversary: they seemed to slide off an invisible barrier that shielded him. The Adversary grimaced distastefully at the drool, but continued regardless. 'I will aid you in this, Fenris, for I have accelerated a process I had hoped to avoid, for it is wasteful, and many souls will be lost to me in the process. Souls that I could have harvested, but needs must. For though this may take longer, the end results come closer that much faster.'

Fenris was fascinated now, for he loved strategy, and the destruction of humankind had always been dear to him. Ragnarok was due to be his greatest achievement but he was thwarted in that particular endeavor by the

Valhallarans: Odin the All Father and his brood, along with all his sycophants and subordinates. To be a part of the Adversary's grand scheme was almost as satisfying. Almost.

'What do you have planned, my liege?' Fenris was almost panting with anticipation.

'Simple really, too simple, if I'm completely honest. Humanity has teetered on the brink of global meltdown for so long. With a little persuasion from us, they have built and gathered about themselves weapons of such foul mass destruction that they fear ever using them – foolish and pointless. They may have no intention of using them but I have. That was why I gave them the clues and the blueprints for such a devastating capability. My possessed have infiltrated every level of their social structure as well as their governments, religious institutions and military structures. You don't honestly think they came up with all those ideas on their own, do you? Silly puppy, no, no, they had a little push. And now, I've given them another little push, or should I say…' the Adversary began to chuckle as he envisaged his handiwork, '…I've encouraged them to push a little something. As we speak, my minions should be entering their launch codes and sending their nuclear angels flying. Okay, it might mean that half of humanity is wiped out, but it will make my task that much easier. As long as the Earth dies and I am there to harvest her soul, that will be sufficient.'

The Adversary turned to Fenris and the Dread Wolf Lord recoiled in fear at the look in his lord's eye. He saw the end of all things there, and for the first time, Fenris felt real terror.

'Listen carefully, dog; you'll probably hear their screams from here.' At that moment, the Adversary himself stepped across that magical threshold between lucidity and madness and he threw back his head and roared his laughter long into the oncoming night.

ᚦᛗᚪᚠᚾᛟᛗ ᚱᛋᚠᚱᛋ

Sure enough, across the Earth, in every city that still stood; and across the rolling countryside, even that which had been scourged by invading demons and was scorched beyond life; in every country from Alaska to Australia; vapor trails could be seen rocketing skyward from silos the world denied existed. Missiles launched what should not have been armed or pointed anywhere, let alone launched. But man was renowned for his deceit and self-denial, the veneer of civility tightly wrapping cruel barbarism. And once he was capable of building such powerful weapons, he was loath to let them go. It was as if he could unlearn how to build them, to forget they ever existed. But that was not to be, and now he was to fall prey to his own machinations and greed as well as from entities far more powerful and corrupt than he could imagine, with ambitions that should make humanity tremble in its bed at night and wish fervently it had never left the cave.

Battles that were in mid-flow stopped and every creature paused to look skyward. The demons who saw the event capered and cackled at the sight, aware to an extent what was occurring. Though not fully cognizant of their lord's intent, they knew enough to seek the shelter of the nearest portal. For though they were not of this world and the weapons of man could do them little harm, it would be painful and uncomfortable all the same.

The Angelic Host also saw the atrocity that had been set in motion and they simply watched in despair, knowing there was little they could do now to protect humanity. This was the attack they had hoped to avoid and prevent from taking place, for even they would be powerless against such elemental devastation. Everything that had gone before was now for nothing and the next couple of hours would decide the fate of worlds. Even if some desperate and brave few managed to enter any abort codes now, it would be too few, too late.

Mortalkind was dumbstruck. Many couldn't believe what they were seeing. Others dropped to their knees and prayed to whoever they felt was listening. Some got religion fast while others yet simply wept and sought out loved ones. And yet more knew they were far from both home and those they loved. These lost souls simply sat and waited for the inevitable, hoping it would be quick and painless, yet in their hearts they knew it would be neither.

Out across the Great Pacific Ocean, four riders reined in mid-flight. The fabled Horsemen of the Apocalypse stared long and hard at the missiles that criss-crossed across the sky like some obscene weaver stitching the end of the world high in the sky. They watched the rockets for a few more moments before turning to each other. Something silent and unspoken passed between them and they each saluted the other, as though they didn't expect to see one another again. Then, as one they turned, and with a direction apiece, sped off much faster than any mere human missile, intent on their objective and with one purpose only.

So Ends

THE ADVERSARY
FOUR HORSEMEN OF THE APOCALYPSE SAGA: BOOK ONE.

LOOK OUT FOR BOOK 2 OF
THE FOUR HORSEMEN OF THE APOCALYPSE SAGA

THE EMERGENCE

COMING SOON, FUTURE PERMITTING.